THE WAR OF
VENGEANCE

WARHAMMER CHRONICLES

- **THE LEGEND OF SIGMAR** -
Graham McNeill
BOOK ONE: *Heldenhammer*
BOOK TWO: *Empire*
BOOK THREE: *God King*

- **THE RISE OF NAGASH** -
Mike Lee
BOOK ONE: *Nagash the Sorcerer*
BOOK TWO: *Nagash the Unbroken*
BOOK THREE: *Nagash Immortal*

- **VAMPIRE WARS:
THE VON CARSTEIN TRILOGY** -
Steven Savile
BOOK ONE: *Inheritance*
BOOK TWO: *Dominion*
BOOK THREE: *Retribution*

- **THE SUNDERING** -
Gav Thorpe
BOOK ONE: *Malekith*
BOOK TWO: *Shadow King*
BOOK THREE: *Caledor*

- **CHAMPIONS OF CHAOS** -
Darius Hinks, S P Cawkwell &
Ben Counter
BOOK ONE: *Sigvald*
BOOK TWO: *Valkia the Bloody*
BOOK THREE: *Van Horstmann*

- **THE WAR OF VENGEANCE** -
Nick Kyme, Chris Wraight & C L Werner
BOOK ONE: *The Great Betrayal*
BOOK TWO: *Master of Dragons*
BOOK THREE: *The Curse of the
Phoenix Crown*

- **MATHIAS THULMANN:
WITCH HUNTER** -
(June 2018)
C L Werner
BOOK ONE: *Witch Hunter*
BOOK TWO: *Witch Finder*
BOOK THREE: *Witch Killer*

The Gates of Azyr
Chris Wraight

Hallowed Knights: Plague Garden
Josh Reynolds

Eight Lamentations: Spear of Shadows
Josh Reynolds

Overlords of the Iron Dragon
C L Werner

Black Rift
Josh Reynolds

Legends of the Age of Sigmar
Includes the novels *Fyreslayers, Skaven
Pestilens* and *Sylvaneth*
Various authors

Nagash: The Undying King
Josh Reynolds

The Realmgate Wars

War Storm
Nick Kyme, Guy Haley and
Josh Reynolds

Ghal Maraz
Josh Reynolds and Guy Haley

Hammers of Sigmar
Darius Hinks and C L Werner

Call of Archaon
David Annandale, David Guymer,
Guy Haley and Rob Sanders

Wardens of the Everqueen
C L Werner

Warbeast
Gav Thorpe

Fury of Gork
Josh Reynolds

Bladestorm
Matt Westbrook

Mortarch of Night
Josh Reynolds and David Guymer

Lord of Undeath
C L Werner

WARHAMMER® CHRONICLES

THE WAR OF VENGEANCE

**NICK KYME
CHRIS WRAIGHT
C L WERNER**

BLACK LIBRARY

A BLACK LIBRARY PUBLICATION

The Great Betrayal first published in 2012.
Master of Dragons first published in 2013.
The Curse of the Phoenix Crown first published in 2015.
This edition published in Great Britain in 2018 by
Black Library,
Games Workshop Ltd.,
Willow Road,
Nottingham, NG7 2WS, UK.

10 9 8 7 6 5 4 3 2 1

Produced by Games Workshop in Nottingham.
Cover illustration by Johan Grenier.
Map by Nuala Kinrade.

The War of Vengeance © Copyright Games Workshop Limited 2018. The War of Vengeance, Warhammer Chronicles, GW, Games Workshop, Black Library, Warhammer, Warhammer, Age of Sigmar, Stormcast Eternals, and all associated logos, illustrations, images, names, creatures, races, vehicles, locations, weapons, characters, and the distinctive likenesses thereof, are either ® or TM, and/or © Games Workshop Limited, variably registered around the world.
All Rights Reserved.

A CIP record for this book is available from the British Library.

ISBN 13: 978 1 78496 693 5

No part of this publication may be reproduced, stored in a retrieval system, or transmitted in any form or by any means, electronic, mechanical, photocopying, recording or otherwise, without the prior permission of the publishers.

This is a work of fiction. All the characters and events portrayed in this book are fictional, and any resemblance to real people or incidents is purely coincidental.

See Black Library on the internet at

blacklibrary.com

Find out more about Games Workshop
and the world of Warhammer at

games-workshop.com

Printed and bound by CPI Group (UK) Ltd, Croydon, CR0 4YY

It is an age of legend.

In the elder ages when the world was young, elves and dwarfs lived in peace and prosperity. Dwarfs are great craftsmen, lords of the under deeps, artificers beyond compare. Elves are peerless mages, masters of the dragons, creatures of the sky and air. During the time of High King Snorri Whitebeard and Prince Malekith, these two great races were at the pinnacle of their strength. But such power and dominion could not last. Fell forces now gather against elves and dwarfs. Malekith, embittered by his maiming in the Flame of Asuryan, seeks to destroy them both but still darker powers are also at work. Already strained, disharmony sours relations between them until only enmity remains. Treachery is inevitable, a terrible act that can only result in one outcome... War.

The dwarf High King Gotrek Starbreaker marshals his throngs of warriors from all the holds of the Karaz Ankor, whilst the elves, under the vainglorious and arrogant Caledor II, gather their glittering hosts and fill the skies with dragons.

Mastery of the Old World is at stake, a grudge in the making that will last for millennia. Neither side will give up until the other is destroyed utterly. For in the War of Vengeance, victory will be measured only in blood.

CONTENTS

The Great Betrayal   11
Nick Kyme

Master of Dragons   363
Chris Wraight

The Curse of the Phoenix Crown   633
C L Werner

THE GREAT BETRAYAL

Nick Kyme

SINS OF THE ANCESTORS

I

Thunder rolled across the slopes of Karag Vlak, shaking the earth for miles. Fire wreathed the sky, warring with the furnace at the mountain peak that glowed hot and angry through swathes of pyroclastic cloud. Shadows lurked within that grey smog, drifting against the wind on membranous wings…

Eclipsed by the mountain, two great hosts had gathered on a blasted plain of scorched rock studded with the corpses of petrified trees. Death had changed this place. Pastureland had become a sprawling battlefield of skulls, flattened by war engines and thousands of booted feet. Air tasted like ash and the rivers were veins of smoking acid. Mordant horns and harrowing death cries supplanted the shrill of birds, the bray of elk.

In the middle of this carnage, a soaring monument of stone reached into the fiery sky. It was called the Fist of Gron, so named for its ugly, knuckled shape and reputedly after the dwarf king who had supposedly shaped it with his bare hands. Once it might have been a magnificent mountain pinnacle but some past cataclysm during the shaping of the world had reduced it to a flattened edifice. Other than the lesions of dead forest puckering the landscape, it was the only feature for miles.

And like the swell circling the eye of a maelstrom, a great battle raged around it. Thurgin Ironheart eyed the enemy charging at his throng across the hellish plain and scowled.

The dwarf was part of the second vanguard, summoned from his place at the foot of Karag Vlak where the rest of the host was encamped. He and his warriors were to fill the gap left by the throng of Karak Drazh. Thurgin had already lost sight of their shields, the sigils of the Black Hold trodden underfoot in the eagerness of the enemy to shed more blood.

'They are swift,' he said, drawing a nod from his nearby kinsmen. Thurgin felt the tremor of hoofbeats through his heavy black boots and iron-wrought armour. Runes of warding fashioned into the breastplate began to ignite in a chain of forge-bright flares that emblazoned the metal as the enemy neared. The fierce effigy of his dragon-faced war helm caught the flicker of fire. His short emerald cloak stirred in a foul wind rolling off the mountain. Muttering an oath to Grungni, he gripped the haft of his rune axe.

They would need an ancestor's blessing this day.

Never before had dwarfs waged war against such a foe. All of the orcs and goblins festering beneath the world could not come close in number to the horde riding down upon them now. The cavalry were but a small part of it.

Two hundred feet away from bloodying his axe and Thurgin growled an order. Despite distance and the clamour of the battle, his words carried to every warrior in the throng.

'Sons of Grungni, lock your shields!'

It was a resounding shout, made louder by the rune magic of his war helm, and a call to arms from which there could be no turning back.

Dwarfs do not turn back. In Khazalid, the language of the *dawi*, there is no word for retreat.

Across the slopes of Karag Vlak, ten thousand dwarfs of Karak Izril obeyed.

They were but the first rank.

Drums beat, horns blared. Eight more armies marched slowly into the fray. Here was where the fighting grew fiercest. Several massive regiments of infantry had already engaged farther down a long, rippling line. Thurgin's throng were coming forwards like the end of a gate with their hinge a half-mile to their left, about to close on the cavalry charging at them.

Amidst the clash of arms, Thurgin saw the banners of Kadrin, Vlag and Eight Peaks amongst those of his own hold. Thousands of dwarfs fought hammer and axe against the enemy hordes. His heart swelled with pride at the sight, even though he knew it might be his last. Other holds joined in as the dwarfs came together as one, but it was to the standard of the High King that Thurgin's eye was finally drawn.

Almost a mile away, standing upon the Fist of Gron, Thurgin saw him.

It was said the High King could break the stars. To witness the rune blade he wielded in a two-handed grip, splitting heads as if they were rotten barrels, Thurgin could believe it.

There was no time left to worry about the fate of the High King. Thurgin's march had brought his warriors into the fray. The horns lessened and the drums stopped beating as the dwarfs of Karak Izril waited silently for what they knew would happen next.

Less than a hundred feet away, the enemy came fast and hard on hooves of silver flame.

Thurgin felt the solidity of his clan brothers at either shoulder and smiled.

This would be a good day for the dwarfs.

Vengeance would be theirs.

He shouted, voice louder than a hundred war horns, '*Khazuk!*'

The throng of Karak Izril answered, its many ranks adding to the fury of their reply: 'Khazuk!'

Axes and hammers began to beat shields, rising in tempo as the riders closed.

'Khazuk!'

Thurgin slid the ornate faceplate over his eyes and nose until it clanked into place, and the world became a slit of honed anger.

His brothers' chorus resonated through his helm, chiming with the clash of arms.

'KHAZUK!'

It meant *war*.

War had come to the enemies of the dwarfs.

Glarondril the Silvern spurred his riders to greater effort. Standing up in his stirrups, he let the fire of the angry mountain reflect in his gleaming armour. Without a helmet, his long white hair cascaded down the back of his neck like a mane of frost. His eyes were diamond-hard, his jaw set like marble.

The enemy was close; a thick wedge of mailed warriors that seemed to stretch the length of the horizon, clutching blades and shields.

Twenty thousand noble lords at his command, armour glittering with the falling sun, lowered their lances.

They had raced hard and far to reach this hellish plain. Glarondril would not be found wanting on the slopes of the mountain. He would see the battle through to its end, even if that meant his death. Whispering words of command to his mount, he drew the riders into a spear tip of glittering silver.

'In the name of the Phoenix King,' he roared, unable to keep his battle-lust sheathed any longer. A sword of blue flame slid soundlessly from his scabbard. 'For the glory of Ulthuan!'

The enemy were so close... Glarondril saw their hooded eyes, shimmering like moist gemstones, and smelled the reek of their foul breath, all metal and earth.

'None shall live!'

The blue-fire sword was held aloft as a thicket of lance heads drew down before the charge.

Thurgin felt his body tense just before the moment of impact.

'Hold them, break them!' he roared. 'No mercy! Kill them all!'

Here before them was a foe worthy of dwarf enmity.

The shield wall dug in, backs and shoulders braced. All fifty thousand in this single throng came together. The muster from Karak Izril was large, but far from the largest of the holds. Deeper into the plain, Thurgin knew there were others similarly embattled. He prayed to Valaya for their souls as well his own and that of his men.

Behind the thick infantry formations, he heard the slow tread of the *gronti-duraz*. Through the dense earth he could feel the tremor of their footfalls as the low, sombre chanting of their masters animated them. Thurgin was glad to have the stone-clad behemoths at his back.

Above, lightning cracked the sky as magical anvils were made ready.

On the far mountain flank to Thurgin's left, the bolt tips of ballistae twinkled in the dying light through a rolling fog. They looked like stars.

Dwarfs did not need the stars, or the sun. They were dwellers of the earth, solid and determined. They would need those traits today, as they would need all the craft of the runesmiths and the engines of the guilds to overcome the horde upon the plain.

They were foul and wretched creatures that the dwarfs would drive from the Old World forever.

At last the enemy reached them, a collision of barbed lances and mewling steeds against dwarf shields and tenacity.

As he raised his axe to strike, Thurgin knew no quarter would be given.

He would ask for none.

Glarondril and his knights swept into the armoured horde, piercing flesh and shattering bone. Severed heads fell from the necks of his foes as he swept around his blazing blue sword in a killing arc. A jab disembowelled another, as hundreds of lances struck flesh, impaling dozens with every vengeful thrust.

'I am the Master of Dragons,' he roared. 'Behold your doom!'

Incandescent fire spewed from the jaws of the elven mounts. It rose in a tide that burned their enemies to ash. No defence was proof against the Dragon Princes of Caledor. No foe, however determined, could resist their charge. The few who did survive found their attacks repelled harmlessly by dragonscale harder than plate. The beasts snarled in contempt, crimsons, ambers, emeralds and azures, a myriad of colour and fury, tearing at limbs with fang and claw.

Hundreds of the enemy died in the first seconds, spitted by lances, devoured by the dragons or burned alive, their corpses left to ruin in the sun. What began as a contest swiftly became a slaughter.

A leader, his armour thicker than the rest, bellowed a challenge at Glarondril who accepted without hesitation.

'For the king!' he shouted above the eager roar of his mount, as he took the enemy leader's head.

'For the king!' urged Thurgin, chopping into the riders blunted on the dwarfs' wall of shields. A spurt of ichor splashed across the dark lacquer of his vambraces but he ignored it, thumping with his shield and hacking with his axe. The runes on the blade flared like star-fires as it hewed through iron-hard skin like it was parchment.

Though the foe pushed and pressed, using every ounce of their depraved strength, the dwarfs held back the tide. Utterly implacable, the shield wall didn't budge and the enemy cavalry buckled as they rolled against it. Riders in the rear ranks, unable to arrest their momentum, barrelled into those in front. The enemy's formation rippled, mounts and riders sent sprawling only to be crushed by those that followed in their wake, or butchered by dwarf axes.

Thurgin knew they had weathered the worst of it, and now what they had to do next.

'Forward!'

Fifty thousand booted feet stomped in unerring unison. The enemy resisted at first, but once the dwarfs had overcome the inertia caused by the broken bodies underfoot they were unstoppable. The throng of Karak Izril moved slowly but inexorably. Like a landslide, and with the same momentum, they cascaded over the cavalry and destroyed it. Already smashed against the dwarfs' resilience, the riders scattered. Harried without mercy by the triumphant dwarfs, the enemy cavalry had lost two-thirds of its warriors before the charge was ended. Thurgin himself had accounted for no fewer than fifteen of the creatures.

Seeing no gain in pursuit, he called the throng to a halt. His chest was heaving and there was a burning sensation in his shoulder from the violent axe-work, but it was a good pain.

Taking a moment to look around, he realised the battle was perched on a dagger's edge. A heavy toll had been taken of the enemy, but they were numerous and their will bordered on fanatical.

Lifting up the faceplate of his dragon helm, Thurgin's eye was drawn upwards to a vast shadow approaching him and his warriors from out of the sun. Not one of the throng of Karak Izril so much as flinched.

'We have the east flank,' he called out. An elven dragon rider, leading his scaled host, answered with a clenched fist and a broad, warlike smile.

Glarondril landed gracefully and bowed in the saddle to the thane-lord of Karak Izril. So too did his beast.

'Well met, Thurgin son of Brak.' He wiped the ichor from his sword before sheathing it. Behind him, almost twenty thousand dragons lowered their heads in respect to their allies. Each of their riders, every one of them a prince, nodded.

The dwarfs slammed their fists against their breastplates, raising a mighty clamour.

'High prince,' answered Thurgin, thumping his own chestplate and the angular rune engraved upon it. 'I am always glad to see the Master of *Drakk* and his host.' He gestured to the mound of sundered daemon corpses strewn around them. They were ugly creatures with hell-red skin, hooves and coiling horns that jutted from canine skulls. Foul steam rose off their broken bodies as the slow dissolution of their natures rendered them down to nothing but essence.

'I am especially glad,' Thurgin went on, 'when his intervention crushes my enemies so gloriously and hands us a piece of the field to hold on to.' He gestured to the slain host littering the ground for a hundred feet or more in front of them.

Glarondril regarded the daemon corpses with disdain.

'We had best make the most of our good fortune then,' remarked the elf, already spurring his mount.

'Indeed...' Thurgin turned his eye northwards where the bulk of the daemons festered and gibbered. 'Those two fiends won't kill themselves, now, will they?'

Even in the distance the leaders of the horde were easy to discern as they towered above their vassals: the feathered sorcerer and the bloated lord. Each was a prince of daemons with the innumerable hosts of Chaos at their command.

As the daemons retreated on one corner of the battlefield, they swelled in another. Thurgin saw them, the bulk of the cavalry he had butchered, the remnants left by Glarondril and his dragons, gathering around the Fist of Gron. And on that flat spur of rock was High King Snorri Whitebeard and the Elf Prince Malekith, alone and besieged by hell.

II

A sea of red-skinned death surrounded the king of the dwarfs and the prince of the elves. Though the Fist of Gron was over a hundred feet across, they could see the creatures capering and undulating below them because the horde stretched so far back onto the plain. Had they both stood in the middle of the flat, featureless rock that capped the Fist, Snorri and Malekith would still have seen them.

As it was they stood at either end, close to the edge, as determined warriors would defend a wall during a siege. But it was the braying, the animalistic moans and lascivious promises emanating from beneath them, that told the nobles their enemies were climbing up to fight them.

'They are eager,' shouted the High King, clashing his hammer and axe together in a challenge.

'Try not to be as keen, old friend,' the elf prince replied. 'They are coming.'

Snorri and Malekith faced away from each other, but each knew that their counterpart was smiling.

This was the war to end all wars, the final battle against the daemons and the power of Ruin. Here, history was being made. Malekith and Snorri were its architects. But although legendary, this was not the first time that Chaos had challenged for mastery of the Old World.

Long ago the hosts of Chaos had come from the north. An icebound, unforgiving land, the north was thronged with feral tribes and great primordial beasts. These creatures were the first amongst the servants of

Ruin, the denizens of the glacier caves and frost-bitten valleys quick to bend their knees in worship. Succour was granted without mercy, their bodies reshaped into horrific forms, just as their souls were cast to damnation. Through a great gate, from a hellish netherworld where all the laws and fabric of nature were mutable and perverted, Chaos spilled into the mortal realm.

Its essence had bled into the lands beyond, turning trees into claws, rivers into arteries of blood and natural beasts into abominations. Like shadows, wisps of half-seen smoke or nightmares witnessed in periphery, the daemons marched alongside these beasts. On leathery pinion, on hoof or claw, slithering on their bellies the monstrous horde had swept across the Old World devouring all before it. Bloated on corruption, swollen with mutation, it could not be allowed to endure.

Grimnir was the most warlike of the dwarf ancestor gods. Legend told that he had closed the Chaos Gate himself and been doomed by the very deed. Left behind by Grimnir's sacrifice, his fellow deities Grungni and Valaya passed from the mortal realm and went back into the earth, never to be seen again. But even the might of the ancestors could not prevent the canker of Ruin escaping. Disaster was averted, destruction of all life forestalled for a time, but Chaos lived. It bred and permeated the very cloth stitching reality together. It became pervasive, an invisible stain that would only spread with the passing of millennia.

Statues and memories were all that remained of the ancestor gods now. Even their lesser children were dust, with only scant temples to remember them. Such numinous beings could not exist forever and so it fell to their scions to try and rid the world of Chaos...

Snorri Whitebeard unleashed a bolt of lightning through the haft of his hammer. It sparked and cracked with all the fury of the ancestors, luminous and burning. A tide of hell-spawn that had come crawling over the lip of the flat rock where he made his stand was sent reeling. Blackened and smouldering, the creatures pitched over the edge and did not return. Sulphur-stink tainted the air as they were banished, the unreality of this place the only thing keeping them from dissipating immediately.

It had been a verdant valley once, the rich volcanic soil of the mountain giving life to acres of forest. All that had changed with the coming of Chaos. A blasted landscape, scorched black and seized in the grip of a half-frozen waste, was all that remained.

A mire of corpses piled up around the foot of the rock, putrefying with the taint of Ruin. From the steaming carcasses that were dried to husks and broken open by the baleful sun further abominations arose. Dewy eyelids blinked and nictitated in the light. Tentacles, claws and fleshy protuberances burst from skin-taut bodies eager for transformation. Carapace, chitin and malformed bone swaddled beasts already overrun with corruption that advanced against the elves and dwarfs.

These were the spawns of Chaos, hell-ravaged abominations birthed by fell sorcery of the darkest kind.

Uttering a cry to Khaine, the elven war god, Malekith speared a basilisk through its gullet. Viscous ichor spewed arterially from the wound. Mercury-swift, the elf prince leapt forwards and decapitated the beast without pause with his blade, Avanuir. Its dead, collapsing mass crushed several lesser beasts and swept many others to their doom as it fell.

Hundreds more of the wretched creatures now littered the rock where the lords of the dwarfs and elves made their stand. Daemons of every malformed persuasion and aspect had fallen beneath their weapons.

With a grunt, Snorri kicked a corpse over the edge. If they allowed the bodies to accumulate both elf and dwarf would soon be slipping on tainted entrails. Malekith's dragon had not borne them here just to die ignominiously for no purpose.

''Tis thirsty work,' remarked the dwarf in a moment of rare respite. Snorri licked his lips, smiling at the elf prince who hurled his spear into the belly of a bloated troll. Fire ignited along the haft, immolating the beast.

'We'll toast our victory later,' Malekith replied, pointing to the southern edge of the rock where a horde of glaive-wielding beasts had just appeared. It was like an ever-lapping tide, with Snorri and Malekith acting as breakwaters. Horned and cloven-hooved, heat bled off the daemons' muscled bodies in a gory steam. Malign intelligence flickered in their pit-black pupils. It warred with a terrible, consumptive rage.

Attracted by the scent of power emanating from the dwarf and elf, the daemons came on in droves. Eight became sixteen then over twenty as more and more of the daemons wanted to taste the flesh of true heroes. Like sharks drawn to blood, an insatiable hunger motivated them.

'*We are the devourers...*' they said as one in a horrible collision of voices patched together from a thousand different shouts of anger and wrath.

Grinning wickedly they began to circle the lords, beckoning them towards death and damnation with the tips of their hell-blades. Loping between the bloody daemons were brass-collared hounds, bigger and more brutish than any normal canine and with a vaguely reptilian aspect.

In seconds, the edges of the flat rock were festooned with daemons and the lords were surrounded.

Snorri backed up, snarling with wrath palpable enough to make the abominations pause.

'*We shall feast upon your mortal soul...*' promised the daemons. A hound leapt at the dwarf with an echoing roar.

But it would take more than a daemonic dog to fell the High King. 'Then chew on this,' he said. Silver fire flared, too fast to truly see, and the hell-beast was cut in half.

'Tasty?' asked Snorri, brandishing the head of his gore-stained axe at the other monsters.

Three more hounds sprang after the first, but were swiftly struck by a flight of pearlescent arrows. Every shaft was a heart shot.

Snorri only half turned, giving Malekith a sidelong glance.

The elf nodded to the dwarf, lowering his bow and stowing it to draw Avanuir.

'That's a debt I'll have to repay now,' said the High King. Snorri grinned at the elf, showing two rows of crag-like teeth within the forest of his long beard. 'We stand before the world's ending, elfling.'

Malekith gave the dwarf a wry glance, but his attention was partly on the daemons advancing across the Fist of Gron. He lost count after fifty, and was acutely aware he had retreated several paces. Elf and dwarf were almost back to back.

'You sound almost pleased.'

'Aye, think of the saga it will make. Immortality awaits!'

Malekith didn't sound convinced. 'Not if there is no one left alive to write it, and all existence has come to an end.'

'Good point,' the dwarf conceded. 'Let us hope not then.'

Snorri eyed the daemons as he would dung upon his hobnailed boot, swallowing back a bitter taste in his throat at their stench. A cage of iron-hard, blood-red monsters surrounded them and its bars were tightening.

'We need room to fight,' he muttered, then hefted both his rune weapons and beckoned to the daemons. 'Come on then!'

In one gnarled fist the dwarf had a gromril axe, its face etched with three angular runes. In the other he had a hammer, a lightning bolt embossed upon the head in gold. Thick links of gilded mail swathed his broad, muscular body. His arms, dark from the forge and the earth, were bonded with torcs and vambraces. A red, fur-trimmed cloak fell from slab-like shoulders armoured with pauldrons fashioned into the faces of ancestor gods. He wore no helm, for he wanted his enemies to see his fury, but carried a crown upon his brow instead. Runes inscribing every inch of his armour shimmered. Flawless rubies, verdant emeralds and pellucid sapphires studded every ring and bracelet.

I am the High King, they said. *I am Lord of the Dwarfs and my vengeance is terrible. Behold! For your doom has come.*

Snorri beat his chest with a clenched fist.

'Khazuk!'

It was not meant as a challenge, but a death sentence.

The daemons heard neither but attacked as one, hounds and masters both. They were a crimson tide, of rage, hate and a desire to end all things.

Snorri cried out to Malekith as the daemons rushed them, 'Hold on, elfling!' and brought his rune hammer crashing down on the rock with all the potency of a lightning bolt.

Tremors rippled from the point where the dwarf had struck, cracks jagging outwards in an ever-expanding crater of sundered earth. Stone split, sending teeth of razor-edged rock into the daemons, scything into hellish flesh and spilling their tainted ichor.

Malekith was fast as quicksilver, darting between the spears of rock thundering out of the ground, running ahead of the quake. He weaved around the lazy blow of one daemon, severed the head from another. A third he impaled, before swinging the twitching corpse around to bludgeon three more. Destruction from the dwarf's hammer rained around him, but did not touch the elf. Not one scratch.

Avanuir took a heavy toll, almost acting as an extension of the elf's will and fury. Not to be outdone, the dwarf king weighed in with his axe, smashing into anything that had survived his first titanic blow.

Howling, bleating, furious, the daemons were slaughtered.

A heavy pall of dust engulfed the survivors, their balefire eyes the only thing visible at first. The storm presaged a seismic crescendo, an aftershock of power that cast the rest of the bloody daemons back over the edge of the rock. They fell screaming, raging before being dashed to paste or impaled on the upraised blades of the monsters below.

Malekith was crouched down, his head bowed. He held on to his spear haft, using it to anchor him to the rock until the storm had passed. With the tremors fading, he rose to his full height again.

The elf prince was as impressive as the dwarf.

A long coat of ithilmar mail draped his lithe but honed body. Nearly twice as tall as the High King, his face was thin and pale but noble. There was wisdom in his eyes, born of the esteemed bloodline of the greatest *asur*, but coldness too that the dwarf did not fully understand. At times, it bordered on cruelty. Angular, almost almond-shaped, the elf prince's eyes were concealed behind a tall, conical helm that left only his mouth visible. A mane of griffon hair cascaded from the peak and ran the length of Malekith's back.

Snorri was tired. Breathing hard, the dwarf leant his forehead against his hammer's pommel and bent one knee to rest. It was almost genuflection. The oath on his lips had been spoken to Grungni, so it was as if he were praying at the altar of his own rune-crafted hammer.

The hand on his shoulder lifted him, and brought strength back to his weary limbs.

The dust was receding, spiralling away on the hot breeze. But through the slow dispersion of the cloud, claws could be seen and heard reaching for the summit of the rock.

'Relentless bastards, aren't they?' the dwarf remarked, raising his chin.

Malekith pulled his gore-streaked spear from the ground. In his other hand was Avanuir. Although it had reaped many monstrous heads during the battle, the silver sword's blade remained untarnished. Just a part of its magic – along with its brutal killing edge.

'Old friend,' said the elf, 'I think it is almost time for us to depart.' With the spear's tip, he pointed to the battlefield below where their armies warred against the Chaos hosts. Judging by the fury of the unfolding melee, the clash had reached a tipping point.

'Aye, lad, you may be right,' Snorri admitted, deciding to slake his lust for grudgement on the beasts below. Weary, he got to his feet.

Malekith laughed. It was a hollow sound, but had genuine mirth.

'*Lad*, am I? You ever manage to amuse me.'

'*Old*, am I?' Snorri replied, his grin as broad and wide as an axe blade.

Though he was far the younger of the two, an age of living beneath the earth, of sweating in the forges and furnaces of the underdeep, had left the dwarf with skin like baked leather. Unlike the elf, he was not immortal, although relatively long-lived.

'See there?' The elf hastened to the edge of the flat rock, thrusting again with his spear. He kicked at a daemon that had come close to the lip, giving it little thought as it plummeted hundreds of feet to its doom.

Snorri joined him, hacking into the face of another beast that had reached the edge of the Fist. The dwarf followed the elf's pointing spear tip. Crow's feet at the corners of his eyes deepened as he squinted into the fading sun.

'A breach in their lines.'

Through the mad swell, the pitch and yaw of the battle, it was difficult to see at first, but the ranks of the Chaos host had thinned. Where before a seemingly impenetrable tide of monsters had barred the way for the elves and dwarfs to reach the feathered sorcerer and the bloated lord, now there was a gap. A slim gap. A slim hope, but hope it still was.

The dwarf's plan was straightforward. Use them both as bait.

His thane-kings and the other lordlings of the elves too had argued against it but Snorri would not be swayed, nor Malekith who saw its virtues at once. The elf's dragon had brought them high above the battlefield to the Fist of Gron where all the foul daemons of Ruin could see and taste them. Eager to kill the elf prince and the dwarf king, the horde would flock to them, but in their eagerness would leave their daemonic masters less well protected.

'Your ruse has worked, old friend.'

'Of course it worked, I am a dawi!'

Malekith laughed again, but this time it was deep and hearty.

'Fighting at your side, I do not think I have ever been more at peace,' he said, flashing the dwarf a warm smile.

Snorri frowned at him.

'You find your solace in the oddest of places,' he shrugged, 'but then you are an *elgi* and as strange to me as the sky.'

Snorri grew stern. Despite this relative victory, the plan would only succeed if their armies held and could maintain the breach until he and Malekith arrived to lead them. The High King gazed out from the Fist of Gron, trying to gauge how the dwarfs were faring. They were fighting hard, thane-kings leading their warriors from the slopes of the distant mountain into the heart of the daemonic hosts and their beasts. On the vast left flank, lightning speared from runic anvils in their dozens and turned the monsters into ash. Immense pillars of flame rolled out from other runic war engines. Daemons and beasts caught up in the conflagration were swiftly rendered to charred hunks of tainted meat. Earth trembled as runesmiths in their hundreds called forth powerful quakes that opened up great chasms in the ground, swallowing scores of monsters before closing ominously.

Behind the stout phalanxes of dwarf warriors leading the attack, Snorri saw giants. Creations of stone and metal, these ancient golems were slow to rise and quick to slumber. Only the most powerful runelords could rouse them. Like the anvils, they were magical machineries fashioned by the supreme artifice of rune masters. The craft to forge them anew was lost, but the gronti-duraz lived still. It meant 'enduring giant' in the dwarf tongue.

On this great day when elf and dwarf stood together united in purpose, they had woken in their hundreds. The sight brought a tear to the old dwarf king's eye. It was to be their final battle, for the magic to animate them was getting harder and harder to craft, seeping away like a draught through a slowly widening crack.

From the craggy flanks of Karag Vlak a horn blast resounded, seizing the High King's attention. Ballistae gathered in serried ranks turned the air dark with flights of bolts the size of lances. Farther up the mountainside, mangonels and onagers hurled stones. Chunks of rock etched with runes of banishment and daemon-killing crashed and rolled amongst the horde. Beasts and daemons alike were crushed and skewered by the deadly rain pouring from the ranks of war machines.

Though monsters of every stripe had been unleashed against the armies of Snorri and Malekith, it was a plague-ridden tide that faced the dwarfs. Even high above the battlefield, Snorri could see hundreds of horned and hunchbacked daemons. Tallymen, he had heard them named. One-eyed, bloated bellied, the stench of their decaying flesh assailed his nostrils all the way up on the Fist of Gron.

Lesser, maggot-ridden beasts loped alongside them in their thousands. Some had once been men. Slug-like beasts with gaping maws like cages of acidic slime slithered behind them. Daemonic tallymen rode on the backs of the beasts, rusted bells ringing at their shrivelled necks. Diminutive, wide-mouthed daemons, covered in boils and pustules, swarmed like a rancid sea. They gathered at the edges of the horde, giggling like manic children.

'Such horror...' breathed the High King of the dwarfs, knowing even this was not the worst of it. Snorri followed the diseased ranks of the enemy until he saw the bloated lord.

Behind its pestilent legions there loomed a malevolent creature, as cankerous and rotten as its vassals. Clad in rags and strips of flesh, a cloud of flies buzzed around it like a miasma. Tattered wings hung from its emaciated arms and a flock of rotting crows perched on its hulking shoulders, cawing malevolently.

Alkhor, it had named itself. Defiler, it boasted. Tide of Pestilence and Harbinger of Nurgle, it claimed. None of which were its true names, for daemons would never relinquish those.

Disgusted, Snorri saw a throng of warriors attack the beast and his heart swelled with pride. The banner of Thurgin Ironheart fluttered on the breeze. Snorri clenched a fist as a flash of fire tore down the daemon prince's flank. For a moment it burned, and the dwarf dared to hope... But then the rent flesh began to re-knit, hideous slime filling the wound and resealing it.

Alkhor's foul laughter gurgled on the breeze. Its crow host cawed and chattered as a stream of utter foulness retched from the daemon's ugly mouth.

Thurgin and his clansmen were overwhelmed, drowned in a stinking mire of vomit. Dwarf skeletons, half clad in rotting plate and scraps of burned leather, bobbed to the surface of the miasma. Hundreds died in seconds, their gromril armour no defence against Alkhor's disgusting gifts.

'That creature needs sending back to the abyss, as do all its debased kind,' said Malekith.

Deep as an abyssal trench, a roar split the heavens. It brought an answering cry from the elf prince before he declared to the dwarf, 'The war hinges on the next few moments.'

Snorri's jaw clenched. The elf was right.

On the other side of the vast plain, the elves fought a very different foe. Lurid, gibbering creatures cavorted in unruly mobs. Bizarre, floating daemons dressed in skirts of transmuting flesh spat streamers of incandescent fire from their limbs. Feathered beasts, bull-headed monstrosities and hell-spawn wracked with continuous physical change roved next to the daemons.

'They were all once men,' said Snorri, 'the barbarian tribes of the north.'

Malekith looked grim. 'Now they are monsters.'

Overhead, the sun was eclipsed as a massive shadow smothered the light.

Lifting his gaze, the prince of the elves saw a massive host of dragons coursing through the red skies. He longed to join them, his fist clenched as he watched the princes of Caledor and their mounts clash with flights of lesser daemonic creatures.

Amidst the swathe of dragonscale, he saw the smaller forms of eagles circling with the dragons. They picked apart the hellish flocks so the larger beasts could bring their fury to bear on the Chaos infantry. No less proud, the belligerent cries of the eagle riders carried through the battle din to the glittering elven warriors below.

He recognised one of them, noble Prince Aestar. He was keen-eyed and raised a quick salute to his lord, which Malekith returned before turning his gaze on the elven warriors below.

A large phalanx of knights, riding hard alongside scores of chariots, hit a thick wedge of pink, gnarled daemons that blurred and split apart as they were killed. Malekith gaped in disbelief as smaller blue imp-like abominations sprang from the ashes of their larger dead hosts and swarmed over the mounted elves. Victory looked far from certain for the knights, who were on the verge of slowing down and being overwhelmed when a conclave of Sapherian mages riding pillars of storm-cloud rained enchanted death down on the daemons. The creatures squealed in pain and delight, before the knights ended them and the mages flew off to confront a coven of sorcerers riding screaming discs of flame.

It was madness, a desperate struggle where the fates of not just lives but souls were at stake.

'There...' Malekith gestured to the second daemon lord, the feathered sorcerer. 'The creature is drawn into the open at last.'

'Like poison from a wound,' snarled Snorri. 'We must act swiftly,' he said, with half an eye on the edges of the rock where more beasts had begun to appear.

The feathered sorcerer was a creature of mischief and convoluted machination. Though they had never seen its true form, for it wore many, it had chosen an imperious aspect and was swathed in varicoloured flesh-cloth. Beneath its cowl, there was the suggestion of a beak. In one claw the daemon prince clutched a staff of obsidian carved with the faces of the damned. Souls were enslaved within its haft, ever screaming, ever changing as the Architect of Fate moulded them to its will. Unlike Alkhor, it did not attack but merely watched. But as the elves pulled open the threads of its legions, the daemon would soon have to act.

A massive shadow loomed above Malekith, and he averted his gaze from his enemy to crane his neck and search the skies. Something was approaching through the choking cloud, the thump of its wingbeats like peals of thunder.

From below the rock shook, the earth underfoot trembling as if in fear as something massive neared the summit.

'Time to leave,' said the elf.

'I crave a moment longer...' Snorri stared straight ahead at the massive claw that had just reached up over the edge.

After a long climb, a cyclopean brute had gained the Fist of Gron's flat summit.

A second claw joined the first and slowly a massive, tusked head came into view. It snorted, releasing a drool of snot from its blunt, scarred snout. Tiny eyes, hooded by a sloping brow, glinted like rubies shot through with dark veins of anger. Its hide-wrapped chest was brawny and swathed in a thick fur. Scales colonised its abdomen, swallowing muscular forelegs and then back legs as the shaggoth heaved itself up.

'I saw it earlier,' Snorri confessed, 'when we were at the edge together, lingering behind the lesser beasts.'

Malekith had put some distance between them both, so the dwarf had room to fight. He shook his head.

'You were waiting for it, weren't you?'

As if bored with the exchange, the shaggoth bellowed and thumped its chest. It hefted a cleaver as large as a tree in one meaty fist. Plates of armour, shields and pieces of cuirass taken from dead heroes, wrapped its torso. A shoulder guard fashioned from battered war helms hung from strips of sinew lashed around its neck, back and chest.

'Not exactly,' the High King lied.

Snorri swung his rune axe in a practice arc, eyeing with dangerous belligerence the massive brute that had just crested the rock. He had fought one of these creatures before with Malekith at his side. It was many years ago. He had been a younger dwarf then, and his friendship with the elf was in its infancy.

'No, you wanted to kill it,' Malekith protested, circling around to try and reach the monster's blindside.

'Well... it has climbed such a long way to taste the bite of my axe.'

'There'll be plenty for you to kill below. More than enough to satisfy any battle-lust,' the elf reminded him.

'Aye, but I want this one,' said the dwarf, catching the monster's reflection in the blade of his axe.

Scenting blood, the shaggoth threw up its head and roared at the lightning wracking the sky. Its ululating challenge was eclipsed by another as an even larger beast armoured in carmine scales descended on the shaggoth like an owl upon a rat. Hide and metal plate tore open like parchment. Fire spewed from the dragon's jaws in a red conflagration that set hair aflame and sizzled flesh. The shaggoth recoiled in agony, realising the larger monster's dominance, but Malekith's dragon raked it with sword-long claws and clung on. Strips of meat and sinew ripped away from the shaggoth's body as it fought desperately to free itself. A cleaver blow went wild and the dragon chewed off the other monster's arm, releasing a font of spewing gore from the point of dismemberment. Then it bit down on the shaggoth's neck, tore out its throat and the brief one-sided brawl was over.

The slain monster staggered back, not quite realising it was already dead, and fell off the rock to the earth below.

Spreading its wings, the dragon unleashed a deep-throated bellow that prickled the High King's beard.

'No need to shout.'

'Hope there are no hard feelings, old friend,' said the prince with a wicked smile.

Snorri glowered at the beast, but his wolfish grin returned quickly. 'Consider that one I owe,' he said. 'Our friendship is worth more than the stolen scalp of some shaggoth.'

The dragon growled in empathy and Snorri laughed despite the beast's formidable size and presence.

Malekith muttered a heartfelt greeting to his mount that Snorri didn't catch. As he approached where it was perched on the edge of the rock, the dragon lowered its serpentine neck so the prince could stroke it.

Snorri frowned, then sighed. 'Another of your customs I cannot fathom, elfling.'

Ignoring him, Malekith swung up onto the saddle and looked down. 'We've lingered long enough,' he said, nodding towards the smoke-choked battlefield. 'Our warriors have need of us, old friend.'

Through the murk and the carnage, the elves and dwarfs were fighting hard but their strength was finally waning. A last effort, a determined push that looked chaotic from above, widened the fissure in the daemons' ranks a little farther. Beyond it there lurked the lords of the host.

'The sorcerer is mine,' snapped Malekith, before proffering a gauntleted hand to the dwarf.

Snorri declined.

'I can make my own way,' he replied. Sheathing his axe, he began to swing his hammer above his head. The lightning rune engraved upon it started to glow, and the heady aroma of the forge filled the air. 'Step back,' he warned.

Malekith and his beast obliged, watching the hammer's arc grow wider and wider.

The dwarf frowned in consternation.

'Why so grim-faced?' asked the elf prince, as his dragon sent a belt of flame over the north edge of the rock. A cacophony of screeching told them the beasts climbing up it had been destroyed.

'Because I *hate* being storm-borne...'

Snorri smashed the hammer into the earth. A flash of lightning, a dense clap of thunder and the High King was gone, carried off by the power of the hammer's ancient rune magic. Just a patch of scorched earth was left behind, a tiny circle where the dwarf was kneeling.

'Always with another trick beneath your beard, eh, old friend?' Malekith chuckled to himself. 'Ride the lightning,' he whispered, kicking his heels into the dragon's flanks. With a single beat of its huge wings, the elf prince soared skywards. His mount screeched a final curse at the encroaching hordes as they reached the flat summit of the Fist of Gron too late.

Elf and dragon breached cloud and smoke, ascending to the higher heavens. Below, glimpsed through a greying fog, the rock was overrun. Like an anthill swarmed by its denizens, the Fist of Gron was engulfed as a red sea rose up to claim it. The anguished hell-cries of the teeming masses followed him all the way back to the elven battle line.

III

High King Snorri Whitebeard emerged at the edge of the battle through a jagged tear of light. Tendrils of lightning still played across his pauldrons and rivulets of power spilled over his breastplate as the magic he had employed was slow to dissipate.

The cohort of five hundred hearthguard who greeted him tried not to appear shocked at his sudden arrival, for the elder rune on the High King's hammer was slaved to his throne, the earthing point for its magic. Only half hiding his smile, enjoying the little piece of theatre, Snorri ascended the stone steps of the immense throne awaiting him.

An artefact from an ancient age, forged when the ancestor gods still roamed the deeps of the world, the Throne of Power was unique. It bore the Rune of Eternity, believed to have been inscribed upon its high back by Grungni. The dwarf name for it was *Azamar*, a rune so potent that nothing in existence could destroy it.

Fifty paces ahead of the High King were the backs of the gronti-duraz lumbering alongside the warrior clans and brotherhoods. Another hundred paces beyond them were the daemons and one of their masters. Snorri eyed the bloated lord with vengeful relish just as the stone-clad giants began to part, letting him through.

'Thronebearers.' The High King's voice was a deep rumble as he spoke to his retainers. 'Bring me to war.'

'Khazuk!' Grunting with effort, four burly dwarfs lifted king and throne aloft. Singing their deathsongs, they began to march.

The hearthguard fell in beside them. Thanes borne on their own war shields ordered their clansdwarfs to gather around the king's throng as he passed them, flanked on either side by the gronti-duraz. Snorri nodded to them, though the creations of metal and stone could not respond.

Vagrumm, his standard bearer, bellowed above the din of tramping boots and clashing shields to announce him.

'For Karaz-a-Karak! In the name of the ancestors and the High King!'

'Khazuk!' the throng replied.

A last bulwark of mail parted before the High King, the vanguard of the dwarf army hearing their liege-lord's return and rejoicing. Their ranks bowed aside only to reform again behind the hearthguard as slowly they reached the front where the fighting raged.

No sooner had he joined the front, than Snorri was immediately embattled.

A daemonic tallyman flung itself at the High King but was cut in half before it could land a blow. Rotten viscera sizzled on the ground but turned into mist where it touched the Throne of Power, the rune of Azamar flaring brightly. Another daemon was smashed asunder by the thronebearers as they pushed against the horde, trying to throw them back.

Hearthguard were hacking great inroads into the daemonic ranks, whilst the other thane-kings wrought similar carnage on either side of the king's throng.

It was wide, a two-hundred-foot hammer-head driven deep into the heart of the enemy. With Snorri leading them, the dwarf advance was inexorable and devastating. His sheer presence, and the innate resistance of the dwarfs, seemed to drain the creatures of Chaos, and as the fell magic drenching the plain waned, so too did the corporeal bonds binding the lesser daemons to it. Plague-infested corpses began to dissipate, cast back into the Realm of Chaos. Sloughing away, burning down to bone and ash, dissipating into smoke, hundreds of daemons surrendered to instability and were banished.

The tide turned.

Like an armoured plough scything a field of pestilential wheat, the dwarfs slew every Chaos beast that came before them until the High King was face-to-face with the bloated lord himself.

Alkhor chuckled at this reckoning. The bloated lord was many times larger than Snorri and towered over the dwarf until its shadow eclipsed the entire Throne of Power. It seemed to relish the fight to come.

Snorri was only too happy to oblige. Feet braced either side of his ancestral seat, he stood up to level his axe at the daemonic prince.

'Now you are mine.'

IV

Malekith flew low across the daemon ranks, his dragon spitting fire. Since leaving the Fist of Gron, he had made straight for his war host and the feathered sorcerer they fought against.

A hideous clutch of hell-spawned creatures spat tongues of iridescent fire at the elf prince but their aim was poor and he evaded the barrage. Issuing a mewling challenge, half plea, half roar, the beasts snapped their malformed jaws in frustration.

The dragon snarled back, despising the foul stench of the hell-spawn.

'Burn them,' Malekith whispered.

Liquid sulphur drooling from the dragon's snout burst into flame and streaked across the battlefield to engulf the Chaos beasts. They recoiled, reduced to little more than a dark silhouette amidst all the haze and smoke. Against such fury, the spawns' charred remains capitulated into ash. What remained of their mutated bodies sank into a heap.

One of Malekith's lieutenants, Klarond, saluted. They had been struggling against the monstrous spawn until the prince of Nagarythe's timely intervention.

'For Anlec and King Bel Shanaar!' roared Klarond, stabbing his sword into the air. The cheer from his warriors drew a sneer to Malekith's lips which he hid well before soaring back into the sky.

As he ascended he was met by Glarondril of Caledor. A host of dragons circled with the prince, the other nobles of the mountainous realm.

'I see no daemon lord, Malekith,' said Glarondril, an edge to his voice.

Malekith ignored the thinly veiled slight and instead surveyed the battlefield.

'It is here somewhere.'

His eyes narrowed, alighting on the dwarf throng where the king fought his own daemon lord. Many of the hearthguard lay dead around his feet, and one of the king's thronebearers could no longer fight.

Turning his gaze back to the dragon host, Malekith gestured to a trio of eagle riders that had just joined the flight.

'My lords,' he said, recognising again Prince Aestar as he addressed them, and glancing darkly at Glarondril, 'come with me.'

Malekith arrowed out of sight a moment later, piercing the cloud layer in seconds. Avian shrieks behind him told the elf prince that Aestar's eagle lords had followed.

The dwarf king looked beleaguered.

'I am coming,' he said, and urged his dragon to fly faster.

V

Ropes of mucus drooled from the bloated lord's mouth. Its teeth were blackened nubs, rotting in the gum. Its breath was beyond foul, and rose from its maw in a noisome gas the dwarfs fought hard to ignore. Worst of all was the daemon's laughter. A hideous chuckle burbled from its lips, echoed mockingly by the crows perched upon its shoulders and fluttering around its corpse-like body. Alkhor was laughing when its jaw distended to impossibly wide proportions and it unleashed a stream of filth.

Snorri brandished his hammer and a shield of lightning sprang up to protect the king and his charges. The deluge seemed unending, a veritable torrent of puke and acidic bile from the very pit of the daemon's stomach. It spat and crackled like cooking fat against the runic shield, burning to smoke and sulphurous vapour that clung to armour, skin and hair. Merciful Valaya was by Snorri's side, as the foul slop ceased at last and the High King was left alive and miraculously unharmed.

The hearthguard fighting either side of the throne were not so fortunate. Dwarfs died in their droves, their armour melted, skin and bone rendered down to nothing, sloughed away by the disgusting miasma. Above the fading screams the stentorian tones of Haglarr Grudgekeeper, who had served the High King for centuries, could be heard recording each and every name and the reckoning that would follow.

'Heed that, beast,' snarled the High King, 'your infamy shall be remembered. I shall reckon it here and now. You'll burn for this.'

Lashing out savagely, Snorri carved a notch into Alkhor's plague sword. The daemon's bulk belied its swiftness as it parried the High King's axe and the runes upon it flared in anger at this denial of their power. A blow like that should have snapped the daemon sword in two, but the wretched weapon was ensorcelled. Rusted and pitted with serrated teeth, the glaive looked ancient and broken but was far from it. Encrusted with aeons of filth, Snorri knew just by looking at it that the slightest cut from the weapon's blade would fill its victim with a cornucopia of disease. Flesh would blacken, bones would crumble and organs liquefy until all that remained was a soup of corruption.

Seven brave dwarfs had already succumbed to that fate. Many more had been devoured by the daemon, swallowed into its belly. With every morsel, the bloated lord swelled until it had become a behemoth of utter foulness.

Shouting his defiance, Snorri was determined it would grow no further.

A chip of tainted blade came loose like a rotten tooth as the dwarf yanked out his axe. He swung the rune weapon around, circling the plague sword. Snorri went to attack again when an unholy swarm spilled from Alkhor's widening mouth and engulfed him.

Bloated flies, the daemon's host of tiny familiars, crawled over his eyes and armour, and scurried into his beard. They bit his skin, buzzed in his ears. Suffocated, blind, Snorri spat out a wad of insects trying to burrow into his mouth and uttered an invocation.

'*Zharrum!*'

Lightning arced from the haft of his hammer, drawn into a thunderhead that wreathed the king in a furious storm.

A shriek of agony, louder than the storm, split the air. It took a moment for the High King to realise it had come from the fly swarm, speaking with one voice as they burned and died. The enchanted fire had lifted the malaise, and Snorri shook the insects from his beard, brushed them hurriedly from his armour and breathed again.

Alkhor loomed, mocking the dwarf with its gurgling laughter. Its plague sword was raised for a cleaving blow. Blinking away the filth crusting his eyes, Snorri thrust upwards with his rune hammer and crafted a lightning bolt from the storm that speared the daemon's bloated chest.

Mirth became pain, the face of the daemon contorting as rune fire devoured and purified its flesh. It staggered then slumped, legs giving way to agony and bringing it within striking distance of the High King.

'I said you would burn!' Snorri roared, and slashed Alkhor open like a boil.

A slew of foulness erupted from the wound in the daemon's stomach. Half-digested corpses, chunks of armour and cloth, scraps of corroded leather and the remnants of skeletons eroded by the daemon's intestinal acids spilled out.

'Don't touch it,' warned the High King, and his retainers stayed back.

Alkhor staggered again. Unable to regenerate, the daemon clutched its wound, spitting bile and curses at the dwarf who had hurt it. Pathetically, it began to sob.

Unfurled from its back, a pair of tattered fly-like wings started to beat.

But Snorri wasn't finished with it yet.

'Closer, filth,' he growled, stepping down from his throne, 'so I can take your ugly head.'

As Snorri's booted feet hit the ground, Alkhor's sobbing turned into derisive laughter.

'*Foolish little creature*,' it burbled and tugged at the edges of the wound the dwarf had made. From within the rotten ropes of intestine, the sacs of pus and putrefying organs, a welter of tentacles burst forth. One wrapped around the High King's arm, the other pinned his leg. A third quested for his neck but he swatted it with his rune hammer before it could strangle him.

Each of the tentacles was swathed in sharp teeth that champed and gnawed at Snorri's armour. Slowly, they began to drag the dwarf into Alkhor's gaping maw.

Rising in the saddle, Malekith put the bloated lord firmly in his sights – along with Snorri entangled in the daemon's intestines, losing his fight for survival. Malekith was about to even the odds.

Digging his feet into the stirrups arrested the elf's descent and the dragon pulled up sharply, its long neck angling downwards and nostrils flaring. Trails of smoke extruded from the corners of its mouth, carried away on the breeze.

'I hope that armour of yours is as impervious as you claim...'

Inhaling a deep, sulphurous breath, the dragon unleashed fire.

Flames roared hungrily across the daemon's wretched body, burning away pestilence and purging rot. Clods of fat, festering slabs of skin sizzled and spat. Alkhor squealed as the tentacles rippling from its stomach were reduced to charred meat, writhing like headless vipers.

'*Htarken...*' it pleaded, but the feathered sorcerer did not appear.

'So that is your name,' the elf prince muttered.

The daemon pulled away, its tattered wings beating furiously and spewing gouts of filth in its desperate attempt to escape. Slowly, Alkhor began to rise. Its body was still smouldering, shrinking as the dragon fire consumed it.

Snorri swung and missed. He cursed the daemon's cowardice, hurling vengeful insults as it fled.

Malekith flew his dragon low and into the dwarf's eye line.

'Are you hurt, old friend?'

Snorri looked rueful, but otherwise uninjured.

'Only my pride. Killing that thing will salve it.'

A feral smile turned the corners of Malekith's mouth as he set his gaze on the fleeing daemon. Spurring his mount, he was about to pursue when he had to pull up sharply to avoid a burst of incandescent light exploding in front of him. Blinking back the after-flare, the elf saw a figure emerge from the sudden luminance. Clad in varicoloured robes, held aloft on feathered wings, Htarken barred Malekith's path.

The elf reacted as quick as thought but his thrown spear evaporated into mercury before it could impale the daemon. Its outstretched claw and swiftly spoken incantation was enough to destroy the weapon. Htarken returned its talon to the folds of its robes, yet made no motion to attack.

All the while, Alkhor was escaping. Thinking quickly, Malekith turned to the lord of the eagle riders who had just arrived from on high.

'Prince Aestar,' he said, thrusting his sword in the plague daemon's direction, 'slay that thing!'

Nodding grimly, Prince Aestar soared through the clouds after the daemon, his brothers close behind. Malekith was left to face Htarken.

He would not be alone. A conclave of three Sapherian mage lords rose up beside the prince on pillared coruscations of gold.

'You are finished, daemon.' He gestured to the valley below where the hell-hosts were slowly dissipating, their mortal followers fleeing with the dissolution of their immortal allies. 'Chaos has been defeated.'

'*Has it?*' Htarken spoke with a hundred different voices at once. Some were not even voices at all. They were the crackle of fire, the howling of the wind or the breaking of wood. They were cries of slaughter, pleas for mercy and the gibbering laughter of the insane. Birds, beasts, dwarfs and elves all collided in an unsettling union that put the prince's teeth on edge.

Malekith grimaced as the sound of Htarken's 'voice' echoed in his mind. Like a cancer, it sought to take root and destroy him from within.

'*Change,*' said the daemon, with the prince reeling, '*is inevitable. Even with all your many gifts, the heritage of your bloodline, you cannot fight entropy.*'

Malekith wondered why the mages had not yet banished this thing, and then he realised they were transfixed. Seized by a sudden palsy, they trembled as all the horrors of change were visited upon them. As the minds of the mages died, so too did the pillars of fire holding them up.

Htarken had them now, bound to puppet strings. And they danced, they jerked and spasmed until they exploded into transmuted globs of flesh and flailing limbs. They were loremasters of Hoeth and the feathered sorcerer had vanquished them as if they were nothing more than apprentices.

'*Fate is mine to manipulate,*' said the daemon. '*I have seen yours, elf. Would you like to know it?*'

Malekith was about to answer when a terrible pain seized his body. He convulsed, clutched at his skin.

His dragon mewled in fear and confusion.

'I am...' Malekith tore off his helm, ripped at his gorget and cuirass, 'on fire! Isha preserve me!'

'*All endings are known to me. Every skein of destiny is mine to behold. I see past, present and future. Nothing is occluded. Your doom has c–*'

Agony lessened, the fires in the elf's mind faded to embers.

As he opened his eyes, Malekith saw a rune hammer lodged in Htarken's chest. The daemon clutched at it feebly, arrested in its sermonising.

A gruff voice called from below.

'You'll find it hard to speak with dwarf iron in your gut.'

Relief washing over him like a balm with the dissipation of Htarken's sorcery, Malekith nodded to his friend.

Snorri was not done. He outstretched his hand and the hammer's haft began to quiver. As if snared by an invisible anchor the daemon came with it, drawn down by the runecraft of the weapon, unable to remove it from where it had impaled its ribs and chest.

'*I am master of fate...*' Htarken was weakening, his many voices becoming less multitudinous with every foot he descended. '*I see all ends... I see...*'

'Bet you didn't see this, hell-spawn,' Snorri snarled through gritted teeth. The daemon was almost in front of him. He readied his axe in one hand, drew in the hammer with the other.

Htarken was weeping... no, *laughing*. Its spluttering mirth paused for agonised breaths and to spit ichor from its mouth. The hood fell back in its pain-wrecked convulsions, a savage parody of what it had done to the mages, revealing a grotesque bird-headed fiend. Narrow eyes filled with pit-black sclera glared over a hooked beak.

'*I am oracle, architect and thread keeper...*' it gasped, every second bringing it closer to the bite of the dwarf's axe. Htarken coughed, its laughter grew deeper and its struggles ceased. '*Your doom is certain, you and your pathetic races. Chaos has come and already a change is upon you. Feel it warp your bones, the very course of your bloodlines. It will shape the future and I will be there to witness it. Htarken the Everchanging shall stand upon the ashen corpses of you all and exult. Doomed...*' it cawed, eyes widening in a sudden fervour. '*Doomed, doomed, doomed, doom–*'

'Elfling!' Snorri cleaved the raving daemon with his axe as Malekith plunged Avanuir into its heart.

Htarken screamed a thousand times all at once as it was cast back into the abyss. An inner fire consumed it, possessed of chilling heat that made the elf and dwarf recoil.

In a flare of light, the last gasp of a candle flame before its air has run out, Htarken was gone and left only colourful ash motes in its wake.

Malekith felt his heart beating hard in his chest like a drum. His arm was shaking where he held Avanuir and he had to lower it to keep from dropping his sword.

'Isha...' he breathed and turned to the dwarf.

Snorri was on one knee, holding himself up with his axe as his chest and back heaved up and down.

A shaft of sunlight blazed down from the sky, lancing through the bloody cloud that was slowly turning back to white. Snorri looked up into it and let the warmth bathe his face.

Malekith took off his helm to wipe the sweat from his brow. He smiled. Snorri was nodding.

'Good,' he said, licking the dryness from his lips.

With their leaders banished or fled, the hell-hosts were dying. The lesser daemons were gone, the beasts and thralls were slowly being destroyed by the triumphant armies of the elves and dwarfs.

Snorri sighed as if a heavy burden had been removed from his shoulders and tramped wearily up the stone steps of his throne where he sat down heavily.

'Thus ends the threat of Chaos to the Old World,' he said. 'We have followed in the footsteps of our ancestors, of Grimnir and Grungni and Valaya.'

'Of my father Aenarion and Caledor Dragontamer,' said Malekith as his dragon bowed low to let him leap from the saddle and be at the dwarf's side.

They stood shoulder to shoulder, the lords who had challenged darkness and cast it back to hell.

'You look tired,' said the elf.

Snorri slumped against the throne.

'I am.'

Still clutched in one hand, his rune hammer drooled black smoke from a cleft in its head. Malekith knew the weapon's name was *Angazuf*, which Snorri had told him meant 'sky iron'. In banishing the daemon it had been ruined.

Snorri looked sad to see its runic strength diminish; the hammer was older than some hold halls.

'What else has been lost to this fight, I wonder?' he uttered, suddenly melancholy.

Around them the battle was ending. With the defeat of the Chaos hordes, order was returning. Life would return in time, but this would forever be a tainted place. For the touch of Chaos is a permanent taint that cannot ever be entirely removed.

Above them, Karag Vlak was quiescent, its anger spent like that of the dwarf king.

Around the mountain and before it, elves and dwarfs lay dead in their thousands.

But it was for his friend that Malekith's eyes betrayed the most concern.

There was rheum around Snorri's eyes. Age lines threaded his face, gnarled skin and lesions showed on his hands. Like his rune hammer, he was broken. The elf wondered just how much this last fight had taken out of the dwarf, how badly Alkhor had really wounded him.

'Don't look so afraid, I am not dead yet,' growled the king.

Silent as statues, his thronebearers and hearthguard were grim-faced.

Malekith smiled, though it was affected with melancholy. He looked around at the battlefield, at the dying and the dead.

'We have paid a great price for this,' said the elf, finally answering the dwarf's question. 'Here we witness the passing of a golden age, I fear.'

He watched the elves and dwarfs as they fought together to cleanse the battlefield of the last remnants of resistance. Some had already begun to celebrate victory together and exchanged tokens and talismans. For many, it would be the last time they would see one another.

So different and yet common purpose had formed a strong bond.

'But perhaps we can usher in a new one. Either way, let us hope this is an end to hell and darkness.' He added, without conviction, 'To war and death.'

'Aye,' Snorri agreed, 'it is the province of more youthful kings, I think.'

Malekith nodded, lost in introspection.

'I had expected more joy, elfling,' said the dwarf. He leaned forwards to clap Malekith's armoured shoulder. 'And you say that we are dour.'

The elf laughed, but his eyes were far away.

'We should feast,' he said at last, returning to the present and leaving his troubles for now, 'and honour this triumph.'

'Back at Karaz-a-Karak, we will do just that, young elfling.' Some colour had returned to the dwarf's cheeks at the prospect of beer and meat. 'And yet you still seem moribund. What is it, Malekith? What ails you?'

'Nothing...' The elf's eyes were fixed again on a dark horizon, his mind on the remembered fire that had ravaged his body. It felt familiar somehow. 'Nothing, Snorri,' he said again, more lucidly. 'It can wait. It can certainly wait.'

ONE

RAT CATCHING

The tunnel was dank and reeked of mould. Darkness thicker than pitch was threaded with the sound of hidden, chittering things. Far from the heat of the forges, here in the lost corridors of the underway, monsters roamed. Or so Snorri hoped.

'Bring it closer, cousin. I caught a whiff of their stink up ahead.'

Morgrim held the lantern up higher. Its light threw clawing shadows across the walls, illuminating old waymarker runes that had long since fallen into disrepair.

'Karak Krum,' uttered the older dwarf, his face framed in the light. A ruddy orange glow limned his black beard, making it look as if it were on fire. 'The dwarfs there are long since dead, cousin. No one has ventured this deep into the Ungdrin Ankor for many, many years.'

Snorri squinted as he looked at Morgrim over his shoulder.

'Scared, are you? Thought you Bargrums had spines of iron, cousin.'

Morgrim bristled. 'Aye, we do!' he said, a little too loudly.

Two dwarfs, standing alone in a sea of black with but a small corona of lamplight to enfold them, waited. After what felt like an age, the echo of Morgrim's truculence subsided and he added, 'I am not scared, cousin, merely thinking aloud.'

Snorri snorted.

'And who do you think you are, oh brave and mighty dawi, Snorri Whitebeard reborn?' said Morgrim. 'You have his name but not his deeds, cousin.'

'Not yet,' Snorri retorted with typical stoicism.

Grumbling under his breath, Morgrim traced the runic inscription of the waymarker with a leathern hand. There was dirt under the nails and rough calluses on the palms earned from hours spent in the forge. 'Don't you wonder what happened to them?'

'Who?'

'The dawi of Karak Krum.'

'Either dead or gone. You think far too much, and act far too little,' said Snorri, eyes front and returning to the hunt. 'Here, look, some of their dung.'

He pointed to a piled of noisome droppings a few inches from his booted foot.

Wrinkling his nose, Morgrim scowled. 'The reek of it,' he said. 'Like no rat I have ever smelled.'

Snorri unhitched his axe from the sheath on his back. He also carried a dagger at his waist and kept it close to hand too. Narrow though it was, he didn't want to be caught in the tunnel's bottleneck unarmed.

'Make a point of sniffing rats, do you, cousin?' he laughed.

Morgrim didn't answer. He glanced one last time at the runic marker describing the way to Karak Krum. Passed away or simply moved on when the seams of gold and gems had run dry, dwarfs no longer walked its halls, the forges were silent. Merchants and reckoners from Karaz-a-Karak had brought tales of a glowing rock discovered by the miners of Krum. It had happened centuries ago, the story passed down by his father and his father before him. It was little more than myth now but the stark evidence of the ancient hold's demise was still very real. Morgrim wondered what would happen if the same fate ever befell Karaz-a-Karak.

Snorri snapped him out of his bleak reverie.

'More light! This way, cousin.'

'I hear something...' Morgrim thumbed the buckle loose on his hammer's thong and took its haft. Leather creaked in the dwarf's grip.

From up ahead there emanated a scratching, chittering noise. It sounded almost like speech, except for the fact that both Morgrim and Snorri knew that rats could do no such thing.

Morgrim turned his head, strained his ear. '*Grobi*?'

'This deep?'

In this part of the underway, the tunnel was low and cramped as if it hadn't been hewn by dwarfs at all. Such a thing was impossible, wasn't it? Only dwarfs could dig the roads of the Ungdrin Ankor that connected all the holds of the Worlds Edge Mountains and beyond. And yet...

'A troll, then?'

Snorri looked back briefly. 'One that talks to itself?'

'I once encountered a troll with two heads that talked to itself, cousin.'

Snorri shot Morgrim a dubious look.

'No. Doesn't smell right. Can tell a troll from a mile away. Its breath is like a latrine married to an abattoir.'

'Reminds me of Uncle Fugri's *gruntis*.'

Snorri laughed, and they moved on.

A larger cavern loomed ahead of the dwarfs, unseen but with the shape and angle of the opening suggesting a widening threshold, the scent of air and rat together with the sound-echo hinting at a vaulted ceiling. Dwarfs knew rock. They knew it because it was under their nails, on their tongues, in their blood and ever surrounded them.

It was not merely a cavern ahead of the two dwarfs, where the tunnel met its end. It was large and it was a warren infested with rats.

Snorri could hardly contain his excitement.

'Are you ready, cousin?' He brought up his axe level with his chest and clutched it two-handed. There was a spike on the end of it that could be used for thrusting, a useful weapon in a tight corner. For the last mile the dwarfs had been forced to stoop, and the prospect of standing straight was abruptly appealing. At least, it was to Morgrim.

'As ready as I was when you defied your father's wishes, slipped your retainers and dragged me along on this rat hunt.'

'See,' Snorri explained, inching closer to the cavern entrance, 'that's what I like about you, Morgrim. Always so enthusiastic.'

Snorri touched a finger to the talisman around his neck, muttered, 'Grungni...' and peered around the edge of the tunnel.

Several large rats were gathered in the middle of a vaulted chamber. It might once have been the old entry hall to Karak Krum. Gnawing frantically at something, chattering to one another in high-pitched squeaks and squeals, the creatures seemed oblivious to the presence of the dwarfs.

'Are they wearing rags?' Morgrim was so incredulous he shone the lantern closer.

'*Hsst!*' Snorri hissed, scowling at his cousin. 'Douse the light!'

Too late, Morgrim shuttered the lantern.

One of the rats looked up from its feast, fragments of calcified bone flaking from its maw as it screeched a warning to its brethren.

As one the others turned, snarling and exposing yellowed fangs dripping hungrily with saliva.

Snorri roared, swinging his axe around in a double-handed arc.

'Grungni!'

The first rat fell decapitated as it lunged for the dwarf, its head bouncing off the slabbed floor and rolling into a corner. At the chamber's edges it was dark, so dark the dwarfs could not see much farther than the glow of the lantern.

Snorri cut open a second, splitting it from groin to sternum and spilling its foul innards, before Morgrim crushed a third with his hammer. He battered a fourth with a swing of the lantern, the stink of the rat's burning fur enough to make him gag as it recoiled and died.

'Two apiece!' Snorri was grinning wildly, his perfect white teeth like a row of locked shields in his mouth, framed by a blond beard. The heritage of his ancestors was evident in the sapphire blue of his eyes, his regal bearing and confidence. He was prince of the dwarf realm in every way.

Morgrim was less enthused. He was looking into the shadows at the edge of the chamber. It was definitely the old entry hall to Karak Krum.

Mildewed wood from thrones and tables littered the floor and a pair of statues venerating the lord and lady of the hold sat in cobwebbed alcoves against the east and west walls, facing one another. Sconces, denuded of their torches, sat beneath the statues, intended to illuminate them and the chamber. They were all that stood out at the periphery of the hall, except for the glinting rubies now floating in the darkness.

Morgrim cast the lantern into the middle of the chamber where it broke apart and flooded the area around it with firelight. Scattered embers and the slew of ignited oil illuminated a truth that Morgrim was aware of even before he had unhitched his shield.

'More of them, cousin.' He backed up, casting his gaze around.

Snorri's bright eyes flashed eagerly. 'A lot more.'

The dwarfs were surrounded as a score of rats crawled from the darkness, chittering and squeaking. To Morgrim's ears it could have been laughter. 'Are they mocking us?'

Snorri brandished his axe in challenge. 'Not for long, cousin.'

His next blow cleaved a skull in two, the second caving a chest as the rat reared up at him. Snorri killed a third with a thrown dagger before something leapt onto his back and put him on one knee.

'*Gnhhh...* Cousin!'

Morgrim finished one off with a hammer blow to the jaw, and broke its back as it fell mewling. He then kicked ash from the sundered lantern in the snout of another, before using his shield to batter the rat that was clawing and biting at Snorri's back.

Scurrying and scratching rose above the din of blades and bludgeons hitting flesh, the squeals of dying rats.

'Bloody vermin,' Snorri raged, throwing another rat off his arm before it could sink its teeth in.

A score had become two score in a matter of minutes.

Morgrim smashed two rats down with his shield, staved in the head of a third with his hammer. 'There are too many. And big, much bigger than any rat I've ever seen.'

'Nonsense,' Snorri chided. 'They are just rats, cousin. Vermin do not rule the underway, we dawi are its kings and masters.'

Despite his bullishness, the prince of Karaz-a-Karak was breathing hard. Sweat lapped his brow, and shone like pearls on his beard.

'We must go back, get to the tunnel,' said Morgrim. 'Fight them one at a time.' He was making for the cavern entrance from whence the dwarfs had first come, but it was thronged with the creatures. A mass of furry bodies stood between them and the relative safety of the tunnel.

'We can kill them, Morgrim. They're only rats.'

But they were not, not really, and Snorri knew it even if he would not admit this to his cousin. Something flashed in the half-light from the slowly fading lantern that looked like a hook or cleaver, possibly a knife. It could not have been armour, nor the studs on a leather jerkin – rats did not wear armour, or carry weapons. But they were hunched, broad shouldered in some instances, and some went on two legs, not four. Did one have a beard?

'The way back is barred, we must go forwards,' said Morgrim, the urgency in his tone revealing just how dire he thought the situation to be.

Reluctantly, Snorri nodded.

The two dwarfs were back to back, almost encircled by rats. Eyes like wet rubies flashed hungrily. The stink of wet fur and charnel breath washed over them in a thick fug. Chittering and squeaking wore at the nerves like a blunt blade working to sever a rope.

'Remember Thurbad's lessons?' Snorri asked. A slash to his cheek made him grimace but he cut down the rat who did it. 'Little bastard, that was a knife!'

Morgrim's voice suggested he was in no mood for an exam.

'Which one, cousin? There are many.' He kept the rats at bay with his shield, thrusting it against the press of furred bodies trying to overwhelm him. His hammer was slick with gore and he had to concentrate to maintain his grip, thankful for the leather-bound haft.

'Choose your battlefield wisely.'

'Our current situation would suggest we did not listen very well to that particular lesson, cousin.'

Snorri grunted as he killed another rat. Dwarfs were strong, especially those that descended from the bloodline of kings, but even the prince's fortitude was waning.

'We can't fight a horde like this in the open,' he said, swiping up a piece of broken wood with his off hand.

Morgrim was trying not to get his face bitten off when he said, 'And you could not have thought of this *before* we were surrounded?'

'Now is hardly time for recriminations, cousin. Do you have any more oil for that lantern?' he asked, preventing any reply from Morgrim who didn't bother to hide his exasperation.

'A flask.'

'Smash it.'

'What?'

Each reply was bookended by grunts and squeaks, the swing and thud of metal.

'Smash it, cousin. There.' Snorri pointed. 'Next to the stairway.'

'What stairway? I can see no–'

'Are you blind, cousin? There, to your left.'

Morgrim saw it, a set of stone steps leading further into darkness. The prospect was not an inviting one.

Snorri was still pointing with the piece of wood. 'We can – *arrrggh!*'

Morgrim dared not turn, but the sound of his cousin's pain made him desperately want to.

'Snorri?!'

'*Thagging* rat bit off my fingers… Throw the *chuffing* flask, Morgrim!'

It was risky to stow his hammer, but Morgrim did so to take the flask of oil from his belt and toss it. The heavy flask sloshed as it arced over the bobbing rat heads and smashed behind them in a scattering of oil and clay fragments.

Despite his wounding, Snorri still clutched the piece of wood in his maimed hand and thrust it into the dying embers of the lantern fire the dwarfs had rallied next to. Dried out from the many centuries down in the abandoned hall, it flared quickly, a spattering of spilled oil and the moth-eaten rag still attached to it adding to its flammability.

Snorri didn't hesitate – his grip was already failing – and hurled the firebrand into the expanding pool of oil. It went up with a loud, incendiary *whoosh*, throwing back the rats clustered around it. Clutching their eyes, they squealed and recoiled, opening a path to the stairway.

Once he was sure his cousin was behind him, Morgrim was running. He didn't bother to pull his hammer, and even threw his shield into the furred ranks of the rats to buy some precious time to flee. Snorri outstripped him for pace, his armour lighter and more finely crafted, and he reached the stairway ahead of Morgrim.

'Down!' shouted Snorri.

Still running, Morgrim replied, 'What if the way isn't clear?'

'Then we're both dead. Come on!'

The dwarfs plunged headlong down the stone steps, heedless of the way ahead, the way behind bracketed by flames. As swiftly as it had caught light, the lantern oil burned away and went from a bonfire to a flicker in moments.

The rats were quick to pursue.

Halfway down the stairs, which were broad and long, Snorri pointed with his maimed hand. Even in the semi-darkness, Morgrim could see he had lost one and a half fingers to the rat bite.

'A door, cousin!'

It was wood, probably wutroth to have endured all the years intact and bereft of worm-rot. Iron-banded, studs in the metal that ran in thick strips down its length, it looked stout. Robust enough to hold back a swarm of giant rats, even rats that wore armour and carried blades.

Snorri slammed against it, grunting again; the door was as formidable as the dwarfs had hoped. Morgrim helped him push it open, on reluctant, grinding hinges.

The rats were but a few paces away when the dwarfs squeezed through the narrow gap they had made and shut the door from the other side.

'Hold it!' snapped Snorri, and Morgrim braced the door with his shoulder as the rats crashed against it. He could hear their scratching, the enraged squeals and the squeaks of annoyance that could not have been a language, for rats do not converse with one another. Frantic thudding from the other side of the door made him a little anxious, especially as he couldn't see Snorri any more.

'Cousin, if you've left me here to brace this door alone, I swear to Grimnir I'll–'

Carrying a broad wooden brace, Snorri slammed it down onto the iron clasps on either side of the doorway.

'You'll what?' he asked, catching his breath and wiping sweat from his glistening forehead.

Off to seek easier pickings elsewhere, the din from the rats was receding. Snorri smiled in the face of his cousin's thunderous expression.

After a few moments, Morgrim smiled too and the pair of them were laughing raucously, huge hearty belly laughs that carried far into the underdeep.

'*Shhh!* We will rouse an army of grobi, cousin...' Morgrim was wiping the tears from his eyes as his composure slowly returned.

'Then we'll fight them too! Ha! Aye, you're probably right.' Snorri sniggered, the last dregs of merriment leaving him. Wincing, he looked down at his hand and became abruptly sober. 'Bloody vermin.'

'I have never seen the like,' Morgrim confessed. He pulled a kerchief from a pouch upon his belt.

Snorri frowned at it. 'What's that for, dabbing your nose when you get a bit of soot on it? Are you turning into an *ufdi*?'

Morgrim's already ruddy cheeks reddened further. "Tis a cloth,' he protested, 'for cleaning weapons.'

'Of course it is,' Snorri muttered as his cousin proceeded to wrap it around his bleeding hand. His smirk became a grimace as Morgrim tied the cloth a little tighter than necessary.

'For now, it will suffice as a bandage,' he said. He looked at the dark stain that was already blossoming red all over the kerchief. 'It's a savage bite.'

'Aye,' Snorri agreed ruefully. 'I've half a mind go back in there and retrieve my fingers from its belly.'

'Bet you would as well.' Morgrim was exploring their surroundings, looking for a way onwards and preferably back to a part of the underway they knew. 'That *would* be half-minded,' he mumbled, attention divided. 'Ha, ha!' he laughed, turning to face his cousin. 'Half a mind, to go with half a hand.'

Snorri scowled. 'Very funny. Haven't you found a way out of here yet?'

'There's a breeze...' Morgrim sniffed, venturing forwards. Without the lantern, even with the sharp eyes of a dwarf, the darkness was blinding. 'Coming from somewhere–'

Splintering rock, a loud *smack* of something heavy hitting stone and then a grunt arrested Morgrim's reply.

It took Snorri a few moments to realise this *was* Morgrim and his cousin had fallen into some unseen crevasse.

'Cousin, are you hurt?' he called, only for the darkness to echo his words back at him. 'Where are–'

Hard, unyielding stone rushed up to meet him as Snorri slipped on the same scree that had upended Morgrim. Daggers of hot pain pierced his back as he went down and he cracked his skull before the ground slid from under him and he fell.

Another thud of stone hitting flesh, this time his, like a battering ram against a postern gate. He felt it all the way up his spine and his left shoulder.

Groaning, Snorri rolled onto his right side and saw Morgrim looking back at him with the same grimace.

'That bloody hurt,' he said.

Morgrim eased onto his back, looked up at the gaping crevasse above. Dust motes and chunks of grit were spilling down from above like rain.

'Must have fallen thirty, forty feet.'

He pushed himself up into a sitting position.

'Feels like a hundred.' Snorri was on his back, rubbing his swollen head.

'Nothing to damage there,' said Morgrim. He tapped the helmet he wore. A pair of horns spiralled from the temples and a studded guard sat snug against the dwarf's bulbous nose. 'Should wear one of these.'

'Makes you bald,' Snorri replied, prompting a worried look on his cousin's face. A small stone struck Snorri's brow and he grimaced again.

'See,' said Morgrim, getting to his feet and helping his cousin up. 'Enough lying down.' Once Snorri was vertical again, he brushed the dirt off his armour and checked he still had his hammer. 'We need a way out.'

Without the lantern, it was hard to discern exactly where they had fallen. Doubtless it was one of the lower clan halls of Karak Krum, but there was precious little evidence of that visible in the shadows that clung to the place like fog.

Snorri sucked his teeth.

'A pity you chucked our lantern oil.'

Morgrim bit his tongue to stop from swearing. Instead he looked around, sniffed at the air. 'I smell soot,' he said after a minute or so, then licked his lips. Another short pause. 'Definitely soot.'

Snorri frowned, and went to recover his axe from where he'd dropped it when he fell. 'All I can smell and taste is grit.' He spat out a wad of dirt, hacking up a chunk of phlegm at the same time. 'And rat,' he added.

Morgrim's face darkened. 'No rat I have ever encountered spoke or carried a blade.'

'That is because rats can't do such things.' Snorri tapped him on the forehead and made a face. 'Perhaps you need a tougher war helm, cousin.'

Morgrim wasn't about to be mollified. 'I know what I saw and heard.' His face grew stern, serious. 'So do you. There is more than grobi and *urk* in these old tunnels. Who can say what beasts have risen in the dark beneath the world?'

Snorri had no answer to that. He hefted his axe and gestured roughly north. Even when lost, if a dwarf is underground his sense of direction is usually infallible.

'Nose is telling me it's that way.'

'What is?' asked Morgrim, though his cousin was already moving.

'Something other than this thrice-cursed darkness.' He paused. 'And your talking bloody rats,' he added, before stomping off.

Groaning under his breath, Morgrim followed.

◀ TWO ▶

WHISPERS IN THE DARK

Snorri and Morgrim knew there was something in the Ungdrin Ankor, vermin maybe, but definitely an enemy the dwarfs had not faced before. Tales abounded, they always did, told by drunken treasure hunters. Few dwarfs, barring the credulous and the gullible, beardlings in the main, believed such tall stories. But myths made flesh were hard to refute. Morgrim was reminded again of the stories of his father, of the glowing rock unearthed by Karak Krum's miners. He brought to mind the faces of the savage creatures they had just escaped and decided there was something alarmingly familiar about them.

The two dwarfs spent the next few minutes in silence, listening for any sign of the rats' return.

After passing through a vast open cavern, its narrow stone bridge spanning a bottomless pit and its ceiling stretching into darkness, Morgrim asked, 'How is your hand, cousin?'

Snorri kept it close to his chest, taking the axe one-handed as he walked. Blood stained the metal links of his armour where it had bled through the makeshift bandage. Regarding the wound, he sneered, 'Think you need thicker pampering cloths.'

Morgrim ignored the gibe, reading the pain etched on his cousin's face. 'Looks in need of a redress.'

They had left behind the chasm chamber with its narrow, precipitous span and walked a long gallery with a high ceiling. Errant shafts of light cast grainy spears in the darkness from clutches of *brynduraz*. Such a rare mineral was worthy of mining and Morgrim had wondered then whether the clans of Karak Krum had left willingly – or moved at all. Long stalactites dripping with moisture that reflected the brightstone made the dwarfs duck occasionally, and a chill gave the air a bite.

'Hurts like Helda just sat on it wearing full armour,' Snorri complained, wincing as the ruddy cloth was re-tightened.

Morgrim laughed out loud.

Helda was one of many would-be consorts that Snorri's father had attempted to *arrange* for the young prince. She was of good stock, *too* good in Snorri's opinion given her impressive girth. A dwarf lord was said to be worthy to marry a *rinn* if his beard could wrap around her ample bosom at least once. Snorri doubted Helda would ever find a mate able to achieve that feat. If she did it would be a longbeard and past the age when siring an heir was amongst the dwarf's concerns. In fact, one night with Helda would likely test the poor sod.

Her father, the King of Karak Kadrin, was a strong ally of Karaz-a-Karak and had offered a sizeable dowry from his personal coffers to secure the union but Snorri had objected and then declined. Comely as she was, he had no desire to bed such a walrus and continue the Lunngrin bloodline. Besides, he had eyes for another.

'She was a broad girl,' admitted Morgrim, wiping tears from his eyes as he finished binding the wound anew.

'As an alehouse, cousin.'

'And a face like a troll.'

'Trolls are prettier.'

Morgrim was holding on to his sides, which had begun to pain him, when he saw the light. It was faint, like a distant fire or a partly shuttered lantern.

And it was moving.

'Hide!' he hissed. Both dwarfs moved to the opposite edges of the gallery and hugged the walls.

Snorri gestured silently to his cousin, asking him what he had seen.

Morgrim nodded to the lambent glow in the distance. The reek of soot had grown stronger too.

Dawi? Snorri mouthed.

Morgrim shook his head.

Not this deep.

Karak Krum was a tomb in all but name. It only harboured creatures and revenants now. It fell to the dwarfs to find out which this one was.

The blade of Snorri's axe caught in the light from the brightstone, signalling his intention.

Nodding slowly, Morgrim drew his hammer and followed his cousin as he crept along the opposite side of the gallery. All the while the patch of light bobbed and swayed, but never got any closer. Tales were often told to scare beardlings of cavern lamps or *uzkuzharr*, the 'dead fires' of dwarfs long passed who were slain in anger or because of misfortune. Such unquiet spirits did not dwell with the ancestors, nor did they eat at Grungni's table, but were destined to walk the dwarf underworld. Jealous of the living, they would lure young or foolish dwarfs to their deaths, drawing them on with their light and their promises of gold. Often these dwarfs were found at the bottom of chasms or crushed to death under a rock fall.

Snorri and Morgrim knew the stories, they had been told them too during infancy, but now they were faced with such an apparition made real. The dwarfs kept it in their eye line at all times, using the eroded columns at the sides of the tunnel that held up the ceiling to hide behind. The tunnel led them to another room. It was small and had once possessed a door, which stood no longer. Only rusted hinges and wooden scraps clung to the frame.

It was a temple, obvious from the icon of Grungni carved into the wall, and had no other visible exits. A figure clad in a simple tunic, hose and chainmail was kneeling down inside. Old, if the bald pate and greying locks were anything to go by, he was muttering whilst casting rune stones onto the ground in front of him. A lantern was strapped to his back via some leather and metal contrivance and shone brightly without need of a flame. Its light gave him an unearthly lustre. Seen side on, he appeared to be conversing quietly with someone out of view.

Snorri mouthed, *Not alone*, and the two dwarfs crept closer until they could hear what the old dwarf was saying.

'*Dreng tromak, uzkul un dum?*' the old dwarf asked. 'Are you sure? Nah, cannot be that.' His low, sonorous tones made Snorri think of slowly tumbling rock.

'*What?*' Morgrim hissed, but Snorri pressed his finger to his mouth to silence him.

Casting the stones again, the old dwarf muttered, '*Dawi barazen ek dreng drakk, un riknu...*' It was Khazalid, the language of the dwarfs, but archaic to the point where it was almost incomprehensible. 'Not what I was expecting,' he said, looking up at his companion, who was still obscured from sight. 'Any ideas?'

Morgrim had reached the very edge of the temple and gestured to the old dwarf's 'companion'.

It was a stone statue of Grungni.

'He's mad,' hissed Morgrim, frowning.

Snorri nodded. He recognised some of the old dwarf's words, which now seemed prompted by their arrival. *Death* and *doom*, he knew. Also there was *destiny* and *king*.

Uzkuzharr lure their victims with promises, and their malice is as old as the earth, the words of his mentors returned to him.

'*Uzkul un dum.*' The old dwarf nudged a rune stone with his knuckle, arranging it above another. '*Dreng drakk... riknu...*'

The markings were ancient, wrought from chisel-tongue and hard to define.

Suddenly, the old dwarf turned, fixing them with a narrowed eye.

'I see a dragon slayer in my presence,' said the old dwarf, reverting to more common Khazalid. 'One destined to become king.' His eyes were slightly glazed, as if perhaps he was still unaware of their presence.

'Ears like a bat!' hissed Morgrim, hammer held ready.

Hackles rose on the back of Snorri's neck. His tongue felt leaden, and he tasted sulphur. He hefted his axe in two hands, glad when his voice didn't quaver. 'Stand, creature. Make yourself known.'

In the glow of the lantern, the strange dwarf looked almost hewn from stone, no different to the statues of Karak Krum's fallen king and queen. Snorri had heard Morek the runesmith speak in whispers of dwarfs that dabbled in magic, the wild unpredictable kind not bound to metal, of the slow petrification of their bodies and the cruelty it bred into their souls.

Not all dwarfs honoured the ancestors any more. Not since the Coming of Chaos in the elder days. Snorri knew his history, of legends about clans that fled the Worlds Edge Mountains to a land of everlasting fire and who swore fealty to a different god entirely, a father of darkness.

No dwarf in their right mind would venture this deep alone. Snorri and Morgrim were only there by misadventure, but the old dwarf had clearly come here deliberately. Perhaps he sought to profane the temple. Perhaps it was not a dwarf at all but some unquiet spirit of the lost dwarfs of Karak Krum.

Snorri's skin felt suddenly cold and he suppressed a shiver. He edged forwards, caught a reassuring glance from Morgrim who was just behind him.

Axe at the ready, Snorri called out, 'I said, rise and make yourself known. You are in the presence of the prince of Karaz-a-Karak.'

'I see a great destiny,' said the old dwarf, both cousins in his sight but looking right through them. 'A king one day.'

Snorri partly lowered his axe without thinking. Another step brought him within a few short feet of the old dwarf.

He uttered a choked rasp.

'*My* destiny? King?' The desire in his eyes and his tone betrayed him.

'One who will lift the great doom of our race, he who will slay the drakk...' said the old dwarf, half lost in his prophetic reverie and, muttering the last part. '*Elgidum...*'

'Drakk?' Snorri's axe went up again. 'What drakk, old one? Is there a beast in these tunnels?' He glanced around, nervously. Morgrim did the same.

'I see nothing, cousin,' he hissed, but was deathly pale and clutched his hammer tightly.

Anger burned away Snorri's fear like fire banishes ice, and he returned to the old dwarf.

'Who are you? Speak now or I will–'

'You will what, brave prince?' asked the old dwarf, regarding him properly for the first time, groaning in protest as he struggled to his feet in the light. 'Kneeling is a young dwarf's game,' he mumbled under his breath. 'Would you stab an unarmed dawi, then?'

Like a veil had lifted from his eyes, Snorri balked as he recognised Ranuld Silverthumb, Runelord of Karaz-a-Karak and part of the High King's Council.

'Lord Silverthumb, I...' He kneeled, bowed his head.

So did Morgrim, who caught a flash of azure fire in the runelord's eyes before he looked down.

Ranuld sighed wearily. 'Arise, I have no desire to strain my neck and back further by looking down on you pair of *wazzocks*.' He scowled at the two dwarfs who got up apologetically. 'And sheathe your weapons,' snapped the runelord. 'Did you think me one of the *dawi zharr*, mayhap? Or an *uzkular*? Ha, ha, ha!' Ranuld laughed loudly and derisively, muttering, 'Wazzocks.'

Snorri flushed bright crimson and fought the urge to hide his face.

'What was that prophecy you spoke of?' he asked.

Lord Silverthumb grew angry, annoyed. 'Not for ears the likes of yours!' he snapped, and a shadow seemed to pass across his face. Snorri thought it looked like concern, but the runesmith was quick to recover and wagged a finger at them both.

'Choose your own fate. Make your own. Destiny is just about picking a path then walking it.'

Shaking his head, Morgrim asked, 'What are you doing down here in these ruins, lord? It's perilous to venture here alone.'

Ranuld gaped in sudden surprise, glancing around in mock panic.

'Danger is there?' he asked. 'From what, I dread to know? Might I be stabbed in the back by my own kith and kin?' He scowled again, his face wrinkling like old leather, and sneered scornfully. 'I came here in search of magic, if you must know.'

The look of incredulity on Morgrim's face only deepened.

Snorri was also perplexed, his silence inviting further explanation.

Ranuld raised a feathery eyebrow, like a snowfall upon the crag of his brow. 'And you two are supposedly from the blood of kings. Bah!' He stooped to retrieve his rune stones, chuntering about the thinning of dwarf stock and the dubious practice of *krutting*, when one consorts with a goat.

Snorri got over his awe quickly. 'What do you mean? How can you simply *look* for magic? It isn't like a lost axe or helmet. It can't be touched.'

Ranuld looked up wryly as he put the last of his rune stones into a leather pouch and drew its string taut. 'Can't it? Can't you?' Straightening up, grimacing as his back cracked, he jabbed a gnarled finger at the prince like it was a knife.

'I am... um–'

'No lad, you are Snorri, son of Gotrek, so named for the Whitebeard whose boots your beardling feet are unworthy of, let alone his name. I do not know who *um* is.'

Snorri bit back his anger. He had stowed his axe, but clenched his fists.

'Venerable one,' Morgrim stepped in calmly, 'we are not as wise as you–'

'But have a gift for stating what is obvious,' Ranuld interrupted, turning his back on them and taking a knee before the shrine. 'Never any peace,' he grumbled beneath his breath, 'even in lost years. Overhearing words not meant for ears so young and foolish...' Again, he frowned.

Morgrim persisted, showing all proper deference. '*Why* are you looking for magic?'

Finishing his whispered oath to Grungni, Ranuld rose and grinned ferally at the young dwarf.

'*That* is a much better question,' he said, glancing daggers at Snorri. '*This*,' he said, rubbing the dirt and air between his fingers, 'and *this*...' he smacked the stone of the temple wall, 'and *this*...' then hacked a gob of spittle onto the ground, just missing Morgrim's boot, '*is* magic. Some of us can feel it, beardling. It lives in stone, in air, in earth and fire, even water. You breathe it, you taste it–' Ranuld's face darkened, suddenly far away as if he was no longer talking to the dwarfs at all, '–but it's changing, we're changing with it. Secrets lost, never to return,' he rasped. 'Who will keep it safe once we're gone? The gate bled something out we couldn't put back. Not even Grimnir could do that.' He stared at the dwarfs, his rheumy eyes heavy-lidded with the burden of knowledge and all the many years of his long life. 'Can you feel it, seeping into your hearts and souls?'

Morgrim had no answer, though his mouth moved as if it wanted to give one. 'I... I do not...'

As if snapping out of a trance, Ranuld's expression changed. As fiery and curmudgeonly as he ever was, he barged past the two dwarfs and into the long gallery. The runelord was halfway down when Morgrim shouted after him, 'Where are you going now?'

'Didn't find what I was looking for,' Ranuld called back without turning. 'Need to try somewhere else.'

Morgrim began to go after him. 'It's fortunate we found you, old one. Let us escort you back to the underway.'

'Ha!' Ranuld laughed. 'You're lost, aren't you? Best help yourselves before you help me, *werits*. And find me, did you? Perhaps I found you? Ever consider that, beardling? And this *is* the underway, wazzock.'

'No part of it I know.'

'You know very little, like when it's a good time to run, for instance,' Ranuld replied, so distant his voice echoed.

'Wha–'

A low rumble, heard deep under their feet, felt through their bones, stalled Morgrim and he looked up. Small chunks of grit were already falling from the ceiling in vast clouds of spewing dust. Cracks threaded the left side of the gallery wall, columns split in half.

Morgrim had spent enough time in his father's mines to know what was about to happen.

'Get back!' He slammed into Snorri's side, hurling the dwarf off his feet and barrelling them both back inside the temple.

The roof of the long gallery caved in a moment later, releasing a deluge of earth and rock. Thick slabs of stone, weighed down with centuries of smaller rock falls, speared through the roof from above and brought a rain of boulders with them. A huge pall of dirt billowed up from the sudden excavation.

Though he tried to see him, Ranuld was lost to Morgrim. It wasn't that he was obscured by falling debris, rather that the runelord simply wasn't there any more. He had vanished. It was as if the earth had swallowed him. As the storm of dust and grit rolled over them, Morgrim buried his head under his hands and prayed to Grungni they would survive.

Blackness became abject, sound smothered by an endless tide of debris. Stone chips, bladed flakes sheared from a much greater whole, cut Morgrim's face despite his war helm. He snarled but kept his teeth clenched.

Tremors faded, dust clung to the air in a muggy veil. Light prevailed, from above where the ceiling had caved in. It limned the summit of a pile of rocks no dwarf could ever hope to squeeze through.

Snorri coughed, brought up a fat wad of dirty phlegm and shook age-old filth from his hair and beard. Clods of earth were jammed in his ears, and he dug them out with a finger.

'Think most of Karak Krum just fell on top of us.'

'At least we are both alive, cousin.'

Snorri grunted something before spitting up more dirt.

Morgrim wafted away some of the dust veiling the air. 'What about Lord Silverthumb?'

'That old coot won't die to a cave-in, you can bet Grungni's arse he won't.'

Morgrim agreed. For some reason he didn't fear for the runesmith. The old dwarf had known what was going to happen and left them to be buried. If anything, he was more annoyed than concerned.

Barring the mucky overspill from the cave-in, the temple was untouched. Its archway still stood, so too its ceiling and walls. Grungni sat still and silently at the back of the room, watching, appraising perhaps.

Morgrim touched the rune on his war helm and gave thanks to the ancestor.

Snorri was already up, pulling at the wall of rock that had gathered at the only entrance to the temple. It was almost sealed.

'Did you also bring a pick and shovel when you picked up the lantern, cousin?' he asked, heaving away a large chunk of rock only for an even larger one to slam down violently in its place. A low rumble returned, the faint suggestion of another tremor. Motes of dust spilling from the ceiling thickened into gritty swathes.

'Leave it!' Morgrim snapped, reaching out in a gesture for Snorri to stop what he was doing. 'You'll bring the whole upper deep down on us. It'll flood the chamber with earth.'

Snorri held up his palms.

'Buried alive or left to rot in some forgotten tomb,' he said, 'neither choice is appealing, cousin. How do you suggest we get out?'

'Use a secret door.'

'Would that we had one, cou–'

Snorri stopped talking when he saw Morgrim hauling aside the statue of Grungni. Behind it was a shallow recess in the wall that delineated a door. It was open a crack and a rune stone had been left next to it that caught Morgrim's attention. He pocketed it and gave the door another tug.

'Get your back into it,' Snorri chided.

'How about yours?' he replied, red-faced and flustered.

'I'm wounded,' said Snorri, showing off his half-hand.

Morgrim spoke through gritted teeth and flung spittle. 'Get your chuffing arse over here and help me move this thing.'

Together, they dragged the door wide enough to slip through. Musky air rushed up to greet them, the scent of age and mildew strong enough to almost make them gag. A long, narrow darkness stretched before them. The gloom felt endless.

'We can stand here,' said Snorri, pulling out his axe, 'or we can go forwards. I vote for the dark.'

'Aye,' nodded Morgrim, and drew his hammer.

They had gone only a few feet when Snorri asked, 'What did he mean?'

'About magic? Chuffed if I know.'

'No, about my destiny. It being great and "lifting the doom of our race" and "he who will slay the drakk"? Those words were meant for me, I am sure.'

'Agreed,' said Morgrim, 'but you're the son of the High King of Karaz-a-Karak, of course your destiny will be great.' Morgrim led the way, following veins of gemstones and ore in the tunnel walls.

Snorri snorted, his disdain obvious.

Morgrim barely noticed. 'Feels like we're going up... Does it feel like we're going up?' He stopped, trying to get his bearings even though there was supposedly only one way for them to go.

'A great doom...' said Snorri. 'Are we headed for war, do you think?'

'Why do you sound as if you want a war? And against whom will you fight, eh, cousin? The urk and grobi tribes are diminished, dying out, thanks to your father. Ruin left the land long ago. Will you fight the rats, the vermin beneath our halls? Our enemies are dead. Don't be so quick to find others to take their place. Peace is what I want, and a mine hold of my own.'

'Fighting is what I am good at, cousin.' Snorri peered down the haft of his axe, all the way to the spike at the top. 'I can kill a grobi at a thousand yards with a crossbow, or at a hundred with a thrown axe. None are better than I with a hammer when used to crush skulls. In that, in the art of killing our enemies, my father and I are very alike.' He lowered the weapon and his eyes were heavy with grief when he met Morgrim's gaze. 'But he has already defeated them all and left no glory for me. I stand at his shoulder, nothing more than a caretaker who will sit upon a throne and rule a kingdom of dust.

'So when you ask why I want war, it is because of that. As a warrior I am great but as a prince of Karaz-a-Karak, I am nothing. At least before my father.'

Morgrim was stern, and a deep frown had settled upon his face. A small measure of respect for his cousin was lost.

'You are wrong about that. Very wrong, and I hope you learn the error of it, cousin.'

Grunting, unwilling to see Morgrim's pity or think about his father's shame, Snorri walked on.

'Ranuld Silverthumb is the most vaunted runelord of the Worlds Edge. If he says a doom is coming then we must prepare for it.' He thumped his chest, stuck out his pugnacious chin. 'Dragon slayer, I was so named. King because of it. *That* is a legacy I wish to inherit, not one of cowing to the elgi and the whims of other vassal lords.'

Morgrim fell silent, but followed. The old *zaki* had said many things during his casting.

One word stood out above the others.

Elgidum.

It meant *elfdoom*.

THREE

SHADOWS ON THE DWARF ROADS

Murder was always better conducted under moonlight. This night the moon was shaped like a sickle, curved and sharp like Sevekai's blade as he pulled it silently from the baldric around his waist. Unlike the moon, its silver gleam was dulled by magwort and edged with a verdant sheen of mandrake.

Fatal poisons, at least those that killed instantly, were a misuse of the assassin's art in Sevekai's opinion. Debilitate, agonise, petrify; these were his preferred tortures. Slaying a victim with such disregard was profligate, not when death inflicted upon others was something to be savoured.

Crouched with his shadowy companions behind a cluster of fallen rocks that had sheared from the looming mountainside, Sevekai considered something else which the moon was good for.

Stalking prey...

It was a bulky cart, high-sided and with a stout wooden roof to protect whatever was being ferried. Two stocky ponies pulled the wagon, its wheels broad and metal-banded to withstand the worst the dwarf roads had to offer.

In truth, the roads were well made. An army could march across them and have no blisters, no sprains or injuries to speak of at the end of many miles. Dwarfs were builders, they made things to last.

Some things though, Sevekai knew, would not endure.

As the trundling wagon closed, four guards came into view. Like the driver, they were dwarfs with copper-banded beards and silver rings on their fingers. Fastened to a hook next to the driver hung a shuttered lantern that spilled just enough light to illuminate the road ahead. The dwarf had kept it low so as not to attract predators. Unfortunately, no manner of precaution could have prevented this particular predator crossing his path.

Sevekai took the driver for a merchant – his rings were gold and his armour ornamental. It consisted of little more than a breastplate and vambraces. Each of the guards wore helmets, one with a faceplate slid shut. This was the leader.

He would die first.

Heavy plate clad their bodies, with rounded pauldrons and a mail skirt to protect the thighs and knees. No gorget or coif. Sevekai assumed they'd removed them earlier in the journey. Perhaps it was the heat of the day, a desire for cool air on their necks instead of stinging sweat. So close to home, they had thought it a minor act of laxity.

Sevekai smiled, a cold and hollow thing, and silently told his warriors, *Aim for the neck.*

The hand gesture was swift, and heeded by all.

Most of the dwarfs carried axes. One, the leader, had a hammer that gave off a faint aura of enchantment. Sevekai was not a sorcerer, but he had some small affinity with magic. Some had remarked, his enemies in fact, that he was lucky. Not just average good fortune, but phenomenal, odds-defying luck. It had kept him alive, steered him from danger and heightened his senses. For a murderer, a hired blade whose trade was killing other people, it was an extremely useful trait to possess.

Other than the hand weapons, a crossbow with a satchel full of stubby quarrels sat within the merchant's easy reach. It was leant against the wooden back of the driver's seat with the lethal end pointing up. That was another error, and would increase the merchant's reaction time by precious seconds once the ambush was sprung.

Six dwarfs, three of them.

The odds were stacked high against the stunted little pigs.

Clouds crawling overhead like ink in dirty water obscured the moon and for a few seconds the road turned black as tar.

Sevekai rose, as silent as a whisper in a gale, his shrouded body dark against darkness. The sickle blade spun, fast and grey like a bat arrowing through fog, and lodged in the guard leader's eye-slit as the wagon hit a rock and jumped.

With a low grunt, the dead dwarf lost his grip on the side rail and pitched off the wagon. To the other guards, in what few breaths remained to them, it would have looked as if their fellow had fallen off.

'Ho!' Sevekai heard the merchant call, oblivious to the fact there was a black-clad killer arisen in his midst and but a few feet away. Hauling on the reins, the dwarf drew the wagon to a halt with a snort of protest from the mules.

That was another mistake.

In the time it took for the merchant to turn and ask one of the other guards what had happened, one of Sevekai's warriors had crossed the road. Like a funeral veil rippling beneath the wind, the warrior crept along the opposite side of the wagon and rammed his dagger up to the hilt in a guard's neck. Sevekai couldn't see the kill, his view was obstructed by the bulky wagon, but he knew how it would have played out.

Kaitar was a late addition to his band, but a deadly one.

Two guards remained. One had dismounted to see to his leader; the other looked straight through Sevekai as he searched for signs of ambush.

You have missed... all of them, swine.

Sevekai drew back his hood for this dwarf, let him see the red and bloody murder flaring brightly in his dagger-slit eyes.

The dwarf gasped, swore in his native tongue and drew his axe. One-handed because of the rail, he should have gone for his shield. It would have extended his life expectancy by three more seconds. That was the time it would have taken Sevekai to close the gap, draw his falchion and dispatch the dwarf with a low thrust to his heart.

Instead he threw his second blade, already clutched in a claw-like grip.

Bubbling froth erupted from the dwarf's gullet, staining his lips and beard a satisfying incarnadine red. He gurgled, dropped his axe and fell face first into the dirt.

The colour spewing from the dwarf's neck reminded Sevekai of a particularly fine wine he had once drunk in a lordling's manse in Clar Karond. Generous of the noble to share such a vintage, but then he was in no position to object given that his innards had become his *out-ards*. Hard to take umbrage when you're fighting to keep your entrails from spilling all over the floor.

The last guard fell to a quarrel in the neck. It sank into the dwarf's leathery flesh and fed a cocktail of nerve-shredding poison into his heart. Death was instantaneous but then Verigoth was an efficient if predictable killer.

That left the merchant who, in the brief seconds that had been afforded to him, had indeed reached and gripped the crossbow in his meaty fist.

Sevekai was upon him before the dwarf had drawn back the string.

'Should've kept it loaded,' he told the snarling pig in a barbed language the dwarf wouldn't understand. The message Sevekai conveyed through his eyes and posture was easy to translate, however.

You shall suffer.

He cut the dwarf beneath the armpit, a slender and insignificant wound to the naked eye.

After a few brief seconds during which the merchant's grubby little hands had constricted into useless claws and a veritable train of earthy expletives had spat from his mouth, the dwarf began to convulse.

Sudden paralysis in his legs ruined the dwarf's balance and he collapsed. Eyes bulging, veins thick like ropes in his cheeks and forehead, the dwarf gaped to shout.

Sevekai leapt on the dwarf like a cat pounces upon a stricken mouse it has nearly tired of playing with. Before a single syllable could escape the lips, he cut off the beard and shoved it down the dwarf's throat. Then he stepped back to watch.

The dwarf bleated, of course he did, but they were small and pitiful sounds that would scarcely rouse a nearby elk, let alone bring aid of any value or concern. From somewhere in the low forest a raven shrieked, emulating a death scream the dwarf could not make.

'Even for a race like ours, you are cruel, Sevekai.'

'It's not cruelty, Kaitar,' Sevekai replied without averting his gaze from the convulsing dwarf merchant. 'It's simply death and the art of crafting it.'

Teeth clenched, upper body locked in rigor, choking on his own beard, the dwarf's organs would be liquefying about now. With a final shudder, a lurch of defiant limbs still protesting the inevitable, the dwarf slumped still.

Sevekai knew he had no soul, save for something cold and rimed with frost that inhabited his chest, and he regarded the dwarf pitilessly. Despite the artistic flourishes, this was simply a task he had been charged to perform. The theatrics were for the benefit of the others to remind them of his prowess as an artful killer.

Satisfied with the deed, he addressed the night: 'Leave no sign,' and the two assassins on the road stepped back as a slew of arrows thudded into the dwarf corpses.

Pine-shafted, flights woven from swan feather, the arrows were not typical of Naggaroth. Not at all.

When it was done, four more warriors dressed in similar black attire stepped into view.

Sevekai was stooping to retrieve his sickle blades, replacing them with elven arrow shafts, when Kaitar asked, 'And this will fool the dwarfs?'

'Of course, they won't bother to look for subterfuge. They *want* a fight, Kaitar,' Sevekai explained.

'What of the poisons?'

'Gone before the bodies are found.' Sevekai looked up as he punched the last arrow through the dwarf leader's eye. 'If you hear hooves, what do you think of?'

'Horses,' said the deep-voiced Verigoth, a smirk on his grey lips. Like the others, he'd descended from the ridge to appreciate the carnage.

Sevekai smiled, colder than a winter storm. 'And when you think of arrows?'

Now it was Kaitar's turn to smile. 'Asur.'

FOUR

WHAT LIES ABOVE...

'It's as mysterious to me as it is to you, cousin.' Morgrim looked behind them, but saw only darkness. 'How far have we walked?' Taking off a leather gauntlet, he ran his hand along the wall of the tunnel and then licked his fingers. 'Tastes familiar.'

'*Zaki,*' said Snorri, using the Khazalid word for 'mad wandering dwarf'. During the long walk in the dark, his mood had improved and the dour silence between them ebbed until all was well again. Destiny, his to be specific, was still on the dwarf prince's mind, however. 'You are probably right, cousin. The old fool was likely senile.' He tilted his head, thinking. 'Then again, the words of a runelord are not easily ignored. Are we still lost?'

Pain flared in Snorri's jaw. He grimaced, staggered by the sudden blow. Glaring at his cousin, he asked, 'What was that for?'

Morgrim was big, even for a dwarf. His father was bulky too, from a lifetime spent in the mines. Broad of shoulder, stout of chest and back, he had a chin like an anvil and a head like a mattock. Snorri was leaner, though still muscled, and surrendered half a foot in height to his cousin. Bare-knuckled, strength for strength he would not prevail against him.

'It was either that or I hit you with the hammer,' said Morgrim.

'I'm just glad you didn't butt me with that bloody helmet of yours.' Snorri rubbed at his chin, wincing at the slowly swelling bruise. 'Take my bleeding eye out with one of those horns. Big buggers. What was it, a stag?'

'Beastman. Much larger than a stag, cousin.' Morgrim smacked his fist into his palm. 'Are you done talking about destiny, or do you need some more sense knocking into you?'

Snorri held up his half-hand; the bandage was dark crimson but the wound had clotted. He slowly nodded.

'Me one-handed, weakened from blood loss and being almost buried alive... Reckon you'd have a decent chance of beating me.'

'Aye,' said Morgrim, unconvinced it would be any sort of contest, and slapped his hand against the wall. 'See this?'

Snorri did.

'I know what stone is, cousin.'

Morgrim glowered at him. 'Use your eyes, *wattock*. I know this place. We are no longer lost.'

Snorri frowned, and regarded their surroundings.

'How can that be? We've not long been...' His voice tailed off, claimed by the darkness which was lessening by the second. Ahead, the crackle of brazier fire resolved on a breeze redolent of shallow earth and the upper world.

A dwarf's nose can discern much in the subterranean depths. He can tell the difference between the deep earth where he makes his hold, that which harbours veins of gold or precious minerals, and shallow earth, the loamy soil best for crops and farming. Unless he is one of the *skarrenawi*, those who 'live under sky', a dwarf has no interest in such things, but he knows earth and can tell it apart.

Other smells, carried by the breeze, drifted into being. There was grass, leaf, stone dried by the sun, the scent of animals and warm water.

Morgrim nodded as he saw the recognition in his cousin's expression. 'It's the *Rorganzbar*.'

'Cannot be,' said Snorri. No matter how hard he stared at the way they had come, he couldn't find the doorway through which they had entered the tunnel. 'We were far from the northern gate.'

'During the fight, we could have got turned around?'

Snorri raised an eyebrow, dubiously. 'And ended up over fifty miles in the wrong direction? Are you sure that helmet of yours didn't take a heavier hit when the cave collapsed? Perhaps you hurt your fist on my jaw and the pain of it has addled your mind?'

'How else would you explain it?'

Taking a last glance at the darkness behind them and the firelit shadows now glowing ahead, Snorri said, 'I cannot.'

The Rorganzbar was the name of the northern gates that fed into the upper world from the Ungdrin Ankor. Such passageways were falling out of use, for dwarfs had little need for what lived above ground, but they were fashioned anyway during times when trading with other races was more common. Elves thronged the Old World now, returned after a war, some matter of kinstrife the dwarfs did not really understand. So too did the skarrenawi, the dwarfs of the hills who had chosen to eschew solid earth and stone for the promise of sky and the warmth of the sun. *Elgongi* some mountain dwarfs called them, 'elf-friends'.

It was meant as an insult.

As they reached a vast stone gateway, the truth of where they were could not be denied. Runic script along the tall, square pillars of the northern gate confirmed Morgrim's suspicions.

'*Rorganzbar*,' read Snorri, hands against his hips. 'Well, I'll be buggered.'

* * *

Numenos hailed them with a shout. Gifted with tongues, the black-clad warrior made it sound like the screech of a crow.

Sevekai found the scout at the summit of the ridge, crouched low in his chosen rookery. He was gesturing for them to climb up and meet him.

A quick glance around at the ambush site revealed that all was in readiness. Blades and quarrels had been gathered, corpses left with asur arrows in their bellies instead. Stowing his own weapons, Sevekai ran up the craggy ridge in long, loping strides. The others followed silently in his wake.

As he crested the rise, he went low and hunkered down behind a cluster of fallen rocks. Numenos was waiting for him, the slit of his mouth curved upwards like a dagger.

'Fresh meat,' he hissed, and pointed higher up the mountainside, through a gap in a patch of sparse forest, where a second pathway wended above the one where they had laid their ambush.

Two walkers, dwarfs and nobles judging by their attire. They were armed, but looked as if they had already been in a fight, and they were alone.

Killing merchants in cold blood was one thing, murdering the sons of some thane or king was another entirely. It went against orders, and Sevekai was nothing if not a dutiful soldier.

'Tempting, but too risky. The dwarfs will look more closely at their deaths.'

The black-clad warriors were peeling away from the summit of the ridge, back into the night, when Kaitar crept up behind Sevekai and gripped his shoulder. It was light, like a breath of wind brushing against him at first, but with a fearsome strength.

Sevekai snarled but his wrath died in his throat when he looked into Kaitar's eyes. They were fathomless black, as deep pits of cruelty as he'd ever seen.

'Two scalps like that are worth a hundred wagons,' he purred without insistence, like he was stating an irrefutable fact.

Despite his earlier misgivings, Sevekai could see the sense in his words and the eagerness for spilling more blood in his followers. He wondered briefly if Kaitar was trying to usurp his leadership but could see no concealed blade, no desire for command in his eyes. He only exuded a frightful ennui, something dark and shrivelled that Sevekai couldn't reach.

He turned to Numenos. 'How many more asur shafts remain?'

'Enough to stick two stunted pigs.'

Sevekai held his gaze then nodded. Licking the dryness from his lips, moistening his throat so his voice wouldn't catch, he said to Kaitar, 'We kill the nobles.'

Fashioned of heavy stone, the door to the Rorganzbar needed at least two dwarfs to push it. From the outside it was hard to find, even for those looking for it. Crafted in such a way that it blended in with its surroundings, only a dwarf who knew the exact place and correct height at which to stand could ever hope to find the way into the underdeep through the Rorganzbar.

Snow, light for the time of year, dappled the crags and grassy heaths as the dwarfs stepped outside. The door closed behind them, shut by its own weight in a clever piece of dwarf engineering.

Before them, a long and narrow path that wound around the foothills of the mountains. Above, the towering peaks of the Worlds Edge so high they were lost in thick cloud. Amongst them was Karaz-a-Karak, hold hall of the High King and their home.

It would be a long walk back.

'See that crag over there?' Morgrim pointed. 'The one shaped like a tooth?'

Snorri nodded, mastering a sense of agoraphobia washing over him. A lifetime spent living under the earth where there was no sky apart from the vaulted chambers of the ancestors and the great hold halls had bred a fear of the upper world and all its vastness.

'I see it, cousin,' he gasped, not used to the crispness of the air.

'That's Karak Varn, and in that deep depression where the mountains and hills thin...' He gestured again. Snorri nodded. 'Black Water,' said Morgrim. 'We head south from here, and try to pick up the Silk Road then the Dwarf Road down from Black Fire Pass. Follow it all the way back to hearth and hold.'

'Where I hope there's meat and beer waiting for us and a fire to warm my feet.' Snorri laughed, as the two began to walk. 'You have been ranging with Furgil, I see.'

Thane of pathfinders, Furgil knew the roads and byways of the overground world well, better than any in Karaz-a-Karak. An expert tracker, he was seldom below the earth and spent much of his time under sky instead.

'You'd do well to heed some of his wisdom, cousin.'

Snorri shrugged. 'For a skarrenawi, he is not so bad, I suppose. But what need have I for trees and sky?' He kept his eyes down on the road, on the earth, but his gaze drifted.

Hills undulated below, covered with thick forests of fir and pine, hardy even in winter. Elk and goats watched the passage of the dwarfs nervously from shadowed arbours and brush-choked glades. Deep within the forest, near to the low road, a crow cawed. This close to the mountain there were tors, thickly veiled with rock. Throughout the ages, much of the mountainside had slipped, creating crag-toothed valleys and boulder-strewn fields.

Snorri was glad to feel the solidity of the road underfoot. Strong and flat, it wended around the mountain out of respect. By contrast, the lands beyond it were wild and ragged. This was the domain of the skarrenawi, dwarfs who had left the mountain long ago to find fortune and sovereignty amongst the foothills. Their gilded cities had a dwarf aesthetic. Squat structures of stone and petrified wutroth, resilient to the elements and fortified against attack from beasts and urk or grobi, they had stood for centuries. Outposts dotted the lands of the low hills and plains but the larger cities were few. Kazad Kro was chief amongst them but there was also Kazad Mingol and Kagaz Thar.

Three kings were there of the skarrenawi, but Snorri's father believed there would be more before the century was out.

In truth, the prince knew little more about them. His father had often remarked on how numerous the skarrenawi had become, of their flourishing trade with elves and men from distant lands he did not remember the names of. They were distinctly un-dwarfish names and so Snorri had no interest in them.

'Have you ever visited the hill forts?' asked Morgrim, following Snorri's gaze.

'Once. My father brought me to a council with Skarnag Grum, though I think he just wanted to remind the fat noble of who was High King. Two hundred hearthguard and retainers travelled with us and father was carried upon his throne.'

'Are they like us?' Morgrim asked. Though he knew Furgil, he had never been to the hill forts.

'They are dawi... of a fashion. Their skin is lighter and softer. Fairer haired, too, and with shorter beards, but they are decent forgesmiths and can drink almost as well as a proper hall-dweller. Though I cannot fathom why any son of Grungni would prefer sky over earth. It is unnatural.'

'Perhaps they will soon outnumber the dawi of the mountains and establish more forts.'

'Ha!' Snorri shook his head ruefully. 'Between the elgi and the skarrenawi, the lands beyond the Worlds Edge will be thronged. It already feels crowded as it is.'

Morgrim nodded, 'I know many amongst the clans, my father included, who think the elgi have encroached too far into the empire. Some believe we would be better–'

'*Hsst!*' Snorri held up a clenched fist. He stooped, looking up into the sky where the clouds conspired to obscure his view. Thunderheads were boiling and a low rumble echoed dully above them.

''Tis a storm, nothing more.'

'Nah, there is something else...' His eyes narrowed and he turned his ear to listen. 'Can't you hear it, a smack of something hitting air?' He released his axe, and met Morgrim's questioning gaze. 'Wings, cousin.'

Morgrim's brow furrowed. He heard it too.

'Something big...'

'And strong enough to defy the wind.'

Unslinging his hammer, Morgrim searched the sky but the growing storm was thick.

'Perhaps old Silverthumb was right about that drakk.'

Snorri scowled. 'Unless dwarfs have learned to fly, we need to leave the road. Now.'

FIVE

SKY SHIP

The great rock *Durazon* commanded an unparalleled view over the lands neighbouring Barak Varr. Below the flanks of the mountain, several miles down, tributaries ran like veins of crystal, bleeding from the nearby Black Gulf in shimmering ribbons of azure. They fed valleys and farmland, filled the wells of the lower deeps and birthed three mighty water lanes – Blood River, Howling River and Skull River.

Heglan Copperfist, so named for his father who had discovered a vast seam of the ore and made his fortune trading it with the other clans, had sailed all three rivers. An engineer, Heglan had constructed the *grubark* he used to ply these waters himself and had travelled as far as Karak Varn and Black Water.

Now his mind was occupied by an entirely different enterprise, one that forced his gaze upwards.

Great birds of prey circled in a platinum sky. Screech hawks and crag eagles, the majestic griffon vultures or talon owls, the red condor or the diminutive flocks of peak falcons, Heglan knew them all by size and appearance. Amongst his studies in engineering and the lessons of his guildmasters was an interest in ornithology. Some in the guild believed it to be an unhealthy one.

For as long as he could remember, ever since he was a beardling and his grandfather Dammin had taken him to look out at the wider world from the Durazon, Heglan had believed a ship could be made to fly. Not by growing wings or some such aberration, but by sailing the clouds.

Here, many hundreds of feet up in the high peaks, he would do just that.

Few dwarfs ventured onto the Durazon. Though it was over a hundred paces across, it ended in a crag which led to a sheer, vertiginous drop that for a people who lived most or all of their lives underground was uncomfortable. Not so for Heglan; he relished the sense of freedom he felt standing on this rock that jutted from the flanks of the Sea Hold.

'Sun stone' was its literal name and an apt one at that. The rock was wide and flat, perfect for what Heglan needed, and turned gold in summer when the sun was high and pierced the cloud veil. Winter was ending and the rising sun was obscured by storms rolling in from the south-west. Better days for flying would certainly come but with the guild's patience almost exhausted, Heglan had no choice but to demonstrate his invention now. Frowning at the spreading path of darkness creeping towards them, he just hoped the weather would hold.

From the lofty heavens and the avian beasts he so envied, Heglan's eyes were drawn downwards.

Arcing from peak to peak, resolute against the rigours of weather and war, were the skyroads. It was whilst crossing the passage from Barak Varr to Karak Drazh that inspiration first struck like a hammer swung by Grungni himself. Stone-clad bands that crossed the mountains through belts of thickening cloud and raucous gales, the skyroads had stood for thousands of years. Ever since the earliest days of the dwarf empire these lofty conduits had enabled those brave enough or surefooted enough to traverse between the holds.

Few did, because most believed a dwarf's place was below the earth. Unlike the underway, however, the skyroads were not the lair of monsters. Great eagles and other flying beasts were a menace but stocky watchtowers punctuating the long spans provided warning and protection. Trolls and greenskins couldn't touch these vaulted pathways.

Some engineers had even built ships to travel across them, great propeller-driven longboats that carried cargo and dwarfs by the score. Wind shear made widespread use of these 'sky ships' untenable as many had been torn off the skyroads in a strong gale and dashed on the ground far below. But despite its dangers, upon such a bridge a dwarf could literally walk the skies.

For Heglan it was as close as he could come to doing just that.

Until today.

'Quite a sight, aren't they?' said Nadri, breathing deep as he regarded the monolithic skyroads.

'Aye, they most certainly are, brother.'

'I have heard standing upon them a dwarf can see the entire kingdom, from Karak Izril in the south to Karak Ungor in the north.'

Like his brother, Heglan inhaled a full breath of the high mountain air and closed his eyes, remembering.

'Indeed he can, but such a magnificent vista will pale compared to what I have in mind.'

Nadri clapped Heglan on the shoulder.

'Ever with your head in the clouds, eh, Heg?'

Unlike his brother, who wore a leather apron with a belt of tools fastened around his ample waist, Nadri was more finely attired as befitted a merchant guildmaster. His tunic was gilded and he wore a small travelling cloak fashioned from the very best *hruk* wool of the mountains. His leather boots were supple and tan. The many rings upon his fingers shone in the occluded winter sun.

Nadri stroked his ruddy beard. It was well preened and beautifully studded with silver ingots that bound up locks of his hair.

'Father would have been so very proud,' he said, and gripped Heglan's shoulder a little tighter.

Lodri Copperfist was dead, slain by urk over a decade ago during one of the High King's purges of the mountains. Grief had brought his only sons closer, despite the very different paths they had taken.

'He loved the skyroads, Nadri. Just like grandfather.' Heglan's beard was unkempt, more brown than red and tied together at the end with a leather thong. Most casual observers would not think them kin, but the bond between the siblings was stronger than gromril.

For a moment, Heglan was overtaken by a wistful mood. In his mind's eye, he soared through the heavens with the wind on his face, buffeting his beard as he flew. Birds arced and pinwheeled beside him, the sense of freedom overwhelming...

Burgrik Strombak brought him back to the ground with a stamp of his foot.

'Earth is where dwarfs are meant to be,' he said, a pipe stewing between clenched teeth. 'Under it or over it, but never flying above it.'

The engineer guildmaster cut a formidable figure. Two mattock-like fists pressed against his broad waist and a thick leather belt filled with tools crossed his slab chest. Strombak knew engines like no other dwarf of Barak Varr. Most of the sea wall defences on the side of the hold that faced the Black Gulf were his design. A circular glass lens sat snug in his left eye, which he used to scrutinise the young engineer before him.

'What about the sea, master?' asked Heglan, bowing deferentially. 'Dawi can sail the seas too, can they not?'

'You ask me that question in a Sea Hold. Have you hit your head, Heglan Copperfist?'

Heglan bowed again, deeper this time. 'I only meant that the horizons of our race have broadened before and will again.'

Scowling, Strombak leaned in close. 'You are fortunate King Brynnoth can see a military use for this machinery of yours.'

Heglan shook his head. 'No, master. Its intended use is for trade, prosperity and peace, not as an engine of war.'

'We'll see.'

Strombak sniffed contemptuously and stomped over to where Heglan's creation was docked. It had taken sixteen mules and twice as many journeymen to get it up the Merman Pass and onto the Durazon.

It was a ship, a vessel of dark lacquered wood and gilded trim. Incongruous as it was, sitting on the mountain plateau atop a curved ramp, the small wheels attached to its hull arrested by stout wooden braces, it was still magnificent. If he thought so, Strombak did not give any indication.

'And sea is not air, though, is it,' grumbled the old engineer, chewing on his pipe and feeling the smoothness of the wooden hull beneath his grizzled fingers. 'Wood is stout,' he said, 'that is something at least.'

As well as the braces against its wheels, the ship was also lashed to iron rings driven deep into the rock so it wouldn't sway in the wind. A small vessel, it could take five passengers including its captain, but had a hold that would accommodate twice that again in wares for trade. Presently, twenty casks of *grog* sat in the ship's belly from the brewmasters' guild, bound for Zhufbar.

Spry for an old dwarf, Strombak clambered up the ramp and tugged on the rigging.

'Strong rope,' he mumbled. 'Might hold in a decent gale.'

Strombak pulled out the pipe and chewed his beard. It was black with soot from his workshops and resembled a fork in the way the strands of it were parted by bronze cogs and screws. A leather skullcap covered his bald pate, which he revealed when he removed the cap to wipe his sweating brow. Runes of engineering, telemetries and trajectories, parabolic equations and yet more esoteric markings lined his skull in knot-worked strands.

He paced the length of the ship, appraising its rudder and sneering at the absence of sweeps. Sails jutted horizontally from the sides and with the effigy of a dragon carved into the prow it had the appearance of some alate predator, albeit one fashioned from wood and metal.

Sat astern was a small tower, where its captain was already installed and at the wheel. Three large windmills surmounted masts that stuck out from the deck, angled slightly so as not to be perpendicular to the ground.

'Never have I seen a more awkward-looking ship,' Strombak muttered. He turned away, as if he'd seen enough, and addressed Heglan. 'You'd best get on with it. Guilders are waiting.'

Behind the engineer guildmaster were three other dwarfs of the engineers' guild, the high thane of Barak Varr himself and his retainers, and a contingent from the merchants' guild who had funded the enterprise. Every one of the assembled nobles and guilders, some thirty-odd dwarfs, was silent.

Nadri stepped back and joined his fellow guilders.

Heglan licked his lips to moisten them. He glanced at the ship's captain to ascertain his readiness. A vague nod didn't do much for Heglan's confidence at that moment.

'*Tromm*,' he uttered, crafting a deep bow to the lords as he gave the traditional dwarf greeting for veneration of one's betters and elders. 'High Thane,' he added, rising but turning to the entire assembly. 'With your permission, Lord Onkmarr.'

The high thane nodded dourly.

King Brynnoth was away in Karaz-a-Karak attending a council of the High King and had left Onkmarr in charge as regent until his return. Unlike

Brynnoth, who had a ribald manner and was as gregarious as any king of the dwarf realm, Onkmarr always seemed slightly put upon. Perhaps it was the fearsome rinn he had taken as his wife. Certainly, his posture was more stooped, his humour more acerbic, ever since he had made a union with her.

Premature age lines furrowing on his brow like cracks in weathered rock, Onkmarr looked as if he wanted nothing more than to return to his hall and his business. Especially if that business was sitting by his fire, seeing to the affairs of the hold and staying out of his wife's way. With the exception of Nadri, the entire assembly appeared eager to get Heglan's demonstration over with.

'Go on, Copperfist,' grumbled Strombak, 'make your oaths and hope they're good ones.'

Heglan nodded, clearing his throat to speak.

'Thanes and masters of Barak Varr, vaunted guilders, we stand on the precipice of a momentous discovery. Ever have the dawi been lords of the earth–' nods and muted grunts of approval greeted this proclamation, '–and the clans of Barak Varr are lords of the sea too.' This brought further bouts of agreements and much chest puffing, especially amongst the engineers. 'But now, with this innovation,' a word that elicited grumbles of disapproval and reproachful glances, 'we can be lords of the sky too.'

Heglan stepped back so the attention of the dwarf nobles was on the ship. He whispered behind his hand to the captain.

'*Turn the propellers...*'

Having missed his cue, the dwarf in the tower pulled at some levers and the three windmills attached to the masts began to rotate.

'*Skryzan-harbark*,' Heglan declared. 'The first ever dawi airship!'

Six burly dwarf journeymen in short sleeves and leather aprons were on standby next to ropes that fed to the braces impeding the vessel's wheels. Another two stood ready with axes to cut the lashed sails.

At a sign from Heglan, the sails were freed and the wooden stops removed.

Creaking wood made him wince as the ramp took the weight of the ship and it rolled onto the curve. Propellers were beating furiously now as the captain tested the rudder experimentally as he pitched towards the edge of the cliff.

It got a decent run up, needing to gather speed before the Durazon ended and all that sat beneath the ship was air.

'Grungni, I beseech you...' muttered Heglan, hiding his fervent oath from the other dwarfs as the airship plunged off the end of the ramp at pace. It rolled on for almost fifty feet, wheels spinning, propellers turning like mad. And with sails unfurled, Heglan's creation launched off the edge of the rock and soared like an arrow.

He fought the urge to shout for joy, content to clench a fist in triumph at the skryzan-harbark's inaugural flight instead.

Surprised but approving mutterings issued from the throng of guilders and nobles in a rumbling susurrus of speech as they beheld the flying ship.

'Valaya's golden cups, lad,' breathed Strombak, unable to hide the fact he was impressed. 'I did not think you would do it. The ship is small, but if you can get this to work we can enlarge it.'

Bowing his head, Heglan's voice was low and deferential at such high praise. 'Tromm, my master. This is just a trial vessel. I have plans for bigger versions.'

Clapping the young engineer on the shoulder, Strombak stepped back to discuss the incredible ship with his fellow guilders.

Disengaging himself from the other merchants, Nadri joined his brother and slapped him heartily on the back. 'It is a marvel, Heg, a true wonder to help usher in a prosperous new age.'

Heglan barely heard – he was watching the realisation of a dream.

'See how the sails billow and catch the wind?' he said. 'And the way it achieves loft and forward motion.'

'It is...' Nadri's smile turned into a frown, '...listing, brother.'

At the same time a look of horror was slowly creeping its way onto Heglan's face.

A heavy gust of wind, driven hard and fast through the peaks, pitched the airship to one side. The sails bulged like an overfull bladder, straining against the rigging, and the dragon prow listed awkwardly as if the ship was drunk on too much grog.

'*Compensate, compensate...*' Heglan urged the captain, who was lost from view but evidently struggling at the controls.

Ugly and portentous, the sound of snapping rigging resolved on the breeze and a deep crack fed down one of the masts. The ship began to turn on its axis, pulled and buffeted by the wind.

'Grimnir's hairy arse, no...' Heglan could see the danger before it unfolded fully but was powerless to avert it. He would have run to the edge of the Durazon in the vain hope that his proximity to the ship would somehow guarantee its continued flight if Nadri hadn't held him back.

Buoyed on the harsh thermals whipping up from below, slewed by the biting wind, the ship lurched. The dragon bit upwards, briefly righting itself before yawing dangerously the other way. Pulled back and forth at the whim of the elements, there was nothing the captain or Heglan could do. With a loud crack, made louder and more resonant as it echoed around the peaks, one of the masts snapped. It split in half and speared the deck, releasing a fountain of dark beer from the grog in the hold. Like a lance in the belly of a beast, the skryzan-harbark was wounded. At the same time, one of its sails sheared in half, plucked from its bearings and scattered like sackcloth on the wind.

'Girth of Grungni, no.'

But all the sworn oaths of the dwarf ancestors couldn't stop the encroaching storm from ripping Heglan's dreams apart. Utterly helpless in his brother's arms, all he could do was watch. Like a pugilist that had taken too many licks, the vessel was thrown about and battered by the storm. Slowly the airship began to lose height and sank deeper and deeper into the valleys below. Cloud partly obscured it but soon parted to reveal crags, encroaching from the lower peaks and jutting spurs of rock. Bitterly, Heglan wished he had the foresight to launch the skryzan-harbark over the sea-facing aspect of the hold. Pitching into the waters of the Black Gulf, the vessel could be rescued. Hitting one of the lower peaks or the hard earth of the plains, it would be smashed to splinters.

Below the jagged fingers of rock, the thick spires of stone that could impale the airship and rip it right in half as it fell, were boulder-strewn heaths. Scattered farms dotted the landscape but it was largely barren aside from old burial mounds and trickle-thin streams. Plummeting now, loft decreasing more swiftly with each passing moment, but no longer spinning, the airship slipped through the forest of crags and spires.

Only earth awaited it, packed tight and resilient by the winter. It would be like hitting the solid rock of the mountainside.

Heglan cursed again. Foolish sentiment had got in the way of prudence. Heart ruling the head, it was a mistake he had made before. Nostalgia to release the airship from the Durazon and honour his grandfather Dammin's memory had left him undone.

He wept openly at the thought, but could not take his eyes off the vessel he had so doomed. Striking the edge of the last crag, just the smallest of nicks, the hull was torn open in an explosion of splintering wood.

Every blow brought a wince to Heglan's tear-streaked face.

'Valaya, please be merciful...'

But the ancestor goddess of healing was not listening. Her gaze, deep within the earth, did not extend to sky and cloud. Thunder and storm were Grimnir's domain, and he was ever wrathful.

Entangled with the rigging, the other sails ripped open and dragged much of the hull with them. Deciding upon discretion rather than valour, the dwarf captain at the wheel leapt from the tower and hit the ground a few seconds before the stricken vessel. He landed with a heavy bump, but otherwise survived unscathed.

The same could not be said for the skryzan-harbark.

Prow first, the airship ploughed an ugly furrow into a rugged patch of farmland. Its proud dragon head smashed upon impact, split down its skull as if killed by some mythical dragon slayer. The hull broke apart like a barrel divested of its bands, and the ship's three masts jutted at obscure angles like broken fingers.

Bruised, in both pride and rump, the dwarf captain looked down at the wreckage that had finally settled in the valley and then up at the Durazon. Too far to see anything, he limped off furtively.

Heglan's wrath almost overflowed. He hoped the dwarf below would feel its heat as he looked on disconsolately.

Impelled by what was left of their perpetual motion, two of the propellers still spun. The rudder flapped like a dead fish, hanging on by one of its hinges, the stern jutting up in the air in an undignified fashion.

Free of Nadri's grip, Heglan sank to his knees and held his face in his hands.

'I am finished,' he breathed, letting his fingers trawl down his cheeks, pulling at his beard in anguish.

'*Dreng tromm*,' muttered Nadri, shaking his head. 'I am sorry, brother. I really thought it would work.'

'It should have worked, but I didn't take into account the wind shear, the vagaries of weather or that wazzock, Dungni.'

Adding insult to already stinging injury, the grog from the sundered hold began to leak through the jagged gashes in the wood. It reminded Heglan of blood. His magnificent machine was dead, his dream was dead, so too his tenure as an engineer of Barak Varr.

Strombak was not kind with his reproach as he stomped over to him.

'Gather it up, all of it,' he growled under his breath. 'You have disgraced this guild with your invention and your enterprise. Such things are not for dawi! Tradition, solidity, dependability, that's what we strive for.'

Heglan begged. 'Master, I... Perhaps if–'

'*If*? If! There is no "if". Dawi do not fly. We live under earth and stone. Do not tread in the same shameful footsteps as your grandfather. Dammin was thrown out of the guild, or is your memory so short that you've forgotten? Keen to endure the Trouser Legs Ritual too are you, Heglan son of Lodri?'

The rest of the assembly was leaving, chuntering about the wilfulness of youth and foolhardy beardlings. First to go was the high thane, already descending the Merman Pass on his palanquin-shield. He left without word or ceremony, pleased to leave the draughty plateau no doubt and enjoy the fire in the hearth of his hold hall.

Unable to rise from his knees, Heglan answered Strombak with his head bowed, 'No, master. I only wish to be an engineer of the guild. I am a maker, a craftsman. Please don't take that from me.'

The scowl on Strombak's face could have been chiselled on, engraved much like the runes on his tools, but it softened briefly before Heglan's contrition.

'You're not without skill, Heglan. A decent engineer, aye. But you're wayward, lad.' He gestured to the sky, 'Head up in the clouds when it should be here–' he stamped his boot upon the rock, '–in the earth. We're not birds or elgi, we're dawi. Sons of Grungni, stone and steel. You'd do well to remember that. Not like your grandfather. He *was* gifted–' Strombak's voice became rueful, '–but he squandered it on foolishness and invention.'

Heglan remained silent throughout his chastisement. Strombak left a long pause to glare at him, measuring him as he would a windlass, crank or a mechanism, to see if what he was saying was sinking in. He grumbled something inaudible, an expression not a word, then sighed deeply.

'Another misstep and you'll be cast out, sworn to secrecy about all you know of our craft.' Jabbing a leathery finger at Heglan, he said, 'Change your ways or change your profession! Barrel makers and hruk shearers are always looking for guilders. Now,' he added, drawing in a long breath that flared his nostrils, 'gather up that mess and use it to fashion something that works, something tried and tested. Tradition, not progression, lad – *that* is the dawi way.'

Heglan nodded – there was little else he could do – and was left alone with Nadri.

On the Durazon, the winter sun was dying as the storm from the southern peaks eclipsed it. Black clouds were gathering, billowing like wool across the sky and full with the promise of thunder.

Wearily, the engineer picked himself up. It felt as if he'd been beaten by a mob of urk.

'Bloody Dungni, son of Thok!' he spat, his shame giving way to anger. If his glare could kill then the dwarf captain sloping back towards the outer gate of the hold would have died at once. 'Drunken bloody *bozdok*. The clod handles a ship like a grobi grabbing at a hruk. Grungni's arse, I'll see this lodged with the reckoners.'

Nadri looked on grimly, at Dungni and the wreck scattered like kindling across the lowland.

'Stoke that furnace, brother. A dawi without fire in his gut is no dawi at all,' he said, and whistled at the devastation. 'Not much to salvage?'

'Ruined, brother,' said Heglan his voice barely louder than a whisper. 'There is nothing left. Nothing.' He seemed to sag, sinking lower than when he was on his knees. 'Bugger.'

A muted cough broke the brief silence that had fallen between them. Nadri turned at the thinly veiled signal.

'Krondi?' he said, addressing one of the merchants who had also remained behind but who was anonymously waiting at the gate to Merman Pass.

'My thane.' Krondi bowed deeply. He was a grizzled dwarf, who had seen much battle in the wars of the High King against the urk. Fair-bearded, he never really fit into the mould of a merchant but had been part of the guild for almost a decade. 'We are expected in Zhufbar in just over two weeks.'

'Aye,' said Nadri, 'and a stop to make at Karaz-a-Karak beforehand. I am well aware of our commitments, Krondi.'

Krondi bowed. 'Of course, my thane.'

Nadri narrowed his eyes at the other merchant. 'Is our passenger ready to travel?'

'He is. Our wagons stand ready to depart at your word.'

Nadri looked down at the wreck in the valley again. 'Then it would not do to keep him waiting,' he said to himself beneath his breath before regarding Krondi again. 'Ride on ahead and pass on my assurances to the king's reckoners that he'll get what he's owed. Gildtongue has never reneged on a bond of trade, tell them.'

Though Nadri's family name was Copperfist, he was known as 'Gildtongue' by his fellows in the merchants' guild on account that his every word turned to gold. So successful was he as a trader that he had holdings and wealth that some kings would envy. Of course, in Karaz-a-Karak the hoard of any merchant would always be bettered by the High King.

'I need you to leave me two carts with mules and drivers, Krondi.'

Krondi bowed again and left down the Merman Pass without further word.

'You risk much by not making full delivery, brother,' said Heglan. 'Don't let my failure drag you down.'

'Don't be a wazzock, Heg. By Valaya's golden cups, I'm helping you pick up the pieces of your ship. There is no argument to be had.'

Heglan looked about to protest, but there would be no changing Nadri's mind and so he capitulated. He cast a final glance at the wreckage, the vessel into which he had poured his craft, his sweat and his heart.

'I could have made it fly,' he uttered, the strength of his voice stolen by the wind.

Nadri tried to be consoling. 'You did, brother.'

'That wasn't flight, it was a slow fall.'

'Don't be too disheartened, Heg. At least you are still of the guild.' Nadri was heading towards Merman Gate. From there, they'd travel the winding pass all the way to the upper hold gate, just above the first deep.

Heglan waited until Nadri had passed under the Merman Gate and was out of earshot.

'I *will* make it fly, brother,' he said beneath his breath. 'For Dammin and Lodri Copperfist, I shall do it.'

Heglan and Nadri were already back inside the hold, through the fastness wall and more than halfway down Merman Pass when a bell tolled. It was a warning signal from the sea wall at the other side of Barak Varr.

Through the glass lens the waters of the Black Gulf undulated like a desert of obsidian. Tiny breakers, errant spumes of white foam, exposed the lie of that misperception. In the storm darkness it appeared endless, stretching to an infinite horizon. In truth, it was vast and the Sea Hold of Barak Varr was its only bastion-port.

A flotilla of *ghazan-harbarks*, six in all, plied the gulf. A signal had roused them and together they looked for enemies.

Nugdrinn Hammerfoot perched on the prow of one of the ships, and scoured a small stretch of the Black Gulf that was lapping at the flanks of the Sea Hold. He had a brass telescope pressed to his left eye and peered hard through the lens. Three beacons were lit in the watchtowers, which meant three dwarfs had seen something approaching the gate. A warning bell was tolling, warring with the persistent ringing in the captain's ears, but thus far the horns had stayed silent.

Cessation of the bell and the clarion of horns meant danger approached and the many defences of the sea wall would be levelled at the intruders. Batteries of ballistae and mangonels stood sentry upon the wall, as well as a hefty garrison of Barak Varr quarrellers. If the ghazan-harbarks were the hunters then the warriors on the sea wall would be the spear to slay whatever predator was lurking in the darkness beyond their lanterns.

'Bori, bring the lamp forwards,' he said, one meaty fist wrapped around a length of rope to steady him, one clutching the telescope to his remaining eye. The other was patched, a small oval of leather studded with the ancestor badge of Grungni.

O'er earth and sea, the great miner sees all, Nugdrinn would often say and tap his eye-patch. In other words, just because he only had one eye didn't mean he wasn't watching. 'Shine it here, lad.' He pointed with the telescope. 'Here. Quickly now.'

Nugdrinn had been a sailor all of his life. Born and raised in Barak Varr, there was no ship he could not sail, no ocean he dared not face. Unlike many dwarfs, even those of the Sea Hold, he was at peace with a stout hull and the waves beneath him, so whilst on the gulf his instincts could not be more honed. They were telling him something was out there, lurking in the dark.

Nugdrinn wanted to know what it was.

Lantern light washed over the water, casting it in ruddy orange. It was as if a fire was burning beneath the waves, just about to emerge and swathe the Black Gulf in conflagration.

Beasts lurked in the deeps, way down in the cold ocean darkness. Tales abounded of tentacled kraken and vicious megaladon, the dread black leviathan and the unearthly Triton. Such stories were spun by drunken sailors looking to enhance their reputation or angling for a pint of grog at the listener's expense, but Nugdrinn knew first hand there was some truth to them.

Out in the deep ocean he had seen... *shadows* lurking just beneath the waves, too vast and grotesque to be some mundane predator. Issuing from miles below, he had heard the call of beasts, abyssal deep and full of malice.

One moonless night, many years ago in the waters of the far north, he had witnessed the hide of some gargantuan beast slowly disappearing beneath the waves. Returning with the holds of their three grubarks brimming with the gold of the northern king, Nugdrinn had glimpsed the monster from a distance. By the time he had the telescope to his eye, the beast had sunk beneath the water but several sundered ships were left in its wake.

It was a chill night. Frost clung to the deck, resolved as a ghostly pale mist in the captain's breath. Ice cracked as the dwarfs' ships ploughed through it. Nugdrinn's teeth chattered and not just from the abominable cold. It took several minutes to find the courage to sail close enough to the scene of devastation to look for survivors. It took less time for them to discover there were no crewmen amongst the broken hulks. Only blood remained, and carnage.

Stooping to hook a broken piece of debris that carried the clan's sigil so he might bring word of their demise to their kin, Nugdrinn saw a great blackness through the gaps in the floating remains of the ship. Too late, he recoiled but by then the beast had scented his fear. It came crashing out of the waves stinking of old blood and the cold dank of death. With its single gelatinous eye, the beast fixed on Nugdrinn. Its first bite took apart the grubark, tore a great cleft from the hull and doomed it. Under such incredible pressure, the deck violently split apart and sent a dagger-sized splinter into the dwarf's eye. Nugdrinn screamed but had enough about him still to try and scramble back up what was left of his ship before a second bite claimed his foot.

Half blind, Nugdrinn roared. He bit his lip, used the pain to stop himself from passing out. Blood gushing from the ruined stump of his left leg was already freezing, sealing up the wound. A deeper cold was spreading through Nugdrinn's body when the other dwarfs attacked. Crossbow bolts, some with their tips drenched in oil and then lit, hailed the beast. Thick-bladed throwing axes gouged its flanks. Piercing its blubbery hide, the barbed quarrels drew a bleat of pain from the beast's puckered maw, which was champing up and down on the rapidly disintegrating hull. A noisome stench rolled from its gullet, redolent of putrefaction and the slow rot of the half-frozen dead.

A second barrage of axes and quarrels forced the beast under but it had claimed Nugdrinn's foot and his eye.

Anger and a desire for retribution kept him alive until the dwarfs reached Barak Varr some months later. A mattock head was forged by Guildmaster Strombak to replace the piece of his limb he had lost and so Nugdrinn became 'Hammerfoot' to ever remind him of what he owed the beast.

The memory of that night still brought a tremor to his hand that made the view through his telescope quiver, if only slightly. Nugdrinn took a stronger grip of the rope, glad his rune axe was looped to the belt around his waist.

'Is it you, daemon?' he asked the water. 'Has the gulf spewed up a monster from the watery hells of Triton's cage?'

The water didn't answer.

Instead, the amber glow of the lantern crept across the waves until it found something to alight on.

Nugdrinn snapped shut the telescope and pulled out his axe. He'd fight the beast one-handed, lashed to the prow.

'Come forth then,' he bellowed, vying against the roar of the water that was in a foaming frenzy with the wind peeling off the northern peaks. 'And I'll take from you what you took from me in recompense.'

His ghazan-harbark pitched and yawed but Nugdrinn barely noticed. Adrift on rough water was akin to walking to the experienced captain. His face was slick with spray, little diamonds of seawater clinging to his beard. A rime of salt layered his upper lip and he licked it.

'I taste blood on the water, fiend,' he promised. 'I'll open up yer belly and release those poor lost souls you devoured. I'll cut yer until your entrails spill into the black and are swallowed whole by the briny deep. Come forth!'

For such a monster to be found so close to Barak Varr was unheard of, but Nugdrinn wasn't about to shame the ancestors by doubting it.

A shadow, half-revealed in the lamplight, became more distinct as its identity was unmasked at last.

Nugdrinn lowered his axe, and let his ire cool.

'Douse the lamp,' he said. His heart thundered, and his breath quickened in his chest.

It was wood floating on the gulf. Just a piece of hull, a chunk of stern or prow, some vessel broken out in the deep ocean and washed up on the shores of Barak Varr.

It was nothing. Yet, as the urgency and fervour fled his veins and left him cold and trembling, Nugdrinn could not shake the feeling that there had been something out in the gulf.

But the bell tolled on and no horn was heard on the rough black waters.

'Douse the lamps,' Nugdrinn said again, retreating back to the deck and wondering what they had missed.

Blood magic was never predictable. It was a roiling mass of archaic forces drawn together through murder and slaughter, a hound brought to the leash but never fully at heel. Dhar, the Dark Wind, was capricious but the deeds that could be wrought through its manipulation were great and terrible. Drutheira knew her art well, however, and had practised much. She knew, as all sorcerers must, that dark magic always required sacrifice. The dead druchii warrior with her throat cut, spilling arterial crimson all over the deck, was testament to that.

Most of the blood from the corpse had been wasted, but there was enough to fill a ritual bowl in the middle of the deck. From it tendrils of ruddy smoke quested like the tentacles of some abyssal horror. They enveloped the raiding ship, occluded it from sight. Thus clouded could the dark elves pass by the watchtowers of the dwarfs and gain passage through the Black Gulf into the rivers of the Old World proper.

Two other witches, Malchior and Ashniel, completed the coven. Lesser sorcerers both than Drutheira, they channelled their mastery into her and she became a conduit that articulated the power of the whole. Sweat dappled her brow, intense concentration written upon her face as she maintained the casting all the way through the gate markers that led them north. As one the triumvirate muttered their incantations through taut, bloodless lips as the other warriors looked to the sea wall and hoped the enchantment would hold long enough for them to pass by.

At the stern of the raider ship, a dark elf stood ready behind the vessel's reaper. The single bolt thrower would find itself quickly outmatched by the battalion of ballistae arrayed against it, so too the twenty or so warriors armed with spear and shield at the ship's flanks. Their fate was in the hands of Drutheira and her witches.

Slowly, agonisingly so, the sea wall faded from sight and the dark elves left the Sea Hold behind them with the dwarfs unaware of them ever having been present in their waters.

Drutheira let out a pained breath, the evidence of her body's trauma revealed in the dark flecks on the hand that she used to cover her mouth.

The others sagged, visibly drained. Ashniel wiped a trickle of crimson from her mouth, whilst Malchior staunched his bleeding left nostril with a black cloth he then secreted back into his robes.

'*Dhar* is a hard mistress,' he remarked, coughing into his hand. When he wiped it away quickly with his sleeve there was blood on his palm.

'Does the sight of blood on your own skin upset you, Malchior?' Ashniel was young and impetuous, but possessed rare magical talent. She also delighted in taunting Malchior.

'I am perfectly sanguine, my little dear,' he replied in a sibilant voice, a savage and murderous glint in his eyes. 'But I would much rather it was your blood.'

Bristling at the obvious threat, she spoke through a dagger-curved grin. 'I could flay the flesh from your bones, here in this very ship.'

Malchior did his best to appear unmoved. 'Ah, the boldness of youth. Such overconfidence for a whelp...'

'Whore-killing dog!' she hissed, summoning a nimbus of dark magic and shaping it in her talon-like fingers.

'Cease your bickering,' snapped Drutheira, dispelling the casting with a curt slash of her hand, 'and know that I am a harder mistress than the Wind of Dhar.' Her wrath faded as quickly as it had appeared, and she narrowed her eyes like a predator to its unwitting prey. 'Save your strength. Both of you. We are not finished, not yet.'

That revelation brought a sneer to Ashniel's blade-thin lips. Malchior tried to hide his dismay behind a viper's charm but failed.

'Whatever our mistress requires,' he purred with a small bow.

Ashniel showed her acquiescence by turning the sneer into a mirthless smile. Drutheira had seen harpies with more humour and resolved to kill the little witch once this was done.

She glanced down at the brass bowl around which the coven was sitting. Together they formed a triangle with Drutheira at its apex. Crimson steam rolled off the sloped interior of the bowl and once it cleared only a residue of the vital fluid remained.

'Vaulkhar,' she called, as if summoning something as mundane as wine or meat, 'I need more.'

The vaulkhar nodded and gestured to two of his crew. A third, who paled when the captain's cold gaze fell upon him, drew his sword but was subdued before he could put up much of a fight. Disarmed, forced to kneel over the bowl, he screamed as Drutheira drew her ritual knife and cut his throat.

Blood, hot and fresh, spilled into the sacrificial vessel.

'Communion...' uttered Drutheira, her voice laced with power, and the three began to chant.

Bubbles rose on the surface of the dark pool as if it were boiling, but no heat emanated from within. Instead an image began to resolve as the fluid thickened. Scarred as if by fire and contorted into a rictus of pure agony, a face appeared in the morass. It had been noble once, now it was ravaged and hellish. Opening its mouth in a silent scream, the face arched back and was consumed.

The bubbling subsided, replaced by ripples, slight at first but growing with intensity as the seconds passed. A pair of tiny nubs, like the peaks of two mountains surrounded by a lake, protruded from the pool. Nubs became horns and the horns crested an ornate helm of jagged edges and bladed ornamentation. It was a barbed piece of armour, sharp and cold. Dripping with blood, its entire surface drowned in viscous gore, a head emerged from the deep red mire.

Unlike before, furnace heat radiated off this manifestation that pricked the skin and brought a grimace of pain to Drutheira's face.

'Dark lord,' she uttered, bowing her head in deference.

Though fashioned magically from congealed blood, her master was no less terrifying. He glowered at the coven, his malice as palpable as the gore-slicked deck beneath them.

At first his words were too thick to understand, spoken in an ancient and evil tongue Drutheira could not translate. Slowly, inexorably, it began to make sense.

'*Tell me of your progress,*' commanded the bloody effigy.

'We cross the borders of the Sea Hold, lord and are even now headed northwards.'

'*And the dwarfs are unaware of your presence?*'

'We passed their defences undetected. The stunted swine could not tell us from the ugly noses on their faces,' she added, allowing a pang of hubris to colour her reply.

'*Don't underestimate them,*' the face snarled, and Drutheira recoiled from its hate and power as if struck. '*Snorri Whitebeard was no fool, and had power. His descendants are worthy of you, sorceress.*'

'No, of course not,' she whispered, abruptly cowed. 'All is as you bid it, lord.'

'*An alliance must not be made between elf and dwarf. They must destroy one another utterly.*'

'It will be as you will it.'

'*See that it is.*'

Rivulets were streaking down the effigy as the magical communion lost potency. Like wax before a strong flame, the blood was slowly melting back into the pool from whence it emerged.

'What is your command, lord?' asked Drutheira, concealing her relief at the spell's ending.

'*Our allies are already abroad. The shade Sevekai and his band await my orders through you. Together, enact my plans I have given to you. See the asur undone by their own nature.*' As the face sloughed away, its words became slurred and indistinct. The horns had already gone, collapsed into the pool along with much of the jagged helm. Even the eyes had bled away to nothing, the head caving in shortly after until only the mouth remained. '*Yours is but a piece of a much greater plan. Sevekai is to be your scout, your herald. Use him. Fail me and you need not return to Naggaroth...*'

Like the final exhalation of breath from a corpse, the voice gurgled into nothing but the threat remained as real and immediate as a knife perpetually at her throat.

Drutheira swallowed, imagining the caress of that steel, and drew on hidden reserves of strength to speak.

I am drained, she said into the minds of her coven. Her eyes were closed. To the warriors aboard the raider ship it would appear as if she were meditating.

We all are, Ashniel replied, as precocious as ever.

Drutheira kept her annoyance at the interruption from her face.

That is why when we reach the shore we will kill every elf aboard this ship and steal the vigour from their blood.

Storm clouds billowed across the mainland, presaging the chaos to come.

At the prow of the ship, the vaulkhar snarled orders to the crew. Unbeknownst to him and his warriors, the coven shared a conspirators' smile.

Malekith had spoken and they would enact his will or they would die.

SIX

MASTER OF DRAGONS

A great roar echoed across the peaks. It split the storm in two like a jag of lightning cuts the sky in half and leaves a ragged tear behind it.

Sheltered beneath an overhanging spur of rock, the dwarfs kept their eyes on the heavens. Morgrim's ached from not blinking.

'I still don't see anything.' He had to shout against the wind, which had grown into a tumultuous gale. Drifts peeling off the mountains skirled through the pass and swathed the rocky clearing where they hid in grubby grey-white.

Flecks of snow clung to Snorri's beard like ugly, malformed pearls. He spat through clenched teeth. 'If it is a drakk, I will spill its heartblood and paint the ground red with it.'

Angular runes on his axe blade began to glow as he summoned their power with a muttered oath.

'Two dwarfs with fate on our side against a beast that can raze entire towns with its breath and lay siege to a hold single-handed,' said Morgrim. 'I'd say the odds are with us, cousin.'

Snorri did not reply. His gaze was fixed, the grip around the haft of his axe like stone.

The whip of battered air drew nearer, a low and steady *thwomp* of vast, membranous wings driving against the gale. To maintain such a rhythm, the dragon must be incredibly strong.

Morgrim cried out as a shadow seen through cloud darkened the sky.
'It comes!'

A crack of lighting flared behind it and framed the beast in silhouette.
'Gods of earth and stone...'

The dragon was massive.

Snorri edged from beneath the craggy overhang, squinting against the snow hitting his face. He spat out a lump of frozen mulch and snarled, 'I'll turn its skin into a scale cloak...'

The dragon breached the clouds, tendrils of mist rolling off its muscled silver torso. A long, serpentine neck ended in a snout like a blade, fanged and drooling iridescent smoke. Unfurling its wings, the beast's shadow eclipsed the dwarfs and the entire clearing where they were standing. Like two metal sails, its mighty pinions shimmered as star-fire. Talons like sword blades extended from its feet, and eyes akin to flawless onyx glittered hungrily as it saw the morsel before it.

'Make a tankard of its hollowed out skull...'

No dwarf, however skilled, could hope to defeat such a monster.

Morgrim grabbed for Snorri to haul him back but missed. 'Cousin, wait!'

'Destiny calls!' shouted Snorri and roared as he lifted his axe.

It was the single bravest and most foolish thing Morgrim had ever seen.

Thinking of all the things he had wanted to achieve and that would now be denied him, he sighed, '*Bugrit...*' and then charged after Snorri.

Pressing against the rock, Sevekai prayed to all the dark gods that would listen.

The beast had speared through the storm like a streak of ithilmar, bellowing with such intensity it put the elf's teeth on edge. Heart thundering in his chest, he dared a glance around the edge of the rocks where he and his warriors had gone to ground as soon as they had seen the dragon.

Killing the dwarfs now would be impossible, but then also hardly necessary given what they faced.

Kaitar was crouched beside him but seemed unmoved by the terrifying monster in their midst.

'Was the fear siphoned out of you as an infant, Kaitar?' asked Sevekai. 'Or are you simply too dull-witted to realise how imminent all of our deaths are?' He was about to withdraw, the dwarfs were good as dead anyway, when Kaitar put a hand on his chest.

Sevekai glared daggers at the elf but didn't raise a hand against him.

'A little hasty, I think,' he hissed, nodding towards the dragon.

As the beast landed, its claws pulverising rock, it lowered its head, revealing an elven warrior mounted on its back.

Silver-helmed with lance in hand, he looked like a prince of the ancient days when Malekith and Snorri Whitebeard both still walked the earth. Behind the dragon visor concealing his face, the elf lord's eyes glittered like emeralds.

Fastened to an ornate saddle of white wood and bone was a shield depicting an unsheathed sword. He bore the same device attached to the crown of his war helm.

He raised his hand, voice resonating through the mouth grille of his silver dragon mask. 'Hail, dwarfs of Everpeak,' he said, using rudimentary Khazalid and referring to Karaz-a-Karak by its common name.

Morgrim lowered his hammer, but not completely. Snorri was less keen to relent and maintained his belligerence before the monster.

The elf noble leaned forwards in the saddle and whispered to his beast, although his words carried on the storm.

'Easy, Draukhain.'

'State your business, elfling,' Snorri demanded.

The elf lord stowed his lance, its crimson pennant flapping in the fierce wind. Bowing, he raised his visor. Despite his ostensible geniality, he still sounded imperious.

'I am Imladrik of Caledor, Master of Dragons and Prince of Ulthuan, Lord of Oeragor. I bear you no ill-intent, lord dwarfs.'

Despite the offer of peace, Snorri was pugnacious. '*Dragon* master, eh? I slay dragons, elfling.'

Imladrik raised a gauntleted hand. The knuckles were fashioned as scales, the fingertips like talons.

'I am an ally to you. I mean no harm,' he assured them.

'Be calm,' Morgrim hissed to his cousin through clenched teeth, looking sidelong at the creature drooling sulphur and smoke.

Snorri hissed back, 'I won't be cowed by this elgi and his beast!'

'No, but you may be eaten, cousin!'

'A lot of titles for an elgi,' Snorri scoffed. 'I'm surprised you can remember them all. And you should be more concerned about who wants to harm who, elfling.'

Morgrim tried not to groan, but put a hand on his cousin's arm until he lowered his axe.

'You are far from Oeragor, Prince Imladrik,' he said, eager to defuse the situation once he'd calmed Snorri down. 'I am Morgrim, son of Bardum, thane of Karaz-a-Karak, and this–'

Snorri stepped forwards and thrust out his chest.

'I am Prince Snorri Lunngrin of Karaz-a-Karak, heir to the dwarf kingdom. You are upon my sovereign soil, elgi.'

Imladrik bowed, betraying no hint of reaction to the goading Snorri was attempting.

'I meant no offence, my lords. Through the storm, I saw travellers on the road. Once I realised you were dwarfs, I decided to descend and see if I could offer you a ride. It is a long way back to Everpeak, and since it is where I am bound...'

'Indeed it is a long way,' Morgrim agreed, thinking how his feet would ache after such a trek, and looked at his cousin who had yet to take his eyes off the dragon.

'A ride, eh? On the back of that beast? Is that what you're suggesting, prince?'

'It is faster than going on foot,' Imladrik replied without condescension.

The storm was dying out, the winds abating and the snows thinning until they were little more than errant drifts carried on the breeze. In the north-east, the sun was rising again, easing some warmth back into a cold winter's morning.

'It seems Kurnous favours us, my lords,' the elf prince added, gesturing to the improving weather. 'But I still think you'll reach Everpeak faster on Draukhain's back.'

Morgrim turned to his cousin and whispered, 'I have never ridden on the back of a dragon.'

'With good reason.' Snorri looked askance at the beast. 'They are fell and dangerous creatures. Not to be trusted, much like their masters.'

Elves were possessed of incredible hearing and Imladrik had heard every word exchanged between the dwarf nobles, but if he thought anything of it he did not show it. He merely smiled impassively and waited for them to make their decision.

Morgrim was insistent. 'I have no desire to walk back to the hold when I can as easily fly.'

'And I have no desire to be devoured by some beast of the lower deeps whilst my back is turned!'

Morgrim smiled.

'You are afraid.'

'I am not. I am scared of nothing. I am the son of the High King, a destined dragon slayer I might add.'

'Then ride the dragon and we'll be back in the hold hall before supper,' said Morgrim. 'I for one would like to get out of this thrice-damned cold and feel a fire on my skin, have meat in my belly.'

Snorri licked his lips at the prospect of meat. It had been a while since he tasted beef, smelled roast pork or elk. Stonebread was fortifying but it lacked flavour, in fact any taste at all.

'And what of beer?' Morgrim pressed. 'I would drain the brew-houses dry with my thirst.'

At the mention of ale, Snorri began to salivate and had to wipe his mouth.

All the while, the elf prince looked on.

'I've heard Jodri has uncasked a golden reserve and plans to serve it to the kings at the *rinkkaz*.'

'Which is another matter, cousin,' said Morgrim. 'Your father is expecting you at the council of kings.'

Snorri's expression darkened at mention of the High King. 'Aye, isn't he always.' He turned to Prince Imladrik. 'Very well, elfling, we shall accept your offer of transportation but mark me well,' he said, pointing rudely with an accusatory finger, 'any falsehood will mean the death of both you and your ugly beast.'

Imladrik bowed again, as he would in court. 'As gracious as you are direct, my dwarf prince.' At some unseen, unheard command, Draukhain went down on its forelegs and laid its neck upon the ground so the dwarfs could climb aboard its back. 'There is room enough on my saddle for two.'

'Does he trawl the skies often, looking for wayward travellers below?'

Snorri muttered behind his hand. He kept his rune axe loose in the sheath in case he needed it in a hurry.

'I doubt it, cousin, but I do know if you try his patience further we will be going back to Karaz-a-Karak charred to our very boots. Now shut it and get aboard!'

Snorri grumbled some expletive but reluctantly followed Morgrim as he approached the dragon.

Despite his fear, Sevekai edged forwards to try and better hear what transpired between the dragon rider and the dwarfs. An elf of Ulthuan, especially a prince, this close to the dwarf kingdoms was unusual. That he flew alone without his army or any retainers was stranger still.

Whatever the reason, it did not appear that the dwarfs were imperilled after all and that meant Sevekai still had a duty to perform. He silently drew a sickle blade from his baldric.

Verigoth interceded. 'What are you doing?' he hissed.

Sevekai bit back savagely, 'Don't question me, druchii! I've gutted people for less.'

'Perhaps Verigoth is right, brother.' Kaitar slipped between them, a finger on Sevekai's blade hand.

He sheathed it, incredulous that this was the second time Kaitar had touched him and the wretch still wasn't dead.

'We can get closer, listen in. Even if we cannot kill the nobles or their asur ally, we can discern their plans.'

Verigoth and the others looked no more enthusiastic about this plan than the previous one, but probable death was at least preferable to certain death.

'If we are discovered,' hissed Sevekai, glancing at the dragon then back at Kaitar, 'our dark lord's plans could be jeopardised, and I have no desire to engage the interest of the beast.'

Kaitar grinned, a faint resonance to his voice Sevekai hadn't noticed before. 'Then we creep softly and silently, like shadows.'

'Like shadows,' repeated Sevekai, eyes locked with Kaitar's.

Slowly, the dark elves detached themselves from their hiding place and began to creep closer.

Morgrim had already mounted the beast by the time Snorri was ready to do the same. Though he had agreed to ride upon the dragon's back, the dwarf prince kept his distance.

'Be careful, cousin,' he said, as Morgrim climbed a length of white hemp lowered by the prince. It was thin and Snorri had expected the rope to snap, but it proved equal to Morgrim's considerable mass.

'Must be bound with steel,' he muttered, but detected an aura shimmering off the rope.

Imladrik gestured to him, offering the saddle as one would welcome a stranger in their house. 'Your turn, my prince.'

It was then Snorri realised he had no desire to ride this beast, to fly amongst the clouds. The very thought of it brought an unpleasant acerbic tang to his mouth, but he swallowed it down, knowing he could not be outdone by his cousin.

'We are hall dwellers, not dragon riders,' he grumbled, cinching his belt up and reaching for the proffered rope.

The faint tang of spoiled meat, the scent of dust and ancient fire-baked plains, quite incongruous in winter, suddenly tainted the breeze.

Inches from grabbing the rope, Snorri's fingers seized. A second later and Draukhain reared up, its bulk smacking the dwarf onto his rump. It roared, spitting a plume of flame into the air and swinging its head around as if searching.

'Grimnir's teeth!' Snorri scrambled to his feet, reaching for his rune axe. 'Never trust an elgi! Never trust a drakk!' he spat, ripping the shimmering blade from its sheath.

Flung back in the saddle, Imladrik was trying to steady the beast. He muttered words of command and reprimand, but in a language neither dwarfs, nor most elves, could understand.

Morgrim was pitched off the dragon's back. He rolled, grabbing at the beast's spines to try and arrest his fall, and ended up dumped on the ground next to its thrashing tail. An errant flick caught his helm and he staggered, trying to back away. Like Snorri, he had drawn his weapon.

Not understanding what was happening, together the dwarfs circled the beast.

Snorri's expression was murderous as he briefly met his cousin's gaze. There was more than a hint of self-satisfaction in his eyes.

'You offer us safe passage on your drakk,' he said to the elf, 'and then it tries to kill us!'

'Lords, please.' Imladrik was still struggling to calm Draukhain, though his verbal goads had lessened. Instead, intense concentration was etched on his face as an entirely different war of wills played out.

'What is he doing?' whispered Morgrim, swinging his hammer around in a ready grip.

Snorri wasn't listening. His teeth were clenched. 'If dawi were meant to fly, Grimnir would not have taught us how to kill wyverns and drakk. Any creature with wings is no friend to a dawi,' he spat.

Ignorant of the dwarfs circling him and his mount, Imladrik closed his eyes and began to sing. A soft, lilting refrain echoed across the clearing. Though the elf's words rarely rose above a whisper, they were resonant with power and potency. Each syllable was perfectly enunciated, every string of incantation precisely exacted.

At first Draukhain resisted, reacting to whatever it was that had ignited its predatory wrath. But slowly, as the pattern repeated and Imladrik wove the dragonsong tighter and tighter around it, the beast was soothed and its head bowed. Anger still burned in the black pits of its eyes, but it was fading to embers.

When he was done, Imladrik sank a little in his seat as if his armour was suddenly heavier. When he removed his war helm, his face was gaunt and dappled with beads of sweat.

'My sincerest apologies,' he began, a little out of breath, 'He has never done that before, except in battle. Something enflamed his anger, I don't know what.'

'Perhaps it was a hankering to taste dwarf flesh,' Snorri chided. 'I warn you, my meat is bloody tough!' He brandished his axe meaningfully. 'And my *rhuns* are sharp.'

Mortified, Imladrik put his palms together in a gesture for peace and calm. 'Please, it was a misunderstanding.'

Snorri wasn't about to back down. The beast had accepted Morgrim without complaint, but railed against his presence. It was a matter of wounded pride now, a sin that the prince of Karaz-a-Karak had in abundance.

'And if we'd have been aloft when another "misunderstanding" took place? What then, eh? Cast to the earth like crag hawks pinioned by a quarreller's bolt, left to be dashed on the rocks as a red smear.' He thumped his chest. 'I am dawi born, stone and steel. If you wish us dead then fight us face-to-face, you dirty, thagging elgi.'

It was a step too far. Morgrim knew it and went to say something but no words could take back his cousin's insult.

Imladrik paled, and not from the exertions of his dragonsong. He had to bite back his anger, covering it with a low bow. His eyes glittered dangerously when he rose again, as hard as the gemstones they so closely resembled.

'I deeply regret this, and offer apology to you both. I shall convey the same remarks to your father, the High King,' he said to Snorri alone, 'but you have much to learn of elves, young prince. Much indeed.'

Obeying a snarled command, Draukhain speared into the air and emitted a roar of sympathetic anger. With a few beats of its mighty wings, both dragon and elven prince were gone, lost to the cloud and the endless sky.

'That was foolish,' said Morgrim. He had followed the dragon's searching gaze to a cluster of rocks outlining the clearing but could see nothing amiss amongst them.

'Foolish was it?' Snorri turned, but when he saw the look on his cousin's face his vainglorious pride deserted him. He muttered, 'Perhaps I did speak out of turn.'

'Your words were callous, cousin, and ill-considered.'

Snorri looked to his boots, then to his half-hand. His anger, self-directed, rose again. 'My father has said something similar to me often. Are you going to rebuke me constantly as he does, cousin?'

'I...' Morgrim met Snorri's hurt gaze and knew the prince was just lashing out. The High King was a hard taskmaster, tougher on his son than even his most veteran generals. It would be difficult to bear for any dwarf. In the end, Morgrim relented. 'No cousin, I will not. But without wings to take us back to hearth and hold, we have a long journey ahead of us. I don't think we'll make the rinkkaz. Your father will be wrathful, I fear.'

'Let him,' the prince snorted. 'I would rather walk the road in my boots, facing urk and troll, even my father's anger, than risk life and limb on the back of a drakk.' He stomped off down the path, slinging his axe onto his back and swearing loudly with every step.

Morgrim decided not to reply and fell in behind him to let his cousin vent.

The return to Karaz-a-Karak suddenly seemed much longer and more arduous.

Crouched in a thicket of dense scrub, Sevekai fought to catch his breath. When the dragon had reared up, he had fled with the others back down the ridge.

The ambush site was close by, as yet undiscovered.

Killing dwarf merchants in the darkness was something he had a taste for, but he was no dragon slayer. In truth, the creatures terrified him. Even those slaved to the will of the druchii he treated with wary apprehension. It had taken him all his willpower to stay hidden when the beast had bayed for their blood.

Verigoth was still shaking and took a pinch of *ashkallar* to calm his nerves. The narcotic was fast-acting but the tremors still remained.

'Did it see us?' he asked.

Sevekai shook his head, reliving the moment in a waking nightmare.

'We'd already be dead if it had,' he breathed. His gaze fell on Kaitar, who was watching them all impassively. 'Are you not disturbed at all, Kaitar?'

He shrugged, as bizarre and incongruous a gesture as he could make in the circumstances.

'We are alive. What is there left to fear?'

Numenos had taken out his blades to sharpen them and calm his shattered nerves. Though his body still trembled, his hands were steady. It spread slowly up his arms, to his neck and back.

'Is it ice or blood you have in your veins, druchii?' he asked, glancing up from his labours to regard Kaitar.

'Neither,' Kaitar answered with a laugh.

Watching the exchange keenly, Sevekai couldn't tell if he was joking or not.

Mirth changed to murder with the shifting of the breeze on Kaitar's face. 'We should go back and kill those two dwarfs.'

Sevekai shook his head. 'That door is closed to us.'

'The beast is fled,' Kaitar pressed.

With a flash of silver, Sevekai's sickle blade was at Kaitar's throat. His voice was thick with threat. 'I said no.'

Kaitar raised his hands, showing Sevekai his palms in a plaintive gesture. 'As you wish.'

Glaring at him for a moment longer, Sevekai lowered his blade and returned it to its place on his baldric. He addressed the warband. 'The storm is abating,' he said, gesturing to the breaking cloud. 'We will need fresh attire by the time the dawn breaches it.'

Before sailing to the Old World, his mind was implanted with Malekith's sorcery. Into Sevekai's mental pathways, he had poured memories of the secret trade routes of the dwarfs, those learned many years ago when he had befriended their High King. Snorri Whitebeard was long dead, so too Malekith's affinity for dwarfs. Only cruelty remained, and a desire for vengeance against those who had wronged him and cast him from his rightful throne.

Sevekai felt these desires vicariously like hot knives in his mind as he sifted through the scraps of memory he needed to fulfil his mission. Failure was not something he dared countenance. Killing the dwarf lords would have garnered favour but his spine was not up to the task of returning to the clearing. An image resolved in his mind's eye, a sheltered passageway of rock and earth, high hills and scattered forest. He had never seen the trail before yet it was as familiar to him as his own hand, or the blade he wielded with it. A second vision revealed a face: a woman, a sorceress, and a name to go with it.

Drutheira.

She was to be their overseer. Sevekai scowled inwardly, and wondered if she had requested this duty. It would not surprise him in the least.

'We move now,' he said.

They needed to find elves first, some asur to kill and steal from before they ambushed again or met up with the sorceress.

It would be as it was before, only this time they would be brazen and leave a survivor.

'Follow me,' said Sevekai, the route burning brightly like a torturer's fire in his head. 'We have elves and dwarfs to kill.'

Snorri and Morgrim were skirting the foothills when the dauntless peaks of Karaz-a-Karak towered above them through mist and cloud. Monolithic ancestor statues tall as the flank of the mountain loomed into view, silently appraising the nobles with stern stone countenances.

Shading his eyes from the sun, Morgrim looked up in awe. 'I see Smednir and Thungi, sons of Grungni and Valaya.'

Several hours had passed since their encounter with Imladrik and his dragon, but the memory of it remained – as did the burning insult Snorri felt at the beast's sudden change in temperament. But to the prince's credit, he kept it hidden.

Snorri followed his cousin's gaze, then looked further across the mountain to an eagle gate, one of the lofty eyries through which the honoured brotherhood of the Gatekeepers kept watch on the upper world. Beneath and beside the chiselled portal hewn into the very mountainside were more dwarf ancestors.

'And there is Gazul and your namesake Morgrim, at Grimnir's side.'

All of the ancestors, their siblings and progeny were rendered as immense cyclopean statues around the flank of Karaz-a-Karak. Crafted in the elder days, they reminded all of the Worlds Edge of the hold's importance and closeness to the gods.

With the hold in sight, the mood between the cousins began to improve.

'More than once, I thought we were bound for the underearth and Gazul's halls,' said Morgrim.

'Bah, not even close, cousin. You fret too much.' Snorri slapped him on the back, grinning widely. He thrust his chin up, breathed deeply of the imagined scent of forges and the hearth he would soon enjoy. 'Lords of the mountain, cousin. Both of us. Ha!'

Morgrim's own declaration was less ebullient. 'Lords of the mountain, Snorri.' He looked down at his cousin's ruined hand. 'And with the wounds to prove it.'

Snorri sniffed. 'A scratch, Morgrim, nothing more than that.' When his eyes alighted on a figure waiting on the road ahead, his smile faded. 'Oh bugger...'

'Eh?' Morgrim was reaching for his hammer when he came to the same realisation as Snorri. 'Oh bugger.'

Furgil Torbanson, thane of pathfinders, stood in the middle of the road with a loaded crossbow hanging low at his hip on a strap of leather. At the other hip he carried a pair of hand axes in a deerskin sheath. In place of a helmet, he wore a leather cap of elk hide, three feathers protruding from the peak. Lightly armoured, most of his attire was rustic, woven from hardy wool and dyed in deep greens and browns as befitted a ranger.

He was not a dwarf given to saying much, but his eyes gave more away in that moment than his tongue ever would. 'You have been missed, lords of Everpeak.'

Four other rangers blended out of the foothills. Dressed in the same manner as Furgil, they also carried various pots and pans about them. One also had a brace of conies tied to his belt, another had a pheasant.

'Are we having a feast?' Snorri ventured hopefully.

'No young prince, we are not,' said a stern, unyielding voice from farther up the road. When a hulking, armoured warrior, much larger than the rangers, stepped into his eye line, Snorri groaned. 'Thurbad,' he muttered, nodding to the captain of the hearthguard. 'I take it my father sent you to bring me back?'

'He did.'

Thurbad's brown beard was resplendent where the rangers' were scratchy and unkempt. His gromril armour shone, though the cloak around his shoulders achieved much to conceal it. A chest plate inscribed with a dwarf face glowered at them both from within the folds of the ranger cloak. His honorific was 'Shieldbearer', a name he had earned time and again in service of his liege-lord.

'And I also assume that my father is not happy with me?'

Thurbad's chin, much like the rest of his granite face, was like a slab of rock.

'He is not.' He looked down, noticed the prince's bandaged hand and frowned.

'Lost some fingers to a rat,' Snorri explained.

Thurbad's frown deepened.

'It was a *big* rat.'

'You'll go to a temple of Valaya and have your hand seen to before going to the High King,' said Thurbad. His tone made it clear there would be no argument.

'And after that I'll feel my father's wrath?'

Thurbad's jaw twitched then clenched at what he saw as disrespect.

'Yes, young liege, then you will feel the High King's fury like a furnace fire has been lit under your arse. Follow. Now.'

With a curt word he dismissed the rangers, who were led by Furgil into the wilds.

Armour clanking, Thurbad stalked away. Not far from the road, a cohort of hearthguard was waiting.

Morgrim waited until Thurbad was out of earshot before he spoke. 'Not quite the welcome home we had envisaged, cousin.'

'I would almost rather be back with the drakk,' Snorri moaned, dragging his feet after Thurbad and his warriors.

SEVEN

HEARTH AND HOLD

Thurbad left them as soon as they had passed through the great gate and were safely inside the outer entrance hall of the upper deep. A vast echoing chamber had greeted the dwarf nobles, a very dark and sombre place with its gloom leavened partly by immense brazier pans aloft on chains suspended from the vaulted ceiling. The glow of fiery coals cast a lambent light across statues, inscribed columns and yawning archways. It barely reached the ceiling, the creeping tongues of fire lapping less than halfway up the columns, but cast enough of a glow to make the inlaid gemstones sparkle like a firmament of lost stars embedded in a stony sky.

At the back of the chamber, across a sprawling plaza of stone slabs, was the *Ekrund*. This monstrously broad stairway was the outer marker that led to the lower deeps and the hold proper. Stout-looking Gatekeepers, the same brotherhood who watched the eagle gates, glared like stone golems from their posts, barring the way below to the uninvited.

At its flanks, half hidden in shadowy alcoves, were the hearthguard. Though ostensibly the bodyguard of dwarf nobles, the warrior veterans were arrayed in force to safeguard the many retainers and dignitaries the kings and regents of the other holds had brought with them as part of their entourages.

Treasure keepers, shield carriers and lantern-hands, oath-makers, lore-keepers, reckoners, banner bearers, weaponsmiths and gold counters, muleskinners and their mules, wheelwrights, bards, brewmasters, cooks and consorts all hustled together more than a thousand strong. Like any regal lord a dwarf king had need of many servants, but such retainers were never admitted to the great halls. Despite the masses, the grand entrance hall was not even close to full. Yet dwarfs favoured closeness to their kith and kin, and so the entourage of each king and regent chose to stand together.

They were watched keenly by quarrellers, the king's own, from a lofty perch of stone overlooking the entire chamber. Both Snorri and Morgrim knew that two hundred and fifty of the Eagle Watch were tasked with the safeguarding of the outer entrance hall. There were no better marksmen in the realm, not even the rangers.

As soon as the nobles had set foot inside the hall a doleful voice had boomed out, resonating through a speaking horn.

'Prince Snorri Lunngrin, son of Gotrek, of clan Thunderhorn,' it announced, and then 'Morgrim Bargrum, son of Bardum, of clan Ironbeard,' shortly afterwards. This had continued, until each and every one of the new arrivals was accounted for, named and recorded.

All had bowed, even Snorri, to the speaker and showed their respect as one.

'Tromm,' they intoned.

Standing behind a pulpit of stone, raised above ground level by a thick dais, was one of Karaz-a-Karak's lorekeepers. A thick, leather-bound tome sat on the lectern in front of him and he called the names of each and every visitor, be it dwarf, elf or otherwise, that entered or left the entrance hall. This he then recorded in his book for the later use of reckoners or chroniclers. With all the retainers currently in residence, there was little wonder the lorekeeper was hoarse.

'And so we are named,' said Morgrim as the hearthguard departed.

'Are you not seeing me to the temple then, Shieldbearer?' Snorri asked of Thurbad.

The hearthguard captain did not look back. 'I've charged your cousin with that duty, my prince.'

'Let it be known that Thurbad Shieldbearer did make grudgement against the heir of Karaz-a-Karak,' said Snorri in a petulant tone under his breath.

'You'd be wise not to bait him, cousin.'

'Aye, I reckon my next lesson in axecraft or hammer throwing will be a hard one.'

'I have no doubt at all.'

Morgrim gestured to the myriad retainers thronging part of the hall. He noted some bored but stoic faces.

'The rinkkaz must be well attended and many hours old.'

'It will last for days, cousin,' Snorri moaned, striding purposefully towards the Ekrund, 'days. You had best get me to my priestess. I think I'll have need of some fortification before seeing my father again,' he said with a wink.

'I do not envy him, cousin,' said Morgrim, 'not at all.'

At the entrance to the temple of Valaya, the dwarfs parted ways.

Snorri regarded his bandaged hand. The blood had long since clotted, making a mess of the wrappings Morgrim had used to staunch the bleeding.

'You are not half bad as a nurse, cousin. Shave your beard and perhaps they'd have you at the temple if the miners' guild doesn't work out for you.'

'I see your humour has returned,' Morgrim answered dryly.

'Only, if you do, make sure you don't tend *my* battlefield injuries. I would rather it be a rinn that bathe my cuts and clean my wounds. One in particular, in fact.' A flash of mischief lit up Snorri's eyes at this last remark.

'Ah, and now I see why.'

'She has been waiting for me, I am sure.'

Morgrim groaned, removing his horned helmet to massage his forehead in exasperation.

'Tenacious as ever then?'

'Would you not be with a rinn like that? She is no Helda.'

'*That* we can agree on. You do know that priestesses cannot be betrothed to any dwarf, noble or not?'

'Who is talking about marriage here, cousin?'

The Valkyrie Maidens, temple warriors of Valaya, glared scornfully at the prince from behind their half-faced war helms but Snorri seemed not to notice.

Morgrim rubbed his eyes, as if a persistent headache he thought gone had suddenly returned to haunt him.

'I bid you farewell and good luck,' he said. 'I'll go and find what news there is to be had of the hold. Try and keep it in your trousers.'

Snorri grinned. 'I make no promises.'

'Do you ever wonder, cousin, whether the reason you want her is because you cannot have her?'

'There is nothing I cannot have, cousin,' said Snorri, laughing as he was ushered silently through the gate and into the temple. 'I am the prince of Karaz-a-Karak!'

'You are a fool.'

Elmendrin's scowl was fiercer than some ogre chieftains Snorri had met. She was slowly removing the makeshift bandage, and regarded the chewed nubs of his fingers beneath. 'They were bitten off?' she asked, reaching for a salve and bidding an attendant to bring a bowl of clean water.

'I was rat hunting in the lower deeps of Karak Krum,' Snorri explained, smiling broadly and looking into Elemendrin's eyes. 'Sapphires do not sparkle as brightly,' he said in a low voice.

They were more like steel as the priestess pierced the prince with a gimlet gaze.

'Rats?'

Snorri's brow furrowed and he tried to gesture with his arms.

Elmendrin snapped at him. 'Sit still!'

'But they were big rats, massive, and carrying blades.'

She scowled again. The expression seemed near fixed in Snorri's presence. 'Vermin do not bear weapons. I see no hero before me, I see the spoilt son of a king with a swollen ego.' She examined the hand further. 'At least your cousin has bound it properly. The wound has clotted.'

Carefully, she began dabbing the stumps of Snorri's fingers with cloth and ointment. He winced, receiving another reproachful look from the priestess.

'It stings,' he complained.

Elmendrin rolled her eyes and continued cleaning the wound.

The temple of Valaya was a simple enough chamber. A place of healing, it contained baths and ranks of cots. But it was also a place of worship and the statue of the ancestor goddess stood proudly at the back of the room, overseeing the work of her handmaidens. Valaya was depicted wearing robes, over which was a skirt of chainmail. She bore no helm, though she was a warrior goddess, and her long plaits fell either side of her ample bosom. Her hands were clasped beneath her chest and a gold circular plate sat in front of the statue, engraved with the goddess's rune.

Low lantern light painted the temple in hues of deep red and orange. The air was thick with the smell of unguents and healing incense. There were also several large beer barrels filled with the kind of restorative no dwarf would ever refuse or doubt the medicinal properties of.

Several priestesses roamed about, bringing fresh water from the wells or salves and balms from the stores. There were a few other injured dwarfs being tended, miners mostly, but due to the size of the chamber the prince had Elmendrin all to himself. A fact he intended to make the most of.

'I have many scars,' he said, 'from the many battles I have fought in.'

Elmendrin kept her eyes on her work. 'Indeed.'

'See here,' said the prince, twisting to show off a jagged red mark down his left side. 'See...' he repeated. With an exasperated sigh, Elmendrin looked up.

Snorri smiled. 'From an urk cleaver, wielded by a chieftain. I cut off his head and mounted it on my banner pole. During the wars of my father, I killed many urk and grobi, milady. See how it has made my arm strong...' Shirtless, his armour resting at the side of the cot where he was sitting, Snorri flexed his bicep and was gratified by the bulge he saw.

Elmendrin was unimpressed.

'I do not know,' she said, turning back to tending Snorri's hand, 'why you have removed your upper garments when it is just your hand that is injured.' Wound cleaned, she began to rebind the ruined fingers with fresh bandages, muttering imprecations to Valaya as she did so.

Snorri leaned in to whisper in her ear, 'Would you like me to remove the lower garments too?'

Elmendrin met his gaze, their lips not quite touching. The prince's confidence eroded with the sudden prospect of intimacy. She purred, 'Not unless you wish to be a prancing ufdi for the amusement of your father's court, a bard with the voice of a beardling.' She held a pair of prising tongs, the kind used to extract chips of wood or metal from a wound, and held them close to the prince's crotch.

Snorri paled. 'Not the *dongliz*...' he said, and recoiled.

She smiled humourlessly, set the prising tongs down. 'I thought not.' Elmendrin finished tying off the bandage, binding it over tightly and bringing another wince to the prince's face. 'There, it is done. May Valaya bless you and keep the wound from festering. It'll be a while before you can shoot a crossbow again, my prince.'

Snorri examined the finely tended wound. 'Aye, you might be right at that. My sincerest thanks, milady,' he said with genuine affection.

Despite her prickly veneer, Elmendrin blushed and turned away to wash her hands. Heat was radiating off her skin and she felt a tightening in her stomach.

'I am sorry, I–' Snorri began, slightly flustered. 'What I mean to say is I–' He reached out to touch her shoulder, admiring the way her violet robes framed her stout body and the flaxen locks bound into a ponytail that draped down her back.

She was broad chested, with a short stubby nose and strong cheekbones, a fine rinn and a worthy wife of any king. But it was her fire that Snorri so admired, her kindness and poise lacking in some dwarf women, some of whom had greater and longer beards than their dwarf men. He had spoken none of this to Morgrim, for to do so would damage the image he had worked to cultivate in his cousin's eyes. But here, alone with Elmendrin, he had no need for such disguise.

Alas, he also found that words deserted him.

'Do not speak further, my prince.' Her head was bowed when she faced him, but she met his gaze furtively.

'Let us not be prince and priestess,' he said, swallowing his sudden anxiety. 'Rather, we could be Snorri and Elmendrin.'

Elmendrin was about to answer, her lips framing a word, when another voice intruded.

'I heard of your wounding, Prince Snorri,' said a warrior in the garb of a reckoner. He wore chainmail over a leather hauberk and pauldrons of black leather, and carried an iron helmet in the crook of his arm. A small leather book along with several scroll cases was fastened to his broad belt. There was room for an axe too, or hammer, but its loop was empty. No weapons of any kind were allowed in the temple of Valaya. It was a sanctuary devoted to healing and protection, not a place to shed blood in anger. 'But I did not realise it went beyond your hand. Were you also stabbed?' the reckoner asked.

Annoyed at the interruption, Snorri stood up and started to dress. As he hauled on his overshirt, he replied, 'Just my hand, Grimbok.'

Forek Grimbok was removing his leather gloves, tucking them into his belt with the rest of his trappings, when he said, 'Then why is it you need to remove your garments and armour?' He looked to Elmendrin, sketched a quick bow. 'Sister.'

'Forek,' Elmendrin replied.

The reckoner was lean, with a thin face for a dwarf and an aquiline nose. His black beard was neatly trimmed and tidy, but still retained its length. His accent was cultured, for as well as reckoning for the king, he was also a gifted ambassador and negotiator.

Snorri met Forek's iron gaze without flinching. 'I asked the lady Elmendrin to rub salts and salve into my back and neck. When fighting all day in your armour, a dwarf tends to develop a tightness in the shoulders that requires the tender mercies of the priestesses. But I doubt you would be aware of that given the reckoners' deeds are generally confined to seeking recompense from other dwarfs, or am I wrong?'

Forek's face reddened at the obvious slight but he didn't bite, not yet. 'I serve your father, the High King,' he said, 'as do you, Prince Snorri.'

Snorri laughed. 'You and I are not so alike as that, reckoner.' He strapped on his armour, attached his vambraces. 'I assume you're here to take me to him.'

Livid with barely contained anger, Forek's next words almost came through clenched teeth. 'Indeed I am. You have much to explain.'

'Not to you, Grimbok,' said Snorri, flashing a smile at Elmendrin that elicited a scowl from the priestess.

Forek gave her a warning glance, escorting Snorri from the temple in silence.

'I know you covet my sister,' he hissed once they had their weapons and were headed for the Great Hall.

Snorri kept his eyes forwards, nodding to the clan warriors and guilders they met along the way. 'It's the only thing I like about you, Forek.'

'What, my sister?'

'No. Your boldness. One day it's going to get you in trouble.'

'Threats do not become a prince of Karaz-a-Karak, my lord.'

Snorri laughed, loud and hearty like they were two old friends sharing a joke. 'It's not a threat.'

Anything further would have to wait. Thurbad Shieldbearer waited at the end of the corridor, muscled arms folded across his chest. He had removed his vambraces and torcs banded his brawny skin instead.

As Snorri approached, he stepped aside without a word and the iron-banded doors into the Great Hall opened with an ominous creak of hinges.

EIGHT

ARROWS AND BLADES

A bead of sweat creeping down his back, a half-glimpsed shadow at the periphery of his vision, a waft of noxious odour, the scent of perfume gone before it was fully resolved. Furgil recalled the sensations he had experienced when they'd found the nobles on the Old Dwarf Road.

He knew these mountains, knew the hills and even the forests though he loathed their shaded arbours and sinister groves. In the wilderness, the lands beyond the hold halls of the mountains or the fortresses of the hills, there was much to be wary of. Danger lurked in every crag and narrow pass, in each wooded glade and weathered hollow. Creatures made their lairs in such places, hungry primitive things that preyed on the isolated and the lost.

Never venture into the wild on your own.

Save for the rangers, it was a rule many followed. But death was a patient hunter and all it took was a moment of recklessness, a wrong turn on the wrong trail, and all the guards and precautions would not matter.

Even during times of peace, these were untamed lands. The Old World would never know true peace. Its citadels and bastions of civilisation, whether they were above or below ground, ruled by elf or dwarf, were merely lanterns in a dark and turbulent sea. Some were even less than that, merely candles guttering in the storm. Furgil had known of many outposts, isolated hamlets and villages where a stake wall, a watchtower and a warning bell were poor defence against being consumed by the darkness.

Beasts and greenskins, giants, trolls and even dragons had descended upon such tenuous places and wiped them from existence.

Knelt with his hand upon the earth, a fistful of dirt clenched to his palm, the thought of unending peril did not bother Furgil. It was the way of nature. It was balance and order, albeit a brutal one. He understood it and that made it tolerable to the dwarf.

But something else lurked in the shadows, something that was not part of this order. It was a foreign object, a thing that had made the ranger's skin crawl and his beard bristle. Ever since he was a beardling, Furgil did not like to be watched.

Out on the Old Dwarf Road, he had sensed the presence of several watchers, of eyes regarding them with harmful intent. If asked, he could not explain how or why he knew this. It was a survival instinct he had cultivated whilst ranging the wild lands beyond the dwarf kingdoms, and it had saved his life on more than one occasion.

Almost without thinking, he touched the scar that ran from his neck all the way down to his chest. Invisible to a casual observer, Furgil felt the evidence of the wound with every breath. The beast responsible was dead. Its gutted carcass was a trophy in his private chambers, a reminder of always listening to instincts, especially when they screamed danger.

Furgil felt that sensation anew now and got to his feet. The earth had a strange aroma, the scent of narcotic root and dank metal. There was another smell too, old and ashen. Throwing the fistful of earth away, he dusted off his hands and descended the slope beyond the ridgeline into the heavy forest below.

A fourth smell intruded on the others. It clung to the breeze like a plague, filthy and rank. It was piss and dung, mould and the stink of wet canine fur. Once off the road, their spoor was not hard to find. It wasn't as if they were trying to conceal their tracks.

A talisman hung around Furgil's neck. It carried the rune of Valaya and he beseeched for her protection as he entered the wooded glade. The deep forest triggered a sense of disquiet in the ranger. East of Karak Norn was the Whispering Wood, the Fey Forest. He had never entered that place, nor would he unless his life or that of an ally depended on it, but he had seen what was bred within its arboreal borders. Such a beast now adorned Furgil's wall, a many-antlered creature with too many eyes and reeking of musk, fever sweat clinging to its hide like a second skin...

It was no fell beast the ranger now tracked, though. The snuffling of canine muzzles and the shrieking, clipped speech of greenskins were proof of that. Nor were these the watchers he had felt earlier, for they were much subtler creatures.

The rest of his rangers had disbanded across the hills, searching for the watchers too. Furgil was alone.

He sneered, 'Grobi...' when he saw what was waiting for him in the wood.

Three greenskins and their mounts, mangy malnourished wolves, had dragged something off the road and were now worrying at it with tooth and claw.

Silently, Furgil unslung his crossbow and released the studs that looped his hand axes to his belt.

He didn't kill the creatures straight away, but waited to ensure there were no scouts or any lagging behind. Only when he was certain he had all of his prey in his sight, did he bring the crossbow up to his eye and shoot.

A bolt through the head killed the goblin instantly. It collapsed off the back of its wolf, much to the amusement of its fellows who thought it was drunk. When they realised it was dead, they looked up from their feast and began to chatter nervously, drawing crude blades and cudgels. By then, Furgil had loaded another bolt and sent a second rider to meet the first. This time the bolt tore out the goblin's throat and it died slowly but in agony.

A third bolt – and by now Furgil had given away his hiding place – killed a wolf. Its death howl sent a shrill of fear through its brethren, who reacted by snarling at the dwarf.

A flung hand axe killed a second wolf, as it sprang at the ranger without its rider.

The last died when his second thrown axe caved in its flank and sent spears of shattered ribcage into its soft organs.

Rider and mount parted in a fury of curses and flailing weapons. More or less unscathed, the goblin got to its feet, jabbing at the dwarf belligerently with its sword. When it realised its cousins were dead and so too their wolves, it shrieked and fled.

Furgil didn't run after it. Calmly, he slipped a bolt into his crossbow and drew a bead on the goblin's back. Obscured through thick woodland, scampering erratically and at pace. He counted the yards in his head. Nigh on two hundred by the time he had the stock to his cheek and sighted down the end of the bolt.

A difficult shot for most dwarfs.

Not for Furgil. Even the Eagle Watch was in awe of the ranger's skill with a crossbow.

The goblin pitched forwards moments later, the barbed tip of a quarrel sticking out of its eye.

With all the prey dead, Furgil recovered his weapons and went over to see what they'd been gnawing on. He left the quarrel he used to kill the last goblin, resigned to picking it up later in favour of examining whatever carrion had nourished the wolf pack.

The meat was badly mauled, but he caught scraps of tunic, a piece of bent-out-of-shape mail and even a broken helm. Judging by the chewed-up boots, the amount of ragged limbs, he estimated three bodies. Snagged between the wolves' jaws was some ruddy and blood-soaked hair. In the slack mouth of another, tough and leathern flesh.

Kneeling by one of the corpses, a scowl crawled across the ranger's face. His fist clenched of its own volition.

They were once dwarfs.

Furgil was picking through the bodies, searching for talismans, rings or other icons that would identify the dead, when the crack of kindling behind him made his heart quicken. Cursing himself for a fool, his hand got as far as the crossbow's stock when he felt the press of cold steel at his neck.

'Twitch and this dirk will fill your flesh up to the hilt,' uttered a deep voice in the ranger's ear.

A smile creased Furgil's lips as he recognised the speaker.

'You've spent too long in the mountain, brother,' said the voice again, as the blade was lifted from Furgil's neck. 'It's made you rusty.'

'Has it?' Furgil turned around and looked down at the throwing axe in his other hand, poised at the ambusher's crotch.

Rundin smiled broadly, revealing two rows of thick teeth like a rank of locked shields.

'But I have more friends than you do,' he said, sheathing his dirk as four hill dwarfs emerged out of the forest.

Furgil lowered his axe. 'Never did like the deep wood,' he said, and made Rundin laugh.

'That is true enough. Up you get,' he said, clasping the ranger's forearm in the warrior's grip and heaving him to his feet.

The two embraced at once, clapping one another on the back and shoulder like the old friends they were.

Rundin was a slab of a dwarf, broad and muscular like a bear but also lean enough that he had a light, almost lupine, gait. Tanned skin spoke of days spent beneath the sun, roaming the wilds, and a mousy beard unadorned with ingots or rings suggested a down to earth temperament.

'Been too long, son of Torban,' said Rundin, adjusting the thick belt around his waist. Scabbards for several dirks, daggers and long knives were fastened to it, and another belt that sat across his barrel chest had a sheath for the great axe on his back.

With a look, Rundin dismissed the other hill dwarfs who melted away silently. 'Unwise to leave our backs unwatched,' he said.

Furgil nodded, his mood suddenly serious. 'The truth of that sits before us, brother.'

He gestured to the carrion feast, bidding Rundin to kneel down beside him as he continued his investigation of the corpses.

'Dawi?' The leather hauberk he wore creaked as Rundin crept down beside Furgil. He lifted his leather helm – there was an iron raven icon on the band around the forehead – to wipe away a lather of sweat.

'I'd say merchants by what remains of their garments and trappings.'

'Agreed. Though this one wears heavy armour and there are calluses from haft work on the hand.'

'Dreng tromm...' Furgil breathed, and shook his head. He looked up. 'They did not meet their end here.'

'Aye, did you see it too?'

'That I did, brother.'

Easily missed amongst the carnage, the broken shaft of an arrow protruded from one of the dead dwarfs. It was buried deep into his back. The other half was snagged to his mail jerkin, partly concealed under the dwarf's body. It had swan feathers and the shaft itself was fashioned from white pine.

'Elgi,' said Rundin, face darkening.

'Aye. We need to find that ambush site.'

A bird call echoed from beyond the forest borders.

'One of your men?' asked Furgil, rising.

Rundin nodded.

It seemed they had already found where the dwarfs had died.

Three more dwarfs grew cold on the road.

They were face down in the dirt, surrounding a sturdy wagon with two dead mules. Some still clutched weapons in their hands. Drag marks in the earth, scattered stones at the edge of the road revealed where the three the goblins had taken had come from. Unlike their clansmen in the deep wood, the others were more or less intact. Decay had yet to set in, so the deaths were recent. Judging by dwarfs' cold skin, the stiffness of their limbs and fingers, Furgil reckoned they had been dead a few hours.

Arrows stuck from their backs, same white pine shafts, same swan-feathered flights. No goblin could loose with such a bow. Definitely elves.

The thought brought a concerned expression to Furgil's face.

'Elgi slaying dawi?' He released a long breath through his nostrils, trying to imagine the rationale for what he was seeing. 'Hard to countenance, brother.'

Rundin and Furgil were not brothers, though their bond of friendship was as strong, if not stronger than some siblings. They had shared the same clan once, several years ago. Both were Ravenhelms, though Furgil had been stripped of that honour by King Skarnag Grum and thrown out of the lands of the hill dwarfs upon pain of death.

Unbaraki, the king had denounced him. It meant 'oathbreaker' and there was no greater insult that could be levelled at a dwarf.

Furgil had spoken out against Skarnag, for his greed and his isolation of the hill dwarfs. A seat on the high council had given the thane of the pathfinders a voice. With it he had condemned himself to banishment and shame by a bitter, petty king.

Fortunately for Furgil, the High King of the Worlds Edge Mountains agreed with the pathfinder and so he returned to the mountain from whence his clan had departed many centuries before.

Worst of all was that Rundin knew it and had said nothing in his friend's defence. Furgil had warned him not to, for then there would be no one to ensure the prosperity of the hill dwarfs. Loyalty to a corrupt ruler was the price Rundin paid, but devotion would only go so far.

In the solitude of their own thoughts, both dwarfs remembered this thorn between them. It had long since been removed but the memory of it was still bleak.

Furgil paced around the wagon.

'Five heavily armoured guards and a merchant guilder at the reins.'

Sweeping quickly across the scene, crouching and darting as he gathered further signs and markers, Furgil described what had happened.

'No fight occurred here, no battle. The dawi were killed quickly, without mercy. See how the crossbow is loaded but this satchel is full of quarrels. And here... The warrior's axe is still looped to his belt.' He gestured to the wagon itself. 'Unused shields still clasped to the sides.'

Rundin was crouched down, both hands resting on his thighs.

'An empty wagon this close to the hold means they were returning home. Why attack a caravan without wares to steal?'

'I don't think they were merely thieves,' said Furgil, though he had also noticed the little white bands around the dead dwarfs' fingers from stolen rings, the red-raw marks on their wrists where gilded bracelets had been forcibly removed.

Looking up from examining one of the dead guards, Rundin asked, 'What then?'

Furgil touched the swan-feathered shaft of an arrow. It had punched right through the dwarf's platemail as if it were parchment.

'This was cold murder, but I know of no elgi that would ever do such a thing.'

Rundin frowned, remembering something. 'From the watchtowers of Kazad Mingol there have been reports of black-cloaked strangers abroad on the hills. None have yet managed to get close enough to challenge them. When I read the missives that arrived at Kazad Kro, I assumed it was just because of the increased trade with the elgi.'

'Feels different,' said Furgil, suddenly glad that a ring of four hill rangers surrounded them. 'On the Old Dwarf Road, I felt... *something*.'

'Like being watched.'

Furgil met Rundin's gaze. The recognition in the warrior's eyes sent a chill down the ranger's spine.

'Just so.'

The earlier storm had almost passed, but the sun beaming down through the winter sky was neither warming nor comforting. Furgil stood up, deep in thought, his face creased with concern.

'Can you return the bodies to Karaz-a-Karak, Rundin?' he asked.

'Of course, brother. Are you not going back, then?'

'Not yet. I have to find out who these watchers are and what, if any, role they played in this slaughter. Dead dawi on the Old Dwarf Road this close to Everpeak is brazen, but I must go back to the High King with more than just questions and suspicions.'

Rundin got to his feet. 'Need some company?'

Furgil eyed the deep wood, his gaze sweeping across the ridgeline, the low hills, rivers and the crags. They could be anywhere, travelling under any guise. Killing a dwarf on the threshold of his own domain took skill; killing six who were armed and looking for danger took something much, more dangerous than that.

The ranger was about to break one of his own rules. He plucked an arrow from one of the bodies, placed it carefully in his satchel for when he'd need it later.

'No. I'll travel faster on my own.'

The raider ship was several miles behind them, sunken to the bottom of the river bed, its crew likewise. Weighed down by their armour, over a dozen exsanguinated bodies would putrefy and succumb to the slow rot of the dead.

Drutheira and her coven had been swift about the murder of the vaulkhar and his warriors. Gorged but not yet slaked, the witches' power swelled with the stolen blood. The way north would be long and not without peril, but there was much to do beforehand. Not least of which was finding Sevekai and his warriors.

Its presence burned into Drutheira's mind as if by a brand, a settlement was visible on the next rise. Fortified with an outer wall, tower and gate, it was a permanent outpost. Elf and dwarf banners hung from its crude battlements, fluttering on a low breeze blowing in off the distant gulf.

Malchior had not walked far when he began to moan. 'I am not a pack mule, Drutheira.' He adjusted the rough satchel on his back and it clanked with the swords and spears within. 'Could we not have stolen some horses? What merchant travels on foot anyway?'

Malchior no longer had the pale skin of a druchii, nor did he wear the arcane trappings of a sorcerer. A white skullcap enclosed his head, and a skirt of light lamellar mail clad his body. There were vambraces, shin greaves, calfskin boots and a travelling cloak that attached to small pauldrons on his shoulders. Healthy sun-kissed skin described a rough but noble face.

He still wore a viper's smile, no enchantment could conceal that, but his appearance was already different from the one that had sailed into the Black Gulf from Naggaroth.

'And why must I be the beast of burden when *she* carries nothing?'

Ashniel had undergone a similar transformation, but wore a circlet instead of a skullcap with a diadem at its centre. Her distaste at the pearl-white robes beneath her breastplate was obvious in the sneer on her face. She grinned darkly at Malchior's displeasure, though.

Drutheira flashed a deadly glare at Malchior. 'Because I need her abroad in the settlement, doing the dark lord's work. You are welcome to explain to him why you disagree with that.'

Malchior fell silent, but Ashniel was unafraid to show her disgust.

'My skin crawls with this pretence.' She too carried nothing save for the jewelled athame at her waist and the small flask concealed beneath the belt of her robes.

'Silence,' hissed Drutheira. Her own disguise was akin to that of her coven, albeit more impressive and ostentatious. She had no skullcap or circlet, but wore a gilded cuirass and a velvet cloak with ermine trim. She'd kept her raven hair, masquerading as a noblewoman with two servants. Her eyes were on the outpost and the guards occupying its tower and in front of its gate. Dwarfs *and* elves; it was a strange sight to behold such apparent harmony. Each of them carried either a bow or crossbow.

'We can be seen from this distance. Do not fail me here,' she warned them both, her voice changing mid-sentence. Gone were the barbed tones of the druchii and in their place the more lyrical, lilting cadence of the asur.

'Besides,' she said, allowing the slightest dagger of a smile. 'What need have I of horses when the two of you carry all of my wares and do my bidding?'

Malchior hid his sneer behind a bow, though Ashniel was more brazen and showed her displeasure openly. Drutheira could not have cared less.

'Remember your roles,' she said, hiding her contempt for the nearest guard behind a warm smile. She purposefully kept her eyes off the archers in the tower, as not to do so would arouse potential suspicion. 'We are weaponsmiths, servants of Vaul from across the sea and the rugged hills of Cothique.'

'Must we play as rural peasants, Drutheira?' whined Malchior. 'Why not vaunted nobles of Saphery or Lothern?'

'Because nobles of Ulthuan would not be caught dead in a hole like this,' she said through her teeth. 'And they would certainly possess horses. Of course, if you want to be flayed then by all means please continue complaining.'

Malchior spoke no further, but gave a deathly glance to Ashniel who didn't bother to hide her amusement.

As she approached the gate Drutheira tried to ignore the nocked bows, the ready swords and axes loose in their scabbards. She made the rune of *sariour* with her empty hands, adding a shallow incline of the head in mellow greeting.

Sariour symbolised the moon, its aspect that of a crescent. Especially to merchants and traders, it meant 'fortune' and would be taken as a positive sign by the guards. But like most elven runes, it had a darker interpretation too. For sariour also signified 'evil deeds' and 'destruction'. The obvious duplicity, the plain threat it embodied amused Drutheira greatly as they passed through the gate and into the settlement without incident.

It was as much a backwater as its exterior suggested but large, with at least a hundred elves and dwarfs trading with one another from wagons, stalls and pitched tents. A few less ephemeral structures could be found farther from the gate. One, an ale house, was wrought from stone. A blacksmith's was little more than a stone hut, but its anvil and furnace were in constant use. There were also barrack houses and inns, little more than huts themselves but a roof and four walls for weary travellers who needed a night's rest in a bed and not on the hard ground of the road.

An impromptu market had grown up around a bell house that Drutheira assumed was the domain of some kind of alderman or outpost captain. There were several other structures too, fashioned from wood and at the periphery. Some of these were of elven design and bore such devices as rampant Ellyrian stallions and the rising phoenix of Asuryan.

Above the archway framing the gate a sign swung in the wind on two lengths of chain. *Zakbar Varf* was written in chiselled runescript. It meant 'Wolf Hut' or 'Wolf Wall'. Drutheira decided that 'hut' was a more accurate description of the place.

A dwarf trader with a cadre of guards and wagons in tow and not long arrived himself aroused her attention.

'This way,' she muttered. As she was walking towards the dwarfs who were unhitching their wagons and stretching the stiffness from their backs, she gripped Ashniel's arm. Drutheira's eyes held the fiery intensity of flaming coals.

She hissed, 'You know what needs to be done?'

Ashniel nodded slowly.

'You have everything you need?'

Again, she nodded.

Drutheira held the young witch's gaze a moment longer, saw the hatred and ambition in her almond-shaped eyes.

She released her, taking a mote of pleasure in the grimace of pain Ashniel failed to conceal.

'Good,' said Drutheira.

Like a shadow retreats from the approach of the sun, Ashniel crept away from the others and blended into the crowd.

Silently, Drutheira conveyed a final order to Malchior and the two druchii closed to speak to the dwarfs.

'Greetings, traveller,' she said to the dwarf merchant, smiling politely.

He had a grizzled face, more at home on a battlefield than a trading post, and his fair hair showed up the grease and dirt. He grunted a reply of sorts.

Drutheira tried not to sneer. Fortunately for her, the dwarf was busy with his wagons and paid little attention.

'Are you here to trade, ah...?' she invited.

'Krondi,' said the dwarf, handing a barrel of something to one of his fellow traders. There were runes scorched into the hard wood that Drutheira didn't understand. 'Krondi Stoutback.' He turned and firmly shook her hand.

'Astari.'

Such physical greetings were not common amongst elves and Drutheira was unable to hide her surprise and discomfort.

'Apologies for the muck,' said the dwarf, misunderstanding. Belatedly, he wiped the palms of his hands on his tunic. 'Been a long way from Barak Varr. On the road like on campaign, grime tends to get ingrained. Easy to forget it's there.'

Drutheira smiled again and fed some sorcery into the gesture.

'That's perfectly all right. *Barak Varr*?' she asked, struggling a little with the pronunciation.

'The Sea Hold,' Krondi explained, pointing roughly south with a leathery finger. Under the nail was black with dirt and Drutheira fought to hide her disdain.

She also remembered the bastion the dwarf spoke of, and its defences. She masked her interest with another question.

'You were a soldier then? A warrior for the king, perhaps?'

'Aye, milady,' said Krondi, warming to the elf as his companions unloaded the wagon. Drutheira noticed one dwarf, far off at the head of the wagons, remained seated. He was also hooded and kept to himself, more than most dwarfs usually did. Not a merchant, nor a guard. This was something else. She tasted power and resolved to keep her distance.

'I fought for the High King,' Krondi went on proudly, 'and my own king, Brynnoth of the Sea Hold.'

Gently putting her arm around him, hiding the urge to gag, Drutheira led the dwarf to where Malchior was waiting. She briefly searched the bustling crowds for Ashniel but the witchling was nowhere to be seen. Allowing a half-smile she said, 'Here, then you'll know the value of a good blade.'

Krondi began to detach himself, waving Drutheira off.

'Not here to buy,' he said, shaking his head as if trying to dispel an itch, 'but to rest and pick up provisions, possibly sell, before heading on.'

She made a hurt expression, her eyes mildly pleading. Again, she used a little sorcery to enhance her charms. 'At least look at what I'm offering before you dismiss me, Lord Stoutback.'

Krondi laughed. 'I'm no lord, but I'll take a gander at what yer peddling.' He nodded to Malchior who simply bowed and then unrolled his satchel. Unbeknownst to the dwarf, he was incanting silently beneath his breath.

As the leather satchel was unfurled, a rack of stunning ithilmar weapons was revealed. Jewelled daggers, short swords and spear tips were arrayed in rows. There were shimmering axes, both for felling and throwing, and a few smaller pieces of armour.

One in particular caught Krondi's eye.

'Is that…?' He breathed and looked again, closer. 'Gromril?' There was a glint in Krondi's eye as he met Drutheira's, but also something else. Anger?

'How did you come by this?' It was less of a question and more of an accusation.

'A gift,' said Drutheira, drawing closer. Her eyes shone with power. 'I take it you're interested then?'

Krondi went back to the gromril blade. It was a sword, an uncommon weapon amongst dwarfs, who preferred hammers and axes. There were no runes, but the star-metal it was forged from was unmistakable.

'How much?' he asked, his gaze fixed on the blade.

'Only a fair price. Does anything else catch your eye?'

'I'll take everything. All of it,' he said gruffly.

Drutheira smiled thinly, and bade Malchior to wrap up the leather satchel.

'You have made a considerably wise decision.'

She met Ashniel on the outskirts of the settlement, away from prying eyes and ears.

'Were you successful?'

'Of course.' Ashniel presented the athame dagger. Its blade was fire-blackened and the pearlescent gemstones had dulled to the lustre of bare rock. She then showed her mistress the flask, empty of its contents.

'You used all of it, on the ale *and* wine?'

An evil smile curled Ashniel's lips. 'Even the water.'

'Then there's nothing further for us here.' Drutheira looked to the distant horizon and the storm rolling across it. She could almost hear the thunder of hooves.

Several miles from Zakbar Varf, a host of riders dismounted from a barge. They were hooded and twenty-five strong. Three more such bands were alighting from their own ship nearby. In a hidden grove, a few miles from the trading settlement, they would gather. Sharpening their blades and spear tips, they would wait for nightfall and then ride out.

NINE

RINKKAZ

Over eight hundred dwarfs crowded the room and still it echoed like a tomb.

The Great Hall of Karaz-a-Karak was the single largest chamber in the entire hold. A small town could fit into its vastness. A vaulted ceiling stretched into a gem-studded darkness overhead and columns broad enough to be towers punctuated miles-long walls against which monolithic statues of the ancestors glowered. There was a stern austerity to the hall, despite its roaring hearth and the dusty banners that stirred gently on the hot air.

Three runes arranged in a triangular formation and confined by a circle of copper and bronze sat in the middle of the dwarf gathering. Each rune was wrought from gold and when the light caught them in a certain way they shimmered with captured power. They were devoted to the chief ancestors: Grungni's rune of oath and honour; Valaya's of hearth and hold; and Grimnir's of wrath and ruin. Each described an aspect of the dwarf race, their very essence which made them sons and daughters of the earth. If lore and legend was to be believed, the magic within the runes had been put there by the ancestors themselves. It was latent power, but would protect the dwarfs when needed.

Gotrek Starbreaker looked upon those runes now and tried to remember their lessons.

A dry, rasping voice uttered from parchment lips intruded on the High King's thoughts.

'Such a rare gathering of kings and thanes is a strong sign of a liege-lord's strength, even though they bicker like beardlings.'

The voice put Gotrek in mind of forgotten halls, lost holds and leather-bound tomes caked in dust.

Looking down from his throne, he met the rheumy eyes of the oldest dwarf in Karaz-a-Karak, he of the longbeards who was simply called 'the Ancient'.

'Tromm, old one.' The Ancient was wise beyond reckoning, his age uncounted and unknown except by the High King's Loremaster. 'Should it not concern me that my vassal lords snap at each other like jackals?' he asked in a sideways fashion. He needn't have been so surreptitious, for the dwarf nobles were not paying any attention.

The rinkkaz was a sacred oath that bound all kings. Barring recent death, war, plague or invasion, the council of kings was observed by all of the dwarf holds and occurred every decade. But it was also a chance to settle old scores or revive grudges that were never truly forgotten. For every rinkkaz, which often lasted several days, the incumbent High King would allow a period of *grudgement* for the other kings to vent some spleen. It made later discussion swifter and more amiable.

Gotrek was patient. He had to be. The Ancient never answered quickly and always considered every word. He would often say, at length, it was why he had lived for as many centuries as he had. In the end his breath came out of his wizened mouth like a pall of grave dust.

'Better they bite at one another than sharpen their teeth on your hide.'

Leaning over, Gotrek whispered conspiratorially, 'They would find it leathery and tough if they did, old one.'

The Ancient laughed at that, a grating, hacking cough of mirth that brought up clods of phlegm.

Gotrek slapped him on the back, loosening whatever was lodged in the old dwarf's throat, and received a nod of thanks. He regarded the throng in front of him.

No fewer than seven dwarf kings, not including the High King himself, were in attendance. If a king could not be present at the rinkkaz then a delegate, an ambassador, lord or high thane, even a regent, was sent in his stead. Only the kings of the hill dwarfs were absent, a fact that was noticed by all.

'Yet again, Skarnag makes his insolence plain to the realm...' muttered Ranuld Silverthumb. The runelord was seated on the opposite side of the High King, wisdom and knowledge to his left and right. Only the captain of the hearthguard was closer, but the imposing figure of Thurbad was absent for the moment. 'Wazzock.'

Since their expatriation from the Worlds Edge Mountains, Skarnag Grum and his fellow lords had not once attended the rinkkaz.

'He might surprise us yet,' muttered Gotrek, though without conviction. His gaze strayed to the distance, where he could just make out the bronze doors to the Great Hall, but he wasn't about to hold his breath in expectation of them opening.

Bedecked in his finest runic panoply, a staff of wutroth and banded gromril clenched in his left fist, a helm of gilded griffon feathers upon his beetling brow, Ranuld cut as stern a figure as his liege-lord.

'I'd suggest we march on Kazad Kro and bring the rinkkaz to his gates if it were not for my weary back and legs.' Ranuld grimaced as he said it, and Gotrek smiled to himself. The runelord was much more hale and hearty than he let on. 'Besides,' he added, thumbing over his shoulder, 'the Ancient would never make it.'

A snorting, nasal dirge was coming out of the old dwarf's mouth. None in the hold could snore so loudly.

Ranuld frowned, waggled a finger in his ear. 'Like a boar rutting with an elk.'

Gotrek stifled a laugh then asked, 'Did you find what you were looking for in the old halls?'

The runelord shook his head, 'No, my High King.'

Ranuld Silverthumb was amongst the High King's royal retinue and occupied one of ten seats reserved for the high council. At Gotrek's edict, all of his advisors were present including his Loremaster and Grudgekeeper, both of whom scribed in leatherbound books cradled on lecterns in front of them, thick parchment pages cracking as they were turned. As well as the Master of Engineers, who sat with a thick belt of tools around his waist, there was also the Chief of Lodewardens, he who was responsible for the mines and therefore much of the hold's wealth and prosperity, and the Chief of Reckoners who ensured that grudgement was meted out and reconciled on the behalf of the clans of Karaz-a-Karak, including the royal clan of Thunderhorn, against other clans and other dwarfs if needed.

Disputes were commonplace for a race that valued honour so highly and held grudges so easily. Dwarfs would seldom forgive; and they would never forget. Therefore a record and a means of settling disputes was needed in order for their culture to function without constant wars breaking out between the clans. As High King, Gotrek was fierce but also wise. He had mediated many grievances between his clan lords and those of his vassal kings. His rise to power was not only assured through the greenskin purges of his early reign, but also the agreements he brokered between the northern and southern kings when the former encroached on the latter's territory by mistake. Blood was shed, for dwarf clans are not above fighting one another, but not so much that the warring nobles could not be reconciled.

Many years later the grudges on both sides were still remembered. It was echoed by the fact that all the northern kings sat on Gotrek's left and the southern kings his right. He wondered absently where the kings of the hill dwarfs would have sat, should they ever have graced his hall with their presence.

Gotrek had made his disdain for Grum's insolence plain to all, and only current matters prevented him from taking steps to redress it. From atop his Throne of Power, seat of the High Kings since before Snorri Whitebeard's days, he glowered. Clan bickering had turned to matters of the realm. It was a subject that had cropped up often during the rinkkaz, and Gotrek felt its unwelcome weight upon him like a cloak of anvils.

Ever since they had returned to the Old World, the grumbles from the other kings had been the same.

Elves.

No one wanted war with them, but then no one especially wanted peace either. Of all the liege-lords of the dwarf realm, it was Gotrek who had extended the hand of friendship most readily. Like his forebears, he recognised the nobility and power of the elves. There was also the honour of heritage and ancestry to uphold. For was it not Snorri Whitebeard himself who had made an ally of the Elf Prince Malekith and even called him friend?

Who were they not to maintain such a fine tradition?

'They encroach too far onto my lands,' griped Thagdor. As he puffed up his chest, the King of Zhufbar clanked in his ceremonial armour. The majority of the kings and their delegates were smoking pipeweed. Thagdor was no exception, and a palpable fug of their combined exhalations clung to the lower vaults of the massive chamber in an expansive cloud. Together with the smoke issuing from the roaring fire in the High King's mighty hearth, it muddied the air, obscuring the many warriors Thagdor had brought with him.

A traditionalist, fond of engineering and with a thriving guild, Thagdor was just slightly paranoid. Zhufbar had been besieged by greenskins many times, in the early days before Gotrek had made his war against the creatures and all but eradicated them. It had made Thagdor wary of constant attack, his back perpetually up. A hundred hearthguard had accompanied him into the great hold hall; a hundred and fifty more awaited him above in the entrance hall.

'Every time I step beyond my halls for a stroll, there's a bloody elf wandering about,' he went on. 'I am fed up with it, Gotrek.'

No lord other than Thagdor ever called the High King by his first name during a rinkkaz. There was none more down to earth than the lord of Zhufbar and this extended to the way he greeted his liege-lord, so it was tolerated.

There were mutterings of agreement from Brynnoth of Barak Varr and the fierce-looking Luftvarr of Kraka Drak at this proclamation. The former resembled a sea captain more than a king, with a doubloon eye-patch and a leather cloak festooned with sigils of sea monsters and mermen. Brynnoth had a long, plaited beard that flared out at the ends where it was attached to tiny hooks that tied to his armour.

Luftvarr wore furs and pelts, in keeping with the Norse dwarfs who had to travel vast distances to reach such proceedings. The way to and from the north was perilous in the extreme. Ever since the now fabled coming of Chaos – when monsters had roamed free in Norscan lands – the Norse dwarfs had become largely isolated, but a rare cessation in the storms. A parting of the dark war bands that blocked the way south had allowed this journey. Luftvarr did it gladly, boasting of his prowess and courage to the other kings. His scowl was legendary, said to have killed a stone troll at fifty paces. His beard was rough and wild, his helmet crested by two massive mammoth tusks. Ringmail swathed his muscular body and his arms were bare apart from knotted torcs just below the elbow.

'And what of the rats in the lower deeps?' said King Aflegard of Karak Izril. The Jewel Hold was well known for its wealth and its deep mines. Rich veins of ore ran through its hewn halls, much to the envy of the other liege-lords present.

King Bagrik of Karak Ungor, the farthest of the northern holds of the Worlds Edge Mountains from Karaz-a-Karak, nodded in agreement with Aflegard. He was called 'Boarbrow', an honorific earned because of the mighty pelt he wore over his back and shoulders, beneath which was a red and gold tunic armoured with a coat of silver mail.

Aflegard was as bejewelled as his hold and wore a great many rings and bracelets. It made him appear slightly effete, especially given his silk garments and the fact he was known for trading openly with elves. Every rinkkaz he protested about the rats, claiming them to be more numerous, larger and cleverer with each passing decade. Thus far, his concerns had fallen on deaf ears.

'I have seen them too,' said Thane Brokk Stonefist of Karak Azul. He was no king, not even a high thane, but had been trusted to come in his liege-lord's stead. As militaristic as his king, Brokk's attire was functional and war-ready. His armour was thick plate. He carried a pickaxe and wore a miner's soot-stained features. 'Heard them even,' he added. 'Rats that walk like you or I, noble kings. Rats that can–'

'Bollocks, laddie!' A raucous bellow broke through the fog. King Grundin of Karak Kadrin was on his feet and swearing readily. 'We should be more concerned about the return of the urk and grobi. Ach, there are fekking hundreds of the wee little bastards roaming beneath my halls. What's to be done aboot them, might I ask?'

Grundin's loyalty to Karaz-a-Karak was beyond doubt, but a little needle still persisted between him and Gotrek on account of the High King's son's refusal of his daughter Helda.

'Perhaps you should look to your own ironbreakers to clear your underhalls of the vermin, as we all have,' countered Aflegard.

'Ye dirty little scutter!' Four of the High King's hearthguard had to hold Grundin back from crossing the hall and lamping one on Aflegard's bulbous nose.

'Enough!'

One word, not shouted, but with raised voice, silenced the room.

A grumbling hubbub persisted, but it was impossible to stop a dwarf king from muttering his displeasure.

Gotrek looked down on his vassals and scowled.

'You are kings of the Karaz Ankor, not bickering grobi chieftains. I invite you into my halls, let you eat my meat and drink my beer to discuss important matters of state, not settle old scores.'

Grundin shrugged off the guards with a curse or two then bowed a quick apology. Chuntering, he sat back down.

An impressive feast had been arrayed for the kings, who sat in a semi-circle before their liege-lord, a host of retainers behind them. Adjacent to the Great Hall, through two low archways chiselled with runes and gems, were a pair of large feast halls. Racks of stout wooden tables with short-legged stools and benches sat within. Soon they would be brimming with food and ale.

The vassal lords had been fed already – some still carried their tankards – but the second course was being readied. Roast boar, elk, thick slabs of beef and even fowl were being prepared and cooked for the edification of the High King's guests. The look on Gotrek's face at that moment suggested he wanted to spit on their food and throw them out of his house.

'But what of the elgi problem, my liege-lord?' asked another voice, one that was more cultured and refined than the rest. He had seated himself away from the crowds, at the edge of the semi-circle, so that Gotrek had to crane his neck to speak to him or risk looking as if he was showing disrespect.

Sinking two heavily ringed thumbs into his gilded belt, King Varnuf of Karak Eight Peaks asked, 'Well, my High King?'

Regarding the ostentatiously attired dwarf with his gems and his indecently large crown, Gotrek answered through clenched teeth.

'There are elgi who are guests of this hold, I'd remind you,' he said. 'Not a thousand paces from this very hall in fact. And once the rinkkaz is done with, I'm expecting you all to eat with them too.' He glared at Varnuf before he could interrupt. 'I'll tell you why we tolerate the elgi, why they are allowed to roam in our lands and trade with our merchants. It's very simple. Peace.

'For thousands of years we dawi have fought. We've dug our holds, we've honoured our ancestors, killed urk and grobi and drakk by the score. But now we have peace. For once, our hearths are safe and our wars a distant memory. I could no more expel the elgi than I could oust you all from your own halls.'

That spurred a sudden bout of vociferous complaint, amidst threat of grudgement and invocation of the reckoners.

'Don't be soft in the head,' Gotrek snapped, silencing the ire of some of the more belligerent kings. 'I mean the elgi are staying. They are our allies, and they've given me no reason to believe otherwise.'

'Their ways are not our ways,' Thagdor protested. 'I want 'em off my hills and out of my chuffing sight.'

'You're welcome to move them yourself, Thagdor,' said Gotrek, 'but know that I won't raise a finger to help you and I'll make damn sure none of your fellow kings do either. I won't jeopardise peace.' He shook his head. 'I won't.'

Further grumblings greeted this remark but the High King would not be swayed.

His gaze alighted on Varnuf who said nothing, but merely sank back into his seat. His face was lost in smoke and shadow until the tip of his pipe flared and threw a glow upon a stern and envious countenance.

Ever had the Vala-Azrilungol, the 'Queen of the Silver Depths', been a rival to the majesty and splendour of Karaz-a-Karak. Its halls were vast and impressive, its wealth immense. Varnuf considered Eight Peaks as a rival to Karaz-a-Karak, and himself a worthy replacement for the current High King. He would not do so through dishonourable means, for this was not the dwarf way, but he would also not shirk from the Dragon Crown should it be offered to him.

Gotrek had neither the will nor the strength to continue the argument. It was draining, and he slumped back in his throne.

'The elgi stay. This is my final word.' He surveyed the room with his gimlet gaze. 'And any who gainsay it had best take up their axe and be ready to fight their king.'

TEN

THE HAMMER OF OLD

After leaving Snorri to the tender ministrations of a certain priestess, Morgrim didn't return to his clan holdings as he originally intended. To reach the southern halls of Karaz-a-Karak, even via the mining routes, would take too long and he had no desire to face his father. Not yet.

His mind was occupied by other thoughts.

Morgrim believed in fate, he believed in a reason for everything and everything for a reason. So when Ranuld Silverthumb pronounced a great destiny for his cousin, he was certain of its fulfilment. This in turn troubled him. His concern was twofold: first at what lengths Snorri would go to in order to ensure he attained his prophesied greatness as quickly as possible and second, what that meant for him.

If he was lucky, a dwarf would live a long life; but children were rare and in order for his name to live on, his legacy to endure, it was by his deeds that he would often be remembered. Morgrim had no wife, and no aspirations to find one. He did not wish to be a general or even a king, though his position as the prince's cousin could afford him such a title. Like his father and his father before him, he was a miner. It was a life and profession that suited him, that suited many dwarfs, but one thing about it bothered him.

How would he make his mark?

Such aspirations had never worried him before, but some of Snorri's rampant ambition had rubbed off he supposed. Death had been close in the dilapidated halls of Karak Krum. He'd felt it like a cold breath on the back of his neck. Yes, he and Snorri had laughed about it, but Morgrim saw the look in his cousin's eyes that mirrored his own.

Both of them could have been killed in that lonely place, left to be gnawed upon by rats. Morgrim did not want that as his epitaph. Like any dwarf, he wanted to be remembered.

Perhaps then that was why he now found himself in the Hall of Kings, standing before one of the greatest liege-lords Karaz-a-Karak had ever known.

Every previous incumbent of the Throne of Power was honoured in this echoing gallery of jewel and stone. Thorik Snorrison, slayer of the *ngardruk*; Gorim Ironhammer, he who discovered the mines of Gunbad and Silverspear; and Gurni Hammerfist, he who was father of Gotrek and defeated the orc warchief Huzkalukk... with only one hand. Legends all, but it was the alcove-chamber of Snorri Whitebeard that was the largest and most venerated.

An immense statue of the High King of the Karaz Ankor, rendered in his full panoply of war and hewn from flawless marble, stared out into the darkness of the deeper hall.

The Hall of Kings was a place of veneration, of quiet imprecation to the spirits of the great ancestors. Some came to beseech wisdom, others fortune and better times. Occasionally, dwarfs would speak their grudges before these effigies of stone or swear oaths of vengeance or fealty.

Morgrim did none of these things, for he did not come to the Hall of Kings on his behalf but rather he came to plead for another.

'Tromm, High King Whitebeard,' he uttered, bowing his head sombrely to remove his helm before taking a knee in the shadow of the cyclopean liege-lord of Karaz-a-Karak. 'I come to you on behalf of another. Though he carries your namesake, and proudly, he does not have your temperance.' Breathing deeply, he said. 'Let him heed the wisdom of his ancestors. By Grimnir, he has courage but let him be brave enough to not let pride ruin a father's love and respect. Let him find inner counsel against reckless abandon. Let him live to see his destiny realised. For this I make my oaths to the gods, to hearth and hold.'

Morgrim raised his eyes, returning the great horned war helm to his head.

Hard marble stared back at him.

The ancient king had not stirred. No magic had animated his stern countenance, which was as unyielding as winter earth. His jaw was still fixed. His fists were still clenched.

But Morgrim hoped his words were heeded anyway. Oaths made, he began to appreciate the rest of what lay inside the alcove-chamber.

Though his weapons and armour were locked away in the treasure vaults of the lower deeps, protected by rune seals and stern-faced ancestor guards, there were other artefacts of Snorri Whitebeard's reign. Banners describing his conquests and deeds swathed each of the chamber's three walls. Trophies of the terrible monsters he had slain were hung up on spikes of iron between them.

Some of the scaled flesh of Gnaugrak was missing, supposedly cleaved off to fashion a wondrous cloak given as a gift to one of Snorri's vassal lords. It was said it had taken the king and over fifty of his ironbreakers to impale the dragon's heart. On the opposite wall, the spiked head of a massive orc chieftain. Preserved in oils and unguents, the greenskin still leered, though the gums around its shattered tusks were slowly succumbing to rot. It neighboured a crushed giant's skull and beside that was a flayed troll carcass, doused in fire-salt to prevent regeneration. Morgrim doubted that even without the salt, the beast would ever be able to re-knit its skin and bones, or grow its organs anew. Stranger things had happened though.

Bones of other creatures, griffons and shaggoths, great tuskors and iron-hided manticores, fimir and wyverns described a bloody legacy that stretched into centuries. But it was to the broken hammer, incongruous amongst the grisly trophies, that the dwarf's eye was drawn.

'What must it have been like to live in such days?' he wondered aloud, reaching out for the weapon.

Its power had been drained long ago, during one of the last great battles of the age. A jagged cleft raked down the head and split the haft, evidence of where a daemon's evil had broken it. Tentatively, Morgrim went to trace his finger down the hammer's mortal wound, imagining it reforged before he took his hand away.

'A different time...'

Morgrim turned sharply at the voice in his ear. What he saw standing in the entrance of the alcove-chamber, almost fifty paces away, was a friend.

A look of incredulity crumpled Morgrim's face as he recognised the warrior before him.

'Drogor?'

The dwarf was dressed in furs and lizard hide, a bronze pauldron over one shoulder and a helmet with a flanged crest in the crook of his right arm. On his left side was a mace, also bronze, with a heavy gem affixed to the pommel. He looked weather-beaten, his skin sun-kissed and a peaty brown, but he wasn't old. White, wiry hair ran a ring around his balding pate and his long moustaches drooped like the exhausted tentacles of some leviathan cloud. His beard was bound in a bronze ringlet, etched with the snarling visage of a serpent. A cloak of exotic feathers cascaded down his back.

Drogor was staring intently at the statue and the hammer above it in what Morgrim took to be reverence. At mention of his name, the dwarf smiled and nodded.

'By the ancestors, I thought you were dead!' Rushing over, Morgrim clapped his errant friend in a firm embrace, slapping his back and shoulder.

'I went south with my clan, Morg,' said Drogor, coughing as Morgrim crushed the air out of him. 'I didn't venture north to the Wastes.'

'Of course... I just didn't expect to see you again.' He shook his head in disbelief. 'There's been no word from Karak Zorn in many years, and last we heard...'

At this remark, Drogor nodded grimly.

'Aye, there are worse things than sun and jiggers the size of your fist in the endless jungle. Ziggurats that claw at the sky, and beasts...' He shook his head, as his gaze was drawn far away as if back beneath the sweltering canopy. 'Like you have never before seen. Creatures of tooth and scale, of leather pinion and tusk, chitinous bone plates that repel crossbow bolts like paper darts.'

Drogor's hand was shaking, and Morgrim clutched the fingers to steady it.

'It's all right, old friend,' he said, his voice soothing, 'you are returned to Karaz-a-Karak, but I am surprised you are back at all. How long did you travel from the Southlands to get here? How many long years has it been?'

Clans Bargrum and Zarrdum had been staunch allies for many decades, across two generations without bloodshed or a grudge made. Miners and fortune hunters, the Zarrdums had left Karaz-a-Karak over twenty years ago and gone south to be reunited with their cousins in the sunny climes of Karak Zorn.

Finding his composure again, Drogor said, 'We were many months travelling on perilous roads. Fifty of us ventured out, our pack mules brimming with saurian gold. Of that expedition, I alone remain.'

'What happened?'

Drogor's expression darkened further. 'Having survived the jungle with just under half of my father's warriors, we reached the borders of Karak Azul.' His eyes narrowed, remembering 'Foolishly, we thought we would be safe in the shadow of the mountain but we were wrong. An ambush, old friend. Archers, hidden in the crags and raining steel-fanged death upon me and my fellow dawi. It was a slaughter.'

Morgrim's jaw clenched at such perfidy. 'Cowards...' he breathed, an undercurrent of anger affecting his voice. 'How did you survive?'

At this Drogor hung his head. 'To my shame, I ran and hid.'

'Dreng tromm... Mercy of Valaya that you lived. There is no shame in retreating from certain death.'

'Then why is it that I wish I had died with my kin?'

Morgrim gripped the shoulder of his old friend, and exhaled a deep, rueful breath.

'Come with me,' he said, after some thought. 'I must meet my cousin outside the Great Hall but then we can find an alehouse and drink to the honour of your slain clansmen.'

Nodding solemnly, Drogor said, 'I don't think I have ever met your cousin, the great prince of the Karaz Ankor. I much look forward to it.'

'I warn you,' said Morgrim as he left the alcove-chamber, 'he takes a little getting used to.'

Drogor smiled. 'We have time, old friend.'

ELEVEN

RETURN OF THE PRINCE

During times of war, a king's duty to his hold and his peoples is very clear. Conflict against a different race, a different creed unites clans, it brings cultures together. It was no different for the dwarfs. But Gotrek had fought his wars, or so he hoped. He had defeated the greenskins, harried them to the point of extinction and brokered peace between all the clans of the Karaz Ankor. The dark days were over, at least for a while, and had been for many years.

So, why then did he feel so tired?

It was with a weary reluctance that he dragged himself from his bed or to his feast halls, or even the alehouses of the chief brewmaster. War made a king lean, sharp like the razored edge of an axe blade. Gotrek felt blunt like a hammer, but without its purpose and directness.

Though he didn't want to admit it, especially to himself, peace was wearing him out. Despite his protestations to the other kings who still argued and fought him and each other, he would prefer war but was wise enough to realise the folly of that desire. Weary of constant negotiation and compromise in the search for harmonious co-existence with the elves, he just wanted a good clean fight to blow away the dust he felt gathering between his bones. It provoked a maudlin mood in the High King.

I am atrophying, becoming a living ancestor bereft of his tomb.

In the minds of some, he had invited an enemy onto their shores, to camp and build cities outside their holds. Tempers were already frayed. It wouldn't take much of a spark to ignite something more serious than mere discontent and pugnacious bellyaching.

War was easy. It was simple, the need obvious. Survive or die. Kill or be killed, they were hackneyed words but with good reason. Truth shouted loudly from every syllable. Give him greenskins or giants, even dragons run amok in the underway, even the Grungni-damned rat creatures he was hearing so much about of late. But not elves, not them, and not peace. At least not one as fragile as this. It was as if their very natures fought against it, that no matter how he reasoned, no concession would ever satisfy the lords of both races.

Looking over to the only two empty seats on the high council, below and in front of the Throne of Power, Gotrek sagged. One was for his queen, beautiful Rinnana, who had died some sixty-three years ago whilst giving birth. Perhaps that was why the weight fell so heavily upon his shoulders? Shared, it would be halved. As it was, it was an anvil big enough to forge a sword for a giant.

'*My love...*' he murmured, and prayed to Valaya to bring him fortitude.

The other empty place brought a scowl to the High King's face. His errant son was wayward yet again.

As if summoned by the thought, a creaking sound invaded the penumbral gloom of the Great Hall as the massive bronze doors yawned open. A quartet of figures entered, striding quickly, armour clanking, down the mosaicked walkway that led all the way to the ancestor runes and the Throne of Power.

There was a shallow enough gap in the semi-circle of nobles for the late entrants to pass through. None spoke, not even to grumble, during the many minutes it took for the dwarfs to cross the hall. All looked, though, sucking on their pipes thoughtfully, glaring through exhaled smoke.

Thurbad led the small throng, his face as grim as a thundercloud. He stopped when he reached the ancestor runes and took a knee. Slamming a fist against his armoured chest, he waited for the High King to bid him rise and then announced who he had escorted into the chamber.

'Tromm, High King,' he said, bowing his head before meeting the king's gaze again to add, 'Prince Snorri Lunngrin of Thunderhorn.'

'Tromm, Thurbad.' Gotrek nodded his respect to the captain of his hearthguard. 'You may take your place.'

Snorri stepped forwards from between a pair of silent warriors, crafting a shallow bow that smacked more of rote than respect.

When he continued forwards, the High King raised his hand.

'Not you, my son,' he said, fierce and cold as winter storm. 'You have not earned the right to be by my side.' He nodded to the back of the semi-circle where room had been left for Skarnag Grum. 'That's your place, back there.'

Snorri looked over his shoulder, and frowned.

No one spoke. Even the Ancient's snoring had dulled to a low susurrus of heavy breathing.

'In the seat of the skarrenawi? Thagging hill dwellers?'

The frown became a scowl.

Gotrek mirrored it, only his was born of centuries of grudges. He had perfected it, forged it into a weapon to make all but the staunchest vassal lords quail.

'Sit down,' he said, snarling the words through his teeth. 'Now, and disrespect me no further.'

Snorri glared, every inch his father's son, about-faced and planted himself down in the seat reserved for Skarnag Grum. It took a few minutes to reach the back of the throng, and silence was with the prince during every step. He didn't speak to the lesser nobles around him when he sat down, he didn't even look at them. His eyes were on his father, arms folded and brow jutting to display his displeasure.

Like any good father who is trying to teach a lesson to his son, Gotrek ignored him and turned to his Loremaster instead.

'Missives?' he asked, requesting any letters or messages from the more distant holds unable to attend the rinkkaz.

Clearing his throat, the Loremaster's stentorian voice boomed without need of a speaking horn.

'From Krag Bryn, King Drong does send word of elves setting up a colony on the borders of his lands.'

This brought renewed consternation from certain vassal kings, especially Bagrik of Karak Ungor, which Gotrek silenced by slamming his fist upon the arm of his throne.

Turning to a fresh page, the Loremaster continued, 'At Silver Pinnacle, King Borri Silverfoot of Karaz Bryn makes a detailed record.' The Loremaster waited for permission to relay it, which Gotrek gave him with a nod.

'"More of the grey men were sighted in the southern reaches today, wandering lonely upon the hills and fens that border our hearth and hold. As their numbers grow, so too does my concern at their presence. A dark cloud lingers over the barrows and cairns beyond our walls, where a party of rangers went missing several weeks past. I have instructed the gates to be shut and sealed, the guard doubled at night. No more dawi shall leave my halls come the fall of darkness. Fell winds blow across my lands that reek of death, even in the deep earth we can smell them and are reminded of our own mortality. I pray to Valaya they will soon abate."'

The Loremaster looked up from his reading.

'There is nothing further, High King.'

A perturbed look creased Gotrek's brow. Beyond sending a message of support, there was little else he could do for the Lord of the Silver Pinnacle.

'Carry on,' he breathed, still deep in thought.

'Karak Zorn makes mention of riches in the far south where the sun is hot enough to cook a dawi in his armour. Several have fallen to exhaustion and wells have dried up across the hold. Forays into the deeper jungle have encountered "saurian beasts". A gathering of these creatures is mentioned and an attack upon the hold itself.'

The crease on Gotrek's brow deepened. It seemed the dwarfs were assailed by enemies familiar and unknown. At least Karaz-a-Karak and the Worlds Edge were mercifully spared from fighting.

Shutting his great leatherbound tome, the Loremaster looked up. 'That concludes all of the missives, High King.'

'Tromm, Loremaster.' Gotrek switched his attention to the assembled lords, regarding his son with a reproachful glance.

Some of the kings and thanes had caught the waft of cooked meat, the malty flavour of hops from freshly uncasked ale. Several licked their lips, stomachs groaning in anticipation.

'Business is concluded,' he declared. 'The feast halls are prepared. Eat. Drink.' He shooed them off, as if tired of seeing their faces.

None took offence, but rather tromped off in their masses to the nearby feast halls, drawn by the emanation of smells.

Snorri was left alone, sitting before his father and the high council. The young prince was surprised to see Ranuld Silverthumb amongst the venerable dwarfs and glowered when the runelord winked at him.

'Leave us,' Gotrek said firmly, but with an underlying weariness.

It took many minutes for the council to depart, during which time Snorri locked his gaze with that of his father. Should the two of them ever attempt a staring competition, a victor would be tough to predict and the contest itself would last for days, perhaps even weeks.

When they were properly alone, the sounds of merriment echoing distantly from the feast halls, Gotrek beckoned his son to him.

Fighting to keep his temper, he rasped, 'Where were you?'

Snorri's nostrils flared and he licked his lips. 'Father, I have been on the road for many hours. My stomach is empty. Can we not discuss my absence before there is nowt but scraps at the feast table?'

'Answer me!' Gotrek rose to his feet, hands clutching the arms of the throne; their knuckles white, he gripped so hard.

Snorri was about to when Gotrek raised his finger, stopping him. 'And I warn you, boy, give me any more of your flippancy and I will come down off this throne and beat some respect into you. I swear to Grungni, I will do it,' he said, settling back down and speaking more calmly. 'Now where were you?'

Snorri swallowed back a lump of trepidation in his throat. 'In the Ungdrin Ankor, in the hold halls of Karak Krum.'

The anger returned to the High King's face, manifesting as a flush of vermillion to his cheeks and nose. His beard bristled.

'That place is forbidden to the dawi.'

'Morgrim and I, we only–'

'With good reason!' Gotrek bellowed. 'There are dangers in the dark beneath the world, fell creatures we dawi have no interest or business in provoking.'

'Provoking?' said Snorri, becoming bolder. 'The Karaz Ankor is our sovereign territory. We dawi are masters of earth and stone, is that not what you have always told me?'

'Aye, it is, but–'

'Then what do we have to fear of the dark, father? Whatever lurks in the ruins of Karak Krum should be mindful of us, not the other way around.'

Gotrek was shaking his head, descending the throne. 'You have much to learn, my son. And do not think I won't have words with your cousin and his father too, though I know whose idea this little adventure was.'

'I venture beyond our borders because you will not. Every day parts of our hold are surrendered to urk and grobi who have returned in number since the purge. Beneath the halls of Karak Krum, I saw rats, father. Rats! They walked on two legs and spoke with one another.' Snorri brandished his bandaged hand like a badge of honour. 'We barely escaped with our lives.'

'Precisely why you must do as I bid, as your king bids.'

'Ignoring the enemies at our gates won't make them disappear, father. We are besieged, if only you would look beyond your fragile peace with the elgi to see it. Or are we to look to them for our protection now? Resting on past laurels, what would my mother think?'

Gotrek raised a fist. His teeth were clenched tight as a sprung trap.

Despite himself, Snorri flinched.

'I am your father, Snorri, but you should choose your next words very carefully indeed.'

Snorri bowed, and knew he had gone too far. 'Tromm,' he uttered. 'I am sorry, father. I didn't mean it.'

Unclenching his hand, letting his arm fall by his side, Gotrek sighed and turned his back. 'Yes, you did.'

'Please father, I...'

'It's all right,' said Gotrek, waving off his son's protests like they were flies. 'Do you not think the same thoughts have entered my head?' His eyes lingered on Rinnana's empty seat. 'How I miss her...'

When he faced Snorri again, there were tears in Gotrek's eyes but he mastered his voice to stop it from cracking as he put both hands on his son's shoulders.

'One day the throne will be yours,' he said, staring into Snorri's eyes, 'and I would have it that you're ready to rule when that day comes. Being king is not about warring and killing, it is about keeping your realm and maintaining peace for as long as you can. It is the hardest thing you'll ever need to do as king. Killing is easy. Any fool can make war and slay his enemies. Keeping a realm once it is intact is much more difficult. Don't be so eager to take up axe and hammer, my son. It might be a while before you can put them down again and I can tell you they grow very heavy in that time.'

'I *am* ready, father,' Snorri said in a small voice, 'if you would but see it. There is none amongst all the champions of the holds that can best me with axe or crossbow. Nothing scares me, nothing. I would purge the very Ungdrin Ankor of monsters to prove that I am a leader, a worthy successor.'

Gotrek let go, and began to pace.

'Have you got chuff in your ears, for I can think of no other reason why you have heard nothing I have said.'

'Father, I have–'

Gotrek stabbed a finger in the direction of the feast halls.

'Sitting in there, Varnuf of Eight Peaks covets my throne. He would not seize it or try to take it from me by nefarious means, but nonetheless he believes he would be a better High King than I. He wants war with the elgi because it is popular amongst the other kings, and he also seeks to undermine me at every turn. We dawi are honourable, but we are also envious, greedy creatures. One always wants what another has, be it his gold or his armies, even his hold.'

'Then declare grudgement against him. Tie your beards together and fight Varnuf. Show him who the High King of the Karaz Ankor is. I'll do it now, father. Challenge him in your name.' Snorri began to turn.

'No! Do not suggest it. Do not even dare. If the only way a king can maintain order is to pummel his fellow lords into submission, his would be a short rule. Stand down or I shall put you down, by Grungni I swear it.' Such was the intensity in Gotrek's eyes that the prince shrank from it and was rooted to the spot.

Snorri rallied quickly. 'Can I do nothing that meets your standards, father? Without chastisement and being brought to heel? Ever do my achievements fall short. What must I do to earn your respect?'

Gotrek sighed again, like he was a bellows and all the air was escaping from within him.

'Not this.'

'Then what? What must a son do to gain his father's favour? He who vaunts all others above him out of spite.'

Gotrek had no answer. He dared not speak in case in his anger his words betrayed him.

'You are a great king, my liege.' There was a grimace of inner pain on Snorri's face as he spat the words. 'But you are a poor father.'

He turned around and stalked from the Great Hall.

Breathing hard, heart pounding in his chest, Gotrek watched him go.

It was several moments before he could speak again. When he did, it was to ask a question of the shadows.

'Why won't he heed me?'

From the darkness, a smoke-wreathed figure answered.

'He is still young, and burdened with the weight of expectation,' said Ranuld Silverthumb. Hidden from sight, he watched the prince keenly. 'Do not be too hard on yourself, my liege.'

Gotrek's shoulders slumped and he broke out his pipe to draw deep of its calming embers. 'I am striving to leave him a legacy of peace, of a lasting realm unfractured by war and death. Yet he is more belligerent than ever.'

'Were you so temperate when you mustered your armies during the greenskin purge? Or when you knocked Grundin and Aflegard's heads together? What about the time when you journeyed to Karak Vlag and fought King Huskarr for his fealty?' Ranuld emerged from the darkness to add his smoke to that of his king's. 'You have fought your wars, my liege. Not only that, you won them all and have carved a great legend for the book of deeds. When Grungni calls you to his hall, you will sit at his table.' He gestured to Gotrek's departing son with his pipe. Snorri had only just reached the doors and slammed them on his way out. 'Not so for Snorri Lunngrin, now Halfhand.'

Gotrek laughed. 'Is that what they're calling him now?'

'His cousin thought of the name.'

'A worthy honorific, I suppose. He said there were rats in the deeps of Karak Krum, who walk on two legs not four.'

'And who speak.'

Gotrek turned to Ranuld Silverthumb, but the runelord was not mocking him.

'And who speak, yes.'

'It was a rat that gnawed off your son's hand.'

The silence held an unspoken question that the runelord answered.

'There *are* creatures in the deeps of Karak Krum, but they are not rats. At least, not as we know them.'

'I'll have the ironbreakers look into it. Borin can muster the lodewardens and seal up the underway. No dawi will set foot in there again.'

Ranuld said nothing. His mind was far away, lost to some unfathomable thought.

'He'll need a gauntlet for that hand,' said Gotrek.

'My apprentice shall fashion one under my tutelage.'

Gotrek half-glanced over his shoulder, one eyebrow raised. 'And the other?'

'*Az* and *klad* as you requested, my liege. But it will take some time. Master runes always do.'

Gotrek's gaze returned to the distant bronze door of the Great Hall.

'I hope he is worthy of it.'

'That, my liege,' said Ranuld, slowly disappearing back into the darkness, 'is not up to you.'

TWELVE

OLD MAGIC

Morek had been listening to the rinkkaz from an alcove behind his master. Dutifully, he remained silent throughout the summit with his head bowed.

As Ranuld Silverthumb returned to the shadows he strode past his apprentice, uttering a single word.

'Come.'

Morek followed, marvelling at how the statue of Smednir slid aside as his master worked the earth runes on the hidden doorway it concealed. Like many of the lesser ancestors, Smednir dwelled in the penumbral darkness that haunted the edges of the Great Hall. Few knew of the statue's presence, let alone the existence of the hidden passageway that lay behind it.

Lost in thought as he counted the six hundred and thirty-four steps of the spiral down into the first of the deeps, Morek started when his master spoke.

'You are prepared for what is before you, runesmith.'

From Lord Silverthumb's tone, it was difficult to tell whether it was a question or even one that he wanted answering.

'I am, master.' The feebleness of his own voice surprised Morek.

Ranuld Silverthumb barked back at him.

'I know you are, wazzock. I have made certain of it, sure as steel.'

Morek fell into silence again at the sudden rebuke, which only earned further reproach.

'Have you no tongue, zaki? Bitten off by a grobi hiding under that last step was it?'

Morek resisted the urge to look back to see if there actually was a greenskin crouched under the last step. Their echoing footfalls, clacking against the stone, seemed louder in that moment.

Smoothed by the rivulets of water trickling from some underground lake or stream, the walls of the stairwell were also chiselled with runes of warding and disguise. None but a runesmith, or someone who was accompanied by one, could enter this place and not lose his way. By their natures, dwarfs were secretive but there were none more clandestine about their craft than the runesmiths. Other than its enchanted sigils, there was little else to distinguish the long, winding, descending corridor.

It was wide, massive in fact like so much of the subterranean Karaz Ankor. There were precious few sconces with lit braziers and those that did grace the coiling tunnel did so with a flickering, eldritch flame.

Occasionally, the hewn face of Thungi, lesser ancestor god of runesmiths, would glare at them from some sunken reliquary or shrine. Lord Silverthumb seemed to ignore it but his lips moved in silent oath-making as he passed by the patron of their guild and profession. Morek felt cowed by every stony glance, feeling more unready and unworthy than his master surely already believed. After the four hundred and fifty-eighth step, he found his voice again.

'No, master. But I am unsure of what you want me to say.'

Lord Silverthumb grumbled another insult under his breath, hawked and spat as if the stupidity of his apprentice left a bitter taste in his mouth.

'Aren't you wondering,' he said, 'why I brought you to the rinkkaz?'

'I... um...'

'You are the second ufdi to refer to yourself as "um" in as many days.' Ranuld Silverthumb came to an abrupt halt, bringing Morek to a stop too. So sudden was it that the apprentice nearly tripped and fell trying to avoid clattering into his master, who stood in front of him like a craggy bulwark and glowered.

'Come here,' he snapped, and seized Morek's chin in an iron grip that had more in common with a vice than a dwarf's fingers. Even the gnarled leathern skin of the runelord chafed and the apprentice barely stifled a yelp.

Lord Silverthumb pulled open Morek's eye, using thumb and forefinger to check the sclera. His own eyes narrowed as he made an observation.

'Are you a doppleganger wearing the flesh of Morek as a dwarf would wear a coat of mail? Hmm, well? Speak, fiend, if that's what you are!'

Ranuld Silverthumb let him go, carried on walking.

'No,' he said, 'I think you are him.'

Morek shut his open mouth, an answer no longer needed.

His master continued. 'I shall tell you then why I brought you.'

Scents and sounds wafted and emanated from below as they closed on the deep. Morek discerned metal, the heady aroma of soot, the tang of heat pricking his tongue. Hammer rang on anvil, creating a monotonous but dulcet symphony that had oft been used to send beardlings to sleep. But there was something further... Old stone, dank, but which had seen and endured more than one age of the slowly turning world. Every time Morek placed his hand upon it to steady himself when a step was too broad to descend safely without being braced he felt the resonance within the rock, the sweat and earth of the dwarfs who had also once traversed this passage. Magic was thick in the air, and not just on account of the runes engraved into the walls. It saturated the corridor, bound to the rock, to the earth.

'Master?' Morek ventured after a few minutes of silence.

Lord Silverthumb scowled, flashed a scathing glance in his apprentice's general direction. 'What is it now, wazzock? Always talking... chatter, chatter, chatter,' he said, mimicking a flapping mouth with each of his hands. 'You're no better than a rinn.'

Reddening beneath his beard, Morek said, 'Why did you bring me to the rinkkaz, master?'

Lord Silverthumb sniffed either with regret or rueful derision, Morek couldn't tell which.

'Do you know how old I am, Morek?' he asked.

'I... um...'

'Again with this "um". Our noble ancestry has been watered down to a clutch of would-be lordlings and princes who when confused can only think of "um". You and the prince, "ummers" both. Must be chuffing catching or something.'

Ranuld Silverthumb had lit a pipe and was blowing intricate smoke rings in the shape of runic knotwork through the flickering half-darkness. 'I am venerable,' he said, and now he sounded weary, thin like old parchment or a threadbare tarp stretched too wide over its frame. 'The oldest living runelord of the Karaz Ankor. Knowledge is my legacy and I am to bequeath it to you so the greatest secrets of our craft do not die with me. But I am yet to be convinced if such power is for your generation of dawi. If I pass on my wisdom to you, I will be putting god-fire into your hands, Morek. Are we not too belligerent, so that such a thing would destroy us? But if I don't, and allow this power to fade, to be consigned to dust and memory, then the dawi will fade as well. One is a slow demise, the other a flare of fire, ephemeral but bright.'

The talk of mortality and destruction sent Morek into a grim quietude. He got the impression of a great weight upon his master, a burden of which he had confessed but a little. Of course, he knew there was much below the forge halls, in the lowest deeps of Lord Silverthumb's chambers, that he had never been privy to. Giving of knowledge, especially that which comes also with power, implied trust – but not only in the wisdom of the receiver, but also in his ability to keep such power safe and for what it was intended. How many had fallen to corruption and ruin where the pursuit of power was concerned?

Known as 'Furrowbrow', after his father and his clan, entire harvests could have been planted in the deep ripples lining Morek's forehead at that moment.

Ranuld Silverthumb seemed not to notice his apprentice's dilemma.

'The High King has asked for a weapon and armour for his son. A gift if he is worthy of it, and token of his father's esteem. Gotrek Starbreaker too, you see, has a legacy to hand down. All of us, we dwarf lords, carry that burden. You will forge them, az and klad, inscribe the master runes and speak the rites.'

Morek briefly bowed his head. 'Tromm, master. It is a great honour.'

'No, apprentice, it is your *duty*. To me, to your king, to your race. Legacy, lad, is all we veterans have left to us in the end.'

The last fifty steps were descended in silence until Morek asked just before they reached the lower deep, 'You were gone for several days, master... Did you find what you were looking for?'

Lord Silverthumb shook his head. 'No, lad, I didn't. Old magic is getting harder to find.' He scratched his beard as if pondering why. Unable to reach an answer, he carried on. 'But I fear the world is changing because of it. Something lurks in the air, the earth. I fear it will change us, that it *is* changing us even now.'

Morek frowned and the furrows deepened. 'Old magic?'

Ranuld Silverthumb shrugged. 'Magic is magic, I suppose. It's what's done with or can be harnessed with it that makes some of it feel old. We dawi know magic. Its dangers are known to us too, so we trap it within stone and steel in order to control it, lest it control us and we become as stone.'

Morek didn't fully understand, but chose to ask no further questions. His master had answered; he had to fathom its meaning for himself.

They were walking the slab-stoned passage that led to the iron forge where the clattering of hammers sounded and bellows wheezed in time with every strike of metal against metal. Bordering the threshold of the forge hall, Lord Silverthumb's expression darkened as a cloud passing over the face of the sun.

'Trouble is coming. It's been coming for thousands of years but we'll see it in our lifetime, Valaya have mercy. A great doom, lad, and a terrible darkness from which there may be no light.' With the premonition bright like azure flame in the runelord's eyes, he retreated into himself but spoke his inner monologue aloud. He rasped, voice barely rising above a whisper, 'A gathering must be made, a conclave of the runelords.' He shook his head, his faraway eyes no longer seeing the fuliginous dark of the forge or the lambent orange glow of embers at its yawning cavern entrance. 'Won't be easy. Some might be dead, others lost or asleep. Some can sleep for years at a time. It feels like an age since I last slept... Ancestors, all of us. Too old, too thin and past our time. Been centuries since the last conclave, but the wisdom of the ages can no longer be left to slumber. I fear it will be needed in the end...'

Ranuld Silverthumb blinked once and his voice returned to as it was before. 'What are you staring at, wazzock? Look like you've seen one of those talking rats those two ufdis were blathering about.' He snapped his fingers and made Morek jump. 'Wake up, *wannaz*. Now,' he added, heading into the forge, 'Snorri Lunngrin, now Halfhand, needs a gauntlet fashioning. Find him before you begin the rune rites, examine his wound and see what's to be done.'

Morek was half agape, unable to follow his master's capricious nature in the slightest.

'Well, go on then, zaki,' said Lord Silverthumb, shooing his apprentice away like he was a beardling. 'Bugger off and find the prince. And do it fast, the anvil calls.'

Ranuld had brought him all the way down to the *grongaz* only to dismiss him and send him back up its steps again. He was about to ask why but his master was gone, swallowed whole by soot and shadow.

Scratching his head, more furrow-browed than ever, Morek went to look for Snorri Halfhand.

For Ranuld, the dark brought with it a sense of peace. Even with the hammers of the grongaz flattening and shaping, he found tranquillity in his own domain. Breathing deep of the soot and ash, of the metal and the heat, he sighed.

The words spoken in the ruins of Karak Krum had come unbidden. They were also not meant to be heeded, but fate had other ideas it seemed. Briefly, he hoped he hadn't begun a landslide with his trickling rock. Deciding it was done and could not be undone, he sagged in his ceremonial armour and began removing it. Unbuckling straps, uncinching clasps, he walked over to a stone effigy of a dwarf's body. There he released the breastplate, followed by the rest of the cuirass. Resting it reverently on the armour dummy, he took off his helm and did the same with that. Then he grabbed a leather smock, stained with the evidence of forging, streaked black and scorched with burns. He passed through a dark chamber, beyond his forging anvil. No other smiths were present, Ranuld was alone. The sound of hammers echoed from the upper deeps, from the foundries and armouries above. Passing a weapons rack, he took up his staff and looped a hammer to his belt.

Smoke parted before him and the firelight of the forge itself cast deepening shadows, pooling in his craggy features. Through a narrow aperture in the stone, he crossed a small corridor to a door hewn from petrified wutroth. Ranuld merely presented his staff and a sigil hidden upon the door's surface glowed. With the scrape of rock against rock, the portal parted wide enough for the runelord to enter. A muttered incantation and the solid door closed behind him again, sealing off the new chamber like a tomb.

It was dark within, darker even than the rune forge, and no sound reached its confines. Warmth radiated from inside, even standing at the threshold. Lifting his staff, Ranuld ignited the first braziers set into the flanking walls. Like ranks of fiery soldiers they came alight, first six then ten then twenty then a hundred. A chain of fire burst into life down both walls and threw an eldritch glow upon the contents.

'*Duraz a dum...*' he intoned, releasing a breath of awe.

No matter how many times he had seen them, they never failed to impress him.

Six immense anvils sat in front of Ranuld, arranged in two ranks of three. Silver flashed in the brazier light, the anvils capturing the potency of the magic used to ignite them and using it to set their own runes aflame.

Ranuld read each and every one, careful to speak them in his mind and not aloud. The rune hammer in his belt hummed with the proximity of the artefacts, and the runelord patted the weapon to calm its spirit.

Anvils of Doom were one of the single most powerful weapons the dwarfs had in their arsenal. Legend held that Grungni had forged them in the elder days, as a means of harnessing the elements. Mastery over lightning, earth and fire were the reward of any runesmith dedicated and skilled enough to mount an Anvil of Doom. Six more resided in each of the major dwarf holds of the Worlds Edge Mountains, presided over by their chief runelords.

Muttering oaths to Grungni and Valaya, Ranuld ran his hand over the surface of one. Its inner glow grew brighter still and a thin veil of lightning crackled across the metal. It fed to the others, leaping from anvil to anvil until all six were wracked by the same storm. Shadows that were impenetrable to the brazier light retreated before the magic and revealed further runic artefacts in silhouette and half-light, immense war gongs and battle horns the size of ballistae. Behind them, at the back of the chamber slumped onto their haunches, were statues. Stone golems, like the other artefacts in the room, were relics of the elder days. Even with the unfettered fury of the anvils crackling loudly before them, the golems did not stir. Magic was leaving them, fading just like the knowledge which had created it.

A last artefact caught Ranuld's eye, a massive war shield turned on its edge and polished to a mirror sheen. Runes circled around a plane of pellucid silver in which the runelord could see his own image reflected back at him. He tried not to linger on the thought that he looked older than he remembered, so much so that he almost didn't recognise himself any more.

'A great doom, indeed,' he muttered, recalling his earlier vision, and recaptured the lightning of the anvils back into his staff where it would dissipate harmlessly.

Approaching the shield, he spoke an incantation under his breath and the silver shone, rippling like a pool.

Only the *Burudin* were capable of harnessing its power. There were eight ancient lords of the rune that yet lived in the dwarf realm and one of those belonged to the expatriate hill dwarfs of the upper hold-forts. Over the centuries, many had perished through war or old age. Ranuld had known each and every one, just as he knew their like would not return and he, like the remaining Burudin, would be the last of an era.

Feldhar Crageye, Negdrik Irontooth, Durgnun Goldbrow, these were the ancients that Ranuld sought next. Agrin Fireheart was second in venerability only to Ranuld. He had already answered the summons and was on his way from Barak Varr, but more were needed.

Ungrinn Lighthand, Jordrikk Forgefist, Kruzkull Stormfinger... Leagues upon leagues separated the distant holds but through the shield that would be as nothing. Ranuld wondered how many more would heed the call and come to the conclave. With regret, he realised that some would not, that some would already be dead. Old magic was leaving the world, never to return. And like all who are privy to secret knowledge, he feared what would happen when it did.

THIRTEEN

REUNIONS

Even as the bronze doors slammed violently in his wake, Snorri felt the first pangs of regret. His ire, so quick to rise in the Great Hall, cooled quickly when faced with the quiet introspection of what he had done and said.

Bringing the name and memory of his mother into the argument was low. He regretted that, but couldn't retract it.

Pride and the slightest undercurrent of persistent annoyance kept him from turning around and apologising immediately, but a lot of those words, although harshly given, were true.

Gotrek Starbreaker was Lord of the Underdeep, High King of all the dwarfs, and he cast a long shadow. Snorri felt eclipsed by it. He had wanted to tell his father about the prophecy he had heard, of his foretold greatness, how he had fought the ratkin in their warrens and the threat they might mean for the hold, but instead he had chosen to swagger in and expect his place to be waiting.

Being discarded at the back of the assembly, in the seat reserved for the hill dwarfs of all creatures, had been a barb too hard to excise before they had exchanged words. Now they could not be withdrawn, as every dwarf knows. In any other circumstance, a grudge would have been made against Snorri but a father was not about to do that to his son.

Instead he would endure his wrath, and hope that like his own it faded.

Neither, of course, would admit they were in the wrong. It was not the dwarf way.

In the end, Snorri was glad the flickering darkness barely leavened by the ensconced braziers hid his face, although he could still feel the cold glare of accusation from the hearthguard that had been waiting outside.

The veteran warriors were not the only ones waiting for him upon leaving the Great Hall. A familiar figure approached from farther down the corridor, moving with long and light steps like a dancer. Warm and welcoming, his face did not mirror the dwarf's even slightly. A scowl distorted Snorri's expression, only partially hidden by his beard. He had at least removed his axe for the audience with his father and looked slightly less belligerent than the last time he had seen Prince Imladrik.

In lieu of his armour, the elf wore pearl-white robes trimmed with the fire-red commonly associated with Caledorian princes. A circlet of silver with a sapphire in the centre replaced his war helm and he carried no visible weapon. Clean and dressed, he had obviously been at Karaz-a-Karak for several hours already, perhaps even days. As the elf walked down the wide corridor towards him, Snorri wondered for what purpose.

No elf would ever be invited to the rinkkaz. Even in the pursuit of peace his father wouldn't break that sacred oath. Imladrik's presence in the hold halls must be for some other reason. Whatever the cause, Snorri found he resented it just as he resented the prince. After the dragon had turned on him, Snorri felt ridiculed and secretly blamed the elf for what happened. It only affirmed what he had always suspected, that you could never trust an elf or its beast.

Though he walked the hold halls unarmed, Imladrik had several retainers who were waiting for him at the threshold of Everpeak. Each was fully armoured, helmed and wore a long sword scabbarded at the waist. Short cloaks of dragon hide hung from their backs, not trophies but rather the honourable leavings of shed scales from the oldest and mightiest of the drakes.

The retinue reminded Snorri of elves masquerading as dragons, hoping perhaps to yoke some element of their obvious power. It drew a sneer to his lips at the sheer hubris of the notion.

Master of dragons and dragon lackeys, thought Snorri, allowing the bitter curl to grow for the prince's benefit. Heading towards the Great Hall, the elf was obviously here to meet with his father. More talk of peace and harmony, no doubt. Snorri's fists clenched.

'We meet again, Prince Lunngrin.'

Snorri didn't return the nod of greeting, nor did he dawdle to exchange pleasantries.

'You will find him in a foul mood, elfling.'

One of the guards stiffened at the flagrant disrespect but Imladrik quietened her with a glance.

'I hope to bear news that will improve it, then.' Imladrik's reply was diplomatic, but fashioned so that he wouldn't seem to be cowed in front of his warriors.

'Doubtful,' Snorri replied, hiding well his desire to know the elf's business. 'He is a curmudgeonly bastard, slow to calm down.'

'I see *you* possess his fiery spirit too.'

Snorri ignored the comment as they passed each other. 'You'll have to leave your entourage outside,' the dwarf said, thumbing over his shoulder at the formidable hearthguard standing sentinel before the doors.

Imladrik stopped as Snorri walked on. A light clanking refrain from his warriors sounded as they did the same, circling the prince protectively.

'Tell me something, lord dwarf,' he said, 'what is it exactly that I have done which offends you?'

Snorri considered walking further. In the end he stopped too but left his back to the elf.

'You left your island and came here.'

'Your father wants peace, so do we,' he called to the dwarf's slowly departing figure.

Snorri's reply echoed back. 'My father wants many things. And not all of your kind desire peace. That's what concerns me, dragon master. You're squatters, nothing more. The Old World belongs to the dwarfs and will do always.'

The elf didn't answer. There was nothing he could say, though it took all of his resolve not to rise to anger as the dwarf wanted. Instead he carried on in silence, ruminating on all he had heard.

'I will not be the last dwarf to speak it, either,' said Snorri to himself, and went to find Morgrim.

Alehouses were sombre places, more akin to temples than bawdy drinking holes. Sitting by the roaring hearth, the air thick with the reek of hops and wheat, dwarfs came here to worship. For aside from gold, there were few things the sons of Grungni vaunted as highly as beer. But they were also discerning creatures, and would not put up with swill or any brew which they deemed weak or unworthy of their palate. Grudges, bloody ones, had been made for less than a brewmaster who served another dwarf a poor beer.

As Snorri entered the hall, a dozen pairs of eyes looked up at him, glittering like jewels. Several of the dwarfs acknowledged the prince, uttering a sombre 'tromm' in Snorri's direction. Others were too lost in grim reverie to notice.

A strange gloom pervaded in the drinking hall where scores of dwarfs clasped gnarled fingers around foaming tankards of clay and pewter. It was a half-light, a gloaming that settled upon patrons and furnishings alike. Long rectangular tables filled the main hall, surrounded by stout three-legged stools and broad benches. An antechamber, the brew store, fed off one side of the expansive drinking hall and was festooned with wide, iron-bound barrels. Every barrel was seared with a rune describing the beer's name and potency. Only the ones behind the bar and the alehouse's brewmaster were tapped.

Brorn Stoutnose was cleaning his tankards with a thick cloth behind a low wooden bar. Deliberate, exact, there was ritual to the task he performed and he muttered oaths to the ancestors as he did it. Several other cloths, one for drying, one for polishing, another for wringing, sat snugly beneath a thick belt girdling an impressive girth nurtured by many years of dedicated quaffing. Nodding at the prince of Karaz-a-Karak, he gestured with raised chin to one of the low tables where two dwarfs were in hushed conversation.

'Of all the brew halls in the karak, you managed to find the soberest,' said Snorri.

Morgrim looked up sternly from his tankard, which he'd only half drained, but couldn't suppress a wry grin. 'I see you escaped your father's wrath more or less intact.'

At mention of the High King, Snorri's face darkened. 'Words were exchanged,' he said, and read from his cousin's face that Morgrim knew some of those words were regretful.

'Did you tell him about the rats of the underdeep?'

'The elgi sit at the forefront of his mind, and the precious peace he has fought so hard to win. I even saw that elfling prince on his way to the Great Hall.'

'Imladrik?'

'Yes, but not his drakk. I cannot even imagine where he would have stabled such a creature.'

'Likely it nests in one of the peaks. He must have business with your father.'

'Indeed, but what?' Glancing over to the other stool, Snorri addressed the dwarf sitting opposite his cousin. 'And who might you be?' He took in the bronze pauldron, the sigils on his belt and armour. 'Strange trappings for a dawi.'

Morgrim introduced them. 'This is Drogor...'

'Of Karak Zorn,' said Drogor, rising to offer a hand to the prince. 'My lord.' His eyes flashed in the firelight from the hearth. 'I can see the blood of kings in you.'

Morgrim clapped Snorri on the back, so hard it made the prince's eyes bulge a little.

'This is Snorri Lunngrin, Prince of Karaz-a-Karak.'

Drogor bowed deeply. 'I am honoured, my lord.'

'Karak Zorn in the Southlands?' asked Snorri, ignoring the flattery. His eyes narrowed, only half shaking the other dwarf's hand. 'How is it you are here, yet your king was absent from the rinkkaz?'

'Drogor is only here by the mercy of Valaya, cousin,' said Morgrim.

'My party and I were ambushed south of Karak Azul,' Drogor explained. His eyes dipped slightly. 'I alone lived to tell of it.'

'Dreng tromm,' uttered Snorri, suspicions fading. 'Was it grobi?'

'They were... archers, cousin.'

Snorri regarded Morgrim sternly.

'Elgi?'

Morgrim shook his head then looked at Drogor, who answered, 'Perhaps. The arrows were not crude enough for grobi or urk, though I didn't wait for the killers of my kin to reveal themselves.'

Snorri's gaze was on the table at the two slowly warming tankards of ale, but he wasn't thirsty. When he looked up, his face was creased with concern.

'I'm sorry for your loss, but you should seek an audience with my father and tell him what happened to you and your kin,' he said to Drogor. 'There has been no word of Karak Zorn for years, and then there is the matter of your ambushers.'

The sound of a door opening arrested the dwarfs' attention.

A familiar figure had just entered the alehouse, and was looking around.

'Furrowbrow,' Snorri scowled. 'What does he want?'

When the runesmith's gaze alighted on their table, he began to walk towards them.

'Looks like he wants you, cousin,' said Morgrim.

Folding his arms in a gesture of annoyance, Snorri said, 'Aside from his master, I have never known a more saturnine dawi.'

'He is certainly dour,' agreed Morgrim.

'Why the perpetual frown though, cousin? Perhaps his gruntis are too tight, eh?' Snorri leaned over to speak to Drogor. 'What do you think, Dro...'

But the dwarf from Karak Zorn was gone. Snorri thought he saw him at the back of the drinking hall, disappearing into a pall of pipe smoke, lost to the gloom.

'Let's hope that wasn't because of something I said,' Snorri remarked, and turned to face Morek Furrowbrow.

'My lords,' uttered the runesmith, bowing. Though he was Ranuld Silverthumb's apprentice, Morek was older than both the nobles. Grey hairs intruded on his dun-coloured beard and at his temples. Wrinkles under his eyes suggested a lack of sleep, but also a weight of years yet to burden the other two dwarfs. And then of course there was his forehead and the lines of consternation worn there almost continuously.

Peering past the two nobles, Morek scrutinised the darkness at the back of the hall. The alehouse was over half full and there were many patrons who chose the anonymity of that part of the drinking hall, but Morek's eye was fixed upon one and one alone.

He couldn't say why.

'Who was that dwarf?' he asked.

Morgrim glanced over his shoulder. 'Which dwarf, this place is full of– Ah,' he said, realising who the runesmith meant. 'An old friend, come back from Karak Zorn.'

Morek glanced at Morgrim. 'The Southlands? I thought that hold was cut off from the rest of the Karaz Ankor.'

Snorri chipped in, 'Yes, the Southlands. An expedition made it to Karaz-a-Karak, if you can count one dwarf as an expedition that is. Are you here to see me, runesmith?'

Regarding Snorri askance, Morek said, 'At the behest of my master, I am to fashion a gauntlet for you. Given your injuries, I need to see your hand in order to forge one that fits.'

Snorri showed off his bandaged wound and smiled. 'Well, it won't need all the fingers.'

Morek wasn't really listening. His eyes had returned to the shadows at the back of the drinking hall, but the dwarf from Karak Zorn was gone.

FOURTEEN

CITY OF THE HILL KING

Perched like an ugly bird of prey on a rocky tor, the city of the hill dwarfs glowered down on the boulder-strewn valley around it with disdain. Its watchtowers and stout walls offered a peerless view that stretched for miles, all the way to the edge of a treeline where the forest became a sea of fir and pine. Flanked by jutting crags of rock, the only way to gain an audience with the king of the hill was to climb. After the High King of Karaz-a-Karak had visited with two hundred of his warriors, Skarnag Grum had commanded the old sloped concourse demolished. Back then entire wagon trains, two abreast, with mules and trappings, could be let up to his gates. Now, if Gotrek Starbreaker returned to try and cow the hill king in his own hall again he would do so without his throne and all his retainers.

A narrow path wended the last few hundred feet to the city gates, but even this was treacherous. A long fall awaited any dwarf who slipped on the scree underfoot and sharp rocks that bullied onto the trail at intervals made safe navigation difficult. The hill dwarfs mainly used ropes and baskets dangled from the walls to send and receive supplies. It was awkward, but Skarnag Grum would have it no other way.

Defensively, the approach to Kazad Kro was both well watched by scores of crossbowmen but also forced attackers and visitors alike into a single file.

Its message was simple, *Leave us alone*. Although King Grum did welcome trade, he preferred it to camp outside his halls. Tents and temporary lodgings were a common sight ringing the borders of Kazad Kro. Anything so long as the gold kept flowing into his coffers.

Krondi had felt far from welcomed as he made his last weary steps into the city. A fat tongue of gold shimmered underfoot in the light of a low sun. Here, in the kingdom of the hill dwarfs, the streets were literally paved with gold. Flagstones and viaducts of the soft metal were everywhere, a proud boast and a declaration of wealth. To Krondi it looked wasteful and ostentatious. He had been on the road for three days already, with the sore back and the blistered feet to prove it. But despite his fatigue he would not allow the rough threshold of Kazad Kro to deter him from seeking out the justice of the king. According to its captain, Zakbar Varf was under the auspice of the hill kings and any charge of poor dealings or a plea for reckoning would have to go to them.

Not since his old campaigning days had Krondi felt the same wrath and desire to enact vengeance against an enemy as he did now. Of the party that had left Zakbar Varf, he alone had walked the long road to the summit of Kazad Kro. Every step he took, his ire for the indignity visited upon him at the trading outpost had increased.

After what felt like another day, he had at last reached the great gilded gate of the city. A huge effigy of the king was emblazoned upon it in relief, and the guards on the wall had granted admittance reluctantly. Wary eyes had watched him as he passed beneath the vaulted stone arch, and an escort of warriors had met him as soon as he set foot into the city proper. Krondi didn't know what had transpired when the High King had come to Kazad Kro but it had certainly soured the attitude of some of its citizens.

For outsiders, hill dwarfs were hard to distinguish from those who lived beneath the earth under the mountains, but Krondi could see the differences well enough. Fairer haired with sun-baked skin, they stood a little taller or less stooped on account of the fact they didn't spend all of their days crawling through tunnels. But they weren't as broad and the layer of soot and grit commonplace under the nails of all but the best preened of dwarfs wasn't present in the hill folk.

In spite of these differences, Krondi had still felt a kinship with them as he passed through their smithies and fletchers, markets and jewel-cutters, and hoped the king would have the same empathy for his mountain brethren too.

Sadly, the old dwarf campaigner would be disappointed.

Krondi was now kneeling in the hold hall of the king himself, his back still aching, his feet still sore and his pride more wounded than ever.

'Lower...' the voice uttered again, hoarse with age or overuse, putting him in mind of a crow by the way it rasped. It wasn't hard to imagine beetling little eyes like black pearls, the suggestion of a hooked beak in the shape of the king's nose, the avian sweep of his cheekbones and receding hairline, black fading to pepper grey at the fringes.

'I am as low as I can get.' Krondi attempted to stoop further, but a sharp pain in his knee prevented him sinking much more than another inch or two.

Evidently dissatisfied, the crow-king squawked again, 'Rundin, help this dawi show the proper obeisance.'

Krondi glared up under his eyebrows, muttering an oath. The hill king stared back, bird-like and imperious. Something glittered in his dark little eyes. It might have been pleasure.

A heavy-armoured dwarf behind Krondi put a meaty hand on his shoulder. It felt like a mason's block. Leaning, exerting a little pressure as he did so, the warrior whispered into Krondi's ear, 'I'm sorry, brother,' and pushed.

Failing to hide a grimace, Krondi sank another half a foot.

'Am I to kneel or genuflect?' he grumbled under his breath.

'Better,' said the king. 'Now rise.'

The dwarf called Rundin tried to help him back up, but Krondi shook off his hand. 'I can manage well enough,' he snapped, to which the other dwarf merely nodded and stepped back. 'And he is not my king,' he hissed between his teeth.

Skarnag Grum sat upon a gilded throne. A long stairway of stone steps led up to it, crested by a circular dais engraved with runes. Beringed fingers, festooned with gems, clacked loudly against the golden arms of the throne as the king vented his impatience. A jewel-encrusted gold crown sat upon his head, so large and grandiose his neck was braced with an aureate gorget to support it.

Though his gilded trappings, his armour and royal vestments shone, the king did not. Unlike most of the other hill dwarfs, Skarnag Grum's skin was pale and waxy. Krondi fancied if held up to the light of a lantern you would see his bones and organs through the thin parchment of his flesh.

Overlong nails and black-rimmed teeth spoke of matters occupying the king's mind that exceeded the necessity for personal grooming. Even his beard, also festooned with gems and ingots of precious metals, was unkempt.

Apart from his warrior protector, Krondi and the king were alone in the grand hall of Kazad Kro. Like its liege-lord it was opulent, with tall shining columns of stone and a wide aisle of silver flagstones that led to the vaulted throne itself. Banners and tapestries lined the walls, hinted at by the flickering embers of brazier pans suspended from the high ceiling on gold-plated chains. Furs and silks lay strewn in a penumbral gloom not so far removed from the dwarf halls beneath the mountains, though some of the materials were distinctly elven in origin.

Krondi's warrior instincts had not been completely dulled by his time as a merchant under Nadri Gildtongue and though he could not see them, he felt the presence of further guards lurking in the darkness and knew then why the hill king had devised his hold hall in this way.

'Speak then,' said Grum, wafting his hand disinterestedly in Krondi's vague direction. 'Time is precious, dawi.'

Krondi was still trying to work out if the hill king had meant the last word as an insult when he cleared his throat and said in a loud voice, 'Let it be known, on this day did–'

'No, no, no,' snapped the king, scowling and slashing a clawlike hand through the air as if to cut Krondi off from speaking further. 'No declarations, no oaths or grudgement.' He exhaled, as if already tired of the exchange when it had barely begun. 'You have come from Zakbar Varf, yes?'

Shocked at the hill king's flagrant disregard for the accepted tradition of voicing a grievance, Krondi nodded mutely.

'And you claim to have been cheated by elgi merchants?'

Krondi found his voice. 'They said they were weaponsmiths, and it is no claim. It's true, my lord.'

'Liege.'

Krondi frowned. 'Your pardon, my lord?'

'I am a king, High King of the Skarrenawi, and thus you will address me as *liege*.'

Taking a deep breath, Krondi said, 'Yes, I was cheated, my *liege*, and as Zakbar Varf is an outpost of the skarrenawi I have come to seek reckoning against the elgi.'

Dutifully silent until that moment, Rundin stepped forwards to speak on the merchant's behalf. 'I believe there is a case for grudgement here, my king, and can have our reckoners ready in the hour.'

Grum shook his head to dismiss the idea. 'Not necessary,' he said, then eyed the other dwarf sternly. 'Explain to me how you were duped, dawi. What did the elgi do that was so heinous you feel the need to disturb me in my hall and demand restitution? Eh?'

Krondi flushed with anger, but kept his temper. In his battlefield days he had killed for lesser slights against his honour. Shucking off a laden pack he carried on his back, he knelt and unfurled a leather satchel of blades.

Grum recoiled, scowling. 'You dare bring weapons into my hall!'

Rundin interceded again. His hands were raised and he glanced at the darkness behind the throne, giving the slightest shake of the head to the guards Krondi now knew were posted there.

'These are just his wares, my king.' He looked down at the assorted blades, hammers and hafts. 'And a poor lot at that.'

Krondi nodded to the other dwarf, finding him to be honourable and just, much more so than his king at any rate.

'Gold exchanged hands, much of it,' said Krondi, inadvertently piquing the hill king's interest, 'for what was a clutch of battered swords, spears and arrows.'

The weapons were certainly well worn, with chipped blades and blunted heads. Little better than battlefield leavings, it was hard to conceive of why even the most naïve of traders would part with coin for such a sorry cache.

'Did you not inspect them before purchase?' asked Grum, incredulous.

'Of course.' Krondi lowered his voice at an unspoken rebuke from Rundin. 'Of course,' he repeated more calmly, 'but they did not look as this.'

'Then how is it that they do now?'

'What else?' Krondi said, nonplussed at the hill king's failure to grasp his meaning. 'Sorcery. Elgi magic. They enchanted the blades to make them appear to be priceless artefacts.'

Grum tutted. There was more shaking of the head, much stroking of his lank beard. A small gold coin had appeared in his left hand and he was rolling it across his knuckles.

'A bad business,' he conceded, 'for which you have my sympathies.' Grum beckoned to the shadows. Four burly dwarfs in heavy armour and full-faced helms emerged into the hall.

'Agreed,' said Krondi, 'so what is to be done about it?'

The throne bearers were already lifting the opulent hill king and his throne off the ground when Grum turned to the merchant with a confused expression and said, 'Nothing. Fools beget what they beget. I will not waste coin on sending reckoners on a pointless errand. Do I look profligate to you, dawi?'

'Thievery has been done to me!' Incredulous at what he was hearing, Krondi stepped forwards, only for Rundin to impede his path. Instead, he shouted over the warrior's massive armoured shoulders. 'Grudgement must be made...' Krondi scowled as the king was slowly led away and called after him, 'If not against the elgi then against you, Skarnag Grum.'

The hill king raised his hand and the bearers stopped.

'Heed this warning, dawi. Do not return to Kazad Kro and do not threaten me with grudgement in my own halls. Begone, or I will have you thrown out of my gates and off my rock.'

'The reckoners shall hear of this,' Krondi vowed, marshalling his anger but only barely. 'I shall seek the counsel of the High King of Karaz-a-Karak.'

Grum's bearers were moving again, the king's voice growing fainter as they disappeared down the long hall towards his private chambers. 'Do so with my blessing, for Kazad Kro will not hear your grievances further. Rundin,' he called, 'I am retiring to my counting house. Escort the dawi out.'

Rundin was about to oblige when Krondi snarled at him.

'Lay hands on me and it'll be the last thing you do.'

Palms up, Rundin said, 'Leave without a fuss and there'll be no need to.'

Krondi had his back to him when he replied. 'How you can serve a king such as Grum I cannot fathom. All dawi are greedy and selfish bastards, but he is something worse.'

'He is my king,' said Rundin.

'If that is the best you can say of him, you are being loyal to the point of blindness.'

At that Krondi stalked out of the hall.

Rundin was left alone with his thoughts. Silent as a tomb in the grand hall, the distant *chink* of coins being counted in King Grum's treasure room clanged brashly. Beneath it, running as an undercurrent, was another sound. At first it was difficult to place, but Rundin listened hard and was rewarded. Laughter. It was laughter that he heard. Just the odd chuckle, a half-stifled giggle but which soon gave way to raucous hooting and guffawing.

FIFTEEN

WRATH AND RUIN

Skirting the Worlds Edge, the caravan of wagons was deep into the mountain passes now. Despite the fact he rode out ahead of Nadri, Krondi could ill-afford the detour to Kazad Kro especially when it had yielded nothing. His coffers were all but empty, wasted by elven treachery, and he felt the sting of that indignity worse than a dagger in his gut.

Driving the mules hard, he was determined to at least ensure his passenger reached Karaz-a-Karak in good time.

Perhaps it was his obsession with achieving that goal, or possibly some residual anger from his meeting with Skarnag Grum though it was days old, that blinded Krondi to the fact that he had strayed into the sights of a predator. Three days out of the domain of the hill dwarfs and he finally realised they were being tracked.

Cursing himself for ignoring the signs and allowing his good instincts to be clouded by selfish concerns, Krondi turned to his charge who was sitting quietly alongside him in the lead wagon.

'We are being followed,' he said. Krondi glanced over his shoulder, but all he could see was the lengthening shadows of the slowly dipping sun. Nightfall was not far off and they were too far away from Everpeak to reach it before the light died completely. Krondi did not want to still be on the road when that happened.

The old hooded dwarf beside him grunted something, appearing to ignite the smoking root in the cup of his pipe with his finger.

Hailing one of the guards riding at the back of the wagon, Krondi said, 'Keep a sharp eye behind us. I don't think we are alone out here.'

Durgi frowned, gesturing to the twenty or so warriors that rode on the four wagons. 'Only a fool would attack such a well-defended caravan.'

'That is what concerns me. A sharp eye, remember,' Krondi told him, pointing to his eye before returning both hands to the reins.

They were approaching a rocky gorge. High-sided and narrow, it would funnel the wagons into a tight cordon, an ideal position for an ambush.

Krondi tried to search the highlands at the summit of the gorge for signs of warriors. There were only craggy boulders and rough gorse bowing gently in the wind.

He muttered, 'Something doesn't feel right.'

On the path laid before them the wagons would be exposed but at least they would have room to manoeuvre if needed. Through the narrow defile of the gorge they'd be sheltered from the flanks but vulnerable to an attack from above. Making any sort of camp in this terrain was out of the question, so the two choices remained.

Take the path or travel through the gorge?

Krondi chewed his beard then said, 'These mountains are my home. I know them as I know my own skin. So, why then do I fear them all of a sudden?'

'Do you wish me to answer, beardling?' asked the old dwarf with a voice like cracking oak.

'Something hunts us,' said Krondi, urging the mules to greater effort. 'And anything bold enough to attack a party of over twenty armoured dawi in their own lands is something I do not wish to fight.'

'We won't reach Karaz-a-Karak,' said the old dwarf, 'not before they catch us.'

Krondi turned to the hooded dwarf sitting next to him smoking his pipe. His eyes grew a little wider. 'So I am not imagining it. We *are* being followed.'

'Have been for miles, lad.'

Krondi was incredulous. 'Why didn't you say something?'

'What good would that do? Kill us quicker, maybe. No, better to get closer to the hold, better to let them see us and know us for what we are.'

'Their prey?' asked Krondi.

Now the hooded dwarf turned and there was fire in his eyes, of forges ancient and forgotten, of jewels that glitter for eternity.

'No. We are dawi, stone and steel. And we are not afraid. That is what they will see. Strength, lad. Strength and courage of our ancestors.' The flame in the hooded dwarf's eyes faded and he added, 'Slow down, spare the mules or you ride the wagon train into the ground and do our hunters' job for them.'

Krondi nodded, let his beating heart slow also to a dull hammering in his chest.

'I have fought in dozens of battles, fought the urk and grobi, trolls and *gronti*. I am a warrior, not a merchant.'

'Aye, lad,' said the hooded dwarf, 'but this is not a battle. There's no shield wall, no brother's shoulder to lock against your own. We are alone out here in the rising dark.'

The mouth of the gorge was approaching, forking off from the main path.

'What should I do?'

Supping deep of his pipe, the passenger said, 'It doesn't matter. Either way, we will have to fight.'

Muttering an oath to Valaya, Krondi took the gorge.

The skryzan-harbark was ruined. It slumped in Heglan Copperfist's workshop a broken wreck, once a ship and now little more than kindling. Some of the hull had survived intact but the sails had been utterly destroyed, along with Heglan's dreams, in the crash.

Under threat of expulsion from the guild, Master Strombak had commanded him to break the vessel down, strip it for parts, but faced with the reality of that Heglan was finding it hard to imagine such a formerly magnificent creation rendered into anything so prosaic as a stone thrower or heavy ballista. It would be an easy task, Heglan was gifted as an engineer, but that was also why he railed against the fetters of tradition the guild shackled him with.

His entire workshop was littered with designs, plans sketched with sticks of charcoal depicting various flying vessels he one day hoped to build. Incredibly detailed, each parchment schematic was filled with calculations, formulae for wind speed and velocity, theories on loft and chemical equations related to steam and pressure.

Of the engineers, Heglan was the only one to have fitted his workshop with a vast skylight. He had fashioned the glass himself and the massive aperture sat above the wreckage of his airship, letting in the sun to expose its many wounds. Shadows intruded on the scene as Heglan scrutinised through a pall of pipe smoke. Sharp, hooked beaks, arrow-straight wingspans and the suggestion of talons created a fearsome menagerie of silhouettes. Alongside his engineering endeavours, sitting between his many racks of tools, his cogs and half-built machineries, his oils and ropes, nails, bolts, screws, chisels, planes and work benches was his feathered host.

Here Heglan had created an aviary of the creatures of the sky he so wished to emulate. Preserved, meticulously posed and stuffed, there were hundreds. Often he had ventured in the low lands at the edge of the hold or taken a grubark out towards the ocean in the south. Dead birds were a common sight. Heglan had gathered them, studied their musculature, their pinions and the composition of their feathers. A notebook, bound in boar hide, was almost filled to the hilt with his scratched observations and sketches.

'It should have worked,' he muttered bitterly to an uncaring gloom. 'It should have flown.' He approached the wreck. In his tool belt he had a large hammer and a heavy-headed axe for the demolition. Running his hand over the hull, he winced every time he felt a crack or encountered a splinter. Rigging had broken apart like twine, masts snapped like limbs. The stink of spilled grog reeked heavily and spoiled the lacquering of the wood in places.

Shadow eclipsed most of the airship's remains. Heglan kept many of the lanterns doused, lighting just enough in order to work. Cloud obscured the sun and any luminescence that might penetrate the skylight. Heglan preferred it this way. Darkness salved his thoughts and his stung pride.

Nadri had accomplished so much, earning the respect of his guild, his hold and the dwarfs of other holds beyond Barak Varr's borders. Heglan was an engineer, a vaunted profession for any dwarf, but had thus far not achieved his potential. With their father Lodri dead and grandfather Dammin cold in his tomb, it mattered more than ever to honour them. Both brothers felt this keenly, and Nadri had remarked upon it when he had left Barak Varr to try and catch Krondi and the caravans.

'Sons are destined to bury their fathers, Heg,' he had said. 'It's only war that turns that around.'

Heglan had his head in his hands. 'I've shamed them this day with my hubris.'

Nadri gripped his brother's shoulders, made him look up. 'Be proud of what you have achieved. You *honour* them. You will have your moment, Heg. Determination is what made the Copperfist clan what it is this day. Do not forget that. Do not give in to despair, either. We are dawi, stout of back and strong of purpose. We are the mountains, enduring and unyielding. Remember that and you will be remembered, just as they are.'

He gestured to the talisman around Heglan's neck. It was the exact simulacrum of the one that Nadri also wore. Upon it were wrought the names of Lodri and Dammin, a son and father.

Heglan nodded, relieved from his torpor by his brother's words of support.

'But do this one thing for me,' said Nadri, releasing Heglan's shoulders to make his point clear with an outstretched finger.

'Name it, Nadri.'

'Heed Strombak, do not go against your master's will and risk expulsion from the guild. Do that for me, Heg.'

Heglan went to protest, but the look in his brother's eyes warned him to do so would earn further reproach. Reluctantly, he nodded.

Nadri nodded too, satisfied he'd been heard. 'Good,' he said, and clapped him on the shoulder. 'I'm bound for Karaz-a-Karak. Krondi will meet me there and we'll be on our way.' He glanced at the ruined airship, squatting in a forlorn heap inside the workshop. 'I wish I could stay and help you with this, but I am already late.'

They clasped forearms, and Heglan embraced him.

'What would I do without you, Nadri?'

'Likely go mad,' he laughed as they parted.

After that, Heglan had bidden him farewell. Dismissing the journeymen dwarfs who had helped retrieve the broken ship, he had been left alone. There he had stayed in seclusion for two days, pondering Nadri's words and those of Master Strombak.

Almost on the last of his smoking root, he chewed the end of his pipe and regarded the broken ship through a veil of grey. Three days and he had not lifted a finger to break the ship apart. This part of the workshop was sealed, a vault where Heglan could craft in secret and not be disturbed. Other machineries could be fashioned to demonstrate his commitment to his master. This, the plan forming in Heglan's mind inspired by the drawings on his workshop walls, he need never know about.

For the first time in three days, he gripped the worn haft of his hammer. Ever since his grandfather Dammin had shown him the proper way to use one, Heglan had regarded it as a tool to create, not destroy.

Purposefully, he strode towards the wrecked skryzan-harbark.

'I am sorry, brother.'

A dwarf would fly and Heglan was determined to be the first.

Sweat lathered the flanks of the mules. The beasts were gasping, shrieking with fear as Krondi drove the head of the wagon train like all the daemons of hellfire were at their heels.

For all he knew, they actually were.

Of course, daemons did not clad themselves in midnight black, nor did they carry bows, nor did they wear the countenances of elves...

'Curse the thagging elgi and all their foetid spawn!' Krondi shrank into his driver's seat, hunched as tight as he could be and still lash the mules.

Arrows whickered overhead. On the road behind them, three guards lay dead with shafts in their backs. More protruded from the sides of the wagons, jutting like the spines of some forest creature.

Dwarfs armed with crossbows tried to reply in kind but the bouncing wagons, now driven into a frantic charge through the ever-narrowing gorge, made aiming difficult. Even on foot, at full sprint, the elves not only kept pace but were also more accurate.

Durgi took one in the eye. He spun, a rivulet of blood streaking his face like a long tear, before he fell.

Another guard – it looked like Lugni but he died so fast it was hard to tell for sure – gurgled his last breath and also slumped off the wagon. Glancing over his shoulder, Krondi watched their bodies smack off the road like dead cattle and swore an oath to Grimnir towards their vengeance.

Several of the surviving guards were wounded. Some had arrows in their shoulders, others cuts or grazes from near misses. At least all four of the wagons were still intact but the road through the gorge was hard, better suited to travellers on foot than mules and iron-banded wheels.

Krondi cursed himself for a fool again. Then he cursed the elves.

'This road joins the *dawangi* pass to Kundrin hold,' he said to the hooded dwarf, pointing at a fork in the gorge. 'It's little more than a track but we can lose them in there and make for Thane Durglik's halls. Once we have sanctuary behind his walls, we can go back out and hunt these cowards down.'

The hooded dwarf nodded, but didn't stir beyond that. His head was bowed and he was muttering beneath his breath. Krondi did not recognise the words, for they had the arcane cadence of magic.

From the brief glances he'd had and the shouted reports of the guards farther back on the wagon train, Krondi reckoned on six raiders. Twenty dwarfs against six raiders was an uneven contest but the elves had them at range, at the disadvantage of terrain and could pick them off. There was also no guarantee that there weren't more raiders lying in wait. No, to stand and fight was foolish. Better to run and find safe haven. Though all evidence pointed to it, they did not seem like mere bandits either and this was what disquieted Krondi the most.

He was reining the lead mule in, turning the bit so its head faced towards the fork he wanted to take, when a shadow loomed overhead, crouched down at the summit of the high-sided gorge.

A dwarf yelled 'Archers!' before he was cut off by an arrow in his heart. It punched straight through the breastplate, came out of his back and impaled him.

'*Ghuzakk! Ghuzakk!*' Krondi urged the mules that gaped and panted with the last of their failing strength.

The fork that would take them out of the gorge and to the winding trail that led to Kundrin hold was closing.

From above, steel-fanged death came down like rain. Though the dwarfs raised shields, several of the guards were struck in the leg or shoulder. One screamed as he was pinned to the wagon deck by his ankle. When he lowered his shield, a second shaft pierced his eye and the screaming stopped.

A terrible, ear-piercing shriek was wrenched from the mouth of one of the mules on the leading wagon. Moments later the poor beast collapsed and died, unable to go any further. Its companion slumped down with it, similarly exhausted. Krondi was pitched forwards and clung to a hand rail to stay in his seat. Abandoning the reins, for they were no use to him now, he instead concentrated on keeping his shield aloft to ward off the relentless arrow storm. It was studded with shafts in seconds, several of the barbed tips punching straight through the wood mere inches from his nose.

'Thagging bastards!' Krondi leapt off the wagon as it slewed to a halt and nosed into the dirt road with only the collapsed bodies of the mules to slow it. The hooded dwarf beside him made the jump at the same time. Miraculously, the arrows had yet to hit or even graze him.

'Old one,' Krondi called to him, 'here!' Sheltering beneath a rocky overhang, he gestured to the hooded dwarf, who followed.

Despite the furious attack, several of the guards yet lived and were making their way from the wreckage of the other three wagons to join up with Krondi. Two tried to raise crossbows against the archers but were struck down before a bolt was even nocked to string. Of the rest, three out of the original twenty-strong band made it into cover.

An injured dwarf, Killi, was crawling on his belly towards them just a few feet from the safety of the overhang. One of the other guards went to drag him the rest of the way but Krondi hauled him back.

'No, they'll kill you too,' he snapped.

A moment later, three arrows thudded into Killi's back.

Then it stopped.

There was no sight of the elves above or those on the road behind. As if an eldritch wind had billowed through it to carry their enemies away, the gorge was deserted.

Krondi knew they were still there watching. Either they had run short of arrows or they were waiting to see if the dwarfs would venture from safety.

'No one moves,' he told the survivors.

Dwarfs can stay still for hours, even days. During his service in the armies of Gotrek Starbreaker, there was a dwarf Krondi knew, a real mule of a warrior. Lodden Strongarm was his name, a veteran of the Gatekeepers who had stood guard on the same portal into the Ungdrin Ankor for many years. Krondi knew him because he had been the warrior sent to relieve him from his post when the previous incumbent of that duty had died in battle. Three weeks Lodden had waited, unmoving by the gate. He only stirred to sip from a tankard of strong beer or to nibble from a chunk of stonebread, the only victuals he had to sustain him. Like the mountain, Lodden had stood guard and would not shirk or grumble for he had no one to grumble to. Finally, when Krondi had come to take Lodden's place, the old Gatekeeper had grown long in beard, his skin dusted with fallen debris from the mountain to such an extent he looked almost part of it. He didn't voice complaint when Krondi arrived, but merely nodded and returned to the hold.

Waiting was easy for dwarfs. They were mostly patient creatures. This was back when Krondi was young and full of fire. Times had moved on since then. Lodden was laid in silent repose in his tomb, whilst Krondi lived on to lament his loss of youth; but he was not as venerable as the hooded dwarf, whose voice broke through his maudlin reverie.

'Draw your blades,' he rasped, the sound of old oak carrying to every dwarf beneath the overhang. 'They are coming for us.'

Those who still had axes showed them to the failing light.

Krondi drew his hammer, the weapon he had carried since he had been a Gatekeeper. Never in all the years he'd spent campaigning had the haft ever broken.

Darkness filled the gorge as the sun faded, drowning the dwarfs taking shelter at its edges in a black sea. Like shadows detaching themselves from the darkness of falling night, the elves emerged six abreast and filled the narrow road.

From the other side came four more, only this quartet still had arrows nocked and bows unslung. To Krondi's eyes the slender necks and white pine shafts of the bows looked incongruous in the hands of the black-garbed killers.

'There is more to this than mere thievery and murder,' he murmured.

The hooded dwarf answered, a staff of iron appearing suddenly in his gnarled hands. 'They cannot allow us to leave this place,' he said. 'A great doom is coming...'

From the group of six an elf came forwards, evidently their leader. He said something in a tongue unfamiliar to Krondi, though he could speak some elvish, and the four archers fell back.

So they wish to cut us then.

At least it was a better end than dying at the tip of an arrow.

When the six drew long serrated knives from their belts, Krondi knew his earlier assumption was true.

One of the other dwarfs piped up, 'If we fight them, the others will shoot us in the back!'

'Thagging elgi scum!' spat another.

Krondi knew them both. They were brothers, Bokk and Threk. He briefly wondered if their father had any more sons to continue his name.

'Make a circle,' said Krondi. For the old veteran campaigner, memories came back in a red-hazed flood of similar last stands. On each of those previous occasions, fighting beasts or greenskins, dwarf tenacity had won out and he had survived. Somehow this time, it felt different.

The dwarfs obeyed Krondi's command, coming together and raising shields. Only the hooded dwarf stood apart, and Krondi was content to let him. He hadn't asked who the dwarf was and why he needed to be ferried to Karaz-a-Karak, but he'd seen enough, felt enough to realise he was not just some mere warrior.

'Like links in a shirt of mail,' he told the other dwarfs, 'we do not part, we do not break. Stone and steel.'

'Stone and steel,' echoed all three in unison.

Seemingly amused by their antics, the leader of the elves bade some of his cohort forwards. Four night-clad warriors advanced with slow but deliberate purpose.

Krondi saw the glint of stone-cold killers in their eyes, and knew the last stand had been a mistake. It was far too late to do anything about that now. Closing his eyes for a moment, he made an oath to Valaya and then Grungni.

Let me die well, he beseeched them. Finally, he added a remark to Grimnir too, *and let me take some of these whore-sons with me.*

Four elves attacked as one, shrieking war cries.

Ugdrik stepped from the circle, breaking the wall, for the fall from his wagon had damaged his ear drum and he hadn't heard Krondi's command. Sparks flew for a few moments between his axe and an elven blade but poor Ugdrik was quickly gutted on a long knife, his guts spilling all over the road.

The others fared better. Under Krondi's anvil-hard leadership, they repelled the first proper elven attack against their wall. Krondi buried the head of his hammer in the skull of one, which made it three apiece.

Frustrated, the elven leader sent his other warrior into the fight. In the warrior's eyes, Krondi beheld a fathomless abyss of darkness and suppressed a tremor running through his body at the sight. The leader of the elves then hailed his archers to return and waded in himself, a sickle blade held low and by his side.

It seemed the elves did not fight fairly after all, which was no more than Krondi expected.

In a few seconds, what was a short skirmish became a dense melee through which it was tough to discern anything except flashing steel and the reek of copper. Bokk died swiftly, two jagged knives in his back and neck. His fountaining blood bathed Threk in a ruddy mire. He roared, threw himself at one elf, cut him down and wounded another, but a third slit opened the grief-maddened dwarf's neck.

It left only Krondi, the leader and the hollow-eyed warrior.

One of the elf archers went for the hooded dwarf. Embattled himself, Krondi heard a low *whoomf!* of crackling, snapping air, followed by a sudden burst of heat that pricked his bare skin. Screaming came swiftly on its heels. Burning flesh filled his nostrils with a noisome stench.

The hooded dwarf was chanting again, though this time he was much louder. It sounded like an invocation. Between his words, the yelled orders of the elven leader grew more frantic.

Then Krondi realised who he had in his midst and that they would not die after all.

Arrows were loosed by the three remaining archers, but the shafts broke as if they struck a mountainside.

In a momentary respite as the elves' resolve began to fail them and they retreated, Krondi saw the hooded dwarf had one gnarled hand outstretched in front of him, clenched into a claw. Rings upon his fingers glowed brightly in the night gloom and as he brought them into a fist another flight of arrows snapped as if he had been holding them.

Out of shafts, the archers drew blades too and rushed the dwarfs.

Casting aside his cloak, the once hooded dwarf revealed his true identity.

Agrin Fireheart, Runelord of Barak Varr, stood in his armour of meteoric iron. His incantation reached a crescendo as he threw off his disguise and, as he bellowed the last arcane syllable, he brought his iron staff down hard upon the ground. Runes igniting upon the stave which filled with inner fire, a massive tremor erupted from the point where Agrin had struck.

The elves were flattened, their murderous charge violently arrested by the runelord's magic.

A shout split the dark like a peal of thunder. It took a moment for Krondi, lying on his back like the elves, to realise it had come from Agrin's mouth.

Like a dagger blade bent by the smith's hammer, a jag of lightning pierced the sky and fed into the runelord's staff, so bright that the arcing bolt lit up the gorge in azure monochrome. With sheer strength of will, he held it there, coruscating up and down the haft in agitated ripples of power like he was wrestling a serpent.

One of the elves was trying to rise, take up a fallen arrow and nock it to his bowstring.

Agrin immolated him like a cerulean candle. The elf burned, grew white hot... There was a flare of intense magnesium white and then he was gone, with only ash remaining.

Thrusting his staff skywards again, thunderheads growling above him, Agrin was about to unleash a greater storm when a spear of darkling power impaled him.

Slowly he lowered his staff and the clouds began to part, losing their belligerence. A smoking hole, burned around the edges, cut through the runelord's meteoric armour.

It was just above his heart.

Agrin staggered as another dark bolt speared from the shadows at him. Krondi cried out, railing at the imminent death of the beloved runelord of his hold, but Agrin was equal to it and dispelled the bolt with a muttered counter.

His enemies revealed themselves soon after, three robed figures walking nonchalantly through the gorge. A female led the sorcerous coven, sculpting a nimbus of baleful energy in her hands. Krondi was no mageling, but he had fought them before and even he could tell that the female was the mistress. The other two were merely there to augment her powers.

She unleashed the magicks she had crafted and a vast serpent fashioned from bloody light painted the gorge in a visceral glow before it snapped hungrily at the runelord.

Once more Agrin foiled her sorcery, a rune of warding extinguishing on his staff as he brandished it towards the elemental. She shrieked as the enchantment failed, recoiling as if burned, and pressed a trembling hand to her forehead before snarling at the male sorcerer in the coven as he went to help her.

Despite the fresh tipping of the scales against them, Krondi felt renewed hope. He didn't have long to appreciate it as the leader of the elves came at him with a pair of sickle blades. The other was still grounded and watched eagerly from his prone position.

From the corner of his eye, Krondi saw Agrin assailed by dark magic as the three sorcerers vented their power as one. Runes flared and died on his staff as the iron was slowly denuded of its magical defences. Outnumbered, the runelord was finding it hard to retaliate, just as Krondi could only fend off the silvered blades of the elf leader intent on his death.

'Submit,' the elf snarled in crude Khazalid through clenched teeth, 'and I'll kill you quickly.'

Krondi was shocked at the use of his native tongue but knew that some elves had learned it, or tried to.

'Unbaraki!' he bit back, invoking the dwarf word for 'oathbreaker', for these bandits or whatever they were had broken the treaty between their races and sealed the deed with blood.

'Your oaths mean nothing to me, runt. I'll cut your coarse little tongue from your mouth–'

Krondi finally struck his enemy. In the elf's fervour he had left an opening, one an old soldier like Krondi could exploit. Ribs snapped in the elf's chest, broken by a hammer blow that the dwarf punched into his midriff.

Mastering the pain, the elf rallied but was on the back foot as the dwarf pressed his advantage. Laughter issued from somewhere close, though it sounded oddly resonant and was obscured by the near-deafening magical duel between Agrin and the coven.

Like he was swatting turnips with a mattock, Krondi swung his hammer with eager abandon. Kill the elf now, bludgeon him with sheer fury and power, or he would be dead like the others. He couldn't match the elf for skill. Krondi knew this but felt no shame in it, as his father had taught him humility and pragmatism, so that left only brute strength.

His resurgence was only momentary. Dodging an overhead swing intended to break his shoulder, the elf weaved aside and trapped the hammer between the razor edges of his sickle blades. With a grunt the elf cut in opposite directions, shearing the haft apart and disarming the dwarf.

Looking on despairing at his sundered hammer, the weapon that in all his years of loyal gatekeeping had never broken, Krondi scarcely noticed the twin blades rammed into his chest.

'–and then gut you like a fish,' the elf concluded, a grimace etched permanently on his face from the crushed ribs in his chest.

Krondi spat into it, a greasy gob of blood-flecked phlegm that ran down the elf's cheek and drew a sneer to already upcurled lips. The dwarf slid off the blades, life leaving him as he hit the ground. He was on his side and tried to claw at the earth, to catch some of it in his numbing grasp and know he would be returning to the world below and his ancestors. Through his muddying vision that crawled with black clouds at the edges, though the storm had long since cleared, Krondi saw Agrin on his knees.

Teeth clenched, the runelord was defiant to the last but the wound he'd been dealt when his guard was down was telling upon him. It was to be his end.

Agrin met Krondi's gaze across the litter of dwarf and elf dead.

'A great doom...' he mouthed before three tentacles like the arms of some kraken forged of eternal darkness impaled him and then tore him apart. Even meteoric armour couldn't spare the runelord that fate, and so another ancient light of the dwarf race was snuffed out.

Krondi slumped, his final breaths coming quick and shallow. A chill was upon him now, but he heard singing, the crackle of a hearth and the voices of dwarfs he knew but had never met. They were calling his name, calling him to the table where his place was waiting. But as he descended, leaving the world above to embrace those that came before, Agrin's words lingered and seemed to travel through Gazul's Gate itself into the dwarfen underworld.

A great doom...

Sevekai slumped, the pain in his chest from the two broken ribs besting him finally. He scowled at Kaitar who was still lying on the ground, though now more reclining than upended by the dwarf's crude magicks.

'Why did you not aid me?' Sevekai's tone was accusatory. He still held the bloodied sickle blades unsheathed.

'Don't threaten me, Sevekai,' said Kaitar, rising and dusting off his tunic. 'You wanted to kill the runt, you said as much to me with your eyes. If it proved tougher prey than you had first envisaged that is no fault of mine.'

'I heard you laughing when he struck me.'

'From sheer surprise that the runt landed such a blow. You grew overconfident, but it gave you the focus you needed to finish it.'

Sevekai wanted to kill Kaitar. He *should* kill him, plunge his sickle blades into his heart and end the impudent little worm, but he didn't. He told himself it was because they had lost too many of their number already but that wasn't the truth, not really. The truth was that he was afraid of the warrior, of the fathomless black in his eyes, the kind of ennui only shared by converts of the assassin temples, the devotees of Khaine.

Cursing in elvish, Sevekai let it go and turned to the slain dwarfs.

As before on the Old Dwarf Road he was careful, ensuring there was nothing in the murders that would suggest anything other than asur involvement. He suspected most of the stunted creatures wouldn't be able to tell druchii from asur anyway, but it still paid to be careful. Couple this most recent carnage with the acts of killing and sabotage happening all across the Old World and the prospects for continued peace looked bleak. It should have satisfied him. It did not.

Touring the massacre he was genuinely dismayed to see the charred corpse of Numenos amongst the dead, if only because it meant he'd need to find another scout from whoever was left. Including Kaitar and Sevekai himself, only five of the shades remained. Enough to do what still needed to be accomplished but preciously short on contingency. There were other cohorts, of course there were. Clandestine saboteurs were hidden the length and breadth of the Old World.

In his private moments, the few he was afforded and only when he was certain the dark lord wasn't watching, Sevekai wondered at the sagacity of the plan. Unfolding perfectly at present, it would allegedly do much to further druchii ambition but Sevekai could not see that end, not yet. His doubt troubled him more than the thought all of this might come to naught.

'You appear conflicted, Sevekai,' a female voice purred from in front of him. Masking his emotions perfectly, Sevekai averted his gaze from the blank stares of the dead and met her equally cold expression.

She *was* darkly beautiful, wearing a form-fitting robe of midnight black. Her skin was porcelain white but she carried a countenance that was hard as marble with a stare to rival that of a gorgon. Hair the colour of hoarfrost cascaded down her slender back as she near paraded in front of him, her spine exposed in a long, narrow slit down robes that also barely cupped her small breasts. She was lithe and ravishing but sorcery had stolen what youth and immortality had given her. Ashniel, her little protégé witch, had the same snow white hair, but did not carry the subtle weight of age about the eyes, neck and cheekbones.

Lust and wariness warred ambivalently in Sevekai, for the last time he had shared her bed he had left with a blade wound from a ritual athame in his back. Not lightly did one consort with Drutheira of the coven, especially if you ever questioned her prowess as a lover. It was meant as a tease, a playful rejoinder, but Drutheira was not one for games. Some scars, Sevekai knew, went deeper than a blade.

The sorceress's mood was predictably belligerent.

'You also look weathered, *my love*.' No druchii could say 'my love' with such venom as her. A deadly adder could not achieve the same vitriol should it be given voice to speak. 'Are those ribs cracked by any chance? Has your peerless *talent* with your little knives finally been exposed for the parlour trick it really is?'

'I have missed you too, dearest.' Sevekai's smile was far from warm, and had more in kind with a snake than an elf. 'I expected to see you sooner.'

'Other matters required my attention that I do not have to explain to you.'

Though it pained him, Sevekai gave a mocking bow. 'I am your servant, mistress.'

Drutheira was gaunt from spellweaving, but she was also injured. A red-raw scar like an angry vein throbbed on her forehead.

Sevekai gestured to the wound. 'Seems I am not the only one not to have escaped the battle unscathed.' Her hands were also hurt, burned by the dwarf's bound magic.

Drutheira touched the scar, her hands already healing from the minor incantation she'd silently performed, and snarled. Her mood changed again, sarcasm lessening in favour of hateful scorn.

'Little bastard ripped it from my head.'

'Ripped what?' asked Sevekai, briefly regarding the dwarf's corpse. It was hollowed out, as if long dead and drained of all vitality. Dark magic tended to have that effect on the living.

'The incantation, the spell,' Drutheira replied, apparently annoyed at Sevekai's ignorance. 'It was charnel blood magic and he took it from my mind and destroyed it.'

The others in the coven did not speak, but like jackals they examined every detail of her sudden weakness. Drutheira sensed their murderous ambition, spoken on the Wind of Dhar still roiling through the gorge, and was quick to reassert her dominance.

Malchior, her male suckling, was the perfect example. She thrust her hand at him, turning it into a claw, and Malchior was contorted by a sudden agony.

'I see your thoughts,' she hissed, flicking a scathing glance at Ashniel who quailed despite her ostensible truculence.

Veins stood out on Malchior's forehead like death-adders writhing beneath his skin. He fought to speak, to muster something by way of contrition that would make the pain stop. Instead, he managed to stare. His eyes were oval rings of red, burning flesh. Rage, fear, desperate pleading for the agony to end roiled across his face. Spittle ran down his cheek, drooling through clenched teeth.

'I could churn you inside out, flay the flesh off you,' Drutheira hissed, seizing him by the neck of his robe and dragging him to her until mere inches parted them.

She glared, revealing to him the manifold agonies that awaited him, let Ashniel see it too.

'Crippling, isn't it?'

Malchior barely managed a nod. *'Druth...'* Crimson flecked his lips as he tried pathetically to speak.

She leaned into his ear, whispering, 'Do you see how insignificant you are to me?' before she bit his ear and then looked up at Ashniel.

'Excruciating... Would you like to try?'

The young sorceress was already shaking her head. Malchior was on his knees, retching. Drutheira released him, and he collapsed.

'Never put your hands on me again,' she snarled.

Malchior found the strength to breathe then grovel. He nodded weakly.

'I only meant–'

Drutheira cut him off with a raised fist, the promise of further torture.

Malchior bowed and spoke no more.

'Prepare the rite of communion,' she snapped, sneering at them both. 'Lord Malekith will know all that has been done in his name.'

Dismissed, Malchior and Ashniel went to find a sacrifice. Some of the dwarfs yet lived, if only just. Although slowed, their blood would still be fresh.

'Your apprentices, or whatever they are,' said Sevekai, 'are viperous little creatures. You should be careful, Drutheira.'

She pouted at him. 'Is that concern for my welfare I am hearing, Sevekai?'

His face grew stern like steel. 'What are you really doing here? You need no scout through these lands.'

'Performing our dark lord's bidding, as are you I presume. "To each coven a cohort of shades", you remember now, don't you?' She regarded the runelord's desiccated body. 'Fortunate that I arrived when I did, it would seem.'

'Do not expect any gratitude.'

'Must we fight, *lover*?' she purred.

Sevekai laughed, utterly without mirth.

'I still feel your *love*, my dear. It is a wound in my back that is taking its time to heal.' He winced, his mock humour jarring his damaged ribs.

Drutheira stepped closer. 'Then at least let me ease your suffering...'

She outstretched her hand, but Sevekai recoiled from her touch.

'Don't be such a child,' she chided him.

Still wary, he relented and showed her the side of his chest where the dwarf had struck him.

'Now,' she warned, 'be still.'

A warm glow filled Sevekai, just hot enough to burn but the pain was tolerable. When it abated again, his ribs were healed.

'Miraculous...' he breathed.

Drutheira clenched her fist as he smiled and one of the ribs broke as if she'd crushed it.

Crying out, Sevekai glared daggers at her.

'Hell-bitch!'

'A reminder,' she said, all her genial pretence evaporating into an expression of pure ice, 'that I can do that to you at any time.'

'Duly noted,' said Sevekai. Behind, Kaitar was approaching.

Drutheira's gaze snapped to regard him.

'Who is that?' she asked.

Sevekai thought he detected a hint of anxiety in her voice, even fear, but dismissed it almost at once.

'He is no one. Just a shade from Karond Kar.'

She lingered on the distant warrior for a moment, and Sevekai took her interest for lust. He tried not to feel jealous, but his fist clenched at the slight.

Drutheira was still staring.

'What?'

'It's nothing.'

Sevekai's eyes narrowed. 'Drutheira, are you all right?'

'We are not staying,' she said, turning her attention back to Sevekai.

'You have just arrived. Do you tire of my company already?'

'Yes, I do.' She beckoned him. 'Come forwards.'

Sevekai obeyed and like a striking serpent Drutheira cut his cheek with her athame.

'Whore!'

'Now my blood mingles with yours,' she told him. 'In it you will find your purpose.'

Still wincing from the burning pain of the wound, Sevekai saw a host of hidden roads in his mind's eye. Such seldom trodden paths could only be found by those who were given knowledge of them by their keepers. Malekith possessed such knowledge, garnered long ago from an old friend. Given unto Drutheira by the dark lord, she now passed it on to Sevekai.

'We will accomplish more and be less conspicuous if we are apart. My task requires craft that you don't possess, *my love*.' She smiled like a serpent.

'Beguiling dwarf lords and marking outposts for your riders to burn down,' he smirked. 'Indeed, such craft is required for that subtle work.'

'You have your orders,' she snapped. 'See them done.'

Sevekai was still wiping the blood from his cheek. 'You need not worry about that, Drutheira.'

'Just conceal our presence here if you can,' she said, turning on her heel and heading further into the gorge to find the others.

Kaitar had stopped halfway and was standing amidst the corpses. He was just looking, no expression, no acknowledgement beyond what was in his eyes.

Sevekai hailed the others, suspecting that Drutheira was leaving much earlier than she had initially intended. He wondered if it had anything to do with the warrior from Karond Kar.

They hauled the dwarfs off the road, dragged them into the shadows created by the overhanging rocks. Any that still clung tenaciously to life were quickly ended. Others would find them in time, would see the elven arrow shafts sticking out of their bodies and believe the asur had done this.

A fire would sweep through these lands, Sevekai knew. It would be as embers at first, for every flame must begin with a tiny insignificant spark. Soon this would become a blaze, a conflagration that would consume the elves and the dwarfs, drown them in a bloody war from which there would be no return.

SIXTEEN

LET IT NOT BE WAR

Gotrek regarded the broken shaft of the arrow.

Elven.

Definitely elven.

Even a beardling could tell from the white pine, the swan feathers and exquisite fletching. No other race used arrows this good, and the dwarf High King wasn't afraid to admit that.

'And you found this on the road not far from the karak?'

The ranger nodded.

In the shadows behind the High King, the only other dwarf in the room kept his arms folded. Thurbad had listened, and listened grimly, to Furgil's report.

'In the body of a dead dawi...' the ranger added. '*Several* dead dawi, my lord.'

Few dwarfs could range alone in the mountains and the wild lands beyond and return to their hold unscathed. Furgil had achieved that feat but was bowed by the news he brought like a heavy burden on his back as he met Gotrek Starbreaker in his private chambers.

'How many?' The High King still hadn't taken his eyes off the arrow and ran his fingers over the broken shaft in his hands as if some secret would be revealed to him in the process of examining it.

It wasn't.

'Six, my lord.' Grimly, the ranger recounted what he had seen in the woods, the merchant and his guards, the precise nature of the attacks, how there had been no retaliation from the murdered dwarfs. 'It was an ambush in our own territory,' he said, without really needing to.

'Those are our secret trade routes you describe, Furgil. Few who are not dawi know of them.'

'Some of the elgi do, my lord.'

Gotrek's face was set like chiselled stone but the play of emotions visible in his eyes was as turbulent and unsettled as an ocean storm. Returning the arrow, the High King sat down at a broad-legged writing desk. It fitted well with the room's rustic aesthetic, which was mainly comprised of simple wood and stone. This was a chamber for thinking, not entertaining. Solitude was its main function.

Since the rinkkaz, he had dispensed with his regal finery too and wore a simple tunic and leggings. A mail shirt clad his back and chest but he was otherwise unarmoured. He said nothing as he pored over the reports of the reckoners sitting in front of him on his desk. Like his chief scout's, the High King's face was grim.

'According to these–' he picked up a handful of the parchments to help illustrate his point, '–there have been several further acts of disorder in addition to the murder and treachery you describe, Furgil.'

Though he tried, the ranger could not conceal his shock.

'This has happened elsewhere?'

Gotrek nodded, reading off one of the reports.

'A trading outpost sacked and razed not four days ago.' He leafed to another. 'Here, reckoners make claim on behalf of Hugnar Barrelgirth of nefarious dealings that left the merchant out of pocket. Another makes reference to sorcery used to befuddle and extort an honest dawi trader. As of yet,' said the High King, his eyes rising from the parchments to regard Furgil, 'there have been no further deaths.'

Furgil sighed, 'Dreng tromm,' wringing his cap in his dirt-stained hands.

Gotrek returned to the messages from his reckoners. Almost forgetting Furgil was still present, he hurriedly dismissed the ranger.

'Thank you for bringing this to me, Furgil. You have my authority to double all of the ranger patrols on the trade routes. Keep a sharp eye for me, lad.'

Furgil nodded and was gone, leaving the High King alone with Thurbad.

'Thoughts?' he asked the captain of the hearthguard.

'Someone is trying to break down the peace we have with the elgi.'

'Not unexpected, especially when our accord with them is on such fragile ground.'

'Their settlements expand as trade between us grows,' said Thurbad. 'It was only a matter of time before the other thanes objected.'

'Eight Peaks and Ungor pledge their allegiance to "difficult times ahead".' Gotrek held up a pair of missives he had retrieved from the pile amongst the scratchings of the reckoners.

'Very politic of them both,' Thurbad observed. 'They must be seen to support you if they then want to go on and usurp you.'

'Indeed.' Gotrek had taken out his pipe. Upon touching his lips the cup flared into life, casting the rune of *zharr* engraved on it into sharp relief.

'But the attack on the trade routes is troubling. How many know of those roads?'

'Not many, or so I thought. It dates back to the old pact, the one during Snorri Whitebeard's days.'

'The elgi prince, their ambassador?'

'Malekith, aye.'

'Where is the elgi now?'

'Dead, disappeared? I have no idea, Thurbad. The records pertaining to him ended when he left the Karaz Ankor two thousand years ago. They are practically myth.'

'Someone knows.'

Gotrek got up out of his chair and walked over to where a huge map of the dwarf realms was hung up on the wall like a grand tapestry. The map was old, torn in places, burned at the edges and curling slightly. The dark ink etched upon it in certain areas was not so old. In fact, it was very recent.

'I cannot justify sanctions against the elgi for a few acts of disorder.'

Thurbad joined him at the wall.

'Are you asking me or telling me, my king?'

Gotrek left a pause to consider. 'Telling. But I need you to ensure the hearthguard are all armed and ready to act immediately should they be required.'

Thurbad bowed. 'Always, my king.'

Returning his attention to the map where not only the dwarf holds and settlements were depicted, but the elf ones too, he said, 'I hope this is just a spate of disorder, that these are just the rash acts of a few dissenters.'

Gotrek was a wise king. Unlike some, he realised the stark differences between elves and dwarfs would always result in a difficult peace, but unlike others he wasn't willing to go to war with them over it. Fighting the elves for the Old World would harm both races. It was foolish. Despite all of that, he was deeply troubled by everything he had seen and heard.

He pointed to the map with his pipe.

'How many elgi do you think are in my realm, Thurbad?'

'Too many to count easily, my king.'

From the sheer number of settlements, outposts, even cities, Gotrek knew it must rival the dwarf clans. Though he would not speak of it to Thurbad, for the briefest moment he wondered if he had made a grievous error in being so genial to the elves. He wondered if he had allowed an enemy to creep into his hold halls invited and now that enemy was unsheathing his dagger to plunge it into the king's back.

Releasing a long plume of smoke that obscured the crude depictions of holds and cities on the map with an all-consuming fog, he said, 'Have the guildmasters instruct our forges to begin stockpiling weapons and armour.'

'Are we headed for war, my king?'

It was a reasonable question, but one Gotrek chose to answer with flippancy so as not to alarm his captain of the hearthguard unduly.

'Don't be an ufdi, Thurbad. There will be no war between elgi and dawi. There *must* be no war, but I will have our armouries full anyway.'

Slamming his clenched fist against his breastplate, Thurbad left to make his preparations.

The High King was alone.

Gotrek traced a gnarled finger along the sketched trade routes on the map and then the roads and byways to and from the elven settlements.

'Too many to count,' he murmured, echoing Thurbad's words. He prayed to Grungni. 'Let it not be war, noble ancestor. Let it not.'

SEVENTEEN

A CLASH OF ARMS

Sweat soaked his eyes but he dared not blink. A roar filled his ears, muffled by plate, so loud he could barely hear his heavy-beating heart. Steel clashing against steel was a constant drone. The stink of blood, of piss and dung lingered in his nostrils, unfettered by his nose guard. Heat like a second skin cleaved to his body, stealing away breath. Fire burned nearby, the acerbic tang of it on his tongue, the reek of smoke and soot, the crackle and snap as the flames went about their purifying work.

This was battle against a hardened foe, with limbs already numb from the killing that lay around him in chopped-up heaps. Greenskins by the score, too many to tell, too few to matter. But this was no goblin or orc before him with a blade aimed at his chest.

When an attack came, it came like lightning on a clear day. Fast and utterly by surprise. Morgrim snarled in pain, the force of the blow's impact against his shield so hard it jerked his shoulder.

No time to think, just time enough to hurt.

A second strike, overhead and two-handed, kept him on the defensive back foot as he used the haft of his warhammer to parry.

Weather it, endure.

Battered relentlessly, though there was precision and skill to each carefully crafted attack, the dwarf knew he would soon run out of battlefield in which to retreat.

He is stronger than he looks...

So did Prince Imladrik.

The elf was a blur of silver, every thrust and lunge, slash and cut choreographed in a deadly dance for which Morgrim was his unwilling partner. In the brief exchange, several blows had already penetrated the dwarf's armour. A gash below his eye throbbed. His breath was forced and ragged.

The elf was winning.

Corpses lay all about them, putrid and stinking, their spilt blood just as dangerous underfoot as any blade. Broken spear hafts jutted from the earth like bones reaching from the grave. Each was as deadly as a lance if fallen upon. Smashed shields added to the general battlefield detritus. Through his dimming view, Morgrim saw the silhouettes of other figures moving in the battle fog but they couldn't help him.

The dwarf was alone in this.

It was a mercy the elf was not riding his dragon. Should the beast have been involved, it would be a much shorter contest. As it was, Morgrim was hardly making a decent fight of it. Defeat looked all but certain.

He lashed out, caught the elf just below his knee and drew a cry of pain from the prince's mouth. Fevered shouting around the battlefield intensified. Though muffled through his helm, the sound of the elf's discomfort brought a smile to the dwarf's lips. Morgrim roared his defiance, tried to press the slim advantage fate had provided, but Imladrik was a consummate swordmaster and recovered quickly. A dazzling series of ripostes aimed against the dwarf's left side made him overcompensate with the shield, left him exposed on the right. Morgrim narrowly avoided being disarmed as the elf swept his longsword in under the dwarf's guard and tried to hook the hammer away. Twisting his wrist, Morgrim barely caught the blade against his hammer's haft. Shavings of wood and metal cascaded where the elf's weapon bit. He fashioned his resistance into a shoulder barge that caught Imladrik in the chest and drew out a grunt. A hard shove to follow up pushed the combatants apart, and they regarded each other across the charnel field through the eye-slits of their war helms.

Morgrim's, horned and wrought of dwarf bronze, was not only lower but was also bowed compared to the elf's upraised helmet of glittering silver ithilmar.

'If you wish to concede,' gasped the dwarf between breaths, 'then I'll ensure your honour remains intact when my hammer falls.'

Though he hid it well, Imladrik's breathing was laboured too. He lifted the dragon visor of his helmet with a gauntleted hand.

It was the same armour he had worn when they had first met outside Karaz-a-Karak. How different things were now.

'Amusing,' the elf replied. Sweat dappled his forehead. Just a little, but Morgrim saw it catch the light in little pearls of perspiration.

So he does tire.

That at least was some encouragement.

Prince Imladrik went on, 'I would offer you the same courtesy but think you would probably not take it.'

'Aye.' Morgrim spat a wad of phlegm onto the ground. There was a little blood in it from a cracked tooth. 'You'd be right about that, elgi.'

'Thought so,' said Imladrik, lowering his visor before he took up a fighting stance. 'I'll make it quick,' he added with a metallic resonance to his voice.

Shrilling a war cry, the elf leapt into the air – a feat made all the more remarkable for its suddenness and the fact he was wearing a full suit of armour – and launched a piercing thrust that would have split Morgrim's shield and armour as one.

Reacting more on instinct than with purpose, Morgrim hurriedly sidestepped and caught the bulk of the blow against his shoulder. It stung like all the fires of Grungni's forge and he barely held on to his shield. A hammer swing smote air but the elf was gone. Eyes darting, Morgrim caught a silver blur in his peripheral vision but was too slow to prevent the longsword splitting his shield in two. It was hewn from stout oak, banded by iron, and still the elf's sword cut it apart as if it were rotten wood. Such was the power behind the blow that Morgrim lost his footing and his hammer. On his back, barely catching breath, he went to grab the weapon's haft when he felt the chill of elven steel at his neck.

Morgrim slumped, let the hammer go and accepted his fate.

'Grimnir's hairy balls,' he spat, baring his neck. 'You have me, elgi.'

Imladrik's eyes were diamond sharp within the confines of his war helm.

Morgrim growled, 'Finish it, then.'

The elf's belligerent mask slipped.

The dwarf smiled, then broader still.

'Well met, Prince Imladrik.'

Withdrawing his blade, the elf lifted his dragon visor. He was smiling too. Sheathing his longsword with a flourish, he bowed and proffered the dwarf his hand.

'A close match, Thane Morgrim. There is little to choose between elven speed and dwarf tenacity, I think.'

Grunting, Morgrim got to his feet with Imladrik's help.

In the stalls surrounding the arena battlefield the gathered crowd were cheering them both, but Morgrim failed to feel their acclaim.

High King Gotrek had commissioned a vast auditorium of stone and wutroth to be built in honour of a grand feast and series of games that were meant as a way of healing the frayed relationship between the elves and dwarfs in light of the recent 'troubles'.

Known as the *brodunk*, a festival of worship to honour Grimnir and the art of battle, the union of dwarf and elf on this day was hoped to be an auspicious one. In times such as these, with peace hanging by a skein of civility, it needed to be. There were other festivals: *brodag* honoured Grungni and brew-making, whereas *brozan* was the celebration dedicated most to Valaya and the bonds of brotherhood between the clans. In retrospect, perhaps it would have been a better choice to try and coincide the feast with the ancestor goddess's feast day instead.

Upon hearing the news of the caravan attacks and the destruction of Zakbar Varf, many of the thanes had demanded retaliation. Bagrik of Ungor, though now returned to Karak Ungor to meet with ambassadors of Tor Eorfith, had called for calm. He had no wish to disaffect his elven guests before they had even arrived. King Varnuf had kept his own counsel, doubtless seeing where the most favour would fall, whilst Luftvarr and Thagdor demanded retaliation. Thagdor was absent from proceedings but had set up camp close to Karaz-a-Karak to keep a closer eye on what Gotrek would do next. Never one to miss out on celebrating a good fight, Luftvarr had stayed. In any case, the journey back to Kraka Drak was a long one. Above all else, the Norse dwarf king was pragmatic and would always prefer warm food in his belly to an arduous trek north with only trail rations for sustenance. Besides, there was no guarantee the way north would be open to him. And as much as he relished the idea of fighting the northern hordes, for now his place was here and the brewing discord with the elves.

Temperate as well as wise, High King Gotrek had resisted the call to arms. Ambassadors from the elven court in the Old World, of which Prince Imladrik was the highest ranking noble, had assured the dwarfs these were isolated acts of malice to try and undermine peace. They too attended the brodunk. Afterwards, Gotrek had echoed Bagrik in calling for calm and so the axes of his vassal lords remained sheathed for now, but the mood was fractious.

It had taken several days of hard dwarf labour to bring the brodunk into being. More than ever Gotrek was convinced of its need and hoped it would reignite camaraderie and genuine bonhomie between the races. The hold was kept running with a bare minimum of miners and craftsmen, the rest were petitioned to create the stage required for the grand feast.

Mules pushing great, rounded millstones had flattened the ground. Stonecutters, rockbreakers and lodemasters dragging stone from the mines, fashioning pillars and walls, flagstone plazas and wooden stalls had worked days on end to bring the High King's desires to fruition. Many grumbled but respected their liege-lord enough to keep their misgivings private. It was no easy thing to put this burden on his clans, on his hold, but Gotrek did it because he believed lasting peace would only be maintained with sacrifice and toil. These, at least, were not strange concepts to a dwarf.

Flags and banners were nailed up, most bearing the solemn iconography of the dwarfs – the forge, the hammer and axe, the faces of their ancestors – but others depicted dragons, eagles and horses, the imagery of their elven guests.

Mouth-watering aromas emanated from feast halls where dwarf cooks and brewmasters slaved to create victuals for their kin and guests alike. Fluttering in a light breeze coming off the nearby mountains, pennants on the roofs of tented pavilions carried the runes of the elven houses present for the festivities. Other tents sewn together with rough dwarf fabric had the faces of the ancestors stitched in gilded thread and carried banner poles surmounted by clan icons of bronze, silver and gold.

Coal pits provided warmth and light, for the arena was outdoors in order to better suit the elves, a concession which had earned favour from the visitors but not the more truculent dwarf kings. Grundin of Karak Kadrin had been particularly vociferous on this point. There were roasting pits in which boar and elk were prepared for feasting later. Shields describing the clans and warrior brotherhoods festooned the walls of the structure, which was based on a large central arena with several smaller ones attached to it via a series of open tunnels. Even when building an auditorium meant to be open to the elements, dwarfs could still not deny their natural instincts to be enclosed.

At first the elves had balked at the solidity of the auditorium, its stout walls, viewing towers and gates. To the elves it was not so different from a fortress. Certainly, the regal quarters afforded to the dwarf kings in particular were well fortified. Indeed, if attacked, it was highly likely the dwarfs could muster a garrison and defend it like one.

Yes, the clans of Everpeak had gone to great efforts to fashion a stage worthy of their king. It was a pity then that the first major contest upon it had ended in defeat for the dwarfs.

Through the brazier smoke at the edge of the mock battlefield, Morgrim could tell there were more elves than dwarfs rejoicing at the display. One in particular, a stern female wearing crimson scalloped armour, gave Imladrik a nod, which the prince returned. She didn't linger, merely waited long enough to show her quiet applause for his victory before disappearing into the crowd. As was typical of their race, the elves were restrained in celebration but the sense of triumph they evinced was palpable.

It was like a slap in the face for Morgrim. Shame reddened his cheeks and he was glad his helm obscured them. Not daring to look towards the High King's royal pavilion where Snorri and his father were watching, he kept his eyes on his hammer and pretended to tighten the leather straps around its haft.

Imladrik appeared to sense what the dwarf was thinking.

'There's no shame in this. If your shield hadn't broken, if you'd have swung when you tried to dodge... Well,' the elf admitted, 'things could have turned out very differently. If it matters at all, you pushed me to the limit of my endurance, Morgrim.'

They clasped forearms in the warrior's greeting, something not usual amongst elves but common in the dwarfs, resulting in another cheer. Over thirty dead greenskins and one troll, chained to a lump of stone, littered the arena. It was the warm-up act, according to the High King. From their faces, some of the elves had found such wanton butchery in the name of 'entertainment' distasteful.

'You treat them with such disdain,' said the prince, echoing the apparent mood of his kin.

They stood in the middle of the battlefield together, deciding to allow the more raucous spectators to calm before leaving the arena. Armourers from both sides were heading towards them to help them out of their trappings, take their weapons and ensure they were cleaned and readied for the next bout.

Morgrim shrugged, barely glancing at the disappointed faces of his own retinue. 'They're just vermin. Good sport for our axes.'

Imladrik nodded, but Morgrim saw in the elf's eyes that he didn't really understand.

'Grobi are dangerous,' the dwarf said, nudging one with his boot, 'but only in large numbers. True, they have a certain low cunning that–'

A shout from behind the dwarf arrested his explanation. A moment later and a flash of metal glinted off the sun as it sped past the elf. Imladrik avoided the blade out of instinct but need not have bothered. It would have missed him, barely. Instead it struck the shoulder of a goblin that had played dead amongst the corpses. A broken spear tip slipped from the creature's scrawny hands as it collapsed back into the heap of carcasses it had crawled from.

Striding towards them, breaking from the retinue of armourers he had accompanied, Snorri Halfhand's grin was wide and slightly smug.

'Should watch your back, elfling,' he called to the prince, adjusting his weapons belt where a second throwing axe was attached by a leather loop. 'I won't always be there to save your skinny arse.'

He slapped Morgrim on the back, harder than he really needed to.

'Wanted to make him feel better, eh, cousin?'

Snorri didn't wait for an answer and stomped past them. Taking a knee down by the dying greenskin, he muttered with mild surprise, 'Still some life in this one...'

Imladrik turned to the dwarf prince, bowing his head. 'You have my gratitude, lord dwarf. If you had not–'

The *schlukk* of Snorri's axe as it was wrenched from the goblin interrupted him.

'Didn't catch that,' said the dwarf, half looking over his shoulder at the elf. 'Busy getting my axe back.' Looping it back onto his weapons belt, he regarded the greenskin again and thrust a gauntleted finger into the wound.

The wretched creature squealed and squirmed under the dwarf's touch, which only made Snorri dig deeper, a half-snarl contorting his lips. He wasn't dressed for battle, but carried his hand axes anyway. Instead of pauldrons, a regal blue cape armoured his shoulders. A tunic sat in place of a breastplate or suit of chain. His vambraces were supple leather. Morek's mastercrafted gauntlet was the only piece of metal on his body.

Forbidden by his father as punishment for his defiance, Snorri would not be competing.

When the goblin shrieked and crimson geysered from its ugly mouth, Imladrik went to intercede and end the greenskin's suffering swiftly but Morgrim put a hand on his arm.

'This is barbaric,' hissed the elf. 'The creature is no further threat.'

Morgrim simply shook his head.

'Don't be fooled,' said Snorri, and elf and dwarf prince met eye-to-eye with the dying goblin between them. As he withdrew gory metal fingers from the wound, the goblin snarled but Snorri caught its wrist in a steel grip and twisted it before the greenskin could shove a piece of broken blade into his stomach.

It yelped but Snorri kept going until he'd broken the wrist. Then he wrapped his thick fingers around its head and yanked it round to snap its neck.

'See,' said Snorri to Imladrik alone, 'can't be trusted not to stab when your back is turned, no matter how dead you think they might be.'

Though he trembled with anger, Imladrik maintained his composure.

'Your cousin fought well,' he said, his jaw still taut. 'With honour.'

Morgrim was nodding when Snorri interjected and said, 'He doesn't need your false magnanimity, elgi,' before stomping off back towards the royal pavilion.

'My apologies for my cousin,' said Morgrim in a low voice. 'He doesn't realise the effect of his words on others sometimes.'

Imladrik glared at the prince's back as he watched him go.

'It is of no consequence.' He drew his sword, saluted and then sheathed it quickly. 'You honour your kin enough for both of you, Morgrim Bargrum. Tromm...' he intoned, bowing once more before returning to the elven tents with his armourers.

Morgrim went after Snorri but noticed something glinting in the battlefield earth. It was a piece of silver scale, cut from Imladrik's armour. Watching Snorri depart, he was suddenly glad that the father had banned his son from taking part in the games.

An elf death, accidental or otherwise, was the last thing peace needed.

EIGHTEEN

WISE WORDS

Snorri called, 'Come, cousin!', as he tramped across the arena towards the royal pavilion.

A massive stone ancestor head loomed over them, the great god Grungni. Enormous emeralds hewn from the lowest deeps glittered in his eyes and a set of broad steps unfurled from his wide-open mouth like a stone tongue.

Within, lit by the flickering flame of braziers, was the High King of Karaz-a-Karak.

Bedecked in his finest royal attire, a red tunic with a skirt of gleaming gromril mail, matching cloak trimmed with ermine fur and the Dragon Crown of Karaz fixed upon his brow, Gotrek cut a powerful figure sat atop the Throne of Power. Alongside the king, fitting easily in the ancestor's gaping maw, were several of his elders but only those who were capable of leaving the hold and staying awake for the festivities. There was also a place at his side for his son.

Gotrek was in a saturnine mood, rattling heavy rings against the arm of his throne as he awaited the prince's return.

As if sensing his father's displeasure and perhaps even seeking to aggravate it, Snorri slowed as he got closer to the royal pavilion.

'Did you mean to hit him, cousin?' Morgrim asked as he caught up.

'Didn't realise I had,' said Snorri, feigning surprise.

'You are the best axe thrower in all of the karak.'

Snorri smiled wryly. 'It was only a nick, nothing to trouble a master of drakk that is for sure.'

'If he noticed it...'

'Then he is not saying, cousin. Let it go.'

'I cannot.' Morgrim paused. What he asked next wasn't easy. 'Are you deliberately trying to scupper peace with the elgi, cousin?'

His smile faded and Snorri stopped in the middle of the field. He dismissed the dwarf armourers tagging along behind them.

'Why so serious, Morg? It was a jest, a polite reminder that dawi rule these lands, not them.'

'Not *them*? You speak as if they're already our enemies.'

The silence that followed suggested Snorri thought precisely that, to a lesser or greater degree. After a few moments they walked on.

All the humour bled out of the prince, his mood now matching that of his cousin.

'A band of elgi was killed for trespassing on dawi soil a few days ago. I heard my father talking to Furgil about it.'

'Murdered?' Morgrim sounded shocked.

Snorri glanced at him. 'They were uninvited and unannounced, cousin. Given the recent attacks on the caravans, the burning of Zakbar Varf, is it any wonder?'

'Dreng tromm...' Morgrim shook his head. 'It's worse than I thought.'

'Trade has all but ceased with them. More and more of the elgi are going to the skarrenawi now because King Grum has no sense of honour.' Snorri hawked and spat. 'He is barely half dawi as it is, and now he makes himself an *elgongi* to rub in further salt to already stinging wounds.'

'You learned all of this from your father?'

'Aye,' said Snorri, 'as well as speaking with some of the other lords. King Varnuf and King Thagdor have sanctioned heavy embargoes on trading with the elgi. If these "troubles", as my father calls them, continue they will enact outright bans.'

Morgrim's eyes narrowed. 'Aren't Varnuf and Thagdor against your father's petition to keep the peace?'

Snorri nodded. 'By listening to my fellow dawi lords, I'm not going against my father, Morg.'

'But if commerce breaks down between our races, it will lead to but one road after that,' Morgrim warned.

They were nearing the pavilion now and would soon have to part. Morgrim's armour needed tending and Snorri was expected by his father.

The prince's steady gaze told Morgrim he knew what road that was.

'And, cousin?'

'And?' Morgrim was incredulous. 'And? Think of the cost, Snorri, in lives and livelihoods.' He kept his voice low in case others were listening in. 'War will devastate our lands, our clans.'

'Nonsense, cousin. We will expel the impudent elgi with barely any dawi blood being shed. They are merchants and squatters, Morg. Barely a decent warrior amongst them.'

'What about Imladrik? He just bested me in single combat.'

'Bah, you just let him–'

'I let him do nothing. I fought him, as hard as I could, and still he beat me.'

Snorri dismissed the notion with a snort, regarding the broken shield the armourers were taking back to the distant forge.

'For an elgi he has a strong arm, I suppose.'

'You underestimate him, cousin.'

'No, Morg.' Snorri fixed him with a gimlet stare. 'He over-commits when he thinks he has victory, looking for a quick finish. He has no patience, not like a dawi. You should've used that against him, found an opening just before his killing thrust. Then you would not have been beaten.' He shook his head slowly, impressing the import of what he was going to say next. 'He would not have defeated me. I would have broken him apart.'

The two dwarfs parted ways, an uneasy silence between them.

Morgrim's armour needed tending, so did his wounds and battered pride. It was a pity there was no salve in the tent for his unease at his cousin's demeanour. To some it would appear as if the prince believed they were already at war.

As he gave one last look towards the royal pavilion, he noticed Drogor seated within amongst the high thanes and masters. Snorri must have invited him. They had been spending much time together of late, but Morgrim thought no more of it as he headed for the forge.

Liandra's face was a mask of displeasure when Imladrik parted the door of the tent wider and descended into what was known as the 'rookery'. It was dark inside and the air smelled of earth. Though the shadows were thick, they suggested a vastness belied by the apparent closeness of the tent's confines. The ceiling also was incredibly high, even with the sunken floor. Guttering candles did little to lift the gloom, but then elves did not need light to see and nor did the creatures the rookery harboured. It had to be this way, drenched in shadow, to placate these denizens and keep them quiescent.

Imladrik heard their snorting, the hiss of their breath and the reek of sulphur that came with it. Like an itch beneath his skin, a heat behind the eyes, he felt their frustration and impatience, the desire to *soar*. Only through sheer will, born of years of practice and dedication, could the prince shake off his malaise. Otherwise, it would have consumed him as it had consumed lesser elves before him.

Armourers had removed his breastplate, tasset and rerebraces. A servant had also left two missives on the table beside him.

'Letters from home,' said Liandra without looking down. 'I received word from my father, also.'

She glanced at an elf standing nearby clad in silver armour, half cloaked in darkness. He went unhooded, carrying a helmet with a purple feather at its tip under his arm. This was Fendaril, one of her father's seneschals. Bowing to them both, Fendaril left the tent.

'There was no need to dismiss him.'

'Fendaril has other business. Because I'm occupied by this farce, I need him to return to Kor Vanaeth. He has fought in his bout.'

'Very well.'

They were alone.

Setting down his dragon helm on a nearby stool that was altogether too low for an elf's needs, Imladrik silently began to read.

'My brother sends word from Ulthuan,' he said. 'Druchii raids continue.'

'Lord Athinol brings similar tidings.'

Imladrik read the second letter more quickly, before tucking them both into his vambrace. Trying to occupy himself, he started to unbuckle his leg greaves.

'Your son, he is well?' asked Liandra, and Imladrik saw a slight nerve tremor in her cheek as she guessed at the second sender.

'He is.'

'And her also.'

'Yes, her as well.'

Imladrik's scabbard, which contained the sword Ifulvin, was placed reverently on a weapons rack nearby. Lances were mounted on the rack and each of them had names too, etched in elven runes upon their shining hafts.

'Are you going to stare at them all afternoon, Liandra?' the prince asked, changing the subject to ease the tension. Pulling off a boot, he relished the kiss of cool spring water on his bare skin as a servant poured some from a silver ewer.

'I am glad you bested that dwarf,' she said, eager to turn the conversation to more comfortable ground too. Her eyes did not move to regard Imladrik. She lingered at the entrance to the rookery, at the summit of a short set of earthen steps, and peered through a narrow slit in the heavy leather flap. She was fixated on the royal pavilion at the opposite end of the field, the king and all his retainers looking on.

She sneered. 'He was a crass little creature, all dirt and hair. When I first heard that dwarfs live in caves under the ground I scoffed, but now I see the truth of it.'

'I fought a warrior, Liandra. A noble one possessed of a fine spirit. Morgrim Bargrum is a thane of vaunted heritage – you should not be so disparaging.'

'You obviously see something which I do not.' She glanced at him, 'Anyway, I salute your victory, Imladrik.' Liandra raised her sword, which the prince noted was unsheathed.

Despite her caustic demeanour, even in the darkness of the rookery Liandra's stark beauty shone like a flame. Her hair was golden but not akin to anything as prosaic or ephemeral as precious metal – such a thing would fade and give in to the ravages of entropy in time. Rather, it was eternal and shimmered with an unearthly lustre. Threaded with bands of copper like streaks of fire, she had it scraped back and fastened it in place with a scalp lock. Pale as moonlight, her skin was near silvern and her eyes were like sapphires captured from the raging waters of the Arduil.

She was beautiful.

Imladrik had always thought so and the very fact spoke to his poetic soul, much as he tried to deny it. His desires were not for war and battle, though he possessed great martial skill and as brother to the Phoenix King of Ulthuan, it was almost expected. Imladrik wanted peace, which he had. Only it felt like his hands were an hourglass and the fragile accord between the elves and dwarfs grains of sand slipping through it. No matter how hard he tried to seize them they would worm their way between his fingers. Grip too tightly and the glass would shatter, spilling their contents anyway.

Not so Liandra. She desired battle, *ached* for it. Fierce-hearted, especially as she was now clad in her ceremonial dragon armour, she was happiest with a sword or lance in her mailed fist. The blood red of the armour's finely lacquered plates, edged and scalloped, only enhanced her ethereal beauty.

Imladrik removed his other boot before giving her his full attention.

'Petty pride is not worthy of a princess of Caledor,' he told her. 'And you have not even greeted me properly yet,' he added.

Liandra turned and bowed, a gesture that Imladrik reciprocated. There was no physical contact, no handshake or embrace of any kind. It was as if an invisible veil of propriety existed between them that no sword or spear could ever part. Briefly, Imladrik found he was envious of the more tactile ways of the dwarfs, the open and flagrant, even sometimes crass, mores of social greeting in their culture. Elven stiltedness had its place in court. It was dignified, but all too cold between old friends. Perhaps he had spent too long amongst dwarfs, learning their ways as Malekith once did before his fall.

'Congratulations again on your victory,' she said, interrupting his thoughts but only exacerbating the formality of their exchange further.

Imladrik inclined his head. 'Thank you.'

'But it is not pride that makes me glad you defeated the dwarf and showed all of these mud-dwellers our true strength.'

'Do not speak of them like that.' Imladrik was on his feet, and still looked imposing despite the fact he was barefoot and had no armour.

The beasts in the deep shadows of the rookery stirred but he calmed them with a glance. None present, not even the largest, would dare oppose the Master of Dragons.

'*Vranesh!*' snapped Liandra, an eye on the darkness briefly too before she replied. 'I heard them talking, heard what they think of us, our people.'

Pouring a goblet of wine, Imladrik sighed. 'As did I, but that is no reason to hate them, Liandra, not if we are to achieve harmony between our two races.'

'I do not want harmony. I do not like these *dwarfs* or their ways, nor do I understand why you seem to have such an accord with them.' She moved away from the entrance, down the steps and away from prying eyes. 'All this talk of murder, of ambushes in the night, it is just that. Talk. Likely, it was made up by the dwarfs to justify attacks on elves.'

Imladrik looked at her shrewdly. 'And is that what you think, Liandra? Or are these the beliefs of your father?'

'Not only my father, but my brothers also,' she snapped, raising her voice. 'Why wouldn't I believe them?'

'Because they are thousands of miles away on Ulthuan, fighting the remnants of Malekith's forces in the mountains where you wish you could be right now.'

She was on the verge of another outburst when her anger ebbed. 'I am a warrior of Caledor, Imladrik. By my father's side is where I should be.' She lowered her voice, unable to meet the prince's gaze. 'And is it any wonder that I want to kill druchii after what they did, after...' She faltered, but recovered quickly. 'I am here under sufferance, that is all.'

'You're here because your father, despite his misgivings, believes that peace is something worth fighting for and not over. You are his ambassador, a feat beyond the skills or patience of either of your brothers.'

'Do not besmirch them,' she warned.

Candlelight limning the edge of its saurian body, the beast a few feet away from Liandra growled in empathy. It clawed at the earth with its long talons.

Imladrik was not cowed. He had nothing to fear from Vranesh, upraising his palms to placate the princess not her beast.

'I merely speak plain fact and the truth as I see it, Liandra. Just as I see the dwarfs are a noble race who value heritage, tradition and honour.'

'Honour? Really?' She stooped to retrieve a length of thick iron chain that trailed along the ground and into the darkness. 'Where is the *honour* in this? The dignity?'

'The dwarfs built this rookery for us. They cut the earth to allow us–'

'They dug a hole, Imladrik. A *hole*. And then they filled it with chains and shrouded it from the sky. Insult is too light a word, confining noble creatures such as this. The dwarfs should be grovelling at their feet.'

'The High King has organised this brodunk for us, the least we can do is concede to his wishes to see our mounts kept hidden. We are on his lands, these are his people. I can understand his concern.'

Liandra scoffed. 'You even use their tongue like it is your own. Are you sure you aren't turning native on us, Imladrik?'

'I will pretend you did not say that to me, and attribute it to the fact you miss your father and brothers. The dwarfs *are* a good people. We have much to learn from each other. We are just different, our kind and theirs.'

'As mud is to air and sky.'

She mounted Vranesh, getting a foothold in the stirrups and propelling her body up into the saddle. Liandra turned to Imladrik, looking down from her lofty position as the roof of the rookery tent was hauled away by ropes like a tarp from the back of a cart and the light flooded in. A host of dragons, drakes and wyrms of all stripe and hue were revealed, chained to the ground and muzzled. Draukhain was amongst them, easily the largest and most magnificent, lowering his neck under the gaze of his master. All did, recognising Imladrik's mastery and the potency of his dragonsong. Few were left amongst the asur who commanded such respect amongst the dragons. Certainly, none bore his archaic title.

'It is no wonder that blood has been spilled between us and them,' said Liandra. 'The only surprise to me is that it took this long.'

Not waiting for a reply, Liandra whispered a harsh word of command and Vranesh took to the skies. The chain fastening its ankle to the ground broke apart as if it were brittle bone, and the muzzle shattered likewise as the beast uttered a feral roar.

Imladrik watched her disappear into the clouds, an ill-feeling growing in his heart.

'I am sorry, though,' he whispered, but wanting to say it out loud, 'about your mother.'

NINETEEN

FATHER AND SON

Drogor clapped Snorri on the shoulder from where he sat behind the prince. Since he'd entered the royal pavilion, his father had said nothing to him and this was the first act of recognition the prince had received since taking his seat... aside of course from the High King's toady, Grimbok. Preened and plucked as ever, the reckoner had been particularly obsequious during the brodunk and cleaved to Snorri's father's side like a limpet. Like a narrow-eyed crag-hen, he scoured the clans watching the tournament, his dirty little book of reckoning ever chained to his belt. In fact, he had only averted his gaze from the crowds to give both Snorri and his new friend a withering glare as the prince had joined the royal party.

Mouthing the word *ufdi*, Snorri had ignored him after that, including his muttered rejoinder. Drogor had laughed. It was a burbling sound that rattled in his gut, but was not so loud that it woke or roused any of the High King's guests that were sitting with him.

Since making his acquaintance in the drinking hall, Drogor had been Snorri's near-constant companion over the past few days. Regaling him with tales of Karak Zorn, of scaled monsters that lurked in the torpid jungles of the Southlands and of ziggurats of pure gold that stretched all the way to the sun, Snorri had found his company a welcome respite from Morgrim's continual lectures about duty and the decency of elves. Several were sat with the High King and did not look best pleased by the fact. Snorri ignored them too.

As Prince Imladrik was the Elf King of Ulthuan's representative, he was afforded a seat in the royal pavilion but had yet to sit in it because he was still taking part in the brodunk. Along with the presence of the elves, this was another reason for Snorri's distemper.

At least Morgrim had stopped urging him to heal the rift with his father, which was some small respite, but then he had barely seen him to talk to at length. Other, more conciliatory voices had the prince's ear now.

'Saw what you did out there,' Drogor whispered. 'That axe throw...'

'Heh.' Snorri grinned, enjoying the quiet acclaim. 'Yes, a little closer than I had intended.' Given who was sitting nearby, he lowered his voice still further. 'The elgi moved quicker than I thought.'

'Not close enough to my unpractised eye, my lord.'

'I think drawn blood might have put a dampener on the brodunk, Drog.'

A brief pause suggested Drogor thought that would be no bad thing at all.

'You should be out there competing against the elgi, my lord.'

'Aye, but I am not.' Snorri half turned so he could see the other dwarf. 'And stop calling me "my lord". It's overly formal. Use "my prince" instead,' he said with a wry smile.

Drogor chuckled, but the smile he wore didn't quite reach his eyes, which glittered like endless dark pools in the dim light of the pavilion. He leaned in closer, pointing across the field to the elven rookery.

'See there,' he hissed, 'the elgi rinn lurking in the darkness?'

Snorri nodded.

'Not stopped glaring at you or your cousin since she clapped her narrow little eyes on you. What do you think she is saying?'

Surprised that Drogor could even see that far, let alone know it was an elf female that was looking at them, Snorri squinted but couldn't tell much of anything.

'How I am supposed to know.'

'It doesn't look friendly. She scowls, like she just stepped in something.'

'Perhaps our rugged earth disagrees with her.'

'That or the fact she is surrounded by dawi,' said Drogor. 'I see the same expression in many elgi faces.' He glanced askance at the elven lords in the royal pavilion. They appeared too self-absorbed to pay much attention to the High King, let alone any other dwarf sitting with them. 'I do not think they can be trusted.'

Now Snorri turned all the way around, earning a reproachful glance from his father who was trying to look interested in the brodunk but who had a host of other matters on his mind.

'What are you saying, Drogor?' Snorri asked.

'That elgi and dawi should not mix. We are too different.'

'Aye, as solid rock to an insubstantial breeze.' Supping on his pipe, he returned his attention to the battlefield.

'Bad enough having skarrenawi around.' Drogor pointed at the champions taking part in the next event, an elf and a hill dwarf Snorri had heard of.

The prince clenched his teeth a little.

'They are not so bad.'

Rundin Ravenhelm was well known to him. Skarnag Grum had made him his captain and chief reckoner. He seldom left Kazad Kro, on account of the king's paranoia no doubt. This, then, was a rare occasion. Obviously, Grum had sent him here as his champion to uphold what little honour the hill dwarfs had. Snorri felt his annoyance at his father for barring him from the brodunk anew – he would have dearly liked to measure himself against this Ravenhelm.

'Perhaps not,' hissed Drogor and shrank back into the shadows.

Snorri watched as the elf and hill dwarf readied their weapons, the former carrying a silver longsword and wearing an eagle-winged helm, while the latter bore a finely crafted rune axe and went unhelmeted in lacquered black leather armour.

'He is bold, for certain...' muttered the prince and could not help but admire the hill dwarf. Half turning again, Snorri was about to reply to his friend but Drogor was gone.

The air was hot and thick inside the iron forge, drenched with the smell of soot and ash. Morgrim breathed deep of it, letting it fill him like a balm. In the murky depths, he found Morek casting an eye over his warhammer.

After a few words of incantation, a silent rite performed in the air, the runes of the hammer glowed and were still again.

'What are you doing here, runesmith? Surely the karak has enough metalworkers and foundry dwarfs to run the forges for the brodunk?'

It was true. There were several other dwarf smiths roaming the gloomy confines of the forge, working the bellows and hammering out the dents from the armour and blades of all the combatants. Morek Furrowbrow was the only runesmith.

'I am here at my master's behest to deliver the gauntlet to Prince Snorri and ensure its fit was a good one.'

'I saw it earlier. A fine piece of craftsmanship indeed, but why do you linger now?' Morgrim sat down on a stone bench and began to take off his armour. It was a slow process, made slower by the fact that every piece coming off his body was accompanied by renewed pain at the battering Imladrik had given him.

'I merely wanted to watch some of the bouts. Seemed wasteful not to lend my skill in the forge tent. Master Silver thumb will summon me as soon as he is ready. Then I shall commence my master work.'

Morgrim nodded, satisfied with the runesmith's explanation.

Morek gripped the hammer's haft to test the leather bindings, swung it around his wrist a few times gauging its balance and heft. His deftness surprised Morgrim. There was not only forge-skill in the runesmith's hand. He had the hammercraft of a warrior too.

'All is well?' asked Morgrim.

Through the tent flap, the clash of arms sounded again as the next bout began.

'Solid as ever, the *rhuns* on the blade potent as the day they were wrought.'

'You wield it better than I.'

'I doubt that.' Morek set the hammer down. 'But I've spent my entire life around weapons. I know something about how to use them.'

'Indeed you do.'

Morgrim was removing his war helm. Stinging sweat made him blink and he ran a gnarled hand through his soaked hair. Summoned from the healing tent, a priestess of Valaya had entered the forge and waited nearby to provide ministration. Once he was done smoothing his scalp, he beckoned her.

'It availed me little though, I'm afraid,' Morgrim told the runesmith as the priestess dabbed his facial cuts with a damp cloth from a bowl of water. 'I hope I did not dishonour its craft.'

Morek shook his head. 'Not at all. I saw you fight. The elgi is a fine warrior.'

'You are one of few other dawi at this brodunk that thinks so.'

'I know metal and flame, and nothing of the politics surrounding elgi and dawi,' the runesmith confessed. 'I saw a little of the rinkkaz but much of it was beyond my grasp to negotiate. Certainly, I do not envy the High King in his task. As dawi, we pride ourselves on tradition and heritage. It is one of the cornerstones of our culture. Tradition it seems must be eased if we are to maintain peace, but many of the lords are stubborn. My master is concerned with legacy and what is left behind for others when he and his kind are gone. I think perhaps that the High King is too.'

Morgrim eyed him shrewdly. 'You understand more than you think, runesmith.'

Looking up from tending a piece of battered armour, Morek was about to try and mend Morgrim's shield but discarded it as scrap.

'You'll need a fresh shield.'

'With a shoulder and arm to go with it,' Morgrim replied, wincing as his pauldron was removed along with the padding and chainmail beneath, an ugly purple bruise revealed beneath all three. 'He hits like a hammer.'

Once he was no longer armoured, the priestess approached with a bottle of rubbing alcohol to ease Morgrim's suffering. He stopped her before she could apply it.

'Waste of grog that, milady,' he said, and gently took the bottle from her. 'Use salts instead.'

She did.

Grunting as he eased the stiffness from his back, Morgrim drank a belt of the dirty liquor and grimaced at the taste.

'Packs a kick like a mule.'

'You are as unrefined as that ale, Morgrim Bargrum,' Morek informed him.

'I am.'

The bruise on Morgrim's shoulder was ripening nicely as the priestess applied the salts.

'Do you have another bout?' asked Morek.

'Anvil lifting.'

'Not even the sense you were born with.' He laughed. It was an all too rare expression in the runesmith that lifted the furrows of his countenance.

Outside the forge tent, a resonant shrieking rent the air as the dragons took flight. Morgrim watched them ascend, fear and awe warring for emotional dominance within him. Through the peeled-back leather flap, it was difficult to see much but he fancied he could make out Imladrik's beast and the prince saddled on its back. He was like a glittering arrow of silver fire, behind the flight of dragons at first but quickly gaining on the leader before overtaking her and assuming the tip of their formation.

Though he had humbled him in front of his king and peers, Morgrim bore no grudge against Imladrik. The elf had fought fairly and honourably. Again, as he had so many times in recent days, he found Imladrik to be even tempered and moral. Unlike many elves who could be haughty and arrogant, even disdainful, there was much to like about him. It was just a pity that Snorri could not see it.

'An anvil lifting an anvil, eh?' he said to Morek, reaching for happier thoughts and looking back over his shoulder.

The runesmith wasn't listening. Something else, or rather someone else, had got his attention. The frown returned to his brow as his face clouded over.

'Is that your old friend?'

'Who?'

'The dawi from Karak Zorn.'

Morgrim looked but couldn't see Drogor amongst the crowds.

'Possibly, though he's been spending more time with my cousin of late.'

Morek turned to him. 'With the prince?'

'Yes, my *cousin*. That's what I said.' Morgrim tried to find Drogor again but it was like looking for chalk dust in an ancestor's beard. 'Is something wrong?'

Morek was leaving.

'My master will be waiting.'

Left alone with the priestess, Morgrim sighed. 'I'll never understand runesmiths.'

A commanding voice got Snorri's attention. 'Son of mine,' said Gotrek Starbreaker, not even deigning to glance at the prince, 'see here a lesson in axecraft.'

Even as the High King spoke, goblins were scurrying into the arena armed with knives and cudgels. Furgil and his rangers had rounded up the creatures, caging them until this very moment.

Sitting a short distance from the High King, Forek Grimbok was busy speaking with the elven lords. Using a mixture of elaborate hand gestures and a halting dialect, the reckoner described to them what was about to happen next. As Snorri listened to the crude bastardisation of Elvish and Khazalid tumble and crash off Forek's tongue like weighted anvils, he smiled. For a dwarf, Forek sounded like a very good elf.

The reckoner need not have bothered with the convoluted explanation. It was a waste of effort. Snorri could have explained the outcome of the fight with a single word.

Slaughter.

The elf and the hill dwarf had unsheathed their weapons and went to opposite ends of the arena, the former releasing his longsword with a perfunctory flourish, whilst the latter merely fastened a tight grip around the haft of his axe. Both combatants looked determined on what they were about to do. Despite himself, Snorri found himself admiring the toughness of the elf. He seemed less airy than Imladrik, a warrior not a statesman, a slayer not a conciliator.

Perhaps it would not be such dull entertainment after all.

In the middle of the arena were the greenskins, penned off from the two fighters by a cage. Wrought of heavy iron, spikes decorating the points of intersection on the latticed metal, the goblins were well secured. Capering and hooting, biting each other and rolling around in the muck, the greenskins did not seem to understand what was about to happen to them.

Snorri did a rough count in his head and reckoned on close to eighty greenskins on the field. Furgil must have been busy to capture so many for the brodunk.

'All the grobi at once?' he muttered, intending to keep it quiet, but the High King had sharp ears like a wolf's and heard him anyway.

Gotrek jabbed his son playfully in the side.

'Would you balk at such a feat, lad?'

Snorri affected a dismissive air. 'They are just grobi. I could kill a hundred on my own, but since you have banned me from taking up an axe...'

'Ha!' Gotrek's bellowed laughter woke some of the sleepier members of the elder council and sent tremors of unease through the elves, for which Grimbok hastily apologised. 'And that is not about to change because of your petulance. Remember why you are sat here and not out there fighting alongside Lord Salendor.'

'Is that his name, the elgi?'

'Aye lad, and he is a brutal bastard of a warrior. You just wait and see.'

Snorri had already made that same assessment.

'Sounds like you admire him, father.'

'I respect him, as should you. They are not so thin boned and soft of spine as many dawi think.' He eyed the elves again at this remark, as if testing that theory by sight alone. He need not have been so cautious, for the elves did not understand him. True Khazalid was beyond even their most gifted ambassadors. Even so, Gotrek leaned in closer to his son, nudging him conspiratorially. 'Tell me, what do you think of the skarrenawi? You have seen him fight.'

Gotrek pointed at the hill dwarf. He was crisscrossing test swings over his body to loosen his shoulder. Every loud *whomp* of his blade through the air drew a cheer from the small crowd of hill dwarfs that had gathered at the arena side.

'Years ago,' said Snorri, recalling a similar feast time. 'He was decent with an axe.'

'Now I know you are lying, son.'

Snorri was disinterested and had no qualms about giving his father that impression. His gaze wandered over to the healing tents, where the priestesses of Valaya practised their battlefield ministrations.

The High King seemed not to notice and went on, 'Rundin son of Norgil is the skarrenawi king's champion. He shuns the rinkkaz but sends his axe-battler to humble our warriors in the brodunk. Petty, King Grum, very petty,' he grumbled.

'What does it matter if he does? Let me go over there and show him up for the pretender he is. The skarrenawi do not care about us, why should we care about them?'

'Spoken like a true wazzock,' Gotrek said angrily. 'Does nothing I say ever sink into your thick skull, Snorri? The skarrens are our kith, if not kin. They are dawi, albeit of a different stripe. You should care about them, for the day may come when we need them. Relations between our two disparate clans, hill and mountain both, are important. Grum is the problem, not the skarrenawi.'

'Yet you do nothing when he thumbs his teeth at you.'

'Diplomacy is a delicate business, lad,' the High King replied, though he agreed with his son that something needed to be done to bring Grum back in line. Bad enough dealing with elves and the ambitions of King Varnuf, without adding the hill dwarfs to his list of immediate problems.

Snorri scoffed, his gaze drawn back to the healing tents where it lingered in hope.

'Skarnag Grum is an oaf and a glutton, grown fat on excess,' he declared, lowering his voice to add, 'I've even heard rumours of an elf consort.'

Forek, who had evidently been earwigging, nearly spat out his ale and ended up tipping most of his tankard over his finely tailored tunic.

'I seriously doubt that,' said the High King, though there was a glint of amusement in his eye as Forek did his best to apologise to the elves and wipe down his attire at the same time.

'If I could beg your leave, my liege,' he began, coming over. 'I need to–'

'Yes, yes,' Gotrek told him dismissively, 'just go. You don't need me to tell you when to go for a piss, Grimbok, neither do you for this. Away.'

Bowing profusely, crafting a dagger stare at Snorri who was finding it hard to maintain his composure, he left the pavilion to get cleaned up.

'Bit of an ufdi, that one,' Gotrek said behind his hand to Snorri once the reckoner was gone. 'But he's good with words and the hardest bastard reckoner in the Karaz Ankor. Grimbok has settled more debts than any other for this hold.'

Snorri wasn't really listening. His attention was on the healing tents.

'Do not look for her,' said the High King. Though his tone was stern, it was also paternal. 'She isn't there, son.'

Turning away ostensibly to watch the tournament, Snorri feigned ignorance. 'I look for no one, father. My eye merely wandered for a moment.'

'See it does not wander back then.'

Snorri didn't answer but his face was flushed.

'Don't take me for a fool, lad. I know for whom you hold a torch. It is as glaring as Grungni's heart-fire. A pity that Helda was not more to your liking,' he mused briefly, 'a marital union between Karaz-a-Karak and Karak Kadrin would have been very useful about now. Though I trust him to be an ally, Grundin is a thorny hruk at the best of times. If we could have bonded his daughter and his clan to ours...'

'Father,' Snorri implored, 'she was–'

Gotrek waved away his protest. 'The size of an alehouse and with a face like an urk licking dung off its own boots. Yes, I know, lad. But the rinn you want is not for you. She is sworn to Valaya and as such is off limits, even to the son of the High King.' He gestured in the direction of another tent put up nearby. 'Besides, her brother would not look on it favourably either.'

Snorri opened his mouth to protest, but Gotrek silenced him.

'Off limits, lad,' he told him again, but for all that the mood between them was improving. 'Now, let's watch this son of Norgil and see if he's as good as he claims... for a skarren, anyway.'

Father and son smiled together, and Snorri found he was glad of the rare moment of bonding. There had been precious few of them recently.

In the arena, the cage was lowered into a thin trench through some mechanism fashioned by the engineers' guild and the goblins were finally released. Twin war cries in Elvish and Khazalid curdled the air.

Before it was over, there would be much blood.

A foul mood was upon Forek Grimbok as he entered the healing tent.

Several dwarf warriors taking part in the various games had laughed at him as he strode across the field and the memory of it still simmered. His breeches were wet from the spilled tankard, and it looked as if he'd pissed himself. Their derision only worsened when they realised it was beer that Forek had wasted. One even offered to sup it from his sodden garments, until the fearsome reckoner had glowered at him. At that the half-drunken clanner had sobered up and left quietly with his friend.

Grimbok might enjoy the finer things that life had to offer, he might enjoy the silks the elves brought from far-off lands and keep his beard trimmed, maintain neat and pristine attire, but he knew how to crack skulls too and had done so often during his tenure as reckoner.

It was warm inside the healing tent, and light from suspended lanterns cast a lambent glow over cots and baths. In the centre stood Valaya, a small stone effigy of the ancestor goddess removed with respect from one of the lesser temples and brought here to watch over the wounded. Her rune-emblazoned banners hung from the leather walls.

During the course of the games so far, there had been mercifully few serious injuries to trouble the priestesses. Therefore he was surprised to see his sister Elmendrin tending to the wounded. She was carrying an armful of fresh linen bandages to a wooden trunk.

'Were you planning on wringing that out into your tankard later, brother?' she teased, gesturing to his soiled tunic.

'An unfortunate accident,' Forek replied formally, cheeks reddening. 'I thought you were performing rites in the temple?' he asked, looking around for something to swab his tunic with.

Elmendrin proffered a clay bowl and a sponge she picked from the trunk, which Forek took and proceeded to dab his tunic with.

'Scrub it,' she chastised, showing him how until Forek got hold of the sponge again to save his expensive attire from ruination.

'You are such an ufdi, Forek,' she said, smiling.

A dwarf in a nearby cot sniggered. He had one foot up, exposing a missing toe.

'Never was much of a dancer,' he said.

Forek scowled back before returning his attention to his sister.

'So why are you here, then?'

'Another of the priestesses came down with *kruti* flu, so I took her place.'

The scowl turned into a disapproving frown.

'*He* is here, but I daresay you've already noticed that.'

'Who?' asked Elmendrin as she started to wash a batch of soiled, ruddy bandages in a pewter tank.

'Halfhand.'

She paused, failing to suppress a small smile. 'Is that what they're calling him?'

'I don't need to tell you–'

Elmendrin turned sharply, cutting off Forek in mid-stream.

'No brother, you *don't* need to tell me anything. I am here to perform my duty, not to fawn over the High King's son,' she snapped. 'For good or ill, Valaya has sent me here.'

Forek sagged down onto an empty bench, holding his hand up apologetically.

'Sorry, sister. I am drawn, that is all.'

Indignation became concern on Elmendrin's face and she went to him and sat down.

'You look very troubled,' she said, resting her hand on Forek's shoulder. 'Tell me.'

'I am tired, worn like metal overbeaten by the fuller,' he confessed, using his knuckles to knead his eyes. 'Failing to reckon the many misdeeds done to dawi by elgi has left me ragged. Reports flood in daily of more attacks, more unrest, and our kin grow ever more belligerent.' He met her worried gaze with a look of fear in his eyes. 'I can see but one outcome.'

'But what about the brodunk? Surely it will help salve whatever wounds these troubles have caused between our peoples.'

'Weak mortar to mask the cracks, sister. Nothing more.'

Remembering the other priestesses moving quietly around the healing tent, Elmendrin whispered, 'I had no idea it was this bad.'

'Few do. My every effort is bent towards urging the clans not to retaliate unless they know for certain who the bandits responsible for this perfidy are.'

'Surely the High King can restrain them.'

'Not for much longer. Relations with the elgi are worse than ever.'

She pursed her lips, unsure how to ask her next question. 'And what do you think? About the elgi, I mean?'

Forek looked down at his boots, worry lines deepening the shadows on his forehead. 'I think the world is darkening, sister.'

Elmendrin rubbed her brother's back and held his hand.

'They will be caught. This will stop and the bloodshed will end,' she assured him. 'Elgi do not want to kill dawi, nor dawi kill elgi. It is madness.'

'And yet the killing does not stop. Only the other day, a band of rangers from Karak Varn slew a band of elgi traders bound for Kagaz Thar. Aside from hunting bows, they were unarmed but did not speak much Khazalid and could not explain why they had blundered onto the sovereign territory of the Varn. With all that has happened, what else could they do but kill them?'

Elmendrin rubbed his back harder, fighting back her tears. 'It will pass. It has to. You always see the worst, Forek, but that is just how Grungni made you.'

Forek gripped her hand and she embraced him warmly.

'Not this time, sister.'

He let her go, and her eyes followed him all the way to the flap of the tent. Forek turned just before he left. 'I need to return to the king.' He smiled, but it was far from convincing. 'You're right, sister. All will be well again soon.'

Elmendrin watched him go and the silence of the healing tent became as deafening as a battlefield in her ears.

TWENTY

A HERALD OF DOOM

As Snorri watched the fight unfold he began to recognise some of the differences between elf and dwarf in the way that they fought. Despite his obvious disdain for the elves, he had always studied them in war, what little he had been able to garner in these times of peace anyway. Salendor was an odd exemplar of their method.

He fought more like a dancer than a warrior, but with a brutal edge that many elves lacked. His face was an impenetrable mask of concentration. It betrayed no weakness, nor did it show intent. Every blade thrust was measured and disguised, fast as quicksilver and deadly as a hurled spear with the same amount of force.

Goblins fell apart against Salendor's onslaught. Heads, limbs and torsos rained down around him in a grisly flood of expelled blood and viscera. He weaved through the bodies, never slowing, always on the move. No knife touched him. No cudgel wielded by greasy greenskin hands could come close. He was like a cleaving wind whipping through the horde, and wherever he blew death was left in his wake.

Where Imladrik fought with precision, a swordmaster in every regard, Salendor improvised, broke expected patterns and unleashed such fury that many of the goblins simply fled at the sight of him advancing upon them.

The hill dwarf was a different prospect altogether. He brutalised like a battering ram, gladly taking hits on his armour, wearing the savage little cuts of the greenskins like badges of honour. As well as his axe, he fought with elbow and forehead, knee and fist. Rundin reminded the prince of a pugilist, wading into the thick of battle. Utterly fearless, his axe was pendulum-like in the way it hewed goblin bodies. Never faltering, rhythmic and inexorable, it carved ruin into their ranks. Where the elf used as much effort as was needed, the hill dwarf gave everything in every swing. His stamina was incredible.

From what he knew of the son of Norgil, Rundin was not given to histrionics, yet he flung his axe end over end to crack open a fleeing goblin's skull and earn the adulation of the crowd. It was indulgent, and Snorri suspected that Grum had instructed him to entertain with this obvious theatre. It left the dwarf vulnerable but he used a long left-handed gauntlet to parry then bludgeon until he seized his axe and began the killing anew.

Seeing the artifice of the gauntlet reminded Snorri of his own finely-crafted glove. Through it, he recalled the pain of his wounding by the rats beneath the ruins of Karak Krum and of Ranuld Silverthumb's prophecy. Scowling at the memory, he wondered how he was supposed to fulfil his great destiny *watching* other people fight.

Flowing like a stream, Salendor moved through a clutch of goblins. He cut them open with his longsword, spilling entrails, then sheathed the blade and drew the bow from his back in the same fluid motion.

It appeared that Rundin was not the only one told to put on a show.

Arrows seemed to materialise in the elf's hand, nocked and released in the time it took for Snorri to blink. One goblin about to be felled by the hill dwarf's axe spun away from the blow with a white pine shaft embedded in its eye.

At the edges of the arena, a dwarf loremaster announced the kill for the elf. Tallymen racked the count and held up stone placards decorated with the *Klinkerhun* to describe the score.

It was close, but Salendor had the edge by one.

Only six goblins remained.

Beside the prince, the High King shifted uncomfortably in his seat.

'It is tight...' he murmured.

'What does it matter who wins?' said Snorri. 'Elgi or skarren, we lose on both counts.'

That earned a look of reproach from his father. 'I would rather it be a dawi, be that of the mountain or hill.'

'You should have let me fight,' said Snorri, his sudden petulance betraying the better mood that had been growing between him and his father. 'Then the victor would not be in any doubt.'

Gotrek showed his teeth. They were clenched but did not bite. Instead, he fixed his attention on the end of the bout.

Around the arena, the mood was tense but raucous. In tents draped in mammoth hide, Luftvarr hooted and roared with every goblin slain. On the opposite side, Varnuf was more considered and watched keenly over the top of his steepled fingers. Grundin and Aflegard mainly glared at each other, their attention returning to the fight only when prompted by the reaction of the crowd to something particularly noteworthy. Brynnoth, ever the gregarious king, vigorously supped ale with his thanes as they exchanged commentary. The closer it became, the more he drank. It was fortunate that the king of the Sea Hold had an iron constitution from imbibing vast quantities of wheat-rum.

Rundin had pulled one back, but Salendor was quick to riposte, unleashing the last of his arrows to pin a goblin through the heart.

It left four greenskins with the elf still one up. Rundin took two at once, earning a loud bellow of approval from King Luftvarr. Even Grundin clenched a fist. The hill dwarf tackled them before Salendor could run them through with his sword. In using the bow, the elf lord had put too much distance between his quarry and was now paying the price for that.

Swift as a lightning strike, the elf thrust his blade through a greenskin that rushed him in desperation, making it even. One goblin remained, flanked by the two bloodstained champions who looked ready to rush it from opposite ends of the arena.

'The elgi is quick,' hissed Gotrek, glancing up as Grimbok returned to the fold.

'Aye, but the son of Norgil has an eagle-eye when he throws that axe,' the reckoner replied.

Snorri folded his arms and said nothing.

Both warriors advanced on the lonely greenskin, who looked back and forth, scurrying one way and then the other before it realised there was no escape.

'Kill it!' bellowed Brynnoth, banging down his tankard and swilling out some of the dregs.

The goblin shrieked once, clutching its emaciated chest, and slumped down dead, its heart given out.

Silence descended like a veil, settling over the dumbstruck crowd.

Eyes wide, wondering if he had ended the creature with his voice alone, Brynnoth looked down at his tankard and belched.

Some of the elves looked around at him, disgusted and incredulous at the same time.

Both combatants met one another's gaze. The loremasters scoring the bout paused, unsure what to do next. They looked to the High King.

Snorri laughed out loud, his mirth echoing around the arena crowd who were still stunned into bemused silence.

'The grobi kills itself,' he declared. 'Expired by its own fear!'

He laughed again, raucously and derisive. 'Incredibly, both elgi and skarren found a way to lose.'

'That's enough,' snapped the High King. 'You dishonour yourself and the hold.'

'I am merely stating facts, father.' He gestured to the stone placards, the same Klinkerhun inscribed on each now the loremasters realised they had no choice but to score one kill apiece. 'A tie is a win for neither.'

Grimbok began to clap, slow and loudly. When he got to his feet, some of the elder council took up the applause. When the thanes of Everpeak joined in it grew to a clamour. Brynnoth roared with drunken laughter, the king and thanes of Barak Varr hammering their tankards with aplomb. Setting aside their grievance for now, Grundin and Aflegard urged their respective quarters to clap and holler.

Much to Grimbok's relief, elves were celebrating too, not only the ambassadors but those retainers who had accompanied the nobles of their houses. There was a rare mood of camaraderie and community fostered as both races seemed pleased with the result.

From the Norse dwarfs, Luftvarr shouted, '*Runk!*' and his boisterous warriors took up the call.

'Runk, runk, runk!'

The chant spread to other quarters, dwarfs from the other holds echoing their northern cousins eagerly.

'Runk?' one of the elf ambassadors queried to Grimbok.

'It means a thrashing, noble lord,' he explained. 'Such as that given to the grobi by our champions.'

The elf didn't look as if he really understood.

Snorri leaned in, enjoying the swell of aggression manifesting around the arena.

'It also means brawl, ufdi,' he grinned.

The elf ambassador lifted his eyebrows to ask an unspoken question.

'Ahh...' Grimbok began but then cringed as the first punch was thrown.

King Luftvarr decked one of his thanes, a heavy blow that knocked the other dwarf out cold. Seconds later, the entire Norse quarter were fighting.

Drunk, still feeling the vicarious belligerence of watching the brutal combat, dwarfs from other holds started brawling too. Unlike the Norse, it was less brutal, more wrestling than boxing as such.

'Runk, runk, runk!' they bellowed as one, a deafening refrain that set the elves on edge.

Tankards were spilled over, tables upended as most of the onlooking dwarfs revelled in a good, honest scrap. Musicians began piping, drummers beating out a tune to accompany the brawling.

Grundin was slapping his thighs, supping on his pipe and blowing out smoke rings. The King of Karak Kadrin looked as if he were enjoying this spectacle much more than the bout itself.

Sloshing ale hither and thither, Brynnoth seized a boar-skin drum from one of his musicians and joined the chorus.

Even Varnuf was laughing, though whether in genuine merriment or at the elves' obvious discomfort was difficult to ascertain.

Unsure at the sudden development, Lord Salendor merely bowed to his kin and stalked from the arena. Rundin clapped with the drummers' beat, dancing a little jig much to the roared acclaim of his fellow hill dwarfs and the other mountain clans too.

Throughout it all, Gotrek remained pensive. Like his chief reckoner, he recognised the unease of the elves and dearly wanted the runk to subside, but to do so would harm his standing with his own kin. This was customary amongst the dwarfs and as their High King he would not stop it.

'The elgi, my liege...' Grimbok began. He had sat back down and was no longer clapping. He looked as unsettled as the High King.

'I know,' said Gotrek, impotent to do much of anything in that moment.

'Sire–' Grimbok persisted.

Gotrek snapped, head turning on a swivel to face the reckoner.

'I know!'

'They are leaving, my king.'

Without a word, the elf ambassadors had risen from their seats and were filing out of the royal pavilion with their retainers in tow.

'Should I...' Grimbok was getting to his feet.

'No, sit down,' chafed the High King. 'These are our ways, dawi ways. If the elgi cannot stomach that, then... well, I will not change our customs for outsiders.'

'*Outsiders*, my king?'

'Yes! That is what I said. The elgi are–'

Whatever Gotrek was going to say next remained unspoken when a hearthguard strode up the stone steps of the royal pavilion, interrupting him.

Thumping the left breast of his cuirass, the warrior took a knee and removed his war helm.

'Rise, hearthguard,' said the king. Out of the corner of his eye, he noticed the elves still lingered and were looking at the warrior too. 'You are Gilias Thunderbrow, aren't you?'

'Aye, my king,' the warrior said, standing up. 'Sent by Captain Thurbad with a message from the entrance hall of the upper deep. He bade me come swiftly.'

Around the arena the din from brawling was dying out as all attended to the lone hearthguard. Without his helm, which now sat in the crook of his left arm, to conceal it, the warrior's face was grim.

'Bad news, is it, Gilias?' Gotrek exchanged a dark look with Grimbok, for he already knew the answer to his question.

'Aye, my king,' the hearthguard replied. 'Bleak as winter.'

TWENTY-ONE

THE COMING OF WAR

Except for the High King's guards, Nadri Gildtongue stood alone in the entrance hall of Karaz-a-Karak.

The merchant guildmaster from Barak Varr paid no heed to the mute ranks of quarrellers and hearthguard that surrounded him. Silence persisted like that of a tomb. It only served to echo his darker thoughts. He closed his eyes... Snatched glimpses of what he had seen in the gorge returned.

The dead everywhere... their blood soaking the earth...
Krondi... Poor old Krondi... His friend, who hadn't stood a chance...
And a husk that was once a dwarf...

Sending the rest of the wagons on their way, Nadri had travelled to Everpeak by himself with a single mule and cart.

The great gate opened, arresting Nadri from his black reverie, admitting a pair of kings and their retainers. One of the liege-lords advanced ahead of the other and embraced the guildmaster warmly.

'Nadri,' said King Brynnoth, stepping back to clap the dwarf on the shoulders. 'I am relieved to see you alive and in one piece.'

Nodding, Nadri said, 'Tromm. I have bleak tidings, my king.'

'Tell us, lad,' said Gotrek, moving into a patch of brazier light.

Nadri bowed deeply to the High King, but then recoiled sharply when he saw the other members of the party who had entered the hall behind them.

'Elgi!' he hissed.

Eyeing first the guildmaster and then the elves shrewdly, Brynnoth raised his hand for calm.

'Easy, Nadri.'

'All is well here,' added Gotrek, nodding silent thanks to Thurbad who had been waiting in the shadows. 'Prince Imladrik is an ally of the Karaz Ankor.'

'What harm befell you, guildmaster?' asked the elven prince.

Nadri's face contorted into a mask of fury. 'It was not me who was harmed. Agrin Fireheart lies dead, so too my kith and kin. A noble friend,

Krondi Stoutback was amongst them.' He wept without shame. Some of the dwarf retainers tugged or gnawed at their beards.

Brynnoth wore a snarl as he stepped away from the elves to his guild-master's side.

'*Thagi!*' he spat. 'Agrin Fireheart was runelord to my hold, a near ancestor of the dawi. His death is perfidy beyond reckoning.' He glared at the elves. 'Something must be done.'

'I agree,' said another voice from farther back in the hall. Varnuf had entered through the great gate. Gotrek scowled when he saw the King of Eight Peaks.

Snorri was with him.

'Did you bring him here?' he asked belligerently of his son.

'I came of my own accord,' Varnuf interceded, 'to find out what dire matter would demand such hasty attention. I see now I was right to do so.'

Gotrek noticed one of the elves, a female, reach to her sword but a fierce glance from Imladrik stayed her hand. The High King could see why they were suddenly paranoid. The dwarfs had them surrounded.

'Be calm, all of you,' he said. 'This is still my hold and I am still High King of the Karaz Ankor.'

Varnuf's eyes narrowed slightly at that remark. Gotrek expected nothing less.

'Then expel the elgi from our halls and lands, father,' Snorri urged.

'I will not!' roared the High King.

All the dwarfs present, even the other kings, lowered their eyes in acknowledgement of his superiority. All except Snorri.

'They kill dawi by the score, take our gold, cheat our merchants and burn our settlements to the ground and you still wish to treat with them?'

The elf female could contain her ire no longer and spoke out. 'Our people have been slain too. Fort Arlandril was burned and innocent asur murdered. It is not just–'

'Quiet, Liandra!' Imladrik glowered at her, but retained some of his composure to address the High King. 'Liege-lord,' he said, 'this heinous act will not go unpunished. Allow me to send riders to find these bandits and bring them to justice.'

Gotrek was shaking his head. His shoulders sagged, as if defeated.

'It has gone beyond that, my prince. Deaths of merchants are one thing but the slaying of an ancient is something else entirely. I must think on this. Decide upon a course of action.'

Snorri was incensed. 'What is there to think about? Banish the elgi and draw arms against them.'

The stony expressions of Brynnoth and Varnuf suggested they agreed.

Liandra went for her sword again. Several of the elf retainers did likewise and this time Imladrik did not forbid them. Unsheathed elven steel shone brightly in the lamplight.

Only Prince Imladrik stayed his hand.

A ripple went through the hearthguard as they tightened their fists around axe hafts. Above in the higher vaults of the chamber, bow strings were tautened. Thurbad held the warriors in place.

Gotrek met the prince's gaze, and there were storm clouds boiling in the High King's eyes.

'Tell your kin to put up their swords,' he said levelly. 'Tell them to do it now, my prince.'

Imladrik did so, immediately. None argued, for they could see the hopelessness of their situation.

'Please, High King,' Imladrik implored, 'let me–'

'You will do nothing! Nothing!' Gotrek raged. 'This is a dawi matter, now. It shall be dealt with by my hand. Leave.'

Imladrik's face clouded over. 'High King?'

'I said leave. Take your elgi and leave this place. I will guarantee safe passage back to your settlements, but you cannot stay here. Not now.'

Realising there was nothing more to be said, the elf prince bowed and did as the High King had ordered.

Liandra and the other elves followed. The great gate was still open and no one barred their exit. All of the dwarfs watched them go, not taking their eyes off them until the gate was sealed again and sanctity had returned to the entrance hall.

'Why does it feel as if you just gave quarter to an enemy?' said Brynnoth.

Varnuf remained pensive.

'We should have killed them,' muttered Snorri. 'Send a message to–'

Gotrek struck him across the jaw, hard enough to put the prince on his knee.

'Shut your mouth,' snarled the High King, 'and do not dishonour me further with your idiotic talk.'

Snorri was hurt, but mainly his pride. 'Father, I'm... I'm sorry. I didn't–'

'Save your contrition.' Gotrek was shaking his head. 'To think I have raised such a son.' That barb stung worse than any blow ever could. Gotrek turned to Thurbad. 'Gather the rest of the kings, round them all up and bring them here. I will have counsel immediately.'

None opposed him. None dared. With a final glance at his son, who rubbed his jaw painfully, Gotrek stormed from the entrance hall and down into the Ekrund.

A grim and sombre mood pervaded in the Great Hall.

Agrin Fireheart was dead. Worse than that, he had been slain by elves. *Elves.*

It went beyond merely killing. Agrin was a runelord, an ancient, one of the few. His like would not grace the earth again. In one fell and heinous act of callous murder, Barak Varr had lost its closest link to its ancestors.

Gone were the retainers, the guards and lesser thanes; only kings remained. The Grand Hall echoed with their lonely presence, and shadows crowded the small group of dwarfs encircling the High King.

'His body shall be recovered. Furgil and his rangers shall see to it,' he told the only member of the assembly who was not of regal birth.

Nadri Gildtongue bowed. Tears were yet to dry on his dusty cheeks and ran in streaks down his face. In lieu of speech, he chewed his beard. Clothes torn, lathered in mud, stinking of sweat, the merchant cut a sorry and dejected figure.

King Brynnoth nodded to his fellow king.

'Tell them as you told me,' he said to Nadri, indicating the other kings who had only just arrived back at the hold, 'of how you found him and the rest of your kin.'

Nadri nodded, but the words did not come. Grief had thickened his tongue, and the long moments spent waiting for the other lords of the Karaz Ankor to arrive had forced him back to bleak thoughts.

Brynnoth gripped the merchant's shoulder paternally.

'Come on, lad,' he urged. 'All here present need to hear this.'

Swallowing hard, Nadri met his king's steady gaze and found his courage.

'I was three days, maybe less, behind Krondi,' he said. 'We were driving wagons to Zhufbar, but Krondi carried a passenger that was bound for Karaz-a-Karak, so we agreed to meet there and continue on together.'

'Agrin Fireheart was whom your friend was ferrying, yes?' asked Varnuf. For once the King of Eight Peaks seemed without agenda and shared a worried glance with Gotrek.

'Aye, lord,' said Nadri, 'but he did not know. I thought it better if the ancient travelled in secret. It seems my plans were for naught, though.' Face clouding over, he was about to lapse into another deep melancholy when Brynnoth brought him back.

'Keep going, lad.'

Licking his lips, Nadri went on.

'Following Krondi's trail, I became concerned when I reached the ruins of Zakbar Varf. The trading post had been burned, many dawi were dead but, by Valaya's mercy, Krondi was not amongst them.' He wiped an errant tear at the memory. Some of the dwarf kings began to tug their beards in anger. Luftvarr had almost stuffed his entirely into his mouth in order to fetter his Norscan wrath. 'But I moved with haste, eager to make sure of my friend's safety and that of his charge and his warriors.' Nadri's face darkened further and from looking down at his boots forlornly, he met the gaze of the High King who listened quietly. 'Upon reaching the gorge, not twenty miles from the hold gates, I was disabused of that hope.'

All eyes were on the merchant now as a strange air of stillness settled over the kings like a funerary veil.

'At first I saw a guard,' said Nadri. 'He'd lost a boot. It was a few feet from his body. Arrows studded his back, splitting his mail and greaves like paper. They were white-shafted, long and with fanged tips.'

Gotrek weighed in at that point. 'My chief scout found similar arrow shafts at the site of another ambush several days ago.'

'D'ya think these were tha same wee *dreks* that killed this one's kin?' asked Grundin. The King of Karak Kadrin went unhelmeted and his bald pate shone like a coin in the lambent light.

Despite their dispute, Aflegard stood beside him, smoking his pipe in quiet contemplation. Dwarfs were a passionate race that were quick to anger, but slow to forget, and never forgave. No one could hold a grudge like the sons of Grungni. In their language, there were more words for vengeance and retribution than any other. But in this, when kith and kin were attacked by outsiders, they were united. Feuds could wait when others warranted the axe first.

Gotrek nodded. 'It is very likely. Furgil has increased the rangers' patrols and all roads around the karak are watched day and night, but no one has seen these bandits. No one.'

Nadri spoke up. He was shaking his head. 'They were not bandits, High King. What I saw in that gorge was no skirmish. Agrin Fireheart was a master of the rhun. He could wield the elements through his craft.' The merchant clenched a fist as if reliving the final moments of the runelord. 'He brought lightning and thunder to the gorge. Though there were no bodies of elgi, I saw the black marks they had left where Agrin had scorched their skin. No mere bandit could match such a power. Only one thing I know could do that.'

'Sorcery,' uttered Aflegard, the word bitter in his mouth. He chewed the end of his pipe, leaving an indentation in the clay from his clenched teeth.

'Aye, magic of the darkest kind was unleashed against Agrin,' said Nadri, weeping again, 'and he was undone by it.'

And there the merchant's story ended.

Brynnoth patted him on the back, saying, 'Well done, lad. Well done,' in a soothing tone.

Silence fell upon the hall, leavened only by the dulcet crackle of braziers.

Each of the kings looked at one another, their eyes revealing more of their inner thoughts than their tongues ever would.

Luftvarr's were red-rimmed. The King of Kraka Drak was almost apoplectic. Others maintained a more guarded countenance, though it was fairly obvious that Varnuf was waiting for Gotrek to do or say something. His expectant gaze bordered on disparaging before the High King had even spoken.

'Thurbad...' Gotrek intoned to break the quietude.

Like a stone sentinel, the captain of the hearthguard emerged from penumbral shadow.

Gotrek addressed Nadri. 'You'll be escorted safely from the karak back to the Sea Hold. Thurbad will see to it.'

Brynnoth nodded again to his High King, knowing that he would need to remain behind for further talks. To make a decision in haste now would be foolish, but something would have to be done.

Gently taking Nadri by the arm, Thurbad led the merchant out of the hall and left the kings to ruminate.

'Snorri,' said the High King as Thurbad was leaving. Gotrek did not deign to look at his son. 'You may go too.'

About to protest, Snorri clamped shut his mouth and marched from the Great Hall in barely veiled disgust.

'He's a fiery wee bastard, yer son,' Grundin remarked when the prince was still in earshot.

Gotrek lowered his voice, only looking at Snorri with his back turned and walking away.

'He is a headstrong fool with much to learn.'

'And even more to prove, it would appear,' added Varnuf.

'Not so different from his father during his early reign,' said Brynnoth, to which Aflegard nodded.

'I care not!' Luftvarr had spat out his beard. It spewed out with a spray of sputum. Gobbets still clung to it like dirty little pearls but the Norse king seemed not to notice. 'My warriors stand ready to fight. Elgi have slain dawi in cold blood, and this time a lord of the rhun. No answer to that could ever end in peace, so tell me this, king of the high mountain – when do we make war?'

TWENTY-TWO

LEGACIES

The surface of the *dokbar* faded from pearlescent silver to ash grey, its activation robbing it of its lustre and plunging Ranuld into shadow. Like the massive runic shield, his surroundings were a dark mirror to his thoughts. Through the gate between holds he had warned the others. He hoped it would be enough to spare them a similar fate. The magic in the runes inscribed around the dokbar's edge were fading. Soon it would speak no more and his voice would no longer be heard across the leagues.

Much as he had feared, old magic was leaving the world. As the secrets of the old lore diminished, so too did what the dwarfs used to be. Ruin was changing them, as slowly and inexorably as the tide erodes the face of a cliff and exposes its inner core to further decay.

Ranks of gronti-duraz surrounded the runelord but were not good company, no salve to his grief. Still dormant as they were, he alone did not possess the craft to reanimate the stone giants and breathe magical life back into their runes. He needed others to achieve that feat. It was one made harder by what had happened at the borders of Everpeak.

Since leaving the Great Hall after the rinkkaz, Ranuld had remained in the forge but he had felt the passing of Agrin Fireheart like a physical blow. Scattered coals, a fuller lying strewn and uncared for, still littered the floor above. Intent on his work in another chamber of the forge hall, Morek had not heard them fall.

Another light had faded, snuffed out by a great doom that would douse all the lamps should it be allowed to run unchallenged. Ranuld knew not what he could do to stop it, only that he must.

Hope lay in those younger than he and the ancients he had summoned to his conclave. Age and wisdom were giving way to youth and passion. All he could do was help temper this young steel into a blade that would cut through the encroaching shadow.

Weary, Ranuld left the vault and went back to the forge itself, drawn by the sound of hammering.

Morek was toiling at the anvil. Sweat lathered his muscled frame and he wiped a gloved hand against his brow to soak up the worst of it on his face.

'Star-metal is not so easy to shape,' uttered the runelord, causing his apprentice to turn.

A partially formed blade, slowly being cogged into shape and then to be edged and fullered, lay upon the anvil. Morek stared at it forlornly.

'It is unyielding, master.' He sounded breathless; the sinews in his arms were taut enough to snap and his muscles bunched like overripe fruit grown too big for its own skin.

'Like the *karadurak*, it must be coaxed into giving up its secrets,' Ranuld told him. 'Strength is not enough. Any oaf can whack a hammer with enough force to split a rock, it will only respond to skill. And much like splitting ever-stone, meteoric iron, *gromril*, can only be forged by a master smith. Are you such a dawi, Morek of the Furrowbrows?'

'I think so, master.'

Ranuld scoffed. 'Werit. Think? Think, is it? *Think!*' He bellowed, 'You must *know* it. Az and klad will not forge themselves.'

'Master, I...'

'And to think it is to you who I must pass on all my knowledge... Kruti-eating *wanaz*, I should take the hammer from your hand this instant and use it upon your stupid head! Ufdi!'

'Please don't, master.'

'Wazzock,' spat the runelord. His eyes narrowed on his terrified apprentice then to the slowly bending star-metal he had clamped against the anvil. An axe blade was visible, and once it was finished the runes could be struck. 'Hit it again,' Ranuld told him, watching sternly as Morek worked the meteoric iron.

'Gromril is the ore of heroes and masters. It is only they who can wield it, only they who can craft it.'

Morek kept going, hammering relentlessly, slowly building up a rhythm that Ranuld felt resonate in his very soul.

'It requires an artisan's touch to tame and temper. No mere metal-smith can do it. Let them forge shoes for mules or rivets for scaffolds. Theirs is not the way of the rhun. That is the province of our sacred order alone, of which you are a part.'

Hammering, Morek became entranced and the star-metal began to bend to his will.

Ranuld lit up his pipe, took a deep draw as he sat back to regard his apprentice.

'The rhun is slow, so too the metal that bears it. Many weeks it can take just to make a single ingot. Forge its angles sharp and tight, imbue it with the magic of our elders and become a master.'

The ring of metal against metal was almost hypnotic now. Morek had transcended from the 'now' to a place of creation, the rites of forging tripping off his lips like a chant.

'Aye,' said Ranuld, 'now you *know*, lad. Now you can see.'

Slowly, a smile crept up at the edges of his lips. Morek was learning.

'As one light dies,' he said, 'another ignites.'

Even the skies presaged a storm. Grim, black clouds crawled across the sun to blot out the light. Imladrik felt the cold pull at his clothes and seep beneath the plates of his armour. But it was not just the sun's absence which chilled him. The look in the High King's eyes was like ice when he had dismissed Imladrik and the other elves. Suppressing a shiver, he dug his heels into Draukhain's flanks, urging the beast to fly lower.

Karaz-a-Karak was a bitter memory. He cursed inwardly that blades had been drawn in the High King's hold hall and wondered if there was any turning back from the course they were set upon now.

The prince's retainers were on their way back to Oeragor, where he would join them just as soon as he had made this last flight with Draukhain. Others would return to Athel Maraya, Kor Vanaeth and even the vaunted spires of Tor Alessi. After what little he had heard in the entrance hall, Imladrik had decided to track the dwarfs leaving Everpeak. Not those going to Barak Varr but the rangers who had been ordered to recover the bodies of the slain. He wanted to see where it had taken place, and know what had happened in order to make sense of it. One of the dwarfs' runelords was dead. It was unlikely a bandit's arrow had killed him. Imladrik suspected something darker was at work and intended to find out the root of it. The only way to do that was to go to where Agrin Fireheart had died.

The prince's dragon snorted and growled, behaving more belligerently now than when it had been surrounded by dwarfs. It felt the prince's ire and frustration, echoing and amplifying it.

'Peace, Draukhain...' Imladrik soothed, inflecting his voice with a mote of dragon mastery. The beast eased, piercing a layer of cloud.

Below, the rangers were gathering up the bodies of the dead, wrapping them in cloth and placing them reverently on the back of a cart. As funerary transportation went, it was hardly fitting. Imladrik stayed within the lower cloud layer, wreathed in its grey tendrils so if the dwarfs should look up they would not easily see him. The last thing peace needed now was the sighting of a dragon prowling the scene of a foul murder. But then perhaps peace was beyond them at this point. He hoped fervently that this was not the case, and wondered how much his brother knew or cared about what was unfolding on the Old World. Not for the first time in recent weeks, Imladrik wondered if he should return home. The letters he had received at the tournament were still tucked in his vambrace. Their words were burned so indelibly in his mind that he had no need for either any more.

Rising again with a beat of Draukhain's powerful wings, Imladrik found he was not alone when he returned to higher skies.

'Can you smell that reek?' asked Liandra from the back of Vranesh. The beast was small in comparison to the mighty Draukhain but the two dragons recognised each other as kin, snarling and calling to one another in greeting.

Liandra wrinkled her nose. 'It is dark magic. Like a canker on the breeze, the stench is unmistakable. The Wind of Dhar has been harnessed here.'

Though her lips moved, Imladrik heard the words in his mind as though they were standing side by side in a quiet room and not aloft and far apart in a turbulent sky.

He calmed Draukhain, for the depth of the beast's greeting cries would build to the point where the dwarfs below could hear them and think they were under attack.

Liandra frowned. 'What are you doing here?'

'Flying.' Imladrik was in no mood for an inquisition. 'Why did you follow me?'

Beyond his dragonsong, which was potent, Imladrik had no magical craft to draw upon. He had to shout, but Liandra heard him easily enough.

'You can speak normally,' she told him. 'The enchantment works both ways.' She reined Vranesh in a little, for the dragon could smell the dwarfs far below them and wanted to better taste their scent. Like its mistress, the beast neither liked nor trusted the dwarfs. But also like his mistress, he had even less love for dark elves.

Imladrik would not be distracted and asked again, 'Why did you follow me, Liandra?'

'If I said it was to make sure you weren't going to do anything reckless, like try and talk to the dwarfs, would you have believed me?'

'No.'

'Then I did it to find out what you were doing. You entire household leaves the dwarf lands, headed for Oeragor, and yet you, their prince and master, go west after a trail of rangers. I wanted to know why you would do that, Imladrik.'

'And do you?'

'You don't believe that asur did this.'

'No elf of Ulthuan I know uses the Dark Wind. Those that do are rounded up as traitors and executed.'

A darkness flashed across Liandra's face at a bitter memory.

'You think it was druchii?'

'You do not?'

They circled one another, the wings of their mounts flapping lazily but their nostrils flaring as the wind grew steadily more vigorous. It was buffeting Liandra's hair, releasing her gilded locks into the air like flecks of brilliant sunshine.

'Storm is coming,' she said, gazing into the heart of a thunder-head growing on the horizon.

Imladrik maintained a neutral expression. 'You didn't answer my question again.'

'I do not think it matters whether the druchii are involved or not. But I can taste Dhar like ashes in my mouth. Whatever was unleashed down there in that gorge left a mark.'

'A powerful sorceress then,' said Imladrik, partly to himself. 'It is worse than I first thought.'

Liandra nodded. 'And something else too, something I cannot quite see.'

Imladrik was keen of sight. He looked through a patch of thinning cloud and saw that the dwarfs had collected their dead and were moving on.

'Would a closer look make it any clearer?'

'I would rather not descend into the gorge,' she told him, and there was a note of fear in her voice.

'The dwarfs are leaving. If we land at the ridge on either side and climb down into the gorge, they would not see us.'

Despite the prince's reasoning, she looked far from certain.

'I would have thought of all people, you would be the most keen to find out if there are druchii abroad in the Old World. It might have a bearing on whatever happens next. You are no friend to the dwarfs but I also know you do not want another war for our people.'

She peered down through the clouds for a few seconds before conceding. 'We must be swift.'

The dragons dived a moment later, Draukhain in the lead with Vranesh a few feet behind. In keeping with Imladrik's plan, they perched on the ridges of the gorge on either side. The elves then dismounted and climbed down. They met in the middle in a scrum of scattered, broken blades and patches of churned earth.

'It was a brutal fight,' said Liandra. She was crouching down, running the earth between her fingers.

'That is plain even to my mundane sight,' said Imladrik. 'What else do you feel?'

She closed her eyes and took a deep breath.

'Dhar saturates this place. It has been tainted by it. Three sorcerers, one much more potent than the others...'

Imladrik kept his voice low, but his gaze was intense. 'How can you tell?'

'Each crafts the wind of magic subtly differently. Such a thing leaves a trail of essence behind it if you know how to look for it.'

'And what of the other thing, the enigma you spoke of?'

She screwed her eyes tighter. Her fists were clenched at her sides. Liandra's already pale skin drained further, leaving her cold and corpse-like. She shuddered, wracked by a sudden convulsion that threw her off her feet and onto the ground where she spasmed.

'Liandra!' It was as if Imladrik's voice was lost through the veil of a waterfall, distant and muffled.

Reaching her side, he shook her hard, pulling her up onto her knees again.

'Liandra!' Rubbing her arms, trying to beat some warmth back into her, Imladrik didn't know what else to do. 'Come back to me,' he urged and was about to strike her when Liandra's eyes snapped open again.

She flushed at the look of concern on Imladrik's face. When the prince recognised it too he backed off.

'Are you hurt?'

She struggled to her feet but refused any help.

'We cannot linger here. It's not safe.'

'Liandra?'

She was already climbing back up to the ridge, finding trails no dwarf ever could and moving with a grace and swiftness that would seem impossible over such rugged terrain. Equally as nimble, Imladrik gave chase.

'Liandra...' He grabbed at her arm, and she snapped it away with a muttered curse.

'Even with a dragon to protect me, I do not want to feel a crossbow bolt in my back,' she said.

'The dwarfs are gone, and I doubt they would shoot us without cause.'

'Did you not see as I did in the dwarf hall? They want retribution for this. Even if their king is wise, they are not. They are a vengeful and greedy people, Imladrik. It is time you realised that. It might not be tomorrow, or even next year, but a war is coming to our people and there is nothing you can do to prevent that.'

Imladrik was about to respond but knew she was right.

Perhaps he had lingered too long in the Old World with the dwarfs. His brother was calling him back. He had received several letters from the Phoenix King petitioning for his return. Standing there looking at Liandra, he also realised something else.

'You hate them, don't you.'

'The druchii,' she sneered, 'yes. They killed my mother, there is much in that for me to hate.'

'No, not just that. You hate the dwarfs too.'

She nodded without hesitation.

And just like that, Imladrik saw how far apart the two of them had become. He wanted harmony, a peaceful accord between their races; Liandra wanted war. Either against dark elves or dwarfs, it didn't matter.

'I did not notice it before,' he admitted. 'I think I was blind somehow, but you are a supremacist, Liandra. Whether from your bloodline or the horrors you have endured in the past, you have become intolerant of every race except for your own.'

'I am my father's daughter,' she answered defiantly. Her face softened and she added, 'You are leaving, aren't you?'

Imladrik looked resigned. 'Yes. With Malekith's forces stirring in the north, my brother has need of me to marshal the warriors of the dragon peaks.'

'I wish I could go back with you, but my father forbids it.'

'Don't be so eager for bloodshed, Liandra. It is not as glorious as you think it is.'

'I only want to be by their side... my father's and brothers'. But if there are druchii here, I *will* find them,' she promised.

'Don't give in to hate, Liandra.' Imladrik paused, unsure of how to ask his next question. He decided to be direct. 'What did you see, when that palsy stole upon you?'

Her face paled a little at the memory.

'I don't know.'

'Nothing born of Naggaroth?'

She shook her head, which only made the prince's frown deepen. Their enemies were gathering, it seemed.

Though she was a little further up the rise, Imladrik was much taller than her and looked down on the princess. As their eyes met, they drew close enough to touch. She gently put her hand upon his cheek. The metal of her gauntlet was cold, but the warmth of the gesture was not.

'You are such a noble man, Imladrik.'

The prince's face darkened as he thought of those who waited for him back on Ulthuan, and the feelings stirring within him as he looked at Liandra despite everything.

'No, I am not.'

'Love is not love when the choice is made for us,' she said, cradling his chin before leaning in to kiss him delicately on the cheek.

He didn't stop her but didn't know how to respond either. She did all the talking for him.

'If this is to be farewell then I would have you know what I think of you, my prince.'

She touched his chest once, her armoured fingers lingering against his breastplate just where his heavy-beating heart was drumming. Then she carried on up the rise without another word.

Imladrik let her go. He didn't return to the gorge but summoned Draukhain from the opposite ridge, leaping onto the dragon's back as it flew beneath him.

He flew into the storm, his mind troubled. If the dark elves really were abroad in the Old World then the High King of the dwarfs must be told. Arriving at the gates of Everpeak on the back of a dragon after being banished would only create further discord. A subtler method was needed. Reining Draukhain, Imladrik headed west in the direction of his retainers. He needed a swift messenger, one the dwarfs would not try to kill or capture on sight. Praying to Isha, he only hoped he would not be too late.

TWENTY-THREE

SKULLS

Bone fragments peppered Snorri's armour as he shattered the goblin skull with a warhammer.

Kicking off the bone chips still littering the flat rock he was abusing, the dwarf prince went to grab another skull when he saw Morgrim watching him from the archway.

'Quite an impressive collection you've got, cousin,' he said, indicating the fifty or so flensed greenskin heads Snorri had piled up. Several days old, they were the gruesome leavings from the brodunk. The dwarf prince had severed the heads himself. Stuck in the earth next to them, nigh hilt-deep, was a broad-bladed knife. It was flecked with goblin blood. There was no sign of the skin or flesh.

'Threw it over the edge for the screech hawks,' said Snorri, as if reading his cousin's mind. 'I've heard they like the taste of grobi.'

Morgrim closed a heavy wooden door behind him, and stepped out onto a rocky plateau. Surrounded by a low wall punctuated by crenellations, it was one of the eagle gates of Karaz-a-Karak; just without its Gatekeeper, whom the prince had dismissed for some solitude.

Morgrim sucked in the mountain air, relishing its crispness.

'Didn't think you liked the outdoors,' he said.

Snorri lined up another skull and smashed it with a heavy blow, like he was hewing timber for the hearth fire.

'I'm learning to live with it. I'll be seeing a lot of it in the coming months.'

'You think we'll go to war, then?'

Another skull capitulated noisily beneath Snorri's hammer.

'It's inevitable. Every dawi knows it. It's only my father that won't acknowledge it.'

'He doesn't want a war.'

Snorri looked up from his bludgeoning. 'You think I do?'

'You're out here smashing grobi skulls, venting your anger, cousin. I think you have some pent-up aggression.'

'My father talks when he should be strapping on az and donning klad. I am frustrated, Morg. And I don't understand why he cleaves to the elgi so much. What have they ever done for us but cause trouble?' No longer in the mood, Snorri tossed the hammer down and sat on a different rock. He rubbed his shoulder to ease out the stiffness. 'Every day brings news of more murder and theft, yet my father does nothing. He hides in his Grand Hall, bickering with the other kings. Right now the elgi are nothing, just a few thousand warriors and the odd drakk, scattered across disparate settlements. We could defeat them in a month and reclaim the Old World as our own.'

Morgrim picked up where his cousin had left off, choosing a particularly ugly goblin skull to split.

'You make it sound so simple.'

'It is! It's easy, Morg. If an enemy threatens you, take up az and klad, step into his house and kill him. Drogor can see it, why not you?'

Morgrim looked down at the skull he'd just sundered. 'Drogor is not the dawi I remember.'

'You were little more than beardlings when you knew each other. Despite what our ancestors say, dawi can change.'

Morgrim took another skull. 'Not that much.'

'He is a little strange, but I just put that down to his ordeal to reach the karak or living under hot sun for the last twenty-odd years. Southland jungles are no place for dawi.'

'Aye, perhaps.' Bone fragments exploded furiously across the ground. 'I can see why you enjoy this.' Swinging the hammer onto his shoulder, Morgrim hefted a third skull. This one had belonged to an orc. 'He certainly hates elgi.'

'Wouldn't you if they'd slain your kin? And is that such a bad thing?'

'I do not doubt his cause, but if he turns your mind towards similar thoughts then yes, it is bad.'

Snorri scowled. 'I'm no puppet, Morg.'

Two-handed, Morgrim split the orc skull in twain.

'I know that, cousin. I'm sorry.' He took off his war helm to wipe the sweat dappling his forehead. 'Thirsty work.'

'I have ale...' Snorri pulled a damp tarp off a modest-sized barrel he'd kept in shadow beneath the tower wall. He handed Morgrim a pewter tankard. 'And hoped you would find me up here.'

Taking a long pull of the foaming brew, Morgrim said, 'Tromm, but that is fortifying.'

'*Drakzharr*, one of Brorn's special reserves.'

A companionable silence fell between them as they supped together, the sun on their faces and a light wind redolent with the scent of the earth filling their nostrils.

Morgrim breathed deep as he took a long swig of the liquor.

'Been too long since we did this.'

'Aye Morg, it has. I am sorry too. My father...' Snorri bit his lip to keep back his anger. 'He treats me like... like...'

Morgrim smiled reassuringly.

'Like his son, Snorri. And that means he judges you harshest of all dawi.'

'Why won't he let me show him what I am capable of? I am of the Thunderhorn clan, of Lunngrin blood. I am Whitebeard's namesake, by Grungni, and yet he favours elgi over his own kin.'

Morgrim shook his head. 'No, cousin. He does what he must to hold on to the peace he's fought so hard to create.'

'And what if I want war?' Snorri's eyes were crystal clear as he said it. 'What if what Drogor says is right and the elgi cannot be trusted? Is it not better to strike first?'

'When have you ever known a dawi to strike first, cousin? Besides, Drogor seems full of bile. Be wary that you do not heed him too much.'

'He is your friend.'

'Not one I recognise.'

'What is it you can see that he and I cannot? You have befriended this Imladrik–' Snorri tried but failed to keep the sneer from his face, '–and of all the elgi, he at least seems honourable, but the rest... this elgi woman and the other, this Salendor...'

'Imladrik is the ambassador of the elgi king, the one who resides across the sea. If anyone speaks for their race, would it not be him? Why do you see the others as enemies? They are acting no different to you, cousin. Your belligerence and mistrust is a mirror which they reflect back.'

Snorri smirked. 'Have you been talking with Morek, cousin? You sound as cryptic as the runesmith and his master.' Finishing the drakzharr, he wiped his mouth and poured another. 'A drakk slayer, one destined to be king. That is what Ranuld Silverthumb prophesied.'

'I remember,' said Morgrim.

'Only elgi ride drakk and they are supposedly our allies. How then must I go about killing one if that will always be true?'

'Nothing with prophecy is ever clear. Even Ranuld Silver-thumb doesn't know its meaning and he is runelord of Karaz-a-Karak. Do you think you can decipher it so easily?'

'Times are changing,' said Snorri, looking off into the high peaks where dark clouds had started to gather, wreathing the pinnacles of the mountains like smoke. 'I can feel it, Morg.'

There was a danger of the conversation souring again, so Morgrim sat down, clapping his cousin on the shoulder to dispel any growing tension. 'These are hard times for everyone,' he said, 'but I am still hopeful that a peaceful outcome to the troubles can be reached.'

Snorri paused in his supping, eyes darkening.

'It may already be too late for that.'

Incredulity deepened the lines in Morgrim's face. 'The High King is still in council, so how can that be so when no decision has been made?'

Snorri met his cousin's questioning gaze.

'Varnuf and Thagdor have already mustered armies. They wait in the hills and valleys not far from Karaz-a-Karak. Luftvarr too has over two thousand dawi warriors awaiting their king's return. And I reckon there will be others too.'

'And what do you plan on doing, cousin?' Morgrim had set down his tankard, the ale more bitter than it was previously.

'Several clans see as I do. Regardless of the council's decision, I am marching on the elgi. We attack now or regret our temperance at length.'

Morgrim was on his feet. In his haste he kicked over his tankard, spilling the precious brewmaster's ale. He barely spared it a glance.

'Varnuf is a rival of your father's, so too Thagdor of Zhufbar. Luftvarr is just a savage. How can you be thinking about throwing your lot in with them, possibly against the High King's wishes? It is beyond reckless, cousin.'

Snorri stood up too. 'It is reckless to do nothing, *cousin*. The elgi have enjoyed our understanding and flouted our hospitality for too long. We must show them who the true lords of the Old World are. My father *will* declare war. What other choice does he have?'

'And if he doesn't?'

Snorri's eyes were hard as granite. A harsh wind tossed the curls of his beard, making him appear even more belligerent.

'Then I shall declare it for him.'

TWENTY-FOUR

WAR COUNSEL

No decision ever made by a dwarf came easily. One that must be debated by a dynasty of dwarf kings was near impossible to reach a consensus over.

Debate raged in the Great Hall. Tempers were fraying after the news of Agrin Fireheart's death had got out. The High King had made no attempt to conceal it, but the furore it had created was increasing the number of worry lines upon his brow tenfold.

All of the kings from the brodunk were there. Thagdor had also travelled from his encampment to be at the council. Only Bagrik, who had long since returned to Karak Ungor, was absent. There were other nobles of the dwarf realms, of course: the lodewardens of Mount Gunbad and Silverspear, too busy at their mineholds; the southern kings of Drazh and Azul, too distant. Both Brugandar and Hrallson had sent emissaries for the rinkkaz, both of whom had returned to their holds and not attended the brodunk. There was no time to request the presence of them or their liege-lords. The same was also true of Karak Varn and its king, Ironhandson. Fledgling holds, those of the Black Mountains and Grey Mountains, would also not be present and so the decision whether or not to make war with the elves would be decided by but a few.

The King of Zhufbar was unperturbed by that and took his opportunity to speak eagerly.

'We must fight the elgi. What other choice do we have now?' Thagdor asked of them all. 'Dead merchants, theft and thagi across the length and breadth of the Karaz Ankor. Settlements burned, and now rhun lords slain by sorcery. What's next? Besiegement of our holds and lands? Will I wake up tomorrow from my bed to find a host of elgi outside my gates?' The King of Zhufbar paused for breath. 'I bloody won't. I'll kill the sods before it comes to that.'

Luftvarr thumped his chestplate, declaring, 'Elgi cannot be allowed to stay in the Old World. I have warriors, two thousand strong, ready with *az un klad* to kill the elgi traitors!'

The Norse king's declaration was met with rousing approval from Brynnoth who burned with retribution for the slaying of his runelord, but it was Varnuf who spoke up next.

'None of us want war with the elgi...' he began, waving off protests from the more belligerent kings, but eyeing Gotrek in particular, 'but anything less would be seen as weakness on our part now.'

Brynnoth tugged at his beard, unable to say much of anything. His eyes said enough. He wanted blood.

'We should not be hasty,' counselled Aflegard, tucking his thumbs into the jewelled braces he wore across his paunch. 'I can spare no warriors for war, and it would be unwise to attack the elgi before we know who the perpetrators of Agrin Fireheart's death were.'

Grundin stepped in to cut off some of the more pugnacious kings before they could voice further tirades. 'For once, I find myself in agreement with the ufdi king. He's thinkin' aboot his purse, though–' Grundin snapped. 'Ah, shut it ya wazzock!' before Aflegard could open his mouth to deny it. 'We all know ye trade with the elgi. Am no sayin' you're a traitor or even an elgongi, just a miserly bastard, protectin' his hoard.' The King of Karak Izril looked far from placated but Grundin ignored him so he could carry on. 'But I dinny think we should be killin' elgi fer no good cause. Ach, I know that Agrin lies cold. Dreng tromm, I know it, but I canny see how declaring war on the pointy-eared wee bastards is ginny change that.'

Brynnoth glared, unconvinced and swung his murderous gaze over to the High King, who so far had only listened.

'Trade with the elgi ends. Now,' Gotrek declared to all. 'We shut our borders to them until such a time as the fighting stops and we can return to the negotiation table.'

'Negotiation,' said Thagdor, brandishing his fist. 'I'll negotiate with the buggers at the end of my chuffing axe, I will.' He shook his head and the copper cogs attached to his beard jangled. 'There can be no treating with these elgi, none at all. I won't do it,' he said, folding his arms as if that was an end to the matter.

'See this?' Gotrek brandished a slender note in his meaty fist, the parchment too thin and smooth to have been made by a dwarf. 'Written by the hand of a prince and brought to mine by a bird,' he said. 'Can you imagine such a thing? How different are we, the elgi and the dawi?' He laughed without genuine humour. 'As mud is to the sky, I have heard said behind our backs. This Prince Imladrik is an honourable warrior and ambassador to his king. He claims another race did this.' He paused to read a word from the note, finding the pronunciation difficult. '*Druchii.*'

'What is this *druchii*?' asked Thagdor, unconvinced.

None of the kings were.

'A darkling elgi,' said Gotrek, unsure himself. 'Some murderous but distant kinsman, bent on mischief. I do not know.'

'Elgi is elgi!' snapped Grundin. 'Ach, the pointy-eared bastards will say anything to save their silk-swaddled arses.'

Mutters of approval from the other kings greeted the lord of Kadrin's outburst.

'There was betrayal here,' said Gotrek to quieten the murmurs of his vassal lords, eyeing Brynnoth in particular, 'and mark me that retribution will be meted out, but I cannot sanction war against all elgi on account of the deeds of a few, especially when there is any doubt.'

'You may not be able to stop it,' answered Varnuf dangerously.

Gotrek swung his gaze onto the King of Eight Peaks. 'Speak your mind plainly, Varnuf,' he told him, his voice level and laden with threat. His knuckles cracked as he seized the arms of his throne.

'Forces already muster north of Karaz-a-Karak.' His eyes widened and a slight smile tugged at the corners of his mouth, barely visible beneath his long beard. 'And they are making ready to march.'

'Aye,' said Aflegard, ignorant of what was happening between the other two kings, 'and I've heard talk of elgi laying siege to the skarrens too.'

'Ach, that's a lot of shite,' said Grundin, scowling at the effete dwarf. 'You would jump at your own shadow, ufdi.'

Aflegard was puffing up his chest, about to reply, when the High King bellowed.

'Silence! Both of you.' He glared, then returned his gaze to Varnuf. 'Any vassal lord of mine who marches on the elgi will be answerable to me, whether these so-called *druchii* exist or not. Is that plain enough?'

The mood around the Great Hall was fractious. The kings did not look keen to submit easily. Varnuf had read it well and chose then as his moment to act.

'Dawi lie dead and you ask us to do nothing,' he said. 'What will stopping trade achieve? How will shutting our borders and roads stop the killing? It will not. It will send a message to the elgi that we are soft, that they can kill our kith and kin, and that we will let them.' He stood up to address the gathering. 'I won't stand by and allow murder and destruction to continue in my lands, our lands, without response. *Our* lands,' he reaffirmed, nodding to all, 'not theirs, not the elgi's.' He looked at Gotrek, who glowered, and pointed a beringed finger at the High King. 'When you vanquished the urk and grobi–' Varnuf bared his teeth, revelling in the bloody memories, '–rendered them so low that they would never threaten our kingdoms again, I would have followed you into the frozen north itself. A king of kings sat upon the Throne of Power then. He did not fear war. He was stone and steel with the wisdom of Valaya upon his brow, Grimnir's strength in his arm and Grungni's dauntless courage.'

There was regret in Varnuf's eyes and hurt too, as if from a sense of betrayal. 'Now, all I see before me is a scared dawi who no longer has the stomach for a fight. What value has peace, if it is bought and paid for with our deaths?'

A shocked murmur ran around the chamber like a flame as each of the kings shuffled back. Alone of all them, Varnuf stepped forwards. He had unhitched the hammer from his belt.

Gotrek was already on his feet and had done the same. He knew what was coming and couldn't help but think back to what his son had said to him all those nights ago in this very hall.

'Speak the words then. Do it now or by Grungni I shall descend from this throne and crack open your skull, Varnuf of the Eight Peaks.'

Varnuf did not just speak the words, he snarled them. 'Let it be known that on this day, Varnuf of Eight Peaks did pronounce grudgement on Gotrek of Karaz-a-Karak.'

Aflegard stifled a gasp, but only so Grundin wouldn't clout him for it.

The others looked on solemnly, waiting for the High King's answer.

'So be it.' Gotrek unclasped the cinctures and torcs binding his beard, unfurling it like a belt of cloth as he stepped from the dais of his throne and onto the chamber floor.

Vanruf had done the same. Like Gotrek he had also removed his crown.

Both dwarfs wore no armour beyond that which was ceremonial and had no war helms either. Their hammers were not runic, but they were well fashioned from hewn stone and could crack bone easily enough.

Thurbad was not present, so Gotrek turned to another ally to officiate.

'Grundin, come forth,' he said, gripping the full thickness of his beard in one meaty hand and proffering it to the northern king. 'Bind us,' he said, staring into Varnuf's eyes as he too gave Grundin his beard.

'You two are proper wazzocks…' muttered the King of Karak Kadrin.

'Tie it tight,' said Gotrek, the leather grip of his hammer creaking in his clenched fist.

Grudgement was a solemn oath pledged by kings and lords. It was a trial by combat and could also end in death, though no dwarf would ever condone the slaying of his own. This was a matter of honour and for such things a dwarf would shed blood, even kill if necessary. By the binding of beards did both combatants commit to the fight. There could be no flight, though some had tried only to end up with their brains dashed upon rock or their necks severed by a heavy-bladed axe. Only death or the cutting of the beard bond, the *trombaraki,* could end such a duel.

'Hammers then,' muttered Varnuf, swinging a few half circles to loosen up his shoulder.

'Aye, hope you have a harder head than you look.'

'Hope yours is not as soft as your stomach,' Varnuf bit back.

Once grudgement was declared, accepted rank and station counted for naught. Two dwarfs entered this deadly compact and only one would be standing at the end of it. Alive or dead was at the victor's discretion.

Tired of talking, Gotrek nodded to Grundin. The northern king backed away and so grudgement could begin. All the kings had done the same, leaving a small arena for the two dwarfs to fight in.

'It's not too late, Gotrek. Relinquish your throne and I will take us into this war.'

'You're a damn arrogant fool, Varnuf. And there can be no backing out, not once grudgement is pronounced. But you can do me one favour...'

'Name it, your tongue may be incapable of speech after I'm done with you.'

'Stop talking and swing. I have a kingdom to protect.'

Varnuf roared, yanking on his beard and dragging Gotrek towards him. His blow glanced the shoulder of the High King, who grunted but was unbowed, planting his hammerhead into the other king's gut. Beer breath exploded violently from Varnuf's mouth and he almost retched, but managed to smack his haft against the High King's nose.

Blood streaming from his left nostril, Gotrek dropped to a crouch, bringing down with him Varnuf who hadn't properly squared his feet. Rising, Gotrek uppercutted the King of Eight Peaks in the jaw, and Varnuf snapped back immediately because of the beard binding and took a sturdy elbow smash in the cheek. He kneed Gotrek in the stomach, forcing a pained shout, but the High King had fought in many grudgements before and thumped Varnuf hard and repeatedly in the kidneys.

Thrusting his shoulder, Varnuf barged Gotrek onto his heels.

Battered, both kings tried to retreat for a breather but their beards were well tethered and they lurched back into striking range.

Haft to haft they rained a score of heavy blows on one another, hitting so hard as to create a rain of splinters. Varnuf resorted to a punishing array of overheads, which Gotrek parried with both hands braced against his hammer. He grimaced as the last breathless blow fell and he managed to lock their weapons together.

'Let me tell you something about when I purged the grobi and the urk,' Gotrek growled when the two were inches apart and face to face. Sweat was pouring off both kings, sheeting their foreheads and darkening their tunics across the chest and armpits.

'Go on,' hissed Varnuf, straining against his opponent's guard.

'Well,' said Gotrek, 'I didn't do it cleanly.'

The King of Eight Peaks's face went suddenly blank.

'Uh?'

Letting all of his resistance go, Gotrek quickly stepped aside as Varnuf's momentum took him forwards. There was just enough beard length to get behind him and swing his hammer haft into the other king's crotch.

For want of a better word, Varnuf yelped. It was so brief, so small a noise that it was missed by most of the spectators, but Gotrek heard it. Then he exhaled, a long, deep, agonised groan that echoed around the Great Hall and had every king present wincing.

'Reet in the *dongliz*,' whispered Grundin with a pained expression.

'Bugger me,' gasped Thagdor.

Most of the other kings crossed their legs.

Varnuf staggered. His eyes were watering and he tried to shuffle around to face Gotrek before collapsing. He half crouched, half slumped, held up by his bound beard.

Gotrek turned to Grundin, who was standing nearby with an axe.

'Cut it,' he said, and watched as Varnuf fell into a heap. 'Eh,' he added, giving the King of Eight Peaks a nudge so he looked up at him. 'My balls are solid rock. That's why I sit on that throne. That's why I am High King.'

Varnuf nodded meekly, and whispered, 'Tromm.'

Gotrek looked away.

'Brynnoth,' he said, singling out the lord of the Sea Hold. 'You'll have vengeance for Agrin Fireheart. I swear to Grimnir, he will be revenged, but not like this. We will find the truth of this first, if it was these druchii that the elgi prince spoke of.' Then he shifted his attention to the others, regarding each king in turn as he uttered a final edict. '*I* am High King. Gotrek Lunngrin of the Thunderhorn clan, Starbreaker and slayer of urk. My deeds eclipse all of yours combined as does my will and power. Do not defy it. Here in these lands, my word is law. Obey it or suffer my wrath. Defend your borders and sovereign territory. Close your gates and hold halls to the elgi. No trade will pass between us. All dealings with them will cease. An elgi upon our roads will be considered trespass and you may reckon that to the very hilt of our laws, but we do not march.' He shook his head slowly for emphasis. 'We do not go to war. It will ruin us. Ruin the dawi and the elgi for generations.' He let it sink in, let the silence amplify the resonance of his words before adding a final challenge.

'Will anyone else gainsay me?'

None did.

Gotrek was alone again as he went down into the grongaz. Amidst the smoke and ash, he discerned the glow of fire and heard the clamour of a single anvil. So he followed the sound. Passing through a solid wall of heat, he found Ranuld Silverthumb watching his apprentice.

'He works a master rhun,' said the ancient dwarf without looking up from his vigil.

'My son's az un klad?'

Ranuld supped on his pipe, took a deep pull. 'Aye,' he said, expelling a long plume of smoke. 'You have given your word on the elgi?' he asked after a moment or two of watching Morek's hammer fall. It was rhythmic, measured. It rang out a dulcet chorus resonant with power. The very air was charged with it. Gotrek's beard bristled, and the torcs and cinctures he had entwined in it grew warm to the touch.

'I have,' he said. 'Though it was not easy to do. My heart says fight, my head says not to. What would you do, old one?'

'I think I am not High King, therefore my opinion is moot.'

'But I value your counsel.'

'Of course you do, I am the oldest runesmith in the Karaz Ankor. My wisdom is worth more than your entire treasure vault, but it still matters not what I think. I see greed amongst our kin, an obsession towards gold gathering and hoarding. It was not always so. Once dwarfs crafted and were not so driven by the acquisition of wealth. What good is a hoard of gold to a dead king, eh?'

'Tromm, old one, but Agrin Fireheart was one of your guild. Would you not see him avenged?'

'Aye, one of the oldest, and his name shall be remembered. I mourn him but do not want revenge against all elgi for his death.' Now he met his king's gaze, showing the hard diamonds of his eyes. 'A great doom is coming, and it is this which I fear. Elgi may be a part of it, though I think it is but a small part. I foresee destinies forged in battle and a time of woes.'

Gotrek looked away, searching his heart and his conscience.

'I must do everything to prevent a war. It will destroy us both. The elgi are not as weak as some suppose them to be, though that is no reason not to fight them. They have been friends to the dawi. I will not cast that aside cheaply.'

'And we have precious few allies in the world when our enemies are amassed around us above and below. You are rare, Gotrek Starbreaker.'

Gotrek raised an eyebrow questioningly.

'We are changing, all of us, dawi and elgi both. You, like me, are hewn from elder rock. Less prone to change. I have seen another who is of similar stock. Stone and steel. He shall become king when you are dead, the slayer of the drakk.'

'I don't understand, old one.' Gotrek frowned. 'My son will be king when I am gone. It is his legacy.'

Ranuld said nothing further, and returned to his vigil.

'Will it be ready soon?' Gotrek asked, listening to the anvil, aghast at the lightning strikes cutting the air with every blow against it.

'He works the magic,' said Ranuld, gesturing proudly with his pipe. 'It will take time, but with patience anything is possible.'

'And should I show patience now?'

'That is something a king must answer for himself.'

TWENTY-FIVE

THE KING OF ELVES

Oeragor was a fading memory, as was his urgent flight across the Great Ocean, through the storms and on to the verdant pastures of his home. His army had gone ahead, led by the dragons but ensconced in a great fleet of elven galleons. Alone, it had been a hard journey for the prince through a succession of unearthly storms. Something unnatural persisted about the blackened clouds and the roar of the wind. He had hoped to find his warriors again, catch up to them before they reached home but the storm was all consuming. Though it was difficult to tell for certain, shadows lurked within those clouds. Bestial faces, the visages of the daemonic and the monstrous, loomed over Imladrik during his flight. They mocked and cajoled, raged and encouraged. The elf prince shut his eyes and tried to close off the rest of his senses to them.

More than once, Imladrik had faltered until a growl from Draukhain steeled him against the voices. He chanted the names of Isha, Asuryan, Kurnous, invoking the blessings of the elven gods to ward him against the unnatural tempest that had set about them.

It grew angry, and Imladrik had been forced below the clouds to keep from being struck by lightning or ripped out of the saddle by hurricane winds. He reached the borders of the island with his nerves hanging by a thread. Never had he undertaken such a perilous journey, but after almost two weeks he had reached his ancestral lands alive and intact. And like a dream, the memory of the faces in the storm faded to nothing but a wisp of remembrance that Imladrik would only recall in his deepest nightmares.

A thick bank of cloud parted to reveal an island of verdant pastures, soaring mountains and crystalline rivers. Ports and fleets of ships resolved through the mist, together with sprawling forests and glittering towers. It shimmered, like an image half seen through a haze of heat, though the air was cool and refreshing. Imladrik breathed deep.

At last, he was home.

Ulthuan.

It had been years since he had last set foot upon the magical isle.

He had travelled south borne by Draukhain, across the harbours of Cothique where doughty merchantmen and sailors aboard catamarans pointed up at the sky at the passing of the dragon. From there Imladrik went east, skirting the Chracian mountains and letting Draukhain have his head amidst the cloud-wreathed peaks. Though he couldn't see them from so high up, he knew the vigilant woodsmen of that land would be abroad in the dense forests and narrow passes through the cliffs, ever watchful for invasion.

Imladrik's thoughts had strayed to Liandra and he had to banish them at once. His mind also wandered back to the carrier-hawk, soaring into the mountain fastness of the dwarfs, bringing his message to the High King. He hoped the words would hold some meaning, that a chance yet remained to avert a war. If it brought the dwarfs to the negotiating table then that at least would be something. Perhaps if they were willing to treat, he might be allowed to return to the Old World again and heal two rifts at once.

First he flew over the Phoenix Gate, the great bastion wall that sat on the borders of Chrace and Avelorn, its purpose to defend against invasion from the north across the hills of Nagarythe. It was a monolithic structure of pale stone and encrusted with jewels. The gilded image of the rising phoenix was emblazoned upon its vast and towering gate, a bulwark against attack. Silent guardians patrolled its battlements, grim-faced and clutching their halberds with fierce intent. Its neighbour, the Dragon Gate, was equally magnificent. Bordering Avelorn and Nagarythe, it was well garrisoned by spearmen and archers. The buttressed walls were scaled in keeping with its draconian aesthetic and the effigy of a soaring drake of Caledor was engraved upon the gate itself.

Even seen from high above, the gates were impressive. To Imladrik they looked nigh-on impregnable, which was just as well given the enemy they had been erected to repel. Many were the battles fought against the dark elves beyond their borders.

Once across the Phoenix and Dragon Gates, Imladrik was reunited with his army as he had set down on the plains of Ellyrion where his host were making ready for the next stage of their journey. He didn't stay, for he had business elsewhere, but instead took a steed from one of the horsemasters who had been there to receive him and rode back to the borders of Nagarythe and Avelorn until he reached his destination. During that time he was regaled with familiar sights, sounds and smells, a cavalcade of sensations that whispered 'home'. Except for Imladrik, this was no longer a place he understood.

This was no homecoming for the prince, it was more like a trial.

Dark arbours drenched in shadows gave way to thicker brush, thorny branched pines and an altogether denser arboreal gloom. These were wild lands, heavily forested, and beasts lurked in the mountains brooding overhead. A small war party moved through the thickening forest, fleet of foot and lightly armoured but wary.

A tall warrior dressed in tan and crimson led the modest group. Leather-clad, he carried a long bow and had a quiver half full of arrows strapped to his back. He was lithe, with almond-shaped eyes and a mane of golden hair tightly bound in a ponytail behind his neck.

Sighting prey, the warrior stopped and signalled silently to his companions to do the same. One was a burly-looking woodsman with thick furs draped over his back. He had drawn a hunting knife and a large double-bladed axe sat in a sheath between his shoulders, haft sticking up. The other laboured under a red hauberk, not as used to the forest as the other two. A short sword slapped against his thigh and three more quivers full of arrows were slung over his shoulder. Despite his shorn hair, which was night black, he was sheened with sweat.

'I see you...' whispered the leader, silently drawing an arrow and nocking it to his bow in a single seamless motion.

Scenting danger, the great stag realised it was being stalked. Raising its mighty antlered head, it snorted the air and the muscles bunched in its legs as it made to flee.

The swan-feathered shaft made almost no sound as it was released into the air. It sped swiftly in a white blur, dagger sharp and lightning fast. It pierced the great stag's heart, killing it instantly.

'Ha!' King Caledor looked pleased with his kill. A fine mist was coming off the beast, a fever sweat that was fading to nothing as the heat of its body expired.

'Flense it, woodsman,' he said to the fur-clad brute, who nodded. 'I want fur, flesh and meat. Spare nothing except for the head, which I shall take as a trophy.'

'See, Hulviar,' said Caledor to the other elf, gesturing to the woodsman who was quickly about his task. 'Chracians do have their uses.'

'Ever since your father's time, they have been the protectors of the king, my liege.'

'Yes, the White Lions,' Caledor sneered, 'but *he* is just some peasant.'

If the Chracian heard his noble lord, he was wise enough not to show it.

'How many is that today?' Caledor asked.

'Seven, my liege. You have denuded this part of the forest.'

Caledor's eyes narrowed and he smiled self-indulgently. 'Indeed, I have.'

The sound of branches snapping underfoot had the king raise his bow again, and Hulviar draw his sword.

'Who goes there?' demanded the retainer.

The woodsman had work to do, and continued with it. Besides, he had been aware of the intruder several minutes ago and knew it was no threat.

'Stand down, Hulviar. I am no great stag to be skewered by my brother's wayward arrow,' came a voice from the gloom.

Another warrior emerged into the clearing where the woodsman was butchering the dead stag.

'Khalnor,' said the warrior, who received a warm nod of greeting from the Chracian.

The king smiled so broadly that it filled his face, if not quite his eyes.

'Never forget a name, do you, little brother?' Handing the long bow to Hulviar, Caledor went over to the warrior and embraced him.

'A lesson you would benefit from learning,' he chastised mildly.

Caledor whispered, 'I can always call them peasant, can I not, Imladrik?'

There was amusement in the king's face that Imladrik hoped wasn't genuine.

'I have returned, brother.'

'For which you have my thanks.' Caledor let him go, favouring his brother with another half-smile, before walking from the clearing.

Imladrik followed. He was still clad in his dragon armour, though he'd removed the greaves and wore only the cuirass and vambraces.

'When I received your missive, I was under the impression that the skirmishes had escalated to something more serious and yet here you are... hunting.'

'It is good sport during this part of the season, brother, and as you can see...' Parting the thick bracken, Caledor stepped into another clearing where several more high elves pored over a map stretched across a white table. It sat beneath a tented pavilion where servants decanted wine and served silver platters of truffles. 'My advisors keep me well apprised.'

Imladrik joined them at once as Caledor slumped upon a plush couch to remove his boots and hunting apparel.

He nodded to the assembled lordlings, greeting them all by name. To a man, they responded in kind, showing Imladrik the same amount of deference as their King.

Though he thought he had kept it hidden, the prince noticed his brother's scowl at the way the other nobles and warriors treated him. Imladrik was beloved.

'He seeks inroads through the Caledorian Mountains and Ellyrion,' he observed, fathoming the situation instantly without need of assistance from any of his brother's advisors.

'Lord Athinol requires reinforcement,' said Caledor idly. 'More swords and spears to watch the passes. Every day more Naggarothi scum penetrate our watchtowers.'

'I am dismayed to hear that,' Imladrik said honestly, 'but unfortunately I bring further bad tidings.'

Caledor frowned, as if sensing his hunting trip was about to be curtailed.

'Relations with the dwarfs have soured.' Imladrik looked up from the map to regard his brother, who was sipping from a silver chalice.

'Hardly a surprise. What of it?'

It took all of Imladrik's composure to bite back his exasperation. 'Our colonies in the Old World are in danger. There have been murders, I believe by druchii, designed to foment ill will between our two races.'

Caledor sat up, but held on to his wine.

'Again, I cannot see how this is of import to Ulthuan. We have our own problems to deal with.'

'There are over eighty thousand elves in the dwarf realm, with more arriving every day. Trade has been completely suspended by their High King.'

'And still I do not see the imperative here,' said Caledor. 'Malekith has been beaten. Sorely. But he is not vanquished. Did you not hear what I said about our borders, brother?'

'I did hear it, but I am talking about the prospect of a full scale war on foreign soil.'

'With the mud-dwellers,' Caledor laughed, loudly and derisively. 'Let them return to their holes and tunnels. Our lands here in Ulthuan are threatened and I have need of generals to protect them.' He nodded to Imladrik. '*You*, dear brother.'

'I do not think this problem should be ignored.'

Caledor rose to his feet, shedding the leather armour for a close-fitting tunic of blue velvet. 'And so why did you return if matters are so dire?'

Though he found it hard to admit, Imladrik was jaded. He thought his years spent in the Old World, living amongst and trading with the dwarfs, had fostered a culture of understanding. That assumption had been dashed when the High King had refused his aid, expelled the elves from his lands and shut his gates.

'My presence there was not helping the situation.' It was a half-truth.

Caledor seemed not to notice or care.

'Let the colonies look after themselves. We have other vassals better suited to that task, do we not?

'There is Lord Salendor of Athel Maraya and Lady Athinol of Kor Vanaeth, amongst others. In them I pledge my trust and confidence, but they do not share my temperance.'

At this remark, Caledor smirked. 'And how is the Caledorian princess?'

'Well, but belligerent as ever.'

'Much like her father then,' Caledor added by way of an aside. 'Tell me, brother, have you seen your wife or have you yet to divest yourself of your army?'

'Yethanial awaits me in Cothique.'

Swilling the last of his wine around the chalice, Caledor tried to appear nonchalant. 'How many did you bring back with you, brother?'

'Ten thousand warriors and a head of fifty dragons,' Imladrik stated flatly.

'Quite a host. And Oeragor, it flourishes?'

'Less well without my presence, but yes.'

'A pity, but the needs of Ulthuan must come first.'

'Of course, brother.'

'What is it they call you again?' Caledor asked, feigning interest in his empty chalice. 'Ah yes, that was it... *Master of Dragons*. Such a curious little honorific and one I have never really understood.'

'It's ceremonial, and a tad archaic. I am the last Master of Dragons.'

Caledor sniffed, mildly amused. 'And they should be mastered, shouldn't they?'

'Our bond with the drakes is a harmonious one, forged of mutual respect.'

'Indeed,' Caledor replied, though he did not sound convinced. His disdain for dragons was well known, his opinion of their servitude to the elves a matter of some consternation amongst the older drakes. Fortunately, it was also one that had yet to be debated.

Imladrik got the sense that Caledor had discovered what he needed to and was rapidly losing interest in their conversation. This was confirmed when he changed subject.

'I want to show you something, Imladrik,' said Caledor, turning his attention to his retainers. 'Hulviar.'

The retainer nodded, evidently prepared for his king's theatrics as he tossed a scabbarded blade which Caledor caught and drew with ease.

'It's a sword, brother,' observed Imladrik, nonplussed.

Caledor showed him the edge, the runes upon the flat of the blade and how it shone in the dappled sunlight coming through the forest canopy overhead.

'Sapherian steel,' he said. 'As light as goose down but deadlier than a Chracian's axe blade. I had it made.'

Caledor turned the weapon in a series of intricate moves, rolling it over in half-swings and switching from hand to hand in a dazzling, but vainglorious display of swordsmanship.

'Impressive,' said Imladrik without much enthusiasm. 'You dropped your scabbard,' he added, stooping to pick up the scabbard from where Caledor had carelessly discarded it.

The king took it and sheathed the sword, obviously upset with his brother's apathy.

'You have had a long journey,' he said, 'and must be tired, which explains your mood, Imladrik. Return to Cothique, see your wife and then come to Lothern and my court. We have much to discuss.' He was already turning his back when he added, 'You have six days.'

Imladrik bowed, albeit curtly and lacking in deference. His brother the king had measured the threat he posed to his rule and had positioned him here to neutralise it. Imladrik cared not for the trappings of rulership. He didn't lust for power or standing and so was happy to oblige.

Mounting his horse at the edge of the deeper forest, his thoughts were troubled nonetheless, but not by that. The maps and charts strewn upon the war table showed the dark elves had made extensive inroads into Ulthuan.

Attacks were obviously increasing and together with that, he suspected, was dark elf involvement in the Old World. Imladrik wondered just how spent a force Malekith really was.

A war with the dwarfs would decimate the high elves, take them to the brink of destruction. After that, it wouldn't take much to push them over the edge and into oblivion.

TWENTY-SIX

THE GATHERING THRONG

A vast force of dwarf warriors had gathered on the shores of the Black Water.

Early morning brought with it a dense fog that rolled off the mirror-dark sheen of the lake-filled crater in a grey pall. Cloth banners, topped by icons of bronze and copper, fluttered in the wind. The standards of the brotherhoods were metal only, forged from gold and silver, and sat apart from the clans. The debris of over two hundred extinguished campfires littered the high-sided gorge where the dwarfs had sung songs, supped ale and eaten roast beef and pork, elk and goat the night before. What began as bawdy drinking ditties, the lyrical mottos of the clans and the sombre litanies of the brotherhoods, became a rousing war chant that disturbed crag eagles from their eyries and sent greenskins for miles around scampering in fear of death.

Khazuk! was the cry that pealed across the Black Water, in the shadow of Zhufbar where fifteen thousand warriors had assembled. Several hours later with the sun just reaching up over the peaks, the echo of their belligerence had still to fade.

War was coming to the elves, and the dwarfs would bring it to them.

They merely awaited the order of their general to march.

Snorri paced the edge of the lake, fancying he could discern the shadow of bestial creatures moving languidly in its fathomless depths. He was arrayed in his full war panoply, a winged helm fastened to his belt by its chinstrap, and chuntered loudly.

Most of the other dwarfs couldn't hear him. They were too busy making preparations themselves, sharpening axes, tightening the bindings on hammers, fastening armour plates and tying off vambraces. Colours were unfurled, icons presented to the sky, horns and drums beat in a warm-up staccato. The clan warriors jostled and joked; but the brotherhoods, the longbeards and ironbreakers, the hearthguard and runesmiths, wore grim faces, for they all knew what they were about to undertake.

So did Snorri, and it was this thought as well as respect for his father that warred within him.

'They gave us no choice,' said a voice from behind him.

Snorri started. He had thought he was alone.

'Drogor...' he said, as if just speaking the dwarf's name made him weary.

'But,' said Drogor, coming closer, 'if you were to halt the march, no one would brand you a coward. You were merely fulfilling the wishes of your father and High King.'

'I am not my father's vassal lord, for him to command,' Snorri snapped. 'I have a destiny too.'

'A great one,' Drogor conceded, bowing his head in a gesture of contrition. 'I meant no offence, my prince, only that you should not feel forced into action.'

'We will march, by Grimnir,' Snorri scowled. 'This has gone on long enough. If my father lacks the courage to do something then I, as heir of Karaz-a-Karak, will.'

'Justly spoken, my prince.'

Snorri frowned. 'Drogor, please. To you I am Snorri, not "my prince".'

Drogor bowed again as if at court. 'As you wish, Snorri.' He smiled. 'Shall I see to the preparations of the warriors?'

Snorri nodded. 'Yes, do it. Begin the muster and send runners to Thagdor and Brynnoth, even Luftvarr. I want to speak with all three before we leave Black Water.'

'As you wish.'

Drogor departed just as another dwarf was coming into view, emerging through the lake fog which was thick as pitch.

Morgrim gestured to Snorri's winged war helm. 'Didn't think you needed one.'

'I like the wings. Makes me look important,' Snorri replied, grinning. 'Or perhaps my head has grown soft, cousin.'

'Perhaps it has,' said Morgrim, glaring after the Karak Zorn dwarf. He seemed to blend with the mist, becoming spectral until he was lost from sight completely. 'I hope he is not giving you more bad counsel.'

'He is a dutiful thane and valuable advisor,' Snorri replied with a little bite to his tone.

'*Thane* is it now?'

It had been several weeks since the High King's pronouncement that all trade would be suspended with elves. Armies were mustering too, and the weapon shops of all the holds toiled day and night churning out armour and war engines for what Gotrek hoped would be a stockpile of materiel he would never need to call upon. Short of declaring outright war, it was as far as the High King could go to assert his authority as well as present a clear warning to the elves. His edict had been welcome news, but for many did not go nearly far enough. Snorri counted himself amongst that number and in Drogor found an ally more willing to listen to his concerns than his peace-favouring cousin. Nonetheless, he had wanted Morgrim by his side in this and so here they were, together, if at odds with one another.

'Aye, thane. He has no hold, no clan. I will make him a clan lord of Karaz-a-Karak in recognition for his deeds and loyalty. It is only honourable and right.'

'Then why do you look so troubled, cousin?'

'Because I am about to go to war against the wishes of the High King and am painfully lacking in warriors.'

'You have over fifteen thousand axes, if the loremaster's tallying is accurate.'

'Aye, but none from Eight Peaks and no word from King Varnuf.'

'He was at the council of kings with your father.'

'And, no doubt, my father has convinced him it was not in his best interests to support me. Musters take time, all dawi know that, but three weeks is enough to send a missive or a war party.'

'Perhaps he saw sense as you should do.'

Snorri roared, 'What, to sit on my arse as elgi kill kith and kin with impunity?' Some of the dwarfs nearby looked up as the shout resonated around the gorge, and the prince lowered his voice. 'I can be idle no longer. I said if my father did not declare war then I would. Once it's begun, he will see I was right and have no choice but to call the clans to battle. I know it.'

'I hope you are right.'

'If you do not believe in this then why are you here, Morg?'

Morgrim was already turning his back, disgusted by what he saw as warmongering for its own sake. Snorri wanted to prove his worth and the only way he could see of doing that was to wilfully go against his father and pick a fight with the elves.

Snorri called after his cousin. 'Well? If you don't want a fight then why come here bearing az un klad, eh? Why are you here, Morg?'

'To stop you from getting yourself killed, you ufdi.'

He walked away and Snorri, though he wanted to apologise, to take back his words, could only watch.

With one last look at the stygian depths of the Black Water and the endless darkness within, he went to meet the kings. Heart-sore and weary beyond fatigue, his armour had never felt so heavy.

He did not want to defy his father but what choice did he have? Destiny, his destiny, was in the balance. Snorri *would* be king and this would cement his legacy. Gotrek had purged the greenskins, he would kill the elves.

Two kings with their ceremonial hearthguard awaited Snorri beyond the mist-shrouded shores of Black Water. Brynnoth of Barak Varr was bedecked in scaled armour of sea green. A teal leather cloak, emblazoned with images of mermen and other sea beasts, was cinched to his shoulders by a pair of kraken-headed pauldrons. His war helm bore a nose guard studded with emeralds and carried an effigy of a sea dragon as its crest. Snug in its belt loop was a broad-bladed axe with a toothed edge like the fangs of some leviathan.

Thagdor's armour was less ostentatious. He favoured a simple bronze breastplate over gilded chainmail. His vambraces were leather and sewn with the images of hammers. An open helmet with a slide-down faceplate sat on the table beside him and his hammer was strapped to his back, the haft jutting out from behind a cloak of purple velvet.

From where he'd been stooping over the table, Brynnoth looked up. He scratched the hollow under his eyepatch as Snorri approached.

'My prince,' he said, sketching a short bow.

Thagdor did the same, but was less deferential to the young heir of Karaz-a-Karak.

'So when are we getting bloody going then?' he asked. 'My boots are rough as a troll's arse I've been standing around that chuffing long.' Thagdor thumbed over his shoulder to where a large cohort of dwarfs was gathering. 'I've got nigh on seven thousand beards mustered behind me, lad, and they want a bloody good scrap.'

The sun had risen higher in the last few minutes and was slowly burning away the morning mist, revealing the full glory of the dwarf throng.

Thagdor had brought the bulk of the army and a great many siege engines, but then they were practically on the doorstep of Zhufbar. It was mainly clan dwarfs and miners, but with a strong cohort of hearthguard. Sailed up from the Sea Hold across the Skull River were another five thousand dwarfs of King Brynnoth's throng, many of which were longbeards roused to battle by the tragic death of Agrin Fireheart. The rest came from Luftvarr, two thousand Norse dwarfs who just wanted a decent fight, and the clans that were loyal to Snorri in Everpeak. Others had pledged their allegiance to his cause too. Hrekki Ironhandson of Karak Varn and dwarf throngs from Karak Hirn were to meet them at the edge of Black Fire Pass.

The route was inked out on the parchment map lying on the table. South across the fringe of the mountains, along the hills and rocky tors until reaching the mouth of the pass. From there, with some twenty thousand dwarfs in tow, north-west to the first elven city of Kor Vanaeth. Only by attacking a settle-ment of some significance would the dwarfs make clear the elves were no longer welcome in the Old World. Snorri meant to sack Kor Vanaeth, to raze it to the ground utterly. It was a long march, one that would take several weeks with mules and trappings, but the prince was patient. He had waited this long for his father to act and been content to watch as the High King did nothing. Now, he would show his mettle and seize the destiny that had been foretold to him by Ranuld Silverthumb.

'We are ready,' he said huskily. It was no small thing to defy his father, but Snorri kept telling himself the dishonour of it was outweighed by the indignity of standing by and letting elves kill dwarfs without retribution.

Brynnoth gripped the young prince's hand. There were tears in the dwarf king's eye. Salt stained his beard and a briny odour emanated off his clothes.

'Thank you, lad,' he whispered. There was fire in Brynnoth's gaze too, fuelling his desire for vengeance at Agrin's death.

Nodding, Snorri slipped free of the sea king's hand and signalled the call to march.

Drums and horns echoed around the gorge, followed by the raucous clanking of armoured dwarfs moving into position.

To the outsider dwarfs might appear stunted and slow, but when properly motivated they are quick and direct. Such a fact had often caused their enemies to underestimate them, and believe them cumbersome creatures when the opposite was true.

'Luftvarr of Kraka Drak,' Snorri called, seeing the Norse dwarf king who looked up at the prince from brawling with his warriors. 'Do you stand with me?'

Brandishing his axe into the sky, Luftvarr roared and his huscarls roared with him, a belligerent chorus that shook the earth from the surrounding mountains.

'Khazuk!' they cried as one, before the king silenced them to speak. 'Luftvarr think this will be a mighty runk... Ha, ha!' His warriors laughed with him and kept going until they were ranked up in the order of march.

'I hope you know what you're doing trusting to those savages,' muttered Brynnoth.

'I can heel them easily enough,' said Snorri, eyeing the berserkers with a wary look. 'Luftvarr just wants to kill elgi, we can all empathise with that.' He tromped off to join the Everpeak dwarfs at the head of the army. Who he saw there when he reached them was unexpected.

Standing by Morgrim's side, dressed in a travelling cloak and wearing a light suit of mail, was Elmendrin Grimbok.

'Come to wish us on our way, priestess?' Snorri uttered coldly, and tried to deny the heavy beating of his heart at the sight of the dwarf maiden. 'War is no place for rinns,' he said, 'despite the warriors you have brought with you.' A small band of ironbreakers, clad in gromril with their faceplates down, stood back from the maiden, together with two more priestesses from the temple. Snorri glared at Morgrim before she could answer. 'I assume you are responsible for this?'

Elmendrin stepped in front of him.

'He merely told me where you would be mustering. I chose to come here of my own accord. The warriors are for the protection of my sisters who insisted on accompanying me.'

'What would your brother say, I wonder?' Though he tried, Snorri could not help it sounding petulant.

'Since he is with your father, trying to find a way to maintain peace with the elgi, I would not know.' She paused, searching for some mote of conscience in the prince's eyes. 'I would speak with you, Snorri Lunngrin.'

'It's Halfhand.' He brandished the gauntlet. 'And I am here,' said the prince, 'so speak. Though be quick, I have an army to lead.'

'So I can see.' She scowled disdainfully, then gestured to where one of the encampment tents had yet to be taken down. 'I would prefer to talk alone.'

Snorri smirked. 'Finally want to get me alone do y–'

'Stop it!' Elmendrin snapped, and there was venom in her eyes that told Snorri his remark had been an unworthy one. 'You are acting like a wanaz.'

He capitulated at once. 'Tromm, I'm sorry. We can talk, but I cannot linger.'

'That's all I ask,' she said, and headed for the tent.

Snorri turned to his cousin. 'Morg...'

'I'll keep them here until you return,' he said, gripping Snorri's shoulder before he left. 'Listen to her. Please.'

Snorri nodded. He caught Drogor's gaze as he went after Elmendrin – he was standing with the Everpeak dwarfs and had an intensity about him that disquieted the prince. Shrugging off a profound sense of urging to expel the priestess, he followed her into the tent.

She had her back to him as he entered the narrow angular chamber. It was gloomy inside and the canvas reeked of sweat and stale beer. Snorri found it embarrassing that she should have to endure this, and felt suddenly crude and ungainly in his armour.

'I would offer you something, but the victuallers have packed it all up. Not even a crumb of stonebread remains.'

'We've recently eaten. It's fine.' She was wringing her hands, clearly nervous.

Snorri wanted to go to her, but knew it was not his place.

'It has been a while since I last saw you,' he ventured awkwardly.

'You had lost some fingers to a rat, if I remember.'

Snorri looked to his gauntlet, tucking it behind his back as Elmendrin turned around to face him.

'It was a *big* rat,' he said, frowning.

She smiled, but all too briefly and all too sadly for it to warm the prince.

'I thought... I mean, I saw you at the brodunk, did I not?' he asked.

'Yes, you did. I was in the healing tent, tending to the wounded. You seemed to be on better terms with your father then.'

Snorri's face darkened and he half turned away. 'My father doesn't know me. He sees only a petulant son, who must be kept in his place.'

'He sees what you show him,' said Elmendrin.

The scathing glance Snorri was about to give her faded when he realised she wasn't remonstrating with him.

'He loves you, Snorri,' she told him.

Snorri sagged, and his pauldrons clanked dully against his breastplate.

'And I him.'

'Then don't be so pig-headed, you stubborn, obstinate fool. Look beyond your own selfishness and see what this will mean. If you make war on the elgi, you will invite devastation on us all and estrange your father into the bargain. Is that what you want? Is that why you are here?'

'It's my destiny.'

'To kill wantonly to satisfy your need to be honoured by your father? Do you think he will clap you on the back and tell you how proud he is of you for defying his will? He will not respect you for this. He will despise you for it. So will I,' she whispered.

Snorri had no answer. In his heart, he thought what he was doing was right. Some small part of him knew it was to serve selfish needs, but he assuaged that guilt with the certain conviction that he was acting on behalf of the greater good. Confronted by the hard truths from Elmendrin, he wasn't so sure.

'Hearth and hold, oath and honour,' she asked. 'Whatever happened to that?'

'Wrath and ruin, that is what we must do in times of war.'

'We aren't at war. Not yet.'

'Not yet, indeed.' Snorri started pacing, exasperated but also conflicted. Elmendrin had a way of clearing his thoughts, easing away the fug of doubt and guilt that fostered his belligerence. 'What would you have me do?' he asked, pointing to the entrance of the tent. 'Out there, fifteen thousand dawi await my command. At Black Fire Pass another five thousand will join us. It is too far gone to turn back now. I cannot.'

'You are the prince of Karaz-a-Karak, what can *you* not do?' She came over to him, touched her fingers to his arm, and drew the gauntleted hand out of hiding from behind Snorri's back. 'Losing a few fingers is one thing, but the consequences of a reckless decision here are far worse. Stay your armies. Show what kind of a king you will be, one who calls for calm when all others are losing their heads, one who is not afraid to take the hard path if it is the best of all roads, a king who puts his people before himself.'

Though Elmendrin was proud, by far the proudest dwarf woman he had ever known, Snorri saw the tears in her eyes and knew she was pleading with him. He willed her not to get onto her knees. He didn't want that.

In the end he sighed. 'Brynnoth will not be pleased, nor Luftvarr.'

Morgrim was waiting at the entrance to the tent. Evidently, the army was waiting but could do so no more. He had overhead the last part.

'I'll tell them both,' he said.

'No, Morg, it should fall to me.'

Snorri was on his way out when he turned back to Elmendrin.

'Though I sheathe my axe today, war *is* coming. My father knows it too, though he would deny it to all but his own heart. Peace cannot endure, but I won't break it. Not yet.'

Then he left and so did Morgrim, who gave a nod to the priestess, left alone in the gloom.

'Thank you, cousin,' said Morgrim, walking by Snorri's side as he went to address the throng. 'For heeding her, I mean.'

'It will do no good,' said the prince. 'None of this will. I meant what I said, war will come. Dawi and elgi are too different, it's only a matter of time before we start killing each other for real.'

'Then why disband the army if that's what you believe?'

'Because she asked me to, and I'm not disbanding us.'

'What then?'

'There is a fortress at Black Fire Pass, large enough to hold a force this size. I plan to garrison it and set up pickets along the mountains.'

Morgrim stopped him. 'You're waiting, aren't you?'

'Isn't that what we dawi do best?'

'Do you really think there can be no peace between our races?'

Snorri favoured his cousin with a stern glance. 'None.'

'And what of the kings? They have holds and will not wait for war to begin.'

'None will march without me. Even Luftvarr is not so bold as to go against my father without the presence of his son. Thagdor will return to Zhufbar, and Brynnoth to Barak Varr. But both will leave warriors in my charge. The Norse will probably go back to Kraka Drak whilst the way remains open, but I'd prefer to be without the savages anyway. The rest will remain here for as long as it takes, a bulwark against further elgi aggression.'

'So this is a shield wall now, is it? One to keep the elgi out.'

'We'll lock our shields for now, but we will become a hammer when needed and mark me, cousin, it *will* be needed. The only difference now is that when I do eventually march it will be at the head of a much larger throng. Word will be sent to the lesser mountains and when my father sees how many have come to my banner, he will have no choice but to throw in with me.'

They had reached the army, fifteen thousand dwarfs waiting silently for their prince to lead them. Even the Norse were quiet but the scowl on King Luftvarr's face suggested he suspected all was not as it had been before the prince had entered the tent.

An oath stone was embedded in the earth in front of the throng, set there by Snorri's hearthguard. These warriors were as dour as any of Thurbad's praetorians but they believed that war was the only answer to the elves and had thrown in with the young prince. Snorri nodded grimly to them as they parted their armoured ranks for him. Just before he climbed the oath stone, he saw Elmendrin's silent departure back towards Everpeak. He watched her for a few moments but she didn't look back, not once. In her absence he felt his anger returning, and found he was drawn to Drogor who waited in the front rank of the Everpeak dwarfs.

'While our axes remain clean, there is still hope for peace,' said Morgrim, wrestling Snorri from the other dwarf's gaze.

Snorri looked down on him before he addressed the army, clutching in his gauntleted fist a large speaking horn handed to him by one of the hearthguard.

'Peace died in that gorge, cousin. It died when Agrin Fireheart was murdered. A wall of shields has risen up in answer. With you by my side or not, Morg, I shall kill the elgi and drive them from the Old World. Whether now or in ten years, war is coming. And I will be ready for when it does.'

TWENTY-SEVEN

GOLD AND GRUDGES

There was a glint in the eye of the hill dwarf king that only came upon him when he was in his counting house surrounded by his most precious possessions. Of late, they had diminished and it was for this that he scolded his goldmasters.

'Every year for the last eight my hoard has lessened.' Grum cast around, gesturing to the piles of treasure, the ingots, doubloons, crowns, pieces, gemstones, bracelets, torcs, mitres and chains that festooned his counting house. Sets of scales were abundant, all carefully balanced and their amounts meticulously logged in stacks of leather-bound volumes that lined the bookcases on the walls. They were hard to see, not just because vast mounds of accumulated treasure obscured them but because of the sheen that was emanating from all the gold. It hurt the eyes to look upon it, though Grum's were bird-like and narrow as if the mammonistic king was well used to the sight and had evolved to compensate for it.

Uncharacteristically, his eyes were wide at that moment as he thrashed in a fit of conniption.

'It should accrue, not diminish!' He thumped the arm of his throne with a gnarled, bony fist. 'Explain yourselves! Why aren't you bringing more treasure to my coffers? Why aren't I getting any richer? Eh?'

There was a fever in the king's expression and the chief of his goldmasters balked before it as he made his excuses.

'Since the High King of Karaz-a-Karak suspended all trade with the elgi–' He didn't even get chance to finish his sentence before Grum interrupted with another bout of apoplexy.

'*I* am High King of this city, of the skarrens. I care not for the whims of Gotrek bloody Lunngrin. He is not my lord and master. Let him be concerned with the mountain. If he has taken umbrage with the elgi then that is his business. Our gates remain open to their gold and business.'

In his anger, Grum knocked over a pile of coins with his kicking leg and scattered them across the floor. His gaze followed them for several moments, drawn to the tinkling, glittering pieces inexorably. A little patch of white froth bubbled at the corner of his lip.

'Well then?' he raged, as if coming out of a trance and remembering where he was and the matter at hand.

'Our gates have remained open, High King,' said another of the goldmasters, an enthusiastic understudy wanting to curry favour, 'and we continue to extend invitation to elgi traders to treat with us but they do not wish to trespass onto dawi lands for fear of persecution. The Hi-, er... *King* of Karaz-a-Karak has petitioned greater and greater numbers of rangers and reckoners to patrol dawi borders. Travel is almost impossible.'

'Enough!' snapped Grum, staggering to his feet to dismiss the ineffectual goldmasters. 'Get out, all of you! Especially you,' he added, jabbing his finger at the one who had seemingly lost his tongue. 'Bloody mute! Out!'

Bowing profusely, the three goldmasters backed away and out of the counting house.

'Idiots,' hissed Grum before they were gone, stacking coins as the old familiar veneer slid across his face. Eyes beginning to glaze over, a dumb smile pulling at the corners of his mouth, he almost didn't hear Rundin speaking.

'...are right, my king,' he was saying.

'Uh? What?' Grum asked, slightly dazed. When his gaze fell on his champion and protector, he became more lucid. 'Who are right?'

Rundin was standing by his master's side, arms folded, his expression neutral at all times.

'Your goldmasters, my king. All of the major roads are closed to trade, especially to elgi. What little gold is coming in to Kazad Kro is from the Vaults and the Grey Mountains, but that is not enough to sustain previous yields.'

Grum slapped a page of his ledger, leaving a greasy palm print on the parchment. Scrawled Klinkerhun daubed every leaf in a feverish script.

'I can see that, Rundin. The numbers never lie.' He carried on counting, mumbling, 'Gotrek is a selfish wazzock.'

'My king...' Rundin ventured after a minute of listening to his liege-lord lay one coin atop another.

'There is more?' asked Grum, agitated, licking his bottom lip as he slowly created a gleaming tower of stacked coins.

Rundin nodded. 'Cessation of trade with the elgi these past eight years is because of a much larger problem.'

'I fail to see any larger problem than that which my goldmasters have already presented.' Once again, he returned to his counting.

'War, my king. There is talk of war with the elves.'

Grum's face screwed up like an oily rag. 'Over what, some petty trade disputes? Bah! Gotrek must have been supping from the dragon.'

'No, my king.' Throughout the exchange Rundin's tone had never wavered from stolid and serious, but now he showed his incredulity at just how little his liege-lord seemed to be aware of the greater world. 'Murder and death, sabotage and destruction. The burning of Zakbar Varf was just the beginning. Kazad Mingol bore witness to a skirmish between a band of its rangers and elgi warriors. No fewer than sixteen shipments from Kagaz Thar have gone missing in the last three months alone. Grudges longer than the gilded road running through our city litter our *dammaz kron* and continue to accumulate. And that is not to mention the grievances of our mountain kin.'

'No,' Grum uttered flatly.

'No?'

'I will not have war. It is bad for business.' He gestured to the massive hoard of treasure in his counting house. 'See how it already hurts my coffers? I won't countenance it. War is expensive. It means shields and armour, and axes, provisions. If the elgi are as belligerent as you say then we will shut our gates to all and wait out Gotrek's little feud.'

'I fear it has gone beyond that, my king. We may have no–'

Grum slammed his fist down on the arm of his throne and glared at his champion.

'Are you determined to defy me, Rundin?'

'I would never do that, my king, but if Gotrek Starbreaker declares war upon the elgi then we must, as dawi, answer.'

'Must... *must!* I am High King and shall not bow to him. I do not recognise his authority. Let mountain dawi deal with mountain dawi problems, why should I be dragged into it, why should our people be dragged into it?' Grum's eyes narrowed as he found the leverage he needed to mollify his champion. '*Your* people, Rundin. You wouldn't want to see them ravaged by a war that is not theirs to begin with, would you?'

Rundin bowed his head, knowing he had lost.

'Of course not, my king.'

'You are loyal to me, are you not?' asked Grum, leaning forwards as if to scrutinise the champion's veracity.

'I am, my king.'

'And swore oaths to defend me and protect my rule, yes?'

'I did.' Rundin knew it, he knew it all, but could not bring his eyes up from his boots.

Leaning back, Grum returned to his counting.

'Find me more gold, Rundin. You're good at that. Seek it out in the rivers and hills, bring the elgi back to our table to make trade.'

'As you wish, my king.'

Thumping his chest, Rundin took his leave.

He met Furgil on the outskirts of Kazad Kro, below the city's rocky promontary. It was a wasteland outside. Gone were the encampments, the bustling market town of trade that had grown up around it. A few disparate, determined traders from the Grey Mountains and Vaults had set up their stalls and wagons but would stay only briefly. Threat of imminent war had chased all others away. Either that or it was the constant patrols of heavily armed rangers that had dissuaded them.

The chief scout of Everpeak looked more grizzled than most. He was not alone and led a large band of rangers. Some had injuries and one of the dwarfs carried two crossbows.

'A skirmish,' Furgil explained, when he saw Rundin regarding the state of his warriors. 'Lost Bori and took some cuts.'

'Elgi?'

Furgil nodded.

'Seems your king has extended invitation to trade still, but hadn't reckoned on the fact that his liege-lord has rangers patrolling the roads and overground routes.'

'He will not fight,' said Rundin, 'if it comes to war.'

'Been eight years, brother, and the killing keeps on rising. We haven't returned to Karaz-a-Karak for months. War will come, Rundin. Too much bad blood running in the river now. We stand on a precipice.'

'Aye, brother. But the skarrenawi will not march.'

'What of Kazad Thar and Mingol?'

'Them neither. King Grum rules both with iron.'

Furgil spat onto the ground. 'Grum rules nothing except that treasure chamber he sits in all day. *You* are the one the skarrens respect, not him.'

'What are you saying, brother?' asked Rundin, a dangerous look in his eye.

'Ah, calm yourself. You know what I'm saying.' Furgil turned on his heel and the other rangers went with him. 'If Grum sits on his arse, Gotrek will be coming for his head when he's done with the elgi,' he called.

Rundin had no reply to that. He let Furgil go, hoping it wouldn't be the last time he saw his friend.

A canker wormed at the heart of Kazad Kro and all the skarrens, it stank to the sky and though he didn't want to admit it, Rundin knew he would have to be the one to cut it out.

Gotrek Starbreaker had never felt so powerless.

For eight years he had cooled the ire of his vassal kings, for eight years he had shackled them to peace. And for eight long, arduous years his efforts had come to naught.

He was drowning, in more ways than one. The sheer amount of parchments, scrolls and stone tablets was staggering. Gotrek's private chambers were full of them. His desk groaned under their weight despite its broad wooden legs. Hunched and grim-faced, he looked almost gargoylesque as he peered over the piles of missives and declarations of grudgement laid out in front of him. The tankard he had supped from was long empty, his pipe cold with its embers long dead. From across the Karaz Ankor, kings, thanes and lodewardens expressed their continued dissatisfaction at what they described as elven 'dissension' and 'belligerence'. Attending to them was not to be a brief task, even for a dwarf.

Trains of reckoners were dispatched daily from Everpeak alone, seeking recompense for misdeeds, and rangers thickened the byways and roads of the hills and lower slopes of the Worlds Edge Mountains until nothing could get through without their prior knowledge.

And still disorder persisted.

Dwarfs and elves were not meant to live together, it seemed.

Some of the disparate clans, those from Mount Gunbad and Silverspear, took the lawlessness as sanction to attack elven settlements, gold-greedy miners looking to fatten their hoards with stolen treasure. Warriors from the distant holds of Karak Izor and Karak Norn had clashed directly with elven war parties in minor skirmishes. Such incidents were few and far between, but as the last decade had ground on the frequency of such skirmishes had worryingly increased.

Gotrek condemned it, sought recompense from the elves, but thus far his messages had remained unheeded. In turn he urged the clans to close their gates and stay within their holds, and forbade any dwarf of Everpeak from violent action.

In the deeps, the forges slaved night and day to fashion weapons, armour and machineries. Thus far, it was stockpiled in the voluminous Everpeak armouries but Gotrek knew the day was approaching when it would have to be broken open and used to furnish his armies.

It had been a desperate hope that forcing distance between the dwarfs and elves would see matters improve or at least not worsen between the two races.

That hope had been dashed on bloody rocks and it was to falter further still.

'And here,' he said wearily, a rasp in his throat from the many hours of reading aloud to his Grudgekeeper who was on hand with the hold's book of grudges. 'At Krag Bryn and Kazad Thrund did elgi come from across the sea and slay the great King Drong the Hard, leaving his queen Helgar without a husband. Let it be known on this day...' Gotrek trailed off, taking a moment's respite to rub his brow.

Seeing his chance, the Grudgekeeper massaged his aching shoulder and flexed his fingers.

For days they hadn't left the chamber. It was the latest stint in what had become a regular accounting of the misdeeds of elves over the last few years. The grudge from Krag Bryn was almost three years old and Gotrek was only just getting to it now. He balked at what else he would find.

'How many more are there?' he asked the statue at the door of the room.

'Three more vaults, my king,' uttered Thurbad in a sonorous voice. 'And there are reckoners gathering in the entrance hall.'

'How many of them?'

The captain of the hearthguard didn't betray a tremor of emotion. 'Almost two hundred.'

Gotrek rubbed his eyes with fingers black from ink. Try as he might, he could not smooth out the worry lines across his forehead. He picked up another missive, waving away the Grudgekeeper who was still waiting for the High King's edict concerning Krag Bryn.

'Bagrik is dead,' he muttered, it not seeming so long ago that the King of Karak Ungor had enjoyed the hospitality of his hold. 'Slain by elgi, his queen now a widow too. Two kings of dawi dead, and a host of elgi lordlings too no doubt.' He seized a fistful of parchments, scattering and displacing others much to the Grudgekeeper's obvious but quiet dismay. 'Grievances the length and breadth of the Worlds Edge...' Gotrek sighed deeply, worn out and tired of peace. 'Is it any wonder my son has left the karak, and garrisons the keep at Black Fire Pass?'

'There is still no word from him, my king,' offered Thurbad, 'but my hearthguard report he has yet not left the fastness. Should I tell them to stop him if he does?'

Two hundred of Thurbad's warriors had left with the prince, ostensibly in support of Snorri's war. In truth, the High King had sent them to keep a watchful eye on his son. The wayward clans of Everpeak, he would deal with later. Their thanes would be punished for their transgression. Such things had waited for eight years, they would stand to wait a little longer.

'I am sorely tempted to join him, Thurbad.' Gotrek paused, as if considering just that, then shook his head. 'I'd rather he had hearthguard protecting him as not. I doubt they could stop him anyway. How many dawi does he have allied to his banner?'

'Almost thirty thousand warriors.'

'Dreng tromm... and he holds?'

'For now, my king. He does.'

Gotrek muttered, 'Perhaps he's learned some temperance after all.' He sighed again, trying to exhale his many worries. 'We stand upon the brink of war,' he croaked in a tired voice that suggested decades, not years, had passed since he ceased trade with the elves.

The two other dwarfs in the room did not answer. What could they say that wasn't a facile reminder that their High King was right?

Gotrek rose to his feet.

'High King?' asked the Grudgekeeper, uncertainly.

'I am done with grudgement for today, Haglarrson. Seal the *kron* and have these grudges gathered up for my later reckoning.'

Haglarrson the Grudgekeeper nodded mutely, still unsure what was happening.

Gotrek directed his attention to Thurbad. 'Dismiss the reckoners. All of them.' He was leaving, and the captain of the hearthguard followed him in perfect lockstep.

They walked into the Great Hall, its large and empty vaults echoing with the footfalls.

Gotrek snarled, 'This is blatant transgression by the elgi. They flout any chance at peace with their arrogance! Dawi lie dead and cold in my lands, Thurbad. Tell me how should I make answer to that without dooming us all?'

'I cannot, my king. All I can do is serve the karak.'

Gotrek stopped. He gripped Thurbad's shoulder.

'And a more brave and noble servant I could not wish for, Thurbad.'

'Tromm, my king...' he said, bowing. 'Is there anything further?'

Gotrek nodded. 'Yes, bring me my Loremaster and that reckoner, Forek Grimbok. I have need of his silvern tongue.'

'Should I tell him what it is concerning?' Thurbad asked.

'Tell him I need him to go to the King of the Elves on Ulthuan,' said Gotrek. 'Tell him I need him to prevent a war.'

Forek Grimbok's heart pounded like a boar-skin drum. He knelt before the Throne of Power, head bowed, his left arm tucked against his chest.

'Tromm, High King...' he uttered to a largely barren room.

'Look at me, reckoner.'

Forek tilted his head up to meet the gaze of the High King. His mind was reeling already with the task before him. Pride swelled his heart and he tried to master it for fear it would overwhelm him.

'You are my most gifted ambassador. If anyone can wrench a peace from this mess, then it is you. But make no mistake, Grimbok, I want an apology from the elgi for their transgressions, nothing less.' He waved the robed dwarf on his left forwards. 'My Loremaster has a missive you must present to the King of the Elgi. It is unsealed. Read it, digest its meaning and know my mind before applying the wax. Put it in the elgi king's hands and his alone. Do you understand?'

'I do...' Forek croaked, cleared his throat then tried again. 'I do, my king.'

'Good. It will be up to you to impress upon him that misdeeds have been done unto us by the elgi, but that I am not without forgiveness and such misdeeds can be undone in the eyes of the Karaz Ankor.'

'Yes, my king.' Forek took the letter and secreted it inside his tunic.

'Now rise and let Thurbad tell you of your journey ahead.'

The High King gestured to the captain of the hearthguard, a mass of armoured muscle who was standing by his right.

'Twenty of my best warriors will accompany you,' said Thurbad.

Behind Forek, the hearthguard bristled with strength and threat. Only one amongst them wasn't wearing his full-face war helm, a flame-haired warrior who stepped forwards into the reckoner's eye line. 'Gilias Thunderbrow is their leader and will be your shadow.'

The one Thurbad had introduced as Gilias bowed, before steeping back and donning his war helm.

'A ship will carry you across the Great Ocean and you will have the runelord Thorik Oakeneye in your party. He will meet you at Barak Varr and shall ensure you reach the land of the elgi.'

With the salient details of the journey revealed, the High King took over again.

'This is our last chance, Grimbok. Of all the dawi of the Karaz Ankor you know the elgi best. Bring me back peace and a measure of contrition with which I can placate the other kings.'

'By Grungni, I swear I will try.'

'You must succeed, Grimbok. Many dawi lives are depending on it.'

'Y-yes... of course, my king. When do I depart for Ulthuan?'

The High King's eyes were like two chips of hardened diamond.

'Immediately.'

The fastness of Black Fire Pass was bleak and cold. Known to the dwarfs as *Kazad Kolzharr*, which simply meant *the fortress of black fire*, it was a stout keep of hewn stone with a broad, thick gate bound by strips of iron and sentinelled by a quartet of stocky watchtowers. It offered a peerless view of the mountains and a wide aperture into the lands west, all the way down the Old Dwarf Road.

'I heard Ranuld tell that in ancient days the road was paved with gold and shimmered like fire in the sun.'

'Poetry isn't really my strength, cousin.'

Snorri's mood was as bleak as the weather and their surroundings as Morgrim joined him on the wall.

The dwarf prince was peering into the west through a spyglass at the arrow-sharp pinnacles of the elven cities several hundred miles away. They were distant and indistinct but he could make out the rough shape of Kor Vanaeth and knew the names and positions of several others from the map spread in front of him. Two large rocks kept the fluttering parchment from blowing away in the high wind coming off the mountains. Winter nipped at the air and a light frost rimed the battlements and glistened on the grasslands below.

'He said that gold-gathering put paid to the gilded road, to all the golden byways of the Karaz Ankor,' said Morgrim, stoking up his pipe. 'That it was dawi, not urk or grobi, that picked the great shining roads clean.'

'It's a myth.' Snorri put the spyglass away, braced his hands against the wall. Apart from the hearthguard manning the watchtowers, they were alone.

'Perhaps,' admitted Morgrim, blowing out a plume of grey-blue smoke. 'But we *have* become greedy.'

'Is it greed then that brings thirty thousand of the *kalans* to Kazad Kolzharr?'

'Some, yes. For you, cousin, I do not think so.'

'I have a score to settle with my father then, do I?'

'Do you deny it?'

Snorri turned to face him. 'Why are you here, Morg? You claim it is to watch my back, but is that all?'

Morgrim slapped the battlements with the flat of his gauntleted hand. 'You are as cold as this stone, Snorri. The last few years have hardened you. I am here because I am hoping to catch a glimpse of the dawi I once knew...' Morgrim met his gaze. 'My cousin and friend.'

For a moment, Snorri's tough, weather-beaten face softened. Since the garrisoning of the fortress at Black Fire Pass they had seen the musters of the elves, their horse guard and warriors scouting as far as they dared in dwarf territory. The pointy-ears did not believe in peace. Just as the dwarfs did, they knew that war was inevitable. It merely remained to see who would cast the first spear.

After eight years, after honouring his promise to Elmendrin and suffering the oathmaking of King Brynnoth and Thagdor, Snorri had decided it would be him. Regardless of what his father wanted, he would march on Kor Vanaeth and destroy it.

Word had reached the fastness that the High King would attempt one last act of diplomacy before committing to war. In his heart and his head, Snorri knew this would fail.

'The dawi you knew, he stands before you, cousin. But if I am to accept the mantle of High King one day, I must seize destiny for myself. I must slay the drakk of which Ranuld Silverthumb spoke. I must defeat the elgi.'

'Is there nothing I can say to keep you here behind these walls? If not for your father's wishes, what of Elmendrin?'

'My father chases a foolish dream, one that ended long ago. And as for her... She...' Snorri faltered, looking down. 'She is–'

'My prince,' uttered a voice from the other end of the wall.

To Morgrim's ears it seemed to be closer, but Drogor had barely mounted the battlements and was striding towards them.

Like the cousins, he wore full armour, plate over mail with a thick furred cloak to ward off the cold. He wore his battle helm from Karak Zorn, the one with the saurian crest, and lifted the faceguard to speak further.

'Our runners have returned,' he said, with a small nod of acknowledgement for Morgrim who reciprocated reluctantly.

Drogor was clutching a piece of parchment and presented it to the prince. Snorri read it silently, his expression hardening with every line.

'The elgi have mustered a large force on the outskirts of Kor Vanaeth.'

'Apparently, their spies have discovered your intention to attack them and are making ready their defences,' said Drogor. 'It's possible they will ride out against the kazad, my prince.'

Snorri snapped at him, 'Do not call me that, Drogor. How many times must I tell you?'

Drogor bowed. 'Apologies, Snorri. I am your thane, you are my prince, one day to be High King. It feels dishonourable to address you any other way.'

Snorri returned to the letter.

'Rangers have been attacked on the road and a band of reckoners put to flight.' His eyes widened in shock, quickly narrowing to anger. 'Priestesses of Valaya were amongst their number.'

'What?' asked Morgrim. 'What were priestesses doing this far from the hold? It makes no sense.'

Snorri glared at his cousin. 'Eight years ago they came forth from their temple, did they not?'

'Elmendrin was not amongst them?' Morgrim betrayed more than mere concern.

Snorri gave him a wary glance before reading on.

'No, she is back at Everpeak, but they would undoubtedly be her maidens.'

Morgrim frowned, unconvinced. 'Valayan priestesses abroad on the road? It makes no sense. Let me see that letter.'

Snorri handed it over but it broke apart in his metal fist, fragmenting like ash.

'Odd,' he said. 'I've never seen parchment do that before.' He looked at it for a moment then cast it over the wall, where it was caught by the wind and borne away.

Morgrim turned to Drogor, who was waiting patiently for the prince's orders.

'Where is this runner now? I would speak with him.'

Drogor grew solemn, though his eyes remained cold and lifeless. 'He is dead, shot with elgi arrows.'

Morgrim sneered. 'I see.'

'Is there a problem?'

'Nothing that cannot be rectified.'

'It matters not,' said Snorri. 'Slaying rinns and priestesses, it cannot go unanswered any longer.' He was stern, and he spoke through a portcullis of clenched teeth. 'Gather the clans. All of them. And send word to Brynnoth and Thagdor. This time I won't be dissuaded. We march on Kor Vanaeth.'

'What about your father? He sues for peace, and any warmaking that we do here could–'

'Let him!' Snorri roared. 'He's knows it's over, as well as I. Peace is dead, has been for eight years.'

'And while peace fails, what will we do?'

Snorri's face was as pitiless as knapped flint, and just as unyielding. 'What we should have done years ago. Kill elgi.'

TWENTY-EIGHT

THE SEA GATE

Towering cliffs, thronged with shrieking gulls and carved with the likenesses of the ancestors, loomed over Forek Grimbok and the hearthguard.

'Is that it?' he asked the armoured warrior standing next to him at the ship's prow.

'Aye,' murmured Gilias, tightening his grip on his axe haft instinctively. 'The Merman Gate, entryway into Barak Varr, the Sea Hold and realm of King Brynnoth.'

The pair of cyclopean statues were fashioned seamlessly into the rock face, depicted wearing fishscale armour and fin-crested war helms. One was female and carried a trident in her left hand; the other, male, bore an axe that he held across his chest.

'Magnificent,' breathed Forek.

Insisting they make all haste to Barak Varr, the High King had petitioned the King of the Sea Gate to both receive them and send a vessel to bear his emissary to the hold. Though dwarfs were not fond of water-borne travel, preferring solid rock as opposed to a leaky deck beneath their boots, Forek and his retinue had adjusted quickly.

Over the last eight years relations had soured between the two holds. Brynnoth did not believe in peace, but he also did not believe in denying his king and so had acceded to Gotrek's request.

The most direct route from Everpeak to Barak Varr was Skull River, one of several large tributaries that joined the Black Gulf. The river widened as it met two shoulders of jagged rock that formed the monolithic cliffs that had glowered down on them several miles out. The sweeping crags arched over an immense gate of bronze, green with verdigris and clinging seaweed. A dwarf face, with a sea serpent coiling from its open mouth and an ocean wyrm perched atop its helmet, was emblazoned across it that split in two as the gate opened.

Either side of the gate was a tower, a garrison of dwarf quarrellers within each and a journeyman engineer to pump the crank that worked the mechanism which opened it. The reek of salt and the open sea hit them in a wave as soon as the bronze gate was breached.

Like his retinue of hearthguard, Forek looked up as they passed under the archway but saw the faces that regarded them were far from friendly.

'Why do I feel a chill in this wind all of a sudden?' he asked, determined not to flinch against intimidation.

'They are Gatekeepers,' explained Gilias, 'and not prone to warm welcomes. Barak Varr and Karaz-a-Karak are not on the best of terms at the moment.'

'King Brynnoth knows who his allies are,' Forek assured the hearthguard. 'He would not have aided us if he felt otherwise. Grudgement for Agrin Fireheart will be done, but not until the truth is known. A war would eclipse all hope of that. It would be petty and unworthy of the runelord. Brynnoth knows this.'

'You seem very sure,' said Gilias.

Mist wreathed the passage of the grubark in a white, impenetrable fog but the hearthguard rowed unerringly, one of the warriors working the tiller to keep the rudder straight and their small ship from falling foul of the banks.

'I will make certain of it upon making the shore,' said Forek. He tried not to breathe too deep of the briny air, already feeling a little nauseous with the gentle rocking of the boat.

'Here.' Gilias uncorked a flask of tarry liquid and offered it to the reckoner. 'This'll calm your stomach.'

Forek took a grateful swig, gulping back the fiery liquid and trying not to cough. He was used to 'gentler' brews, not the harsh muck enjoyed by the king's protectors.

'Tromm,' he said, nodding thanks, 'that feels better al–'

Forek stopped mid-sentence, his mouth suddenly agape. The mist had thinned and parted, revealing the majesty of the Sea Gate.

Massive columns surged upwards from dark water, decorated with immense statuary and brazier pans of burning coals as broad as a hundred shields laid edge to edge. The columns supported a vast ceiling of rock, a natural cave that served as Barak Varr's dock. The rune of *bar* – that which means 'gate', and is a potent symbol of protection – was emblazoned upon slabs of rock, towers and minarets, portcullises and keeps built into the cave wall. Tips of spear-sized quarrels could be seen poking out through arrow slits and stone throwers mounted on rotating platforms were angled towards them in a blatant threat.

Barak Varr was a hold that took its defence very seriously, and even a vessel that had encroached this far into its borders was not guaranteed continued safe passage.

Somewhere a bell was tolling, its sound solemn and echoing. A hold was still in mourning for its venerable dead, and it only made the cavernous chamber more desolate. Ordinarily it would be bristling with vessels from across the Old World: strange barques of dark-skinned merchants, the skiffs of Southland traders and even elven catamarans had all been seen at the Sea Gate before. Not so any more. Impending war had seen much of the trade dry up and now only a few dwarf vessels occupied the yawning expanse of black water.

'It's like a graveyard,' remarked one of the hearthguard, until Gilias silenced him with a look.

Forek agreed, the doleful bell ringing in the distance to announce them. His reckoning days had never brought him to Barak Varr before. Perhaps it was on account of the strong bond between it and Everpeak that this was the case. But whatever he had expected, this was not it.

As they were ushered towards a jetty, several warriors wearing scaled mail and carrying axes and crossbows met them. Their helmets were almost conical, fashioned into the simulacra of a sea dragon's snout, and had a pair of jagged fins protruding from either temple. Shields strapped to their backs were scalloped at the edges and their axe blades were flanged like a trident's teeth.

'Quite a show of force,' murmured Gilias, careful to keep his voice low.

Forek muttered, 'Once King Brynnoth has received us, all will be well. They are just wary of dawi not of their hold.'

As soon as they set foot on dry land, Forek whispered an oath of gratitude to Valaya for her deliverance and then one to Grungni for creating the earth.

Two figures not part of the throng of warriors awaited them on the flagstoned shore. As soon as Forek saw one of them he realised why there were so many warriors.

'That is High Thane Onkmarr.'

'You sound surprised,' said Gilias as they walked along the jetty to the creak of wood bending beneath the weight of so many armoured warriors.

'I am.'

The other dwarf Forek didn't know. He was dressed in black leather armour over a scruffy-looking tunic. The eyepatch he wore, together with the mattock head he had instead of a foot, marked him out as a ship's captain but the reckoner thought he looked more like a pirate.

'If Onkmarr is here then that can mean but one thing.'

'Which is?' hissed Gilias as they neared the edge of the jetty.

Forek replied in the same guarded tone, 'That King Brynnoth is not.'

Heglan awoke to a hammering against his chamber door.

He was face down in a scrap of parchment, ink smears on his cheeks from where he had fallen asleep pressed against his still-wet scribblings, exhaustion forcing him to eschew his bed in favour of the first available place to collapse.

At first he was disorientated. This last session in the workshop had been the longest, several weeks in isolation with only stonebread and strong beer to sustain him. Dawi had survived on less, he had told himself at the outset of his labours. His avian menagerie startled him and he gasped aloud at the talons of a crag eagle bearing down from on high. Belatedly, he came to his senses, still slightly fuddled by strong drink but at least now able to make out someone calling his name.

'Heg? Open the door, brother. Heg?'

Tripping on a stuffed griffon vulture that had fallen from its perch, he stumbled to his feet and hurried over to a crank that would seal off the hidden vault where he kept his secret labours. Setting the mechanism going, he quickly gathered up the scraps of parchment he had been sleeping on, rolled them up and stuffed them in a drawer.

By the time he reached the door and opened it, the vault was shut and Nadri Gildtongue looked less than impressed.

'What are you doing, Heg?' he asked bluntly.

'I was sleeping, brother. What's your excuse for being here?'

Nadri barged his way in and began to look around.

'I haven't seen you in months. I've spoken to your guildmaster,' he said, rifling through tools and sketches, drawers of cogs and nails and bolts. 'Your absence has been noted.'

'If you tell me what you're looking for perhaps I can help you find it.'

'You are doing it again, aren't you?'

'Doing what?'

'Building the airship. I am no wazzock, Heg, do not treat me as one.' Nadri rapped his knuckles against the room's back wall. 'What is behind here?'

Heglan feigned confusion, but inwardly stifled a pang of anxiety. Nadri was certainly no fool. 'It is a wall, brother. Solid rock is behind it.'

'Every other surface in this workshop is covered in designs and formulae and notes. You have papered it in parchment scribblings, Heg. Yet this wall is barren.' Nadri shook his head, his face clouded by anger. 'Don't lie to me. Show me what you're hiding.'

Heglan closed his mouth – protesting his innocence would be pointless now – and opened up the vault.

The skylight beamed weak winter sun onto the hull of a magnificent ship. It was lacquered black, fully restored and even larger and more impressive than before. Gone were the rotary sails and the sweeps, but there was more rigging and a sack that looked like a stitched animal bladder draped the deck.

'It's unfinished but an inaugural flight is close, I think.' Heglan's eyes widened, his hangover all but forgotten in his excitement. Like an artist with his latest masterwork, he relished the opportunity to show it off.

Nadri was less enthused but couldn't hide his awe.

'It is incredible, Heg. But you will be expelled from the guild for this. Strombak will see to it that you are given the Trouser Legs Ritual and kicked out.'

'When he sees what I have crafted, when he witnesses its first flight he will–'

'He doesn't care, Heg! He will expel you and further shame will be heaped on the Copperfists. First Grandfather Dammin and now you... Our father, Lodri, will never be allowed at Grungni's table. He will wander forever at Gazul's Gate.' Nadri tugged on his beard, fighting back the tears in his eyes. He rasped, his voice choking, 'Dreng tromm, brother.'

'The skryzan-harbark will fly, Nadri. I know it. And when it does our family's shame will be expunged, our seat in the Hall of Ancestors assured. Please don't tell Strombak what I am doing, not yet. I must–' He stopped, as if seeing his brother for the first time since he'd entered his workshop. 'Wait... why are you wearing your armour?'

Nadri was clad in ringmail. A helmet was tethered to his belt by its strap and there was a small round shield on his back, an axe looped by his waist.

'It's why I came to find you, brother,' he said with a hint of melancholy. 'King Brynnoth is going to war. Our kalan marches with him.'

Heglan was shaking his head, fear for his beloved brother lighting his eyes. 'No. You are a merchant, not a warrior.'

'We are all warriors when the horn blows calling us to war. The elgi are to be held to account for Agrin Fireheart's death at last.' Nadri's face darkened, his mouth becoming a hard line. 'And I shall seek vengeance for Krondi.'

'But war? When did this happen?' asked Heglan.

'It is happening now, brother. The king has already left Barak Varr and another two thousand dawi of the kalans follow in his wake.'

'But what of trade, who will bring gold into the Sea Gate if you are at war?'

'There is no trade! It ended years ago and has been drying up ever since. The only currency now is that of axes and shields, war engines to break open the elgi cities. It's why Strombak has not been to find you. He is in the forges, as you should be, fashioning weapons for our king.'

Like a hammer blow had struck him on the forehead, filling his skull with a sudden realisation, Heglan went from being stupefied to urgently casting about his workshop.

Nadri frowned. 'What are you doing now?'

Heglan was ferreting around in drawers and racks, sweeping aside tools and materials. 'Looking for my axe,' he said. 'I'm coming with you.'

Nadri went over and held him by the shoulders to keep him still.

'No, brother. You are staying here. Finish your airship. Strombak will definitely cast you out of the guild if you tell him what you've been up to now. Realise grandfather's dream. It might be your last chance.'

Worry lines creased Heglan's brow. 'Why are you talking like this? A moment ago you were chastising me.'

'I changed my mind. You were right. Nothing will be the same after this,' he said, sombrely.

Heglan grew fearful as he saw the fatalism in his brother's eyes.

'You are coming back, aren't you?'

'I hope so.'

'You have to come back. Father is dead, mother too. You are my only family, Nadri.'

'And you mine, Heg.'

They embraced awkwardly, Nadri's armour unfamiliar on his body and getting in the way.

'Keep it secret, Heg,' he said.

Heglan was weeping. 'Dreng tromm, Nadri...'

Nadri held him behind the neck, pressed his forehead to his brother's.

'*Karinunkarak*,' he murmured.

'Karinunkarak,' Heglan replied in a choked whisper.

It meant 'protect and endure', but words were not shields or armour.

Detaching himself from his brother's embrace, Nadri met Heglan's gaze one last time and then left the workshop.

The door slamming after him arrested Heglan from his reverie. He turned to regard the airship, a masterwork waiting for its artisan to finish it.

Seizing a hammer that he'd spilled onto the floor, he locked the door to his chamber and went to work.

Onkmarr had wasted no time in getting Forek and his retinue on their way. They didn't leave the dock and certainly had not been granted admittance to the Sea Hold itself. Instead, as the high thane and regent left them, the Everpeak dwarfs were guided by the rough-looking captain to where his ship was berthed.

It was a massive vessel, engraved with runes along its hull and festooned with rows of sweeps along either flank. A vast paddle sat at the stern that could pivot back and forth like a rudder, but there were no masts, no sails to speak of. It was armoured in plates of metal, the heavy wood of its structure thick and well lacquered. Three bolt throwers, one at the prow where Valaya's effigy looked stern in her warrior aspect and two more to port and starboard, provided obvious protection but in addition to them were racks of crossbows and harpoons that Forek could see jutting up above the bulwarks from below. A crew of leather-skinned, weather-beaten dwarfs hoisted barrels and other provisions up a ramp onto the deck. They too were armed.

'A mission o' peace never looked so tooled up, eh?' the captain remarked over his shoulder as he led his passengers up another ramp. The swarthy-looking dwarf grinned, revealing several gold teeth, as he noticed Forek looking at his missing foot. 'Ah, don't let that bother ye, lad,' he said in a gravel-thick voice. 'I needs hands to steer a ship, not feet. And as you can see, I have both of those.' He patted a broad black belt, a rune axe looped on one side, spyglass on the other. The dwarf sea captain gave a shallow bow. 'Nugdrinn Hammerfoot. I'll be the zaki taking you across the Great Ocean.'

Halfway up the ramp, Forek shook the dwarf's proffered hand and felt whale grease and spit between his fingers.

'This is your ship?' he asked, for want of a better reply.

'Aye, the *Azuldal*,' he said proudly. 'Come aboard.'

Up on deck, the *Azuldal* looked even more fortified. It was a keep, just one that floated on water.

'There are no sails?' Forek asked, noticing a hooded figure sitting at the ship's forecastle. He faced in the direction of the sea, clutching an ornate staff in both hands.

'That's right, lad. Paddles, oars and solid dawi grit is how we'll make passage.' He jerked a thumb at the mysterious passenger. 'Oh, and a little rhun won't hurt us either,' he added in a conspiratorial whisper.

This must be Thorik Oakeneye, Forek supposed, the runelord who would help them reach Ulthuan.

'How many times have you travelled across the Great Ocean before, Captain Hammerfoot?' Forek asked, still beguiled by the runesmith.

'Never.' He was already shouting to his crew, getting them to make ready for depature. With a creaking refrain, the paddle at the ship's stern began to turn and the long sweeps pierced the dark water as they started to pull.

'Then how do you know you can successfully navigate it?' asked Forek urgently.

Nugdrinn scratched under his patch at his missing eye.

'I don't, but that's where the adventure comes in, lad.' His good eye narrowed as he caught on. 'You look concerned. It's not the navigating that should worry you, it's the blood-hungry creatures of the deep.' He laughed, loud and hearty, stomping towards the helm.

Forek watched him go, only vaguely aware of Gilias Thunderbrow's warriors making ready behind him. He felt a hand upon his shoulder.

It was Gilias. The hearthguard's eyes followed Nugdrinn limping up every step of the helm until he reached the ship's wheel.

'Thorik Oakeneye will guide us, but he will keep us afloat. Don't worry.'

'I'm not worried,' said Forek, unconvincingly.

Gilias laughed. 'Of course not.'

Nugdrinn was pointing at the horizon with a grubby finger.

'We're under way!' he cried, 'To the land of the elgi with all haste!' He looked down at Forek. 'You should tie yourself down, ufdi. It'll be a rough passage, I'd warrant. Ha, ha!'

'He's mad,' he hissed to Gilias.

'He'd need to be to venture where we're going.'

'Aren't you concerned?' he asked the hearthguard.

'No,' he said. 'I am more concerned with what happens if you fail.'

Forek could find no argument with that, and as the *Azuldal* pulled out of Barak Varr and drove towards the Black Gulf, he wondered what would await when they arrived on Ulthuan.

If they arrived on Ulthuan.

TWENTY-NINE

HUNTED

Heavy rain peeled off the hood of Sevekai's cloak, teeming in rivulets of dark water that pooled at his already sodden feet. Brooding clouds overhead showed no sign of abating and an ever-present thunder promised worse weather to come.

The skull-headed rock seemed to glower down at him, presaging darker times ahead. Sevekai glared back, unimpressed.

'Hell's Head indeed,' he muttered. 'You'll need to summon more than just rain to kill me, spirit.' He cursed with all the names of the dark elf gods of the underworld. It had been days, but still no sign. 'Boredom might, however,' he admitted.

Crouched in the lee of the Hell's Head crag, there was little else to do but wait. She said she would be there and though it went against every instinct he possessed he had to trust her.

A biting wind was blowing off the mountains, chilling the air and turning the rain to sleet. Drawing his cloak tighter around his body, Sevekai tried to imagine warmer climes.

'Why are we still here?' moaned Verigoth. The grey-pallored shade looked more sullen than usual. 'Our task is finished. The asur will soon be at war. Why must we remain?'

Sevekai didn't have the heart to tell him they would not be returning to Naggaroth any time soon, that Malekith had left them here to rot or find passage back to the frozen island for themselves. No, it wasn't a lack of heart; he just preferred the other dark elf to suffer.

'We are here because our dark lord wills it.' A raven had perched on the overhanging rock, seemingly oblivious to the rain, and cawed at the bedraggled warriors. Flitting from one settlement to the next, often sleeping on bare rock or under shadowed trees, they looked ragged. Verigoth wasn't alone in his displeasure. At least they were alive. For now. If *she* got her way, the other bitch making Sevekai's life torment, then the situation might change. 'And even this far from his court, do not think for a moment that his eye isn't ever watchful.'

In truth, though, Sevekai had begun to wonder the same thing. Not why they were still here, but rather why they were in the Old World at all. What would a war between elves and dwarfs achieve? It would not restore the druchii to glory. Not for the first time he considered his position but was wise enough to keep his misgivings hidden beneath his surface thoughts. Drutheira might be close and reading his mind. Worse still, Malekith could be listening.

The raven took flight, and Sevekai prayed to the gods of the underworld that it wasn't a Naggarothi messenger.

For the last eight years, ever since murdering the dwarf wizard or whatever he was, the shades had gone to ground. Occasionally they had resurfaced to attack a band of dwarfs or ambush a caravan. Discord needed to be nurtured if it was to flourish into something as permanent and debilitating as enmity. Sevekai had curtailed their activities deliberately. Flames had been fanned, they merely needed to watch and see where they spread. The dwarf king had shown more resilience than he had expected in resisting a declaration of war. In part, this forced the shades out of hiding, but the other mud-dwelling lords had fomented the inevitable war nicely with their bigotry and greed.

The message from Drutheira came as a surprise. He had neither seen nor heard from her since they had been reunited in the gorge. They were evading a band of dwarf rangers – heavier patrols along the roads had made travelling more difficult – when her face had manifested in the rotting intestines of a dead raven. Perhaps the one on the rock earlier had been looking for its mate.

She had bidden Sevekai meet her at this place, and wait there until she arrived. The sending was so incongruous, so unlike her in its tone and desperation that he decided to believe the witch. Any chance to see Drutheira squirm, whatever the cause, was worth taking. And, besides, there was something more than lust which compelled him.

The others didn't chafe much. Likely they hoped she would spirit them away with sorcery. Sevekai let them believe that, even though he knew that though Drutheira was powerful she did not possess that kind of craft, even with her lackeys. Only one of the party seemed sceptical.

'You still think she will come?' asked Kaitar.

Sevekai met the cold bastard's gaze and suppressed a shudder, telling himself it was caused by the wind.

Losing Numenos at the gorge had been a blow. Now they were five, and could ill-afford to lose anyone else, but he wished bitterly there was one less of their number. Verigoth was rumoured to have a witch elf for a mother, his pale skin indicative of Hag Graef, the lightless prison city. Hreth and Latharek were twins from Har Ganeth, City of Executioners, and as hard as druchii came but even they looked ill at ease around Kaitar.

Sitting in a circle around a guttering fire that was more smoke than heat, every face was forlorn.

All except for Kaitar. He was smiling.

'I see little to be pleased about,' said Hreth, a dangerous edge to his tone.

'Perhaps he likes the rain,' suggested Latharek, smirking with his brother.

Kaitar grinned, showing perfect teeth. Ignoring the brothers, he turned to Sevekai. 'You didn't answer my question. Will the witch still come, because if not...'

Sevekai didn't look up. 'She'll be here.'

Hreth got to his feet, rain hammering against his cloak and running down the broad-bladed knife he wore at his hip. 'Where is it exactly you hail from again, Kaitar?'

Kaitar didn't look back. 'Many places, none. It doesn't really matter.'

'I think it does,' said Latharek, standing up next to his brother.

Sevekai edged back, hand slipping furtively to his sickle daggers, but otherwise content to let it play out.

'You don't want to know where I am from, Hreth,' Kaitar answered, staring into the embers of the fire which seemed to spit and flare into life.

Hreth would not be dissuaded. 'I have been to many of the dark cities but never met one such as you.'

Latharek joined in, 'Yes, you are barely druchii at all.'

Kaitar laughed, goading Hreth.

'Something amuses you?'

'Only your foolishness.' He looked up from the fire.

Sevekai licked his lips, anticipating violence. Verigoth remained still and silent.

'Sit down,' Kaitar told the brothers.

Eight years had frayed tempers, stoked discontent to the point where it was about to spill over into something more lethal. Perhaps this was how Malekith had intended to deal with his errant scouts, by having them kill each other.

'Now,' Kaitar added.

Sevekai's skin tingled and he thought he detected a slight resonance to the warrior's voice.

Hreth and Latharek sat down as ordered, as if pole-axed and struck dumb.

'That's better,' said Kaitar. 'Is that any way to behave when we have guests?' He turned to Sevekai, who couldn't stop his flesh crawling nor the itch behind his teeth. 'You were right.'

'About what?' Sevekai asked.

Kaitar pointed to the tip of a craggy rise.

'She did come.'

Drutheira had arrived with Ashniel and Malchior.

Sevekai gave Kaitar one last look before greeting the witch.

'Enter, stranger...' He gave a mock bow, masking his discomfort with absurd theatrics.

Drutheira did not appear to be impressed.

'We do not have much time,' she hissed, glancing at the brooding sky overhead. Now he saw them up close, Sevekai thought the coven looked more ragged than his own tattered followers.

'You've been prettier, my dear,' he said, betraying a mote of concern at Drutheira's appearance.

'Like a cold one sniffing blood,' she spat, seeming not to hear the gibe. Her fingers were thin, almost like bone, and her sunken cheeks reminded Sevekai of a cadaver that had yet to realise it was dead. 'It has taken all of my power to stay hidden.'

The two at her side bristled at this.

Her power?

Sevekai could almost hear their thoughts, slipping porously through their hateful eyes.

'The elf woman? I thought we had eluded her years ago.'

Drutheira rounded on him, snarling. 'She is a mage, idiot! Such creatures cannot be eluded. She has found my magical spoor, tracked me, dogged me without relent.'

'Then you must flee.'

'I *am* fleeing, my *love*,' she said, 'to you. I need you to kill her for me.'

Now Sevekai laughed. 'And her beast too, I suppose?' His face hardened. 'You reap your own harvest, Drutheira. Leaving a stain on that gorge was a mistake, one that will hound you to the edge of the Old World.'

'Do you know how many settlements I have razed to ash over the last eight years?' she asked, fashioning a coruscating orb of dark energy in her hand. 'And my wrath is far from spent.' The orb writhed as if constricted in Drutheira's grip, oily tendrils coiling and uncoiling in agony, eager to be unleashed.

Sevekai stepped back.

'This black horror will strip flesh from bone,' she promised. 'I saved your miserable life in that gorge. That dwarf would have killed you all had I not intervened. *Now*,' she said, the summoning receding into trailing smoke that left a dark scar on her open palm, 'the balance of that must be accounted.'

'What makes you think I can kill her?'

'You are not fixed in her eye. She won't see the blade until she's already dead from its poison.' She cast another glance skywards, imagining the beat of heavy wings, a shadow overhead...

Sevekai smiled.

'You *are* weak, aren't you?'

Drutheira came close, so only he could hear her.

'She has hunted me for eight years, Sevekai. I am exhausted,' she said, with a furtive glance at her predatory cohorts, but they were just as wasted. Drutheira's voice dropped to a whisper. 'She will kill me.'

Appealing to the heart of an assassin is no easy thing but despite their ostensible enmity Sevekai did not want harm to come to the sorceress.

'I know a hidden path, one that will take us south, beyond the mountains and to the coast. There is a ship waiting in dock that can take us to the Sour Sea and from there we'll make our way back.'

Drutheira dragged Sevekai close and hissed, 'I will not make it that far. She must die.' Her face darkened, blackness pooled in her sunken eyes and a shadow of a grin lifted her features. 'You have no choice.'

Sevekai threw her off.

'Another dagger in my back, Drutheira?' he snarled. 'You led her here deliberately.'

All of a sudden, the sorceress did not appear so weak or desperate.

'I'm sorry, *my love*, but our survival depends on us working together. Our dark lord has decreed it. I need the elf bitch dead. She is interfering with my plans.'

Murderous intent flashed over Sevekai's face.

'How close?'

'A day, if that. It is Malekith's will that the dragon rider dies.'

The shade shook his head, 'And here I was thinking all I had to be concerned about was the rain.'

'And one other thing,' Drutheira said, keeping her voice low as her gaze lit on Kaitar. '*That* is not a druchii.'

With the coming of the dream, she smelled smoke and heard the crackle of fire...

Cothique was burning.

Liandra ran through the streets, crying out for her mother, desperate to see her father and brothers. She was young, too young to wield a sword or spear. Not like them. They would have killed the raiders, put them to flight, but the warriors defending Cothique were all dead and only women and children remained.

A terrible clamour raked the air, and it took a few minutes for Liandra to realise the sound belonged to gulls, screaming as the air in which they flew was set aflame.

The port was ablaze, half-burned bodies face down in the water from where they'd tried to douse themselves. Quarrels protruded from their backs like spines.

Everything was haze and shadow, muffled by the flames, clouded by the smoke. Liandra coughed, bringing up a ropey phlegm that spoiled her summer dress. She was crawling before she realised she had fallen, hands and knees in the dirt and blood. It sluiced down the streets in a river.

Somewhere, she couldn't tell precisely in her dark occluded world, a horn was braying. Liandra knew that sound, just as she knew the raiders were taking flight, their black galleons brimming with slaves. Lothern had answered, their ships had come and sent fear running through the hearts of the druchii.

Reaching out, half blind with smoke, Liandra found the edge of a broken cart. She began to crawl beneath it when an iron-hard grip seized her ankle. She screamed as she was pulled, looking back through tear-streaming eyes into the face of a wraith.

Though her brothers had told her tales, she had never seen a druchii before. He was pale, his features so like and yet unlike her own; appearing sharper, as though she would cut herself on his nose or cheekbones.

She screamed again and the druchii laughed, drinking in her terror. His face was painted in cruel, angular runes that made Liandra's eyes hurt, or that might just have been the fire. She kicked wildly, connecting with the druchii's face, and he snarled in anger at her. She tried again, but he caught her ankle, twisted it hard until she thought she might pass out from the pain.

'Khaine's hells are reserved for little ones like you,' the raider hissed, drawing a curved dagger with serrated teeth along its edge.

His breath smelled of blood.

She struggled, looking around for help, but there was no one. Only fire and smoke. The warriors from Lothern would not reach her in time. Gutted on a druchii's blade or a prisoner on their foul ships, either way she was as good as dead. But Liandra was a princess of Caledor, she had a warrior's heart and fire in her veins to fuel it. She would not die without a fight.

A heavy punch to her jaw put the fight out of her and she mewled like a milksop farm girl, blacking out for a second. When she opened her eyes again, the dagger was all she could see, filling her eye line. She noticed the blade was black, or rather, stained that way.

She wept. 'Mother...'

The druchii grunted, the dagger falling from Liandra's sight, a grimace marring the raider's porcelain features. A woman stood over him, a broken spear haft clutched in her shaking hands.

'Get off her, you bastard!'

Liandra wept again, even as the druchii parried a second swipe of the spear haft and disarmed its wielder with ease. 'Mother...'

'Run!' she cried to Liandra, urging her daughter with all the swiftness of Kurnous. 'Flee, Liandra!'

Even as the druchii closed her down, seized her flailing fist and plunged the dagger deep.

Time slowed, the smoke and flame so thick Liandra could hardly breathe any more, the figures a few feet in front of her reduced to hazed silhouettes.

One crumpled and fell. It brought a word half-formed to her lips that she was unable to speak.

Mother.

The druchii turned. Something dark and vital shimmered on the edge *of his blade. It dripped to the ground, as the last ounces of Liandra's innocence bled away with it.*

Horns were braying.

Lothern had answered, but their call came too late for her mother.

Heedless of the danger, the druchii advanced on her. He got three steps before an arrow punctured his chest. Another pierced his throat and he gargled his last words through a fountain of blood.

Then he fell, and Liandra was alone.

The archer hadn't seen her. No one came.

She stayed there in the ruins of Cothique, surrounded by smoke at her mother's side, until the fire died and all that remained was ash.

Liandra awoke with a sudden start, awash with feverish sweat.

She breathed deep, trying to abate her trembling, soothing Vranesh who was similarly distressed. The high mountain air was crisp and cold. It chilled her, but she relished it, found it calming.

'Mother...' The word escaped her lips without her realising, and terror was subdued by a hard ball of iron that nestled in her heart.

Eight years she had been hunting. As soon as she learned of the druchii's presence in the Old World, and she felt the resonance of the Wind of Dhar in the gorge to confirm her, she had not rested. Kor Vanaeth was left to one of her father's seneschals. He was a good man, a dependable warrior, but not one in whom Liandra could confide.

Not like Imladrik.

Every since the day they parted ways, she had ached for his return. Not once had she gone back to Kor Vanaeth, preferring the cold solitude of hunting dark elves. She cared not for the imminent war. It didn't matter to her who had killed the dwarfs. None of that mattered now. She just wanted revenge.

And her prey was close.

She breathed deep of the mountain air again... and smelled smoke, heard the crackle of fire.

A tremor jerked her heart and she gasped, reliving the dream all over again. Then fire turned to ice in her veins.

She wasn't dreaming. The fire was real. Smoke carried on the swift mountain breeze.

Kor Vanaeth was burning.

THIRTY

A HURLED SPEAR

By the time the armies of Barak Varr and Zhufbar had reached the fortress at Black Fire Pass, it took thirteen days for Snorri Halfhand's throng to meet the elves in pitched battle.

It took less than three hours to defeat them and send the survivors fleeing back to their city.

Now, Kor Vanaeth was surrounded by almost forty thousand dwarfs. Like an ingot of iron clenched in the tongs, they would hammer the elves against the anvil until they broke.

On a dark heath strewn with battered shields and snapped spear hafts, a conclave of dwarf lords had gathered to decide upon their siege tactics. Frost crisped the ground underfoot, showing up spilt blood that glistened like rubies in the light snowfall. It made the earth hard and the grass crunch like shattered bone.

'We could just wait them out,' suggested King Valarik of Karak Hirn. 'Set up our pickets and let the elgi starve.' Two great eagle wings sprouted from his war helm and a suit of fine ringmail clad his slight frame. A short cape of ermine flapped in the wind, revealing the haft of his mattock slung beneath it on his back.

A susurrus of disproval emanated from the gathered lords. Valarik was youthful, his hold barely founded. It was only natural the older, venerable kings would take exception to his idea.

'They already look beaten.' There was a glint in King Hrekki Ironhandson's eye. It sparkled like the tips of his bolt throwers in the low winter sun.

A gust of cold air ghosted from Snorri's mouth as he exhaled.

'Because they are.' Like many dwarf kings, a vein of greed as thick and beguiling as any motherlode ran through Ironhandson. He licked his lips as he imagined the plunder inside the elf city that would swell his coffers.

Snorri didn't feel it. He only wanted to show his father he was wrong and that the elves were a threat in need of ousting from their lands.

Thagdor certainly thought so.

He regarded the lines of battered but defiant spearmen, the rows of dishevelled elven archers upon the wall with disdain.

Their horse guard were all dead, the silver-helmed riders smashed against a bulwark of dwarf shields. The King of Zhufbar had revelled in this, for they were his shields.

'Aye, as bloody weak and feeble as I thought. We should've done this years ago.'

Why then, thought Snorri, *do I not feel it?*

He expected satisfaction, a sense of righteous vengeance, but all that filled him was a terrible emptiness, which he could fill with neither gold or violence.

He had gathered the kings together, standing behind the serried shield walls of almost forty thousand dwarfs, to plan the assault. It only occurred to him now that the battle required little in the way of strategy. The dwarfs possessed an overwhelming advantage in terms of their numbers. They could simply march on Kor Vanaeth and not stop until it was rubble under their stomping boots.

The left flank contained the bulk of Karak Varn's war engines. Ironhandson was particularly proud of them, a battery of fifty stone throwers and half that again in ballistae. Untouched in the pitched battle, his engineers and journeymen made ready to unleash them now.

Brynnoth said nothing. He had come to the council as requested, but cared not for tactics. Like most of the clans of Barak Varr, he just wanted revenge. Dwarfs are patient creatures, but eight years had begun to seem a long time coming for Agrin Fireheart's retribution.

Snorri recognised the merchant Nadri Copperfist amongst the king's retinue. Doubtless, his place there was because he had found the runelord and desired vengeance of his own. A merchant no longer, he had left the name Gildtongue behind and become a warrior. Before it was over, Snorri suspected many more would have to do the same. Rope makers, lantern-bearers, barrel-wrights, muleskinners, gold-shapers, rock-cutters, brew-hands, all the dwarfs of the clans would set down the tools of their various trades and take up their axes in this cause.

His father had seen that. After eight years, Snorri was only just beginning to see.

'We should let the elgi surrender,' said Morgrim. His mail hauberk was chipped in places, some of the rings split and dented from elven lances. A worn shield hung over his back and a hammer, stained dark crimson, was looped in his belt. Pleading eyes regarded Snorri from beneath the mantle of his horned helmet as his cousin sought to end the fight.

Snorri held his gaze for a moment before casting it over the city. Every one of the elves had retreated behind its walls. His rangers had estimated somewhere in the region of eight thousand warriors still lived and were able to fight. Mainly spearmen and archers; the cavalry were either dead or would be no use during a siege. There were bound to be sorcerers too, but the prince was unconcerned. Both Brynnoth and Thagdor had brought their runesmiths.

'They won't surrender, cousin,' said Snorri. His burnished breastplate shone dully in the sun as if lacking some of its former lustre. It came with a winged helm that the prince kept in the crook of his arm, and had a shirt of mail beneath it. His axe was unsullied and sat upon his back in its sheath. His iron gauntlet flexed. 'And nor would we let them. We must send a message. Elgi are not wanted in these lands. They are trespassers and interlopers, and won't be tolerated any more.'

Morgrim lowered his voice. 'You think it will end here? You've made your point, cousin. Let them go.'

He half glanced at Drogor who was standing stock still beside his cousin, eyes front.

Snorri shook his head.

'Can't do that, Morg. The elgi have enjoyed our mercy long enough. Agrin Fireheart lies eight years dead and that must be accounted for. There are entire chapters of grudges devoted to the acts of murder and sabotage perpetrated by these thagging pointy-ears. Have you forgotten Zakbar Varf?'

'That was a trading settlement, *this* is a city!' Morgrim bit his tongue, struggling to rein in his exasperation. He urged, 'Please don't do this.'

Snorri paused, betraying the slightest chink in his resolve.

Drogor's grip tightened on his axe haft, and the prince hardened again.

'It's already done,' he said, thinking about the elven corpses littering the battlefield behind them. He signalled to King Ironhandson. 'Bring it down,' he told him. 'By Grimnir, bring it all down.'

Greed lighting his eyes like a bonfire, the King of Karak Varn raised his fist.

Horns blared, drums beat, warriors clattered their shields.

'Khazuk!'

Hurled stones and flung bolts thickened the air, whistling in a murderous clamour.

The inevitable war had finally begun.

Fighting outside the gate to Kor Vanaeth was fierce.

Nadri hacked his blade into the elven wood, finding it much more unyielding than he would have first believed.

In their eagerness to kill elves, and their greed, the dwarf army had not bothered to hew down the trees for battering rams. Instead they would use their axes to cut the city gate down, for surely an elven gate would be easy to breach?

The last hour had proven the falsehood of that, but even as the arrow storm raining down on them from above claimed yet more of Grungni's sons, the gate was slowly beginning to buckle.

Wrenching his axe loose, Nadri saw and heard a crack split its length all the way to the keystone above.

'It yields!' roared King Brynnoth, shielded by his doughty hearthguard.

Within a few paces of his liege-lord, Nadri struck again, urging his clan to greater efforts. He had killed many elves in the earlier pitched battle, and saw their faces with every blow against the gate. Bloodied grimaces, terror-etched or dead-eyed, they rattled him to the core. Then he remembered Krondi, gutted like a fish, and his grip hardened to chiselled stone.

Hammer-armed dwarfs from the Sootbrow clan thumped the cracks, widening the breach with each successive blow. Miners by trade, the Sootbrows worked with steady momentum like they were at the rock face hewing ore.

'*Ho, hai, ho, hai...*'

Their labouring song was mesmeric. Even when one of their number was felled by an arrow and gargled his last, they did not pause or falter.

The war machines were silent. King Ironhandson had ordered an end to the barrage as soon as Prince Snorri had blown the signal to march. Nadri had been glad of it, muttering an oath to Krondi as they advanced on the city. How far away his life as a merchant seemed now. He spared a brief thought for Heg before the arrows started flying, hoping his brother was still safe in the Sea Hold.

With a sickening splintering of wood, the gate broke apart. A forest of spears glittered on the other side. Behind them, a host of angry and defiant elven faces.

Shields up, the dwarfs barged forwards. Some spears found a way through, skewering mail or splitting plate. With their shields facing elven aggression in front of them, the dwarfs were vulnerable to arrows from above. Even when over a hundred dead littered the gateway, the sons of Grungni did not relent.

Unable to hold back such a determined tide, the elf spear line buckled and the dwarfs poured in.

An elven lordling wearing shining silver scale, a feather of amethyst purple poking from the tip of his helmet, and riding a white horse, raised his sword to urge the garrison of Kor Vanaeth on. Archers mounted on the steps loosed the last of their remaining shafts into the courtyard that was clogging quickly with elven dead.

Nadri took an arrow in his shoulder before he raised his shield to block three others. Head down, seeing mainly booted feet and the skirts of elven scale mail, he swung like a blind man in a bar fight. The hard *thwack* of his axe blade hitting flesh then bone was the only sign he was still in the fight. A spear tip glanced off his helmet, setting a ringing in his ears and a dense throb in his skull. Blood pulsing, heart thundering, he lashed out and was rewarded with a half-strangled scream.

Sweat filled his nostrils, some his own, some his warrior brothers'. He heard their grunting, the muttered curses.

'*Thagging elgi!*'
'*Dreng elgi!*'
'*Uzkul, uzkul!*'

No way out of the melee, surrounded by the din of battle and dying, Nadri roared his own war cry.

'*Krondi! Dammaz a Krondi!*'

A brief cessation to the killing allowed him to look up. The elves were retreating further into the city, but their numbers and formation were scattered. Most of the archers had emptied their quivers so abandoned their bows in favour of knives.

Nadri saw a spearman brought to his knees by one of the hearthguard. Another smacked the elf around the face, his neck snapping wildly to the left before he slumped down and was still.

A second clutched the air, his spear wrenched from his grip before the hammers were upon him, silencing his screams.

Spurring his mount the lordling rode at King Brynnoth, who had demanded to lead the attack personally, uttering a battle cry to his elven gods.

The king of the Sea Hold shoulder barged the steed, thudding his armoured bulk into the beast's chest and stealing away its breath. With a shriek, its ribcage cracked; heart failing, the horse collapsed and bore its rider with it.

Brynnoth showed no mercy as he cut off the lordling's screaming head.

That was almost an end to it.

Seeing their commander slain was enough to break the elves. Those who could, ran; those who couldn't, surrendered. Several of the pleading elves died before Prince Snorri entered the fray to call a stop to it.

Nadri stood in the middle of the carnage, breathing hard, an ache in his back and shoulder where the arrow remained.

'Get the healers to look at that,' said a voice behind him. He half turned and saw the Prince of Karaz-a-Karak. He was about to kneel when the prince stopped him.

'You've fought and bled, by Grimnir,' he said.

For Agrin Fireheart, the dwarfs of Barak Varr had been given the honour of breaking the gate, and it didn't take forty thousand to sack a city of eight. Some of the walls had collapsed, weakened by stone throwers, brought down by grapnels, but the incursions of the other dwarfs had been mild compared to the effort of the Sea Hold clans.

Prince Snorri met Nadri's gaze. There was steel there, and stone.

'No son of Grungni who has fought this day kneels to me. Go find a healer, lad. The deed here is done.'

He walked on, several of his thanes in tow.

Nadri had expected to feel satisfaction, a sense of closure, even relief. He felt none of these things. Looking around at the corpses, the greedy looting that followed, he found he felt nothing at all.

* * *

A warrior of the hearthguard hurried over, his heavy armour clanking. He'd run a good distance, heaving and gasping in his suit of plate and mail, lifting his visored helm to speak.

'My prince.'

Snorri took the proffered spyglass, nodding thanks, before aiming the device at the sky. The lens was grimy, smeared by dirt and smoke. Snorri had to rub it with his thumb to clear it, and tried not to rush.

'What do you see?' asked Drogor, sidling up beside him.

The pair of them were beyond the borders of the city, which was still burning. Once the brief siege was over, Snorri had returned to the heath where he could plot his next move. He'd had a map in his hand, his eye on the road to Tor Alessi, when the hearthguard had interrupted.

'It's large, moving quickly and against the wind,' he told Drogor. He peered for longer, squinting for a sharper look. Then he put down the spyglass and yelled to one of the Karak Varn engineers. 'Bolt throwers!'

The dwarfs followed the prince's pointing finger, the master surveying the sky with a spyglass of his own. 'Drakk!' he bellowed to his kinsmen, prompting frantic scurrying as spear-tipped shafts were loaded into cradles, windlass cranks turned and sighters levelled.

'Did he say "drakk"?' asked Morgrim, joining them. Behind him, the dwarfs of Karak Varn had begun loading carts and wagons to ferry their plunder back to the hold. King Ironhandson's booming laughter overwhelmed the crackle of the inferno gutting the city as he saw his treasure hoard swelling.

Brynnoth and his warriors had come together, apart from the rest of the army. Heads bowed, listening to the sonorous tones of their king, they were holding a vigil for Agrin Fireheart.

'None other,' uttered Snorri, his voice full of loathing. 'I *hate* drakkal.'

Morgrim squinted but couldn't make out the beast or its rider clearly enough. It was a dark shape, sweeping between clouds of smoke.

'It could be Prince Imladrik.'

Snorri turned on him. 'Your pet elgi?'

'He is a friend to the dawi, and to me.'

'All elgi became enemies as soon as we crushed that army.' Drogor thumbed over his shoulder where the shattered horse guard still lay bleeding and broken. Most were probably dead by now. 'Do you think he'll still clasp your hand in a warrior's grip when he sees this?'

Morgrim ignored him, looking to his cousin.

'We cannot loose.'

Snorri clenched his teeth, considering Morgrim's request, but in the end had to shake his head.

'Can't risk it. That drakk will burn our camp to cinders, cousin.'

'We are at war now,' Drogor reminded them. 'Our stone was cast and more will be needed.'

Morgrim bit his tongue. He hoped it wasn't Imladrik. Not since the bro-dunk had he seen the elf prince, and despite the discord between their peoples, he still regarded him as a friend. He warranted that friendship would be tested if Imladrik saw what had transpired at Kor Vanaeth.

The low rumble of cracking stone presaged the collapse of the gatehouse, leaving the entire city razed and brought to rubble. A cheer rose up from the dwarfs of Zhufbar who were presiding over the demolition. Morgrim tried hard not to despise them for it.

Bolt throwers cranked to the highest possible elevation, the master of engineers looked over expectantly at the prince.

'The drakk!' bellowed one of the engineers, his crew trembling with fear at the sight of the monster.

A bestial shriek, chasm deep and full of hatred, echoed across the sky. It was a challenge. If the dragon rider was Imladrik, he had seen the carnage by now and had chosen to attack. Morgrim unslung his hammer, the runes flaring bright across its head.

Snorri ran out into the open ground, snarling to match the beast.

'Hold fast, let it come!' He swung up his axe, brandishing it at the sky and the winged shadow rapidly closing. 'Face me!' he roared. 'I am the *dreng drakk*. Taste this steel, for it will cleave you unto death!'

Morgrim ran after him, grabbing Snorri's arm. 'What are you doing?'

'You wanted me to hold off the bolt throwers, that is what I am doing.'

'Don't be an idiot.'

Snorri glanced at Morgrim over his shoulder. 'Still want to shake hands with the elgi?'

He looked back at Drogor, but the Karak Zorn dwarf hadn't moved and was watching the sky. Morgrim scowled before standing at his cousin's side.

'Get back,' Snorri warned. 'I don't need your arm in this fight.'

Morgrim was resolute. 'I am your cousin, blood is blood. Here I will stand.'

'Move! It comes for me.' His gaze flicked between his cousin and the growing shadow in the sky. The beat of heavy wings resolved above the wind.

'Then give the order to loose,' said Morgrim. 'That beast will burn us where we stand, unless you plan on slaying it with a single throw of your axe.'

Snorri looked like he was considering it.

'Don't be a stubborn fool. I don't want to die here.'

Something redolent of ash and sulphur tainted the breeze.

'Dragon's breath.' Morgrim readied his shield, knowing it was too late to retreat now.

So too did Snorri, but the prince had long embraced his fate.

'Let it come!' he shouted, hefting his battle axe. 'I'll kill it!'

The dragon dived, scales shimmering like fire in the sun. Like a red blade ripping through a bank of snow-shawled cloud, it angled towards the prince.

Shouts were coming from other parts of the field as more and more dwarfs heard and saw the beast.

A roar like a discordant bell pealed out of the heavens as dragon and rider cried in unison.

King Ironhandson was being barrelled away from danger by his warriors when he jabbed a finger towards the sky.

'Loose!' he cried. 'Bring the monster down!'

Some dwarfs hid behind their shields, others scurried behind carts and wagons. A few drew their weapons and rushed to the prince's side.

Fumbling their war machines, the engineers of Karak Varn unleashed a volley but by then the dragon had pulled out of its dive and climbed for higher skies. Every shaft went wide of the target.

Snorri raged.

'No! Come back,' he roared. 'Come back and face me, beast!'

'It's gone, cousin,' said Morgrim, pulling Snorri back.

'I could have killed it,' he spat, 'and fulfilled my destiny.'

'You will,' said Drogor, his eyes on the sky following the departing figure of the dragon. His voice was calming, and the two cousins climbed down from their heightened emotions at once. Both regarded the Karak Zorn dwarf as he turned his gaze on them.

'Not yet, but soon my prince. Now, we must march.'

Snorri shook his head as if coming out of a daze.

'Yes...' he murmured, blinking twice in close succession. 'Gather the kalans, sound the horn. We march for Tor Alessi.'

Tears streamed down Liandra's face, and Vranesh wailed in empathic anguish.

Kor Vanaeth was gone, sundered to ruins, and Fendaril was surely dead. She had failed her people, obsessing over vengeance and a desire to punish all druchii for what they had done. Her father knew she was volatile. Only now did she realise why Lord Athinol had sent her to the Old World. Soaring into the high skies, she welcomed the loneliness and the chill in her bones. It numbed her from feeling.

She had seen an army outside her city. Others would come, compelled by greed. Though her desire to return and take out her anger on the dwarfs was strong, she resisted. The other cities would need to be warned.

Tor Alessi was the greatest of them, so she would go there first.

Urging Vranesh, she tried to push the images of Kor Vanaeth from her mind but they burned, just as the city had burned, and would not fade.

THIRTY-ONE

A SHAMING

They were ugly creatures, the king decided.

Bulbous noses, ruddy cheeks, their jutting foreheads and brutish feet. Every cobble-booted step as they walked down the long aisle towards the throne put his teeth on edge. And the smell... Caledor held a pomander up to his nose to smother the worst of it. Sadly, it could not hide the dirt or hair of the beasts.

Caledor could easily believe they lived in holes in the ground.

So incongruous in his pristine hall, amongst the fluted archways and pale stone. The throne room of the palace at Lothern was so smooth and perfect. These *dwarfs* – even the name was lumpen – were just... gnarled.

He leaned over in his throne.

'They seem humbled,' he remarked, considering the sober expression of the one in front. Like the rest, he had a long plaited beard which was no doubt crawling with lice and other vermin. 'Do they seem humbled to you, brother?'

Imladrik was standing beside the throne, one hand on the hilt of Ifulvin, the other behind his armoured back. Though he wasn't wearing a helmet, his face was hard as steel as if masked by one.

'They look proud to me. Defiant.'

Caledor shook his head. He wore robes, white as swan feather with a gold trim, and reclined like a dilettante. No effort had been made to adopt the mantle of the warrior king. In fact, since the dwarf vessel had found its way into the harbour of Lothern, little effort had been made at all.

Ushered from the city to the Phoenix King's court, few words beyond those which were necessary had been exchanged. A cohort of spearmen had shadowed the dwarf ambassador and his small retinue, the rest of the dwarfs staying behind with their crude-looking ship.

Word had come from the High King, brought by eagle riders, that he wished to parley. Amused, Caledor had granted his request. Less than two weeks later, the dwarfs had arrived. A fast crossing across the Great Ocean. Apparently, they had navigated its many perils through the efforts of their veteran captain and a dwarf wizard of some description. His mages had dismissed the feat as hedge magic, or some baser sorcery, but the fact remained that they had reached Ulthuan as swiftly as any elf vessel.

'I think they looked humbled,' Caledor reasserted, 'even grovelling.' He reached for his goblet, supping deeply and regarding the approaching dwarfs over its gilded rim.

There were six in total. Five were warriors, armed and armoured despite Imladrik's protests to the contrary, but one carried no weapon and wore a tunic and cloak. Obviously, this was their ambassador. He clutched a letter in his grubby little hands.

As the dwarf delegation came to within ten feet of the throne, Imladrik raised his hand and a line of spearmen stepped between them.

'That's far enough,' he said.

Caledor waved him down.

'Nonsense!' he cried. 'Let them come closer. Is this any way to treat guests of our court?'

If the dwarfs understood his mocking tone, none of them showed it.

Pausing in his theatre for a moment, Caledor looked to Hulviar who was standing on the opposite side to Imladrik.

'They *can* understand us, can't they, Hulviar?' he muttered.

'My lord,' one of the dwarfs spoke up.

The ambassador stepped forwards as the line of spearmen parted. He bowed.

'I can speak elven, if only rudimentarily.'

Caledor snorted, laughed. His eyebrows arched incredulously.

'Then you are a clever pig, aren't you?'

The ambassador became indignant. 'I am no pig, my lord.'

'You dig holes in mud where you then live, and protest you are not swine?' Caledor smiled haughtily. 'Intriguing. What do you make of my court?' he asked, gesturing expansively to the columns of white marble decorated with statues of griffons rampant, brooding dragons and majestic eagles. Banners and tapestries hung along the walls, which were punctuated by fist-sized rubies and sapphires. It was austere, but it was also magnificent.

'A fine antechamber, my lord.'

A nerve trembled in Caledor's cheek, the king unable to tell if the dwarf was now mocking him.

'Is your sty so much grander then?'

'I am no pig,' the ambassador repeated. 'I am Forek Grimbok, dawi of Karaz-a-Karak and representative of the High King.' He brandished the letter. 'And I bring his terms in this missive.'

Caledor arched an eyebrow, half distracted by drinking his wine. He drained the goblet and gestured to a nearby servant to bring another.

'Terms?' he said, focusing his full attention back on the dwarf.

'Yes,' said the ambassador. 'For peace. That is why we are here. That is why we have travelled across the Great Ocean from the Old World.'

Caledor smiled, nodded. '*Peace*, is it? Where was this peace when Kor Vanaeth was attacked? Does your *king* have an answer for that in his letter?'

The ambassador struggled to hide his surprise. News about Kor Vanaeth had arrived only that morning, sent by Liandra Athinol, the city's custodian.

'It does not,' admitted the dwarf. 'Nor have I heard of such an attack.'

'Burned to the very stone,' said the king, dangerously.

Some of the other dwarfs shifted uncomfortably at the obvious change in mood. Several of their hands strayed to the hilts of their axes.

Imladrik hissed through clenched teeth, 'You should have let me disarm them.'

'Don't be silly, brother,' Caledor admonished. 'Forek, here... that is your name, isn't it? Yes, that's what you said. Forek, here, has said he knew nothing about it. Nor, apparently, did his king. It seems his subjects are roaming his lands killing and sacking cities according to whim. Is that about right, Forek?'

The ambassador's jaw hardened. He eyed the spearmen either side of them, caught the gaze of another dwarf who merely shook his head.

'I have said I know nothing of that.' He showed the letter again. 'Again I say, here are my High King's terms.'

Caledor leaned back in his throne.

'*High* king? Seems an odd turn of phrase for such a diminutive race.'

'He is lord of the Karaz Ankor, greatest dawi of the realm!'

'Yes, yes, I understand.' Caledor waved away the impassioned protests of the ambassador. 'Well then, you had better read these terms before more cities are put to the torch, hadn't you?'

The ambassador looked momentarily confused, but then cleared his throat and was about to read when Imladrik stepped from the throne's dais and took the letter.

'Tromm,' he muttered under his breath with a nod to the dwarf, who replied in the same way.

He glared at Caledor, who seemed disinterested but there was a glint of something unpleasant in his eye, an idea forming that Imladrik hoped would not come to fruition.

The Master of Dragons read swiftly. His expression darkened further when he was done.

'Well then,' asked Caledor, 'what are the dwarf king's terms?'

Imladrik met his gaze, knowing the response before it was given.

'He asks for recompense and apology for the hostilities directed at his people. Furthermore, he demands a cessation to all further violence against the dwarfs.'

'A long letter for such a short list of terms,' said Caledor.

'There is more, which you would not be interested in, my king.'

'You are right about that, brother. The griping and posturing of these mud-dwellers is not my concern.'

He nodded to Hulviar.

'Seize them!' snarled the seneschal.

Twenty spearmen levelled their weapons at the dwarfs, but the warriors were ready with axes drawn and smashed several of the tips aside.

One dwarf was pierced in the back and side before he could swing. Another was brought to heel with three points at his neck. A third was pinioned in the leg and couldn't move. A fourth was similarly trapped. The fifth, their leader, rolled beneath the jabbing spears and came up to bury his axe in an elf's shield. The blow split it in two, breaking the elf's arm and drawing blood.

The ambassador cried out, 'Gilias!' as the dwarf advanced on another spearman, barging into him and bearing the elf down.

'They mean to kill us!' cried Gilias.

Caledor was up and out of his throne in an eyeblink. His sword, by his side until that moment, was now drawn and sunk halfway up the long blade into Gilias's chest.

The dwarf grunted once, unable to comprehend what had happened at first, then he spat a stream of blood and collapsed.

Caledor turned to his spearmen, who had completely subdued the dwarfs.

'Hold them,' he said.

They were chewing and tugging their beards, moaning in their crude language and glaring first at the king and then at their fallen kinsman, his life pooling beneath him.

'Thagi!' shouted the ambassador. He'd balled his fists but with a spear tip at his neck was powerless to do anything.

Caledor rounded on him.

'Brother, wait...' Imladrik tried to intercede but the king pushed him aside.

'You burn my cities,' he said to the dwarf, 'and come here expecting apology and recompense? I do not give apologies, *pig*, I grant pleas. You and your kind are worthy of neither.'

'Let us go,' the ambassador warned. 'And allow us to bear Gilias Thunderbrow's body back to his kalan, you thagging pointy-eared bastard.'

Sneering, Caledor looked Forek up and down. He reached out to seize his beard, pulled it hard until the dwarf ambassador winced.

'You are an uncouth creature,' he told him, smiling cruelly.

'I cannot be a party to this,' said Imladrik, shaking his head, and went to leave before his brother's command rooted him to the spot.

'You'll stay and witness this,' he said. 'I want you to see what your lassitude has bred in these pigs.'

Imldrik glowered, but he obeyed.

'Let us go,' said Forek. 'What are you going to do?' There was fear in his voice that warred with the anger.

Caledor released the fistful of hair in his grasp.

'You know, I am not ignorant of your ways,' he said, backing off.

Hulviar had drawn a long dagger from his belt. So had several of the spearmen who were otherwise unencumbered by pinning down the dwarfs.

'I understand you place great importance in your beards, is that right?'

'Brother, no,' Imladrik warned.

'Stand fast!' snapped Caledor, whirling around to glare at him before returning his attention to the dwarfs.

Forek glowered, tears of rage welling in his eyes.

His voice was barely above a whisper as he pleaded, 'Do not do this. I beg of you.'

'Now, he pleads. Now, he begs,' said Caledor. 'Too late, pig. My brother was right. You are proud and defiant.' He raised his finger as if finding the answer to a question that had so far eluded him. 'But I know how to humble you.'

'Please...'

'Caledor...' Imladrik warned him again.

'Silence, brother. I am your king, now do as bidden.'

'Please,' said Forek. 'Dreng tromm, it is our legacy, our ancestry. It will bring great shame on my clan, on all our clans.'

Caledor's eyes were cold and pitiless as the stone of his hall as he regarded the ambassador.

'Shave them. Every lice-infested inch.'

Hulviar and the other elves that had drawn their daggers came forwards. The dwarfs struggled, but were held by the spearmen.

'Dreng tromm, dreng tromm,' wailed the ambassador, and he and his retinue broke out in a raft of curses in their native tongue.

Caledor returned to his throne to watch.

The elves were not kind in their ministrations. Skin was cut, punches thrown and blood shed on the pristine white of the Phoenix Court.

The dwarfs fought, they gnawed and kicked and scratched, but to no avail. The elves held them and did not let them up until every bruised and savaged inch of their faces was shorn.

Throughout the shaming, Caledor looked on impassively.

'See, brother,' he said, watching the dwarfs squirm and quail, 'I said they were humbled.'

He turned to Imladrik, but the Master of Dragons was already walking away.

THIRTY-TWO

THE RUNES FAIL

In the deeps below Everpeak the clang of hammer hitting anvil resounded. For the last eight years and more it had done so with barely more than a moment's respite.

Morek spoke the rites with sonorous solemnity, broke the karadurak, tempered the star-metal and from it fashioned such artifice as only happened once in a generation.

Hissing vapour rushed from the barrel. A gromril blade, its runes refulgent in the forge flame, came forth from its raging depths.

'*Drengudrakk,*' he intoned, naming the weapon clutched in his gauntleted hand.

Ranuld Silverthumb, looking on from the shadows, merely nodded.

'Tromm, Morek,' he uttered, 'and so the rhun is struck and the rite spoken. Metal has come from fire and water, bound by the rituals of earth and air. All the four elements are bound within, trapped by meteoric iron sent from the vaults of heaven.'

Morek looked exhausted, lathered in sweat and soot, his chest, face and fingers burned. But he was exultant.

Bowing his head, Ranuld told him, 'You are now a true master of the rhun.'

A grimace stole upon the runelord's face and he clutched his shoulder suddenly, teeth clenched tight in his mouth.

'Master!' Morek went to him at once, the blade left upon the anvil, but Ranuld stopped him with his upraised palm.

'No,' he rasped, his anguish almost palpable. 'Set it properly. Do it!'

Morek was caught by indecision. He looked once to the blade and then to his master, who was doubled up in pain.

He was by Ranuld's side a moment later, helping the venerable dwarf to his seat in the forge.

'Pipeweed...' he gasped, pointing fervouredly at a small stone box resting on a shelf.

Morek left him to retrieve the box.

Hands shaking, Ranuld opened it, took the pipe and the weed from within, stoked the cradle and lit it.

After a few draughts, his hands steadied, the pain eased and he breathed again.

His eyes were watering, from the seizure or something else, Morek could not tell. He regarded his apprentice with a crestfallen expression, shaking his head.

'What is it, master? Are you–'

'Wazzock!' snapped the runelord. 'Look at that,' he said. 'Look!'

The rune axe upon the anvil had a tiny fissure running through the metal. It was cracked, ruined.

'The magic was not properly bound,' Ranuld told him. Struggling but refusing any help, the runelord got to his feet and shuffled off. 'You should have left me. The rhun is all that matters. Legacy is all I have left to give.' He turned, snarling, 'Let me die next time, and save your worthless concern.'

He tromped from the forge, headed for the deeper vault where Morek was forbidden.

'Not ready,' he chuntered to himself beneath his breath. 'Not nearly ready.' Slowly shaking his head, he disappeared into the soot and smoke. Before he was lost to the darkness completely, his voice rang out, 'Again, do it again.'

Morek slumped to his haunches, regarding the broken metal on the anvil.

Taking up his tongs, he gripped the sundered blade and returned it to the fire.

Speaking through the magic of rune stones was not so easy. Ranuld leaned heavily on his staff, standing before the dokbar, and saw little of Thorik Oakeneye. It was as if some great arachnarok, like the beasts that once roamed the deeps, had spun its silken threads across the shield's surface and obscured it from sight. As if he were trapped at the bottom of a long well, Thorik's voice was muffled and echoed. As Ranuld listened, his expression clouded.

Thorik spoke of a 'great shaming', of 'misdeeds' and 'foulness beyond countenance'.

Throughout his report, which must have taken a great deal of strength to send, Ranuld tugged his beard, muttering, 'Dreng tromm, dreng tromm...'

Perfidy beyond reckoning had been done.

When Thorik was finished, Ranuld looked his fellow runelord in the eye.

'The conclave must gather at Karaz-a-Karak.'

Thorik nodded.

'As soon as I reach the Sea Hold, I will make all haste.'

'War has come, unleashed by the arrogance of youth,' Ranuld said. 'The gronti-duraz must walk. Together we will wake them from slumber.'

'Tromm, my lord.'

'Tromm,' uttered Ranuld, bowing his head as Thorik faded and the dokbar returned to silver once again.

Regarding the silent ranks of stone golems, Ranuld prayed to Grungni that they would listen.

THIRTY-THREE

MUSTERING THE THRONG

'Stand aside!'

Rundin's voice was laced with threat, but the three goldmasters did not yield.

'King Grum has insisted he not be disturbed,' protested one.

'War has come to the Karaz Ankor,' said Rundin. 'All dawi must stand and fight, including the skarrens.'

'Edicts of the mountains do not bind the hills,' said a second.

'I am the king's protector,' declared Rundin, shoving aside the dwarfs, who were wise enough not to resist.

'He is alone, what does he need protecting from?' asked another.

Rundin threw open the doors to the counting house, sparing the goldmasters a final scathing glance.

'Himself,' he answered, stepping inside.

The counting house was dark, even the lamps had been doused, and it stank of sweat. Another stench accompanied it, something acerbic that stung the nostrils.

Rundin's nose wrinkled when he identified what the smell was.

'Grungni's oath...' he muttered, realising just how far his king had fallen.

Skarnag Grum was crouched naked before a candle flame, surrounded by gold. He almost bathed in it, watching the coins trickle from his grasp, delighting in the way they flashed as they caught the light.

'*Gorl* is *galaz* is *gorlm* and *bryn*...'

In Khazalid there were over four hundred different words and expressions for gold. Grum was reciting every single one in a fevered cantrip.

'...is *konk* is *ril* and *frorl* and *kurz*...'

'Valaya's mercy,' Rundin breathed, stepping into the corona of light cast by the candle. 'What has become of you, my noble King Grum?'

At the mention of his name, the king of the hill dwarfs looked up with rheumy, manic eyes.

'Run-din.' His mouth struggled to form the word, drooling saliva.

Holding back his anguish, Rundin knelt beside the king.

'Yes, my liege,' he said, cradling his cheek like a father to a beardling. 'It is me.'

Capricious as winter snow, Skarnag Grum recoiled from his protector, his face a mask of accusation.

'Why are you here?' he snapped, gathering his gold to him, spilling piles of it and snatching at the errant coins. 'You want my gold, don't you? You want it!'

Rundin stood up, shaking his head.

'No, my liege,' he said calmly. 'But you must leave this place. Come with me now.'

Skarnag's eyes narrowed. 'So you can slip in when I'm absent. You have the look of a *skaz* about you, Rundin.' He stood, a filthy loincloth the only scrap of clothing to preserve a shred of dignity. 'My protector turned skaz,' he said, jabbing a finger, 'coveting my gold from afar, waiting for his chance to steal it! Is that it? Eh? Eh!'

Rundin did not want to see any more. He turned around, the king cursing his every step until he sank back down amidst his hoard.

Wiping the tears from his eyes, Rundin paused as he reached the door. Skarnag Grum was still muttering,

'And *renk* is *glam* and *hnon* is *geln* and *bruz*...'

The goldmasters were waiting for him on the other side, their faces caught between fear and admonishment.

'There will be consequences for what you did,' said one.

'Defiance of the king is an act worthy of grudgement,' said another.

Rundin did not meet their eyes. Such wretched dwarfs who had so utterly failed their king were unworthy of his attention.

'Whatever that dawi was in there,' he said, leaving the goldmasters in his wake, 'he is not our king.'

Beyond the Great Hall, which led from the counting house, a long gallery was thronged with hill dwarfs. News had travelled fast of King Gotrek Starbreaker's declaration of war. Clans were amassing, unsure what to do, waiting for the orders of their king. Orders that Rundin knew would not come.

'Kerrik Sternhawk!' he bellowed at one idle-looking warrior. 'Follow me.'

The dwarf obeyed at once. He was fresh-faced with barely a growth of beard, a youth but one that Rundin knew he could trust.

'Thane Rundin?' asked the beardling, falling into step with the king's protector.

'You are the Kro's fastest runner,' he said. 'I need you to convey a message of the utmost importance and secrecy. Can you do that?'

Kerrik looked concerned and confused as they left the gallery and walked out into the light, but nodded immediately.

'Good,' said Rundin. 'Relate this exactly as spoken...'

* * *

Tracing his finger across a narrow line on the map, Snorri sucked his teeth.

'Elgi will be thronging the roads,' he said.

'And if the last army we fought is any gauge, the numbers will be greater,' Morgrim suggested.

'They are bloody greater the closer we get to Tor-chuffing-Alessi,' snapped Thagdor, finding the elf words difficult to pronounce. Since they were not dwarf holds, they had not bothered to name the elf cities in Khazalid. It had seemed unimportant.

Since Kor Vanaeth they had met the elves in battle three more times. On each occasion the dwarfs had been victorious, but on each occasion they had taken losses.

During the last engagement, a band of swift, bow-armed riders had destroyed several of the Karak Varn war machines. In another, over two hundred clansmen had died to the combined sorcery of three elven mages.

The rearguard, made up of clans from the Sea Hold, had been harried for over six days during the last march. Eighteen warriors lay dead as a result. Despite the best efforts of their rangers, the dwarfs could not bring the perpetrators to heel.

Arrows were the worst – the elves possessed uncanny accuracy. Digging graves for dwarfs slain by arrows had delayed Snorri's army by several days already.

Snorri turned to King Brynnoth, who had promised further reinforcements from Barak Varr.

'Any news from your hold, my king?'

'Some,' he said, chewing on a thigh bone he had divested of the meat several minutes ago. 'Four wagons bearing arms and armour were lost whilst crossing the Vaults, a grudge against Dammin Cloud-eye for his ineptitude,' he grumbled. 'Another message speaks of foraging in the forest for wood and provisions when the throng was attacked.'

'Attacked?' asked Morgrim. 'We are close to the forest, our route might take us into the neighbouring Grey Mountains.'

Brynnoth's face reddened. 'Said it was haunted by unquiet spirits. Trees came alive, they reckon.'

'I have heard similar tales from our cousins of Karak Norn,' uttered Valarik fearfully, making the protective sigil of Valaya.

Snorri frowned, unconvinced. Thagdor had to stifle a laugh.

'Who leads this throng?' asked the prince.

'Ungrim Shaftcleaver,' said Brynnoth. 'A trusted thane of my hold, or so I thought.'

'Perhaps he was addled by the sun?' suggested Drogor. 'I have seen such things happen before in the Southlands.'

'In winter?' said Thagdor, incredulous.

Snorri exhaled ruefully. 'It doesn't matter. Tell Shaftcleaver to get his warriors here as quickly as he can. We are now thirty thousand dawi, just over, and there's still a long way to go to the elgi city.'

'Which route do we take then, cousin?' asked Morgrim. 'The passes through the mountains, risking the wrath of the Fey Forest?' He glared at Thagdor, who stopped chuckling to offer an apology, before carrying on, 'Or march down the Brundin Road and walk right up to their gates?'

'I'll happily ruddy knock at their doors,' boasted Thagdor.

'Aye,' agreed Ironhandson, who was still sore over the wrecking of his war engines. 'Let them see us coming. Likely the pointy-ears will soil themselves first and then flee.'

Snorri doubted that. The elves were not as soft-skinned and callow-hearted as any of the dwarfs had believed.

Crouched over the map, his lords arrayed around him, he found he was at an impasse. Though he would never admit it, he had given little thought to what might happen after Kor Vanaeth. So far, he had simply marched onwards, headed for Tor Alessi and fighting whatever stood in his way. Now he had three kings at his behest, as well as their armies. Thirty thousand of his kinsmen were relying on his judgement and leadership. How Snorri wished his father was there at that moment, and felt a prick of regret at their parting and his actions since.

'Which is it to be then, lad?' asked Thagdor, stabbing at the map with his finger. 'Road or mountain pass?'

Snorri rubbed his beard. Both ways were perilous, and so far no rangers had returned from their scouting to offer any idea of the sort of numbers the dwarfs faced at Tor Alessi. It was their largest settlement, but Kor Vanaeth had fallen easily enough. Surely, this Tor Alessi would capitulate in similar fashion.

'Cousin,' muttered Morgrim, 'you must make a decision.'

Snorri answered through clenched teeth, 'I am thinking.' He had settled on a course and was about to tell his generals when a shout came from deeper in the camp. Through the parting throngs, there hurried a beardling, a runner.

'Prince Snorri,' he gasped, struggling for breath. The youth kneeled until Snorri told him to get up and spit out whatever he had come to tell him. 'Rangers, my liege,' said the youth, 'from Karaz-a-Karak.'

At some instinctive sign Snorri looked up over the runner's shoulder and beheld a face he hadn't seen for some time. Despite the obvious tension associated with the ranger's arrival, he smiled.

'Tromm, Furgil.'

Supping deep of the black beer in his tankard, Furgil smacked his lips and sighed.

'Been a while since I had the taste of proper ale on my tongue,' he said. 'Grog has been all we had to sustain us for the last two weeks.'

The pathfinder had arrived in camp with nineteen other rangers, all well-worn and travel-weary but clearly having seen little actual battle. Apparently, they had skirmished with orcs and goblins of the mountains, even seen a band of elven riders in the distance, but little else. Wisely, their enemies were moving away from the dwarf holds of the Worlds Edge. Should they not, they would be trampled by a shield wall of some fifty thousand dwarfs or more. Warriors were amassing; the High King had called the clans and declared war.

When he had heard of the ambassador's shaming, he and his guardians, Snorri had spat numerous oaths of vengeance. Grimbok was no friend to him, but he was a dwarf and no son of Grungni should endure such mistreatment. When his apoplexy had passed, he fell into a deep introspection, chewing at his beard as his father might have done in a similar situation.

Snorri reclined on a leather-backed throne sitting in the lee of his tent. A hearthguard stood nearby, eyes fixed on the horizon line that presaged storm. Grey, black clouds streaked low and fast, swelling with each passing moment and filling the sky with an endless gloom.

'A wretched day to march,' said the prince, drawing on his pipe. He was fully armoured, only his war helm resting against the leg of his throne, and shifted uncomfortably in his full panoply of battle. 'I would prefer a steam bath and the attention of a buxom rinn.'

'Wouldn't we all,' remarked Furgil, taking another pull of the black beer and leaving the foam to evaporate on his beard. 'Except the bath, of course. An annual *dunkin* is just fine for me, my prince.'

'Am I still your prince?' Snorri asked curtly. 'You have brought message of my father, his intention to make war, but said nothing of his mood.'

The tent was pitched on a rugged hillock that offered a decent view of the encampment. With his back to his lord, Furgil swept his gaze across the numerous snapping pennants, clan icons and banners that were mounted on the army's tents. Dwarfs were massed outside them, some sparring, others merely sitting. They encircled fires, clutching tankards like he was, smoking or muttering. Some recounted grudges, others sang songs or bemoaned the weather and the air. Dwarfs were not so fond of air, at least not that which smelled of grass and river and bird. They longed for heat, for ash and smoke, for the reek of the deep earth.

There were a host of machineries, mostly under tarp but some being tended by engineers and their journeymen. He saw ballistae and catapults of varying size and girth. Many bore the rune of Karak Varn.

'You have gathered quite the host,' said Furgil, turning to face Snorri at last, 'and, yes, you are still my prince and always shall be.' He bowed his head, low in respect and fealty. 'Your father is angry,' he said, 'and asks me to bid you wait for his army to reach you before marching further.'

Snorri scowled. 'I will not be cowed by him, Furgil. When you return, you must tell him that. This–' he gestured to the throng of dwarfs below, '–is *my* army. He may have declared war but it is I who have waged it first.'

'As you wish, my prince. I merely convey the message.'

Snorri's scowl turned into a questioning frown, and he leaned forwards. 'Have all the holds mustered?'

Furgil nodded, draining his tankard before answering. 'Aye. As well as the clans of the capital, your father the High King has Karak Drazh and the mining clans of Gunbad and Silverspear with his banner. Even Varnuf of the Eight Peaks marches, along with the holds of the south. North, there's King Grundin and a contingent from Karak Ungor who have already suffered from elgin perfidy.'

Snorri raised an eyebrow in query.

'Bagrik, their king, was slain by treachery,' Furgil explained. 'The length and breadth of the Worlds Edge, even the Vaults, the Grey and the Black, are bound to this war.'

'Not all the realms of the dawi, though,' said Snorri, his eyes never leaving the ranger who lowered his gaze in shame.

'No, not all. Not yet.'

'You know something my father and I do not?'

'Only hope, my prince. Hope in an old friend to do what is right. That is all.'

Snorri laughed. 'I expected my father to be less understanding.'

'Oh, make no mistake, my prince, grudges against Thagdor, Brynnoth and Valarik have been writ. Retribution for their transgression will be taken in wergeld or actual blood, the Starbreaker has avowed it, but not until the war is done.'

'They best hope it claims them, then,' muttered Snorri, knowing well his father's wrath.

Furgril merely nodded.

'Tromm for the beer, but I should be on my way.'

Snorri didn't answer immediately. His mind was elsewhere, back during his carefree days of adventuring with Morgrim in the lower deeps. He glanced down into the encampment, knowing his cousin was somewhere below, preparing for the march. It would have to wait, Snorri decided.

'Tell my father we will hold here for a week but no more. If his throng hasn't reached us by then we will have to march.'

'I'll tell him, my prince.'

Furgil was already on his way, signalling to his rangers who waited silently for him below, when Snorri called out to him.

'You are a loyal servant of the Karaz Ankor, Furgil. It's a pity your countrymen are not like you.'

Furgil paused but didn't answer. He left as quietly as he'd arrived, headed east to the host of the High King.

'Summon my war council,' Snorri said to the hearthguard once Furgil had gone.

THIRTY-FOUR

WAR OF THE BEARD

'That is what they are calling it, my king.'

'Even for elgi that is bold,' said Gotrek. 'They mock us with the very name of this conflict.'

Thurbad didn't disagree, so just nodded.

After a short rest in the Mootlands of the half-folk, the army of Karaz-a-Karak and its vassal lords was preparing to move on. Furgil had recently returned bringing news of the prince's intention to wait for his father. A week was not long, however, and winter ground made for a difficult march, even for dwarfs. Time could not be wasted if they were to meet Snorri's deadline.

Gotrek cast a mantle of red velvet, trimmed with eagle feathers, over his shoulders. Thurbad attached the pauldron pins, then tightened the clasps of the king's gromril armour so it hugged his waist.

He groaned. 'Been too long vacillating in my throne room,' said Gotrek. 'Must have gotten fat.'

'Winter padding, my king.'

Gotrek smirked at the hearthguard, who hadn't even paused to acknowledge his joke.

'Aye, something like that.'

He would have preferred a hold hall, a roaring hearth at his back as he donned his armour, but out on campaign a tent would have to suffice. Gotrek scowled at its weakness, wishing for solid stone above and about him. The wars with the greenskins and the monsters of the Ungdrin were vicious affairs, cramped, brutal and close up, but at least they were beneath ground. Sky and forest were not to the High King's liking, and made him uneasy.

'Should I have marched before now, Thurbad?' he asked candidly.

Now the hearthguard paused, halfway to buckling a leather weapons belt.

'You may speak your mind,' Gotrek told him. 'Have no fear of grudgement.'

Thurbad looked the High King in the eye. 'No, my king. You did what was necessary to protect the Karaz Ankor. A calm head should always prevail over a rash one, or so my father always said.'

'Then he was a wise dawi, your father.'

'Tromm, he was.'

'It would have spared Grimbok his fate, your hearthguard too and the life of Gilias Thunderbrow, if I had thrown in with my son and marched.'

'He is in the Hall of the Ancestors now,' said Thurbad. 'I could wish no more for him than that. As for the others...' He looked away for a moment, and Gotrek knew he was picturing the wretched dwarfs, their beards shorn, their ancestry taken from them. Even in death, their shame would cling to them like a miasma, bound forever to Gazul's Gate through which the unquiet could not pass.

Gotrek put his hand on the hearthguard's shoulder.

'We will avenge them.'

Thurbad nodded, buckled the High King's belt and stepped back.

'You are klad, my king,' he said, handing Gotrek his axe.

'To think,' said Gotrek as he took the weapon in his hands, 'we were once allies.' He ran his thumb over the blade, drawing a ruby of blood that ran all the way along the axe's gromril edge.

'Will you punish him, my king?'

'Snorri did what he thought was right. He predicted war and war we have got, sacking the elgi settlement didn't cause that. It was already done when our kin died on the road and Agrin Fireheart lost his life. But, yes,' added the High King, 'I will punish him.'

Over fifty thousand amassed in the army of the High King. More were coming from the north and south but would not reach them in time. It wouldn't matter. Gotrek was resolved to meet up with his son and march on Tor Alessi until its walls were down and its people ash on the breeze.

'War of the Beard,' he snorted, suppressing a sneer. 'They are owed, Thurbad. The scales are unbalanced and I mean to redress them with death. It is a different conflict we shall bring to the elgi, not of beards, but a War of Vengeance.'

The kings of Kagaz Thar and Kazad Mingol looked around furtively.

Even surrounded by their warriors, shrouded in the gloom of the shaded glade in the forests beyond Kazad Kro, they looked uncomfortable and slightly afraid.

'Why have you brought us here, beardling?' King Kruk asked of Kerrik Sternhawk.

The liege-lord of Kagaz Thar was dressed in a leather cloak fashioned to look like overlapping leaves. His armour was rough and rugged like tree bark and he wore muddy kohl around his deep-set eyes. An unkempt beard framed an angular face with bushy eyebrows and a flat knot for a nose. Gnarled as oak, bitter as a winter storm, King Kruk was far from happy at being summoned by Skarnag Grum. 'The High King doesn't venture from the Kro. Ever. What is the meaning of this?'

'Aye,' agreed King Orrik. He'd looped his thumbs beneath his belt and rocked back on his heels as he eyed the arboreal gloom nervously. 'In times of war, we should hole up behind walls, shut our tower doors and gates until this wind of conflict passes by.'

The King of Kazad Mingol wore a tall helm that resembled the towering keep from which his hold hall took its name. His beard was long, bound by clasps of iron, and his moustaches curled in blond loops beneath his nose. His teeth seldom parted when he spoke, a portcullis ever shut, his mouth a tight line that rarely broke a smile. Lamellar armour clad his body, and one of his warriors hefted a large shield that bore the emblem of his hold, a tower fort impervious to attack.

'Please,' uttered Kerrik, who could not be further out of his depth if he were swimming the length of the Black Water in full armour, 'all will be explained soon.'

'Three hours we have been here already!' snapped Orrik, glowering at the youth. 'When do you expect *soon* to be?'

'I...' Kerrik looked around but could find no sign or suggestion of his lord. 'I don't know.'

'This is a lot of *krut*,' said Kruk, gesturing to his warriors. 'I have waited long enough.'

'You're leaving?' asked Orrik, his indignation vanishing. 'But what of Grum? You would defy his summons?'

King Kruk paused, as did his warriors. Grum was a fearsome and brutal king. Neither Kruk nor Orrik wanted to incur his wrath, but waiting in the forest for something that might never happen could be just as deadly to their health.

'It does not sound like Grum to me. Why would he leave his counting house, the warmth of his hall to meet us out here?' He leaned in close, hissing. 'There might be elgi, or the Starbreaker's warriors. And I wish for neither an arrow in the back nor to be pressed into the mountain king's horde.'

Orrik nodded, seeing the sense in that.

Both were set to leave when a voice rang out of the shadows.

'Hold,' it said, as Rundin stepped into the light.

'Ravenhelm?' asked Kruk, turning.

Orrik eyed him shrewdly. 'The High King's champion. What are you doing here?'

'Looking for some skarren backbone, but seeing little,' he snapped. 'This beardling has more courage.'

Kruk snarled. 'Be careful, king's thane,' he said, gesturing to his warriors. One hefted his axe until he heard the tautening string of a crossbow.

Orrik looked around. Over twenty of Rundin's rangers surrounded them, though they had yet to take aim. Silent as shadows, they had crept up on the dwarf host without being noticed.

'I brought them so you would listen,' said Rundin.

Grumbling, both kings turned around and settled in to hear what the champion had to say.

'I'm not here on Grum's behalf,' Rundin began.

'Then whose are you here on?' Kruk's eyes narrowed.

'Our people's, the skarrenawi.'

'You mean your own,' said Kruk. 'What are you brewing, king's thane?'

'He speaks of betrayal, dressed in the cloak of patriotism,' spat Orrik, hawking up a fat gob of phlegm at the champion's feet.

'Aye,' said Rundin, advancing on the two liege-lords until they were almost nose to nose. 'I do. But not of mine, of our High King's.'

'Thagging traitor!' Kruk made to move, slipping his hand around the haft of his axe, but Rundin put him down with a swift punch. Now the rangers brought up their crossbows, keeping King Kruk's warriors in check.

'I am sorry, my king,' said Rundin, 'but I need you to listen.' He glared at Orrik who was just releasing the grip of his hammer, adding, '*Both* of you.'

Kruk was rubbing his jaw but got to his feet unaided. Begrudgingly, he conceded.

'Go on then, speak your piece.'

Rundin nodded and stepped back, adopting a less threatening posture.

'Our liege-lord is mad. His mind is lost to the yellow fever.'

Orrik was shaking his head, incredulous. 'What do you mean, "lost"?'

Rundin rounded on him. '*Gorl* and *galaz* and *bryn*. Gold, King Orrik. Skarnag Grum had succumbed to the gold lust. He drools in his counting house, oblivious to his kingdom and his people. I entered in search of counsel and found not a king, but a zaki in his place.'

'Grum has always been covetous, but the fever?' said Kruk. 'I can't believe that.'

'Come and see it for yourselves if you must,' said Rundin.

Orrik sniffed with mild contempt. 'Even if he has succumbed to the fever, what care is it of ours?'

'Our High King is lost, and one of you must take his place.'

The glint of pride shimmered in the eyes of both kings as they weighed up the possibilities. That pride vanished with the champion's next words.

'To lead us into the war.'

'Out of the question!' Kruk was already leaving. He glared at the nearest ranger, daring him to shoot.

Orrik squared up to Rundin. He was taller than most dwarfs, even the champion, but the extra foot he had on him didn't make Rundin balk.

'You're a fool, Ravenhelm. Why would we go to war when we can batten our hatches and seal our gates? We'll weather this storm. It'll blow itself out soon enough.'

'It won't,' Rundin told him. 'You think the elgi will yield? Did you not hear what their king did to our ambassadors? He shaved them, sheared the hair from their faces like they were hruk. If that is his reaction to a banner of peace, what do you think he'll do to a host of dawi under the banner of war?'

Now surrounded by his warriors, Kruk looked over his shoulder. 'The Starbreaker will crush them, send them back across the sea. Why should we get involved?'

'Because we are dawi by any other name!' Rundin declared. 'Our blood runs the same as the mountain clans. We should take up arms, honour them with our pledge of allegiance.'

'For what?' asked Orrik, backing down when he realised Rundin couldn't be intimidated by his size. 'So our throngs can dwindle in the war, so our hold halls can ring empty, their coffers depleting as they're spent on armour and blades? There is no profit in war, not for us, not this way. It is Gotrek at whom the elgi have taken umbrage. Let him fight them.'

'Don't you think that the war will come to us?' Rundin asked of Orrik's back, the other king now departing too. 'I cannot muster the warriors of Kazad Kro or the rest of the skarrens without your help. With it, we can join with Gotrek, end this war quickly. I know it!'

Neither Kruk nor Orrik answered. They were leaving and the rangers would not stop them. No hill dwarf would draw on another, not without grudge.

'It will come to us,' Rundin called after them. 'Not this day perhaps, maybe not for a decade or more, but war will rage and come to our gates. Alone we will perish, but together we have a chance.'

'Go back to the Kro, Rundin of the Ravenhelm,' Orrik replied, slowly disappearing into the wooded darkness. Kruk was already long gone. 'And serve your king as you pledged oath to do so.'

Rundin seethed. His teeth were clenched, his fists tight as his knuckles cracked impotently. 'I serve my people,' he said to the air and the shadows.

'What shall we do, my lord?' Kerrik Sternhawk was at his side, wringing his hands fearfully.

'Go back,' said Rundin. 'There is nothing else *to* do.' He met the beardling's gaze. 'Speak to no one of this.'

'I won't, my lord.'

'I have to convince them, Kerrik, that this is right.'

'What if you can't, my lord?'

'Then we'll all be doomed, lad. Every thagging one of us.'

The rows of dwarfs marching from the flank of the mountain seemed endless.

Soaring high above a thin layer of cloud on the back of Vranesh, Liandra had never seen so many of the mud-dwellers in one place.

Since the sacking of Kor Vanaeth and her arrival at Tor Alessi, she had learned King Caledor had insulted them. Some grievous slight had made their oafish chieftain decide upon war. Liandra relished the opportunity to wet her blade on the dwarfs, mete out her revenge for what they did to her city.

She was tempted to fly lower, harass the dwarf army's flanks and rearguard, spit flame over their war machines, but decided against it. A lucky shot from one of their ballistae could shear Vranesh's wing easily enough, and there were many in the wagon train that followed the armoured dwarf hordes. Doubtless, many more would be marching under the earth, along roads lost to darkness and filth. Perhaps the elves could flood the tunnels and drown a great many mud-dwellers before they even reached Tor Alessi. She decided to suggest it to Prince Arlyr upon her return.

It would almost be worth losing her quarry to see that. The dark elf had been close, the one from the gorge that had left its spoor and eluded her for eight years. In her mind, Liandra had transformed the creature into a spectre of the one that had killed her mother on the burning shores of Cothique. Though the perpetrator of her mother's murder was dead, this spectre represented everything Liandra hated about the dark elves. After the dwarfs had been defeated at Tor Alessi's gates, an outcome of which she was certain, she would resume her hunt.

Dark elf, dwarf, it didn't matter to Liandra. Imladrik was right, she *was* a supremacist, utterly convinced of the asur's superiority over all sentient races. Crushing the dwarfs in the Old World was the first step towards dominion. Then, with a strong and thriving colony on the mainland, the high elves could turn their attention to Naggaroth and the overthrow of Malekith.

Having seen all she needed to, Liandra turned Vranesh about and headed back towards Tor Alessi. In her head, she saw the flames renewed, first at Cothique then Kor Vanaeth. She had seen something else too, a third vision framed in fire, but had banished that one from her thoughts with a shudder. Steel returned quickly, hardening her heart, strengthening her arm and conviction.

'All of them will burn,' she whispered to Vranesh.

The beast growled, low and threatening, its voice lost on the wind.

Several days had passed since their close encounter with the dragon rider. Drutheira had no idea why they had been spared, but she had no intention of wasting her reprieve either. She sat cross-legged in front of a pyre of blood-slicked skulls, hunkered beneath the half-broken roof of a ruined outhouse. It had been a trading post before the dwarfs had razed it. There were no bodies, but the raiders-turned-fugitives had discovered several graves buried in the hard earth.

Behind her, Malchior and Ashniel were flensing the skin and meat off the elf riders Sevekai and his warriors had killed. The small band of reavers had been utterly unprepared for the assassins and died without any fight. Their headless corpses would be left to rot, sustenance for the carrion flock already circling overhead.

She was weak. They all were, and she needed the knives and quarrels of the shades for the communion of blood with her dark lord.

Crimson smoke was already coiling from the piled skulls when she summoned the other sorcerers.

'Come forth, make the circle,' she hissed, her limbs trembling.

Both her fellow coven members looked gaunt and wasted. Their efforts to hide from the dragon rider had been taxing in the extreme. Malchior was weary, but Ashniel managed to make daggers with her gaze.

'Sit. Now,' Drutheira commanded.

Once the circle was made, she began to incant the rites. Red vapour coalesced into something more corporeal and Drutheira felt the chill of Naggaroth knife into her through her robes. She wrapped her cloak tighter, speaking the words of communion faster and faster, Malchior and Ashniel echoing every syllable.

A face half-materialised in the crimson fog but then collapsed as swiftly as it formed.

'No...' Drutheira barely had breath to voice her anguish.

Communion had failed, or rather it was *made* to fail.

She sagged, head slumping into her lap, and wept.

'What is it?' hissed Ashniel, fear and anger warring for supremacy on her face.

Malchior could only stare at the dissipating smoke, caught on the breeze and borne away to nothing. Four blood-slick skulls stared back, grinning.

Drutheira didn't answer. She rose wearily, leaving her cohorts in the ruined outhouse. Snow was falling, peeling off the mountains. It covered her dark cloak in a fur of ice as she crossed the open space, heading towards a shattered building that had once been a stable. Frost crusted her robe where she'd been sat on the ground.

Sevekai was inside, making a fire.

'More riders are coming, my dear,' he said without looking up as the sorceress approached.

The other shades were absent, keeping watch at the edges of the settlement. No more than one night at a time, then they had to move on.

'Hunting us, hunting for them–' he nodded towards the headless corpses of the reavers, '–it doesn't matter. We have to leave soon.'

'Leave?' said Drutheira. 'I can barely walk.'

Sevekai looked up at her.

'Then you'll be captured, and likely killed. The asur have our scent, and war or not they are coming.'

Drutheira stared for a moment, her eyes dead and cold.

'Malekith has abandoned us,' she said simply. 'We are alone, Sevekai.'

Sevekai returned to his fire, coaxing the embers to greater vigour. 'We have always been alone.'

'How long can we stay here?'

'A night, no more than that.'

'I once had a tower, a manse and slaves to do my bidding,' she muttered bitterly.

'I thought *I* was your slave.'

There was a glint in Sevekai's eye that Drutheira didn't care for, but she didn't rise to his goading.

'You said you had a ship,' she said instead, 'south across the mountains at the Sour Sea?'

'There's no way we're going south now, too many dwarfs march that way.'

'How can you possibly know that?'

'Because I skulk in shadows and listen. Armies of dwarfs move north and south towards Tor Alessi.'

'Then what do you suggest? You are the scout, guide us!' she snapped.

'We lay low, find a way to restore your strength and that of your lackeys.' He looked up again, a question in his eyes. 'I suppose you lack the craft to open up a gate right back into Naggaroth, yes?'

Drutheira scowled.

Shrugging Sevekai said, 'Thought so,' and prodded the fire with a shaft of broken roof beam. Then out of nothing he asked, 'What did you mean in the valley, when the dragon rider was close?'

'About what?' Despite herself, Drutheira came down to sit next to him, warming her hands on the fire.

'Kaitar. You said he was not druchii.'

Ever since their reunion, Drutheira and the other sorcerers had kept their distance from the enigmatic shade. He seemed to prefer that too, often scouting ahead, sometimes gone for more than a day at a time.

'He feels... empty, I suppose. Like a vessel of flesh into which something has crept and spread itself out.'

'That is meaningless,' said Sevekai.

'Perhaps, but I can explain it in no other way.'

The shade considered that for a moment before saying, 'I'll admit he has caused me some disquiet. At first I thought he was an assassin, a true servant of Khaine, taken on Death Night and inveigled into my ranks to kill us when our mission was done with.'

'And that has changed?'

'No. I still think he means to kill us, which is why I need your help to kill him first.'

Malice and desire contorted Drutheira's face, and Sevekai revelled in both expressions. Embers thought long extinguished rekindled and flared.

'Kill the shade and the rider,' she purred, creeping closer, her hand straying onto Sevekai's thigh, then further...

'Kill them all,' he murmured, pulling her down and into his embrace.

THIRTY-FIVE

AGAINST THE GLITTERING HOST

Snorri's feet were aching. Even in his boots, robust as they were and made from dwarf leather, the frost-bitten ground had taken a toll. Declining the offer of a palanquin, a throne and bearers to carry him, the prince had joined the ranks at the head of the army. Better they see him that way, as one of them, a dwarf warrior first and a prince second.

'I thought marching in winter was only something mad or desperate generals did?' groaned Morgrim, whose bunions were the size of chestnuts. He and several hearthguard from Everpeak protected the prince's right flank and strode in lockstep with him.

'Who's to say I am not one or both?' Snorri replied. 'Although, if anyone asks I'll say you convinced me do it.'

They shared a fraternal grin, something that had been lacking in their relationship of late but had oddly warmed with the onset of winter.

'We are close, Snorri,' uttered Drogor, on the prince's left amongst a second cadre of hearthguard. Now a thane with holdings in Everpeak come the end of the war, Drogor also carried the army standard after the prince's last bearer was slain by an elven scout during a previous skirmish. It was little more than a raid, the enemy gauging their numbers, but Bron had lost his life as he sounded the alarm.

So many had died already in similar meaningless circumstances. Snorri kept his thoughts on the matter to himself; not even Morgrim or Drogor would know them. It would hurt morale if his kith and kin thought his resolve was wavering.

'Signal a halt,' ordered the prince, and Drogor raised the banner.

Horns blared across the marching ranks, which stopped immediately to the clattering discord of settling shields, armour and weapons. Some of the mules brayed before their skinners quietened them with soothing words. The creaking wheels of wagons, carrying provisions, quarrels, spare shields and helms, were the last sound to abate. Some of the larger beasts towed machineries and these were marshalled by engineers and their crew, smothered in tarps for now but ready to be deployed at the prince's command.

Looking back over his shoulder, beyond the hulking hearthguard, Snorri saw sappers, warriors from over fifty different clans, grey-haired longbeards, quarrellers and rangers, the heavily armoured cohorts of ironbreakers and the dour faces of runesmiths. This was a mustering of some potency, one that would tear down the walls of Tor Alessi with or without his father's help.

True to his word, Snorri waited seven days for the army of the High King to arrive. But his father was late and the prince's patience at an end. The reinforcements from Barak Varr had also failed to materialise, so with just over thirty thousand dwarfs at his banner, he had marched.

On the fifth day, a band of rangers had returned from scouting. Their leader, Kundi Firebeard, had said the elves numbered in the region of ten thousand, including cavalry.

'Heh, what use are horses during a siege?' Drogor had asked.

'I have seen riders charge from a gate to sack machineries, kill their crews,' Morgrim had replied. 'We shouldn't underestimate the elgi knights.'

'It doesn't matter,' Snorri had told them both, 'we are committed to this now. Riders or not, Tor Alessi will fall.'

In the end the prince had chosen the Brundin road, the stories of monstrous trees coming to life and hellish sprites, however far-fetched, enough to dissuade him from taking the mountains. Expecting resistance, the dwarf throng had marched in a tight column with rangers roaming its flanks and rear. They need not have bothered. No elven war host stood in their way. No scouts harried their advance this time. The dwarfs had been allowed to march on Tor Alessi unimpeded.

Several times since they had set out, Morgrim had voiced concern that their haste would mean the High King's army was that little bit farther away.

Snorri had dismissed his cousin's misgivings, stating that thirty thousand dwarfs were more than enough to crack open one elven citadel.

That conviction had not changed.

'Twenty of the hearthguard with me,' said Snorri, gesturing to the last rise. Over that and they would see the port city and its defences relatively close up for the first time. 'You too, cousin.'

Led by the prince the dwarfs climbed up the boulder-strewn ridge, descending to their bellies as they neared the summit in case elven spotters were watching the approach and had ready quarrels to hand.

Snorri was the first to reach the top and peer over the edge.

The city was distant, still another hour's march away, and the dwarf army would be revealed long before they reached it. Bigger than Snorri first imagined, Tor Alessi was erected around a port and used most of the coastline in its defences. Aside from rugged, impenetrable cliffs facing out towards the sea, high walls surrounded a core of inner buildings and there were three large gatehouses. Elven devices, the eagle, dragon rampant and the rising phoenix, were emblazoned on each. Snorri counted three massive towers amongst lesser minarets and minor citadels. There was a large keep, appended in part to the port, and this was protected by a second defensive wall with only one gate. Impressive as it was, what surrounded the elven city surprised the dwarf prince more.

'I did not know it was at the centre of a lake,' said Morgrim, as if speaking Snorri's thoughts aloud.

Snorri reached for a spyglass offered by one of his hearthguard and peered down the lens.

'It's no lake...' he breathed after a few seconds. Putting down the spyglass, he licked his lips to moisten the sudden dryness. 'It's an army.'

An undulating ribbon of almost endless silver surrounded the outskirts of Tor Alessi, a vast host of elves that glittered in the winter sun. Pennons attached to the lances of knights whipped around on the breeze coming down off the ridge and numerous ranks of spearmen stood in ready formation with rows of archers to their rear.

'Grungni's hairy arse...' muttered one of the hearthguard.

Morgrim ignored him, pointing to the elven right flank. 'There,' he said, 'machineries.'

Snorri had seen them during the brodunk, elven chariots drawn by horses. There were at least a hundred in a close-knit squadron, scythed wheels catching the light and shimmering like star-fire.

He cast his gaze skywards and felt suddenly foolish for their attempts at subterfuge. Circling above were flocks of birds. Not like the screech hawks, talon owls or griffon vultures of the peaks, these were giant eagles with claws and beaks like blades.

Snorri lowered the spyglass for the second time.

'Looks like they're expecting us,' he said to the others.

'It explains why the road became suddenly empty,' said Morgrim.

'Because they were all here.'

Snorri got to his feet, seeing no point in stealth any more. 'I am no engineer, but a sight more than ten thousand wouldn't you say, cousin?'

Morgrim nodded slowly, taking in the glittering host in all its shining glory.

'What do you want to do?'

The prince sniffed disdainfully, hiking up his belt.

'First I want to punish Kundi Firebeard for his abject stupidity, then I want to march down there and kill some thagging elgi.'

It wasn't like Kor Vanaeth and the clash for the gate. Nadri had never fought in open pitched battle before. Before the short siege at the elven city, he had never donned axe and shield in anything more than a skirmish. Unlike Krondi had been, he wasn't a campaigner or a soldier; though he knew his axecraft as all clansmen did, he was a merchant. With war unleashed upon the land, Nadri had exchanged gold for blood as his currency.

It was proving a difficult trade.

Two dwarf war hosts had descended the ridge into the teeth of the elven hordes. His liege-lord King Brynnoth led one, his cup of vengeance not even half full from Agrin Fireheart's untimely death. The other was led by Valarik of Karak Hirn, though Nadri did not know him except by sight.

Arrows met them at first, a heavy rain of steel-fanged death that reaped a lesser tally than the pointy-ears had hoped. Dwarfs knew defence as well as attack, and their formations were peerless. Locking shields front, back, to the flanks and above, several large cohorts had weathered the arrow storm with almost no casualties. But for the uncanny accuracy of the elven archers, no dwarf blood would have been spilled at all.

Dismayed at such resilience, the elven lordlings had called for their cavalry. Clarion horns, shrilling much higher than the pipes of Barak Varr, had signalled the charge. The earth shook with the pounding of the knightly horse, and had made Nadri's teeth chatter.

Even in the third rank, behind kith and kin he had known most of his life, he felt the impact of elven lance. It tore into them despite their organised shield wall, raked a great ragged cleft, and left them bleeding. With dogged tenacity, the dwarfs had closed, holding though the urge to run was strong.

Now they were locked with the high-helmed elven knights, matching axe and hammer to longsword.

Sweeping out his arm, Nadri felt more than saw his axe cleave horseflesh. The beast whinnied, its caparison shedding against his well-honed blade. It cut the saddle belt too, plunging the rider into the mass where he slashed wildly for a few moments before he was lost beneath a hail of hammer blows.

Something smacked into his shoulder, and he was about to strike when he realised it was Yodri, a fellow clanner. The old dwarf risked a gap-toothed grin when he saw Nadri's face. The merchant smiled back, grim rather than humorous, before Yodri's expression slackened, the longsword through his neck puncturing his good mood. The blade withdrew with a meaty *schluk!* before it struck down on Nadri, who had enough about him to raise his shield. A thick dent appeared on the underside next to where he'd pressed his cheek. A third blow took a chip off the shield's edge, allowing a narrow aperture through which to see his attacker.

Cold fury lit the knight's face, a snarl growing on his lips with every determined blow. He swung again, Nadri unable to manage any reply, tearing the shield from the dwarf's agonised grasp. Rearing horse hooves put Nadri on his back and he half expected to be ground into paste by them before a heavy shaft punched the beast's flank and sent it and rider sprawling.

'Grimnir's balls, it's a good job them thaggers from the Varn are accurate!' said one of the Copperfist clan that Nadri couldn't place at first.

It was Werigg Gunnson, an old friend of his father's.

Nadri looked to where Werigg was pointing. King Ironhandson's engineers were loosing their ballistae, and the bolt throwers were exacting a heavy price from the knights, whose armour meant little against the thick arrow shafts.

Overhead, there came the heavy *whomp* of stone throwers loosing their cargo. The dwarfs of Karak Varn were neglecting the walls in favour of punishing the stranded cavalry. Through the melee, where the press of bodies and the thicket of limbs had thinned, he saw a swathe of dwarf dead, cut up by the chariots. Here the stone throwers struck next, rewarded for their efforts as one of the elven machineries exploded in a storm of wood, bone and flesh. Blood slicked the flung rock, painting it in a greasy line as it rolled to a halt.

'Either that or the blind buggers are just lucky, eh?' Nadri felt rough hands drag him to his feet and saw a grizzled-looking dwarf facing him. 'Up yer get, lad. More killing to be done.'

Still dazed, Nadri grabbed a shield, not caring if it was his own, and saw the knights had broken off their attack and were retreating towards the city gates. A host of spearmen, out of range of the war machines and thus far unscathed, parted to let them through. Then they closed ranks and lowered their pikes at the badly bloodied dwarfs.

'See,' said the old-timer, hawking up a gob of pipeweed he'd been chewing. 'Plenty more.'

Nadri eyed the determined elven phalanx even as the dwarfs drew back into formation, raising shields as the arrow storm began anew, and groaned.

His retinue of hearthguard just below, Snorri surveyed the battle from a grassy tor through the spyglass. This was but an opening skirmish and though he had wanted badly to lead it, knew his place as army general was here.

Brynnoth was ever wrathful and had insisted on leading the first attack. Though brave, the clans of Barak Varr were being hammered by the elves. During the skirmish, arrows had killed a great many dwarfs and left countless more for the ministrations of the priestesses of Valaya. Even as the battle raged, the dour warrior maidens roamed the field, dragging back the wounded or silencing those beyond help. Since the initial charge and subsequent breaking of the high-helmed cavalry, the dwarf front line had advanced considerably. Met by a thick wall of heavy-armoured spearmen, their march had now halted. Though difficult to ascertain through the spyglass, it looked like the two forces were at an impasse. From a brutal opening skirmish with a splintered cavalry force, the dwarfs now faced a determined grind.

Snorri smiled despite the grimness of the vista. Dwarfs knew how to fight battles of attrition. Even with their spears and high shields, the elves would soon learn the folly of these tactics. Unwilling to loose directly into the fighting ranks, the elven archers unleashed volleys of arrows in the air and the prince of Everpeak watched their deadly trajectory until they fell amongst the rear ranks. Pushing hard against the backs of their fellow clanners in order to roll the elven line, many dwarfs had their shields front and were struck down. Several ranks lay dead before a proper defence stalled further casualties. Quarrellers attempted to reply in kind, but the dwarf crossbowmen had neither the range nor the accuracy to be effective.

Panning the lens across the melee Snorri found Brynnoth, or at least several of his royal hearthguard, the Sea Wardens, battling furiously in the centre. The king would be amongst them, at their heart, and strong as he was the elves were showing no signs of capitulation. Several large cohorts, including those from Everpeak, were ready as reinforcement. With almost a third of his army committed already, Snorri was reluctant to feed any more into the grind.

He considered employing the war machines to thin the elven ranks, but the proximity of dwarf warriors made it too risky. Without the need to punish the knights, they were standing dormant so Snorri gave the signal for them to be brought forwards and batter the walls instead.

A drum beat was followed by the raising of banners down the line until the message from the prince was conveyed to Ironhandson and his throwers. A few moments later and a cascade of bolts and boulders assailed Tor Alessi's walls.

Snorri followed their descent through the spyglass, grumbling in dismay as an arc of lightning tore one stone from the sky, disintegrating the missile in a shower of debris. Several more went the same way as the elves revealed their mages, casting fire and ice from their fingertips to blunt the dwarf barrage. A few missiles struck but the damage they caused was negligible to a city that size. Bolts from the ballistae were snatched out of the very air by flocks of the great eagles, the massive birds of prey snapping them in their vice-like claws before diving down onto the machineries themselves.

Engulfed by a swarm of flapping feathers and flashing silver beaks, dozens of dwarf crewmen and engineers lay dead before Ironhandson restored order with his rangers and saw the beasts off.

'It is harder than I thought,' Snorri confessed under his breath.

'We knew the elgi were tough, cousin, but we are tougher,' Morgrim reassured him.

'Do you think this is their entire force?'

Morgrim frowned, watching the battle from afar without the benefit of the spyglass, and shook his head.

'The city will harbour a second army, I am sure.'

'We have to crack the gates anyway,' suggested Drogor, his grip tight on the banner where it snapped in the breeze. 'A stern push would sweep this force away and let us bring the fight to the walls.'

'Lay siege?' asked Snorri, looking askance at the Karak Zorn dwarf.

'No, forge a hammer and break down the gates. Once inside the elgi's resolve will waver.'

Snorri rubbed his bearded chin. The entire throng on the field was engaged. Two thick lines of infantry cut and hewed at one another with neither willing to yield. The arrows levelled the scales for the elves, preventing the dwarf line from a concerted push, but the clans were gaining ground on the walls.

'It's not a bad idea.'

Morgrim disagreed. 'Patience is more prudent, Snorri. We grind the elves down, then retreat to our lines and lay siege.'

'I want this over quickly. No elgi rabble is going to defy me.'

Drogor said, 'Perhaps Morgrim is right. Hurt the elgi at the gates, sound a retreat and surround them.'

Morgrim was nodding, surprised that his old friend was agreeing with him.

'Besides,' added Drogor. 'It's likely your father will have arrived by then with the army from Karaz-a-Karak. There would be no shame in leaning on his larger throng.'

His mood souring swiftly, Morgrim tried to intercede. 'That is not what I meant, cousin–'

'Enough!' The spyglass snapped shut, revealing the anger-reddened features of the prince. 'I will not have my father come here and see this place intact. It will be rubble by the time he reaches the field.' Snorri donned his war helm, the feathered wings fluttering in the breeze. He spoke at Morgrim, glaring around the nose guard. 'I'm ordering the reinforcements in. Sound the clarion. I'll lead them myself.'

Shield forwards, shoulder locked, Nadri was pinned. He found himself in the third rank of the Copperfists, pushing hard against the wall of elven spears. In such tight confines, there was no room for axe work, save for those chopping frantically at the front. Several dwarfs had already fallen to spear thrusts, their anger blunted on high shields over which almond-shaped eyes glared with contempt.

Unlike the fight against the knights, which was a maddened frenzy of plunging lances and flailing horses as the cavalry sought to rip the dwarfs open, this was a strength-sapping grind. Heave and push. Heave and push. Dwarf and elf shoved against one another, pressing with all the weight of their formations until one bent and broke.

So far, the contest was evenly matched.

Impossible to tell for sure, but Nadri felt like it was the same across the line. One shield wall had met another, though the elven forest of spears was making hard work of it for the dwarfs. As warriors died on both sides, those behind filled their place. From the front rank, which was brutal even from his position two rows behind, Nadri heard a grunt. Another dwarf had fallen, arterial crimson jetting from his neck and blinding the one behind him who also died to a quick thrust from the white-haired champion leading the cohort of spears.

Suddenly and without realising, Nadri was at the front. A jabbing spear was turned aside by an instinctive parry with his axe haft. A sword blow fell against his shield and stung his shoulder with the impact. He roared, invoking Grungni and Grimnir, thrashed out with his axe. Scale mail parted, shearing off like autumn leaves, and a spearman crumpled trying to hold in his guts. As another warrior took the elf's place, the champion was pushed closer. His sword flashed, an eldritch blade that bore glowing elven runes of power.

Nadri met the attack with his shield and his defence was almost cloven in half.

Spitting some curse in elvish, the white-haired champion swung again. This time Nadri ducked and the rune sword shaved off the sea dragon device on his helmet.

Like his kin, the elf was dressed in blue-grey robes, his armour like polished azure, only metal and much more unyielding. He wore a conical helm, a star-pattern emblazoned on its nose guard, with a shock of horsehair protruding from the tip.

'Uzkul elgi!'

A shout came from further down the line, a few places to Nadri's right. Whilst the other dwarfs fought, their champion, Vrekki Helbeard, stepped forwards. He was pointing at the white-haired elf with the spiked tip of his mattock. The weapon was dark with blood.

Nadri felt a hand grip his shoulder and then heard the gravel voice of Werigg Gunnson in his ear.

'Let him through, lad,' he said. 'Helbeard challenges the elgi.'

'How, in this?' asked Nadri, fending off another thrust that nearly took off his ear.

As the challenge was met, the pressure on the dwarfs leavened. Vrekki shouldered up the line and was standing alongside Nadri, the elf champion facing him.

The fighting hadn't ceased, it merely allowed for the passage of the two warriors so they might meet in combat. No order was given to let through, it was merely *understood*. Vrekki threw the first blow, taking a chunk from the elf's shield, and the crushing pressure of the grind returned in earnest.

Through the frenzy, Nadri caught slashes of their duel, although to refer to it thus would not be accurate. Vrekki fought two-handed, using the thick haft of his mattock to parry. Like the elf, he had runes too, and they flashed along the shaft of his weapon and the talisman he wore around his neck.

To Nadri it seemed like many minutes but it was over in seconds.

Vrekki battered the white-haired champion hard, hurling blow upon blow against his shield. It looked like he was winning, until having soaked up all the punishment he was willing to, the elf thrust from beneath the guard of his shield and pierced poor Vrekki's heart. The champion died instantly, his mouth formed into an inchoate curse.

With their thane's death, Nadri felt the Copperfists falter. A ripple, almost impossible to discern, fed down their ranks. The elves felt it too and pushed. Two spears came Nadri's way at once. He parried one, but the other pierced his chest, just below the shoulder, and he cried out. The white-haired champion had discarded his shield and fought only with his sword. Pinioned and in agony, Nadri was an easy kill. But before the deathblow came, he flung his axe. It turned one and a half times in the air then embedded itself in the elf's face, splitting his nose in two and carving into his skull like an egg.

He fell, brutally, and the momentum shifted again.

There was a cheer of 'Khazuk!' of which Nadri was only vaguely aware, before the push came again. It pressed him into the spear that was pinning him and he roared in pain and anger. Unarmed, there was little he could do but hold up his shield and pray to Valaya it would be enough. At either side, though he couldn't move to look properly, he felt his fellow clanners hacking with their blades.

'Take it, lad!' Werigg bellowed from behind, a hammer slipped into Nadri's grasp which he used to smash the spear haft jutting from his chest. The immense pressure of the other dwarf's considerable bulk levelled against his back followed swiftly after as Werigg got his head down and pushed.

The elves were reeling, on their heels and close to capitulation. Like a ship, the dwarfs its starboard, the elves port, the line pitched and yawed as both sides fought for supremacy. More tenacious than they had any right to be, the elves held on.

'Khazuk!' the Copperfists yelled, but still could find no breach in their enemy's resolve.

A foot... two... then three, the dwarfs gained ground by bloody increments but the elves would not yield.

Amazed he was still alive, Nadri forgot the pain from his chest and bludgeoned spearmen with his borrowed hammer.

'Uzkul!' he cried as a splash of crimson lined his face like a baptism, echoing Vrekki, honouring the thane's sacrifice. It was madness, a terrible churn of bodies and blades without end. He wondered briefly if the halls of Grimnir were steeped in such carnage.

A horn rang out, so deep and sonorous as to only be dwarfen, dragging Nadri from his dark reverie.

The elf line trembled, just the lightest tremor at first but then building to a destructive quake. Like a tree hewn at the root and felled by its own weight, the spearmen buckled. It was as if they bent at the middle and were funnelling into the hole where Snorri had forced his wedge of gromril.

Hearthguard were tough, implacable warriors and Snorri had rammed a cohort of a hundred right down the throat of the elven infantry. To see them broken so utterly by the prince's charge stirred Morgrim's blood, but it was also reckless.

'You did this,' he said, a grimace revealing his displeasure.

'I did nothing but agree with you, old friend,' said Drogor with a plaintive tone, though his eyes flashed eagerly to see such carnage wrought upon the elves.

'He has overstretched and left himself vulnerable.'

Drogor appeared nonplussed, gesturing to the elf ranks.

'The elgi are in flight, I can see no danger. Your cousin has done what Brynnoth could not, and broken their ranks.'

'Aye,' snapped Morgrim, 'and he will not stop until he's reached the walls and torn apart the gate. That, or until he's dead. You goaded him.' He was nodding, a distasteful sneer on his face. 'You drew him into this fight by mentioning his father.' Morgrim turned to the other dwarf, the rows of silent hearthguard Snorri had left behind unmoving like statues behind them. 'Why?'

'Snorri, our prince, will do what he wants. It was he who brought an army to these gates, who forged the will of no less than four kings into a throng capable of challenging the elgi in their greatest citadel. Do you really think I, a lowly treasure hunter from the Southlands, could do *anything* to affect the mind of a dwarf capable of that?'

Morgrim snarled, turning away.

'Signal Thagdor's clans. I want Zhufbar prepared to march in support of the prince.'

Drogor didn't react. His face was set as stone as he lifted the banner.

The elves were running, but to Snorri's annoyance their flight was not a rout.

Shields as one, spears to the fore, the elves retreated in good order. At the head of the hearthguard, Snorri battered at them. He carried no shield, and instead wielded an axe in either hand.

Hacking away a desperate lunge with the short haft of his hand axe, he buried his rune axe in the attacking elf's torso. Silver scale and blood shed from the warrior like he was a gutted fish. Snorri whirled, cleaving the forearm of another, splitting apart his shield. A stomp forwards with a heavy boot and he cut the groin of a third elf, bifurcating the spearman all the way to the sternum. A shoulder barge put down a fourth before the prince took a shield smash to the face, which he shrugged off with typical dwarf resilience.

'Harder than that, you kruti-eaters,' he spat, hewing down another.

For all the carnage he wreaked, him *and* his hearthguard who were just as merciless, the elves maintained their ordered retreat.

'Stand and fight, thagging cowards!' Snorri raged at the disappearing spearmen, who were edging closer and closer to the wall and the gate.

Within a hundred feet of the defences, the archers took aim again and loosed. With the measured retreat of the spearmen, gaps had begun to appear in the fighting. It was no longer a tightly packed melee with heaving, pushing ranks; rather a patch of open killing ground had materialised between the two forces that was thronged with the dead and dying.

A shaft struck Snorri in his shoulder guard but he ignored it, ignored that the tip had pierced metal and meat. One of the hearthguard took an arrow in the neck, an impossible shot between helm and gorget, and died gurgling his own blood.

Seconds after the first arrow, another shaft hit the prince in the thigh. He cursed once, snapped it and drove on.

'Into them,' he bellowed. 'By Grimnir's wrath, we'll overrun the gates!'

A cheer rang out from the nearby clans, but the hearthguard were stoic in silence, determinedly sticking to their task.

The elven shield wall returned, spears levelled like spikes. At some unseen signal they stopped falling back and solidified again, hoping to bulwark the dwarfs against a cliff face of high shields.

Charging, impelled by their prince, the dwarfs hit it hard. Several warriors, not expecting the sudden shift, were impaled and the brutal melee renewed. As elf and dwarf clashed at close quarters, jabbing, hacking, cleaving, the arrow storm continued unabated. Hearthguard warriors lifted their shields to protect the prince, whilst the pushing back ranks were pinioned. Like an anvil the dwarf line had come together, some three thousand warriors of the clans and brotherhoods, fighting shoulder to shoulder against a thin, glittering line of elves. Attrition was simply the reality of war for dwarfs, they weathered it well, used it to break the most determined and numerous of foes. Here against elven skill and discipline that strategy was being sorely tested.

Caught between the will of the spears and the volleys of the archers, the dwarfs were taking a beating.

Snorri tried to change that single-handed. He ploughed into the enemy ranks, splitting them down the middle. A champion, some elven lordling with a shimmering spear and armour of gilded metal, went to impede him. The prince cut him down like he was a common soldier.

Elves recoiled from the vengeful prince. Dwarfs followed him, King Brynnoth leading a determined charge of his own, Valarik too. Like a swelling tide, the sons of Grungni puffed up their chests and became the hammer.

Such discipline the elves possessed, not like the ragged tribes of the greenskins or the feral beasts of the dark wood, but even their resolve was buckling in the face of the dwarf onslaught. And just as it felt as if they were about to break for the last time and surrender the field, white mantlets decorated to look like overlapping swan feathers tilted to reveal the deadly reason why the elves had drawn their enemy on.

Bolt throwers, rank upon rank of them, but not like the dwarf machineries for these racked a quartet of bolts at a time, unleashed a devastating salvo.

'Mercy of Valaya...' Snorri breathed, as the spear-thick arrows descended.

Horns were blowing. Nadri heard them above the whipping report of the elven bolt throwers raining down death upon them. Despite the terrible barrage, the Copperfists continued to advance. As they closed on the wall, barely twenty feet away and almost beyond the minimal range of the elven reapers, Nadri saw the gate open into Tor Alessi. There were more warriors within, hard-faced veterans wearing long skirts of mail, adorned with jewelled breastplates and carrying immense two-handed swords.

The spearmen retreated into the relatively narrow aperture, walking backwards unerringly, spears outstretched as they condensed their long shield wall into a tight square of blades angled in every direction.

Without the bolt throwers to skewer them relentlessly, Nadri felt a tremor of relief through the ranks, but it was short lived. Murder holes opened in the walls above, manned by pairs of archers who had fallen back into the city before the spearmen. The storm returned, thickening the air with hundreds of feathered shafts.

Nadri's shield sprouted more than a dozen arrows in a few seconds.

The hand-to-hand fighting had all but ceased, the spearmen retreating faster than the dwarfs could keep pace and the archers making them pay for every step.

A flash of light and the stink of burned flesh heralded a magical attack. Turning their efforts from destroying the deadly cargo of the siege engines, the elven mages had their eyes fixed on the advancing dwarfs.

From nearby came chanting, a doleful, sombre refrain that fizzled out a second lightning arc before it could strike. Incandescent serpents of amethyst, spears of luminescent jade, the enchanted manifestation of dragon-kind spitting crimson flame, came at the dwarfs in a sorcerous hail that the runesmiths were hard pressed to repel.

Nadri grit his teeth, barely fighting, merely marching against the attack. He felt the hairs on the back of his neck spike, tasted copper in his mouth and smelled the reek of brimstone in his scorched nostrils. The dwarfs resisted, calling upon their natural resilience to harmful magic, channelled it back to the earth, back to rock where it would be safe and dormant.

The king's banner was aloft; he saw it above the throng, flapping defiantly. It was an order to charge, to run at the gates and bring them down while the elves were in retreat, but the arrow storm was unrelentingly heavy. A pity Werigg had no words of encouragement, but Nadri felt the old solider at his back, his hand on his shoulder if not gripping quite so tight now the battle pressure had lessened.

They got another foot before a second horn was sounded, followed by the beat of drums. The banner dipped, away from the gates. A signal to retreat.

Nadri couldn't decide if he felt indignant or relieved. They had bled so much to reach this far and gain so little. The bellowed command from one of the thanes further down the line confirmed it.

'Retreat!'

Nadri was confused. He had always believed there was no word for 'back', 'give up', in Khazalid. Seemed he was wrong, they all were.

'That's it,' he called over his shoulder. 'Werigg, we lived, we–'

The old soldier's glassy eyes staring back unblinking supplanted Nadri's relief with grief. Werigg's hand was still upon his back, seized with enough rigor to keep it there, his body pressed into the throng unable to fall. A dark patch blotted his armour, running stickily over the mail. A spear tip was lodged in the middle of it, broken off at the end. Nadri remembered the one in his chest, the second one he'd deflected, unknowingly, into Werigg's gut. A mortal wound. As the dwarfs peeled away and the throng parted, Werigg fell and Nadri wasn't able to catch him or carry him. Borne away by the urgency of the crowd, he couldn't stop and the old soldier was lost from his sight.

Snorri cursed, he cursed in as many foul ways as he knew, spitting and raging as the retreat was sounded. He turned briefly, looking over his shoulder to see the throng from Zhufbar heading back to the encampment at the edge of the battlefield. He also saw Morgrim, arms folded after issuing the command.

Cursing again, Snorri flung his hand axe in a final defiant gesture and it stuck in the thick wood of the elven gate like a promise.

We'll be back, it said, *the killing isn't done, we are not done. Battle has only just begun.*

He seethed, marking the face of each and every elf that looked down on him with haughty disdain from the city walls.

'Khazuk,' he screamed in promise. 'Khazuk!'

But the elves didn't understand, nor did they care.

THIRTY-SIX

PREPARING TO LAY SIEGE

Once the withdrawal from outside the city began the hail of arrows ceased, the elven reapers returned behind their mantlets and the mages to their towers. It was not a benevolent act towards a respected foe; it was a pragmatic one. The elves were not so foolish as to believe they had won. They knew enough of dwarfs to realise they would come again. Arrows were finite, so too the strength of a wizard. Both needed conserving if they were to hold the city.

From inside his tent looking out onto the field, Snorri glowered. He chewed his beard and muttered, trying to excise his feeling of impotence with the clenching and unclenching of his fists.

A young priestess was tending the wound in his shoulder, packing it with warm healing clay, but he ignored her. Since the retreat, he had spoken to no one.

Morgrim approached, invading the prince's solitude. Over an hour had passed since Snorri had glared at him upon the army's disappointing return, and as the injured were patched up and armour mended by the forges he decided it was time to confront his cousin.

The foulness of his mood was etched across the prince's face. 'Don't you understand what "do not disturb" means?' he grumbled.

'Aye, and I understand what would have happened had you fought on,' Morgrim replied curtly, surprising Snorri with his choler. 'Eight hundred and sixty-three dead, the reckoners are still tallying the injured. What were you going to do if you had reached the walls, climb them with your axe or hack open the gate?'

'If needs be, by Grungni. I'll make those elgi pay.'

'What price do you think they owe you, cousin? Was the *rhunki* lord a friend of yours, was he known to you or even of your hold? We all mourn for Agrin Fireheart but this goes beyond that.'

Snorri leaned forwards, fighting back the pain as he felt his injuries anew and scowling at the priestess who scowled back.

'It was an affront to all dawi, what they did. Slaying a rhunki of such venerability...' He shook his head, rueful. 'My father should have declared war there and then.'

'And now we come to the root of it,' said Morgrim, folding his arms.

'Meaning?' asked Snorri, sitting back before the priestess clubbed him.

'Your father, the High King.'

Snorri's expression darkened and he dismissed the dwarf maiden trying to tend to him with a curt word. She glared but relented. 'What is it with these Valayan rinns?' he griped.

Morgrim went on. 'Ever since you heard that prophecy in the ruins of Karak Krum, you have railed even harder against him. You made this cause your own, this war, to slight the High King, declare grudgement if I am wrong.'

Snorri seethed, fists balled, and looked like he might spring from his throne and knock his cousin onto his back. Anyone else but Morgrim and he would have raised fists, but after a minute he climbed down from his anger.

'He who will slay the drakk, he who will be king, those were his words. Am I still to believe them, cousin?'

Like heat from the cooling forge, Morgrim's ire dispersed in the face of Snorri's humility. 'You are prince of Karaz-a-Karak, heir to the Throne of Power and the Karaz Ankor. Your destiny is great as are you, cousin. Don't let this feud with your father get in the way of that. Embrace him again. Show him you are the High King's regent he needs you to be.'

Holding Morgrim's gaze, Snorri slowly nodded and then looked across to the killing field where a host of broken shields, shattered helms and axe hafts remained. Both sides had allowed the other clemency to remove their dead but the earth was soaked with blood that would not be so easy to excise. And amidst all of this carnage, Tor Alessi still stood like a defiant rock in the storm.

'They are harder than they look,' Snorri conceded.

'Aye,' Morgrim agreed, following the prince's eye.

'Gather the other kings,' said Snorri. 'We need a different strategy.'

'Such as?'

'What we should have done when we first got here. Lay siege.'

The prince's decision was met with unanimous approval. Even King Brynnoth, whose eagerness to kill elves hadn't lessened much since Kor Vanaeth, was in agreement. The dwarfs would do what they did best; they would wait.

For the rest of the day, whilst blacksmiths repaired armour and weapons, healers tended and the victuallers and brewmasters kept the army fed, bands of rangers ventured into the nearby forests. They returned with cartloads of wood and at once the dwarf engineers and craftsmen began to fashion battering rams and siege towers. Raw iron had been brought from the holds for just such a purpose and once they were done with arming the clans, the blacksmiths began labouring to reinforce the wooden siege engines. Stout ladders were made too, along with broad, metal-banded pavises and mantlets for the quarrellers.

Every dwarf in the throng had a trade and every dwarf was put to the task. Unlike most armies who possessed dedicated labour gangs to achieve such a feat, barring the warrior brother-hoods dwarfs could call upon their entire host and so the engines went up quickly. From their tents and around the flickering glow of cook fires came the sound of deathsong, sombre on the breeze. For their enemies or themselves, the sons of Grungni accepted either.

It put Nadri in a grimmer mood than in the aftermath of the battle. He hadn't seen Werigg amongst the dead, and barely knew the old warrior anyway. Yet it burdened him, especially the callousness of his death. Seeking to stymie his grief, Nadri had looked to other tasks to occupy his mind. His father, Lodri, was a miner and lodewarden. He knew rock and metal, and had passed some of that knowledge on to his sons. The ex-merchant, a trade to which he doubted he would ever return, was hammering the roof of a battering ram when a voice intruded on his thoughts.

'Stout work.'

Nadri kept labouring, carefully beating the plates with a mallet and then using a hammer to drive in the iron nails that secured to its frame.

'I said stout work.'

Looking up, Nadri reddened at once when he saw it was Prince Snorri Lunngrin addressing him, his retainers and bodyguards close by.

'It'll need to be to turn those elgi arrows, but thank you, my liege.'

'I saw you at Kor Vanaeth, didn't I?'

'You have a sharp eye, my liege. Yes, I fought at the gate.'

Snorri seemed to appraise him. 'You're not a warrior, though.'

'No, my liege. I am a merchant but took up az and klad to fight the elgi for my king.'

'And you shall be remembered for it. What's your name, dawi?'

'Nadri Lodrison, my liege. Of the Copperfist clan.'

'Tell me, Nadri, do you have any kin, a rinn or beardlings back at the Sea Hold?'

'A brother only, my liege. Heglan. My father died during the urk purges of your father, Gotrek Starbreaker the High King.'

At mention of the name, the prince visibly stiffened.

'He does not fight, your brother?'

'He's an engineer, my liege, fashioning war machines for the army of Barak Varr.'

That was a lie as far as Nadri knew but he saw no reason to reveal that Heg was trying to build a flying ship. Unless the master of engineers had discovered his workshop and then he might be toiling in the mines instead. A sudden pang of regret tightened Nadri's stomach at the thought of his brother, but he was glad too, glad Heg didn't have to endure all of this. At least not yet. 'And I would dearly like to see him again,' he added in a murmur.

Snorri nodded, genuinely moved by such fraternity. 'You will, Nadri. The elgi will break against our siegecraft and the war will be over. Grungni wills it, Grimnir demands it and Valaya will protect us throughout.'

'Tromm, my liege.' Nadri bowed his head, whilst the prince echoed him and continued on his tour of the siege works.

'I just hope I am alive to see it,' he whispered when the prince was gone, and returned to his hammering.

'It was a good idea to tour the ranks,' Morgrim muttered in Snorri's ear.

'Aye, there's not only pride that needs salving after a beating like that.'

The dwarfs were passing through a throng of blacksmiths' tents, and the air was pleasingly redolent of ash and smoke. The ring of metal against anvil was soothing and brought with it a small measure of home.

Only Drogor seemed unmoved. 'Were we beaten, though?' he asked. 'I see dead elgi littering the outskirts of the city, not just dawi.'

Morgrim grew belligerent. 'We *were* bloodied, kinsman. Badly.'

The three were accompanied by one of the hearthguard, a flame-haired brute called Khazagrim, who bristled as he remembered the battle. Otherwise, he was silent and only present to protect the prince against elven assassins, should any try to kill him.

'It didn't look like defeat to me,' said Drogor.

'I didn't say we were defeated. I–'

'Enough bickering,' Snorri sighed. 'The elgi city stands, and we must find a way to bring it down. Simple as.'

They left the forging tents and came upon the edge of the camp where the war machines were covered under tarp and chained down. It was an impressive battery of machineries. Heavy stones lay piled in stout buckets, thick bolts were lashed together with rope and racked in spear-tipped bunches. Runes and oaths of vengeance were engraved upon every one. They were grudge throwers now, carven with dwarfen vitriol. Enough to bring down a city, or so they all hoped. A small group of warriors guarded the engines and bowed low to the prince and his entourage as they passed by.

'Three towers, high walls, a keep and a well equipped garrison, it's not exactly an urk hut is it now,' Morgrim chafed, once they were out of earshot. 'We need to pummel it, soften the elgi until they're ready to break, then assault. Tunnellers too. I'd suggest three.'

'Thom, Grik and Ari,' said Snorri, naming the three tunnels. 'Clan miners are already setting to the task, the Sootbacks, Blackbrows, Stonefingers and Copperfists.'

'How soon until they're fully excavated?' asked Morgrim.

'Several days.'

'Our siege works will be ready for a first assault within the hour,' said Drogor. 'We could have the walls down by nightfall if we push hard. Tunnels would finish them off.'

The glint in Snorri's eye as he ran a hand over the carriage of one of Ironhandson's stone throwers suggested he liked that idea, but Morgrim was quick to dispel it.

'We should rest and attack at the dawn, wait until the tunnels are more advanced,' he said.

'A night attack would terrify the elgi,' Drogor countered.

'Having seen their discipline, I doubt that. In any case, our forces are spent and would do well to rest.' Morgrim tried to keep the argument from his tone.

'We'll bombard them instead,' Snorri declared, slapping the stone thrower's frame with the flat of his hand. He turned to Drogor. 'Have the king of the Varn bring his war machines up and assail the walls. No sleep for the elgi this night,' he grinned.

Drogor bowed and went immediately to find Ironhandson. Like many of the kings he had retired to his royal quarters until needed.

'Hrekki won't be pleased at being disturbed,' muttered Morgrim. 'He'll be on his fifth or sixth firkin by now.'

Snorri was dismissive. 'Let him moan,' he said. 'Not all dawi of royal blood have gone to their beds for the night.'

The cousins had reached the edge of the camp and Snorri mounted a rocky hillock so he could gesture to the distant, brooding figure of Brynnoth.

The king of the Sea Hold was crouched down, a plume of pipeweed smoke escaping from his lips that trailed a vaporous purple bruise across the twilit sky. The silhouette of his ocean drake helm sat beside him, a predatory companion. Though he had borne the brunt of the fighting, he had yet to remove his armour or accept healing of any kind.

'He is marred by this,' Snorri observed, striking up his own pipe.

'Do you think any of us will not be by the time this is over, cousin?'

Snorri had no answer, contemplating as he smoked.

'How's the hand?' Morgrim asked after a short-lived silence.

'Hurts like a bastard.' What Sorri's reply lacked in eloquence, it more than made up in its directness.

'I watched you fight. Never seen you better, cousin.'

'Even with a gammy hand – ha!'

Snorri looked askance at his cousin, but Morgrim was in no mood for jests.

'You *want* to kill the elgi, don't you? It's like you hate them, Snorri, and don't care what you have to do to vent the anger that comes with it.'

Again, Snorri fell to silence.

'Keep at it and it'll kill you, cousin. That's why I pulled the throng back. It was the only way to get you to stop.'

The alarum bell pealing out across the camp interrupted them. All three dwarfs drew their weapons. Even Brynnoth was up.

'Elgi?' the king of the Sea Hold called.

'Could be an attack?' suggested Morgrim, put in mind of an elven sortie from the gates.

Snorri shook his head at them both. 'Our look-outs would have seen it before it got this close, that's the camp alarum.'

They ran down off the hillock and back through the entrenched war machines. From deeper in the camp there came the sound of further commotion. A horn was braying and there was the beat of distant drums tattooing a marching song.

'Not elgi,' breathed Snorri, his face thunderous.

Morgrim espied banners, waving to and fro above the throngs. They bore the red and blue of the royal house of Everpeak.

'The High King,' he said.

Snorri was already scowling. 'My father is here.'

The war machines from Karak Varn had been brought forwards and were loosing their deadly cargo by the time the High King's royal tent was up and Gotrek seated upon his Throne of Power. A single dwarf was granted audience with him, but the meeting was far from cordial.

In the half-light of the tent, Snorri returned the fierce glare of his father with one of equal reproach.

'I did what I did for the Karaz Ankor, and would do it again,' he pledged.

Supping on his pipe, Gotrek merely glowered.

The High King's tent was festooned with banners and statues of the ancestor gods. All three were represented in chiselled stone, each a shrine of worship for when Gotrek wanted to make his oaths. They were shrouded, smoke clouding the room in a dense fug, drowning out the light from hanging braziers and lanterns. A thick carpet of rough crimson material, trimmed with gold, led up to the High King's seat. Even though he wasn't yet clad in his battle armour and instead wore a travelling cloak of tanned elk hide over tunic and hose, he still cut an imposing figure. A simple mitre with a ruby at its centre sufficed in place of his crown, but Gotrek's rune axe was nearby, sitting in its iron cradle, shimmering dully in the gloom.

'Have you nothing to say to me, father?' Snorri had expected wrath, reproach, even censure. The silence was maddening. He snorted angrily, 'I have a war to fight,' and was turning when Gotrek spoke at last.

'A little profligate, my son,' uttered the High King in a rumbling cadence, 'to loose the mangonels and onagers so indiscriminately.'

Biting his tongue, Snorri faced him again but wouldn't be baited.

'The elgi will not rest during the barrage. Come the dawn, when we attack, they'll be tired. Weaker.'

'Hmmm...' The High King grumbled into his beard, then let the silence linger.

It was the Ancient who had once said, '*In talks or negotiation of any kind, only speak when necessary and let silence be your greatest weapon. For in quietude your opponent's tongue will reveal more than he wishes in seeking to fill it.*'

Snorri knew the tactic, but spoke anyway.

'Are *they* strictly necessary, father?' He gestured to a small cadre of warriors at the side of the High King. At first, the prince had thought them to be hearthguard. Certainly, they wore the armour and trappings of these veterans. But even Thurbad amongst their ranks, the High King's ever-present shadow, was not enough to persuade Snorri that these were not singular dwarfs of a different order.

There were seven in total, clad in gromril plate, wearing war helms with full-face masks and a mailed smock that went from armoured chin to chest, draped over the gorget like a beard of chain. No skin was visible on a single one, and for a moment the prince wondered if they were truly alive at all or some runic golems brought to life by Ranuld Silverthumb.

In the end, the High King revealed nothing and merely dismissed them with a nod.

Thurbad led the warriors out of the tent, and father and son were alone.

'Attacking Tor Alessi alone was an unwise move,' Gotrek uttered flatly.

Snorri bristled but held his temper again. 'You were late.'

The High King made no such concession and bellowed, 'And you are reckless! Starting a war without any thought to the consequences. Rushing in like a fool. You are a beardling playing at being a king, and I will have you kneel before me as your liege-lord.' He sat up in his throne. 'Do it now, or I'll put you down myself.'

Snorri thought about protesting but saw the wisdom in bowing to his father and his king.

'I acted for the benefit of the Karaz–'

'No! You acted for your own self-interest, Snorri. You attacked a city, destroyed it, and threw us into war.'

Snorri glared, unprepared to capitulate completely. 'War was inevitable, father. I merely struck first.'

'I forbade you.' Gotrek was on his feet, two steps down from his throne. 'And you mustered an army. And you played on Brynnoth's grief, drew him and three other kings into this.' He shook his head, snarled. 'I daresay Thagdor and the rest were easily convinced.'

'They saw as I did.'

'And they'll be punished for that. Grudges laid down in blood.' Taking a long pull of black beer, Gotrek exhaled an exasperated breath. He sat back down again, wiped his beard. 'By seeking to unite the clans, you have divided us.'

Snorri frowned, confused. 'But now you've declared war, the dawi are one.'

'Because of you, I have to sanction four of my vassal lords. If you were not my son, I would have killed you for such a transgression.'

Snorri got to his feet, and the High King roared.

'Don't defy me further. Kneel down!'

'I will not, father!' He thumped his chest. 'I regret nothing. Nothing! You've grown old sitting in that chair. Peace has softened you, made you weak. We've already been invaded, our holds and borders both. The skarrens flourish, their king mocks you, and we ignore it. I was wrong about the war, about it being inevitable. We were already *at* war, a war of wills. Ours versus the elgin's...' Snorri's tone became pleading, 'and we were losing, father.'

The prince let his arms drop to his sides. He lifted his chin, pulling aside his beard to expose his neck.

'So, do as you will. But I didn't divide the holds or the clans. You did, when you put the crown of Karaz upon your head and did nothing. Kill me, if the *Dammaz Kron* demands it.'

Gotrek's fists were clenched like anvils, his chest heaved like a battering ram. Wrath like the heart of Karag Vlak boiled within him.

'I cannot,' he growled through a shield wall of teeth.

'Come, do it! If that is your will, but promise me you'll destroy these elgi and drive them from the Old World.'

'I cannot!' he snapped, standing.

Snorri took three paces until he was before his father at the foot of the Throne of Power.

'Why, father? Mete out your retribution.'

'I cannot,' he hissed.

'Why?'

'Because I cannot lose my only son!' The anger died as quickly as it had erupted and the High King sagged, his face a fractured mask of weariness and remembered pain. 'Your mother, my queen, is dead, and when she passed half my heart went with her, dreng tromm.'

Releasing a shuddering breath, Gotrek gripped Snorri's shoulder. Tears glistened in his eyes. The High King's voice came out in a rasp.

'I am afraid. This war will destroy us if we let it. I fear it will destroy you too...'

'Father...'

They embraced, and the bad blood between them drained away.

'I'm sorry, father. I should not have defied you. Dreng tromm, I should not–'

'Enough, Snorri.' Gotrek held Snorri's face in his hands. He clasped his neck, bringing their heads together, and closed his eyes. 'It doesn't matter now. I have been a poor father. I tried to teach you, but was over harsh. I can see that now. I am an old fool, who almost forgot he had a son.' He pulled back, meeting Snorri's gaze. 'We will break the elgi together, and take back the Old World.'

Snorri nodded, wiping away tears with the back of his hand.

'Now,' said the High King, 'tell me of the siege preparations. We have a city to sack.'

THIRTY-SEVEN

THE FIRST SIEGE OF TOR ALESSI

For six days, Liandra's morning had begun the same.

Clanking armour as the wearers stomped in unison, the stink of their bodies potent on the breeze, the reek of their dirty cook fires, their furnaces, the soot and ash that seemed to paste the very air, making it thick and greasy. Worst of all were their voices, the crude, guttural bellowing, the flatulent chorus as they rose from their pits, the holes they had dug or the tents they had staved for sleeping in.

'Khazuk!'

She knew this word, the one they were bleating now, together and in anger. It put her teeth on edge, made her want to unsheathe her sword and begin killing. Liandra did not speak Dwarfish, she found the language base and flat like much of what the mud-dwellers built, but she knew a call to battle and death when she heard it.

Every morning it was like this and every morning, and deep into the night she had endured it. Now, at last, she would get a chance to do something about it.

In a high vault of the Dragon Tower, she looked out onto the battlefield beyond the walls of Tor Alessi at the dwarf host. They marched in thick phalanxes, shields together, axes held upright like stunted ugly statues.

Stout-looking siege towers rolled between the squares of armoured warriors. On a ridge line far behind the advancing army she saw their bulky war engines, strings tautened, ready to loose. Several carried score marks, the deep gouges of eagle claws. There were fewer now than the dwarfs began with, but still a great many remained. A thick line of crossbows sat in front of the machineries, a little farther down the incline, taking shelter amongst scattered rocks.

It would not avail them, elven eyes could see and kill a dwarf hiding in rock easily enough.

And they were digging. How like the mud-dwellers to burrow underground like small-eyed vermin. Like the rocks, there was an answer to that too. She had spoken with Caeris Starweaver and knew of his plan to sunder the tunnels with the dwarfs still in them. Liandra sneered; they were persistent creatures, seemingly content to batter at Tor Alessi's walls until they broke. Given time, under such constant pressure, they probably would, but then she knew what was coming across the sea and what would happen when it arrived.

She looked towards their own forces and saw the disciplined ranks of spearmen arrayed on the wall. Behind them and below were ranks of archers, their spotters in position between the spearmen to guide their arrows. Several mages had joined the warriors on the battlements and there were small cohorts of Lothern axemen between the spears too. For doubtless, the dwarfs would try to climb again and a heavy blade severs rope more easily than a spear tip.

Some of the refugees from Kor Vanaeth, a pitiful number, swelled the elven host. They were positioned at one of the gates. From the disposition of their forces, the dwarfs looked to be assaulting all three at once. It had taken much resolve not to take flight on Vranesh's back before now and burn a ragged hole in the mud-dwellers' ranks, but that would not win the battle. She needed to choose her fights more carefully than that.

'Princess Athinol...' One of Prince Arlyr's retainers was waiting for her in the tower's portal. He cast a fearful glance into the stygian dark of the vast tower at the hulking presence spewing sulphurous ash into the chamber.

Arlyr was commander of the Silver Helm Knights and like all young lordlings, he was impatient to sally forth, but required a distraction.

Liandra had decided to be much more than that.

'Tell him I am almost ready,' she said, donning her war helm and turning from the battlefield. It wouldn't be long before she'd see it again, this time on leather wings and spitting fire.

Dull thunder rumbled from above, shaking the roots of Ari and spilling earth on the miners. They were close, almost to the wall. Six days of hard toil had almost come to fruition.

Nadri wiped a clod from his brow, spitting out the dirt before hacking down with his pick. It was tough work, but preferable to the battlefield. A muffled clamour was all that reached them from above, and even that was barely audible through the digging song and the thud of sundered earth.

'*Ho-hai, ho-hai...*' Nadri joined in with the sonorous refrain, reminded of the attack on Kor Vanaeth's gate. Rise and fall, rise and fall, his pick-axe was almost pendulous. The diggers cut the rock, the gatherers took it away in barrels to shore up the foundations. Runners brought stone flasks of tar-thick beer. Used to the finer ales, Nadri found the brew caustic but at least it was fortifying. Every miner took a pull and their spirits and strength were renewed. They cut by lantern light, the lamps hooked on spikes rammed into the tunnel walls with every foot the dwarfs dug out. Just a few more and they would breach.

Behind the miners were a wedge of the heaviest-armoured warriors Nadri had ever seen. He had heard tales of the ironbreakers, the dwarfs that guarded the old tunnels and forgotten caves of the Ungdrin road, but had never seen one face to face. Up close, they were imposing and seemingly massive. Hulking gromril war plate layered their bodies and their beards were black as coal, thick and wiry. Hard, granite-edged eyes glinted behind their half-masked helms, waiting for the moment when the digging was done and the fighting would begin.

Rest over, Nadri gave the flask back to the runner with nodded thanks, and returned to the rock face.

Soon, very soon now.

The iron ramp slammed down into the breach with enough force to knock the defenders onto their backs.

The dwarfs raised shields immediately as they were met by an arrow storm.

Morgrim roared as if voicing his defiance could turn the shafts aside, and ploughed forwards.

'Uzkul!'

The reply came as a roar of affirmation from Morgrim's warriors, who surged alongside their thane into a host of elven spears.

It was the third assault in six days. The dwarfs had used probing attacks after the night bombardment, picking at weak points, gauging the strength of the defences and defenders. The east gate was deemed the most likely point of breach, it was the most distant of the routes into the city and therefore less well fortified. For the last three days, Gotrek Starbreaker had amassed forces in the east, concealed by trenchworks. Stray barrages from the stone throwers had weakened the gate house around the towers. Great clay pots of pitch were being readied to weaken it further.

Morgrim took the north wall, volunteering to lead a cohort in one of the siege towers and onto the very battlements of Tor Alessi. It was to be a hard push – the High King wanted the elves to think this was the main point of assault. Morgrim was happy to oblige.

Half-sundered by their war machines, chunks of battlement broke away as the dwarfs tramped over it. One poor soul lost his footing and fell to his death many feet below. No one in the front ranks watched him but a grudgekeeper in the rearguard called out the dwarf's name to ensure he would be remembered.

'Uzkul!' Morgrim yelled again, bludgeoning a spearman's skull as he fended off another with his shield. He drew one elf in, butting him hard across the nose and splitting his face apart. Another dwarf finished the spearman when he dropped his guard, recoiling in pain.

An axe blade dug into his weapon's haft and Morgrim shook it free, snarling. He kicked out, snapping the elf's shin with a hobnailed boot, before burying his hammer head into the warrior's neck. Blood fountained up in a ragged arc, painting a clutch of spearmen who pressed on despite their disgust.

Morgrim smashed one in the shoulder with his shield and took a spear in the thigh for his trouble. Smacking it away before the wielder could thrust, he incapacitated the second elf with a low blow to the groin. The backhand took a third spearman in the torso. A dwarf warrior next to him fell in the same moment before one of his fellow clansmen stepped in to take his place.

Somewhere in the frenzy, Morgrim and his warriors gained the battlements. Elves came at them from either side, wielding spears and silver swords. The small knot of dwarfs, desperately trying to expand outwards and establish a foothold, was quickly corralled.

Barely before Morgrim had Tor Alessi stone under his feet, a fair-haired captain carrying a jewelled axe and a small shield hit him hard. Daggers of pain flared in his shoulder but the runes on the dwarf's armour held against the elf magic and Morgrim kept his arm. He replied with an overhand swing, denting the elf's shield before uppercutting with his own. Spitting blood, the elf's chin came up and Morgrim barged into him, barrelling the captain over the battlements and to his death. It only seemed to galvanise the other elves further.

The dwarfs gained maybe three feet. It was tough going. Arrows whistled in at them from below, piercing eyes and necks, studding torsos like spines. Out the corner of his eye, Morgrim saw Brungni spin like a nail, three white shafts embedded in his back. The inner side of the wall was open, and a yawning gap stretched into a courtyard below. It left the dwarfs dangerously exposed, a fact Brungni learned to his cost. In his death throes he handed off the banner to Tarni Engulfson before falling into a riot of elven spears below.

'Don't drop that,' Morgrim warned.

The young dwarf nodded, clutching grimly to the banner pole.

A hastily-erected line of shields protected the battling dwarfs from the worst of the elven volleys but it made fighting to the front and rear more difficult.

Farther down the wall, Morgrim saw another siege tower reach the battlements. A plume of flame fashioned into an effigy of a great eagle engulfed it before the ramp was even released, burning the dwarfs within. Cracking wood, the sound of splitting timbers raked the air as the tower collapsed in on itself, killing those warriors waiting on the platforms below. It tumbled slowly like a felled oak and was lost from Morgrim's sight.

There would be no reinforcement on the wall, not yet.

He lifted his rune hammer to rally the spirits of his warriors. By now it was a familiar cry.

'Uzkul!'

Death.

* * *

Gotrek watched the battle from atop his Throne of Power.

Below, his bearers were unyielding, their strength unfailing. It needed to be; throne and king were a heavy burden in more ways than one.

Several of the siege towers had reached the ramparts of the north wall and two of the gates were under assault with battering rams and grappling hooks. A sortie of elven horse riders had stalled the third assault, Thagdor's longbeards currently waging a contest of attrition with the high-helmed knights.

Gotrek would have bet his entire treasure hoard on the victors of that fight, but it was hard to smile when the elves were making them pay so dearly for every foot.

From the east flank, quarrellers maintained a regular barrage from behind their mantlets. Behind them on a grassy ridge, the war machines continued to loose with devastating effect. Several sections of the wall were broken and split, but not enough to force a breach. They needed the tunnels to undermine them, bring the foundations crashing down into a pool of fire as the dwarfs burned the elven stone to ash.

Zonzharr was potent dwarf alchemy that could reduce even the stoutest rock to blackened dust. The miners had pots of the stuff, hauled into the tunnels by pack mules, ready to be rolled down to the rock face when the digging was done.

Overhead the sky darkened as the elven mages practised their foul art. Summoned fire blazed into one of the siege towers, burning it to a scorched stump. A second conflagration followed but dispersed against the solemn chanting of the runesmiths.

Most of the elder lords of the rune had not joined their kings in battle. Mysteriously, they were nowhere to be found, some having left their holds for places unknown. Gotrek knew better than to question it. Ranuld Silverthumb had been runelord of Everpeak for as long as he could remember, from before even his father Gurni had reigned. The servants of Thungi had their own ways the High King could only guess at. If the ancient lords were absent, it was for good reason.

It did not mean the dwarfs were without magic of their own, however.

'There is one more weapon in my arsenal,' said Hrekki Ironhandson whom Gotrek had joined on the hillside not far from the war machines.

'Summon it and its keeper,' said the High King. His eyes never left the battlefield, for somewhere in the chaos was his only son.

Snorri fought at the east gate under a mantle of iron. The stout shaft of a battering ram swung between his cohort of warriors, smacking fat splinters from the wood.

'We'll make a dirty mess of their door,' he promised, shouting to be heard, 'and then we'll make a mess of them. Khazuk!'

'Khazuk!' chimed the warriors together, heaving the ram back for another blow. The end was fashioned into the simulacrum of an ancestor head, Grimnir, his beard wrought into spikes. It gored deep, tearing at the gate.

Boiling oil, alchemical fire, swathes of arrows all fell upon Snorri's warriors but they didn't even flinch. These were hearthguard, king's men, and they would not shirk from the deadliest of battles. Either the gate would fall or they would.

A prickling sensation in Snorri's beard made him look up. The view was narrow, and the prince caught snatches through the slits between the tiles in the roof.

'Spellcrafter,' he growled.

Above, an elven mage was conjuring. She wore a pale robe, emblazoned with stars, and a moon-shaped circlet sat upon her brow. But it was the crackling staff to which Snorri's eye was drawn, and the tempest waxing around it.

'Spellcrafter!' he roared this time, inciting a dour chorus as the dwarfs invoked earth, stone and metal to retard the harmful magicks.

A hundred dwarfs clamouring at the east gate chanted in unison. It began slowly but grew into an almost palpable wall of defiance. A hundred became two hundred, then three hundred until all the warriors assaulting the east gate were united in purpose.

But elven sorcery came from the Old Ones, it was High magic and could not so easily be undone. Eldritch winds were already clawing at the hearthguard, tugging at their limbs, buffeting them into their fellow dwarfs. The chant faltered. Rain lashed down, sharp as knives, impelled by the gale. The slashing deluge turned the ground beneath the dwarfs' feet to sludge. Several warriors were fouled in it, some even to their necks. Easy prey for the archers whose arrows flew with storm force, piercing armour like it was parchment.

Despite his best efforts, Snorri could feel his body sinking into the mire. Hail stung his face, opening a cut on his cheek. He reached out, letting his hand axe hang by the thong on his wrist, hauling a hearthguard to his feet.

'Up, brother,' he growled. 'Stone and steel.'

'Stone and steel, my prince,' the breathless hearthguard replied.

Snorri turned, and roared to the others, 'Heads down and heave!'

One warrior was blown free of the ram's protective mantle. The elven archers seized upon him, pinioning the dwarf with a dozen arrows before he could so much as raise his shield. Another, sunk almost to the waist, was left behind and fought defiantly until a shaft took him in the neck and he spat his last.

'Thagging bast–' Snorri began, but the tempest had them now.

Rivets fixing the mantle to the ram frame were loosening. A flap of metal swung up briefly before clamping down again. In those few seconds, four hearthguard warriors lay dead with arrows jutting from their bodies.

Wrenching his boots free of the mud, Snorri stepped up to take the place of one. Clutching the iron handle of the ram, he pulled it back.

The hefty wooden log lurched, swinging wildly in the gale. Its violent backswing almost pushed the prince out from the mantle. The wind was rising, building into a fist of elemental force that would punch the roof of the battering ram clean off.

Drowned in mud or condemned to death by elven arrows, neither was a favourable ending worthy of song. The gate was weakening, Snorri could hear it even above the storm in the protestations of the wood. A few more solid hits and it would buckle. But only if there was time before the battering ram was torn apart.

Behind them to the south, distant thunder was booming.

Snorri groaned under his breath, 'What now?' before he realised it had come from the dwarf ranks.

Lightning sheared through the storm dark a moment later. It struck the elven battlements, a second arcing bolt spearing the elven mage. Her death scream echoed loudly before her scorched body crumpled and the tempest lifted.

Snorri tried not to be relieved. There was no time for it. A minor reprieve, nothing more. The real fight lurked behind the gate, and he planned to smash it wide open.

'Khazuk!'

Twenty hearthguard heaved and the ram swung back.

Grimnir snarled and the angry god swung forwards, baring his teeth.

But the east gate held.

Fundrinn Stormhand called the lightning back. He was standing on an Anvil of Doom, feet braced apart. Great runes of power crackled and flashed across the anvil's pellucid silver surface, and the storm lived briefly in the runesmith's eyes, in the rivulets of magic coursing through his jagged red beard before earthing harmlessly.

But as soon as the storm lightning had faded, Fundrinn was calling fresh elemental power into being. It began as a mote of flame in his outstretched palm but as he spoke the rune rites the fire grew until the runesmith could no longer hold it and was forced to set the conflagration loose. What began as a flaming wind swelled into a tidal wave of burning vengeance, a score of spectral dwarf faces snarling and biting at its fiery crest.

Fundrinn cried out, '*Zharrum!*', coaxing and shaping the raging inferno with sweeping arcs of his runestaff. '*Zharrum un uzkul a elgi!*'

Across the battlefield, a second voice bellowed. It spoke unto the deep earth, making oaths of the great ancestors. One of the anvils of Zhufbar rolled forwards, impelled by the will of its keeper Gorik Stonebeard, and joined the magical convocation. He had no staff, but carried a rune hammer. As he smacked the hammer head down upon the anvil, the deep earth answered and a rippling tremor shuddered from beneath him.

'*Duraz um uzkul a elgi!*'

The tremor rolled outwards at the invocation, building in ferocity, splitting the ground underfoot.

The lords of Karak Varn and Zhufbar crafted in perfect magical concert, unleashing hellfire and earthquakes against the elven host.

Gotrek felt their power through his beard, in his fingertips, along his teeth, and grinned.

'Burn them, bring them down!'

Liandra was barely in the saddle when the quake hit. Dust and grit spilled from the vaulted ceiling of the Dragon Tower, shaking its walls violently.

'Vranesh!' she urged and the beast tore up into the vaults, head down, smashing through the roof. There was no time to guide the dragon through the narrow aperture of the tower. The small minaret that served as Vranesh's rookery was collapsing. Mere appendage to the grand tower itself, it would still have buried dragon and rider.

Exploding from the shattered tower, Vranesh exulted and Liandra with him as he tore into the sky. Empathic joy rippled through the elf's body, and she embraced a thrill of violent intent as she beheld the dwarfs below.

'*Higher, higher...*' she coaxed, guiding Vranesh into the ice cold skies, daggering through cloud until they were lost from sight. There they roamed, Vranesh trailing tendrils of smoke from his maw in hungry anticipation.

In the solitude high above Tor Alessi, Liandra's thoughts returned to Imladrik. She remembered their last conversation in the gorge, the widening gulf she felt growing between them, and wondered where he was now and if he had thought of her since then. For a moment, the iron grip she had on her lance loosened and she considered that vengeance would not be an adequate substitute for her grief. Then she thought of Kor Vanaeth and her people, dying at the hands of the cruel dwarfs, and her resolve became a thing of unyielding ice.

Liandra leaned over in her saddle, roving the enemy army with her eyes for a target.

'There,' she hissed. 'Dive, Vranesh!'

Silver lightning breached the cold winter cloud as a beast of old myth fell upon the war machines.

Gotrek had barely ordered his bearers forwards before the dragon had torn up three engines and devoured their crew. Snapping wood, torn metal and shouting dwarfs merged into one discordant sound. Screwing up his courage, a thane of the Varn rushed at the beast with his rune axe trailing fire, but was dispatched by a lance strike through the heart before he'd done much more than heft the blade.

An elf maid, armoured in dragon scale. She gutted three more dwarfs before her eyes met with the High King's. Bolt throwers further down the line of war engines were already turning as the elf's beast started in on the quarrellers. It led with its forelegs, gouging a deep, ruddy furrow in the dwarfs' ranks, their hand axes and crossbow bolts unable to penetrate its dragonscale.

Gotrek snarled at the nearest ballista crew, knowing he wouldn't reach the elf dragon rider in time to save the quarrellers from being devoured by her mount. 'Shoot that elgi bitch!'

Its strong pinions flexing, the dragon took flight with its rider as the first of the iron shafts flew, cutting air. She dodged a second volley too, the beast snapping one in mid-flight before it turned to spew fire.

Heat ten times more potent than a forge furnace washed over Gotrek and his charges, but the magic of the Throne of Power kept them safe. Singed but alive, he glowered through a wall of flickering haze at the fleeing beast and its rider.

'Crozzled my bloody beard,' he growled. 'Drakk,' he said as the fire died, now just a a blackened ring on the hillside. 'I hate drakk.' He rapped on the arm of his throne with a ringed fist. 'Forward. We make for the east gate. Furgil and the others best be ready. Thurbad,' said Gotrek, looking down to his captain of the hearthguard and the seven iron-bearded warriors that accompanied him. 'Gather fifty warriors, including the steelbeards. You're with me. Leave the rest.'

'But you'll be open to attack, my king.'

'Aye,' said Gotrek, eyeing the dragon as it dived down to spew more fire, 'and if we're lucky, she'll take the bait.'

On the north wall the fighting had grown fiercer. Elf and dwarf lay dead and dying upon the battlements, gutted and staved in, broken and cleaved. Two great civilisations were destroying one another, yet no one cared to notice.

Morgrim's hammer felt heavy as he bludgeoned but not from the heft of the weapon, he could wield it all day and night if needed. It was the blood upon it, the slaughter that weighed the dwarf down.

A screech that resonated across the sky, tearing it open, shook Morgrim from his reverie. An upper tower had collapsed and something leathern and terrible had shot out from it like a battering ram.

'Drakk!'

His warriors cried out and balked when they saw the dragon smash through the tower roof. Pieces of stone, shattered chips of tile cascaded onto them but were a paltry shower compared to the deluge that slammed down into the elves amassing in the courtyard. Fixed on the beast, the dwarfs barely paid any heed. One abandoned all thoughts of defence altogether and found a spear in his gut for his trouble. Another jumped off the battlements, mind crushed by fear. Dwarfs were a hardy race, and their history with dragons was long and bloody, but such primordial beasts were terrifying even for the sons of Grungni.

Morgrim marshalled his courage, still fighting hard with an eye on the sky as the beast wheeled above. 'Hold fast!' he yelled at the clanners. 'Stone and steel!'

Gritting their teeth, the rest of the dwarfs gripped their axe hafts and fought on.

Through maddened slashes of the battle, Morgrim saw the dragon savage the war engines before turning its wrath onto the High King. His heart quickened for a moment when his liege-lord was engulfed by flame but then returned to normal when he saw the High King was unscathed.

Soaring skywards, the beast pulled out of bow range before coming down hard on the tunnellers. Dragon fire stitched across their ranks, igniting the pots of zonzharr and pushing a ferocious inferno down Grik's gullet. Morgrim was forced away before he could see more, but the image of burning dwarfs staggering from the tunnel mouth was etched into his mind.

With the wrenching of stone Grik collapsed, releasing a pall of dust and trapping the survivors inside with the fire.

Below the western gatehouse, Nadri toiled at the face of Ari. Strong elven foundations were making the last few feet hard, but it meant they were close. Hacking with their picks and shovels, the miners had carved out a subterranean cavern that was wide enough to admit a small army. With over four hundred ironbreakers waiting silently in the wings, it needed to be.

They were led by one of the Everpeak thanes, a foreign-looking dwarf whom Nadri had seen with the prince on several occasions and so assumed was part of his inner circle. Unlike the ironbreakers, his armour was light and of a strange design, depicting effigies of creatures Nadri wasn't familiar with. The thane seemed to be waiting for something, as though he knew they were about to breach.

A lodewarden called the sappers back. The time for digging was over, fire would do the rest. Lighting the zonzharr, the miners at the end of the tunnel retreated and took shelter behind barriers of wutroth. With a grunt, three dwarfs from the Copper-fist clan rolled the great clay urn of the zonzharr down the tunnel. When it smashed against the end it immolated the base of the gatehouse wall in a flare of angry crimson fire. A cheer went up as the foundation rock broke apart, dumping earth and flagstones into the gap the miners had hewn with their pickaxes.

'Khazuk!' The chant resonated through the ironbreakers' closed helms as they rushed through the breach, led by the thane.

Nadri and the other sappers stood aside to let the cavalcade of armoured bodies through.

Jorgin Blackfinger, lodewarden of Barak Varr, climbed onto a boulder so he could be seen and heard by all the clans.

'Ready for another tough chuffing slog, lads?'

Nadri bellowed with his fellow clanners. 'Ho-hai!'

Nearly two hundred miners followed behind the ironbreakers, brandishing picks and shovels. The light streaming through the breach was hazy, thick with grey dust, but the clash of blades was clear enough.

The elves had lost their gatehouse, a part of it at least, but their warriors were ready and willing to defend the breach. And above the carnage of the battle, a sound, deep and resonant... A primordial roar.

Snorri heard the dragon rather than saw it. Enclosed beneath the mantle of the battering ram, it was hard to see much of anything other than the back of the dwarf in front and the shoulder of the one to your side.

Words spoken what seemed like an age ago returned to the young prince, plucking at his pride.

Dawi barazen ek dreng drakk, un riknu.
A dragon slayer, one destined to become king.

Snorri felt the pull of destiny. It was slipping through his grasp.

He tried to turn, find the beast through the slit of vision afforded to him beneath the mantle, but it was impossible. The ram was moving under its own momentum, him with it. Apparently, fate was too. All he caught was snatches of sky, of armoured dwarfs embattled.

The beast cried out again, a rush of flame spat from its maw easy to discern even above the din of the assault. Burning flesh resolved on the breeze.

Trapped in the throng, battering at the east gate, Snorri railed.

But there was nothing he could do.

And then, like a magma flow breaching through the crust, the gate cracked apart and the dwarfs flooded forwards. Snorri went with them, hurled along by furious momentum. Behind him, he heard the shouts of other warriors joining the fray.

The goad was obvious. Liandra saw it as clearly as the lance in her armoured grip. She imagined ramming it through the old dwarf king's heart, the one who lorded over the others on his throne of dirty gold. She would make him suffer, but would have to do it soon. Fires caused by the mud-dwellers' crude magic lit Tor Alessi like lanterns honouring some perverse celebration. For all that she burned, the dwarfs could visit it upon the elves threefold. She needed to redress the balance and was about to rein Vranesh into a sharp dive when the west gatehouse collapsed.

Like armoured ants, dwarfs scurried from below and attacked her kinsmen. She watched an entire cohort of spearmen, injured and confused from the destruction, wiped out by the mud-dwellers in seconds. More were coming, spilling up from the earth like a contagion, a spouting geyser of filth running amok across Tor Alessi's west quarter.

Liandra hesitated, torn by indecision. She wanted the dwarf king, to gut him like a wild boar on her spear. But the defenders at the west gatehouse were failing. They needed time to restore order, something to regain some momentum.

Spitting a curse, Liandra turned away from the king and went to the aid of her dying kin.

After a welter of colourful swearing, Gotrek gave up on the dragon rider and ordered the host of Everpeak to march. Reacting to the gatehouse collapse, elven reserves stationed behind the city walls were swarming to the west quarter to try and staunch the dwarf incursion. Gotrek gave them just long enough to become entangled in the fight there before he nodded to his horn bearers to herald a second assault.

The east gate was breached, but the throng there led by Snorri hadn't penetrated far. That was about to change. As the deep, ululating clarion call boomed out dwarf forces hiding amongst the rocks came forth, led by Furgil. The pathfinder had done well to conceal an entire host. Combined with Snorri's clans and the throng of the High King, it was an army large enough to overrun the entire eastern wall let alone its gate.

Gotrek despaired at the thought of it. They had gone from peace... to *this*.

'So arrogant...'

'My king?' asked Thurbad, as the rest of the throng joined them in serried ranks to begin the march. 'You mean the elgi?'

'No, Thurbad,' Gotrek replied. 'I mean us.'

His raised his axe and the dwarfs marched on the east gate.

Through a fog of dust and spilling rock, Nadri clambered out of the breach and up to the surface.

Ironbreakers were already fighting as well as several cohorts of clan warriors led by King Valarik. Seeing the imminent destruction of the wall and gatehouse, the lord of Karak Hirn had urged his throng towards it. The elves were quick to counter, and by the time most of the miners were shoulder to shoulder with their kith and kin, the fighting around the breach was ferocious.

Nadri was still blinking the grit out of his eyes, adjusting to the light, when a shadow roared overhead. Though he didn't see it, the very presence of the thing above filled his gut with ice and made his limbs leaden. The reek of sulphur wafted over him, burning his nostrils, and he heard the crackle of what sounded like a furnace being stoked only much louder, much deeper.

Someone shouted; he couldn't make out the exact word, but it sounded like a warning. Then a heavy weight smacked into him, bore him down until day became night and Nadri tasted hot armour on his tongue a moment later. Something was burning. There were screams, smoke, the stench of scorched meat, but it wasn't boar or elk. It was dwarf. The roar came again, resounded across the breach.

A gruff voice told him, 'Stay down, until the monster has passed.'

Blood flecked Nadri's cheek. It was warm and wet. After a few seconds hunkered in the dark, he realised it belonged to one of the ironbreakers shielding him. He went to move, trying to find the injured warrior, but the gruff voice spoke again.

'Hradi's dead. Stay down.'

Shouting this time, heard through a press of armoured bodies that were slowly crushing him. Nadri couldn't breathe. Terrified, he'd been holding his breath and only now realised that he couldn't draw more into his lungs. He also couldn't speak to let his saviours know they were killing him.

More shouting and the screech of something old and primordial. It was above him, squatting on the rubble. Nadri could almost see it. He caught a glimpse of scale, a tooth, a baleful yellow eye.

Shadows lingered at the edge of his sight, growing deeper as he crept closer to oblivion. Singing, he heard. It sounded distant and at odds with the battlefield. He tasted beer, rich and dark, and smelled the succulent aroma of roasting pork.

'Heg...' It was all he could think of to say, though he wasn't sure whether the name had actually passed his lips or he had merely imagined speaking. Either way, it was the last word of a wraith, Gazul beckoning him towards the gate, darkness closing in all around...

It was like an anvil being lifted off his back. When he came to, the pressure was gone and Nadri heaved a long, painful breath into his gut. Hours must have passed; the sky above, what little he could see through the smoke, was darkening. He saw the suggestion of walls, a ruined tower, and remembered he had fallen on the battlefield inside the elven city. It took almost a minute before he got up, and even then he only sat. He'd lost his pickaxe. A host of dead ironbreakers surrounded him, cooked in their armour. Their champion's face was etched with a grimace. They had protected him, in life and death. Deeper into the west quarter of the city, not that far from the breach, a battle was ongoing. Nadri heard shouts to the east, too, and the clash of arms at the northern gate that still held.

His dead saviours weren't alone. Nadri saw a dwarf he recognised, despite the horrendous burns. Exotic-looking armour was half-melted to his face. A veneer of soot clad his body like chainmail. Tendrils of smoke spiralled from his mouth. The rest of the brotherhood had advanced deeper into the breach, the miners too. Nadri and the others had been left for dead, except he was a sole survivor.

'Heg...' This time he knew the word was spoken aloud, and felt tears fill his eyes at his miraculous escape. Even surrounded by death, for the first time Nadri believed he might see his brother again. He was rising, pushing himself up on pain-weary limbs, when something nearby moved.

It coughed, or at least it sounded like a cough but such a thing wasn't possible. Then he saw the soot, flaking away like a second skin, the flesh beneath pristine and untouched by flame. Nadri gaped and would've grabbed for his weapon but the pickaxe was gone, lost in the chaos, and he was too paralysed to reach down for an ironbreaker's axe. Most were fused to their gauntlets anyway.

'Valaya,' he breathed, staggering backwards from the thing that also lived. 'What are you?'

White teeth arched into a pitiless smile and a voice that was several but really no voice at all said, 'Nothing you would understand, little dwarf.'

Dusk was painting the horizon, creeping towards the battlefield with soot black fingers. They had held the breach for several hours, drawing the elves away for an attack on the east gate that had yet to breach much farther than its outer defences. Nightfall was approaching rapidly and with it the end of the sixth day and the third assault.

For all that they pushed and pressured, the dwarfs could not sack the city – though it burned badly, there were fires everywhere and even the dragon rider had been put to flight when the heavy ballistae from the Varn had pierced its wings and sent it fleeing.

Snorri raged. For every elf he cut down another took its place, two more ready after that and then three, four. It was endless. And these foes were not like greenskins or the beasts of the forest, or the terrors of the deep places or the high mountains; they were disciplined, determined and utterly convinced of the righteousness of their cause.

Only one thing gave the young prince heart as he heard his father's war horn sounding the retreat – the elves were wearying. Only a dwarf could match another dwarf in a war of attrition. Dwarfs were stubborn to the point of self destruction. Entire clans had wiped themselves out in proving that point to a rival or out of grudgement. Elves were strong, there could be no denying that now – only a fool would, and Snorri was no fool – but they were not dwarfs, and in the end that would prove their undoing.

So as the throngs departed, leaving the ragged breach in their wake and the elves to contemplate how they might secure it before the dawn's next attack, Snorri was smiling.

And what was more, the dragon still lived.

For now, the battle was over and Morgrim toured the field of the dead with shovel and pickaxe. As before, the elves granted the dwarfs clemency to tend to their injured and dead, and the dwarfs reciprocated. But even with this tenuous agreement, Morgrim eyed the silent ranks lining the walls of Tor Alessi with something that approached trepidation.

His attention returned to the battlefield as an elf apothecary passed close by to him. Morgrim gave her little heed, but noticed there was no malice in her eyes, just a desire to ease suffering. Considering the dwarfs' own healers, he wondered just how different they really were to one another when blades and pride weren't getting in the way.

Shrouded in cloaks of deep purple, a silver rune emblazoned on the back, were the priestesses of Valaya. They roved in pairs, administering healing where they could and mercy where they could not. Morgrim thought it was the least he could do to help bury those beyond help. Though the ground was hard from the winter frost, despite the heat from the dwarf forges softening the earth, it was purifying work. There was rejuvenation in good, honest, toil, even though it was grave digging. To wield an axe for something other than bloodletting came surprisingly welcome to him.

A veritable sea of carnage stretched out in front of Morgrim. Acres of land were littered with broken shields; notched blades and spear tips; the sundered links of chainmail, rust red and still sticky; split pieces of elven scale, blackened by fire; shattered war helms with severed horns or their horsehair plumes aggressively parted; and the bodies of course, there were a great many bodies. One stood out above the others, which in itself was remarkable.

Despite the dead dwarf's expression, Morgrim recognised him. It was the miner Snorri had spoken to before they had laid siege, Copperhand or Copperfinger. Copper something, anyway.

The poor bastard, like so many others, had given his life for hearth and hold. But unlike the remains of his kinsmen, this dwarf was unscathed. There were cuts and bruises, some of which were likely from digging, for he had the trappings of a tunneller. No killing blow that was obvious, though. It was his face that drew Morgrim to the dead dwarf's side. Etched in such utter terror and disbelief. Fear had stopped the dwarf's heart; he clutched his chest in rigor mortis as if it might have burst had he not.

'Dreng tromm...' breathed Morgrim, gripping a talisman that hung around his neck.

'I've seen others who died with fear on their faces,' said a female voice.

Morgrim turned, half-crouched by the deceased, and saw Elmendrin.

'Tromm, rinnki.' He bowed his head.

'Always so respectful, Morgrim Bargrum,' she said, returning the gesture. 'What is it the warriors call you? Ironbeard? Grungni-heart would be more appropriate.'

Unused to flattery, Morgrim reddened. He gestured to the corpse.

'You see something different in this one?' he asked.

'Yes, he is dead *from* fear itself. But it's as though something just reached in and crushed the beating heart in his chest.'

'My reckoning was not quite so exact, but this dwarf's death is unique.' He looked out over the killing field. Other grave diggers had joined him, together with the priestess. Morgrim even thought he saw Drogor. The dwarf from Karak Zorn was brushing soot from his shoulders, having doubtless had a near miss when the dragon had burned the attackers at the west wall. Not many survived that assault. Indeed, Morgrim was surrounded by some of its victims as a dozen eagle-eyed elven archers kept a bead on him from the ruined battlements not ten feet away.

'He can't be buried here,' Morgrim decided, hoisting the dwarf onto his back.

Elmendrin helped him.

'King Brynnoth's tent is not that far,' she said. 'His grudgekeeper has been busy naming the dead all evening. Looks like a long night ahead of us.'

At the edge of the dwarf encampment, rites for the dead could be heard being intoned by the priests of Gazul. Morgrim had seen the solemn service many times before during battle, when tombs could not be built nor bodies returned to their holds. Instead, the dwarfs would bury them in the earth according to their clans. Shoulder to shoulder they would meet Grungni as warriors, the honourable dead. Barrows of earth would shroud them, dug by the surviving clans as Gazul's priests uttered benedictions and incantations of warding. Every dwarf war caravan carried tombstones and these rune-etched slabs would be placed upon the mounds of earth where the fallen were buried. If the ground proved too hard to dig or the army fought on solid rock or tainted earth then the dead would be burned instead and their ashes brought back in stone pots for later interment. These too were carried by Gazul's priests on sombre-looking black carts. So did the dwarfs attend to their dead, even when far from hearth and hold.

'Does Snorri know you're here?' Morgrim asked, as they started walking. A dozen bowstrings creaked at the dwarfs' departure.

Elmendrin looked down at the ground. 'No. And it must stay that way.'

'I doubt your presence will be a secret for long.'

'Perhaps, but for now I want to do my work, fulfil my oaths to Valaya. Besides,' she said, 'Snorri has more important things to worry about than me.'

'I think he would argue that.'

'Which is precisely why I must go unnoticed by the prince.' She allowed a brief pause, then looked up at Morgrim. 'The war has changed him, hasn't it?'

'All of us are changed by it, and will continue to be.'

'Not like that, I mean,' said Elmendrin.

Morgrim regarded her curiously.

She answered, 'It's made him better, somehow. As if he was forged for it.'

There was a sadness in Morgrim's eyes when he replied. 'I think that perhaps he was, that all his petulance and discontent stemmed from a desire to fulfil that for which he was made.'

'I thought so,' said Elmendrin, moving off to help one of her sisters. 'Do one thing for me, Morgrim Bargrum.'

'Name it,' he called out to her.

'Try to stop Snorri from getting himself killed.'

He didn't answer straight away, watching Elmendrin disappear back in to the mass of dead and dying. There were tears in his eyes when he did.

'I will.'

THIRTY-EIGHT

THE FLEET FROM ACROSS THE SEA

The elf was painted head to toe in filth. His silver armour was muddied, his cloak torn and smeared in dung, his alabaster skin grimy and dark with a peasant's tan. Dirty white hair framed a narrow face, pinched with anger.

'Doesn't look happy, does he?' Snorri jerked his thumb at the dishevelled noble behind the cage.

'Would you be, if you were boarding with the mules?' King Thagdor laughed, loudly and raucously, until the High King approached, dousing the northerner's mirth.

'His name is Prince Arlyr, of Etaine.' Gotrek struggled with both foreign words, but spoke them anyway before turning his glare from Thagdor to the elf. 'And apparently he has nothing to say beyond that.'

'Why are we gathered here?' asked Brynnoth. 'Surely your tent would have provided better accommodation.'

They were standing next to the mule pen at the rear of the encampment, near its edge. Skinners were hustling the beasts in and out of the cages to haul machineries or cart raw metal for the new rams, but none cast an eye towards the kings.

Several bedraggled-looking elves, stripped of their weapons and armour, walked alongside one train. They were Arlyr's warriors, put to use gathering firewood for the furnaces and watched keenly by Furgil's rangers.

The same question as asked by the king of the Sea Hold lingered in Valarik's eyes too, though the lord of the Horn Hold had not the courage to speak it. All of the kings, barring Brynnoth whose desire for vengeance still blazed hotter than his shame at defying the High King, felt chastened just to be in Gotrek's presence. The High King's ire was volcanic but kept dormant for now. None of the liege-lords wanted to be there when it erupted, and so conducted themselves as if that possibility was imminent at any time and by treading gingerly they could abate it.

Last of the kings was Hrekki Ironhandson. The lord of the Varn was slow to arrive, having trekked across from the opposite end of the field where his war machines and much of his army was mustered. He nodded to the other lords, and only once he was within the circle of kings did Gotrek continue.

'Quicker to say it here, and I want to look into this one's eyes when I do.' His attention returned to their elf prisoner, who glowered back at him.

'To say what, father?' asked Snorri.

Not since the assault on the sixth day had the dwarfs enjoyed the same level of success in breaching the elven city. Tor Alessi had abandoned its outer wall and retreated, closing its ranks further, repositioning its bolt throwers, mustering even more archers.

Even buoyed by their apparent success, the dwarfs had been unable to penetrate any further. The rubble made it impossible to bring in siege towers and excavation teams were quickly pinioned by arrows as soon as they tried to clear the ground. The elves had left pockets of murderous scouts in shadowed alcoves and secret chambers that ambushed the dwarf attackers, foiling assaults before they could begin.

Tor Alessi had shrunk, and like a trap closing around the elves inside, it had armoured them.

Snorri didn't understand the tactic. Yes, it retarded the dwarfs' efforts, but they had already established that winning a war of attrition was playing into their hands. What did the elves have to gain from waiting and pulling in their necks, besides a slow death?

When the young prince got his answer, it was not to his liking.

'We must retreat,' said Gotrek flatly.

'Do what?' asked Thagdor, incredulous.

Snorri was speechless.

Brynnoth fought down a belligerent snarl. Of all the kings, he had seen the most battle and bore the wounds to prove it. None present had greater right to question the High King's reasoning than Brynnoth, but the lord of the Sea Hold stayed silent.

'Elgi have been sighted coming across the sea in a great fleet.' Gotrek eyed the elven noble and saw everything he needed in the lordling's supercilious expression to know what his scouts had told him was true, that it wasn't some trick or glamour, that the elves were trying to keep them embattled until reinforcements could arrive. 'Could be two hundred ships, maybe more. Drakk too, eagles and magelings. A war host that puts even this city's sizeable garrison to shame. That's right, isn't it, elgi?'

Prince Arlyr glared, and spat something in his native tongue before flashing a condescending smile.

'I think he's trying to mock you, Gotrek,' observed Thagdor.

Gotrek smiled back. 'Yet he's the one covered in donkey shit.'

'Caught between the city and the arriving army, we would be hard pressed,' admitted Snorri, seeing the sense in what his father was saying but inwardly chafing at the need to retreat. 'How close is the fleet?'

Gotrek turned his gaze from the elf to look at his son. 'Furgil says they're close enough that some of the machineries will need to be left behind if we're to make good our escape.'

'Grimnir's balls, those engines are not cheap,' moaned Ironhandson. 'I'll lose a fortune if we leave them.'

'You'll do it and be glad that I don't further balance your accounts, Hrekki,' snapped Gotrek, referring to the king's existing debt in the great book of grudges.

Knowing what was best for him, Ironhandson backed down.

Thagdor balled his fists against his hips and sighed. 'Bugger me. They're right sneaky, them elgi bastards.'

'Aye,' Gotrek agreed. 'Tor Alessi is their anvil, the fleet their hammer. We'd be crushed.'

Snorri was scowling. 'This is wrong. Escape? We're running? From *them*?' He jabbed a finger at Prince Arlyr, who appeared to be enjoying the debate more than the dwarfs. 'The wall is breached in at least two places and there are fires that will last well beyond morning.'

'Aye,' said Gotrek, 'and for fourteen days we've knocked on their door and for fourteen days been repelled. Can anyone here think of a fastness the dawi could not crack in two weeks of hammer?'

None could.

'But, father...'

'But nothing,' Gotrek began, harshly at first, but softened quickly. 'I feel your frustration, but this isn't over. We were naive to think the elgi could be so easily broken. They obviously want to stay here very badly. We'll need to beat that out of them, but all meat must be tenderised before it's cooked and eaten. Just so happens that elgi is a little tougher to chew than we thought.'

'So that's it then?' said Snorri. 'What about Varnuf and Grundin, Aflegard and the rest of them?'

Valarik looked down at this boots.

Ironhandson shook his head.

'I've sent runners north and south,' Gotrek told them, 'but so far none have returned bearing word of the other kings. We cannot rely on them for reinforcement.'

'So we're going back to the mountains?' Brynnoth didn't sound pleased.

Gotrek nodded. 'To gauge the elgi's strength, and their keenness for a fight. Admit it or not, we've underestimated this enemy, and are already counting that cost. War won't be over in a single siege.' He turned to his son. 'How many did your cousin say we'd lost thus far?'

Snorri's face darkened. 'Close to three thousand dawi, father.'

'Dreng tromm...' breathed Valarik, whilst the other kings except for Brynnoth shook their heads at the thought.

'We return to the holds,' Gotrek told them all, 'and make strategy for a long war. This is far from over. It has barely begun.'

'And what about little lord dung boots over there?' asked Thagdor, gesturing to Prince Arlyr.

Gotrek fixed the elf with a cold stare that robbed the lordling of all his defiance.

'Oh, I can think of something.'

Liandra was knelt by Vranesh, tending to the dragon's wounds in one of Tor Alessi's ruined courtyards, when the dwarfs' message came sailing over the wall. It landed with a wet *splut!*, rolling awkwardly until it came to a halt by a spearman's boot. The elf looked down at the severed head of Prince Arlyr and was promptly sick. To see such a noble lord so brutally abused had turned the young warrior's stomach.

Horns rang out, summoning the garrison commander, Lord Impirilion.

When Arlyr's body was flung over the walls next, engraved in vengeful dwarf script, Liandra could not have been less surprised.

'They are leaving,' she told one of Lord Impirilion's retainers.

'How do you know?'

She laughed humourlessly, pointing at the headless corpse. 'What do you think that is?'

The retainer looked nonplussed at the body.

'It's a parting gift,' she told him, getting to her feet. 'Can you fly, my beast?' she asked the dragon.

Vranesh growled in affirmation.

'Where are you going?' asked the retainer. 'What about Lord Impirilion?'

'I have no business with the garrison commander, and you have no need of me here now the fleet has arrived. I will return to Kor Vanaeth. There are still people who are living like wretches in its ruins.' She swung into the saddle. 'This is not over. Far from it, and we need every bastion if we are to defeat the dwarfs on their own soil. Rest assured, this is but a taste of the war to come,' she said, a flash of excitement in her eyes as she took to the skies.

For now, fighting the dwarfs took precedence over her other concerns. Liandra's prey would have to wait, the druchii would have to wait, but not too long.

THIRTY-NINE

TWO DECADES OF WAR

The foothills north-east of Kazad Kro were swathed in darkness. It wouldn't last; a pale sunrise was already breaching the horizon, smearing it in washed-out yellow. In less than an hour it would be vibrant and ochre, blazing like the summer. Light would paint the land, revealing the ruination, the barrows and the churned earth of over twenty years' worth of battles.

Rundin had played no part in any of them. He had trekked from his city, walking over forty miles to reach this place, which was little more than a clearing of scattered rocks.

'Took your time,' said a familiar voice, the speaker squatting on one of the collapsed menhirs surrounding Rundin.

'Just because we are not at war doesn't mean I have no other duties to attend to, brother.'

Furgil smiled, jumping down from his rocky plinth, and went over to Rundin.

The two dwarfs embraced, clapping one another on the back with genuine bonhomie. Two decades was not so long to a dwarf, but their reunion was heartfelt.

'Good to see you, Rundin.'

'And you, Furgil. How fares the King of Everpeak?'

'Troubled, as he has been for the last twenty years or more. The third siege has failed, Tor Alessi yet stands and other cities are mustering greater and greater armies of elgi. Reinforcements would be generously received, I am sure.'

At this remark, Rundin averted his gaze to the stone circle.

'And I would grant them, had I the power to.'

Furgil grunted at that, suggesting Rundin already did, but chose not to press. Instead he asked, 'And what of the skarrens, my former kinsmen?'

'Trade has come back, after a fashion. Not with the elgi, of course, but dawi from the Vaults and the Black Mountains. They bring talk as well as trade,' he ventured.

'Such as?' Furgil was typically guarded, and Rundin faced him again to gauge his humour.

'That the south is embattled, and that Gotrek is reluctant to bring full force of arms to bear against the elgi.'

'He is wise, our king. All-out war would destroy our race, as it would theirs. Hope still remains that some agreement can be reached, or that the elgi will lose heart and give up.'

'I also hear their king has no intention of leaving the Old World, that he is as arrogant an elgi as one could possibly be.'

'You hear much, old friend.'

'That sounded almost like an accusation, Furgil.'

The pathfinder shook his head. 'Not at all, but I'm surprised at your keen interest in the war, given the skarrens' abstention from it.'

'Not my choice.'

Furgil lit his pipe, allowing the silence to stretch before asking, 'How many from the hill clans are there now? Eighty thousand, more?'

'Is that why you're here, why you requested we meet? Does Gotrek want the skarrenawi for his throngs?'

'You know he does,' said Furgil. 'I just wanted to see if you did.'

'And do I?'

Furgril didn't answer, but asked another question instead. 'He still mad, is he? Your "High King", the Grum?'

Rundin's face darkened, first with anger then shame when he realised he had no rebuttal. His voice lowered to just above a whisper, as if to speak louder would somehow heap further disgrace upon the truth.

'Lucidity comes and goes with the fever, but he's locked in the counting house most days now. I think the gold-masters are puppeting him, but there's little I can do about that unless Kruk and Orrik change their minds. And for over twenty years they've shown no sign of doing so. Both are saying the war is over.'

Furgil scoffed, watching the first rays of dawn spear across the lowlands and slowly scrape against the mountainside. "Tis far from over. I know longbeards that've slept for more than twenty years. This is nothing. High King Gotrek is mustering again, so are all the kings. You'd do well to join us. Don't think the elgi will know the difference between dawi and skarren when their armies come calling, and don't expect protection from your kith and kin in the mountains if you're not prepared to take up az un klad.'

Rundin bared his teeth. 'I don't like threats, Furgil, especially from those whom I consider friends.'

'It's no threat, it's a fact.' The pathfinder's defiance lessened, the edge to his words dulled. 'Go back to Kruk and Orrik, convince them that this is the right thing to do. Please, Rundin.'

Rundin didn't answer, he just watched Furgil go and wondered what he would have to do to get his people out from under the yoke of Skarnag Grum.

In the Great Hall a huge map of cured troll hide described the entire realm of the dwarfs and was laid out on an octagonal table of dark wutroth. It had turned from a throne room into a chamber devoted to war. Around the map, several kings and thanes of the Karaz Ankor were discussing strategy.

'And there is still nothing from the south, I take it?' Thagdor looked almost smug, despite the scar he now wore on his face. 'Bloody soft.'

'King Hrallson is besieged, you northern oaf,' snapped Brugandar. The King of Karak Drazh was the only one of the liege-lords south of Everpeak that had made the rinnkaz. He was a severe-looking character, with a wiry beard the colour of iron and a face just as unyielding. Drazh was known as the 'Black Hold' on account of its munificent mines and quarries. Coal was its principal export, but it also yielded much in the way of metal ore. In fact, Brugandar looked more like a miner than he did a king, just with all the bearing and confidence of one.

His declarative insult incited a raft of angered murmuring from some of the kings. All knew the elves had made solid inroads to the south. Varnuf of the Eight Peaks had done well to keep them at bay for this long but even his vast armies were not inexhaustible.

Finding only fools amongst the northern kings, Brugandar turned to the head of the table and the High King. His tone changed abruptly to one of the utmost respect. Although he had not personally fought in the first siege of Tor Alessi, he had lent many warriors to the cause.

'Liege-lord,' he intoned, 'what about Karak Kadrin? Can we expect much from King Grundin and his throngs?'

Elbows leaning on the edge of the map, Gotrek looked over his steepled fingers at the many flags and icons representing elf and dwarf armies, as well as their bastions and holdfasts. There were a great deal on both sides, and the sight of this aged him further than the last two decades had. A war without end was the very thing he had fought so hard to avert, and now here they were.

'Musters in the north must continue without interruption,' he said. 'And as requests to the mines at Silverspear and Gunbad have gone unanswered, I can only assume those greedy bastards have decided that digging is preferable to fighting. We are alone in this.'

'Three times we've marched on those walls,' said Valarik, 'and three times we've failed to take the city. What else can we throw at it?' The king of the Horn Hold had grown older too, but with experience and wisdom. For its part in the conflict thus far, Karak Hirn and its king had earned great respect amongst the lords of the Worlds Edge.

'Dawi bloody grit and chuffing determination is what!' said Thagdor, thumping the table. 'They'll yield, they have to at some point.'

Ironhandson was unmoved by the King of Zhufbar's typically demonstrative outburst and stroked his beard thoughtfully. 'What of the garrison at Black Fire? Does your son bring any news, High King?'

Gotrek raised his eyebrows, arrested from whatever dark reverie had claimed him for the last few minutes. Snorri was not at the rinnkaz. Upon the third defeat at the gates of Tor Alessi, he had gone back to the fortress at Black Fire Pass, Kazad Kolzharr, to act as his father's eyes and ears beyond the mountains.

It had been weeks since his last runner to Everpeak.

The High King was about to speak when Thurbad entered the war chamber and every pair of eyes within it turned to alight upon him.

'Lords,' he addressed the assembly, before approaching Gotrek. 'A message from the Kolzharr, my king.' Thurbad handed over a piece of slate the size of his fist.

'As if Valaya's own hand had a part in it,' said Ironhandson, marvelling at his own apparent prescience.

Gotrek ignored him and took the slate.

Silence fell in the Great Hall as everyone present watched the High King read.

'"Our rangers bring word that the king of the elgi has been sighted,"' Gotrek began aloud. '"Tired of impasse, he has taken to the field at Angaz Baragdum with a sizeable army. I shall meet him and give battle."'

Gotrek put the slate down, still staring at the Khazalid engraved upon it.

In the end, Thagdor broke the silence.

'Well this is what we've been waiting for,' he said. 'Not since this bloody war began has the elgi king shown his pointy ears. Now, we have a chance to kill the bastard and send the rest of 'em running for their ships.'

Brugandar was nodding. 'I agree. This is a mistake, born out of elgi arrogance. We must seize upon it.'

Gotrek wasn't listening. He turned to Thurbad, who was waiting dutifully behind him.

'Did the runner say if my son had already left the keep?'

'Two days ago, my king. He marches with his cousin and most of the garrison.'

'So, we won't reach him before he gets to Angaz Baragdum.' Gotrek knew the answer before it was given, and didn't care that his face betrayed all of his concern for his errant son.

'No, my king. We will not.'

A horn blared in one of the lower deeps. Its doleful echo carried all the way to the Great Hall, signalling the miners to the rockface. To Gotrek, it sounded like a death knell.

Had he believed his cousin would listen, Morgrim would have told Snorri to wait. True, the rift with his father had scabbed and healed over the last few years but the young prince was still convinced the only way to achieve the great destiny he so craved was to seize it for himself.

Slay the drakk, become king.

He had spoken of little else since word had come to Black Fire Pass that the elf king was in the Old World and marshalling an army.

'I am surprised,' said Snorri, marching at the head of an army twenty thousand strong.

'Cousin?' asked Morgrim, from Snorri's left. Drogor, ever dutiful and silent, was on his right holding up the banner.

'That Elmendrin is not here to dissuade me.'

There was hope in the prince's voice, not that the priestess would convince him not to fight the elf king but that she would be there before he did to see it.

'She would not wish this for you,' Morgrim answered.

'Of course she would. Elmendrin understands legacy and its importance. I don't want to usurp my father, I just want to ease the burden of kingship from his shoulders. Ending this war will let me do that.'

'Twenty years ago we were going to end this war, cousin. Seems we only started it, though.'

'Aye,' Snorri sighed. The attack on Kor Vanaeth had been rash, but necessary. 'But it was right that we did. Kill or capture the elf king and the war ends, though, Morg. *That* I know.'

'Do you wish she was here, Elmendrin I mean?' Morgrim asked.

Most of the Valayans had returned to Everpeak after the third siege. A handful remained at the keep, but Elmendrin was needed back at the capital.

Snorri nodded. 'It would have been good to see her again, but her brother takes up much of her time these dark days.'

At this, Morgrim looked down. All who had returned from the ambassadorial mission to Ulthuan had come back with deep scars. None more so than Forek Grimbok, and even then not all had made it. Gilias Thunderbrow was dead, slain through elven treachery. Morgrim thought this must trouble Forek the most. Few dwarfs had seen him since he had come back. In fact only the High King and his closest advisors knew where the shamed dwarfs were now, and the priestess who ministered to them of course.

'I knew she was there, you know,' said Snorri.

'Where, cousin?'

'At the first siege. I saw you talking with her as she tended the wounded.'

Morgrim frowned. 'And you wait until now to mention it?'

Snorri shrugged. 'Seemed as good a time as ever. Besides, we have been busy.'

The war had thrust the cousins apart for the last few years. Ever since the end of the first siege and the retreat, both Snorri and Morgrim had returned to their clans to prepare further musters. The elves had surprised them with their discipline and the size of their armies. Not content to merely soak up the dwarfs' punishment, the elves had gone on the offensive. Several lesser holds had been attacked, particularly in the south. Most notably Karak Azul had sustained serious damage to some of its upper deeps during one assault. King Hrallson was still refortifying his walls and sealing off the damaged areas, which had become infested with greenskins and giant rats, if the rumours were to be believed.

Morgrim had gone south to bring reinforcement, and turned back the elf army camped on Azul's doorstep so its clans could return to their forges and fashion the engines and armour the dwarf war effort so badly needed. Snorri had greeted him warmly upon his return, but couldn't entirely conceal his jealousy at his cousin's success.

Now, it seemed he was just glad to have him back at his side.

'What did she say to you in the field of the dead, Morg?' he asked.

Morgrim snorted with amusement. 'She asked me to try and keep you alive.'

Snorri clapped him on the back. 'Well, you've done your task well then.' He laughed. 'Do you ever wish we were back in the ruins of Karak Krum chasing talking rats, eh?'

Morgrim laughed too but stopped when he saw the seriousness in his cousin's eyes. 'Every day,' he muttered soberly.

Snorri slowly nodded.

'Lords,' Drogor interrupted. 'The Angaz Baragdum is over the next hill. We should be able to see the elgi throng arrayed.'

'And they us,' noted Snorri, signalling a halt. He turned to one of his rangers, who was outriding at the edge of the army. 'Any sign?' he called.

'The skies are clear, Prince Snorri.'

'No eagles, that's a good thing,' Snorri said to himself.

Morgrim drew close to him as the dwarf column ground to a halt with a clattering of armour. 'Are you certain of this plan?'

'Arrogance has brought the elgi king to this place. He must be made to realise the folly of that, and when he does he cannot be allowed to escape. For the same reason we strike now and do not wait, you must do what I've asked you to next.' Snorri smiled, gripping Morgrim's armoured shoulder with his gauntleted hand. 'Do not fear, cousin. Drogor is by my side. Neither I nor the banner will fall this day.'

Not entirely convinced, Morgrim summoned his warriors. He gave Drogor a parting glance but could find no clue as to the Karak Zorn dwarf's thoughts. His own were fraught with concern that he would not be there to temper the prince's eagerness. Certainly, Drogor would not do it.

Half the army would go with Morgrim. Sheltered by the foothills, they would take the wide and rugged path east, come around the back of the enemy and close off any route of escape. Dwarfs knew the mountains better than anyone; they could sneak up on elves easily enough. It would leave Snorri with only ten thousand to face whatever host the elf king had amassed. According to their scouts, it was considerable.

Before he left, he said to Snorri, 'Hold them until I get there, cousin. Hold them and only then engage the king.'

'Aye.' Snorri grinned. 'I'll cut off his pointy-eared little head.'

FORTY

THE SPILLING OF NOBLE BLOOD

No ceremony, no celebration of any kind had greeted the army of Barak Varr when it had returned to the Sea Hold. Led by Brynnoth, a battered and brutalised king, the dwarfs were a returning tide, washing up on the borders of the great fastness with all the detritus that had survived the siege of the elven city.

No, as Heglan remembered that day, just as he had remembered it every day since, it was more like a funeral procession. All along the Merman Pass, trailing back down to the shipyards many miles behind, were dour-looking clanners shouldering biers of shields the colour of the ocean. Upon them were their fallen brothers. And there had been a great many. At first, Heglan had hoped some of the warriors had remained with the High King to garrison the lesser citadels but the mood was too sombre, too withdrawn and bereft of hope for that to be true. A defeated force had returned to Barak Varr, carrying its dead. But they clung to something else too, a very familiar emotion to Heglan now – vengeance.

That sight, the returning dwarfs, the warriors lain in silent repose upon their shields, had stayed with him for over twenty years. It was his waking thought, his last memory at night, at least when he managed sleep. During the dark hours, Heglan's workshop became his refuge. He laboured until exhaustion claimed him and sent his mind into an agonised hell of remembrance. Running down to the Merman Pass, barging the gathered crowds from his path, ignoring their curses. Watching the procession pass, listening to the weeping, the declarations of revenge, the wailing of the women. An impenetrable line of hearthguard prevented the crowd from approaching closer than the edge of the road. With every bier that passed by, Heglan's hope grew, until he saw the eighty-first shield and the dwarf dead upon it.

Unmarked by war, no wound to be seen, Nadri Lodrison was a cold corpse.

Heglan had lost his brother, and in that fateful moment of realisation became the last of his line. Few of the clan Copper-fist returned, and though some spoke words of conciliation, Heglan heard not of it. Instead, a tiny fire grew into being inside his stomach. Quickly it became a fist of flame then a blaze, until the conflagration of his hate and desire for retribution was born.

Sheltered in his workshop, bent towards dreams of invention and prosperity, he had been untouched by the war. With Nadri's death, it had gouged him and left a gaping wound behind. From the sky and the sun, Heglan retreated downwards to the earth and the desolation of his brother's tomb.

Cold stone pressed against his forehead. Heglan opened his eyes, returning to the present. He could smell grave dust and dank, though whether this was real or a trick of his grief-stricken conscience he could no longer tell. Somewhere in the back of his mind, a doleful tolling announced the dead.

'Copperfist...' a gruff voice intruded on the funerary bell.

Heglan looked up to see sky and sun, not the hollow dark of a tomb.

'Yes, master.'

Burgrik Strombak was standing behind him, arms folded.

'I was wrong.'

Dark against the sun, driving against the wind and rising, the skryzan-harbark flew. It was an airship in every sense, with a huge leather bladder of gas attached to masts with stout rope giving the vessel the necessary buoyancy. There were rudders and paddles, barrels of ballast to alter loft and direction. Great turning whirls, like windmills, provided impetus and power. It was the single most impressive piece of machinery any dwarf had ever constructed and it had launched from the Durazon like a soaring crag eagle. But the dream for Heglan was flawed, forever so, tainted by the fact that his brother would never get to see it.

He had found a captain too, and Nugdrinn Hammerfoot steered the airship like he was born to it. In another time, Heglan would have been expelled from the engineers' guild for such rampant diversion away from tradition but times were changing, and with them the attitudes of the dwarfs. The Sea Hold had ever been a bastion of invention and progress, looked down upon by some of the traditionalists of the Worlds Edge. No good could come of the new, of the untried, untested. Dwarfs were creatures of earth, grounded in stone and steel. They did not reach for sky and cloud, and yet...

'Is it ready?' asked another, and Heglan turned to address his king.

Brynnoth didn't meet his eye, he kept his gaze on the airship as it returned to the Durazon. It grew larger by the moment, transforming from a shadow silhouetted against the sun to a behemoth with a dragon-headed prow and armoured flanks of copper in the shape of scalloped wings. It was a beast in every aspect, powerful, intimidating, brutal, and seemed to almost growl at the dwarfs as it landed on claws of steel.

'I still need to arm it, my lord.'

'Bolt throwers?' suggested Strombak with an appraising eye. 'It wouldn't support a catapult.'

'Yes, and something else I've been working on.'

Strombak raised an eyebrow, but Heglan didn't elaborate. The weapon wasn't ready yet and he wouldn't reveal it until it was, even to his guildmaster.

Heglan was not a warmonger. It had never been his intention to create something with the purpose of killing. Exploration, technological achievement, the mapping of the skies had always been at the forefront of the engineer's mind, but unfortunately death had a way of making peaceful men warlike.

'It's a marvel,' Strombak conceded, in spite of all his reservations.

'No,' said King Brynnoth, a darkness in his eyes that had never lifted since Agrin Fireheart. 'It's a war machine.'

Strombak nodded, sucking on his pipe as he turned to its creator. 'And what will you call it, lad?'

Heglan's eyes mirrored the king's.

'*Nadri's Retribution.*'

Snorri was not impressed. Ranks of spearmen hiding behind high shields that protected their scale-armoured bodies marched into formation before the dwarfs. On the opposite flank was a host of elven cavalry, the shining-helmed knights clasping lances and riding barded steeds. Archers occupied a slight rise, but there was little to distinguish the army save for a small retinue of warriors bearing long-hafted glaives and shimmering like fresh-forged gold in their heavy plate.

Estimating twenty thousand men, Snorri wondered what the king of the elves hoped to achieve with such a paltry show of strength. He had yet to see the great lord himself and suspected he was as craven as many dwarfs made him out to be.

Angaz Baragdum was an iron mine long fallen out of use. Its old quarries and tunnels went deep into the earth, and its heath stretched into a vast plain of grassy tussocks far south of Black Fire Pass. The elf king had arrived in the Old World by sea, though not across the Sea of Claws like the bulk of his fleet. He had gone south, presumably along the Black Gulf to alight so far away from Karaz-a-Karak. Perhaps he wanted to oversee what remained of his forces still encamped at the edge of Karak Azul, or he might have been leading a spearhead to attack the dwarfs from their southern borders. It mattered not. Regardless of his rationale, the elf king had made a grievous error in coming here. Snorri was determined to ensure he realised that.

The young prince cast his gaze over the field where the elves and dwarfs had pitched. Little advantage would be gained from the sparse terrain, but it better suited the dwarfs who could make their battle line strong by keeping their clans together.

'Shoulder to shoulder,' Snorri muttered to Drogor, who lifted the banner.

A horn clarioned and then came drums as the dwarfs drew together, slowly locking their shields.

'Hold here!' yelled Khazagrim, the prince's chief hearthguard.

'You see him yet?' asked Snorri, scrutinising the sea of elven silver.

'Perhaps we should advance further, a show of aggression to goad the elfling out?' suggested Drogor.

Khazagrim looked for his prince's sanction. Snorri nodded, but said, 'Keep us out of their archer range for now. Don't want those pointy-eared bastards sticking us before I've seen their king. Until I'm sure the coward is even–' The words stuck in Snorri's throat as three elves mounted on horses broke off from the host and rode towards them. Flanked on either side by his standard bearer and knight protector was an elf who could be none other than the king, the one they called Caledor.

'What is he doing?' asked Snorri, reaching for his axe.

Drogor raised his hand for calm.

'I think the elgi wants to talk.'

'Talk?' Snorri was nonplussed. 'About what?'

'Surrender?' Drogor suggested, before looking the prince in the eye. 'What should we do?'

Snorri scowled at the sheer arrogance of the gesture, that the elf king thought parley was still on the table. He considered having his quarrellers shoot the elves down but dismissed it at once as dishonourable.

'We meet them,' he replied, deciding he would not be outdone by an elf. If an elf could stride boldly into his enemy's midst and demand parley then so could a dwarf.

'Is that wise?'

'No, but I'll not have that pointy-ears show me up on dawi ground. Khazagrim, you're with me.' He turned to Drogor. 'Throng holds here, but be ready.'

'Tromm,' said Drogor, bowing.

Snorri stomped off with Khazagrim.

The elves had been waiting for several minutes by the time the dwarfs reached them.

King Caledor muttered something in elvish to his protector who smiled and nodded back.

'Something amuses you, elgi?' Snorri snapped, his half-hand resting on the haft of his rune axe. 'A joke to lighten the mood, is it?'

The banner bearer leaned forwards in his saddle to look down on the diminutive dwarf retinue.

'The Phoenix King remarks on your stature, and how it must take interminably long to get anywhere and do anything. He wonders if you are faster at digging than you are walking?'

Snorri bit his tongue. He could feel Khazagrim trembling with anger next to him, his leather gauntlets creaking into fists.

The elf king was sneering, but despite his levity his blue eyes were like chips of ice. He had the look of a hunter about him, and carried a long spear as well as sword and bow. Tendrils of golden hair slipped from beneath his helm and here Snorri paused. For the war helm sitting upon Caledor's brow was shaped to resemble a dragon. His entire armoured body was fashioned thusly, wrought in fire-red plate and silver scale akin to the hide of such a beast. Edged in gold, the king's armoured skirts carried further effigies firmly establishing the aspect he wanted to promote.

Words spoken what seemed like an age ago now returned to the young prince.

Snorri's lip curled into a snarl. '*Drakk...*' he breathed, and felt the touch of destiny upon him. It was no beast at all that Ranuld's prophecy spoke of, but an elf, *the* elf. All thoughts of negotiation evaporated.

The elf banner bearer looked confused at this declaration, turning to his liege-lord. His comment elicited another bout of sarcastic humour.

For his part, Snorri jabbed his finger in the elf king's direction.

'You,' he said, before turning to prod at his own chest, 'and me.'

Smiling, King Caledor trotted forwards on his steed.

'Are you challenging me, mud-dweller?' he asked in perfect Khazalid. 'Do you mean to say I have brought all these warriors and only you and I will get to fight? Seems a pity.'

Snorri was taken aback. 'You speak our tongue?'

'When I must.' He scoffed, apparently amused at the prince's boldness. 'I came to answer your plea for surrender, but it seems dwarf stupidity really *is* without limit.'

'Aye, and elgi arrogance is boundless too. By Grungni, you will meet me on the field of battle and we'll settle this honourably.'

Looking Snorri up and down, the elf king frowned. 'Are you certain you want to do this? I am the Phoenix King of Ulthuan, greatest warrior of this age.'

Now it was Snorri's turn to smile. 'We have many names for you, elgi, but king is not amongst them. The Coward, the Friendless, He Who is Frightened of Loud Noises. My favourite is the Goat Worrier, for you have the hunter's eye.' Jabbing a finger back at the elf king, Snorri bared his teeth in a mocking grin and bleated at him.

Caledor's expression hardened at once to chiselled stone.

'Have your shovels ready,' he told the prince, 'for they will soon be needed.' Turning his horse around, Caledor rode off to prepare for the duel and took his scowling retainers with them.

Snorri nodded as he watched them go.

'Well,' he said to Khazagrim. 'I thought that went well.'

As they rode back to the army, King Caledor turned in the saddle towards his seneschal.

'Hulviar,' he said, 'as soon as I have cut that imp down signal the attack. Every dwarf on this field shall die today.'

'All of them, my king?'

'Every last one. They attack my cities with impunity, a message must be sent. It's why we are here and why I must miss the beginning of the hunting season. Soon as it's done, we return and these dwarfs will go back to their holes in the ground. See them dead, Hulviar.'

Hulviar nodded grimly and went to ready the Silver Helms.

Rain battered at Morgrim's forces as they slogged through the foothills in an ever-thickening mire. The summer storm had come from nowhere, splitting the sky with dry lightning in the east and hammering them with a downpour in the west.

'Have you ever seen the like of this?' Morgrim remarked as rain teemed off the nose guard of his war helm, trickling down his face and beard.

Tarni, his banner bearer, shook his head, spitting out a mouthful of the sudden deluge.

Ahead in the road, Morgrim saw one of the rangers had returned and was beckoning them onwards. The dwarf pointed to a high cliff of rock that hung over the trail and would grant some respite from the storm.

Morgrim nodded, though he had no idea if the ranger had seen him or not. He waved his army on. 'Forward, to the crag,' he yelled, and horns blared down the ranks to relay his order. Their clarion was answered a moment later by a peal of thunder that shook the earth underfoot. From the sky there came a jag of pearlescent lightning. Bright as magnesium, Morgrim had to shield his eyes from it, and when he looked back the bolt had struck the cliff face, shearing off a chunk that had collapsed across the road and buried the poor ranger with it. There was no sign of the dwarf and no sign of the trail either. The way ahead was cut off.

'Should we go around?' asked Tarni, shouting to be heard.

Harsh sunlight was blazing through the sheeting rain, making it shimmer and flash. Morgrim nodded, and with little choice the dwarfs trudged back. All the while they were delayed Snorri fought alone.

Snorri rotated his shoulder to loosen the muscles and hefted his rune axe one-handed, gauging the weight.

'Shield or hand axe?' asked Drogor, proffering both.

Snorri was sitting on a stout wooden throne as Khazagrim made sure his armour was secure. The hearthguard was tightening a vambrace when the prince answered, 'Shield.' His gaze was on the distant elf king who was undergoing similar preparation. Behind him, the elf army waited silently. 'Against that spear, I'll need a shield.'

Drogor nodded.

'Do not be nervous, my prince,' he whispered as he came close to strap on Snorri's shield.

'I am not,' Snorri snapped. 'I will end the war, claim my destiny. It is written.'

'Yes, but perhaps you should wait for your cousin. No one would think less of you if you did, my prince.'

Snorri narrowed his eyes. 'I've asked you before not to call me that,' he said.

Drogor smiled but there was no warmth to it, no feeling at all. 'But that is what you are, a prince.'

'I...' Something disturbing had just happened, a tiny seed of doubt had been planted that was already taking root.

Drogor was still smiling that deadened smile. It chilled Snorri like a winter's breeze, but there was no time left to question it. Horns were blowing on both sides, the call to arms. The duel was about to begin.

Snorri stood, his armour clanking as it came to rest. It felt heavy all of a sudden, his axe haft greasy in his armoured fist.

'My prince?' asked Khazagrim.

Snorri was still looking at Drogor.

'Go and meet your destiny, Snorri Halfhand,' he said.

'Come,' the prince said to Khazagrim, trying to banish the malaise that had settled over him like a shroud. The elf king was already striding to the middle of the battlefield. Silence reigned, interrupted only by the wind and a distant summer storm.

'Strange weather,' Snorri remarked. Even his own voice sounded distant to him.

'Aye,' he heard Drogor answer, in a way that suggested he did not find it strange at all.

Eyeing the horizon behind the elf army, Snorri looked for his cousin as if just the sight of Morgrim would steady his inexplicable nerves. But Morgrim wasn't there. Snorri was on his own.

The few hundred feet to the middle of the battlefield felt like leagues. Sweat lathered Snorri's face. It dripped off the end of his nose, and made him want to remove his winged helmet. His heart was racing, faster than it should be, and he had to suppress a tremor in his injured hand as phantom pain he hadn't experienced in years returned.

'I call you forth to face grudgement, elfling,' said Snorri, trying to bolster his fractured resolve. 'Let it be known on this day that Prince Snorri Lunngrin did meet Caledor of the elgi in honourable combat to settle the misdeeds of his race and exact recompense in blood.'

Caledor was sheathing his sword after making a few practice swings. He had decided on his spear to open with and made a quick thrust before turning to the prince.

'Were you speaking, little mud-dweller? I didn't hear you all the way down there, I'm afraid.' He settled into a ready stance, spear held in one hand. 'Shall we begin?'

Snorri was incensed, his momentary fear eclipsed by rage, and he roared, 'Elgi bast–'

The spear lashed out like quicksilver, ripping open a gash down Snorri's face and splitting his war helm apart. Dazed, the prince half spun then staggered, almost losing his footing. A second blow, a downstroke with the haft, put the dwarf on his back.

The elves cheered, whilst the dwarfs were stunned into silence at the abrupt turn.

Snorri raised his shield, fending off a flurry of jabbing thrusts. The last went straight through, pinning his shoulder before the spear was withdrawn in a welter of his blood.

Crying out, Snorri punched back with the remains of his shield, swinging his axe wildly so he could regain his feet. Laboured breaths that felt like knives sheared from his mouth. His armoured chest heaved and ached. The elf king hadn't even broken a sweat and stared coldly at his prey.

'I knew you dwarfs were weak,' he said. 'You are diggers and labourers, not warriors. You have erred here, and you will die for it.'

Snorri charged, with a cry of 'Grungni!', but found a spear in his thigh arresting his forward momentum. He jerked to a halt, and felt the ground rush up to meet him, smacking into his back like a battering ram and pushing the air from his lungs. Snorri reached for his axe, but it was no longer in his hand, nor was his shield. As the elf king glowered over him, he was defenceless.

'My father will–' The words died as Caledor left his spear pinning Snorri to the ground and opened the prince up with his sword.

'Sapherian steel,' he told the dwarf, showing Snorri the bloodied blade. 'Deadly.'

Numbing cold spread through the prince's body, a deepening chill that would freeze him unto death. He thought of his father, of the destiny that would not be his, of Morgrim and Elmendrin. Until the very end, he fought, spitting blood and mouthing curses at the slowly fading figure of the elf king. It would do no good because Gazul had Snorri now and would take him to his gate.

Snorri Halfhand was dead.

Morgrim barrelled over the rise and saw Snorri fall.

'No!' Half rasp, half shout, the thane's agony echoed across Angaz Baragdum. It incited a riot in the dwarfs, who came forwards to protect the body of their prince. Too late, though, for the elf king had cut Snorri's arm from the elbow and brandished it like a trophy to his warriors.

Elven riders were already spurring their horses and beginning to charge. They had not yet seen Morgrim's army.

'Uzkul!' he bellowed, consumed by wrathful grief. 'Crush them!'

Led by Khazagrim, the hearthguard surged forwards to protect the prince. Several were cut down by Caledor before the elf king withdrew on a horse brought by his banner bearer.

Engaged by foes from behind, the knights' charge failed to materialise and they faltered.

Laughing, and only pausing to cast Snorri's severed arm into a deep, flooded quarry, the elf king signalled the retreat. In disarray from seeing their prince so savagely struck down, the dwarfs were unable to contain them. Morgrim had abandoned the plan and was forging towards his cousin with all haste, driving through the enemy and hacking down any elf that got in his way. His hammer was crimson by the time he reached Snorri's side.

A ring of armoured hearthguard parted to let him pass.

Battle din faded in the distance as the last few skirmishes between the fleeing elves and pursuing dwarfs subsided. Morgrim looked down on his cousin's broken, mutilated body and wept.

Snorri was already ashen. A grimace of defiance etched upon his face, he looked far from at peace. In pursuit of destiny, he had died an ugly, painful death.

'Dreng tromm...' uttered Morgrim, sinking to his knees.

'He would not listen,' said a voice beyond the hearthguard.

Morgrim looked up and through his tears fixed Drogor with a steely glare.

'Speak plainly,' he rasped.

'I told him to wait.'

'And is that what you did, Drogor? Did you wait? I saw the throng rooted to the spot whilst my cousin was cut apart. Why did you not aid him?'

'I was forbidden, and by Grungni's oath I couldn't believe what I was seeing. It happened so quickly, the elgi king striking our prince down like he was a beardling.'

'And heaping further ignominy on him by cleaving his arm! Gods, Drogor, he will wander Gazul's underworld a cripple because of this!'

'Perhaps with your army to reinforce us...'

Morgrim's face darkened further. 'We were delayed. By Valaya, the very elements turned on us.'

'They can be capricious.'

Morgrim glared but Drogor had already lowered his gaze.

'It is I that failed the prince, Morgrim, not you. I am sorry.'

Bustling through the throng, Khazagrim returned, preventing further recrimination.

'The elgi have fled, back to their ships,' he said. 'We won't catch them now.'

Morgrim shook his head in disbelief. 'And so we suffer further indignity. Gather the throng. We're going back to Karaz-a-Karak to bring the High King the body of his son.'

FORTY-ONE

AWAKEN MY WRATH

Gotrek's face was as cold as the marble slab upon which his son was lying.

The tomb was hewn by Everpeak's finest craftsmen, and the hoard of a lesser king would have been needed to fashion it. Opulent yet austere, it was a monument to dwarf grief and a reminder of a father's abject failure.

'It should be me,' he said to the dark.

Thurbad answered. 'You could not have known the elgi's intentions, my king.'

His granite features stained by tears, Gotrek looked up to a shaft of hazy yellow light breaching the ceiling. It peeled back some of the shadows that had settled like a veil upon this sombre place. Statues, great monolithic effigies of the ancestors, were revealed in it. They looked down sternly but benevolently on the High King, who still found it hard to meet their stony gaze. The rest of the vast chamber was lost to echoing darkness, a hollow tomb of broken vows and empty promises.

'He was to be my heir, Thurbad. I never wanted this for him. I strove to carve out a kingdom that he could rule in peace and prosperity.'

'Yours has always been a just rule, my king.'

Gotrek sagged. He was only wearing a furred cloak, simple tunic and breeches, but he felt the weight of Snorri's death like twenty suits of chainmail. Old hands gripped the edge of the marble tomb for support.

'Fathers should not bury sons, Thurbad. This is not the way of things. It should be me lying upon this slab in grim quietude. It should have been me that met the elgi king at Angaz Baragdum.' The High King let out a long breath that shuddered with the power of his grief. 'He baited us. Snorri went to meet him on the field and could not have known he was stepping into a trap. It reveals something to us, though,' Gotrek added, his back straightening as he found inner reserves of strength.

'What is that, my king?'

'This Caledor, son of kings, is arrogant. To believe he could set foot in our lands, slay my son and return without retribution... It will be his death when I meet him on the field. Throughout this sorry affair, I have held on to the belief that war could be averted. Even when the first battles were fought, when cities were burning, I clung to the hope that we could still find a way out of conflict and return to some measure of civility. That has ended with the death of my son.' His fist clenched like a ball of iron. 'I will level the full might of the Karaz Ankor against these interloping murderers. No elgi will be safe from my wrath, for it has been awakened by this perfidious deed! Every axe, every quarrel and bolt and hammer shall be bent towards the destruction of this enemy in our midst. Vengeance will be done. So swears Gotrek Starbreaker!'

The grongaz echoed like a tomb. Ranuld Silverthumb embraced the silence gratefully, hunched in deep contemplation before the statues of the gronti-duraz. Morek was gone, bound for Tor Alessi and the fourth siege. For his endeavours fashioning the axe and armour of Snorri Halfhand, Ranuld had granted his charge the use of an Anvil of Doom and bestowed upon him the title of 'master runesmith'.

Great had been the undertaking to forge the prince's rune weapons. After fashioning the axe, Morek had left the hold in search of what was needed to begin his labours on the armour. Scarred was the young runesmith now, and more furrowed than ever. For the blood and scale of monsters, jewels that could only be found in the dark, forgotten places of the world, were required to craft such an artefact. Rites were not enough; like all magic, rune forging needed ingredients. Since his return, he had not spoken of his journey nor would Ranuld ask him to. The runelord had his own dark travels to remind him of such endeavours.

Over two decades of toil had changed him, and Morek was apprentice no longer.

And though the death of Prince Snorri had grieved them both, Ranuld allowed himself a sigh of relief. Perhaps the old magic was not dead after all. Perhaps there were those that could still wield it when his like was gone forever from the world. The tremor in the old runelord's heart told him his thread was thinning, that soon it would become so frayed that the tendrils of his life would unravel and snap, and then Grungni would welcome him to his halls.

Soon... he prayed.

Elves were gathering. The death of the High King's only son had galvanised and emboldened them. Gotrek would retaliate. Death would be the only victor, and once again Ranuld was reminded of the darkness that infected the Old World. It came from the gate in the north and could not be gotten rid of now that it was closed. He had to endure, at least until the conclave was concluded and the stone giants roused from their millennia of slumber.

Ranuld opened his eyes, saw the axe and the armour, knew at once who would bear them into battle now.

'*Dawi barazen ek dreng drakk, un riknu...*' He spoke the ancient words of the prophecy aloud. 'He who will slay the dragon, and become king.'

Four other runelords, ancients all, nodded in agreement.

Feldhar Crageye, Negdrik Irontooth, Durgnun Goldbrow.

Last of all was Thorik Oakeneye, he who had taken the place of Agrin Fireheart in the Burudin. The runelord of Barak Varr carried his own darkness from all he had seen on the island of the elves.

More were needed – the conclave was not yet complete. Around a circular table of stone, three empty places remained.

'We know his name,' uttered Feldhar Crageye of Karak Drazh, stroking the forks of his black beard and squinting through his good eye, the other shrouded by a stone patch.

'Aye,' said Negdrik Irontooth, grinning to reveal metal-plated bone. '*Elgidum*.'

The blond-maned Durgnun Goldbrow nodded. 'The elf doom.'

'The dawi known as Ironbeard,' concluded Thorik Oakeneye.

A vein of fire ran through the dragon-slaying axe lying on the table before them. Its master runes shone, eager to be ignited; so too the armour alongside it, which was impervious to flame. Fate not design had guided Morek's hand in their creation.

'Let it be known,' said Ranuld Silverthumb, folding his arms, determined not to make another mistake. 'Morgrim Bargrum will be the one to lift the doom of our race.'

EPILOGUE

Sevekai awoke in a feverish sweat. The nightmare was already fading, evaporating in the chill night like the heat from his cooling skin.

A darkling forest. A frantic flight into a barren glade filled with such a terrible gloaming. The trees alive, and the chittering, snapping refrain of their pursuit...

'Hush, my love...' soothed Drutheira. Her hands upon Sevekai's half-naked body were like pricks of fire against his icy skin.

'Did you see it again?'

Sevekai nodded weakly.

'It is always the same.'

'Visions always are.'

Sevekai turned to face her, lying naked next to him under their furs.

'You believe it is real? That the dreams are prophecy?'

Drutheira was playing with her hair, more coquettish and much less the viper than she had once been. Strange, Sevekai thought, that their alliance had brought them to this place in their relationship. 'Perhaps,' she conceded, but was unconcerned. 'It was a vision that brought us here, was it not?'

They had left Athel Maraya several months ago, bound for the mountains, when the dwarfs had begun to amass near its borders and their subterfuge as refugees of Kor Vanaeth had started to slip. For one, Sevekai was glad of it. By the nature of their work, spies and assassins needed to blend in to their surroundings, to escape notice, to become nothing more than backdrop. For twenty years, since the dragon rider had left them alone, he and the others had done just that. Asleep until their dark master chose to wake them again. If ever.

Escape was unconscionable. Malekith was silent and travel almost impossible without armed escort. Even for a warrior as gifted as Sevekai, the passage south would have been difficult. They would lie low until summoned again, and if not they would try to endure until the war ended or Malekith attacked and conquered Ulthuan.

The dark dreams had been recent. Drutheira believed they presaged the will of their lord and that he would make himself known to them again soon. She was right, at least about the latter. One night, as they were sleeping fitfully in their bed, Malekith had returned. Seemingly possessed, Drutheira had risen from slumber. She had gone off into the night and killed the innkeeper of their lodgings, slit his throat wide until it painted the wall in the dark lord's image.

Malchior and Ashniel had risen too to form the blood communion with their mistress.

Orders were given, and they had all left that night, meeting at the outskirts of Athel Maraya.

'There are times,' said Sevekai, as his breathing slowly returned to normal, 'that I wish we could have stayed.'

'Stayed where?' asked Drutheira, carving out a graven rune upon the floor of the cavern. She had left the warmth of their bed to do it and was crouched naked in the half-light.

'In Athel Maraya, or perhaps some other city.'

'After the ritual slaying of that slave, that would have been unwise,' hissed a voice from the shadows.

'Kaitar.' Sevekai didn't even try to hide his vitriol.

The other dark elf nodded. He looked to Drutheira.

'Are you close?'

The sorceress had finished her malediction and spoke words of power unto it.

'It is here, the creature we seek. Deeper in the bowels of the earth, it slumbers.'

Sevekai glanced around at the cavern, the endless rock surrounding them. He had forgotten how deep they had already penetrated into the mountain.

'We must go further into the dark?'

'Yes, but Bloodfang is near.'

Sevekai was on his feet, getting dressed. 'I'll rouse the others.' He looked over to Kaitar but the shade was already gone. In all the years they had been travelling together, he couldn't remember ever seeing him sleep.

'I have not forgotten our pact,' he said to Drutheira.

'Nor I, my love,' she purred, uncoiling to reveal the curves of her sinuous body.

'We will still kill him, and the dragon rider?'

'Why else do you think Lord Malekith has brought us to this place?'

'I honestly don't know.'

'Yes,' said Drutheira, slithering to her feet. She padded over to touch Sevekai's arm, sliding her hand behind his back and whispering in his ear. 'We shall kill them both. Soon, my love. Very soon.'

CHARACTERS

THE DWARFS

Karaz-a-Karak
Gotrek Starbreaker – High King
Snorri Lunngrin 'Halfhand' – Prince
Morgrim Bargrum – Thane and Snorri Lunngrin's cousin

Ranuld Silverthumb – Runelord and one of the *Burudin*
Morek Furrowbrow – Runesmith and Ranuld Silverthumb's apprentice

Elmendrin Grimbok – High Priestess of Valaya
Forek Grimbok – Reckoner

Thurbad Shieldbearer – Captain of the Hearthguard
Furgil – Pathfinder and Chief of Rangers

Barak Varr
Brynnoth – King of Barak Varr
Nadri Gildtongue – Merchant Guildmaster
Burgrik Strombak – Engineer Guildmaster
Heglan Copperfist – Engineer
Nugdrinn Hammerfoot – Sea Captain of Barak Varr

Northern kings
Grundin – King of Karak Kadrin
Thagdor – King of Zhufbar
Luftvarr – King of Kraka Drak
Bagrik Boarbrow – King of Karak Ungor
Hrekki Ironhandson – King of Karak Varn

Southern kings
Varnuf – King of Karak Eight Peaks

Aflegard – King of Karak Izril
Brugandar – King of Karak Drazh
Hrallson – King of Karak Azul

Lesser dwarf lords
Valarik – King of Karak Hirn
Drong – King of Krag Bryn
Borri Silverfoot – Lord of Karaz Bryn
Drogor Zarrdum – Thane of the Lost Hold of Karak Zorn

Runelords
Feldhar Crageye – Runelord of the *Burudin*
Negdrik Irontooth – Runelord of the *Burudin*
Durgnun Goldbrow – Runelord of the *Burudin*
Agrin Fireheart – Runelord of Barak Varr and one of the *Burudin*
Ungrinn Lighthand – Runelord of the *Burudin*
Jordrikk Forgefist – Runelord of the *Burudin*
Kruzkull Stormfinger – Runelord of the *Burudin*

Hill dwarfs
Skarnag Grum – 'High King' of Kazad Kro
Rundin Torbansonn – Champion of the Skarrenawi
Kruk – King of Kagaz Thar
Orrik – King of Kazad Mingol

THE ELVES

The Asur
Caledor II – Phoenix King
Imladrik – Prince of Caledor
Liandra – Princess of Caledor
Hulviar – King Caledor's seneschal

The Druchii
Sevekai – Shade
Kaitar – Shade
Verigoth – Shade
Numenos – Shade
Hreth – Shade
Latharek – Shade

Drutheira – High Sorceress
Malchior – Sorcerer
Ashniel – Sorceress

Dragons
Draukhain
Vranesh

KHAZALID

THE LANGUAGE OF THE DWARFS

Az – Axe
Az un klad – Donning one's weapons and armour, readying for battle

Bar – A fortified gateway or door
Bozdok – Unhinged as a result of constantly banging one's head on low roofs and pit-props; 'cross eyed'
Brodag – A festival of worship to honour Grungni and the art of brewmaking
Brodunk – A festival of worship to honour Grimnir and the art of battle
Brozan – A festival of worship to honour Valaya and the bonds of brotherhood between the clans
Bugrit – An invocation against ill-luck uttered by a dwarf who has banged his head, hit his thumb, stubbed his toe or some other minor misfortune; usually repeated three times for luck
Bruz – Gold that has a purplish tinge only visible by twilight
Bryn – Gold that shines strikingly in the sunlight; anything shiny or brilliant
Brynduraz – Rare mineral, a stone that glows in darkness
Burudin – The sacred order of runelords of the dwarfs

Chuf – Also 'chuff'; a very old piece of cheese a miner keeps under his hat for emergencies; a declaration of exasperation, usually in response to foolish, stupid or remarkable behaviour

Dammaz kron – The Great Book of Grudges
Dawi – Dwarfs
Dawi zharr – Fire dwarfs
Dokbar – Gate of 'seeing'; a runic artefact of the elder ages used to commune with dwarfs from distant kingdoms
Dongliz – Nethers; the parts of a dwarf's body impossible for him to scratch
Drakzharr – A potent dwarf beer, a special reserve

Drek – Wastrels or bandits; also far, a great distance; great ambition or enterprise

Dreng tromm – A lament, usually in response to some terrible act or misadventure; literally 'slay beard' in that it refers to the act of a dwarf pulling out the hairs of his own beard

Drengudrakk – Dragon slayer or honoured title bestowed of any dwarf who has killed a dragon

Dunkin – Annual bath traditionally taken whether needed or not

Elgi – Elves

Elgongi – Elf friend; a mild insult

Frorl – Dusty gold with a farinaceous layer obscuring its brilliance

Galaz – Gold of particular ornamental value

Geln – 'Get gold' that is borrowed from others but not returned

Ghazan-harbark – Paddle-driven dwarf sea vessel

Ghuzakk! – Imperative shouted to mules, goats or beardlings to get them to move faster

Gorl – Gold that is especially soft and yellow; the colour yellow

Gorlm – 'Green' gold, which has achieved a patina of age

Glam – Especially shiny or silven gold whose appearance belies its actual meagre worth

Gronti-duraz – The stone giants, runic golems of the dwarfs; literally meaning 'enduring stone'

Grunti's – Dwarf undergarments (usually soiled)

Grobi – Goblins

Grongaz – Runic forge

Gronti – Giant

Grubark – Oar-driven dwarf sea vessel

Hnon – 'Rainbow gold'; in certain subterranean light this gold captures a myriad of hues

Hruk – Breed of dwarf mountain goat

Kalans – Clans

Karadurak – Enduring stone through which the most potent of runes can be crafted

Karaz Ankor – Mountain Realm, the lands of the dwarfs

Karinunkarak – Gesture of protection and farewell, usually invoked when a dwarf is about to go to war

Klad – Armour

Klinkerhun – Common runes or 'chisel runes'

Khazuk! – War cry of the dwarfs, 'the dwarfs are going to war, the dwarfs are on the warpath'
Konk – Gold that is ruddy in colour; a large and bulbous nose
Krut – A discomforting disease contracted from mountain goats
Kruti flu – A discomforting disease contracted from mountain goats
Krutting – A 'practice' frowned upon by all dwarfs
Kurz – Pitted gold, very dark in colour

Ngardruk – A heinous beast of dwarf legend
Rhun – Rune, word of power
Renk – Gritty gold, often veined with lesser minerals
Ril – Gold ore that shines brightly in rock
Rinkkaz – Gathering of dwarf kings at the behest of the High King
Rinn – A lady dwarf or king's consort
Runk – A one-sided fight; a sound thrashing!

Skarrenawi – Hill dwarfs; literally dwarfs of the sky
Skaz – Thief
Skryzan-harbark – Dwarf airship or zeppelin

Thaggi – Treachery or murderous traitor; sometimes also spelled 'thagi'
Tromm – Beard, but also used in respectful greeting or as a way of showing respect to another dwarf
Trombaraki – The act of cutting another dwarf's beard during a duel of grudgement; a weakling gesture; a cowardly act

Ufdi – A dwarf overfond of preening and decorating his beard; a vain dwarf; a dwarf who cannot be trusted to fight
Unbaraki – An oathbreaker, the very worst insult a dwarf could level at another dwarf
Urk – Orc or enemy; also fear, to be afraid of, to retreat
Uzkul – Bones or death, usually to the enemies of the dwarfs
Uzkular – Undead
Uzkuzharr – 'Dead fires', the unquiet spirits of slain dwarfs

Wanaz – A disreputable dwarf with an unkempt beard; an insult
Wattock – An unsuccessful dwarf prosector; a down at heel dwarf; an insult; a credulous dwarf
Werit – A dwarf who has forgotten where he has placed his ale; a state of befuddlement; a foolish dwarf
Wazzock – A dwarf who has exchanged gold or some other valuable item for something of little or no worth; a foolish or gullible dwarf; an insult
Wutroth – Wood from ancient mountain oak

Zaki – A crazed dwarf who has lost his sanity and wanders above and below the mountains aimlessly

Zharr – Fire

Zonzharr – Potent dwarf incendiary; highly volatile, often used in sieges and blasting tunnels

MASTER OF DRAGONS

Chris Wraight

I
DRAGONSONG

ONE

Arian saw the three black, wedge-shaped sails on the eastern horizon and his heart went cold. They emerged out of nowhere, taut triangles of sable in the dawn sun-glare, moving fast against a running swell.

'Full sail!' he shouted.

The crew were already complying. Sailors hauled to unfurl the buffeting mass of white sailcloth. The fabric filled out, catching the brisk easterly, making the ship jerk forwards in the water and cutting a line of foam through the waves.

The *Ithaniel* was not a warship; she was a light cutter, a dispatch-runner, a jack-of-all-trades employed by Lord Riannon to pass missives and personnel between the hawkships of the main fleet. She was fast, but not the fastest. She carried two quarrel repeaters – one fore, one aft – and a complement of thirty spearmen amidships.

None of that would make much of a difference, for Arian had seen the look of the sails coming after him. He knew the manner of ships they belonged to, and why they ran fast through the contested northern ocean.

'How long have we got?' asked Caelon, the master's wind-bitten face screwed up against the glare.

'We can beat west,' said Arian, 'hard as Khaine's blades. Might stumble into one of Riannon's patrols.'

Caelon didn't look convinced. 'Anything else?'

'Move the bow-fixed repeater aft. We'll loose a few as they close. Might even take one out.'

'It will be done.'

'They'll come up fast,' warned Arian. 'I've seen this before. We'll need to jig around like a hare or they'll eat the wind from our sails before noon.'

Caelon ran a nervous hand through his long brown hair. He was from Chrace, a veteran of many battles and didn't quail easily, but the odds did not favour them and he knew it. 'And the cargo?'

Arian smiled coldly. 'The cargo. Perhaps we'd better let him know. If he's awake, that is.'

Caradryel of the House of Reveniol was a light sleeper, easily disturbed by the sway and creak of a sea-going vessel. He habitually used the morning hours to recover his equilibrium; unconsciousness, as he was fond of remarking to himself and others, was his natural and optimal state. Involuntary assignment to Riannon's war-staff had not succeeded in altering the habits of a short lifetime, something he was perfectly aware did not endear him to the duty-minded crew.

For all that, by the time the captain had made his way down to his cramped cabin, Caradryel was awake to receive him. The prince pushed himself upright, smoothing silk sheets over his knees. His pale blond hair fell about his shoulders, stiff from salt and sun and badly in need of beeswax and lustre-oils.

The barbarism of war, he reflected sadly.

Arian had to duck as he entered.

'Bad news, lord,' he said, glancing sidelong at the crumpled sheets with poorly hidden disapproval.

'I heard the commotion,' said Caradryel. 'The cause?'

'Three druchii raiders, closing fast. We're no match for them, I'm afraid, and they have the weather on us.'

'Regrettable. How long have we got?'

'A few hours. We're bearing hard west, but unless Mathlann conjures something they'll overhaul us before sunset.'

Caradryel drew in a long breath. He would have to put in an appearance on deck, which was an irritant. 'Thank you for informing me,' he said. 'Given the circumstances, I think the best we can do is put up a creditable fight. Do you think we'll take one down with us?'

'I've mounted the repeaters aft,' said Arian. 'If they fail to spot them we might get a scalp.'

'Very good. I'd have done the same. And I assume we're now bearing full sail?'

Caradryel enjoyed seeing the look of exasperation on Arian's face when he enquired about nautical matters. Both of them knew that his experience of commanding a ship of any kind was somewhere less than negligible, though the game of pretending otherwise amused Caradryel almost as much as it annoyed Arian.

'Of course,' said Arian stiffly. 'We have archers in the high-top and spearmen arming in the prows. If you have any further recommendations, though, do be sure to pass them on.'

Caradryel bowed. 'I certainly will. Now, if you will give me just a few moments I will join you on deck. It may take me a while to choose a robe.'

Arian stayed where he was. 'You realise, lord, how serious this is?'

Caradryel gave him a steady look. 'I do indeed.'

'I cannot see a way out of this. The druchii are not merciful captors. You may wish to make... preparations.'

Caradryel smiled. 'Captain, you deserve better than ferrying princelings between the fleets. Calm yourself – I have no intention of dying under traitors' blades.'

Arian looked unsure how to reply. Caradryel maintained the smile – the polished, courtly smile that had carried him smoothly through a hundred encounters and came as easily to him as sleeping.

'For they are such grotesque blades, are they not?' Caradryel added. 'No taste, our fallen kin. No taste at all.'

The hours did not pass quickly. The three dark-sailed hunters steadily hauled the gap closed, sailing with reckless skill through a wind-chopped sea. Arian drove the *Ithaniel* as hard as he had promised to, straining the rigging and almost losing the mainsail twice. The crew worked as hard as he did, for they all knew the odds; only at the very end would they take up bow, blade or spear, ready to fight to the last, knowing that captivity would be far worse than a clean death in combat.

Arian leaned over the railing of the ship's sloping quarterdeck, watching the foam-edged wake zigzag away towards the enemy. On either side of him stood two big repeater crossbows, each one wound tight with iron-tipped bolts. The shafts were huge – as thick as his thigh and longer than he was tall.

By then he could make out the detail on the lead druchii corsair: a rune of Khaine on a satin-black ground, elaborate and gauche. It looked like a spatter of blood on dark glass, glistening wetly in the strong sun.

Like most of those now serving in the Phoenix King's navy, Arian was not old enough to remember the time before the Sundering. Horror and grief had thinned the ranks of those who had been there at the time, eight hundred years ago during the dark days when his race had cracked itself apart. Arian could, though, remember the subsequent years of horrific bloodshed. He could remember believing, long ago, that a reconciliation would somehow be found.

Now he entertained no such dreams. He knew, as all on Ulthuan surely knew, that war would now be with them for as long as any could foresee. Most of the druchii who crewed the corsair ships would not have been born in Ulthuan and would have only a sketchy knowledge of their ancient home. Most of the crew he commanded had never known a world in which the druchii were not mortal enemies from a frozen land across the oceans. The two sundered kinfolks now looked at one another and saw nothing more than an enemy, as alien now as the greenskin had always been.

How far the sons of Aenarion had fallen.

'They sail like maniacs,' observed Caradryel.

Arian hadn't heard him approach. He remained poised on the railing, eyes fixed out to sea. 'They know what they're doing.'

'If you say so. Why not explain it to me?'

Arian pointed out the lead vessel. It was still too far out for a bolt-shot, but every buck of its prow brought it closer. 'That's the one they want to close first. Caelon's spied grapples in the bow and it's stuffed with troops. I'd guess fifty, maybe more.'

'And the two others?'

'They'll eat our wind,' said Arian grimly. 'They'll swing out as they get closer, cutting our sails flat. When we're hooked by the lead corsair they'll close back for the kill.'

'I see. Anything you can do about that?'

Arian had to hand it to the prince: his tone was one of amiable curiosity, unmarked by the slightest tremor of fear. He might have been discussing the merits of the wine from his father's vineyards. 'Caelon knows this ship better than his own wife,' said Arian. 'We'll slip the trap for as long as we can, praying the wind drops or we spy ships of the fleet.'

'And what, do you suppose, are the chances of that?'

'I would not lay money on it.'

'Then we are hoping for the miraculous.'

'You could say that.'

Caradryel laughed. It was a light, unaffected sound, and it made several of the deck-hands turn from their labours. 'I should not fret, captain,' he said. 'The miraculous has a way of following me. Always has. Should you wish to, you might give thanks to the gods for having me amongst your crew this day. In any event, try not to look so worried – it is not, as they say in Lothern, *good form*.'

Caradryel could only watch as the corsairs did exactly what Arian had predicted. They ran fast, dipping through the pitch of the waves before crashing up again with spiked prows. More details became visible – curved hulls glossy as lacquer, black pennants fluttering around bone-like mastheads, ranks of warriors in ebon armour, crowding at the railings, eager for the boarding to come.

Caradryel withdrew from the quarterdeck and walked unsteadily towards the prow. As he did so he scoured the western horizon. The sky was clear, the wind remained strong, the seas were empty.

Dying here will annoy my father, he thought to himself as he drew his sword from its scabbard. *That, at least, is something.*

His blade had not been well cared for and showed signs of rust along the edges. Caradryel had never been a warrior. He had never been much of anything, though that had never shaken his inner confidence. He had always assumed that his time would come and his path would open up before him like the petals of a flower.

'Bolts!' came a cry from the high-top, and spearmen on either side of him crouched down low. Caradryel followed suit, pressing himself to the deck. A second later the air whistled with crossbow quarrels, some of them thudding hard into the wood, some sailing clear.

Before Caradryel could react, the *Ithaniel* opened up with its own bolt throwers and the recoil shuddered down the spine of the ship. Spray crashed up over the prow, salty and death-cold. He pushed his head up from the deck and saw two black sails standing off, eating up the wind just as Arian had predicted. The other one had tacked in close, bursting through the heavy swell like a pick hammered through ice.

Another volley of bolts screamed across the deck at stomach-height, barely clearing the rails. Caradryel saw a spearman take a quarrel in the midriff, another catch one in the thigh. Several shots scythed through the sailcloth, slashing it open and cutting the ship's speed. Archers mounted in the masts let fly in return. Caradryel couldn't see the results of their shots, but he guessed they would be meagre.

He kept to his hands and knees and crawled towards the high prow. He heard the aft repeaters loose again, followed by the *crack* of wood splintering. For a moment he thought Arian had scored a hit, but then the *Ithaniel* bucked like an unbroken stallion and slewed round hard.

Caradryel was thrown over to the nearside railing, still ten paces short of the prow. He stared back down the length of the ship. Spearmen were running towards the quarterdeck. The lead corsair was now right on the *Ithaniel*'s stern and loosing grappling hooks.

Caradryel gripped his sword two-handed and wished he'd paid more attention to the expensive lessons he'd been given back in Faer-Lyen. For all that, fear still eluded him. He'd never found it easy to be afraid. The overriding emotion he felt was irritation, a nagging sense that something was *wrong* – that dying in the middle of the ocean on a nondescript errand-runner was not how he was meant to leave the world.

'Repel boarders!' came Arian's powerful voice from the quarterdeck, followed by a commendable roar of determination from the spearmen around him. Caradryel watched them form a knot of resistance, their speartips glinting in the sunlight. 'For Asuryan! For the Sacred Flame!'

Then, as the *Ithaniel* fell away and the corsair warship rose up on a rolling wave-front, he saw the foe revealed – ranks of druchii swordsmen, four-thick along the pitching railing of the enemy decking, poised to leap as the grapple-hooks pulled tight. Caradryel saw them jostling to get to the forefront – they outnumbered the asur by at least two to one, and that was before the other two ships drew alongside.

Caradryel started to stagger back the way he'd come, teetering along the tilting deck with sword in hand, certain he'd be no use but belatedly determined not to cower in the prow while fighting broke out at the other end of the ship.

Such a waste, he thought, gripping the blade inexpertly and thinking of the fine silks of his robe, the ancient towers of Faer-Lyen in the mountains, the future he'd planned out in the courts of Lothern, Caledor and Saphery. *Such a stupid, terrible waste.*

He made it less than ten paces before falling flat on his face, slammed down against the deck by sudden wind and movement. He tasted blood on his lips and heard an echoing rush in his ears. He cursed himself, angry that he'd already tripped over his own feet.

But then he lifted his head and saw the reason he'd fallen.

He had not tripped. Amid the sudden screams he had just enough wit to realise that his role in the combat had suddenly become entirely irrelevant, and that no one else – druchii or asur spearman – had any further part to play in what now unfolded. The battle had been snatched away from them, swatted aside contemptuously by power of such splendour that it made the world itself around him seem diminished into nothingness.

Caradryel hardly heard the sword fall from his fingers. He barely noticed that his jaw hung open stupidly and his eyes stared like a child's.

It had all changed. In the face of that, and for the first time in his short, privileged life, Caradryel at last learned the heady rush of true, undiluted fear.

Arian didn't see it coming. Caelon didn't see it either, nor did the sharp-eyed archers in the masts. Very little escaped the eyes of the asur, so it must have moved fast – astonishingly fast, faster than thought.

The druchii were slow to react, but even when they did it was painfully inadequate. Whoops of relish changed into screams of terror just before it hit them, snapping the grapple lines and whipping the rigging into tatters. Arian saw some of them leap into the water rather than face it. He'd fought druchii before and knew they were no cowards, but he understood the panic. What could they do? What could they possibly do?

He barely held on to his wits himself. Part of him wanted to bury his head in his hands, cowering against the decking until it shot clear again.

'Fall back!' he shouted, somehow dragging the words out of his throat. 'Man the sails and pull clear! Pull us clear!'

He didn't know if anyone heeded him. He didn't even turn to look. All he could do was watch, gazing out at it as if newborn to the world and ignorant of all its wonders.

As long-lived and mighty as the children of Ulthuan were, some powers in the world still had the heft and lineage to overawe them.

'Dragon,' he whispered, the word spilling reverently from his cracked lips. It might have been the name of a god. 'Holy flame. A *dragon.*'

Caradryel pressed himself up against the railings, trembling and useless.

The wind itself had changed – it was as if the elements of air and fire had suddenly burst into violent union. The ships rocked crazily, thrown around like corks by the downdrafts from splayed wings.

The noise was the most terrifying thing. The *Ithaniel*'s spars shivered and the water drummed as if under a deluge. The sound was unforgettable – the mingled screams and battle-cries of a thousand mortal voices, locked together and blended into a pure animal bellow of rampant excess.

After the noise came the stink, a charred-metal stench like a blacksmith's forge, hot, pungent and saturated with the wild edge of ancient magic.

And then, finally, how it looked.

Its body was taut like a hunting hound, ribbed with steely plates, vivid, glistening, a shard of a jewel hurled into the heavens. It twisted in the air, flashing a long sapphire-blue hide. Its wings shot out like speartips, splayed with membranous skeins of bone-white flesh. Its tail was prehensile, snapping and flicking; its jaws gaped, blurry from heatwash and snarls of smoke, lined with teeth the length of a mortal's arm, crowned with drawn-back horns and tapers of ridged armour.

It was immense. Its shadow compassed the druchii corsair-ship, and its wingspan alone dwarfed the slack sails, turning what had been a daunting hunter into a drifting hulk.

Caradryel dragged himself upright, heart beating hard. As he did so the dragon came around for another pass. Flames thundered from its gaping jaws and hit the centre of the druchii vessel, punching clear through, shattering and carving, before exploding in a ball of steam as seawater gushed through the breach. The dragon swooped past and its tail lashed out, striking the reeling corsair amidships and breaking its spine. The warship wallowed in a flaming whirlpool for a moment before sinking fast, pulled down below as if grasped by greedy hands.

The dragon surged away after the remaining two ships. They had both turned hard into the wind and were beating a furious retreat, but it was hopeless. Caradryel steadied himself against the *Ithaniel*'s railing. The dragon reached the first corsair with a single wing-thrust, shooting across the water faster than a thrown spear. It vomited another burst of flame then pounced on the remains, seizing a mast-top in its maw and savaging it. The ship broke apart in a flaming tumble of splinters and shards.

Then the second. A score of heavy wing beats, a diving attack, a lash of the long sinuous tail, and it was over. All that remained of the corsair squadron was a miserable collection of bobbing flotsam. Those druchii not killed by the flames went under quickly, dragged down by their armour. A few deck-slaves clung to the wreckage, shivering from the shock, the cold, the awe.

Caradryel was unable to do much more than observe. The sight both scared and thrilled him – the exhibition of such power went far beyond anything he had seen before. The dragon's movements were almost lazy in their effectiveness, as if the creature were barely summoning up more than a token effort. As he gazed up at the wheeling wingtips Caradryel found himself lost in the arrogance of it. It was primordial. It was astonishing.

He knew then why it made him afraid: he couldn't control it, couldn't *hope* to control it. It was as pure and mindless as the storms that raced down from the Annulii. Caradryel had never encountered anything that he truly believed he couldn't control, whether through manipulation or flattery or the careful use of well-placed bribes. A dragon, though... Only a fool or a demigod would try to master that.

The creature came to a halt before the *Ithaniel*'s prow, maintaining its position in mid-air with a heavy sequence of downbeats. Its long, lean head rose high above the mast-top and its tail slashed through the waves below. Hot, metallic air washed across the decks, making the sails fill and flap.

Arian was the first to recover. He stood up in the prow, looking tiny under the shadow of the beast.

'My lord!' he cried, saluting. 'Our thanks!'

It was then that Caradryel saw the figure mounted on the dragon's shoulders. He wore silver armour chased with black runes and a tall helm crested with drake-wings. A heavy crimson cloak hung around him, pooling in the muscle-hollows of the dragon's hide. One silver gauntlet rested on the dragon's neck, the other held a naked blade.

He looked like a figure out of ancient legend – an avatar of Aenarion brought back to life.

'Where are you headed?' the dragon rider called. His voice rang clearly across the waves – a calm, authoritative voice, coloured with the aristocratic accent of Caledor.

'Lothern, lord, on business for the Lord Riannon.'

'Then make your way. More druchii will taint these waters before the sun sinks and I do not have the leisure to slay them all.'

Arian bowed. 'We had not been warned of corsairs, nor did I dream to see a dragon rider aloft. Is something amiss?'

The dragon rider laughed wryly. 'Amiss? That depends on your point of view. The Phoenix King returns to his throne, hence the seas are alive with intrigue and dragons are on the wing. Our meeting here was by chance – on another day you would have been alone with your assassins.'

'Caledor returns!' cried Arian. 'You bring great tidings, lord.'

The dragon rider didn't reply. His steed beat its wings fiercely, bearing them both higher and away from the ship. Caradryel found himself wishing they would linger. The spectacle of it all – the dazzling, bejewelled creature of the high airs, the aura of raw magic bleeding from its armoured flanks – it was a heady, intoxicating presence.

A few powerful downbeats, though, and the dragon was spiralling away from them. Mere moments later it was little more than a speck of glittering blue against an empty sky.

The *Ithaniel* drifted on the open sea, alone again, surrounded by the blackened evidence of the dragon's power.

Arian stirred himself. 'Lower the boats,' he ordered, moving down from the quarterdeck. 'Take aboard survivors. Slaves will be freed; druchii taken to Lothern. With haste! We must be under sail again soon.'

Spearmen and deck-hands shook themselves and stumbled back to work. The ship was quickly thick with activity as repairs were made and wounds bound up. Tales of the dragon could wait until they were safely in port.

Amid it all, Caradryel remained motionless, staring up at the heavens, his hands still clutching the rails.

That is true power, he thought. *That is greatness. The one who controls such power controls the world.*

He didn't notice Arian coming up to him, a wide grin on his face. The captain stooped to pick up Caradryel's discarded sword and handed it to him, blade-first.

'Dreaming?' he asked. Many lines of anxiety had fallen away from his face.

Caradryel took the sword and sheathed it self-consciously. 'A dragon rider,' he said, trying to affect disinterest. 'How unexpected.'

Arian laughed. 'We were honoured. Did you not see the livery? You were in the presence of the king's brother.'

'Imladrik?'

'And you missed your chance for advancement.'

'The Master of Dragons,' Caradryel remarked. 'What great fortune.'

Arian turned away, a smile playing on his lips. 'I thought you didn't believe in fortune,' he said, heading back up to the prow to oversee the retrieval of the boats.

'I don't,' murmured Caradryel, too soft for hearing, his mind working hard.

TWO

Imladrik sat loosely in the saddle, no longer giving directions to his mount but letting him find his way amid the paths of the skies. Draukhain headed south-west, gliding languidly. The destruction of the druchii squadron had been a trivial task for one of his breeding and his enormous lungs worked as rhythmically as ever, untroubled by the diversion, drawing in the chill wind and transmuting it into fiery exhalations.

The work may have been easy but the orders had been an insult. Dragons were rare and perilous creatures; to turn them into celebratory attendants of Caledor's homecoming was an ignorant misuse of power.

You are angry.

Draukhain's mind-song echoed in Imladrik's head like one of his own thoughts.

Not angry, Imladrik returned. *Weary.*

Weary? I have borne you aloft a hundred leagues. Draukhain snorted, sending flecks of smouldering ash cascading over his immense shoulders. *I am weary; you are angry. You rage against your brother who commands you.*

Ah. You read my thoughts now.

I do not need to. This anger is a waste – it serves no purpose.

Imladrik shifted in the saddle. After hours of flight his limbs were tight and his muscles raw. The ocean glittered below him, a shallow curve extending in all directions, glossy with reflected sunlight. Soon the sun would begin to dip, descending in golds and reds towards the western horizon, but for the moment the world looked pristine, awash with light, just as it must have done in the dawn following creation.

My brother shows disrespect, mind-sang Imladrik. *To you, great one. He does not understand you.*

How many are left who truly understand, kalamn-talaen? *Do not judge him for that.*

Kalamn-talaen: the little lord. A whimsical title, one the dragons used to distinguish between Imladrik and the great-grandsire of his bloodline,

Caledor Dragontamer, whom they called *kalamn-kavannaen*, the great lord. Imladrik had heard their minds burst into joyous celebration at the very mention of the Dragontamer – perhaps he had been the only mortal other than Aenarion to command their total respect. The rest of the asur, Imladrik included, were merely indulged, as if in homage to that one undying example of greatness.

It is not like you, Imladrik returned, *to be so magnanimous.*

No, it is not. Draukhain snorted again, producing a gout of glutinous smoke that rolled across his sapphire-scaled skin. *But I am in a good temper this night.*

For the ending of so many druchii?

Maybe so. Or maybe the golden sun on the sea, or maybe your company. Who can tell?

That brought a smile to Imladrik's stern face. *I am glad one of us is, whatever the cause.*

They flew further west. The first cliffs of Ulthuan became visible as a blurred line of dark grey against the horizon. The rock-ramparts grew in size, steadily accumulating detail and definition. Soon the eastern curve of the Annulii could be made out, vast and gold-glittered and crowned with ice.

Where shall I bear you, then? sang Draukhain, dipping his head and sweeping closer towards the scudding wave-tops.

Do you have to ask? returned Imladrik. His mind-voice, unguarded for a moment, was a mix of yearning and resignation. He didn't mind giving that away – Draukhain was hard to deceive, even for one with his command of dragonsong.

A deep, grinding sound rumbled up from Draukhain's belly. Imladrik knew how to interpret the sound, for he understood the great dragon's soul nearly as well Draukhain knew his own: the creature approved, was reassured, understood his reasons and wished him well for much earned repose and restoration. All these things could be divined from a single harmonic. Dragons were creatures of music and instinct, more eloquent in gestures than they were in words.

Draukhain banked over to the left, pulling fractionally to the south, aiming towards the high peaks, to the realm of Cothique.

We shall be there before the sun sets, sang Draukhain.

Do not hurry, returned Imladrik, watching the last of the light on the water as it flickered beneath him. *Enjoy the remains of this day. You have earned it, even if none but I will ever know it.*

She was not waiting for him. She never lingered on the balcony, staring up into the skies for his return, pining like a maiden for her lover in the poetic romances of Avelorn. Her work was too important, too all-consuming for that.

When he found her at last, after slipping through the gates of Tor Vael and up the echoing stairways, she was doing what she always did, so absorbed in it that the rest of the world might have been a fiction spun in the minds of others.

Imladrik paused at the entrance to her chamber. She was bathed in the light of dusk from the open window, framed against a darkening vista of high mountain-slopes. She was seated, her shoulders stooped over an angled caelwood writing table.

Imladrik leaned against the doorframe, his movements silent, his breath shallow. He watched her trace the shape of runes against parchment, working the quill deftly. He saw her grey eyes latched on to her work: twin vices of concentration. He saw her hands moving. He saw her slender frame crouching over the desk, and regretted the tight curve of her spine. He had warned her about it often, offering to have a new chair made, pleading with her not to work for so long without rest.

His lips twitched into a smile. She never listened. She had always been stubborn – not angry, never irritable or shrewish, just stubborn – like the hard, dark rock of his homeland.

'My lady,' he said softly.

Yethanial's head jerked up. She glared at him, startled as if roused from a deep sleep.

Then she leapt up, her grey robe rustling around her. Her pale face brightened and the grip of exertion fell away from her features.

'My lord!' she cried, her voice ringing with joy.

Imladrik laughed, pushing himself away from the door to meet her. They embraced, clasping one another tight.

As he pressed against her, Imladrik drew in her familiar aromas of homecoming: coarse woollen fabric, inks that stained her fingers, crushed petals of the seaflower he had placed in her hair before he'd left. He guessed that he would smell of sweat, brine and dragon. Yethanial professed never to mind that; he doubted whether he believed her.

'I was not expecting you,' she said, nestling her face into his shoulder.

'I told you I would return before nightfall.'

'Then I did not listen.'

'You never do.'

He pushed her away, holding her at arm's length to get a better look at her.

He thought then, not for the first time, how different they were. Imladrik knew well enough how he looked: tall, broad-shouldered, his body tempered into hardness by the demands of riding the great drakes. He knew how severe his features were, hewn roughly, so he'd been told, like the white cliffs of Tiranoc. He knew his long hair, a dull bronze like his mother's, hung heavily around his shoulders, pressed flat by the dragon-helms he wore in battle.

Yethanial, by contrast, was like a dusk-shadow: slight, her limbs as lean as mages' wands, her glance quick and her smile quicker. In every movement she made, the sharpness of her scholar's mind spilled out. In her eyes it was most unavoidable – those steady grey eyes that seemed to look within him and prise out his innermost thoughts.

It was her eyes that had snared Imladrik long ago. He had gazed into them on the windswept cliffs of Cothique during their long formal courtship and revelled in their elusive, darting intelligence. Now, after so many years together, they still had the power to captivate.

'The flower I gave you,' he said.

Yethanial's hands flew to her head, searching for what remained of it. 'It was lovely. I cherished it. But, somehow–'

'Somehow, during the day, you forgot it was there,' smiled Imladrik, taking her hands back and pressing them gently into his own. 'Your work consumed you. What are you doing? May I see it?'

Yethanial looked apologetic. 'Not finished, of course.'

She led him to the desk. A battered leather-bound book rested, clamped open, on the left-hand edge. Next to it was a pinned leaf of heavy vellum, fresh-scraped and as white as bone. She had been working on it, transcribing text from the flaking pages of the book. Only a part of one page had been completed, but Imladrik could see the emerging pattern of it. She had traced out runes carefully, leaving spaces where gold leaf and coloured inks would be applied. The text had been painstakingly drawn in black ink, and several discarded quills littered the floor around the writing desk.

'These books were not well-made,' she said, glancing at the open volume. 'But their contents are precious. When I am done I will take this to Hoeth to be bound. They can create books that will last for as long as the world endures.'

Imladrik looked at the script. It wasn't in Eltharin, even though the characters were familiar. 'I cannot read it,' he said.

'Few can. It was written before the time of Aenarion – we only have copies of copies. The speech is called *Filuan*. These are poems. I find them beautiful.'

Imladrik tried to decipher something of them, but made no progress. He was not a gifted loremaster – only the language of swords and of dragons had ever come easily to him. 'What do they speak of?' he asked.

'The same things our poets speak of,' she said, running a finger lightly down the edge of the vellum. 'Love, fear, the shape of the world. They must have been very like us. I would hate their words to be lost forever.'

Imladrik considered asking her to translate some for him, but decided against it. He would pretend to appreciate it, she would see through him, and a small cloud of irritation would come between them. He had long ago resigned himself to their fundamental differences.

'I wish I could understand it as you do,' he said softly, pulling her close again. 'I feel like a barbarian out of the colonies.'

'You are a barbarian out of the colonies.'

'I miss you, when alone up there.'

'Then stay,' said Yethanial. 'We can dwell wherever you wish – Kor Evril, Tor Caled, an empty barn in the mountains.'

'Anywhere but Elthin Arvan.'

'What is there in Elthin Arvan?'

Imladrik almost replied. He could have said: freedom, open lands as wild as at the dawn of creation, dark woods that stretched from horizon to horizon, untouched by the hand of civilisation and rich in both peril and majesty. Then there was Oeragor, the city he had founded but not seen for over twenty years, a half-finished sanctuary he had hoped to turn into a desert jewel for the two of them to grow old in together.

But he said nothing. They had covered this ground before and he knew when to retreat from a hopeless cause.

'I am back now,' was all he said. 'My duties are here.'

Yethanial rested her head in the crook of his shoulder. It was an almost childlike movement; one of trust, of contentment.

'That gladdens me,' she said.

Dawn brought rain, hard and slanted from the east. It drummed against Tor Vael's lead roofs and gurgled down its granite walls.

Imladrik awoke before Yethanial. He slipped soundlessly from the sheets and opened the shutters of her bedchamber. The view from the window was dove-grey and rain-blurred. In the east he could make out the smudge of the ocean. Nowhere in Cothique was far from the sea.

He breathed deeply, inhaling the salt-tang. He felt rested. He stretched, feeling long-clenched sinews in his back and shoulders unfurl.

'My lord,' said Yethanial, sleepily.

Imladrik smiled, turning. 'My lady.'

She sat amid a pile of linen, looking flushed with slumber. He went over to her, embraced her, kissed her, smoothed her grey-blonde hair from her brow.

'Hungry?' he asked.

'As if starved for a year.'

Imladrik sent for food. In the time it took the servants to prepare it, the two of them rose and dressed. They broke their fast in an east-facing chamber of the old tower. The rain lashed against the glass of the windows and the wind sighed around the walls as they ate, making the fire in the grate gutter and spit.

Imladrik leaned back in his chair. The kitchens at Tor Vael cooked food the way he liked it: plain. He swallowed the last of a round oatcake and reached for a goblet of watered-down wine.

Yethanial had been as good as her word; she ate ravenously, like a scrawny mountain wolf at the end of winter.

'It troubles me,' said Imladrik.

'What troubles you?'

'That you do not look after yourself when I am away.'

Yethanial shrugged. 'Too much to do.'

'You have servants here.'

'Yes, and I have been cooped up with them for too long. Tell me of the real world.'

Imladrik took a cautious sip of wine. 'What do you wish to know?'

'Everything.' Yethanial crossed her arms, waiting.

'Well, then. My brother heads back to Ulthuan and Lothern runs with rumour. They tell me he has won his war in the colonies, that the stunted folk are defeated, and that we can at last turn our attentions to ridding the world of druchii.'

'The stunted folk are defeated? Should I believe that?'

Imladrik leaned forward, his elbows on the table. 'Have you ever met a dwarf?'

'I have read accounts.'

'Scrolls do not tell the truth of it.' Imladrik felt his mind roving back over the past, the years he had spent in the wilds. 'Imagine, somehow, if rock were to come to life, growing limbs and a heart. Imagine that every virtue of rock – durability, endurance, hardness – were somehow condensed into a living thing.'

Yethanial smiled affectionately. 'Language is not your gift, my lord.'

'It is not. But think of it: a race of stone, as resolute as granite, as unyielding as bedrock. That is the dawi.'

'Dawi?'

'What they call themselves.' Imladrik shook his head. 'And they are not defeated. Menlaeth has killed one of their princes, but dozens more remain under the mountains. I have seen those places. I have seen halls of stone larger than our greatest palaces. I have seen their warriors gathered around the light of ritual fires, each one wearing a mask of iron and carrying an axe of steel.'

Imladrik looked down at his hands. Speaking of such things took him back. 'They can never be defeated,' he said. 'Not there, not in their own realm. I tried to tell my brother that.'

Yethanial listened carefully. 'I am sure he took account of that.'

Imladrik's lip twitched in a wry smile. 'I met the dwarf prince he is said to have killed. Halfhand, they called him. A brave warrior, though headstrong. The dawi will hold a thousand grudges against us now, and they will never stop.'

'But they will have to relent soon, no? They cannot fight us forever.'

Imladrik's smile remained on his lips. 'Relent? No, I do not think they have a word for that.' He took another swig of wine. 'I read the tidings from Elthin Arvan. They tell me that Tor Alessi will soon be attacked again. There are dozens of dawi thanes, all with their own armies. Athel Maraya is exposed too. It is only arrogance that makes us believe these places are invulnerable.'

'But here we are told–'

'Here you are told that the war will be over in a year, the colonies will expand and the dawi will soon be suing for peace on their knees.' Imladrik looked into his goblet sourly. 'It is lunacy. At Athel Numiel even the infants were butchered, so they say. Menlaeth has set the fire running; I hope he understands the inferno that will come of it.'

Imladrik put the goblet down. 'I love my brother,' he said, his jaw tight. 'Or I try to. He is the mightiest of all of us, the crown is his by right, but...'

Yethanial rose from her chair and hastened to his side. She knelt beside him, catching his hands in hers and pulling them to her lap. 'You do not have to pretend, not with me.'

'I never pretend.' Imladrik shot her a bitter smile. 'The dragons see through it, so I lost the knack. Believe me, I do not envy him. He has our glorious father to live up to, and I would not wish that on anyone.'

'You both have that to bear.'

'My name will not be in the annals. When I remember to, I pity him. I wish to help him, but he takes no counsel.'

Yethanial's mouth twitched into a smile. 'Remind you of anyone?'

Imladrik gave a hollow laugh. 'I am surrounded by the stubborn. Why is that? Do I attract them?'

'Some of them.' Yethanial stroked his hands. The touch was soothing. 'I have made you melancholy. I did not mean to.'

Imladrik slipped his hands free and reached for her, pulling her towards him. 'No, it is me – I have let the past intrude. I was over there for a long time.'

Yethanial nodded, looking up at him with sad knowledge written in her features. 'It has been over twenty years. How much longer will you need before you let it go?'

Imladrik didn't reply. He knew that his face would give away his answer if he spoke.

I will never let it go.

Yethanial reached up to press her hand against his heart. 'I am not a fool, my lord. I know enough, but it is over now. You came back, and the gods know we have enemies enough in Ulthuan to keep you busy.'

Imladrik nodded. They were the words he needed to hear.

'Whatever you left behind,' she said, 'whatever part of you that remains there, think of it no more. Think of me. Think of the realm you are charged with defending, for you are loved here on Ulthuan. Your troops would march beyond the gates of madness if you led them there. Remember that.'

Imladrik lowered his forehead against hers. 'And you are loved more than life itself,' he said. 'You remember that.'

'Always.'

They remained like that for many heartbeats, their limbs entwined. They said nothing as the rain ran down the glass and the gusts shook the stonework. For all the world outside cared, they might have been an image of Isha and Kurnous, frozen outside time.

But they remained mortal. Time passed, and the clatter of servants coming to retrieve the silverware broke their communion. Yethanial extricated herself before they entered, smiling bashfully, kissing Imladrik on the cheek and taking her place at the table.

Imladrik retrieved his wine, swilling it in the goblet before taking a draught. He felt unsettled. Duties would call for him soon – orders relayed from Lothern and Tor Caled, demands on his time, requests for aid. Part of him wearied of the burden of it, but part of him wished for nothing more. His duty would take him away from Tor Vael, away from Yethanial, but also from the emotions that preyed on him whenever he was forced to confront them.

Whatever you left behind, he told himself, looking up at her and wishing his smile could be more carefree, *whatever part of you that remains there, think of it no more.*

THREE

Liandra stood, shivering, in the hills above Kor Vanaeth. Her robes were heavy from rainwater and hung like dead weights.

She ran a grimy hand through her copper hair.

Mud, she thought grimly, gazing across her domain. *Filth. Every year it gets dirtier. What in the name of Isha am I still doing here?*

As the years had passed, it had become harder to answer that question. The colonies were a hard place to live in for one of her breeding. The landscape was heavy with sludge, an endless grind of snarled, twisted, muck-thick forest. Everything was washed-out, mouldering, greying at the edges.

Stubbornness, she concluded, glowering at a rain-washed sky. *I cannot bear to see them win.*

She looked down at Kor Vanaeth's walls, half a mile away. Some sections hadn't been completely rebuilt, though years had passed since the dawi had razed it. It had been hard to attract artisans back, and harder still to secure the materials they needed. The stonewrights of Tor Alessi were busy with the city's own immense defences and were loath to spare any of their fellowship for outlying fortresses.

Liandra began to walk, retracing her steps down the rain-slushed path into the valley. Her robe-hem dragged behind her, sodden.

When her father had founded Kor Vanaeth it had housed over thirty thousand souls. The streets had burst with life, spilling beyond the boundaries of the walls and into the forest.

Hard to remember that now. Fewer than five thousand had returned. Most had done so out of loyalty to Liandra's father, though a few saw opportunities to advance themselves amid the rubble. Some dark-eyed souls had just suffered too much and wanted to take something back.

Twenty-five years. So much work, and so little to show for it. They were vulnerable still. If another army swept down the valley, even one half the size of the one that had destroyed them before, not a single stone would be left standing.

Liandra felt her fists clench. The movement was almost involuntary; she had caught herself doing it more and more often.

I am changing. This war is changing me.

Sometimes she awoke angry, fresh from vivid dreams of slaughter. Sometimes she awoke in tears with images of the slain crowding in her mind. And sometimes, more often than she liked, she awoke after dreaming of him.

The years had not dulled the loss. It was for the best that he had gone back to Ulthuan. He belonged amid its refined spires of ivory, just as she belonged in the wilds of the east, doused by the rain and up to her ankles in blood-rich filth.

'My lady.'

Alviar's voice made her start. She hadn't seen him approach, trudging just as she had done up the steep hill-path from the valley. That was sloppy; her lack of sleep was beginning to take its toll.

'What is it?' she demanded, more sharply than she'd intended.

Her steward bowed in apology. 'You asked me to tell you when we had word from Tor Alessi.'

'And?'

'Messengers are here. They bring greetings and news from the Lady Aelis. Do you wish me to summarise?'

'If you please.'

'Aelis agrees with you: now that Caledor has gone, the dawi will be quick to rally. She has tidings of new armies gathering in the mountains. She asks you to join her. She says she cannot promise to protect Kor Vanaeth when fighting resumes.'

Alviar was so dutiful. He spoke like a scribe reeling off trade accounts. Liandra had preferred Fendaril, but he, of course, was dead.

'What of Salendor?' she asked.

'Lord Salendor is already at Tor Alessi, along with the Lords Caerwal and Gelthar. In the absence of the King, a war council has been formed. They call themselves the Council of Five.'

'Those are four names, Alviar.'

'They hope for yours to be added.'

'Do they, now?'

'Salendor in particular, they tell me,' said Alviar.

'Salendor is a brute,' said Liandra. 'He understands the dawi, though. He knows how to fight them. If he wants me to be there then I should perhaps consider it an honour.' She pressed her lips together ruminatively. 'Do you remember, Alviar, when Caledor left us?'

'Clearly.'

'He thought he'd won the war for us. I heard him say it. *Now finish the task*, he told us. I felt like laughing. No one would tell him the truth. He left for Ulthuan with no idea of what we face.'

'I should say not.'

Liandra clasped her hands before her, pressing her chilled flesh against the rain-wet fabric of her robe. 'We accomplished so much here. I cannot leave now. I was not here when the dawi came the first time, and that weighs on my heart.'

'Shall I tell them that?'

Liandra shook her head slowly. 'No. No, I will give it more thought. You offered them lodgings?'

'Of course. As much comfort as we could make for them.'

Liandra breathed in deeply, looking around her, sucking in air that tasted of damp and rot. 'So what would you do, Alviar?'

'I would not presume to have an opinion.'

Liandra smiled. 'None?'

'You are a mage of the House of Athinol. You require the counsel of princes, not stewards.'

'Princes may be fools, stewards may be wise. But you speak truth – I've been starved of equals ever since...'

She trailed off. It was still hard to say his name.

'Enough,' she said. 'Return. Tell them they will have their answer soon.'

Alviar bowed and withdrew, retracing his steps down the shallow slope towards the city.

Liandra watched him go. When he was gone she resumed her vigil, alone at the summit, watching over the city of her father as the cold wind whipped at her robes.

Now finish the task, she mused.

Sevekai ghosted through the deep dark. His movements were silent. Years in the wilds of Elthin Arvan had only honed his already taut physique; his reactions had always been sharp, now they verged on the preternatural.

The others were still on his heels, just as they had been on every fruitless trail since leaving Naggaroth: Verigoth with his pallid skin and dewy eyes; Hreth and Latharek, the brutal twins, their glossy hair as slick as nightshade. The two sorceresses, Drutheira and Ashniel, prowled ahead, lighting the way with purple witch-light. Malchior, their counterpart, brought up the rear.

A whole party of assassins, gaunt from the wild, buried deep in the twisting heart of the Arluii. They were lean from hunger, their skin drawn tight over sharp bones. Elthin Arvan had not been kind to them. Why should it have been? After what they had done to it, a measure of hatred was richly deserved.

Only Kaitar looked untouched. Kaitar the enigma, Kaitar the cursed. Sevekai loathed him. There was something deeply wrong with Kaitar. His eyes were dull, his manner disquieting. None of the others liked Kaitar; he himself seemed to care little either way.

Sevekai avoided Kaitar's gaze, just as he had done for all the years they had suffered one another's company. It had been surprisingly easy to work with someone and barely exchange words. Their routine tasks – slitting throats, administering poisons, squeezing tender flesh – lent themselves to a cold, mute kind of pragmatism.

Now, though, after so long without word from the Witch King, Drutheira had taken matters in hand. It could not continue as it had been. They had done what was required of them and had now been forgotten. So she had taken them south, then up into the peaks, then down again, deep down, burrowing through cold, lost shafts of feldspar and granite. Sevekai could only guess how far they were underground now. He liked the chill of it, though. It cooled his limbs and made him feel languidly murderous.

'Be still,' whispered Drutheira from ahead.

The druchii froze. Her witch-light died away, plunging them into darkness.

Sevekai switched to a state of high awareness. Twin blades slipped soundlessly into his hands. He tensed, feeling the muscles of his arms tighten and the hairs on the back of his neck rise.

For a few moments, nothing changed. Then, from far away, from far down, he heard it – a long, low rumble, as if the mountain itself stirred. Then silence.

'What is this, witch?' whispered Kaitar. His voice gave away his uncertainty. That in itself was unusual; Sevekai had never heard him sound uncertain before.

'I told you,' replied Drutheira. 'The weapon.'

'The *weapon*,' he repeated. 'I asked you before what it was.'

Drutheira's voice remained perfectly calm, perfectly poised. Sevekai had to hand it to her: she knew her craft. 'Do you doubt me, Kaitar?'

Sevekai smiled wolfishly. He could just make out the ivory glow of her bleached-white hair. She was savagely beautiful, as cruel and fine as an ice-goad.

'No more than you doubt me,' said Kaitar. 'Tell me what you know, or I go no further.'

'Just what have you sensed down here, Kaitar?' asked Drutheira, her voice intrigued. As she spoke, a soft blush of colour spun into the void, lighting up her alabaster cheek. 'What worries you?'

'You do not wish to provoke me.'

'Nor you, me,' she said, before relenting. 'It is a relic, one that will cause the asur more pain than we have ever caused them. If that does not stir your curiosity then maybe you are in the wrong company.'

Sevekai saw Kaitar's face flicker between doubts.

'Maybe I am,' Kaitar said, 'but you could retrieve it yourself. There is no reason for me to be here.'

'Why do we wait?' hissed Malchior from the rear of the party, unable to hear what was being said. 'We need to move.'

'Yes we do, so do not be foolish!' snapped Drutheira to Kaitar. 'Without me to guide you, you'd stumble down here for days. I'd happily watch you starve but I need every blade for what's to come. If you had doubts you should have voiced them on the surface.'

Kaitar hesitated. Still, the uncertainty; Sevekai enjoyed that.

'So be it,' Kaitar muttered at last, drawing a curved knife. 'Take us down. But this blade will be at your back.'

'And this one at yours,' said Sevekai, shifting his weight just enough to prod the tip of a throwing dagger into Kaitar's tunic.

Kaitar turned to glare at him. Sevekai shot him a frigid smile.

'Watch your step,' Sevekai warned. 'The stone's slippery.'

Slowly, deliberately, Kaitar sheathed his blade again.

'Very good,' said Drutheira mockingly. 'Now, if we may?' As she turned back down the tunnel Sevekai caught the look of capricious enjoyment she gifted him.

They crept onwards, going near-silently, treading with feline assuredness in the black. The tunnel wound ever deeper, switching back and plunging steeply. It became narrow, barely wide enough to take two abreast, clogged with stalagmites and glossy tapers of dripping rock.

A second rumble ground away in the depths, then faded. Sevekai's heartbeat picked up. He knew something of what they sought, but not everything – Drutheira was miserly with information even with her allies. Kaitar said nothing further, but Sevekai could sense the tension in him. He kept his daggers to hand, poised for use. Slipping one between Kaitar's shoulders would be no hardship – he just needed the faintest of excuses.

The air began to heat up. Sweat ran down Sevekai's temples. He felt minuscule trembles in the rock as he walked, as if the entire underworld shivered in anticipation.

'It lies in the chamber beyond,' said Drutheira. 'Go silently. Follow my lead.'

Then she set off, creeping through the pitch darkness.

The tunnel floor sloped downward steeply, then levelled out. Sevekai could sense the roof opening up. The floor became flatter, as if made level by mortal hands.

'Go no further,' said Drutheira, halting them. 'This is the place. I think we may risk a little magic – the sight is worth it.'

Her staff flared, throwing out a curtain of purple-blushed illumination. Sevekai shaded his eyes against the glare, then peered cautiously through his fingers.

They were on the lip of a vast, perfectly circular chasm. It must have been a hundred feet across, as dark and clotted as the maw of Mirai. A narrow ledge ran around the perimeter, barred by cracks and heaps of rubble. Other tunnel entrances were visible at intervals, leading off to Khaine-knew-where. The cavern roof soared away above them, lost in shadow.

One by one the druchii crept out onto the ledge, going warily. Latharek hung back, hugging the near wall, looking sickened by the precipitous drop.

'Behold its chamber!' cried Drutheira, sweeping her staff-tip around her and throwing light up the walls.

Huge pilasters loomed up over them, each one carved with immense runes of containment. Sevekai could sense the magic bleeding from them like a physical smell, sulphurous and metallic.

As soon as he saw the runes, Kaitar turned on Drutheira. 'Dhar,' he snarled, reaching for his blade.

Drutheira smiled wickedly. 'What did you expect?'

Kaitar sniffed. It was an odd gesture – like a dog hunting the scent of its prey. His eyes suddenly widened. 'No. Do not do this.'

Drutheira shrugged. 'A little late, I fear.'

Her staff exploded with power, sending crackling lines of energy lashing out against the pilasters. The aethyr-force slammed into the runes, shattering them. A rumble like thunder welled up from the chasm depths, sending loose rubble clattering down the sides of the shaft.

Sevekai staggered, nearly losing his footing. Kaitar's head snapped around. He looked terrified.

'What do you fear, Kaitar?' asked Drutheira, her violet eyes glittering with mirth. 'No druchii fears Dhar.'

Kaitar's face changed into something bestial. 'Fool!' he slurred. 'You cannot control it!'

'You have no idea what I can control,' said Drutheira imperiously.

Kaitar went for her, lunging out with his blade. Latharek was closest. He tried to block Kaitar, ducking low to shoulder him off the ledge. Kaitar lashed around, grabbing Latharek and hurling him away. Off-balance, Latharek tumbled clear over the chasm edge, screaming as he plummeted.

Drutheira fled along the ledge, hurrying around to the far side of the chasm, her staff still blazing. More runes shattered, sending fragments spilling into the vault. The stone walls trembled again, rocked by something huge and muffled from far below.

'You cannot stop this!' cried Drutheira.

Kaitar went after her. Malchior attempted to seize him but Kaitar twisted away from his grip. Hreth darted at him next, blade in hand. For a moment Sevekai thought Hreth got a dagger to stick, but Kaitar somehow angled away at the last moment. They grappled on the edge of the ledge, blows flying furiously, before Kaitar punched his dagger into Hreth's stomach and wrenched it free with a flourish.

Something terrible had happened to Kaitar – his eyes gleamed with unnatural light, his limbs moved with ferocious speed. He was demented, raving, slavering with fear and fury. Whatever Drutheira was doing had made him crazy.

Sevekai went for him, dagger in each hand. Kaitar parried with his blade, desperate to get past and go after Drutheira. In the flurry of jabs Sevekai managed to wound him, stabbing a dagger-point deep into his arm before pulling sharply away.

It should have stopped him. It should have severed tendons, sliced muscle. Kaitar merely grunted and rushed at him faster. Sevekai got his blade to block just as Verigoth came at Kaitar from behind, dropping a throttle-cord over his neck and yanking it tight.

Kaitar's eyes bulged and his cheeks went purple. Verigoth dragged him back from the brink and for a moment Sevekai thought he'd pinned him. Then Kaitar's hands flew over his shoulders and grabbed Verigoth by his armour. With a ferocious lurch, Kaitar doubled over and hurled Verigoth headfirst into the chasm.

That was impossible. That was *madness*. Verigoth was strong – the strongest of them all – and he'd been thrown overhead like a child.

By then Drutheira had reached the far side and begun destroying more runes. Kaitar's gaze switched back and forth: Ashniel and Malchior blocked him from the left, Sevekai and the wounded Hreth from the right. He looked like a trapped animal.

Sevekai twirled his daggers in his hands and advanced again. Kaitar let slip a strangled growl and crouched down against the stone.

Then he leapt.

If any doubt remained that Kaitar was more than mortal, the leap quashed it. Sevekai could only watch as Kaitar flew high into the air, his limbs cartwheeling, propelled by some unnatural strength far out over the drop. He flew straight at Drutheira, his eyes blazing with anger, his arms outstretched to grasp her. She watched him come with a playful smile on her pale lips.

'Impressive,' she murmured.

But just as Kaitar reached midway, a column of fire thundered up from the depths, spearing out of the gloom and engulfing him in a gale of flame. He screamed – a horrific, otherworldly sound that rang round the chamber.

Sevekai dropped to his knees. The heat was incredible, pressing against his face like a vice. After the long trek in the dark, the sudden brilliance made his eyes sting.

Drutheira revelled in it. Her robes flapped about her.

'*This* is the weapon!' she crowed. '*This* is the weapon!'

Sevekai had no idea what she was talking about. He shrank back from the heat and the noise, just as all the others did.

An instant later the fires gusted out and something vast and dark surged up out of the chasm, rising on a tide of ruin, wreathed in oily smoke. With a twist and snap of immense jaws it ended Kaitar's wretched screaming. A hard bang echoed around the vault, like a steel hammer falling on an anvil. Cracks shot across the walls and rubble rained down from above.

The creature kept rising, buoyed by an updraft as hot as a forge. Vast wings stretched out, bat-skin black and pierced with chains. Ophidian flesh snaked and coiled on itself in the flickering gloom.

'You *know* me, creature!' cried Drutheira. 'You know what I am. Listen to me! The druchii have returned. Listen! We have come to reclaim what is ours.'

Sevekai looked on, unable to do anything but cower. A solid mass of curled, distorted black flesh loomed high up over them, hovering across the face of the chasm. Its hide glistened in the witch-light, reflecting from a thousand tight-woven scales. Ragged wings brushed against the shaft's wall. He saw spines, curved teeth crowded along a jagged jawline and talons the length of an elf's body. Gold chains, some broken, hung from an armoured torso, and iron runes had been branded and hammered into its flesh.

A dragon. A black dragon. One of Malekith's own creations, as warped and ruined as anything to emerge from his embittered mind.

'Your will is broken!' shouted Drutheira, speaking in the tone of command she used when spellcasting. 'Your mind is enslaved. You are *ours*, creature.'

The beast hissed at her, and flickers of blood-red flame danced across the void.

'Do not resist!' warned the sorceress. 'You belong to the druchii. We never forget. We never release.'

That brought a sudden gush of flame and a roar that made the whole shaft shiver. Flames kept coming after that, guttering and snorting, breaking the murky darkness with a dull glow of crimson.

'Serve me!' commanded Drutheira, raising her staff fearlessly. 'Serve *me!*'

The beast screamed back, but it did not attack. If it had chosen to it could have wiped her out just as it had consumed Kaitar. Its jaws opened and closed, revealing a long, lolling tongue the colour of burned iron. Its eyes – slits of silver – flashed furiously.

Sevekai saw the truth then: the powerful magicks that had cracked and twisted the creature's mind still held. It would not attack. It writhed, snorted and flailed, but its fires stayed subdued.

Drutheira smiled savagely. 'You know who your masters are. You sense us. You *smell* us.'

It screamed at her again, and echoes rang around the vault. Drutheira pointed the staff directly at it. 'The wards are broken. When I call, you answer.'

The dragon's wings thrashed, sending acrid air washing over the ledge. Its tail scythed, swishing in dumb frustration. Sevekai could only marvel at the imbalance: such a monster, held in check by a fragile, white-haired sorceress. Whatever magic had been used to crack the creature's mind must have been of astounding strength.

'Go!' cried Drutheira, raising her arms. 'Break out! Your will is mine! Your power is mine!'

The dragon coiled in on itself, writhing in a paroxysm of rage. Its eyes rolled, its jaws clamped shut.

Then it obeyed. With a clap of ebony wings it surged upwards, climbing fast. Sevekai saw then that the cavern had no roof – it was a shaft soaring upwards, carving through the heart of the mountain like an artery. The dragon ascended rapidly, lighting up the walls in a corona of red. The wind whistled in its wake, howling up out of the depths before falling, eventually, back into echoing silence.

Sevekai crept to the edge and risked a look down. He could barely make anything out, though the shaft stank of death. Hreth, lying next to him, gurgled weakly. His innards were visible between blood-drenched tatters of clothing.

Drutheira was breathing heavily and her pale cheeks were unusually flushed.

'So what did you think?' she asked, calling out to them over the gulf. 'Magnificent, eh?'

Malchior scowled back, his expression dark. 'You let it go.'

'It'll come when called. Unlike some, it is *utterly* faithful.'

Sevekai smiled wryly and got to his feet. Ashniel picked her way around the ledge toward Drutheira. 'What now?' she asked.

'To the surface,' the sorceress replied. 'It will be waiting.' As she spoke, the cavern shook again. The cracks that had opened after Kaitar's death widened. 'And we should hurry – this place is perilous now.'

Ashniel and Malchior hastened to follow her. Sevekai, following suit, felt the stone tremble under his feet.

'Wait!' called Hreth, dragging himself along the ledge. 'Some help, brother?'

Sevekai glanced at him scornfully. Shameful enough to be defeated; bleating about it compounded the crime.

'Sorry, brother,' he replied coldly. 'I think you would slow me down.'

More rumbles broke out, echoing dully from the depths. Sevekai broke into a jog, gliding surely across the uneven ledge surface. When he got to the tunnel entrance Malchior and Ashniel had already gone through, but Drutheira was waiting.

'You planned it all?' he asked her. 'For Kaitar?'

Drutheira placed a finger on his lips. 'Later, I promise. For now, trust me.'

Sevekai grinned. 'Not an inch.'

More cracks opened up, snaking up the height of the chamber. A low growl welled up from the deeps, prising what remained of the pilasters from the rock walls.

'We need to move,' said Sevekai.

'So we do.'

Drutheira slipped into the tunnel and hurried up the incline.

Sevekai took one last look at the chamber. Chunks of rock were beginning to fall freely, splitting from the mountain and tumbling into the shaft. Whether as a result of Drutheira's magic or Kaitar's violent death, the whole shaft was falling in on itself. Hreth still struggled on, stuck on his hands and knees as debris rained around him.

Sevekai couldn't resist a wintry smile. It was always pleasant to witness the demise of a rival.

Then he turned on his heels and raced into the tunnel, following Drutheira back into the dark.

FOUR

Lothern was not the oldest of the dwellings of the asur, nor the wisest, nor the most steeped in the thrum and harmony of magic, but it was the most magnificent, the most imposing, the most martial, the most sprawlingly and gloriously worldly.

Clusters of bone-white spires soared into the air, each reflected in the deep green of the lagoon that lapped before them. Immense statues of the gods stared out across the waters, their golden faces cast in expressions of austere superiority. Crystal coronets shimmered under the glare of strong sunlight and the sky blazed a clear blue, washed clean by the rain squalls and now as pure as a mage's spyglass. A thousand aromas rose from cargo heaped high on quaysides, and every crate, barrel and sackcloth was branded with the esoteric mark of far-off realms and colonies.

The royal fleet lay at anchor in the glassy lagoon. Each warship had been decked out in red and gold, their sails furled and their pennants rippling in the breeze. Mail-clad troops lined every thoroughfare, and their chainmail sparkled.

The waterfront rang with boisterous celebration. Crowds thronged along the long quayside, pushing past one another to gain position. All eyes looked up at the greatest spire of them all – the truly colossal Phoenix Tower, rearing up sheer above the water's edge, its flanks as pure as ivory and its crystal windows flashing in the sun.

Caledor II stood on the Tower's ceremonial balcony, a clear hundred feet from ground level, and drank the vista in. The acclamation of his people made his heart swell. Adulation was good for him. It vindicated everything he had done since setting sail from the same quayside six years ago.

They worship me, he thought, gripping the marble railing with silver-edged gauntlets. *Just as they worshipped my father, they worship me.*

Seldom had so many of the fleet's eagleships been concentrated in one place. The fortified cliffs that surrounded them, all bristling with turrets and banners, added to the sense of excess, of overflowing command, of invulnerability.

Nothing in the colonies would ever compare to Ulthuan, not even if the asur laboured there for a thousand years. Nothing would ever shine so vividly, or be filled with as much vivacity, or give harbour to so many of the Phoenix King's dread vessels of war.

Lothern was the heart of the fleet; thus, Lothern was the heart of power.

'Good to be back, my liege?' asked Hulviar, standing beside Caledor on the balcony. The seneschal wore his ceremonial armour, piped with gold filigree and lines of inlaid jewels.

'I can breathe this air without gagging,' replied Caledor, waving at the crowds below. Every movement he made seemed to elicit fresh cheers. 'My boots are free of mud. Best of all...' He smiled contently. 'No dwarfs.'

'Indeed,' agreed Hulviar with feeling. 'So will you address them now? They have been waiting a long time.'

Caledor gazed out indulgently. He felt reluctant to do anything to break the spell of massed veneration. Kingship was in large a matter of theatre, of display, and moments such as these were priceless.

Still, though. They wouldn't wait forever. 'Sound the clarion.'

Hulviar motioned to an attendant in the shadows. A moment later a fanfare rang out, cutting across the water and stilling the crowd to an expectant hush.

'I will be heard by them all?' whispered Caledor.

'The mages are prepared,' said Hulviar. 'Speak as comes naturally, my liege; the deafest of them will hear as if they were alone with you.'

Caledor placed both hands on the railing and pushed his shoulders back. He knew full well how resplendent he looked – artisan-fashioned armour of ithilmar and silver, a heavy cloak of sky-blue, long blond hair pulled back from his brow by the winged crown of the Phoenix Kings.

'My people!' he cried, and they cheered again. Soldiers along the terraces clashed their blades against their shields, sending an echoing wave of noise rolling across the lagoon.

Caledor couldn't prevent a fresh smile. The occasion called for dignity, but he was enjoying himself too much.

'My *people*,' he said again, waiting for the hubbub to die down. 'I return to you at the start of a new dawn for Ulthuan. Not since Aenarion's time have we known such victory. The druchii fall back under our relentless onslaught. The Witch King cowers in his frozen land, knowing his fate draws ever closer.'

That brought heartfelt cheers. Every soul gathered below would have lost someone to druchii raids; hatred for Malekith never needed to be stoked.

'But I need not tell you this – you know the truth of it. I come here this day to tell of victory in the east, for we have triumphed! We have triumphed over the mountain-folk. The stunted creatures of Elthin Arvan are defeated, and I myself, Caledor the Second, slew the son of their High King in single combat.'

Hulviar reached into a pouch at his belt and withdrew a shrivelled, stinking hunk of dried flesh. He handed it to the King, who lifted it up for all to see.

'They called him "Halfhand",' said Caledor, swinging the trophy from side to side as if it were a piece of meat brought back from the hunt. 'No longer – I call him "No-hand"!'

Snorri Halfhand's severed hand, cut from his arm at the wrist before the remnant had been thrown away, dangled from Caledor's grasp. The grey flesh was a mess of black, dried blood, the fingers little more than maimed stumps. At the sight of it the crowd burst into contemptuous laughter.

'They came to this realm and I cut off their beards,' Caledor went on, revelling in the reception. 'They did not take that lesson well, so I went to their realm and cut off their hands. When *will* they learn? Will we have to slice off every extremity, one by one?'

More laughter.

'So much for this *War of the Beards!*' Caledor said, flinging the severed hand back at Hulviar. 'The stunted ones dared to challenge their betters, and thus have been bloodied. They will think twice before assaulting our colonies again. Should they now sue for peace and come before me on their knees, we shall be magnanimous. But if they dare, if they *dare*, to rise up against us again, we shall visit vengeance on them *a thousandfold*.'

Laughter was replaced by roars of approval.

'We shall root them out of their holes and drag them into the sunlight,' Caledor promised, warming to his theme. 'We shall burn their mines and flood their holds. We shall seize their goods and make prisoners of their wives – though what use one might have for such creatures, I have little idea.'

More laughter, crude this time.

'So I tell you: rejoice! Rejoice in the valour of our legions, in the strength of our fleets, in the matchless spellcraft of our mages. No force of the world can stand against us. First will the dawi fall, then the druchii, just as any power must fall that sets itself against the chosen ones, the children of Aenarion!'

The cheering was thunderous.

'From henceforth, this day shall be known as the Day of the Severing. It shall mark our crushing of the dawi in their own domains. Until the sun sets, do no work. Drink wine, feast well, revel in your leisure: you have laboured hard in the years since my father's death, now take your ease and bask in the glory of his son's accomplishments.'

He leaned forward, stretching out his fists.

'I told you that a new dawn has broken over Ulthuan,' he cried. 'It shines on the reign of *Caledor the Second*.'

That brought the loudest cheers of all. Soldiers resumed their shield-clanging salute; whole bunches of flowers were hurled up at the tower's stonework. Caledor basked in it all, smiling benignly, waving regally, before finally, just as the prepared casks of strong wine were opened along the waterfront, withdrawing from the balcony's edge.

He passed into a gilt-and-mirror chamber to the rear, followed by Hulviar. The cheers from the quayside went on and on, persisting even after glass-paned doors were closed against the noise.

'That went well,' said Caledor, taking the crown from his brow and handing it to a waiting attendant.

Hulviar drew the strings tight on the bag containing Snorri's hand and dangled it with distaste. 'What do you wish me to do with this, my liege?'

Caledor pulled his gauntlets free and discarded them. 'Whatever you will. Feed it to your swine, throw it into the sea, I care not.'

Hulviar gave him an uncertain look. 'You know, of course, that his father still lives? And his cousin? They're sure to seek vengeance.'

'Of course. They shall meet the same fate.'

'Our lords in Elthin Arvan are not so sure. They make requests for more arms. They are worried.'

'What would they have me do? Go back again? Nursemaid them?'

Hulviar leaned closer. Aside from a couple of attendants who knew how to keep their eyes and ears to themselves, the chamber was empty; even so, he kept his voice low. 'Far from it. You have already been away six years, and that is a long time for the throne to be empty. You know how these things work, my liege: the court grows restive without a strong hand to guide it.'

'Is this a lecture coming?' asked Caledor, irritably. The address had been a triumph; he had no desire to be dragged back into intrigue, something of which there seemed to be an infinite supply in Lothern. 'If so, make it short.'

'Your homecoming has been a success, my liege,' said Hulviar. 'Your position is strengthened, but you are not the only popular name in Ulthuan. Before you returned there was another on the lips of the rabble.'

'Imladrik.'

'Your brother has won renown against the druchii – they have no answer to his dragons. Some whisper that he would wear the crown well, too.'

'Who whispers this?'

'No names, my liege, just rumours. But they persist.'

Caledor shot Hulviar a flinty look. 'My brother has no ambition for the throne. Anyone who knows him would tell you that.'

'Just so, but that – if you will forgive my saying so – is neither here nor there. Others can use Imladrik whether he wishes them to or no.' Hulviar's face was almost apologetic. 'Your brother is the greatest dragon rider of our age, but no statesman. He can be made into a figurehead.'

The beginnings of a scowl formed on Caledor's smooth brow. The joy of his homecoming felt soured, and that darkened his mood. Even now, just at the moment of triumph, the tangled skeins of his family history were ripe to pollute it all. 'Then he must be sent away again,' he muttered. 'He professed to love the colonies; he can mire himself in war there.'

Hulviar nodded, looking satisfied. 'A judicious course, but he will not go willingly. He has taken up residence in Tor Vael.'

'Tor Vael,' said Caledor, scornfully. 'His dreary wife's tower. So *unalike*, those two.'

Hulviar shrugged, as if to say, *what can one do?* 'He seems to find it amenable.'

'He has had the run of it for too long. I shall send messages there. He will not refuse an order.'

'Indeed he will not, but I understand he is not there: he goes to commune with the drakes. Perhaps it would be best to meet him in person, in Kor Evril.'

Caledor shook his head with irritation. 'I love my brother, Hulviar, but the age of the dragons was drawing to a close even before our great-grandsire walked the mountains. He would do better to devote himself to his own kind.'

Hulviar smiled. 'As you have done, my liege.'

'Quite,' agreed Caledor, already preoccupied by the arrangements he would have to make to secure his position. 'See that all this is put in motion, Hulviar. Your advice spoils my mood, but I see the sense of it.'

'It shall be done,' said Hulviar, bowing smoothly.

Sevekai loped along, keeping his head low. Drutheira, Malchior and Ashniel went ahead, guided by their flickering staffs. The tunnels wound their way tortuously up through the mountain's core, worming like maggot-trails in rotten meat. It was hot, dust-choked and treacherous underfoot, but the druchii went as surely as night-ghouls, never pausing, never missing a footing.

So Drutheira had known Kaitar was tainted. She'd kept the knowledge to herself, as close and devious as ever. Sevekai admired that. He admired her perfect calmness in the cause of deception, the effortless way she discarded those who blocked her path back to Naggaroth. He wondered whether the day would come when she tried to dispatch him, too. That would be an interesting challenge, a potentially enjoyable test. Drutheira was powerful, for sure, but he had tricks of his own, some of which he'd kept secret even from her.

He noticed light growing around him. The purple flickers of witch-fire died out, replaced by a thin grey film on the stone. They were jogging up steeply now, angled hard against the heavy press of heart-rock.

'Stay close,' warned Drutheira. 'The dragon flies.'

The tunnel opened up around them. Sevekai caught sight of its entrance – a jagged-toothed mouth, opening out on to a screen of grey.

They ran for it, emerging into the pale light of an overcast day.

They were on another ledge, high on the shoulder of a narrow gorge. Vast, blunt peaks crowded around them with their heads lost in mist. The Arluii mountains were always bleak and rain-shrouded.

Sevekai leaned against the cliff at his back, catching his breath. The ledge was not wide – a few yards at its broadest. To his left it wound higher up, clinging to the gorge-wall like throttle-wire. To his right it snaked down steeply and headed into the gloom of the gorge. Straight ahead was a plunge into nothing. Fronds of mist coiled over the lip of the brink, gusting softly in the chill wind.

'So where is it?' demanded Malchior, turning on Drutheira with a face like murder.

Drutheira looked at him irritably. 'Give it time.'

'We had it in our power,' Malchior insisted. 'Down there. Why did you–'

Before he could finish, a thin cry of anguish rang out over the gorge. They all looked up.

Far up, part-masked by cloud, the black dragon was on the wing. It flew awkwardly, as if flexing muscles that had been cramped for too long.

Sevekai let slip a low whistle. 'Ugly wretch,' he said.

Drutheira laughed. 'Ugly as the night. But it's ours.'

The dragon circled high above them, unwilling to come closer, unable to draw further away. Its screeches were hard to listen to.

Ashniel gazed up at it with the rest of them. 'So what now?'

'This road leads east,' said Drutheira. 'It will take time to break the beast. But when we do–'

She didn't hear the wheezing until too late. None of them did, not even Sevekai whose ears were as sharp as a Cold One's.

He burst out of the tunnel mouth, limping and bleeding with a blade in hand. Sevekai whirled around first, seeing him go for Drutheira. For a moment he thought it was Kaitar, then he saw Hreth's familiar expression of loathing. Left for dead, somehow he'd clawed his way back up to the surface.

Hreth leapt at Drutheira, who was standing on the lip of the ledge. Sevekai pounced instinctively, catching him in mid-leap. The two of them tumbled across the rock. Sevekai felt blood splash over him from Hreth's open wounds.

'Kill it!' cried Drutheira, but he couldn't twist free to see what she was doing. Hreth's fingers gouged at him, scrabbling for his eyes. Sevekai arched his spine, shifting Hreth's weight, ready to push him away.

He caught a brief glimpse of Hreth's face rammed up close to his own. It was just like Kaitar's had been – dull-eyed, hollow, staring. Sevekai suddenly felt a horrific pain in his chest, as if something were sucking his soul from his body.

A wave of purple fire smashed across him, hot as coals. Hreth flew away from him, shrieking just as Kaitar had done. He crashed into the cliff face, burning with witch-light, before springing back at Sevekai.

Sevekai dropped down and darted to one side, but Hreth grabbed his tunic and dragged him to the brink. Another bolt of witch-light slammed into Hreth, propelling him over. With a terrible lurch, Sevekai realised he was going over too.

He tried to jerk back, to shake Hreth off him, to reach for something to grab on to, but it was no good – a final aethyr-bolt blasted Hreth clear, dragging Sevekai along in his wake.

For a moment he felt himself suspended over nothing. He saw Hreth's maddened grimace, felt the spittle flying into his eyes.

'Sevekai!' he heard someone cry – it might have been Drutheira.

Then everything fell away. He tumbled through the void, breaking clear of Hreth and plummeting alone. He had a brief, awful impression of rock racing by him in a blur of speed, the wind snatching at his tunic and a howling in his ears.

Something hit him on the side of the head, rocking it and sending blood-whirls shooting across his eyes. After that he knew no more.

The highlands above Kor Evril had the look of a land cursed. Cairns of ebony littered the steep mountainsides. Little grew. The winds, as hard and biting as any of the Annulii, moaned across an empty stonescape, stirring up ash-like soil and sending it skirling across stone.

Only those of the bloodline of Caledor had learned to appreciate the Dragonspine's stark rawness. Fissures opened up along the flanks of the high places, sending noxious fumes spewing into an unspoiled sky. Foul aromas pooled in the shadows, gathering in mist-shrouded crevasses and lurking over filmy watercourses. The air could be hot against the skin or as frigid as death, depending on which way the capricious wind blew. It was a land of extremes, a battleground of elemental earth, harsh air and raging ocean.

Imladrik stood before the cavern's wide mouth, breathing heavily. His cheeks were flushed from the climb into the Dragonspine, his body lined with sweat. A stench of burning metal rose up from the charred soil. Kor Evril was far below, miles away, down in the fertile lands to the south-east. It had taken two days to reach the cavern, a long, painful slog on foot.

Now at his destination, his eyes shone. He felt invigorated. The sensations, the smells, the incessant low rumble of steam and wind – they were the things he had been born to. Something in his blood responded to it – he had always felt the same way, ever since his father had taken him into the peaks as a child.

'This is the forge of our House,' the great Imrik had told him. 'This is where we were tempered. As the sea is to Eataine and the forests are to Avelorn, the fire-mountains are to Caledor. Forget this truth, and we lose ourselves.'

Imladrik had taken the words to heart, returning to the Dragonspine whenever he could. Even during times of warfare he had made the pilgrimage, renewing himself, reciting afresh the arcane vows he had made so long ago.

A dragon rider was a restless soul, condemned to rove the passages of the air for as long as the bond existed between steed and rider; if he had a home on earth, a true home, then it was the Dragonspine.

'Such a thing has not been seen for many years,' Imladrik said. 'We are honoured, Thoriol.'

Imladrik's travelling companion stood close by. Thoriol tended to his mother in looks, with pale colouring and slender frame. Only his eyes were the same as his father's – emerald, like summer grass.

Thoriol said nothing. He looked doubtful, standing dutifully beside his father, the collar of his robe turned up against the heat rolling down from the cavern entrance.

'I remember my first summoning,' said Imladrik, lost in the memory. 'We tell ourselves that we choose them, but of course they choose us. We are like swifts to them, our lives flitting across the path of theirs.' He smiled broadly. 'But who can tell? Who really understands them? That is the majesty of them: they are an enigma, an impossibility.'

Thoriol drew in a deep breath, wincing against the foul air. He looked paler than normal. 'You are sure this is the place?' he asked.

Imladrik put a reassuring hand on his shoulder. 'I have been watching this peak for ten years. When I saw the first signs, I thought of you. Others have been studying for longer, but – forgive my pride – I wanted you to have the honour. New blood is so rare.'

'And if...' Thoriol broke off. He looked nauseous. 'And if it does not choose me?'

'*She*,' corrected Imladrik. 'Can you not tell from the way the smoke rises? She is a queen of fire.'

Thoriol tried to calm himself. 'I sense nothing. Nothing but this foul air.'

'I taught you,' said Imladrik proudly. 'The songs will come. You have my blood in your veins, son. Take heart.'

Imladrik drew himself to his full height. He was clad in the silver armour he wore when riding Draukhain, embellished with a drake-winged helm and crimson cloak. The runes inlaid into the metal seemed to smoulder, as if aware they were close to the foundries where they had been made. Thoriol, wearing only brown acolyte's robes, looked insubstantial.

Both of them carried swords. Imladrik bore Ifulvin, Thoriol an unnamed blade from the armoury. Once he became a rider it would be rune-engraved and named.

Imladrik raised his blade before him in a gesture of salute.

'Soul of ancient earth!' he cried. 'Wake from sleep! Let your spirit rise, let your heart beat, let your eyes open.'

Thoriol mimicked his father's movements. He shut his eyes, mouthing the words he had been taught in Kor Evril. A thin line of sweat broke out on his brow.

Imladrik felt the familiar thrill of power shudder through him. The cavern mouth gusted with fresh smoke, swirling and tumbling over the dark rocks.

You know my voice, he mind-sang. *You sensed my presence in your long slumber. Come now, answer the call. I have been calling you since you first stirred. Listen. Awaken. Stir.*

The gusts of smoke grew stronger. The air before the cavern entrance seemed to shimmer from sudden heat, and a low hiss emerged.

Thoriol held his ground. Imladrik heard him begin his own dragonsong, haltingly at first, then more assuredly. He had a clear voice; a little tremulous, perhaps, but greater command would come in time.

My will is before you, mind-sang Thoriol. *Bind your will to mine. Our minds shall be joined, our powers merged. We shall become one mind, one power.*

Imladrik felt his heart burn with pride. He remembered singing the same words, many years ago, just as nervous and uncertain as Thoriol was now. It was a momentous thing, to summon and bind a dragon. Once forged the link could never be broken; the names of a dragon rider and his steed ran down together in history: Aenarion and Indraugnir, Caledor Dragontamer and Kalamemnon, Imrik and Maedrethnir.

'She approaches,' Imladrik warned, maintaining the summoning charm but letting Thoriol's voice take over the harmony of the song. 'Do not waver now, I can feel her mind reaching out to yours – seize this moment.'

Thoriol kept singing. His words were clearly enunciated, echoing through the aethyr with perfect clarity. *Our minds shall be joined. Our powers merged. One mind, one power.*

The shadows at the cavern entrance shuddered, shook and were broken. A golden shape, sinuous and dully reflective, slid slowly into the shrouded sunlight. It uncurled itself, stretching out lazily, extending a curved neck atop which rested a sleek, horned head. A pair of golden wings unfurled, splayed out to expose rust-red membranes blotched with black streaks. Two filmy eyes opened, each slitted like a cat's.

The dragon's back arched. Like all her kind, she was massive – many times the height of the figures that stood before her. Her shadow fell across them, throwing down an acrid pall of hot air and embers.

Imladrik gazed up at her. She was magnificent. Though only half the size of the great Draukhain, she still bled that mix of raw potency and feral energy that was the truest mark of the dragon-breed. Her hide glistened as if new-forged metal. Her enormous heart, still sluggish from her long slumber, began to pulse more firmly.

Thoriol took a step closer, his blade raised. Imladrik could sense his trepidation. Every fibre of his being longed to help him, to ease the passage between them, but this was something Thoriol had to do for himself.

The stirring of a hot-blood, a Sun Dragon, was a rare thing, and such spirits were hard to tame. Though they couldn't match the sheer power of the Star Dragons or the cool splendour of the Moon Dragons, they brought a wildness and vivacity that thrilled the heart of any true Caledorian. This one was young, perhaps no more than a few centuries. Imladrik could sense her fearlessness, her savagery.

At that instant, he knew her name: Terakhallia. The word burned on to his mind as if branded there.

Our powers merged. One mind, one power.

Thoriol's mind-song continued. His voice became more powerful. Imladrik listened with pride. Terakhallia drew closer, taking cautious steps down the slope towards the young acolyte. Her great head lowered, bringing her jawline almost down to the level of Thoriol's sword. For a moment the two of them stayed like that, locked in the mystical dragon-song, bound by a symphony as old as the winds of magic.

One mind, one power.

Then, without warning, Terakhallia belched a gout of ink-black smoke, coiled her tail, and pounced into the air. The downdraft was tremendous, knocking Thoriol to his knees and nearly sending Imladrik reeling.

Thoriol cried aloud. The bond was cut.

'Father!' he gasped, instinctively, his blade clattering across the stones.

Imladrik recovered himself and watched, grimly, as the serpentine form rippled up into the heavens. Terakhallia's golden body flashed in the sunlight. Her blood-red wings flexed, propelling her upwards like an arrow leaving the bowstring. It was over so quickly. Once aloft, a dragon moved as fast as a stormfront, thrusting powerfully on wings the size of a hawkship's sails.

Imladrik felt his heart sink. For a moment longer he watched the Sun Dragon gain height. He had the power to call her back. If he chose, he could command her; alone of all the asur living, he could have summoned her back to earth.

But that would have been unforgivable. He would not do it, not even for his son.

Imladrik glanced at Thoriol. As he did so, catching the boy's anguish, he felt a pang of remorse.

'Why?' asked Thoriol, standing up again with difficulty. 'What did I do wrong?'

Imladrik shook his head. 'Nothing, lad. They are wild spirits. Some answer, some do not. It has always been that way.'

Thoriol's face creased with misery. The exertion of the dragonsong was considerable; he looked suddenly drained, his shoulders slumped, his blade discarded. 'I knew it,' he muttered. 'It was too soon.'

Imladrik went over to him. He knew the pain of a severed link, of a bond that was not completed. 'There will be others, son. Do not...'

'You *knew!*' cried Thoriol, his eyes wide with anger. 'You knew. Why did you even bring me?'

Imladrik halted. 'Nothing is certain. Dragons are not tame.'

'Neither am I.'

Thoriol pushed past Imladrik, ignoring his lost sword and limping down the slope, away from the cavern entrance.

'There are others!' Imladrik called after him.

Thoriol kept on walking. Imladrik watched him go.

Was he too young? he asked himself. *Did I push him too fast?*

He went over to the sword and picked it up. The steel at its tip was scorched from Terakhallia's fiery breath. The Sun Dragon was long gone, free on the mountain air. She would not return for many days, and when she did her soul would be even wilder, even harder to bond with.

Imladrik felt failure press on him. Perhaps their spirits had been misaligned. Perhaps the boy needed more time. Perhaps he himself was to blame.

He tried not to let himself consider the alternative, the possibility that burned away in his mind like a torturer's blade: that Thoriol did not have the gift, that unless the fates granted Imladrik and Yethanial another child, mastery of dragons would die with him and the House of Tor Caled would never produce a rider again.

I could not live with that.

Moving slowly, his heart heavy, Imladrik began to walk. He would have to hurry to catch Thoriol; when the boy's temper cooled, they would talk, discuss what had happened, learn from it.

Even as he thought it, though, he knew that the failure would change everything. Something new was needed, and he had no idea what it would be.

Imladrik shook his head, pushing against the ashen wind and picking up his pace. His mood of exhilaration had been doused; the descent to Kor Evril would be harder than the climb.

FIVE

Drutheira stared out at the sun setting over the Arluii. Neither of the others had spoken to her since the grim trek down from the gorge, not even Ashniel. Occasionally she had caught them looking sidelong at her, but the accusatory gazes had quickly fallen away. They were still scared of her. Sullen, but scared.

Now, crouched around a meagre fire and with the wind snatching at their robes, the questions came haltingly.

'You're sure you finished it?' asked Malchior.

'Of course I'm sure,' snapped Drutheira.

'But Hreth–' started Ashniel.

'It wasn't Hreth. Khaine's blood, even you could see that.'

'Kaitar,' said Malchior.

'Yes. Or whatever was inside Kaitar. And we banished them both.'

Drutheira found it hard to concentrate. Her mind kept going back to the final glimpse of Sevekai as he sailed over the edge. The Hreth-thing had been little more than a grasping bundle of ashes by then, but Sevekai had been alive.

She shouldn't have cared, and didn't know why she did. They had shared a bed together, of course, but Drutheira had shared the beds of many druchii and not mourned their deaths a jot. Their relationship had been neither close nor deep; they had been thrown together by their orders, both refugees in the grime of Elthin Arvan seeking a way home, so she should have cared as little for Sevekai's death as she had for all the other many deaths she had either caused or witnessed.

Perhaps it was the fatigue. She felt like she had been crawling across the wastelands forever, hunted by both dawi and asur, forced to creep into mountain hollows and make temporary homes in the trackless forest like any common bandit. Even the simple task of getting back to Naggaroth had proven beyond her. For the first time in centuries, she felt vulnerable.

Are we still capable of loyalty? she mused, watching the sun sink lazily towards the western horizon. *Do we even remember what it is? Could we go back?*

She knew the answer to that even as she asked the question. They had all made their choices a long time ago; she certainly had. Sevekai had been so young – he'd had no knowledge of the Ulthuan that had been, the one that she had fought alongside Malekith for mastery of. He could never have known how deep the wounds ran; he had not lived long enough to learn to hate purely, not like she had.

For a long time hatred had been enough to drive her onwards: hatred of the asur, hatred and contempt for the dawi, hatred of those in Naggaroth who had plotted and connived to see her exiled to the wretched east in pursuit of a mission of thankless drudgery. Now, perhaps, the energy of that hatred had dissipated a little.

I am exhausted, she admitted to herself at last. *Unless I find a way to leave this place, to recover my spirit and find fresh purpose, I will die here.*

'So what of Kaitar, then?' came Ashniel's voice again, breaking Drutheira's moody thoughts. 'Still you tell us nothing.'

Drutheira glared at her. The three of them sat on blunt stones in a rocky clearing. The fire burned fitfully in the centre of the circle, guttering as the mountain wind pulled at it. Mountain peaks, darkening in the dusk, stretched away in every direction. The Arluii range was big, and they were still a long way from reaching its margins.

'What do *you* think he was?' asked Drutheira.

'Daemon-kind,' said Malchior firmly.

'How astute,' said Drutheira acidly.

'But why?' asked Ashniel. 'Kaitar was with Sevekai for years. He followed orders, he killed when told to. Can you be sure?'

'You saw it leap. It was a shell. As was Hreth.' She poked at the fire with her boot. 'Banished, not killed. You never truly kill them.'

Malchior kept looking at her, a steady glare. 'How long did you know?'

'A while. Sevekai guessed it too.' Drutheira suppressed a glower. Malchior was a thug, not half as clever as he supposed, and explaining herself to the two of them was tiresome. 'But none of my arts would divine it. For as long as the orders from Malekith were in force I couldn't move against him, but it has been over a year now since I was able to commune. Time to test Kaitar's mettle, I thought.'

Ashniel snorted. '*Test* it?'

'If he had been druchii the dragon would not have harmed him. Up until then, believe me, I was not certain.'

'So it was all for him,' said Malchior. 'The dragon in the dark.'

'I've been hunting that dragon for thirty years. An opportunity presented itself: skin two slaves with one knife.'

The dragon still shadowed them. She had not yet attempted to ride it – it was too soon. Its spirit was wild and frenzied, damaged like a cur beaten too often by its owner. The only thing stopping it from killing them all was the bond of magic placed on it hundreds of years ago.

Urislakh, it had once been called; the Bloodfang. The black dragon still answered to that name, though only grudgingly, as if unwilling to remember what it had been in earlier ages.

She didn't know where it was at that moment. Possibly aloft and out of sight, possibly curled up in some dank crevasse hissing out its misery. The beast would come back when Drutheira summoned it – her leash was long, but it was still a leash.

Ashniel still looked pensive. 'So what does it mean?' Her frail, almost fey features were lit red by the firelight, exposing the hollowness of her cheeks. The rose-cheeked bloom she had once worn when in the carefree courts of ancient Nagarythe had long since left her. 'Was Kaitar one of Malekith's creatures?'

Drutheira shook her head. 'Daemons serve their own kind. We have been duped.'

She let the words sink in. It was a shameful admission. No greater crime existed in Naggaroth than to be made a fool of, to be deceived by a lesser race; and of course, to the druchii, *every* race was a lesser race.

'But for what?' asked Malchior, speaking slowly as his mind worked. 'What was its purpose?'

'Who knows?' said Drutheira impatiently. 'Maybe it was watching us. Maybe it was whispering everything we did to its dark masters. Maybe it was bored by an eternity of madness. You should have asked it before we killed it. Perhaps it would have told you.'

Malchior flushed. 'Don't jest.'

Drutheira sneered at him. 'I wouldn't dream of it. We have already been made fools enough.'

'So you care not.'

'Of course I care!' she shouted. The firelight flickered as her sudden movement guttered the flames. She collected herself. 'It still lives, somewhere. We have lost four of our number. The asur and the dawi will kill us when they find us. That is it. That is the situation. Of course I care.'

Neither Ashniel nor Malchior replied to that. Ashniel chewed her lower lip, thinking hard; Malchior stared moodily into the fire. Drutheira watched them scornfully. Their minds worked so sluggishly.

'Then what do we do?' asked Ashniel eventually.

Drutheira sighed. The sun had nearly set. Shadows had spread across the clearing and the air had become chill. She felt weary to her bones. 'What we have been trying to do: get back to Naggaroth. I cannot commune, so we must get to the coast. Malekith must be told that he has daemons amongst his servants.'

Malchior looked up at her, his eyes bright with a sudden idea. 'We have a steed.'

'It will not bear us all,' Drutheira said. She watched the last sliver of sunlight drain away in the west. In advance of the moons rising, the world looked empty and drenched in gloom. 'In any case, I did not raise the beast merely to test my suspicions of Kaitar. We have more than one enemy in Elthin Arvan.'

Her eyes narrowed as she remembered her humiliation, years ago, at the hands of the asur mage on the scarlet dragon. The pain of it had never diminished. The long privation since then had only honed the sharp edge of her desire for vengeance.

'We cannot leave yet,' she said, her voice low. 'Not until I find the bitch who wounded me.'

She smiled in the dark. She could sense Bloodfang's presence, out in the night, curled up in its own endless misery.

'And we have a dragon of our own now,' she breathed.

Liandra heard the voice before she awoke. It echoed briefly in the space between waking and sleep – the blurred landscape where dreams played.

Feleth-amina.

She stirred, her mind sluggish, her body still locked in slumber. Then her eyes snapped open and her mind rushed into awareness. She had been dreaming of Ulthuan, of fields of wildflowers in the lee of the eastern Annulii, rustling in sunlit wind.

Feleth-amina.

Fire-child: that was what the dragons called her. The dragons always gave their riders new names. They found Eltharin, she was told, childish.

Liandra pushed the sheets back. It was cold. Nights of Kor Vanaeth were always cold, even in the height of summer. Shivering, she reached for her robes and pulled them over her head. Then, barefoot, she shuffled across the stone floor of her chamber to the shuttered window.

Feleth-amina.

It was Vranesh's mind-voice. Those playful, savage tones had been a part of Liandra's life almost as long as she could remember. The two of them had been bonded for so long that she struggled to recall a time when the link had not been present.

Where are you? she returned, fumbling with the shutter clasp.

You know. Come now.

Liandra opened the heavy wooden shutters, revealing a stone balcony beyond. Starlight threw a silver glaze across the squat, unfinished rooftops of Kor Vanaeth. Her tower was the tallest of those that still stood, though that was hardly saying much.

Vranesh was perched on the edge of the railing, waiting for her. The sight was incongruous – Liandra half-expected the balustrade to collapse under the weight at any moment.

I was asleep, she sang, still blurry.

You were dreaming. I could see the images. Your dreams are like my dreams.

Liandra rubbed her eyes and reached up to Vranesh's shoulder. Familiar aromas of smoke and embers filled her nostrils.

Do you dream? she sang.

I have known sleep to last for centuries. I have had dreams longer than mortal lifetimes.

Sleep to last for centuries, sang Liandra ruefully, settling into position and readying herself for Vranesh's leap aloft. *That would be nice.*

The dragon pounced. A sudden rush of cold wind banished the last of Liandra's sluggishness. She drew in a long breath, then shivered. It would have been prudent to have worn a cloak.

'So what is this?' she said out loud, crouching low as Vranesh's wing beats powered the two of them higher. 'Could it not have waited?'

Below them, Kor Vanaeth began to slip away.

It could have waited, but the mood was on me. You have not summoned me for an age, and I grow bored.

Liandra winced. That was true enough. She had been over-occupied with the rebuilding for too long and, in the few quiet moments she had had to herself in the past few months, she had known it.

Forgive me, she said, her mind-voice chastened.

Vranesh belched a mushroom of flame from her nostrils and bucked in mid-air. The gesture was violent; it was what passed for a laugh. *Forgive you? I do not forgive.*

Imladrik had told her that. Liandra remembered him explaining it to her, back when she had asked why the dragons suffered riders to take them into wars they had no part in.

'They do not suffer us,' he had said. 'They have no masters, no obligations, no code of laws. They do what they do, and that is all that can be said of them. These things: blame, regret, servitude – they have no meaning to a dragon.'

'What does have meaning to them?' she had asked.

She could still see his emerald eyes glittering as he answered. 'Risk. Splendour. Extravagance. If you had lived for a thousand ages of the world, that is all you would care about, too.'

I cannot remain here all night, she sang to Vranesh. *I will freeze, even with your breath to warm me.*

Vranesh kept going higher, pulling into the thinner airs. *You will be fine. I wish to show you something.*

The stars around them grew sharper. Wisps of cloud, little more than dark-blue gauzes, swept below. The landscape of Elthin Arvan stretched away towards all horizons, ink-black and brooding. Faint silver light picked out the mottled outlines of the forest – Loren Lacoi, the Great Wood. The trees seemed to extend across an infinite distance, throttling all else, choking anything that threatened their dominance.

You are changing my vision, sang Liandra.

Not my doing.

Liandra smiled sceptically. Vranesh had only a semi-respectful relationship with the truth.

Let us call it coincidence, Liandra sang.

Something had definitely changed. She could see far further than usual and the detail was tighter. She almost fancied she could see all the way to the Arluii range, or perhaps the Saraeluii, impossibly far to the east.

Tell me what you can see, sang Vranesh.

Liandra narrowed her eyes as the dragon swung around, giving her a sweeping view of all that lay beneath them. Stark sensations crowded into her mind. The intensity was almost painful.

'I see lights in the dark,' she said softly, speaking aloud again. 'Just pinpricks. Are they watchfires?'

They are the lights of cities, sang Vranesh.

'Ah, yes. That is Tor Alessi, along the river to the coast. And Athel Maraya, deep in the forest. How is this possible? And that must be Athel Toralien. They are like scattered jewels.'

What else do you see?

'I see the forest in between them,' said Liandra. 'I see the whole of Elthin Arvan resisting us. We are invaders here. The forest is old. It hates us.'

Vranesh wheeled back round, pulling to the east. Her body rippled through the air like an eel in water, as sinuous as coiled rope. *It does not hate. It just is.*

Like the dragons, Liandra sang.

There are many things we hate. What else do you see?

Vranesh flew eastwards. The dragon's speed and strength in the air were formidable. Liandra doubted any were faster on the wing, save of course the mighty Draukhain. Ahead of them, blurred by distance and the vagaries of magical sight, reared the Saraeluii. Liandra had visited them many times, always in the company of Imladrik. Those mountains were truly vast, far larger than the Arluii, greater in extent even than the Annulii of home.

They daunted her. The dark peaks glowered in the night, their flanks sheer and their shadows deep. She had never enjoyed spending time in those mountains – that was the dawi's realm, and even before war had come it had felt hostile and strange. She looked hard, peering into the gloom. She began to see things stirring.

I see armies, she sang, slowly. As Vranesh swept across the heavens in broad, gliding arcs, she saw more and more. *Huge armies. I see forges lit red, like wounds in the world. I see smoke, and fire, and the beating of iron hammers.*

It was as if the entire range were alive, crawling like a hill of angry insects. Pillars of smog polluted the skies. The earth in the lightless valleys shook under the massed tread of ironshod boots.

Endless, Liandra sang, inflecting the harmonic with wonder. *So many.*

Vranesh swung around again. *Now you see what your scouts have seen. You see why you are needed. The storm is coming. It will roll down from those mountains soon and it will tear towards the sea.*

Liandra sighed. She understood why the dragon had shown her such things. *Kor Vanaeth cannot stand*, she sang.

I did not say that. But you should think on where your powers are best employed. You should see what choices await you.

Liandra's mind-voice fell silent. She had always known that hard decisions would come again. Like water returning to the boil, she felt her ever-present anger rising to the surface.

They killed thousands at Kor Vanaeth, she sang bitterly.

They did. We both saw it.

Liandra clenched her fists, just as she always did. The gesture had become habitual. *I wish for nothing but to see them burn.*

The druchii first, sang Vranesh. *Now the dawi. Can you really kill them all?*

The night seemed to gather itself around her as the dragon soared. It toughened her resolve, helped her to see things clearly. Salendor was already preparing to march, to bring the war back to the stunted ones before they could seize the initiative. Perhaps he was right to.

I cannot, she sang savagely, feeling the lava-hot energy of the beast beneath her. *But you can.*

Sevekai awoke.

For a long period he didn't try to move. The spirals of pain were too acute, too complete. More than one bone was broken, and he saw nothing from his left eye. A vague, numb gap existed where sensations from his limbs should have been.

At first he thought he might have been blinded. Then, much later, the sun rose and he saw that he had awoken during the night. Little enough of the sun's warmth penetrated down to the gorge floor, though – the difference between night and day was no more than a dull, creeping shade of grey.

When he finally summoned up the effort to shift position, the agony nearly made him pass out. He tried three times to pull himself to his knees. He failed three times. Only on the fourth attempt, dizzy with the effort, did he drag himself into something like a huddled crouch.

He was terribly, horribly cold. The shade seemed eternal. The rocks around him were covered with thin sheens of globular moss. Moisture glistened in the underhangs, dripping quietly. When he shivered from the chill, fresh pricks of pain rushed up his spine.

Awareness came back to him in a series of mismatched recollections. He remembered a long trek into the mountains with the others. He remembered Drutheira's black-lined eyes staring into his, the raids on trading caravans deep in the shadow of the woods and then the dull-faced visage of Kaitar.

Kaitar.

That name brought a shudder; he couldn't quite remember why. Something had been wrong with Kaitar. Had he died? Had something terrible happened to all of them?

Sevekai's forehead slumped, exhausted, back against the rock. He felt his lips press up against moss. Moisture ran into his mouth, pressed from thick green spores. It dribbled down his chin, and he sucked it up.

It was then that he realised just how thirsty he was. He pushed himself down further, ignoring flaring aches in his back and sides, hunting for more water.

Only when he had trawled through shallow puddles under low-hanging lichen and licked the dribbling channels from the tops of stones did he feel something of a sense of self-possession begin to return. He lay on his back, breathing shallowly.

He had fallen a long way. He could see that now, twisting his head and gazing up at the sheer sides of the gorge. A hundred feet? Two hundred? He should be dead. The rubble that had come down with him alone should have finished him off.

Sevekai smiled, though it cracked his lips and made them bleed. It was all so ludicrous.

Perhaps this is death, he thought. *Perhaps I shall haunt this place for a thousand years.*

He looked up again. As his senses became sharper, as his mind put itself back together again, his thoughts became less fanciful.

For fifty feet or so below the ruined ledge he'd fallen from, the rock ran straight down, a cliff of granite without break or handhold. Then, as it curved inwards towards the gorge's floor, it began to choke up with a tangled mess of briars, scrub and hunched trees. Down in the primordial gloom, a mournful swathe of vegetation had taken hold, clinging on grimly in the perpetual twilight. It was dense and damp, overlapping and strangling itself in a blind attempt to claw upwards to the light.

For all its gnarly ugliness, that creeping canopy was what had saved him. As Sevekai gazed upward he could see the path he had taken down – crashing through the branches of a wizened, black-barked shrub before rolling down across a clump of thornweed and into the moss-covered jumble of rocks where he now found himself.

It was still unlikely. He should still have died.

He let his head fall back again. He could feel the heavy burden of unconsciousness creeping up on those parts of him that still gave him any sensation at all. Night would come again soon, and with it the piercing cold. He was alone, forgotten by those he had trekked up into the mountains with. He knew enough of the wilds to know that strange creatures would be quick to sniff out wounded prey in their midst. He was broken, he was frail, he was isolated.

A crooked smile broke out again, marring the severe lines of his thin face. He felt no fear. Part of him wondered whether the plummet had purged fear from him; if so, that would be some liberation.

I will not die in this place, he mouthed silently. He did not say the words to encourage himself; it was just a statement of belief. He knew it, as clearly as he knew that his body would recover and his strength would return. The scions of Naggaroth were made of hard stuff: forged in the ice, sleet and terror of the dark realm. It took a lot to kill one – you had to twist the dagger in deep, turning it tight until the blood ran black.

He had killed so many times, had ended so many lives, and yet Morai-Heg still failed to summon him to her underworld throne for reckoning.

Even as the light overhead died, sending Sevekai back into a dim-lit world of frost and pain, the smile did not leave his face.

I will not die in this place.

SIX

Yethanial looked up from her work, irritated. She had slipped with her last stroke, jabbing the tip of the quill across the vellum. The servant was well aware of his crime, and waited nervously.

'I told you I was not to be disturbed,' said Yethanial.

'Yes, my lady, but he would not accept my word. He is highborn, and refuses to leave.'

Yethanial looked down at her work again. At times she wondered why she cared so much. No one other than her would ever read it.

'Tell him to wait in the great hall,' she said. 'I will see him there.'

The servant bowed, and made to leave Yethanial's chamber.

'Wait,' she said, lifting her head. 'What did you say his name was?'

'Caradryel, of the House of Reveniol.'

'I have never heard of it.'

'From Yvresse, I believe.'

Yethanial shook her head. 'There are more noble houses in Ulthuan than there are trees in Avelorn. What does that tell us?'

The servant looked uncertain. 'I do not know, my lady.'

Yethanial shot him a scornful glance. 'Deliver the message. I will come down when I am ready.'

He was waiting for her in Tor Vael's great hall. 'Great' was somewhat optimistic; the space was modest, capable of holding no more than several dozen guests, bare-walled and with only a few drab hangings to lighten the stonework. The fireplace was empty and had not been used for years. Yethanial did not often entertain guests; as she had often complained to Imladrik, she found their conversation tiresome and their manners swinish.

The present occupant lounged casually in one of the two great chairs set before the granite mantelpiece. His long blond hair was artfully arranged, swept back from a sleek face in what Yethanial supposed was the latest fashion in the cities. He wore a long robe of damask silk, a burgundy red with gold detail. It looked fabulously expensive.

Yethanial walked up to him. He did not rise to greet her.

'My servants tell me you will not leave,' she said.

Caradryel raised a thin eyebrow. 'That is not much of a greeting.'

'I have important work. State your business.'

He settled into the chair more comfortably. 'Ah, yes. The scholar-lady. You are spoken well of in Hoeth.'

Yethanial paused. 'Hoeth? You bring word from the loremasters?'

Caradryel laughed; an easy, untroubled sound. 'Loremasters? Not my profession, I'm afraid. I only use parchment to light fires.'

Yethanial folded her arms. She knew that she must look impossibly drab next to him in her grey shift and barely-combed hair, and cared nothing for it. 'Then you are running out of time here.'

'Something I am sure you must be short of, so I will come to the meat of it.' He pushed himself up higher in his seat. 'I was serving in the fleets, sent there by a father who despairs of my ever performing gainful service to the Crown. He is wrong about that, as it turns out, but that is not something you or he need worry about. My time aboard ship turned out to be instructive, though not in the way he hoped for.'

'I am just burning to know how.'

Caradryel flashed her another smile – the effortless, artful smile of one who has spent his life flitting through the privileged circles of courtly classes. 'I saw a strange thing. We were attacked by corsairs. I have never been one to scare easily, being of the view that my destiny is almost certainly a great one and thus the gods have a clear incentive to keep me alive, but I admit that I did not like the way the situation looked. I had made my preparations to meet death in a suitable manner when, quite unexpectedly, salvation came out of an empty sky.'

Yethanial struggled to control her impatience. Caradryel clearly enjoyed the sound of his own voice and fancied himself a storyteller. She could see the steady confidence radiating from his languid frame and wondered what, if anything, justified it.

'A *dragon rider*, my lady,' Caradryel went on. 'Rare enough even on the fields of war. Vanishingly rare in the open seas. When the shock of it had faded, I reflected on that. I could not help but feel that my earlier judgement had been vindicated: I am being preserved for something special. That is a comfort to me, as you might imagine.'

'Or a delusion.'

'Quite; time will tell which. But here is the thing: the rider was your husband, the King's brother. When this became known, the crew of the ship fell into the kind of fawning adulation that is embarrassing unless directed at oneself. And that prompted me to think further on it.'

'Any brevity you can muster would be welcome,' sighed Yethanial.

'Our beloved ruler, Caledor the Second, has returned to Ulthuan. His victory in the east has bolstered his strength at court, but he is not without enemies, who think him vain and unwise. Factions exist that wish for an end to the fighting in Elthin Arvan. They would not move against him openly, but there are other things they can do to undermine a king. I know how the courts work, my lady, and so does he. The crown does not suffer rivals. Caledor will act; he may have already done so. Your husband, you should know, will not be suffered to remain in Ulthuan.'

Yethanial smiled thinly. 'And you understand all of this from one chance encounter at sea.'

Caradryel shrugged. 'That was the start of it. I have friends in all sorts of interesting places, and they tell me the same thing. A story is being whispered all across Ulthuan, passed from shadow to shadow.' He gave her a sad, almost sincere, smile. 'Lord Imladrik will be sent back to the colonies, my lady. Nothing can prevent it.'

Yethanial felt her face grow pale. 'Is this why you came?' she demanded. 'To pass on tittle-tattle and gossip?'

'Not at all. I can do that far more productively in Lothern.' Caradryel rose from his chair and bowed floridly. 'I came to offer my services.'

For a moment, Yethanial was lost for words. As she struggled, Caradryel kept talking.

'They say your husband is the greatest dragon rider since the days of the Dragontamer. Having seen his prowess at first hand, I have no doubt they are right. When it comes to the arts of state, though, he is a neophyte. My guess is that he thinks statecraft beneath him, as do you. You despise the likes of me; you think us gaudy parasites on the real business of life. Of course you are right: we are parasites. But necessary ones.'

Caradryel fixed her with a serious look, the first he had given her.

'I can help him,' he said. 'I can guide him. When he is alone in Elthin Arvan, beset by enemies on both sides of the walls, I can give him counsel. Believe me, he will need it.'

Yethanial's surprise ebbed, giving way to anger. Caradryel must have been half her age, and yet felt free to lecture her as if speaking to a child. She drew closer to him, noticing for the first time that she was taller.

'Save your counsel,' she said coldly. 'It, and your presence here, are not welcome. I do not know to whom you have been speaking, nor do I care to. My husband's business is here in Tor Vael and it is no one's concern but his and mine. You clearly have little regard for the sensibilities of this house, so let me enlighten you: three dozen guards stand ready on the far side of this door. Should I order it, they will rip those robes from your back and drive you all the way back to Yvresse for the sport of your long-suffering subjects. I am close to giving that order. If you disbelieve me, feel free to provoke me further.'

Caradryel met her gaze for a little while. His blue eyes flickered back and forth, as if testing her resolve, or perhaps his own. Eventually they dropped, and the smile melted from his face. 'So be it,' he said, adopting a breezy, resigned tone without much conviction. 'I made the offer. That is all I can do.'

Yethanial said nothing. For some reason, her heart was beating hard.

Caradryel bowed. 'I was told you were a shy soul, my lady, much taken up with books. I see that you have been undersold.' He started to walk away. 'Should you change your mind–'

'I will not change my mind.'

'Just in case, I can be found at Faer-Lyen. You will not have to look hard; I have many friends who know me well.'

'How fortunate for them.'

Caradryel smiled again ruefully, reached the doors, and took the handle. He almost said something else, but seemed to change his mind. He bowed, turned on his heel and slipped through them. As he departed, his damask robes gave a final flourish.

Yethanial watched him go. Only once the doors had closed did she look down at her hands. They trembled slightly.

She had spoken as firmly as she was able, something she disliked doing. Perhaps it had fooled him. She had not fooled herself, though. His prediction had shaken her; his assertiveness had shaken her.

She stirred herself, ready to climb the stairs to her chamber and start the process of writing again. As she prepared her mind for the labour, though, she knew it would not come easily this time. The moment had gone. Other thoughts would preoccupy her now, ones that she had believed consigned to the past over thirty years ago.

Lord Imladrik will be sent back to the colonies, my lady. Nothing can prevent it.

That was not true. It could not be true – those days were done with, over.

Yethanial moved away from the fireplace, forcing a measure of calm onto her speculating mind. She pushed Caradryel's infuriating smugness from her thoughts, returning to the labour of scholarship that had occupied her before his interruption.

I will not permit it. I have my dignity.

She reached the stairs and started to climb, her grey robes whispering across the stone.

Nothing can prevent it.

Imladrik had never loved Kor Evril. Its walls were dark, hewn from the volcanic rock that riddled Caledor and gave the kingdom its untamed aspect. They were as old as the bones of Ulthuan, having been raised in the days when Aenarion still walked the earth and daemons sang unchecked in the aethyr.

He preferred the open sky. Walls made him restless; towers made him feel confined. Perhaps it was the dragons that had done it to him; once one had ridden on the high paths, circling under the sun with the whole world laid out like a crumpled sheaf of parchment, the confinement of mortal chambers became hard to bear.

Imrik, his father, the one known to Ulthuan as Caledor I, had warned him of it. 'They say steed and rider become alike,' he had said. 'They get into your mind, the dragons. Beware of that: they are creatures of another world. Never believe you control them. They only come to you if they see themselves already inside you – the dragon becomes you, you become the dragon.'

Imladrik knew the truth of that. He had started to speak like Draukhain, even to think like him. When they were apart, which was most of the time, he would sometimes catch himself pondering strange images of far-off mountains or shorelines. He knew then that Draukhain was on the wing, perhaps thousands of leagues distant, and that the great creature's mind was reaching out to him.

Did he share such an understanding with any of his own kind. With Thoriol? With Yethanial? He wanted to say that he did.

But he had never shared their minds as he had shared Draukhain's. He had never become one with them, lost in the joy of flight, of killing, in the perfect freedom that had existed since before the coming of the ancients and the ordering of the earth into its mortal realms and jealousies.

At times he felt like one of the poor fools who sipped the nectar of the poppy, forgetting themselves, gradually slipping from the real world. They, too, lost themselves in dreams. How different was he to them? If he wanted to, could he break free of it?

Possibly. But the question was moot; he would never want to.

He approached Kor Evril's gates on foot. A clarion sounded and the heavy wooden doors swung inwards. Guards raced out to greet him, bowing the knee and lowering iron spear tips in homage. They bore the colours of his House – crimson, bone-white, black.

Imladrik strode past them, barely checking his stride. 'Where is my son?'

'He has not been seen, my lord,' replied one of the guards, hurrying to follow him. 'I thought he was with–'

'He was,' said Imladrik grimly. 'He chose to descend alone.' He walked briskly through the narrow streets, ignoring the startled looks of his people. They stared at him from narrow windows. They were not used to seeing their lord travel without an escort, with the black dust of the mountain caking his robes and with two swords in his hands. 'He was not seen on the road?'

'He was not,' said the guard. 'I will send out patrols.'

'No need. I know where he has gone. I will go after him myself.'

The guard bowed, struggling to keep pace as Imladrik pushed up towards the citadel's main tower. 'My lord, there is something else.'

'Make it brief,' snapped Imladrik, maintaining his pace. His failure with Thoriol still rankled. The ceaseless war with the druchii would call him away again soon, so he needed to make his peace before then. The two of them needed to speak, like a father and son should. His duties had always taken him away. That was the cause of the rift – it could be healed, given time, given patience.

'The King is here, lord,' said the guard, looking up at Imladrik's stern face with some trepidation. 'He arrived last night.'

By then Imladrik was approaching the central tower, his own keep, and he could see it for himself. Two banners hung over the gateway: one the gold and white of the Phoenix Kings, the other the pale blue of Caledor II.

He felt his heart sink. He gazed up at the high window, knowing that Menlaeth would have installed himself in there with his entourage, waiting for his subject to come to him.

It was a petty indignity. Imladrik paused, toying with the idea of turning on his heels. He was the inheritor of the title once carried by his illustrious ancestor, and need bow to no living monarch.

'My lord?' asked the guard, hovering uncertainly. 'Shall I send word that you are coming?'

Imladrik briefly glanced up at the sky – a wistful look. He half expected to see Draukhain up there somewhere, spiralling in the emptiness, his long sapphire body twisting in perfect freedom.

The dragon becomes you, you become the dragon.

'Do no such thing,' he said dryly, pushing the doors open and walking inside. 'I shall announce myself. It is always nice to give my brother a surprise.'

Imladrik's audience chamber was a long, many-pillared space, lit by tall arched windows that sent clear bars of sunlight across the stone floor. At the far end stood a low dais, upon which sat a throne of obsidian. Imrik's old battle-standard hung behind the throne, scorched at the edges. The dragon's-head device had faded over the years.

Caledor filled the throne out pretty well. His fur-lined robes spilled over the arms. His longsword, Lathrain, rested against the obsidian, still sheathed in its ancient wound-metal scabbard. Hulviar, the king's seneschal, crouched on the steps to one side, wearing a high-collared jerkin of worsted wool and a thick cloak.

Imladrik smiled to himself. Hulviar had always felt the cold.

'Brother,' said Caledor warmly, rising from the throne and coming to greet him.

Imladrik met the embrace, kissing his brother on both cheeks.

'You look terrible,' Caledor said. 'You *smell* terrible. Have you been rolling in charcoal?'

'I have been in the mountains,' replied Imladrik, thinking much the same about his brother's primped and perfumed attire. 'It takes its toll.'

'Your people told me you were up there,' said Caledor, returning to the throne and brushing his robes down. 'I asked when you would return and I was told that no one knew. It could be tomorrow, it could be in a month, they said.'

Imladrik stood upright before the dais. He could feel his muscles ache from the long hike down but did not send for a chair. 'What do you want, Menlaeth? I am tired, I have much to do. If you'd wanted me I could have come to Lothern.'

'I know, brother, but are you not grateful? *I* have come to see *you*. Not every King would have made such an effort. Can you imagine our father doing it?' Caledor's face clouded. 'Can you imagine him ever pulling himself away from his wars long enough to speak to either of us?'

'No, I cannot.'

'Now I am back from wars of my own, and it has been too long since we spoke. So I am here, and I am glad to see you, though I am not sure I would have waited a month for the privilege.'

Imladrik glanced at Hulviar, who studiously ignored his gaze. 'I heard your reception in Lothern was worth seeing.'

Caledor inclined his head modestly. 'It was. And our passage across the seas was equally splendid, thanks to the escorts you arranged. I am grateful.'

Imladrik paused. Was he being sarcastic? He couldn't read his brother's expressions any more. For that matter, he couldn't read anyone's expressions any more. 'Please, Menlaeth,' he said. 'Tell me why you are here.'

'Very well,' said Caledor. 'I am sending you back to Elthin Arvan.'

Imladrik stood stock still. The words hit him hard. For a moment, he thought he might have misheard. Then he thought that Caledor might have misspoken. Then he realised that no error had been committed – that was what he was being told.

'This is an honour for you,' Caledor went on. 'The dawi are easy prey: we will have victory after victory. I have seen for myself the glory it brings. You too will earn a reception in Lothern, and they will greet you as they did me – like a god.'

'Madness.' The words seemed to spill out of their own accord. 'You were barely there a year. You have seen only a tithe of their strength.'

Caledor shot him an indulgent look. 'No doubt! No doubt there are thousands more, and you can root them out, one after the next. You can take the dragons, too, as many of them as will cross the ocean. Imagine when the dwarfs see *them*. I don't think they truly realise what a weapon they are.'

'They are not weapons,' said Imladrik, his voice low.

'Of course, no, they are not: they are ancient and wonderful beings. I forget that sometimes, so it is good to have you here to remind me.'

Imladrik struggled to keep his anger down, mindful of where he was and whom he spoke with. 'I cannot go back,' he said. 'Not now. We are taking the war to the druchii. A thousand plans are in motion. My troops–'

'–will serve just as ably under another commander,' said Caledor coolly. 'And what is this "I cannot"? Is that how you were schooled to talk to Kings?'

'I am used to Kings making wiser choices,' said Imladrik.

Hulviar pursed his lips. Caledor's face went a shade paler.

'This is not a request, brother,' he said, his tone frostier. 'I am still the regent of Asuryan in this realm. Unless, that is, you can think of a better candidate.'

Imladrik laughed, suddenly understanding. 'Is *that* what this is about? You should find yourself abler counsellors.' He took a stride towards Caledor, and his metal-shod boots clinked on the stone. 'I have no desire to sit on your throne, nor to wear your crown. By the gods, I have no desire to lead armies at all – if duty did not demand it I would happily spend my days in the Dragonspine. Forget those who whisper in your ear; we are winning the war against the druchii, and I will not leave it.'

Caledor's face flashed briefly with anger. '*Will not?* Let me remind you, brother, of how things stand. I have the mandate of the Flame. I built the fleets that spread our power over the world. I broke the grip of the corsairs. I slew the prince of the stunted folk and sent his armies reeling.'

Imladrik listened to the litany wearily. Perhaps it sounded impressive to his brother; to his own ears, it sounded painfully insecure. Both of them knew that their father had been gifted the title 'Conqueror' by the people. Caledor II was desperate to make a similar mark in the annals and so threw himself into one battle after the other, neglecting all else but war. That might fool the rabbles of Lothern and Tor Alessi, though it fooled no one who had actually known Imrik.

'And *you*,' said Caledor, almost scornfully. 'The Master of Dragons. What *is* that, even? An old title from a dusty lineage. They are *dying*, Imladrik. They have been dying for centuries and nothing will halt it. You have wasted your life with them, trying to coax out a little more ore from a mined-out shaft.'

Imladrik met his gaze evenly. 'You know nothing of them.'

'So you have always told me, but by Khaine, brother, your piety riles me! You speak of mystical nonsense and then expect me to take you seriously, and in the meantime there are real wars to be fought. My gold buys the making of a thousand warships. Every day we ferry more soldiers to Elthin Arvan – you think it happens by itself? And all the while you commune with your... creatures in the hills.'

'I will not go.'

Caledor rose from the throne. Imladrik saw the brittleness there: the raised veins in his neck, the tight line of his jaw. So it had ever been with him, always just one step away from battle-rage.

'Then I order it,' said Caledor through gritted teeth. 'I order you to Elthin Arvan. You will wage the war against the dawi. You will not return until their forces are broken and the colonies are secure.'

'We *do not need* to fight them!' Imladrik shouted, struggling to curb his exasperation. 'You *provoked* them, time and again. They are proud, they do not suffer slights, and you shamed them. You shamed them in the worst possible way, and you do not even know it.'

By then they stood only inches apart. Imladrik was the taller, the leaner, but Caledor was the stronger. Thus it had always been with them – the older brother staring up at the younger.

'And what of you, brother?' Caledor spat, his eyes flat. 'You will speak up for anyone but your own kind. They killed thousands at Kor Vanaeth, thousands more at Tor Alessi. At Athel Numiel they butchered infants for sport. What would you have me do – roll over for them? Beg for mercy?'

Imladrik shook his head in disgust. 'The war is a sham. It always has been. Our father would never–'

'Do *not* mention him!' Caledor's voice rose in fury, skirting hysteria. 'This is not his time! It is *my* time! It is *my* time!'

Imladrik pulled back as if burned. The frenzy in Caledor's voice was disconcerting. 'Gods, listen to yourself. What has happened to you?' He forced himself to relax, his fists to unclench. 'Just *think*. We can take the war to the druchii, just as we were always meant to: my dragons, your ships. There need be no jealousy between us. I have always been content to follow you. Come, you know this.'

Caledor hesitated then. His face remained taut, locked in outrage, but something else flickered across it: embarrassment, perhaps. Imladrik hardly dared to breathe.

Then Hulviar's silky voice broke the silence.

'This is false policy,' interjected the seneschal. 'We will lose the colonies. My liege, recall the determinations made–'

Imladrik whirled on him. 'Silence!'

Hulviar recoiled, raising his hands in self-defence. By then, though, the damage had been done; Caledor's resolve returned.

'You will go to the east,' Caledor ordered, his voice firm again. 'Either you will go by your own will or you will be sent there under the custody of more dependable subjects. You are mighty, brother, but even you cannot defy the will of the Crown. If you try, it will break you.' His voice lowered, just a little. 'I do not wish to break you.'

Imladrik's heart beat hard, the blood thudding in his ears. The twin swords in his hands felt heavy. He felt the potential in them, and for an instant imagined the storm he could unleash if he chose to.

Caledor did not waver. Imladrik stared down at him, his mind a torment of emotions, his face a mask. Then he looked away.

'You are the Phoenix King,' he said, softly.

'And your brother,' added Caledor, relenting a little with a half-smile.

Imladrik turned away, ready to stride back down the length of the hall. He shot a withering glance at Hulviar, then started to walk.

'For what's it's worth,' he said.

SEVEN

Thoriol lay back against the cushions, feeling his muscles relax. Soft lute music filled the background, calming him, easing the tensions that had filled his mind during the long descent from the mountains.

He didn't like to think back over the journey. He had taken a steed from one of the hardscrabble settlements just outside Kor Evril and ridden along stony tracks down to Lothern, weathering incessant salt-thick wind until Eataine's gentler land had taken hold.

The country of Caledor had always left him cold, and he had never understood what his father saw in it. To his eyes, it was all black rock and smouldering craters, scoured by the elements and beset by legends of past glory. In comparison to Cothique, his mother's land, where grass-crowned cliffs stood proudly against the ocean and the air was sweet from the woodlands of Avelorn, it seemed a meagre, desolate place.

As a child Thoriol had been proud of his father's lineage. He had boasted to his playmates about it, enjoying it when they had stared back at him, mouths open, as he had told them stories about the great dragons. Some of them had even been true.

Thoriol smiled as he remembered. It was hard not to smile. After nearly half a decanter of *heliath* the whole world seemed essentially benign.

He looked around him. The house of pleasure was much like most of the others he had spent time in, though, this being Lothern, more richly appointed. Long drapes of diaphanous silk hung from high ceilings, wafting from the gentle movement of bodies. The tinkle of a fountain sounded from somewhere close by, part-masked by the hum of conversation. He saw lissom figures drifting in and out of the various private chambers, both male and female, all with the flushed cheeks and sparkling eyes that spoke of exotic consumptions. The light was subdued; a dim cloud of reds and purples, thick with curls of smoke.

Thoriol shifted on his couch, enjoying the give of it against his skin. After so long in the saddle it felt good to be somewhere more civilised. You had to be discreet – such places were secretive by nature – but if you knew the right palms to press it was always possible to find what you were after.

The failure with the Sun Dragon barely troubled him now. It had troubled him, badly, just after it had happened. For a time he had allowed himself to be tortured by familiar feelings of inadequacy, the same feelings that had dogged him ever since he had been old enough to understand that his boastful tales of dragons and battles would need to be replaced one day with deeds of his own. After a while even his old playmates had stopped thinking of his heritage as a blessing – none of them had had such achievements to live up to as they reached gingerly towards adulthood.

Thoriol had his mother's temper in so many things. He had loved the books she had shown him as a child, poring over them, tracing the runes on the parchment, committing the sacred words to memory. He had imagined he would end up as a loremaster like her, locked in some isolated tower studying the mysteries of the aethyr or the poetry of the sages.

But his mother had never pushed him to follow that path, and when his father had begun to school him in the lore of the dragon riders, she had supported him.

'This is important,' she had told Thoriol, smiling reassuringly. 'Think of it: you are the heir. One day you will ride the great ones into war. Part of me envies you, for I will never understand them, but do this for him. Do this for both of us.'

He had wanted to tell her then, but somehow the words never came. As the months passed it had become harder to change course. His tomes of lore had been left in Tor Vael, slowly mouldering – after that he had worked to grow used to the cold and the hardness of life at Kor Evril. He had studied diligently, memorising the rites of summoning, learning the mental disciplines, spending hours in caverns in an attempt to decipher the tremors and hisses that gave away the rousing of a dragon below.

On some days he had truly believed he could master it. There had been times – not many, but they had existed – when he had looked up into Caledor's bleak skies and seen the raw beauty in them that so excited his father.

But he had never truly fooled himself. He had always known the truth, and had festered away in resentment of it. There had been times when he had wanted to shout it out aloud, to rage at his father who had worked so patiently with him.

'Can you not see it?' he had wanted to yell. 'I have no talent for this! You know every nuance of these creatures – are you no judge of my own?'

Throughout it all Imladrik had never been cruel, never domineering; it was just that he had never understood, not even for a moment, why one of his bloodline would not leap at the chance of becoming a dragon rider. Imladrik was doing what a father should – passing on the keys to greatness, schooling him, nurturing the talent that surely lay somewhere buried deep within.

Thoriol took another long draught of *heliath*.

At least the deceptions were over. That, along with much else, was a comfort.

'You are new here,' came a lilting voice close to his ear.

Thoriol turned to see a hostess curled up on the couch next to him. She had dark hair, as straight as falling water, and almond-shaped eyes. The scent of cloves rose from her high-collared dress.

'True,' he replied, propping himself up on an elbow to get a better look at her.

'Is everything to your satisfaction?' she asked.

'Quite, thank you.'

'I can fetch more *heliath*. Or a dream-philtre.'

'Dream-philtre?'

She smiled conspiratorially. 'The poppy.'

'Ah. I thought that was... prohibited.'

'You have a trustworthy face. I believe you can keep a secret.'

Thoriol laughed. 'I keep many secrets.'

'Tell some to me?' the hostess asked. 'I am as discreet as the night.'

'I'm sure.' Thoriol held his goblet up to the diffuse light. The cloudy blooms from the lanterns reflected in the cut crystal. 'I did not come here to talk. I came here to forget.'

'We can help you with that. We can help you with anything.'

Thoriol saw his reflection in the glass. He gazed at it wearily. 'Can you help me to escape?'

'That is a speciality.'

'You do not know whom I am escaping from. He is powerful. Very powerful.'

'Many powerful figures come through these doors,' said the hostess.

Thoriol found himself looking at her lips as she spoke. They were such soft lips.

'They are all much the same as one another,' she added, 'once you get under the robes.'

Thoriol laughed again. For some reason, he found himself wanting to laugh at almost everything she said. 'I like you.'

'I am glad. Tell me more about where you wish to go.'

'As far as possible,' said Thoriol wistfully. 'I would go where nobody knows me. I would spend my days with no expectations. I would take time, I would think. Perhaps I would reconsider some choices I have made. Perhaps I would change a great deal.'

The hostess nodded. Her hair shimmered strangely as her head moved, as if it were a single sheet of silk.

'Do you see that one, over there?' she asked, pointing directly ahead of her.

Thoriol followed her manicured fingernail. In a booth opposite lounged a tall elf in a white gown. He was drinking from a goblet, watching the people move around him absently. He had a blunt face for one of his race, by the look of it bitten by a life in the open air. A scar ran down his right cheek, pale and raised.

'What of him?' asked Thoriol.

'I think you might get along,' replied the hostess.

'Maybe we would.'

'Perhaps I might introduce you.'

'Maybe you should.'

The hostess smiled at him. It was a comforting gesture; almost maternal. 'Your glass is empty. More *heliath*?'

Thoriol looked at his goblet. He hadn't noticed that he'd drained it. 'What was the other thing?'

'A dream-philtre. I can get that for you. Just ask.'

Thoriol lay back on the couch, stretching his arms lazily. A languor spread throughout his body, warming him pleasantly. 'That would be nice.'

The hostess placed her hand on his arm lightly. 'Whatever you wish,' she said. 'You are amongst friends here.'

Draukhain plunged through the night sky. He let slip a grating roar, like metal being dragged across an anvil. He was in a savage mood.

Imladrik gave him his head. He too was in a savage mood.

Together they wheeled and dived above a seething mass of cloud. The layers below them were unbroken, lit vividly by the stars and the world's moons. An undulating carpet of mingled silver and green rippled towards the curve of the horizon. The two of them might have been in another dimension of the universe, locked away from the world and sustained only by starlight and infinity.

I feel your wrath, sang Draukhain. *The last time you summoned me you were angry. Is this how it will be from now on?*

Imladrik laughed harshly. The wind raced through his bronze hair. *Your spirit is wrathful too.*

Because you are, kalamn-talaen. *You are angry; so am I.*

Imladrik had kept his son's sword with his own and the two scabbards hung at his belt, clattering against Draukhain's heaving hide. The dragon flew very, very fast. Every so often Draukhain would unleash his potency to the full. Even after centuries steeped in dragons and their ways, Imladrik could still be taken aback by it.

You awaken this in me, Imladrik sang. *You are wild.*

Draukhain grunted, dropping low and skimming across the landscape of vapour. *Believe that if you wish*, he sang, inflecting the harmonies with sceptical humour.

On Ulthuan I am equable, sang Imladrik. *I live a modest life. I sleep on the ground beside my troops.*

You say that as if it were something to be proud of.
It is.

Mortals, snorted Draukhain contemptuously. *Modesty is perverse. Revel in the superiority you have been given.*

Imladrik laughed again. *And be more like you.*

It would improve you.

It would improve my mood.

They hurtled into the north-east, swinging far out over the cloud-wreathed ocean. They had left the rugged shoreline of Chrace behind them a long time ago; now all that remained below the cloud-veil was open sea, black as pitch. No birds flew so far out, no ships plied those waters.

I have been ordered to the east, said Imladrik.

Good. I grow tired of the Annulii.

It is against my will. Duty compels me.

Draukhain let a long stream of fire wash over his body, rolling amongst it as he powered through the air. *I will never understand your obsession with duty.*

I know you won't.

You could disobey.

I could. It would break Ulthuan apart, and the druchii are not slow to take advantage of weakness.

At the mention of the dark kin, Draukhain let fly with a furious spout of smoke-edged flame. Nothing, save perhaps the daemons of the earth, was more likely to rouse a drake to fury than the mention of the druchii, who enslaved and broke dragons whenever they were able.

That is the one thing I will miss, sang Draukhain. *Every druchii that dies under my claws makes me live a little more.*

You may find some to kill in Elthin Arvan.

Not enough of them. But still – I am glad we are going. I will bring terror to the wilds.

Imladrik smiled grimly. Draukhain was perfectly capable of that. All the dragons under his command brought terror in their wake. They were perhaps the only weapons they had that the dawi didn't understand.

But dragons were not 'weapons' – he had admonished his brother for saying the same thing.

I will not fight this war the way he wishes me to, Imladrik sang. *He thinks the dawi will crumble on the first charge. I know they will not. I have seen their stone halls. We could break against those holds for eternity and they would never crack.*

Draukhain rolled to one side, pulling across a buffeting squall of wind and angling expertly along in its wake. *I would relish taking apart a hold,* he sang. *It would be vengeance for all my kind they have slaughtered. They think of us as beasts – did you know that?*

I did. And many asur think the same way about them. He looked up at the stars above them, cold, distant and uncaring. *That is the easiest step to take: to see one's enemy as an animal.* He thought of Thoriol, and winced inside. *None of us are brutes. We should not even be fighting.*

But we are. That cannot be changed now.

Perhaps, perhaps not. That shall be my first battle.

Draukhain began to sheer downwards, dragging his wings closer to the thick carpet of moonlit cloud. *So when shall we commence this? Shall I bear you to Elthin Arvan this night?*

Imladrik shook his head. *Not yet, great one,* he sang. His mind-voice became low, almost reluctant. *Did I say my first battle? No, I have one more ahead of me before I leave. Take me to Tor Vael.*

Yethanial awoke with the first rays of sunlight bursting through open shutters. She had slept poorly – just a couple of hours, her mind unable to break itself away from the worries that circled endlessly in her head. For a moment she stared groggily at the pale grey arched window. She could smell salt on the breeze, and something else too: charred metal.

She pushed herself free of the sheets abruptly, suddenly worried that something in the kitchens had been left to burn. Then she remembered what else in her life routinely smelled of a blacksmith's forge.

'My lady,' said Imladrik from behind her.

She turned to face him. 'How long have you been there?'

Imladrik came over to join her on the bed. 'Not long. I did not wish to wake you before the dawn did.'

Yethanial smiled cautiously. 'My lord,' she said and reached for him.

Imladrik pulled back.

Yethanial frowned. 'What is it?'

Imladrik rarely looked truly uncertain. He had an understated confidence that resonated with those around him; it was one reason why he was popular with his troops. In the absence of that, Yethanial felt her anxiety return.

'Where is Thoriol?' he asked.

'I thought he was with you, in Kor Evril.'

'He did not come back here?'

'No. What happened?'

Imladrik seemed to slump inside. 'He failed with a drake. He blames me. He may be right to. It was not the proper time.'

Yethanial reached for his hand. 'He will recover, though? It does not always succeed the first time – that is what you told me.'

'I do not know. For the first time, I begin to doubt.' He looked up at her. Again, uncertainty was etched deep on his face. 'He might never do it.'

'He is young. He can turn his mind to anything.' She tried to smile, to make light of it. 'Perhaps he might become a scholar. Would that be so bad?'

'It might have been something I did. Perhaps I pushed him too fast. The summonings come easily to me; I forget that others need more time.'

'You are hard on yourself. Did your father ever give as much time to you? You have devoted yourself to that child, and when he comes to his senses the two of you will speak and this will be forgotten.'

'We will not speak.'

'Why not?'

'Because I will not be here.' Imladrik's face took on a grimmer aspect; it was the way he looked before taking his leave for the next battle.

Yethanial withdrew her hand. Caradryel's final words to her entered her mind. 'What do you mean?'

Imladrik looked at her steadily. 'I have been ordered back to Elthin Arvan.'

Yethanial felt as if her stomach had been turned inside out. 'Refuse,' she said, her voice hard. 'Refuse him.'

'I cannot.'

'You can.' Her shock made her sharp. 'You can refuse anything you like. You command *legions*. You command mages, you command ships, you command dragons. Tell Caledor to finish his sordid war for himself.'

Imladrik looked back at her, his face an agony of understanding. He did not need to be told such things. 'That is why I cannot refuse. He will not change his mind. If I oppose him, my troops will remain loyal. War will come to Ulthuan. I will not see that.'

Yethanial wanted to rage at him. His resignation was infuriating. 'I don't believe you,' she accused, pushing herself angrily away from him. 'You could do it if you wished.'

'He is the King. He has the mandate of the Flame.'

Yethanial got out of the bed and strode over to where she had discarded her robe the night before. She wrapped it around herself. 'He is your jealous brother. He is a fool.'

'Listen to me.' Imladrik rose too. 'This is a chance to mend the damage he has done. He thinks that by sending me away I will be mired in fighting for years. He thinks I will do as he would, and take the fight to the dawi, but I will not. He does not know them as I do. I can end it. Think on it, Yethanial: I can *end* it.'

She shot him a scornful look, reaching up to tie her hair back. 'Did you think that up on your way here?'

Imladrik stiffened. 'Do not use those words.'

'And what words do you expect me to use?' she shouted, surprising herself with her vehemence. 'Do you expect me to say: my blessings go with you? Is that what you want? You will not get it! You belong here, with me, with those who love you.'

'You think I *wanted* this?' Some colour returned to his cheeks, some wounded pride.

'Yes! Yes, I think you did want this! Half your soul has been there, ever since you came back. You could not scrub its mud from your hands, you could never forget what you did there.'

'Yethanial, you are–'

'You could never forget *her*.'

As soon as she said it, she wished she could gulp the words back down and bury them deep. She stared at Imladrik, her mouth open, her eyes still flashing with anger. Imladrik stared back at her. Silence fell between them, tense and febrile.

'That was unworthy,' said Imladrik at last. His voice was soft, though it too resonated with anger.

'Was it?' asked Yethanial.

'If you understood me at all, you would know it.'

Imladrik pushed his cloak back from where it had fallen over his shoulder. His expression was dangerous – like a thunderhead curdling on the horizon. He said nothing more, just turned and walked from the chamber. As he left, he kicked the door closed behind him, making it slam and shiver in the frame.

Yethanial stayed where she was, frozen by the emotions running through her.

Why did I say it? she thought, as angry and confused with herself as she was at him.

Then she remembered Caradryel again.

He will be sent back to the colonies, my lady. Nothing can prevent it.

She rushed at the door, yanking it open and going after him. There were things she needed to tell him. Parting on such terms would leave a wake of bitterness. It would weaken him, and it would weaken her.

But by the time she had run down the stairways and across the empty hall and pushed her way through the great gates, she was too late. She stood on the wet grass, her robe rippling around her in the morning breeze, watching the long tail of Draukhain disappear into the far distance, already high out over the sea.

She watched the dragon for a little while longer, then the haze of the horizon defeated her.

'Sundered again,' she breathed, ignoring the shouted queries after her welfare from the guards on the walls. She heard them hurrying after her, no doubt with cloaks and hoods to ward against the dawn chill.

She felt cold to her soul, though the elements did nothing to worsen that. Some words, some thoughts, could not easily be taken back.

EIGHT

Caradryel sat alone. The ornate surroundings of Faer-Lyen's private dining hall surrounded him. A long polished table stretched away into the distance, set with polished silverware and decked with terraces of candles. He'd taken pleasure in such things in the past. Now they did nothing but expose his inadequacies.

He would have to find something to occupy him soon, some scheme or diversion. He might arrange an assignation at court – it had been a while – or manage the destruction of a rival's career. The arts of state were like a ritual game, with pieces scattered across the board in complicated webs of power. Move one, and the whole pattern shifted.

Caradryel was good at the game. He knew which cords to pull, which ears to whisper in, which beds to slip into and out of and which palms to press with gold, jewels or daggers. The fact that his father saw no value in such prowess was neither here nor there; slowly, with glacial patience, Caradryel had built up a formidable cadre of loyal retainers, dotted around the Houses like thieves in the basement of a grand old mansion. One day he would call the favours in. It amused him sometimes to contemplate what would happen after that. Perhaps he would find himself exiled from Ulthuan in disgrace, perhaps end up on the Throne.

He knew the source of his ennui. The affair with Yethanial, he could see now, had been a miscalculation. It was no good trying courtly suavity on the likes of her – she was a scholar, a dealer in the purity of words and thoughts. He should have been more humble, less cocksure, then perhaps he might have swung it.

It was a shame. He had managed to persuade himself that a spell in Elthin Arvan would be just the thing; he could have ingratiated himself with his new master and extended his network of patronage to the colonies. He could have observed the war first-hand and gauged how best to take advantage of the many opportunities that such things invariably delivered. Most of all, he knew he would have enjoyed the simple pleasures of seeing something different. Even Ulthuan, the most spectacular and varied realm in all the world, became dull after a while.

He took a sip of wine, and a low chime sounded from the far end of the dining chamber.

'Come,' he said lazily, only mildly interested.

The doors opened and a servant padded in.

'Your pardon, lord,' he said, bowing. 'A lady awaits.'

Caradryel's lids barely lifted. 'Mirielle? She's early.'

'From Tor Vael, lord.'

Caradryel's heart skipped a beat. 'Khaine's eyes, you fool, show her in.'

By the time the servant had withdrawn, summoned Yethanial and brought her up to the dining chamber, Caradryel had seen that the table was cleared of food and the platters replaced with a heap of serious-looking scrolls.

He rose to greet her as she entered, affecting a look of disinterested welcome. Yethanial wore grey robes and a grey hood, making her look almost ghostly. She didn't so much as glance at the piles of parchment he'd carefully arranged.

'This is a surprise, my lady,' he said.

'Is it?' she asked, her voice resigned. 'I thought you knew everything.'

'By no means. Are you well?'

Yethanial laughed sourly. 'He has gone. Just as you said he would.'

'Ah, I'm sorry. I didn't think it would come so soon.'

'I hope you can take some satisfaction from being right.'

'Believe me, that's not how I take satisfaction.' Caradryel motioned towards a chair. 'Will you sit?'

'I had much to think about after he left,' said Yethanial, ignoring the offer. 'At first I determined to ignore you. I supposed that if, as you told me, knowledge of Caledor's orders was widely shared, then you were nothing more than the boldest of any number of gossip-merchants.'

Caradryel bowed humbly.

'But then I gave the matter thought,' she went on. 'I have a tendency to disregard your sort. I find the games played in Lothern tiresome, and so assume that all the highborn do. This has evidently been a mistake. Perhaps I should have paid them more attention, and thus avoided a snare.'

'I am flattered that you think so.'

'I asked around about you. Believe it or not, I have contacts of my own, some of whom have the ear of the powerful.'

'I do not doubt it. What did they say?'

'Listen to me now. Do not interrupt. My husband is heading to Elthin Arvan alone. He wishes to end the war, not to prolong it, and for this reason those already there will resist him at every turn. He has respect from those who fight but few allies among those who command. You offered your services to me. Having no better options, I am taking up the offer. I wish you to go to Tor Alessi and work for Tor Caled. I can pay you anything you wish.'

'That will not be nec–'

'I said do not interrupt. If you accept, you will be required to perform three duties. First, advise the Lord Imladrik. Follow his commands, see that he achieves what he has set out to, give him sound counsel. Second, report back to me on all matters of import. Ships ply between Lothern and Tor Alessi, so this should not be difficult, though do it secretly. My husband is no schemer. You may struggle to understand this, but he has a noble soul and will do nothing unless he sees the good for Ulthuan in it.'

'So I under–'

'Third, I wish to hear details of anything concerning the dragon riders. There is a mage among them, her name is Liandra. At one time she and my husband… worked together. No doubt she is still active in the defence of the colonies. Other riders will follow my husband to Elthin Arvan, and they should be watched too. Make this a priority. Dragon riders are a strange breed, hot-blooded and affected by the wills of the beasts they ride. They must not have influence over him.'

'Liandra? Of the House of Athinol?'

Yethanial gave him a wintry smile. 'You seem well-informed. I hope, for your sake, that you are. I find this work, this *deception*, distasteful. It would not take much for me to change my mind and call a halt. Should you prove unequal to the challenge, or should you not fulfil these orders in every particular, I shall have no hesitation in cutting you off and leaving you stranded there.'

'I have no doubt of it.'

'Make no mistake, Caradryel of Faer-Lyen: when in the right mood, the Lord Imladrik is the most dangerous warrior of this age of the world. Though I may not look it, I have strengths of my own and am quite capable of visiting retribution on those who would harm us. We make a formidable pairing, and we will continue to do so, whatever fleeting difficulties may come between us. You should be aware of this before agreeing to take the assignment. You should be aware of your peril.'

Caradryel had to fight to stop himself smiling. The notion, so recently entertained, that he might struggle with boredom over the coming months now seemed impossibly quaint.

'I understand,' he said, his face as serious as his mood was buoyant. 'And I have already given the matter all the thought I plan to. So here is my answer: you may consider me, my lady of Tor Vael, your most humble servant.'

Liandra strode along the curving corridors of the Tower of Winds. The quality of the stonework around her was finer than at Kor Vanaeth, but still far cruder than that found in Ulthuan. Tor Alessi was the largest and the mightiest of the asur settlements in the east, but it still couldn't mimic the elegance found in her race's homeland. The whole place had been built for defence, with three concentric circles of high walls and heavy bulwarks over the gates, and the aesthetics had suffered as a result. The city had been besieged three times since the war had broken out and each battle had left its scars. In the lulls between fighting the walls had been made thicker and higher, every time further ruining what symmetry remained.

The Tower of Winds stood at the westernmost point of the city, where the walls ran up to the sea and enclosed the deep harbour below. It had survived mostly unscathed, being too far from the perimeter for the dawi's catapults and stone-throwers to make much impact. Even so, the lack of finish in its interior spoke of the hard times that had fallen on the city. Metal finishings had been stripped out and melted down for weapons, glass had been pushed out of window frames and replaced with iron grilles, sacred images of the gods had been removed from their proud stations on the walls and taken into the catacombs for safekeeping. What remained in place was stark, functional, pared-down.

For all that, the white stone still shone in the light of the setting sun, and the banners of the gathered armies still fluttered proudly in the sea-wind. The city had never been more heavily populated – as the principal landing for the Phoenix King's armies, it hummed with the constant tramp of soldiers' boots and the clatter of unloading cargo.

Tor Alessi was battered, roughened at the edges, but still proud.

Like us all, thought Liandra.

She reached the twin doors to the Council Chamber, where two Sea Guard sentries waited on either side. They pushed the doors open immediately, and she went inside.

The Council Chamber took up the full width of the Tower's topmost storey. The floor was polished marble, deep black and veined with silver, and the rune Ceyl had been engraved in the centre of the floor, picked out in iron and inlaid with pearl. Five thrones surrounded the rune, each one facing inwards, each hewn from obsidian and surmounted with the crest of a royal house. Sunlight poured in through narrow barred windows.

Four of the thrones were occupied: Lady Aelis of House Lamael, Lord Salendor of House Tor Achare, Lord Caerwal of House Ophel and Lord Gelthar of House Derreth. One remained to be filled.

'Welcome, Liandra,' said Aelis, rising from her throne. The Mistress of Tor Alessi was wand-thin, with dark hair pulled back from an austere face and bound with silver wire. 'We are glad you decided to make us complete.'

Liandra bowed. 'I was honoured to be asked,' she said, taking her seat as Aelis resumed hers. 'Have I missed much?'

'We were waiting for you,' said Salendor. His stocky frame made him look too big for his seat, and his dun-red cloak was still caked with mud, as were his tall leather boots. His magestaff rested loosely in his hand.

'I came as swiftly as I could,' she said. 'Much needed to be done at Kor Vanaeth.'

'You wasted your time, then,' replied Salendor. 'It will never stand a second attack.'

Liandra retained her composure. She knew what he was doing; in a way, it was a compliment. *He tests me. He wishes only warriors on this Council.*

'We will be ready, when they come again,' she insisted, her voice quiet but firm. 'We have been blooded once, and may bleed again, but we will never retreat.'

They held one another's gaze for a moment, her blue eyes locked with his. Then he grunted and looked away.

'That is why we are all here,' interjected Aelis calmly. 'We know they are coming again. A month, a few weeks, maybe. The question is: how shall we respond?'

Liandra stole a glance at the other two members of the Council. Caerwal and Gelthar were both the very image of asur nobility: slim, impeccably dressed, their robes lined with gold and their lean faces placid. They did not look like they would rush into battle with the relish of Salendor. For that matter, they did not look like they would do anything with relish.

So that is how this works: Salendor and myself are the hotheads, they are the cautious, and Aelis will adjudicate.

'We have more power in Elthin Arvan now than when the King was here,' said Gelthar, speaking ponderously. 'We must install the legions here, in Athel Maraya, Athel Toralien. Then we wait.'

Salendor snorted. 'We *wait*. Your counsel never changes, Gelthar. What would it take to prompt action from you?'

Gelthar remained implacable. 'Why give up our advantage? Let them wear themselves out in endless sieges.'

'Each siege has cost us,' said Liandra.

'It has,' said Caerwal bitterly. 'Gods, it has.'

'And when did this become the asur way of war?' demanded Salendor, exasperated. 'This is craven counsel.'

Gelthar pursed his lips. 'Enlighten us, then. What is yours?'

Salendor sat forward in his throne. 'Muster the legions at Athel Maraya. Strike now. Meet them under Loren Lacoi before they get to us here.' He shot a furtive glance at Liandra, as if already looking for her agreement. 'They move slower than a crippled carthorse. We can choose where to engage them, how we engage them.' He smiled rakishly. 'If we choose, we can *crush* them.'

Gelthar sniffed. 'Your counsel, too, never changes.'

Aelis looked at Liandra. 'Your people have suffered as ours have. What is your view?'

Here it is. My chance to play the part assigned to me.

'My view?' she asked. She could feel Salendor's impatience, and ignored him. 'It is this: whenever our race has been threatened, we have ridden out. We have never waited for our lands to be burned first. We are the masters of the world; if we do not defend what is ours, then we do not deserve the title.' She allowed herself to look at Salendor and caught the look of approval in his face. 'We must strike first. Caledor has bought us this brief lull. Let us use it.'

Salendor could barely contain himself. '*Hear* her, my lady,' he urged Aelis. 'It is only caution that keeps us back. They sowed the seeds of this war; now let them reap the harvest.'

'And throw away our greatest asset,' said Gelthar wearily. 'The walls they have never yet breached.'

'We *wither* inside them!' cried Salendor.

'They preserve us,' said Gelthar.

'They did not preserve Athel Numiel,' said Caerwal coldly. 'It had high walls, but they did not stop the slaughter there. They *murdered* my–'

'Enough.' Aelis held up her hand again, stilling the argument. She inclined her head to one side, as if listening for something.

'Do not stifle–' started Salendor, but Aelis silenced him with a glare.

'Be still,' she said. 'Do you not hear it?'

For a moment, Liandra sensed nothing. The first thing she noticed was a tremor in her mind-harmony with Vranesh. She felt the dragon's sudden emotion flowing into her body, as if the resonance of a musical instrument had made the hairs on her neck rise. The sentiment was a powerful one; at first, she assumed it spoke of alarm, and she half-rose in her seat.

Then she discerned its true character – *joy*, of a pure kind, like a child recognising its mother and rushing to greet her.

By then the noises that Aelis had heard had become more obvious. From far below the Council Chamber, dim but growing in volume, crowds were crying out in fear and wonder.

Liandra pushed herself from the throne and rushed to the western wall of the chamber, followed by the others. She pulled open a pair of doors leading to the tower's balcony and stepped out into fresh air.

The five of them lined up on the balcony's narrow platform, suspended high above Tor Alessi's narrow, teeming streets. Below them, a tangle of whitewashed buildings crowded and clustered its way towards the harbour, a half-ring of stone enclosing a basin of deep blue water. Dozens of warships swayed on the waves, their masts seesawing as they were buffeted. Across the entire city, from the high ringed walls to the summits of its many spires, tight-packed throngs peered up into the skies.

High over the harbour, buoyed by the downbeats of splayed wings, six dragons hovered in mid-air. Vranesh shot up to greet them, snaking around the newcomers and sending columns of flame shooting out in elation.

Liandra knew the dragons' names: Rafuel, Khalamor, Gaudringnar, Telagis, Mornavere. Their mind-voices sang to her like a choir, overlapping and pushing against one another. They were magnificent, as huge as watchtowers and blazing with colours: gold, emerald, ivory, amethyst, wine-red. The air around them shimmered with heat and magic, as if they had carved their way into the realm of the senses from beyond the veils of madness. For all that, they were no daemon-kind – they were flesh, bone and blood, as superb and pristine as fallen stars.

All the drakes carried riders, each one wearing heavy plate armour and carrying a rune-tipped blade. They were nearly as splendid as their steeds, and she knew their names too: Heruen of Yvresse; Cademel of Eataine; Selegar, Teranion and Lania of Caledor. She could sense their gathered power, filling the air around her and making it tremble.

One drake hovered apart from the others, and they all paid deference to him. The mighty Draukhain arched his long neck high, holding perfect position with ease. Sunlight flashed from his sapphire hide, making it dazzle and shine like a coat of ithilmar. Even from such a distance Liandra could smell the burnt backwash of his movements. The furnace of his lungs sent out curls of fire and smoke like garlands; the aroma was almost as familiar to her as Vranesh's.

Atop Draukhain's churning shoulder-blades sat the Master of them all, the scion of the Dragontamer, the one whose name she still hesitated to recall lest it brought pain back with it. She tried to look away, but it was futile; her eyes were drawn ever upwards, scanning up to the silver armour with its black runic warding, the crimson cloak that draped across dragonhide, the naked longsword. She thought for an instant that she caught an intense flash of green eyes under a heavy silver helm, and had to grip the railing of the balcony to keep her poise.

She had forgotten the aura of power that he carried with him. None but a fellow dragon rider could truly know the command Imladrik possessed; only one of their esoteric fraternity could understand what it took to earn the allegiance of a creature like Draukhain.

Once, long ago, Vranesh had told her how her own kind saw Imladrik.

He is the dawn and the dusk, she had sung, respectfully, with none of her usual flippancy. *He is the sun and the moon. Where he goes, we will go; when he passes, so shall we. He is the kalamn-talaen. He is the Master.*

Liandra tried to look away, and failed. She felt old emotions rising to the surface, breaking the mask of certainty she had learned to wear over the last thirty years.

Salendor, standing at her side, seemed to feel nothing but elation. He turned to her, his face alive with fresh hope. 'Imladrik!' he cried. 'Drakes! The King has sent us rare weapons! Now the dawi shall know fear!'

Liandra tried to smile. All she could think about was the figure atop the sapphire dragon: what he had been to her before, what his return to Elthin Arvan foreboded.

'They are not weapons,' she said faintly, her heart already twisting in anguish.

II
DRAGONFIRE

NINE

The time had come.

The wait had passed quickly by the reckoning of his people, but still every day spent in preparation and argument had seemed like an age. The mountain-realm was huge and sprawling, home to hundreds of holds, mines, bulwarks, citadels and quarries. It took time to reach them all, to pass on the news, to wait for anger to boil up within the deliberate minds of the dawi.

But now the time had come. Given enough of it to consider the wrong, given enough to reflect on it and compare it to the wrongs of the past, they became angry. They started muttering in the deep places, hammering away at the walls in unsettling rhythms. They chanted in the lightless halls and stoked the eternal fires of the forges. They smelted iron and beat gromril, they marched along the winding ways of the Ungdrin, they poured out onto the causeways of the great Karaks, their faces masked by helms, accompanied by the booming call of war-horns.

He had kindled a fire in the deep vaults. Then he had watched it grow, rippling out into every corner of the dawi empire until it became a roaring inferno. The Lords of the Dwarfs had been roused from their torpor. No dissenting voices had been raised, no old grudges had been unearthed, no rival claim to the leadership of this anger had emerged. They were united in slow, cold fury and the rock itself rang from their ironshod treads. A dozen armies already marched; more would follow.

The time had come.

First hundreds came, then thousands, then tens of thousands. His own host snaked along the ice-bitten road to Karaz-a-Karak and down towards the forest-lands of the elgi who had brought such hatred upon their own heads.

Morgrim Bargrum, kin of the High King, cousin to the slain Snorri Half-hand, the Uniter, the one they were already calling the Doom of the Elves, stood on a high spur of rock and watched his army grind its way west.

The sky above him was leaden and bloated with rain. Lightning flickered across the northern horizon, broken by the massive shoulders of far peaks. Dull light glinted from chainmail, from axes, from the tips of quarrels and from the iron of the great standard poles.

Morgrim rested on his axe-handle, his chin jutting and his beard spilling over his crossed hands. His bunched-muscle arms, each one tattooed and laced with scars, studs and iron rings, flexed in time with the tramp of boots. His heavy helm sat low on his brow, pocked with precious stones and draped with a curtain of fine mail.

Like all his kind, he was hard, angular, solid, immovable. The cross-hatch rune *zhazad* had been daubed on his forehead in his own blood, now dried a dark brown by the chill mountain wind. His eyes glittered darkly under the shadow of furrowed brows. His boots were planted firmly, locked against the stone as if one with it.

The host was immense. Not since the days of forgotten wars had so many of the dawi marched under one banner. Many of them had torn their beards, ripping hair from flesh in savage mockery of what had been done to the ambassadors in Ulthuan. Many more had painted their armour plates with blood, just as Morgrim had done. Dwarf blood was thick. It dried fast, cleaving to steel like lacquer. Even as the rain fell, coursing over hunched shoulders in runnels, those bloodstains remained vivid.

Morgrim watched his regiments creep down towards the lowlands. He watched the tight squares huddle together, ringed with shields and toothed with speartips. He watched grim formations of longbeards, roused from their lethargy by the anger he had birthed. They marched slowly, their grey eyes fixed unwaveringly on the horizon, their lips unmoving. He watched smaller formations of bulkier warriors covered from head to toe in thick plates of gromril, clanking like infernal machinery. He watched hammer-holders stride down the causeway, each one thronged around a great lord of battle. He watched heavy battle standards swinging among them, all adorned with the runic emblems of holds picked out in gold and bronze.

It was just one army of many. More would follow, gathered together in the booming halls of deep fastnesses and sent forth into an unsuspecting world.

All of this Morgrim watched in silence. It was not an army of containment, or of exploration, or of defence. It had no other purpose than destruction.

In my name, cousin, he mouthed silently. *You will be avenged.*

The time had come.

'*Tromm*, lord,' came a throaty voice at his shoulder. Morgrim did not need to turn to see who it was.

'*Tromm*, Morek,' he said, all the while watching the host march on. It would be many hours before the vanguard cleared the foothills, and many more hours before the rearguard passed his vantage. 'Have you come to summon me down?'

'Summon you? I would not dare.'

The Master Runesmith was far older than Morgrim. His beard was flecked with grey like the down of a hunting peregrine, and his eyes were sunk deep into leather-tough skin the colour of burnished copper. He carried an ancient runestaff topped with gromril and wore master-crafted armour of interlocking plates.

'Look out on them,' said Morgrim, his voice as gruff and spare as a *drakk*'s exhalation. 'Look at what we have done, then tell me: what does your heart say?'

Morek did as he was bid. He cast his deep-set eyes over the slowly moving host. It looked like a river of molten iron creeping down the flank of the mountains. As the light began to fail and the shadows lengthened, the iron darkened.

'It says that this thing cannot be stopped,' Morek said. 'It tells me Halfhand did not die in vain. He saw through the elgi – even his father did not see so clearly. They set this fate in motion, they shall bear the pain of it.'

Morgrim grunted. He could feel the dull thuds of a thousand footfalls, echoing up through the stone beneath his feet.

We have made the mountains tremble.

'I did not want this,' Morgrim said, his voice low and dark, as it had been ever since Snorri had died. 'Let the records state that.'

'They will.'

'But now it is settled, I feel the blood of the ancients grow hot within me.'

'As do we all.'

Morgrim bared his teeth – a tight, warlike grimace, one that made the lined skin of his face crack and flex. 'My axe thirsts.'

Morek glanced at the blade. Its runes were inert. 'It has not been proved yet.'

'You made it. It will answer.'

Morek hawked a gobbet of spittle up and spat on the ground. 'And Drogor?'

Morgrim's expression briefly faltered. 'What of him?'

'Where is he? None have seen him for months.'

'I care not.' Morgrim found the mention of Drogor an irritant. He did not want to be reminded of that baleful presence, one that had hung around his cousin like the stench of carrion. There had always been something strange about Drogor, though it had been hard to say quite what it was. His eyes had been... dull.

'He came from nowhere,' said Morek. 'Now he returns to nowhere, and no one, it seems, wishes to speak of it.'

'I never liked him,' said Morgrim dismissively. 'Snorri listened too closely to him. Those who remain are pure.'

Morek pursed a pair of cracked lips. 'That they are – for now. But beware: your armies will hold in one piece only as long as their anger remains. You must bind your thanes strongly until they can face the enemy. Even

Gotrek struggled to control them, and while he remains grieving he cannot help you.'

'Fear not,' growled Morgrim, his slab-heavy face glowering under the sky. 'They sought a leader, one who would deliver their axes to the elgi. With Snorri's passing, that is all I live to do.' His lips twisted into a half-snarl then, disfiguring features that had once been mild-tempered. 'I will permit the elgi to leave these shores, if they choose the path of sense. But if they stay to fight, then I swear by Grimnir I will choke them all in their own thin blood.'

Morek nodded sagely.

'That would be worth seeing,' he said, his voice thick with relish.

Imladrik stood before the Council of Five. They regarded him with a mix of wariness and awe. At least, four of them did; the fifth didn't lift her eyes from the floor.

'So here we are together,' said Aelis, clasping her hands. 'At last.'

Imladrik regarded her coolly.

She thinks I should have made this Council my priority. Let her think away; the world has changed, and they will have to get used to it.

'My apologies for the delay,' he said. 'You'll understand I had many things to detain me.'

The chamber around them was deep in the Old City, down in the heart of the first colonists' settlement. The stonework was more refined than in the Tower of Winds, the wood more cleanly carved, for it had been raised in a more carefree time when the thought of war between close allies would have been impossible to conceive.

'You have kept us waiting, my lord,' said Salendor. 'We have armies garrisoned here, in Athel Maraya, in forward stations. All they need is orders.'

Imladrik knew he had to be careful around Salendor. The warrior was clearly itching for a fight and no doubt saw him as the one to deliver it. Imladrik could sense the brutality coiled within him, the eagerness to spill blood, and he could also sense the fine-honed mind, the moral clarity. Salendor was a serious proposition, but a dangerous one.

'I know where our armies are,' Imladrik said. 'And they will wait a little longer for orders.' He turned to Aelis. 'The defences here are impressive. Everything you have done is impressive. I have not come to sweep it away and start again – I am here to work with you, not against you.'

'That is good to hear,' said Aelis. 'We have not always had... wise governance out here.'

Imladrik just resisted the temptation, nagging away at him since he'd entered the chamber, to glance over at Liandra. She hovered, dressed in crimson as ever, on the edge of his vision. They had not spoken since his arrival. Though he would never have admitted it to anyone, that was the true reason he had put off meeting the Council – Yethanial's words still burned in his memory.

'There has been division between you,' Imladrik said. 'This cannot continue – we must speak with one voice.'

'We have all we need,' said Caerwal. 'One choice remains: to meet them here, or march east and face them in the wilds.'

'The judgement is a fine one,' said Aelis.

Imladrik could sense Liandra's mind-voice on the margins. He didn't need to ask what side of the debate she was on. 'Yes, it would be,' he said, 'were we committed to war.'

Silence followed that. Imladrik waited for his words to sink in.

'My lord,' started Salendor cautiously, 'we have been at war for nearly thirty years.'

'Hardly,' said Imladrik calmly. 'We have been shown only a tithe of their strength.'

Salendor looked perplexed. 'These are the opening moves of the game. We are ready for what will come.'

'We are ready?' asked Imladrik. 'You sound sure. I hope you are. I hope you remain sure when your woods begin to burn. I hope you remain sure when our people begin to die in earnest, and I hope you remain sure when the corpses are piled high between the ocean and Karaz-a-Karak.'

Salendor looked taken aback. Still Imladrik did not seek to catch Liandra's eye.

'This is a lull,' Imladrik continued. 'My brother's victory wounded them, but we know it will not last. You gave me two choices, but I give you a third: pull back from the precipice. Close the wound. Talk to the dawi.'

Again, silence. When the next voice broke in, Imladrik had to work hard to keep his expression neutral.

'They will not listen,' said Liandra.

Her speech was just as he remembered it – hard-edged, louder than most, flavoured with the rough tones that spoke of a long time away from home. For a moment he could have been dragged back in time, to the long conversations they had shared while on the wing together, the tips of their steeds' pinions nearly touching. He could have recalled how her mind-voice had sparred with his, approaching that strange intimacy that a dragon rider shared with his steed.

It was harder than he had expected, to hear that voice again.

'You are sure?' he asked, unwilling to contradict her directly. Not yet.

'With respect, we have tried this,' interjected Salendor, clearly making an effort to retain his temper. 'They do not talk. They slaughter.'

Caerwal also looked unconvinced. 'That is the truth. If you had been here during these last years–'

'I have been in the colonies longer than any of you,' said Imladrik firmly. 'I founded Oeragor in the east before the towers of this city were raised, beside which thirty years away is nothing. You are free to dispute with me, Caerwal, but never presume that I know not of what I speak.'

Caerwal looked chastened, and fell quiet.

'War may come,' Imladrik went on. 'It may be too late to prevent it, but I will try. That is my first order: keep the defences in order, but no armies will march. Messages will be sent to the dawi. Snorri Halfhand is dead, but I knew his cousin in happier times – if I understand anything of them, he will be the first to seek vengeance, and of all of them he was always the mildest.'

Salendor shook his head in frustration. 'Your brother killed Halfhand. You know how they are – his rage will blind him now. The father, too.'

'Perhaps,' conceded Imladrik. 'If so, it will be a mark against us, for Snorri was a noble warrior when I knew him. For that reason I will make the attempt. We *must* make the attempt: we cannot be as blind as them, for we are the children of Aenarion and the fates hold us to a higher standard.'

He saw Aelis looking at him doubtfully. None of the others spoke in support of him. He had not expected them to do so; this counsel was always going to be unpopular with those who had suffered most.

'Then how will you achieve this?' asked Liandra. The tone of her voice was strange. 'The dawi kill any of us they come across, even under banners of truce. The rules of war have long since ceased to apply in Elthin Arvan.'

Imladrik turned to her. Her face was just as he remembered it – framed by a shock of copper hair, pale and vigorous, her blue eyes rich and glittering.

'It will not be easy,' he admitted, 'but no paths are free of danger, and I will not believe their minds are fully closed, not yet, not until I have seen it with my own eyes. They were a proud people, one in which honour once dwelt.'

'So you always counselled,' replied Liandra, 'even before the war started. Things change, though, my lord. People change.'

Imladrik held her gaze. 'The core of them remains the same. That never alters.'

'Does it not, my lord?'

'It cannot.'

They looked at one another for a little longer. Imladrik thought she might speak to him directly, mind to mind, just as they had once done freely.

In the event, she said nothing, and her eyes fell away.

'If this is the will of the Crown,' said Aelis slowly, breaking the awkward silence, 'then of course it shall be done, just as you command.'

Imladrik nodded. 'Good. Then our business is concluded here. This is our last chance for peace, my lords; let us ensure it does not fail.'

'And, despite all, if it should?' asked Salendor sceptically.

'Then, my Lord of Tor Achare, you shall have the slaughter you desire,' said Imladrik wearily. 'And when that is done, when the world lies in ashes around us, we can reflect at length on what follies may be committed by the wise, and what horror may be unleashed by those who once only worshipped beauty.'

After the Council had dispersed Imladrik made his way to his chambers. He had taken up residence in one of the smaller towers, pressed tight against the inner wall as it curved round towards the harbour. Its windows faced west, back across the seas to Ulthuan. The accommodation within was modest: a few rooms in the lower levels in which to receive guests, a couple more devoted to charts and ledgers, a private suite at the summit in which he slept and meditated.

Tor Alessi's citizens treated him with a muted reverence. They parted to allow him passage along the narrow streets. Mothers brought their children out to witness his presence, as if that would confer some sort of protection on them. Soldiers bowed low; mages doffed their staffs.

He found the whole exercise ridiculous and irritating. His father, ever the consummate mythmaker, had appreciated deference, viewing it as an essential tool of kingship. His brother loved it for other reasons – it eased the constant doubt that nagged at his jealous soul. Imladrik, who had never wanted anything more than solitude and the clear air of black-flanked mountains, had come to hate it. In that, at least, he was of a mind with his wife.

Yethanial had been in his dreams ever since he had left Tor Vael. After their last meeting he had headed first to Lothern to take counsel from the commanders of the fleet, then to Caledor to summon his dragon riders. Only then, days later, had he embarked across the ocean at the head of the speartip of drakes.

In the days since then he had thrown himself into making sense of the sprawling web of armies committed to the defence of the asur territories. Communications in the wilds were difficult and estimates of the enemy strength, their movements and deployments, were confusing and contradictory. All that had kept him busy, which was good.

But if his days were full, his nights were empty. He would lie for hours on his shallow bunk, knowing sleep was far away, remembering Yethanial's look of reproach. He would turn her words over in his mind endlessly, worrying at them, picking them apart. He had never felt more alone. Draukhain was no comfort; like all dragons, he found mortal attachments trivial.

They are a fortunate breed, Imladrik thought. *To care only for freedom, to care nothing for confinement. As for us, we are nothing but the sum of our confinements.*

Imladrik reached the doors to his tower. The guards bowed low long before they needed to.

'My lord, tidings from Ulthuan,' reported one of them, a tall Sea Guard officer with a competent, soldierly look. 'Sent by swift dispatch from Cothique.'

Imladrik raised an eyebrow. 'Very swift. What news?'

'A single passenger. He awaits within. I checked his credentials.'

'Very good. No disturbances, please.'

'By your will.'

Imladrik passed inside and the doors locked closed behind him. Though he could not see them, he knew that archers had been stationed all around the tower. Units of spearmen were deployed nearby and a mage was on duty at all times in a neighbouring spire, all of them watching against attack. Centuries of warfare, open and clandestine, against the druchii had made the asur protective of their commanders.

His guest waited for him in the room beyond the entrance hall, lounging in a low chair by the fire. As soon as Imladrik entered he got to his feet, showing off a flurry of damask robes decorated with fabulously complicated images of serpents and seawyrms. His hair was straw-blond and arranged impeccably across slender shoulders. His face had a certain sharpness to it, but his smile came readily enough.

'My Lord Imladrik,' he said, bowing floridly.

Imladrik looked at him steadily. 'You were sent from Ulthuan? Who sent you?'

'I sent myself.'

Imladrik drew a seat up before the fire.

'You had better explain.'

'My name is Caradryel of the House of Reveniol, latterly in the service of Tor Caled. Though you will not remember it, we have met before. You did me the not insignificant service of saving my life when our ship was attacked by druchii. That placed me in your debt; since then, I have been searching for a way to repay it.'

Imladrik regarded Caradryel doubtfully. His speech was polished, but there was something... slippery about it.

'Latterly, though, I was fortunate enough to be presented with a way to remedy matters,' Caradryel went on. 'I learned you had no counsellor. This is, you might say, my speciality. I have a facility for the arts of state – negotiation, diplomacy, persuasion and inveiglement. I flatter myself, but to my mind there really is none better. So there it is: in this, you have my service.'

Imladrik couldn't suppress a twitching smile. Caradryel had front, that was certain.

'Interesting,' Imladrik said. 'Perhaps you can tell me why I should prefer your service to my officials stationed here, all of whom have sworn oaths to the Crown and to my security?'

Caradryel shrugged. 'They are competent enough, no doubt. Two things count against them. First, they are loyal to the Crown, not to you. I have no especial fondness for your royal brother, if I am truly honest, but have every personal reason to see you prosper. You might even say that it has become my vocation.'

'And the second?'

Caradryel smiled. 'None of them are as good as me. Not remotely.'

'You are not short of confidence.'

'Modesty is a waste of everyone's time.'

'I know someone who would agree with you,' said Imladrik. 'Myself, I have always thought it the mark of nobility.'

'I make no claim to be noble. Far from it. Still, I am the best offer you'll have out here.'

'So you clearly believe.'

'Perhaps you should ask how I got myself in here. Do you really think I had anything like the right credentials? Other supplicants have been waiting days for an audience and yet I arrived on the quayside yesterday evening with little more than the clothes on my back.' He smiled to himself, drawing a few tattered leaves of parchment from his robes' pocket. 'Your guards are thorough and honest, but they need to check the provenance of official seals more carefully. Honestly, I could have been *anyone*.'

'So you are a trickster,' concluded Imladrik. 'Tor Alessi has a thousand of them. Work quickly: your audience is drawing to its conclusion.'

Caradryel nodded to himself. 'You dislike subterfuge. Easy enough, for someone who can walk into any chamber in Ulthuan he pleases, though it has its uses for the rest of us. Here, though: perhaps this will speak more eloquently on my behalf.'

Caradryel took one of the leaves of parchment and handed it over.

Only a few words had been written on it, in a clear, elegant hand that Imladrik recognised only too well.

Though we parted at odds, my thoughts remain with you. The bearer of this message comes with my blessing. He is boastful and tiresome, but will serve you. Y.

Imladrik looked at it long and hard. Though none but he would have known it, the Eltharin characters had been written in such a way as to conceal a second meaning amid the words, something that Yethanial had long delighted in doing. *Trust him*, the hidden text said, lost amongst the swirls and loops of the runic script.

'Boastful *and* tiresome,' said Caradryel ruefully. 'I thought that a little harsh.'

'She finds the company of most people tiresome,' said Imladrik, reading the message again. 'Do not take it personally.'

Seeing Yethanial's calligraphy before him sharpened the sense of loss. He could imagine her, bent low over the writing desk, painstakingly drawing each character with the attention to propriety and order that characterised all her work. Beauty existed in everything she did – the kind of raw, bleak beauty that was prized in windswept Cothique.

'We spoke at length before I set sail,' said Caradryel. 'She understood what I understand: that Tor Alessi is a den of wolves, ready to tear apart your plans as soon as you make them clear.'

'My wife does not concern herself with statecraft.'

'Perhaps not,' said Caradryel, 'but she is a good judge of character. I approached her thinking I would persuade her easily; by the end, I was the one being examined. She is a formidable soul, if you will forgive me saying.'

'She is. She always has been.' Imladrik leaned back in his chair, feeling fatigue bite at his shoulders and wondering what to make of the figure before him. 'If she had not vouched for you, all your honey-tongued words would have made little difference. But she did, and so you give me much to think on.'

Caradryel's face become serious. 'Think on it as much as you wish, my lord, but time is not on our side. I know what is happening here. I know that you wish to halt the war, but most in this city do not – they will work to frustrate you at every turn, even as they smile to your face and bow before you. You cannot fight them openly, because they will not contest you openly. Salendor is one; there may be others. If you truly wish to bend the city to your will, then we need to act now.'

'I have done so. The orders have been issued.'

'Ah, but will they be carried out?'

Imladrik smiled coldly. 'Have a care, Caradryel. I am not some simpleton ripe to be lectured – I am your master. Remember that.'

'Master?' asked Caradryel, slyly. 'So we do have an arrangement?'

'Perhaps. Some tasks that need to be performed are difficult; I had not yet decided who to assign them to. One in particular might serve as a test: perform it well, and I will look on your application with favour. I need to contact someone. It must be done quietly, and it must be done quickly. It will be dangerous.'

'Perfect,' said Caradryel. 'Who?'

'His name is Morgrim Bargrum,' said Imladrik. 'He was a friend, once.'

'A dwarf?'

'If our scouts have it right, he is marching towards us even as we sit here. He will not be coming to talk.'

Caradryel smiled, though a little less assuredly. 'A challenge, then. We will have to change his mind.'

'To change a dwarf's mind,' Imladrik remarked dryly. 'If you can achieve that, my friend, then I may start to believe your boasts.'

TEN

Thoriol woke late. The sunlight hurt his eyes and he squinted against it, holding his hand up to the window. There were no drapes. He had no idea why.

He felt sick, as though the floor were pitching under him, and let slip a weak groan of wine-sickness.

He opened his eyes wider, getting used to the glare slowly. It was then that he realised the floor really was moving. For a few moments he had no idea what was happening. A stab of panic shot through his stomach.

Then he smelled salt, saw the narrow window in one wall of the chamber, and felt the rough planks of decking beneath him.

At sea, he realised, which made him scarcely less panicked. *How, in the name of Isha…?*

He pushed himself into a seated position, head hammering from the rush of blood. The wine-sickness at least was no illusion – he felt like vomiting.

So he did. He managed to get to the far corner of the tiny cabin before his guts rebelled, then retched for a long time, leaving a foul puddle of saliva-strung bile against the curved wall of the ship's hull.

Finishing made him feel only a little better. His whole body felt shivery and feverish. He had a dim recollection of a female elf with silk-like hair offering him something, but he couldn't remember what it was. It had smelled good, that he did recall.

Hands shaking, he clawed his way back to where he'd awoken. He'd slept in his robes, the same ones he'd worn coming down from the Dragonspine. He peered cautiously at the window again. The movement of the horizon made his nausea worse.

What day is this? How long have I been asleep?

He got to his feet, bracing uncertainly against the movement of the cabin around him. The space was barely big enough to house him and he cracked his head on the low roof. Cursing, he fumbled for the clasp on the door. After a few false starts, he managed to push it open, and staggered out into a larger space beyond.

Three figures turned to face him, all seated around a long table covered in charts. Leaf-shaped windows ran down the two sides of a larger cabin, each running with spray as the ship pitched.

'Good morning,' said one of them, looking at Thoriol with a smile.

Thoriol stared back at him. The elf had strangely familiar features: a scar on his right cheek and a blunt, tanned face. For a minute he was taken back to that evening in the House of Pleasure. How long ago was that? Last night?

'Who are you?' Thoriol managed to blurt out. He had to grasp the doorframe to keep from falling. 'Where am I?'

The elf with the scar motioned to his companions, who rose silently and left the cabin by a door at the other end. Then Scar-face beckoned Thoriol to join him at the table.

'Come,' he said. His voice had an earthy quality, rich with the accent of Chrace. 'You look like you could use a seat.'

In the absence of better options, Thoriol tottered over to the table, collapsed onto the bench and slumped to his elbows.

'Who are you?' he asked again, feeling like he might be sick a second time.

'Baelian.'

Thoriol stared stupidly, wondering if that should mean something to him. 'That all?'

Baelian shrugged. 'What do you want to know? This is my ship. The archers aboard are my company. As are you, of course.'

'As am I,' Thoriol repeated. He felt thick-headed. Some of what Baelian said resonated faintly with him, as if he'd dreamed of it a long time ago. 'I have no idea what has happened, but I warn you, sir, my father is–'

'Yes, you explained all of that,' said Baelian. 'Do you not remember?'

Thoriol managed to summon up the energy for a cold look. 'Obviously not.'

'You had taken a lot of it. Your first time, perhaps? It can do that to the unwary.'

As Baelian spoke, some recollection began to filter back through Thoriol's addled mind. *The dream-philtre. The poppy.*

'How long have I been out?' he asked nervously.

'Three days.'

Thoriol felt dizzy. He stared at the rough grain of the wood, trying to latch on to something certain. 'If you have taken me against my will,' he said, as deliberately as he was able, 'you will suffer for it.'

Baelian laughed. He pushed back, hands behind his head. 'Do I look like the kind? This is what you *wanted*, lad. You may not remember it now, but you will.'

As Baelian spoke Thoriol began to have the horrible feeling that he had done something very rash. His memory began to come back in slivers – he recalled speaking to Baelian in the House, watching the scar with fascination in the light of the lanterns.

'Why don't you remind me?' Thoriol suggested. 'That might save some time.'

'As you wish.' Baelian reached across the table and rifled through some leaves of parchment before drawing one out. He pushed it across to Thoriol. 'Your scroll of warrant. You signed it before we left Lothern.'

Thoriol stared at the sheet. It was covered with a dense screed of runes and had a wax seal at its base. Just above the seal he could see his own scrawled handwriting.

'We spoke for a long time,' explained Baelian. 'You wanted to escape, I made you a proposal. You were very keen to take it up. It'll all come back in time.'

'What does this mean?' Thoriol asked, struggling to decipher what he'd been given – the words seemed to swim before his eyes.

'You are a member of my company of archers. You've had the training, you know how to use a longbow. The pay's good, and in gold. You'll get it, too: ask anyone. Nothing to worry about, lad. You wanted to escape, and this is your chance.'

Thoriol ran a shaking hand through his blond-grey hair. His nausea got worse with every revelation. Some of what Baelian told him resonated, some of it didn't.

'You took advantage,' Thoriol accused, putting as much authority as he could into his voice. 'I was not in my right mind. You have no hold over me.'

Baelian looked amused. 'Is that right? That's not what the parchment says.'

'I had taken a... dream-philtre.'

'A dream-philtre? I'm shocked. You know they're prohibited?'

Thoriol looked up into Baelian's eyes and saw the mockery there. 'So that's how this works.'

Baelian sighed. 'Look, lad, this can be as easy or hard as you make it. You're one of the company. You can't change that, not until I release you, but you're no slave. Like I say, you'll be paid, you'll be trained. The captains aren't too picky about who serves these days, not with two wars running at once, so you'll be fine. Anyway, I look after my own.'

Thoriol barely listened. Already thoughts of his father's vengeance were running through his head. He guessed that this Baelian didn't fully understand who he'd taken on; telling him again would do no good, as he'd surely not convince him now. A familiar voice of derision echoed through his head.

You are a failure. You have failed again. And this time you are on your own.

'So where are we going?' he asked. He had to plan, to think, to recover. He was of the House of Tor Caled, the lineage of the Dragontamer – something would turn up.

'Where do you think? Where the fighting is.'

For a moment, Thoriol had a terrifying vision of Naggaroth – a land he had only heard about in hushed whispers. He knew that his father had campaigned in the seas off the frozen coasts, and there were rumours that asur raiding parties had penetrated the interior. Even before Baelian spoke again, though, he realised how stupid that idea was.

'The *colonies*, lad,' said Baelian. 'A long way from Ulthuan. You should be happy – you can make a fine fortune in the east, and whatever you're running away from back home won't follow you out there.'

Thoriol nodded wearily. So that was that – a single night's indiscretion, and he'd allowed himself to be hoodwinked into a stint in the wilderness. Once the ship made landfall he'd have to think hard on how to get out of it.

'Tor Alessi?' he asked, trying to picture how the next few weeks were likely to unfold.

'Where else?' said Baelian. 'Or, as you'll start to think of it soon, home.'

Thoriol smiled acidly. The stench of vomit was beginning to seep from his cabin, mirroring his mood. It was hard to think of a way in which he could have got things more badly wrong.

Of course, there was one silver lining; though by means he'd never have chosen, he was getting almost as far away from his father as possible.

That was something.

'You will *break!*' screamed Drutheira, slamming her staff on the rock at her feet.

Bloodfang reared up before her, forty feet in the air, its body snapping and twisting like a fish caught on a wire. Flames gusted and flickered, covering the black dragon in a nimbus of ash and light.

From her cliff-edge vantage high over the northern scarps of the Arluii, Drutheira could see its anguish – its jaws were twisted and torn, its eyes stared wildly. Every so often it would swoop down, flames licking at the corners of its mouth, ready to snap her up in a single bite.

She stood firm, staff raised and feet apart, knowing the creature could not break its magical bonds. Bloodfang would always pull out at the last moment, doubling back on its length, screaming with frustration and shooting back into the sky.

The beast's misery radiated out in front of her, a pall of anguish that seemed to stain the air itself, the agony of a great and noble mind laid to waste by the slow arts of the Witch King. Though she knew little of dragon-lore, she understood well enough what a mighty feat it must have been to enslave one of the famed fire-drakes of Caledor.

She wondered what exactly must have been done to break its spirit. Had it been raised from an egg by Malekith and tortured from birth? Or had it somehow been lured into the Witch King's clutches once full-grown and imprisoned in secret? She could not imagine what torments must have been applied, perhaps over decades, to turn what had been born as a creature of ecstatic fire into such a twisted, ruined horror.

Bloodfang's wings were ragged and punched with holes. Some bore the marks of hooks or iron rings. Its scaly hide was dull, as if caked with soot. Only its eyes still flashed with intensity – they were a white-less silver, and were painful to gaze at for too long.

Black and silver: Malekith's favourite colours. Truly, he had left his imprint heavily on the world.

'Break!' she commanded again.

Purple-edge lightning forked out from the tip of her staff, crackling around the hovering dragon and causing it to roar in fresh pain.

'You *know* my voice now,' hissed Drutheira, applying more power to the halo of dark energy dancing around her. 'Resisting will only bring you *more pain*.'

Bloodfang screamed at her, flicking the barbed point of its tail within a few feet of her face. Pain was the only thing its ruined mind truly understood.

Drutheira withdrew the sorcerous lightning, freeing Bloodfang from the lash of it for a few moments.

'Come, now,' she said, her voice softer. 'This can end. What remains for you, should you resist? You cannot go back to your kind now – they would rend you wing from wing. We are your guardians now. We are your protectors.'

That made Bloodfang scream again, though the strangled tone was different – almost a sob, albeit one generated from iron-cast lungs. Its wings beat a little less firmly; its body writhed with a little less frenzy. Its huge head, gnarled with tumours of black bone and horn, slumped lower.

Drutheira smiled. 'That is better. We may yet come to understand one another. Come closer.'

Malchior and Ashniel were nearby – she could sense their sullen presence – but neither came out into the open, for they had neither the power nor the will for this work and did not wish to risk inflaming the dragon more than necessary.

It hates us, thought Drutheira as the battered creature sank a fraction further in the sky. *It hates us, and needs us. Truly Malekith has excelled himself with this: he has taken our self-loathing and given it form.*

She lowered her staff and the last of the lightning flickered away, dancing across the bare stone like scattered embers. Drutheira took a single step towards the dragon, which continued to descend even though its fear and anger had clearly not gone away.

'Give in,' Drutheira urged.

Despite herself, she couldn't resist admiring the beast's damaged magnificence. Up close its sheer size was daunting. It stank of charred flesh and old blood, every downdraft of its wings sending a charnel mixture of ancient kills to waft over her. The thought of enslaving such power was faintly ridiculous – the beast could slay her with a casual twitch of its talons.

But it wouldn't. That was the genius of sorcery.

'Give *in*,' she breathed, watching the long neck bow in exhausted submission before her.

It came closer. She saw long trails of hot tears running down its cheeks and almost let slip a cry of joy. Her whole body tensed, ready for the most dangerous moment – Bloodfang's will had been ground down further, but the spark of rebellion had not been entirely extinguished.

Just a little closer, she thought, inhaling deeply as the wings washed pungent air across her. *A little... closer...*

Bloodfang's jaws reached the level of her shoulders. She snatched the staff up again and it blazed into purple-tinged life. The dragon tried to jerk away but it was too late – snaking curls of aethyric matter locked on to its neck, lashing fast like tentacles.

Drutheira launched herself into the air, leaping high and pulled upward by the crackling lines of force. The long whips of coruscation acted like grapple-lines, hauling her onto the creature's bucking neck and over to the rider's mount at the junction of its shoulders.

It all happened so quickly; before Bloodfang could lurch away from the cliff-edge Drutheira had straddled its nape. She planted her staff firmly, driving the spiked heel into the dragon's flesh. It screamed again, snapping its body like an unbroken steer's, trying to dislodge the goading presence on its back.

'Ha!' roared Drutheira, her eyes shining. She held her position, hanging on tight to the wing-sinews that jutted out on either side of her.

Bloodfang raced into the air, corkscrewing up into the heavens, screaming all the while in an incoherent mess of anguish. The wind raced past, pulling Drutheira's white hair behind her and making her robes ripple wildly.

She grabbed the golden chain that ran from the dragon's huge neck and yanked as hard as she could. Bloodfang's collar jerked back, wrenching the drake's head up and slowing its ascent.

Drutheira felt a hot surge of elation. The beast's scent filled her nostrils; its agony filled her mind. She could almost hear the creature's inner voice echoing in her own thoughts – a jumbled, maddened stream of half-thoughts and half-words.

'You know your master!' she cried, seizing the staff again with her right hand and twisting the spike in further.

Bloodfang roared in pain, but its spasms grew less violent. It came around, swinging back towards the cliff edge. Below them the land fell away in a steep drop towards the range's northern fringes. Drutheira caught glimpses of huge swathes of land spreading out into the distance – tracts of forest bisected by the grey ribbon of a mighty river snaking west towards the sea. The view thrilled her. Never before had she seen so far. It felt like she was the queen of the earth.

Far below, she saw Ashniel and Malchior creep from their hiding places to stand and gawp at her. She laughed to see that – they looked tiny, like insects crawling across dirt.

'And what do you say now?' she cried, hoping her voice would carry over the continued bellowing from her enraged mount.

They said nothing. Perhaps they could not hear her, or perhaps they had nothing to say. Drutheira turned away from them, uncaring. She had the vindication she needed: the dragon had been broken again. It would take time to learn how to command it properly, to force it to fight again, to trust it to respond to her commands.

In the meantime, the ascent into the heavens continued to make her heart beat with elation. She yanked on the chain, forcing Bloodfang to climb higher. The mountains extended out below her, a rumpled landscape of broken granite and snow-streaked summits. The wind around her was as cold as Naggaroth, as pure as hate.

Unbreakable, she thought to herself, sensing the massive power undulating beneath her and already planning what she would do with it. *Unstoppable.*

Sevekai crouched low, feeling his boots sink into the soft earth. They had been badly worn by the months he had spent in the wilds – the leather had split along the soles, letting in water and irritating the sores that clustered on his feet.

He was still sick. His chest gave him spasms of pain every time he breathed and his left leg was badly swollen. Vision had only properly returned to one eye; the other wept constantly. He was famished, chilled, often delirious.

For all that, things had improved since his awakening at the base of the gorge. Water had been plentiful in that dank, sodden chasm, so his strength had returned in gradual slivers, eventually enabling him to drag himself down under the cover of the trees. Refusing to countenance even the possibility of dying, he had grimly pulled himself like a worm along the forest floor, sniffing out anything that looked remotely edible.

He had had some successes – a thicket of wild rythweed that he'd been able to chew on, followed by a collection of sour crab apples left rotting under wind-shaken boughs. He'd made some mistakes, too: an appealing clump of milk-white fungi bulging in the shadow of a rotting log had made his stomach turn and given him blinding headaches and two days of vomiting.

Still, with every tortured step he'd taken since then a little more of his native strength had returned. His ordeal had begun to feel almost like purification – his body had been driven down to a whipcord-lean frame of sinew. When he stooped to drink at a stream, he saw a sunken, cadaverous visage staring back at him from the water and only slowly recognised the reflection of his own face. Everything came to him vividly, as if the world had been scrubbed clean and somehow made more real.

When not travelling he slept for long periods, drained by even the most mundane tasks. When he slept his dreams were lurid. He saw Drutheira in them often, and imagined they were still together.

'I am glad you survived, my love,' she told him.

'Where are you?' he asked.

'Far away,' she said. 'Keep moving. Keep walking.'

Sevekai did as his dreams commanded. Sometimes crawling, sometimes limping, he picked his way down from the gorge. The landscape of the Arluii never stopped being unforgiving: as soon as he negotiated one rock-filled defile he would be faced with a fresh wall of broken cliffs. Get around that, and he would have to plunge back into thick tangles of knotweed or negotiate treacherous, icy river-courses. A circlet of blunt peaks reared over him the whole time, vast and uncaring, cutting off the light of the sun and making his bones ache from the cold. He began to hate them.

Time passed in a strange way. He started to suspect he was sleeping for much longer than he ought to. Sometimes he would awaken and the world around him would look altered, as if too much time had passed, or sometimes not enough. Whenever he saw more clumps of mushrooms he ignored them; even his ever-present hunger did not make him desperate enough to risk more sickness.

Gradually, painfully, the severity of the mountains began to lessen. He staggered into a hinterland rising from a bare land of blasted grass and tumbled boulders. The wind moaned across them, snagging at the stone. He stumbled onwards, barely noticing which direction he was heading in, his feet falling in front of one another in a numb, automatic procession.

When he finally dropped to his knees he was faintly surprised to feel soft earth under his flesh, not rock. He lifted his head groggily and saw a hillside running away from him, fading eventually into a wide valley studded with scraggly vegetation. He twisted his neck to peer over his shoulder, back to where the outriders of the Arluii loomed up hugely against a darkening horizon.

Where am I? he asked himself, knowing that he had no means of answering.

He looked back down the slope. Ahead of him, a few hundred yards away, the scrub began to thicken into the tight foliage of Elthin Arvan's forest country. The further he went, he knew, the thicker it would get. Elthin Arvan was covered in forest, a cloak of wizened and grasping branches.

Such landscape was all he knew of forests – few trees grew in Naggaroth, and he was too young to have witnessed the blessed glades of Avelorn. When Drutheira had scorned the ugliness of the east, Sevekai had seldom understood her; next to the icy wastes of home, Elthin Arvan was teeming with life. Something about the smell of it appealed to him – the mulchy, sedimentary tang that never left the air.

He curled his fingers into the earth, watching the black soil part between them.

I can barely remember Naggaroth. And if I could... He smiled grimly, making his swollen gums ache. *Would I want to go back?*

A sudden noise ripped him from his thoughts. He instantly adopted a defensive crouch, ignoring the protests from his tortured limbs. For a few moments, he couldn't see what had made it.

He screwed his eyes tight, scanning the scrubland before him. His left hand reached down for the throwing dagger strapped to his boot. He hadn't heard the sound of a single living thing since waking. The sensation was strangely unnerving. His heart raced; his hand trembled slightly.

Then it came again, from ahead of him and to the left, a hundred yards away, lodged amid the jumble of bushes and boulders – like a hoarse cough, but far lower and richer than a druchii's voice.

Slowly, Sevekai crept towards the sound, keeping low, staring hard at the thicket of branches ahead. The lessons of his long training returned to him. His heart-rate slowed; his hands stilled.

Then he saw it: a stag, standing still amid a thicket of briars. It was young, its limbs slender and its flanks glossy. It looked directly at him, antlers half-lowered in challenge, nostrils flaring.

Sevekai froze. He could smell its musk and the scent made him salivate – it must have been weeks since he'd eaten more than berries. He clutched the hilt of his dagger tightly, preparing his muscles to throw.

Something nagged at him. Something was wrong. The stag just stood there, watching him. It should have bounded away, darting back into the cover of the trees.

Sevekai reached down gingerly and pulled a second dagger from his belt. A blade in each hand, he slunk a little closer, keeping as low and silent as possible.

He needn't have bothered. The stag stayed where it was, perfectly aware of his presence. Two black, deeply liquid eyes regarded him steadily. Its ribcage shivered as it breathed.

What are you waiting for?

Sevekai paused. Everything felt disconnected, as if he was in a dream. He sniffed. He picked up no taint of Dhar, but then he hardly had Drutheira's facility for sensing it.

A few more steps and he was into throwing range. He hesitated for a moment longer, perturbed by the creature's lack of movement.

Something is wrong.

Then, sharp as a snake-strike, he threw. The first dagger went cartwheeling through the air before *thunking* heavily into the beast's shoulder. The stag buckled, baying, and at last kicked free of the briars.

By then Sevekai was already moving. One hand loosed the second dagger, the other reached for a third. Every throw was perfectly aimed: one after the other, the long steel blades bit deep, carving through the beast's hide.

The stag managed to stagger on for a few more yards before tripping over its buckling legs and collapsing heavily to the ground. Sevekai caught up with it, grabbing it by its shaggy nape and using the last of his blades to slit its throat. He pulled the knife across its flesh viciously and a jet of hot, wine-dark blood gushed out, drenching his clothes.

The smell of it intoxicated him. He grew dizzy, both from the exertion and from the thick, viscous musk enveloping him. He reeled, falling down against the animal's heaving shoulders.

Blood splashed against his chin. Almost unconsciously, he sucked greedily on it. As soon as the hot liquor passed his lips he felt a sudden swell of energy. He plunged forwards, cupping his hands under the torrent and gulping more blood down.

The thick, earthy taste of it made his vision swim, but he kept going – it felt as if life were flowing into his limbs again, heating him, strengthening him. He drank and drank, tearing at the wound's edge with his teeth, gnawing at the raw flesh in his famishment.

He did not stop until the flow had slowed to a dribble and the stag's eyes had gone glassy. Then he pulled free, his hands shaking again, chin sticky with residue.

He felt nauseous. He sank down on his haunches and stared about him. The empty land gazed back, still scoured by the wind, still as broken and grey-edged as it had been. In the distance loomed the Arluii, a wall of solid darkness against the low sky. Behind him, the land fell away into the bosom of the gathering woodland.

It took a long time for his breathing to return to normal. Practical thoughts began to enter his head – to make a fire, to butcher the carcass, to preserve more for later, to clean the blades.

He did none of those things. He just sat, his face and hands as bloody as Khaine's. Something like vitality had returned, though it was bitter and hard to absorb.

The blood of the land.

He didn't know where those words came from. They entered his head unbidden, just as so much had entered his head unbidden since the fall.

Now you have drunk the blood of the land.

He began to shiver again, and wondered if some of the poison from his blades had got into the stag's bloodstream. His stomach began to cramp, and he curled over, coiled up next to the corpse of the stag in a bizarrely tender embrace. A curtain of shadow fell across his eyes. The shaking got worse. He tried to still his teeth's chattering, and failed.

So cold.

His eyes fluttered closed, his fists balled, his neck-cords strained. Cradled amid the limbs of the beast he had killed, Sevekai screamed. Then he screamed again.

It was hard to tell how long the screaming lasted. He nearly blacked out from it, but when the spasms finally eased he found he could lift his head. Lines of saliva hung, trembling, from his bloody chin.

Ahead of him, no more than ten paces distant, a crow was perched on a briar. It stared at him just as the stag had done, eerily unmoving.

Sevekai looked at it for a long time. Then, without quite knowing why, he held up his hand. The crow flapped across, alighting on his wrist and digging its talons in.

'Well met, crow,' said Sevekai, his voice cracked and hoarse. It sounded like someone else's.

The crow nodded its sleek head. Then, unconcerned, it began to preen.

Sevekai got to his feet. His head was light but the worst of the blood-agony had passed. He stood for a while, looking down into the valley, holding the crow like a falconer holds his hunting-bird.

For the first time, perhaps, in many years, something like certainty descended over him.

'It has changed,' he said, surprising himself. 'Blood of Khaine, everything has changed.'

ELEVEN

The chamber was dark, lit only by a few wall-mounted candles. Four bare walls enclosed an empty stone floor, a single door served as entrance and exit, and there were no windows.

Liandra waited impatiently. It was hard to resist the urge to pace up and down, like some prisoner in a cell. It wasn't just her current surroundings; ever since arriving at Tor Alessi she had felt confined. The huge city bore down on her, shutting her in, cramping her movement. Every so often she had fled the walls for a short time, taking Vranesh out on the sudden, vigorous flights the dragon loved. They had circled high up, going as far east as they dared, hoping against hope to see the first glimpse of the dwarf army marching through the forest.

But she could not always be on the wing. Membership of the Council brought duties with it: fresh troops arriving at the harbourside every day, and every shipful needing to be garrisoned and supplied.

It had initially been exhilarating to see the huge strength of the asur legions being landed at Tor Alessi. It had felt for a time as if the real power she had craved for so long had finally fallen into her lap.

That feeling had not lasted. She was not in command, not truly; Imladrik gave the orders, locked away in his isolated tower overlooking the sea, taking no advice and heeding no requests for fresh Council meetings. The enormous strength at his disposal was kept behind the walls. No armies were sent out into the wilds. No regiments were spared for outlying fortresses such as her own Kor Vanaeth.

For a long time she had held her tongue, biding her time. Surely, she reasoned, Imladrik would come to her. As the long days passed, however, it became clear that he would not.

Liandra had almost gone to the tower herself. She had walked halfway there, rehearsing what arguments she would make to him.

'Kor Vanaeth can be defended,' she had planned to say. 'Give leave for two regiments, that is all – two regiments and a battery of bolt throwers. The rest I can manage.'

She had never made it. As she had walked, her pride had got the better of her. Liandra had never begged, not even to him. Her father, still in Ulthuan fighting the druchii, had taught her that. If Imladrik had softened and turned away from the sacred savagery of his calling, then that was his loss; she would play no part in it.

Since then she had made no fresh attempt to contact him. She had festered, her frustration with enforced inaction growing with every wasted day. At times it felt like her heart was hammering at her ribcage, inflamed by imprisonment.

If he had not come back we would be marching by now, she thought, watching the candles burn low. *If he had not come back, the battles would have started.*

She heard a noise outside the door. Boots shuffled for a moment, then a key rattled in the lock. The door opened, exposing a cowled silhouette.

'Did anyone mark you?' asked Liandra.

'What do you take me for?' replied Salendor, slipping inside and closing the door. He pushed the cowl back, revealing coarse, battle-scarred features.

'As yet, I don't know,' said Liandra irritably. She hadn't wanted a meeting with him, not outside the confines of the Council and certainly not in the city, but Salendor was not an easy person to delay for long.

'I know your mind, Liandra,' he said, leaning against the wall. 'You and me, we are spirits of the same temper.'

'So you believe.'

'I can see it in your face. You chafe here. You've fought the dawi, just as I have, and you know what must be done.'

'And if I do?' Liandra stared at him defiantly. 'What does it matter? We have our orders.'

Salendor laughed. 'You care nothing for orders.'

Liandra bristled. It was tiresome to have a reputation for impetuosity, forever likely to tear off on some reckless charge into danger. Doubly so when it was true.

'Dragon riders,' Salendor went on casually. 'Gluttons for bloodshed, the lot of you. All but him. Why is that?'

'He is capable of it,' said Liandra.

'So they tell me, but I've seen no evidence. If not for his bloodline, I might suspect he had no stomach for a fight.'

'Then you would be a fool.'

Salendor shot her a shrewd look. 'None know him better than you, eh? I heard that too. Tell me, what passed between you when he was last here?'

'Why did you wish to see me, Salendor?'

'You know why. Peace is not possible. He might put off war for a few months, maybe years, but not forever.'

Liandra said nothing. Salendor was right, of course, but there was no point in confirming it.

'So we have two choices,' Salendor went on. 'First, we can change his mind.'

'Impossible,' said Liandra. Despite herself, a little sadness sank into her voice. 'Trust me, there is no turning it.'

'Then you know what must be done: we make other arrangements.'

'That could mean anything.'

'It means *acting*,' said Salendor. 'He can talk with them for as long as he wishes, but there will be no peace if we do not allow it.'

'You would not dare.'

'*We*, Liandra. You and me. Forget the rest of the Council – they would not stir if the world was ending around their ears. Gelthar is obsessed with defence and Caerwal... I do not understand Caerwal. His people have been butchered and still he hesitates. But you know the truth – we are *warriors*. We have already blooded the dawi, we will do so again. Think on it: my forces will follow my orders. Add yours, and near half the armies of Tor Alessi would march on our word.'

Liandra closed her eyes wearily. She could already see images parading before her – legions of spearmen coursing through open gates, picking up speed as they charged towards dug-in ranks of iron and bronze, surmounted by the raging wingbeats of dragons sweeping east. She saw herself at the head of it, as glorious and unstoppable as Isha, festooned in flame and underpinned by fields of steel.

'You do not know me,' she said softly.

Salendor lost his smile. 'What?'

Liandra opened her eyes. 'If you came here asking me to oppose him, then you do not know me.'

'So you spurn the offer.'

'It is no offer!' she said, her eyes flashing with anger. 'You give me nothing but revolt, something the humblest archer captain would blush to consider. I had heard you were a tactician, my lord, not a gutter-thief.'

Salendor pushed clear of the wall, suddenly looking dangerous. 'You dare to–'

'I dare nothing!' cried Liandra. 'And neither do you – we are just following our instincts, doing what we were trained to do. Do you think Imladrik is a simpleton? His troops would fight for him until their last breaths – *none of them* will stir to support you. You might as well ask them to fight with the druchii.'

Salendor took a single step towards her, his right fist clenching. For the first time Liandra saw just how powerfully built he was. 'Then you are in his thrall, just as I feared,' he said. 'What were you, then – his lover? His whore?'

'Say no more,' hissed Liandra, her own fists balling. A stray flicker of fire rippled over her flesh. 'I swear by holy Isha if you say another word I will kill you.'

They stood facing one another, hearts beating powerfully, eyes locked together. Liandra saw the desperation in Salendor's battle-scarred face.

For a moment she thought he might goad her further, just to test whether her threats meant anything.

Then, slowly, grudgingly, he backed down. 'They were unworthy words,' he muttered. 'I should not have spoken them.'

Liandra unclenched her own hands, feeling the burn from where her fingernails had dug in. He had dragged her close.

Salendor shook his head with frustration, looking like he wanted to punch the walls. 'But by Khaine,' he spat, 'he drives me to it. He does not answer my pleas. He will not bend. He will damn us all.'

Liandra looked at him coldly. All at once, Salendor's rage seemed ignoble to her, like the rantings of a child kept from his sweetmeats rather than the noble fury of a son of Ulthuan.

'You have said what you came to say,' she said. 'No word of it shall come from my lips. Now go.'

Salendor hesitated. 'I will not make the offer again,' he warned.

'You should not have done so now.' Liandra ran her hands through her hair. She felt weary, tainted. Despite the insult, some of what he had said hit near the mark. 'Salendor, I know why you suffer. On another day, in another war, perhaps I might have listened. But know this: I can never oppose him.'

Salendor looked at her grimly. 'So there it is. I made the attempt.' He started to leave, then halted. 'He has some hold over you, I see that. I will not ask you again, but beware. Memories are a poor guide.'

Liandra didn't reply. Salendor shrugged, withdrew down the length of the chamber and stalked back outside.

She waited for a long time after that, standing still as the candles burned down, leaving a suitable interval before following him out into the city. She had lost track of time and had no idea whether the sun had gone down.

It didn't matter. Salendor's words still echoed in her mind.

He has some hold over you, I see that.

Perhaps he had, once, but that was a long time ago. The more she thought about it, the more she doubted whether it had ever been true.

Caradryel rode uneasily. The guards Imladrik had sent to escort him were from his own personal retinue: Caledorian, each with a dragon-winged helm and riding a powerful black charger. Twenty rode within Caradryel's eyeshot; twice that were in bow-range, fanning out through the trees in a wide, almost silent arc.

Even to Caradryel's untrained eyes they were quite obviously deadly. Their captain, a sour-faced killer named Feliadh, had made no secret of his contempt for his feckless-looking charge. Feliadh had ridden ahead during the entire journey, conversing with his troops in a local dialect and avoiding standard Eltharin. The days had thus passed in a procession of weary, wordless rides followed by lonely and windswept camps.

Every so often the party would encounter bands of scouts returning from the east. Some looked relatively unscathed; others had been savaged, down to one or two survivors. Feliadh would ask them for news, which was always the same.

'They're on the march,' the scouts would say, voices wary. 'They're cutting down the trees as they come. We couldn't see an end to them. No end at all.'

Feliadh would calmly ask them the most direct route towards the dawi vanguard, ignoring the incredulous looks on the scouts' faces.

'If you really wish to...' they would begin, and then reluctantly offer directions.

Caradryel had lost count of how many such encounters they had had. Six, seven, maybe. With each one they passed a little further away from the security of Tor Alessi's hinterland and a little further into the dark, uncharted morass of Loren Lacoi.

The Great Forest, they called it. 'Great' referred to its size, not its beauty. Caradryel had been prepared for neither: the utterly huge expanse, nor the stinking ugliness of it. His horse's hooves sank deep into sucking slicks of mud. They ploughed through swarms of biting flies and had to cut through choking walls of briars. Strange noises welled up out of the shadows, echoing in the murk like laughter.

It was worse at night. Caradryel slept badly, huddled in his damp cloak and trying not to hear the whoops and calls of the distant gloom.

'Why are we fighting over this?' he muttered once to himself.

Feliadh overheard him. 'You have not been to Athel Maraya, my lord,' he said.

'Should I have?'

'Lord Salendor's realm,' Feliadh said, his voice full of admiration. 'Filled with the light of a thousand lanterns. Only Avelorn is more beautiful. One day this whole forest will be as Athel Maraya is now.' He glanced around them, scanning across the gnarled and bloated knuckles of the tree-branches. 'That is why we came here: to turn this filth into something that reflects honour to Asuryan. Do you not see that?'

Caradryel grunted something like agreement, though the pious tone in Feliadh's voice annoyed him.

That had been days ago. Since then they had pressed on, skirting south of the sprawling port-city of Sith Rionnasc and along the northern shores of the wide River Anurein. On the south-western horizon loomed the distant Arluii; ahead of them was nothing but forest.

They came across no further bands of scouts, and no living settlements. Once they passed through an abandoned Kor, its walls black and broken. Another day they stumbled across mine workings, long since deserted though still bearing the angular runes of the dawi over heavy stone lintels. Feliadh went cautiously through the ruins, wary of an ambush. None came. The war had driven its old inhabitants away long ago, just as it had in all the smaller dwellings. Now only the great fortified cities remained – islands in a sea of unbroken wilderness, guarded by high walls and watchful towers.

They passed into a long, snaking valley overshadowed by marching terraces of pines. A stream, half-stopped with rocks and silt, ran uncertainly down its base. Above them the sun struggled to clear a screen of white-grey cloud, casting grey light weakly over a dripping vista.

Caradryel shivered. Feliadh remained up ahead, his shoulders rolling easily with the gait of his steed. The Caledorian horses trod with uncanny skill, making almost no sound as they moved along the valley floor. The only noise was the faint moan of distant wind and the crack of twigs under hooves.

He tried to relax in the saddle. The trek was beginning to exhaust him. If it went on much longer, he might have to speak to Feliadh and demand a change of tack.

The first quarrels came out of nowhere – the first Caradryel knew of them was when a Caledorian outrider bent double, clutching at his breast and coughing blood.

The guards around him immediately drew their blades.

'Truce!' Feliadh roared, his harsh voice outraged. The captain's standard-bearer brandished the white flag wildly.

Caradryel struggled to control his mount. More quarrels scythed across the open space, sending the beast into a panic. Cries rang out as the darts found their targets. Caledorian outriders spurred their horses up the slopes, seeking out the sources.

'Where *are* they?' Caradryel blurted out loud, drawing his sword but seeing nothing to attack. The enemy must have been dug in, waiting for them with the patience of statues.

'We come under flag of truce!' shouted Feliadh again. Caradryel saw him spur his horse onwards, pushing further down the valley. He made no attempt to hide.

Typical Caledorian, thought Caradryel grimly. *More bravery than brains.*

He dug his heels in, forcing his skittish horse to stagger up the stony incline away from the river. Pine trunks surrounded him, mottled with shadows. He heard the dull *clink-thunk* of a crossbow mechanism working. Without thinking, he threw his body forwards, causing his steed to stumble. A dart whistled past his left shoulder, tearing the fabric of his cloak.

Caradryel hauled on the reins, yanking his mount's head around. For a split second he thought he caught a glint of armour in the undergrowth, but then it was gone, lost in a swirl of movement and shadows.

The Caledorian knights were more successful in unearthing hidden attackers, and the clash of steel against iron rang down from the upper slopes. Caradryel heard one of them shouting out an Eltharin battle cry before it was drowned by a sudden shout of *Khazuk! Khazuk!*

Nothing was in the open; everything was hidden. The Caledorians made heavy work of the defence, hampered by the trees and the terrain. Caradryel saw another one go down, the shaft of a quarrel shivering in his neck, but others gained higher ground and began to hunt down the crossbowmen.

'Truce!' bellowed Feliadh from further ahead, his voice increasingly forlorn amid the cries of aggression from all around. More quarrels fizzed between the trees, some clanging from shields or thudding into the trunks.

A few moments more and the encounter would be a bloodbath. The dawi either couldn't hear Feliadh or didn't care. Caradryel felt fear rise up his throat, ready to choke him. That would be a disaster – only he had the means of preventing a slaughter, and he was almost too scared to try it.

'*Khazukhan!*' he cried, standing in the stirrups and flinging his cloak back. If a dart were aimed at him now, he'd stand no chance. '*Imladriki a elgi tarum a grikhaz Morgrim Bargrum! Morgrim Bargrum! Imladriki a elgi!*'

Almost as soon as the words left his mouth, a horn sounded from high up the valley slopes. It was an unearthly sound – a brazen dirge that made the ground vibrate.

The rain of quarrels stopped immediately. Some of the Caledorians responded with cries of victory, thinking their counter-charge had routed the attackers, but Feliadh was astute enough to see what was going on.

'Hold fast!' he ordered, hauling his own steed round and hastening over to Caradryel's position. 'Do not pursue! Pull back!'

The rest of the riders did likewise, drawing together again, their swords still drawn and their manner wary. Three did not return; several more carried wounds or dented armour plates.

For a long, terrible period, nothing happened. The dwarfs seemed to melt back into the earth. The wind moaned down the valley, the needles rustled in the pines.

'What was that?' whispered Feliadh, keeping his eyes on the forest around them.

'Honest answer?' replied Caradryel, his heart still beating hard. 'I'm not exactly sure. Imladrik made me memorise it.'

Feliadh raised an eyebrow. 'Well memorised, then.'

Another horn-note sounded, a fraction higher, still with the thrumming reverberation that seemed to lodge in the bones. All around them, from just a few paces away to a hundred yards up the wooded slopes, dwarfs rose from the undergrowth. There must have been over a hundred of them.

'By the Flame,' breathed Feliadh, gazing at them.

Caradryel felt slightly sick. The trap had been artfully laid. If the Caledorians had kept up the pursuit they would have been overwhelmed, however bravely they fought. He had never seen such a display of stealth.

The dwarfs said nothing. They stood like graven images amid the bracken. Caradryel found it hard to tell one from another: they were all stocky, broad-shouldered, bearded and clad in thick plates of armour that overlapped across their burly chests. Dark eyes glinted from under the brow of iron helms.

Now that he saw them in the flesh, Caradryel at last understood some of what Imladrik had told him in Tor Alessi. When the asur called them the 'stunted folk', that implied something missing, something unfinished. He saw how false that was: they were almost as broad as they were tall, as sturdy as tree-roots and as heavy as ingots of pig-iron. They stared back at him without the slightest shred of fear or wonder. No doubt existed in those dark stares, just disciplined, regimented hatred.

They will never forgive, he realised. *They will never give in. They do not know how to.*

Eventually, one of dawi made a move. The dwarf broke ranks and waded towards them through knee-high undergrowth that reached his waist. His beard was steel-grey, plaited and folded up in a baroque array of knots and tassels. His exposed biceps were a patchwork of scars, tattoos and iron studs. Unlike the crossbow-wielders, he carried a warhammer, the head of which was beautifully engraved with runes and dragon-head knotwork. His helm was open-faced and crowned with drake-wings just like the Caledorians, though his were bulky and blunt in comparison.

When he was a few paces away he rested the hammerhead on the ground before him, folded his hands over the hilt, and leaned on it. His eyes, sunk deep under bristling brows, surveyed Feliadh's troops with calm disdain.

'Who here speaks Khazalid?' he demanded. His voice was deep and hoarse, as if clogged with coal-dust.

Caradryel swallowed. His usual self-assurance would not help him here. 'None do,' he said, edging his horse to the fore of the Caledorian group. 'I was given the words by another.'

The dwarf chuckled. It sounded like loose stones tumbling down a ravine. 'So I thought. You speak like a stupid child. We barely understood you.'

Caradryel bowed in apology. 'Forgive me. I had little time to learn. I had hoped to speak in… other circumstances.'

'No doubt,' said the dwarf. 'Thank your pale gods that we heard the name Imladrik – that is all that saved you.'

'He wishes to pass a message to his friend, Morgrim Bargrum,' said Caradryel. 'We had hoped to find him here.'

The dwarf scowled. 'If they were friends once, they are friends no longer. But if you carry terms of surrender we will hear them.'

Caradryel paused. This was difficult. 'Imladrik's tidings are for Lord Morgrim alone,' he said, trying to sound authoritative without being haughty. 'Unless, that is, it is he to whom I am speaking.'

The dwarfs broke into a barking, growling fit of laughter, filling the valley with their bizarre and guttural mirth. Caradryel could feel Feliadh's annoyance, and placed a hand on his forearm to restrain him.

Laughter is good, he thought, studying the chortling dwarf before him carefully. *I will endure a thousand insults if it gets us to where we need to be.*

'Your mind is as slow as your speech, elgi,' mocked the dwarf. 'You think we would risk Morgrim in the vanguard? You speak to Grondil of Zhufbar, slayer of your sickly kinfolk, and I ask you again: what are your tidings?'

Caradryel recalled what Imladrik had told him of the dawi.

'They despise weakness, and they despise arrogance,' Imladrik had told him. 'Steer a path between the two: never show frailty, but never insult them. Everything they do is a challenge. Give in to it, and they will hold you in contempt; ignore it and they will assume you mock them. Remember: they kill anything that mocks them.'

Caradryel swallowed.

'Grondil of Zhufbar,' he said. 'I am Caradryel of the House of Reveniol. I serve Imladrik of House Tor Caled. He commands me to speak only to Morgrim. You have us at your mercy and may slay us at your pleasure, but for all that none among us will break our vows. I will speak with Morgrim alone, or I will die here in this valley. They are the choices: you, my lord, have the decision.'

For a moment, silence. Caradryel felt a chill run up his arms. His stomach felt weak. The words 'die here in this valley' had slipped out rather easily.

Then Grondil chuckled again, and shook his head. 'Elgi amuse me,' he said. 'So serious, all the time. And you love your fine words.'

He shot Caradryel a sly, intelligent look.

'I'll take you to Morgrim,' Grondil said. 'Though you'll have to watch your scrawny backs with him – he doesn't have my sense of humour.'

Thoriol emerged into the sunlight, blinking and stumbling. He carried his gear slung across his back, just like the others. They were dressed the same way: loose-fitting white robes trimmed with a deep crimson. Baelian's company shouldered their longbows casually, used to the cumbersome lengths of yew and silk-spun bowstrings. Thoriol remembered enough of his training to use the weapon but struggled to look proficient with it.

'It'll come,' Baelian had told him during the crossing, grinning as ever. 'Soon you'll forget what it was like not to carry one.'

Thoriol gazed up at the soaring spires of Tor Alessi, glistening white in the strong sunlight. Gull-shrieks filled the air. Behind him, the length of a gangplank away, the *Resurviel* bobbed on the quayside. Harbour-hands were already crawling all over her, furling sails and stowing lines.

Baelian's company assembled on the stone quay, all twenty-four of them. Crowds pushed past them as Baelian attempted to call them to order and speak to the harbour official. Everything in the waterfront seemed to be in constant motion – a carnival of unloading, loading, shouting, moving and hauling. The wind was stiff and thick with salt. The aroma of it was different to Ulthuan – fewer spice fragrances and somehow... dirtier.

While Baelian argued with the official, Thoriol let his eyes wander across to the towers rearing up ahead. Some of them still bore the scars of ballista strikes. Banners of the King and various noble houses rippled in the breeze, exposing images of trees, horses, sea-serpents and hawks.

Everything was martial, hard-edged and poorly finished. Tor Alessi seemed to have no purpose to it but war.

Eventually Baelian turned away from the official, his scarred face tight with irritation.

'Fools,' he spat, rolling up some parchment and stowing it under his robes. 'This place is full to bursting and they're running around like startled pheasants. Useless.' He started to storm off, then turned and gave Thoriol a significant glance. 'Stay together. I've got us lodgings in the lower Eliamar quarter. Let's not get lost in the crush, eh?'

Thoriol smiled dryly. The captain had little to worry about – Thoriol had no plans to make an escape any time soon. Despite himself, he had found himself rather enjoying his reacquaintance with the archery he had learned as a youth. He'd taken a surprising degree of pleasure in handling the long yew bow, in stringing it and leaning in to the pull.

It came back quickly. He remembered how he'd taken hunting bows into the forests west of Tor Vael, and how proficient he'd become at bringing back a haul for the larders. He'd always had a quick eye, and enjoyed the lightweight spring of the weapon; far more elegant than a sword or an axe. Only later had that enjoyment faded, and he'd never had the chance to become expert with the battlefield weapons of the asur companies – long, slender bows with a range of over two hundred yards and a fearful delivery. The effort required just to bend those bows was considerable, and after days of practice on the ship he was only capable of matching his counterparts' most elementary efforts.

For all that, the process had been oddly cathartic. The others had accepted him readily, showing little or no interest in his origins but willing to help him learn. They shared watered-down wine, bread, hard cheese and olives, discussing the potential for riches in the east, the prospects for the war against the druchii, tales – implausible or otherwise – of love affairs in Saphery and Avelorn.

After the worst of his sickness had abated, Thoriol had found himself more at ease in their company than he would have imagined possible. His early reticence had earned him the moniker of 'the Silent'. Despite opening up a little since then, the name had stuck, and he saw no harm in it.

He had made friends: Loeth, the tall one from Tiranoc; Taemon, the intense brooder from Chrace; Rovil and Florean from Eataine, good-natured, jovial and as close as brothers.

They did not judge him, except in jest. They accepted the strange gaps in his history without question, for most of them had similar missing pieces from their own half-told lives. They did not talk of arcane matters or the deep counsel of kings, but they laughed often, and seemed to have few cares beyond the acquisition of prestige, the payment in gold coin every month, and the care of their bows and quivers –about which they were all fastidious.

So the crossing had not been as arduous as Thoriol had feared. He still rankled over the deception that had brought him there, and remained wary of the ever-smirking Baelian, but he could not pretend that it had been unbearable.

Now, looking at the teeming mass of asur around him, letting the rough-edged splendour of Tor Alessi sink in, feeling the firmness of solid ground under his feet for the first time since passing out in Lothern, he smiled ruefully.

The world was a strange place. For the time being, he would see where the current path led. Thoriol the Scholar was long dead, confined to a past that he could not talk about. Thoriol the Dragon rider had always been a fiction, something that he'd known deep down would never amount to much.

Thoriol the Archer, though. It had a certain ring to it. Perhaps not enough for him to tarry with it for more than a few weeks, but a certain ring nonetheless.

'Lost in thought?' came a familiar voice just ahead of him. Rovil was grinning at him.

'Always lost in thought,' said Taemon sharply.

'Or seasick,' said Loeth. 'Though that won't be a problem now.'

Thoriol said nothing, happy to live up to his new name, but smiled back amiably.

Then he pulled his hood up against the chill sea-wind, taking care to avoid the crush of bodies around him, and followed his companions up the winding streets from the waterfront to whatever future awaited him in the city.

TWELVE

Caradryel sat on a low, rough-hewn bench, resisting the urge to scratch his neck. He kept his back straight and his hands clasped loosely in his lap, trying to project the kind of elegant disinterest that he supposed the dawi would expect him to display.

Since arriving at the dwarf camp he had felt eyes all over him, scouring him like some slab of precious metal ready for the hammer. They were subtle, though; they never looked at him straight on, but only from under heavily lidded eyes. He could never quite meet their gaze – they turned away, quick as cats, muttering impenetrably into their plaited beards.

He'd done his best to observe them in return, making mental notes of their habits and demeanour. Their physicality was quite astonishing, from the tightly corded muscles of their exposed forearms to the heavy tread of their ironshod boots. They crashed through the undergrowth like bulls, growling, expectorating and grumbling the whole time. Yet, when they truly wanted to, they could slip into the shadows like wraiths, sinking into an almost trancelike stillness.

They smelled strongly, though not in the bestial, unclean way he'd imagined they would, but more of burned things: metal, leather, embers. If anything, they reminded him of the faint aroma he'd detected from Imladrik, the residue from the drakes he rode.

They had treated their guests well enough – curtly, with plenty of snide remarks on elgi weakness and moral cowardice, but no physical violence. That gave Caradryel at least some hope that things were not as far gone as they might have been. Grondil had escorted him and the Caledorians to a clearing some five miles from where the ambush had been laid. On the way they'd passed several heavily armoured columns of dwarfs marching west. They didn't so much march through the forest as annihilate it, smashing aside the grasping branches and treading the splinters into the mud. Now Caradryel sat alongside Feliadh and the others, waiting; ignored by the dozens of dawi warriors that came and went across the clearing, though their hostility was palpable on the air, hanging like a stink of contagion.

Perhaps, he admitted ruefully, thinking back on his grand plans for ingratiation, *on this occasion at least, I may have overreached myself.*

'Who is the one sent by Imladrik?' came a voice then from the far side of the clearing.

Caradryel's head snapped up. A dwarf had emerged from the trees, flanked on either side by a retinue of axe-wielders in iron battle plate. Unlike most of the others he wore no helm, and his black beard spilled openly across his finely worked breastplate.

Something about his eyes, the way he looked straight at Caradryel in the way that none of the others did, gave away his status. Those grey eyes had the fixed certainty of command that he'd only witnessed before in Imladrik. Like him, this dwarf walked with a kind of unconscious air of confidence. Also like him, there was a bleakness to him, an austere mien that lined his face and gave his wrinkled skin a greyish sheen.

'I am,' Caradryel said, rising from the bench and bowing.

The dwarf lord looked at him for some time before snorting. 'You're no warrior,' he observed.

'Indeed not.'

'Why did he send you?'

'I perform these things for him. My service is with words, not with blades.'

'I can see that.'

Caradryel worked hard to maintain a deferential manner, fully aware of his danger. Out of the corner of his eye he saw the heavily armoured guards regarding him carefully, as if yearning to find an excuse to strike.

'Imladrik spoke to me highly of the dawi,' Caradryel said.

The dwarf lord grunted. 'Imladrik,' he repeated slowly, as if savouring the bitter taste of the word. 'He is here again, on this side of the ocean?'

'He is at Tor Alessi.'

'Why did he not come himself?'

'For the same reason, I imagine, that you do not walk in the vanguard.'

The dwarf nodded slowly. 'Once he rode freely all the way to Karaz-a-Karak. He was our guest at the Everpeak. Did you know that?'

'They were freer times.'

'They were.'

The dwarf lord gestured to his retinue – the faintest movement of a finger – and the armoured warriors withdrew a few paces, crossing their arms and glowering on the edge of the clearing.

'These are my *bazan-khazakrum*,' he said to Caradryel. 'Each has sworn a death-oath and would lay down his life a dozen times over before any harm came to me. They find your presence an insult.'

Caradryel resisted the urge to glance at them. 'I regret that.'

'Perhaps you think that your status will be enough to protect you.'

Caradryel could sense Feliadh and the others tensing up and willed them not to do anything stupid. Caledorian hot-bloodedness was an asset on the battlefield but a handicap for this sort of work.

'I understand the point you are making,' he said.

'Do you?' The dwarf lord drew closer to him. 'What point am I making?'

'What happened to your ambassadors was shameful,' said Caradryel. Those words, at least, were no deception – Caledor had been stupid to humiliate the dwarf embassy and all but the most blinkered of his ministers knew it. 'Imladrik regards it as an unforgivable crime.'

'Unforgivable, eh?' The dwarf lord came closer still. His forehead came up to Caradryel's chest, but somehow the disparity in height did nothing to alter the unequal relationship of threat that existed. Caradryel felt ludicrously skinny next to the solid mass of flesh and iron that stood before him. He could smell the dwarf's breath – a meaty, beery aroma. 'Imladrik knows we never forgive anything, so that's not saying very much.'

Suddenly, with a jerk of speed, the dwarf grabbed Caradryel's long blond hair and yanked him down to his knees.

'Shall I rip these golden locks from your head?' he hissed, pushing his face towards Caradryel's in a snarl. 'Shall I shave your head and send you limping back to Tor Alessi?'

Caradryel grimaced, feeling his scalp flex, hoping Feliadh had remained completely still. The dwarf twisted his fist further, half-pulling a clump free, making Caradryel gasp.

Then the pressure released. The dwarf let him go, shaking a few loose tresses from his gauntlet in disgust.

'We do not do such things,' he muttered. 'We leave that to savages.'

Caradryel caught his breath, still on his knees.

The dwarf lord glared at him coldly. 'So what do you have to say to me?'

Caradryel looked up. 'You are Morgrim?'

'I am.'

'Then I am instructed to tell you this. Imladrik knows of the wrongs done to your people. He laments the death of Snorri Halfhand. He grieves for the loss of trust between our peoples, and understands that much blood has been shed on both sides, but still believes that an unwinnable war between us may be averted. He wishes to speak to you, as he once did, to explain what we know of this conflict's origins.'

Morgrim looked at him wearily, as if he'd hoped for something better, but did not interrupt.

'There are things about my race you do not know,' Caradryel went on. 'We are divided. This war is part of that.'

Morgrim laughed harshly. 'You say this now, when your cities are besieged. You say this now, when our strength is revealed and you realise the folly of shaming us.'

Caradryel wanted to stop him there, to point out that however strong the dwarf legions were they had nothing to compare with the flights of dragons, and that Imladrik's embassy was sent not from weakness but from strength, and that Tor Alessi had been turned into an anvil on which even the mightiest of hosts would break like foaming surf.

But he said none of that – it would have done no good.

'So what can Imladrik offer?' demanded Morgrim, his eyes flashing with anger. 'My cousin lies dead. Some of my people now live only to see the elgi driven into the sea – what shall I say to them?'

Caradryel clambered back to his feet, brushing the soil from his robes. Just as he had done before, he aimed to find the balance – not craven, not arrogant, not supine, not threatening.

'Imladrik knows you will march on the city. He knows your people demand vengeance and knows you are sworn to deliver it. All he asks is that, for the sake of your old friendship, you speak to him once before giving the final order. He will meet you, under flag of truce. He requests nothing more – no assurances, no treaties – just the chance to speak.'

Morgrim's grey eyes flickered, for the first time, with less than certainty.

'That's all?' he asked.

Caradryel risked a nod. 'If he has any further tidings, he has not shared them with me.'

Morgrim shook his head and turned away. 'This army is drawn from all the holds,' he muttered. 'There is no dam capable of holding it back now.' He snapped his gaze back to Caradryel. 'It is too late. It cannot be stopped.'

Caradryel met his glare evenly. 'He told me you would say that, and so told me to reply thus: The runes never lie, but nor do they compel. Nothing is fated.'

That held Morgrim's attention. The dwarf pondered the words for what seemed like an age.

Caradryel watched him, saying nothing. He had heard it said that dawi minds were slow, like those of simpletons or children, but he saw the lie in that immediately. Morgrim was no fool, and if his thoughts worked with more deliberation than an elf's then perhaps that was to his credit. Caledor had a quick tongue and a ready wit, but it had not made him a wise king.

Finally Morgrim's face lifted again.

'The march continues,' he announced. 'I swore an oath to bring this army to Tor Alessi and I will not break it.'

He drew close to Caradryel again, the familiar breath-stink of meat and ale wafting over him.

'But I will think on your words,' Morgrim said, making it sound more like a threat. 'By the time you smell sea-salt, you will know my answer to them.'

Final preparations had been made. The great hawkships of the fleet put to sea again, packed with ballistae and Sea Guard units to keep the supply routes open. The last repairs were made to the city's battlements and bulwarks. Standards bearing the runes of war – Charoi, Ceyl, Minaith, Urithair – were slung from every parapet and balcony, rippling down the pale stone in a riot of blues, reds and emeralds. Tor Alessi's many walls stood proudly against the desolation of the land about them, rising up like spars of dirty bone from the scorched and scoured earth below.

They will drown in their own blood, observed Draukhain, wheeling high above the tallest of the towers. *The city is impregnable.*

Imladrik gazed down at the sprawling fortress below, not sharing the dragon's assessment. To be sure, the defences were awe-inspiring – taller, thicker and more heavily manned than at any time since the city's foundation – but he'd seen what the dwarfs could do when their blood was raging.

Our strength is not in the walls, he sang. *I hope, though, that they will prove enough of a deterrent.*

Draukhain laughed, pulling hard round and swinging over the sea. The long, maundering coasts extended far into the north, their smooth strands broken by rocky dune country.

So restrained, the drake mocked. *You really are not much sport.*

The sun blazed strongly, making the sea sparkle and lifting the worst of the gloom from the nearby forest. Imladrik turned his head to the east, watching curls of mist rise from the brooding treeline. It looked like the woodland had somehow contracted, pulling together like an inhalation before the storm.

Just on the edge of sensation, he almost felt something, like a faint whiff of burning, or the distance-muffled sound of iron boots crashing through rotten wood.

Consumed by it, he missed Liandra's approach, coming out of the sun-glare some hundred feet above him, riding the high airs with her habitual carefree abandon. He only sensed her at the last minute, just as she swung alongside him, her red steed trailing a long line of hot smoke behind her.

'My lord!' cried Liandra, saluting him. Her copper hair buffeted out behind her, her robes tugging at her body in the wind.

He saw her then just as he remembered her – a creature of fire, a spirit of the raw heavens, unbound and vivacious. It was as if the past had suddenly come alive before him, his memories crystallising out of empty skies.

'My lady,' he responded, immediately wincing as he remembered how he and Yethanial played at such exchanges. 'I did not know you were aloft.'

Liandra laughed. She was close enough now for him to see her face light up in amusement – the narrowing of her eyes, the wrinkling of her freckled skin.

'No,' she replied. 'I don't suppose you did. You've been busy since you got here, lord. Too busy to speak to me, it seems, or to know very much of what I am doing – no doubt you've had weightier matters on your mind.'

The familiar insolence – he'd missed it.

'I have been busy,' he admitted, giving Draukhain his head and speeding further up the coastline. Vranesh struggled to match the pace and was soon spitting sparks of effort from her flame-red maw. 'As you should have been too.'

'Oh, my duties have been many. I have thousands of spears under my command, all waiting for orders to march. They have been waiting a long time.'

'I know,' said Imladrik. He was not blind to their frustration. 'And if I have my way they will be waiting longer still.'

Do you really think you can halt it? Liandra sang, her voice appearing in his mind as suddenly and as clearly as Draukhain's did.

That stung him. It was an intrusion, an unwelcome reminder of how they'd once conversed.

'You always wanted to fight them, Liandra,' he responded aloud, pushing Draukhain harder. The wind raced against him, making his crimson cloak ripple. 'You wanted it even before Kor Vanaeth.'

'No,' she replied, shaking her head vigorously. 'I did not. I came with you to the mountains and tried to understand them. Remember this – they started the killing.'

Imladrik let slip a weary laugh. 'Oh, they *started* it. Then that makes everything clear.'

You make it sound as if our races are equals, she sang. *You make it sound as if they could actually hurt us, if we had a mind to prevent it.*

Draukhain swung round again, enjoying the speed and exchange. He seemed to be goading his younger counterpart a little, daring her to match his mastery of the air. Imladrik let him.

'You are all the same,' said Imladrik wearily. 'You, Salendor, my brother: you think we are bound to destroy them. You are all wrong.'

Are we? Or is it you, my lord, who is afraid?

Imladrik spun around, hauling Draukhain back on himself in mid-air, rearing up in the sky like a charger on the battlefield.

'Afraid?' he asked, incredulous.

Liandra laughed again. 'Of battle? You know I do not mean that.' She was struggling to keep Vranesh on a counter-trajectory to match Draukhain's dazzling change of angles. *You are fearful of what would happen if you unleashed yourself, if you allowed yourself – for one moment – to let slip the shackles she has placed on you and became what you know you should be.*

Only then did Draukhain's flight dip from perfection. Imladrik's mind flickered, momentarily, out of focus.

What do you mean? he sang, inflecting the harmony with warning.

That you are a dragon rider, lord. You always have been. You have fire in your blood but you will not light the kindling. As Liandra spoke her eyes glittered, as if she was both thrilled and appalled by what she was saying.

You think you love her – you have persuaded yourself you do – but you are wrong. She has tamed you.

Imladrik rose in the saddle, angling his staff towards her, feeling a hot wash of anger building behind his eyes.

'Foreswear those words!' he cried, feeling Draukhain respond instantly. The dragon's vast wings fanned the air into a whirl of ashes and flame-flickers. Raw aethyr-fire rippled along his staff-length, crackling angrily.

Liandra glared back at him, her face twisted in both delight and fear.

'I take back nothing, lord!' she shouted across the gap between steeds. 'The truth needs to be told!'

Imladrik spurred Draukhain towards Vranesh, and for a moment, just a moment, he teetered on the edge of attack. He could already see the outcome – the tangled clash of talons, laced with the quick burn of actinic magic. He had a splintered image of himself, wreathed in anger and lightning-crowned majesty, cleaving the air apart and casting the Sun Dragon down and into the sea.

At the last moment he pulled away. Draukhain turned, pulling out of the encounter and swinging back out seawards, and he caught a glimpse of Liandra's defiant, terrified face staring right at him.

The dragons spun apart, wings beating and tails writhing. Draukhain quickly took up the dominant position, his shadow falling over the smaller Vranesh and turning her vivid red scales into a dull, dried-blood colour.

Is this what you intended? Imladrik sang, controlling his mighty steed with some difficulty. *To make me angry? You would risk that, knowing what it means?*

Liandra's resolve dissolved then – she was like a child who'd pulled at the tail of a cat and now had to contend with the claws.

'Something had to stir you!' she cried aloud. 'You are *dead!* You treat me with contempt, like some lordly conquest which now means nothing to you – a toy, thrown aside now that you have taken up loftier things.'

'I never dishonoured you,' said Imladrik.

Then Liandra laughed for a third time, and the sound was bitter. 'No, you did not. I do not believe a day has passed when you have not kept your honour, my lord.'

Imladrik said nothing. The words cut him deeply, especially coming from her. He knew what they all wanted of him, and he also knew what *she* wanted of him – the two things were much the same. Just as he had done years ago, he felt the tug of desire, the pull towards oblivion. The dragon responded to it, growling like a blast furnace lighting up.

It would be so easy. He could give in this time, forgetting about windswept Tor Vael, forgetting about Ulthuan and its survival. The two of them could do what they had resisted before and take the fight to the enemy together. They could sweep east at the head of Caledor's armies, burning a furrow through the forest until the flames licked the very ramparts of Karaz-a-Karak.

He saw Draukhain and Vranesh flying in dreadful unison, the Master and Mistress of Dragons searing through the air like vengeful gods, cracking open the halls of the dwarfs and exposing the deeps within. He could cut loose at last, unlocking the cage that kept his true nature sealed behind layers of control. He could unfurl, giving into the second soul that whispered within him and finally, just for once, forget duty and embrace *pleasure*.

He felt the words form in his mind, ready for the song that would seal things.

I long for it. I long to bring ruin on them, with you by my side. I would wage war until the end of the world with you, caring for nothing but death and splendour.

In the end, though, it was Liandra that turned away, as if suddenly afraid of what she might goad him into doing. Vranesh's head dipped, and the two of them started to circle back down, gliding through the twisting air currents.

'But you are right, of course,' she said bleakly. 'You are always right.'

Imladrik followed her. The fury ebbed from him, but only slowly.

You deserved better than silence, he sang.

That halted her. Vranesh slid round, angling so that Liandra could look back up at him. She gave him a proud look.

'I did.'

'And do not think, even for a moment, that I had forgotten.' Imladrik came down to her level, easing Draukhain's bulk alongside the slender Vranesh. 'We are all the children of Aenarion, Liandra. That is our downfall. We have only ever been defeated by ourselves.'

Tor Alessi was by then barely visible, a speck of white stonework on the long shore. They could have been alone, the two of them, lost in an edgeless sky.

'Do you not think it would be easier for me to give Salendor what he wishes?' Imladrik asked softly. 'I know what it would bring – victories, to begin with. For a time we would hurt them. Our thirst for vengeance would be slaked, and we would revel in it.'

Draukhain was circling Vranesh now, turning in a wide falconer's arc as Imladrik kept speaking.

'But then the long grind would begin. Athel Maraya would burn. Athel Toralien, Sith Rionnasc, Oeragor – they would all burn. We would throw our finest into those flames and they would wither. Even the dragons would grow sick of it as the years wore on; they would no longer heed our songs, leaving us alone against an empire of mindless fury.'

Liandra listened warily, as if he was spinning some deception around her.

'And who would gain from this?' asked Imladrik. 'You know whose hand was behind the war – the same that grasps the sceptre in Naggaroth. I will not see that happen. I will not let our desire for vengeance give him what he desires.'

She never looked away. Her expression never changed: sceptical, bruised, disappointed.

'You sell us short,' she said.

'That is your judgement,' said Imladrik.

'Then I must warn you, lord,' said Liandra, nudging Vranesh closer. 'You are wrong. This course leads to ruin. We must strike now before they gather more strength.'

Imladrik nodded. 'I know your view, though it changes nothing.'

'So what, then, of us?'

Imladrik felt his stomach twist. The burn of desire was still there – for another life, one that he had only glimpsed in brief intense snatches. Above it all, though, hovered Yethanial's calm presence, the one who had sustained him, the one his true soul cleaved to when away from the heady madness of the dragon.

'That moment has gone, *feleth-amina*,' he said, forcing the words out. 'We have both taken vows.'

Liandra looked at him for a little longer, her face flushed. He couldn't decipher her expression – it could have been anger, or maybe humiliation, or simply disbelief. They hung there for a while longer, their steeds' wings making the air thrum, before her expression finally hardened again.

'You may have done, my lord,' she said. 'For myself, I vow nothing.'

Then Vranesh arched, twisted, and shot down towards the sea. She went quickly, like a falling stone, plunging down towards the sparkling waters.

Imladrik watched her go, motionless in the air, letting Draukhain hold position and giving him no orders.

For a long time he said nothing at all. The wind pulled at his hair. He felt wretched, more wretched than he could remember being – even the brisk push of the salty air felt stale and old.

I like her, sang Draukhain eventually. *I always did – she has a heart after our own. Are you sure you are right in this, kalamn-talaen?*

Imladrik's eyes remained locked on the diminishing figure of the flame-red dragon as she spiralled out over the ocean.

No, great one, he sang bleakly. *I am not sure about anything.*

'Draw!'

Thoriol bent into the pull, using his whole body to lever the arrow on to the string. Alongside him on the battlements his company did likewise; alongside them a hundred other companies the same. With a ripple of steel points, the battalions of an entire wall-section pulled their bowstrings tight, angling the heavy yew shafts and holding position.

Thoriol felt his muscles tremble as the tension bit. He'd become far more proficient than he had been, but the effort of using the longbow was considerable and he was less comfortable with it than his companions. They could work a longbow for an hour and register little fatigue, whereas he was struggling after several flights.

He gritted his teeth, desperate not to lose face. Loeth stood beside him, calm as ever.

'Release!'

The order was a relief – Thoriol loosed his arrow with the others, watching as the dense hail of darts soared up into the sky and arced down to the plain beyond.

The sight was a stirring one. Their wall-section was nearly fifty feet above the level of the plain, facing due east. The arrows clustered together in a thick cloud, whistling through the air before jabbing down into the sodden earth far below. The range was impressive – over a hundred and fifty yards, with each dart falling within a wide band. Thousands of arrows already stood at angles in the mud, the results of many previous volleys.

'Draw!'

If Thoriol had counted correctly, this should be the last one. He'd already reached for his arrow in the rack before him and had it ready. He grasped the string with three fingers, feeling the single-feather fletch brush against his knuckle. The nock slid up against the silken string, and he pulled it tight using his bodyweight as a counterbalance.

At such ranges the aim was not as important as the timing. The task was to fill the air with a thick cloud of arrows, all hammering earthwards in a single block. The defenders of Tor Alessi knew from experience that dwarf armour was extremely tough and so single shots were rarely effective. The only thing that troubled units clad in steel plate was a veritable flood of darts, clogging the air and rattling down against them in a dense cloud. At such concentrations there was every chance of hitting an exposed joint or sliding through a narrow eye-slit, and, even if the majority of arrows wouldn't register a kill, the flight as a whole would badly hamper any advancing formation.

'Release!'

Thoriol let fly, watching with satisfaction as his arrow soared upwards with the others. The air thickened with shafts again before they swooped down in unison, tracing a steep arch towards the plain below.

It was a sight to gladden the heart of any true son of Ulthuan. When the final assault came it would be even grander – thousands of archers arranged across the entire stretch of parapets, raining steel-tipped ruin on the advancing host. To that would be added the shuddering flights of ballista bolts and the arcane snarl of magecraft.

Thoriol smiled. For the attackers, it would be like walking into a hurricane. He found himself almost desperate for them to arrive, just so he could witness it.

'Stand down!'

The order rang out from the tower at the far end of the parapet. All along the battlements archer companies leaned heavily against the stone, shaking down aching arms and counting their remaining arrows. A trumpet sounded as dozens of basket-carrying menials hurried out of the gates below, ready for the laborious process of retrieving the arrows and carting them back up to the armoury for re-use.

Loeth smiled at him amiably. 'You're keeping up, Silent.'

Thoriol nodded. 'Seems that way.'

Baelian pushed his way towards them, moving carefully along the crowded parapet.

'It'll be harder when we're doing it for real,' he warned, looking with guarded approval at Thoriol and the others. 'Think your arms are aching now? They'll be shredded by the end, and that's before you see what the bastards will be hurling up at us the whole time.'

Rovil laughed. 'From fifty feet down?'

'Don't be a fool,' snapped Baelian. 'Last time they breached the walls in nine places before we drove them out.' He swept his scarred gaze across them, wagging a calloused finger in their direction like an old loremaster with his pupils. 'Be *careful*. Remember your training. If they break through anywhere close to you, reach for your knives and fall back in good order. It's not your task to stop them up close – that's what the knights are there for.'

Thoriol looked away then, his mind already wandering – Baelian had given them the same speech many times.

As he did so, he caught a familiar whiff on the air, like burning embers. He craned his head, shading his eyes with one hand against the glare of the sun. He'd known ever since arriving that dragon riders were among Tor Alessi's defenders but he'd made no effort to find out anything about them – the memory of the Dragonspine was still too raw for that and he'd had plenty to occupy him with the archery work.

But as he looked up then, though, he saw it – the massive sapphire drake, the one he'd seen over Tor Vael and Tor Caled a hundred times. It was dropping fast, descending into the forest of spires behind them with an echoing clap of huge wings. A moment later and it was gone, lost in the vastness of the upper city.

He felt his stomach twist.

'That is Imladrik's dragon,' he said, blurting it out even as Baelian was still speaking.

'So it is,' smiled Loeth. 'What did you expect? I've seen him aloft twice since we dropped anchor.'

Florean nodded enthusiastically. 'A monster. A true monster.'

Thoriol turned to Baelian. 'Then... he's here?'

'Of course he is.' Baelian looked at him steadily. 'He commands the army.'

Thoriol almost felt like laughing, but not from mirth. Even the simple task of escaping his father seemed to be beyond him. A familiar sinking sensation fell over him: the embrace of failure.

He started to say something, but Baelian's look silenced him. The archery captain shot him a glare, the meaning of which was obvious.

No one needs to know but you and me.

Thoriol clammed up.

'Are you all right, Silent?' asked Florean. 'You've gone pale.'

'I'm fine,' replied Thoriol. 'Gods, but my arms are sore.'

They could believe that, and so the moment passed. The archers gathered up their arrows into quivers and checked their strings for damage. Loeth reached for a pot of beeswax and began to rub at a splintered section of his longbow – it would need to be replaced, but the bowyers were already working flat out and spares were hard to come by.

As the company fell into its familiar routines Baelian drew Thoriol to one side.

'You've made a place for yourself here, lad,' he said, his voice low. 'Don't do anything foolish.'

Thoriol didn't know how to reply. Thoughts of escape had faded days ago, replaced by the enjoyment of – for the first time – actually doing something worthwhile well. The fact that his father was in the city, no doubt preoccupied with the enormous task of organising its defences, shouldn't have made a difference to anything.

But it did, of course. It tarnished the whole exercise, putting into relief just how incongruous it was that he, the son of the King's brother, had ended up serving in the rank and file of his armies.

He was about to mumble something inconsequential when his attention was broken for a second time. Clarions, whole groups of them, began to sound from the tops of the highest towers. A rustle of movement followed, then the rising clamour of voices raised all along the battlements.

Thoriol looked out across the plain just in time to see the collectors hurrying back to the gates, escorted by spear-carrying riders who hadn't been there a moment ago. The clarions continued to sound, joined soon afterwards by ringing blasts from the city's huge central keep.

His gaze snapped up to the edge of the forest, only a few miles distant but hazy in the strong sun. He saw nothing moving there, but the sight nevertheless filled him with foreboding.

'So they've been sighted,' Thoriol said quietly.

Baelian stared out in the same direction, eyes fixed on the horizon.

'Sounds like it,' he agreed. 'Better get those arms limber again, lad. Looks like you'll be using them soon.'

THIRTEEN

The dwarfs on the march were like a slow avalanche battering its way down a mountainside. They made little effort to skirt around obstacles or difficult terrain – they ploughed through it, never changing pace, keeping their heads low and their arms swinging in unison. In their wake they left a wasteland of hacked stumps and trampled-down foliage, a scar on the forest as wide as fifty warriors marching shoulder to shoulder.

Behind those pioneers came the builders. Wooden bridges were thrown up over gorges; earthworks were hurriedly put up to shore the road's margins; the stubbornest obstacles were simply demolished by a whole phalanx of bare-chested workers using axes, hammers, shovels and long-handled hods.

Caradryel had plenty of time to watch the dawi at work, and what he saw gave him plenty to think about. Even the lowliest worker applied himself with almost fanatical zeal. He saw dwarfs staggering under their own weight in rubble, shining with sweat, refusing any help until their portion of the labour was done. He saw others carrying atrocious wounds and still working on, shrugging off levels of pain that would have had him in bed for a week.

The dwarfs seemed consumed by a kind of low-level mania that drove them west, ever west, obliterating anything they came across on the way. He found their single-mindedness both repellent and admirable. An elf would have found a more elegant route, taking care to conserve strength for the battle ahead. Something about the dawi's utter disregard for such considerations made him uneasy.

He had spoken to Morgrim on and off during the trek towards Tor Alessi. The dwarf lord was busy for most of the time with his thanes and warlords and spared himself as little as they did, marching to and fro amongst the armoured columns tirelessly, taking counsel and ruminating with them long into the night. Dwarf discussions seemed to involve an inordinate amount of beard-tugging, ale-drinking and low grunting – even about seemingly trivial matters.

Slowly Caradryel had come to realise why Morgrim kept himself so busy.

The dwarf army, which was far, far bigger than he'd been led to believe, was composed of forces from many different holds. Each one was led by its own prince or thane, many of whom were older than Morgrim and had trenchant views of their own. Seniority was a powerful thing with them, and Morgrim had to work incessantly to keep the whole messy, fractious, temperamental caravan on the road.

Caradryel found himself admiring the dour warrior. Morgrim was driven and irascible, obviously haunted by the death of his cousin and the need for blood-vengeance, but he could keep his head when he needed to, cajoling and arguing with a deft mix of forcefulness and tact.

'Does it make you nervous?' Morgrim had asked Caradryel on one of their few conversations together.

'What, lord?'

'Being surrounded by those who wish to kill you.'

Caradryel thought for a moment. 'In truth, I have never found myself to be universally popular,' he said eventually. 'So, no.'

Morgrim didn't smile. It was rare to see him smile, and when he did it was a cynical gesture, bereft of warmth.

'Morek tells me I am wasting my time with you,' said Morgrim. 'He says you should have been sent back to Tor Alessi with an iron collar round your neck.'

'Morek is your counsellor?'

'My runelord.'

'I'm glad you didn't listen to him.'

Morgrim picked his nose and flicked the results to the floor. 'You know what I despise about you elgi?'

Caradryel didn't offer a suggestion.

'Your lack of seriousness,' said Morgrim. He held up his axe. 'This is Morek's finest work. He spent decades crafting the symbols into this metal. He bent his neck over it, honing, tapping, seeking. He never smiled, never made an unworthy remark – he worked until it was done. Now the power within it almost scares me.'

Caradryel thought of all the wasted, half-finished endeavours he'd embarked upon in his life, only to discard them when something more appealing came his way.

'This land rewards such work,' Morgrim went on. 'It is a serious land. You can carve a living here, if you work at it, but it will never repay sloth. I've seen the way you people look at the grime under the leaves and I know what you think of it, but we cherish every shadow, every pit. It is our place. You should not have come here.'

'We have been in Elthin Arvan for a thousand years,' countered Caradryel carefully. 'There is room enough for both of us, is there not?'

Morgrim hawked up a gobbet of phlegm and spat it messily. 'I don't think so,' he said.

Caradryel paused before speaking again. 'If I may, then, lord – a question.'

Morgrim grunted his assent.

'Why are you not sending me back to Imladrik? Why are you entertaining his proposal at all?'

'Because of who he is.' Morgrim drew in a long breath. The leather-tough skin around his eyes creased as he remembered. 'He never looked down on us. He did not scorn our food, nor our caverns, nor call us stunted. When I showed him the vaults of the Everpeak he remained silent. He bowed before the great image of Grimnir, and for a moment I could not tell whether it was elgi or dawi who stood there.'

When Morgrim spoke of Imladrik, his harsh voice softened a little, losing its cold edge of disdain.

'I looked at him and I saw one of us,' Morgrim said. 'A soul that understood the path of duty.' Morgrim glanced at Caradryel. 'He learned Khazalid. He spoke it well, for an elgi. It took him twenty years, he told me, to master the greeting-forms, but he did it. I know of no others of your kind who have even tried, let alone succeeded.'

As Morgrim spoke, Caradryel remembered the ephemera of Yethanial's patient scholarship at Tor Vael. He had wondered at the relationship between the two of them back then, struck by how pale and grey she seemed next to his vigorous dynamism, but perhaps there was something more profound there than appearances.

'His brother is a fool and my people will rejoice when his neck is cut,' continued Morgrim. 'But my cousin was not wise-tempered either.' The dwarf's nose crinkled as he attempted what passed with him for a smile. 'What might have been, if Imladrik and I had been the heirs? Perhaps none of this foolishness.'

He looked sidelong at Caradryel.

'But all we have are the things set before us, and I will tell you this: I respect him for the reason I do not respect you. He is *serious*.'

Caradryel remembered how, despite himself, that accusation had wounded him. Alone among all the insults and contempt he'd faced from that dawi, that one had somehow struck home.

Perhaps, he thought, *if I somehow make it out of here alive, I will have to address this. Perhaps I have been playing at life for too long.*

Now though, days later, the march was coming to an end. Caradryel had taken his place beside Feliadh again. He and the other Caledorians walked by his side, leading their horses, looking dishevelled from the long trek but otherwise unharmed. For the last few hours the trees had been thinning out around them, gradually giving way to a bleak country of grass, sea-wind and loamy earth.

The dwarf vanguard pulled together, forming up into squares of impeccably ordered warriors. Morgrim and his *bazan-khazakrum* hearthguard had forged their way to the forefront, taking the combined standards of the army with them – a heavy-set collection of banners bearing stylised images of forges, hammers, flames and mountains.

'Now we see where this game has led us,' whispered Feliadh to Caradryel.

Caradryel nodded, keeping a careful watch on Morgrim's progress ahead.

'We will indeed.'

They crested a low tussock of tufted grass and sucking mud, beyond which the plains running down the sea suddenly opened out before them. Caradryel breathed in deeply, relishing the brine on the brisk air.

The sun was low in the east behind them, still pulling clear of the morning mists over the forest. Elthin Arvan's coastline was visible in the distance, a line of barred silver crowned with piled seaborne clouds. The huge, proud outline of Tor Alessi broke its emptiness, jutting up from the plain in a mass of spear-sharp towers and soaring walls. Runes on its walls could be made out even from such a distance, picked out in gold and emerald, glowing warmly as the waxing sun caught the gilt tapestry.

Caradryel saw the city then as the dwarfs around him must have seen it – huge, bristling with arms and magic, a fastness unrivalled by any the elves had built in all their colonial lands. It looked indomitable, as solid as the Phoenix Throne itself.

If Caradryel had been one of those dour-faced, iron-clad warriors his spirits might have faltered then. Somehow, he doubted theirs would.

'So what do we do now?' asked Feliadh. The Caledorian had started treating him with a good deal more respect since the events of the ambush.

'The Doom of the Elves has made his arrival,' Caradryel said dryly. 'Now we wait for the Master of Dragons to make his.'

Alviar walked along Kor Vanaeth's main thoroughfare. Loose soil and straw clung to his boots – the stone paving that had once made the roads a pleasure to walk on had long since been ripped up for repairs to the walls and citadel. Everything that had any military use had been taken, including ornamental stone lintels, bronze statues, even articles from the temples.

Alviar had disapproved of that at the time, as had most of the citizens. Liandra had been most insistent, though. She always was.

If he was honest, Alviar had never truly agreed with the decision to repopulate Kor Vanaeth. It was too small, too isolated, too enclosed by the forest. He would have been happy enough to follow Liandra to Tor Alessi or Athel Toralien, to start a new life in one of the truly big fortresses, the only places where a modicum of safety was still preserved.

He smiled as he remembered how Liandra had replied when he'd first suggested that, years ago. He'd never been able to repeat what she said in front of his four children, but the sight of her with eyes blazing, cheeks scarlet and spittle flying remained seared on his memory. She hadn't agreed.

Given all of that, it had been a disappointment when she'd accepted the summons at last to go to Tor Alessi. Right up until the end he had hoped she'd find a way to ignore it, but then Alviar supposed that it was hard to resist the Council for long.

She'd been torn about it, at least, which boded well for her return.

'I will come back,' she had promised him.

'I know you will, lady,' he had replied.

'And I will bring reinforcements too. It's long past time Tor Alessi released some of its defenders – they can hardly house the troops they've got.'

'That would be good, my lady.'

Then she had gone, taking wing on that flame-red dragon of hers. Alviar had watched her go, wondering if anything she'd promised would be delivered.

Since then, nothing. Vague reports had reached them of dwarf armies on the move again, but all had been from the north. Alviar had done what he could in the meantime: overseeing the last of the repairs to the walls, ensuring the soldiers he did possess were in a good state of readiness for whatever might come. They knew that attack was likely, particularly if the dwarf forces started to splinter as they had done so many times in the past, so he'd sent messages to Tor Alessi warning of the imminent danger, despite little faith they would be received.

He looked up at the citadel ahead of him. It rose from the patchwork of houses like a tree-stump from the soil, streaked black from old fires. If all failed, the entire population could retreat to that redoubt, the only part of the old fortress that had remained intact after the dwarf attacks.

Alviar narrowed his eyes, running his gaze along the battle-ments. He thought he should really send someone up to ensure the ballistae were all in perfect condition and safely stowed before the next storm came in.

He was about to turn away, making a note to himself to have a word with the watch commander, when something else caught his eye. It was high up in the eastern sky – a lone bird with a strange, halting flight.

He paused, wondering for a moment what it was. Then, as the speck of darkness grew larger, his heart missed a beat. For all its ungainliness it was coming at them fast. Far, far too fast.

'Sound the alarm!' he shouted, breaking into a run. 'Man the walls!'

He made it as far as the citadel gates before it hit them. The stench was incredible – a rolling wash of hot putrescence, like a boiled corpse. He staggered, losing his footing and colliding heavily with the stone doorframe. From behind him he heard screams as others looked up into the skies and saw what was bearing down on them.

Hands trembling, Alviar pushed his way through the citadel doors and scrambled up the spiral stairway beyond. As he raced up the steps they seemed to shiver underneath him.

He reached the bell tower and caught hold of the long chain, yanking it frantically. That was the signal – it should bring the soldiers to their stations on the walls and summon everyone else to the sanctuary of the citadel.

Alviar rang it furiously for a few seconds longer, his heart pounding and his pulse racing.

It had been huge. Huge, and... *wrong*.

Then he tore out of the chamber and up to the citadel's summit. As he ran he started praying that the ballistae were manned and that they'd managed to get a few bolts away. He didn't know whether anything they had would do much against that monster, but they should at least attempt a defence.

He burst out into the open at the top of the stairwell, slamming the wooden door back on its hinges as he emerged on to the wide, flat rooftop. He was instantly reassured – several dozen guards were already there on the ramparts, hauling the heavy ballistae and bolt throwers into firing angles and shouting furiously at one another. The wind whipped across him, as hot as a desert sandstorm and flecked with eerie snarls of flame.

'Where is it?' he yelled, twisting around as he ran, his neck craned up into the skies.

It was a superfluous question. The black dragon headed straight at them, less than a hundred feet away and tearing towards the citadel's summit. Green and purple energies laced around it, dripping like molten metal from its outstretched maw. Alviar caught a blurred impression of massive jaws pulled wide and a pair of silver eyes blazing with madness before he threw himself on to the stone and covered his head with his hands.

He heard a throttling roar that made the stone beneath his chest judder, then felt a sudden rush of air being inhaled into massive lungs. The stink intensified – a foul mix of mortuary scraps and magic. Amid all the roaring and the terror he thought he caught a woman's voice, screaming out words that he couldn't understand but that somehow amplified the paralysing dread that gripped him tight.

That, though, was the last of Alviar's fear-fractured impressions. A second later the jets of flame came, tempests of addled fire that crashed across the citadel's battlements like breakers against a prow, immolating everything like the vengeance of Khaine and sealing, for a second time, the doom of Kor Vanaeth.

The doors were barred with spiked iron bands and weighed the same as a fully laden trade cutter. Somewhere within the cavernous gatehouse, chains the width of wine barrels clanked taut around wheels, then pulled.

Imladrik watched them draw to the full – first a slit, then a window of daylight, then the wide vista of the plains beyond.

His mount was skittish under him. The horse could smell dragon, and that always unsettled them. He placed a reassuring hand on its neck and whispered the calming words that Yethanial had taught him.

Twenty ceremonial riders passed through the archway ahead of him, each decked in dazzling ithilmar and carrying pennants with the emblems of Ulthuan and Caledor. Aelis rode on his left side, Salendor on his right. Gelthar and Caerwal came behind, along with three battle-mages.

Liandra had still not returned from wherever Vranesh had taken her. Imladrik could have remained preoccupied, but the time had passed for that.

One battle at a time.

They rode out. Ahead of them, a mile from the walls, the dwarfs had taken up positions. Their army stretched across the eastern limit of the plain in a long arc. Imladrik could see regiments digging in: some carrying huge warhammers two-handed, others with axes or stubby crossbows. Their armour glinted dully in the sun, exposing intricate knotwork engraving on the helms and pauldron plates.

He tried to estimate numbers. Fifty thousand? Sixty? There might be more still marching through the forest to join them. In any case, it was a brutally large muster.

Thin columns of smoke were already rising from the dwarf encampment, marking the fires that they would drink and eat around, working one another up into battle-readiness with old tales of heroism and grudgement. Once those tales might have concerned Malekith and Snorri Whitebeard, though they would do so no longer, and for that Imladrik was thankful.

The Sundering was largely unknown to the dwarfs. If they had ever been curious about the affairs of Ulthuan they would no doubt have uncovered the truth soon enough, but they were an insular race with little concern for internal elgi politics. For their part the asur had never made reference to it. In the early days many assumed Malekith would be defeated quickly. Only slowly had the dreadful truth become apparent – that the split would linger for as long as any could foresee, and that the Witch King was far too powerful to be reliably defended against, let alone destroyed.

After that the asur kept the truth from the outside world, guarding their shame like an oil lantern in the wind, sheltering it from prying eyes and hoping that, somehow, it could be contained. When the strife in Elthin Arvan had first come, Imladrik had sent Gotrek letters, hinting at the truth, still constrained by the need for secrecy and veiled with vagueness. Perhaps he should have been more explicit.

Ahead of him the dawi banners hung limply. Everything about them was blunt, grim, heavy. As the elves approached the dwarf lines, crossbow-bearing guards stomped out to greet them. Behind them came a company of foot soldiers wearing thick plates over chainmail, their helms carved into grotesque representations of dragon-faces. Imladrik pulled the reins gently, and the party came to a halt.

The dwarfs assembled, crossbows levelled, saying nothing. An uneasy silence descended, broken only by the distant sounds of campfires crackling and supply wagons being unloaded.

Imladrik removed his high helm, exposing his face to the enemy.

'*Tromm, dawinarri,*' he said, bowing respectfully. '*Ka ghurraz Imladriki na Kaledor.*'

The wind whistled. For many heartbeats, no one spoke.

'Your accent has got worse.'

The voice came from behind the lines, hidden by the grim wall of steel and iron. Imladrik thought it sounded harsher than it had once done; back then, Snorri had always been the angry one, his cousin the voice of calm.

'I have not had much time to practise,' Imladrik called out, resisting the urge to scan along the lines to see where Morgrim was hidden.

He did not have to wait for long. The guards shuffled to one side, and the iron-clad hearthguard replaced them. Then their ranks parted, exposing two figures standing within their midst.

One was grizzled with age, his long beard flecked grey and his stance hunched. He carried a thick-shafted stave crowned with an iron anvil, the head of which seemed to shimmer as if in a heat-haze. Imladrik did not recognise him, though he knew well enough the marks of a runesmith.

The other one he certainly knew, though time had not been kind to the memory. Morgrim's helm and armour were smeared with blood, daubed in ritual marks of vengeance. His eyes had darkened and his previously open face had withdrawn into a scarred, tight visage of distrust. His boots and cloak were travel-worn, his fine armour splattered with the mud of the road. He carried an ornate axe, studded with runes. It looked new-forged.

Imladrik dismounted, though even on foot he still towered over the dwarf lord.

Morgrim did not bow. 'You sent me a fool,' he said.

'He came to me recommended,' said Imladrik.

'By whom?'

'Someone I trust.'

Morgrim grunted. 'We did not harm him,' he said, in a voice that indicated he regretted the fact.

'Then what of his tidings? Do we have leave to talk?'

'My thanes counsel against it. They are hungry to see your walls in rubble. They ask me what you can tell us that we haven't heard before.'

'Little, perhaps,' admitted Imladrik. 'But not nothing. We used to speak often, you and I. Back then your cousin was the one who wouldn't listen.'

A shadow fell across Morgrim's face. 'His death is the cause of this.'

'He should have been buried in the Everpeak with honour. He should have taken his place beside Grimnir, and should have done so intact.'

As Imladrik spoke, one of his guards dismounted and bore him a rosewood box inlaid with silver renditions of the dwarfen runes of kingship. Imladrik passed it to Morgrim, stooping as he delivered it.

'I brought this from Lothern, where it should never have been taken. It is presented to you in reverence, in the hope that it may be returned to where it belongs.'

Morgrim glared up at him suspiciously for a moment. Then he opened the catch. A withered hand lay within, cushioned on silk and bound with fine linen. Its fingers had been severed at the first knuckle.

Morgrim stared at it for a long time. When he next spoke, his voice was thick.

'I would have brought our armies to Ulthuan to retrieve this.'

'I know.'

'And you think you can buy my goodwill with it?'

'It was not intended to buy anything,' said Imladrik, knowing the danger of mortal insult. 'I give it to you now before fighting makes it impossible, so it may be returned to his father in Karaz-a-Karak and interred with the *grondaz* rites. I would have it known that Snorri Halfhand, greatest of dawi princes, can still grasp an axe in the afterlife.'

Morgrim nodded slowly. 'Aye,' he said grimly. 'It would be fitting.'

Then he glared up at Imladrik again.

'It can never go back to how it was,' he said. 'My army will remain on these plains, preparing for battle. But I will listen. Perhaps you can tell me something new, perhaps not: I make no promises.'

Imladrik bowed, feeling a surge of relief wash over him. He felt like thanking Morgrim, knowing the risks the dwarf lord ran to make such a concession, but that would have been fatal – dwarfs cared nothing for gratitude, only debts, loyalty and payment.

So instead he rose to his full height and withdrew slowly, never taking his eyes off Morgrim's conflicted face.

'So be it,' he said. 'The last chance to end this madness. By Asuryan, let us not waste it.'

FOURTEEN

Liandra drove Vranesh hard, pushing her towards the far-off peaks of the Arluii. Her steed was happy to comply. As ever, their moods were intertwined, amplified and echoed in one another's minds with every movement and gesture.

She knew she should turn back. Her foray out over Loren Lacoi had given her a hawk's eye view of dawi columns moving close to Tor Alessi's hinterland – the vanguard of the main force would not be far behind it. On another day, she might have ordered Vranesh down, raking the slow-moving formations with a burst of dragonfire. She would have enjoyed that – it would have been a release after so long holding back.

Imladrik, of course, wouldn't have allowed it. His restraint was maddening. Liandra knew what he was capable of if he chose to unlock the power coiled tight within that proud, buttoned-up exterior. She had seen it for herself, and the memory still burned within her.

But she had made herself weary now telling others of his potential, even Salendor had stopped believing her.

'It doesn't matter how much you *tell* me this,' he'd complained, smarting after her rejection of him. 'Weak elves tell good stories.'

Salendor was within his rights to be sceptical – very few had ever seen dragon riders in action. The drakes were rare and majestic beasts, kept away from the battlefield by their riders unless the need was great. Salendor could have no idea what would happen when they were let loose. He could have no idea how contemptuously Draukhain or Vranesh could carve through the mightiest of defences, leaving nothing but molten armour fragments in their wake.

The dawi did not understand it either. It was centuries since dragons had gone to war in Elthin Arvan – no dwarfs now lived who would have witnessed them unleashed to the full. They had only ever hunted miserable cave-dwelling wyrms of the eastern mountains – the colossally powerful Star Dragons of the Annulii were another proposition entirely.

It was all so *frustrating*.

He is a fool, sang Vranesh in sympathy.

Liandra laughed bitterly. *You've changed your tune.*

Who but a fool would spurn the chance to mate with you?

It is not about mating, she sang back, affronted. *Gods, you can be crude sometimes.*

Then what is it? Vranesh sounded genuinely interested.

I see the things we could accomplish together. It was hard to conceal emotions from the dragons – they sniffed them out like prey. *He sees it too, but holds back.*

Because he is promised to another?

That is not all. Liandra's mind-voice was hesitant; she didn't like thinking of Imladrik's motivations. *He has his father's example to think of.*

Imrik, sang Vranesh with approval.

Indeed. Think on the lesson of Imrik, and you will understand both his sons.

Vranesh dipped a little lower, pulling clear of a long grey cloudbank. Ahead of them, still many leagues distant, the grey profile of the Arluii pocked the southern horizon.

His father refused to draw the Sword of Khaine, even though it would have ended the war, sang Liandra. *Caledor believes this was weak, and has spent his life trying to erase the shame of it. He would go to war with his own shadow if it offended him.*

And kalamn-talaen?

He thinks otherwise. Liandra looked out at the vast spread of Elthin Arvan, regarding it with the mix of hatred and devotion that she had always felt. *He thinks we carry the seeds of our destruction within us. He yearns for nothing more than to give free rein to the dragon, but dreads what it will do to him. He does not want to become another Aenarion.*

Liandra gripped her staff tightly. *I am his Sword of Khaine*, she sang. *That is the problem.*

Vranesh snorted her contempt. *Foolish.*

Liandra nodded slowly. *It is. We are a foolish race.*

Vranesh angled steeply, pulling closer to the land below. Liandra peered over the creature's shoulder, scouring the unbroken forest for signs of movement.

When will you order me back to the city? sang Vranesh. *Not that I am in a hurry – I enjoy the chance to stretch my pinions.*

Liandra was about to reply, to begin the long journey back, when something suddenly struck at her soul: a sharp pain, like a dagger-thrust. She winced, tensing in the saddle.

'What is that?' she asked aloud, voice tight with pain.

Vranesh had felt it too – the dragon instantly gained altitude, powering aloft with an urgency she hadn't employed for a long time.

East, Vranesh sang.

Liandra twisted around, feeling the pain intensify. Only slowly did she recognise the cause: echoes of agony in the aethyr, souls shrieking in pain, all wrapped in the poisonous embrace of Dhar magic.

'Kor Vanaeth,' she breathed, her heart suddenly chilling. 'Blood of Isha – my people.'

By then Vranesh was already flying hard, thrusting east, picking up speed with every powerful wingbeat.

Liandra reeled, clutching her breast as more waves of misery impacted.

She had always had a sympathetic link with her adopted home, but this was different. The pain was being shouted out across the aethyr like a beacon in the night. Someone wanted her to feel it.

Abomination, snarled Vranesh. The dragon's voice was twisted in fury. *I sense it.*

Find it, gasped Liandra, trying to shake off the sickening pain and summon up her own anger. *Find it, run it down. By Isha's tears, you shall have the bloodshed you seek.*

The tent's canvas walls swayed in the wind, buffeted by gusts that came off the western ocean and straight across the plain. It was an elaborate construction, a storeyed collection of fabric-walled chambers erected around a scaffold of thick wooden poles and taut hemp ropes. Imladrik had had it prepared weeks ago, hoping that it would be used for such a purpose; erecting it had taken just a few hours.

The site was equidistant between the dwarf camp and the city walls. No more than a hundred delegates were permitted within half a mile of it, fifty from each opposing force. Despite the precautions, the atmosphere of tense antagonism was palpable. Dwarfs glowered at their elgi counterparts; the asur glared back at them with equal suspicion.

Imladrik didn't like to see it, but he wasn't surprised.

So are the dreams of our fathers diminished.

He sat at the centre of a long table covered in white linen. He had come in his ceremonial robes rather than armour as a gesture of trust. Aelis, Gelthar, Caerwal and Salendor sat on either side of him, all similarly garbed.

There was still no sign of Liandra. He had sent messages to her quarters. She might, of course, have been unaware that the dawi had finally arrived, but he doubted it. Whatever her feelings about remaining in his presence, she should not have stayed away.

Perhaps that vindicated everything he had done. He wished he could feel surer.

Opposite them, sitting at a similar table, were the dwarfs. Three lords, in addition to the runesmith, sat with Morgrim. Imladrik didn't know them or recognise their livery; they had been introduced as Frei of Karak Drazh, Grondil of Zhufbar and Eldig of Karak Varn. They were neither princes nor kings, but thanes, advisers to their hold-master. Each looked ancient, as knotted and weathered as oak-stumps.

For all of their grandeur, there could be no doubt who dominated the chamber. Morgrim brooded in the midst of them, his countenance hanging like a funeral pall over the proceedings. He still wore his fabulously ornate battle plate with its swirling curves of knotwork decoration and bronze-limned detail, looking ready to unclasp his axe at any moment.

Still, he was there. That was something.

'So,' Imladrik said, inclining his head toward Morgrim, who made no move in return. 'Three sieges have taken place here. It is my hope we may avoid a fourth.'

Grondil grunted, Eldig looked bored, but none of them spoke. From either side of him Imladrik could sense the wariness of his own side: Salendor disdainful, Gelthar wary, Caerwal silently hostile.

'We came here for vengeance,' replied Morgrim. 'It will not be halted by words we have heard before.'

'Things have changed,' said Imladrik. 'I suspect much.'

'Suspect?' Morgrim's tone was dismissive.

'More than suspect.' Imladrik motioned to one of the servants standing in the margins of the chamber, who unfurled a long sheet of parchment and held it aloft.

'This is a map of our homeland,' said Imladrik. 'I had it drawn with every detail. You can see the extent of Ulthuan here. Note the scarcity of land between the mountains and the sea. So it was that the asur first came to Elthin Arvan, to escape the boundaries that fate had enclosed us in.'

Morgrim's eyes flickered over the parchment, taking in the detail quickly.

'Observe the land to the north-west,' Imladrik went on. 'The race who live there we name the druchii, the dark ones. They are driven by a pleasure creed which turns their minds, blighting them with sadism. For seven centuries we have warred with them. For more than a generation we have kept this war secret, shamed by it even as we strive to end it. Over the years it has changed us: we have become a harder people. We remember our fight against the daemons with pride, but this secret war has caused us nothing but shame.'

Morgrim looked back at him doubtfully. 'What is shameful about war?'

'Because the druchii were once one with us,' said Imladrik. Admitting it, even after so long, was still painful. 'Their master was our greatest captain. He will be known to you in your annals. His name is Malekith.'

The runesmith Morek grunted in recognition. 'We do remember. He was a friend of the dawi.'

'He was once,' said Imladrik. 'He was many things, once.'

Morgrim placed his gauntlets on the table before him with a soft *clunk*. 'This is your business, elgi. We have no concern what battles you make for yourselves.'

'So it would be, had the war not spread to Elthin Arvan. We have always tried to prevent it. Even in times of peace we maintained a watch on the seas, knowing that the Witch King would covet our cities here just as he covets those in Ulthuan. Athel Toralien was his once, and he is jealous over what he believes has been taken from him.'

As he spoke, Imladrik kept a wary eye on the dwarfs before him. They made very few gestures and gave away almost nothing, though they were still listening, which was good.

'Druchii can pass as asur with some ease; even my own kind cannot always tell them apart. I tried to warn Gotrek of it, but by then he was in no mood to listen. They have certainly been here, perhaps in small numbers, but enough for what they were sent for.'

Morgrim leaned forward. 'And what is that? Enough hints – tell us what you suspect.'

'Agrin Fireheart,' said Imladrik. 'The spark that started this. They killed him, not us. The trade caravans, the first attacks; we were not responsible.'

That brought a change: Grondil shook his head angrily, Frei rolled his eyes. Morek leaned over to Morgrim and whispered something in his ear.

'You're telling me that these... druchii were to blame?' Morgrim asked, pushing the runelord away. He pronounced the word awkwardly.

'In the beginning, yes.'

'There were a hundred skirmishes,' said Morgrim sceptically. 'Dozens of attacks in the first years. We *know* they came from your colonies.'

'That did happen. Tempers flared, some lords were foolish.'

'Foolish!' snorted Grondil.

'And we also were attacked by dwarfs,' said Salendor, his eyes flat with hostility.

'All suffered,' admitted Imladrik, giving the Lord of Athel Maraya a sharp look. 'All of us did.' He turned to address Morgrim directly. 'You remember how much your High King tried to restrain your warriors, how much I attempted to keep my own back, and how we both failed – could that have happened if other forces were not at work? Think back: were there no voices in the holds whispering from the start? Strangers, perhaps, who somehow gained the ears of the already-willing?'

He might have imagined it, but Imladrik thought he caught a flicker of recognition from Morek then – the briefest of sidelong glances.

'I will not try to convince you we were not to blame,' said Imladrik. 'Believe me, I regret plenty, including things that happened before I went to Ulthuan. All I will say is this: other powers were active, powers that have wished to see us brought low ever since the Sundering. And if that is the case, should we not stand back, just for a moment, and consider what that means?'

His eyes remained fixed on Morgrim's.

'Warriors have died,' Imladrik said. 'Some fights have been without honour, and I understand the need for grudgement, but the *Dammaz Kron* makes provision for deception, does it not? This is my case, lords. Deception has taken place, poisoning the way between us. We can restore it, if we choose – it requires patient work, a little more understanding.'

Imladrik sat back, waiting for the response. He hardly dared to breathe. It would have been in character for the dawi to flatly refuse any further discussion – the information was new to them and they did not like tidings they could not personally verify.

The runesmith leaned over to Morgrim and they conferred for a few moments in whispers. They needn't have lowered their voices – even Imladrik could not understand much of the Khazalid they used. After that, Morgrim took views from the three other thanes. They took their time, grumbling and muttering in their guttural tongue with stabbing gestures from armoured fingers.

Imladrik watched all the while. None of his companions said anything; they sat erect in their seats, their faces calm. Of all of them, Caerwal looked the most uneasy, which surprised him. Salendor's hostility, for the moment, had been replaced by curiosity.

Eventually Morgrim leaned forward again. His expression, as much of it as could be read under the ironwork of his helm, had not changed.

'We are not stupid,' he said. 'Nor are we blind. We know that you have your divisions. Perhaps we did not appreciate how deep they ran.'

Morgrim didn't bother looking at or addressing the others; he spoke to Imladrik alone.

'But you cannot think this is enough. Halfhand was slain by your own Phoenix King. The blood has been bad for too long to wave away with half-truths.'

Imladrik bristled. 'They are not half-truths.'

'Then prove them.'

Imladrik was about to ask, wearily, what would satisfy him when Morgrim shot him a rare look, one almost reminiscent of the way he used to be before, free of the patina of bitterness that now clouded his every move.

'But neither let it be said that the dawi do not know their own laws,' he said. 'You are right about the *Dammaz Kron*.'

He still didn't smile, though. Perhaps he was no longer capable of it.

'So tell us more about the druchii.'

Drutheira brought Bloodfang around for another pass, thundering towards the devastation that had once been Kor Vanaeth. The dragon had exceeded her expectations – once given a channel for its misery it had poured the full measure of woe on to its target, ravaging the asur settlement as if the place were somehow responsible for its life of torment.

The defenders had done their best. Some had even managed to loose a few bolts from eagle-shaped launchers atop the citadel's central tower.

One had sheered close, nearly punching a fresh hole in Bloodfang's already ragged wings, but that was the best they had managed before the dragon had razed the rooftops, sweeping the whole rabble of artillery pieces from their places in a single, scything run.

After that the battle was ludicrously one-sided, something Drutheira took an exquisite pleasure in. The dragon's columns of flame ripped roofs clean from walls; its raking claws tore deep into towers and bulwarks, collapsing masonry into clouds of spiralling rubble. Arrows clattered uselessly from its armoured hide, igniting as they shot through the waves of flame that swathed the beast.

Drutheira hung on tight throughout, clutching the bone-spur before her one-handed and enjoying the violent swerve of the plunging attack. Her other hand brandished her staff, but aside from adding a few aesthetic touches she left the destruction to the dragon.

Magnificent, she thought, lurching to one side as Bloodfang shouldered aside another watchtower, crushing it into clouds of flaming dust. *Truly magnificent.*

By then little remained of Kor Vanaeth aside from its crudely fashioned central citadel. Shattered walls and dwellings lay smouldering and stinking. Whole streets had been demolished in the rush of claws and fire, their inhabitants roasted as they scampered for sanctuary. A porcine smell of cooked flesh hung over the sorry remnants, sweet and cloying and utterly delicious.

'The fastness,' Drutheira snarled, cracking her staff over Bloodfang's writhing neck.

The dragon roared its hatred, twisting its long jaws around and snapping at her, but the defiance was all for show – Drutheira dominated the creature entirely now, like a kicked cur goaded into the hunt. Bloodfang rolled awkwardly in the air, twisting its sinuous body and powering towards the citadel.

The survivors of the first attacks had barricaded themselves in there, trusting in its thick walls and heavy-beamed roof. Retreat had been the only strategy open to them, but it hemmed them in and sealed their doom. Bloodfang threw itself at the citadel's smoke-darkened flanks, hurling cascades of fire across the stonework. Narrow windows exploded as raw dragonflame washed across them, showering the ruins below with blood-coloured glass. The dragon reared up and slammed directly into the walls, latching on with all four claws and grinding into the stone.

Drutheira was nearly thrown from her seat by the impact and had to scrabble to hold her place. 'Not so clumsy!' she cried.

By then, though, there was no stopping it. Perched halfway up the steep citadel walls, the dragon started to tear its way towards the soft interior, ripping the thick shell open and sending stone blocks thudding to earth.

A buttress collapsed, sending cracks racing across the reeling fortifications. A huge sandstone lintel dissolved into debris as Bloodfang's tail slammed into it, further weakening the structure. Drutheira heard muffled screams from within.

They would be cowering now, huddled in the deepest recesses and praying for deliverance. That was fine – it was what she wanted them to do. To turn those screams into aethyr-born echoes was the most trivial exercise of her art. The preparations had already been made, the blood-sacrifices performed. The death of Kor Vanaeth would echo in the hearts of any who cared for it.

Bloodfang grabbed a mighty block of wall-section in its jaws, ripped it free and flung it to one side. The heavy chunk of stonework sailed through the air before thumping down amid the destruction, rolling twice and toppling into the skeletal frame of some burned-out dwelling.

That left a gaping wound in the citadel's outer fortifications. Drutheira could make out torchlit movement within – a score of desperate defenders with what looked like long pikes, backing up in the face of Bloodfang's bludgeoning entry.

Drutheira couldn't help but laugh. It was like watching ants rush to staunch the breaches in their nest. She ran her fingers along her staff, pondering about adding some agony of her own to Bloodfang's relentless assault – perhaps they would be more amusing to watch with their skins pulled inside out.

'Burn them,' she ordered, her eyes going flat with delight.

But Bloodfang did not obey. The dragon pounced clear, dragging half the wall-section with it. The sudden movement caught Drutheira off-guard, and she rocked in her seat, nearly slipping for a second time.

'What are you *doing*?' she shrieked, snatching her staff up to strike the creature's flesh.

Bloodfang climbed fast, pulling away from the burning wreckage, its huge lungs wheezing from the sudden effort. Drutheira felt a shudder pass through its body, like a ship turning too rashly in a hard swell. She twisted around, scanning the rapidly tipping horizon for what had got the creature spooked.

It didn't take long. She wondered how she hadn't sensed it earlier.

'There she is,' she hissed, projecting witch-sight into the north-west.

Still far off, half-lost in the gloom of the dusk, a scarlet dragon was tearing towards them, burning up the air around it in its haste and fury. The creature came on fast. Terrifyingly fast.

Drutheira felt a sharp thrill of excitement shudder through her. A *real* dragon, not the ruined, sorcery-spoiled monster she had charge of. This should be interesting.

'Away,' she ordered, seizing control again, swinging around and into the south-east. Bloodfang responded, weeping fire and anguish, its silver eyes rolling with battle-madness. Together they raced from the ruins, out over the forest and towards the Arluii.

Drutheira looked over her shoulder. She no longer needed witch-sight to see the blazing dragon on her tail – it devoured the air between them, racing along hungrily, its wings a smoke-clouded blur.

Come to me, then, thought Drutheira greedily, watching the dragon rider's vengeful progress. *The last time you pursued me I was alone, but now I have such delightful toys.*

She struck Bloodfang hard, goading it onwards.

To the mountains, you and I. For the reckoning.

FIFTEEN

The meeting broke up in the evening, just as the shadows began to lengthen. Caradryel had watched it all with interest, hanging back in the margins and taking care not to become conspicuous.

It was good to be back among the civilised; the stench of the dawi had become wearisome. The food they had given him had been all but inedible – heavy sourdough breads slathered in some form of meat dripping washed down with the bitterest, darkest, foamiest liquid he had ever imbibed. He'd struggled to keep it in his stomach, though he couldn't deny it had given him endurance to keep marching.

Imladrik had been appreciative of his efforts in bringing Morgrim to the table, though there had been little time for the two of them to confer since his return. Caradryel had not been able to pass on properly his worries over division within the dwarf ranks, though Imladrik would surely have guessed much of it. Most of the dawi army was thirsting for blood still; it would take only the merest hint of a spark to light the fire again.

'Worry about our own people,' Imladrik had told him. 'That is your task now.'

Since then Caradryel's eyes had been firmly fixed on the asur delegation. He'd watched Gelthar try his best to hide his uneasiness, Caerwal his impotent hostility, Aelis her frustration at being sidelined. They were all of them chafing for one reason or another, though their noble-born discipline worked hard against rebellion.

As he had been from the start, Salendor remained the worry. The warrior-mage had scowled and frowned his way through the proceedings, interjecting unhelpfully and coming perilously close to overriding Imladrik twice. The dwarfs must have noticed, though of course they gave no sign of it.

Now, as the various contingents left the main tent and made their way warily back to their respective camps, the fragile air of amity withered again. Asur guards looked on stonily as the dawi trudged out of the marquee and back to their increasingly settled battle-lines.

Morgrim was the last to go.

'Until tomorrow,' Imladrik told him, bowing.

'Until then,' Morgrim replied, nodding brusquely.

After that the tent remained occupied only by asur council members. Servants milled around them, removing the linen drapes and the pitchers and salvers that had been served during the day. Caerwal talked animatedly with Aelis – something about reparations for Athel Numiel – Gelthar with Imladrik. Only Salendor was missing.

Caradryel withdrew from the tent and made his way across the rutted plain towards the city. In the failing light Tor Alessi looked even more massive and unlovely than it had when he'd left it. He reached the gates, showed his medallion of office to the guards and passed under the archway.

Inside the walls Tor Alessi hummed with activity. Its streets were crowded, just as always, swollen with soldiers hurrying to their stations or back to barracks. Caradryel pushed his way through the jostling throngs. No one paid him any attention – he was just one more official on just one more errand.

Salendor's mansion close to the quayside was well-guarded and not easy to observe unseen. By the time Caradryel reached it – an extensive, many-towered edifice near the waterfront, encircled by high walls – torches were being lit against the gathering dark. He could see the masts of ships in the harbour, black against deep blue.

Caradryel pulled back, letting the shadows of the nearside wall envelop him. The roads were still busy, dense with movement just like every street and alleyway in the entire fortress. He watched the gates of Salendor's mansion for a few moments. No one came in or out. A soft glow of lanterns spilled from the upper windows, but no figures were silhouetted against the glass.

He withdrew, walking back the way he had come until he reached a nondescript-looking building set back from the quayside road, three storeys tall, square and heavily built. The smell of grain emanated from it and piles of empty sacking slumped against the stone. Like so many of the harbourside buildings it had long since been commandeered for supply storage, which made it ideal for the purposes Caradryel had put it to.

He slipped a key into the lock and went inside, climbing up a steep stairwell past stacked grainsacks and wine barrels. The third floor was largely empty. As he entered, a figure at the window turned hurriedly to look at him.

'It's me,' said Caradryel, joining him. 'Anything to report?'

Geleth, one of his many agents in the city, relaxed. 'He's had visitors.'

'From Athel Maraya?'

'Hard to tell.'

Caradryel peered out of the window, keeping his head low against the sill. Salendor's mansion was quiet, enclosed within its high walls and insulated from the bustle outside.

'How long has he been back?'

'He arrived just ahead of you.'

Caradryel nodded. There was nothing, nothing at all, suspicious about Salendor's movements – every member of the Council had supplicants and counsellors calling in a steady stream, even more so since the preparations for battle had been stepped up. Unusual, though, to receive them here, rather than his formal lodgings near the Tower of Winds.

Caradryel scanned the mansion frontage. It was an old design, less functional than the buildings on either side of it, with something of the old flamboyance of Athinol. It looked like the two wings ran back a long way from the frontage, part-hidden by the walls of the mansion's neighbours. He could just make out lantern-glows from a long way back, though the windows themselves were almost totally obscured.

'How many guests entered by the main gates?' Caradryel asked.

'A dozen or so.'

'And left?'

'Half that.'

Caradryel nodded. 'So they're being put up, or there's another way out.' He pushed himself to his feet. 'Keep watching the gates. Try to spy an insignia if you can.'

He walked back down to street level, wondering where best to start in the maze of alleyways and narrow streets that zigzagged around the mansion. He matched the unconcerned gait of those around him, letting his eyes wander over the buildings that loomed up into the early evening sky.

It would have been pleasant to linger, had circumstances been different. The soft light on the stone, the chatter of the crowds, the smell of cooking from a dozen different windows, it was all agreeable enough.

Following a hunch, Caradryel ambled into a very narrow alleyway that ran at an angle away from the main street. Just as he had expected, after a while it doubled back, enclosed on either side by tall stone walls with few overlooking windows. He smelled the dank, briny smell of seawater puddles and felt layers of moist dust under his boots. Soon he was in a labyrinth of capillary footways, all of them hemmed in by a close press of tenements. The hubbub of the main thorough-fares fell away into a low, distant hum.

Then, fifty yards ahead, he saw a shadow flit from a side door, a door that might very well have led out from one of the mansion's rear wings. Caradryel lengthened his stride. The shadow went ahead of him, neither hurrying nor tarrying. It wore a cloak with a red lining.

Caradryel began to catch up, and checked his pace – he needed to see where Salendor's guests were coming from before he challenged them. He slipped around a sharp corner only to stare down an empty path. Too late, he realised he'd missed a narrow opening twenty paces back, and retraced his steps just in time to see his quarry reach the end of another meandering alleyway.

Caradryel broke into a jog, cursing himself for carelessness. The end of the alleyway opened out on to the main quayside thoroughfare, as busy as all the others. Caradryel emerged breathlessly from the shadows, peering back and forth.

Crowds milled close by, a mix of soldiers in full armour and harbour workers in loose woollen tunics. Caradryel pushed his way through them, trying to catch sight of the figure he'd been chasing.

Sure enough, a way ahead and separated by a throng of unconcerned passers-by, he caught half a glimpse of scarlet fabric, quickly lost in the press. He pushed towards it, shoving his way past those in his path, but it soon became hopeless – the volume of bodies around him reduced his progress to a crawl.

Mouthing a curse under his breath, Caradryel elbowed his way over to the waterfront where the mass of bodies was thinner, trying to decide if he'd learned anything of importance.

He concluded that he probably hadn't, not enough to report back to Imladrik with at any rate. Something was going on. He resolved to make enquiries on his return as to the whereabouts of the dragon rider Liandra. If she was still missing by the morning and messengers were colluding with Salendor, wearing what might or might not be the livery of Kor Vanaeth... well, that would be of some interest.

It would not be worth divulging to anyone else, at least not in the absence of anything like proof, but it was the start of something, something that might grow.

His face fixed in a frown of concentration, Caradryel started walking again. He had much to think on before the dawn.

Fatigue had no hold on Liandra, nor on Vranesh. The dragon tore through the night sky as fast as she had ever flown, eating up the leagues in an attempt to run down the abomination before them. There was no complaint nor query from her mind-voice, just a blank, animal hatred that crowded out all else.

It is ruined! Vranesh cried out, her song discordant with pain. *What have they done to it?*

The horror in Vranesh's mind polluted Liandra's own, making her hands shake with rage.

I know not, great one, she sang back, holding back tears of empathetic anger. *Believe me, we shall end it.*

Kor Vanaeth's desolation still hung in her mind's eye, inescapable and damning. She had hardly paused over the ruins, unwilling to lose the abomination's trail. The city was gone now, destroyed for a second time, and from this there would be no rebirth. The walls might have survived an attack by the dawi, but a dragon was another matter. The wreckage of the assault spread for miles into the forest – there had even been signs of a slaughtered dwarf warband amid the trees. The fact that the creature's rampage had been indiscriminate gave no comfort.

The stink of Dhar hung over the dragon's trail, tainting the air with a residue of putrid over-sweetness. The aroma was horribly familiar to Liandra, instantly bringing back memories of a hunt she had ended a long time ago. Like a nightmare dragged back into the world of wakefulness the same stink of sorcery had re-emerged, more spiteful than before and now borne on tattered, tortured wings.

Death will be a mercy for it, Vranesh sang, still enraged.

Mercy for the beast, replied Liandra grimly. *For her, nothing.*

The abomination was still fast. It must have once been a truly magnificent creature, a rare scion of the Dragonspine with few peers, for the black arts of the Witch King had not robbed it of its native speed. Even Vranesh, counted among the swiftest of the drakes, closed on it only slowly.

The hours passed in a bleak procession, marked only by twin flames in the night, the two of them tearing across the sleeping world like burning stars. When the clouds rolled over them at last, cutting out the light of the moons and dousing them in perfect darkness, it felt as if the earth and sky had been swept away, leaving them alone in a void of pure hatred, pursuer and pursued, hunter and prey.

Only with the dawn did the gap close. The black dragon seemed to tire as the sky in the east lightened, finally slowing as the mist-pooled mountains below were picked out by the shafts of gold. The two drakes came together, poised over the high peaks, wings splayed and claws unfurled.

Now we have them, Vranesh sang, her mind-voice little more than a growl.

Liandra leaned forward in her seat, sending flickers of aethyr-fire snaking along her staff.

Fight well, beloved, she sang.

Fight well, feleth-amina, came the reply.

Imladrik slept little, troubled by dreams in which both Yethanial and Thoriol had appeared before him accusing him of things he had done and things he had not. Waking from them to find himself in a besieged city on the edge of eternal war was almost a relief.

Dawn brought a sobering vision to the east of his tower. Morgrim's host had continued to grow, digging in across several miles of open countryside. Massive engines of war had been dragged up out of the trees – ballistae, trebuchets, siege towers, as well as other huge constructions he had never seen before. Whole regiments of infantry engaged in exhaustive dawn-drills before his eyes, swinging hammers and axes in unison across ranks a hundred wide. Every so often booming war-horns would sound, prompting a massed *Khazuk!* response which made the earth shake.

Imladrik watched them for a long time, scouring for signs of weakness, marvelling at the vast swell of bodies, all encased in thick armour or draped in coats of close-fitting mail. They went with a swagger, fully aware of their destructive potential. Self-doubt did not come easily to a dwarf – they knew just how deadly they were when gathered together in numbers.

After that he dressed and prepared for the day. He made his way down to the plain in the company of his ceremonial guard. Caradryel was waiting for him at the gatehouse, and the two of them walked out to the great tent together.

'Any news from Liandra?' Caradryel asked.

'Not yet. I am choosing to be generous, and assume she does not know that the dawi are here.'

Caradryel looked sceptical. 'It is still a desertion, is it not?'

'As I say, I am choosing to be generous.'

'Have you asked Salendor about her?'

Imladrik gave him a hard look. 'Why would I do that?'

'Perhaps you should. Just gently.' Caradryel looked ahead to where the cluster of tents shivered in the early morning wind, and grimaced. 'Another day of this. Blood of Khaine, I wonder if I'd prefer the fighting.'

'What of Salendor?'

'He's been busy, talking to all sorts of people.' He gave Imladrik a wary look. 'I think he's close to the edge.'

'Then keep an eye on him. I can handle the others, but I still need your eyes and ears. Do you need more money?'

Caradryel looked mildly insulted. 'I'll come to you if I do.'

They reached the tent, its canvas walls glossy with dew. Two guards in the livery of Silver Helms stood to attention, clasping their fists against their chests in homage.

'Does it ever get wearing?' asked Caradryel as they passed within. 'Being saluted by everyone?'

'I live for it,' said Imladrik, not really in the mood for Caradryel's flippancy.

The dwarfs were waiting for them in the central chamber, sat as they had been the day before, looking just as mutely murderous. Aelis, Salendor, Gelthar and Caerwal were there likewise, waiting for Imladrik to take his place.

'My lords,' he acknowledged as the elves rose to greet him. He bowed to Morgrim and the dwarfs, then took his seat. Caradryel took his place on the margins, sliding effortlessly into his habitual state of near-invisibility.

Imladrik reached for a pewter goblet filled with watered-down wine and took a sip. Then he clasped his hands before him and drew in a long, quiet breath.

'So,' he said, already feeling weary. 'Let us begin again.'

The black dragon coiled in the air ahead of them, no longer trying to escape and adopting a defensive posture. Its long ebony body snaked in an S-curve before hunching over, claws raised and jaws open.

Vranesh gave it no time to prepare – she hurtled straight at it, preceding her attack with a wall of crimson flame. The dragons collided in a blaze of mingled energy, lighting up the peaks in vivid, crimson-edged relief.

Vranesh powered through the inferno, raking out with her foreclaws, but the other dragon twisted away, doubling back on itself to escape the rush of talons. Liandra caught a fleeting glimpse of her opponent – an ivory-skinned druchii in torn robes. The sorceress looked emaciated, her staring eyes hollow with fatigue and deprivation.

They tumbled apart, each creature already coiling for the return. Vranesh was quicker, and managed to loose another gout of magma-hot flame before the abomination could bring its jaws around.

The blast hurt it – Liandra heard its screaming even over Vranesh's frenzied roars – but the black dragon somehow pushed through the intense heat and loosed a barrage of its own. Vranesh plummeted, letting dragon-fire shoot over her arching spine before thrusting back up for a bite at the enemy's trailing tail. By then the abomination had powered away again, swinging about in mid-air and drawing in breath for a third fire-blast.

The speed of it, the intensity of it, the *noise* of it – was incredible. At first Liandra could do little more than hang on as Vranesh wheeled, bellowed and dived. Her counterpart seemed even more unsteady. Perhaps she was still new to the dragon; if so, that gave Liandra an edge.

In close, great one, she urged, regaining her balance and angling her staff for attack. *The rider is the weakness.*

Vranesh hardly needed telling. The dragon shot forwards, tail flicking out and her wings slamming back. As the enemy raced in close, Liandra unleashed her art.

'*Malamayna elitha terayas!*' she cried, feeling her staff shudder as lightning crackled out from its tip.

Golden aethyr-fire shattered across the abomination's mottled hide, showering both creatures in clouds of stinking black blood. The beast screamed again, this time with genuine excruciation, and launched itself directly at Liandra, evading Vranesh's jaws and aiming to pluck her clean from her mount.

Vranesh was equal to the move, plunging down again and rolling away, but only just – Liandra had to throw herself to one side to evade the talons before Vranesh pulled them both out of danger.

Again, Liandra commanded, pushing singed hair from her face and righting herself for a second pass. Her heart was thumping, her eyes shining. The mountains wheeled and swung below them, lit by the angry glow of the dawn sun. Vranesh swooped, angling her attack to scrape across the abomination's wings.

Then Liandra felt it: a sudden plunge of pain in her spine, as if a metal bolt had been hammered in. Vranesh sensed it and tried to pull out at the last moment, but it was too late. As if forewarned, the black dragon pounced, ripping its foreclaws across Vranesh's extended neck.

Liandra reeled, feeling herself go dizzy. The abomination made the most of the confusion, tearing and clawing, trying to bring its ragged maw to bear.

Her vision swimming, it was all Liandra could do to summon a fresh brace of lightning-bolts and hurl them into the monster's face. That knocked it back, giving Vranesh the chance to pull out of the attack.

The witch, sang the dragon.

No, gasped Liandra, tottering in her seat and peering down at the mountains below. *From the earth.*

Vranesh immediately plunged towards the horizon, blood trailing behind her in a long stream. Liandra could feel the depth of the wound in the dragon's neck as clearly as she felt the pain in her own body.

Forcing herself to concentrate, she scoured the landscape below. Rocky crags sped by beneath them, snow-crowned and empty. She could hear the wheezing breath of the dragon racing after them and ignored it.

She is not alone, Liandra sang, gaspingly. *She drew us here.*

We must withdraw.

No! The vehemence of her denial surprised even her. *This is the chance – I will not lose it.*

Even as she sang the words she saw them – two robed figures standing on the very lip of a high crag below them, each one chanting, their staffs running with black-purple illumination.

Vranesh thrust towards them immediately, corkscrewing and undulating to avoid the abomination's pursuing fire. Liandra felt fresh stabs of pure pain explode within her and fought to maintain consciousness. Her staff felt impossibly heavy in her hand, and an almost overwhelming urge came over her to let it fall away.

Fight it! sang Vranesh, bucking hard to her left to evade a spitting column of dragonfire.

Liandra gritted her teeth, feeling sweat sluice down the nape of her neck. Her hands shook as she summoned aethyr-fire back to her.

You are a daughter of Isha, she recited to herself as the edge of the crag raced towards her. *You are a daughter of Isha.*

She could see their faces now – two druchii sorcerers, one male, one female, each bedecked in tongues of dark fire. At the last minute, faced with the crimson hurricane of fire and flesh barrelling towards them, they broke, sprinting back along the crag-top and seeking shelter.

The sudden cessation of their pain-magic revived Liandra. Her staff sprang back to life, shimmering with pent-up golden fire.

'Asuryan!' she cried aloud, swinging her staff around her head before hurling its tip in the direction of the fleeing sorcerers.

The air shook as the fire blazed free, streaking after the druchii and detonating around them in a hard crack. The entire crag-top exploded in a roar of shattering stone.

Vranesh pulled up at the last moment, claws scrabbling through the breaking summit. With an echoing boom the crag began to collapse, dragging whole chunks of slush and granite down the far side. Liandra swayed in her seat as Vranesh's momentum carried them both over. The pain had gone, but the abomination was still hurtling after them, snarling close on Vranesh's tail.

Did we get them? she asked, twisting her head to catch sight of the sorceress – she could smell and hear the dragon but no longer see it.

Vranesh didn't reply. Her huge breaths were strained. A hot aroma of burned copper rose from her torn neck-scales as she thrust up skywards, more laboured than before.

Then Liandra caught sight of the enemy, still close but hovering forty feet clear, strangely indecisive, as if the loss of the sorcerers had given its rider doubtful pause.

Liandra's eyes narrowed. She crouched low across Vranesh's straining shoulders, her staff still rippling with power.

Now we take her, she snarled.

SIXTEEN

'You have given us *nothing!*' accused Grondil, flecks of spittle flying. 'You say you do not think of us as fools. Well, you have a strange way of showing it.'

Caradryel watched the dwarf lord rage. The display was impressive, full of the red-cheeked, fist-slamming bravado the dwarfs employed when they wished to get a point across. Grondil had stood up to speak, though the difference in height, as far as Caradryel could see, was slight.

Caradryel glanced over at Imladrik, sitting calmly waiting for the tirade to finish.

'What would you have me do?' Imladrik replied. 'Summon the druchii before you?'

Grondil glowered. 'It would be a start.'

'Enough,' muttered Morgrim irritably. 'You have made your point.'

Grondil glared at Morgrim for a moment. Then, grudgingly, he sat down again.

Morgrim looked tired. Caradryel guessed that he had been engaged in many long sessions of argument with his thanes during the night. Morgrim had very little to gain from any cessation in hostilities but plenty to lose; perhaps the strain was getting to him.

'Grondil speaks the truth,' said Morgrim. 'We can talk around this as much as we like, but we will always come back to the same issue. You ask us to believe you, to trust you, yet trust is just the thing we do not have.'

Imladrik raised his hands in a gesture of hopelessness. 'We've talked ourselves hollow over this. Your people in the high places, mine in the lowlands. There is room for us to live alongside one another.'

'For now, perhaps,' said Morgrim. 'But in a year, when memories have faded? What shall I tell the High King – that we had the chance to destroy our enemy when he was weak and instead let him recover to come after us again?' He shook his head. 'You must give us more. There is a blood-debt on your head.'

Caradryel had been watching Imladrik's exchanges for so long that he'd almost forgotten the other members of the Council. Against the odds, it was Caerwal who spoke up then, his blank face uncharacteristically animated.

'Blood-debt?' he demanded bitterly. 'What of my people? Who will pay the price for the slain at Athel Numiel?'

Eldig snorted. 'Perhaps it was not dawi who killed them. Perhaps it was these druchii. After all, who can tell?'

Caerwal shot to his feet. 'Do *not* dishonour them!' he shouted, his cheeks flushing.

Grondil and Eldig both stood up and started to shout back. Caradryel glanced at Imladrik again and their eyes met. Imladrik gave him a weary look that said *this is hopeless*.

Then, just as the entire chamber dissolved – again – into a series of bawling matches, a lone elf slipped in to the tent from the asur side and sidled up to Salendor. He wore the livery of Athel Maraya, and in all the commotion no one gave him a second glance.

No one, except, for Caradryel, who observed carefully. The elf stooped low and whispered something in Salendor's ear. Then, just as silently and with as much discretion as before, he rose to his feet and ghosted back out. Salendor sat for a while, pensive, no longer paying much attention to what was going on around him but staring down at his hands.

'And so what do we have left to talk about?' demanded the runelord Morek amongst the hubbub, his old voice cracked and cynical.

'Everything, *rhunki*,' urged Imladrik, still trying to rescue something from the wreckage. 'If we could just calm ourselves...'

'That is wise counsel,' said Salendor, suddenly lifting his head up and looking around the chamber. At the sound of his voice, the space fell quiet. 'We have been arguing for hours and achieving nothing. Perhaps some time apart would be beneficial.' He glanced over at Imladrik, seeking his approval. 'Some wine, some food.'

Imladrik considered that for a moment, seemingly torn between pressing on and cutting things short before they descended into a brawl.

'Very well,' he said resignedly. 'We will adjourn. But, my lords, I implore you to *consider* what has been offered here. Reflect on it. Let us hope we may convene in a better temper.'

The session rose. As servants filed into the chamber with refreshments, Salendor quietly made his way to the entrance and walked outside.

Caradryel got up and followed him. As he neared the canvas opening, Imladrik broke free of an animated discussion with Caerwal and called him back.

'Where are you going?' he asked.

Caradryel nodded in the direction of the city. 'Salendor,' he said, and that was all that was needed.

Imladrik looked distracted, no doubt already thinking of ways to salvage the upcoming session. 'Are you sure you're–'

'Leave him to me,' Caradryel said. 'You worry about the dawi.'

Imladrik nodded. 'Very well, but if he's ready to move...' He paused, his face looking almost haggard for a moment before hardening again.

'You know what to do,' he said, and turned away.

The land raced past in a blur. The two drakes dived and soared, each snapping at the other as they tried to find purchase, neither landing the decisive blow.

Drutheira had been reduced to hanging on grimly. The crimson mage was far more powerful than she'd guessed. A dragon – a *real* dragon – was also far more powerful than she'd guessed. Her own mount was bigger and more steeped in sorcery, but its erratic mind made it a haphazard and flailing combatant.

She had no idea where they were. The hours of flying had left her disorientated and exhausted. The Arluii were long behind them, a hateful memory now consigned to the north. Seeing her companions on the mountaintop swatted aside so easily had been like taking a kick to the stomach – they should have been able to cripple the mage at least. Perhaps their powers had withered during the long years of the hunt, or perhaps they had just got careless.

A sun-hot burst of flame rushed past her. Bloodfang wheeled down to its right, tilting clear of the blast, its chains clanking as it spun away from the danger.

'Back!' she cried, driving the spike-point of her staff into the creature's neck again, though it did little good. 'Do not run!'

Bloodfang had long since ceased responding to her commands. The beast had been badly mauled, first by dragonfire and then by talons – the pain seemed to have driven what little sanity it possessed into abeyance.

Drutheira glanced over her shoulder. The red mage was close behind, just as she had been since the fight over the mountains, her face fixed in a mask of hatred, her staff still glittering with nascent sunbursts of power.

Drutheira raised her own staff, dragging up yet another gobbet of raw Dhar potency, dreading the pain it would bring her.

'*Kheledh-dhar teliakh feroil!*' she shrieked, her voice cracking, and launched a trio of spinning black stars at the red dragon.

The creature evaded two of them, pulling up high with a sudden thrust of its wings and arching over the star-bolts, but one impacted, cracking into its exposed chest. The bolt detonated with a sick *snap*, making the air around it shudder and bleeding out lines of oil-black force. The star-bolt clamped on, sprouting slick tentacles that gripped and ripped like a living thing.

The red dragon bucked and twisted, bellowing in pain, nearly throwing its rider off and falling further behind.

'Now!' Drutheira screamed at her wayward steed, wishing she could grab the monster's head and force it to see what she had done. 'While it is wounded!'

The red dragon's roars of pain must have penetrated into even Bloodfang's pain-curdled mind, for it responded at last, switching back mid-air and inhaling for a fresh blast of dragonfire.

By then the asur mage had done her warding work, ripping the sorcerous matter clear of her mount's flesh and casting it away. Bloodfang lurched into range, its massive wings thrusting like bellows, fire kindling between its open rows of yellow teeth. The red dragon responded as best it could, uncoiling its wracked body and summoning up flame-curls of its own.

Bloodfang slammed into it, hurling a raging stream of dragonfire at its torso and following up with scything swipes from its extended forelegs. The two beasts crunched together, meeting with an echoing crack of bone.

Drutheira's mount ripped into the other drake's already ravaged neck-armour. Claws and tail-barbs flew back and forth, dragging and biting. The two creatures grappled with one another, rolling over and over in the skies, retching fresh dragonfire into one another even as their jaws bit deep into fissured armour.

Blood splashed across Drutheira's face as she gripped tight, trying to keep her head as the world whirled around her. She caught fractured glimpses of her adversary doing the same thing, lost in the savagery of the dragons unleashed at close quarters.

Drutheira had lived through a hundred battles, but the viciousness of this one took her breath away. Both creatures were consumed with primal bloodlust, far beyond reason or mortal understanding, roaring into one another like hounds on a stag. Bloodfang was the bigger, the heavier and the more powerful – its muscles rippled under steel-hard armour as its claws punched out – but the crimson dragon was still the quicker and more cunning, writhing out of the reach of its enemy's jaws and biting back with attacks of its own.

Drutheira swung around in her mounted vantage, getting a brief glimpse of open water far below them, but dared not shift position further to get a better look. She gripped Bloodfang's bucking neck two-handed, no longer able to use her staff, summon magic, or do anything other than weather the storm.

'*Elemen-dyan tel feliamor!*'

The words somehow rose above the deafening roars, piercing the confusion like a sudden shaft of sunlight. Drutheira snapped her head back up and what she saw took her breath away.

The red mage was standing – *standing* – on her steed's back, bracing herself with one hand while the other whirled her staff around her head. Her poise and balance were incredible, as if she could somehow anticipate every movement her mount was making and adjust for it ahead of time.

Drutheira tried to drag herself into an attacking posture, to kindle her staff and summon up some kind of response, but Bloodfang's violent movements made it impossible and she fell back heavily against a bulge of heaving wing-muscles.

Then the world exploded around her. The red mage launched her magic: a coruscating bloom that blistered the air and ripped into the glimmering world of the aethyr beyond. Drutheira heard a sudden clap, followed by a howl of wind and the tart stink of burning. Bloodfang, agonised by a sudden burst of aethyr-brilliance, twisted its massive head over to bite at the source.

'No!' cried Drutheira, hauling on the beast's chains. 'Do not–'

It was too late. Bloodfang's massive, sore-encrusted jowls closed on the mage's incandescent staff-tip even as she thrust it out. Its point drove up through the roof of the creature's mouth cavity, searing clean through flesh, gristle and bone.

The red dragon spun away, breaking free of Bloodfang's throttling embrace and powering back into the open sky, leaving the mage's flaming staff embedded in the black dragon's maw.

Drutheira tried to clamber up towards her steed's head to retrieve the lodged staff, but it was hopeless – she had no command of such work, and Bloodfang had been driven into a frenzy of spasms.

The length of spell-wound ash kept burning away, crackling like lit blackpowder. Bloodfang's mouth was now smoking, and not from the creature's native fire-breath. It arched, clawing at its own face, lost in a hell of pain and confusion as the staff worked its way in towards the brain.

Drutheira clung on, hoping against hope to find some way to pull things back from the brink. The scarlet dragon made no attempt to come at them again – Drutheira caught a fragmentary glimpse of it limping through the air, bleeding profusely, head lolling with exhaustion.

That was the last she saw of it, for Bloodfang plummeted further, losing height with every jerking wingbeat. Its neck thrashed about, its head shook back and forth, its limbs extended rigidly, stiff with pain.

'Fight it!' screamed Drutheira, seeing how fast the world below was racing up to meet them. Now it was clear where they were – out over a wide strand of water that glittered in the sun. Bloodfang was heading right for it, perhaps unable to gain loft, perhaps somehow aiming to douse the agonising fire that raged in its skull.

Drutheira watched helplessly as the dragon's eyes turned from silver to gold before exploding in a splatter of flaming liquid. The skin around its jaws broke open, exposing taut cords of sinew within. Bloodfang's own furnace-like innards now worked against it, feeding the inferno that raged down its neck and into its lungs, hollowing it out, purging the ancient sorcery that had sustained it and turning it into a flesh-bound caldera.

Drutheira had seen enough. Struggling still against the dragon's tumbling flight, she pushed herself out over a shoulder-spur, almost losing her staff in the process. With a sickening lurch she saw how far she had to fall – over sixty feet, though dropping fast.

Bloodfang seemed to sense that she was abandoning it and twisted its blind head round a final time. Even amid its anguish the dragon managed a final burst of fireborn hatred. Drutheira pushed herself clear, leaping from her steed as the flames screamed over her. The heat was intense, sweeping across her back and shoulders, but mercifully brief. For a terrifying moment she felt the world open up below her and the whistling surge of the air racing past her cartwheeling limbs.

Then came the splash and booming rush of impact. She plunged deep below the surface, her robes billowing around her, bubbles swarming into her face and making her gag. She had a sudden terrible fear of hitting the bottom and tried to kick against her momentum. Something snagged against her left ankle and her heart-rate spiked, driven by panic.

Somehow, though, she managed to push up again. She thrashed her way to the surface and her head broke through. She drew in a desperate breath before ducking under again, gulping and spluttering, then pushed back up, her cheeks puffing.

As she emerged she saw Bloodfang go down. The creature was howling, wailing in abject degradation as its face melted away from the bone. Its wings had gone limp, fluttering like a shroud as its chained body rolled earthwards.

The dragon hit the water a hundred feet from her, crashing down with a gargling roar and sending out waves like the wake of a warship. Foam surged up around it, vapourising instantly as its sorcerous flames were finally doused. Its huge tail whipped out a final time, sending spray flying high, before it too was dragged under.

Drutheira caught a final glimpse of the dragon's ruined head, gasping for air, before the hissing waves closed over it, then all was lost in a welter of steam and bloody froth.

The waves from the impact hit her next, nearly swamping her and sending her back under. Her limbs felt like lead weights and her flame-seared flesh smarted – it was all she could do to flail away, blundering towards where she supposed the shore must be.

The sky above her remained empty, with no sign nor sound of the red mage. She swam on, doggedly pulling into calmer waters. Soon she was amongst reeds, then she felt soft mud under her feet. She hauled herself upright, wading through the shallows, breathing heavily.

Standing knee-deep, she looked around her. The shoreline was empty – a parched scrubland of ochre soils and meagre bushes. The sun beat down hard from a clear blue sky, already warming her sodden body.

Her breathing began to calm down, the shaking in her hands eased. There was still no sign of the red mage. The asur's steed had been horribly wounded; perhaps it too had fallen to earth.

Bloodfang, though, was gone. Against all expectation, Drutheira felt a pang of remorse at that.

She shook her head irritably.

It was a beast, she remonstrated with herself. *A dumb, mad beast. May the day come when all the dragons are so enslaved.*

She started to wade again. A silty beach drew closer, covered in a scum of algae and beset by clouds of flies. Beyond that, desolate land stretched away from her. She could see bare hills on the eastern horizon, their crowns baked butter-yellow and dotted with sparse vegetation. Already she felt thirsty, and the heat was growing. The sky remained empty, devoid even of birds.

Perhaps I killed them both.

Her head was light. Already the past two days of unremitting combat felt like some crazed, poppy-fuelled dream, and she still didn't know quite what to make of it.

It had not gone how she had expected, and certainly not as she had planned, but she was alive. That was the important thing: she was bruised, alone, exhausted, but alive.

'So then,' she said out loud, sweeping her dark, hollow eyes across the strange landscape before her. 'What now?'

Caradryel made his way quickly to the city. Just inside the gatehouse he caught up with Feliadh, who was waiting for him with a dozen of his troops in tow.

'Is it time?' Feliadh asked.

'It is,' replied Caradryel. 'Where did he go?'

'Into the Merchants' Quarter.'

Caradryel nodded. 'Then we follow him there.'

They went swiftly. Caradryel let his hand stray down to the long knife at his belt, and cursed himself for not bringing something a little more useful.

The Merchants' Quarter was not far, though the name had long since ceased to signify anything meaningfully mercantile. The old storehouses and market squares had been given over to supply depots and training grounds, and like everywhere else in the city the place was crawling with soldiers.

'Who has responsibility for this place?' asked Caradryel as they made their way deeper into the warren of streets.

'The Lord Caerwal,' said Feliadh.

'Really? Interesting.'

They reached a ramshackle courtyard near the centre of what had been the clothiers' market. One of Feliadh's soldiers was waiting for them at the junction of two narrow streets.

'He went in there,' said the soldier, pointing to a nondescript tower a few yards down the left-hand street. 'I counted six with him.'

Caradryel glanced at Feliadh. 'I'd rather not wait. Can you handle six?'

Feliadh smiled condescendingly. 'Worry not,' he said, patting the hilt of his ornate Caledorian longsword.

The captain took the lead. Feliadh walked up to the tower and tried the door. It swung ajar as he pushed it, revealing a shadowy hallway on the other side.

Caradryel took a deep breath. This kind of work was not something he enjoyed – the prospect of blood, real blood, being shed made him nervous in a way that was hard to hide.

'Let's try to make this clean,' he said, drawing his knife. 'Remember – Imladrik wants proof before we take him in.'

Feliadh gestured with a forefinger and his troops drew their blades.

'For Ulthuan,' he said quietly.

Then he plunged inside, barging the door open and charging into the hallway. Caradryel followed closely, trying his best not to impede the movements of the Caledorians around him.

The space beyond the doorway was deserted, but a stairway rose up steeply on the far side. Light and noise came from the upper storey – the sound of voices raised in anger.

Feliadh raced up the stairway two steps at a time, reaching another landing with a heavy wooden door on the far side. An elf was slumped on the floorboards, unconscious. As Caradryel jogged past him he noticed the crimson edge-livery on his rumpled cloak, then Feliadh shouldered the door open.

'Lower your blades!' he roared as he and his soldiers bundled inside. 'In the name of Imladrik of Caledor, lower your blades!'

Caradryel was next inside, his heart thumping heavily.

It was a large, sunlit chamber. A long table ran down its centre at which half a dozen elves in loremasters' robes were seated. Maps, campaign plans and other documents covered the surface. Six soldiers in the armour and colours of Athel Maraya stood protectively around the loremasters, their swords hastily raised at the intrusion.

Salendor stood at the head of the table with mage-staff in hand. He looked furious.

'What is this?' he demanded.

Caradryel pushed his way to the front of his party. The Caledorians fanned out defensively around him.

'My apologies, lord, but I have been tasked with ending this.'

Salendor looked at him incredulously. 'And who are you?'

Caradryel stiffened. The contempt in Salendor's voice was withering.

'Imladrik's agent,' he replied, producing the seal of office he'd been given. 'Please do not resist – it will be easier on everyone.'

For a moment Salendor looked too outraged to speak. Caradryel worked hard to retain eye contact with him, painfully aware of how dangerous the mage could be and hoping Feliadh's troops would have his measure if things turned difficult.

'Do not *resist?*' Salendor laughed harshly. 'Blood of Khaine, you have no idea what you've stumbled into.'

Caradryel walked over to the table and grabbed a handful of parchment pieces. He could see instructions scrawled in Eltharin outlining attack routes, all leading to the dawi lines. It was a pre-emptive strike, one designed to destroy the fragile truce.

'This is the proof, my lord,' said Caradryel. 'I have been observing you for some time.'

Salendor raised an eyebrow, and a dark humour played across his lips. 'Have you, now? And you truly think you can bring me in?'

Caradryel swallowed. 'Know that I will do my duty,' he said, gripping his knife tightly.

Then Salendor laughed. He motioned to his guards, who all stood down and sheathed their weapons.

'You're a damn fool,' Salendor sighed. 'And two steps behind me.'

Even as Salendor spoke, Caradryel noticed that the seated figures were not in the same livery as those standing – all of them wore cloaks lined with red, just like the one slumped on the landing outside. They also looked horribly afraid.

'I don't–' he started, suddenly doubtful.

'No, you don't,' said Salendor. 'Tell your Caledorian savages to put their knives away. We are on the same side.'

Caradryel hesitated, unwilling to lose the initiative, but as he looked more closely at the situation his confidence drained away.

'I was alerted to this by one of Caerwal's adjutants,' said Salendor, leaning against the table. 'A loyal one, but I took some time to establish that, because it is important to be *sure*, is it not?'

Caradryel began to feel distinctly foolish. 'The messenger at your mansion.'

'So you have been watching me. I suppose I should be flattered.' Salendor looked over the rows of seated loremasters and his expression changed to contempt. 'I argued against Imladrik's plans – you'll know that. I tried to persuade the others to join me – you might know that too. But you think I'd be stupid enough to try *this*?'

Caradryel stared down at the attack plans. They involved named regiments from the city. 'Then who–'

'Caerwal. Have you not seen the way he is? He lost half his people at Athel Numiel and will never forgive it. Even as he sits in that tent his loremasters have been planning to end it all.'

Caradryel sheathed his knife, feeling a little nauseous, and motioned for Feliadh and his company to do the same. 'When?'

'Any time. Six regiments, all sent against the dawi right flank. Suicidal, but it would have brought the war he wanted. Look, you can see the plans here. You can even check the garrison sigils if you wish.'

Caradryel looked down at his hands. 'My lord, I owe you–'

'Do not insult me. Learn from it.'

Caradryel really had very little idea what to do after that. He felt deeply, profoundly foolish – like a child suddenly exposed at playing in an adult world. Various responses ran through his head, none of them remotely satisfactory.

He started to say something, but the walls suddenly shook, rocked by a new sound that burst in from outside. Caradryel reached for his knife again, staring around him to find the source.

Salendor tensed, as did his guards. An abrupt tumult rose up from the plain. Horn-calls followed it, harsh and dissonant, and the volume of noise quickly mounted.

Caradryel hastened over to the window, followed by Salendor. He opened one of the heavy lead clasps and pushed it open.

Up on the parapets, sentries were rushing to the bell-towers. Their hurried movements spoke of surprise, perhaps some fear. A great boom of drums rang out from the east, soon joined by rolling repetitions. He knew what that was, just as every asur who had spent any length of time in Elthin Arvan did.

Caradryel turned to Salendor, his smooth face going pale.

'The dawi,' he murmured.

Salendor nodded. 'Indeed,' he said, closing the window and making for the door.

'Where are you going?' asked Caradryel, hurrying after him.

Salendor halted at the doorway. The disdain had not left his face. 'It was always bound to end like this. Caerwal has not succeeded, but someone else has. Do what you will – I have more important tasks now.'

As he spoke, the floor throbbed from the chorus of low drumming that now rolled at them from beyond the walls. Caradryel heard the tinny response of clarions, followed by the metallic clatter of soldiers beating to quarters in the streets outside.

Salendor strode out of the chamber, his cloak swirling imperiously around his ankles. His guards followed him.

Feliadh glanced enquiringly at Caradryel. 'What now?'

Caradryel looked around him. Caerwal's loremasters all waited, mute and fearful, knowing the penalty for what they had done. Outside, the drumbeats picked up in tempo and volume, matched by the strident tones of bronze war-horns.

Caradryel's shoulders slumped. Everything he had worked for had just dissolved, and for reasons he did not yet even understand.

'Chain them,' he said miserably, drawing his knife again and looking distractedly at the dull edge. 'Then report to me.'

Feliadh saluted smartly. 'And where will you be, lord?'
Caradryel smiled coldly. 'On the walls,' he said, already moving. 'Fighting.'

SEVENTEEN

The pain was astonishing. It wasn't physical, though her body had been battered badly on the way down. It was spiritual torture, as exquisite as any devised by the debased courts of Naggaroth. Liandra wanted to scream out loud, to rage against the fortune that had brought her such agony, but somehow managed to bite her tongue.

Tell me you can restore yourself, Liandra sang.

Vranesh could barely summon the strength to open her eye. It stared at Liandra from just a few feet away, immense and glossy like a golden pearl.

Do not be foolish, the dragon replied. *My fire is gone.*

Liandra caressed the dragon's long neck. It felt like her heart was being torn out. She could feel Vranesh's mortal pain, burning in her own body like an echo.

I would go there with you, Liandra sang.

You cannot.

I would be the first.

Vranesh attempted a laugh. A rolling pall of greyish smoke spilled from her open jawline, sinking into the dry earth and drifting away.

She was right – the fire had gone.

What it is like? asked Liandra, desperate to keep speaking, as if that alone could somehow postpone the moment.

We are there as we were before you entered the world, sang Vranesh. *Before the shaan-tar came to tutor you, before strife came from the outer dark. The eldest of us remember. I will see them again, the names of legend.*

Liandra inhaled deeply, breathing in the remnants of Vranesh's scent. The ember-charred musk was weaker, tinged with the hot stink of blood. The dragon was covered in it, its scales sticky and matt with clogged dust.

The land they had crashed into was a desolate one: sun-hardened plains of baked earth and sparse-brush hills. The heat was oppressive, as if sunk into the air like dye in cloth.

Liandra had little idea where they were. For the long hours of pursuit all that had mattered was vengeance – running down the druchii witch. At least that had been achieved.

Vranesh's voice entered her mind again then, reading her thoughts. *She is not dead.*

I saw her hit the water.

The abomination, yes, sang Vranesh. *Not the rider.*

You are sure?

I can hear her still. Vranesh's long mouth twisted at the corners in a reptilian grimace. *She is fearful and alone, but alive.*

Liandra almost stood up then. She almost walked straight out into the heat-shimmer plain, once more driven with that thirst for revenge that had dogged her since first taking the drake-saddle.

But she didn't. She remained where she was, cradled in the massive claws of her mount like a child in the arms of her mother. Her cloak lay about her in singed tatters.

We will hunt her, then. When you are ready.

Vranesh did not smile that time. The dragon let out a long, long sigh, as sibilant as steel sliding across steel. *You do not listen. You have never listened.*

I do not–

Silence! Vranesh snapped. *No time remains.* The dragon tried to lift her head and failed. More blood bubbled in the corners of its mouth, popping like tar. *Kill the witch if you must, but remember where the real battle lies. All that matters is the song sung between our peoples. If the kalamn-talaen falls then the bond will be broken.*

Liandra did not want to hear the words. Imladrik, for so long an obsession with her, had become an unwelcome reminder of the past, something to be put away and forgotten.

He will not–

Listen! He is the last. Though maybe you can learn. Vranesh blinked – a slippery movement with a leathery inner eyelid – and fixed her obsidian pupil on Liandra. *Do not waste yourself out here. You will be needed. Preserve yourself.*

Liandra felt the words stab at her. *I would follow you,* she said again, tears of anger spiking in her eyes.

Perhaps you might. Perhaps you, out of all of them, might.

Then more grey smoke poured out of Vranesh's blackened nostrils, flecked with black motes. The huge eye lost its glossiness, and a sigh like winter wind escaped from bloodstained jaws.

I loved you, fire-child, Vranesh sang.

Then she was gone. The mind-presence disappeared from Liandra's thoughts, snuffed out in an instant. Although the pain went with it, the hollowness that came in its place was almost unbearable.

Liandra rocked to and fro, balling her fists. For a moment it felt as if she were going mad, or maybe sinking into the same death-trance as her mount.

The tears would not come. She had never been able to cry from grief, only from anger or frustration. Now, alone, stranded on the edge of the world, her companion sundered from her at last, she just rocked steadily, eyes staring, consumed by horror.

Only much later did the first howl come – a rending wail that burst raw from her throat. Then more cries, each shaking with loss, each sent up into the uncaring, empty skies above.

She lost track of herself, consumed by a grief so total if felt as if the world were swallowing her into its heart. It might have been hours before she returned to her senses.

When she finally did so the heat was still there with the harsh sunlight, and the yellow earth that was as dull and lifeless as the corpse of the dragon beside her.

Liandra rose unsteadily to her feet. She stared at Vranesh. The dragon's crimson wings were ripped and limp; the mighty chest deflated.

There were rites for such occasions, ways of preparing the body for the afterlife, but they required time, strength and the use of a magestaff, none of which she still possessed. In their absence Vranesh's mortal shell was ripe for carrion or plunder.

Liandra collected herself, stilling the shuddering that made her breaths short. She extricated herself from the dragon's clutches, working quickly now that she had some purpose, moving her hands in old patterns, murmuring words she had not used for decades. Even so, they came back quickly to her, just as if they had always been waiting.

The air around Vranesh's corpse seemed to thicken, to fill up, to clog. The raw blood-colour faded, replaced by a dun-yellow miasma. The serrated curve of the creature's spine sank, fading into the profile of the sandy dune beyond. The claws, talons and eyes disappeared, replaced by the shadow of rocks or the struggle of desiccated vegetation.

By the time she was finished all that remained was a vague hump in the landscape, bulbous in places but otherwise one with the stark earth around it.

The deception was a minor cantrip – no determined traveller would be fooled by it, and it would dissolve at the first hint of a counter-spell. Liandra guessed that few travellers passed through such a place, though, let alone mages. By the time her illusion wore off, only heat-bleached bones would remain, themselves already sinking into the sand.

She brushed her hands on her robes. Her blood pumped a little less strongly now, anguish replaced by a sense of exhaustion. Her mind still felt empty, bereft of the voice that had once shared it. Her intense grief, for all it might have been weak, had also been cathartic.

She looked around her. To the south lay the long firth where the abomination had gone down. To the north and east lay a wasteland, as vile as it was hot.

She would need to find drinking water, some shade, possibly food. Her arts would help her a little, but not much – she would need to work hard to stay alive.

Liandra started to walk, heading towards the nearby reed-beds. She guessed it was an inlet of seawater, but it was a start. As she went, she struggled to turn her thoughts away from Vranesh and on to the task at hand.

It wasn't easy, but it was possible.

'First, to survive,' she breathed out loud, picking up her pace and leaving the dragon-corpse behind. 'Recover strength. Learn what manner of place this is.'

Her eyes glittered darkly, remembering the witch.

'Then vengeance.'

The summit chamber of the Tower of Winds was full. Armed guards posted themselves wherever there was room; mages shuffled about, preparing spells that would not be ready for hours. A few loremasters tried to stay out of everyone else's way, apologetically shuffling parchment maps and requisition ledgers.

None of them dared to take a step within the inner circle of thrones. Four figures stood there, ignoring the seats, seemingly oblivious to the hubbub around them.

Both Aelis and Gelthar seemed subdued. Imladrik couldn't have cared less about the wretched Caerwal, whose plans would have been uncovered by Caradryel if they hadn't been by Salendor. The only consolation he took from the whole sorry affair was that his most potent general had remained loyal and still stood at his side. As things had turned out, that might prove the most important point of all.

But Liandra – where was Liandra? Her disappearance had gone from being regrettable, to curious, to worrying. She had always been impulsive, but Imladrik couldn't believe she would have actually deserted, not when things were so poised.

It was too late to do anything about that now.

'Are they marching yet?' demanded Salendor, his blunt expression hard to read.

'They will be soon,' said Aelis.

'What changed?' asked Gelthar, obviously still shocked. 'We were talking. I thought we might be getting somewhere.'

Imladrik shook his head. It felt as if events were running away from him. 'We were.' He slammed his fist into his gauntlet, a gesture born of pure frustration. 'This was not Caerwal's work – something else has riled them.'

'We can find out,' said Salendor.

Imladrik turned on him. 'How?'

'A sending. It may do no good, mind.'

Imladrik felt like laughing. It could hardly make things worse.

'Make it,' he ordered. 'I must speak with him, just one more time.'

Salendor placed his staff before him, holding it two-handed and resting the heel against the marble floor. He closed his eyes and rested his forehead against the tip. A greenish bloom rode up from the centre of the marble, coiling like oily smoke. Strange noises echoed from it – the clash of metal against metal, shouting in a strange tongue, the rush of wind from another place.

Imladrik watched distastefully. A sending was a crude thing, a simulacrum and a sham, but it was the only course left to him. The plain beyond the walls now seethed with dwarfen warriors and the great tent had been abandoned. With the gates having been sealed, no elf now walked outside the walls.

Perhaps, he thought, they should have stood firmer – made some kind of principled stand at the site of the talks. But Imladrik had seen the looks in the eyes of the dawi once the war-horns had started blowing, a look he recognised from a long time ago. There had been no time, no means of responding. The only sensible thing to do had been to withdraw to the city until it was clear what had changed.

Sensible, but hardly heroic.

Salendor's spell took firmer shape. The green cloud reached chest height and spread out across the floor. Within the swirling centre images began to clarify. Like an eye sweeping across a confused panorama, fleeting glimpses of dour faces flickered in and out of focus. The harsh tones of Khazalid rose and fell, fading as the roving search cast about for its target.

Salendor began to sweat. 'They are aware of me,' he said, his eyes still closed. 'That damned runesmith...'

'Do not lose it,' warned Imladrik.

The cloud's restless movement paused and the images within its centre sharpened. Imladrik saw faces looming up out of the gloom, like weeds slowly rising to the surface of a lake.

One swam to the forefront.

'Master Runelord,' said Imladrik, recognising Morek's grim visage.

The dwarf glared back at him, eyes out of focus, as if struggling to see through the sending's magical depths. He raised his runestaff and the anvil-head sparked with energy.

Then Morek's face was gone, replaced by a blurry image of Morgrim. The dwarf lord glowered at Imladrik, squinting hard.

'Sorcery,' he spat. 'This will not be forgotten.'

'What is happening, Morgrim?' asked Imladrik. 'Your war-horns are sounding. Your warriors are moving.'

Coarse laughter sounded from somewhere behind Morgrim; perhaps Morek's.

'I believed you,' Morgrim said. 'For the sake of the past, I believed you. Grimnir's beard, I should have known better.'

Imladrik drew closer, peering with difficulty through the miasma. 'I don't understand. What has changed?'

Morgrim didn't reply immediately. He gazed back at Imladrik, scrutinising him as if for a sign of deception. Then, finally, he spat on the ground and shook his head.

'Maybe you do not know,' he growled. 'Warriors from Karak Varn, attacked as they marched to the muster, their bodies still lying unburied in the great forest.'

They were the words Imladrik had dreaded hearing.

'This was not our doing,' he said, though he knew it would sound empty.

'No, nothing in this war seems to be,' said Morgrim dryly.

Imladrik could hear hurried mutterings all around him as his loremasters tried to ascertain the truth of what Morgrim was saying. It was a futile quest – no reports of a break in the truce had come in, not even rumours.

'Tell me where,' said Imladrik. 'I will investigate, you have my word. If there has been–'

'North of Kor Vanaeth,' said Morgrim. 'A woman – a sorcerer – on a dragon. She came on our warriors with no warning.' Morgrim jabbed a stumpy finger in accusation. 'Who but the asur ride dragons? Who among you commands them?' He was getting angrier with every word. 'This is the greatest insult – I *believed* you. For just a moment, you made me trust again.'

Imladrik felt light-headed.

Liandra.

'I did not order this,' he protested. 'Why would I?'

'You know what?' said Morgrim, his voice as bitter as wormwood. 'I no longer care. I listened to your excuses for two days. I told my thanes to keep their blades in their sheaths. I told them that you were in control of your forces, that you alone were worthy of respect among your faithless people. I told them to listen while you spun stories of druchii, even as others warned me that it was lies and fakery designed to buy time to land more legions.'

Morgrim was getting worked up, his eyes burning and his movements agitated. He had been made to look a fool in front of his thanes, something Imladrik knew he could never forgive.

'If you can't control your beasts, then you are to blame,' Morgrim went on. 'I sacrificed much for you, but no longer. Enough talk. We are coming for you with axe and hammer now. We are doing what we came to do: raze your walls and destroy your city.'

Imladrik saw the mania in his eyes even through the distortions of the sending. Morgrim was in his full battle-rage now, fuelled by the burning sense of injustice his race took so much trouble to cultivate.

'It was one dragon rider, Morgrim,' said Imladrik quietly, though he knew it was almost certainly futile. 'Just one. Can you vouch for all the warriors under your command?'

Morgrim nodded angrily. 'I can. They are already marching, elgi. A blood-debt of a thousand gold ingots hangs around your neck. I plan to claim it myself: for Snorri, who was right about you from the start.'

Even as he finished speaking, the sending began to dissolve. Imladrik heard chanting from somewhere – the runelord, now working to banish the hated elgi magic from his presence.

'This is the end, Morgrim!' Imladrik cried. 'You give Malekith what he wants!'

'No, *govandrakken*,' snarled Morgrim, his face fracturing into flame-like slivers as Salendor's magic finally gave out. 'It is what *I* want.'

Then the images gusted away, snuffed into curls of emerald smoke by Morek's command of the runes.

After that, no one spoke. Salendor recovered his poise, breathing heavily. All in the chamber had heard the words. They stood still, waiting for Imladrik's response.

Imladrik stared at the floor. Nothing but despair came to him. The hard truth, the one he had tried so hard to resist, had asserted itself once more.

This was the moment. This was when it all turned. No fellowship would exist between the two races again, not after this. He would be the last of his kind to gaze on the giant, rune-engraved images of Grimnir and Grungni, to peer into the gromril shafts and see the glittering metal hacked from the very base of the earth, to witness the ancient iron-bound tomes in the libraries of the runelords.

The world would be poorer for it. It would be colder, darker and less glorious. Even as he contemplated it, reflecting on a future bereft of harmony and riven with suspicion, he could feel the cold vice of hopelessness around his heart.

Imladrik lifted his head, looking first at Salendor.

'We tried,' he said, quietly. 'When I stand before Asuryan I can at least say that.'

Salendor nodded perfunctorily, but it was clear his counsel had not changed. 'And now, lord?'

'The path is clear,' Imladrik replied, his voice heavy. 'Look to the walls. Ensure the bolt throwers are trained. Let us hope they withdraw when our strength becomes obvious.'

'And if they do not?'

'Then they will die, Salendor,' said Imladrik coldly. 'If they force me, to the last warrior I will kill them all.'

EIGHTEEN

Thoriol ran up the steep stairway, taking the steps two at a time. Moving fast was difficult with bow in one hand and quiver in the other – the constant jostling from those around him made it even harder. The entire city was in motion, with troops rushing to their stations under the echoing blare of trumpets. The noise from the war-drums outside was deafening – a grinding, rolling hammer-beat that made the air shake.

The rest of Baelian's company raced alongside him, Florean in the lead with Loeth close behind. The captain brought up the rear carrying his own bow, a heavy yew-shaft tipped with silver that he'd carried into battle for sixty years.

They ran up another winding stairwell, making the torches gutter as they swept past, before spilling out on to the east-facing outer wall. The ramparts were wide – over twelve feet – but were already filling with bodies.

'Down here!' cried Baelian, his voice impatient, directing the company to their allocated place. 'Faster!'

Tor Alessi's walls rose up in three concentric layers: an outer curtain that soared up from the plain for over a hundred feet, smooth and pale with only one land-facing gatehouse; then an inner sanctuary wall that rose even higher, ringing the inner city with its clustered spires and mage-towers; and finally the ultimate bastion, a truly cyclopean cliff of ice-white masonry that protected the mightiest central citadel.

The mages had been stationed up there, their bright-coloured cloaks rippling in the wind and their staffs already shimmering with power. Eagle-winged bolt throwers had been mounted on the next tier down. Some of those war machines were gigantic, carrying darts hewn from single tree trunks and bowcords the diameter of a clenched fist. The archers were stationed on the outer perimeter, thousands of them rammed close along the long, winding parapets.

It was a daunting sight, a majestic display of Ulthuan's glory. The banners of the King and the many asur kingdoms blazed clear under the powerful evening sun, draping the walls in a garland of vivid runes. Thoriol knew thousands more warriors waited within the cover of the walls, ready to advance swiftly if the perimeter were breached. Many of those were regular spearmen detachments, but he'd seen more heavily armed companies waiting in reserve, all clad in high silver helms and wearing ithilmar-plate armour. The entire city was teeming with violence, suppressed for so long but ready, at last, to unleash.

Thoriol slammed his quiver on the stone in front of him, hefted his bow to shoulder height and adjusted position, placing his left foot forward and preparing for the first draw. Only then did he look out beyond the battlements, across the plains that had been until that day empty of life and movement.

All had changed. Marching figures now filled the wasteland, teeming like flies. They were advancing slowly, arranged in long ranks of tight-packed infantry. He couldn't begin to guess how many there were – the entire eastern fringe of the plain was dark with them. They marched in rhythm to the incessant beat of the war-drums, swaying in perfect unison under stone-dark banners. Some regiments were clad entirely in close-fitting metal plates; others had donned chainmail hauberks; still more wore heavy breastplates over leather jerkins, their warhammers and battle-axes clutched two-handed.

Behind the front ranks came the war machines – huge and grotesque devices of iron, bronze and wood, dragged into position on massive spiked wheels or metal-bound rollers. Thoriol saw stone-throwers, pitch-lobbers, trebuchets, ballistae, battlefield crossbows, grapnel hurlers and other things he had no name for. Each was massive, towering over the hordes that milled around them, crowned with beaten war-masks and mighty iron rune-plates.

Brazier pans glowed angrily under the open sky, polluting the clear blue with snaking columns of dirty brown. The war-horns kept on blaring, overlapping with one another in a cacophony of hard-edged, intimidatory clamour. None of the dwarfs spoke. None of them chanted or sang – they just tramped across the plain, sweeping with remorseless slowness, surrounding the city in a closing vice.

Thoriol swallowed. He could feel his heart racing. Those on either side of him tensed, ready for the order to draw. Some of the archers were veterans of a hundred engagements and kept their faces stony with resolve; others were scarce more experienced than Thoriol and their nerves were evident even as they attempted to hide them.

The dwarfs came on, closing to five hundred yards of the walls. At such a distance Thoriol could clearly see the details on their armour – the sigils, the battle-runes, the daubs and spots of blood. Every tattooed and bearded face was twisted into hatred, warped by a single-minded desire to break the walls, to drag them down, to drown the city in blood.

So many.

Then, with no obvious order given, the host stopped. Every dwarf halted his march and stood perfectly still. The war-drums ceased. The horns stopped. For an awful moment, the entire plain sank into a fragile silence.

It seemed to go on forever. As if in some bizarre dream, the two armies faced one another across the empty land, uttering no words and issuing no challenge.

Then, as suddenly as the dwarfs had stopped, each raised his weapon above his head. Tens of thousands of mauls, axes, short-swords, flails, war-hammers and crossbows pointed directly at the walls, each one aimed in ritual denunciation.

Khazuk! came the cry – an immense, rolling, booming challenge. Every wrong, every grievance, was distilled into that one word and hurled up at the white walls of the city like a curse.

Khazuk!

The din of it was incredible, a roar that seemed to fill the heavens and the earth. Thoriol had to work hard not to fall back from the parapet edge, to creep into the cool shade of the stone and escape the horror of it.

Khazuk!

The third shout was the greatest, a mighty bellow that felt as if it would shatter crystal and dent stone. In its wake the war-horns started up again, underpinned by the frenzied beating of drums. The host began to move once more, but this time the shouts of challenge did not stop. Tor Alessi was besieged by it, surrounded by the maelstrom.

'Hold fast,' warned Baelian. His voice was as steady as the granite around them. Thoriol wondered if anything scared him.

Four hundred yards. Trumpets sounded on the elven battlements, almost drowned by the surge of noise out on the plain.

'Prepare,' ordered Baelian, just as hundreds of other company captains did the same. Tens of thousands of archers stooped for their first arrow, fixing it against the string and preparing for the draw.

Three hundred yards; just on the edge of their range. Thoriol held his stance, feeling like his muscles were about to seize up. He felt nauseous, and swallowed hard.

A second trumpet-blast rang out.

'Draw,' ordered Baelian, notching his own arrow.

Thoriol heaved the string to his cheek. He held it tight, feeling the feathers of the arrow's fletching against his forefinger.

Two hundred and fifty yards. Optimal range. The dwarfs must have known it, but they just kept on marching, still chanting, shouting, challenging and making no effort to evade the storm to come.

This was it. This was the culmination of everything he'd been working for, the final fruits of a foolish flight to Lothern away from the deadening hopes of his father.

Perhaps he might catch sight of me in all this, thought Thoriol dryly. *Perhaps he might approve. Perhaps, for once, I might make him proud.*

Then the final trumpet-blast, the signal to release. Up until now it had all been a mere shadow-play, a rehearsal, a toothless precursor.

'Let fly!' ordered Baelian.

As one they loosed their arrows, and the sky went dark.

Drutheira woke with a start. For a moment she had no idea where she was or what she was doing. Sevekai's face had been in her dreams again, chiding her for leaving him. She hadn't had visions of him for a long time, not since Bloodfang's presence had been in her mind.

It unsettled her. Sevekai was gone, dead, his body rotting at the foot of a mountain gorge. He had no business still affecting her, skulking in her dreams like a spectre of Hag Graef.

It was dark – pitch dark. For a moment she feared she'd slept far into the night, but then, as her awareness returned, she remembered having to tie strips of her cloak around her eyes to blot out the sun. She ripped them off and the light came back as intensely as ever, burning like a brand thrust into her face.

Blinking heavily, she gradually remembered where she was: a shaded hollow under a tumbled cliff of red-brown stone, the best shade she'd been able to find. The cliff wound its way south-east, following the course of an old dried-up river. She'd followed it, unable to stomach the brackish seawater where she had waded ashore and unable to find more promising tributaries.

So far all she'd found was damp mud caking in the heat. The need for liquid was becoming pressing – despite the oppressive warmth she was no longer sweating, and her head felt thick and clogged.

It had been foolish to fall asleep. More than foolish – dangerous.

She looked around her, squinting against the hard light on the rocks. No sign of movement, pursuit or tracks.

Drutheira pushed herself to her feet, collecting her staff and leaning on it heavily. For the first time ever she regretted having spent so long cultivating the arts of Dhar at the expense of all else. It might have been nice to conjure up something to drink. She could have fooled herself easily enough with chimeras of wine or ice-cool water but the effects would not last. The only things her sorcery could genuinely construct out of nothing were destructive – the bolts of aethyr-lightning that tore through armour, the snarls of unnatural flame that crisped flesh and melted eyes.

It suddenly struck her as so pointless, so *wasteful*. Out here, in the parched hinterland, she was no better than any mortal.

Drutheira started to limp, keeping to the shade of the cliff to her left. Ahead of her the path wound along the foot of the cliff, choked with loose stone. To her right ran the base of the dry riverbed, the far shore of which rose up again a few hundred yards distant in another cliff face. Its twin rock-tumbled edges were far apart, enclosing a shallow dusty bowl between them, but they gradually drew closer together the further she went.

In time the riverbed narrowed to a gorge. The sun sailed westward, still horrendously hot. Drutheira's mouth became too dry to open without pain. Her lips cracked and bled, and she breathed through her nostrils as sparingly as possible.

The passing hours gave her no fresh indication of where she was. She remembered vague rumours of a vast land to the south of Elthin Arvan. Malekith had been interested in it, saying that he sensed some strange and potent magic brewing there, but that had been decades ago and Drutheira suspected he didn't truly understand what he was speaking of. As far as she was concerned the place she was in had no magic about it at all, let alone strange and potent magic. It was a forgotten land, a between-place wedged amid greater realms, no doubt destined to remain barren forever.

She caught sight of bushes clustered in the lee of the nearside gorge-wall. They were harsh, dense things – black-leaved, bristling, no more than five feet tall – but it was a hopeful sign. It might even mean water.

She picked up her pace, ignoring the protests from her strained leg-muscles and forcing herself to keep going. She had another day, perhaps two, before the thirst would get her, and she had absolutely no intention of meeting her end in such an undistinguished place.

It was then that she sensed it, hovering close, barely noticeable but wholly unmistakable.

Drutheira crouched low, hugging the rock wall once more and letting its shadow slip over her. She scanned the landscape around her, sniffing, her eyes wide and her senses working hard.

She is close, she thought, recognising the stink of the asur. She could not see or hear any sign of the dragon, but the aethyr-presence of the red mage was definitely hanging on the wind.

The sunlight made it hard to see much at distance – dazzling out in the open, causing the air to shake and shimmer. Drutheira did not move for a long time, hoping her adversary would betray herself first.

Can she detect me? she wondered. It was possible that, in her diminished state, Drutheira's aura would be less obvious to a fellow magician than in the normal run of things. Dangerous to rely on the chance, but something not to ignore either.

She crept onwards, hugging the shadow of the gorge, her eyes sweeping around at all times, her staff ready. The scent faded, replaced by the wearyingly familiar tang of burned earth. Perhaps she had been mistaken, or perhaps the dragon rider was still aloft, miles away now, her scent carried by the wind.

Then she saw something else, lodged in the thick tangle of black-leaved bushes ahead – a flicker of red, barely visible, quickly withdrawn. Drutheira tensed, wondering if she had the strength for a summoning.

The asur mage was there, somewhere, crouching or lying among those dark branches. Was she waiting for her? Or was she, too, lost in the wilds and seeking some respite from the beating sun?

The more Drutheira watched, the more her conviction grew. She screwed her eyes up, letting a little sorcery augment her already-sharp vision. Something was hidden in the bushy cover, clad in red, prone on the ground as if exhausted. Drutheira tasted the nauseating tang of Ulthuan mingled with the hot metal aroma of dragon.

Drutheira broke into a lope, going as silently as her training enabled. She flitted across the gorge-floor, body crouched low and robes whispering about her.

She was soon amongst the bushes, ignoring the sharp jabs from the thorns as they ripped through her clothes. She raised her staff quickly, kindling dark fire. Ahead of her, only half-obscured by a tight lattice of thorns, was her enemy: out cold on her back, her pale freckled face staring up at the sky, unmoving.

Drutheira pounced, forgetting her fatigue as she crashed through the final curtain of spines, jabbing her staff-heel down at her enemy's heart.

The metal tip hit the ground hard, jarring Drutheira's arms. It bit into nothing – where Drutheira had seen a body, there was now just a stained patch of earth, as dry and desolate as every patch of earth in the whole Khaine-damned place.

Too late she caught a fresh stink of magic, tart in her nostrils like acid.

Illusion!

She felt something hard crack into the back of her head and staggered to her knees. She tried to get up again, to twist around and bring her staff to bear, but another blow followed, flooring her.

Tasting blood in her mouth, she rolled over, feeling the staff slip from numb fingers. Her vision was swimming, already shrinking down to blood-tinged blackness.

Standing above her, real this time, loomed the red mage, her hair hanging limp in the hot air, her face streaked with dust, smoke and gore. She looked half-dead. Her right hand clutched a fist-sized rock, one that dripped with Drutheira's own blood.

'I–' started Drutheira, not knowing what to say, her voice cracked and empty.

That was all she managed. The red mage slammed the rock down again, this time into Drutheira's forehead, snapping her skull back against the ground and making her mind reel in pain.

The last thing she heard before passing out was Eltharin, the hated tongue of her enemy, but one which she unfortunately understood all too well.

'At last,' hissed Liandra, her voice heavy with exhilaration, readying the rock again. '*At last.*'

Imladrik stood alongside Salendor at the summit of the inner parapet, watching grimly as the dwarfs assaulted all along the eastern walls. The two of them had said little for a long time.

The dawi had assaulted Tor Alessi three times in the past and had been driven back three times. In the early years of the war, though, the armies on both sides had been smaller and expectations different. The dwarfs had expected to demolish the walls; the elves had expected to defend them with ease. In the event the walls had always held, but at terrible cost in desperate defence and hurried counter-attacks. The proud dawi infantry had been mauled by the volume of arrows, while the equally proud asur knights had been hacked apart whenever they had been caught in the open.

Other cities and holds had suffered, but both sides knew that Tor Alessi was the key to the war. While the deepwater harbour endured the Phoenix King could land fresh troops in Elthin Arvan at will; if it fell then the remaining elven Athels and Tors would be vulnerable, each one ripe to be picked apart in turn. So it was that the dwarfs had come for it again and again, scarcely heeding what it cost in blood and gold.

'Will they break in this time?' mused Salendor, watching as more siege engines were hauled into range through a veritable hail of arrows. Some of the asur darts were flaming, and where they kindled the massive war machines collapsed in columns of burning ruin. The battlefield was studded with them, like sacrificial pyres to uncaring gods.

Imladrik shook his head. 'Not while I command.'

Far below them, a heavily armoured column of dwarf infantry was getting bogged down as it tried to force a passage to the gates. The dawi held their shields above their heads, making painful progress with admirable determination, but still they came up short, choked by their own dead and mired in the bloody mud.

'Arrows will not hold them forever,' observed Salendor.

A volley of bolt throwers on the second level opened up, hurling their payloads through the smoky air. The bolts ploughed into the advancing infantry ranks, or lanced into war engines, or collapsed trebuchets in welters of splintered timber.

'Trust to the walls,' said Imladrik calmly.

Salendor looked sceptical. 'Perhaps.'

Even as he spoke, the first stone-throwers reached their positions. Imladrik watched dwarfs run out bracing cables and hammer them into the yielding soil. They threw up massive bronze shields in front of the delicate mechanisms before loading rough-cut stones into the cages and pulling the iron chains tight.

Three of them loosed, almost together. Their lead weights thumped down and their hurling-arms swung high. Three rocks, each the size of a hawkship's prow, sailed through the air before crashing into the parapet of the outer wall. One exploded into fragments without causing much damage. The second smashed a rent in the outer cladding before sliding down the smooth exterior. The third punched straight through the ramparts, dragging dozens of archers with it and careering on into the towers and winding streets beyond.

'That's just the start,' said Salendor bleakly. 'They have bigger ones.'

'Then you had better instruct the mages to take them out, had you not?'

Salendor gave him a significant glance. 'Dragons would do it faster.'

'Yes, they would.' Imladrik did not look at Salendor as he spoke. The plain was pressed tight with bodies, punctuated by rains of arrows and returning strikes from the war engines. Soon the dawi would gain enough ground to install bolt throwers of their own. They might even force their way to within axe-range of the stonework.

'Will you go aloft, then?' asked Salendor, doing well to control his impatience.

Imladrik pressed his lips together calmly, and kept watching. Salendor had no idea what he was asking. None of them did.

'Instruct the mages to take down the stone-throwers,' Imladrik said coldly. 'Leave worrying about the rest to me.'

More war engines swayed into position. Several were blasted apart by strikes from the wall-mounted bolt throwers, others were fatally pinned by hundreds of flaming arrows, but more than a dozen made it to join the first three and then the onslaught began in earnest. Rocks, spiked iron balls, flaming phials of runesmith-blessed fire, all were flung at the walls in a swinging, pivoting barrage.

The dwarf advance, though bloody, had not been reckless. The most heavily armoured infantry units had soaked up the earliest swathes of arrow-flights, risking casualties but secure in the knowledge that many of the iron-clad warriors would endure. That had bought time to establish the heavier wall-breaking engines. Now that the defenders had been forced to concentrate on multiple targets, the intensity of the dart-storms at ground level lessened, and the iron-clad battalions began to crawl forwards once more.

Tor Alessi began to burn. As the sun wheeled westward, fires kindled by the rain of rune-fire projectiles erupted into life, resisting every effort to put them out. Explosions flared up on the walls where they impacted, adding columns of twisting smoke to the growing film of murk in the air; others burst out within the city itself, drawing troops away from the perimeter to fight the stubbornly persistent blazes.

Morgrim watched the carnage unfold from his vantage in the centre of the plain. He could not lie – it made his heart swell.

The bickering and hesitation was over. He didn't know what he would have done if the elgi had not broken the ceasefire. He knew full well that warlords within his own host had been planning similar acts of sabotage, but remained confident he could have prevented them.

Perhaps there was something to Imladrik's fanciful tales. It didn't matter any more. So many acts of cruelty had been committed that the need for grudgement was now overwhelming. Even if he had withdrawn his own army from Tor Alessi, others would have come in time. He knew of musters in the mountains to the east, each one already setting off toward other asur outposts – Athel Toralien, Athel Maraya, Oeragor. There was no way he could have stopped all of them even if he had wanted to.

And he did not want to. He wanted the dwarf armies, all of them, to succeed. He wanted the elgi gone, banished back to their strange and unnatural island, their taint wiped from the honest earth of the dawi homeland. Only then could the wounds of the past be healed, old poisons withdrawn, new mines delved.

It all starts here, he thought grimly. *May Grimnir curse us if we falter now.*

Morek lumbered up to him, his staff acrid with discharged energies.

'*Tromm*, lord,' said the runelord, bowing low.

Morgrim nodded in acknowledgement. As he did so, strange flashes of light lashed out from Tor Alessi's summit. Morek and Morgrim watched as magefire in all hues – emeralds, sapphires, rubies – spiralled down into the dawi front lines, tearing them up like ploughs turning a field.

Morek regarded the development sourly. 'Their magic is as flighty as they are,' he muttered.

A siege tower, the first to come near the city's gatehouse, ignited, its crown exploding as magefire kindled and bloomed on its protected shell. Flames raced unnaturally through the heavy leather shrouds and timber bracing-beams, streaking down the structure's core. A few seconds later and it was little more than charred scaffolding, its deadly cargo leaping to safety as the wooden platforms and ladders disintegrated around them. More trundled onward to take its place.

'Deadly, though,' observed Morgrim.

His voice was distracted. For some reason he couldn't take the loss of a few siege towers and trebuchets as seriously as he ought. Something nagged at him, dragging his mind from the conduct of the battle.

'Where are the dragons?' he asked at last, out loud though not speaking to anyone but himself. Everything he had been led to believe, not least from Imladrik himself, told him that the drakes were the most potent weapon the asur had.

Morek looked up at the walls contemptuously. 'We have killed wyrms before.'

The grip around the city tightened. Morgrim saw miners finally reach the base of the walls just south of the gatehouse. He saw more war engines pull into position and begin to unload their deadly contents. He saw fires burst into life on the parapets, sending smoke boiling up into a wearing sky. The light was beginning to wane and turn golden as the sun began its long slow descent towards the ocean. As the shadows lengthened, Tor

Alessi looked battered, proud, and doomed, ringed by a veritable sea of ground-deep loathing.

'So we have,' he said softly. 'But keep your runesmiths aware, *rhunki*. The drakes will fly. Only then we shall truly see Imladrik's mettle.'

NINETEEN

'They're coming!'

The shouts of panic were superfluous – Thoriol could see perfectly well that they were coming. Everyone along that section of the parapet could see that they were coming. That didn't stop the shouts, though. Loosing arrows into the skies was one thing; going face to face with the enemy was another.

Magefire rippled through the air like strands of crystallised starlight, spinning and flickering in the dying day. Arrows still flew, though less thickly than they had done. Thoriol wondered just how many thousands of darts had been loosed – how many warehouses had been emptied and how many quivers discarded. His own arm muscles were raw with effort despite the increasingly frequent breaks the company had been forced to take. Using a longbow was not like twanging a hunting bow – it was exhausting, back-bending work.

The endless flights had hurt the enemy. He could see the piles of dead on the flat below, bent double, twisted. No enemy, no matter how well armoured or disciplined, could march through such a storm without taking damage.

But the advance had not been halted. The dwarfs had come closer and closer, wading stoically through their own dead, shrugging off the slamming impacts of mage-bolts and quarrel-shots, all the while hurling their strange guttural abuse up at the defenders.

Now the outer walls were reeling. Some sections had been shattered by the stone-throwers, opening breaches that were desperately reinforced by thick knots of spearmen. The dwarf vanguard brought ladders and grapnels with them; once the parapets were blasted clear by the trebuchets a hundred hands would start to climb and a hundred pickaxes would begin to swing. As soon as one ladder was knocked back another two would lurch up again, propelled by burly arms from the boiling mass of bodies on the plain.

Thoriol's own wall-section had weathered the storm. No impacts had shaken their parapet and no rune-magic had been slammed against the foundations. Throughout it all, several hundred archers had been able to maintain regular volleys against the throng below with only their own exhaustion to fight.

It couldn't have lasted. The next big impact was less than a hundred yards from Thoriol's position. He felt the whole wall shudder as the battlements were shattered by a tumbling ball of rock. Cracks snaked like lightning along the stone, and a massive chunk of masonry toppled inwards, breaking up and raining down on the buildings below. The screams of those caught in the disintegration were mercifully short-lived.

Dwarfs homed in on the damaged section. Bolt-thrower quarrels lanced into the crumbling stonework, smashing more pieces free. Arcane-looking caskets crashed amid the residue, bursting with the hateful fire that seemed to kindle on anything. Grapnels followed, some thrown up to haul warriors onto the walls, others used to drag more slabs of facing stone away. With terrible speed the breach was widened and lowered, enough for siege-ladders to start clattering into position against the trailing edge.

The asur defenders were not idle, though. Spearmen from the city's interior clambered up across the ruins, forming dense spear-lines just in the lee of the breach. They spread out across the rubble, overlooked on either side by the still-standing wall-ends. Soon asur and dawi were fighting furiously amid collapsed stonework, just as they were doing across a dozen other breaches.

'For Ulthuan!' roared Baelian, rushing along the parapet to gain a vantage over the broken section. Other archers did the same, eager not to let the spearmen down below take the brunt of the dwarf assault unaided.

Thoriol was swept along in the crush. He barely had time to snatch his quiver before he was standing on the brink, his boots grazing the edge of the precipitous drop. His companions closed by on either shoulder, all drawing their bows.

'Aim well!' cried Baelian.

The wall had not come down cleanly, and long slopes of detritus lay on either side of the breach, serving as a ramp for troops of both sides. Dwarfs clambered up one side, spearmen the other.

Thoriol notched his first arrow and pulled the string taut. The dwarfs were a few dozen yards below him, their attention fixed on the spearmen ahead of them. Thoriol screwed his right eye closed and lowered the point of his arrow just in front of a dwarf warrior lumbering up the steep bank of rubble. He let fly, and the dart thunked heavily into the dwarf's chest. It was enough to send him toppling backwards and into his comrades.

More arrows fizzed down from both sides of the breach. Baelian sent a shaft into the eye-socket of a bellowing dwarf champion – a breathtaking feat of marksmanship. Other darts found their mark, pinning the dwarf advance back and giving the spearmen space to advance across the open wound and pull reinforcements up in their wake.

Thoriol's heart pumped strongly again. Fear ran hard through his veins, though tempered with something else, something wilder and more elemental.

Excitement? Am I truly exhilarated by this?

He could smell them, they were so close. He could hear the wet *shlicks* of the arrows biting into flesh. At such range the elven shafts were utterly deadly, capable of stabbing through all but the very thickest plates of armour.

He notched a second arrow, then a third, watching with grim satisfaction as each found its target.

But the dwarfs were not liable to stumble blindly into a slaughter. Crossbow-wielding warriors crouched low in the rubble and aimed up at the archers on either flank. Soon the air was filled with the snap and whistle of bolts. Thoriol ducked down as one flew past him, almost snagging his trailing shoulder.

Still kneeling, he notched another arrow. Just as he lifted his bow to take aim, he heard a strangled cry. Turning to his right he saw Baelian stumble forwards, a quarrel sticking proudly from his throat. The company captain, at the forefront as always, must have presented a tempting target.

Baelian managed a final look in Thoriol's direction. The scars on his face writhed as he struggled to breathe. Then he collapsed, falling over the edge of the parapet and down into the rock-choked breach below. His body hit the rubble hard; soon it would be under the boots of the advancing dwarfs.

For a second, Thoriol was dumbstruck. Baelian had seemed invincible, immune from the fear and filth of battle.

'Let fly!' came Loeth's voice, thick with rage.

The others leapt to obey. Thoriol felt fury surge up in his breast. For the first time, he was angry rather than scared or thrilled.

Ignoring the danger, he stood up straight, drawing his bow with a savage expertise he would never have considered possible during the crossing from Lothern.

'For Ulthuan!' he cried, sending another arrow spinning into the line of advancing dwarfs. Even before it had found its target, he was reaching for another.

Salendor rose up to his full height at the very edge of the precipice. Below him the walls fell away in three vertiginous cliffs, each one towering over an ocean of fire and turmoil. He felt the hot wind rush across his face, laced with ashes and magic. As the sky darkened to dusk he felt power well up within him once more, swelling to the flood, ripe to burst from the tips of his calloused fingers.

The winds of magic raced around him, swirling and eddying with increasing force. Aethyr-essence crackled in the air, snarling with semi-sentient fervour. On either side of him other mages cast their battle-spells. Bolts of vivid, rubescent force shot out into the gathering dark, sweeping past the burning towers and slamming through siege towers, clusters of ladders and knots of enemy fighters.

For all its potency, the magefire was not unopposed. Salendor could feel the deadening effects of the dwarfen runesmiths countering every attempt to raise fresh magic. He could sense their dreary chanting, stilling the vital winds of magic and making them listless. In the wake of such work it was hard to pull the requisite power from the aethyr, to drag it into the world of the senses and make it do its work.

Salendor grimaced, feeling the physical pain of the summoning. His lungs ached from chanting the words, his hands bled from gripping his staff. The siege had become a gruelling test of endurance, a clash of two equally deadly and equally implacable enemies. The entire lower levels of the city were now furiously contested, the many breaches in the walls glowing like a ring of embers. Vast blankets of smoke hung over the lower city, brooding across sites of slaughter. Every so often another war engine would ignite, exploding in an angry bloom of crimson, or another watchtower would crumble under the relentless onslaught of the stone-throwers, dissolving into yet more shattered masonry.

Salendor whirled his staff around his head, using the growing momentum to add to his summoning. The winds whipped up around him, sparking and surging. Soon he had his target: a battering ram being dragged up to the main gates, covered in metalwork protection and warded by powerful runes of destruction. Though the sigils were carved in the dawi tongue Salendor could sense their malign power well enough.

'*Othial na-Telememnon fariel!*' he shouted, dragging an aethyr-mark out from behind the veil. His staff burst into blazing silver light and he loosed the fire, sending it snaking down through the burning towers. The magical beams homed in on their distant target unerringly, spiralling through the chaos before smashing into glittering shards across the battering ram's housing. Each shard burrowed deeper into the metal plates, dissolving iron and pulverising timber.

Lit up by silver explosions, the battering ram made an appealing target for the surviving archers. First a flaming bolt hit it, then several pitch-dipped arrows impacted. With its thick outer shell compromised, the barbs tore deeper into the mechanism within.

The battering ram's progress ground to a halt. Soon the entire structure was listing, its immense axles broken, its back aflame.

Salendor grunted with satisfaction. That would set them back.

His satisfaction did not last long. The gatehouse was relatively secure, but elsewhere the situation was deteriorating. More breaches in the outer perimeter had been inflicted. One looked particularly bad – a huge gouge in the stonework with dawi actually clambering up the ruins. He could just make out valiant clusters of archers clinging to the two ragged edges, pinning the invaders back. A bold stand, but precarious.

His fellow mages were tiring. One of them, Eialessa of Eataine, as powerful a spellcaster as he had ever seen, looked out on her feet. Several of the others had pale faces and sunken eyes.

'Where are the damned dragons?' Salendor asked aloud, tilting his head to the heavens. Imladrik had been gone for hours – it was becoming absurd. 'Where is the lord of this city?'

Nothing but darkness and tattered clouds answered him. The sky was streaked with sullen red glows, interspersed with occasional sharp flashes of magelight.

But then, finally, he sensed a change on the air. Something stirred, a rush from the west, the echo of something very, very high up.

He saw nothing. The sky remained dark and mottled. The fires continued to burn, adorning Tor Alessi in a corona of sullen anger.

For all that, Salendor could not suppress a smile.

'Ah,' he breathed, raising his staff once more, forgetting his fatigue and remembering anticipation. 'Now, my stunted friends, we shall see.'

Imladrik pushed Draukhain higher. The first pinpoints of starlight clustered on the extreme eastern horizon, glowing in a deepening sky. It was perishingly cold. The other dragons coursed and wheeling around him, wings rigid for the glide. Telagis's emerald wings glinted in the dusk as he swept past Draukhain, bowing his head in submission as the greater drake's shadow fell across him. Imladrik could sense the dragonsong of the other riders, whispering to their mounts, holding their immense power in check.

Down below, far below, his city burned. He could see the flare and pulse of the flames, barred by black lines of smog and ruin. The sun still shone in the west but was setting fast, making the tips of the waves looked like burnished bronze.

Why do we wait? sang Draukhain. The kill-lust was high in him; Imladrik could sense it pressing on his own mind.

I am preparing myself, Imladrik replied. *It has been a long time since you and I went to war.*

Nonsense. We have been killing druchii for months.

They are different.

Draukhain snorted. *Bonier, perhaps.*

Imladrik looked down, peering through the layers of drifting smoke. The vision was hellish, like the opening maw of Mirai in the depths of the gathering night.

The dragon knew well enough why they paused. Draukhain knew almost everything about him – the shape of his moods, the tenor of his thoughts. Sometimes Imladrik wondered if keeping secrets from his mount was even possible. Some things had been surrendered a long time ago – the right to a solitary mind, the right to an undisturbed sequence of mortal thoughts.

I do not wish this to be a slaughter, Imladrik sang.

Then do not ask me to unfurl my claws at all.
I am serious. We must drive them from the walls, but limit our wrath to that.

Draukhain flexed his pinions, preparing for the dive that would take them hurtling into the battle below. *Even now, you harbour dreams of ending this?*

Imladrik smiled bitterly. *Not any more, but they are not daemons. Kill in proportion: that is the maxim.*

Proportion! sang Draukhain contemptuously. *Aenarion would have laughed to hear it.*

And look what became of him.

Draukhain spilled a savage, metal-grating noise from his smoking jawline. *Then we hunt.*

Imladrik rested his blade on the dragon's shoulder bone-spur and tensed for the shift.

Aye, Draukhain – we hunt.

He gave the mental order. His mind connected with those of the five other riders, and for a moment they were locked in silent communion. He felt the hot presence of the Caledorians, so similar to his own; he felt Heruen and Cademel prepare for the dive. He saw the varicoloured wings pull in tight, their iridescence furled.

For a moment all six dragons teetered on the brink, their riders sitting back in the saddle. Then the steepling fall began, and the drakes shot earthwards.

Imladrik felt the wind race past him. Draukhain took the lead position, racing down like some gigantic falcon, already breathing heavily with an iron-furnace rattle in his lungs. Gaudringnar followed closely, shadowed by the swift Rafuel.

Tor Alessi rushed up towards them, rapidly growing in size. Imladrik held his position carefully, watching as the three lines of walls separated and became individually visible. He picked out the flashes of magefire in the pinnacles and the staccato delivery of the bolt throwers. He saw the fires burning along the parapets in the lower city, throbbing and flaring in the gathering dusk.

Draukhain growled with joy. By then he could smell the dawi. He extended his wings again and began to sweep into the attack run.

Hunt well, sang Imladrik to his companions, knowing that once the dragons were amongst the enemy they would each fight alone. That was ever the way with them: they were solitary predators.

The summit of the Tower of Winds shot past, the first of the tall towers to be reached. The drakes split, cascading like lightning across the city. Imladrik caught sight of Salendor standing on one of the highest platforms. The mage-warrior looked elated, and saluted him as he passed.

Then Draukhain plunged down further, snaking through the thud and shriek of projectiles and beating his wings harder.

The walls, sang Imladrik, gripping tight against the push of the wind. *Drive them from the walls.*

Draukhain powered towards the nearest breach, the clap of his wing-beats like thunderbolts. The dawi did not see him coming until far too late. Even then, what could they have done? Run? None of them were fast enough. They had scoffed at the legend of the drakes and now their mockery would kill them.

Imladrik guided the dragon towards the largest of the rents in the eastern flank of the city – a huge hole in the stonework the width of a hawkship's sails. Dwarfs were battering away at a thinning line of elven defenders, pushing gradually into the lower city.

Draukhain *roared*, making the residual bulwarks of the twin wall-ends shake further. In a spiralling flurry of dislodged stone, he crashed into the dwarf front rank.

It was like being hit by a tornado. Dawi were hurled into the air by the impact, plucked and dragged from the rubble by Draukhain's claws or slammed clear by savage downbeats. The lashing tail accounted for dozens more, sweeping them from their positions and sending them cartwheeling, broken-backed, into the seething mass beyond the walls.

Then the fire came. Draukhain twisted around, still airborne, spewing a massive, writhing column of dragonfire that crashed across the stonework like clouds tearing around a mountain summit. Even the staunchest of the dwarfs fell back in the face of that, clawing at terrible burns as they staggered clear.

Imladrik rose higher in his seat, riding the swerve of his mount. He bent his mind to the task of dragonriding, adding his consciousness to Draukhain's own, melding his awareness with that of the mighty drake. They were like twin entities bound within a single gigantic physical frame.

Draukhain snapped his wings back and thrust clear of the breach, leaving a trail of smouldering carnage in his wake before pushing out into the horde of dawi beyond. Staying low, he punched into them like a ploughshare breaking into soil, blasting blue-tinged sheets of flame across the reeling lines before plucking the most defiant of them from the earth and flinging them high.

All across the beleaguered city the tale was the same. Each dragon hit the attacking armies at once, devastating the vanguard and driving deep into the supporting troops behind. These drakes were no drowsy, gold-hoarding wyrms of the eastern mountains – they were Star and Moon dragons, the most powerful beasts in all natural creation, sheer engines of destruction, avatars of primordial devastation. The dawi had never seen the like, and they shredded them.

Imladrik felt the lust for killing swell up within him. The taste of dawi blood came to his lips as splatters of gore streaked across his silver helm. A savage smile half-twitched on his lips, teetering on the brink of spreading.

Retain control, he sang, guiding Draukhain further into the press of dwarf bodies. He could see siege towers up ahead, all ripe for destruction.

Draukhain hurtled low over the battlefield, raking the oncoming hordes. The dwarfs who attempted to rally were first bludgeoned with dragonfire, then gouged by Draukhain's jaws and talons, then swept aside with the disdainful flicks of his immense tail. Crossbow bolts clattered harmlessly from the dragon's scaled hide. Axes and warhammers were wielded too slowly to make an impact; even those that connected did little more than bruise Draukhain's armour.

Imladrik nudged his mount and the dragon climbed a little higher, thrusting clear of the struggling infantry lines and up towards the first siege tower. The dwarfs mounted on its flanks behaved with characteristically insane bravery, holding their positions and loosing a whole flock of quarrels at the approaching monster.

The pitiful scatter didn't even slow them. Draukhain flew straight into it, smashing through the upper platforms and bursting clear of the far side in a rain of broken spars and planks. The entire structure blew apart, flayed into splinters by the thrashing tail and crushing wings. By the time the dragon wheeled back around for a return pass, nothing remained but dust, corpses and crackling firewood.

Back to the walls, sang Imladrik, struggling not to give in to the powerful urge to slay with abandon. Part of him wished to drive onwards, to carve a gorge of slaughter between the bloated flanks of the enemy all the way to the baggage trains. Part of him wished to push on towards Morgrim himself, to punish him for his lack of imagination.

You become the dragon; the dragon becomes you.

But he had to resist, to retain command. Draukhain swung about, angling hard over the disarrayed dwarfs and powering back towards the burning city. Imladrik spied another breach in the outer walls and marked it mentally. He could make out iron-clad infantry labouring in the ruins, driving up a long slope of rubble to get into the city beyond. He saw lines of elven spearmen facing them from the interior, supported by archers perched precariously on the half-ruined walls either side.

This would be simple – another clean sweep, driving the dwarfs back out onto the plain and picking them off. After that the assault could slow: the walls would be secured and the dragons could take up stations above them. The lesson in power would be enough – even Morgrim, stubborn as he was, would have to pull back in the face of it.

As Draukhain arrived at the breach, though, the dragon suddenly pulled up sharply.

What is it? sang Imladrik, looking about him concernedly in case some stray barb had somehow penetrated the dragon's armour.

Your blood is on the walls.

For a second, Imladrik had no idea what he meant. The dragon soared higher, clearing the breach before banking tightly over the eastern wall-end.

Imladrik looked down. Several dozen archers still manned the intact ramparts overlooking the ruined section. Several more lay on the parapet surface, their light armour pierced with quarrels.

I do not under– began Imladrik, then broke off.

Draukhain dipped lower and broke into a hover, his massive body held immobile with all the poise of a kestrel.

I sensed it, sang Draukhain. For once, his voice was neither sarcastic nor wrathful. *Your blood.*

Reluctantly, fearing already what he would see, Imladrik peered into the lambent shadows. One of the archers, the one closest to him, had had his helm knocked from his head. Imladrik recognised the face even amid the fire and murk. For a horrific moment he thought he spied Yethanial there, her bruised features twisted in pain.

Then, in a moment of no less horror, he saw the truth. It was Thoriol, prone, his robes wet with blood, his eyes closed and unmoving.

'What madness–' he started, before being shocked into silence.

The surviving asur on the walls stared up at him, their faces fearful. The surviving dwarfs beat a hasty retreat under the whirling shadow of Draukhain's wings, summoned away by frantic signals from the battlefield.

Imladrik was unable to take his eyes from the scene. Thoriol lay awkwardly on a broken slab of marble, his hand still half-holding a longbow. He was dressed in the manner of a common archer. The last time Imladrik had seen him he'd been arrayed in the acolyte's robes of Tor Caled.

He should have been in Caledor. He should have been *safe*.

Draukhain began to labour in the skies. Imladrik could sense the itch for combat become restive. He looked back over his shoulder, over to where the sea of dwarfen warriors marched, their momentum stalled but their numbers still formidable. The other dragons wheeled and dived at them, lighting up the dusk with blooms of consuming fire.

And then, distracted, Imladrik felt his long-kindled bloodlust boil over. He felt the spirit of the dragon surge through his limbs, animating them with a dark, cold fire. He saw the pale, bruised face of his only son before his eyes.

They have done this. They dragged me here. They caused this war. They laid waste to this land. Damn them! Damn their stubborn, ignorant, savage minds!

Draukhain responded instantly, rising higher against the backdrop of swirling smoke. The beast's animal spirits burst into feral overabundance. Fires sparked into life between his curved fangs. His pinions spread, splaying out like a death shroud.

'Damn them!' roared Imladrik, giving in at last, feeling the hot rush of exhilaration take him over. '*Damn them!*'

His blade became hot in his gauntlets, searing like the cursed steel of the Widowmaker itself. He felt the blood of Aenarion throb in his temples.

The runes on his ancient armour glowed an angry arterial red, responding instantly to the preternatural powers unleashed across the sacred silver.

Draukhain pounced, sweeping out into the dark with a magisterial surge. Imladrik levelled his sword-tip over the ocean of souls before him. He no longer saw them as worthy adversaries to be curtailed. All he saw in that moment, his soul twisted with blood-madness, was *prey*.

The other dragons sensed the change in mood. They dived into the enemy with renewed fervour. The lowering sky fractured with bursts of fresh flame and cries of dawi agony. The asur behind the walls, also sensing the vice of restraint lifting, began to pour out through the gaps in the walls. They spilled out on to the plain, murder glittering in their eyes.

Amid them all and above them all, mightier than all others between the mountains and the sea, came the Master of Dragons, unleashed at last, his brow wreathed with darkness, his countenance as severe as Asuryan's, his soul burning with the madness of Khaine.

They have done this, he sang, his mind-voice icy. *Leave none alive.*

TWENTY

Grondil strode onwards through the morass of blood and churned-up mud. It swilled over his shins, dragging at him, though he barely noticed the pull.

Up ahead the walls of Tor Alessi burned a vivid red in the darkness. Trails of fire shot up from the trebuchets and bolt throwers, streaking out in the night. The noise of battle was deafening – a frenzied melange of drums, shouting, screams, magefire explosions.

'To the breach!' he roared, blind to all else. His hearthguard strode with him, weathering the storm of arrows that whined and clattered about them. He had no idea how many had managed to follow him thus far. The battle-ground had dissolved into a vast scrum of straining bodies and labouring war engines, all formation lost in the churning melee at the base of the walls.

The sudden arrival of the dragons had changed nothing. They soared and dived into the host, lighting up the sky with flashes of iridescence. Their power looked phenomenal, but that did not concern Grondil. No opponent, however towering or malevolent, had ever truly concerned Grondil. They all drew breath; they could all be killed.

His contingent was still fifty yards short of the walls and making heavy weather of the march. The shells of ruined trebuchets burned in the mud around him, grisly monuments amid a press of straining bodies. The attack was faltering; it needed something decisive to turn the tide.

'The breach!' he bellowed again, swinging his warhammer around his head. The walls ahead had been hammered into semi-ruins, exposing the soft innards of the city within. If a salient could be pushed into the city's perimeter, sheltered by the walls and out of the sweep of the dragons, that might be enough. Grondil could already see the jagged edges of the stone-work picked out in the firelight, swarming with defenders trying frantically to shore up the defences. Axe-blades flickered in the half-light, rising and falling like picks at a coal-face.

He tried to run, to break into the charge that would carry him to the fighting. His armour clattered around him, weighing him down. He stumbled, falling to one knee, tripped by jutting debris left in the mire. Hot air rushed across his back, scorching him under his armour. A tart stench of ashes clogged his nostrils, followed by a sharp scent of blood.

Cursing, he twisted round to beckon his contingent onward, and his jaw dropped.

They had gone. They had all gone, swept away as if scooped out of the ground by the hands of some daemon of the earth. All that remained was a vast crater of scorched soil, thick with blackened corpses. In the centre of it writhed a gigantic creature, a golden dragon with wings unfurled, its serpentine tail coiling around it, its long neck arched above him.

Up close, it was colossal. Grondil had never seen a living thing so enormous. He almost lost his grip on his hammer.

The rider on the dragon's back lowered a sword in his direction. It danced with a strange, elusive light that made Grondil's eyes smart.

He didn't wait for it to explode into life. He pushed himself up from the mud and broke into a charge.

'Grimnir!' he bellowed, holding his weapon two-handed and scouring the creature's hide for a weak spot. All he saw was a screen of glistening golden armour, flawless in its protective coverage, splattered with great streaks of dwarfen blood like honour markings.

Before he could get within strike-range the dragon belched a searing blast of flame. It overwhelmed him, raging across his plate armour, worming its way into every joint and crevice. He staggered on for a few more paces, blinded by the heat, hoping to land at least one blow before his strength gave out.

The heat suddenly ebbed. Grondil reeled, trying to squint through the pain, to somehow get into position for a swipe.

But the dragon had taken flight again, hovering just a few yards above the wreckage of Grondil's company. The downdraft of its huge wings was acrid and gore-flecked. For a moment longer Grondil stayed on his feet. He dimly heard shouts of alarm, of retreat. Somewhere close by, something exploded with a dull *boom* – a siege engine, perhaps.

The beast loomed over him, magnificent and terrible, out of reach of his warhammer, impervious to anything he could throw at it. Blood sluiced down Grondil's armour. Delayed by shock, he felt the onset of the burns he'd taken, waves of pain that swelled across his whole body. Then, as if as an afterthought, the dragon turned in the air, switching back sinuously, its tail sweeping round in a casual arc. The heavy end-spine caught Grondil square in the chest, hurling him back through the air, driving his breastplate in and crushing the ribs beneath.

Grondil thudded back to earth twenty paces distant, sliding on his back, his spine arched in pain. Through blood-wet eyes he saw the dragon climb higher into the air, its body a dazzling mottle-pattern of crimson and gold.

It snaked higher, graceful and unconcerned, its rider already searching for fresh prey.

Grondil felt oblivion creep up on him. His limbs went cold. He couldn't lift his hammer. The whirl of battle around him became muffled, as if underwater. He kept his eyes fixed on the heavens, trying not to slip away too soon.

He would have raged then, if he had been able. Not against his own death, which meant little to him, but for what the dragon had done to the army about him.

Grungni's beard, he thought, aghast at the cold realisation even as his mind slipped into darkness. *We cannot beat them.*

Morgrim watched the dragons with a slow and growing sense of awe. He had witnessed such creatures before, of course. He had even come close to riding one – the very sapphire monster that was currently ripping his armies into shreds – but he had never seen one unshackled in battle. Only his ancestors in the days of glory, back when Malekith had fought alongside Snorri Whitebeard, would have witnessed such terrible carnage.

He stood grimly amid his faltering legions, resting on his axe, staring fixedly at the bloodshed.

'We cannot hold them!' cried one of his thanes – he did not even notice which one. Warriors were hurrying into position all around him, reserves suddenly pressed into action and charging out across the battlefield. He heard the bellows of captains exhorting their troops to move faster, to fight harder, to bring the damned *drakk* down.

None of them, not one, considered falling back. Faced with a terror greater than any living dwarf had faced, they just kept advancing, hurling themselves into the fiery maw of it with death-oaths spilling from their lips.

We never learn.

Morek limped up to him out of the darkness. The runelord's grey beard was flecked with ash and blood, his staff leaking a thick dirty smoke.

'The *drakk*...' he began, his gnarled face wide with shock.

Morgrim nodded. 'I can see, *rhunki*. I can see it all.'

Out across the far side of the raging battle, the elgi had pushed out of their citadel, emerging in strength from the breaches his own war engines had carved into the outer walls. Their infantry were formidable enough – well-organised squares of mail-clad spearmen supported by cavalry squadrons that moved steadily across the ceded ground. On their own such soldiers would have been a worthy test.

But the dragons... they were something else. Morgrim stayed where he was, saying nothing, in silent awe of their supremacy, their matchless arrogance, their contempt.

Some madness had taken hold of them. They crashed to earth in flailing whirls of claws and tails, crushing everything beneath them, before launching back into the skies with broken bodies trailing in their wake. They smashed siege engines apart. They belched gobbets of coruscation that melted all but the gromril masks of his best equipped elite. Bolts fell harmlessly from their armour. No axe or blade seemed to bite. Those that stood up to them died and, since no dwarf ever ran from danger, that meant whole regiments were wiped out with horrifying speed.

As the sun finally met the western horizon, casting crimson rays across the fields of death and sending long barred shadows streaking out from the base of the towers, the dragons still glittered like jewelled spears, their scales flashing vividly like the coloured glass in the shrine of Grungni.

He remembered Imladrik telling him of the Star Dragons. Morgrim had scoffed at the description.

'We know how to kill *drakk*,' he had said.

Imladrik had laughed. Back then, they had often laughed together. 'Even daemons struggle to live against a Star Dragon,' he had replied. 'On this occasion, my friend, you do not know of what you speak.'

I did not. Truly, I did not.

The runesmiths were struggling as they attempted to drag up rune-wards that would do something to halt the dragons' rampage, the elgi mages in the city were freed up to send their own magics whirling and bursting into the shattered dawi formations. Everything had been overhauled, turning with agonising swiftness from the long grind of a city siege into the sudden slaughter of a rout.

'We cannot fight this,' said Morgrim quietly. With every second that passed more of his host was being hammered into the ground. He could smell the blood on the air, thick as woodsmoke.

'There must be a way,' Morek insisted, still breathing heavily from whatever summoning he had been attempting. His staff looked as if it had been retrieved from a magma-pit; even Morgrim could see that the power had been burned away from it.

'There will be a way,' agreed Morgrim. 'But not this day.'

Morek looked at him doubtfully. 'The thanes will not retreat.'

'They will, because I will order them to.' As he spoke, Morgrim felt a sense of resolution he had never felt before, not even after Snorri's death. The bloodshed inflicted by the asur was so outrageous, so wild, performed with such abandon that he could scarcely believe he had once entertained notions of making peace with them. Under their veneer of superiority they were as bloodthirsty as any lurking creature of the mountains. They were animals.

Morgrim drew his axe and held the blade up before him. It reflected the gold dusk-light dully, picking out the intricate knotwork on the metal. He pointed it up at the distant figure of the sapphire dragon, still tearing across the battlefield and lashing tongues of flame down on the warriors beneath its massive span.

'I *curse* you,' he cried, his voice as withering as gall. 'I curse you in the name of immortal Grimnir and the spilled blood of my people. By my blade, I shall find you. By my blade, I shall hunt you down and I shall end you. This is my oath, made in the name of my cousin, made in the name of vengeance, which shall bind us both until death finds us.'

Morgrim's arm shook as he spoke, not from weakness but from fervour. His battle-axe whispered its own response – a sibilant *yes*, barely audible over the clamour of the field. The runes glowed angrily, throbbing from the steel like torchlight. Morek watched, awe-struck.

'It is alive,' he said, staring at the blade. 'You have awakened it.'

Morgrim felt the truth of that. The dragons had kindled something, unlocked something. He remembered Ranuld's prophecy, the mumbled words under the mountain. He could feel Azdrakghar humming between his fingers.

The battle was already lost, ripped from his fingers by the arrival of the dragons, but other battles would come. The dawi would learn, growing stronger and more deadly even as the elgi crowed over their reckless slaughter.

'Do what you can to shield the fighters,' he said coldly. 'We will retreat – for now. Vengeance will come.'

Even as he said it, the word struck him as absurd. How many causes for vengeance had there already been in this messy, dirty war? How many more would come before the end, piling on one another in an overlapping maze of grudges and resentments?

It mattered not. For the present, all that mattered was keeping what remained of his forces intact, preserving them and holding them together. Then the counsels would begin, the recriminations, the renewed oaths. All of them would home on to one thing, and one thing only.

How do we kill the dragons?

Morek hesitated a moment longer, loath to be part of anything but pure defiance. To fall back, even temporarily, was anathema. Eventually, though, even he bowed his grizzled head.

'It will be done,' he said.

By then, Morgrim was no longer listening. He had turned his mournful gaze back over the battlefield. It was rapidly turning into a charnel-pit.

We will learn, vowed Morgrim, watching the blistering attack runs of the sapphire drake and marvelling at its unmatched destruction. *We will learn, and then we will come back.*

He felt the axe shiver in his fist.

This is not the end.

Imladrik had no idea how much time had passed. Hours seemed to go by in which he had no awareness of anything at all, though they might well have been mere moments amid the combat. Everything melded into a blur, a long smear of violence. His vision was ringed with black, filmy with the blood that had splashed into his face and across his helm. All he heard was the rush and roar of the dragon, the mighty wall of noise that thrummed and raged in his ears.

The sun had gone. Flying through the flamelit dark was like flying through the recesses of a dream. Brilliant explosions of dragonfire and magelight briefly exposed a desolate waste of mud, bone and broken weapons. Tattered standards flew from splintered poles, bearing the images of mountain holds. Every so often Draukhain would spy a living soul and go after it, bearing down like a falcon pouncing on a hare.

The core regiments had gone. They had been smashed open, first by the dragons and then by the vengeful spear battalions that had emerged in their wake. The battlefield had been thinned out, harrowed, flensed.

He remembered the screams. Hearing dwarfs scream had been a strange experience – it took a lot to make a son of the earth open his throat and give away his agony.

All of them had fought. He had admired the hardened units in the centre of the advance on the gate – they had resisted for the longest, striding towards him with utter fearlessness as he glided in for the kill. Their thick plate armour had given them some protection from dragonfire and their blunt warhammers and mauls had been able to crack with some force into the hides of the ravening drakes.

He didn't remember how long it had taken to kill them all. The whole recollection was little more than a mix of blind wrath and delirium. Draukhain had raked into them again and again, tearing up the ground beneath their feet and shaking them in his jaws like a dog with its quarry. Imladrik had been a part of that, guiding him, fuelling his rage, amplifying the annihilation.

At some point the war-horns had sounded again, marking the retreat. That didn't stop the killing. The dragons raced after the withdrawing columns, harrying them, picking off the outliers and tearing them to pieces in mid-air. The dwarfs never turned their backs. They left the field in good order, facing the enemy the whole time, stumbling backwards over terrain made treacherous by blood-slicks. They left behind huge baggage trains, each composed of dozens of heavily laden wains and upturned carts. When the dragons got in amongst the ale-barrels, the night was lit up with fresh explosions and racing channels of quick-burning fire.

Only when they reached the cover of the trees did the worst of the slaughter break off. The dragons wheeled up and around again, hunting down those still out in the open. The asur infantry, seeing the assault begin to ebb, established positions out on the plain, unwilling to break formation by pursuing the dawi into the shadows of the forest.

It was then, slowly, that Imladrik began to recover his equilibrium. He felt the swell and dip of the mighty muscles beneath him and smelled the smoky copper stench of his mount. He saw the stars spin above him and the gore-sodden earth stretch away below. For the first time since the kill-lust had taken him, he truly took in the scale of the destruction.

He allowed Draukhain to carry him across the face of the plain. They flew in silence, the roars and battle-cries stilled.

He could not count the dead. Thousands lay in the mire, spines broken and armour cracked. They stretched from the walls right up to the eaves of the trees, half-buried in muck and slowly cooling gore.

Draukhain still flew strongly. His spirit burned hot. A palpable sense of satisfaction emanated from his blood-streaked body.

Imladrik said nothing. His heart was still beating far faster than usual. His breathing was shallow and rapid. His palms were scorched even through his gauntlets and his sword still glowed red.

The dragon did not slow until they reached the walls again. He flew low over the asur on the plain, who whooped and saluted as they soared overhead, before rising up towards the Tower of Winds.

No, sang Imladrik, his first words since giving the order to unleash the drakes. *The walls.*

Draukhain understood, and banked steeply, heading back towards the breach where he had first sensed Thoriol. In a few moments he had found the spot again and hovered over it. Menials were already at work clearing the bodies from the stonework, labouring under the light of torches brought up from the lower city.

Imladrik guided Draukhain to the breach. The parapets were almost clear; only a few sentries from the archer companies remained, and they cowered in the dragon's shadow, awe-struck.

'Where are the archers who were stationed here?' demanded Imladrik, finding it strange to hear his mortal voice out loud again. His throat was raw and painful.

One of the sentries, shading his eyes against the fiery presence above him, stammered a response.

'Th-they withdrew to the healing house. With the others.'

'Their wounded?'

'They took them. The captain died. Two others died.'

'Who lived?'

'Loeth did, lord, and the Silent, and–'

'The who?'

'Thoriol, the Silent, lord.'

A desperate hope kindled. 'Go to the healing house now. Find the captain of the guard and tell him to place a watch on it. Tell him that Imladrik orders it, and will be with him soon.'

The sentry bowed, and fled.

Then Draukhain rose up once more, spiralling higher, his tail curling around the charred and semi-ruined spires.

Where now? the dragon asked.

Imladrik drew in a long, weary breath. He felt sick. He saw Yethanial's face before his mind, calm and grey. Then he saw Liandra's, the polar opposite. He wanted to be furious with her still, but sheer exhaustion got the better of him.

The Tower of Winds, he sang gloomily.

He knew why such torpor affected him: it was always the same after the brief releases of power. Every action had its price, and losing control exacted a heavy burden.

Draukhain thrust upwards, his flight as effortless as ever. The dragon could have flown for days and never grown weary. He was a force of nature, a shard of the world's energy captured and given form; for such as him a night's carnage was of little consequence.

You have done what they asked of you, Draukhain sang, in a rare concession to Imladrik's disquiet. *This is the end. We shall hunt them all the way back to their caves now.*

Imladrik laughed hollowly. *Ah, great one. No, this is not the end. This is just the start.*

Draukhain's long neck swung to and fro in a gesture uncannily like a mortal shaking his head. *You will never be satisfied.*

No, probably not.

They reached the open platform just below the tower's topmost pinnacle. Salendor was there, as were Aelis, Gelthar and many other mages. The spellcasters looked on the edge of collapsing. A raw aroma of aethyric discharge hung on the air like snuffed candles.

Salendor was the first to salute Imladrik. He looked genuinely impressed, his hard expression softening into something close to relieved remorse.

'Hail, lord! You did as you promised.'

Draukhain drew close to the platform's edge. Imladrik pushed himself from his mount, stumbling awkwardly as he touched down on to the stone. His joints were raw and stiff, his limbs wooden. Servants rushed to aid him and he waved them away.

'You doubted the drakes,' Imladrik replied, allowing himself to take a little satisfaction in Salendor's rare humility.

To his credit, Salendor bowed. 'I did. And their master.'

Imladrik turned to Aelis. 'Any word of Liandra?'

Aelis shook her head. As she did so, Imladrik felt a warmth at his back, running up his spine. The air stirred, rustled by an ember-hot wind.

He turned. All six of the dragons were suspended above the platform, five of them still bearing their riders. They held position in a semicircle, heads lowered, spines arched steeply. They hung in perfect formation, huge and terrible, making the robes of the mages bloom and flap from the beat of their wings.

Before the battle each one had been a different colour, as glorious as new-mined precious gems. Now they were all red, covered in the blood of the slain, dripping as if dipped in vats of it, glistening in the light of the fires like raw sides of meat.

'They salute you, lord,' said Aelis, her eyes shining with wonder.

Imladrik saw then how he must look to the others. He too was drenched from head to toe in blood. He too looked like a visitation from some other world, one of reckless savagery and unlocked murder.

He didn't know what to say. The dragons' fealty, for the first time, embarrassed him. In the light of what he had done, his failure, his loss of control – it felt like a mockery.

You become the dragon, the dragon becomes you.

'Enough,' he said, turning away from them and beginning to walk. His heart was heavy, his footprints dull crimson smudges on the marble. 'My son is here. The boy has need of me.'

III
DRAGONSOUL

TWENTY-ONE

Yethanial woke suddenly. She had only been asleep for a short time, retiring early after a long and gruelling session at her writing desk. Ever since Imladrik had gone her mind had struggled to retain its focus. She dreamed of him often, imagining him at the heart of battle, mounted on that damned creature that made his moods wild and dark.

Her chamber was still lit by half-burned candles. The windows rattled from the wind, a strong easterly. She sat up, rubbing her eyes. Sleep, she knew, would be elusive now.

It could not go on. She had tried to pretend that all was well for too long. She reached out to the table by her bed and rang a small brass bell.

A few moments later her maidservant entered, bowing as she drew close to the bed.

'I asked you for word of my son,' said Yethanial.

'There has been none, lady. Not for many days. The master-at-arms believes...' The girl trailed off, uncertain whether she should go on.

'That he is no longer on Ulthuan,' said Yethanial. She had come to the same conclusion herself, but unwillingness to countenance it had prevented her from acting. 'We must accept that he is right. And if he is not on Ulthuan, then there is only one place in the world he would have fled to.'

She reached for a scrap of parchment – there were always several lying close to her bed – and began to write with an old quill and half-clotted ink.

'I have stayed here long enough, pining like some useless wife. I am not some useless wife. I am a daughter of Isha with the blood of princes in my veins.'

She handed the parchment to her servant. 'Take this to the harbourmaster at Cothmar. Ensure he finds me a good ship – fast, and with room for a dozen guards. Take my house seal so he knows who asks him. I will travel tomorrow and will be at the quayside by noon.'

The maidservant bowed again, taking the parchment. 'How long will you be gone, lady?'

Yethanial sat back against her bolsters, dreading the long night ahead.
'I have no idea. Long enough.'

The maidservant left, hurrying as she went. Yethanial heard her echoing steps as she skipped down the stairs. Soon after she heard the slam of doors and the creak of the great gates, followed by the drum of horses' hooves in the night.

She hated the thought of leaving. She hated not being in Ulthuan, and hated the thought of a long and dangerous sea crossing. Caledor, had he known, would almost certainly have forbidden it.

Yethanial lay back, pulling the sheets around her. It could not be helped. Even if she had not had such dreams she would have made the crossing, for the sake of her son if for nothing else.

It had always been Thoriol who had drawn them together – he, in the end, remained the strongest bond between them.

One by one, the candles in her chamber blew out, gradually clothing the room in darkness. Yethanial lay there, her mind alert and unsleeping, her hands loosely clasped over the counterpane. Even when the last one guttered out, little more than a pool of wax in the silver holder, she was still awake, her grey eyes shining with resolve.

Liandra shaded her eyes against the horizon-glare. For a moment she didn't believe it – just another mirage on the baking world's edge, a false hope born from desperation.

Then it didn't go away. She looked closer, squinting into the distance. It stayed put, tantalisingly so.

A city. *The* city. One she had never visited but had known must be close: Oeragor, Imladrik's own, thrust out into the utter margins of asur territory in Elthin Arvan and raised from the choking desert in defiance of all reason.

Drutheira didn't say anything. It would have been hard for her to do so with a gag ripped from her own robes wrapped tightly around her jaw. The druchii's eyes were red-rimmed, her stance slumped in the heat.

Every so often on the long trek east she had fallen, no doubt from genuine fatigue. On those occasions Liandra had waited patiently for her to get up, neither helping nor hindering. The druchii witch didn't like to show weakness and would struggle to her feet again when she could. With her arms bound tightly, her tongue clamped and her staff shattered she was no longer a threat, just an encumbrance.

Killing her would have given a modicum of satisfaction. Over the past two days Liandra had come close. Once, in the middle of the night as the campfire burned low, she had reached over to the witch's slumbering form, knife in hand, just a hair's breadth away from plunging the point into her throat.

It had not been mercy that had held her back. In a strange, shadowy way Liandra felt like the dark elf had been part of her life for a long time, an integral part of the struggling tale of the colonies. Drutheira was a dark mirror to her, a spectral counterpart of Liandra's own fiery presence.

When she had first come round from her deep unconsciousness, the witch had smiled thinly.

'So you won,' she had said, as if that was all there was to it.

It had been unutterably eerie to look into the violet eyes of her quarry. The hatred Liandra felt for her was too intense to generate even a token response. She stayed her dagger-hand, though.

Perhaps she had learned something from Imladrik after all, and saw the larger canvas spread out before her. The witch *knew* things: she knew why the druchii had been active, why they had been sent, how many were still in Elthin Arvan. Her very existence was the proof Imladrik needed. If Liandra could bring her back to Tor Alessi alive then the dream of a settlement was not yet dead.

All of which, though, meant nothing if she failed to keep her alive.

Liandra hauled Drutheira along behind her on a length of cord taken from her belt. The witch was in a far worse state than her, ravaged by what must have been months out in the wild. Liandra never untied her and never let her speak again, but soon stopped fearing her powers.

The first day was the worst. Plagued by terrible headaches from the sun, progress amounted to little more than putting one foot in front of the other. All Liandra had to guide her was old memories and a vague sense of *rightness* – like all the asur mageborn she could sense the echoes and resonances of her kind even from immense distances, shimmering amid the aethyr like the whispers of overheard conversations. Many times on that trek she stood still, eyes closed, letting her mind rove ahead of her, seeking out the source of the faint aura of familiarity.

Such work was easier in the absence of Vranesh's huge influence. With the dragon gone, Liandra's mind seemed to work more surely. Once the worst of the grief had subsided she found her moods calming down, settling into the analytical patterns required for survival. She still missed the drake's voice – unbearably so, at times – but it was impossible not to also notice how much freer she felt once out of its shadow.

It wasn't until the third day that she began to give up hope. The hard land yawned away from her in every direction, a semi-desert of scree, dust and thorny bushes that gave neither shelter nor moisture. Both of them suffered. Drutheira's eyes were permanently half-closed and puffy, her breathing little more than a soft rattle. They spent most of the morning struggling down a winding defile and having to clamber over boulders twice their size. Only at the end of it, after miles of solid torture, did the landscape finally open up again.

Liandra looked east, and her heart sank: the land was as featureless and barren as the rest. But then she saw them, hard on the edge of her vision: spires, hazy in the distance, glinting like ivory in the sun.

'Oeragor,' she breathed. It was the first word she had spoken aloud for three days.

Drutheira stood beside her, swaying, looking like she had barely any awareness of where she was. Liandra glanced coldly at her. 'They will welcome you there, witch. Always a chamber to be found for the druchii.'

They started to walk again. After the initial euphoria wore off the precariousness of their position reasserted itself. Liandra went steadily, trying not to breathe too heavily, feeling the solid heat hammer at her back and shoulders. She had wound fabric from her cloak over her head, but though it protected her skin from the worst of the sun, it made her feel claustrophobic and stuffy. Every time she looked up the spires seemed to be just where they had been the last time – too far away.

After several hours of trudging she realised she wouldn't make it. Her heart was labouring like an old carthorse's. Her throat was so bone-dry she could no longer swallow and her lips were split and bleeding. The towers remained just where they had been all along: within eyesight, still too far.

Drutheira was in even worse shape. When Liandra stopped the witch fell to the ground and stayed there. Liandra couldn't be sure she was breathing and couldn't be sure that she cared. She sank to her knees, wondering just how long it would take for the sun to fry her into wizened ashes. There was no shelter, no moisture, just open miles of horrific, bleary, seamy heat.

She closed her eyes. After a while, oddly, she began to feel better. The heat on her shoulders felt a little less intense, the air a little less stultifying. Perhaps, she thought, this was what dying felt like.

She opened her eyes again and looked up, half expecting to see the skies unravelling into waves of pure sunlight. Instead she stared straight up into the jaws of a huge creature, hovering above her on massive wings like a golden eagle's. A cruel curved beak snapped at her less than an arm's length from her face. She smelled the tart scent of animal breath on the wind.

For a moment she thought she was hallucinating. Then she saw the rider mounted on the back of the beast – asur armour lined with black and bronze – and realised what it was: a griffon, magnificent in leonine splendour.

'I would have slain you for a dwarf,' called the rider, shading her with his beast's wings. He landed and dismounted, bringing a gourd of water with him. Liandra saw the sigil of Oeragor – a black griffon rampant on an argent field – embroidered on the fabric, and would have smiled if her mouth still worked.

She drank, just a little, letting the griffon-rider hold the gourd for her. The water was cool, almost painfully so.

'We do not see many travellers out in the Blight,' he said. 'If I had not been aloft–'

'Don't,' croaked Liandra. 'I do not wish to think on that.'

'And your companion?'

'Druchii.'

The griffon rider started, hand leaping to the hilt of his sword, but Liandra shook her head weakly.

'Captive,' she rasped, forcing the words out. She began to feel dizzy again, and struggled to keep her poise. 'Bringing... to the city. Take us there. Lord... Imladrik...'

That was all she got out. Black spots appeared before her eyes and she felt her head go thick.

The griffon-rider gazed at Drutheira doubtfully, then back to Liandra.

'I can take you to the city,' he said, tipping the gourd up for her again. 'Though Imladrik is not here, nor has been for many years.' The rider had a young, lean face, one that was both serious and mournful. 'Would that he were. I fear you have not found much sanctuary here.'

Liandra drank greedily. She barely heard the words; all she knew was that she had cheated death – again. That made her happy, almost deliriously so.

'There is little time,' she said painfully. 'Use it well. Take us both.'

A fire burned in the heart of the forest, as tall and broad as the great oaks that crowded around the edges of the clearing. It roared and crackled, sending sparks trailing high up into the night sky and skirling above the treetops.

During the journey west the dwarfs had lit no fires, mindful then of the need for stealth. Now that need had passed.

Morgrim's surviving thanes sat around the blaze, their armour limned a deep orange. Grondil had gone, last seen charging into the path of a golden wyrm, swinging his warhammer wildly around his head and yelling obscenities at the top of his voice. Frei had survived but his arms were both broken, rendering him furiously weaponless. Many others were lost.

Those who remained stared moodily into the flames. Morgrim could see the wounds they had all sustained – deep wounds from speartips or dragon-claws. Frei had lost almost all of his incredibly finely crafted armour, ripped from his back by one of the beasts. He'd been lucky to survive, broken arms or no, though Morgrim knew Frei didn't see things quite like that.

They were consumed with shame. Their cheeks glowed red, their hands rubbed one another, knuckle over knuckle, wearing at their anguish. The dirges had not stopped; even now Morgrim could hear them from the trees, murmured around lesser campfires by the warriors he had brought to the face of ruin.

As for himself, Morgrim felt nothing but resolution. He had felt it ever since leaving the mountains – only Imladrik's doomed attempts to halt the violence had shaken that certainty. There was a kind of purity in adversity and, now that they had been so comprehensively ravaged, all that remained was to fight on. There was nowhere to go, no further questions to ask, nothing left but unbreakable stubbornness.

Which is, after all, what we are known for.

'And so what now?' asked Frei, his voice thick with weariness.

Morek spat on the earth. 'Back to the holds. Muster again, then we strike. Like a hammer on the metal, they will break eventually.'

'No, *rhunki*,' said Morgrim quietly. He remained staring at the flames, appreciating the heat of them against his exposed skin. 'We will not go back.'

Morek looked at him with surprise. To contradict a runelord was rare.

'What do you think will happen when we return?' Morgrim asked, speaking slowly, almost sonorously. 'We could assemble a host three times the size and the result would be the same. The *drakk* are too strong. I should have listened to Imladrik. I took it for boasting, but he was too noble for that. Grimnir's eyes, he was trying to *warn* me.'

The other thanes looked at him warily. They didn't like talk like this.

'We cannot fight them like this,' Morgrim said. 'We must find another way.'

Frei laughed bitterly. 'And what way would that be? Can you now fly in the air? Can you shoot flame from earth to sky?'

'Don't write that off,' said Morgrim, utterly serious. 'But for now? We must forswear Tor Alessi. We must, for the moment, forget the oaths we took there.'

The thanes began to mutter amongst themselves. Even Morek looked perturbed. 'We cannot forget them,' he warned.

'We can let them rest. There are other ways to hurt them.' Morgrim never took his eyes off the flames. They were reassuringly alive to him, like flickering remnants of the ancestor gods he had worshipped his whole life. 'How many *drakk* do they have? I saw six. If others exist, they are over the sea. In one place, those six can destroy any army we create.'

As he spoke he lifted his eyes from the fire and studied the reaction of his surviving thanes. 'That is the key: one place. They cannot be everywhere. They cannot defend Tor Alessi and Athel Toralien, Athel Maraya and Sith Rionnasc, Tor Reven, Kor Peledan or the hundred other fortresses they have built. If we cannot defeat them in one battle then we shall defeat them in a thousand small ones. We must split ourselves, fracture our armies into pieces. Every King shall lead his host, every hold shall work on its own; no grand host will be assembled, not until the very end.'

Morgrim's jaw clenched. 'This is *our land*. Why do we fight like they do, out under the sky, lined up to face their magics? We are *tunnellers*. We can melt into the stone, sink back into the soil. We need no hosts pulled together in the open for the *drakk* to fly at.'

His eyes went flat as he envisioned it.

'We can mount endless attacks, one after the other, directed at every fortress they possess. They will turn most of them back. They will kill many more of us. But some will get through. One by one, the walls will fall. We can make this world a hell for them, one in which the suffering never ceases.

They fight well, the elgi. They fight better than any warriors I have ever seen. But do they *suffer* well? No one suffers like the dawi. We will make *this* the battleground – they will be broken on the anvil of our suffering.'

He finished. The silence was broken by the low roar of the fire and the murmur of the dirges. The thanes listened. They digested. They reflected.

Morgrim leaned back, clasping his hands together. They would need time. The High King would need time, as would the other warlords and captains who were already marching towards their future battles. Word would spread out, travelling like wildfire along the mud-thick lanes of the deep forest, gradually spreading from mouth to mouth until the whole world was running with it.

Morek shook his head. 'I don't know,' he muttered.

That was good. A runelord would never simply agree; there needed to be deliberation, debate, rumination. As a start, given the circumstances, Morek's stance was admirably open.

Morgrim determined to say no more that night. He would listen to the others, knowing that in time his counsel would prevail. He had seen the way the war must now be fought. In time the others would too.

A thousand tiny battles, each one grinding into the bedrock of the earth, each one a new wound on the weary face of the elgi empire.

He was already planning his next move. Before dusk the following day he would be marching. His army would splinter, each shard heading in a different direction, and he would make his own way among them, no longer the leader of many holds but the warlord of one.

He could see the spires of his prey in his mind, rising from the dry lands to the south, the fragile citadel created by his enemy.

For revenge, for the deaths of Tor Alessi, that one would be the first to burn.

Sunlight angled into the marble chamber from high glass windows. Low beds ran along the walls, dozens of them, each occupied by a wounded highborn. Incense burned in suspended thuribles, a soft fragrance of lavender and marjoram designed to mask the underlying tang of blood. Attendants came and went, feet shuffling on the stone, pale robes brushing.

Thoriol lay on his back, staring at the ceiling. His whole side throbbed with a dull pain, worse when he moved. His chest and stomach were swathed in bandages, some of them bloody.

He had only sketchy memories of how he had arrived there. He didn't remember falling during the battle; he had pushed to the forefront, determined to avenge Baelian's death. He'd loosed two, maybe three, arrows, thinking that they'd all found their marks.

After that, very little. The dwarfs had been massing in numbers and one of them must have loosed a crossbow bolt at him. He had dim recollections of a burning night, of shouting and hurrying. He'd awoken briefly in a crowded chamber, its floor strewn with bloody straw and smoking candles. Someone had leaned over him, pulling his face around to get a better look. He remembered the pain being much worse then.

Then he'd awoken in the marble chamber with very little idea how much time had passed. His dressings had been changed and healing oils applied to his wounds. The attendants had treated him with the sort of unconscious respect he'd enjoyed as a dragon rider's acolyte in Tor Caled, not with the peremptory instruction an archer enjoyed.

He tried to pull himself further up in his bunk, to ease some of the discomfort in his side. As he did so he saw two figures approach, and his heart sank.

'Awake, then,' said the first of them. The Master Healer was an old man from Yvresse, bald as an infant, prone to smiling, his fingers stained from the herbs he crushed during the night hours. 'I do not think you will be with us much longer.'

Thoriol ignored him; his companion was another matter.

'How did you find out?' Thoriol asked his father.

Imladrik looked tired. Incredibly tired. His skin was raw, as if scrubbed hard with pumice to remove some terrible stain, and his long hair hung listlessly around his face. 'Draukhain recognised you,' he said. 'He can sense the Dragontamer's bloodline.'

Thoriol winced. 'Then you brought me here.'

'Others took you from the walls. I sent for you once I knew you lived.'

'You should not have taken me from my company.'

'If you had not been brought here you would have died,' said the Master Healer placidly. 'Two quarrels pierced your flesh, one deeply.'

Imladrik turned to the Healer. 'Thank you, Taenar. I think I might have some time alone with my son now.'

The Healer bowed and withdrew, his slippers padding on the marble. Once he was gone Imladrik sat at the end of the bed. As he did so his whole body seemed to sag.

'Why, son?' he asked.

Thoriol had dreaded the question ever since he had awoken on that first morning, out at sea with his head hammering. It was all so random, all so unplanned. Not for the first time, he had no good answers.

'I was deceived, at the start,' he said, opting to be as truthful as he could. 'Then I thought I'd been given another chance. Where is the rest of my company?'

'I do not know. I can ask Caradryel to bring them to–'

'No!' Thoriol exhaled with irritation. 'No, they will not want that. Do you not understand?'

'No, I do not understand.'

'It would terrify them.' Thoriol didn't want to explain. 'They were all running away, for one reason or another. I will find them myself.'

Imladrik looked at him with concern. It was an expression Thoriol recognised very well – the look of strained worry, of doubt, one that said *are you sure that is wise?*

'You are not one of them,' Imladrik warned. 'You are a prince. It could not have lasted.'

'You do not know them.'

'Of course not. Do you think I know a fraction of those who serve under me?'

Thoriol struggled to control his irritation. 'They were good soldiers.'

'No doubt, but you are better than them.'

'Why? Because I am Tor Caled?'

'Yes.' Imladrik's voice was soft but his expression was unbending. 'We do not choose our path, son. You may think you can deny your bloodline and take up a longbow, forgetting every privilege you have had, but believe me the gods will punish you for it. You were born to higher things.'

Thoriol laughed sourly. 'You saw what happened in the Dragonspine.'

'You failed. Once. Do you think that every rider succeeds on his first attempt? Don't be weak. You are throwing everything away.'

That stung. 'Do you know how many dwarfs I killed on the walls? I was *of service*. For the first time in my life, I did something worthy.'

'I have ten thousand archers,' said Imladrik, still struggling to comprehend. 'I have one son.'

'Yes, you do, so let me choose this.'

'Did you not hear me? Choice is for lovesick swains. There is no choice; there is duty.'

Thoriol felt like screaming. All his life it had been the same, the relentless pressure to fulfil the potential of his ancestors.

'It is not as if I wish to remain idle,' he protested. 'I can fight! I will fight.'

'You placed yourself in danger.'

'But the dragons are dangerous. Magic is dangerous.'

'You do not belong there.'

'I do not–'

'I *will not lose you!*' Imladrik shouted, losing control for just a moment before reeling it in again. He clenched his fists, balling them into the coverlet.

Thoriol said nothing, stunned. His father rarely raised his voice; he rarely needed to.

Imladrik took a deep breath. Fatigue hung heavily under his eyes in black rings.

'You are the destiny of the House,' he said, quietly, recovering himself. 'My brother is a fool and a warmonger – he has no issue and will not live out the storm he has set in motion. Only you will remain, Thoriol. Only you.'

That was hard to hear. It had always been hard to hear. He had never wanted any part of it, though even to think such a thing seemed churlish in the light of the sacrifices that had been made.

That had ever been his curse, ill-fitted for the life the gods had ordained for him. His father would never understand, being so consumed by the path he had taken, so entranced and absorbed in the dragons that gave him his power and his reputation.

Before he could reply, though, Imladrik rose, pushing himself heavily from the bunk as if he carried the weight of the Annulii on his shoulders.

'You need rest.' He looked shaky on his feet. 'Gods, I need rest. I should not have raised my voice. But promise me this: stay here. Do not seek them out. We will talk again and find some way to make sense of all of this.'

Thoriol watched him, wondering if anything he had said, now or at any other time, had ever made much of an impression on his father. Perhaps he should have tried dragonsong.

Imladrik extended a hand awkwardly, then let it drop. 'I am glad you are recovering. For a moment, during the siege...' A wintry smile flickered. 'We will talk again.'

Thoriol nodded weakly, knowing that they would and yet doubting that anything much would be said.

'So we will,' he replied, his voice unenthusiastic.

TWENTY-TWO

Death just wouldn't find Drutheira. She felt as if it had been snapping at her heels for years, but the final cut was never quite made. If she had been of a sentimental disposition she might have suspected fate was preserving her for something or other, but she wasn't, and so she didn't. It was all luck, blind luck, and of a particularly sadistic kind at that.

At least her jailors had given her something to drink. The asur treated her roughly but Liandra had been insistent that she wasn't to be harmed and her orders had been followed with typical assiduousness.

So noble, the asur; so *proper*, in thrall to the rules that bound them into their stultifying patterns of decay. Their reasonableness drove her mad. If the situations had been reversed they would all have been writhing in agony pits by now, their skin hanging from their flesh and their eyes served up on ice for the delectation of the witch elves. They would have begged to tell her everything they knew before the end, which would at least have been amusing for her if not actually useful.

Her detention in Oeragor had been luxurious in comparison. Once she had recovered enough bodily strength to swallow her food unaided she had been strapped into a metal chair deep within the citadel's dungeons. Warding runes had been engraved in the walls, sapping any residual sorcery that might still have lurked in her battered body. A dozen guards stood outside her cell at all times, two of which were always mages. When the asur entered to give her food they glared at her with stony, hatred-filled eyes, clearly itching to do her violence but never giving in.

She could not move, she could not use her art, she could not even speak unless the gag was taken from her scabrous mouth. The whole thing was a humiliation; a spell of honest torture might have been preferable.

Liandra didn't deign to speak to her for two days. When she finally did descend to the dungeon, closing the door behind her with studious relish, Drutheira wondered whether death had found her at last. She certainly didn't blame the mage for wanting to kill her – the antipathy was, after all, entirely mutual.

Once again, though, her expectations were confounded. Liandra looked sleek and rested, freshly supplied with a new staff and pristine mage's robes. She ripped Drutheira's gag free, checked her bonds were secure, then stood before her, arms crossed. For a long time she did nothing but examine her, as if trying to ascertain whether the pitiful creature before her could really have been responsible for so much suffering.

'No questions?' Drutheira croaked eventually. Her strained voice sounded odd in the dank, echoing cell.

'What could you tell me,' said Liandra coolly, 'that I do not already know?'

Liandra's voice was a surprise: it was temperate, restrained even. Everything Drutheira knew about Liandra promised impetuosity, but perhaps being deprived of her creature had bled the fire from her.

'Plenty, I judge,' Drutheira said.

Liandra's expression didn't change. It was contemptuous more than anything.

'You were sent to Elthin Arvan by Malekith,' she said. 'We were guarding the sea-lanes, so the best you could do was land in secret. You were here for years, hiding out in the wilds, doing nothing. Only when orders from Naggaroth came did you act, starting the violence that turned the dawi against us. You killed the dawi runelord. You ambushed the trade routes.'

Drutheira couldn't help but smile. When listed like that, the tally of achievement was rather impressive.

'We didn't do it all,' she said. 'Plenty of you wished for war.'

'You are right. I was one of them.'

'Then you should be pleased.'

'How little you understand us.' Liandra crossed her arms, threading the staff under an elbow. 'You sit there, smirking, content in small malice. Nothing you have done here will hasten Malekith's return to the Phoenix Throne. He will remain an outcast for the rest of his days, howling his misery into the ice.'

Drutheira inclined her head in putative agreement. 'Maybe, but he has his war. Nothing can stop that now.'

'You know less than you think. They are talking again, and the dwarfs know of the secret war. All they need now is proof, and that is why you have been suffered to live – so I can drag you to Tor Alessi where, under the hot irons, you will be made to speak. Truth-spells shall be wound around you. All shall hear it. Your last action, before I finally kill you, will be to weep for the ruin of all you have sought to achieve.'

Drutheira couldn't prevent a faint quiver of doubt showing on her face then. Liandra might have been lying, of course, but she sounded unnervingly confident. Recovering, Drutheira glared back defiantly.

'Wishful,' she said. 'You know the chance has long gone. I sense the hatred boiling away within you even from here – you *loathe* the dawi.'

Liandra drew close to her then, so close that Drutheira could smell the fragrance of her robes and make out the freckles on her pale cheeks.

'I do,' Liandra whispered, bending over her almost tenderly. 'I wish to see every last one of them driven back into the mountains, but how much more do I loathe *you*.'

The intensity of hatred then was unmistakable. Drutheira tried to pull her head away but her bonds held her tightly.

'When you burn, witch, I shall be watching,' Liandra whispered coolly. 'For the sake of those you killed, I will *revel* in your agony.'

Drutheira couldn't look away. Two blue eyes glared at her from the gloom, unwavering in their passionate intensity.

For the first time in a long while, no words came to her: no acid riposte, no withering put-down. She was alone, shackled, held in the vice by those who hated her, and there was nothing much left to say.

Then Liandra sneered, her message delivered, and withdrew. The mage swept from the chamber, not looking back, and slammed the heavy door behind her.

Alone again in the darkness, Drutheira heard the bolts lock home. Then silence fell again, as complete as the outer void.

This, I admit, she thought to herself mordantly, *is getting difficult.*

The drum beat with a steady, driving rhythm. Even as the dark trees clustered close, their shaggy branches hanging low across the path, the beat continued – heavy, dull, dour.

Morgrim enjoyed the sound of it. It reminded him of the beating of hammers in the deeps, the ever-present sound of the sunken holds. Its steady pace spoke of certainty, resolve, persistence.

He marched in time with it, as did all of his retinue. Five hundred dwarfs of the *bazan-khazakrum* kept up the punishing pace, hour after hour, pausing only for snatched meals of cured meat washed down with strong ale. They carried their supplies on their backs, not waiting for a baggage train to keep up with them. Every warrior matched the stride, none falling behind, none pressing ahead.

The constant exertion helped Morgrim forget. While he was moving, his breathing heavy and his arms swinging, he could consign the memory of Tor Alessi to forgetfulness. Only in the few hours of sleep he allowed himself did the images come back – the flaming fields, the stink of burning flesh, the cries of alarm. He would awake in the cold dawn, his eyes already staring, his fists clenched with anguish.

'Onward,' he would growl, and all those around him would drag themselves to their feet once again.

Dwarfs could cover a phenomenal amount of ground when the occasion demanded. They were not quick in their movements but they were relentless. No other race of the earth had such endurance, such capacity to drive onwards into the night and start again before first light. Freed of the straggling demands of his huge army, Morgrim's warband had made good progress, led from the front and hauled onwards by his indomitable will.

Morek kept pace just as well as the others. He swayed as he strode, his cheeks red and puffing, his brows lowered in a permanent scowl of concentration.

'How many miles?' he asked, several days into the march, the road still thickly overlooked by foliage. His hauberk was thick with mud, his cloak ripped and sodden.

'No idea,' replied Morgrim, maintaining pace to the hammer of the drum. 'Why do you ask?'

Morek snorted. 'Because Tor Alessi is at one end of the world and Oeragor is at the other. I do not mind the exertion, but was there not a closer prize?'

Morgrim hawked up phlegm and spat it noisily into the verge. 'There are many closer prizes. Soon they will all be burning.'

'That is not an answer.'

'Then because it is *his*.' Morgrim's voice shook with vehemence. He was tempted to stop then, to call the march to a halt and remonstrate with the runelord, but resisted. Every minute was vital. 'It is his place, the one he built. It will hurt him.' He glared at Morek. 'Enough of a reason?'

Morek nodded, his breathing getting a little more snatched. 'So it is a private war with you now.'

'It is, and if you have issue with that there are other warbands you could join.'

Morek shook his head wearily. 'Gods, no. I made an oath.'

Morgrim looked ahead again. 'Good. While we march, recite your rune-craft. I will need it.'

He knew he spoke harshly; the runelord deserved more. His mood was dark, though. He could feel Snorri's casket rattling against his jerkin, bound to his chest with chains of iron. Imladrik had no doubt intended the return of Halfhand's remains as a gesture of goodwill. Now, in the aftermath of what had been unleashed, it felt like an insult.

'I sent word to every thane under the mountains,' he muttered. 'They are all marching. Frei has taken half his hold to Sith Rionnasc. Others are heading through the forest. Others are marching under Brynnoth of Barak Varr. His army is the one we will join. He will support the new way of war – he was ever a wily soul and he knows how best to skin the elgi.'

Morgrim didn't mention the other reason he wished to join forces with Brynnoth's armies. Rumours had been whispered through the candle-lit corridors of Karaz-a-Karak for months, sometimes with scorn, though often with interest. Brynnoth had done something interesting in Barak Varr, something that held greater promise of taking on the elgi than the campaign of scorched earth he now advocated. He'd heard stories of airborne machines, held aloft only by sacks of air and carrying weapons of fiendish invention. That was interesting. The two of them needed to talk, and to accomplish that he needed to get to Brynnoth.

For now, though, retaliation needed to be decisive, extensive, and, above all, swift.

'You think we will be in time?' asked Morek. 'Last I heard he was close to his muster weeks ago.'

'We will be in time,' said Morgrim dismissively. 'We will make rafts for the river and drive up against the current. We will march into the Ungdrin when we find it again. I will burn myself into the ground if need be, but we will be there.'

Spittle flew from his mouth as he spoke. Anger was only ever a finger's breadth under the surface with him, ever ready to erupt. The axe weighed heavily on his back at such times, as if daring him to draw it.

Morek scratched the back of his neck, still marching, looking as if he had his doubts but was too prudent to voice them.

'The runes,' he said, glancing at the axe. 'Do they still answer?'

Morgrim nodded. Azdrakghar had felt alive since Tor Alessi, resonating through his armour in its strapping. 'It growls like a caged wolf.'

'The *drakk* woke it,' said Morek. 'Snorri thought–'

'Do not mention him,' snapped Morgrim sharply. 'I grow tired of hearing his name. For too long we have used it, making it stoke our anger. Do we not have enough reasons of our own to hate them?'

Morek stared at him. 'I only meant–'

'It is my blade. Snorri was wrong, it was forged for me. It was forged for the *drakk*. You knew this when you made it.'

Morek shook his grizzled head, puffing hard. 'I don't know. Even Ranuld didn't know. If it has a destiny, I cannot see it.'

'I can,' said Morgrim, his grey eyes narrow. He kept marching. 'I see it as clear as moonlight.'

'So here we are again.'

Imladrik sat in his throne at the summit of the Tower of Winds. Three of the other thrones were occupied.

Caerwal was no longer there. Neither was Liandra, whose whereabouts had still not been established. Word had come in regarding the fate of her fortress: Kor Vanaeth lay in ruins, its surviving people heading towards Tor Alessi. A dwarf column nearby had also been destroyed. Both sites, Imladrik had been told, bore the marks of dragonfire.

He didn't know why she'd done it. Hatred – for him or for the dawi – didn't seem enough. The betrayal hurt him deeply, the more so given the uncertainty over her motives. He'd been tempted to take Draukhain east and find her. Perhaps there were still things they had to say to one another.

Or maybe she had extinguished any trust they still had. As surely as if she had slipped a dagger into Morgrim's chest, Liandra had ensured the war could never be stopped.

Whatever I may have done to hurt you, he thought bitterly, *I deserved better than that.*

'We are victorious,' said Aelis. She looked reinvigorated. The flight of the dragons had given them all hope again. 'Thanks to you.'

Gelthar, who sat one place to her left, also looked content. His troops had been first out onto the plain once the dwarf retreat had started.

Of all of them, though, it was Salendor who had been most vindicated by events. The mage-lord was at pains not to make too much of it, but his satisfaction was hard to hide.

'Then the question is: what now?' asked Imladrik.

'Go after them,' said Salendor bluntly. Then he laughed. 'Did you expect any other counsel? Morgrim's army is broken.'

'They are ripe for destruction,' agreed Gelthar. 'Now is the time.'

Aelis shot her companions a tolerant look. 'Have you learned nothing, lords? We will offer our views here, discuss them for an age, and then Imladrik will overrule us.'

Imladrik smiled wryly. 'So you understand how this works at last.'

In truth, his position was a strange one. His policy of restraint had failed spectacularly, just as they had all warned him it would. On the other hand he had demonstrated the full ambit of power at his command, which had daunted even Salendor. He couldn't decide quite what that made him.

A fool? A saviour? Possibly both.

'You have another idea,' said Salendor.

Imladrik leaned back in his throne. 'Place yourself in the mind of our enemy. What will he be thinking?'

'Vengeance,' said Gelthar. 'They will come back at us.'

'Yes, but how? They are not stupid. We have exposed our greatest strength to them, and they have felt just how powerful that is. They will not repeat their mistake.'

'What can they do?' asked Aelis lightly. 'They have no answer to your drakes.'

'They will find one. Even now they will be thinking on it. As I say, they are not stupid.'

'They will disperse,' said Salendor quietly.

All turned to him. Imladrik nodded fractionally. For all their differences, he had always known that Salendor was the most tactically astute of his captains.

'Six dragons,' Salendor went on, speaking thoughtfully. 'Overwhelming together, but they cannot be everywhere.' His voice grew in certainty as he considered the options. 'I would send my warriors in every direction.

Forget this place – they cannot take it now. But what of Athel Maraya, or Athel Toralien?'

'Quite,' said Imladrik. 'If we had a hundred dragons then we could consider engaging them, but even Aenarion did not command such numbers. This is their land – our numbers are divided between here and Ulthuan. We do not know how many warriors they have under arms, but it is surely many times what we can muster.'

Aelis's brow furrowed. 'Then what is to be done?'

'The dragon riders will be sent out,' said Imladrik, 'one to each great fortress. Regiments will travel to the frontier citadels. They must leave immediately, for the dawi move fast when the mood is on them. They disperse; so do we.'

Gelthar looked unconvinced. 'That is thinning our forces. No early victory can come from this.'

'You are right,' said Imladrik. 'We will be fighting for years.' He had resolved not to labour the point, but it was worth stating again, just to underline why he had worked so hard to avoid it. 'This will be the shape of the war now: brawling over scorched earth, each of us as exhausted as the other. History shall judge us harshly for it.' He shook his head in frustration. 'And Liandra most of all.'

The others looked awkwardly at one another.

'You cannot believe that,' said Salendor.

'Then where is she?' Imladrik demanded, trying not to let his frustration spill out too obviously.

'I do not know.'

'She went to Kor Vanaeth. We know this.'

'And only the word of our enemy condemns her,' said Salendor, 'I will not doubt her loyalty, not until we know more.'

'So sure,' observed Imladrik, looking at him carefully. 'No qualm at all?'

Salendor looked back confidently. 'None.'

Part of Imladrik wanted to believe him. Any thread of hope that Liandra was not responsible would be clung to.

For all that, he remembered how she had been when they had last spoken.

We must strike now before they gather more strength.

'The truth will out,' was all he said. 'For now, we have preparations to make. We cannot remain gathered here while the fighting spreads across Loren Lacoi. Salendor, you must leave for Athel Maraya and prepare for attack – they will surely be there soon. Gelthar, take Athel Toralien and order its defences. Aelis, command of Tor Alessi will be returned to you. Each of you shall have dragon riders: two remaining here, two for Athel Maraya, one for Athel Toralien. A lone drake will be a match for all but the mightiest armies, and the memory of their blooding here will not fade quickly.'

Things had changed since he'd first arrived. They nodded readily enough, accepting his orders. Even Salendor voiced no objection.

'And you, lord?' asked Aelis. 'Where will you go?'

Imladrik did not know the answer to that. A dozen places had already sprung to mind: remaining in Tor Alessi; joining Salendor at Athel Maraya; heading to his own citadel of Oeragor on the edge of the wasteland; returning to Ulthuan to petition for more troops and dragon riders. The final option was the least palatable but also the most prudent: it would give them the best chance of survival in the storm to come. It would, though, mean leaving the conduct of the war to others and abasing himself before his brother.

'Where the war takes me,' he said. Even then, though, locked in discussion of strategy, Liandra's fate burned on his mind. 'Asuryan, no doubt, will determine.'

TWENTY-THREE

Liandra headed across the piazza feeling, if not exactly content, then certainly partially satisfied. The days since her recovery had passed quickly, dulling some of her lingering grief over Vranesh. It had taken an almighty effort of will not to kill Drutheira when she had spoken to her last, but the witch's unmistakable reaction to the news of what Liandra intended had almost been worth it on its own. Vengeance would come in time and would be all the sweeter for the wait.

She reached the western end of the piazza, passed under a shaded portico, and ascended a long train of stone stairs. It had not taken long for her to recover from her ordeal out in the wasteland, especially since Oeragor's people had plied her with medicinal draughts and restorative tinctures.

Their care had been welcome, but now impatience was beginning to drive her again. She was mindful of the fact that her disappearance from Tor Alessi had been sudden. Imladrik would not know why she had gone; he might attribute it to her awkward outbursts during their last conversation, perhaps even cowardice in the face of the dwarf advance. The matter needed to be settled quickly, not least as she had no means of knowing how the talks were faring, nor indeed if they were even still in progress.

As ever, the lack of certain knowledge was troubling. For far too long she had been guessing at shadows and half-truths, just as they all had. Such was always the way in Elthin Arvan, a land of enormous distances, choked by forests and hampered by lurking dangers under the shade of every branch.

At the end of her climb she reached a sunlit chamber with arched colonnades around the edges. She passed across a marble floor, up another spiral stair and into the interior of a large octagonal tower. By the time Liandra emerged at the topmost balcony she could feel the pricking of sweat in the small of her back.

She had not quite recovered, then; not yet.

A tall figure in long ivory robes waited for her, standing against the balcony railing and staring out northwards. His hands and face were tanned a rich light brown, much like the rest of Oeragor's population. It was an attractive counter-point to the washed-out colouring of temperate Ulthuan.

'How is our guest?' the tall elf asked.

'Talkative,' she replied. 'Not that I am much interested in what she has to say.'

Kelemar, Regent of Oeragor, nodded in satisfaction. 'I am glad you're happy, though I warn you my people are not. There has been talk of breaking into the dungeons and dragging her out.'

'I can understand that. Believe me, I will rid you of her as soon as I may.'

Kelemar looked back out over the balcony's edge. 'That would be appreciated, but I don't know how you'll do it.'

Below them lay the tight-packed towers of Oeragor's northern slopes. The city had been built at the heart of the wide, sun-baked plain and the buildings clustered together as if for protection from the elements. Every surface was whitewashed. The walls gleamed under the sun, making Liandra's eyes water if she looked at them for too long.

It was not a large settlement. She had often wondered why Imladrik had chosen such a site. Oeragor's foundations had been sited over a deep well of pure spring water, an oasis amid the bleakness; so it did at least have enough to drink, as well as a surplus to irrigate some modest gardens and terraced plantations. The city stood on the site of a truly ancient road, one that predated even the dawi presence in Elthin Arvan, though none could say who had made it or why. Its population numbered some five thousand, almost as small as Kor Vanaeth though far more remote. Even with recent reinforcements it stood at a little over seven thousand, leaving plenty of room within the whitewashed walls for more.

Liandra once asked Imladrik why he had adopted the far-flung location. He hadn't been very forthcoming.

'We cannot restrict ourselves to the coast,' he'd said lightly. 'We must push into the wild places, taming them one by one.'

It wasn't much of an answer. Liandra had always suspected he'd had designs on making the place his home one day, a refuge away from the scheming of Ulthuan and the grimy hardship of the coastal colonies. She could certainly imagine Draukhain out here, coasting effortlessly over the empty lands, his sky-blue hide sparkling in unbroken sunlight.

Even if that were true, though, she knew he'd never be given the freedom to pursue the dream. Caledor had summoned him back to Ulthuan to oversee the everlasting war against the druchii, then given him the command that had taken him to Tor Alessi. One way or another, his brother had frustrated any plans Imladrik might have once had for Oeragor.

And of course there was his wife, the scholar-lady of Tor Vael. Liandra could not imagine her willingly uprooting and coming to the desert. The relationship between the two of them had always been a mystery to her, one that perhaps only they themselves truly understood.

But that was uncomfortable to think about.

'You say the roads north are still too perilous?' Liandra asked, shading her eyes as she looked out over the honey-yellow landscape.

'The dawi are marching. They have emptied their holds to the east, destroyed our outposts all across the northern edge of the Blight.'

'The Blight. I can see why you called it that.'

'Nothing else seemed appropriate. You were lucky to last out there for as long as you did.'

Liandra pushed a stray length of copper-blonde hair from her face. She could already feel her skin tightening in the heat. 'Why stay here, Kelemar? What keeps you?'

'Because we were ordered to. And because we have our task here: to turn the barren land into a garden.'

Liandra had thought much the same of Kor Vanaeth. Elthin Arvan was dirty, dangerous and feral, but the vision of the colonists had been to tame it, to make it a paradise. If they were fighting for anything noble, that was it.

'And, of course, it is Imladrik's place,' Kelemar went on. 'We are all his people. We would work ourselves into the dust for him.'

Liandra shook her head gently. 'Why is this? He inspires this... devotion.'

Kelemar pursed his lips in modest disapproval. 'In the early days he laboured with us here. He carried stones on his back with the rest of us. He could have followed the life of his brother and lived in a palace in Lothern. Whatever it was that took him away from us, we know he did not choose it.' He smiled regretfully. 'Does that give you your answer?'

'There's some secret to it, to be sure.' She found herself wishing to change the subject and withdrew from the bal-cony's edge, pulling out of the direct sunlight. 'So the passage north is closed, and there is nothing to the south, west and east but empty rock. I need to find some way to reach Tor Alessi.'

'I think you have missed your chance. The dawi will be here soon.'

Liandra looked out north again, seeing no more than haze and heat-shimmer.

'How long?'

'A few days, if we are lucky.'

Liandra drew in a deep breath. Oeragor was a world away from Tor Alessi, where, she had to assume, hostilities were still suspended. To end up stranded in some sweaty skirmish on the margins of civilisation while the real war in the west had been interrupted... The frustration was almost unbearable.

'There will be a way,' Liandra said, doggedly. 'The witch cannot die here. I do not intend to die here. By Isha, there *will* be a way.'

Caradryel pushed back in his chair, feeling irritable and at a loose end. He hadn't slept well for days, kept awake both by his memories of the siege – which were terrible – and his frustration at how the events beforehand had turned out.

Everything he had touched had turned to swill. Confidence, a quality he had never struggled to lay hold of, was in short supply. He had considered speaking to Imladrik about it, perhaps even suggesting that his service had been a mistake and he would be better employed back in Ulthuan.

That, of course, would have been a mistake. Having offered his assistance so brazenly, Caradryel knew there would be no backing out of it now.

In the days since the siege had ended he had barely exchanged a dozen words with his master. Imladrik had looked exhausted in the aftermath of the battle, his face drawn with a dull kind of horror. He'd remained punishingly busy, striding from one end of the city to the other to oversee repairs, rebuilding and restocking. Given the damage inflicted, it would be weeks before full order was restored.

Beyond the walls, the battlefield reeked. Mists rolled in from the sea, turning everything mouldy and sodden. Huge funeral pyres had been constructed to dispose of the dead but they had burned sullenly, leaving thick shrouds of foul-smelling smoke suspended in the air around them. Days later the plain still smouldered under grey clouds, its soils blackened and clotted.

Caradryel had found few things to occupy himself during those days. He had followed up on a few loose ends from the Caerwal affair. He had ensured that his informants were paid, and had kept several of them on to ensure he knew what was going on while the city slowly recovered its equilibrium.

Many of the regiments were now being prepared for marches elsewhere. The dragons flew constantly in the skies over the harbour, as if giving visible reminder of the might of Ulthuan before the troops were sent off into enemy-infested swamps to an uncertain fate. It felt as if everything was unwinding, slowly dissipating like the smoke over the slain.

He tipped his chair on to two legs and swung back on it lazily. When the knock came on the door of his chamber, he nearly sent it – and himself – toppling over.

'Come,' he snapped, righting himself and brushing his robes down.

The door opened and Geleth entered with a female elf in tow. She looked like a beggar, her shift dirty and ragged, her hands and face dirty from the road.

'My lord,' said Geleth, bowing. 'Something I thought you might wish to hear.'

Caradryel shot a superficial smile at the newcomer. 'Welcome. Be seated.'

She remained standing. She had a hunted look in her eyes. Her hands turned over one another in a nervous pattern.

Caradryel glanced at Geleth, who returned a look that said *give her time*.

'Perhaps you would like some wine?' Caradryel tried again. 'Something to eat?'

The elf shook her head. 'Are you Imladrik?'

Caradryel just about suppressed a smile. 'No, not really, but if there is something you wished–'

'I came here for Imladrik.'

'He has many things to worry him. The best way to get a message to him is to entrust it to me. So, let us see if we can get things started. What is your name?'

She looked uncertain. For a minute Caradryel thought she might make a break for the doors.

'Alieth,' she said.

'Good. Alieth, where are you from?'

'Kor Vanaeth.'

Caradryel raised an eyebrow. 'Kor Vanaeth was destroyed.'

Alieth's face flickered with momentary anguish. 'It was. I walked here.'

'On your own?'

'There were others. Not many.'

Caradryel found himself getting interested. Geleth stood calmly by her side, saying nothing.

'You should sit,' Caradryel said, motioning to a chair opposite him. 'You look like you need it.'

Gingerly, Alieth shuffled over to it, perching on the edge as if afraid it would fall apart.

'You are among friends,' Caradryel went on. 'Tell me everything. No dwarf can get to you here.'

She shook her head. 'It wasn't the dwarfs.'

'What do you mean?'

'Kor Vanaeth. It was not destroyed by the dwarfs. We never saw them.'

Caradryel frowned. 'The reports we have–'

'They are wrong. That is why I have to speak to Imladrik. We know he is close to the Lady.'

'Liandra?'

Alieth nodded. 'We came because we had nowhere else to go. When we arrived here we heard rumours.' She frowned. 'Foul rumours. They are saying the Lady broke her commands, that she caused the dwarfs to attack. It is lies.'

Caradryel crossed his legs and leaned forwards, listening carefully. 'Tell me everything. From the beginning. Can you do that?'

'We were attacked. A black dragon ridden by a sorcerer. She destroyed the city. The Lady came to our aid, and they fought above us. I saw it. I saw the red dragon take on the black, driving it out over the mountains.'

'A black dragon?' asked Caradryel. He'd never heard of such a thing.

Alieth nodded vigorously. 'A monster, covered in chains. The Lady pursued it. That was the last we saw. Some tried to follow, but they moved too fast.' She started to rub her hands together again. 'Imladrik must know. The Lady is in danger. There were no dwarfs at Kor Vanaeth.'

'Please calm yourself. If what you say is true–'

'It is true.'

'–then I will pass it on to Lord Imladrik. Are you prepared to vouch under oaths to Asuryan?'

Alieth nodded firmly.

Caradryel reached out and rested his hand on hers. It was a tender, reassuring gesture, one he had always been proud of.

'Then I want you to keep remembering,' he said soothingly. 'Think carefully, hold nothing back. Lord Imladrik will be made aware, but first you must tell me what happened next.'

Alieth began to speak again then, a little more fluently as she gathered confidence, explaining how she and her companions had survived the onslaught and subsequently made their way through the forest towards the coast.

Caradryel listened, making mental notes of the portions he would pass on to Imladrik. Even as he did so, though, another, more encouraging thought made its presence felt.

This will make me useful again.

So it was that as he listened, despite the impropriety of it, despite his attempts to quell it, Caradryel could not help a furtive smile creeping along the corners of his elegant mouth.

Night fell, though the skies above Tor Alessi remained blood-red from the fires. Labourers worked tirelessly, building as fast as their exhausted limbs would allow. Detachments of soldiers still prowled the streets, though their numbers had been thinned following losses and reassignments.

The world's moons rode high in a cloud-patchworked sky. A lone dragon flew lazily to the north, its black outline stark against the silvery feathering of the heavens.

Thoriol did not spend time watching it. His whole body throbbed. It felt as if his wound had opened up again; a hot, damp sensation had broken out just under his ribs.

He didn't stop walking. He limped through the dusk, ignoring those around him just as they ignored him. He passed fire-scarred walls and piles of rubble. Somewhere in the distance he heard weeping. There had been weeping every night since the siege and the passing of time did little to lessen it.

Thoriol kept going, averting his face from the glow of the torches.

It had been easy to deceive the Master Healer, who was more adept at creating poultices than he was at reading intentions. With all else that had transpired, the few guards there had been preoccupied with other matters and were not looking for a lone charge seeking to evade their attention.

In any case, there was little they could have done to stop him leaving. He was a prince of a noble house, the Dragontamer's House no less, and they would have been bound to accept his orders if he'd been forced to give them.

For all that, Thoriol had been glad no confrontation had taken place. Giving orders was not, and had never been, his strength.

He limped down a long, crooked street in the south quarter of the lower city. It looked different to the last time he'd been there. Then again, much of the city looked different. The buildings seemed to crowd a little closer, their pointed roofs angling like furled batwings into the night.

He found the door he was looking for, and paused. Two narrow windows shone with hearth-rich light from within. He could hear voices from the other side, voices he recognised. Someone was laughing; a tankard clinked.

Thoriol smiled. His father was wrong. He did not understand such things. Comradeship, *companionship* – Imladrik had never known such closeness. He'd probably never fought alongside another living soul in his life, save for the great beasts that carried him into war.

Thoriol reached for the door and rapped hard. He heard more laughter, the sound of something being knocked over, then it opened.

'Greetings!' said Thoriol, trying to look carefree against the pain of his wound.

Taemon stood in the doorway. His mouth opened. It took him just a little too long to close it. He stood there, stupidly, a tankard in one hand, the door-latch in the other.

'Well?' asked Thoriol good-naturedly. 'Are you going to let me in?'

Taemon stammered an apology and stood aside. Thoriol limped into a crowded chamber. Loeth sat in a chair by the fire, his leg bandaged and raised on a stool. Rovil stood over the mantelpiece, looking as if he'd just been speaking. Florean sat across a rough table. He'd been carving the skin from an apple, knife still in hand.

All of them stared at Thoriol as he entered. Their laughter stilled.

'Silent?' asked Loeth, squinting up at him as if unsure it was really him.

Thoriol nodded, grinning. Already he felt better; the marble chambers of the old city now seemed like some kind of fleeting aberration. 'They would not tell me where you were, but I hoped nothing had changed. What happened to your leg?'

Loeth looked down at the bandages, as if seeing them for the first time. 'Dawi quarrel,' he said uncertainly. 'Thigh. But it's healing.'

Thoriol gazed around the room. He smelled the familiar aromas of rough wine, straw, cooked meat.

None of them spoke. The fire spat. Rovil stared at the floor; Florean kept his knife in hand, frozen in the act of peeling appleskin.

'Well?' asked Thoriol, wanting to laugh at their shock. 'Have you all lost your tongues?'

Taemon closed the door and stood against it, arms folded. 'Where have you been?' he asked.

That was the first sign. Taemon's voice was blunt with suspicion.

'They took me to the old city.'

'That's what we heard,' said Rovil.

'But I'm back now,' said Thoriol.

'So you are,' said Taemon.

Thoriol looked back at them all. The chamber felt suddenly chill.

'What is this?' he asked, maintaining a smile with some effort. 'I know Baelian has gone, but–'

'Yes, Baelian has gone,' said Loeth. He plunged his dagger into the table. 'He was not taken to the upper city. He was burned out on the plain.'

'I didn't know that.'

'No, you didn't.' Loeth didn't make eye-contact. He just kept staring at the dagger hilt. 'Why would you?'

'I was wounded.'

'You were highborn,' said Taemon.

Thoriol felt his cheeks flush. They had never spoken like this, not even on their first meeting out at sea. 'Does that matter?'

'Lying does,' said Florean.

'He didn't–' began Rovil, trying to soften the tenseness in the room, but he was soon talked over.

'Did you fancy some sport, then?' asked Florean. 'See how the rustics live? I hope it was worth it.'

Thoriol's heartbeat picked up. 'That's not how it was.'

'Why don't you tell us, then?' asked Loeth. 'How was it?'

'It was Baelian. He was recruiting in Lothern. We spoke, but my memory is hazy. I don't even remember agreeing to join, but–'

Taemon smiled coldly. 'He took advantage. You were wine-stupid and you made promises he held you to.'

'Yes,' said Thoriol. 'That's it. But after that, I worked at it. You saw that I did. It wasn't about lying, it was about being... honest.'

Loeth shook his head dismissively, smiling in disbelief. 'Your *father*, Thoriol. Your father is Imladrik.'

'And?'

'You truly do not see, do you?' murmured Taemon. 'They won't permit this, and when they come after us it won't be you that suffers.'

'I can prevent that.'

Loeth laughed harshly. 'No, you can't. And even if you could, here's the thing. We don't want you here.'

Rovil looked uncomfortable then. Even Florean looked a little embarrassed.

Thoriol felt like he'd been struck in the stomach. His father's last words to him seemed to echo in his mind.

You do not belong there.

With a sinking, almost nauseous feeling in his innards, Thoriol realised how right he had been. Again.

'I don't understand,' he said, though he did, perfectly.

'It's not just a game for us,' said Taemon. 'We can't leave when the blood starts running. You can.'

'And you lied,' said Florean.

'Baelian did too, but he's dead,' said Loeth. 'There's no place for you here any more.'

A tense silence fell. Rovil almost said something, his honest face contorted with unhappiness, but a glare from Florean cut him off again.

'Then it seems I misunderstood,' said Thoriol stiffly. 'You should know this, though: I never lied.'

'You hid the truth,' said Taemon, as unbending as ever. 'What's the difference?'

Thoriol scanned across the room, seeing nothing but hostile faces. They wanted him gone. Not until he left would the drinking start up again, the flow of jests and jibes that would last long into the night. It was a curiously wounding experience, far more so than the quarrel-gash in his side.

'I won't say anything of this,' he mumbled, pulling his robes about him and walking back to the door. 'And... I wish you fortune.'

'And to you,' said Rovil. No one else spoke.

Then Thoriol ducked under the lintel and was out into the night again. The door closed behind him with a dull *click*. Few people were abroad; the street was quiet, no one paid him any attention.

He looked down the mazy passages, the ones that led deeper into the lower city. There was nothing for him there. Then he turned the other way, facing up the slope towards the spires and interconnected towers of the old city. Their pinnacles reared up like stacked arrowheads, sharp black against the sullen red of the sky.

They looked alien to him, like reminders of a harsher world he had almost managed to leave. Now they beckoned him back, as inexorable as the tides.

Not much use fighting it, he thought.

Slowly, his feet heavy, he started to retrace his steps, back up to where the highborn – his people – conducted their lives.

TWENTY-FOUR

The first dwarfs were sighted on a cloudless morning following a rare lull in the heat. A griffon rider circling high above Oeragor's northern marches was able to convey some useful tidings: a dozen lightly armoured scouts moving through the Blight. They weren't going quickly; they were marking out the approaches, frequently stopping and conferring with one another.

After that, three more riders were dispatched north. They all came back with similar stories – the first tendrils of the dawi host were moving within range, creeping down from the foothills and out on the plains. The numbers reported steadily rose: a few dozen, then a few hundred, then many hundred, then more.

On hearing the news Liandra went down to the dungeons again. She did not enter the witch's cell but ensured that Drutheira's guard was doubled and that they would not leave their posts without explicit instructions from her.

'If the dawi get this far, kill her,' she had told them. 'Do not untie her, do not ungag her, just kill her.'

Then she headed back up to the northern watchtower, going as quickly as she could. The noises of preparation followed her all the way there: the thud of hammers, the tinny rattle of swords being drawn from armouries. In a way it was a relief to hear it again: things were moving.

Kelemar was waiting for her at the summit of the tower, along with Celian, captain of the griffon riders. Both were already wearing their armour – light plates of steel over silk undershirts, open-faced helms, no cloaks. The heavier garb of regular spear companies would have been hopelessly impractical in such terrain; lightness and movement were the keys to warfare out in the blighted lands.

'Here at last,' said Kelemar as she arrived. It took Liandra a moment to realise he was referring to the dawi, not her.

'Are they ready for battle?' she asked.

Celian nodded. 'Very much so.'

That was the final confirmation. 'Then it has all been for nothing,' said Liandra wearily. 'Salendor told him the dwarfs would not listen to reason.'

Kelemar reached up to wipe a line of sweat from his brow. 'Maybe this army has not heeded its commands – there is more than one dwarf lord under the mountains.'

'Maybe,' said Liandra grimly, unconvinced.

She felt sweat on her hands as she gripped her staff. Facing the enemy without her dragon would be a new experience, and not one she relished. Even to use magefire without Vranesh alongside her felt... wrong.

'Any numbers yet?' she asked, screwing her eyes up against the glare.

'Twenty thousand,' said Celian flatly.

'Really?'

The captain nodded. 'At least.'

Liandra smiled wanly. 'Perhaps I should not have asked.'

'You could leave,' said Kelemar. 'No oath of fealty compels you.'

Liandra turned on him, incredulous. 'Are you jesting?'

'I merely–'

'Well, do not. Never again.' Her face hardened. 'I have never run from battle.'

Celian leaned out over the balcony railing, shading his eyes. 'And there they are.'

Liandra and Kelemar turned, following his outstretched hand. There was very little to see – just a faint plume of dust on the north-western horizon. It looked strangely innocuous, a wisp of wind gusting across the powdered earth.

It would grow. Steadily, slowly, just as it had been at Tor Alessi, the dawi would tramp out of the wilderness, their armour caked in filth from the road, their standards hanging heavily in the air.

Liandra thought then of the vast armies that Vranesh had shown her from afar, crawling in the shadow of the peaks, pouring out of the ground like tar sliding up from a well.

'So it starts again,' she said grimly.

Brynnoth, King of Barak Varr, was both irritated and intrigued. The orders had been given, the front ranks of warriors were already within sight of the elven fortress.

He had been looking forward to the fighting. Taking Oeragor would eliminate the elvish presence on his southern flank, freeing up forces for the more serious campaigns in the west. Oeragor might not have had the prestige of Tor Alessi, but it was an important step nonetheless. Brynnoth wanted his name in the book of victories, and he wanted Barak Varr taken seriously alongside the larger holds of the mountains.

He wouldn't have held up the advance if the name he'd been given had been anyone else's. A part of him remained sceptical – Tor Alessi was a long way away. When he finally saw the incoming party hove into view, though, he saw it to be true. Morgrim Elgidum stood before him, sweltering in the heat.

Brynnoth laughed, partly from disbelief.

'You are lost, lord?' he asked.

Morgrim didn't smile. 'You are already attacking?'

'The advance has begun.'

'Then I will fight with you.'

'I thought you were–'

'Things have changed.'

Brynnoth puffed his cheeks out thoughtfully. Morgrim looked fatigued. His whole troop looked fatigued. If they truly had come all the way from the coast... well, he'd have been fatigued too.

'So I see,' Brynnoth said. 'Your axe with mine, then; it will be an honour.'

Morgrim limped closer. 'Do you have the new machines?'

'New machines?'

'The ones that fly.'

Brynnoth smiled. 'Ah, Copperfist's devices. So you've heard about those. No, they're not ready. May never be.'

Morgrim grunted. 'When this is over I need to speak to him.'

Brynnoth decided he didn't like the way he was being addressed. Morgrim was a prince, one held high in the runelords' estimation, but Brynnoth was lord of an entire hold.

'I'll decide that,' he said. 'You could tell me why you wish to. You could also tell me why you're here at all.'

Morgrim looked at him sourly. '*Drakk*. The elgi are using *drakk*.'

Brynnoth snorted. 'And?'

'They kill faster than anything I've ever seen. What war machines do you have?'

'Ballistae. Bolt throwers. They're being rolled up towards the city.'

'Keep them back. Angle them steeply and save them for the skies. We weren't prepared for them – you should be.'

Brynnoth narrowed his eyes. 'What happened?'

'They tore us apart.'

Morgrim's expression was thunderous. Brynnoth decided not to press the matter. 'I'll heed the warning then,' he said, 'but there are no *drakk* here.'

'For now.'

Morgrim's own soldiers stood shoulder to shoulder around him, as grim-faced and battered as their master. A runelord leaned on his staff some way distant, looking nearly at the end of his strength.

They didn't look capable of adding much to his own forces, all of whom were in prime condition for the fight. Adding a few hundred exhausted refugees from a failed campaign didn't seem like much of an asset.

Still, it was Morgrim.

'Then we should march,' said Brynnoth. 'Or do you need rest?'

Morgrim gestured to his warriors, all of whom took up their weapons and fell into formation.

'Just show me the elgi,' he growled.

Caradryel raced up the stairs to Imladrik's arming chamber. The news had reached him late that Imladrik was leaving the city; he hoped not too late.

He pushed his way past the guards at the doors and entered the chamber breathlessly. Imladrik was still there, fixing the last silver pauldron in place, his tall helm placed beside him on a stool.

'My lord,' he said, bowing.

Imladrik acknowledged his presence with a curt nod. 'You're out of breath.'

'I didn't know you were leaving so soon.'

Imladrik reached for his long cloak and draped it over his shoulders. 'The dawi are moving. We should too.'

Caradryel sat down heavily on a chest made from varnished Lustrian hardwood. His breathing took a while to return to normal.

'I have news,' he said.

Imladrik looked at him coolly. 'More reliable than your last?'

Caradryel flushed. He would not be allowed to forget about Salendor any time soon. 'I trust so. It concerns Liandra.'

Imladrik turned on him, suddenly interested.

'Refugees from Kor Vanaeth have got here,' said Caradryel. 'They told me she was in combat with a black dragon and pursued it over the Arluii, heading south-east. They swear on Asuryan's Flame she had nothing to do with the dwarfs killed there.'

'A black dragon?'

'So they said. I've never heard of such a thing.'

Imladrik looked distasteful. 'They exist. Creatures of the druchii.'

'She did not desert, though: that is the important thing.'

For a moment Imladrik's expression became almost desperately hopeful. 'How reliable is this?'

'They all said the same thing. A sorceress on a black dragon, attacking the fortress before being driven off by the red mage. I believe them.'

Imladrik reached for his sword. 'Where did their fight take them?'

'They don't know. South, over the mountains.'

'Anywhere, then.' Imladrik took his helm under his arm and walked towards the doors, fully armoured and ready for his steed.

'Should we not search for her?' asked Caradryel, following him.

'Elthin Arvan is vast.' Imladrik's voice was flat.

'But a druchii dragon! Is that not worth–'

'Just stories. The dawi are real, and they are here.'

'But you cannot–'

'Enough.' Imladrik kept walking, out of the chamber and up another flight of stairs. 'Liandra was always reckless. She should have been here, with us, when the city was under siege. I will not leave the war now.'

Caradryel followed him uneasily. 'Oeragor is out there,' he offered. 'She might have made it that far.'

'And if she has?' Imladrik emerged at the top of the tower and donned his helm. A large courtyard extended out around them, open to the skies. 'I do not choose my battle-grounds on a whim.'

Caradryel looked up just in time to see the giant sapphire dragon descending to the courtyard, its wings a blur of motion. He retreated in the face of it, his robes flapping and his hair streaming. He'd not been so close to it since the first encounter out at sea, and the experience was almost overwhelming. He retreated to the far edge of the courtyard and pressed his back against the railings.

The dragon landed impossibly lightly, its huge talons barely scraping the stone beneath it. Its long, inscrutable face didn't so much as glance in his direction. Imladrik walked up to it casually, placed a foot on its crooked foreleg and hoisted himself up into position.

'So where will you go?' Caradryel called up to him.

Imladrik did reply, but by then the dragon was already moving, thrusting heavily and coiling up into the air. The response was lost in the downdraft of smoke-flecked turbulence.

Caradryel watched him go, overcoming his fear of the beast just enough to admire its smooth, powerful movement up into the heavens. He felt a pang of envy then, just for an instant, seeing the flash of sunlight on the creature's sparkling flanks and hearing the low growl of its breathing.

Soon it had gone, undulating into the distance, thrusting through the heavens with its ever-astonishing speed and grace.

Caradryel pushed back from the railings and walked around the courtyard's edge.

It was a good vantage. He could see out over the plain to the east, the cluster of spires in the old city to the north, the deep blue curve of the ocean to the west. Only one ship broke the waves – a light warship carrying full sail and working hard.

Caradryel screwed his eyes up against the distance. Few ships had come to Tor Alessi since the days of constant reinforcement; more recently the flow had been the other way, with heavy troop galleons setting off up the coast to Athel Toralien and the other coastal fortresses. This ship was heading in from due west, straight out of the open seas.

Caradryel watched it, wondering whether it brought any interesting news. He pondered whether he should head down to the harbourside. He was about to demur when he made out the emblem on the ship's sails: the mark of House Tor Caled, picked out in gold, shining in the sun just as the dragon's scales had done.

It was then he knew who was on that ship, and it made his mind up for him. Hurrying again, he passed down the stairs and into the tower, wondering what possible errand could have brought Yethanial of Tor Vael away from her books and over to Elthin Arvan.

They came out of the dust, a rolling tide of iron and leather, bodies pressed close together, standards swaying to the rhythm of hide drums.

Liandra watched them come, standing on the upper battlements with Kelemar and her fellow mages. Not many of them: just five besides her, and she far surpassed the others in power. Aside from the griffon-riders and some battle-hardened Chracian warriors sent east a decade ago, Oeragor's defences were modest, designed for stray incursions of greenskins.

The dwarf army closing in on them was more than an incursion. The front ranks came on quickly, wading through the ochre dust, kicking it up and tramping it down. A vast rolling cloud came with them, rearing above the army like a protective mantle.

They brought wall-breaking engines with them, ballistae mounted on huge platforms and battering rams on rollers. They had crossbow units, axe-wielders, hammer-bearers and ironclad maul-bringers. The mismatch between the attackers and the defenders was almost ludicrous. Oeragor was like a lone spur of rock thrust out into a rising tide, isolated and ripe to be overwhelmed.

Kelemar watched them stoically.

'Signal the archers,' he said. 'Let fly at two hundred yards.'

A messenger ran down to the parapet. Clarions rang out with the signal, and all across the ramparts longbows were notched and raised. The few bolt throwers mounted on the walls were primed, loaded and swung into position.

The gates were the weak point. Even though they had been reinforced with terraces of granite and cross-braced iron beams, that was the place where the outer stone barrier broke its smooth uniformity. Five hundred of Kelemar's best troops waited on the other side of it, crouched in the shade, waiting for the inevitable breakthrough.

Liandra looked up to the skies. The griffons were aloft, hugging the central towers and circling slowly. Their riders would not venture far from the walls once the assault began, restricting themselves to counter-attacking runs until the armies were grappling at close quarters. No sense in being torn to pieces by quarrels before getting a chance to land a claw.

The dwarf vanguard ground closer. The tumult from the drums and war-horns became all-consuming, forcing the captains on the walls to shout at their own troops just to be heard. Infantry squares spread out across the northern face of the city, extending in either direction as far as Liandra could make out through the swirling dust. The air became thick with it, surging up over the ramparts and coating the stone.

'Perhaps he was right,' said Liandra softly to herself, thinking of Imladrik. Now that she saw the scale of the dawi host in the full glare of daylight, the sheer immensity of just one of their many armies, she found herself wondering whether anything could prevail against them for long.

Then the long grind would begin. Athel Maraya would burn. Athel Toralien, Sith Rionnasc, Oeragor – they would all burn.

'Did you say something?' asked Kelemar.

Liandra shook her head. 'Just preparing myself.'

The dwarfs marched to within bowshot. The orders went out, and Liandra watched the archers loose their arrows, angling the shafts high so they plummeted down hard in a solid curtain. It was an impressive enough show, and some dwarfs in the front ranks stumbled.

Not nearly enough, though. The army kept coming through the onslaught, its pace hardly dented. Bolt throwers opened up, sending heavy quarrels whistling directly into the front ranks. Wherever they hit they tore furrows in the infantry formations, scattering dwarfs and throwing up fresh plumes of dust.

They kept coming. The hammer of the drums became almost unbearable. The heat, the dust, the blare of the war-horns – it was like being thrust into the maw of insanity.

Kelemar took up his helm, fixed it in place and drew his longsword. He held the blade up to the obscured sun.

'For Asuryan, Ulthuan and Tor Caled,' he said, his voice steady. All around him his retinue did the same, raising their blades through the murk.

He turned to Liandra, a resigned expression on his face.

'I'll take my place at the gatehouse now,' he said. As he spoke the stonework around him trembled – the front rank of dwarfs had made it to the foundations. 'You have all you need?'

Liandra raised her staff, the one she'd been given after her rescue from the Blight. 'It will do.'

'Then Isha be with you, lady.'

Liandra inclined her head. The first shouts and screams of combat drifted over from the walls.

'And with you, lord.'

As Kelemar left she turned, raised her staff, and kindled the first stirrings of aethyr-fire along its length. Ahead of her rose a sheer wall of rage, a heat-drenched surge of focused violence, repeated in rank after rank of implacable dawi warriors, all now surging towards the walls like jackals crowding a carcass.

She ignored the tight kernel of fear in her breast, ignored the avian scream of the griffons as they swooped into the fray, ignored the murmured spells of the mages around her, and prepared her first summoning.

It was about survival now.

'For Ulthuan!' she cried aloud, and her staff blazed with light.

TWENTY-FIVE

Imladrik rode east. Below him the forest passed in a smear of speed. The endless trees looked like waves on the ocean, infinite and without permanent form, a swathe of dirty grey-green under a cloud-pocked sky.

Draukhain had sung little since their departure from Tor Alessi. The dragon seemed in contemplative mood.

So you will leave, then? the creature sang eventually.

I need more troops, I need more dragon riders. Only the King can grant me those.

He will not do so willingly.

No, he doesn't grant anything willingly.

In the far distance the mountains rose up, their vast peaks little more than claw-shaped marks on the edge of the world. Draukhain exhaled a gobbet of black smoke from his nostrils. He was flying fast, though comfortably within his capability.

You know, of course, that Ulthuan is in the west? he sang, sounding amused with himself.

Imladrik sighed. Like everything he had done since arriving in Elthin Arvan, his current course felt far from wise. It was driven by necessity, though; by loyalty, and by a hope he hardly dared entertain.

Oeragor is my city. I should have gone there at the start of this.

What can you do there now? Too far to help.

Not for you, great one. Imladrik peered ahead of him, as if he could see out across the Arluii and into the great Blight, the semi-desert that separated the temperate northern lands from the lush and mysterious south. *It should be abandoned, its people escorted to the coast. I will oversee this, then go to Ulthuan. To Tor Vael, then to Lothern. The arguments will begin again.*

Draukhain's head dipped, his shoulders powering smoothly. The ivory-skinned wings worked harder, scything through the air.

Always arguments with you.

So it seems. Imladrik shook his head. *I need to breathe the air of the Dragonspine again, if only for a short time. I need to think.*

Draukhain discharged a growling fireball in approval. *Good. Good. I will breathe it with you.*

Imladrik watched the forest slide underneath him, mile after mile of featureless foliage. The dream of taming it, of turning it into a fragranced land of beauty, now seemed worse than foolish.

This has nothing to do with the fire-child, then? asked Draukhain, impishly. *Nothing.*

You mean that?

Imladrik did not reply. It was impossible to lie, almost impossible to dissemble. In truth he didn't know what he would do if Liandra were still alive. The reports of a druchii abomination might have been true, they might have been false. He had tried to persuade himself, and Caradryel, that he didn't care and that his first duty was now to the war, but the arguments were weak. Possibilities wore away at him, eating into what little sleep he could muster.

This flight was a final act of duty, a last display of responsibility before the war would consume him utterly. Yethanial had been right – Elthin Arvan made his moods dark, however hard he tried to counteract it. Once Oeragor was evacuated he would return west, rebuilding the bridges he had let fall into ruins. Thoriol, Yethanial, Menlaeth – they were the souls he needed to cleave to. They were his blood-ties, the ones whose faces he saw in his dreams.

This will be the last ride to Oeragor, he sang, remembering how much labour it had been to create and how many plans he had once had for it. It had been years since he had even seen it. *Let us try to enjoy it.*

The gates buckled, struck from the outside by the first kick of the ram.

Kelemar, waiting with his knights in the inner courtyard, steeled himself.

'Stand fast!' he cried, watching the wood tremble and splinter.

Above him on either side the walls rang with the clang and crack of combat. Ladders were already appearing on the ramparts, each one thrown up by iron-clad dawi gauntlets. Rocks sailed high over the parapets, crashing into the towers beyond and sending rubble cascading down to the streets.

The ram thudded into the gates again, bending the bracing-beams inwards with a dull boom.

Kelemar tensed, ready for movement. His best infantry stood around him, all ready for the charge. They would have to meet the dawi at speed, trusting to the charge to repel them. Once the dwarfs were inside the battle was lost.

On either flank of the courtyard stood two rows of archers, bows already bent. In the centre stood the swordsmen. All held position, hearts beating hard, waiting for the inevitable crack of timber.

The third impact broke the braces, sending tremors running along the stone lintel and shivering the doors. Dust spilled out of the cracks in ghostly spirals. The roar of aggression from the far side grew in volume – a hoarse, guttural chant of detestation.

'On my command,' warned Kelemar, seeing the nervous twitches of those around him.

The battering ram crashed into the gates a fourth time, smashing through the centre and slamming the ruined doors back on their tortured hinges. Broken spars tumbled clear, rolling across the stone flags like felled tree trunks.

'Let fly!' cried Kelemar.

The archers sent a volley out at waist height. The arrows spun through the debris, finding their marks with wet *thunks*. Some dwarfs made it through, stumbling into the open over the broken timbers; many more were hurled back, throats and chests impaled.

'For Ulthuan!' roared Kelemar, charging at the breach.

His troops echoed the shout, sweeping alongside him in a close wave of steel. Kelemar made the ruined doors and swung his blade into the reeling face of a dwarf warrior, already hampered by an arrow sticking from his ribs. The sword bit deep, angled between helm and gorget, spraying blood out in a thick whip-line of crimson.

More dwarfs clambered through the ruins bearing axes, mauls, hammers. They pushed the yard-long splinters aside, backed up by the brazen blare of war-horns.

Kelemar barrelled into one of them, kicking him backwards before plunging his blade point-forwards into his stomach. The dwarf's armour deflected the blade, sending it pranging away, and Kelemar nearly stumbled. He caught a cruel-edged maul swinging low at his legs and just managed to twist clear. One of his own knights then cracked a blow across the maul-bearer's face-plate, throwing him on his back where he was finished off by a third.

The melee sprawled onward across the ruined gates, a desperate pack of grappling, thrusting and stabbing. The elves gained the initiative, and their charge carried them under the shadow of the gatehouse. Helped by the steady torrent of arrows from the walls, they pushed the dwarf vanguard back out into the sunlight.

Kelemar drove onward, nearly decapitating a dwarf with a vicious backhand strike. Swords whirled on either side of him, spun and thrust with disciplined speed. The counter-attack pressed out further. More dwarfs piled into the breach, charging out of the dust like iron ghosts.

They seemed to fear nothing. They didn't move as fast as his own fighters and their reach was far less, but every blow was struck with a heavy, spiteful intent. Kelemar saw his troops begin to take damage – bones smashed, armour dented, swords shattered.

'Hold here!' he bellowed, hoping they could drive the dawi back far enough for the engineers to erect some kind of barricade across the shattered doorway. He pivoted expertly, using his bodyweight to propel his blade across the chest of another dwarf, biting clean through the chainmail and into flesh beneath.

It was only then that his gaze alighted on the dwarf beyond. This one was taller than the others; broader, too. His armour was all-encompassing, lined with gold and covered in blood and dust. He strode into battle with a dour, heavy tread, a huge axe gripped two-handed. He didn't roar his contempt like the others; he just waded silently through the throng around him, striking out with chill deliberation.

Kelemar rushed to engage him, seeing he was the linchpin and knowing he needed to buy more time. He closed in, throwing a wild swipe across the dwarf's right pauldron.

The dwarf met the strike with his axe and the two weapons rang together, resounding like bells as the metal bit. Kelemar's arms recoiled; it was like hitting an anvil.

The dwarf counter-swung, aiming for Kelemar's midriff. Kelemar got his sword in the way – just. He staggered backwards, aware out of the corner of his eye that his troops were beginning to take a similar beating.

The counter-charge was faltering. Kelemar pressed forward, whirling his blade around to where it could be slid into the dwarf's gorget. The manoeuvre was done well, as quickly as he had ever done it.

It was too slow, though, and too weak. The dwarf thrust his body into the blow, hurling his axe-head savagely upwards. Kelemar's blade was ripped from his grasp by the viciousness of the dwarf's strike.

Bereft of options, Kelemar grabbed a dagger from his belt, aiming for the dwarf helm's narrow eye-slit. By then the axe-head was already sweeping back, careering through the air two-handed. Kelemar didn't even feel pain as the edge cut deep into his chest; only seconds later, as his innards spilled out across the dust, did the raw agony bloom up within.

Kelemar fell, coughing blood, eyes staring sightlessly at the dark runes on the dwarf's axe-blade. If he'd had any self-awareness left he might have consoled himself that to fall to such a master-crafted blade was no shame; he had stood no chance, not against a weapon forged to take down the mightiest of living beasts.

His head cracked against the hard ground, just as those around him fell to the remorseless advance of the dawi vanguard. He didn't see the ladders finally find their purchase on the ramparts above, nor the last of the gate-doors kicked aside, nor the first rank of knights beaten back into the breach.

For a while the dwarf who had slain him stood over the corpse, as if ruminating on the kill. His axe dripped with blood, his breastplate and gauntlets ran thickly with it.

Then Morgrim Bargrum lifted his head, pointed Azdrakghar through the ravaged gatehouse, and broke into his stride once more.

'Khazuk!' he roared, at last joining in the wall of noise created by his war-hungry warriors. '*Khazuk!*'

Liandra hurled another flurry of star-bolts into the advancing knot of dwarfs before retreating further up the stairway. The front rank collapsed in a burst of crimson fire, their armour cracking and splitting. Dwarfs tumbled down the steep incline before toppling over the stone balustrade and down to the dust below.

More quickly arrived to replace them. Uttering grim dirges to their ancestor gods, the dawi advanced remorselessly. They stomped their way up the stairs, helm-shaded eyes burning with fury.

Liandra fell back again, already summoning up more aethyr-fire. Her palms were raw, her breathing ragged. The watchtower she'd been aiming for loomed up at the summit of the open stairway. Ahead of her, past the square at the stairs' base, was a scene of pure destruction. She could see dwarfs crawling all over the city's multi-layered thorough-fares and bridges, slaying at will, driving the remaining defenders back into whatever squalid last stands they might be able to muster.

The battle for the walls had been a nightmare – a doomed attempt to hold back whole battalions of implacable attackers. They had clambered over every obstacle, destroyed every barricade, surged up a hundred ladders and demolished entire stretches of wall with their damned stonebreakers.

She had no idea where the other mages were. She'd seen one of them dragged down into the rubble after a wall-collapse, his screams lingering thinly before being suddenly cut off. After the gatehouse had been taken the order had come to abandon the outer perimeter and fall back towards the central tower, but the retreat had been anything but orderly. Blood was everywhere, splattered against the hot stone like a gruesome mural.

Somehow Liandra had made it to the centre of the city, fighting the whole way with her ever-diminishing band of defenders. The Caledorians with her had fought well but they were hopelessly outnumbered. The watchtower was her last refuge – a squat, four-sided building at the summit of the wide stairway, still occupied by archers and with the emblem of Tor Caled hanging limply from the flagpole.

She retreated further up towards the doorway, now less than twenty feet away, her robes ripped and her staff spitting sparks.

Closer to hand, the dawi clustered once more at the base of the stair, ready to pile upwards towards the tower. Liandra slammed her staff on the ground before her.

'*Namale ta celemion!*' she cried, angling the staff-point and dragging more aethyr-energy from the sluggish winds of magic.

A nest of crimson serpents crackled into life, spinning from the tip of her staff and flailing outwards. Liandra swung the staff around twice before hurling the writhing collection down at the dawi labouring up the stairs.

The snakes scattered across the foremost, clamping on to the joints of their armour and burrowing down like leeches. They snapped and slithered as if alive, their unnatural skins blazing with arcane matter.

Liandra didn't wait to see if that would halt them – she knew it wouldn't for long – but turned and scampered up the last few steps. A few dozen guards held the doors open for her.

She slipped inside, heart thudding, feeling the trickle of blood running down her forearm.

'Brace it,' she ordered curtly. Soldiers around her hefted the heavy wooden bars into place.

She pressed on, running up more stairs, a tight-wound spiral that ran up the interior of the watchtower. As she went she passed rooms with archers crouched at the narrow windows. They looked low on arrows, and some were already turning to their knives.

At the top level she joined a disconsolate band of swordsmen, all of them streaked with grime and gore, their robes dishevelled and armour cracked.

'Who's in command here?' Liandra asked, limping over to the outer parapet.

Several of them looked at one another for a moment, as if the idea of 'command' belonged to a different age, before the tallest of them replied, 'You are, lady.'

Liandra smiled humourlessly, and peered through the nearest embrasure.

Dust and smoke rose up from the corpse of Oeragor. The gatehouse was now a gaping scar through which marched an endless stream of dwarf warriors. A few islands of resistance remained – clusters of asur defenders holed up in towers or rooftop terraces.

Even as she watched, a griffon-rider swooped on an advancing column of axe-carriers. The huge beast crashed among them, lashing out with claw and beak. Its wings beat ferociously, sending dozens of dwarfs staggering backwards. For a while its lone assault chewed through the oncoming warriors, crushing those within its grasp, flattening others rushing to help. Eerie shrieks of anger rose up above the howl and holler of the battle, a single voice of defiance amid the wreckage of the city.

Then, slowly, the volume of warriors around it began to tell. Liandra watched axe-wielders crawl closer, one by one getting within swing-range. The griffon managed to slay half a dozen more before the blades began to bite. It tried to pounce back into the air but crossbow bolts suddenly scythed out from the shadows. More dwarfs appeared, drawn by the shouts of combat. The griffon was dragged back to earth, its rider seized from the saddle and buried beneath a riot of fists, axe-handles and cutting blades.

Liandra looked away. The screams of the dying creature were hard to listen to, and they went on for a long time. It might have been the last of them. The griffons had accounted for many of the dwarf dead, but it hadn't been nearly enough.

'What are your orders, lady?' asked one of the swordsmen by her side.

Liandra screwed her eyes up against the glare and peered out beyond the walls. Most of the dwarfs' war engines were still out on the plain and guarded by phalanxes of infantry. Almost none had loosed their deadly, steel-tipped bolts. The chassis of the bolt throwers were angled steeply, pointing directly skyward.

'Why so cautious?' she murmured.

She turned to the swordsman. His youthful face was badly bruised, with a purple swelling under a cut eye.

'Give me a moment,' she told him. 'My power will return. I will stand alongside you.'

From below, she heard the first booms as the doors took the strain. She grimaced; the dawi would be inside soon, and that would be an end to it.

'When they come, you will all do your duty,' she said, sweeping her gaze across the chamber and fixing each swordsman in the eye. 'Stand your ground, do not shame our people by giving in to fear.'

She clutched her staff, feeling the dull stirrings of magic under the surface once more.

'They'll take this place, that we know,' she said grimly. 'But, by Isha, we'll make them bleed for it first.'

For a long time Drutheira had heard nothing. The cell was dark, the walls thick. A few dull booms, some muffled shouting from the corridor outside, not much else.

Hours had passed. She began to get very thirsty. It had been a long time since her captors had brought her anything to eat or drink. No doubt they had other things on their minds.

She tested her bonds again, straining against the metal shackles keeping her ankles and wrists locked tight to the chair. She could only move her head fractionally before the chain around her neck pulled tight, restricting her breathing. She'd nearly passed out a few days ago testing the limits of the restraints, and didn't fancy repeating the experiment.

The asur were not careless about such things, which was a shame.

An ignominious end, she thought to herself. *Buried alive in a city on the edge of the world.*

Then she heard a series of thumps above her. She sat perfectly still, letting her acute senses work.

The slit of light under the cell door flickered. She heard more heavy cracks, like iron-shod boots clattering on marble. Voices were raised in alarm and challenge, followed by a sound she couldn't make out.

Drutheira tensed. Either the asur were coming for her or the dawi had penetrated this far down. Neither eventuality was good for her.

The door shivered as something hard hit it. More voices rose, followed by a sharp, wet sound of steel punching into flesh, then a strangled cry.

Locks slid back, chains rattled. Drutheira stared directly ahead, determined to look whatever was coming in the face. If they made the mistake of ungagging her before they slid the knife in then there might still be some way back for her.

The door creaked open. Two asur dressed in the white robes of the city burst in. One of them looked badly wounded, cradling an arm in a sling. The other seemed to need time to steady himself and adjusted slowly to the near perfect dark of the cell.

Drutheira waited patiently. Through the open doorway she could see bodies lumped against the stone floor.

The nearest guard drew a long knife from a scabbard at his calf and loomed over her. Drutheira felt the steel against her cheek, cold as night. She didn't move a muscle. She didn't so much as wince as he pulled the blade across her face, severing the gag and freeing her mouth.

She immediately started to speak – words of power that would burst their eyeballs and shrivel their tongues. Before she could get the spell out, though, the guard clamped a hand over her mouth, leaning close. Drutheira looked up at him, almost amused by the effrontery of it.

'Do nothing foolish,' came a familiar voice.

The guard pulled the linen from his face, revealing Malchior's badly sunburned features.

Drutheira's eye flickered to one side. Ashniel leaned against the cell walls. Malchior withdrew his hand and got to work on the rest of her bonds. Drutheira swallowed. Her throat was almost too parched to speak.

'How?' she croaked.

'With difficulty,' said Malchior, unlocking the clasps at her ankles.

'We nearly died getting here,' said Ashniel weakly. 'And nearly died after we arrived.'

Drutheira raised an eyebrow. So they hadn't been killed by the dragon. How they had tracked her to such a place, and why, were questions for later. The fact they were before her at all was verging on the impossible.

Malchior released the last of the locks. Drutheira got to her feet shakily. For a moment she thought she would collapse again – the blood rushed painfully through her joints – but she managed to remain on her feet.

'You have your staff?' she asked.

Malchior nodded. 'Take robes from the guards. I can do the rest.'

As Drutheira hobbled from her cell into the corridor outside she saw the results of their labours: six corpses cooling on the stone. She stooped over the nearest and began to strip his robes from him.

'Where are the dawi?' she asked, pulling them over her head.

'Everywhere,' said Ashniel.

'This city is dead,' said Malchior flatly. 'We might have waited longer, but the dwarfs are killing everything that moves.'

Drutheira smoothed white linen over her druchii garb. The asur fabric smelled foul. 'Then how are we going to get out?'

Malchior looked at her distastefully, as if he regretted coming after her at all but had been persuaded against his better judgement. 'Deceptions are not as mysterious to me as they are to you.'

As he spoke his features rippled like water under a dropped stone. Ashniel's altered too – she became less conspicuous, little more than a shadow in the flickering torchlight. It wasn't much of an illusion, but amid all the confusion it might suffice.

'Lead on, then,' Drutheira said, bowing slightly. Malchior's cockiness was already beginning to irritate her.

From further up ahead she could hear the sounds of combat – horns blaring, asur crying out in pain and aggression, the heavy *clang* of steel on stone. It might have been nice to linger, to watch a while, soaking in the air of misery, but that would be a luxury too far.

They slipped along the corridor and up a narrow torchlit stair, passing more bodies on the way.

'What is your plan?' Drutheira whispered, limping after Malchior. 'You know some way across that desert?'

Malchior turned back. His face was curiously hard to make out, a shimmering reflection just on the edge of vision.

'We don't have long,' he said. 'If you wish to live, just shut up and follow me.'

He didn't wait for a response before pressing on. Ashniel followed after him. She was clearly in some pain, and said nothing.

Drutheira's eyes went flat. On another day she would have flayed the skin from his palms for talking to her like that. This was not another day, though; mere moments ago she had been contemplating the certain prospect of death. She felt like she'd been doing that for a long time.

'Play at this all you want,' she muttered, shuffling after Malchior, her limbs stiff and aching. 'Once we're out, it won't save you.'

TWENTY-SIX

Imladrik spied the smoke from a long way out and immediately knew what it meant.

Dawi, growled Draukhain, picking up speed.

So fast, murmured Imladrik. He had expected it to take far longer for them to regroup after Tor Alessi, but perhaps that had been a foolish hope. It was not in their nature to retreat.

The dragon powered through the air, faster and faster, picking up truly furious momentum. As he surged towards the burning city, Imladrik could see the extent of the dwarf army that surrounded it.

It was huge. The desert floor was covered in a thick, dark layer of bodies, all converging on the embattled spires at their midst. The rolling sound of war-drums made the air thrum.

Draukhain plunged into the heart of it, his wings driving powerful downbeats like hammers, his jaws already kindling with heart-fire.

Imladrik watched the walls race towards him. They were broken in a dozen places, crushed into wreckage and clogged with the bodies of the slain. He couldn't see any asur defenders still on the walls. Here and there banners of Ulthuan and Caledor flew from tower-tops, but it was clear that the city was lost.

We are too late, he sang, his mind-voice filled with horror.

Not yet, snarled Draukhain, angling down towards the battle. He raced towards the dwarf rearguard still out on the plain, swooping into a low glide.

This time, though, the dwarfs were prepared. A barrage of quarrels flew up from the rank of bolt throwers lined up along the approaches to the city. Brynnoth had taken Morgrim's counsel and saved every one of them.

Draukhain banked hard as the darts whistled past him. They were poorly aimed, but there were many of them. A second wave surged up from the earth, making the air thick with barbs. The dragon narrowly missed colliding with a six-foot-long spiked bolt, checking his surging flight and losing precious speed.

No time, urged Imladrik. *To the city.*

Draukhain obeyed instantly, sweeping across the rows of bolt throwers and powering towards the walls. As he went he carpeted the ground before him in a rolling wave of fire. Several of the war engines burst into flame, exploding as their tinder-dry frames ignited. Others kept up the attack, pursuing the dragon as he sped past, aiming to puncture a wing or sever a tendon.

Imladrik barely noticed the rain of darts. His eyes fixed on the burning spires ahead, desperately searching for some sign of defiance. He thought he caught a flash of magefire and his heart leapt – only for it to be sunlight glaring from dawi armour plates.

The centre, he sang, and Draukhain shot over the walls and thrust towards the tallest towers. Bolts, quarrels and arrows followed them, none biting but several coming close.

A cluster of spires loomed up at them, hazy in the kicked-up dust and smoke. Draukhain weaved through them, loosing tight gouts of flame at any dawi exposed on the surface. He spied a whole phalanx of warriors making their way across a high bridge suspended between tower-tops and pounced after them, climbing steeply and vomiting a column of immolation. They scattered, desperately trying to escape the inundation.

At the last minute Draukhain pulled up. His long tail crashed into the slender span as he soared past, slicing straight through it. The bridge collapsed, dissolving into a cataract of powdered stone and sending the surviving dwarfs plummeting to the earth below.

Imladrik scoured the cityscape. At last, he made out some defenders – asur knights engaged in a fighting retreat towards the huge Temple of Asuryan, just a few hundred of them surrounded by a far larger force of dwarfs.

Down there, he commanded.

Draukhain plunged, tipping left to evade the nearest spire and diving hard. By the time he reached ground-level he was travelling very, very fast. He crashed into the dwarfs, scraping his claws along the ground and dragging dozens up with him, then shooting clear and hurling away those he had skewered. Their broken bodies tumbled headlong before slamming into the walls of the buildings they had ruined.

Draukhain immediately banked hard for another pass, narrowly missing the turret of another tower. The confined spaces of Oeragor's fortress heart were hard to manoeuvre in – with every wingbeat Draukhain risked crashing into a solid wall of stone. Whenever he rose above the line of the tower-tops the bolt throwers would open up again, sending a cloud of darts screaming towards them.

This wasn't Tor Alessi; the dwarfs were not facing battalions of mages and spearmen, nor were there other dragons to rake the bolt throwers while Draukhain slaughtered the infantry. They were alone, a sole dragon and his rider against an entire army, grappling over a fortress that had already been lost.

Imladrik felt like screaming. The hot rush of killing hammered in his temples again, the familiar surge of fury that always came when the dragon was unleashed. This time, though, it was tainted by other things: guilt, frustration. He was too late. He had tarried at the coast for too long, tied up with the business of the war there, dragged down by the complaints and concerns of others.

Liandra. Is she here?

Draukhain thundered down a narrow gap between buildings, his wings brushing at the edges of the stone canyon, covering the cowering dwarfs below in vengeful flames. Then he leapt steeply upwards, swerving away from a looming watchtower before hauling his immense body into the clear.

The bolt seemed to come out of nowhere. As if guided by fate, it scythed through the maze of spires and speared clean through Draukhain's right wing. Its steel tip pierced the hard membranous flesh and lodged fast.

The dragon immediately tilted, righting himself a fraction of a second later. The pain of the blow radiated through Imladrik's mind, a sharp echo that felt as if his own right arm had been impaled.

Down lower! he sang urgently.

More quarrels spiralled through the air, a constant barrage, hurled over the towers by the ranks upon ranks of bolt throwers brought up to the city. They shot above and around them, mere yards away.

Imladrik looked about him, despair mounting. He almost gave the order to pull away then, to power clear of the city's edge and seek respite. There was precious little to save in any case – he needed to *think*.

It was Draukhain that prevented him. The wound seemed to enrage him, as if the sheer impertinence of it somehow pricked his immense sense of superiority. The dragon flew harder, barrelling into the sides of buildings around him and crushing them into rubble. His flames surged out, cascading like breakers against whole rooftops and street-fronts. He roared and bellowed, his tail thrashed, his jaws gaped.

He would take on the whole army, Imladrik knew. He would fly into it, again and again, until one of them lay broken in the dust.

Imladrik looked down then, through the murk and the dirt, trying to make some sense of the milling confusion at ground level. Dwarfs were everywhere, gazing up in either fury or wonder, some running for cover, others angling crossbows in their direction.

Draukhain broke out of the narrow spaces and swung round into a wide courtyard, pursuing a whole company of fleeing infantry into the open. Hundreds more waited for them there, all heavily armoured in iron plates and carrying huge, ornate warhammers. As soon as he saw them Imladrik realised this was the heart of the dwarf army, the thanes and their elite troops at the forefront of the fighting. Dozens of quarrellers crowded the space, jostling to get the first shot away. Bolt throwers had been erected around the courtyard's edge, each one strung tight and loaded.

Pull away, warned Imladrik, seeing the danger. They couldn't miss. Even a blind bowman with a single arrow couldn't miss in that space. *Pull away!*

Draukhain paid no heed. He fell into attack posture – wings splayed, claws out, jaws open. He flew at them in a blaze of fire and loathing, ripping through their ranks like a wolf loosed amid cattle. Imladrik bucked as the impact came, nearly losing his seat. He saw the walls race around in a blur, broken by scattered dwarf corpses, many on fire, others torn into tatters of bloody flesh.

Draukhain thrust upwards, nearing the far side of the courtyard and needing to climb again. Imladrik felt bolts slice into the dragon's side – two of them, each punching deep within Draukhain's armoured hide.

Draukhain twisted in agony, almost crashing straight into the oncoming wall, hampered by his impaled wing. Flames flared out from his outstretched jaws, bursting across one of the bolt throwers and blasting it into ash.

The dragon tried to gain loft, but a fresh flurry of crossbow bolts slammed into his outstretched wings. They pierced the flesh, sending hot, black blood spotting in the air.

Away! ordered Imladrik, glancing up at the sky above. They were hemmed in, overlooked by walls on all sides. This was no place to get bogged down.

Draukhain's claws brushed against the ground. He pounced back at the dwarfs, almost running, his wings rent and bloody. A ferocious swathe of fire burst from his maw, clearing the ground before him. Dwarfs caught in the blaze staggered away, clawing at their eyes or trying to roll the flames out.

The carnage was terrible – Imladrik saw scores dead, face-down in the dust and blood, their armour charred black – but Draukhain couldn't kill them quickly enough.

More quarrels screamed across at them from the far side of the courtyard. Two more found their mark, biting deep in Draukhain's thrashing neck. Imladrik felt the pain of it again, blinding in intensity.

Caught by the impact, Draukhain skidded to one side, tilting over wildly. His shoulder crashed to the earth, digging deep into the stone flags and tipping them up. Imladrik was thrown clear, leaping at the last moment before his mount careered into the side of a terrace. The impact was huge – a *crack* of breaking stone, a shower of masonry over the prone body of the huge beast. Rocks the size of a dawi's chest thudded into Draukhain's flanks, denting the armoured scales.

Imladrik leapt to his feet and spun around, his sword in hand. He twisted his head to see where Draukhain had landed, and saw with horror the half-buried outline of dragon flesh amid a landslide of rubble.

Ahead of him, their formation steadily recovering in the wake of the dragon's ruinous descent, stood the dwarfs. They shook themselves down. They gazed up at the beast, now crippled and in their midst. They saw the lone elf standing before him.

They drew their blades.

Draukhain barely moved – perhaps stunned, maybe mortally wounded. His presence in Imladrik's mind was almost imperceptible. Being without it was terrible, even amid all else, like having his memories excised.

He turned to face the enemy. More than a hundred limped towards him, and others were entering the courtyard. Recovering their poise, they spread out, hemming him in. Some of them started to murmur words in Khazalid – battle-curses, old grudges.

Imladrik gripped his sword tight. Ifulvin was ancient, encrusted with runes of power and forged in the age of legend before the coming of the daemons. The ithilmar felt heavy in his gauntlets; he would have to find a way to make it dance.

'Do not approach him,' came a thick, battle-weary voice from the midst of the advancing dwarfs.

They instantly fell back. The speaker emerged from among them, alone. Imladrik recognised him at once – the heavy-set arms, the embellished armour, the dour air of sullen hatred. He carried his huge axe two-handed, and runes showed darkly on the metal.

The two of them faced one another, just yards apart. The remaining dwarfs fanned out, forming a wide semicircle of closed steel around them. Imladrik could hear Draukhain's broken breathing behind him, moist with congealed blood.

'You,' said Imladrik, gazing at Morgrim and wondering if he was some kind of horrific mirage. 'How are you here?'

'Do not worry about that,' Morgrim replied, swinging his axe around him and striding forwards. 'Worry about this.'

The dragon changed everything. Liandra sensed it coming just before she saw it, magnificent and beautiful, tearing in from the west. For a moment she dared to hope that the others were with him – six dragons would have turned the tide, shattering the dwarf advance and giving them a chance. Even one, though – just *one* – toppled everything on its head.

Then it disappeared, plunging into the mass of spires at the city's heart.

'We have to reach it,' she said, turning from the tower's window and heading for the door. She felt invigorated.

The swordsmen around her stared back in almost comical surprise.

'Lady, do you mean–'

'Do not protest.' She glared at them all, daring one to voice an objection. Only a few dozen remained, plus the archers on the lower levels. They would be lucky to make it half way before being overwhelmed, but that changed nothing. 'Stay with me – I will do what I can to protect you.'

Her staff was already humming with energy. The short respite, combined with Imladrik's presence in Oeragor, gave her fresh hope.

It could be done. They could resist, if only their scattered forces could be given fresh impetus. It wasn't over.

She pushed the door back and jogged down the stairs. The swordsmen came behind her, hastily adjusting their helms. As she descended, Liandra heard the hammering on the outer doors rise in volume. She smelled the musty stink of the dawi on the far side, their ale-heavy sweat and their foul leather jerkins, and felt the thrill of incipient combat burn in her again.

This would be recompense. This would be retribution.

She halted before the doors, watching the timbers vibrate from the impact of the ram. The asur soldiers clustered in her wake, weapons drawn, faces torn between duty and doubt.

Liandra had no doubt. For the first time in a long time she knew exactly what to do.

'*Ravallamora telias heraneth!*' she cried, raising her staff high.

The doors exploded into a welter of light and heat, blasting the shards back and sending the dwarfs on the far side tumbling down the stairway. Sunlight flooded in, dazzling after the shade of the tower.

Liandra charged out, her staff ringing with power, her eyes shining. Behind her came the rest of the troops.

She looked out over Oeragor's ruined towers, and smiled.

'Fighting together, you and I,' she breathed. 'It was always meant to be.'

Imladrik leapt back as Morgrim swung his axe. The swipe was barely controlled – a vicious lunge that nearly sent the dwarf stumbling forwards.

Imladrik backed away warily. For all the hours of flying he felt fresh and in control. Morgrim looked exhausted. To reach Oeragor after the fighting at Tor Alessi he must have marched without pause for days. He had already endured heavy fighting under the punishing heat. Yet, somehow, he was still on his feet.

'You want the honour of killing me yourself,' he said, watching Morgrim come at him again. 'Is that it?'

Morgrim grunted, breathing heavily. 'It is not about honour any more.'

He swung again, moving surprisingly quickly, getting the axe-edge within a few inches of Imladrik's body.

'It is always about honour,' said Imladrik, sidestepping easily. He kept his feet moving fluidly, letting his opponent do the work. 'That is the one thing we share.'

'We share *nothing!*' raged Morgrim, breaking into a charge and switching his axe back suddenly.

Imladrik was forced into a parry, the impact nearly making him gasp. The strength in Morgrim's blows was incredible.

'You are sure about that?' asked Imladrik, pulling his blade away before pressing in close, trusting to the speed of his movements. He battered a few blows across Morgrim's armour before the dwarf pulled away, head lowered.

'You *ride* those creatures,' Morgrim spat. 'You goad them to war. They're vermin. Their minds are poison.'

Imladrik held guard watchfully. Getting through Morgrim's armour would be a challenge – it was all-encompassing, a masterpiece of craftsmanship.

'You should have listened at Tor Alessi,' he said. 'I warned you. Damn you, Morgrim, I *warned* you.'

Morgrim growled, and broke back into a lumbering charge. The two of them exchanged furious blows, one after the other, the steel of their blades sending sparks cascading around them. Imladrik ceded ground, pace by pace, retreating back towards the prone form of Draukhain.

'And I listened!' roared Morgrim. 'By my beard, I listened! That is now my shame.'

Imladrik held his ground, digging in. The blades locked again. This time Morgrim gave ground first. Even his mighty arms, it seemed, were capable of exhaustion.

'Your shame is right here,' panted Imladrik. 'You wanted blood-debt for your cousin, and now you have it.'

'Do not mention him.'

Imladrik parried a fresh thrust and returned a low strike. 'Why not? He blinds you still?'

Morgrim was wheezing now, rolling into contact like a drunken prize-fighter. He said nothing more but worked his axe harder, probing for the way through Imladrik's defence.

'You stubborn soul!' spat Imladrik. 'Snorri has *gone*. He was a fool, just as his killer was a fool.'

They rocked back and forth, trading more blows. Imladrik had to marvel at Morgrim's endurance. Ifulvin nearly buckled under one spiteful lunge, the steel bending under the force of it.

'We had a *chance*,' Imladrik said, breathing hard. 'We could have done better. I told you the truth.'

Morgrim fell back, gasping, his axe held low. 'I watched what your animals did,' he said, his voice ragged. 'You were riding one, so do not preach to me about restraint.'

Then he ploughed into the attack again. The blows were brutal, hurried, devastating. Imladrik fell away, working hard not to be overwhelmed.

'This land is death for you now, elgi,' Morgrim grunted. 'All of you. It will never stop.'

The duel stepped up in intensity. The twin weapons whirled around one another – the axe-blade cumbersome but crushing, the sword-edge rapid but lighter. None intervened, and still Draukhain did not stir, though the city continued to burn around them – a funeral pyre of old hopes.

Imladrik pressed the attack again, his blade blurring with speed. He hammered Morgrim back again, rocking the dwarf on to his heels.

'Caledor will never surrender,' he warned, his voice strained with effort. 'Do you truly think you can kill a Phoenix King?'

Morgrim shorted his disdain. 'His death will end this. Nothing else.'

'And mine?'

'I kill you because I have to. I will kill Caledor for pleasure.'

Imladrik smiled coldly. 'You will have neither.'

He pivoted on his heel, building momentum for a savage crossways swipe. At the last moment he adjusted the trajectory, ducking his blade under Morgrim's lifting guard. Ifulvin cut deep into the dwarf's armour, catching on the chainmail between shifting plates.

Morgrim staggered, and his axe fell by a hand's width. Imladrik hammered another blow in, denting a gromril plate. Ifulvin whirled, moving now with terrible velocity and smashing Morgrim back by another pace. The dwarf's breathing worsened, his head lowered. More strikes scythed down, bludgeoning him back through the dust, nearly causing him to sprawl on his back. Blood splattered across the stone, thick as tar.

It was merciless. None of the assembled dawi moved a muscle – they watched, stony-faced, as their lord was driven across the courtyard. Imladrik kept up the pressure, fighting with peerless artistry, the sun flashing from his helm.

He smashed Morgrim's defence aside with a brutal side-stroke, then rotated his glittering blade on its length, hoisting it over Morgrim's reeling body and holding it point-down. He angled it at the dwarf's shoulder, both hands on the hilt, ready to drive.

As he did so, Draukhain stirred at last, his bloodied head lifting from the rubble of the wall. A wave of hot, bitter air rolled out from his tangled body as he shook his neck, his great eyes cloudy.

The runes of Morgrim's axe suddenly flared. The angular grooves in the metal blazed red-hot amid the bloody patina of the blade. His whole armour surged with power, as if kindled by the awakening of the dragonsoul.

Imladrik plunged Ifulvin down, powering it with all his strength. Morgrim thrust in return, shoving Azdrakghar upwards with both hands, and flames licked along the edge of the blade.

The twin weapons met in a crash of light. A ripple of force shot out from the impact, stirring the dust from the flags. With a crack like ice breaking, Ifulvin shattered. Imladrik felt the force of it radiate up his arms, hard as a hammer on an anvil. He pulled back, amazed, his hands shaking from the impact.

Morgrim roared back at him, heedless, his axe still intact and glowing blood-red. The runes burned like torches. Imladrik saw the blow coming in and desperately jabbed his broken blade in its path, but Ifulvin was swatted aside, its power broken. Morgrim's whole body shook with raw heat-shimmer, a vision of rune-magic unlocked.

Somewhere close by, Draukhain was roaring in thunderous frustration, his coiled body still pinned by wreckage. Imladrik felt the dragon's anger and pain and could have wept from it.

Weaponless, all he could do was watch the axe-head sweep around again, propelled by Morgrim's blind savagery. Its curved edge punched deep into Imladrik's midriff, cutting through the silver armour with a flash of rune-energy. The bite was deep. A wash of pain crashed through him, numbing his limbs. Morgrim pushed the blade in deeper, tearing through muscle.

Imladrik's vision went blurry. He heard Draukhain's strangled roaring behind him even as he sank to his knees. The broken hilt-shards fell from his hand, clattering in the dust.

Morgrim pulled his axe free, dragging a long sluice of blood with it. Imladrik fell forwards, catching himself with his hands.

That brought him level with Morgrim's helm-hidden face. They looked at one another. Imladrik could feel the blood pumping out of him, draining his life away. Morgrim stared back, frozen rigid, as if suddenly shocked by what he had done. He could hear cries of alarm, the discharge of magefire and the groggy snarling of the dragon, still locked in the tangled detritus of its agony.

It was all strangely detached. All he truly saw was Morgrim. Everything else faded into grey.

He wanted to say something. He tried to blurt words out, but none came. Life ebbed from him like water from a sieve.

He closed his eyes. Morgrim was saying something to him, but he couldn't hear it.

He felt the rain of Cothique against his face. He saw the tower of Tor Vael standing against a lowering sky, the light at its summit glowing warmly.

He tried to walk towards it, but even in his delirium he could not do so. The world folded up on itself in darkness.

The last thing he saw was the outline of a drake, high up over the sea, curving in flight out to the west.

He wanted to follow it, but could no longer move.

Liandra saw him fall.

She was running, sprinting with what remained of her escort, her robes and staff still wreathed in flame. The journey into the heart of the city had been horrific – a constant battle with hordes of dawi, all of whom had turned from their slaughter to waylay her. The swordsmen and archers around her had been cut down mercilessly, valiant to the last but wildly outnumbered. On another day she would have stopped to help them.

Not this day. She tore as fast as her legs would carry her, sending a wave of fire coursing out in front of her, burning and blasting any who stumbled into her path. Her desperation made her strong; not since Vranesh had died had she used her power so freely. Her whole body shimmered with it – it spilled from her eyes and mouth, as fierce as sunlight and as hot as coals.

For all that, she was too late. She careered into the courtyard, her boots skidding on the stone, only to see a vista of devastation open up before her.

Draukhain had been brought down and lay half-buried in wreckage on the far side of the square. Dwarfs were everywhere, hundreds of them, most arranged in a loose semicircle around the stricken dragon. Others streamed into the courtyard, attracted by the sights and sounds of combat.

Liandra looked about her. Only a handful of asur remained by her side, panting with exhaustion, their armour hanging ragged from their shoulders. In their expressions was bewilderment – she had led them through the heart of the battle to their deaths. At least at the tower they might have held out for a few hours longer.

'Follow,' she commanded, setting off once more.

Few of the dwarfs noticed her arrival – their attention was on the scene before them. Liandra powered through them, smashing them aside with blasts from her staff. Like a hot iron through water she forged a path towards the centre of the throng, raging words of power throughout, her copper hair flying about her face.

It was only then, right at the end, that she saw him fall. Imladrik collapsed forward, his silver armour dark with blood, his eyes wide with surprise. He didn't see her. It didn't look like he saw anything but the dwarf who had killed him.

Liandra knew who it was – she recognised the armour from a long time ago, though now it bled with the afterglow of unleashed magic.

'Imladrik!' she cried, rushing forwards, heedless of the dwarf arms that reached out to drag her back. The fires about her guttered out, extinguished as suddenly as they had been summoned.

Morgrim barked an order to his warriors. The fighting around her ceased, she was allowed through. Ignoring all else, she fell to her knees, cradling Imladrik's head in her lap, barely feeling the tears that ran down her cheeks.

'Imladrik,' she said again, searching for some small flicker of consciousness.

He was gone. His bruised face was as pale as bone, his unseeing eyes still staring out.

Ahead of her, the vast form of Draukhain struggled to free himself from the wreckage. A foreleg emerged, crusted in dust. The dragon growled menacingly, his eyes flashing with fury.

The dwarfs backed away from it, crossbows raised. Liandra heard the *clunk* of bolt throwers being primed.

Morgrim issued another terse order in Khazalid, and the dwarfs stood down.

Liandra turned on him, half-blind with grief.

'He was your *friend!*' she blurted.

Morgrim looked uncertainly back at her, as if he'd awoken from some dream and no longer knew what it was he'd been striving for. The warriors around him held position, silent as statues.

Liandra turned back to Imladrik, smoothing his eyelids closed. Draukhain managed to drag himself half-free of the rubble, his long tail coiling. The dragon's massive head lowered, dipping over Imladrik's prone body, steam drifting from his nostrils. Even so badly wounded, the beast towered over all else in the square, a crippled leviathan amid the ruins.

Morgrim shook the blood from his axe, stared at it for a moment, then hoisted it across his back.

'This place is ours now,' he said grimly.

Liandra shot him a contemptuous look. 'You could have had it. You could have had anything you demanded. He would have listened.' She turned back to Imladrik. His blood ran across her robes, staining them deep. 'You have killed the only one of us who would have done.'

Draukhain issued a low, grinding growl. The dragon was recovering some of his strength, and pulled another limb from the ruins. He was half-standing now, with only his hindquarters buried.

'Order your beast back, or I will have it killed,' said Morgrim.

Liandra glanced up at Draukhain.

Did you hear that? she mind-sang. *He thinks he can have you killed.*

He may be right, came Draukhain's song, coloured with almost unbearable misery. There was no fight left in the dragon's eyes. The creature stared moodily at Imladrik's corpse, uncaring of the ranks of dawi about him.

Morgrim reached for a casket at his chest. He held it for a while, lost in thought. 'My warriors wish to kill you, too.'

'Do what you will,' said Liandra dismissively, not looking up at him.

'Will the dragon fly?'

Liandra glanced at Draukhain. He was terribly injured, but she had seen drakes recover from worse. 'He might.'

'Then take the body,' said Morgrim.

Liandra stared at Morgrim for a moment. If anything, her hatred for him intensified. 'Your grudge is settled, is that it?'

'Far from it, but we are not animals.'

Liandra shook her head in disdain. 'Caledor will come after you. All of Ulthuan will come after you.'

Morgrim nodded calmly. 'We will meet them.'

Draukhain coughed a bloody gout of smoke from his jaws.

Let me bear him, feleth-amina, he sang. *His place is not here.*

Liandra smiled bitterly. She had never been quite sure where Imladrik's place was. Perhaps he hadn't been, either.

'And the asur who remain?' she asked, glaring at Morgrim again.

'They will be held, once the fighting is over. You may go. For the others, I make no promises.'

Liandra glanced at the few soldiers who had made it with her to the courtyard. They deserved better. Surrounded by dwarfs, their blades lowered, they looked resigned to their fate.

'I know their names,' she said. 'If they are not returned, I will hold you accountable.'

Morgrim bowed. 'So be it.'

Liandra rose, shakily, to her feet. Ahead of her, the dragon hauled itself free. Its flanks glistened wetly. Many barbs protruded from its flesh, each one weeping blood. She had never seen Draukhain brought so low, and that alone stabbed at her heart.

'There is a prisoner in the dungeon below,' she said to Morgrim, stooping to carry Imladrik. 'If she has not been killed already, you should do so. She is a witch.' She hoisted Imladrik into her arms, his feet dragging on the stone. He was impossibly heavy in his armour, but no dwarf came to aid her.

'Elgi crimes are not our concern,' said Morgrim.

'They should be,' she said wearily. 'If you had listened to him you would know why. If you care for anything other than bloodshed, kill her. Kill her and cut the heart from her body. And tell her Liandra of House Athinol ordered it.'

In truth, though, she could not bring herself to care overmuch. Drutheira had done her work. If she lived on she was now a ruined thing, destined for nothing but some petty oblivion. The seeds she had planted had grown into dark fruit and would keep growing now whatever else was done.

She dragged herself over to Draukhain. The dragon dipped his shoulder as low as he could. It was hard work getting the body in position. Several times Liandra nearly slipped, crying out with frustration and anger. Eventually, though, Imladrik's corpse settled in the hollow between the dragon's wings. His cloak hung limply over the armoured hide.

Liandra turned before mounting. In front of her stretched the carcass of Oeragor, destroyed by the dawi who now occupied it. They stood in silent ranks, still bristling with sullen anger. She could tell that they did not want to see her leave alive, but none would gainsay Morgrim.

'You will never know how much he held himself back,' Liandra told him. 'He was the best of us, and you have ended him.'

Morgrim nodded again. The dwarf seemed almost numbed by what he had done. 'He will have a place in our annals. *Govandrakken*. He will not be scorned.'

Liandra shook her head. She could take no comfort from the dwarfs' obsession with records and grudges. More than ever it seemed pathetic to her, a dull rehearsal of rituals that signified nothing. If they could not see what tragedy their stubbornness had unleashed then they deserved the war that would cripple them.

She climbed into position, no longer looking at the dwarfs below.

Can you fly? she asked Draukhain, feeling his pain as her own.

The dragon's legs tensed, ready for the pounce that would propel him aloft. His ravaged wings spread, casting a tattered shadow over the stone.

I will bear you to Tor Alessi, he sang, his mind-voice stricken with a dull kind of emptiness. *But fly? Truly fly? Never again.*

TWENTY-SEVEN

Drutheira re-wrapped the linen around her head again, knowing that it would do little good. The sun seemed to beat down between the weave, torturing her already scarred skin further. She wanted to drink again but their supplies were scant enough. Malchior, Ashniel and she each carried a gourd of gritty water and a few hard loaves – all they had managed to scavenge in the wreckage of the city – and she didn't hold out much hope they would last them long enough.

Ahead of her, Malchior still walked with reasonable fluency. Ashniel was weaker, carrying a couple of injuries. One had been sustained when the red mage's dragon had demolished the mountainside she'd been standing on; the other when her disguise had slipped and an Oeragor guard had recognised her. The knife-fight, Drutheira understood, had been vicious.

'We should look for shade,' Drutheira complained.

Malchior halted, and looked around him. The scrubland ran away from them in every direction, flat, hard and open. 'You see any?'

Drutheira pushed her headdress up a little, squinting in the light. The sun was high in the sky still; it would be hours before the relative cool of dusk. Smoke rose from the northern horizon, now miles away. Oeragor would burn for a long time before they put the fires out. It was fortunate, in a way – slipping out amid all the confusion had been trivial, aided a little by Malchior's subtle arts.

'Walk at night, rest by day,' she said.

Malchior's expression was unreadable; like all of them he'd wound fabric around his face to ward off the worst of the sun.

He reached down for his gourd and took a swig. Ashniel did the same, swaying slightly.

'So how did you find me?' asked Drutheira at last. She'd been putting it off, not wanting to give Malchior the satisfaction, but curiosity got the better of her.

'I could follow you,' said Ashniel quietly.

Drutheira turned to face her, surprised. Ashniel had always been the quiet one.

'I could sense you,' Ashniel repeated. 'Ever since the dragon came. Something in the aethyr.'

Drutheira didn't like the sound of that. If some part of her resonated in there then there were plenty of other things that might be able to track her down.

'It took days to cross the desert,' said Malchior. 'I argued against it.'

'But we needed the dragon,' said Ashniel. 'To get home.'

Drutheira smiled acidly. 'A shame it died, then.'

'It didn't take much art to blend in once we got to Oeragor,' said Malchior, rather pompously. 'Their minds were on other things.'

'By then you knew the dragon had gone,' said Drutheira. 'Why did you still come for me?'

Malchior shrugged. 'We missed your company.'

'We needed you,' said Ashniel, more seriously. 'We know nothing of this land.'

'Neither do I,' said Drutheira.

'You must do. You were in Malekith's circle.'

Drutheira winced. 'Don't assume that means very much.'

Malchior exhaled irritably. 'We need to get away from this Khaine-damned place.' He looked at Drutheira reluctantly. 'You studied the maps longest.'

Drutheira enjoyed the admission, wrung from him like sweat from his headdress. 'That, of course, is true.'

Ashniel looked like she was going to collapse. 'Do we have to do this now? And where are we going?'

Malchior's mouth twisted in scorn. 'South,' he said. 'Everywhere else is crawling with dawi.' He glanced at Drutheira. 'You agree?'

Drutheira nodded.

'Nowhere else to go,' she said. As she spoke, she tried to remember the charts she'd seen so long ago. Naggaroth seemed almost like a dream. 'There was a river marked. There must be one, sooner or later. Vitae, was that it? Some arcane language. Malekith knew something about it.'

'How far?' asked Malchior.

'A long way. We can't walk. We'll need to find somewhere to recover, or try to get to the coast. A boat – that would be useful.'

Malchior snorted derisively and turned away. 'I'll keep an eye out.'

Drutheira looked briefly north again, over to where Oeragor smouldered. The evidence of its ruin was like a premonition, a harbinger of what was to come for all Elthin Arvan. Soon there would be nothing in the colonies but fire, a blaze she had helped to start.

Who would know it, though? Would anyone ever whisper her name with reverence in the hallowed courts of Naggaroth? Drutheira, the destroyer of empires. If she couldn't find a way back, then no one would, and that silence would be worse than death.

Malchior started to walk again. Haltingly, Ashniel followed him. Drutheira took a sip of water before falling in behind them, trying to ignore the residual pain in her joints.

But I am alive, she thought to herself, remembering the malice in the eyes of the red mage, the certainty that she had finally run her down. To be breathing still, to be free, that was more than improbable. *Despite it all, my heart still beats.*

She kept walking. The southern horizon stretched away from them, shaking in the heat. The emptiness looked like it went on forever.

Morgrim hobbled through the streets of Oeragor. He could feel blood sloshing in his boots. His ribs were cracked, his shoulder-blade fractured. When he breathed it felt like dry grass was being shoved down his throat.

Everywhere he went, his warriors saluted him. They raised their fists and bowed their heads. Some of the younger ones shouted *Khazuk!* They all knew what had been achieved. His name would go into the records, carved into the stone tablets buried in the vaults of Karaz-a-Karak. Starbreaker would summon him to the throne. The runelords would honour him. The pall of disgrace that had hung over his bloodline since Snorri's death would lift.

It should have made him fiercely proud. Part of him was. He could still see the carnage caused by the drakes. It felt good to have repaid some measure of pain. Morek's rune-artistry had answered at last, and Azdrakghar had tasted blood.

It was, at least, a beginning.

But beyond that he felt removed from all that had transpired. The long marches had battered his body into submission. He knew when he peeled his armour off, all he would see would be calluses, bruises and blisters. His flesh was now a carpet of them, weeping blood and pus under the hard shell of his battle plate.

He could cope with the pain. It was the other things he found difficult.

Imladrik had been an obstacle. No other elgi commanded such respect. His removal had been necessary, and not just for the satisfaction of grudgement. Morgrim could not have returned to the Everpeak with the Master of Dragons un-defeated and still claimed the title of *elgidum*.

Yet, for all that, his heart remained uneasy. He had tried to speak to Imladrik at the end, though he doubted the elgi had heard him.

'You did not need to fight here,' he had said, almost angrily. 'You did not need to come.'

Then the mage had arrived, bursting into the courtyard with her anger and her witch's fire. The order to release the body had almost been an afterthought. It would certainly not placate any of the asur. In a war that had already seen atrocity unleashed, it would do nothing to restore restraint.

He reached again for the casket at his breast, the one containing Snorri's remains.

All it had been was an exchange. A barter. The dawi understood such things.

'*Tromm*, Morgrim!'

Brynnoth's gruff voice rang out. He was walking towards Morgrim, his armour in terrible shape. An elgi arrow still protruded from his pauldron, the shaft snapped. His grizzled face spread in a wide grin.

'We have broken them!' Brynnoth roared, embracing Morgrim roughly. 'And the dragon! Wings torn to ribbons. That was a mighty feat.'

Morgrim nodded weakly. 'They can be beaten. We know that now.'

'They can, and they will.' Brynnoth's blood was up. He looked ready to march off again that instant.

Morgrim couldn't share his ebullience. 'We should secure the city.'

'Secure it?' Brynnoth laughed. 'From what?'

Morgrim felt like collapsing but kept his feet. He would have to do so for hours. The ale had not even been hauled into the city yet, ready for the hours of ritual drinking and oath-taking to come. 'From ourselves. Let there be no mindless slaughter.'

'Of course not.' Brynnoth looked at him hard. 'Are you all right?'

Morgrim knew he would be. Dawn would come, and he would remember the sacred runes he had sworn over. He would remember his hatred and his pride. He would speak with Brynnoth about the weapons in Barak Varr, and the foundries would soon be ringing with industry. Everything would grind into motion again. They would sweep west, this time knowing what they faced, knowing they could beat it.

In time, all of those things would happen. For now, though, he felt empty, like a clawed-out mineshaft.

'I did not know how victory tasted until today,' Morgrim said, remembering how Imladrik's blood had coursed over his gauntlets. 'It will take some getting used to.'

The three of them sat together in Imladrik's high chamber: Yethanial, Thoriol and Caradryel. The windows were unshuttered and let in the evening light in warm bands of gold.

Caradryel felt awkward. He wasn't sure why he had been summoned. It felt like he was intruding on some private family affair.

'Was he angry?' Yethanial asked, speaking to Thoriol.

The youth shook his head. 'A little. More surprised, I think.'

'He should have been angry.' Yethanial's voice was soft but harsh. 'You have had every advantage. You could have died.'

Thoriol looked resigned. 'So he told me. Look, I see the truth of it, so you do not need to tell me again.'

Caradryel shifted in his seat. Clearly this was something that would be best thrashed out between the two of them.

'My lady, I–' he started.

'Stay where you are,' ordered Yethanial, before turning her severe face back to Thoriol. 'This is not some game we are playing at. None of us gets to choose, not when we are at war. There is *duty*, Thoriol, and that is all.'

She sounded so much like her husband. Thoriol looked chastened, and did not argue.

'I will try again,' he said, lifting his head to return her gaze. 'I can return to the Dragonspine.'

Yethanial looked at him carefully, as if assessing whether he meant it.

'It is not easy,' she said at last. 'Imladrik tells me they wake slowly now, but we need all the riders we can get.'

Thoriol's expression didn't change. Caradryel thought he looked very little like his father; much more akin to the mother.

'And you?' Thoriol asked, his eyes glittering with challenge.

Yethanial bowed her head. 'I should have been here from the start. It was only pride that kept me away.'

Caradryel cleared his throat. 'But a good time to return, if you'll pardon me for saying. Salendor and Aelis are consumed with their own business, and Caledor's gaze remains fixed on Naggaroth. There are opportunities here, lady.'

Yethanial looked at him coolly. 'Opportunities? For what?'

'Power.' Caradryel had never quite got the hang of meeting Yethanial's steely gaze, but worked hard at it. 'Influence. Imladrik destroyed the dwarf host; his prestige has never been higher. We can use it.'

Yethanial looked uncertain. 'I do not follow.'

'The gods' favour is fleeting: one moment all is golden, the next it lies in ruins. You and I both know this war is a disaster, and sooner or later others will realise it. We have armies here, whole legions whose loyalty is now to Imladrik alone. They would do anything he ordered. Anything.'

Thoriol stirred uneasily. 'You mean–'

'Caledor is a fool.' Caradryel said. 'Why apologise for saying it? We need to think to the future. We have what we need here. All that remains is picking the moment.'

A tense silence fell over the chamber.

'This is not why I employed you, Caradryel,' said Yethanial.

'Was it not? I serve the House of Tor Caled, and its destiny is to rule, one way or another. So let me at least point out the possibilities.'

Thoriol shook his head. 'Imladrik will not allow it.'

'Not now, no,' said Caradryel. 'But he knows that no end to this can come while his brother rules. The bloodshed sickens him – he told me so. I think we can persuade him if we need to.'

Yethanial, somewhat to his surprise, did not immediately demur. She thought hard, teasing through the possibilities. Caradryel began to wonder if, of the two of them, she might be the better player of such games.

'The time is not ripe,' she said at last.

'No,' agreed Caradryel.

Yethanial gave him a distasteful look. 'You will need gold?'

'Some. More important is your patronage. Tor Caled is a powerful name; it opens doors.'

Yethanial nodded slowly. 'So you told me before.'

Thoriol looked at both of them uncomprehendingly. 'What are you saying? You talk of duty, and then... this?'

Yethanial shot him a withering glance. 'Have you understood nothing? Your duty is to Ulthuan, to your bloodline.'

Caradryel found himself nodding. 'So she says.'

Thoriol looked like he wished to protest, but his words were cut off by a sudden call of trumpets from the walls. All of them turned to the east-facing window. Caradryel got to his feet, but not as quickly as Yethanial. She hurried over to the sill, leaning out into the dusk air.

A dragon was riding towards the city, its flanks glowing dull blue in the failing light.

'He returns!' cried Yethanial.

Caradryel saw the sudden hope in her face. The soft greyness lifted from her features and her eyes sparkled. For a moment, a fleeting moment, he saw unalloyed joy there, a profound delight that banished her severity. It was transformative, and quite unexpected.

'Why does he fly so low?' murmured Thoriol.

Caradryel looked back out of the window. He had seen Imladrik tear through the air many times and this flight looked nothing like that. The dragon seemed to limp along, dipping frequently. Its wings were ragged. As it neared the walls its tail hung low, trailing feebly.

Caradryel stared harder. An awful feeling crept over him.

'My lady, I think–' he began, but she was already moving, running out of the chamber and towards the spiral stairway leading up to the roof.

Thoriol followed her. Cursing, Caradryel did likewise, taking the steps two at a time to keep up. The three of them broke out into the open, on to the same wide platform where Caradryel had last bid farewell to Imladrik.

The dragon swooped down on them, its flight erratic. Droplets of black blood splattered on the stone.

'Isha, not this...' breathed Yethanial, horror written on her face. She looked like she'd suddenly aged. As Draukhain touched down she hurried over, gathering her robes around her.

Thoriol held back, his face white. Caradryel stayed beside him. The dragon's aroma was awful – like rotten meat mingled with old embers.

He saw Liandra dismount. How she came to be riding Imladrik's dragon was a riddle he knew he did not want to solve. She looked as dishevelled as her steed, her face streaked with tear-tracks over grime and blood. She tried to say something to Yethanial but the grey lady barely noticed her.

Yethanial approached Imladrik's corpse hesitantly, carefully, as if he were terribly wounded and might still get up. Caradryel could see the futility of that – his master lay awkwardly, as slack as sackcloth, his armour dark with blood.

Yethanial's grief then was terrible to witness, so powerful and so complete that for a moment none of them could speak. The dragon wheezed sclerotically, its huge eyes weeping black tears. Across the city, the trumpets were stilled as the celebrating heralds realised that something was terribly wrong.

Thoriol stumbled forward to stand by his mother, his feet shuffling unwillingly on the stone. For a moment the two of them just stood there, staring stupidly, emptily, at Imladrik's body. Then Yethanial's tears came at last – huge racking sobs that made her bend double. Thoriol held her up, his body erect, his face like stone. The two of them clung to one another, grasping greedily as if they could somehow insulate themselves against the truth.

Caradryel looked away, unwilling to intrude further. He felt nauseous.

'What happened?' he asked Liandra.

The red mage looked exhausted. 'Dawi,' she said, coldly. 'They got to Oeragor ahead of him.'

'And you? Where were you?'

Liandra glared at him. 'It can wait.' Her gaze travelled to Yethanial. Sympathy was etched on her features. Sympathy, and perhaps a little envy.

Caradryel felt wretched. Just moments ago the future had been mapped out. His decisions had been vindicated, his path clear.

Now, nothing. He remembered the first time he had seen the sapphire dragon, high above the waves, swooping earthwards like a messenger of the gods. It had looked invincible then, something that no force of the earth could ever vanquish.

Now it slumped on the stone, bleeding like any mortal, still carrying the body of its dead master. Around it huddled the remnants of the House of Tor Caled, one weeping, one silent with shock.

What now, then? he asked himself weakly.

The wind picked up, cold from the west. The east was darkening quickly, sinking into the deep night that made the forest so forbidding. That dark had always seemed contestable before; now it looked infinite and unbreakable.

Caradryel didn't know where to look.

What now? Who will follow him?

But no answer came.

EPILOGUE

Sevekai had no idea how long he'd been on the cusp of it. He didn't know where he was, nor how far he had travelled since leaving the Arluii behind. In the beginning he had tried to remember. He had vague memories of going south, heading down into the lowlands until the trees blotted the sky. Measuring time, though, no longer seemed like something he should concern himself with. The rhythm of the forest was less exact: languorous, shackled to a lower, more eternal measure.

His crow perched on a branch above him, its black eye glinting. It seldom left him now. The others, the ones that had made their way to the forest as he had done, they all had their companions too: Aismarr had a lean hunting dog, as skinny as bones; Elieth had a hawk; Ophiel had a fox that slunk timorously in the shadows. They came and went, these creatures of the wood, but never departed for long. They were like echoes of thoughts lingering under the eaves.

Sevekai watched the others. They bore the same dreamy expression. They had renounced the old passions. None of them hated or loved any more; it was like being half-asleep.

A few of them, he knew, were kin from Naggaroth; just a couple, skulking amid the briars like thieves. They came into the centre of the circle only slowly, just as he had done at the beginning, unable to entirely forswear the hatreds they had been born into.

The forest worked on them, though, just as it did the others. They gradually lost their pale mien and took on a healthier blush. Their tattoos faded somehow. Their oil-slick hair seemed lighter under the green glow of the canopy.

The rest had the healthy light of Ulthuan in their eyes. He didn't know where they had all come from. Neither did they – the old life drifted out of mind and memory so quickly. Some of them had taken on new names. Sevekai, for the moment, clung to his. It seemed important. He didn't know how long he would feel that way.

He didn't even want to hurt them. That was novel.

None of them had penetrated far into the heart of the wood. They lingered on the edge where the light still shafted down between the branches. They heard creaks and snaps from the deep core, buried in arboreal gloom. They heard night-noises – squeals and rustles, low groans that were almost elf-like, though distorted and alien.

What is this place?

He asked that question less often as time went on. At first he had been consumed by it, desperate to know what was slowly altering his mind. He would look at a leaf in the sunlight, seeing its veins standing dark against the translucence, staring at it in fascination. He would breathe deep of the musty soil aroma. He would hear the brush of the branches as the moons wheeled above him.

He never thought of escape. Where would he go?

The wood called them. All of them heard it. Soon they would have to enter, ducking under the curved and twisted branches and stooping into the shadows. He had dreams of what lay in there, waiting for them, though he never remembered them once the sun was up.

Aismarr smiled at him. She was standing a few yards away, her smock stained green and her cheeks ruddy. Sevekai liked the way her hair fell about her face – tangled, flecked with dirt, half-plaited.

'I dreamed of dragons,' she told him.

Sevekai remembered a dragon, though only vaguely. 'Oh? What did it tell you?'

'Their souls are broken,' Aismarr said, sadly. 'Someone has died, someone they loved.'

Sevekai remembered Drutheira then. Of all of them, she was the one he still remembered. He hadn't ever loved her. There had been passion, of a sort, but that was part of the old pattern. Here things were simpler – more direct, more honest. He wondered where she was.

'Then is it time?' he asked. He knew that something would have to change. Some signal would be given and then the deep wood would beckon.

Aismarr frowned. Her hunting dog slunk around her calves, snagging at her smock.

'No.' She glanced over to her left, to where the path ran down like a river into the heart of the forest.

Sevekai followed her gaze. He didn't think it was time either, not yet.

'This is the start,' he said, not really knowing where the words came from. 'The dragonsoul is gone; others will follow. The world must change.'

Aismarr looked at him with shining eyes.

'And then will we enter?' she asked.

Sevekai couldn't take his eyes off the trees. They called to him, though silently, and with neither malice nor affection.

'When the word is given,' he said.

'And what then?'

Sevekai looked back at her. He no longer saw an asur standing before him, just a kindred soul. All of them were kindred souls now.

'Rebirth,' he said, smiling.

CHARACTERS

THE ELVES

House Tor Caled
Menlaeth, called Caledor II – Phoenix King of Ulthuan
Imladrik – Master of Dragons; Menlaeth's brother
Yethanial – Loremaster; Imladrik's wife
Thoriol, called the Silent – Imladrik and Yethanial's only son

The Council of Five
Liandra of Kor Vanaeth – House Athinol
Salendor of Athel Maraya – House Tor Achare
Aelis of Tor Alessi – House Lamael
Gelthar of Athel Toralien – House Derreth
Caerwal of Athel Numiel – House Ophel

Other Asur
Caradryel – House Reveniol
Kelemar – Regent of Oeragor
Baelian – Archer captain
Loeth – Archer
Taemon – Archer
Florean – Archer
Rovil – Archer

Druchii
Drutheira – Sorceress
Malchior – Sorcerer
Ashniel – Sorceress
Sevekai – Assassin

THE DWARFS
Morgrim Bargrum – Thane of Karaz-a-Karak
Morek Furrowbrow – Runelord
Grondil – Thane of Zhufbar
Brynnoth – King of Barak Varr

GLOSSARY

Anurein – River running through the southern reaches of the Great Forest to the sea, later called the Reik
Arluii – Mountain range to the south of Elthin Arvan, later called the Grey Mountains
Asur – The elves of Ulthuan, known to men as High Elves
Athel Maraya – Lord Salendor's lands, located in the heart of Loren Lacoi
Athel Numiel – City in the north-east of Elthin Arvan, destroyed by dwarfs during the early years of the war
Athel Toralien – City on the western shores of Elthin Arvan, ruled for a time by Malekith
Druchii – The elves of Naggaroth, known to men as Dark Elves
Elthin Arvan – The lands east of the Great Ocean settled by the asur, later called the Old World
Ifulvin – 'Bitter-blade'; sword borne by Imladrik
Kor Evril – Imladrik's citadel in the mountains of Caledor
Kor Vanaeth – Settlement east of Tor Alessi founded by Lord Athinol, father of the mage Liandra
Lathrain – 'Wrathbringer'; sword borne by Caledor II, inherited from his father
Loren Faen – Forest south of the Arluii, said to be perilous and enchanted, later known as the Fey Forest or Athel Loren
Loren Lacoi – Forest between the Saraeluii and the coast, bounded on the south by the Arluii and in the north by unsettled wasteland, later known as the Great Forest
Oeragor – Asur city in the far south, chiefly settled by Caledorians of Imladrik's household
Saraeluii – Mountain range to the east of Elthin Arvan, home to the majority of the dwarf holds, later called the Worlds Edge Mountains
Sith Rionnasc – Common name for the port at the head of the River Anurein, later the site of the free city of Marienburg

Tor Alessi – Pre-eminent city of the asur in Elthin Arvan, later the site of the Bretonnian city of L'Anguille
Tor Caled – Home of the House of Tor Caled and the court of Caledor II
Tor Vael – City of loremasters in Cothique; ancestral home of Yethanial
Ulthuan – Homeland of the asur in the Great Ocean

THE HOUSE OF TOR CALED

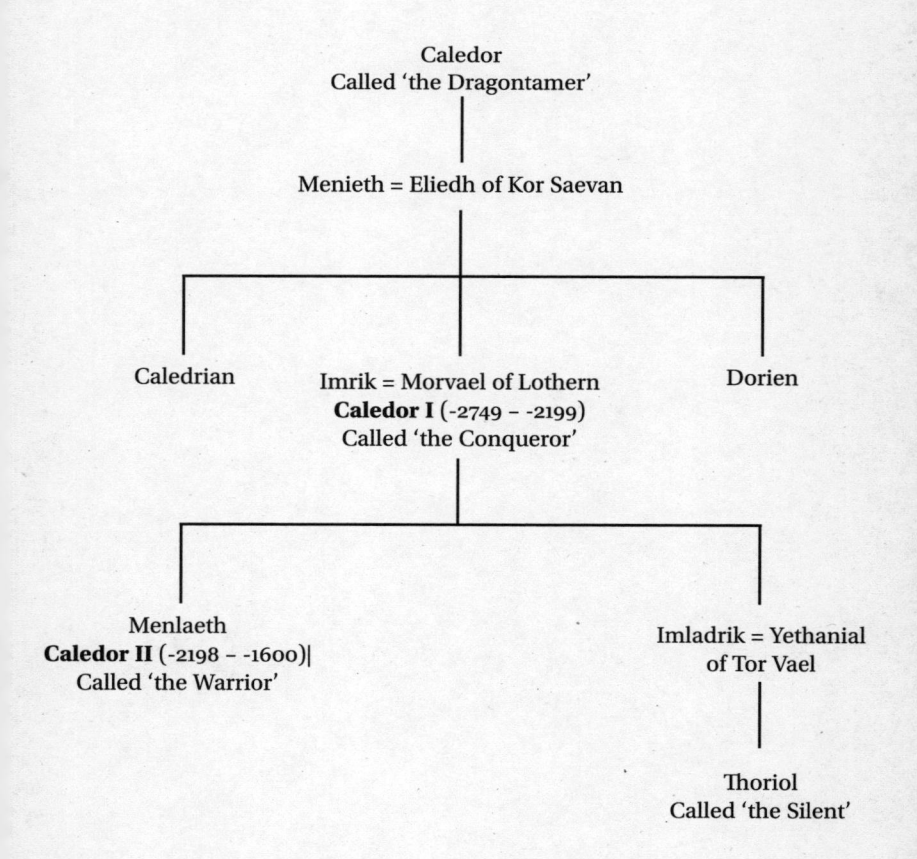

Caledor
Called 'the Dragontamer'
|
Menieth = Eliedh of Kor Saevan
|
—————————————————————
| | |
Caledrian   Imrik = Morvael of Lothern   Dorien
               Caledor I (-2749 – -2199)
               Called 'the Conqueror'
                        |
              ———————————————————
              | |
         Menlaeth   Imladrik = Yethanial
    Caledor II (-2198 – -1600)| of Tor Vael
      Called 'the Warrior' |
                                        Thoriol
                                    Called 'the Silent'

THE CURSE OF THE PHOENIX CROWN

C L Werner

ONE

FIRES IN THE SKY

236TH YEAR OF THE REIGN OF CALEDOR II

'I might be a damn *zaki,* but scupper me if I don't glory in all this.'

Heglan Copperfist smiled at the other dwarf's outburst. He looked up from the airship's broad deck and to the wheelhouse where Nugdrinn Hammerfoot was scratching anxiously at the hollow of his missing eye. The old sea captain had adjusted magnificently to the demands of his new vocation – that of sky captain. Far below them, the snowy peaks of the Vaults peaked out from a mantle of misty cloud, a sight to awe the heart of any *dawi,* moving him to stark terror or, as in Nugdri's case, exuberant jubilation.

The engineer couldn't indulge the same thrill as Nugdri. He couldn't afford to. A grand honour had been given to him, but along with that honour had come a terrible obligation – a grim duty that pressed down upon him with all the weight of the great rock Durazon.

No, he wouldn't fail. He couldn't fail. He was the last of the Copperfists, the last of his line. Only Heglan could redeem the legacy of his grandfather, exonerate the engineering theories of Dammin Copperfist and erase the ridicule and shame that had been heaped upon his name. Only Heglan could bestow upon the arsenals of King Brynnoth and Barak Varr a weapon that could match the might and horror of the *drakk* and their *elgi* masters.

Only Heglan would have the glory of avenging his brother Nadri Gildtongue. Destroying the dragons, eliminating the most devastating weapon in the arsenal of the elgi, would pave the way for a quick and decisive victory against the hated foe. A fleet of airships descending upon Tor Alessi, raining havoc upon the city as the drakk had wrought havoc upon the dawi armies.

In response to Heglan's command, Nugdri coaxed the *skryzan-harbark* still higher. The rest of the crew, down on the main deck, chewed nervously at their beards, eyes locked on the enormous leather sack suspended above them. Filled with buoyant gas, the air-bag was what enabled the skryzan-harbark to defy the pull of rock and earth. Great copper vanes, whirling about at rapid speed, provided the ship's propulsion, but it was the air-bag that was the true triumph of Heglan's invention. At higher altitudes he'd found that gas escaped from the air-bag. A new coating derived from a mix of resin and tar was proving an effective sealant thus far. If the skryzan-harbark were to contend with dragons, Heglan felt it essential that the airships be able to strike from above the monsters. He'd studied birds for many years and one thing had been imprinted on his mind: a predator always swooped down upon its prey from above.

Heglan joined Nugdri on the wheelhouse. 'Glory and danger go together like pick and hammer,' he cautioned the captain. They were climbing into the clouds, the mists of the mountains wrapping around them like a grey cloak. 'The greater the glory, the greater the danger.'

Nugdri stamped his metal foot against the deck, a habit he had that he claimed drew the attention of his ancestors and reminded them to send better luck his way than they had when he'd lost the appendage. 'If you die seeking glory, there's no shame in that.'

The engineer's expression grew sombre. 'There is if others are depending on you,' he stated. 'Pride is a poor excuse to offer the dead.' He turned his head, trying to pierce the clouds with his stony gaze. The skryzan-harbark were wondrous creations, but their mastery of the air wasn't unquestioned. Older and fouler things rode the winds these days.

Signal fires had alerted sentinels in Karak Norn, and from there the alert had passed to Karak Izor and Karak Hirn, finally reaching Barak Varr, the great sea hold, the mighty dwarf bastion on the Iron Gulf. There were few dwarf kingdoms as powerful as Barak Varr and none that possessed the amazing weapons Heglan had devised. It was to King Brynnoth and Barak Varr that the embattled holds in the Grey Mountains and Vaults turned when the elgi were on the march. It was to Barak Varr that the alarm was sent.

The warning had been only one name and one word. *Kazad Thar. Dragons.* That was enough to relay that Kazad Thar was under attack by the hated drakk.

It was rare that any king of the dwarfs made a decision quickly, but it had taken Heglan and Guildmaster Strombak only a few minutes to convince King Brynnoth that the skryzan-harbark must be sent to help the stricken fortress. The hill dwarfs – the *skarrenawi* – were yet cousins of the dawi and it would be an offence to the ancestor gods to abandon any dwarf to the depredations of the elgi and their beasts. Heglan had proven that they could confront the dragons in their own element.

Whether they could win... That was still a question that carried with it considerable doubt. The dwarfs had fought many battles with dragons in their long history, but the gold-grubbing wyrms that threatened their treasure vaults and mines weren't nearly so destructive as the drakk trained by elves. It took a lot to even injure one of those dragons. To kill one would require more weaponry than a single skryzan-harbark could carry. At least, if the airships bore ordinary weaponry.

Test upon test had been made, but even Heglan couldn't be certain that he had the weapons he needed. Ideally, he would have liked to coax one of the drakk out, lure it into a trap and prove the efficacy of their new ordnance under controlled conditions. The war, however, wouldn't wait for his experiments. Year by year, the War of Vengeance became more savage and bitter, the elgi stealing forth from their cities to raid and pillage the scattered mines and outposts of the dawi. Dragons would scorch anything that moved on the roads, forcing the dwarfs to delve new branches of the Ungdrin Ankor to escape their flames. Elgi sorcery had withered the crops and herds that fed many of the strongholds. Elgi ships had even dared to challenge Barak Varr for control of the Iron Gulf and the outlying seas.

The dawi had returned the outrages of the elgi with methodical deliberation. Twilight raids with axe and fire that reduced orchards and vineyards to so much ruin. Bold attacks with hammer and pick that toppled towers and walls. Grim ambushes against elgi knights and soldiers that demonstrated to the arrogant tall-ears the mettle of dwarfish courage and dwarfish steel. The dawi didn't need sorcerers and drakk to fight their battles. To answer the grudgements laid against the elves – the murder of Prince Snorri Halfhand and the unforgivable humiliation of High King Gotrek's ambassadors – it would take dwarfish blades. The blood of the elgi Prince Imladrik was but a drop in the sea of retribution that awaited the enemy.

From his vantage, Heglan could see the artillerists at their assigned stations, each ready to execute the manoeuvres they had drilled for months. Six sleek, bronze-framed bolt throwers were anchored to the mid-deck, three to a side. Metal mantlets shaded each platform, protecting the weapons while at the same time preventing them from being elevated to such an angle that they could threaten the air-bag above. Blockers set into the deck itself likewise arrested any divergence left and right. The bolt throwers required such precautions – their frames were wonders of engineering, designed by Bagdrimm Tallbeard of Karak Kadrin. Fitted to complex swivels, the weapons could pivot from side to side as well as depress or elevate. Each weapon was so expertly balanced that a single dwarf could manipulate it.

It had taken much gold and more flattery for Guildmaster Strombak to secure Bagdrimm's invention for the skryzan-harbark, but Heglan knew it would be worth it. For the airships to be true predators of the sky they needed more than just wings; they needed claws as well. Claws capable of knocking a dragon out of the air.

Claws of fire.

There was pride in Heglan's eyes as he focused on the ammunition positioned beside each bolt thrower. The great ashwood arrows with their barbed, steel heads were only the vehicle for the true bite of the skryzan-harbark. Their real power lay in the small stone pots that would be fixed to each arrow with chain just before it was loaded. The pots were sealed with pitch, a short length of fuse dangling from the mouth. The arrows would strike a dragon hard, but the dwarfs had seen time and again how difficult it was to pierce a drakk deep enough to really hurt it. Thus each missile's barbed head was meant only to hold the shaft in place until the burning fuse touched off the contents of the pot.

Heglan had worked long and hard to find the ideal compound to use. He'd been inspired by 'mine-damp', the explosive build-up of gas that often proved so devastating during the dawi's excavations. He'd tried very hard to find just the right mixture to recreate that destructive power. In the end, he'd been forced to appeal to the engineers' guild, to see if a brother engineer might have the answer that was proving so elusive to him.

The answer was *Tharzharr* – 'thunder-fire' – but it came not from another engineer, but a displaced thane. Drogor Zarrdum, a traveller from the distant hold of Karak Zorn, had brought the secret of Tharzharr to Barak Varr. It was an incendiary of unmatched ferocity, capable of melting its way through solid steel. It was more than merely an explosive: when it was unleashed, it would splash across a target in a burst of green fire, burning its way through whatever suffered its touch.

It was a hideous weapon, but so too were the drakk the elgi employed to reduce dwarf warriors to cinder and smoke. There was no room for sentiment in war, no place for conscience and half-measures. To be victorious, you had to be more ruthless than your enemy. If Heglan ever had any doubts about that, he only needed to recall the name of his ship to cast them aside.

Nadri's Retribution. It would bring retribution. It would make the elves pay in blood for his brother and all the others who had been treacherously killed by the feckless elgi. The Book of Grudges kept by each hold was filled with debts against the elves. The skryzan-harbark would be the vessels to settle those scores.

Lord Teranion had to remind himself that the smell of burning flesh was repugnant, that it should horrify him to the very core of his being. He couldn't exult in what he had unleashed. He had to remember who he was, what it meant to be *asur*. He couldn't allow centuries of civilisation and culture to slip away, shed like a worn-out skin.

The dragon becomes you. You become the dragon.

Teranion recited the old proverb to himself. How many times had he heard that warning spoken by Prince Imladrik? Somehow, no matter how often a dragon rider was told, the wisdom behind the words would fade away. The meaning would recede, all but forgotten until that moment, that instant of horror when an elf felt his identity being consumed by a force so primal it was older than the gods. The arrogance of most elves led them to believe dragons were their servants, that somehow these mighty beasts were beholden to them. The truth was that the best any asur could hope to inspire in a dragon was a sort of tolerant amusement, the indulgent affection bestowed upon a beloved pet by its owner. In all the long history of the elves, there had been only a few elves wise and powerful enough to truly be called Master of Dragons.

Away to the south and east, Teranion could see the forbidding heights of the peaks the dawi called 'the Vaults'. They stood as a stark reminder to him of the monumental task ahead of his people. To destroy the dawi, to bring the dwarfs to their knees, would be like breaking down the very mountains in which they dwelled. It was an effort of such enormity that it made the heart shudder, but was ever such an attempt more necessary? If the dawi weren't brought to heel, then the asur would never know peace again in their colonies. The shining promise of Elthin Arvan would be smothered in the smoke of war.

How, then, to cast down the mountains? One stone at a time! And Kazad Thar, the little hill fort crouching in the shadows of the Vaults, would be that first stone.

At Lord Teranion's urging, Khalamor dived down upon the dwarf hold. Before the lookouts in the crude stone towers spotted the drake, the dragon's fire was already rushing across their walls. Burning dwarfs leapt screaming from the ramparts as Khalamor rushed past. The dragon's long tail slashed out at the battlements, cracking against them like thunderbolts. Rock crumbled and masonry shattered as the tremors of the impact shivered through the fort.

The dwarf warriors still on the walls and towers trained their weapons on Khalamor as the drake circled around. Horns and gongs rang out as the alarm was sounded and terrified dwarfs fled towards the great gates of their hold. Crossbows and bolt throwers sent a barrage of steel-tipped missiles flashing at the dragon in a vain effort to drop it from the sky. Those few bolts that struck the drake lacked the strength and velocity to penetrate its thick scales. The roar that bellowed from Khalamor's jaws was almost scornful as it echoed down upon Kazad Thar.

Their attention fixed upon Khalamor, the dwarfs weren't able to bring their heavy weapons to bear when a second dragon swooped down on them from the opposite side of the hold. Again, dragon fire blasted the ramparts, spilling burning dwarfs down the slopes of their hill. Reptilian claws dug into the wall, tearing a section from its foundations and leaving a great gash in the side of the fort. As the drake flung the crumbling section of masonry earthwards, a burst of flame shot from its maw and into halls its attack had exposed.

Khalamor swept back around, hurling itself at the skarrenawi as they turned their efforts towards fighting Lord Heruen and Mornavere. Teranion felt a contemptuous pity for the miserable creatures in that instant before his steed's fire washed down upon them.

Teranion brought his dragon crashing down upon the gatehouse, pulverising an armoured dwarf warchief beneath the reptile's claws. Khalamor's jaws closed about the frame of a bolt thrower, ripping it from its mount and dragging the weapon and one of its crew away. Ballista and dwarf alike were hurled across the battlements by a turn of the dragon's head, smashing the crossbowmen assembling there. Dozens of dwarfs were crushed by the wreckage, their bodies flattened against the crenellations behind them. For good measure, Khalamor sent a gout of fire chasing after the survivors as Teranion urged the drake skywards.

Below, the walls of the dwarf hold were but so much rubble. Teranion could see Heruen upon Mornavere sweeping above the carnage. A blast of flame erupted from the dragon's jaws, engulfing a group of bearded warriors as they tried to pick themselves from the wreckage. Screams rang out as the dragon fire immolated them. They didn't have a chance, no more than a mouse in the jaws of a fox.

Such was the way of war, Teranion reminded himself. It wasn't all glory; it wasn't all honour. It was dirty and it was despicable. It drew out the most selfless sacrifice from those who fought, and then demanded of them the most remorseless brutality. For only in unrestrained brutality could there ever be an end to the war.

Khalamor dived down upon the burning hold. The dragon's claws ripped into the face of a great stone idol. For a moment, the reptile perched there, spitting fire into the tunnel-like openings to the lower deeps of the dwarf citadel. Teranion noted a score of bearded warriors rushing from behind his steed. At his urging, the dragon whipped its powerful tail around, sending the dwarfs sprawling with broken bones and ruptured organs.

It was all necessary, Teranion reminded himself. This horrific destruction was necessary. Lord Salendor had long urged that the war be extended to the skarrenawi. The hill dwarfs hadn't taken up arms against the asur the way their mountain cousins had, but they still gave the enemy material support. Iron ore, copper, timber, wool, grain – all these flowed from the skarrens to the karaks of the mountain kingdoms. If that flow of resources was stopped, the dawi would find it more difficult to prosecute their war against the asur.

As Teranion urged his dragon back into the sky, he reflected upon the other reason for this vicious attack. The mages in Tor Alessi had scryed some new weapon being developed by the dwarfs. A weapon that could irreversibly shift the balance of power in Elthin Arvan. This attack, therefore, wasn't simply to destroy the skarrens, but to draw out this mysterious threat.

Draw it out and destroy it.

Khalamor leapt from its stony perch, tearing the idol's head from its shoulders. As the dragon began to climb, it let the enormous head crash back to earth. Scores of stunned, charred dwarfs were crushed as the mass of stone slammed into the ground and rolled through their ruined halls.

It was all necessary, Teranion reminded himself again, to preserve the colonies and protect the Asur Empire. So long as he took no pleasure in killing, he could still claim to be civilised.

Nadri's Retribution slowly descended from the clouds, the other airships in Heglan's fleet following after their flagship. As the skryzan-harbark entered the open air, Heglan could see the countryside laid out before him. The vast swathes of lush green forest to the north, the dim wall of the Vaults to the south. Below were green fields and hill country, the lands that had been settled by the skarrenawi.

More than most of the dawi, Heglan could accept the peculiarity of disposition that had made the skarrenawi quit the vaults and tunnels of the Karaz Ankor for the open skies of the lowlands. There was a majesty of the surface world that most of his people were oblivious to, a wonder as profound and magnificent as anything to be found in the roots of the mountains.

Now, however, Heglan found little beauty or magnificence to appreciate. As he looked over the countryside he could see thick pillars of smoke billowing up from the hills. The farms and fields of the skarrenawi were burning. A great smouldering ruin was all that remained of Kazad Thar. The hill fort had been almost razed to the ground, its walls broken open, the halls within blasted with fire and clawed out. Sections of the hold had been scorched with such fiery fury that the walls were as smooth as glass. Other sections were ragged and ripped, scourged by monstrous talons. Columns and pillars, some as much as twenty feet around, lay toppled like the toys of a petulant child. The great gates, which had once stood so proudly, were naught but twisted iron and splinters now, hurled down from the heights to lay crumpled at the foot of Kazad Thar.

A hold of thousands of skarrenawi had been reduced to soot and cinders. Gazing upon it, Heglan felt the blood boiling in his veins. A new urgency wrapped itself around his thirst for revenge. Elgi had done this. Elgi and their thrice-damned drakk!

Heglan pressed his spyglass to his eye, staring down at the shattered husk of Kazad Thar. The charred corpses of dwarfs lay strewn all about the rubble. The dragons made no distinction between dawi or *rinn*, longbeard or child. Pools of bubbling metal were all that remained of the fort's armouries and treasure vaults, and mounds of soot and ash were all that remained of timber and wool. The drakk had taken pains to leave nothing of value behind. Even so, Heglan could see clutches of stunned survivors stumbling about the ruins, trying to excavate the escape tunnels and boltholes where more of their kin might yet remain.

The urge to order his air-fleet to descend and help the survivors gnawed at Heglan's heart. He'd been entrusted with command of the skryzan-harbark by King Brynnoth himself. Not one of Barak Varr's sea captains or thanes, not one of the stronghold's generals or warriors. The king had chosen

Heglan, an engineer, because he knew the machines, knew what they were capable of. Capability meant more than just what the skryzan-harbark *could* do but what they *should* do.

There was only one decision to make, despicable as it felt to Heglan. The survivors of Kazad Thar had to be left on their own. If the skryzan-harbark descended to help, then the airships themselves would be vulnerable to attack.

'Sky-master Heglan,' Nugdri called to the engineer. The hammer-footed captain pointed his hand towards the airship leading Heglan's fleet. There were seven skryzan-harbark, all the workshops of Barak Varr had been able to build since the conquest of Oeragor. Each was a marvel of engineering and invention, but Heglan considered the ship at the fleet's vanguard to be his finest work. It was a great black-hulled behemoth of the air, nearly twice the size of *Nadri's Retribution* and boasting more weaponry than any two airships.

King Snorri it had been named and it was under the command of the late prince's friend and confidant Drogor Zarrdum. Heglan and King Brynnoth had offered the thane whatever price he wanted for the secret of his fire. A flame that burned hotter than *zonzharr* and which could melt steel in the blink of an eye was worth the ransom of a king. Drogor had spurned gold and jewels, however. What he wanted was one of Heglan's airships to command. What he wanted was the chance to strike back against the elgi and avenge the honour of Snorri Halfhand.

Lanterns blinked from *King Snorri*'s aft. The code was a derivation of that employed by the engineers' guild, a system of flashes that conveyed information quickly and efficiently. As Heglan interpreted the message being sent from Drogor's ship, he felt rage boiling up inside him.

'They've spotted what's left of a skarrenawi army, warriors from Kazad Mingol caught rushing to help their kinsmen,' Heglan told Nugdri. 'The drakk burned them on the march. There's a two-mile scorch across the hills where King Orrik's army was reduced to cinders.' The engineer's expression darkened, his eyes taking on a fiery gleam. He raised the spyglass to his eye again and turned his gaze to the north-west. Dimly, he could see what the spotters on the *King Snorri* had seen. There was smoke rising in the direction of Kazad Mingol.

It seemed the outrages of the drakk weren't over. Well, this time the elgi and their wyrms would pay for lingering at the scene of their crimes. This time the dwarfs had the weaponry to hit back.

'Signal all ships,' Heglan bellowed, his voice so loud that he didn't need the bronze speaking horn to be heard by every dwarf of his crew. 'All speed to Kazad Mingol! All artillerists to their stations! We hit the drakk high and hard. We make the elgi know what it means to defile the hearths of the dawi!'

* * *

Two dragons were circling above the shattered walls of Kazad Mingol. They had broken through the outer fortifications, sending great jumbles of earth and stone rolling down the southern face of the hill the stronghold had been built upon. Some of the upper deeps had been exposed by the destruction, great galleries of granite lined with broken pillars and archways. Here and there the titanic statue of an ancestor god towered above the rubble, staring with stony malignance at the flying reptiles as they swooped down and spat flame upon the dwarfs below.

Two dragons: a great monster with scales of alabaster and silver, and a smaller beast with an almost bronzed colouring. The elven riders would have been lost to view upon their steeds if not for the banners fastened to their armoured backs, pennants of sapphire and emerald that snapped and crackled in the wind. Sometimes one of the elves would brandish his lance, shouting at his foes as his steed scattered them in its fury. Sometimes one of the dragons would snatch up a clawful of dwarfs and carry them high into the air before opening its talons and letting them hurtle to the ground far below.

For all their savagery, the dragons worked in concert with each other. When one wyrm dived in to attack, the other would circle overhead, watching for any threat to its companion. Any sign of a ballista being turned towards the marauding dragon, any hint of crossbowmen gathering together to loose a volley, and the watching drakk would snarl a warning to its fellow and then dive down to spit fire upon their foe.

Heglan at once appreciated the mistake the drakk and their riders had made. They'd confined their vigilance to the ground. Secure in their supposed dominance of the heavens, they didn't spare a glance at the sky above. That was an error the murdering wyrms and their elgi wouldn't live to regret.

The engineer barked a command to his signalman, sending prearranged orders to the other airships in his fleet. Three of the vessels would divert northwards and hold themselves in reserve, coming into the fight only if it looked like the dragons would escape. The rest, including *Nadri's Retribution* and *King Snorri*, would circle around and try to engage the drakk from the south-east. The fiery weapons Drogor had provided were vicious things. Like the elements they were named for, the flames wouldn't distinguish between friend and foe. Heglan wanted to strike from such a quarter that he could minimise the risk to Kazad Mingol and its inhabitants. It would be small consolation to them if they were cooked by dawi fire instead of an elgi drakk.

As the airships started their manoeuvres, the dragons noticed them. Heglan cursed when he saw the reptiles turn away from the burning halls of Kazad Mingol. If the drakk had risen to confront the skryzan-harbark, such a tactic would have played into the engineer's hands. The wyrms would have brought themselves within range of the dwarfs' bolt throwers. The pots of Tharzharr would have burned the beasts out of the sky. Instead, the pair of dragons were in full retreat, speeding away towards the north and the elf cities. Several of the airships loosed bolts at their foes, but the shafts fell well short of the mark, spinning downwards to shatter in fiery splendour against the earth.

'After them!' Heglan roared. With what they had seen at Kazad Thar and now witnessed above Kazad Mingol, there wasn't a dwarf in the fleet willing to countenance the escape of the dragons. The monsters and their riders would pay for the havoc they had wrought. They would answer for the grudges born from their rampage!

Nadri's Retribution and the other airships began to descend at an angle, trying to get into range of the dragons below. Smoke from the burning stronghold billowed across the airship's bow, drawing tears from Heglan's eyes.

'Drakk portside!' Nugdri cried out. The captain kept one hand locked about the wheel as he shook his fist at a vast, blue-scaled monster. The dragon was swooping down at the airships, flames billowing from its jaws. The wyrm had been hiding in the clouds, biding its time until the skryzan-harbark were below. In the distance, Heglan could see a fourth dragon diving at the three airships he'd sent to flank the first two wyrms.

It was an ambush! The elgi had been waiting for the skryzan-harbark, waiting for Heglan to come rushing to the defence of the kazads.

Even more infuriating to Heglan was the realisation that so long as the wyrms stayed above the airships, there was no way the dwarfs could bring their weapons to bear against them...

The grim fatalism that had hung so heavy about Rundin's mind on the frantic march from Kazad Kro became pride when he saw the skryzan-harbark appear above Kazad Mingol. Rumours of the wondrous airships of Barak Varr had reached even the halls of the skarrenawi, but he'd never imagined he'd see them for himself. The dawi had come! They had not abandoned their cousins, despite the arrogance of High King Skarnag.

Thinking of his king made Rundin's heart go cold. When the plight of the other hill forts was made known to Skarnag Grum, the High King had ordered almost his entire army to march with haste to the embattled strongholds. From a strategic sense, the king's decree was reckless. From a moral standpoint, it was despicable. Rundin had been there to see his king react to the news that Kazad Thar was being attacked by dragons. Skarnag was thrown into a panic, not from any concern over the misery of his subjects or the untold numbers of skarrenawi being slaughtered by the drakk. No, the miserable, gold-crazed despot was terrified that the dragons would strike his own stronghold and steal his treasure.

That was all Skarnag Grum cared about. That was why the High King of the skarrenawi finally deployed his army. Not to fight the elves and join the War of Vengeance. Not to protect the lands and lives of his subjects. Not to defend the honour of hearth and hold.

Such was the miserable creature to whom Rundin had sworn oaths of fealty, loyalty and service. He wondered if there could be any more shameful burdens a dwarf could take upon himself. He wondered if his ancestors could ever forgive him for the disgrace he had brought upon them when he bent his knee before Skarnag Grum.

'Seven of them,' Furgil cheered as he counted the airships. The ranger captain and a dozen of his followers had joined Rundin's warriors when they were only a few hours into their march. The rangers of Karaz-a-Karak made a welcome addition to Rundin's own pathfinders, helping them scout ahead of the main columns as they made their way towards Kazad Mingol. The plan had originally been to join forces with King Orrik's warriors and then move on to support King Kruk at Kazad Thar.

Instead, they had discovered Kazad Mingol burning. Rundin had been thankful for the caution that had him split his force into three separate columns. If the dragons attacked one, then at least there was a chance the other columns could engage the wyrms.

Now, of course, such caution looked foolish. Rundin couldn't imagine anything opposing the magnificent airships. He was especially impressed with the flying colossus that could only be the flagship. He felt a tingle of pride when he read the golden runes upon its prow. *King Snorri*.

'The elgi will rue this day,' Rundin spat. 'Their treachery has brought doom upon their beasts.'

Furgil nodded. 'Aye, and when the drakk lie burning, the dawi will march upon Tor Alessi. This time their walls will fall and the elgi will be driven into the sea.'

'The skarrenawi will be there,' Rundin vowed. 'After this, Skarnag Grum cannot keep us from joining the war.' Bitterness dripped from the warrior's mouth as he thought of his king's reticence, his all-consuming greed. The skarrens should have been united with their mountain brothers from the beginning.

One of Rundin's warriors thrust his axe skywards, shaking it at the clouds. 'Look! More drakk have come!'

The dwarfs watched as two more dragons swooped down from the sky, diving at the skryzan-harbark from above. Only a heartbeat before, the airships had seemed invincible. Now, with the dragons speeding down upon them, that illusion was broken. As the reptiles flew at the airships, bolt throwers loosed their missiles at the monsters. Massive spikes of wutroth and steel were hurled into the sky, arching upwards. However high the artillerists elevated their weapons, though, they were unable to strike at the dragons above them.

The beasts kept their distance, soaring away from the airships after spewing gouts of flame upon them. But the ships' air-bags had been coated to resist even dragon fire, each blast of the reptiles' incendiary breath breaking apart like a crashing wave against a cliff. If the airships were unable to harm the dragons, then it seemed the dragons were unable to harm the skryzan-harbark.

The brief stalemate was broken when one of the dragons suddenly streaked downwards, flashing directly between the massed airships. The crews were compelled to hold their fire out of fear of hitting their own comrades. Unopposed, the drakk swept towards the mammoth *King Snorri*. Its fiery breath splashed across the stern, protective runes flaring with blinding light as their magic thwarted the caustic blast. The dragon started to dart away, rising back into the sky. Then, before any upon the huge airship could react, the monster turned its ascent into a vicious dive.

Every precaution had been taken to guard the skryzan-harbark against the fiery breath of the dragons, but the same defences couldn't be made against their claws. Talons that could rend steel and crush granite lashed out, digging into the side of *King Snorri*'s air-bag. A stream of greyish gas wheezed from the jagged rent, striking the drakk as it flew past. Buffeted by the escaping gas, the dragon was forced downwards.

The instant the reptile dipped within the elevation of their weapons, the dwarf artillerists loosed a salvo into the beast. The dragon howled in agony as one of the bolts smashed into its side, exploding and throwing green fire across its body. Stricken, the monster wheeled away, but it was in range of the other airships now. Missile after missile sped towards it, each hit resulting in an explosion that cast devouring green flames across its scaly body. Flesh dripped from the beast in a fiery rain as the ghastly fire transformed it into a blazing effigy. Like a falling star, the flaming beast plummeted to earth.

So too did the wounded *King Snorri*. As more gas fled its air-bag, the ship sank through the sky. Two of the other airships followed it, striving to guard their comrades against the threat posed by the remaining dragons.

It wasn't the other dragons that brought destruction upon the immense skryzan-harbark. It was the blazing carcass of the dragon the dawi had already slain. As the beast hurtled towards the ground, it fell past *King Snorri*'s air-bag. Some of the burning flesh dripping from the reptile splashed across the side of the ship.

The next instant, it seemed to Rundin that the entire world shook. There was a roar like the bellow of a dying god, a sound of such booming malignance that the dwarf felt his teeth shiver in his jaw. A burst of light, more tremendous than the sun, seared his vision, leaving him blinking and cursing. Rubbing at his eyes, he forced himself to look skywards.

Through the red haze of his vision, Rundin could see the burning carcass of *King Snorri* slam against the ground. The wondrous ship was nothing but a charred frame that spilled across the plain. Its air-bag was utterly obliterated, transformed into a billowing cloud of fire that blossomed like the petals of some abominable flower. The petals caught the two airships that had tried to protect the stricken *King Snorri*. Green light burst across their decks as the blazing cloud engulfed them. In the blink of an eye, the vessels that had come to *King Snorri*'s aid were crashing downwards too. Their air-bags split as they struck, the gas within jetting forth, igniting as it came into contact with the fires all around it.

'Valaya's Mercy!' Furgil wailed. Rundin wondered if even an ancestor god was equal to the destruction they now witnessed.

The burning gas rolled across the plain like some hellish fog, blasting the land black. One of the columns of warriors from Kazad Kro was caught in the conflagration, reduced to ash and shadow in an instant. Then the fiery blast crashed against the walls of Kazad Mingol. Stone melted like wax; bronze gates and iron shutters evaporated. The dwarfs within King Orrik's halls didn't even have time to scream before the annihilating wave washed over them.

Tears were in Rundin's eyes. Tears for the slaughtered dwarfs of Kazad Mingol. Tears for the massacred warriors of Kazad Kro. Tears for the magnificent airships and the holocaust that had consumed them.

There would be a reckoning for this. Rundin swore by the rage of Grimnir himself that the elgi would be made to atone for this atrocity. 'By the blood of my ancestors, the tall-ears will pay!' he roared. Around him, the stunned warriors of Kazad Kro muttered similar oaths.

It was Furgil who drew their attention away from the burning earth and back to the sky. 'One of the drakk,' he shouted.

Indeed, one of the dragons, perhaps as stunned and confused by the explosion as the dwarfs, was soaring above the devastation. Its flight kept it from the three airships that had been away to the flank of Kazad Mingol, but not beyond the range of the last of *King Snorri*'s companions.

Nadri's Retribution, Rundin read in runes upon the ship's hull. The skryzan-harbark was away to the dragon's flank when her crew loosed its missiles at the wyrm. Staggered by the conflagration, shocked by the sudden annihilation of half their fleet, the aim of the artillerists wasn't precise. Only one of the bolts struck the drakk, a glancing shot that exploded against the beast's wing. Rundin saw the injured wyrm swing away, then start to slip from the sky as the green fire gnawed through its leathery pinion.

'They're leaving!' one of Rundin's warriors cried out. It was true. No doubt stunned and horrified by the destruction they had inadvertently wrought, the airships were in retreat, withdrawing back towards the south and the mountain holds. The elgi and their dragons were likewise gone, driven off by the ferocious display. Only the injured wyrm remained, slamming into the burning ground.

'Then let's finish the job they started,' Rundin snarled, hands tightening about the haft of his axe. Furgil gave his friend a grim nod. The faces of the skarrenawi warriors were no less fierce.

'*Khazuk!*' they cried as they hurried after Rundin onto the hellish plain. There was a dragon that needed killing.

The wyrm was a grisly sight when the dwarfs reached it. The fire from the airship's bolt had scorched its left wing clear to the bone, and shreds of leather and sinew flapped as the beast thrashed and flailed. Splashes of green flame continued to smoulder against its side, gnawing at its thick scales like acid. Sluggish reptilian blood oozed from dozens of wounds, sizzling as it dripped onto the blackened earth. The elgi rider slumped in his saddle, either stunned or slain by the drakk's travails.

Once the dragon would have been an awesome, even terrifying sight. Over sixty feet long from its fanged snout to the end of its bifurcated tail, clothed in dark scales as thick as armour plate, sword-like claws tipping each of its talons. It was the sort of beast that crawled through the oldest legends, dared the boldest heroes. It was a monster birthed in the epic sagas of the most ancient days.

Now it was neither awesome nor terrible to Rundin and the dwarfs who followed him. It was nothing but a vessel into which to pour their hate and fury, an enemy to be destroyed as the first small measure of the debt they would claim from the elves.

'*Khazuk!*' Rundin shouted as he charged across the smouldering ground. Soot covered his armour, the exposed flesh of his face and hands was blistered and raw, every breath he drew scorched his throat, but his hate would not be denied. This wyrm would die and it would die by his axe.

Even through its agony, the dragon sensed Rundin. It reared back, its jaws gaping wide. Rundin flung himself flat as the drakk exhaled a gout of fire. The stink of charred flesh, the screams of burning dwarfs smashed against his senses. Then he was up again, swinging his axe, flinging himself at the monster.

Rundin's axe slashed deep into the beast's jaw, ripping away a great flap of scaly flesh. Reeking reptilian blood gushed down his arms as he worried the blade against the dragon's jawbone. Wailing in pain, the drakk lurched back, throwing its head high and dragging the dwarf after it. Rundin found himself suspended in midair for a moment, then his blood-slick hands lost their grip on the axe embedded in the brute's jaw. Howling in protest, he crashed to the ground.

Rundin scrambled as the dragon brought one of its huge claws stamping down, trying to crush him beneath its foot as he might have crushed a bug. He could see the elf rider, aware now of his peril, trying to direct the monster. For an instant, the eyes of dwarf and elf locked. He knew well the look in the eyes of his foe, that expression of hate so immense it transcended the urge to live. It was the gaze of the warrior who doesn't expect to survive the battle but asks only that he send his enemy into the shadows first.

Before the elf could goad his dragon back to the attack, he was in turn attacked. A hand axe slammed into the rider's side, shearing through the singed ruin of his cloak and glancing from the charred mail beneath. Outrage flared across the elf's lean features. He swiped his hand through the air. In response, the dragon swung out with its claw, swatting the lone dwarf who had hurled the axe at its rider. The strike threw the dwarf through the air, sending him tumbling across the smouldering ground in a tangle of crushed armour and broken bone.

Something inside Rundin shattered as he watched the dwarf who had saved him die. It was the last gesture of friendship Furgil would ever make. There was nothing he could ever do to make amends to the ranger. All that was left was the honour of avenging his sacrifice.

Uttering a howl more bestial than the dragon's own roar, Rundin leapt at the monster. He caught hold of the reptile's horned snout, swinging himself onto the top of its muzzle. The dragon whipped its head back and forth, trying to throw the dwarf loose, but Rundin only tightened his hold, smashing one of his boots into the beast's nostril and digging his foot into the opening. Other skarrenawi were attacking the monster now, running at it from every quarter, hacking at it with their axes, bashing it with their hammers and mauls. A particularly telling strike against its burning side caused the dragon to forget the dwarf clinging to its snout for a moment. As it turned to deal with that enemy, Rundin seized the opportunity to reach down and rip his axe clear from its jaw.

The dragon reared back, hissing in pain as Rundin freed his weapon. While it was still shrieking, he brought the axe slashing across its eye. Muck spilled from the stricken orb, ribbons of jelly clinging to the head of Rundin's axe. He pulled back for another blow.

In that instant, Rundin felt his shoulder explode in pain. He looked over to see the elf standing on the dragon's snout, his sword piercing the dwarf's flesh. There was such a look of murderous fury in the elf's eyes as Rundin had never seen before. As he met that gaze, however, he noticed the blood streaming from the rider's left eye, the same eye as his dragon.

A cruel smile crept beneath Rundin's beard. Maybe he could use whatever magic bound elf to dragon. Viciously, he kicked out with his foot, feeling something snap inside the drakk's nose. The elf lurched back in sudden pain, his hand flying to his own nose.

An instant's distraction was all Rundin needed. As the elf reeled, he swung out with his axe, chopping through his enemy's sword arm. The mutilated elf screamed as his body hurtled earthwards. The empathic bond between him and the dragon caused the beast to rise up, shrieking anew in its agony.

Rundin held tight, watching as the elf was crushed as the dragon came slamming back down. The beast shrieked again as its master was pulverised beneath its weight. The dwarf dug his foot into the brute's nose again and glared into its eye.

'You'll join your master soon enough,' he snarled at the beast. Glancing down at Furgil's shattered body, Rundin released his hold on the dragon's horn. Both hands gripping his axe, the full weight and momentum of his armoured body behind the blow, he brought his blade slamming down between the dragon's eyes.

The dwarf was sent flying as the dragon bucked beneath him. He slammed onto his back a dozen yards away. He could feel the ground shudder as the dragon started after him. The reptile couldn't close the distance, however, before its great bulk slumped against the earth. Blood and brains gushed from the gash in its skull, oozing around the dwarf axe driven into its head.

Rundin glared at the dead monster. Only dimly did he hear the jubilant cheers of his surviving warriors. It was no mean feat to slay a dragon, much less one of the terrible beasts the elgi had brought from across the sea.

To Rundin, however, it was a hollow triumph. It didn't make up for all the dwarf lives he had seen extinguished this day. It didn't make up for Furgil. It would take much more blood – both elgi and drakk – to fill that emptiness.

If the War of Vengeance were to last another hundred years, Rundin didn't think he could ever spill enough blood to balance the scales.

TWO

THE LEGACY OF PRINCES

237TH YEAR OF THE REIGN OF CALEDOR II

What is the secret?

That question had long plagued Thoriol of Tor Caled. It had haunted his thoughts and dreams for years, feeding his feelings of inadequacy and self-doubt. He'd tried to escape – how he had tried. He'd embraced the anonymity of a simple archer, fled across the great ocean to the distant colonies of Elthin Arvan in a fruitless quest for peace.

Destiny was not so easily cheated. The blood of his line seemed to call out to its own. When he'd reached Tor Alessi, his father was already there. Almost alone among the asur nobility, Prince Imladrik had tried one last time to end the war between elves and dwarfs. Morgrim Bargrum and his army wouldn't be dissuaded. After a few days, the dwarfs laid siege to the city.

Unknown to his father, Thoriol had been one of the warriors defending the walls of Tor Alessi. When the dwarfs smashed their way through, Thoriol had been wounded trying to hold the breach. But for his father, he knew he would have died like so many others. It was Imladrik who'd commanded the best healers and mages in Tor Alessi to attend his son's injuries. Thoriol still felt the sting of shame at such preferential treatment.

Resentment had coloured his last meeting with his father. That memory stabbed deep into Thoriol's heart. While recovering from his wounds in the tower Imladrik had spoken with him. At the time, Thoriol had refused to listen, refused to understand. Imladrik's fears about Tor Caled, about the future of their line, had rung hollow to him. All of Imladrik's talk of duty and the obligation of noble heritage had seemed meaningless. Thoriol could see only the advantages and privilege of his highborn status, things he felt himself unworthy of.

Thoriol looked about the room in which he sat, studying the finery of the appointments. Gold and jewels glistened at him from every quarter, set into the delicate woodwork that edged each window and door, inlaid into the feet of silk-cushioned divans and satin-lined footstools. Decanters of wine rested atop a silver-armed bar cabinet, each fashioned from diamond, pearl and ruby. Lush rugs were spread across the floor, their intricate designs woven by master artisans in Eataine employing thread from lands beyond the Capes of Dusk and Dawn. Nowhere in all of Kor Evril was there such finery as that within the Dragontamer's halls.

'Dragontamer.' Thoriol whispered the word, letting it fall like bitter venom from his tongue. His ancestor had been the Dragontamer, mighty Caledor himself, who roused the dragons and forged the alliance between drake and asur. That talent had passed to Imladrik, the one the dragons called *kalamn-talaen:* the little lord. The one the asur had titled Master of Dragons.

How desperately his father had hoped the same affinity coursed through Thoriol's veins. The last time he had been in Kor Evril it had been to accompany Imladrik into the Dragonspine, to attend the awakening of one of the drakes. Thoriol had tried to commune with the dragon as she took wing, tried to employ the ancient dragonsong to establish harmony between their minds. For a brief moment he had dared to share his father's hopes. When the connection failed to manifest, when the dragon rejected his communion, Thoriol had seen the disappointment in his father's eyes. In that instant, he knew there was nothing he could ever do to live up to his legacy.

Now the Master of Dragons was gone, killed by Morgrim Bargrum, the same warlord whose army had besieged Tor Alessi and whose warriors had nearly slain Thoriol. For this feat, Thoriol understood that the dwarfs had bestowed upon Morgrim the title 'Elfdoom'.

The desire to avenge his father was a cold fire deep within Thoriol's heart, tempered only by the understanding that he had neither the skills nor resources to bring about such a reckoning. He was the heir of his father's house, but that was all. He was no great leader of armies. He was no dragon rider. Even the scholarly skills and political acuity of his mother, Yethanial, were beyond him.

The young asur prince looked longingly at the decanters of wine. There was solace there, the peace of forgetfulness and oblivion, if only for a few hours. He shook his head, well aware of how hollow such an escape was. The bottle offered only the illusion of peace, a dull delusion to take the edge from a painful reality. He would find no answers there, only a deeper kind of shame.

A sharp knock on the chamber door drew Thoriol's eyes away from the bar cabinet. A steward appointed in the livery of Tor Caled appeared as the door swung inwards. In a crisp, sharp voice, the servant announced the elf who followed behind him. 'Lord Caradryel of House Reveniol.'

The visitor was a tall, blond-haired highborn, his features handsome but edged with a determination that bespoke either great boldness or great pride. Over the past few years, Thoriol had come to appreciate that Caradryel possessed both qualities in abundance. The prince had taken service with Yethanial, acting as her agent among the great houses of Ulthuan. Sometimes his duties extended as high as the court of Caledor II or as low as the seclusion of the king's nephew.

'My Lord Thoriol,' Caradryel greeted the prince with a courtly bow. As he straightened, he passed a gloved hand across the breast of his tunic, smoothing the rumpled silk.

'My Lord Caradryel,' Thoriol replied with a modicum of civility. Despite the trust his mother had invested in the silver-tongued dignitary, Thoriol couldn't shake his dislike of the highborn. The two of them couldn't be more dissimilar. Thoriol found the privileges of nobility something of an embarrassment. Caradryel revelled in them, savouring each moment, relishing all the ornamental foolishness of courtly courtesy and noble tradition. They were like the moons – Thoriol dark and brooding, Caradryel bright and brilliant.

'It is always an honour to be received with such munificence in Kor Evril,' Caradryel said as the steward closed the door behind him.

Thoriol arched an eyebrow at his visitor's remark. 'I extend no more courtesy to you than I would any other guest.'

'I am certain of that,' Caradryel said. He plucked at the sleeve of his tunic. 'You know, I have an entire wardrobe devoted solely to these visits.'

'Indeed?' Thoriol sank down in one of the divans and waved his guest to seat himself. 'I was unaware that you anticipated your time here with such ardour.'

Caradryel glanced around for a moment, then took a chair that afforded him a view of both the prince and a window looking out upon the mountains. 'There is a distinct atmosphere about this place that never quite abandons a garment once it has been exposed to it.' He smiled and bowed his head in apology. 'It isn't every circumstance where it is appropriate to go about smelling like dragon.'

'You should discuss your wardrobe with my mother,' Thoriol suggested. 'I am sure she has other errands she could entrust you with.'

Caradryel maintained an attitude of affability, letting the slight slide off him with the practised indulgence of a diplomat. Instead, he simply smiled and raised a hand to his neck. 'I fear I am not here as an agent of Lady Yethanial,' he apologised. Gingerly, he lifted a gold necklace from beneath his tunic. Fastened to the chain was a ring of emerald and diamond. Thoriol's eyes fastened upon the ring, gazing on it for an instant in undisguised shock.

'This visit is at the request of King Caledor II,' Caradryel announced. He allowed Thoriol a moment to recover from his surprise at seeing the royal signet. 'I was summoned to the Phoenix Tower three days ago during a visit to Lothern. The king, your uncle, has expressed his desire that you should join his court.' Caradryel raised his eyes to the ceiling, as though trying to recall the king's words from memory, though Thoriol was certain they were as vibrant in the diplomat's mind as though set there in letters of fire. 'He feels that you have spent too much time pining away in the Dragonspine. He believes that your place is with him.'

A scowl of resentment crept onto Thoriol's face. 'Where he can better keep his eye on me,' he growled. For a long time there had been friction between the king and Imladrik, suspicions that the younger brother desired the crown of the elder. Yethanial believed such suspicions had been behind the king's command that Imladrik return to the colonies – an order that had ultimately resulted in his father's death.

Caradryel shook his head. 'I know you don't care for me. The reasons why don't matter. I know you believe me to be duplicitous and opportunistic. Perhaps such judgement isn't entirely baseless. I have become so accustomed to courtly intrigue that I suppose it has seeped into my very bones. Your father's strength was his ability to command. Your mother's lies in her knowledge of lore and history. My strength is bound up in empty flattery and courtly lies. I would ask that you accept that I'm quite talented in my arena.'

'I will concede that you are well versed in intrigue,' Thoriol said, wondering what point Caradryel was trying to make.

'Then perhaps you will also understand when I say to you that there are few asur who can deceive me,' Caradryel said. 'Something, some gesture or word, something said or unsaid, will always suggest their true motivations. I tell you now, Thoriol of Tor Caled, it isn't suspicion behind the king's request. If Caledor was suspicious of you, he wouldn't send me in secret to ask you to join him. He would do as he did when he sent your father away. He would come to Kor Evril with his full entourage. He wouldn't ask in secret, he would command it in public.'

'He is the king,' Thoriol said. 'He can command whatever he wishes. However misguided or foolish.'

Caradryel grimaced at those last words. They were imprudent, even in a place like Kor Evril. 'The wisdom or folly of the king is a subject perhaps best left undiscussed for the moment. You could even say that past mistakes have laid the seeds for future opportunity.'

Thoriol studied Caradryel's face, wondering if the glimmer he saw in the highborn's eyes was genuine or another pretence. 'He is unfit to be king.' They were words that seemed to roll like thunder through the room.

'*Today* he is our king,' Caradryel cautioned. He pointed to the band of white cloth bound about Thoriol's neck, a mark of mourning he still wore years after his father's death. 'When he appears in public, the king shines with splendour. I have seen him in private, however, and I tell you he wears white when he is alone. He mourns the death of his brother in his fashion. I think he questions the decisions that killed your father and the doubts that brought about those decisions.

'The king has no issue,' Caradryel stated. 'Your father's death, I think, has made Caledor think upon his own mortality. He worries about the legacy he will leave behind. He wonders about the future of the House of Tor Caled. *You* are that future. That is why the king asks you to join him.'

'He cared little enough when my father was alive,' Thoriol scoffed. 'What does he expect from me now? What does the king expect me to say that will ease his guilt?'

Caradryel rose from his chair. The diplomatic mask fell away and his face became stern. 'Say nothing,' he warned. 'Listen. Watch. You are being handed an opportunity that is so momentous it terrifies me. You will be ushered into the inner circle of the Phoenix King. You will be privy to his innermost councils, his most private discussions. Blood of Asuryan, can you not understand? He intends to groom you as his heir!'

Thoriol clenched his fist, enraged by the very suggestion. Again, it was the accident of blood not the reward of achievement that was dictating his life. 'I am my father's son,' he snarled.

'Then do what your father tried so hard to do,' Caradryel said. 'Use your influence with the king to save Ulthuan.'

'I have no influence with the king,' Thoriol said.

Caradryel's voice dropped into a warning whisper. 'Then bide your time until you do.'

Even in the quiet solitude of Valaya's temple, the brooding majesty of Karaz-a-Karak made itself felt. It was a climate, an atmosphere all to itself, a sense of ancient honour and monumental strength that fired the blood and made the heart of any dwarf swell with pride.

At the moment, Morgrim was too discomfited to think about pride and magnificence, even that of Karaz-a-Karak. He grimaced behind his beard as a sharp pain throbbed through his body. Inwardly he berated himself for such a display of weakness. He was the great hero of the Karaz Ankor, Morgrim Bargrum, *Elgidum,* Imladrikbane. The slaying of the elf prince was a feat that had fired the heart of all the dawi, from Kraka Drak in the far north to Karak Hirn in the west. Through the many years since the killing of Snorri Halfhand by the elf king, the dwarfs had sought retribution against their foe. They'd laid siege to Tor Alessi four times, razed Kor Vanaeth and Oeragor, sacked Athel Numiel, vanquished armies of elves, seized mounds of treasure. None of it had gone so much as an inch towards settling the grudgement levelled against the asur.

Killing Imladrik was different. The elves had killed the son of High King Gotrek. Now the dwarfs had killed the brother of Phoenix King Caledor II. It wasn't enough to satisfy the call for vengeance, but it was a start, an omen that inspired the whole of the Karaz Ankor. Even after the conflagration that had consumed Kazad Mingol and seen the destruction of Barak Varr's skryzan-harbark, the dawi were still emboldened by what Morgrim had done.

'The wound still pains you?'

Morgrim forced a smile onto his face and started to deny the hurt in his side. One look into the anxious features of High Priestess Elmendrin made him appreciate the futility of such a denial. He might be able to hide his pain from most but there was no fooling a priestess of Valaya.

'When there's a wind from the north, it starts to trouble me,' Morgrim confessed. A gruff laugh rumbled through his broad frame. 'Even in the depths of the Ungdrin Ankor, it troubles me when the wind comes down from the north. Filthy elf magic.'

Morgrim sat upon a stone bench, stripped to the waist so that the priestess might inspect the scar running across his ribs. If a hot poker had been pressed to his hide, he didn't think it could leave a more grisly brand. It was a strange fact that the blow which had inflicted the wound had failed to penetrate the heavy armour he had been wearing. Then again, the elves were a race saturated in magic and sorcery. It only followed that a great leader like Imladrik would have borne a blade with some sort of dire enchantment upon it.

More evidence, as though any were needed, of elven perfidy. Imladrik had been as close to the dawi as any of his breed. He'd known precisely what to say, what to do, to stir doubt in Morgrim's heart. Almost, the elf lord's words had made Morgrim's resolve falter, made him question the righteousness of their war. Duplicitous talk of renegade elgi being responsible for the strife between their peoples! Was it not the elf king himself who had commanded the humiliation of the ambassadors sent to Ulthuan? Was it some mythical druchii who slew Snorri and cut the hand from his corpse?

A low grunt of pain fell from Morgrim's lips as Elmendrin's fingers kneaded his scarred flesh, working the healing salve into his old wound.

'Relax, Ironbeard,' the priestess told him. 'You must rest and give yourself time to heal.'

Coming from anyone else, the advice would have made him laugh. Time to heal? Every hour he spent convalescing in the halls of Karaz-a-Karak was almost as torturous as the wound itself. Years he had spent trying to recover his strength. Years when he should have been out there, leading the dawi in battle. His name had become a rallying cry for the dwarfs, yet the warrior who bore it was left behind in the vaults of the High King. It was left to others to march against the elves. King Thagdor and King Varnuf, their warriors crashing against the walls of Tor Lithanel and Sith Rionnasc. The army of King Bagrik striving to pierce the defences of Athel Toralien. The great thane Brok Stonefist of Karak Azul leading his troops through forgotten branches of the Ungdrin Ankor to attack the enemy where they least expected battle.

Battle! The entire land gripped by war and Morgrim was condemned to watch from the sidelines. Until he was fit again, High King Gotrek had forbidden him to return to the field. A living hero was what the dwarfs needed right now, not yet another fallen lord to avenge. Much as he chafed under his king's command, Morgrim recognised the wisdom of it. Killing him would embolden the elgi at a time when they were being pressed on every front. The elves needed a victory to rally them, something to dull the pain of Imladrik's death and the loss of Oeragor.

Morgrim rested his hand on Elmendrin's shoulder. 'I think I understand now the frustration you must endure.'

'No,' she reproached him, 'you cannot begin to understand. You endure through the hope that your hurt will ease and you will return to the battle. You anticipate taking up your axe and again seeking retribution from the enemy.'

'I do,' Morgrim admitted. 'Azdrakghar hungers for the blood of the elgi and their beasts.' He clenched his fist as he remembered the sight of the elven dragon riders burning his army before the walls of Tor Alessi. The runes had awoken in that moment of rage. The years since had not diminished their ire. 'I would feed my axe well,' he vowed.

Elmendrin dipped her hand into the pot of salve, rubbing more of the ointment into his flesh. 'Such a path is denied to me. However deeply I would drink from the cup of vengeance, I cannot. Even the desire to do so does me shame.'

'You have more cause than most to bring grudge against the elgi,' Morgrim declared. 'Your brother Forek unspeakably disgraced by their king. My cousin Snorri...'

Morgrim felt the tremble that passed through Elmendrin's hand. At once he regretted his words. He knew how close she had been to Snorri. The prince had courted her incessantly, finding any excuse to visit the Temple of Valaya. Sometimes Morgrim had wondered if Snorri's obsession with Elmendrin had played a part in making him so impulsive and reckless. The prince had been brave, but it had been a foolish sort of bravery, the senseless bravado of pride and arrogance. Snorri had often confessed his intention to make Elmendrin his bride, but Morgrim was never sure how much of that desire stemmed from genuine love and how much was simply the knowledge that a priestess was forbidden even to the High King's son.

Looking at Elmendrin now, Morgrim appreciated that whatever Snorri's motivations, the priestess had cared for him. There was such a deep pain in her eyes that he had to hurriedly turn his head, unwilling to shame her by gazing on her sorrow.

'I did not turn from my vows when he was alive,' Elmendrin whispered, her voice so low that Morgrim was uncertain if he was even meant to hear her words. 'How can I break them now that he is gone? Revenge is something I must leave to others.'

Morgrim closed his hand around her own, squeezing her fingers. 'By Grungni, there will be a reckoning. If we must sail to Ulthuan and drag the elf king from his perfumed throne, he will pay for what has been done.'

The priestess drew her hand away. Some of the sadness left her eyes as she looked at the determination in Morgrim's face. 'You do his memory honour,' she said. 'You restored his hand to his tomb. Soon you will restore honour to his spirit.'

Morgrim felt his stomach broil at the mention of Snorri's hand. The hand had been disfigured long ago, bestowing on the prince the title of 'Halfhand'. When the elf king slew Snorri, the villain had contemptuously cut the hand from the corpse and taken it back to his palace as a trophy. Its return to the dwarfs had little to do with Morgrim. It had been restored by Imladrik, an act of contrition on his part for the crimes of his king. Alone of the elf lords, Imladrik had understood what Snorri's mutilation meant and had made the effort to undo such evil.

That was the warrior Morgrim had slain, the hero whose brand he now wore on his flesh.

Elmendrin set the lid back onto the pot of salve. She gathered up the remaining ointments and unguents she had previously applied and replaced them on the wutroth tray. The old poultice she'd removed from Morgrim's side was carefully folded into a tiny square of soiled cloth. Later it would be burned in ceremonial gratitude to Valaya.

'Do I get another of those?' Morgrim asked.

'Not for a few days. The salve must be allowed to work on its own,' Elmendrin answered. A worried look crept onto her face. 'You have visitors,' she said.

Morgrim slipped down from the bench, glancing around for his shirt. 'What?' he barked angrily before remembering where he was and to whom he spoke. He'd been in the hospice for several hours and Elmendrin had never left him. Any visitant would have been cooling his heels for a long time if he'd arrived before the priestess began her ministrations. 'Who is it?' he said, trying to make his voice more respectful than demanding.

'Morek Furrowbrow and... a steelbeard,' Elmendrin said. She didn't look at him as she took up the tray.

Morgrim was barely able to contain himself. Morek Furrowbrow! She'd kept a runelord waiting. Even a king didn't ask a runelord to wait. Before his blood could boil over completely, he considered the rest of her words. Morek and a steelbeard. There was only one steelbeard who would be accompanying the runelord. Anger drained from Morgrim in a surge of sympathy. Years had passed, but Elmendrin was still struggling to accept the dishonour inflicted upon her brother.

After Elmendrin withdrew, a temple acolyte conducted Morgrim's visitors to him. Morek looked thinner than the last time Morgrim had seen him, with more wrinkles at the corners of his eyes and a bit more silver in his hair. The runelord bore his staff, a tall rod of wutroth ringed in bands of iron and copper, and topped with a stone carving of an anvil. Little slivers of light crackled about it every time he brought the steel-tipped stem into contact with the floor.

The dwarf accompanying Morek wore full armour, his face locked inside an enclosed helm of steel. The mask of the helm was cast in the shape of an enraged ancestor, lips curled back in an eternal snarl. A great curtain of gold chains dripped from the mask, falling across the dwarf's armoured chest in a gleaming cascade. With each step he took, a shiver passed through the golden beard, playing upon the subtle differences of hue between each link. The beard had been fashioned from gold gifted by the kings of each hold in the Karaz Ankor, save the lost southern hold of Karak Zorn. Even the skarrenawi kings had sent gifts, all except their greedy 'High King' Skarnag Grum. It was a testament to the great insult the elves had inflicted that even the hill dwarfs felt offended by the disgrace suffered by the steelbeards.

Steelbeards. It was a name bestowed upon the dawi who had been abused in the elf king's court. The name referred not to the metal beards that fell from their masks, but to the grim axes they carried, axes that had been forged to shear elves even more closely than those who bore them had been shorn. The runes inscribed into those axes were the most abominable ever pressed into steel, murderous symbols of such potency that the runesmiths had refused to inscribe them for mere *grobi, urk* and drakk. It had taken the insult of elves to rouse such a fury in the runesmiths and even then there were many who had demurred about their use. Karaz-a-Karak's own High Runelord Ranuld Silverthumb had been one of those who warned against such weapons, proclaiming them to be a curse against not the elgi but the dawi themselves. Ranuld had withdrawn from public view shortly after. Even his apprentice Morek hadn't seen him in over a year.

Morek bowed as he came towards Morgrim. The steelbeard made no such concession. By command of High King Gotrek, the steelbeards were no longer under the authority of anyone and need acknowledge neither king nor thane. That he was here at all was a greater show of respect to Morgrim than the most abject genuflection.

'Forgive my absence, lord,' Morek said. 'I have been away.'

'Looking for more "old magic" for your master?' Morgrim asked. The question put him in mind of that chance meeting with Ranuld deep in the ruins of Karak Krum. The runelord had been searching for what he called 'old magic' at the time. Perhaps distracted by his hunt, Ranuld had muttered a prophecy to Morgrim and Snorri about a future king who would slay the dragon. That prophecy had played no small part in leading Snorri to his death. Many times Morgrim had wondered if he could dare to level a grudge against the runelord for that.

Morek ran his hand along the side of his staff. 'I have been visiting the runelords of the *Burudin* on behalf of my master. After the murder of Agrin Fireheart, the kings are loath to allow the Burudin to stray far from their holds.' An amused cough rumbled through the dwarf. 'Less revered runesmiths like myself are much more expendable.'

'Not to me,' Morgrim said. 'You stood by me at the Siege of Tor Alessi and the Cleansing of Oeragor. I do not forget such loyalty.'

'It is a curious reward you offer in return,' Morek mused, his thumb rubbing one of the iron bands circling his staff. 'Indeed, I am uncertain if it is honour or insult.'

Morgrim looked over at the steelbeard. 'You have explained fully what I want and why?' The steelbeard nodded by way of answer. They were dwarfs of few words, but when they did speak, even kings listened.

'Forek has explained,' the runelord said. 'Most eloquently,' he added with a touch of sadness. Before his humiliation, Forek Grimbok had been the High King's reckoner, his most skilled diplomat and ambassador. 'What I do not know is if what you ask is wisdom or folly.'

Morgrim slapped his hand against his scarred side. 'It's a good blade. Every morning when I wake up, the first thing I remember is how sharp its bite is.'

'Elgi sorcery,' Morek cautioned. 'They are a fearsome people with peculiar ideas about magic and its use. The wise course is to shun their enchantments.' He shook his head. 'No, my lord, if you wish my advice, I tell you to cast the shards into the deepest part of the Black Water and forget it.'

'Is what I ask impossible, then?' Morgrim asked.

Morek smiled and tapped his runestaff on the floor, setting little wisps of light crackling across the metal bands. 'You'll not twist my beard by playing against my pride. Reforging an elven blade is something beyond any swordsmith, but not impossible for a runesmith.' He nodded towards Forek. 'You've even gone so far as to impress the only dawi in the whole of the Karaz Ankor who knows elgi letters well enough to help in the work. Why do you really want this? You say as a symbol of your victory over the elgi, but you yourself are already a symbol of that victory.'

'And that is the problem,' Morgrim said. 'I have become too important as a symbol. High King Gotrek is reluctant to send me into battle now. He worries what my death would do to the war.' He shook his fists in frustration. 'I can't go on like this, locked away like some treasure too precious to spend. Our people are out there fighting! I need to be with them.'

'You think the captured blade of an elgi lord will replace you in the hearts of the dawi? You are Elgidum, the great hope of our people. No enemy's sword will fire their spirits as you have,' Morek reproved him.

'It isn't our people I need to inspire,' Morgrim confessed. He looked over at Forek. 'Our people have enough cause to fight. It is the High King whose spirit I need to inspire.'

Morek frowned. 'The High King has greater cause for grudgement than any of us. He still wears beads of onyx in his beard and stains his cheeks with ash in mourning. Entire vaults in the royal treasury have been emptied to pay for the armies he has set against the elgi.'

'The king fights from sorrow and revenge,' Morgrim said. 'That would be enough for you or I or Forek, but he needs more than that. He fears for the kingdom, fears for the future of the dawi. He needs to fight with hope in a victory worth winning.'

'An elf sword will do all that?' Morek scoffed.

'No,' Morgrim said. 'But it will remind him of what I have overcome. *Who* I have overcome. It will remind him of the warrior who stays sheathed in his halls.'

'Then where will he find this hope you say he needs?' the runelord wondered.

Morgrim's eyes became like chips of granite. 'Let the king send me back into battle, and the victories I bring him will give him all the hope he needs. Reforge Bitter-Blade for me. Let me carry the elf sword to Gotrek's throne and show him that I have already vanquished the best the elgi have to send against us.'

Lord Ilendril scowled as he cast his gaze across the bleak shoreline of sand and scrub. Away across the western horizon, the opposite shore rose, much nearer than the elf lord found comfortable. The Iron Gulf wasn't exactly friendly waters for an elven galley like the *Cormorant*. When he looked at the ship's captain from the corner of his eye, he could see the trepidation there. The captain knew better than to voice such concerns to a highborn like Ilendril, of course. It made things so much easier when a peasant knew his place. It wasn't the captain's business to wonder if the object of this voyage was worth the dangers it entailed. It was simply his duty to obey.

Dismissing the captain's worries from his thoughts, Ilendril studied the barren shore, searching for whatever markers might yet remain of Feillas, the tiny port that had once been the gateway to the city of Oeragor. Even before the fall of Oeragor, Feillas had been destroyed by dwarf warships, annihilated a few years after the Phoenix King struck down a dwarfish prince in single combat.

'There is a ship to starboard.' The words were but a whisper, but they struck Ilendril like a lash. He spun around, forgetting for an instant the detached poise demanded of a highborn. There was no one near him on the deck, no one close enough to whisper in his ear. That left only one possibility. Regaining his composure, he walked across the deck to where a lone elf leaned against the starboard rail.

'Ashelir,' the elf lord said, studying the cloaked figure. Not for the first time Ilendril appreciated why the crew shunned their passenger. The taint of Nagarythe was something unmistakable, a coldness of bearing, a practised furtiveness that coloured the elf's every motion. The steel blades that hung from his broad belt had been forged in Nagarythe. His crescent-headed arrows had been fletched with feathers from Nagarythe's fisher-hawks. His grey cloak, seeming to shift between hues with each breath, was wrapped in the magics of Nagarythe. Nagarythe, the broken land that had spawned Malekith, the Witch King of Naggaroth.

There were few among the asur who tolerated the elves of Nagarythe, however loudly they declared their loyalty. For most, there was little difference between the shadow warriors and the druchii they fought. Ilendril, however, was more pragmatic. If there was one thing he could appreciate, it was the hate one could bear for his own people. In a way, it made Ashelir and himself kindred souls.

'A dwarf ship,' Ashelir said, his eyes still staring out across the sea. There was more than a little magic about the shadow warrior. He couldn't work any mighty spells like the mages of Saphery, but he had abilities that strayed down arcane paths. The lineage of his bloodline strayed to sorcery – at least before the Sundering.

Blood will call to blood. It was an old parable, but one that Ilendril had invested a great deal of faith in.

'They will find us?' Ilendril asked.

Ashelir kept his face towards the horizon. 'If we stay this course.'

'We stay the course,' Ilendril declared. He glanced back at the captain. It would be some minutes before the lookouts spotted the enemy ship. He could pass along Ashelir's warning now, but to do so might cause the crew to decide that flight was the prudent course. Ilendril wouldn't allow their timidity to waste his time and threaten his venture.

'I'll rouse Vithrein from his meditation,' Ilendril said. 'Keep your eyes on the enemy. Warn the captain just before his own spotters catch sight of it.' It was an effort to keep his pace unhurried as he left Ashelir and made his way below deck. It took only a few moments to reach Vithrein's cabin and rouse him from his trance. Ilendril only needed a single word to explain the situation to the other elf.

'Dwarfs.'

The word caused Vithrein's lean, pale features to slip into a grimace. An ugly light shone in the depths of his jade-green eyes. One swift motion brought him to the gem-crusted box lying upon its silken pillow. A gesture of his hand and the lid of the box spiralled open like the petals of a flower. Vithrein reached down and removed a long spur of what looked like charred bone. Ilendril knew the object was a piece of horn. More than that, he knew what manner of creature it belonged to.

As the two elves climbed back on deck, the frightened shouts of the crew struck their ears. The dwarf warship was a dark speck on the horizon. Ilendril felt his heart jump when he saw plumes of black smoke belch from the enemy ship. The dwarfs had spotted the *Cormorant* and were shovelling fuel into their engines.

'My lord, the dwarfs have seen us!' The *Cormorant*'s captain had the dignity not to outright beg as he called to Ilendril, but the highborn caught the note of entreaty in the peasant's voice.

'We cannot outrun them,' Ilendril stated. 'The open sea is behind us. Ahead of us is naught but the neck of a bottle with Barak Varr at the end.' He turned towards the crew as they hurried to tack on more sail and cast stowage over the side. 'By the grace of Mathlann, we are not fated to die in a mud-digger's puddle. I did not bring you so far just so a bearded runt could brag about sinking us in some brewhall burrow. Behold the might of Tor Javril!'

As he spoke, Ilendril made a furtive wave of his hand to Vithrein. The mage sat down upon the rolling deck and brought the horn to his lips. No sound rose from the blackened spur – at least no sound that could be heard by elven ears. The melody Vithrein played was meant for something else.

Long minutes passed. With each breath the dwarf warship came steaming closer. The iron plating of its hull was distinct now, as were the grotesque battlemasks bolted to its sides. Ballistae mounted in the fore and aftcastles could be seen rotating on their mounts, being brought to bear upon the elf ship. Bearded warriors raised their axes and howled their savage war-cries.

The *Cormorant*'s captain came down from the foredeck, hurrying to Ilendril's side. In his alarm, he almost forgot decorum and reached out for the highborn. At the last instant, he pulled back, remembering the insult his common fingers would inflict upon noble flesh. 'My lord, we cannot fight them,' he reported, as though Ilendril were ignorant of so obvious a fact.

'We won't have to,' Ilendril said. Before the captain could question his meaning, the *Cormorant* was rocked by a series of unexpectedly savage waves. Sailors began shouting in shock, pointing at the water. Ilendril followed the captain to the side. Together they watched as a massive shape undulated through the waves, keeping itself just beneath the surface. Great rolls of azure and white, slithering through the water like some vast serpent. Ilendril imagined the captain would be upset if he knew the beast had been following them ever since they'd left port in Ulthuan. Of course, watching the thing speed straight towards the dwarf warship made such deception perfectly justified.

The dwarf ship was still beyond the range of its ballistae when the merwyrm rose from the depths, exploding from the waves with the violence of a water spout. In its first rush, the enormous sea serpent crumpled the vessel's portside plating and smashed its forecastle bolt thrower into the sea. Dwarf warriors rushed at it with axe and hammer, but the great serpent twisted away. Rearing back, the merwyrm spilled itself across the deck, smashing dozens of dwarfs beneath its coils. The enormous head, more like that of a dragon than the bronze effigy mounted to the ship's prow, snapped its jaws around the bolt thrower in the aftcastle, ripping it free in a shower of splinters and twisted metal.

Ilendril fought to remain composed as he watched the mighty merwyrm wreak destruction upon the dwarfs. Sometimes he glanced over at Vithrein blowing upon the horn, directing the mammoth reptile with his arcane melody. The focus and direction of an asur mind married to the elemental might of a sea serpent! If they weren't such contemptible barbarians, he might even find it possible to feel pity for the dwarfs.

A primordial cry, half howl and half hiss, erupted from the merwyrm's maw as its flippers swatted armoured dwarfs into the sea. The dwarfs sank like anchors as they struck the waves. Even as they vanished from sight, the serpent looped another coil of its sinuous body around the vessel. Tightening its hold, the merwyrm began to crush the stout warship.

The elf lord smiled. Vithrein's magic had survived its first test but it would need to do much more before Ilendril was satisfied.

Much more indeed.

THREE

ELVEN BLADES

239TH YEAR OF THE REIGN OF CALEDOR II

She could almost see the hate boiling from her companions, like waves of heat rising from the desert. Every motion, every gesture, every breath was invested with the deepest loathing. It was a testament to how much they needed her that she was still alive. Once that need was gone, the only question would be which of them would strike first. Would it be Ashniel or Malchior? Which of her old acolytes was bold enough?

Drutheira gazed into the flames of the fire Malchior had kindled. The smoke rising from the fire had a bluish tinge, a little something extra for the benefit of the savages native to these forsaken wilds. Over the years enough of the skin-clad primitives had died by sorcery that the rest had learned to give the druchii a wide berth. The blue cast to the smoke would remind them that the sorcerers they feared were yet abroad in these lands.

Wastes, that was what they were: miserable, sun-bleached desolation as far as the eye could see. Even the chill frontiers of Naggaroth were preferable to this brown ruin of dead sand and leafless scrub. That there was life here at all was something Drutheira still found astonishing. Yet there was game enough to be had, fruit of a sort that could be harvested from the thorny scrub and scraggly trees. Somehow, even the packs of tribal humans managed to survive, persisting in lands neither dwarf nor goblin saw fit to inhabit.

'Do you wonder how the war fares?' Malchior asked. The sorcerer sat across from Drutheira, roasting some small creature over the flames. She couldn't be certain if it was a lizard or a rat. She was more worried that her old acolyte was eavesdropping on her thoughts again. It was a bad habit he'd developed as soon as he figured out her powers were too weak to guard against his spying.

'It is of small consequence to us,' Drutheira said. 'Whether it is the asur or the dawi who prevail, the victor will hardly welcome us.'

'Perhaps we should try to contact Naggarond again?' Ashniel's voice carried an almost pathetic hopefulness. Drutheira could almost pity her, if any such emotion were still possible for a druchii. There had been a time when she'd considered Ashniel the more dangerous of her acolytes, more calculating and subtle than Malchior. She'd even been more capable in the black arts, possessing a greater affinity for the dark Wind of Dhar.

'I think our king has heard all he wants from us,' Malchior told Ashniel. His words weren't merely blunt; they were deliberately cruel, punctuated by a sneer and a mocking laugh. He looked over at Drutheira. 'Wouldn't you agree?'

'There is no room for weakness in Naggaroth,' Drutheira declared. 'Even if we were able to appeal to Malekith for help, the act itself would diminish us. Rivals and enemies would see us as easy prey. No, if we are to return, we must do so on our own.'

Malchior tore one of the charred legs from his meal and took an experimental bite of it. He frowned and thrust the carcass back into the fire. 'So you have been saying. We've spent a long time waiting for you to recover your powers and show us the way. It would pain me to think all that time and effort had been wasted.'

Drutheira clamped down on the thoughts that formed in her mind. She'd allowed Malchior to pick too many secrets from her brain already. He couldn't know the truth about her condition. Her link to Bloodfang had been crude and hasty, magic of necessity rather than caution. At the time she'd been arrogant enough to believe she was capable of wielding such power. Only now did she understand the true price she'd paid for her presumption. Alive, she'd poked and prodded Bloodfang's mind, enslaving the beast to her will. That connection hadn't been severed when the dragon was struck down by the asur mage Liandra and her drake. Even now she couldn't break the connection. She could feel Bloodfang lying at the bottom of the sea, its scales rotting away, fish swimming between its bones, worms nibbling away at its flesh. The weight of the sea was constantly pressing down on her, making her head pound with sympathetic pressure. Her magic was yet bound to the dragon's carcass, drawn out of her as though by some blood-sucking ghost.

As she watched Malchior, Drutheira saw the sudden change that came into his eyes. His lips spread in a malignant smile. At once, she knew he'd slipped through her defences and discovered the truth she'd tried to hold from him. 'You disappoint me,' he declared. 'It seems we will have to find a way back without you.'

Drutheira drew the wisps of aethyr that would still respond to her will into a hurried conjuration, an arcane barrier between herself and the sorcerer. She remembered how she'd destroyed the dwarf fire-wizard those long years ago, the mighty death magic she had evoked to bring the creature to ruin. Now it was an ordeal to summon even a fraction of such power.

Malchior's attack took the shape of a jagged spear, a thing of writhing shadows and moaning shades. It flashed from his outstretched hand, shrieking across the camp at her. The hasty ward she'd erected to defend herself crackled, flaring from unseen force to a sparking shell of purple light. The shell fractured as the spear stabbed into it, then crumbled apart as the sorcerer threw more energy into his magic. Drutheira cried out as the arcane shadow seared across her arm. She could feel the flesh wither where it brushed past her, sense the vitality ebbing away as the sorcery sucked some of her life essence out of her.

The sorcerer laughed and began to draw energy into himself for another conjuration. Drutheira knew she couldn't resist another attack. Malchior's next assault wouldn't merely wound her, it would leave her crippled and helpless. She knew him better than to expect a swift, clean death. No, he'd take his time, savouring every scream and every cut.

In desperation, Drutheira looked to Ashniel, hoping that her acolyte would intervene. It wasn't that the sorceress had any more love for her than Malchior, but she had to know what would happen if he prevailed. Bitter rivals, the two acolytes tolerated one another only because they needed each other. Once Drutheira was gone, it was doubtful Malchior would have further use for Ashniel.

Ashniel remained sitting at the edge of the camp. Incredibly, it seemed she was oblivious to the arcane duel being fought only a few yards away. There was a vapid look in her eyes, a lax cast to her features. Like some idiot thing, she just sat there, not even watching what was happening around her.

Then Ashniel's body slumped forwards, exposing the grey-fletched arrow that had pierced her from behind. Sight of that arrow brought a surge of horror rushing through Drutheira's heart. She knew that kind of arrow, had seen them strike down minions and companions many time before. But that had been in lost Nagarythe. To see the same kind of arrow here, in the unmapped wastes of Elthin Arvan, was impossible.

Her distraction made her defence even weaker. The sorcerous shell Drutheira had cast about her body exploded in a burst of shadow as Malchior's magic slammed into it. She was hurled backwards, every inch of her skin feeling as though it had been scalded by a burning coldness. Hoarfrost coated her robe, dripped from her hair, clung to her flesh. It was an agony just to open her lips and try to utter a protective incantation.

Malchior scowled at her. 'I lived in terror of you, once. Now you will live in terror of me. For a time.' He glanced aside abruptly, belatedly noticing the prostrate form of Ashniel and the arrow sticking in her back. It was the sorcerer's turn to attempt a hasty protective ward. His hand had just started the first gesture of his evocation when an arrow whistled out from the barren wastes and transfixed his head. Malchior swayed for a moment as the magic he'd drawn into his body gradually bled away. Then he crashed face first into the fire, crushing his last meal beneath him.

Drutheira took no comfort in her unexpected reprieve. The effects of Malchior's spell were fading away now that he was dead, but they weren't dispersing fast enough. She could barely breathe, much less manage any sort of conjuration. She could only look on helplessly as a shape rose from among the sandy dunes. At first it seemed like part of the dune had become animate and was gliding towards her. With each step a bit more of the illusion was cast aside. The walking drift of sand took on a humanoid outline, then resolved itself into the tall, lean shape of an elf. His enchanted cloak darkened, losing its sandy appearance to become a thing of dull grey, much like the fletching of the arrows in the quiver at the elf's side.

'Yours must have been a long hunt, shadow-crawler,' Drutheira spat at the approaching elf. There was no mistaking the taint that clung to this apparition, the stigma of those of Nagarythe who shunned their rightful king, Malekith, to follow the line of pretenders led by the first Caledor.

'I should have trailed you into the crypts of the Pale Queen,' the shadow declared. Each word was laced with a bitterness that struck Drutheira like a lash. 'Glory to Khaine that my hunt did not demand I go that far.' Grimly, the elf lifted his hand to his face and pulled down the fold of cloth that covered his visage.

Drutheira's eyes went wide with horror as she gazed on that countenance. It was a face that had haunted her darkest nightmares for centuries. 'Ashelir,' she gasped.

A sepulchral laugh escaped the shadow's lips. 'I am pleased you remember me. I had thought you'd forgotten the family you abandoned and left to die when you chased after the usurper and supported his cause.'

The druchii closed her eyes, unable to meet the gaze of her enemy. Shame, something she thought had been burned out of her soul long ago, raced through her veins. 'Now my son comes to kill me,' she whispered. Truly the gods had a cruel sense of humour that she should come to such a finish so far away from the lands that had been their home.

Ashelir drew one of the knives from his belt. For an instant, it seemed he would pounce upon her and sink the blade deep into her heart. Instead, the hate in his eyes subsided. 'I am here for more than revenge,' he declared. 'I am here on behest of my patron. Here to serve the Phoenix Crown and the true king of Ulthuan.' He cut a length of silvery rope from the coil that hung from the lining of his cloak. Sheathing his knife, he tested the strength of the cord.

'I have come for you,' Ashelir said. 'To bring you back to my patron. Alive.'

Drutheira didn't resist as her son bound her hands together. 'It must disappoint you, to have looked forward to this day and be cheated of it because your master holds you back.' She cried out in pain as Ashelir drew the cord tight.

'There will be a great hole inside me when you are gone, witch,' Ashelir snarled. 'Hate and revenge have been my strength for so long, I don't know what I will be without them.'

'Then we have much in common,' Drutheira said.

Ashelir reached to his knife again, caressing its ivory handle. 'The only thing we have in common is the blade that will end your life. Make no mistake, witch, when my patron is finished with you, then you are mine.'

'Khaine himself won't stay my hand then.'

'Riposte! Riposte!'

Thoriol darted to the side as the Chracian came at him again. The warrior's blade flashed towards him, glancing across his shoulder as he swung away from his adversary's strike. Sparks flashed from his pauldron, little flecks of crimson enamel scraped away by the kiss of steel. The prince slashed his own blade at the warrior's back, frowning when his foe twisted away at the last second.

'Feint to your right! The right!'

Each time a new direction was barked at him, Thoriol felt his face turn red. He knew he was indifferent when it came to the sword, but he didn't need to be reminded of it. Not from that quarter, anyway. When his instructors told him he was doing something wrong, it was to make him better. When his uncle did it, it was to emphasise his failings.

When Envaldein came around again, Thoriol deliberately overstepped, thrusting at the White Lion with enough carelessness that the Chracian was quick to jab at his ribs. Thoriol felt the teakwood button fixed to the tip of his opponent's sword slap against his armour.

King Caledor II rose from his golden throne, his emerald robes swirling about his tall frame as he hastened down the dais and across the tiled floor. For a moment, Thoriol saw a touch of alarm on the royal visage, but it was quickly subdued by an expression of disappointment.

The king ignored Envaldein as he stepped past the warrior. After scoring his hit against Thoriol, the White Lion had bowed and laid his sword on the floor. He kept his eyes averted as the king swept past him. The Chracian was an astonishingly skilled swordsman – among the best in all the ten kingdoms – but his king extended to him the same degree of courtesy he might show a dog. It was a display that never failed to disgust Thoriol no matter how often he saw it.

'That was an underwhelming exhibition,' Caledor sighed. 'If you had been crossing swords with a druchii, you'd be dead now.' The king reached out, pulling the button from the point of Thoriol's sword. He frowned as he looked at the blade. 'Hardly an elegant weapon. Your position entitles you to a much finer blade. A sword of ithilmar, keen as the beak of a phoenix and light as an eagle's feather.'

Thoriol bowed his head. 'A gracious offer, my liege.'

Caledor sighed. 'An offer you have already refused.' He tossed the teakwood button on the floor. A file of servants stood along the far side of the room, arrayed to attend their king. One of them hurried out from the line, snatching up the button while it was still rolling and swiftly disposing of it.

'Such ingratitude is unseemly.' The sharp retort came from a thin, pale elf wearing heavy robes of scarlet trimmed in gold. The expression of resentment on the asur's face was undisguised. There was no love between Thoriol and Hulviar, the king's seneschal. The slightest hint of royal disapproval and the mask of polite propriety would slip away and expose the hostility lurking beneath. It was easy enough to appreciate that hostility: before Thoriol joined the king's court, Hulviar had been his closest advisor. Caledor's new interest in his nephew had created competition for the royal ear.

'I am not ungrateful,' Thoriol corrected Hulviar. He held the sword upright, displaying the polished steel of the blade, the intricate lettering that flowed down the edge, the delicate carving of the hilt and guard, the metal dragon with folded wings that served as the pommel. It was many years since he'd been presented with this sword. He had abandoned it once, cast it aside on the slopes of the Dragonspine. He had found it again when going through his father's effects in Tor Alessi.

Thoriol stiffened his back and returned Hulviar's hostile gaze. 'This sword is important to me,' he said. 'No other blade could ever take its place. If I will ever become the warrior my liege wishes me to become, it must be with this blade and no other.'

'And this isn't the arrogance of youthful pride?' Hulviar sneered. Too late the seneschal recognised the trap he'd walked into. His sneer withered when he saw Thoriol turn towards the king.

'This is the sword given to me by my father,' Thoriol told Caledor.

The king was silent for a moment, his expression inscrutable even to Hulviar. At length, Caledor gave the slightest of nods. 'Prove worthy of it,' he said. 'You have a great legacy to live up to. The House of Tor Caled is the line of kings and heroes. There is none greater.'

The veil of propriety was back when Hulviar addressed his king. 'My liege, forgive me, but we have received new reports from the colonies.'

Caledor gestured to the kneeling Envaldein, dismissing the warrior. Slowly, the king retraced his steps to his throne. As he seated himself, he stared out of the arched window that looked eastwards. 'It is always the colonies,' he said. His look was sharp when Hulviar approached the throne. 'And it is always bad news from the colonies. What are these fools doing to let a rabble of mud-dwelling savages vex them so?'

'The colonial council in Tor Alessi reports that the dwarfs have assaulted Athel Toralien again. Dwarf ships also bombarded the waterfront in Sith Remora, the first time they have dared to attack the port. There are also rumours–'

'I care nothing for rumours!' Caledor snapped, his fist crashing against the jewelled arm of his throne. 'It is clear that the council is too incompetent to conduct this war. They have squandered every consideration shown to them. They hide behind their walls and leave these savages free to range where they will.'

'I was there at the Fourth Siege of Tor Alessi,' Thoriol reminded him. 'The dawi are a powerful enemy. One that is not easily challenged.'

Hulviar shook his head. 'They do not seem to challenge the dwarfs at all,' he said. 'They have adopted a defensive mindset. They lose a few dragons to some mud-skulker trickery and they retreat. They don't send word of victories. Instead they plead for more. More warriors. More weapons. More dragons.'

'If they ask for more, perhaps they need it,' Thoriol suggested.

'We have nothing to spare for the colonies,' Hulviar said. 'Everything is committed to the campaign against Naggaroth. Malekith is in retreat – his disciples will not be able to resist much longer.'

'How long can our colonies resist?' Thoriol wondered.

'As long as they are expected to,' Hulviar said. 'Once the druchii problem is resolved, the whole might of Ulthuan can be set against the dwarfs.'

Thoriol directed a cold smile at the seneschal. 'Then you make a good case for them to remain on the defensive. To wait out the dwarfs...'

'We will not wait to punish those animals,' Caledor snarled. 'In their burrows they celebrate the murder of my brother. I will not allow that disgrace to continue. The dwarfs will learn what it means to shed the blood of a prince of Tor Caled.'

Hulviar glanced anxiously at the throne. 'You will draw troops away from the Naggaroth beachhead?'

Caledor nodded. 'We have Malekith in retreat. We can spare the warriors to teach these mud-diggers a lesson.' The king leaned back in his seat, his expression growing pensive. 'More important than fresh troops, however, is fresh leadership. The council has proven their ineffectiveness at prosecuting the war. No war is won through defence. Battle must be taken to the enemy. Imladrik understood that. I know he disagreed with the necessity of war, but he *did* understand how to win that war. The council doesn't.'

'You will send one of your generals to take charge, as you did with Imladrik?' Hulviar asked. 'Perhaps Lord Belicar or Thirian?'

The king laughed, and in that laugh was all the scorn and contempt in his royal body. 'There is no need to draw any of my best generals away from eradicating the druchii. These mud-lickers don't warrant such consideration. Lord Myrion has no pressing duties.'

'Lord Myrion is but a garrison commander in Cothique,' Hulviar objected. 'He's never commanded more than a few companies at one time.'

'He is my choice just the same.' Caledor's voice was cold as he made the statement. 'Myrion chafes under garrison duties. He is eager to do anything to bring glory to his name. Let the colonials try to hide behind their walls with Myrion commanding them. Just let them try! When I cast him upon the shores of Elthin Arvan, I shall be loosing a wild griffon upon the dwarfs.'

Thoriol rushed to the throne, prostrating himself at the king's feet. 'Please, majesty, allow me to accompany Lord Myrion.' His hand clenched about the dragon pommel of the sword at his side.

Caledor shook his head, a hint of sadness in his expression. 'No. Not this time,' he told Thoriol. 'Hunting savages in the wilds is no place for the House of Tor Caled.' Again, he looked through the eastward window, seeming to stare across the ocean to those distant shores. 'It never was,' he added, and just for a heartbeat, Thoriol thought he saw a tear gleaming in his uncle's eye.

A wave of heat rose from the forge, carrying with it a faint flicker of amber light. Rune magic, aethyric power bound into the forge itself. Only a runesmith could work such a forge – only his mind was trained to appreciate the intricacies of dealing with bound magic. A normal smith would find his mind wandering, his imagination seized by flights of fancy inspired by the escaping energies. He would lose the discipline and concentration demanded by his work. Whatever he cast would fail and bring disgrace to his name.

Morek knew how those smiths who had defied convention and attempted to use a rune forge must have felt. Even he, accustomed as he was to binding magic into stone and steel, felt his will put to the test as he laboured over Morgrim's sword. Weird emanations rose from the broken blade, strange harmonies that set his brain pounding and his heart racing. Once, the elven enchantments had even provoked a nosebleed, though he'd been on his guard for such malignant vibrations since.

It had been the better part of a year already and Morek had yet to reforge the blade. Before he started his work it had been necessary to familiarise himself with the sword, to understand the enchantments bound within it. He'd had to study the blade's communion with the rune forge, find a way to bring their disparate vibrations into harmony.

Forek had helped for a time. His command of the elven tongue and elven letters had been of immeasurable help, though Morek was reluctant to confess that to anyone. The former ambassador had deciphered the name of the sword: *Ifulvin*. Morgrim had called it 'Bitter-Blade' and such, Morek understood, was the name's translation. But to work proper magic upon anything it was vital to know its true name. By knowing the sword's name in the elven tongue, the runesmith hoped to tame it, subdue its enchantment enough to bring it under control.

The whole process had been too slow for Forek. His translation work done, the steelbeard had withdrawn. Morek understood that he had left Karaz-a-Karak entirely. Like Morgrim, Forek burned to return to battle, balking at each and every delay. The steelbeard would have gladly followed Morgrim's banner, but with Elgidum restrained by High King Gotrek's order, he had been compelled to seek another general to serve – one who would lead him to battle with the elgi and give him the chance to avenge even a small part of the great shame that had been done to him.

Morek watched the heat of the forge rippling along the length of Ifulvin. If they felt any shame at all, he imagined that the elves would be dishonoured to lose such a sword. He had discovered a grudging admiration for it as he laboured upon it. Far from being the fragile, delicate thing he'd expected, he had discovered a weapon of terrible potency and astounding craftsmanship. Certainly dwarf craftsmanship had proven better – hadn't Azdrakghar broken Ifulvin? – but it was foolish to believe that the elgi swordsmiths were without skill. Ifulvin was a blade built for speed and finesse, as different from the heavy, sturdy axes of the dawi as the mountains from the sea. Perhaps there was a lesson there, something about the psychology of both peoples. The elgi, swift and flighty. The dawi, slow and enduring.

Of more importance to Morek, however, was deciphering the weird magic the elves had infused into the blade. It was frustrating – strange and yet familiar all at once. Perhaps the way the elves used magic was a key to overcoming them. Where a runesmith harnessed magic, bound it into solid shapes, chained it into a semblance of substance, an elf mage worked much differently. They seemed to leave the magic as it was, letting it alter the things it was focused upon rather than having the focus change the magic. It was a difficult concept to work his mind around, as strange to him as learning that fire burned cold or that water could be dry. Deep down inside, his spirit rebelled at the wrongness of such concepts, much less seeing them put into practice.

'This is what keeps you from your duties?'

Morek swung around as the voice smacked across his ears. A flush crept into the runelord's face as he watched his mentor and master march into the crypt-like hall that held the rune forge. Ranuld Silverthumb's long beard was tucked into the broad belt he wore over his fur-trimmed robes. Jewelled torcs glittered on his arms and a circlet of gromril topped by a piece of polished malachite rested upon his brow. Runes sparked from the stones set in the rings he wore, and about his neck hung a ponderous granite pectoral upon which were set several potent symbols of power.

Ranuld would have cast a magnificent image were it not for the wizened appearance of his skin, the drawn look of his face. His eyes weren't as vibrant as they had once been. Morek knew they'd lost much of their lustre when the High Runelord's authority began to be defied. None openly flaunted Ranuld's advice or outright ignored his requests, but they were refused just the same. The kings didn't wish to send their runelords abroad, even to convene the Burudin. The same kings saw no reason not to allow their runesmiths to craft weapons Ranuld told them were too dangerous to forge. Few could comprehend the drive to seek out 'old magic' in the oldest deeps when there were so many more immediate uses for their runesmiths to be put to.

Morek was one of the few who continued to stand by Ranuld and trust completely to his wisdom. He was almost a living ancestor, old enough that he had walked these halls during the glory days of the Karaz Ankor. If a dwarf didn't respect that, then he was unworthy of his beard. It pained him that his master could think he'd defied one of his orders.

'Master, I did as you wished,' Morek explained. 'I have been back for nearly a year now. Do you not remember when I brought back word from the rest of the Burudin?'

Ranuld pressed a hand to the side of his head, kneading his temple as though to stir the memory into being. A confused look came into his eyes. He lowered his hand and pointed at Ifulvin. 'You are recasting an elf blade?' He made a disapproving grunt at the back of his throat. 'Wilful things, elgi enchantments. You have to keep your eye on them every second or they slip away. King Snorri Whitebeard had an elgi sword. A gift from their Prince Malekith. That was... oh... a very long time ago. Before you were born.'

Morek didn't think it was prudent to remind Ranuld that it was before the High Runelord's time as well. These last years, Ranuld's mind had started to wander, losing focus on what he considered petty trivialities. Things like what year it was or what a person's name might be.

'I am fixing this blade for Morgrim Bargrum,' Morek explained. 'He won it in battle with an elgi prince.'

Ranuld nodded, stroking his beard. Strands of hair came away as they caught in his rings. 'Elgidum,' he said. 'He who will slay the dragon and become king.'

Again Morek bit his tongue. He had heard from Morgrim how Ranuld had chanced upon Prince Snorri and his cousin deep beneath Karak Krum. He'd muttered his prophecy then, but had failed to tell Snorri he was speaking of Morgrim rather than the prince. Now Morek wondered if the prophecy was even meant for Morgrim. The only dragons that had been felled in the war were those at Kazad Mingol – one claimed by the crews of the doomed skryzan-harbark and another finished off by Rundin Torbansonn of the skarrenawi.

The High Runelord shook his head, some measure of clarity returning to his eyes. He clapped a hand on Morek's shoulder. 'This war will consume us if we let it,' he declared. 'The old magic is slipping away, sinking too deep for our picks and shovels to follow. It will be a slow death. Excruciatingly slow. We'll cling to past glories and hold our heads high even as we feel everything dying around us.'

'The elgi will not win,' Morek said, trying to reassure his master. 'They don't have the stamina for a long war.'

'Without the old magic we will be lost,' Ranuld persisted. 'It won't matter if elgi or dawi prevails – the Karaz Ankor will be broken.' He fixed his eyes on Morek, as though he could impress his meaning on the runelord through his gaze alone. After a moment, he turned away and started to retrace his steps, returning to whatever secret door had admitted him to the hall.

'I have to call it back,' Ranuld declared, but Morek didn't know if he was speaking to him or muttering to himself. 'I have to make the old magic come back to us. We can't follow it, so it has to come back to us.'

Morek looked back at the rune forge, watching the weird energies rising off the shattered elgi sword. If Ranuld was right and the magic of the runelords was fading, then was the same true of the elves and their mages?

FOUR

THE LORD OF THE TUNNELS

243RD YEAR OF THE REIGN OF CALEDOR II

Steel splintered before the axe's bite, driving slivers of jagged metal into the elf's soft flesh. The elf warrior struggled to bring his shield slamming down onto the armoured hands that gripped the butchering axe, hoping to break the dwarf's assault. Already the effort was beyond the stricken knight. Like those of his steed before him, the wounds he had suffered were too deep, and he was losing too much blood too rapidly to summon any kind of strength into his limbs. Like a weary moth, the asur sagged against the axe, his own sword and shield drooping from his lifeless hands.

From behind his mask of metal, Forek Grimbok glared at the corpse twined around his axe. He kicked at the elgi knight, forcing the corpse to slip away and free his weapon. The knight had made a bold display, rushing to intercept Forek. Surely the elf had seen enough to know what kind of foe he was challenging? Since battle had been joined, the steelbeard had been like some crazed engine of destruction, smashing his way through the carnage, leaving the mangled husks of his enemy strewn behind him, marking his path with their blood.

Forek scowled at the knight's seeming bravery. He wasn't deceived. He knew enough about the elgi to understand something of their ways. The knight was highborn and therefore unimpressed by the dwarf's harvest of mere peasant elgi. He'd thought to make short work of the steelbeard. Perhaps, in that last instant as Forek's axe chopped through his hip, the asur appreciated what a dire mistake he'd made.

All around Forek, the sounds of battle were fading. The fighting had raged for several hours now. The great thane Brok Stonefist had lured an entire elgi army into a carefully laid trap. First the dwarfs had ambushed the asur column on the road, emerging from hidden tunnels, half-forgotten fingers of the Ungdrin Ankor. They hadn't caused much damage, but enough to rile their enemy. When the ambushers retreated and the elgi saw how few they were, it had offended their pride. Angered and insulted, the elgi had chased after the ambushers... and straight into the real trap.

The slaughter had been vicious when three thousand dwarfs emerged from hiding. The elgi couldn't know that the dawi had been in place and waiting for three days among the concealed shafts and pits of an old copper mine. For three days they had bided their time, barely twitching a muscle, becoming as stolid as the stone around them. Then, like an avalanche, they had come crashing down upon the unsuspecting elves.

Cries of 'Khazuk! Khazuk!' rang out from every quarter as the remaining pockets of elgi warriors were surrounded and annihilated. A few of the knights, like the one Forek had killed, had managed to break through the dawi ring. They could have made a good escape, but instead had swung back around to engage the dwarfs. Their charge had faltered almost at once, slamming as it did into an immovable wall of dwarfish steel.

Forek hesitated a moment, cocking his head to one side and listening to the tumult. As High King Gotrek's reckoner, his sense of hearing had been honed to a remarkable degree, able to pick out the whisper of a visiting king halfway across Karaz-a-Karak's great hall. That facility to focus on a single sound amid whatever clamour sought to drown it out now served the steelbeard well. Hefting his vicious axe, Forek hastened across the battlefield. He gave scant notice to the dead lying strewn across the ground, his attention fixated upon the voice he'd picked out from the roar of battle.

The object of his search was standing on a dead elgi stallion, the head of his axe sunk into the animal's side. Brok Stonefist was an impressive sight, clad in rune-etched steel plate, his long grey beard festooned with golden rings and silver combs. A great eagle-winged helm covered his head, its mask dropping down to just below his nose. The thane's steely eyes stared from behind the visor, cold and brilliant as the light of a winter dawn. The thane was almost ancient by dwarfish standards, but the bite of time had yet to steal the strength from his arms or wither the prodigious stamina of a warrior who had spent his youth running messages through the dark tunnels of the Ungdrin Ankor.

Those days were long past. Now Brok was a mighty hero of the Karaz Ankor, the favoured champion of King Hrallson. He'd been leading the warriors of Karak Azul for years, displaying a knack for strategy and cunning that never failed to take the elves by surprise. His unmatched familiarity with the Ungdrin Ankor allowed his forces to move freely beneath the plains, without worrying about elf scouts and flying dragons. He had become something of a bogey to the elgi and the enemy had bestowed upon him the title *Arhain-tosaith*, the shadow from the earth.

At the moment, Brok was much more substantial to his foes, boldly standing before a tiny pocket of elf warriors. The elgi were among the last survivors, clustered around a standard that had grown bloodied and tattered during the conflict. Surrounded on all sides by dwarfs, the enemy remained defiant, brandishing their swords and spears. Perhaps if there had been a bowman among them, they might have dared a shot at Brok, but as it stood all they could do was to shout at their foe.

'They sound upset, whatever that perfumed gibberish means,' Brok laughed, his humour spreading to the warriors around him. He pulled at one of the combs in his beard, scowling at the tiny ring of elgi survivors.

'They are.' Brok's warriors moved aside as Forek strode over to the thane. Many of them clapped their fists against their chest in a gesture of respect to the steelbeard.

Brok was thoughtful a moment. There were some dwarfs who understood Eltharin, but few among the thane's army. He wagged a finger at the surrounded asur. 'Any of that doggerel useful or important?'

Forek listened a moment as an elf wearing a dark purple cloak over his silvery steel plate armour stepped a little away from the others and began to speak. The steelbeard scowled beneath his metal mask. How like the faithless elgi to put their personal pride ahead of all other concerns. Whatever they were, the elgi weren't stupid. They had to know full well the tactical value of what they'd disclosed. They had to know that after this, the forests would burn. Dawi axes would again stand before the walls of Tor Alessi and Athel Toralien and Athel Maraya. They had to know this, but they didn't care. He looked over at the standard the survivors were gathered around, then turned his gaze to the arrogantly defiant elf lord, his swan-winged helm plated in gold and encrusted with gemstones. Around his throat he wore a ruby big enough to choke an ogre. The blade he held at his side was slim, elegant and richly engraved.

No, the elves weren't trying any trickery. Brok's ambush had caught more than an army.

'The one in gold is Lord Myrion,' Forek reported.

Brok whistled in appreciation of the magnitude of Forek's words. 'The general of all the elgi,' he observed. He squinted at the resplendent elf lord. 'Dresses the part, I suppose. Elgi always invest more effort in appearance than substance.' He ripped his axe free from the carcass under his boots and shook it at the elves. 'This isn't some trick to get us to spare them for ransom?'

'It is no trick,' Forek said. He pointed at the standard. 'They want that rag returned to their kinfolk when the battle is ended. That is all.'

A laugh rumbled up from Brok's stout belly. 'So the general wants a family gewgaw sent back to elfland?' He shook his axe at the asur. 'Tell the tall-ears their kin can buy it back from me when I'm done wiping my arse with it.'

When Forek translated the thane's words, it was Lord Myrion himself who replied to Brok's crude abuse. The gold-helmed elf brandished his sword high, heedless of the dozen crossbows focused on him. Myrion's voice rose in a long diatribe. If the meaning of the words was lost to the dwarfs, the tone in which they were uttered wasn't. Growls and grumbles echoed among the bearded warriors.

Forek didn't bother to translate all of Myrion's speech. Even when they had been at peace, he'd found little patience for the flowery extravagance of the elf language. 'He says his gods will curse you if you don't grant him the respect due a foe killed in honour.'

Brok spat into his beard as another laugh shook him. 'Seems to me I haven't seen any elgi gods wandering about lately. They must have more sense than their poncey spawn. At least they stayed back on that damn island where they belong!' The thane pumped his fist in a rude gesture, letting Myrion know precisely what the dawi thought of his gods and their threats.

The elf lord started towards Brok, but his warriors grabbed hold of him, restraining the outraged general. One of them called out to Forek, the elf's voice actually devoid of the habitual condescension exhibited by their race. For a heartbeat, the desperation of that appeal evoked sympathy in the reckoner. Then the memory of what had been done to him crushed any mercy growing within the steelbeard.

'They want you to meet their general in single combat,' Forek told Brok.

Brok swung his axe upwards, letting it come to rest against his shoulder. Puffing out his chest, he climbed down from his morbid perch. 'I killed thirty-six elgi today. One more will be good for my appetite.'

Before Brok could take another step towards the elves, a harsh voice cried out from behind the dwarfish ranks. 'Hold, my lord. The elgi vermin is unworthy of dying on your axe.'

The dwarf warriors parted as a savage apparition stalked forwards. He was a dwarf, broad-shouldered and powerfully built, with a long beard spilling down his chest and a massive axe gripped in his brawny fists. There, however, his resemblance to the other dawi ended. Where the rest of the dwarfs were armoured for war, this one went unshod and bare-chested. Spirals of tattoos marked his skin and iron chains pierced the flesh of each arm, every third link of their length anchored in his body. His scalp had been shaved, only a narrow strip of hair left running down the centre of his head. This had been starched with a stinking mixture of grease and animal fat so that it spiked upwards like a cockscomb.

Every dwarf in Brok's army knew this warrior. He was Rundin Torbansonn of the skarrenawi. Rundin Dragonslayer, many called him, for he had killed an elgi drakk at the fall of Kazad Mingol. Others called him Rundin Oathbreaker, for after that battle he had broken his oaths of loyalty and service to High King Skarnag Grum and led an exodus of hill dwarfs back into the mountains. He was, at once, both a heroic and a despised figure, perpetrator of a great victory and an unforgivable offence.

As he stood between Brok and Forek, both dwarfs could see the ugly brand burned into Rundin's breast, right above his heart. It was the rune of Grimnir, a promise made in flesh by the disgraced hero. The nature of that promise was the most whispered rumour among Brok's warriors.

Many said it meant Rundin had vowed to redeem himself with a life of battle. Others claimed it wasn't life he sought but a glorious death that would eclipse the shame he'd brought upon his own name.

'No elgi is worth a dawi axe,' Brok growled at Rundin. A scowl knotted his brow as he glared into the hill dwarf's eyes. 'Or is it that you think I can't beat him?'

Rundin shook his head. 'You are Ungdrin Ankor Rik, Lord of the Tunnels. Without you, what will become of your army?' He waved his hand at the elves, the chain on his arm clattering as he did so. 'The elgi have lost the day, their army is vanquished. But if they can kill you, they can yet win the battle.'

Brok's anger only increased. 'I can kill that scum and a score like him with one hand tied to my beard! I was gutting urk for King Hrallson before you were a gleam in your father's eye! I've skinned trolls while they were still trying to eat me! You've dishonoured one lord already – I should think that was shame enough for you.'

'I've sworn no oaths to you,' Rundin growled through clenched teeth. 'I fight alongside you because we share an enemy. Don't forget that.'

Forek stepped between the two warriors before their mounting anger could come to blows. 'Don't give the elgi the satisfaction,' he hissed at them. A nod of his masked head drew the attention of both dwarfs back to the clustered asur. There was a look of scornful amusement on some of their faces. Even Lord Myrion was smiling. 'They think us brute savages. Don't prove them right.'

'Then tell this *unbaraki* to step aside and let me kill that grinning dog,' Brok declared.

Rundin's eyes went wide with shock as he heard the slur drop from Brok's mouth. Forek pressed a restraining hand on the hill dwarf, pushing him back before he could answer the thane's insult with a balled fist or the flat of his axe.

'You could best the elgi in fair combat,' Forek assured Brok, slipping back into the courteous flattery of Gotrek's court. 'But would they fight you fair? Rundin is right – killing you would help them, maybe even balance the army they've lost today.' He reached up, his fingers playing across the chains of his gold beard. 'Never underestimate the treachery of elves.'

Brok stepped back, shaking his head in exasperation. 'Gazul take 'em all,' he cursed. 'A volley or two will sort things out.' He turned to give the order to the crossbowmen who had their weapons trained upon the elves.

'No,' Rundin said, the word ringing out like the command of Grimnir himself. He matched Brok's sullen gaze. 'Let me face them. Let me show them the might of the dawi. Let me show them what courage and honour mean.'

Brok tapped the side of his helm with his finger. 'You're a zaki, you know that?' A bitter smile pulled across his weathered face. 'Still, if the elgi kill you, then I'm rid of you both.' He looked at Forek. 'Tell the elgi this lunatic will fight them. If they win, I'll send that rag of theirs back to Tor Alessi.'

It took the steelbeard only a few moments to explain Brok's terms to them. There was no mistaking the disappointment on Lord Myrion's face as he stared at the nearly naked Rundin. Clearly the elf shared Brok's opinion of the hill dwarf's sanity. Angry gestures and words were his response. One of the general's retainers stepped out from the survivors, a long-handled elf axe clasped in his hands.

Forek turned to Rundin. 'The elgi think you are unfit to fight their general. They're matching you against the lowest commoner left among them. It is meant to return the insult they feel Brok is paying them.'

Rundin spat onto the ground, glaring at the elves. 'After I kill him, what then? Will they send the general against me? Or do I have to kill them all?'

'Those are Lord Myrion's personal retainers,' Forek told him. 'Whatever happens, you'll have to kill them all.'

'Grimnir smiles on me,' Rundin said. He slapped his hand across the god's brand, as though to invoke Grimnir's attention. Then, without any hesitation, he charged at the waiting elf.

Even for warriors who had spent decades marching into battle, fighting across the length of the Karaz Ankor and the asur colonies, seldom had they seen such a spectacle. The elf axeman knew his business, coming at Rundin with what seemed an overhand sweep designed to open the dwarf's throat. Before he could connect, however, he spun his body into a rapid twist and set the blade flashing towards Rundin's knees. Impossibly, Rundin was able to react to his foe's feint, bringing his own axe flashing down to intercept the elven blade. Sparks danced away as the weapons ground against one another.

The axeman leapt back, recovering almost immediately from Rundin's block. The elf tried to employ the longer reach of his height and weapon to keep the dwarf at bay, managing to somehow brace himself each time his foe parried, absorbing the shock of the violent collisions with a facility engendered by long experience. Again and again he feinted an attack in one direction, only to pivot at the last instant to send his blade chopping at some seemingly unprotected quarter. Each time, however, Rundin's axe was there to thwart the blow. Even the watching dwarfs were dumbfounded by the Dragonslayer's speed and skill.

When the end came, it was both sudden and shocking. The elf axeman made another of his deceptive assaults on Rundin, bringing his axe low so that he might draw his foe's attention to knee, leg and belly, thereby exposing his upper body. This time, however, Rundin didn't wait to meet the blow, but jumped back. As the elven axe flashed through the space he had occupied, the dwarf's blade slashed at his foe. The longer weapon and the mailed arm that held it were chopped in half, their wreckage rolling across the bloodied ground. Before the maimed elf could even open his mouth to scream, Rundin slammed his blade into his enemy's shoulder and sent him crumpling in a welter of gore.

Looking across from the ruin of the elf soldier, Rundin shook his bloodied axe at Lord Myrion. Then the dwarf raked his thumb across his throat, a gesture of murderous promise that transcended the language barrier. Colour rushed into the elf lord's pale face, overwhelming his surprise at the butchery of his retainer. Shaking off the soldiers around him, the elven general stepped out to meet the hill dwarf.

Myrion raised his blade in mocking salute to the dwarf. Rundin merely turned his head and spat on the ground. Without further preamble, the two combatants rushed at one another.

Myrion's blade was like quicksilver, flying before him in a shimmering skein of deadly ithilmar, moving with such speed that it became a blur to the onlookers, indistinct as a phantom. Its effects, however, were far from phantasmal. Cuts blossomed all across Rundin's exposed flesh. The slashes were shallow, but they bled freely, coating the dwarf's body crimson.

Rundin sounded no cry of pain and did not retreat before Myrion's flying blade. He was determined to press his own attack, yet every time he tried to move forwards, the elf would take a step back. With calculating deliberation, Myrion kept the distance between them, maintained the advantage of his longer reach. He wouldn't make the mistake of his retainer and court disaster by trying to end the contest quickly. No, the elf lord was playing the longer game. Each cut he visited against the dwarf was like a leech sucking away at Rundin's vitality. By inches and degrees he was sapping the dwarf's strength, weakening him, draining his endurance. Only when Rundin was bled down to the dregs, only when he was no longer capable of fighting, only then would Myrion move for the kill.

Beside him, Forek heard Brok utter a disgusted moan as he realised the elf lord's despicable tactics. The thane had no fondness for Rundin, but no dawi wanted to see another dealt such a humiliating death. It was like watching a baited bear being worn down by hounds, a villainous sport Forek had seen the elves indulge in when he'd visited Athel Numiel as an ambassador before the war. It was clear the thane had the same misgiving. Brok looked towards his waiting crossbowmen, the command to loose bolts into the arrogant elf lord almost on his lips. Only the understanding that it would bring further disgrace to Rundin to have his life saved in such manner caused Brok to hesitate.

The decision became unnecessary a moment later. Myrion's lightning blade licked out at Rundin, but this time instead of striking vulnerable flesh it struck much tougher iron. One of the chains piercing the flesh of the dwarf's arms bore the brunt of the elf's attack. A link snapped before Myrion's blade, the razored edge biting through the metal. The frayed end of the chain spilled outwards and snapped against the elf's fingers.

It was a slight, stinging blow, yet its effect was profound. Instinctively,

Myrion drew his arm back from the source of his sudden hurt. For a breath, the elf lord's astonishing defence faltered. There was a pause in that curtain of flying ithilmar he'd woven around himself, a pause as devastating as a breach in any castle wall.

Rundin's axe lashed out as Myrion recoiled. The biting edge crunched into the elf's chest, shredding his silk surcoat and grinding into the armour beneath. The general was sent sprawling by the impact, cast to the ground. Even as he started to rise, to slash out with his sword, Rundin hurled himself at Myrion. Bellowing a feral war-cry, the Dragonslayer leapt upon the prone elf lord. He brought his heavy axe swinging down with both hands clasped about the haft. With the full weight and strength of the dwarf hero behind it, the axe clove into Myrion's gilded helm, splitting both it and the skull inside like cordwood.

The remaining elves cried out in horror and disbelief at the abrupt, brutal destruction of their lord and general. Rundin wiped Myrion's blood from his face and turned to confront them. Before the elves could attack, however, Brok gave the command to loose bolts. The quarrels slammed into the furious elves, piercing their steel armour and puncturing the warriors inside. The first volley put most of them down, a second finished them off completely.

Rundin stared coldly at the dying elves, then at the slaughtered general lying at his feet. Without a word, he turned and stalked back through the dawi ranks. The dwarfs parted respectfully before him, many raising their voices to cheer the skarrenawi's feat. For now, none of them remembered Rundin Oathbreaker. There was only Rundin Dragonslayer now. Killer of elgi. The still-bleeding dwarf paid no notice to their cheers but marched away to find some more obscure corner of the battlefield.

Brok watched Rundin until the hill dwarf was no longer visible. 'Might have shown a little gratitude,' the thane grumbled. 'If I didn't give the command, he'd be lying there next to that elgi snake.'

'That's what he wanted,' Forek said. He was surprised by the sense of admiration that he felt as he said it. 'It isn't victory he wants. It's a death others will remember.' The steelbeard shook the curious mood, turning to regard the dead elf lord and his retainers. Still standing above them was Lord Myrion's standard. 'Are you going to send that back to Tor Alessi?'

Brok frowned as though he had a bad taste in his mouth. After watching Rundin's fight with the elf lord, he had to grudgingly admit that the enemy had been playing on some last chance to kill him and leave his own army in disarray. 'Cast it down,' Brok ordered. He looked at the dead Myrion with his split skull.

'Leave it here with the rest of the elgi garbage.'

The army of Lord Salendor marched along the winding road that had been blazed through the vast expanse of Loren Lacoi. Riding a white mare near to the centre of the column, Liandra felt her attention constantly straying from the warriors around her to the trees flanking the road.

The forest seemed thicker, more wild and overgrown than Liandra remembered it. She'd ridden these trails many times between Athel Maraya and Kor Vanaeth, at least after she'd desisted from riding Vranesh on her errands to the other elf colonies. A dragon, of course, wasn't always in the mood to ferry an asur mage across Elthin Arvan, however indulgent the reptile was of its companion.

They were both gone, of course. Vranesh and Kor Vanaeth. In less than a day, Liandra lost both her city and her dragon. Both of them taken from her by the persistent evil of the druchii. First the traitors had taken her mother when she was still but a child, then they had unleashed one of their black dragons against her city and massacred her people. Then, finally, they had taken Vranesh from her.

Maybe that was why the forest felt so much darker and menacing than it ever had before. Liandra could no longer feel her connection with Vranesh; she no longer had the warmth and security of the drake's ancient power to give her strength and fire her spirit. When Vranesh died, the loss had left a great hole inside her that she didn't think anything would be able to fill. In many ways, the loss of Vranesh had hurt her even more than Prince Imladrik's death. As much as she'd loved him, as close as they had been, as much as they had shared, he had never really been a part of her. There had always been Yethanial, his wife back in Tor Vael in Ulthuan. Thoriol, the splendid son his wife had given him. Draukhain, the awesome drake who shared the dragonsong with him. So many who had shared his life. For Liandra, there had only been Vranesh.

She still blamed herself for Vranesh's death. She had been so focused on revenge, on destroying the black dragon and the druchii witch Drutheira that she hadn't thought about the high cost of vengeance. True, she'd managed to kill the black dragon and subdue the witch, but that hardly made up for the death of a creature as magnificent as Vranesh. She'd left Drutheira captive in the dungeons below Oeragor before Morgrim's army captured it. There'd been some naïve hope that the witch would be proof to satisfy the dwarfs that this war wasn't started by the asur. Looking back, she recognised how foolish that idea had been. The dwarfs would never let facts stand in the way of their grudges. They were too stubborn to ever listen to reason.

Liandra only hoped that Morgrim hadn't made the witch's death a quick one when the dwarfs found her.

A sound from among the trees had Liandra twisting around in her saddle. The spell she'd worked upon her eyes enabled them to pierce the dark of night as though it were bright as midday. She had an impression of motion, somewhere back among the undergrowth, but when she focused there was nothing to be seen. Throughout the ride from Athel Maraya she'd had these 'fancies' – motions caught out of the corner of her eye, yet never anything that lingered long enough to actually be seen.

'Is it not the dawi who are meant to despise the woods?' The question was asked as a half-jest, but there was an undercurrent of genuine concern running beneath. Lord Salendor, Master of Athel Maraya, walked his horse closer to Liandra's. Once, they had both sat upon the Council of Five in Tor Alessi, but that had been years ago. Before Kor Vanaeth had been razed to the ground for the second time. Before she'd lost Vranesh. One of the first things Lord Myrion had done when he arrived in Tor Alessi to take command of the colonies was to remove her from the council, replacing her with Lord Dlryll of Sith Remora, 'leader of a living community, not a vanquished one'.

It was ironic, then, that she should find herself here, riding with an army out to avenge Lord Myrion's death. But that was because she had so few friends left in the colonies and Salendor was one of those few.

Liandra forced herself to look away from the trees, to ignore the furtive motions she was certain wouldn't be there if she actually focused on them. 'I don't despise the woods, but I wonder if they despise us. We have wrought them great injury.'

Salendor nodded and smiled sympathetically. 'A necessary evil. The blight of war.' He gestured to the column of soldiers marching all around them. Three thousand asur warriors drawn from across the colonies and the ten kingdoms, supplemented by their baggage train, were bound to leave their mark on the land. 'Take comfort that we do not despoil the way the dwarfs do. We take what we must, destroy only what is unavoidable. They cut and burn out of simple spite. They ruin what they know we appreciate.'

'But do we?' Liandra asked. 'Do we truly appreciate? We say we do, certainly, and perhaps we even believe it.' She waved her hand at the branches stretching overhead, the green canopy that shadowed the trail. 'We come here as colonists. We come to conquer and reshape, to draw the shapes and sights of Ulthuan out of Elthin Arvan. Look at how you have transformed Athel Maraya, brought it up from the forest to become a glittering jewel.'

'Have you no heart to thrill to the beauty of Athel Maraya?' Salendor wondered. 'Glistening like a tapestry of stars amid the splendour of the forest, towers and obelisks rising from the trees...'

'It is beautiful,' Liandra assured him. 'It is as wondrous as Averlorn and Saphery, but it is the beauty of our land. The harmonies of this land are lost beneath that splendour. To build, first you must destroy.'

Salendor gave her a puzzled look. 'It is a strange mood that moves you this night. I know it isn't the prospect of battle that unsettles you. You are like me, an old warhorse who relishes the chance to strike back, to stand defiant before the enemy. Whoever they may be.' His fingers toyed with the ring that now graced his forefinger. It was similar to the one that had been bestowed upon Lord Myrion and upon Prince Imladrik before him.

'Is it this that disturbs you?' he asked. 'The thought that I am now in command of our armies? Do you think me so unfit for such a role?'

'Never,' Liandra said. 'You are the best among us. Gelthar is too timid, Caerwal too vengeful. Aelis and Dlryll think only in terms of defence.'

'And the Lady Liandra? What are her feelings?' Salendor asked.

'I am... I lack the confidence demanded of a leader,' she sighed. 'I have seen my people massacred and asked myself if I could have prevented it. I have seen friends killed and wondered if it was my fault.' She looked across the ranks of elven spearmen filing down the trail. 'To command, you can't ask yourself these questions.'

Salendor stared down at the ring on his finger. 'No,' he told her, 'if you would be more than a butcher, you must ask yourself these questions all the time. The difference is that you must balance what you might lose against what you might save. You must be ready to spend the lives of a hundred to preserve the lives of a thousand.'

Liandra shook her head. 'Is that why we hunt Arhain-tosaith?'

'Avenging Myrion is the king's decree,' Salendor said, 'but it is far more than that. The dwarfs have been emboldened. They're stirring from their holes again. Scouts say there's a big mass of them gathering in the south, maybe thinking to lay siege to Tor Alessi again. Killing Arhain-tosaith might give them pause, allow us the time to get more troops from Ulthuan.'

The mage reached out and set her hand in Salendor's, giving his fingers a gentle squeeze. 'You have sought this dwarf a long time,' she said. 'Be certain of your motivations. Don't let vengeance cloud your vision.' He felt the shudder that passed through her as she gave the warning. 'After revenge you are always left to count the cost.'

'He is just a dwarf,' Salendor said. The asur lord abruptly pulled away, his face going pale. A strange light was in his eyes, like wisps of scintillating starfire. Liandra was aware of the change for only the briefest instant and then it was gone, but in that instant she felt the aethyric harmonies rippling through Salendor's spirit.

The elf lord had a reputation for his uncanny premonitions. Now Liandra had witnessed one of them as it actually came upon him. Salendor turned from her, ordering his standard bearer to wave his flag and summon his captains.

'Halt the column!' Salendor commanded, waving his captains away to see the order carried out. 'Therial,' he shouted, waiting until the Ellyrian knight rode over to him before saying anything more.

'Bring your riders to the head of the column and remain with them,' Salendor said, his voice so low that Liandra was barely able to hear him from where she was. 'Keep a watchful eye for my signal. At my sign, spur your horses to full gallop and don't stop for anything.' A haunted expression gripped Salendor's features as he added, 'You won't need to be told when to ride back.' Bowing in his saddle, Therial hastened to obey his general.

'What is it?' Liandra whispered as she drew close to Salendor again. 'What did you see?'

Salendor was rubbing at the Eagle Ring, his gaze faraway. 'I saw the roles of hunter and prey reversed. Praise be to Asuryan that I've restored the proper balance.'

Therial's knights moved through the column, the infantry spilling off the trail as they parted for the cavalry. Like a tide of steel, they closed ranks behind the riders. Only when the knights were at the head of the column did Salendor motion to his banner bearer to summon his captains once more. Except for Therial, the officers quickly returned.

'I want a double-file of spears just behind the Ellyrians,' Salendor told them. 'Put your best archers behind the spears. Each bowman is to have an arrow nocked and ready. Implement these commands with discretion. When we resume the march, everything must be ready.'

Long minutes passed. Liandra burned to know what Salendor had foreseen, but she knew it would be useless to press him. Those unfamiliar with magic invariably made the mistake of believing portents and premonitions were quantifiable and readily described things, similar to the mundane senses they knew so well. Magic was different, far more nebulous and vague. A seer could know with certainty the substance of his prophecy but be absolutely at a loss to explain it. Liandra suspected that Salendor was gripped by the same dilemma – knowing what must be done but utterly unable to explain why.

At a gesture from Salendor, his standard bearer slowly moved his colours from side to side. The column began to march once more. At their head, Therial's Ellyrian cavalry lunged forwards at full gallop.

The elven steeds had barely gone more than thirty yards before the ground opened up beneath their hooves. The speed of the chargers carried them over the abyss, though the frightened neighs of the animals echoed through the forest. Behind them, they left a yawning trench five yards across, a great black scar running lengthwise across the trail.

The true menace of the hole revealed itself an instant later. Shouts of 'Khazuk!' rose from beneath the earth. Dwarfs surged up from out of the ground, brandishing their axes and hammers. The deadfall had been intended to drag the front ranks of the asur down to their waiting warriors. Thwarted in that ambition, now the dawi lunged up to meet the enemy.

The dwarfs had expected their foe to be surprised by the sudden ambush. To be certain, many were, but enough recovered quickly to set their spears against the onrushing dwarfs to blunt the initial charge. Behind them, the archers loosed the arrows they'd held at the ready. Few of the missiles pierced the heavy dwarf armour, but enough of them struck home to further blunt the assault.

Commands now rang out across the elven ranks. The captains of those archer companies in the rear hurriedly organised their bowmen to loose volleys into the trench itself. Hundreds of arrows arced over the heads of the elves fighting at the fore of the column to slam down into the dwarfs surging up from the trench. Whatever casualties they inflicted, there seemed no end to the dwarfs. It was obvious that the trench connected to one of their ancient tunnel systems, an underground fortress holding untold numbers of the enemy.

Across the trench, galloping hard, came Therial and his knights. Rushing upon the rear of the dwarfs, the Ellyrians threw the short spears they carried to great effect, striking a goodly number of the foe. Still, the enemy refused to submit. Some of the dwarfs even sallied onto the other side of the trench in a futile effort to confront the Ellyrians. The knights simply galloped away, drawing their enemy after them down the trail until they were far from the safety and reinforcements of the trench. Then, Therial wheeled his knights around and rode the dwarfs down in a brutal cavalry charge.

The fighting at the head of the column only began to falter when Liandra and the other mages in Salendor's army took a hand. Drawing upon the aethyr, the mages sent arcane fire raining down into the trench, scorching scores of the stubborn warriors as they tried to climb out of their holes. They seemed unimpressed by the magical flame, but when one of the other mages evoked a spell that caused the edges of the trench to crumble, it seemed a different matter. Almost at once, the dwarfs began to withdraw, hurrying back into their tunnels before the mages could collapse them on top of them.

When the fighting was over, Salendor hastened to the front of the column. Liandra knew how keenly his warrior's blood had wanted to be there, fighting beside his troops, but the situation had called for a leader, not a swordsman. She watched as the elf lord had his soldiers drag the wounded dwarfs to one side. They'd be tended to and marched back to Athel Maraya as labour for the city's defences, helping to raise the very walls that would defy their kinsmen.

The dead were dredged up from the trench and laid in a heap. The wounded dwarfs swore and cursed at the sight, but Salendor was not to be dissuaded. Carefully, he inspected each body before allowing it to be thrown back into the hole.

One of the dwarfs, unable to control himself any more, rushed past his guards and tried to throw himself at Salendor. Liandra spurred her horse forwards. The animal crashed into the dwarf, pitching him to the ground.

The dwarf's armour was scorched and blackened from the fire, and as he struck the ground, the straps binding his masked helm broke free. Liandra had just drawn her sword, intending to cut down the enemy if he remained defiant. When she looked upon his unmasked face, however, she almost let her sword fall from her hand. The wounded dwarfs gave voice to a piteous moan while many of the elves, those who had been in the colonies long enough to recall the days of peace, gasped in horror.

The face of the dwarf was a ghastly patchwork of scars – old scars that told a woeful story. They were the marks left by a king's imperious humour and the ungentle shears of his court. From cheek to chin, from nose to lip, the dwarf's flesh was a grey confusion of cuts and gashes. Here and there a pathetic patch of white hair stood out among the wreckage, but for the most part what was present bore scant resemblance to flesh, much less a face.

'Is this not a beard worthy of a war?' the dwarf snarled at her in strained yet precise Eltharin.

The words were like a slap across the cheek to every elf who heard them. How many of them had joined in their king's mockery when he derisively called this conflict 'the War of the Beards'? Now, as they stared at Caledor's handiwork, they felt shame at the jest.

Liandra forced herself to meet the dwarf's gaze. 'You... were the ambassador?'

'I have no more words to waste on asur,' Forek growled. 'Strike and be damned!'

Liandra shook her head, slowly returning her sword to its sheath. She had come to despise and hate the dwarfs over the years, nearly as much as she did the druchii. Yet she knew enough about their ways to understand the enormity of the insult King Caledor had inflicted upon their ambassadors. Seeing it for herself only made the insult that much more atrocious.

'I cannot undo what has been done to you,' she said, 'but I will not visit more hurt upon you.'

Fire blazed in Forek's eyes as he heard Liandra's words. 'You already have,' he snarled. 'Your pity is a greater insult than the knives of your king!'

'You have heard my lady's decision,' Lord Salendor declared, walking his horse towards the beardless dwarf. 'Wag your tongue however you like – none here will raise their hand against you. Enough shame has been done to you.'

The dwarf rose to his feet. For a moment, it looked like he would try to lunge at Salendor, but as he stood he began to sway. Blood streamed from a wound in his side. The enraged vitality that had spurred his first effort was gone. 'Your pity is as unwelcome as hers,' Forek spat.

Salendor's gaze hardened. 'It is the last I shall bestow upon a dwarf,' he said. The elf pointed to the heap of bodies stacked at the edge of the trench. 'Tell me, is Arhain-tosaith among them?'

A grisly chuckle spilled from Forek. 'Dead? No, the Lord of the Tunnels isn't dead. He lives, Salendor of Athel Maraya. He lives and one day he will bring your city crumbling down about your ears.'

'Tend the dawi's wound and let him go,' Salendor told his captains. He leaned forwards in his saddle, fixing Forek with his eyes.

'If you see Arhain-tosaith,' Salendor said, 'warn him that death waits for him in Athel Maraya. That is not a threat. It is not a warning.'

Liandra felt her blood go cold when she heard Salendor tell Forek just what his words were.

'It is a prophecy.'

FIVE

FIRES OF HATE AND PROPHECY

250TH YEAR OF THE REIGN OF CALEDOR II

High King Gotrek Starbreaker sat upon his great Throne of Power. The king's beard was still festooned with black beads of mourning even now, two and a half decades after his son was slain by King Caledor II. There were some who whispered that the king's mind was lost to melancholy, that he would never stir himself from his chambers and lead the dawi into battle as he had during the great wars against the greenskins. Some championed more energetic kings like Varnuf of Karak Eight Peaks or Brynnoth of Barak Varr to be appointed High King of the Karaz Ankor.

Such malcontents, however, were careful to keep such whispers far from the halls of Karaz-a-Karak. Only a few minutes in Gotrek's presence was enough to dissuade anyone from the idea that the brooding king was growing weak. Instead, the impression was that of a slumbering volcano, of a tremendous violence waiting to be unleashed.

It was a supreme effort of will on his part to restrain that violence. Every drop of blood, every strand of hair, every thread of sinew in his body wanted nothing but to throw the whole of his kingdom against the elgi. It would be so easy for Gotrek to abandon himself to a campaign of vindictive carnage. That he had the resolve to deny himself, to subdue his own impulses, was testament to his tremendous willpower.

Only when the time was right, when the purpose was clear, could he call the whole of the Karaz Ankor to war. A purpose that served the whole of the kingdom, not the grudges laid out in the Dammaz Kron. Not the wounded soul of a grieving father.

Gotrek laid his hand on the sword resting across his lap. He could feel the subtle energies coursing through the blade, strange and somehow hostile. A fitting reaction from elven magic to the touch of a dwarfish king.

The High King studied the dwarfs gathered before his throne. Morek Furrowbrow had presented the elf sword to him, but he wasn't deceived.

He knew the gift was from his nephew Morgrim. No, he corrected himself, from his *heir,* Morgrim, now that Snorri was gone.

Morgrim was there beside Morek, arrayed in full armour as though Gotrek needed to be reminded of what his nephew wanted. He was a hound straining at the leash, desperate to be set loose. He yearned to return to battle. The question that lingered in Gotrek's mind was what he'd do with such an opportunity.

'Your wound still vexes you?' Gotrek asked.

'I am fully recovered, my liege,' Morgrim replied. Gotrek knew it was a lie. He'd seen the stiffness in the thane when he'd bowed before the throne.

Gotrek stroked the captured blade, feeling its cold metal against his skin. 'The symbolism of your gift isn't lost on me.' He raised his hand, stifling Morgrim's protest. 'Do not argue that it is Runelord Morek's present. He may have reforged it, but it was you who took it from the elgi.' The king leaned forwards, forcing himself to face the third dwarf kneeling before the throne.

The metal mask and golden beard of Forek's helm was a reminder to Gotrek that sometimes a king could ask too much of his subjects, that there were some sacrifices that simply couldn't be asked of anyone. When he spoke to Forek, Gotrek's voice was slow and measured, carefully strained of any hint of guilt that would be unbecoming of a king.

'You bring news from Brok Stonefist?' Gotrek asked. It was no secret that Forek had been campaigning with the energetic Ungdrin Ankor Rik. The Lord of the Tunnels had been engaged in almost constant battle with the elgi, from small skirmishes to assaults against Tor Lithanel and Sith Rionnasc. Brok's slaying of the elf general Myrion had done much to embolden the dwarfs, but Gotrek wondered if it had really been worth it. Myrion had been replaced by Salendor, an elgi who knew both the land and the dawi, qualities his predecessor had lacked. Salendor had proven to be ten times the foe Myrion had been, exacting a terrible cost from the outlying mines and settlements with his lightning raids. This was an elf lord striving not for glory but victory, and he was cautious enough to be satisfied with small conquests that cost his people little in the way of lives.

'*Tromm*, my liege,' Forek addressed the king. The eyes that looked out from behind his mask were as sharp as daggers and Gotrek felt relieved that such a magnitude of hate was reserved for the elgi. 'Brok has conceived a plan that will end the menace of Salendor once and for all.'

Gotrek's expression hardened. Brok had become obsessed with killing Salendor ever since the elf lord's victory over him at the Battle of Blind River. Many times over the years the two had brought their armies into conflict. The bitterness and rivalry of their generals seemed to flow down into their troops. More vicious fighting in the war had yet to be witnessed. Still, despite the ferocity, despite the times when the two generals had actually met in combat, both of them yet lived. Some doom joined the two and seemed to be preserving them until the moment of its fulfilment.

'Brok has promised the death of Salendor many times,' Gotrek observed. 'I have yet to be told that the elgi's head hangs in the halls of Karak Azul.'

Morgrim rose to his feet. 'This time he intends to assault Athel Maraya itself,' he said. 'Forek has explained the plan to me. It is a sound one.'

'Athel Maraya has been attacked before... and by the same general,' Gotrek cautioned. 'The losses to the dawi were heavy and the elgi city still stands.'

'Brok didn't have the troops to penetrate the defences before,' Morgrim stated. 'Now he has King Varnuf and the army of Karak Eight Peaks supporting him. Enough hammers to tear down Salendor's walls.' An ambitious gleam came into his eye as he met Gotrek's gaze. 'If he had the might of Karaz-a-Karak behind him, he would be certain to accomplish his purpose.'

'And who would lead our people?' Gotrek wondered.

Morgrim stiffened. 'I thought that I would command any contingent you were to send.'

The High King pulled at his beard, feeling the beads slip between his fingers. 'No,' he declared. Before Morgrim could protest, he motioned the thane to be still. 'You will not command merely a contingent. Brok is obsessed with the grudges he has laid against Salendor. Varnuf is ambitious and power-hungry – he cares only about seeing my crown on his head. Neither of them will bring our people the victory they need. *You* will be in overall command of the combined army. If Brok and Varnuf cannot agree to this, then you will march back here with your contingent.'

Morgrim's face brightened. 'Then I have your leave...'

Gotrek stood from his throne.

'The time for mourning is done,' he said. 'Now is the time for blood. Now is the time for reckoning.' He looked at Ifulvin, the sword lying at his feet after it had fallen from his lap. 'Now is the time for vengeance,' he declared as he stooped and retrieved the sword. He tossed the weapon to Morgrim.

'It is time you returned that blade to the elgi... one throat at a time.'

Athel Maraya stood in the midst of the Great Forest, what the elves had named the Loren Lacoi. Once it had been more beautiful than anything the asur had dared to build in Elthin Arvan. Its towers and minarets rose among the trees like colossal flowers, their graceful arches and broad balconies accentuating rather than diminishing their arboreal surroundings. Ranks of slender ash trees lined the main thoroughfare and the streets were laid with blocks of agate as smooth and polished as river stones. Beds of flowers were everywhere, sporting an array of colours beyond the limitations of nature, enhanced by careful hybridisation and the even less mundane enhancements of magic.

Ruby and sapphire and emerald shone from the window frames and doorways of each house, nestled among intricate carvings and frescoes.

Tile murals adorned every courtyard and intersection, each vibrant scene depicting some tranquil moment from asur legend and lore. The lamps, wondrous cages of crystal and silver, glittered like a million diamonds when night fell upon the city, the illuminating enchantments bound within those cages making Athel Maraya shine more wondrously than the stars in the sky.

Liandra turned away from the marble balustrade, watching as a liveried servant stepped out onto the balcony. Revenial had been Lord Salendor's own steward before he was sent to attend her. The pale wine standing on the silver tray he carried was a further gift from the elf lord, drawn from his own cellars. She recognised the dusky colour to the bottle and knew it to be from one of the early vintages.

Revenial stopped a short distance from his mistress and proffered her the crystal goblet resting beside the bottle.

'Thank you,' Liandra said after taking a brief sip. Wine, like most beautiful things, had to be taken slowly to truly be savoured. All too soon the beauty could be lost.

'Something disturbs you this evening?' Revenial asked. The steward had always been forthright with Salendor, a habit he'd carried over when he entered Liandra's service.

Liandra took no insult from the servant's familiarity. 'I was thinking about how beautiful Athel Maraya was. Look at it now, marred by the necessities of war. Barracks and fortifications break the symmetry. Flower gardens uprooted to plant crops, trees cut down to form the frameworks for ballistae and chariots, jewels plucked from the houses to buy weapons and armour. And that grotesque stone wall that coils around the city like some titanic serpent. It is a hideous, brutish thing, as hard and ugly as the enemy it was raised to oppose.'

'Beauty is always the first victim of war,' Revenial said. 'It was much the same when Malekith's traitors raged across Tiranoc. People forget beauty when the enemy is near.' He looked away from his mistress, gazing out towards the walls Liandra had called grotesque. 'We learned when fighting Malekith that if you try to save everything then you end up losing it all.'

Liandra turned and the softness drained from her eyes as she looked out at the walls and the army encamped beyond them. For three months the enemy had been laying siege to Athel Maraya. A great host of dwarfs had chopped and burned their way through the forest to menace Salendor's city. The dawi had hurled boulders into its buildings with their catapults, sent cauldrons of boiling pitch raining down on the streets, loosed spears from their ballistae at the high towers.

The elves had returned their attentions in kind. Archers sent volley upon volley flying out from behind the walls to break any dwarf effort to bring ladders and towers towards the city. Mages unleashed arcane malevolence upon the field, withering warriors in their heavy armour with bolts of wizardly lightning or cooking them where they stood with blasts of sorcerous flame. In the sky above, great eagles and griffons prowled the battlefield, spying out the movement and disposition of the enemy.

'He is down there,' Liandra said, feeling a wave of cold hate course through her body. 'The eagle riders saw his standard. Our enemy is no less than Elfdoom himself, the same animal who killed Prince Imladrik.' She shook her fist at the dwarf warriors. 'If I had Vranesh right now, I could fly down there and burn those lice-ridden savages.'

'You have done what you could, my lady,' Revenial assured her. 'You convinced Lord Salendor to send an eagle rider to Tor Alessi and request the aid of Lord Teranion and his dragons.'

'My mistake may have been to allow Lord Salendor to compose the message,' Liandra said. 'I fear he did not impress upon Tor Alessi the gravity of the situation here. He is overconfident, he believes that Athel Maraya can fend off this siege.'

Revenial nodded. 'He clings to the prophecy. He believes only Arhaintosaith can break Athel Maraya. Without the Lord of the Tunnels to lead them, he believes the dwarfs can never defile his city.'

Raising her staff, Liandra sent a bolt of aethyric energy smashing into a boulder flying uncomfortably near to her tower. The magical assault reduced the missile into a shower of pebbles, the tiny stones clattering ineffectually against the rooftops below. 'Prophecy has a way of cheating those who trust in it most,' she warned Revenial. Salendor might be secure in his belief that only Brok Stonefist could despoil his city, but Liandra was confident that Morgrim was equally capable of the feat.

What she didn't understand was why the thane hadn't moved with all of his forces. Thus far, what Morgrim had done amounted to a series of probes, thrusts to test the defences. The real attack was yet to come.

Beyond the walls of Athel Maraya, Morgrim listened to the reports of his thanes. The barrage from the siege weapons was proving ineffectual. He didn't need the thanes to tell him that. Catapults, bolt throwers, they'd been brought against the city before. And, just as before, they hadn't been enough to overcome Lord Salendor and his city. No, it would need a different track to force a way into the city.

'Bring what ammunition you need from the quarry,' Morgrim told the artillerists. During the first siege against Athel Maraya, the dwarfs had excavated a wide expanse of the Loren Lacoi to provide the stone for their catapults. That open wound in the forest was still a rich source of supply for the dwarf war machines. 'Detach the labour you need from the clan dwarf regiments but you are to take no levies from the hammerers and Ironbreakers or from the crossbows.' Morgrim dismissed the artillerists from his tent with a wave of his hand. When they were gone, he turned to Morek Furrowbrow.

'They could lob the Everpeak itself at that city and I think we'd be no closer to conquering it,' Morgrim grumbled.

'Your plan demands the pretence,' Morek reminded him. 'It is a good plan, sound as the halls of Karaz-a-Karak. Give it the time it needs.'

Morgrim scowled. 'Time isn't our friend, and you know it well. The drakk are still licking their wounds after Kazad Mingol, but we can't count on them staying away. Every day we gain is a gift from Valaya.' He clenched his fist and pounded it against the table where his maps and charts were arrayed. 'Brok Stonefist had better deliver on his promises.'

Morek scratched at his brow, giving Morgrim a worried stare. 'You doubt the Lord of the Tunnels?'

'I think he may be a victim of his own legend,' Morgrim said. 'Those of my troops who have done a turn as miners say he should have excavated his tunnels a month ago. I can understand caution, trying to keep the elgi from discovering the diggings, but this…'

'Have you spoken to Brok? Asked him about the delay?'

'It's always the same with him,' Morgrim declared. 'He assures me that his excavations will bring down the walls exactly where we need them to go down. Then he launches into a tirade about Salendor and how his personal honour demands he kill the elgi.'

'You would expect any less from a dawi lord?' Morek wondered.

There was a grave look in Morgrim's eyes. 'I think Brok has become obsessed. There's a fever in him as destructive as gold madness.' He shook his fist at the ground, as though to express his frustration to the Lord of the Tunnels somewhere below his feet. 'Ancestors forgive me, but I wonder if I've placed my whole army at the mercy of a bleeding zaki.'

The outburst had no sooner left Morgrim's tongue than a dirt-covered messenger was standing at the entrance of the tent. The dwarf bowed when the general looked in his direction.

'Tromm, lord,' the dwarf said. 'I bring tidings from Brok Stonefist. He wishes to inform you that you may begin your attack at your pleasure. When you do, he will see to it that the walls are broken.'

'Tell Brok he may expect my command within the next day,' Morgrim told the runner. He waited until the messenger was gone before turning towards Morek. 'When the artillerists get back with their rock, we'll be ready.'

'You don't seem pleased about that,' Morek said.

A rumbling sigh shook Morgrim. 'Brok says he's ready and maybe he is, but I can't escape the feeling that I've put too much trust in him.'

From the balcony of her tower, Liandra watched as another volley of arrows rose from behind the walls, striking a regiment of armoured dwarfs trying to steer an iron-headed ram towards one of the gates. A few of the dawi fell to the barrage, but most were able to scramble into cover behind the ram's immense frame of fresh timber. In taking shelter, however, the dwarfs left the ram itself vulnerable. Unmoving, it presented a prime target for elven magic.

'Shield your eyes,' Liandra warned Revenial. The steward hurriedly covered his face as Liandra raised her staff to the sky. She focused her mind on the swirling currents of the aethyr. It seemed more exacting and difficult to fixate upon those eldritch patterns than it once had been. All the familiar skeins seemed to unravel a little more each time. She might have laid the impression down to her imagination, or a diminishment of her powers after the death of Vranesh, but other mages had confided to her their own growing difficulties practising their craft. It was as if the violence of the war were somehow throwing echoes into the aethyr, disturbing the old harmonies.

Fiercely, Liandra chided herself for her lack of concentration. She could fret over thaumatological theories later. At the moment she had dwarfs to kill. Drawing down the magical essences demanded of her conjuration, she focused them into the head of her staff, letting the energy build. At length, a blast of blinding light leapt from her staff, hurtling down from the tower with meteoric violence. The battering ram was engulfed in flame, the timbers crackling and popping as the bark crumbled from the wood. The dwarfs crowded around the ram shrieked, many of them stumbling away, their clothes and beards aflame. Asur sharpshooters hidden on the walls picked them off one by one, stifling their screams with arrows to breast and brain.

'Magnificent,' Revenial crowed when he looked out and saw the havoc Liandra's spell had unleashed.

'It's a start,' she replied. Liandra could still feel some sense of satisfaction watching dwarfs die. It was easy to remember the first attack on Kor Vanaeth and the fall of Oeragor, even the early sieges against Tor Alessi. The dwarfs had given her ample reason to hate them. Why, then, did she feel a sense of guilt that she did hate them so?

'Khazuk! Khazuk! Khazuk!' The fierce war-cry of the dwarfs rose from the besiegers in a great roar. It was more than simple belligerence. There was a note of jubilation and triumph in the cry. Revenial and Liandra exchanged a confused look.

'What do they have to be so happy about?' Revenial wondered.

Liandra looked towards the Diamond Tower where Salendor was coordinating his defence of the city, wondering if one of the boulders the attackers were lobbing into the city had somehow struck the crystal-roofed tower.

It wasn't the tower that had roused the dwarfs. The cause of their shouting was much closer. The first Liandra and Revenial were aware of it was the tremor they felt pass through the tower. Some instinct drew their gaze away from their own surroundings and out towards the walls. They both gasped in amazement at what they saw.

The walls of Athel Maraya, those grand, colossal fortifications, were swaying and sagging, creaking from side to side like a ship at sea. Dust and rubble trickled down their sides, great clumps of mortar crackling down onto the regiments of archers posted behind them. Some of the sentries on the walls clung to the crenellations, casting aside their weapons in their desperate efforts to retain their footing. Others were thrown, cast off the walls like horsemen from the back of an unbroken stallion. Screaming, they crashed amongst their own comrades, flung at them like an armoured bludgeon and leaving little clumps of broken soldiery all along the perimeter.

Soon a deafening rumble and crash rocked Athel Maraya. The swaying walls came toppling inwards, their immense bulk pulverising soldiers, reducing them to gory smears in the squares and streets. The collapsing walls obliterated the buildings behind them, burying hundreds of elves beneath tonnes of rubble.

Liandra's eyes blazed with outrage. 'Sappers!' she shouted. 'The filthy burrowers set part of their army to excavate beneath the walls and bring them down. That was why there weren't any dawi mages among the besiegers – their runesmiths were focused entirely on hiding the diggers from our divinations and scrying.'

Revenial turned a terrified face towards Liandra. 'What can we do? The dwarfs are in the city. They're through the walls!' He pointed a trembling hand towards the nearest breach.

Looking at the broken walls, Liandra could appreciate the enormity of the attack and the precision with which the dwarfs had wrought such havoc. The walls had been brought down not in one or two places, but six. They'd been sent crashing inwards in each instance, spilling across those structures closest to the breaches and burying whatever defenders might have been able to immediately reach the gaps. Never did the falling walls topple in such a way that they choked any of the wide thoroughfares that stretched across the city. The streets had been left clear for the invaders.

Hidden trenches leading up to the broken walls suddenly disgorged filthy, dirt-coated mobs of dwarfs armed with massive hammers and sharp-headed picks. The very miners who had brought down the walls were now the first to rush into the gaps, defending the dust-choked heaps of rubble until the regular dawi warriors could exploit the breaches and pour into the vulnerable city.

'What can we do?' Liandra threw Revenial's question back at him. 'We can fight and show these brutes that we won't be cowed by their tricks.'

Liandra loosed her magic against the nearest of the breaches. She immolated a burly miner just as he started to pull his pick from the skull of an unfortunate elf swordsman. The screaming dwarf pitched forwards onto his face, blazing away like some obscene candle. The horror-struck dwarfs around him backed away, but Liandra was of no mind to be merciful. Again and again she set her magic against the dawi, sending their burning bodies tumbling down the jumbled debris. A few elf militia scrambled up the rubble, intending to hold the breach until regular troops could be brought up. Quickly they learned how hopeless the effort would be. Dwarf crossbows dropped two of them and wounded a third. Reluctantly, they fell back, conceding the breach to the invaders.

'There! One of the animals is firing the houses.' Revenial was jumping up and down, trying to draw his mistress's attention to the scene unfolding a hundred yards away. Liandra could see a red-bearded dwarf wearing a horned helm playing a lit torch across the wood carvings adorning the doorway of an elven home. The brute chuckled as the carvings began to smoulder and catch fire. Pointing her staff at the vandal, she turned her hate and disgust for the dwarf into a flaming spear of energy that seared through his armour and left him a charred mess strewn across the doorstep of the home he'd set aflame.

It was a fruitless gesture. Liandra could see more and more dwarfs pouring into the city now, many of them bearing torches and pots of pitch. Trees were soon transformed into grisly pillars of flame, flowerbeds became fiery fields. Homes spilled smoke into the sky as their inhabitants burned and screamed. The dwarfs weren't interested in plunder or captives now. This attack had only one purpose in mind: complete destruction. She thought of Kor Vanaeth and what the city had been reduced to when the dwarfs were finished with it.

'Khaine's blood, there are so many of them,' Revenial cursed. 'Even your magic can't kill them all.'

'I won't know until I try,' Liandra growled, raising her staff once more, straining to draw more of the elusive aethyr to her spell.

As the magic swelled within her, Liandra felt the echo of a familiar sensation rush through her. Automatically, she turned her face skywards. There, soaring down upon the stricken city were two of Lord Teranion's precious dragons. The great beasts bellowed in rage as they flew above the burning streets, the primordial roar causing windows to shake in their frames. The dragons made one pass, allowing their riders a view of the overall condition of the battle.

'The dragons have come,' Revenial cheered, giving voice to the exultation racing through Liandra's mind. The dragons had come and now it was the dwarfs' turn to burn.

The huge monsters were diving down, dragon fire billowing from their fanged maws. They struck the dwarfs with almost elemental fury, boiling hundreds of them, melting the armour from their bodies and reducing their flesh to ash.

'There's little more we can do here,' Liandra told Revenial. 'Now that the dwarfs are inside the walls, our place is with Lord Salendor.' As she followed the steward down the steps of her tower, Liandra wondered about Salendor. She wondered if he was still clinging to the prophecy now that Athel Maraya was on fire and Arhain-tosaith was nowhere to be seen.

* * *

The air within the tunnel was foul with dust and the smoke of lanterns. Forek found it nearly impossible to breathe, the temptation to remove his masked helm mounting with each gasp he tried to draw into his lungs. The memory of his humiliation when the elgi rinn knocked him down and exposed his shame was too painful to submit to the temptation. He'd choke before he allowed himself to be disgraced like that again.

A cruel smile formed beneath his mask as the steelbeard recalled how he'd turned elgi pity against them. When he returned to Brok Stonefist, he told the thane what he'd heard. The captives taken by Salendor were to be put to work strengthening and expanding the walls around his city. That had set a cunning plan in Brok's brain, one that had taken years to bring to fruition.

Each time he fought Salendor, a few more of Brok's warriors were taken captive. But some of those who became prisoners did so by design. In ones and twos, Brok had let a few of his miners fall into Salendor's hands. As they worked on the walls, the miners left signs and marks only other members of the miners' guild could read. Signs that told exactly where sappers should dig to exploit the minute weaknesses the dwarfs had connived to engineer and bring the great walls of Athel Maraya crashing down.

Forek had felt the tremors as the walls fell. Indeed, for several ghastly moments it had seemed the tunnel he was in would collapse, such was the violence of the quake. But the tremor had passed and the tunnel remained stable. Brok's miners knew their business and they'd had a long time to turn their profession into a weapon of war.

The Lord of the Tunnels had only disclosed some of his plan to Morgrim Elgidum. While he provided his sappers to undermine the walls, Brok neglected to tell his commander about the other part of his strategy. Forek suspected that Brok was worried about what would happen if Morgrim were to learn that the thane was using the whole dawi army as a cover for his own, private, attack.

The tunnel Brok had his best miners digging was far longer than those that brought down the walls. From the edge of the surrounding forest, he'd ordered it dug clear into the heart of Athel Maraya. While the rest of the army fought for the outskirts of the city, Brok intended to seize its heart. It was there, he knew, he would find Lord Salendor.

'Enough!' Brok's voice echoed through the tunnel. He pushed his way down the line until he was at the front. Around his arm was a coil of thin cord that he had played out ever since the miners had started to dig. Knots in the cord measured the distance. Unless something had gone wrong, the tunnel should have reached the spot he wanted. To be sure, Brok took a long spike of steel and stabbed it up through the roof of the tunnel, piercing the surface above. Hastily, he drew the spike back and thrust a curved tube of bronze into the hole. It was an ingenious device crafted by the engineers' guild, two mirrors set into the angles of the tube reflecting the image of whatever the opposite end was trained upon.

Brok stroked his long beard and gave a satisfied hiss. 'I can see the Diamond Tower,' he said. Withdrawing the bronze pipe, he turned to the expectant miners all around him. 'We're as near as we need to be, lads. Open her up!'

The miners set to the task with an almost bestial fury. Their picks and hammers tore at the roof of the tunnel, tearing a wide fissure. Dirt and the broken tiles from a plaza spilled down on them, but the dwarfs didn't pause in their labour. Inch by inch, the hole they'd made widened.

As light poured down into the tunnel, the warriors who had followed behind the miners came hurrying forwards. Rundin, the fierce Dragonslayer, was the first to leap onto the pick handles the miners held crosswise and be flung up onto the surface. Forek was right behind him, as eager to be out of the stifling tunnel as he was to confront the elgi.

The steelbeard found himself standing in a plaza, the intersection of two tree-lined streets. Great towers rose in every direction, thin and dainty constructions as dwarfs reckoned things, but with a gravity-defying liquidity to their broad arches and engorged spires. Bridges stretched between many of the towers, twisting and flowing above the streets. Forek saw elf bowmen on some of those bridges and hurriedly unslung the shield strapped across his back. He had no fear of fighting the elgi, but he didn't think an arrow in his gizzard would make for a momentous death either.

Rundin seemed to have no such concerns. With a roar, the half-naked skarrenawi charged at a group of elven spearmen who had the misfortune to be marching past the plaza when the dwarfs broke through. They were still in shock at the incredible trespass. Before they could recover, Rundin was among them. One elf fell with his belly opened from hip to rib. A second collapsed in a mire of his own entrails. The third was able to bring up his spear in a futile effort to block Rundin's axe only to have the blade chop through the haft of his weapon and split his breastbone. The murderous carnage broke the discipline of the others. Shouting in alarm, they fled down one of the streets, Rundin and his axe hot on their heels.

The commotion drew the notice of the nearest archers. The bowmen hurriedly nocked arrows and began to shoot at the dwarfs emerging from the tunnel. One arrow glanced off Forek's shield, while another came so near to striking Brok that it became caught in the loose folds of mail hanging from his arm.

'Zonzharr!' Brok cried out as he ducked and tried to make himself less of a target for the archers on the bridges. At his call, the flow of warriors being sent up from the tunnel stopped. Instead, the next dwarfs raised up from the hole were miners. Unlike their comrades, these didn't have candles spitted onto their spiked helms or lanterns fastened to their belts. They didn't bear pick or hammer. Instead, what they carried were crooked metal rods with a strip of leather stretched between the bifurcated end. Into this loop of leather the miners hurriedly set fist-sized globes of iron. A short length of fuse fizzled at the top of each sphere. Hastily, the miners whirled their rods above their heads, swinging them faster and faster. One of them collapsed as an elf arrow struck him, the globe rolling away from his fallen weapon until one of the warriors rushed over and hastily snuffed out the fuse.

The other miners brought the rods to a sudden stop. The momentum they'd built up sent the iron globes hurtling away, up towards the bridges. It was only a moment before the bombs detonated. Filled with zonzharr, a devastating blasting powder, the iron globes wrought brutal havoc among the archers. When a bomb struck one of the bridges, the span was ripped from its moorings and sent crashing to the street below. When one detonated above the bridge, it sent a shower of sparks and flame streaming onto the elves. A few went wide of the mark, crashing instead into the towers themselves, setting fire to the woodwork and nearby trees. Only seldom did they stray, however, for the miners were old hands at slinging zonzharr in this fashion to blast rock from the upper reaches of Angaz Baragdum's open-pit mines.

In short order, the archers were killed or driven into retreat. Brok called his warriors to him, those who had so far emerged from the pit. He wasn't willing to wait for his full force. Like some hunting beast, he seemed to smell Salendor nearby. He wasn't about to let the elf lord slip through his fingers this time.

'We're for the Diamond Tower,' he shouted down into the tunnel. 'Anybody who's coming better get his arse moving! The rest of you bring up pitch and oil. I want this elgi warren burning so bright that Caledor himself will be able to see it from his perfumed throne in elfland!'

The Lord of the Tunnels didn't hesitate a moment longer. Brandishing his axe overhead, he pointed it towards the Diamond Tower. With a fierce cry of 'Khazuk!', his warriors charged after him.

Forek glanced back at the burning towers and trees. In the distance he could see other fires raging in the outskirts. Overhead, a dragon swept past, flames billowing from its maw as it flew towards the walls and Morgrim's besiegers.

Even if the elves somehow managed to repulse them now, there was nothing that could save their city.

Athel Maraya was going to burn.

The streets were a confusion of terror and bloodshed. Liandra's armour was filthy with the gore of the dwarfs she'd cut down with her sword and the dying elves she'd briefly lingered over. There was only so much her magic could do. In the close quarters of the streets a blade was faster than a conjuration, as the dawi had discovered for themselves. Revenial, armed with his own blade, proved a capable fighter in his own right, claiming six dwarfs during the escape from Liandra's tower.

The asur were fighting for every house and every tower, desperately trying to protect their homes and the families cowering inside them. The dawi were equally determined, stubbornly fighting for every inch, heedless of what it cost them. She'd witnessed dwarf warriors crawling over their own dead to force their way into a tower only to put the building to the torch.

Fire burned everywhere. The combined malignity of the dwarf arsonists and the dragons was turning entire streets into infernos. Worse, the flames were blazing away so fiercely that they were creating terrible winds that howled and raged, spreading the fires faster and farther than either dragon or dwarf. Liandra had seen a horrible thing, like a whirlwind fashioned from flame, rise up from the pyre of a field to dance across the district, burning all it touched.

'The Librarium Lacoi!' Revenial howled in a cry of anguish as they hurried through the streets. Liandra froze and turned to stare at the ghastly sight that had overwhelmed her servant. The Librarium Lacoi was engulfed in flame, its skylights collapsing from its tall roofs, its great spire toppling into the conflagration of its main structure. 'Nothing can rebuild Athel Maraya now,' Revenial moaned. 'Even if we win this war, nothing can restore what we've lost.'

'Then we make the dawi pay,' Liandra told him, seizing his shoulder and urging him onwards. 'We make them suffer as we've suffered.' Prodding him ahead of her, they started towards the Aspen Road, the vast parkland that stretched across the city like a belt. They both froze when they saw that the trees were on fire.

Revenial watched the flames as they spread down the belt. 'If that fire isn't quenched, it will consume the outlying districts and then spread to the very core of Athel Maraya.'

'We'll be ringed by fire from within and without,' Liandra observed. 'Every asur in the city will be destroyed.'

A desperate light crept into Revenial's eyes. 'High in the Diamond Tower there's a bell,' he said. 'Lord Salendor had it placed there after the last siege. When it is sounded, it will be the dirge for Athel Maraya. If the bell is struck, it is the order for every elf in the city to abandon it and flee into the forest.'

'Then we have to reach the tower and ring the bell,' Liandra decided, thankful that they were already headed in that direction.

Revenial shook his head. 'Only Lord Salendor can authorise striking the bell,' he said.

Liandra seized him by his tunic. 'He should have done so already,' she snapped. 'That he hasn't done so is proof enough that he's still clinging to delusions about prophecy. His people – *your* people – are all going to die because of him!' She gestured to the spreading flames. 'There's no time to argue with him even if we find him. *I'm* ordering the evacuation. If it comes to it, I'll make my excuses before the Council of Five.'

Revenial nodded his head slowly. 'I will take you to the bell, but you must be the one to strike it.' He looked down at his hands, shame in his expression. 'I have served Lord Salendor too long to betray him now.'

'Lead the way, then,' Liandra said. 'Leave the rest to me.'

Running down side streets and narrow pathways among the copses and groves so far untouched by the flames, Liandra and Revenial were able to avoid the fighting in the outlying districts. The dwarfs were too intent on tearing down everything in their path to bother overmuch about a few stray elves.

As they neared the core of Athel Maraya, Liandra was surprised to find fires raging among the towers and trees. At first she imagined that it had been caused by the dragons, some error made by either reptile or rider. Then she saw the dwarfs rushing about the buildings, giving battle to the asur who tried to oppose them, setting fires when their advance went uncontested.

'The beasts are between us and the tower,' Revenial swore.

A solid block of dwarf warriors was marching across the broad bridge that spanned the Aspen Road. Among them, Liandra saw a figure who had become infamous among the elves: the long-bearded, stout-bellied Brok Stonefist, Arhain-tosaith himself. How the dwarf lord had come to rage and ravage at the heart of Athel Maraya when Morgrim's forces were still fighting past the defences, Liandra didn't know. At the moment it didn't matter. All she knew was that he was here and the effect his presence would have on Salendor.

'We have to find another way,' Liandra said.

Revenial was quiet a moment, then cast a worried look at the Aspen Road itself. Grimly he pointed to the defile, already thick with smoke. 'Maybe we can make it across,' he said. Shunning the bridge with its burden of dwarfs, they climbed down into the smoke, flitting among the aspens as they hurried to the other side of the narrow defile. Towards the east, they could see the fires of the outskirts spreading down the Aspen Road, roaring like some daemonic horror as they devoured the trees. If the wind shifted, the conflagration could spread to the centre of Athel Maraya in a matter of minutes.

Liandra was climbing up the slope at the other side of the defile when she saw asur soldiers marching out onto the bridge to meet Brok's advance. Her heart felt like ice when she saw Salendor leading his troops. The elf lord's banner snapped in the fiery breeze, letting his foe know exactly who it was he faced. Neither bolt nor arrow rose from either of the converging forces. There was too much hate between these foes to take any satisfaction from killing at distance. Only the play of sword and axe would quench the fury of these warriors.

'Lord Salendor,' Revenial gasped. Liandra had to grab her servant to keep him from joining his old master as he marched towards his hated enemy.

'The bell,' she reminded Revenial. 'We have to sound the evacuation.'

One of the dragons flew overhead, diving towards Brok's dwarfs. The flash of Salendor's banner warned the dragon rider off, alerting him that this wasn't his fight. The drake veered off at the last instant, the gout of fire it had been about to send into the dwarfs instead igniting the rooftops of tiered manors and palaces.

Liandra and Revenial hastened to reach the elf-held side of the bridge. The dismissal of the dragon told her all she needed to know about Salendor's intentions. He was fixated upon the premonition, the prophecy that joined his doom with that of the dwarf. As he brought his household guard into battle with Brok's warriors, Liandra knew he wasn't fighting for victory. He was fighting to answer the demands of fate.

As they reached the other side of the defile, Revenial turned to Liandra. 'Help Lord Salendor if you can,' he told her. 'I will attend to the bell.' The steward turned and hurried down one of the desolate streets, soon lost among the ruins of Athel Maraya.

'I'll try,' Liandra promised the departed elf, already knowing her words to be empty. She doubted if it was in anyone's power to free Salendor from the path he was set upon.

The wind shifted, sending the fire roaring down the Aspen Road. Beams and tiles from the buildings the dragon had set aflame came crashing down upon the bridge, slowing the rush of combat as elf and dwarf alike tried to dodge the burning debris.

Only the two warriors at the heart of the conflict took no notice of the fire and smoke. Even now, Salendor was resplendent in his silvered armour and silken cloak, a mild enchantment keeping the grime of war away from his vestment. His sword shone as it slashed and thrust, wove and parried. There was an expression of regret stamped upon his noble features, but in his eyes shone a fierce determination.

His foe was no less determined, but it was there that the similarities ended. Brok's armour was black from soot and ash, his beard stained a dull charcoal colour. The axe the dwarf swung was heavy, ponderous and clumsy beside the nimble elven blade. Again and again, Salendor's sword darted past it to slash against the grimy mail that guarded the thane's body. If the axe was less nimble, it had the benefit of greater strength. The few times Brok pressed home his attacks, Salendor was knocked back, staggered by even the most glancing blow. There was no regret or misgiving in Brok's face, only a primitive, bestial sort of fury.

Liandra cried out to Salendor, begging him to withdraw. She pleaded with him to save himself, to defy whatever doom he imagined he'd seen. He was a valiant warrior and a great leader. The asur needed lords of his calibre to lead them in all the battles to come, to avenge the destruction of Athel Maraya. Members of Salendor's household guard who'd already withdrawn from the fight took up Liandra's entreaties, urging him to end the senseless duel.

Through the air, the dull, dolorous note of the bell in the Diamond Tower rang out, sounding the evacuation of Athel Maraya's survivors. Revenial had honoured his word and broken faith with his old master. Liandra felt shame that her promise to the steward wasn't so easily discharged. The tolling of the bell seemed to antagonise the dwarf artillery beyond the walls. While it sounded, no less than half a dozen boulders were sent hurtling at the edifice. Several struck true and with the sixth, the tower came apart like a rotten tooth, raining chunks of rubble down upon Salendor's estate. Somewhere in that debris would be the body of Revenial and the bell.

The fires roared closer. Now burning branches and leaves were being blown onto the bridge, forcing still more of the dwarfs and elves to disengage and withdraw to opposite ends of the span. Liandra was surprised to see a great body of dwarfs already gathered there, doubly so when she recognised Morgrim and the dwarf ambassador among them. Like the elves around her, the dwarfs were crying out to their champion, urging him to withdraw from the fight.

Like Salendor, Brok ignored every entreaty. His world had narrowed down so that it consisted only of the elf lord who stood before him. Smoke and fire, the burning debris crashing around him, none of it mattered. All he saw was Salendor's sword flashing out to defy his axe. All he wanted was the opening, the opportunity, to drive that axe into his foe's body.

Back and forth the two champions fought. The fires were on both sides of the bridge now. Only the dead shared the span with them; all others had retreated before the advancing flames. At either bank, the onlookers continued to plead with their heroes to disengage, to save themselves.

The fires on the dwarf side of the span caused Morgrim to pull his forces and what remained of Brok's back. Liandra saw them hurrying through the burning streets, retreating before they could be engulfed by the flames they themselves had kindled.

The elves lingered a little longer, but their calls to Salendor went unheeded. The elf lord's sword licked out, hewing one of the wings from Brok's helm. The dwarf's axe raked across the asur's arm, ripping free his cloak. It fluttered there a moment before flying off into the fiery breeze. Elf and dwarf took a step back, glaring into one another's face, then they threw themselves back into the fray.

It was the last Liandra saw of them. In the next instant the bridge, its wooden supports weakened by the fires burning beneath it, shuddered and groaned. With a terrible howl, the span lifted up and then went crashing down into the blazing inferno raging below.

Such was the doom of Lord Salendor and Brok Stonefist. The vision that had haunted the elf lord for so many years.

Liandra turned from the fiery holocaust. Sternly she ordered the grieving warriors of Salendor's household guard to make their escape from the dying city.

More than ever, the elves of Elthin Arvan would need every warrior they could find. The question was, without Salendor, who would lead them?

SIX

CHANGES IN THE TIDE

322ND YEAR OF THE REIGN OF CALEDOR II

It was a strange thing for Thoriol to look out over the familiar vistas of Tor Vael after such a long time. There had been many opportunities to visit his mother, of course, but somehow something had always arisen to interfere with such a meeting. Always some court function, some visiting dignitary who had to be attended, some royal hunt that wouldn't wait. It was as though the king had become jealous of him and didn't want to share him with anybody.

Thoriol would have called such an idea absurd once, just as he had called Caradryel's talk about him being groomed as the king's heir absurd. Now, after nearly a century in the court of the Phoenix King, he knew better than to discount any possibility. His uncle was, by turns, fawningly indulgent and obsessively possessive of Thoriol. King Caledor was proud to display his nephew at the court, to dress him in the finest raiment, to attach him to the most beautiful courtiers and courtesans. He had arranged the finest instructors to be found in the ten kingdoms to teach Thoriol the most intricate nuances of courtly custom, dance and diplomacy. When it seemed to the king that life in Lothern was becoming dull for his nephew, they would quickly leave on an expedition to hunt lions in Chrace or griffons in Cothique. The king was prepared to indulge any whim Thoriol expressed, so long as it kept his nephew close to him.

At last, however, even King Caledor had to concede to Thoriol's desire to again walk the halls where he had played as a child. On past occasions he had always invoked a longing to see his mother again – a tack that typically resulted in the king summoning Yethanial away from Tor Vael to attend the royal presence. This time, Thoriol had invoked the memory of his father. It was something that never failed to make the king bow to his wishes, but it was a tactic that never failed to make him feel ashamed.

Thoriol turned when he heard footsteps on the balcony behind him. He expected to find his mother coming out to check on him. Instead he found that the light tread belonged to Caradryel. The diplomat's expression was as inscrutable as ever.

'What is it that you see out there?' Caradryel asked as he joined the prince.

Thoriol smiled at the question. He'd come to understand Caradryel better during his time among the king's court. He'd even come to appreciate the intricacies of how the diplomat operated – questions such as the one he'd just asked, innocuous things in themselves that could nevertheless reveal the thoughts and intentions of those who answered.

'It isn't what I see,' Thoriol said. 'It's what I don't see.' He leaned against the rail, staring out across the purple horizon. 'How many times I stood here as a child watching for Draukhain to come flying out from behind the clouds carrying my father back home.'

'Lady Liandra writes that Draukhain still makes his lair in the bay of Tor Alessi. A spit of rock they now call "the Dragon's Lament". She says it is piled high with the bodies of the dwarfs he kills when he flies away to hunt.' Caradryel fixed Thoriol with a sympathetic gaze. 'He's refused any rider since your father, even refused the company of his fellow dragons. It takes a great soul to cause a dragon to mourn him.'

Thoriol turned his back on the view, staring back at the tower and the hall where his mother was waiting for him. 'What else does she write?' Even now, he was loath to speak her name, loath to acknowledge the indiscretion his father had shared with Liandra. It would tarnish his memories, and memories were all he had left of his father.

'That is why Lady Yethanial was so eager to see you,' Caradryel said. 'That's why she was so insistent. She wanted to speak to you directly, not convey her meaning through me.'

Thoriol clapped the diplomat on the shoulder, a comradely gesture he would never have spared Caradryel back in Kor Evril. 'Here I thought you were simply weary of playing the messenger.'

Caradryel shrugged. 'It's rewarding work, after a fashion. Where else would I develop such a knack for eluding Hulviar's spies?'

The prince followed Caradryel back into the tower. As he'd expected, Lady Yethanial was seated near the fire, a fur wrap hanging about her shoulders. For some time she had been given to chills, steadfastly refusing the ministrations of either mage or physician. It was always like his mother to think she could find her own answers buried away in some ancient tome of lore.

The other occupant of the room was more surprising. Thoriol had seen Lord Athinol only a few times at Caledor's court. Usually he was away in the east, leading the troops in driving the last scraps of Malekith's followers to their well-deserved ruin. He tried to keep prejudice from his dealings with Athinol, though he found it hard since he knew the silver-haired lord was Liandra's father. To drag him away from the battlefield, his daughter's tidings must be dire indeed.

Yethanial rose as her son entered the hall. With a step that struggled to marry haste and dignity, she walked over and embraced Thoriol. 'It is good to see you home again,' she said.

'Would that the circumstances were more amenable,' Thoriol said. 'But the king would hardly let me stray far from him if they were.'

Lord Athinol rose to his feet, a trace of alarm in his face. 'The king suspects you?'

'Far from it,' Caradryel assured him. 'If Caledor had any misgivings about his nephew he would send him as far from him as he could.'

Thoriol withdrew from his mother's arms, looking to her and then to Athinol. 'I wonder at that,' he said. 'It is certain Hulviar has his suspicions and he certainly has the king's ear. Whatever influence I might have on my uncle, Hulviar's is greater.'

Athinol removed a fold of parchment from the cuff of his tunic, tapping it against his forearm. 'Was it Hulviar then who suggested dismissing Prince Naeir from command of the armies in Elthin Arvan? Liandra tells me that Lord Draikyll has arrived in Tor Alessi to replace him.'

'It could well be,' Thoriol said after a moment's thought. 'I know the king was unhappy with Naeir and considering replacing him. I didn't know he'd chosen Draikyll.'

Caradryel shook his head and started to pace before the fire. 'That's bad,' he said. 'It means Hulviar has planted enough doubt in the king's mind that he's starting to keep secrets from you. He was open enough about the other generals he appointed – at least with you.'

'Is Draikyll's appointment so very different?' Thoriol wondered.

'It is to those of us who still think we can extricate ourselves from this useless war,' Yethanial told him. 'Draikyll is a noble of considerable influence and resources. He is also aware that both his fortune and his influence are waning. The wealth of Elthin Arvan would appeal to him, as would the prestige of being the general who drove the dawi back into their holes.'

Colour rushed into Athinol's face. 'There are enough people who still owe him favours that Draikyll can draw considerable troops and material away from Ulthuan to support any adventure he plans in Elthin Arvan.' He smacked his fist on the side of an ebony writing stand. 'Just when our campaigns against the druchii have a real hope of victory, this has to happen!'

Thoriol looked from Yethanial to Athinol and then to Caradryel. 'I thought you were against war.'

'We war against the dwarfs by choice,' Athinol said. 'The war with the druchii is a matter of survival.'

Thoriol shook his head. 'I don't agree. Perhaps I'm the wrong one to be acting as your spy. I believe the king is right. We can't allow ourselves to be driven from the colonies.'

'The real war is with the druchii,' Athinol declared.

The prince matched Athinol's hostile glare. 'The war is with the creatures that murdered my father.'

'Then you've sided with the king?' Yethanial asked. 'You've taken his side?'

'I don't know,' Thoriol confessed. 'But I have to wonder. If we abandon the lands my father died to defend, then what did he give his life for?'

Ranuld Silverthumb could feel the weight of ages pressing down upon him. The venerable runelord felt as though every minute and every hour was like some parasitic thing, fattening itself upon what vitality remained in him, what magic still coursed through his veins. The old magic, the magic that had carved the first holds from the roots of the mountain. The magic that had brought the great runes to the dawi. The magic that had forged the mighty Anvils of Doom.

The magic that had drawn the *gronti-duraz* from the dark beneath the world.

Generations had passed since the gronti-duraz last stirred. The great stone giants were the greatest accomplishment of the ancients, the pinnacle of the runesmith's art. Their awakening was a secret known to only a few now. Like so much of the old ways and the old magic, there were none among the lesser generations wise enough to be entrusted with such knowledge.

The runelord sank back in his stone chair, feeling the comforting chill of the naked granite through his robes. So few among the dawi really understood. They waged their wars and pursued their grudges, chased after gold and glory, all the time oblivious to the changes all around them. They were blind to the poison sifting through the very air, seeping down into the very rock, sinking into their own bones. The light was fading, but none noticed because there was still enough to let them see.

The younger runesmiths and even some of the elders of the Burudin chose to ignore it. They allowed themselves to be drawn into comparatively petty feuds and vengeance. They let the runes be twisted and warped, put to uses that only a generation before would have been unthinkable. They turned a blind eye to the excesses of the engineers' guild and their reckless experimentation. The destruction of Kazad Mingol should have been enough to stir them from their indifference.

Ranuld sighed. Even the kings were deaf. Claiming to venerate their runelords, they instead denied them their true purpose. They'd defied his every attempt to gather the Burudin, to work the great magic that alone could lead the dawi back to the old ways and warn them away from the doom before them.

The runelord cast his gaze across the darkened hall. He let his eyes linger on the silver war shield. Once it had allowed him to commune with his fellow runelords. Perhaps it might still, if he were to focus his dwindling powers upon it and draw out the enchantments trapped within its runes. But would anyone respond? And if they did, would there be any purpose to it?

He no longer believed there was any use trying to defy the will of the kings. One look at the shadowy hall convinced him of that. The pedestals where the Anvils of Doom rested were half empty. Three of the six had been carried off to war. Not for a single battle, but dragged along through the entire campaign, hauled about like a bolt thrower or rock lobber, like a mere weapon to be used and forgotten.

Ranuld lifted his gaze, looking past the remaining Anvils and to the great hunched shapes that crouched in the darkness. The gronti-duraz, the mighty golems fashioned at the dawn of dwarf kind. The first was said to have been shaped by Thungi himself, ancestor god of the runesmiths. First or last, they were marvels of magic – manifestations of what the dawi had once been capable of.

The runelord looked at the three Anvils, wondering if he dared do what he had in mind with only three of them to magnify his power. Briefly he considered summoning his apprentice Morek. The young runesmith had proven himself a most capable student. Ranuld coughed as a chuckle caught in his throat. What he had in mind was dangerous enough alone. To have some young *wazzock* mucking things up would only make things that much worse.

Besides, he had grown somewhat fond of Morek. He didn't really want to watch him die.

Ranuld squirmed back in his chair, trying to make himself as comfortable as possible. He raised his runestaff, pointing it towards the Anvils. One last time he wondered if he should try what he wanted to do. Wondered if he shouldn't just allow himself and the old magic to fade away.

No, that was never the dawi way. A dwarf was too stubborn to quit, no matter the odds against him. It was the great strength of their kind and also their great weakness.

Letting the runes take shape in his mind, Ranuld let the magic flow through him, flow down the length of his runestaff and into the Anvils. One by one, the artefacts began to glow with power, fingers of golden lightning crackling and dancing across them. Ranuld could feel his blood boiling inside his veins as he continued to feed energy into the Anvils. More and still more, as much as he could summon. As much as he could command.

Blood dripped from his nose, from his ears and mouth, sizzling as it splashed against the cold granite of his chair. Still Ranuld kept channelling the power through him and into the Anvils. More, just a little more! He could smell his beard begin to cook, could feel his skin crackling and sloughing away.

Through the pain of his exertions, Ranuld glanced at those great stone giants crouching in the darkness, those manifestations of the old magic and the old ways. He focused his thoughts upon the great rune, the secret too enormous to ever be written down. The rune that would bring life to unmoving stone. The rune that would make the gronti-duraz walk.

The agony was incredible now. Ranuld heard his teeth burst, one after another, felt their fragments trickling down his beard. They sounded like pebbles as they struck the floor.

His gaze strayed from the golems, intending to see what had become of his teeth. Instead his eyes fixated upon the hand gripping his runestaff. The skin had completely burned away, but what lay exposed beneath was neither flesh nor bone, but blackened stone.

Ranuld slumped back in his chair, breaking the connection between himself and the Anvils. It needed more strength than he possessed to rouse the gronti-duraz, more power than a single runelord could summon.

He watched as the power he'd drawn into them slowly faded from the Anvils. When it was gone, Ranuld tried to stir from his chair. The effort was too great. His legs felt as though they were lead. He looked down at his hand, watching as the petrifaction he'd observed continued to spread.

There were a few secrets he would have liked to pass on to Morek in what time was left to him. Not the great rune that would waken the gronti-duraz, but useful things. It seemed his apprentice would have to learn them for himself, if he ever could.

Ranuld Silverthumb, High Runelord of Karaz-a-Karak, swung his head around, fixing his eyes on the slumbering stone giants. He wanted them to be the last thing he saw before his body was completely petrified and he joined them in their stony slumbers.

Heglan Copperfist looked up from his labours, staring at the stuffed birds that filled his hidden workshop. Few dwarfs had ever been here. His brother Nadri, a handful of others. He knew Guildmaster Strombak suspected the existence of such a workshop, but the master engineer had never pressed Heglan for the details. It afforded Strombak the ability to deny any involvement in Heglan's continuing experiments.

The whole of the engineers' guild seemed divided over the matter of the skryzan-harbark even now. There was one faction that urged Heglan to build more of the airships, perhaps smaller ones that wouldn't cause as much destruction if they crashed. The other faction roared for him to be given the short trouser ritual and cast out of the guild. Heglan suspected that King Brynnoth's continued confidence in the airships was what made Strombak so noncommittal. After the conflagration that engulfed Kazad Mingol, he was certain there was nothing more the Guildmaster wanted than to cleanse his hands of the whole affair.

Heglan appreciated that sentiment more than Strombak could ever guess. After the calamitous finish to the battle, he'd ordered the skryzan-harbark back to Barak Varr. Carefully and deliberately he'd had each one disassembled. Piece by piece they had been brought down into his workshops to be examined, studied and catalogued. In the shock of the conflagration, there had been none to gainsay his decision. It was only later that more calculating voices had risen to point out that while the destruction had been unfortunate, Kazad Mingol would have been destroyed by the dragons in any event. More to the point, the airships had killed one dragon and left a second mortally wounded at a cost that was, after all, quite small compared to the losses inflicted on the dawi armies during the Fourth Siege of Tor Alessi.

Maybe so, but the dwarfs who had been lost had been his dwarfs, the crews that he himself had chosen. That made Heglan feel directly responsible for what had happened to them. Caught in such a ghastly explosion, none of them had any chance at all.

It shouldn't have happened. Heglan had tried and tried to replicate the effects with the materials from the surviving airships. Canvas, wood, gas – nothing would recreate even a fraction of what he'd witnessed above Kazad Mingol.

There was something missing. Some factor he had been unable to work into his calculations. Until he found it, until he discovered what it was and found a way to negate it, he couldn't allow the skryzan-harbark to return to the sky. The danger was simply too great.

Heglan rose from his work table and marched over to the great stone shelves that held the materials he'd been experimenting on. Not for the first time his attention was drawn to the jar of Tharzharr he'd removed from *Nadri's Retribution*'s arsenal.

It was strange stuff to be certain, the discovery of Thane Drogor of Kazak Zorn. The incendiary burned more violently than anything Heglan had ever encountered, short of molten lava. But it didn't merely burn what it touched; it devoured it, gnawing away with its fiery teeth until there was nothing left.

Heglan frowned as he looked at the jar. The impressions of tiny paws were distinct in the dust coating it. Glancing down he saw a rat lying on the floor just behind the shelf, as stiff and lifeless as a board. The sight of the tiny carcass made him reflect on the ingredients that went into Drogor's incendiary.

'Foulstone,' Heglan muttered to himself. It was an ugly green-black rock found in the deeper mines. Normally dwarfs despised the stuff. It had a corrosive effect on any ores near it. Discovering a vein of foulstone meant that any gold or silver in the area would be degraded, perhaps even completely worthless. The stuff was also toxic. Breathing in foulstone dust produced a condition called weeping lung where the insides of the lung were burned and began to fill with pus. It meant a slow and loathsome death for any dwarf.

When foulstone had been rendered down into granules to make Tharzharr, those who handled it had been careful to keep their faces covered. Even then, several had developed wracking coughs and dripping noses.

Another curious property of the stuff was the unnatural way in which it attracted rats. Any shaft with a profusion of rats scurrying around it almost invariably held a vein of foulstone.

Still, for all its nasty properties, every test Heglan had made with the stuff failed to produce the same catastrophic reaction he had witnessed.

'Maybe Drogor could have explained,' the engineer said as he carried the jar back to his workbench. That, of course, was impossible. Drogor had been aboard the great *King Snorri* when it caught fire and exploded. There had been no survivors, not even enough to bring back to Barak Varr and inter in the vaults.

'What makes you think their bones would rest any easier in your musty old vaults?'

Heglan leapt up in surprise as the voice echoed through his workshop. He was alone. He knew he was alone. No one could come in here unobserved. The secret door in his public workshop was something only he knew how to operate. Even if someone had discovered the mechanism, however lost in his experiments he was, he would have noticed the wall rotating to admit an intruder.

'I came by my own method.'

The engineer spun back around, staring at the displays of his birds. A shadow moved out from among them. As it stepped into the light, Heglan blinked in disbelief. It was impossible! He had to be suffering from some kind of delusion, some fantasy brought on by overwork.

'No. I'm quite real,' Drogor said. An amused smile formed on his face. 'Though perhaps "real" is a bit too limited a concept. Ideas like that can be rather limiting.'

Heglan slumped against the workbench, spilling the jar of Tharzharr across the surface. 'You... you're...'

Drogor slowly walked towards the horrified engineer. 'Dead? There we go again with such finite, constrained ideas. You'd be much better off without them.'

'Keep back,' Heglan warned. He drew a heavy iron spanner from his belt, brandishing it as though it were a battleaxe.

The other dwarf paused, his smile growing even wider. 'Do you really think that can stop me if I survived the explosion of my airship?' Drogor laughed. 'Do try to be reasonable. Believe it or not, I came here to help you.'

Heglan rushed the intruder, bringing the spanner crashing against his skull. He could feel the bone splinter beneath the iron, could see the blood and brains rushing from Drogor's scalp.

Drogor's fist slammed into Heglan's chest, throwing the engineer across the room. He slammed into the shelves holding the materials from the airships. He felt one of the shelves crack as he slammed against it. He also felt his spine snap.

'That was rude,' Drogor warned the paralysed engineer. 'I almost think you aren't happy to see me.' He paced across the workshop, finally settling at the workbench where Heglan had been making his studies.

'Your skryzan-harbark are quite clever,' Drogor declared. 'You know, they really could have won the war for your people. The elves could never have roused enough dragons to overcome them. After all, it takes only a year for one of your workshops to turn out a new airship. Do you have any idea how long it takes to rear a dragon from its egg?'

Heglan tried to speak, but all that came from his mouth was a bubble of blood. Drogor frowned at his distress, shaking his head sadly.

'Your kind could still be masters of the air, despite themselves,' Drogor said. 'They could force the elves from your lands and bring a new age of peace.' The smile now stretched across the entirety of his face, more like something ophidian than dwarfish. 'But who wants to see an end to war? Peace is so boring. Yet that's what they want, those who think they'll make more airships without you.'

Drogor leaned across the workbench, his grin becoming still more predatory as he gazed on Heglan. The engineer was doing his best to reach a jar of blasting powder on one of the nearby shelves. The sight brought another laugh from Drogor.

'No need for that, I assure you,' Drogor said. 'No need at all. You see, I came here to show you what happened to your ships. It was the least I could do after all the amusement you've afforded me. I shall truly miss your kind when they're all gone.' Drogor ran his finger through the spilled Tharzharr. 'This is the key, you know. This and the gas you used to lift your ships. But they needed something else. A catalyst. And that, I fear, was something you simply couldn't find on your own.'

Heglan gaped in shock as a grisly blue fire suddenly rose from the centre of Drogor's hand, gyrating and wriggling above his palm as though it were something alive.

'You see, I'm that catalyst,' Drogor stated. He started to move his burning hand towards the spilled explosive, then hesitated. 'We don't have any of your lift gas around, but don't worry, the explosion will still be enough to demolish this workshop and remind your kinsman that they simply aren't meant to fly.'

Drogor's eyes seemed to roll over, changing into the opaque lenses of some vulturine creature. 'Don't trouble yourself about my welfare,' he told Heglan, his smile stretching until it burst his skin. 'You see, I've been through this before.'

Heglan's world vanished in a flash of thunder and light as Drogor slammed his burning claw into the explosive powder.

SEVEN

THE SEA HOLD

335TH YEAR OF THE REIGN OF CALEDOR II

The small flotilla of galleys cast anchor at the mouth of the bay. Far to the south, barely a hint on the horizon, the roofs of Sith Rionnasc reflected the noonday sun. Away to the north there was only the vastness of the Snow Sea, a great expanse that could swallow the six asur vessels without a trace.

Liandra couldn't quite conceal her distaste for the ritual she was witnessing any more than she could hide her loathing of the highborn who was sponsoring it. Lord Ilendril was one of that breed who had been expelled from Ulthuan by the first King Caledor, cast out for their callous, unabashed ambition. She had known some of the disgraced grey lords yet remained in the colonies of Elthin Arvan, but she'd imagined them to be remorseful, not still trying to advance the immoral philosophies that had sent them into exile.

From the aftcastle of *The Sword of Eataine*, she had a good view of what was transpiring. Ilendril's pet mage, a gaunt and pallid creature named Vithrein, sat at the middle of a cabalistic triangle. Two other mages, ones Liandra recognised as former vassals of Lord Caerwal, who had once been imprisoned by Prince Imladrik, stood at opposing sides of the triangle. With her own arcane senses, she could almost see the energies they were feeding into Vithrein, magnifying the aethyric harmonies flowing around the conjurer.

'This won't work,' Liandra said, more to herself than those around her. The words drew their notice just the same. Lord Draikyll had assembled the greatest and most powerful nobles in Elthin Arvan to witness this ritual. The general was depending on this exhibition to bring them into line, to make them enthusiastic supporters of the campaign he'd mapped out. Liandra's doubt made him anxious. She was, after all, a mage and more versed in the possibilities of magic than he was. The general glanced aside at Ilendril, just a hint of accusation in his eyes.

Lord Ilendril took note of the displeasure of his patron. Calmly, he moved down the crowd of noble spectators until he was right beside Liandra. 'Is it that you think it won't work, or that you merely hope it won't work?' He shook his head. 'Clinging to the old ways is no way to build an empire.' Ilendril laughed and looked back at Draikyll. 'Or win a war.'

'It is wrong,' Liandra said.

Ilendril laughed. 'No more wrong than putting a horse in harness or training a hawk for the hunt,' he said. 'Asuryan blessed the asur with minds and souls, the knowledge and ability to bring order from the confusion of nature. We are meant to control the world around us. It is our birthright. The only difference between what we are doing now and what a horse-breaker is doing in Tiranoc is a matter of perception. The prejudices that exist within our own minds.' He smiled at her, laying his hand on her arm in a token of sympathy. 'There is no immorality in power,' he said.

Liandra pulled away from his touch. 'The druchii would agree with you,' she hissed.

Ilendril stepped away, fighting to subdue the outrage her insult had roused. For a moment, he stared at her, his gaze growing colder with each heartbeat. Only when Draikyll called to him did he turn away.

'Begin your demonstration, Lord Ilendril,' the general commanded.

'At once,' Ilendril said, bowing. He nodded to Vithrein on the deck below. The gaunt mage didn't respond, but the low incantation he'd been murmuring suddenly grew louder and more vibrant. Caerwal's mages likewise increased the tempo of their own chanting. The rigging hanging from the masts above snapped in a silent wind as unseen forces spiralled down towards the deck.

Liandra could see the aethyric emanations being drawn down into the three mages. She watched as the two standing outside the triangle fed their power into Vithrein. He in turn transferred the energies into the object that rested along the third face of the triangle. It was a long, curved piece of bone, yellowed with age. A tooth, drawn up from the depths by the net of a Sith Rionnasc fisherman. The focus now of this ritual Ilendril had conceived.

For many minutes, the three mages fed energy into the tooth. Then, with a keening wail, Vithrein ended his conjuration. The other two mages staggered back, slumping against the masts as they tried to regain their balance. Vithrein seemed no less drained than his helpers, but he managed to beckon his master down from the aftcastle before sagging to his knees in an exhausted heap.

Ilendril seemed discomfited by the condition of his conjurers, but he had regained his composure by the time he descended to the deck and lifted the tooth from the silver stand that supported it. Turning back to the assembled nobles, he held the tooth out to them. His gaze lingered on Draikyll and he bowed again to the general.

'What you witness now is no trick,' he declared. 'Those of you who know me also know I have no facility with the arcane arts.' Ilendril nodded to

Liandra. 'My lady will relate the difficulty of what you will witness. It is hard enough to stir a dragon with which an asur is already familiar and in sympathetic harmony. How much greater the difficulties to evoke a creature from the depths with which there is no such harmony?'

Ilendril smiled and raised the tooth to his lips. 'You shall see,' he declared. Moving so that he faced the sea, the elf lord began to blow into the hollowed tooth, sounding it as though it were a flute or horn.

Or whistle.

The Sword of Eataine was one of six galleys in the fleet Lord Draikyll had brought from Tor Alessi to the waters off Sith Rionnasc. Magnificent vessels, lean and sharp, lethal as arrows and nearly as swift, they were the masterworks of Eataine's shipyards. When Draikyll had brought this fleet with him to Elthin Arvan, the colonists had been awed by the tremendous power that would now protect them. Now they would be awed by a far more tremendous power.

Many minutes passed while Ilendril blew a low, dolorous note upon the hollow tooth. The spectators on the aftcastle shifted uncomfortably, some of them whispering to each other about the sorry spectacle of seeing Ilendril publicly humiliated. Liandra felt hope stir inside that it would be a failure.

Then the whispers fell silent and dread returned to Liandra's heart. There was turmoil on the formerly quiet sea. Something immense was rising from beneath, propelling itself just below the surface. Lookouts on the other galleys shouted in alarm; one of the ships listed dangerously to port as the thing from below passed just under its hull. Overhead, the noisy croaks of seabirds became a bedlam of squawks and shrieks.

On *The Sword of Eataine,* all had fallen quiet. Only the voice of a sailor praying to Mathlann intruded upon the silence. The very air had grown pregnant with suspense. The nobles of Elthin Arvan hardly dared to breathe as they stared out across the waves.

Whatever had been swimming towards the galley appeared to have subsided, for there was no trace of its movements now. Yet Ilendril still sounded that fearful note from the hollowed tooth. It was an audible reminder to his audience that this peaceful moment was but the quiet before the storm.

The storm broke in an explosion of foam and spray. *The Sword of Eataine* rolled violently as a gigantic body burst up from the depths right beside the ship. An oily, dank reptilian reek washed across the decks, stifling in its intensity. Liandra and the other nobles were forced to crane their necks back to gaze upon the ophidian head that topped the scaly tower now rising beside the ship.

A merwyrm, one of such size and vastness it might have been the spawn of the famed Amanar. The mighty serpent was hoary with age, encrustations of coral clinging to its spines and caking its horns. The sea birds dived down upon its back, squawking happily as they plucked crustaceans and parasites from its scales.

Ilendril lowered the tooth. Boldly, he walked to the rail of the galley, drawing so near the enormous serpent that he could have stretched out his hand and touched its scaly neck. The elf lord leaned back, fastening his gaze upon the merwyrm's reptilian eyes.

'Dance for me,' Ilendril commanded. For an instant, the serpentine head tilted downwards, a bifurcated tongue licking out from between the jaws. It seemed the merwyrm would devour this impertinent little insect who had the temerity to shout at it.

Then, incredibly, the gigantic body began to sway from side to side, writhing with an unnatural, sinuous grace. Ilendril laughed and flung up the hand holding the hollowed-out tooth. He revelled in the awestruck expressions of his fellow nobles, but most of all, he seemed to savour the look of horror that gripped Liandra.

A merwyrm, conjured up not by some harmony between summoner and summoned, but by use of an enslaving enchantment. Liandra wondered if the others could be so blind that they failed to understand the implications of what Ilendril had done.

Were they all so fixated upon the war with the dwarfs that they couldn't see beyond that?

Nugdrinn Hammerfoot stamped across the deck of *Grungni's Fire*. Around the steamship, a flotilla of dwarf vessels ploughed through the waves, churning the dark waters of the Black Gulf with their great paddle wheels. No simple merchant ships these, but ironclad warships festooned with catapults and ballistae, cadres of warriors waiting below decks to board the enemy. It was the most fearsome command Nugdri had been entrusted with since his captaincy of *Nadri's Retribution*.

War had come to Barak Varr. The Black Gulf just beyond the gates of the sea hold had long been considered a dawi lake, but now that once inviolate expanse was being contested. Up the Black Gulf had come a fleet of elgi ships such as Nugdri hadn't believed could exist. They seemed as limitless as the silver of Karak Azul. When the spotters stationed in the towers far down the neck of the gulf had made their reports, no one had believed them. It was incredible, impossible, that the elgi could muster such strength.

Now that he saw the proof of those reports before his own eyes, Nugdri felt something he hadn't felt since the great conflagration over Kazad Mingol. He felt fear.

The elf sailors seemed to be without any fear at all. Boldly they sailed past the forts along the shore, braving the rocks and bolts set upon them by each citadel's artillery. Without hesitation they danced across the great chains that stretched just beneath the surface of the channel, their barbed links designed to rip the belly out of any ship that sailed above them when they were raised. Every defence the dwarfs threw at the vanguard of the fleet seemed useless. Sometimes an elf ship would suddenly flounder, appearing to fade away as it sank into the darkling waters. More often, however, they sailed onwards without any sign of damage.

Behind the scouting ships, a second tide of elven galleys ravaged the citadels, setting them alight with fiery arrows, pots of alchemical incendiaries and bolts of arcane flame. The sunken chains were severed by elgi magic as the bulk of the fleet pressed onwards, their captains taking far fewer chances with their hulls than those in the vanguard.

'Full speed,' Nugdri growled into the speaking horn set in a brass-faced cabinet on the captain's deck. By some trick of engineering his voice would be propelled down into the engine room below. The stokers would feed still more coal into the hungry belly of his ship and set the great paddle wheel accelerating.

For all the good it would do. Nugdri hated to admit it, but as slight and fragile as the elgi galleys looked compared to the robust dawi ironclads, the enemy had the advantage in speed and agility. One good shot from a catapult would cripple a galley; a solid cast from the grudge throwers on the bigger warships would snap an elgi vessel in two. The problem was closing with the enemy, getting near enough to bring him to battle. The dwarf ships could withstand tremendous violence before taking any real damage. The elves had adopted a different tactic: instead of shrugging off an attack, they preferred to avoid it entirely.

Like jackals nipping at a wounded bull, the elgi made the most of their speed and agility. Always keeping out of reach, the galleys would sail near enough that their archers could loose a volley at the dwarfs. The arrows never struck true, always landing in the sea beside their target, but somehow that was even more infuriating than having them hit. It was unabashed mockery, a scornful insult to the dawi and their martial pride. It was a display of arrogance and disdain that had many a dwarf pulling his beard and muttering curses that would set his ancestors covering their ears.

Goaded beyond endurance, Nugdri's flotilla pursued the elusive galleys. The fragile look of their enemy and their own faith in the strength of their ironclads, made the vindictive dwarf captains cast aside caution. One after another they broke formation to pursue the elves, trying to force them landwards and box them in against the coast.

Nugdri tried to signal his captains back into line, but they were too intent on venting their injured pride against the vexing elves to listen. Soon, he found that he only had five ships following his own. The rest were scattered across the Black Gulf.

Some of the slight galleys continued to plague and torment them, but Nugdri refused to rise to their bait. They were trying to draw him off. He had to discover why. The second wave of elgi warships was still too distant for the ironclads to close with them. Why then were these scouts so intent on holding him back?

The answer came in a display at once both incredible and fantastic. If he'd blinked, Nugdri would have missed the sudden manifestation. As his ironclad thundered onwards, a tall elgi galleon abruptly appeared on his portside, only a few rods away. He could make out the sea-serpent heraldry of the crew, the elaborate detail of its mermaid figurehead, the snap of its triangular sails as they rippled above the decks. Asur archers were already standing on that deck, their captain's arm raised as he prepared to give the command to loose.

Nugdri roared into the speaking horn, ordering the paddle wheel set into reverse, trying to save his ship from the coming assault. Even as he gave the command, another elgi ship manifested from the nothingness. Elven sorcery, a cloak of magic, had concealed the elgi ships, hiding them from sight until the dwarfs were right upon them.

A terrible suspicion struck him as Nugdri glanced over his shoulder. He could still see the scattered ships of his flotilla, but there was no trace of their prey. The captains had been chasing illusions crewed by phantoms, nothing more than mirages conjured by elgi mages. No wonder the galleys had been so bold about exposing the dawi defences! The few that had seemed to be destroyed were nothing more than a further trick to keep the dwarfs from guessing the deception.

Nugdri's crew scrambled to repel boarders while his artillerists and crossbows made ready to return the elgi attack. Their captain stomped his hammerfoot into the socket beside the ship's wheel. Nothing but death would tear him from his post now. If need be, he would go down with his command.

Dawi warriors clashed with elgi swordsmen as the asur swarmed across the railing. The dwarfs had the advantage of brawn and determination, but the elves fought with a grisly grace, seeming to ignore the pitching deck beneath their feet. Where a dwarf axeman missed his strike because of the rolling deck, an elf blade flashed clean and true.

The swordsmen kept to the centre of the ship, for reasons that swiftly became obvious. Elf archers poised in the rigging of their own ships took careful aim and loosed a vicious volley down upon the dwarfs as they moved to surround the invaders. The attack wasn't particularly lethal, mainly resulting in scratched armour and shallow wounds. It was the response that proved deadly. Waiting for the volley, the swordsmen lunged at the dwarfs before they could recover from the abrupt attack. The thrusting blades opened throats and skewered hearts in a brief, murderous melee. In only a few heartbeats, a dozen dwarfs lay bleeding across the deck.

From the forecastles of the elgi ships, bolt throwers launched their spears into *Grungni's Fire,* the enchanted missiles punching through the ironclad hull. Trying to steer his ship to avoid the volley from one, Nugdri found himself in the sights of the other. Shouts from below decks attested to the effectualness of the elgi aim. The steamship was taking on water, though the all-important engine room had yet to be menaced.

Jinking away from the second elf ship, Nugdri felt his heart turn to lead. A third elgi galleon materialised from the nothingness and a volley of flaming arrows slammed down into the deck, setting the planks and clapboards on fire.

Nugdri realised this would be his last battle. He only hoped the elf illusions had been exposed soon enough to benefit the stronghold and allow King Brynnoth to mount a real defence against real enemies.

Of the chances for his own flotilla, Nugdri had no illusions.

From the great rock Durazon, King Brynnoth could look out over the lands surrounding the sea hold. What he saw with his one eye was enough to break a dozen hearts. The Black Gulf had gone from a dawi to an elgi lake. Most of the surrounding citadels had been captured or razed by the invaders; the few that still remained in dawi hands were cut off, the passages connecting them to Barak Varr collapsed by elgi magic. The garrisons were holding out thus far, but the king wondered how long the elves would allow that situation to continue. The defenders of the citadels could resist the elgi themselves and even their magic, but the enemy had other resources to draw upon.

Brynnoth turned his eyes landwards, looking out over the scorched fields and blackened pastures where the dwarfs had grown their crops and herds. 'Drakk did that, two of them working together. Just like Kazad Thar.'

Standing beside his king, High Thane Onkmarr clenched his fists in impotent rage. 'Since we brought the bolt throwers up onto the Durazon, the filthy wyrms have kept their distance. They're eager enough to fight for the *thagging* elgi, but they aren't so keen about dying for them.'

'The elgi have other jobs for their monsters,' Brynnoth growled. 'The wyrms have already driven off armies from Karak Eight Peaks and Karak Hirn. The elgi are spread thin on the shore – if either of those armies had been able to make it through the passes, they could have pushed the vermin back into the Black Gulf.'

'King Varnuf and King Valarik should have coordinated their forces,' Onkmarr grumbled. 'Then at least one of them might have got through. If the elgi could be driven from one side of the gulf then it would open a line of supply. As it stands, even the settlements the elgi haven't burned can't do anything to help us.'

King Brynnoth shook his head. From the top of the Durazon, he'd been able to watch what had befallen those armies. The dragons waited until they were in the narrow mountain passes and then swept down upon them. Boxed into the canyons, with nowhere to escape the dragon fire, the slaughter had been terrible. Both armies had withdrawn when it became clear they couldn't force their way past the dragons and still have enough strength to do the besieged hold any good.

'If we can force the elgi out of the tunnels, we can be reinforced through the Ungdrin Ankor,' King Brynnoth declared, casting his eyes downwards, as though peering through the rock to the deeps far below.

Onkmarr frowned. 'The elgi know it too. That's where they've been clever. They're thin around the gulf, but they've deployed in strength down in the tunnels. So far no relief force has been able to endure the gauntlet of elgi arrows and sorcery waiting for them.' The High Thane pulled at his beard, tugging a few strands away in his fury. 'Worse, the scum are starting to threaten the lower deeps of Barak Varr itself. If we have to confront a simultaneous invasion outside the walls and from right beneath us...'

'It will be a recipe for disaster,' Brynnoth affirmed. The king scratched at the hollow of his missing eye, wondering if some of his detractors weren't right. They claimed that his reckless embracing of unproved inventions had drawn the attention of the elves. If he'd never allowed Heglan Copperfist to build his deranged skryzan-harbark and send them to confront the elgi drakk, it was doubtful the asur would have shown such interest in the sea hold. They hadn't after the destruction of Feillas and Oeragor. It was the skryzan-harbark that had brought them down about Barak Varr's gates.

Briefly, Brynnoth imagined how different the situation would be if he had Heglan's airships to send against the elgi. That, of course, was impossible. The dramatic death of the engineer and the obliteration of his workshop had proven the stance Guildmaster Strombak and many of the other engineers had taken. The technology was too dangerous and unpredictable to pursue, more of a threat to those who used it than the enemy they would destroy.

What a vision it had been though! Driving the elves back into the sea, casting them out of dwarf lands forever. Seeing their drakk brought low, their carcasses burning at the feet of the mountains. Brynnoth would have been the great hero of the Karaz Ankor, his name more revered than that of the High King himself.

Shattered dreams now. Nothing more. His vision had ended in tragedy, and worse, it had brought the full fury of the war upon Brynnoth's head. The king reached up with a trembling hand and pulled the crown from his head. Through his glazed eye he stared at the golden circlet. Never in his four hundred years had the weight of his crown felt so heavy upon his head.

From the tunnels beneath one of the dwarf citadels lining the Black Gulf, Lord Caerwal's forces rushed into the deeps beneath Barak Varr. Mopping up the handful of survivors left by the merwyrms in the citadel had been pitifully easy, but now the elves were finding themselves fighting for every twist and turn in the tunnels. Hundreds of asur lay dead in the passages behind them, the only consolation lying in the hundreds of dwarfs who'd fallen with them.

Yet another corridor and Liandra found herself beset by a fresh surge of dawi warriors. Her blade descended upon the first dwarf to close with her in a flash of crimson and a welter of gore. The bearded warrior collapsed, a warhammer rolling free from his now slackened grip. He clutched blindly for her, trying to drag her down, immobilise her so that his comrades might make short work of her. Grimly, she thrust the point of her sword into the dwarf's throat and ended his struggles.

Even as she rose from the cooling corpse, more of the dawi were rushing down the tunnel, their fierce war-cries ringing across the passage like a giant's bellow. Hammer and axe, pick and sword, the dwarfs threw themselves into the assault. If they faltered, they would withdraw a short distance behind a screen of crossbows protected by tall shields of bronze. With the crossbows to cover them, the dawi fighters would regroup and return to the attack with the wilful stubbornness that characterised their race.

It had become a test of endurance to force the dwarfs back. With each assault Liandra saw scores of the warriors around her brought down. Young seafarers from Eataine, hardened veterans from Chrace, a wispy swordsman who'd been born in Sith Rionnasc barely a century ago. It was all such a waste. Everything these elves might have been, all the things they might have done, all the lives they could have touched, all of it snuffed out hundreds of feet beneath the surface in the black depths of the world, their lifeblood seeping away to stain the floor of a dwarf burrow.

Liandra could suffer no more of this. Taxed and diminished as her magic had become, she couldn't allow this pointless carnage to go on. She had the power to end it, though it would leave her drained and wasted for hours, perhaps even days.

The cry of an elf swordswoman as her arm was lopped off by a dawi axe removed Liandra's last tinge of restraint. 'Defend me a moment,' she told a pair of mail-clad warriors. One look at the mage and they leapt to carry out her order with a ferocity that nearly surpassed that of the dwarfs themselves. Liandra saw one bearded warrior stagger back, his throat opened by a flashing sword. Another collapsed in a gory heap as blood bubbled up from beneath his rent armour.

Then there was no time for thought or consideration of the battle raging around her. Closing her eyes fast, Liandra pulled at the aethyric harmonies, the intangible energies writhing through the air around her. Here, deep within the earth, in the very roots of Barak Varr, the vibrations had a strangely rigid quality about them, as though a wide stream had been funnelled into a narrow channel. It made it easier to latch on to the magic she sought, but at the same time rendered those energies much more difficult to shape and bind to her will. Maybe, at the height of her powers, she would have found it easier. As it was, she felt like a fisherman with some great catch fighting and straining at the end of the line. The difference was, if the catch broke her line, the aethyric discharge would probably run amok and kill every living thing in the tunnels for a league or so.

Liandra heard her heart pounding, felt her blood flowing faster and faster through her veins. Everything inside her was trying to speed up, to find harmony with the racing aethyric current. She knew her heart would burst before it could match that tempo. No, she had to force the current itself to flow. She had to master the magic; she couldn't let it master her.

It was when she was nearly at the limit of her endurance, ready to cast the fish back before it could break the line, that she felt the power swell inside her. The aethyric current, or at least the strand she had drawn upon, was hers. Fixing her gaze on the line of crossbowmen and the thick bronze shields they sheltered behind, she turned those hard-won energies into the force she had envisioned. The incantation that whispered across her lips gave the power purpose and form.

A flare of blinding light seared across the dwarf ranks, howling through them with volcanic fury. The next instant, scores of crossbowmen were screaming, leaping out from behind their shields as the bronze plates turned red-hot and began to drip molten metal across them. Dislodged from their protection, fully illuminated by the afterglow of the magical light, the dwarfs quickly fell victim to asur arrows.

Confusion gripped the other dwarfs. The dramatic display of magic, the sudden and brutal killing of their crossbowmen, these drained the ferocity of their attack. The dawi retreated back down the passage. It wasn't a rout – the dwarfs maintained good order as they withdrew – but it was a retreat just the same. And this time there wasn't a file of crossbows to keep the elves from pursuing their shaken enemy. There wasn't a wall of shields for the dwarfs to shelter behind and regroup.

Liandra took no part in that last, bloody stage of the battle. Drained by her magic, she leaned against the cold stone wall and tried to compose herself. Her heart and blood were still racing at incredible speed, still trying to match the magical current she had tapped into. It took her utmost concentration to force her body to calm itself and to deny the aethyric harmony that sought to draw her in.

When she was composed, the first thing she saw was Lord Caerwal staring at her. His face bore an impatient, arrogant kind of displeasure, but he knew enough about the ways of magic to wait until Liandra was somewhat recovered before voicing that displeasure.

'Do you think that was wise?' Caerwal asked, clearly already aware of what he considered the right answer. Among the asur of Elthin Arvan there was no lord or lady more committed to the war than Caerwal. His every breath was devoted to avenging the destruction of Athel Numiel, the city he'd built and the dwarfs had razed. Anything that obstructed that grim purpose he took as a personal affront.

'No,' Liandra said. 'But it was necessary. Something had to be done to break the dawi formation. Otherwise we might have been days fighting for this miserable stretch of burrow.'

Somehow Caerwal's gaze managed to become even more hostile. 'What use is capturing the tunnel?' he snapped. 'I don't want the tunnel, I want the mud-digger's reservoir! I was depending on your magic to find it, remember? The magic that brought us this far.'

Liandra pushed herself away from the wall, forcing herself to stand steady on her own two feet when she answered the outraged lord. The last thing she wanted was to appear weak before Caerwal, to let him think he owned her the way he felt he owned those who served him. She wasn't one of his servants or stooges. She'd been ordered by Lord Draikyll to attend him – a temporary relationship that would end with the siege.

'What good is knowing where the reservoir is if we can't reach it?' she retorted. She waved her hand at the carnage around them, at the bodies heaped on the floor. 'This is the worst opposition we've encountered since the citadel on the shore was captured. What do you think they're trying to protect so fiercely?'

Caerwal tapped a finger against the blade he held, a sword that Liandra noticed was as clean and polished as the day he'd disembarked on the beach. 'You could be right,' he conceded. He nodded, more to himself than to her. 'Yes, by Hoeth, you may be right.'

Liandra turned from Caerwal, looking instead at the ten bodyguards the lord had brought with him into the tunnels. Like their master, their mail was unblemished by the stains of battle. 'You might join your warriors and see for yourself,' she suggested.

'They have their job and I have mine,' Caerwal said. He patted the golden coffer that was chained to his belt. 'My purpose is more important than killing a few dwarfs.' His face took on a feral, nearly animalistic expression of hate. 'I intend to kill them all.' The expression faded and when he looked back at Liandra there was a smile on his face. 'We'll bide here a time until you are recovered.'

There was no sun or moons to reckon the passage of time by down in the dwarfish deeps, but Caerwal managed with an hourglass fashioned from diamond and powdered manticore heart. There was some measure of enchantment in it – no matter which way it was turned, the sands would flow in the same direction until they had all passed from one sphere to the other. By Caerwal's reckoning then, it was three hours before a messenger came back to them and reported that the way ahead was clear. The dwarfs had been vanquished.

The reservoir was a great chamber carved from the living rock of the mountain. Immense stone faces, the effigies of the dawi's cheerless ancestor gods, scowled down at the elves as they entered the room. A wide shelf of stone ran along the edges of the room, an array of bronze, copper and iron pipes snaking across them to dive into the great basin that dominated the chamber. By torchlight, the water in the reservoir looked almost black, splashing against the sides of the basin in little eddies.

All around the room, dwarf bodies were strewn. They'd put up a fierce fight for this place, doing their best to keep the invaders from capturing the hall. Many had been pierced over and over by asur arrows. Slicks of blood along the floor told where wounded warriors had tried to drag themselves back into the fray.

'It should be easy enough to destroy these pipes,' Liandra said as she studied the vault. 'The dawi must be using them to pump water from the reservoir into the hold.'

'Destroy them?' Caerwal's laugh was the nastiest thing Liandra had heard drop from the tongue of another elf. Even the druchii witch Drutheira hadn't made her skin crawl the way Caerwal's laugh now did.

The elf lord reached to his belt. With a vicious tug he snapped the chain holding the golden coffer in place. An awful light gleamed in Caerwal's eyes as he drew from within it a lead flask. 'I want dead dwarfs, not thirsty ones,' he said.

Liandra shook her head. 'You're going to poison the reservoir,' she said, feeling her stomach clench at the thought.

'This one and all the others I can find,' Caerwal said. He held the flask higher, tapping his finger against it. 'This is powdered basilisk venom. One drop is enough to eat through the bellies of a hundred dwarfs. I'll send thousands to their filthy gods.' Savagely, he upended the flask. A foul-smelling, luminous green sludge dripped out, slithering with syrupy coldness from the bottle to the reservoir. As it struck the water, a luminous sparkle crackled about the slime, wisps of malignant magic that crawled away into the depths. When it was all gone, Caerwal tossed the emptied flask into the basin, watching as it sank from view.

'I have more of the poison for the other reservoirs,' Caerwal said, misjudging the cause for Liandra's disgusted look. 'Without a city to maintain or colonists to support, I have nothing better to spend my fortune on.'

'We call them savages,' Liandra marvelled. She could see a few of the warriors gathered in the reservoir shared her revulsion, but many – too many – had a hateful satisfaction on their faces. That was the real horror of war. Not those killed in the fighting, but those who were made dead while they were still alive.

First Ilendril's ghastly magic that enslaved the minds and spirits of other creatures, now Caerwal's despicable poisons. Liandra turned from the reservoir, making her way back into the battle-scarred tunnel. She had to get away from the smell of blood, the stink of hate. She had to get back to the surface and the clean, open air.

Behind her, she could hear Lord Caerwal calling. 'You'll see, Liandra. I'll poison every mud-eater in this place. I'll turn Barak Varr into the greatest sepulchre in Elthin Arvan!'

High King Gotrek watched as his warriors mustered in the great hall of Karaz-a-Karak. With the mammoth statues of their ancestor gods looking down upon them, ten thousand dwarf warriors bent their knee to the king. There were warriors from Ekrund and Zhufbar, Kraka Drak in the far north and Karak Drazh in the far south. Norse dwarfs and even skarrenawi. All had come to swear allegiance to the High King's banner, to march with him to war.

It was something Gotrek had long desired, a muster not of Karaz-a-Karak or Karak Eight Peaks. Not the drawing together of warriors to fight for a single hold. Not separate armies grudgingly accepting a unified command, yet still pursuing their own individual ambitions and hunt for glory.

The grisly example of Brok Stonefist was a lesson. Most dwarfs couldn't see it that way, but Gotrek did. Brok's stubborn pursuit for his own glory and his own prestige had brought him to ruin. How close a thing it could have been. What if Brok's warriors had been needed elsewhere, needed to be where the army's supposed general, Morgrim, needed them to be? The entire campaign could have become a disaster because of one dwarf's selfish ambition.

The Lord of the Tunnels was revered as a hero now, cheered throughout the Karaz Ankor for his duel with Lord Salendor. He'd earned himself a place in history. Gotrek wasn't so sure he deserved it.

Of course, pride and ambition weren't qualities rare among the dwarfs and certainly not among their lords. The kings of Karak Hirn and Karak Eight Peaks, rather than wait for armies from the other holds to help them break the siege at Barak Varr had instead set out all on their own. The disastrous results had more to do with personal ambition than marauding dragons, though he despaired of ever making the kings see it that way.

Now a third army had been repulsed. King Hrallson's warriors from Karak Azul had tried to reach Barak Varr through the Ungdrin Ankor only to be driven back by elgi magic. And still the lesson wasn't learned. The elves weren't a disorganised rabble like urk and grobi. They were an enemy united in purpose and command. If the dwarfs refused to acknowledge that and adjust to it, then they were doomed to an endless succession of hollow victories and bitter defeats.

The key to changing all of that was arrayed before him in the great hall. From a balcony set between the arms of Grungni and Grimnir, Gotrek gazed across the heterogeneous force that had travelled so far and so long to follow him into war. Over the years and decades, what had started as a trickle had grown into an avalanche.

'Will you lead them?' Morgrim asked. He was alone with his uncle on the balcony. Elgidum had led campaigns many times since the burning of Athel Maraya. He was often away from Karaz-a-Karak waging war in the High King's name. When word of the siege at Barak Varr reached him, however, Morgrim had hastened back.

Gotrek knew his nephew had come to see if the High King needed him to lead an army to relieve the sea hold. When he'd found his liege arrayed for battle, it had surprised him. It had surprised many, but not Gotrek. He knew this day would come, the day when the High King must take to the field of battle.

Failure was what made it possible. The failure of King Varnuf. The failure of King Hrallson. The failure of King Valarik. The failure of King Brynnoth. The inability of any of the holds, Barak Varr, Karak Hirn, Karak Eight Peaks or Karak Azul, to fight off the elves on their own. The eyes of the entire Karaz Ankor were set upon Barak Varr now, watching and waiting.

What they would see was High King Gotrek leading an army not of Karaz-a-Karak but of *dwarfs*. They would see the united power of their people accomplish what was impossible to single kings and single realms.

They would see. They would learn.

'Yes,' Gotrek told Morgrim. 'I will lead them. To hell or victory, I will lead them.'

EIGHT

THE SIEGE OF BARAK VARR

344TH YEAR OF THE REIGN OF CALEDOR II

Standing outside the command tent of Lord Draikyll, Liandra could see the immense reptiles circle above the Black Gulf before flying away. The dragons were leaving. The great drakes Lord Teranion had brought to help Lord Draikyll conquer Barak Varr were abandoning the fight, winging their way back to Tor Alessi. Watching them go, Liandra couldn't shake the sense of longing they evoked. She knew the glory and majesty that came from communing with a dragon, of soaring through the skies on the back of a creature already ancient when the first elf set foot in Ulthuan. There was nothing else that could compare to that experience. In its wake, what was left wasn't so much life as merely existence.

Just knowing that dragons were nearby had somehow made her feel less alone. Sometimes, if she exerted her powers to their utmost, she was able to brush against the consciousness of the dragons. It wasn't like the dragonsong she'd shared with Vranesh, but it wasn't nothing either. She could sense the overall moods of Teranion's drakes, their general attitude to the battles they'd been asked to fight, the continual appeals to their indulgence. This war wasn't their war, after all.

That was never more clear to the elves than it was now. The dragons were leaving Barak Varr, returning to their temporary lairs among the towers of Tor Alessi. It hadn't been the dwarfs who'd made the dragons leave. It had been the asur.

For years now, Liandra had sensed the growing unease of the dragons. The reptiles were becoming distrustful of the asur. If not for the bond that persisted between rider and drake, they would have abandoned the siege long ago. That they had remained this long was a testament to Teranion's persuasiveness, his ability to appeal to the reptilian sensibilities of dragons. It was too simple to think of a dragon's mind in terms like pride and honour, but they were concepts that did evoke those parts of a drake's essence that indulged the entreaties of a comparatively young, weak and fragile creature like an elf. It also held that if something kindred to pride and honour could exist in a dragon, then those qualities could be offended as well.

She knew Teranion had warned Draikyll about using the merwyrm fangs. The magic invested into the fangs was something upsetting to the dragons. Each time Ilendril or one of his confederates had employed one of the fangs to draw a merwyrm into the battle, the dragons had become that much more uneasy.

Draikyll had listened to the dragon riders for a time. It was lack of progress against the sea hold that finally changed the general's mind. He had too many resources tied up in the Black Gulf to countenance defeat, yet with each passing year the risk that the dwarfs would make a concentrated attack against one of the elf cities grew. Tor Alessi could probably hold on its own, but he couldn't be as certain of the others. If he were to lose Athel Toralien or Sith Rionnasc, Draikyll knew he'd be relieved by the Phoenix King. Caledor II would summon him back to Ulthuan in disgrace and all his hopes for advancement and prestige would crumble into dust.

At last, Draikyll threw his support behind Ilendril's magic. The merwyrms were summoned – not one or two this time, but half a dozen of the beasts. They were turned against those citadels that had so stubbornly held out against the asur siege. The sea serpents tore down two of the bastions, using their scaly coils and immense strength to crumble the foundations and spill the towers into the Black Gulf. A third citadel had proven a different problem. The dwarf defenders, fully aware of what had been done to the other garrisons, prepared a particularly hideous surprise for the merwyrms. Among their arsenal must have been a supply of the same incendiary the airships had used over Kazad Mingol.

When one of the largest merwyrms began to coil around their citadel, the dwarfs within detonated their arsenal. The resultant explosion had thrown slabs of stone clear across the Black Gulf, some pieces even smashing into the great sea-gates of Barak Varr, denting their iron faces. The merwyrm had been thrown back into the water, its body wreathed in grisly green fire. Even under the waves, the green flames refused to be extinguished but instead continued to devour the serpent. For the better part of a day, the vast reptile had writhed among the shallows, lashing and flailing as its body was consumed.

As the merwyrm died, Liandra could feel the scorn in the hearts of the dragons. It wasn't empathy for the merwyrm, but a withering disappointment in those who had sent it into the fight.

Liandra stepped inside Lord Draikyll's tent, the brightly coloured pavilion he'd erected on the beach, and tried to explain to the general why the dragons were leaving. It was hard to couch her words in such a way that it didn't sound like she was blaming him for failing to heed the warnings Teranion had given. Draikyll was too much like his king: he didn't understand dragons. He thought they were nothing but beasts, living weapons to be pointed at the enemy and unleashed. It was hard for him to understand an intelligence older and wiser than that of the asur, an intelligence that didn't fawn over ranks and titles with diligent devotion.

Ilendril was there as well, waiting until Liandra was through before speaking his piece.

'With all due apologies to the Lady Liandra, but she makes my case for me,' Ilendril stated. He pointed to the map laid out across the table at the centre of Draikyll's tent. 'Until now, the dragons have kept the dwarfs from making any kind of inroads by means of the mountain passes. They were even able to push Gotrek's first expedition back. With them to watch and guard the overland passes, we've been able to concentrate on keeping the main tunnel network closed to the dwarfs.'

The general brought his golden rod of office cracking down against the table. 'I am aware of the situation and what we've lost by losing the dragons.' He reached over for one of the tiny flags that marked the positions the asur occupied, plucking it from one of the citadels the merwyrms had destroyed. 'In trying to chase the rat from the pantry, we've left the gate wide open for the wolf to come in.'

'Our hand is forced, my lord,' Ilendril agreed, 'but that may be for the best.' He smiled at Liandra before returning his attention to Draikyll. 'The restraint that has held us back is no longer feasible. We have to assault the stronghold and we have to do so in full force.'

'Caerwal fought his way into another reservoir last week,' Liandra reminded the general. 'That makes seven he's poisoned. The dams on the rivers have cut that supply as well.'

'They can still draw water from the gulf itself,' Draikyll stated. 'I don't know how the mud-diggers can drink the stuff, foul as it is with the run-off from their foundries and smelters, but they no doubt have their ways. Anything that might confound us, they find some way to do it. They can play for time here because they know that we can't stay.'

Ilendril pointed his finger at the map, indicating the great sea-gates of Barak Varr. 'The only choice is a full attack. I can have the remaining merwyrms set against the sea-gates. Their combined strength will tear them down and leave the very heart of the dwarf fortress open to us.'

Liandra shook her head. 'The dawi have defences trained on those gates. Your serpents would be torn to pieces.'

'Not before they pull down one of them,' Ilendril stated.

In that moment, Liandra knew she should have gone back to Tor Alessi with Teranion and the dragons.

From the pass above the Howling River some fifty miles from Barak Varr, High King Gotrek watched as the dragons flew away, following them with a spyglass until they vanished in the mists of the mountains far to the north. He lowered the glass slowly, tapping it against the side of the marker stone at the edge of the pass. It seemed too good to be true, yet something in his gut told him that it was no trick. The drakk were well and truly gone.

One of his hearthguard came up to him, offering to relieve Gotrek of the glass if he was done with the instrument. Gotrek waved the warrior back. He knew his bodyguards were eager to get their king back into the safety of the tunnels, back down where the rest of the army was waiting. They didn't like him exposing himself this way, up on the surface where elgi assassins and mages might find him.

Gotrek appreciated their concern better than they knew. At the same time, he was responsible for the vast army he'd assembled – the united command it had taken him so long to forge from the flames of war. It was in answer to his call that his subject kings had set aside their own ambitions and brought armies to join the assault against the elgi invaders. If they failed now, if this campaign ended in disaster, then the damage to the war effort as a whole would be incalculable.

That was why, when some rangers trickled down into the Ungdrin Ankor to report that the drakk appeared to be leaving, the High King himself determined to check the validity of their observations. Now, he felt the thrill of possibility rushing through him. For months the dwarfs had been waiting in the passes, hollowing out old mineshafts and linking them to the Ungdrin Ankor so that they might have a thousand boltholes to fall back to should the dragons descend upon them. To the south he knew the armies of Karak Azul, Karak Drazh and Karak Eight Peaks were likewise lying in wait. Further to the west would be the regiments dispatched from Ekrund and the settlements in the Dragonback Mountains. Northwards, warriors from Karak Hirn and Karak Izor were waiting, secreted among the hills. In all, it was a multitude such as the dawi hadn't mustered in a century. Not under a single command.

Chirps, amazingly like those of a fox calling to its pups, rose from the trees at the mouth of the pass. Gotrek dropped down from his perch on the boulder, brushing off the hearthguard who moved to help him. He might not be as spry as he had been when driving the urk and grobi from the Karaz Ankor, but he was still robust enough to do for himself. Any of his subjects who thought otherwise were quite welcome to mention it to him and see how they enjoyed a cracked skull.

The signal from the dwarf pickets sounded once more, this time from within the pass itself. The hearthguard flipped down the visors of their helms, hefted their axes and formed a wall of steel and muscle around the king. Gotrek peered past their armoured shoulders to watch the pass. He soon saw a lone dwarf rushing up the slope. Unlike the hearthguard, this dwarf wore lighter armour of boiled leather and finely wrought steel chain. His helm was a simple steel bowl with a hammer-shaped spur projecting down over the dwarf's nose. For an instant, Gotrek was reminded of Furgil, his captain of rangers, dead now over a century.

The ranger stopped a few yards from the wall of armed hearthguard. Dropping to his knees, he clapped one fist against his breast and bowed his head. 'Tromm, my liege,' he greeted the High King.

At a gesture from Gotrek, the hearthguard standing in front of him stepped away so that he might have an unobstructed view of the ranger. As they took up new positions, the warriors set down their axes and unslung the shields they carried on their backs. They kept their eyes on the ranger, ready to block any treacherous attack against the king. Tales of elgi illusions were too numerous to be discounted as exaggeration. If the elves could hide an entire fleet with their sorcery, making one of their assassins look like a dwarf should be comparatively easy.

'You bring further news of the drakk?' Gotrek asked.

The ranger raised his face and shook his head. 'No, sire, we have seen no trace of the drakk down in the plains. The last we saw of them they were flying towards the Black Mountains.'

'They kept flying,' Gotrek said, slapping the spyglass against his armoured knee. 'Ancestors alone know why, but they seem to have gone.'

The ranger's face brightened and a smile took shape beneath his grimy black beard. 'They may have been scared off by the fire, my liege,' he said. 'We have been watching the elgi call great serpents from the depths of the Black Gulf to destroy the bastions along the shores. Rather than give the beasts the satisfaction of killing them, one of the garrisons detonated their stores of blasting powder.' The dwarf folded his hand into a fist, then splayed his fingers outwards to illustrate his report. 'Green fire, my liege, just the same as they say consumed Kazad Mingol and killed the wyrms there.'

Gotrek was silent, stroking his beard as he digested this bit of information. 'The elgi, can you see what they are doing? Has there been any change in their deployment?'

'Yes, sire,' the ranger answered. 'The elgi seem greatly agitated. They've drawn many of the warriors they had deployed along the shores back towards Barak Varr.'

A grim chuckle rose from the High King. Everything the ranger reported bore out his gut instinct. He doubted if the elgi would be so perturbed by the destruction of one of their serpents, but the desertion of their drakk? That was another matter entirely. Without the dragons to hold the passes for them, the elgi knew there was nothing they could do to keep the dawi from marching out and joining them in battle.

Clearly the elf general's dreams of conquest died hard. Rather than quit the field, the elgi was throwing everything into one final, brutal effort to take Barak Varr.

It was still a gamble. It might yet be some elaborate elgi deception, a trick to draw out the dawi host. But to play it safe and stand back meant watching Barak Varr be ravaged. The sea hold had already endured so much for so long; Gotrek couldn't accept the shame of letting its people suffer still more.

'Tell my thanes and captains to ready their troops,' Gotrek declared. 'Send messengers to the other kings. We march with the morning sun.' He paused as he waited for the reckoners who'd accompanied his hearthguard out from the mines to copy his words to parchment.

'The elgi have trespassed here long enough. Now, by Grungni, they will leave Barak Varr or remain forever in their graves!'

The great sea-gates of Barak Varr shuddered and groaned. Hundreds of feet high, wrought of iron and bronze, the gates had withstood the worst storms the Black Gulf could hurl against them. Now those titanic portals were confronted by a far different threat, a violence even the most malignant seas couldn't match. The elgi had loosed their merwyrms against the gates, attacking the harbour entrance with all the elemental savagery the colossal reptiles could bring to bear.

King Brynnoth stood on the waterfront, his hearthguard arrayed around him, the seawyrm stylings of their armour tragically ironic given the nature of the enemy that now threatened them. High Thane Onkmarr, his armour black with soot from his inspection of the gate defences, stood once more beside his king.

Brynnoth pushed his finger into the hollow of his missing eye, trying to scratch the nagging itch. His remaining eye was fixed upon the battlements above the sea-gates. He could see the defenders clinging to the shuddering gantries behind the gates, their crossbows aimed through the vents to shoot down into the beasts battering at their defences. On the stone battlements themselves, gangs of shouting dwarfs pushed handcarts along a narrow railway. As each handcart reached the end of its run, it was pitched onto its side, casting a shower of molten lead down the face of the gate. From outside, it would look as though the enormous visages of the ancestor gods sculpted onto the gates were crying tears of fire.

'Nothing could survive such violence,' High Thane Onkmarr assured his king. A thrashing rumble against the gates proved him wrong only a moment later.

'Whatever we do just seems to make them even madder,' Brynnoth cursed. 'By Grimnir, I'd almost welcome their damn drakk into my halls rather than fight these serpents!'

'If the serpents break the gates, that will be the end of them,' Onkmarr declared. 'Half the hold's warriors are here waiting to send those beasts to Gazul's larder.'

Brynnoth turned his attention from the heights to the vast harbourage behind the gates. Regiments of crossbows stood poised along the waterfront, weapons trained upon the trembling gates. Catapults and ballistae had been brought from throughout the hold to form strongpoints within the harbour. Dozens of bolt throwers were ranged at the mouth of each street and passageway. Catapults had been assembled on the piers and docks, anywhere they might have the freedom of movement to hurl their burdens at the attackers. A great grudge thrower, immense blocks of carved stone engraved with runes of woe and havoc resting beside it, had been erected in the hastily demolished fish market, ready to cast a ton of stone at the first serpent that dared poke its head within the walls of Barak Varr.

'We'll stop them before it comes to that,' Brynnoth declared. 'I've already seen to it.' He gestured at the small flotilla of ships poised at the end of the docks. Though no vessel had sailed from Barak Varr since the start of the siege, all had been maintained to a peak of perfection. Early on it had been with the promise that they'd be needed to hunt down the fleeing elgi when the siege was broken. Later, it had simply been a matter of pride and duty that the ships not be allowed to suffer from neglect.

'My liege, think of what you are doing,' Onkmarr said. 'There are many who feel betrayed by your decree. After tending these ships for so long...'

'Let them bring grudgement against a king if they dare!' Brynnoth snapped.

Onkmarr shook his head. 'Most of them won't be able to. They've volunteered to pilot the ships on their last voyage.'

Brynnoth frowned at that last remark, scratching at his missing eye. 'The sacrifice won't be in vain,' he declared. 'Remember how it looked when we watched from the Durazon as the garrison of Bar-Bruz detonated their supply of Tharzharr and killed the elgi snake? The beast had been ripped to shreds and the elgi scattered like rats.'

'The garrison and the citadel were lost to us,' Onkmarr reminded him. 'You should remember what else has been seen from the Durazon. Signal fires telling us that High King Gotrek is leading an all-out effort to break the siege.'

Brynnoth shook his finger in Onkmarr's face. 'That is exactly why we must act now. What pride is left to Barak Varr if it is left to others to rescue us? Gotrek is too soft to be High King, but if I let him rescue my kingdom, I'll be beholden to him. I'll be forced to recant my disfavour of him!'

The king and his thane watched as one of the gates began to distort inwards, a tremendous impact pounding a great dent in the portal. Brynnoth pointed at the stricken gate. 'They won't hold,' he said. 'But we have enough Tharzharr in those ships to blast the serpents into offal. It's been stockpiled ever since the airships were dismantled.'

'Maybe Engineer Strombak and his guild are right when they say Tharzharr is suspect, tainted by its association with the skryzan-harbark,' Onkmarr said. 'They want to do more tests with it to be certain of its–'

Brynnoth cut Onkmarr off with a scowl. 'They want to test and test and test. I may have to suffer the timidity of Gotrek, but I don't have to put up with it from my own vassals.' Angrily, he waved his hand at the roof overhead. 'Go! Climb back to the Durazon and look for sign of the High King. Leave the fighting to those with the stomach for it.'

Onkmarr bowed his head and hastily withdrew. He knew better than to test Brynnoth's temper when the king had his mind set upon a purpose. He could only hope to regain his liege's favour when he was in a less impassioned mood.

Brynnoth turned his eye back to the harbour, chuckling as he considered the ingenuity of his plan. Ten ironclads, loaded to the gunwales with Tharzharr. Fire-ships to ravage the elgi fleet. The plan had been to unleash them under the cover of night, but the elgi attack had forced a change in those plans. Now they would have to use one of the fire-ships to destroy the serpents at the gates and depend upon the shock and confusion from the explosion to cover the other fire-ships as they sailed out into the Black Gulf.

The shriek of twisting metal drew Brynnoth's eyes back to the sea-gates. One of the cyclopean panels was sagging inwards, smashed out of all shape by the fury of the sea monsters. A great ophidian head squirmed through the rent, hissing and howling as it snapped at the dwarfs on the gantry below it. The monster's scales were charred and blackened by the molten lead that had been poured down upon it. Dozens of bolts studded its hide, little rivulets of slimy blood oozing from the wounds. One eye was scorched shut, a blob of shapeless lead hanging from the rim of the socket.

Shouted commands brought hundreds of bolts flying at the monster. Shafts flung from bolt throwers stabbed into its hide; boulders and pots of pitch crashed against its body before splashing down into the water below. The grudge thrower moaned like some vengeful wraith as it cast its massive burden at the serpent. The rune-etched stone slammed into the beast's head, snapping its jaw and smashing the side of its skull. With hideous reptilian vitality, the enormous merwyrm thrashed and writhed, its furious death throes widening the rent in the sea-gates.

As the first serpent died, two more thrust themselves into the breach, clamping their jaws and flipper-like claws onto the twisted edges of the fissure. Savagely, the brutes broke the locks binding the portals together. With a shuddering wail of ripping metal and crumbling stone, the titanic doors began to swing inwards.

Brynnoth raised his fist and a trumpeter blared the signal to the captain of the first fire-ship. The vessel's engine shuddered into life, steam and smoke rising from its stacks as its paddle wheel churned into life. Brynnoth drew his spyglass from his belt, training it upon the ship. He could make out the captain behind the wheel, black beads of mourning already woven into the dwarf's beard. Briefly, the king wondered if the captain was mourning his own sacrifice or that of his ship.

Then the king's gaze was drawn to the lone figure down on the deck where the barrels of Tharzharr were piled. It wouldn't have been strange to see a sailor there, ready to ignite the incendiary once the ship was in range of the enemy. But the figure who stood there wasn't dressed as a sailor.

Indeed, with his strange armour and the feathery cloak hanging from his shoulders, he looked like no dwarf of Barak Varr.

Weird as the dwarf's appearance was, stranger still was the fact that Brynnoth recognised him. He'd met with this dwarf decades ago, offered him a reward for bestowing upon Barak Varr the perfect weapon with which to arm the skryzan-harbark. But it was impossible for him to be here. Drogor had died at Kazad Mingol when his airship was destroyed.

The strange dwarf seemed to feel Brynnoth's eye on him, for he slowly turned around and looked back at the king. There was no question now – it was certainly Drogor's face that smiled at Brynnoth.

Even the mounting fury of the serpents as they broke down the sea-gates couldn't break Brynnoth's fascination as he watched Drogor smash his fist against one of the barrels of Tharzharr. The wood splintered as though it had been struck by a hammer, spilling the black powder across the deck. The captain in the wheelhouse left his post, flailing his arms and shouting at Drogor.

Drogor paid the captain no attention, instead keeping his eyes on Brynnoth. Before the ship's captain could reach him, the thane from Karak Zorn lifted his hand. Purple fire rose from the outstretched palm, flickering and dancing with a malignant energy.

Brynnoth's eye went wide with horror as he understood what was about to happen. He glanced at the other fire-ships, all arrayed in a nice, neat little line. The lead ship hadn't drawn so very far away. An explosion started there would most certainly spread to the others. The havoc the combined detonation would wreak on the harbour was something the king didn't want to contemplate.

Brynnoth spun around to give the order to a nearby regiment of crossbows to strike Drogor down. But even as he turned, the thane slapped his burning hand against the spilled Tharzharr and green fire roared through the heart of Barak Varr.

There had been five hundred dwarfs in the advance when Morgrim led them out from the Ungdrin Ankor and into the tunnel connecting with Barak Varr's lower deeps. Efforts to penetrate into the upper deeps had proven murderous, the elf resistance too well entrenched to dislodge. Unwilling to take such casualties without gaining any ground, Morgrim had left a few hundred warriors in the upper tunnels to keep the elgi occupied while he led his vanguard into the lower passages in the hope that they would find the enemy less established there. If they managed to force a way into the lower deeps, the thousands of warriors in the main body of Morgrim's army would come surging into Barak Varr and block the enemy's route back to the surface. More importantly, the sea hold would be rejoined to the great Underway connecting the whole of the Karaz Ankor.

Such was the plan, at least, but after several hours and dozens of casualties, Morgrim wasn't certain how much progress they were truly making. The elves they faced were tenacious and as he led the vanguard into another underground gallery, the thane found that the enemy had more than swords and arrows to bring to bear.

Morgrim felt the walls shudder around him. Streams of dust and dirt rained down from the ceiling. Farther down the tunnel he heard the roar of crashing stone as part of the roof fell in. The cries of maimed and wounded dwarfs echoed down the passageway.

'That wasn't any natural tremor,' Rundin Dragonslayer said as he helped Morgrim to his feet.

'Aye,' Morgrim agreed. 'The old miners and runebearers with us would have given warning well in advance if it was. Some of them are like mine rats, able to feel the slightest vibration in the rock around them.'

Rundin spat on the tunnel floor. 'Elgi witchery,' he growled, running his thumb along the brand of Grimnir.

Morgrim nodded. 'Their mages bleed like any other elgi.' He turned away from the skarrenawi, peering down the tunnel at the dwarfs ahead of them. A few of those he could see were stumbling about, struck by something more significant than dirt and dust. 'Wounded to the rear,' Morgrim barked. 'All the wounded,' he added. 'I want only fit fighters at the fore.'

There was some grumbling at that reminder of the thane's orders, but he knew they would be carried out. A dwarf would fight with half his body stove-in by a troll unless told otherwise. Such obstinacy was commendable, but impractical. An army needed its best fighters leading the way, not a bedlam of wounded heroes.

Morgrim marched forwards with the twenty hearthguard his uncle had detached from his own bodyguard to defend the Elgidum. Beside him, the savage aspect of Rundin Dragonslayer made for an incongruous sight. Morgrim and the hearthguard bedecked in full suits of plates, the skarrenawi champion wearing only his chains and trousers. As unlikely as Rundin's appearance was, Morgrim knew the hill dwarf to be one of the fiercest warriors in the Karaz Ankor. He'd seen that for himself during the battle for Athel Maraya.

'I'm surprised you aren't up ahead with the scouts,' Morgrim told Rundin. 'Or maybe you've changed your mind about seeking a heroic doom?'

Rundin shook his head. 'Far from it. I just figure that the elgi are certain to throw their very worst at you since you killed their prince. When they do, I'm going to be there and maybe find a death worthy of my ancestors.'

Morgrim shared an anxious look with the closest hearthguard, then glanced back at Rundin. 'That's not exactly comforting.'

'Depends how eager you are to die,' Rundin shrugged. Abruptly the skarrenawi lowered his axe, stiffening like a hound scenting prey.

'Elgi!' a white-bearded runebearer gasped as he came rushing back down the tunnel. Fleet of foot and as cunning as stoats, the runebearers made their living carrying messages through the Ungdrin Ankor. Their work was hazardous in the extreme, fraught with all the dangers of the deeps, from prowling grobi to lurking spiders. Those who survived to become veterans of their trade quickly learned the disciplines of stealth and observation.

Morgrim waved the scout back and tightened his grip on Azdrakghar. The rune axe seemed to throb with anticipation as if it could sense the closeness of the enemy. Soon, Morgrim promised it, soon it would again taste elgi blood.

Dozens of Ironbreakers rushed ahead of Morgrim's bodyguard, a precaution the thane had reluctantly agreed to after his vanguard encountered elgi mages early during the fighting. A strong axe and thick armour were small defence against sorcery as many of his warriors had discovered. As much as he longed to fight, Morgrim knew he couldn't put himself at such risk. An army without a leader was just a mob.

Before Morgrim had gone another twenty yards down the tunnel, the crash of steel sounded from up ahead. A bright flash of arcane fire blazed across his vision as an elgi sorcerer discharged some spell against the warriors he'd sent ahead. A bitter smile worked its way onto Morgrim's face. The Ironbreakers weren't merely warriors; they were all experienced tunnel fighters, used to guarding the deeps beneath each stronghold against the creatures of the dark. The armour they wore was a wonder of the dwarfish forges, fashioned from cold-wrought iron and emblazoned with the rune of Stone to endow them with a protection beyond anything afforded by mundane steel. The enchantment of the rune rendered the Ironbreakers all but impervious to hostile magics. What had defied the crude conjurations of grobi shaman had likewise proven effective against elgi spells.

'Hold.' Morgrim raised his hand, warning the rest of his column to wait. The elgi were clever and sneaky, but there were some things that could be depended upon. One was their utter faith in their sorcery. When their magic failed to perform as they expected it to, it threw them into a panic. Confronted by a company of Ironbreakers, seeing his first spells fizzle away harmlessly, an elgi mage would compound his misfortune by throwing further enchantments against the dwarf warriors. A few moments of such frantic conjurations and the mage would be all but spent – and easy prey for the waiting dwarfs.

It wasn't long before the Ironbreakers in the tunnel ahead began to shout 'Khazuk!' The elgi were so accustomed to hearing the war-cry that they little guessed it was a summons. It was the sign from Morgrim's Ironbreakers that the sorcerous attack had begun to falter.

'Forward, for Grungni and the High King!' Morgrim howled, waving his axe overhead. The dwarf axemen and hammerers behind him down the tunnel roared in answer to his command. Like a single great beast of steel and sinew, hundreds of dwarfs surged up the tunnel and around the bend.

The Ironbreakers were fending off the assault of scores of elgi spears when Morgrim and his hearthguard swept around the corner. Arrows from hundreds of elf archers whistled through the darkness, glancing off shields and helms. A sphere of incandescent fire shrieked out from the shadows, crashing against one of the hearthguard and melting his torso as though it were wax. Bellowing in delight, Rundin charged off into the darkness to chase down the lurking elf mage.

Morgrim couldn't spare any further thought for the death-crazed hill dwarf. A regiment of elf spearmen rushed to block off the tunnel and protect the flank of those who'd engaged the Ironbreakers. The thane was soon beset by elgi warriors thrusting at him with their broad-headed spears, trying to drive him back into the connecting passage.

The elgi effort was fruitless. The hearthguard were too disciplined to break before even their assault. Raising shields to cover their comrades, the hearthguard steadily forced the elves back. Foot by foot, the enemy was pushed down the tunnel. Whenever a spear drew back or an elgi shield lowered, a dwarf axe licked out, smashing armour and slashing flesh. One after another, the spearmen fell, crushed underfoot as Morgrim led his warriors onwards.

The elves, so swift and agile, were out of their element down in the tunnels. In the deeps it was strength and stamina that counted and the elgi simply couldn't match the strength and stamina of the dwarfs. With their arrows and their magic, they might have held Morgrim's warriors at bay, but in close quarters the odds were stacked against them. Too proud to accept the fact, the elgi fought on, those in the rear ranks marching forwards to take the place of their fallen kin.

The dwarfs cut them down with machine-like rhythm, as if farmers cutting wheat with their scythes. For what seemed hours, Morgrim and his warriors fought their way to the Ironbreakers. Scores of elves lay strewn in their wake before they reached their objective. When finally they had smashed their way through their foes, the reunited force pivoted, wheeling so that the whole width of the tunnel became an unbroken wall of dwarfish steel.

'Khazuk!' the dwarfs roared as they drove the remaining elves down the passageway. For a time, the elves tried to hold their position, spearmen forming ranks while the archers behind them tried to pick off individual dwarfs. It was the last gasp of an enemy who already knew it was beaten. When the dwarfs surged forwards, the line of spears was quickly broken. Once they were among the elf ranks, once their enemy's formation was shattered, what had been a battle degenerated into a slaughter.

When it was over, Morgrim surveyed the carnage. The tunnel was a mire of elgi blood. He was shocked at such tenacity. It was true that the elves had fought with surprising ferocity before, but he'd never seen them mount such a stubborn defence. An elf was more likely to retreat if he were looking at certain defeat. These had fought on when there was no hope at all.

Rundin came rushing out from the darkness. The hill dwarf's skin was puckered and burned where an elgi spell had scorched him, but he seemed oblivious to his hurt. 'Elgidum,' the champion cried out. 'Come quickly!'

Something in the skarrenawi's tone brooked no question. For a dwarf who'd accepted the inevitability of his own death to have such anguish in his voice sent a chill down Morgrim's spine. Calling out to his hearthguard to attend him, the thane hurried after Rundin.

The Dragonslayer led Morgrim into a small guard hall off the main tunnel. The room was littered with dead dwarfs and a few elf corpses. Amidst the chaos, Morgrim saw the robed figure of an elgi sorcerer, his head cleft by an axe. Rundin's, unless he missed his guess.

It wasn't the mage that Rundin wanted Morgrim to see. Instead the hill dwarf showed him a wounded dawi leaning against the wall. Morgrim was taken aback when he stared down at the other dwarf. It seemed incredible, but he knew this injured warrior, though it had been more than a century since he'd seen him. It was his old friend Drogor, the adventurer from Karak Zorn who Prince Snorri had elevated to thanehood.

Morgrim started to kneel beside the bleeding dwarf, but Drogor pushed him back. 'No time,' he coughed, blood dribbling from the corner of his mouth. 'You have to stop the elgi.'

Morgrim shook his head. 'They have been stopped,' he told Drogor. 'We're through. The Ungdrin Ankor joins Barak Varr once more.'

'The reservoir...' Drogor said, waving his hand towards a passageway almost lost in the shadows at the far end of the chamber. 'The elgi are... poisoning the water.'

Morgrim cursed into his beard. That was why the elves had been fighting with such tenacity. They were playing for time, waiting so that their comrades could complete this atrocity. The elgi could be driven from Barak Varr and still kill dwarfs with poisoned water.

'Have his wounds attended,' Morgrim ordered one of his hearthguard. Without a second's hesitation, he rushed down the passageway with Rundin and the rest of his bodyguard. He didn't notice Drogor turn his head to watch him go, or the smile that formed on the dwarf's bloodied face.

The reservoir was a crypt-like vault, its high ceiling festooned with a riot of pipes and pumps. At the centre of the chamber was a deep well, the natural pool surrounded by a stone platform. Pillars and columns stretched up the walls to sweep out in broad arches that further strengthened the ceiling, supporting it against the enormity of the hold above.

Morgrim's fury sent him barrelling through the elf guards posted at the entrance to the vault. His arm was gashed by one of the elven blades before he was past them, but he refused to let his wound keep him back. A backhanded sweep of his axe sent the offending elgi sprawling in a burst of blood and teeth. He left Rundin and his hearthguard to finish the elgi warriors. His focus was entirely upon the reservoir and the elf lord standing beside it.

The elf lord turned at the sound of Morgrim's violent entrance. For an instant there was fear on those sharp, arrogant features. His eyes darted from one end of the vault to the other, as though looking for a means of escape. The moment passed, however, and the fear was eradicated by an expression of monstrous hate.

'I am Lord Caerwal of Athel Numiel,' the elf snarled in perfect Khazalid. 'Athel Numiel, whose beauty you animals put to the torch. Whose people you animals put to the sword.' He reached to his belt, removing a golden coffer. 'Now I pay you back in kind,' he hissed.

Morgrim charged at Caerwal as he removed a lead flask from inside the coffer. In a blur, Caerwal's other hand ripped his sword from its sheath and slashed at the oncoming dwarf. The edge of the slender blade slithered across Morgrim's brow. Blood gushed from the cut, dripping into the dwarf's eyes. As he reeled back, Caerwal's boot kicked into his chest, pitching him against the wall.

'Be honoured, dawi,' Caerwal snapped. 'It isn't every mud-digger I let foul my sword with its greasy blood.'

'Let's foul it some more then!' Morgrim roared, pushing himself off the wall and slamming into his foe. Caerwal screamed as the armoured dwarf crashed into him. Sword and flask alike flew from his hands as he was thrown backwards. The flask clattered across the platform to crash against the wall. The sword plummeted into the pool.

Morgrim had his arms wrapped around the elf lord as both of them struck the water. The weight of their armour sent both of them plunging towards the bottom of the pool – if a bottom there was. Caerwal's hands ripped at his helm, finally pulling it free. The dwarf tightened his hold, feeling his enemy's ribs crack. For an instant, the elf's body went lax, then Caerwal's hand was clutching at his beard. The elf tried to gouge his eyes with his other hand, pawing and ripping at him like some crazed beast.

Deeper and deeper they sank. Morgrim could feel the pressure pounding against his ears. He tightened his grip on Caerwal, his fury and disgust at what the elf lord had tried to do lending him a strength he didn't realise he had. He could feel the instant he crushed the last breath from the elf's lungs. A moment more and the hands pawing at him fell limp. With a surge of revulsion, Morgrim pushed Caerwal from him. He could feel the elf's head slap against his boots as the armoured corpse sank down into the depths.

Kicking out, Morgrim tried to fight his way to the surface, using one hand to pull at the jagged wall of the well. The weight of his armour dragged on him, threatening to take him down into the deep. The thought of spending eternity in the company of a murderous wretch like Caerwal filled Morgrim with such horror that he drew the knife from his boot and began slashing the straps of his armour. Mail that had been in his family for generations fell away from his body, hurtling down into the watery darkness. Piece by piece, he cut his armour free, all the while feeling the torturous agony of his burning lungs.

After what felt like an eternity, Morgrim managed to claw his way up the side of the well. When his head broke the surface, when he drew the first breath of air into his starved body, he wondered if he'd ever felt anything more precious. Then he heard the cheer that sounded from the throats of his guards and knew that what he had accomplished, the foul villainy he'd thwarted, was more precious still.

Rundin hurried to the side of the ledge and helped lift Morgrim from the reservoir. The hill dwarf studied the thane's state of undress as he climbed out of the water. In his panic to cut away the armour, he'd slashed his clothes and cut his skin.

'Surely you aren't trying to follow my example,' Rundin said.

Morgrim wrung what seemed a deluge from his soaked beard before answering the hill dwarf. 'Maybe,' he said. 'After all, it is said I am to kill a dragon. When that day comes, I may need to ask you for advice on how it's done.'

Rundin laughed. 'When that day comes, the only way you'll get near a drakk is if I've failed to kill it and the beast has given me a glorious death.'

Lord Draikyll had come to Barak Varr seeking glory. Instead the general had found humiliation and disgrace. There was little question in anyone's mind that he would be relieved of his command as soon as Caledor II learned of his failure. Too many resources had been squandered for anything less than a supreme victory. That would be the decision in Ulthuan.

From the stern of the *Cormorant,* Ilendril watched as the still-smoking sea hold receded in the distance. The siege was over. Threatened by no fewer than four converging dwarf armies and with reports of a fifth reinforcing the hold from below, there had really been no choice. Without waiting for the flames raging behind the sea-gates to subside, Draikyll had given the order to withdraw.

Barak Varr would be a shambles for decades and dwarf ships wouldn't be harassing Sith Remora or any other coastal settlement any time soon. It was a limited success, to be certain and nothing that would appease the expectations of the Phoenix King. However, it might be enough to impress whoever Caledor II sent to replace Draikyll.

Ilendril would be certain to discuss the role the dragons had played in the asur defeat. He'd impress upon the new general that they couldn't depend on creatures that wouldn't obey orders but rather had to be persuaded to fight. They couldn't rely upon the whims of beasts when planning strategy.

Yes, Ilendril thought, he'd pursue that line of reasoning. Then, he would propose an alternative.

Staring down at the fang of the merwyrm he had commanded in the last battle, Ilendril could see the potential for the future. A future when the power of the dragon riders was broken and the glory of exiles like himself was restored.

NINE

HEIR TO THE CROWN

386TH YEAR OF THE REIGN OF CALEDOR II

'The king is in a foul mood.' Caradryel kept his voice low as he walked with Thoriol through the halls of Caledor's palace in Lothern. 'Please keep that in mind when you meet with him.'

Thoriol paused, glancing down the corridor at the royal guards they had passed, looking ahead to the ones at the far end of the hall. None of them were in earshot, but he knew better than to broach untoward subjects anywhere within the palace. The very walls had ears.

Caradryel was making a valiant effort to keep his speech from flirting with his true meaning and true intentions. The highborn diplomat considered King Caledor II to be a reckless fool, an adventurer more concerned with expanding his own personal glory than doing what was right for Ulthuan. There was a growing segment of the asur nobility who were sympathetic to that position. Lady Yethanial and Lord Athinol were but the point of the spear when it came to the disquiet among the highborn.

The expanding crisis in Elthin Arvan was making the situation worse. Lord Draikyll's siege of Barak Varr had been characterised as a wasteful fiasco by Caledor himself. Draikyll was recalled, a new general dispatched to oversee the military situation in Elthin Arvan. Now even the replacement was being recalled, accused of too much timidity in his conduct of the war. The real reason, however, was the dragons.

The dragons. They had become both shield and sword to the embattled colonies. Draikyll had insisted that but for their defection at the siege, he would have taken Barak Varr. Just when he needed them most, the drakes had left the battle and returned to Tor Alessi. Now, the dragons had left even that bastion. They'd flown away, returning to the mountains of Caledor, back to their caves and caverns.

The dragons had left the war.

Thoriol could understand the king's frustration. So much was dependent on the dragons keeping the dwarfs in check. Just the fear of a dragon swooping down on one of their armies had restrained the dawi for a long time. Now, that restraint would be gone. The enemy would feel emboldened to launch campaign after campaign against the asur, to exploit the distress of their weakened foe.

And at home, the voices of dissent saw in the retreat of the dragons a final condemnation against the war with the dwarfs. Yethanial and Athinol hoped that this would be the event to make Caledor sue for peace with the dwarf High King. Even if it meant withdrawing from the colonies.

The very thought of that made Thoriol sick inside. If they abandoned the colonies then they were betraying all those who had fought and died to defend them. He could sympathise with his mother's call for peace, with Athinol's insistence that they turn their full might against the lingering druchii in Naggaroth, but he wouldn't accept that the price for such objectives would be forsaking everything so many had died for. Everything his father had died for.

'I have an advantage over you in that respect,' Thoriol told Caradryel. 'No matter how ugly my uncle's mood, he won't have me executed.'

The jest hardly brought a smile to Caradryel's face, especially in their current surroundings. 'You are the heir of the House of Tor Caled,' he agreed. 'That makes you the king's great hope for the future.'

It was a familiar warning. Caradryel didn't have to say the rest – Thoriol knew the diplomat wouldn't even whisper it while he was within the palace. What went unsaid was the cruel wisdom that, should the king's favour turn against Thoriol then far from being Caledor's great hope for the future, he would become the king's fear for the present. The king's suspicions were what had sent Imladrik back to the colonies. However much Caledor indulged Thoriol, the prince could neither forget nor forgive that fact.

King Caledor II was in the Amber Room of his palace. It was a fabulous chamber, an example of the opulence that attended the Phoenix King. From floor to ceiling, the room was covered in amber. The walls were coated in little polished hexagonal discs of the material, each carefully selected for hue and transparency. The ceiling was covered in tiles of a slightly deeper hue, their thickness creating the illusion of unreachable heights hidden just beyond the semi-translucent skin overhead. The floor was coated in a fine dust of the same amber, persistent enchantments endowing it with a strangely electric cohesion that always reminded Thoriol of the action of iron filings around a lodestone. The dust would sink beneath the tread of a visitor only to restore itself once the intruding foot had passed.

All the appointments within the chamber were adorned with amber, from chairs to cabinets to tables. Even the decanters and goblets were fashioned from amber, and the wine being poured into them by a servant arrayed in an amber-adorned doublet was a magically adjusted vintage designed to perfectly match the colouring of the room. The guards standing at attention on either side of the chamber were likewise arrayed in amber-coloured armour, its unusual sheen precipitated by spells from one of the mages of the king's court. The same magic wouldn't alter the white lion pelts the guards customarily wore, so while they were posted in the chamber they stood watch without the traditional symbol of their warrior brotherhood. Envaldein looked especially uncomfortable when Thoriol glanced his way. Briefly, the prince wondered if his uncle was aware of the insult he paid his guards by commanding them to set aside the distinction and honour of their traditions. If he did, then Thoriol wondered if the king even cared.

Caledor II was easy enough to find amidst his amber settings. He wore a long robe of silver and a heavy necklace of ruby and sapphire. Seated before a game table, he set his ivory pawns against the opposing ebony forces of Hulviar. The king's seneschal, observing some whim of his lord, had adopted black raiment to echo the hue of his pieces on the game board.

The king turned from the game when a steward announced Thoriol. Caradryel, at the moment a mere auxiliary of the prince, went without introduction. He frowned slightly at the indignity, but was careful to compose himself when he felt royal eyes glance his way.

'Dear nephew,' Caledor smiled, rising from his chair and motioning for Hulviar to forsake his turn until such time as the royal presence could again concentrate on the game. The king gave Thoriol an appraising look. 'You have heard about Lord Teranion's betrayal?' The fury in the king's tone was subdued but unmistakeable.

Thoriol was careful about choosing how to answer. 'It is my understanding that only the dragons left Tor Alessi. Lord Teranion and the other dragon riders stayed behind.'

Caledor flung the game piece he had been holding to the floor. 'A pretence!' he snapped. 'The dragons leave and he stays behind? That is supposed to be some astonishing show of loyalty? I am supposed to be impressed by that?' He turned to Hulviar. 'I am certain his show of solidarity with the colonists will go far to easing their minds. Knowing that Lord Teranion stands with them will make the mud-diggers rip at their beards in terror. Honestly, can you think of anyone so useless as a dragon rider without a dragon!'

The moment he made the remark, Caledor froze. He turned back to Thoriol. No apology would ever leave those royal lips, but there was a trace of regret in the royal eyes.

Thoriol kept his expression neutral. His uncle's barb – intentioned or not – had struck home. It was a long time since he had aspired to follow in his father's footsteps. There was no use for it. Try as he might, no drake responded to his dragonsong. The king was right – there were few things more useless than a dragon rider without a dragon.

'They are wilful creatures,' Thoriol said. 'They have a sort of pride and arrogance about them that I don't think any asur can ever really understand. Lord Teranion could be as loyal as Envaldein or Hulviar and still be unable to compel the drakes to do something they have no intention of doing.'

'Then what good are they?' Caledor snarled. 'By Asuryan, of what use is a weapon you can't depend upon? What's next? Must I look forward to the day when the dragons guarding the coast or hunting the druchii decide they've had enough and go crawling back into their holes?'

The king's argument brought back to Thoriol Imladrik's words. How many times had his father cautioned that dragons weren't merely weapons, weren't simply beasts to be goaded into battle? Enough times that Thoriol had grown sick with the hearing of it. Enough times that he had despaired of ever truly understanding.

'They aren't weapons,' Thoriol said, echoing his father's words. 'They aren't beasts or servants. They are allies whose help must be requested, never commanded.'

Caledor was silent, remembering only too well when he'd last heard such arguments – and from whom. It was Hulviar who chose to contest Thoriol's words.

'Allies? Friends?' the seneschal scoffed. 'What kind of ally is it who abandons our forces in the field? What kind of ally is it who deserts our outposts, leaves them helpless before the enemy? Perhaps our mistake was ever trusting the fidelity of such fickle creatures.'

'They yet patrol the coasts and harry the druchii,' Caradryel reminded. 'Perhaps it would be better to hear Lord Teranion's explanation for why the dragons left Tor Alessi before making any decision.'

'If Teranion felt he had any worthwhile excuse to offer, he would have returned with his drake and made his explanation in person,' Hulviar said. 'Instead, he chooses to keep himself in the colonies.'

'As a sign of solidarity,' Caradryel retorted. 'Our people in Elthin Arvan fear that they have been forgotten by Ulthuan.'

Hulviar smiled. 'I have been discussing strategy with his highness. He is of a mind to dispatch a new general to Tor Alessi, Lady Kelsei of Tor Ferrek.'

'With all due respect, my Lord Hulviar, I don't think another general is going to assuage the concerns of the colonists,' Caradryel observed.

'If it is any concern of yours,' Caledor told the diplomat, 'Lady Kelsei will have two thousand troops arriving with her and more at her disposal as and when they can be safely detached from the campaign in Naggaroth.'

Caradryel blinked in surprise. 'My liege, you would withdraw soldiers from Naggaroth?'

'The fighting in Naggaroth is all but over,' Hulviar said. 'Malekith lacks the resources for real war. What we're left with is simply to push the druchii back into the wastes and keep them there until they submit.'

'Would it not be more prudent to bring the campaign to a conclusion before throwing more resources into the war against the dawi?'

A scornful laugh sounded from Caledor. 'You are becoming a contrarian,

Lord Caradryel. From you I hear that these dwarfs are too powerful to dismiss. Then, when I intend to send more forces into the war against them, I am told that they aren't worth the effort.'

Caradryel knew when his counsel was of value and when his words were wasted. He could tell that the king had already made up his mind. Whatever he was told that didn't agree with the decision he'd reached would be dismissed. Or, worse, deemed treasonous.

'It won't be enough,' Thoriol said, stepping towards the king. 'New generals, fresh troops, these have been sent to the colonies before. What they need in Tor Alessi is a more substantial gesture. A sign that Elthin Arvan is very much in the thoughts of Ulthuan.'

Hulviar smiled thinly. 'Surely you aren't suggesting that his highness set aside his duties here and journey to Elthin Arvan? It should be enough that the king has done so once already.'

Thoriol shook his head. 'No, my Lord Hulviar, that is not what I am suggesting. The king's duties must keep him in Lothern. I, however, have no such obligations.' He turned and bowed to Caledor. 'My liege, permit me to sail to Tor Alessi as your emissary. I need have no official position or duties. My presence alone, the presence of the king's nephew, will be enough to tell the colonies that they are still in the hearts and minds of Ulthuan. I will be the living symbol of your promise that they will not be abandoned.'

As he spoke the last words, Thoriol could see Caradryel grow tense. It would be an interesting report he'd have to give his mother and her cadre. They'd thought to use him to speed the War of the Beard to an end. He would still achieve that purpose, but he would do so in a way that wouldn't make a mockery of his father's sacrifice.

The first step would be getting himself to the battlefield. For that, Thoriol would need the king to indulge him one more time. He could see the uncertainty in Caledor's eyes, the hesitance of his uncle to commit his heir.

'It would be imprudent–' Caradryel started to object. Before he could finish speaking, Thoriol received the unexpected support of Hulviar.

'I must disagree,' the seneschal said. 'Prince Thoriol makes a good case for why he must put in an appearance at Tor Alessi. The colonists need something to inspire them, and the prince is quite right when he says it will take more than a new general and a few regiments.' Hulviar bowed to the king. 'For a time, my liege, I think Prince Thoriol should be sent to rekindle the morale of your subjects. To let them know that the eyes of the Phoenix King are upon them.'

Caledor looked as though he would demur. There was a hint of worry on his normally proud features. Unexpectedly, he glanced at Caradryel, almost as though begging the diplomat to offer some rationale that would give him cause to defy the united counsel of both his seneschal and his heir.

'Please, my liege, allow me to perform this service,' Thoriol asked, dropping to one knee. 'For too long I have sat idle. I would not feel useless to my king.'

It was that one word and the memory of his own thoughtless speech that decided Caledor. 'You will go to Tor Alessi as my representative,' he told Thoriol. 'Lady Aelis will be told to extend to you the same courtesies and considerations she would to me.' He stared into his nephew's eyes. 'Restore their courage, then come back to me.'

The king turned and withdrew from the Amber Room. As he departed, Thoriol thought he heard his uncle whisper something.

What he thought he heard the king say was, 'Elthin Arvan has already taken too much from House Tor Caled.'

Reaching up into the misty clouds, the gargantuan peaks of the Worlds Edge Mountains stretched like a wall across the countryside, a megalithic barrier separating the Old World from the Dark Lands beyond. Great stands of pine and spruce clung to the slopes, rising up from between the craggy rocks. Patches of scrubby grass and wizened bushes struggled to find purchase in the shelter of boulders and trees, eking out a precarious existence just between the hills below and the snowline above.

There were twenty of them, climbing down the side of the mountain with a nimbleness that made the native goats seem as clumsy as drunken orcs. Not a branch or bramble did they disturb, not so much as a pebble was kicked loose by their passage. There was barely any sound at all, only the rare rustle of a cloak as the wind pulled at it or the rasp of a boot against a patch of sand. So silently did they move that the birds singing in the trees didn't skip a note.

Watching them from the mouth of a tunnel not a hundred yards away, Morgrim appreciated the enormity of the danger the intruders posed. Elf spies who could move with such eerie speed and silence were a threat that couldn't be understated. It was bad enough that the elgi could spy upon the Karaz Ankor with their sorcery, but for them to feel at liberty to dispatch spies so deep into dwarf lands betokened a boldness that couldn't be tolerated. These spies had to be exterminated. If a single one returned to their cities, if the elgi for an instant thought they could trespass with impunity...

Morgrim closed his hand about the hilt of Ifulvin. Just touching the sword reminded him of his purpose. He was Elgidum. It was his destiny to drive the elves from the Old World and cast them back into the sea.

'You can afford to show them no quarter.' The advice came in a whisper from his left. Drogor Zarrdum, his old friend from Karak Zorn. The thane had been indispensable to him since they'd been reunited in the deeps below Barak Varr, both as a companion and as an advisor.

Even so, at times Drogor's relish at slaughtering elgi was a bit unsettling to Morgrim. Certainly the elgi were an enemy to be fought and conquered, but there was a difference between battle and bloodlust – a difference that Drogor sometimes didn't appreciate.

'Let them get a little closer,' Morgrim whispered back. He turned his head, glancing down the tunnel. There were thirty dwarfs behind him, all with axes at the ready. Across from them, in another mineshaft, were a dozen crossbows. Further down the slope was a patrol of rangers, the ones who had found the first traces of elgi spies.

It was still confusing to Morgrim why the elves had marched across half the countryside to reach the Worlds Edge Mountains and then made their ascent in such a forlorn place. They weren't near Karak Kadrin or Karak Ungor – there were no major passes or trade routes of any consequence for leagues in any direction. Even the Ungdrin Ankor didn't run beneath this part of the mountains. There just seemed no tactical purpose for what the elgi were doing here. They were too few to be establishing any kind of base from which to stage future operations and even if they were, why would they be leaving so soon after making their assent? The rangers had discovered them only a few days ago.

Morgrim chided himself for asking so many questions. They were elgi and it was only right that their treacherous ways should be strange to a dwarf. Wasting energy trying to figure them out was as fruitless as trying to talk to a goblin. The only understanding that could ever exist between them was that of steel!

The violence of his own thoughts surprised Morgrim. Where had such rage come from?

There was no time to question his motives. One of the elves descending the slope abruptly lost his footing. The elgi recovered with a grace and nimbleness that amazed the onlooking dwarfs, but when their foe's slide ended, the elf was in a half-crouch and staring directly into the mine. His green eyes were staring directly at Morgrim.

'Attack!' Drogor shouted, shoving Morgrim to one side as the elf threw a leaf-shaped knife at him. The blade caught Drogor in the breast, the impact knocking him back and into the warriors surging up from the rear of the tunnel.

'Attack!' Morgrim took up the cry. Drawing Azdrakghar, he rushed at the elf who'd thrown the knife. The elgi was already ripping his own sword from its scabbard. Above him, on the slope, the other elves were beset by a volley from the lurking crossbows. Four of their number were cut down, two more staggering from their wounds. The others drew their bows or pulled their swords, reacting to the sudden ambush.

Morgrim could see his warriors fanning out, hastening up the slope to engage the other elgi. They would need to draw the attention of their enemy while the crossbows reloaded. Until then, they would be vulnerable to any charge the elgi mounted. The dwarf warriors had to prevent that from happening.

The elf swordsman was left to Morgrim. There was that much respect that lingered between elgi and dawi that the challenge from one warrior to another would be honoured. Morgrim closed upon the grey-cloaked elf, noticing the seemingly effortless way his foe maintained his footing as he manoeuvred on the uneven ground. It was a stroke of despicable luck that this elgi had tripped up above and sprung the ambush.

Morgrim circled the elgi, waiting and watching for an opportunity. The elf was like a panther, every muscle in his lean frame tensed to spring. Where would the attack fall? When would the warrior decide was the moment to strike? The thin, angular face that glared at Morgrim from the hood of the cloak gave no clue to the thoughts and intentions stirring in the elgi's mind. There was only the stamp of hate and the contemptuous disdain most asur felt for peoples they considered beneath them.

That disdain acted as a warning to Morgrim. He noted the patch of sand, saw the way the elf's foot squirmed when crossing it. From that moment, he knew what to expect. The elf made a few thrusts at him, flashing feints that the thane already knew weren't intended to strike true. His own retorts with his axe were equally half-hearted, just enough to keep his enemy on edge.

When the elf's boot rolled under the little ridge of sand his foot had created, Morgrim threw up his left arm to shield his face. The sand kicked up by the elf spattered across the fending arm, but failed to blind him as the foe had intended. At the same instant, the elf was lunging in with his sword, planning to open Morgrim's throat. He tried to adjust in mid-charge when he realised his foe could still see, but by that time it was too late.

Azdrakghar struck the elgi's waist, the rune axe tearing through the light elven mail to crunch deep into the body beneath. Blood and bile spilled from the grisly rent in the elf's side as Morgrim tore his weapon free. The stricken warrior collapsed at his feet, pawing at the rocks for a moment before falling limp and cold against the earth.

Morgrim was just starting to turn from his stricken foe when a sound from behind him brought him spinning about. He froze in mid-swing, ashamed that he'd almost buried his axe in Drogor's head. His friend noted his alarm and laughed.

'If I'd known you'd be this glad to see me I would have left the elgi knife where it was,' Drogor said. He jabbed his thumb into a tear in his breastplate. The elgi sometimes put enchantments on their blades that allowed them to pierce iron as neatly as flesh. Drogor had been fortunate this blade had penetrated no deeper than it had.

Morgrim shrugged. 'It was meant for me anyway,' he said.

'All the dawi will cry if you fall, my friend,' Drogor cautioned him. 'If Elgidum dies, it is a tragedy. If Thane Drogor of Karak Zorn dies... none will even notice.'

Morgrim was already beginning his climb to join the fighting above. It seemed the worst of it was already past. A dozen elgi were already down. Three others tried to make their escape through the dwarf ambushers, but as they fled down the slope they found a surprise waiting for them. The rangers, concealed as effectively as any elgi scout, emerged from hiding to intercept them. It wasn't long before the only elgi left alive on the mountain were those too badly wounded to fight.

'See to the wounded,' Morgrim told his warriors when he rejoined them. He scowled when he saw the dwarfs ignoring the surviving elves. 'Attend the elgi too,' he warned.

'They will only slow us down,' Drogor said as he watched a pair of rangers trying to staunch the stream of blood coursing from one elgi warrior's mangled leg. 'We should finish them now. There may be other spies about.'

Morgrim frowned at his friend's bloodthirstiness, but decided to put a different rationale for his distaste. 'That's why I want prisoners,' he said. 'I want to know if there are others in the mountains.'

Drogor smiled and shook his head. 'You won't learn anything from these ones,' he declared. Stooping, he reached down to the bleeding elgi and opened the elf's mouth. Blood bubbled over the captive's lips. With a start, Morgrim understood what Drogor meant. Each of the prisoners had bitten through his own tongue when he found himself unable to fight further.

'Bring them just the same,' Morgrim ordered when he recovered from his shock. 'We will leave them in Karak Kadrin.'

'Why? They are no use to us,' Drogor persisted.

Morgrim shouldered his axe and stared at the maimed elves. 'That's exactly why we have to take them with us.'

Shrugging, Drogor turned back to help the rangers attend the wounded elves. For a moment, he stared at a stand of thorn bushes. Quickly he looked away and helped the rangers carry one of their prisoners down the slope.

It was only hours after the last dwarf had withdrawn that a figure emerged from below the thorn bushes. As he threw back his cloak, the garment shifted hue, changing from the mottled black and brown of the thorn bushes to become a dusky grey. The elf gave only a brief inspection of the dead strewn about the slope. The dwarfs had taken their own dead with them and made certain that the elves they left behind were corpses.

Only Ashelir had escaped their notice. It stung his pride that he had hidden himself while so many comrades fought and died, but it would have been a greater disgrace to have failed in his mission.

Reaching under the breast of his tunic, Ashelir felt the ugly piece of bone they'd come so far and risked so much to retrieve. Ilendril assured them it was worth the dangers, that it would change the whole war.

Ashelir cared little for any of that. All he cared was that he was being brought one step closer to the end of his own private war.

Revenge with honour, a dream cherished for so long, would soon be within his grasp.

Thoriol's arrival in Tor Alessi was a bitter one for him. He was greeted with fanfare befitting a conquering hero. Bright pennants bearing the heraldry of Tor Caled fluttered from the spires atop every tower in the city. Flowers were strewn across the piers when the fleet from Ulthuan pulled into port. Crowds swarmed the streets, eager and jubilant, thrilled beyond words to set their eyes upon Prince Thoriol.

He'd only been partially right when he made his case for returning to Elthin Arvan before the king. Tor Alessi was revitalised by his arrival, all the dread and despair caused by the desertion of the dragons forgotten as he disembarked. But it wasn't Thoriol they celebrated. It was the memory of his father, the memory of Imladrik who had come and saved Tor Alessi from the dwarfs.

Grim memories of that battle returned to Thoriol as a chariot drawn by white horses carried him through the streets. In his mind's eye he relived those long-gone days when the smoke of war had choked the sky. He could hear the screams of the dying, could smell the stink of scorched flesh. He could see the dwarfs, massed before the great walls like a sea of steel, their axes glistening in the sun.

He'd nearly died upon those walls when the dwarfs breached them. If not for his father ordering the very best treatment the city could offer his wounded son, Thoriol would not have survived. When his chariot passed the shrine in which the ashes of the siege's dead were entombed, he thought how easily his remains could be there, lying with Baelian and all the others who had been slain defending Tor Alessi.

The asur had extended the walls after that. The dwarfs had tried to attack since, but never in such numbers as when Morgrim Elfdoom had come howling at the gates. Never again had the dawi managed to batter their way into the city. New battlements had been raised two hundred yards before the old walls, a great curtain of stone and mortar twenty feet thick at its base and sixty feet high. Between the curtain and the old wall was a killing field especially prepared for any dwarf who managed to force his way through. Devoid of even so much as a shrub to hide under, the grassy expanse between the walls had been carefully measured so that archers posted on the inner wall could immediately know the distance to any target from where they stood and loose their arrows with unwavering precision.

There was no question in anyone's mind that the dawi would come again. The dwarfs were a stubborn, vindictive people. They could accept no compromise and wouldn't abandon a grudge. They'd come again and again and again. Most everyone in Tor Alessi was resigned to the fact. Many felt the only way they could ever know peace was if the dwarfs were completely exterminated. Even the once passive Lady Aelis, ruler of Tor Alessi, shared that sentiment. After meeting with her, Thoriol realised that his mother had one less ally in the colonies. Yethanial would need to cast her net farther afield if she thought she'd find support for her position in Elthin Arvan. For the colonists, the dreams of building a new life were too grand to sacrifice for a peace that could only come by destroying those same dreams.

It was late in the evening before Thoriol was able to extricate himself from the gauntlet of receptions and soirees that were held in his honour. It was somewhat ironic that Lady Kelsei, now commander of the colonial armies, was barely feted at all by the nobles of Tor Alessi. Tomorrow, tomorrow they would repent not extending full courtesies to her, but this night all they could think of was the hero of the hour.

The hero who as yet had accomplished nothing greater than simply staying alive.

Every passing moment spent among the festivities, listening to the people of Tor Alessi toast his health and express their gratitude had felt like an eternity to Thoriol. They weren't celebrating him; they were celebrating the shade of his father.

That couldn't have been made clearer to Thoriol than with the quarters he had been given. He had been afforded one of the smaller towers, some distance from the Tower of the Winds where the Council of Five gathered, and where Kelsei would have her headquarters. Thoriol knew this building quite well, it was as vivid in his memory as his mother's home in Tor Vael, or his father's citadel in Kor Evril. This was the place Imladrik had taken for his own when he arrived in Tor Alessi. It had been kept as a memorial to him ever since.

The locals called it the Tower of the Dragon.

Thoriol dismissed the servants and Sea Guard who sought to attend him as he made his way into the tower and mounted the steps to his chambers. He was weary, worn out from all the pomp and circumstance of his arrival.

No, he corrected himself, scowling into the silvered mirror standing above the clamshell washbasin in his bedroom. It wasn't ceremony and society that had worn him down. It was trying to smile and maintain a facade of cheer as he listened to everyone around him praising him, lauding him as the great hope of their city and the colonies. Every word, every gesture mocked him more cruelly than he could have believed possible. He had come to Tor Alessi with such a clear vision of what he had to do; now that he found so many ready to follow him, it made him question his motives and his plans.

Who was he to lead anyone? The accident of blood and birth wasn't enough. There needed to be more than that. He only had to think of his uncle Menlaeth, he who was crowned Caledor II, to know that birthright didn't mean one was worthy of power.

Thoriol turned away from the mirror and walked across the richly appointed room. He frowned when he saw a tattered old banner bearing the heraldry of Tor Caled hanging on one of the walls. What battle had the standard been recovered from, he wondered. What great deeds had Imladrik done that day?

Glass-paned doors pivoted outwards at the prince's touch, opening upon a broad balcony. From this height, he could look out across the waterfront and watch the ships returning to the harbour. Even now the docks were bustling with activity, gangs of stevedores helping to unload the supplies that had arrived along with Lady Kelsei's warriors. On the point, a great lighthouse threw its brilliant beam out across the waters, beckoning any wayward fishermen or merchants landwards.

Thoriol followed the path of the beam, but when it illuminated a patch of rock rising out beyond the mouth of the harbour, he found himself captivated. He walked to the edge of the balcony, hands closing tight about the railing. Leaning forwards, he kept his eyes focused in the direction of the rock, waiting for the beam to illuminate it once more.

The light revealed a mouldering heap of burned, blackened armour, mail too small and stout to ever close about the body of an elf. The jumble of armour littered the rocky island, strewn in heaps and mounds, spilling into the waves slapping against the craggy shore. Sometimes a charred skull or bit of bone was thrown into sharp relief by the probing light.

Caledor was wrong to think all the dragons had deserted Elthin Arvan. There was one who had remained, though the fact would hardly reassure the king. Ever since Prince Imladrik's death, his steed Draukhain had refused any overture made by the asur. Even Lord Teranion and the other dragon riders had been unable to appeal to the enormous drake. Draukhain had lost its taste for the war when Imladrik died. In its place had arisen a savage and unstoppable thirst for revenge.

Draukhain hunted on its own, ranging far and wide over the countryside. Thoriol heard the drake would sometimes be gone for months on end, then come flying back over the harbour, its claws filled with scorched dawi armour. It'd drop them on the spit of rock, piling them about the stone rising from the island's centre. It was a stone the dragon had brought from far away, an obelisk that had been salvaged from the ruins of Oeragor. Those who had known the city before its fall said it was the first stone that had been raised there and upon it was chiselled the name of Imladrik and his title, Master of Dragons.

The people of Tor Alessi thought of Draukhain as a loyal dog, mourning its master's memory. Thoriol knew better than that. He might never have shared the dragonsong with a drake, but he knew the majesty of the creatures. Their minds were far beyond those of beasts, alien and strange to any kind of true understanding, even for the wisest of asur. Only the dragon riders came close to any kind of communion with them, and even then it was affectionate indulgence on the part of the dragon, not a true rapport among equals.

Only two elves had ever been accepted by the dragons as equals. Caledor Dragontamer, who had walked through the mists of legend, and Imladrik, who had died on the end of a dwarfish axe.

As he looked out upon the island, at the heaps of armour Draukhain had brought there, Thoriol felt ashamed. Everyone expected him to live up to his father's memory, but how could he ever match the legacy of a hero who could move even a dragon to sorrow with his passing?

'The dwarfs call him *Uzku* – the "Crawling Death" – because his wings are ruined and won't let him soar high among the clouds.' Lady Liandra stepped out from the room behind him. She looked much as he'd last seen her, almost two centuries ago. A little more weathered perhaps, some of the heat in her eyes dimmed by regret, but she was still the noblewoman he remembered, the one who'd ridden Draukhain back from Oeragor with his father's corpse clutched in the dragon's claws.

Thoriol looked at her only briefly before returning his gaze to the island. 'You were the last one he ever suffered to ride him,' he said. 'Is it so painful for them, when the link is severed?'

Liandra joined him beside the rail, following his gaze out to the rock. 'No,' she said. 'It is nothing like the pain we feel if we lose them. To them we are temporary, transitory things. They may become fond of us, feel sad when we are gone, but they know we aren't enduring. Vranesh was fond of me, cared about me, but she didn't love me.' She pointed out to the morbid island. 'He loved your father. That is why he stays, why he hunts the dwarfs. There's an empty hole inside him where your father used to be. He's trying to fill that emptiness the only way he can.'

They were silent for many minutes, the cold sea breeze whipping about them, the briny tang of the harbour stinging their noses, the distant shouts of sailors and stevedores drifting up to them. 'You bribed your way in, of course.' Thoriol didn't look at her when he made the statement.

'It was the most discreet way to see you,' Liandra confessed. 'You are the lord of the hour and all eyes are on you right now. If I'd come to visit you openly, that information would have spread like dragon fire.'

'It is easy to understand how that might become a scandal,' Thoriol said. 'My father's mistress having a liaison with his son.'

Liandra's voice was strained when she replied to his jab. 'I was thinking of the king's spies.'

Thoriol turned and glared at her. 'Of course. Lady Liandra always conducts herself with propriety.'

'If you expect me to apologise for loving your father, then you'll be waiting until the Pale Queen beckons you into her halls,' Liandra snapped back. 'I came to visit you because I thought we shared a common purpose. I thought we had mutual ambitions.'

'Perhaps we do,' Thoriol conceded, 'but that doesn't make us friends.'

'Nor does it have to,' Liandra said. 'Duty and purpose often draw enemies together. Our differences can't be allowed to affect our obligations.'

Thoriol nodded. 'That much we can agree on.' His expression became thoughtful for a moment, some of the hostility draining from his eyes. 'You aren't my enemy, Liandra,' he said. 'I don't hate you the way I do the dawi or my uncle. I'm just... envious, I suppose. Envious of all those years when my father was taken from me and sent here, with you. Envious that you were there with him when he died.' He turned and waved his hand out towards the island. 'I'm envious that you were able to share that with him, that you were a dragon rider, like he was.'

Thoriol shuddered as he turned and withdrew from the balcony. 'I think I would have given anything to have made him so proud.'

The spires and domes of Athel Toralien were glimmering in the last light of the fading sun when Lord Ilendril left his luxurious chambers and hurried by hidden stairs and secret corridors into the cellars far beneath the roots of his tower. The message his steward had brought to him was one he'd been anxiously awaiting for weeks. Now, at last, he could allow his worries to abate. In just a few moments he would have what he'd coveted for so long. Another concealed door, a final flight of steps and he was down in the vault. He barely noticed the other elves who awaited him, his interest at once settling upon the dusty, road-worn figure of Ashelir.

Ilendril clapped his hands together in delight when Ashelir threw back the silken covering and exposed the long, curved length of bone. The highborn's hand slid down the side of the object, savouring the rough caress of its pitted surface. With an expression almost of rapture, he turned and looked at Vithrein.

'Well?' Ilendril demanded.

The gaunt mage closed his eyes, his lips moving in a whispered incantation. A chill swept through the room, a crypt-like cellar deep beneath Ilendril's tower in Athel Toralien. The lanterns flickered as unseen forces pulled at the flames. Rats and spiders scuttled off into the shadows, repulsed by the aethyric stirrings around them.

Vithrein's shoulders sagged. He seemed to wilt into the chair. His attendants, mages formerly in the service to the late Lord Caerwal, hurried forwards to help him. Vithrein waved them back, somehow summoning the strength to give them a reassuring nod. Gradually, he lifted his head and faced his patron.

'The beast lives. Ancient and powerful,' Vithrein said. 'There are some in Ulthuan mightier, but few in Elthin Arvan that are its equal.'

Ilendril's face beamed with delight. Soon, soon a long-cherished dream would be realised. He turned away from the recuperating Vithrein. Snatching up the curved bone from the table, he marched across the dank crypt to the steel cage resting against one of the walls.

The inmate of that cage stirred as she saw the asur lord draw close. The hate that shone in her eyes brought a cruel laugh from Ilendril's lips, the sardonic mockery of one who hears a snake hiss at him and knows he is safe because he's already pulled its fangs.

Drutheira was thin and wasted, her hair matted and torn. A simple shift covered her pallid body, clinging to her like a funeral shroud. The crude garment did nothing to conceal the garish glyphs that had been tattooed across her flesh. Hands and feet, forehead and breast, all were marked by needle and ink. Wards of great potency drawn by a loremaster of Hoeth, the tattoos served to blunt the witch's magical abilities, to cut her off from her aethyric attunement.

'I will soon need your services again,' Ilendril told his prisoner. 'How much torture will it take to make you submit this time, I wonder?' He glanced over at Ashelir. 'I was impressed at the restraint your son displayed the last time. Perhaps I will give him a freer hand.'

Drutheira laughed at Ilendril and at the fury she saw in Ashelir's face. 'No torture this time, asur dog. I'll be happy to speed you to your doom.' She lifted her hand as far as her shackles would let her and pointed to the thing in Ilendril's grasp. 'The creature that belongs to will kill you. You are a fool to even think you can command it. It will kill you, Ilendril, but it will make you know terror first.'

Ilendril sneered at the druchii's threats. 'Instruct Vithrein as you did before. Work your magic, witch. When the dragons are broken, I may even find it in me to be merciful.'

Drutheira laughed again. The druchii were a people alien to the concept of mercy. In Ilendril, she recognised a kindred spirit.

She also saw an elf racing headlong to embrace his own doom.

TEN

BLOOD OF THE DRAGON

393RD YEAR OF THE REIGN OF CALEDOR II

High above the vastness of Elthin Arvan, Lord Ilendril watched as the sprawling greenery of Loren Lacoi stretched away across the horizon. In the distance he could see the sombre, brooding peaks of the Arluii, what the dwarfs called the Grey Mountains. From this height, the broad Anurein river was just a narrow ribbon of silver snaking its way across the landscape. If he strained his eyes, he fancied he could see the farms and vineyards supporting Sith Rionnasc away to the north. Of course, he had no business in the north this day. It was into the dwarf-held south that his destiny led and towards which his steed bore him.

Power! Ilendril had never appreciated just how absurd and juvenile his concept of that word was. Not until Vithrein and the other mages had enchanted the dragon-fang for him. It was only then that the elf lord understood what it meant to truly have power.

He barely felt the cold of the wind as it whipped through his hair and set his cloak billowing out from his shoulders like ebon wings. The tatters of cloud that flashed past left little beads of condensation on his armour, dripping from the steel plate in slithering rivulets, soaking the silken finery of his undertunic and gloves. The air was thin, burning as he drew it down into his hungry lungs. Yet these were but trifling annoyances, obstacles that would be overcome with the proper application of invention and enchantment. Of far more importance was the fact that he'd succeeded.

The reek of wyrm filled his nose, a thick, musky, sulphurous smell that seemed to sink into his skin. Ilendril could feel the dragon's pulse pounding through its colossal body, his bones vibrating in harmony to the reptile's heart. When the beast beat its wings, flexed its claws or turned its head, the elf lord's body shivered at the working of the wyrm's titanic muscles. When he commanded the dragon to vent a blast of fire from its jaws, it seemed to Ilendril that the entire world was engulfed in the roaring flames.

This was power – might beyond that of simply commanding vassals and armies. Strength beyond that of hoarded wealth and lands. It was a power more primitive and raw than even the mage's mystic arts. To harness a dragon was to control a force that was ancient when the gods themselves were new.

Ilendril exulted in the primordial might of the dragon he rode. He could well believe Vithrein when the mage claimed this beast was among the largest and most powerful in Elthin Arvan. Almost two hundred feet from snout to tail, wings that seemed to blot out the sun when they were unfurled, claws like lance heads and fangs like daggers. The wyrm was covered in crimson scales as thick as steel plate, and massive horns swept back from its head to offer further protection to its sinuous neck.

Ilendril closed his hand about the dragon-fang hanging around his neck on an ithilmar chain. Such a small thing, yet it connected him to the wyrm on a level the dragon riders of Caledor could only dream of. It was true, he didn't have that sense of communion the dragon riders always claimed to share with their steeds. He couldn't make sense of the wyrm's mind, only capture vague impressions of the primitive impulses that motivated it. He didn't need any deeper communion than that. He had something better.

He had control.

A dragon rider could only appeal and request the obedience of his steed. There were no better examples of that than the desertion of the drakes during the Siege of Barak Varr and their later retreat from Tor Alessi. The old ways of Caledor Dragontamer left the beasts wilful and independent. It didn't impress upon them their place as servants of the asur.

Ilendril had found magic that would change all that. His ancestors had been cast out of Caledor for seeking such secrets. Now, he had them in his possession. He would prove to all Ulthuan that they were meant to control them and to command the dragons – not as supplicants but as masters.

First he would prove it with the wyrms of Elthin Arvan. Then, when he had the attention of the Phoenix King himself, he would show that the drakes of Ulthuan could be commanded in the same way.

Ilendril wondered what price in fortune and glory could be placed upon a secret that would bring not just an end to the War of the Beard, but give to the asur the keys to conquering the world.

It was a ponderous question, and one Ilendril gave great thought to as he commanded his wyrm to fly him back to Athel Toralien. There was much to do, and the first step was demonstrating for Lady Kelsei the new weapon he had to offer her armies.

Solemnly, Morek Furrowbrow watched as his master, Ranuld Silverthumb, was removed from the chair in which he'd died. It took ten dwarfs with a winch to move the ancient runelord. By some hideous process Morek couldn't begin to understand, his mentor had been petrified. A basilisk's stare couldn't have wrought a more complete petrifaction. Upon discovering Ranuld's body, Morek had given his hand an exploratory tap of his hammer. One of the fingers, extended as though pointing, broke away. From skin to flesh to veins and bone, everything within the finger was still distinct, but it had become solid stone.

Morek looked about the vault-like forge where his master had died. The Anvils of Doom, those precious artefacts of the ancient past, stood upon their pedestals. It was when returning one of the Anvils to its place that Ranuld's body had been discovered. The High Runelord of Karaz-a-Karak hadn't been seen in decades, but that wasn't unusual in itself. Ranuld had been given to long ruminations in private and lengthy sojourns into the forgotten reaches of the Karaz Ankor. His absence was noted among the other runelords and runesmiths, but it hadn't been considered a cause for alarm.

They might never know how long Ranuld had been sitting there in the dark, as lifeless as the hulking gronti-duraz who crouched in the semi-darkness of the vault. What strange process had struck down the High Runelord was of more pressing consequence to Morek. Already there were whispers of elgi sorcery, but he was reluctant to entertain such an easy explanation. If the elgi could dispatch such murderous sendings then how was it that they'd neglected to strike down High King Gotrek or Morgrim or King Varnuf or any of the other great warlords of the dawi?

A chill crept down Morek's spine as he considered other possibilities. Watching the apprentice runesmiths loading Ranuld's statue-like corpse onto a cart, there was no denying the unnatural condition of the body. Some sort of magic had brought the High Runelord to ruin. There were strange, unnatural creatures, it was true, that killed by changing their prey to stone. But if a basilisk or cockatrice had somehow snuck into the halls of Karaz-a-Karak, the brute would hardly have stopped with a single victim. It would have killed again and again to fill its belly, continuing to prey on dawi until it was hunted down and destroyed.

No, there was something more than a simple beast behind Ranuld's death. Morek scratched at his beard, wondering if he dared to draw a connection between his master's strange death and something else that had been nagging at him for some time.

The thane Drogor. Morek had only seen him a few times since his return from Barak Varr. Indeed, it struck the runelord that the thane went out of his way to keep clear of Morek and any other runesmith. He was reminded of the same furtive air when Drogor had first arrived at Karaz-a-Karak and become the friend and confidant of Prince Snorri. Despite his many years with Snorri, Drogor had managed to always be absent whenever Morek called upon the prince.

Now he was back, this time as one of Morgrim's closest companions. It could be simple political expediency on Drogor's part, of course, currying favour with those in power. After all, Snorri had raised him from a nameless adventurer from Karak Zorn to a thane of Karaz-a-Karak. Perhaps Drogor simply sought further advancement by renewing his friendship with Morgrim.

If he could be certain it was so simple a matter as shameless opportunism, Morek would actually be relieved. Such tawdry politicking would be wholesome beside the things he feared.

Maybe it was being so near to Ranuld and recalling his master's frequent talk of 'old magic' that set Morek's mind to thinking about the ancient past. Enemies that were as old as the magic Ranuld had sought to restore. Enemies terrible and malignant beyond the worst outrages of elgi and urk. The old enemies. The eternal enemies.

The undying enemies.

Morek stared about the darkened vault, studying the massive rune forge and the great war-shield lying against the wall. One of the *dokbar*, the fabulously ancient 'windows of seeing' that the runelords of yore had used to commune with their fellows. Ranuld had been one of the few who still knew the secret to evoking the dokbar's rune magic and sending his voice and image to the other dokbars. It was an example of the old magic, just as the gronti-duraz were. Relics of an art that was being lost to the dawi.

As the old magic faded, Morek wondered if the things it had once held at bay might be creeping back into the world. Things endowed with magic of their own. Things with intelligence beyond that of beast and urk. Things that might hide themselves in shapes that weren't their own.

Morek looked at the empty throne. How he wished he could discuss his suspicions with his master. Would the High Runelord dismiss them as baseless or would he find them worthy of concern? And if they were worthy of concern, what would he advise Morek to do?

Morek looked to the slumbering gronti-duraz and shook his head. There were no answers for him here, only the secrets of the dead.

'You should appreciate the *abomination* of what Lord Ilendril is seeking to accomplish.' Liandra was in such a temper that she refused to stay in her seat. Instead she prowled like a lioness through the parlour, her boots clattering as they moved from rug to tile and back again.

Thoriol leaned back in his chair overlooking the window and shook his head. 'I should, but I fear that I can't,' he said.

Liandra rounded on him. 'Your father was the Master of Dragons. He knew them better than any asur alive. *He* would know at once the horror of this thing.' She balled her hands into fists. 'I suspected... I *knew* from the first that Ilendril was going to try something like this. The moment I saw him call a merwyrm from the sea, I knew *this* was what he intended. *This* was why the dragons left Barak Varr. *This* is why they returned to Ulthuan.'

'If they hadn't left us,' Thoriol said, 'then no one would be listening to Ilendril. He wouldn't have Lady Kelsei's ear.'

'You are *excusing this?*' Liandra couldn't keep the disgust from her tone.

'I'm not excusing anything or anyone,' Thoriol told her. 'What I am trying to do is explain why...'

'Do you know that is what the druchii do?' Liandra snarled back. 'I have seen it. They take a dragon and they break him. They torture and mutilate until all that is left is a twisted, tormented thing, and then they force that *abomination* to their will. Ilendril is no better than a druchii to even suggest we do the same. But he's gone far beyond merely suggesting. He's done it. He wants to prove it to–'

'The dragons have left Tor Alessi,' Thoriol reminded her. 'They have left us on our own. Do you understand the panic that has left the people in? They live in dread of the day the dwarfs return to lay siege to the city and there are no dragons to stop them. The people in Sith Rionnasc and Athel Toralien and all the other settlements, they know if they are attacked there will be no dragons flying to their rescue. The people are frightened, and frightened people will grasp at anything and anyone who offers an end to their fear.'

'The mages can conjure phantasms to deceive the dwarfs,' Liandra said.

'How long do you think illusions will be enough to hold them back?' Thoriol asked. 'I was here when they marched on Tor Alessi. I saw them marching out against *real* dragons, marching out even as whole regiments were reduced to ash. No, the dwarfs are too stubborn to meekly turn tail. Once they are committed, they have to be decimated before they will relent. Against that kind of determination, illusions are not enough.'

'Then you are saying we should embrace this?' Liandra cried.

Thoriol caught something in Liandra's eye as she raged about the despicable magics Ilendril had harnessed. It was only there for an instant, but he saw it just the same. It was a look of guilt and shame. He remembered that Liandra wasn't simply a dragon rider; she was a dragon rider without a dragon.

'What worries you more?' Thoriol asked. 'That we will embrace this new magic or that *you* will embrace it?'

Liandra turned on him, her face so filled with outrage that he thought she would come at him with her fists. Then the rage collapsed, sinking beneath the weight of self-loathing. She turned from him, shaking her head.

'You don't know what it's like,' she said. 'You can't imagine the temptation to have that again. To soar above the clouds, to feel the awesome might of a dragon beneath you. *That* is being alive – everything else is just shadows and echoes. To share your heart and mind with something older than the mountains and the seas... There is nothing else to compare.' She looked back at Thoriol, her body trembling with the violence of the emotion that gripped her. 'I yearn for that, to reclaim it for myself. That is what Ilendril dangles before me, the promise that I could be again what I once was.'

Liandra's eyes hardened. 'But it is all a lie. What he promises isn't communion but enslavement. It isn't sharing the power of a dragon but dominating it, commanding it like a huntsman commands his dog. It's a violation of the ancient pacts between asur and dragon, an abandonment of the grace and glory that is the heritage of Caledor Dragontamer. It is... immoral.'

Thoriol nodded slowly. He could appreciate the temptation that drove Liandra's disgust, but she had to understand that it wasn't simply a question of morality, of right and wrong. The war made it so much more than that. 'Without dragons to protect them, many asur will suffer,' he said. 'We can argue all night about whether the colonies should be abandoned or if the king should offer the dwarfs peace on their terms, but the reality is that our people are here *now*. If they aren't protected, a lot of them are going to die.'

Liandra scowled. 'If we abandon principle, if we forsake the ideals that make us who we are, then what is it that we're fighting for?'

'It is the wyrms of Elthin Arvan that Ilendril proposes to harness,' Thoriol said, trying to soothe her. 'The dragons of this land have no compact with the asur.'

'Do you really think it will stop here?' Liandra challenged. 'Can you really believe Ilendril's ambitions are so small? Do you think the king won't be watching?' She pointed to the window, out to the bay where Draukhain's island stood. 'How long before it is the drakes of Ulthuan that Ilendril's supporters decide to harness? Why should the asur ask when they can take?'

The question gave Thoriol pause. Not for the first time he wished Caradryel were with him. The diplomat was far more versed in politics than he was, far more capable of seeing the implications of something like this. Even after all his years at his uncle's court, Thoriol still considered himself a novice when it came to intrigue and deception.

'How would you stop it now?' Thoriol asked. 'Even if you wanted to, how would you stop it? He already has the attention of Lady Kelsei and the Council of Five. You already know the king's attitude when it comes to dragons. What would stop him?'

Liandra came closer to where Thoriol was seated. She lowered her voice, not from fear that there were spies within the Tower of the Dragon but out of deference to the unsavoury suspicions her words would convey. 'I have told you already that this magic of Ilendril's seems similar to the sorcery which commanded the black dragon that destroyed Kor Vanaeth. If any evidence of such a connection could be found and presented to the loremasters in Hoeth...'

'Even my uncle would be forced to condemn it as black magic,' Thoriol said.

'Lord Teranion shares my concerns,' Liandra continued. 'We have both had our agents watching Ilendril's movements. Sooner or later we will discover the source of this monstrous magic of his.'

'And when you do?' Thoriol wondered.

Liandra's eyes were as cold as a glacier. 'When we do, we will expose him.' She turned her eyes back to the window, staring out into the harbour. 'I only pray that when we do, it isn't already too late.'

Kazad Kro squatted upon its hill like some great stone snake. Its massive walls and parapets had been extended over time, coiling round and round until there was no visible trace of the rock upon which they stood. It was the last stronghold of the skarrenawi, the last bastion of a lost people. For centuries the hill dwarfs had toiled, ceaselessly hauling stone to their fortress, expanding its defences, trying to build a barrier strong and mighty enough to keep out the rest of the world. For centuries, it seemed, their strategy had worked. The war raging through the Old World had passed them by, washing around Kazad Kro as though it were a great boulder lying in the midst of a river of blood. Kazad Kro had been forgotten by elgi and dawi alike.

Or so those who had buried themselves behind its walls desperately hoped. After the destruction of Kazad Thar and Kazad Mingol, a great exodus of the skarrenawi had taken place. Led by Rundin Torbansonn, they had renounced their loyalties to High King Skarnag Grum and returned to the mountains and their dawi cousins. Only those too proud and too stubborn to accept the doom of their people remained behind, clinging to their gold-mad king.

Such was Kazad Kro, its once grand halls and bustling markets reduced to a squalor of misery and poverty. The hold was filled to bursting with the remains of the skarrenawi, refugees from across the lands who had once owed fealty to Skarnag Grum. The war, which had bypassed the city, had been more attentive to the surrounding lands. The armies of elf and dwarf alike had trampled the fields and pastures that once supported Kazad Kro. The dawi saw no shame in taking the food of their isolated cousins to feed their own warriors, for the skarrenawi would benefit once the elgi were driven back into the sea. The elgi, by turn, appreciated that anything which gave their enemies support must be destroyed and the fields of Kazad Kro had been razed, great rocks called down from the skies to spoil them and salt sown across what remained. Without crops and herds, the dwarfs within the hold had been reduced to subsisting entirely on the mushrooms they could grow down in their vaults and deeps. The cheese and milk from the few goats kept inside the walls became a precious treasure, and any dwarf who dared strike a goat was summarily and brutally executed by his kindred.

Through it all, through all the squalid despair, High King Skarnag Grum kept himself to his treasure vault, tirelessly counting the gold he had hoarded during better times. His mind retreated back into the days of peace and prosperity, when the wealth of both dwarf and elf flowed through the forts and outposts of the skarrenawi. Sometimes, in the grip of his nostalgic madness, he would order his goldmasters to raise the tax on trade goods or increase the duties on wine and beer. Often he would demand to know why the inhabitants of some settlement burned to ash decades prior had failed to fulfil their monetary obligations to the High King. When such fits came upon Skarnag Grum, his goldmasters shook their heads and made their excuses, none of them willing to break the king's delusions with the terrible reality around them.

And so it sat, forsaken and forlorn – Kazad Kro, the lone citadel of the skarrenawi. Untouched by siege, unblemished by the havoc of attacking armies, the hold endured like its people, stubborn and defiant.

In looking for a site to display the power now at his command, Lord Ilendril could have asked for no better place.

In the chronicles of the asur, the day would be recorded as the Battle of Ilendril's Hill.

In the dwarfs' Great Book of Grudges, it would be known as the Massacre of Malok.

The wyrm circled above the dwarf fortress, its primordial roar smashing down upon Kazad Kro like a thunderclap. Smoke billowed from the dragon's maw, little flashes of flame flickering from between its monstrous fangs. Each beat of the beast's mighty wings sent its reptilian reek rushing into the halls of the skarrenawi.

Again and again the great red dragon soared over the hill fort. The ballistae and rock throwers mounted in Kazad Kro's towers hurled their missiles at the beast, but always the dragon was too high to be within their reach. The bellowing roar deepened into a serpentine hiss, a cachinnation rife with malignant mockery. It was the cruel laughter of a monster confident in its power and in the helplessness of its prey.

Through the refugee-packed halls of Kazad Kro, terror flourished. The skarrenawi were just as capable of stubborn valour as their mountain cousins, but there was a difference between taking a stand against an enemy who could be fought, who at least promised a noble death in battle, and trying to oppose something elemental and ancient. Too many of the dwarfs packed into Kazad Kro had been there to see Kazad Thar razed, to watch the destruction visited upon Kazad Mingol before the conflagration. They knew what a dragon of such size and awful power could do. They had survived it once, and to go through such an experience again cracked such courage as they still possessed.

A riot of fear swept through the fort. Refugees seeking to force their way through the gates, soldiers trying just as forcefully to keep them barred against the enemy. The shrieks of desperate rinns, the wailing of children, the fretful mutterings of elders as they pulled at their beards. Above it all, the loathsome hiss and roar of the dragon, persistent and inescapable.

Then, with the same suddenness with which the monster had appeared over Kazad Kro, the dragon was gone. Lookouts in the towers shouted the news down the passageways, and from there the word was carried into the halls and corridors. The fear and strife of only minutes before dissolved into jubilant laughter and cheers. Prayers of gratitude to Valaya and Grungni rang out. The dragon was gone! The wyrm had fled!

Immediately speculation ran rampant. Rumour quickly established that a dawi army had appeared and driven off the monster. The dragon had retreated when it caught the scent of Morgrim Elgidum, for the great hero of the dawi was prophesied to be a *drengudrakk* and the wyrm didn't want to be the one from which he earned the title of 'dragon slayer'. Then, too, some spoke of Rundin Torbansonn, the exiled hero of the skarrenawi, a dwarf who had already slain a dragon. It was Rundin, naked to the waist and with his head shaved, who the dragon had seen, and in seeing had flown off to find easier prey.

The laughter, the cheers, the rumours and the prayers lasted nearly an hour. That was when the lookouts in the towers blew the great alarm horns, alerting all within Kazad Kro.

The dragon was back.

The wyrm came sweeping down upon the fort in a fierce dive. Its claws were wrapped around a great rock it had ripped from the side of some mountain. As it dived upon Kazad Kro, it released the enormous boulder. Tonnes of rock went hurtling down into the hold's gates, its great velocity and momentum driving it into the iron-banded portals with the ferocity of a volcano. The gates were obliterated by the impact, smashing inwards in a blast of splintered wood and shattered stone. Hundreds of dwarfs, both the soldiers guarding the gate and the refugees who had sought to escape the hold, were pulverised by flying debris. Hundreds more were crushed as the mountain boulder went careening through the halls, grinding dwarfs beneath as though they were grain under a millstone.

Overhead, the dragon reared up, a malefic roar erupting from its fanged maw. A few bolts were flung at it by those skarrenawi still able to answer the beast's rampage, but their aim was too shaky to seriously threaten the reptile. The wyrm's ophidian eyes glared at the most persistent bolt throwers. Uttering a savage hiss, the beast swept down upon their tower.

The dragon crashed into the side of the building, the impact rattling the fortification with the fury of an earthquake. Powerful claws dug into the face of the tower. Like some titanic lizard, the dragon began to pull itself up the side of the fort. At each window and embrasure, the wyrm paused to send a blast of fiery death licking into the room beyond, immolating any dwarf too slow to throw himself down the stairwell.

A few of those dwarfs saw the purple-cloaked rider seated in a golden saddle strapped to the wyrm's back. They noted the callous, imperious cast of the elf lord's face, the tall helm with its sculpted wings and the pearl-fangs that mocked the jaws of the beast he rode. Some few who understood the words of Eltharin and who heard Ilendril's voice, recalled with rage the elgi's vile commands.

'Burn them,' Ilendril snarled. 'Burn the moles in their burrows!'

The dragon obeyed with a spiteful pleasure. Enslaved by the puny creature on its back, the wyrm vented its frustration and rage against the puny creatures before its jaws. The screams of those it scorched, the shrieks of those it crushed, the moans of those it mutilated, these were a salve to its own misery.

When the tower had been reduced to a burned-out cromlech, the dragon threw itself back, tearing a great chunk of the wall away as it ripped its claws free. For an instant, the mighty beast hurtled earthwards, then its immense wings snapped open. With a grace incredible for a creature so massive, the dragon soared away from the smoking tower. Bolts and rocks shot out at it, but it ducked beneath their cast. The dwarf artillerists thought to bring down a fleeing adversary. It was an error from which they wouldn't recover. They thought the monster's outrages were at an end, but they were woefully mistaken.

The carnage had only begun.

Hissing like new-forged steel, the dragon swept towards the smashed gates. Folding its wings as it dived down, it propelled its immense body through the battered defences and into the great hall beyond. Slamming its mighty claws into the granite floor, the wyrm arrested its momentum, bringing itself to a stop just beyond the gate.

For an instant the dragon simply stood there, surrounded by the havoc wrought by the rock it had loosed against the hold, the blood of massacred dwarfs pooling about its feet. The wyrm's nostrils flared and its heart pounded with the intoxicating scent. It wasn't hunger, but something even more primal. It was power, the raw expression of naked, merciless force.

Throwing back its head, the dragon roared, its deafening bellow knocking stones from the damaged ceiling and walls, driving stunned survivors from hiding to flee in mindless terror before it. The wyrm lashed its tail against a nearby pillar, shattering the visage of an ancestor god and sending the entire column crashing down. A cloud of dust rolled across the exultant reptile.

A phalanx of dwarf warriors came marching into the great hall, ponderous door-like shields raised to defend themselves against the wyrm's fire. Crossbowmen hidden behind the advancing warriors loosed their bolts at the beast, groaning in despair when they saw the missiles bounce harmlessly from the monster's crimson scales.

The dragon unleashed a blast of fire at the oncoming warriors. The runes etched into their shields protected the dwarfs from the flames, flaring into brilliance as their protective magic was evoked. But if the fire couldn't hurt the warriors, it could block their vision. It could stifle their advance.

The dwarfs resumed their grim march the instant the fires cleared. Then they saw that the dragon wasn't waiting to meet their axes and spears. During those seconds of blindness, the dragon had reared up, sinking its claws into the already crumbling roof. With a murderous shriek, the wyrm gouged out a great wound in the ceiling and brought the floor above crashing down onto the dwarfs below.

Up through the rubble and debris, the dragon clawed its way into the upper deeps of Kazad Kro. The opulent halls of the guilds and nobles, the richly appointed chambers of the goldmasters, the vast temples of the ancestor gods. One after another they suffered the wyrm's malice. Dragon fire scored the marble walls and pitted granite columns. Those dwarfs of the upper halls, whether they chose to fight or flee, were slaughtered by the wyrm.

Through it all, Lord Ilendril savoured the destruction. Long, so long, had he lusted for this might. The legacy he had wanted so desperately for himself was his now. He hadn't bowed to the fickle hearts of reptilian beasts. He hadn't let his dreams be murdered by the cruel hand of fate. He'd reached out and seized what he wanted from life, claimed what should always have been his. The awesome might of a dragon to command and control. Let the dragon riders of Caledor cling to their foolish traditions of dragonsong and communion. He was a truer master of dragons than any of them.

Searing pain ripped through Ilendril. The fang hanging from around his neck felt as though it were on fire. Blood oozed from his charred cheek and he could feel his skin bubbling and blistering. Beneath him, through him, he could feel the agonies of the dragon.

Looking around, Ilendril saw a lone grey-bearded dwarf raise his strange metal staff and send another blast of lightning searing into his slave's scaly hide. Through the sympathetic pain that stabbed into him, he recognised his enemy as one of the mud-mages of the grubby little dwarf culture. When the runelord moved to assault the dragon again, Ilendril compelled the wyrm to fight past the pain that wracked them. The agony of the rune-lightning was nothing beside the mental daggers the elf sent stabbing into the reptile's brain.

With a howl of agony, the dragon whipped its tail around, catching the runelord and flinging him far across the shattered temple in which they fought. The grey-bearded dwarf slammed into one of the walls, even his rune-etched armour unable to keep every bone in his venerable body from breaking. The runelord crashed to the floor in a jumble of shattered flesh.

Ilendril daubed at his bleeding face with a silken cloth. He wasn't enjoying himself as much as he had only a few moments ago. The magnificent power of his dragon had made him oblivious to his own vulnerability. To die, now, when he was so close to securing his place in the annals of the asur, would be ignominious. Even now, Lady Kelsei and her entourage were watching his progress through the scrying crystals of Tor Alessi's mages. He had so many more important things to think about than simply allowing the dragon to run amok.

Even so, there was still one further thing the dragon needed to do. One act that would impress upon the watching mages that the destruction of Kazad Kro was total and complete.

Exerting his will, Ilendril forced the wyrm to claw its way to the very heart of the fort. There was no toying with the dwarfs now. Every passage connecting to the main hall was brought down by a sweep of the wyrm's tail or collapsed by its powerful claws. Fire turned every warrior who stood before him into a blazing ember.

After more than an hour of slaughter, the dragon reached the core of Kazad Kro. Three dwarfs stood before a great door fashioned from gold. They screamed as the wyrm caught them in its jaws and wolfed them down in great gulping bites. Then the dragon turned to the door again. A heave of its tremendous bulk brought the door and the wall in which it was set crashing inwards.

The treasure hall of Kazad Kor was a testament to the greed and avarice of Skarnag Grum, High King of the skarrenawi. While his domains withered and died, while war raged all around him, Skarnag Grum had withdrawn into his vault, lurking amongst his hoarded gold. Tonnes of it lay piled about the floor, heaped in stacks of ingots and coins, gathered in jumbles of nuggets and mounds of dust. Even now, with the great dragon glaring at him through the ruined wall, the hill dwarf king clung to his gold. Crouching among his coins, he wrapped his arms about the closest stacks, drawing them to him as though he could protect it with his mere presence. A stream of Khazalid obscenities flew from the crazed king's foam-flecked lips.

The dragon glared at the mad, pathetic dwarf for a moment. Then it reared back and unleashed a great gout of flame. The gold heaped about Skarnag Grum melted in the fury of the dragon fire. A wave of molten metal washed over the cursing king, transforming him in an instant into an unrecognisable lump of gold, a precious nugget with a rotten core of burned flesh and scorched bone.

Ilendril stared at the vanquished king and a cruel smile spread across his face. None would contest his power now. He had done more than just give battle to the dwarfs; he had slaughtered one of their kings within his own hall. Let his detractors try to deny his power now.

As he ordered his wyrm out from the crumbling halls of Kazad Kro and back into the open sky, Ilendril's smile might have faltered if he could have read his steed's mind the way those truly attuned to a dragon could. He might have sensed then the lesson the reptile had learned during the massacre: that when the wyrm was hurt, its rider suffered too.

And when the rider suffered, his control over the dragon wavered.

In his pride, Ilendril had named his steed *Ilendrakk* – 'Ilendril's Dragon'. But soon, even the asur would begin to call the wyrm by the name the dwarfs gave it.

Malok, a Khazalid word meaning 'malice'.

ELEVEN

DIRGE FOR ATHEL TORALIEN

445TH YEAR OF THE REIGN OF CALEDOR II

'Khazuk! Khazuk!'

Even out on the bay, the sound of the dwarfish war-cry sent a thrill of fear rushing through Thoriol's blood. His mind retreated back through the centuries to that day when he'd stood on the walls with Baelian's archers against the besieging hordes of Morgrim Elfdoom. It was a sight that was as clear in his memory as though it were yesterday. Every sound, every smell, every touch of that day was imprinted upon his very soul.

It wasn't so easy to forget the day when you should have died.

Tor Alessi had been attacked many times over the intervening years, but never again with such force. The other attacks had been petty, vindictive acts of reprisal staged by individual kings. None of them had mustered the kind of throng that Morgrim had.

Until now. Earlier that day Thoriol had watched from the Tower of the Dragon as the dwarfs again came against Tor Alessi. With the help of a scrying crystal left to him by Lady Liandra, he'd watched the enemy as they advanced. The army outside the walls this time was no rabble drawn from a single hold but a great host of tens of thousands, assembled by none less than High King Gotrek himself. From the walls, the dwarfs could be seen gathering beneath the shelter of the trees.

The High King had marched out on his own, borne aloft upon his Throne of Power by a bodyguard of thanes, their heavy armour gilded and inscribed with runes, their horned helms cast in the semblance of angry ancestors and scowling gods. The king's armour was no less ornate, its dark plates of gromril bound together with links of gleaming gold, mighty runes picked out in lines of diamond and ruby. His long white beard was tucked into a broad belt with an enormous buckle fashioned from a single piece of emerald, each lock of his beard festooned with a line of onyx beads. He was broad of build and shoulder, his arms massive knots of muscle that strained the jewelled torcs wrapped about them. In his hands, he hefted an axe that might have been too big for an ogre to carry. Upon the dwarf king's face was etched an expression of such hatred that even the most prideful of the asur felt an icy tingle of fear along their spines.

The High King's royal procession had stopped a short way onto the field between the walls and trees. Gotrek's voice had barked out, carrying like thunder to the asur behind their fortifications. His words were Khazalid, but there were enough in the city familiar with the tongue to soon translate it. They were words the elves had heard many times before.

'Leave now or remain forever in your graves.'

Not a threat, rather a terrible promise of the destruction the dwarfs would loose against the city.

The dread memory of Morgrim's siege, the knowledge that Gotrek's army would be even bigger than that of his nephew, spurred Lady Kelsei to call upon Lord Ilendril's powers. The once dishonoured and exiled highborn was only too happy to oblige the general. Since the destruction of Kazad Kro, Ilendril had managed to enslave three more wyrms by means of his sorcerous methods. The dragons had been posted all around the colonies, taking the place of the absent dragon riders of Caledor. Now the reptiles were hastily summoned back to Tor Alessi to defend the city in its hour of need.

Fear and despair were driving the asur to embrace powers they had once shunned, to countenance things they'd once deemed utterly immoral. To save Tor Alessi, the asur were ready to blacken their souls.

Thoriol listened to the harsh, guttural war-cry booming out from the besieging army. They were working themselves into a frenzy. For days the dwarfs had taken shelter in their tunnels beneath the trees, safe from the attentions of Ilendril's prowling wyrms. How many more dawi had marched to join the attack it was impossible to say with any real accuracy. Even the mages were unable to pierce the veil of the forest, their magics cast aside by some elder enchantment that hung over the woods like an aethyric fog. There could be a hundred thousand dwarfs under the forest waiting for Gotrek's command to attack.

Desperate moments forced people to desperate measures. Thoriol was never more aware of that truth than the moment he climbed down into a fishing smack and started rowing out to Draukhain's island.

What was he, after all, but the disappointment of Tor Caled? He wasn't the Master of Dragons his father had been. He wasn't the warrior his uncle was. He wasn't wise like his mother. He wasn't even a shrewd politician like Caradryel. He was nothing and he had nothing to offer.

But he could. An awful thought had driven Thoriol across the bay. Draukhain was often absent from its island. If the drake was gone, he would be free to search among the rocks and dwarfish carrion strewn about the isle. All he needed was a broken tooth or a sliver of claw, maybe just a lost scale or chip of horn. He could take what he found back to Ilendril, have him use his magic to make a talisman. Draukhain would be his to command, to bring into the battle against High King Gotrek and his horde.

Thoriol fairly leapt from the boat as soon as he brought it close to the shore of Draukhain's island. He scrambled up the rocks, his hand tight around the hilt of his sword. The sword his father had given him. The sword of a dragon rider.

He would be a dragon rider. He would seize the legacy of his blood, become the great warrior his father had always wanted him to be. He would prove himself a true son of Tor Caled. He wouldn't suffer the whims of beasts to keep him from his destiny.

Through most of the day, Thoriol scoured the island, picking among the charred dead for what he needed. The grisly wreckage of scorched armour and blackened bones was all around him, a seemingly limitless chronicle of carnage and destruction. The first corpse he drew from the piles was fresh enough that some meat yet clung to the bones, sloughing away beneath his touch as he tried to drag the body off. Fighting down his revulsion, Thoriol inspected the mangled dwarf, checking the armour for any rent or tear, studying the decayed corpse for any wound. All that rewarded his attentions were a few sea-worms and a scavenging crab that scuttled out from between the dwarf's exposed ribs.

Crushing his feelings of disgust and nausea, Thoriol pressed on with his search. One body, then two, then three. Again and again he inspected the morbid trophies, the ghoulish hoard the dragon had gathered for itself. A dozen, then two dozen, each body as unrewarding as the last. One by one he shoved them away, hefting them over the rocky shore to sink into the bay. Dozens became scores and still the prince continued his search, roving with eyes and hands across the rotten wastes. Some of the bodies sported golden rings and jewelled necklaces, torcs and belts studded with precious gems, yet it was not for such mundane treasure that the prince hunted. In frustrated despair, he hurled the valuables out into the water. What he had to find continued to elude him as the scores of bodies stretched into a hundred and more. Still the prince wouldn't relent. What was at stake was too enormous to relinquish. The sounds of battle rising from outside Tor Alessi faded away, the cold bite of the sea breeze ceased to sting his skin, the stink of the dead no longer churned his stomach. Nothing mattered now, except the search and the prize.

When he was just beginning to lose hope, when he was just considering abandoning the search and returning to the embattled city, the prince's hand fell upon the very thing he'd been seeking. There, embedded in the breastplate of what had once been a dwarf noble, was a cracked dragon tooth. Planting his foot on the blackened armour, Thoriol worked the fang back and forth, gradually freeing it from the torn metal. He held the fang up before his face, studying it with covetous eyes. Soon he would be there, sailing the clouds on the back of a mighty wyrm, the primordial power of a dragon his to command.

Thoriol turned and looked back at Tor Alessi. He was a hero to them already. Defying the king's orders to return to Ulthuan had enhanced his reputation still further, but he didn't think a simple act of defiance was enough to claim the legacy left by his father. He needed to earn the adoration of Tor Alessi. With the fang he held and the dragon it could command, he would have the power to earn that acclaim.

In his life Thoriol had been forced to make many hard choices, but never one so excruciating as that he had now made. In his mind he could imagine the roar of the wind as he flew through the skies. He could feel the vibrations of power pulsing through his bones, the thunder of the dragon's heart throbbing through his own veins. His ears were filled with the rush of mighty wings, the crackle of searing flames. He could feel the harmonies of the dragonsong, not a lonely unrelieved appeal, but a dream fulfilled, a purpose at last achieved. He could picture the adoring crowds, cheering his valour and his might, crying out their adoration for the prince who had come into his possession, the elf who had claimed the birthright of his blood. Thoriol, the Master of Dragons!

Tears in his eyes, the prince threw the fang out into the bay and watched it plummet to the bottom. Even to save Tor Alessi he couldn't accept a path that defiled Imladrik's legacy and betrayed the ancient alliance between dragon and elf. That was the way of the druchii and if the asur behaved no better than their sundered kin, then they deserved to perish.

Resolved to his purpose, Thoriol turned and started hunting among the dead for anything else Draukhain had discarded. Sooner or later, someone else would think to force the dragon to fight for Tor Alessi and help break the siege. He was determined to remove that possibility.

A strange sound struck Thoriol as he resumed his search. It was a weird, slopping noise, wet and rasping at the same time. He could feel a shiver pass through the rocks under his feet and a few of the helms and shields he'd taken from the corpses and piled into little stacks were set to quivering and rattling.

You do honour to your father.

Thoriol froze, reeling as a deep voice burned itself into his brain. He slumped down atop the charred armour of a dwarf lord, clapping his hands to his head. Again the voice hissed across his mind.

We share the dragonsong of Imladrik. It is the heritage he has left you.

As the prince raised his face he saw the enormous bulk of Draukhain crawling up from the water just beyond the obelisk for Oeragor. The drake's sapphire scales shone with a silky newness, as though the reptile had just shed its skin. The eyes of the dragon studied the forlorn elf.

This is why none of my kind would bear you. They could smell your fate.

With each thought the dragon projected into his mind, the pain lessened. Thoriol briefly wondered if this was how his father had communed with Draukhain. Was there a way to make the drake understand his own thoughts? If there was, it was an art lost to Thoriol.

'Too many of my people don't understand,' Thoriol cried out to Draukhain. 'To save themselves they would enslave what they can't control.'

That has ever been the weakness of your fragile folk. They are too delicate to exist among the elements, so they seek to reshape them. They pull down the mountain to make walls and gates and towers. They cut down the forest to plant orchards and groves. They build a ship so they can contend against the sea.

'Now there are some who would do the same to dragonkind,' Thoriol warned.

Already there are those who have tried.

Thoriol felt the impulse to turn his eyes from the gigantic reptile, looking into the rocks past him. A shudder ran through him as he recognised the ornate armour of Lord Teranion and the high silvered helm of Vithrein lying among the piles of dwarfish dead. He knew at once what must have happened. Instead of exposing the secret of Ilendril's magic, Teranion had instead succumbed to it. The temptation to possess the glories of a dragon rider was too great for him to resist and in the end he had submitted to whatever promises Vithrein made to him.

Strangely, Thoriol felt no sympathy for the dead asur. They had embraced their own deaths when they came to this island and tried to enslave Draukhain. He looked back at the dragon. 'Why did you not kill me? I might have come here to do what they failed to do.'

You are the son of Imladrik.

It was the only explanation the drake would give him, but somehow Thoriol understood. He could feel the bond between them, something more powerful than anything he'd ever known. He felt he was a part of Draukhain and knew that the dragon felt the same. All the doubt and emptiness of his life, the feelings of purposelessness and want... they were gone now. He knew that this was what he'd been waiting for, the role he'd been biding his time to take upon himself.

Slowly, the prince felt himself compelled towards the dragon. He felt an almost primal terror rush through his veins. The image of a bird hypnotised by the glare of a snake rose unbidden, making his heart quake within his breast. His every instinct railed against what he was doing, yet that part of his mind that had ever refused to abandon his father's dream fought back, rebelling with the knowledge that here at last he had found his destiny.

Afraid or elated, Thoriol knew he couldn't tear his eyes away from the dragon's. He could no more defy that reptilian gaze than he could demand the sun to freeze itself in the sky. Closer and closer he came until at last he reached out with his hand and pressed his palm against Draukhain's forehead. The reptile's scales were cold and damp from the sea, seeming to leach the warmth from his touch. At the same time, he could feel the incredible heat burning deep within the drake, the elemental flame that fuelled its fire.

A deep, rolling hiss rasped across Draukhain's fangs. The dragon closed its eyes and its immense body trembled for an instant. Thoriol shivered at the same time, feeling his own heartbeat slow as that of the dragon sped up, each of their bodies struggling to find sympathy with the other. Soon Thoriol could feel the beast's mind coiling around his own, wrapping him in a somehow protective embrace.

'The dawi march against Tor Alessi,' Thoriol told Draukhain. 'Will you defend the city?'

No. The dragon's thoughts swirled through Thoriol's mind. *The city has no interest for me. What I will do is kill dwarfs, make them suffer for what they have done. Make them remember the might of your father. That is what I would share with you, Thoriol of Tor Caled. The tide of vengeance is great enough to bear us both. Together, we will teach the dwarfs what it is to fear.*

Thoriol trembled at the awfulness of the dragon's passion. It was like listening to a thunderstorm explaining its rage or a volcano expressing its hate. It was both terrible and wrong that such elemental power should be so focused and purposeful. And at the same time, he couldn't deny the call of that same power. He knew how Teranion had been tempted, because he felt that same lust pounding through his own veins. The dragonsong was something shared between drake and elf, but never before had Thoriol considered that the call could be issued by the dragon as easily as it could by the asur.

Be the dragon, become the dragon.

Draukhain lashed its mighty tail, toppling the obelisk. Beneath the stone, entombed in a shallow pit, were the gilded saddle and harness the dragon had once worn to bear Imladrik across the world.

Together, Draukhain's mind-voice slithered through Thoriol's brain. As the prince climbed down to retrieve the saddle, he tried to tell himself he did so to save the city, to protect the people of Tor Alessi. In his heart, however, he already knew that was a lie. He would punish the dwarfs for taking his father away. For now, that was all that mattered. Later, later he could think about what it meant to be a dragon rider and to wield such power.

As he lifted the saddle from its hole, Thoriol looked again to the shattered armour of Lord Teranion. He wondered if Liandra's hunt had ended the same way, if her remains too were lying somewhere on the island.

If she had fallen in the end to the daemons of her soul.

The dwarf lords stood within the mouth of the old mine-working, wrapped in the shadows of their refuge. Far below them, beneath the great cliffs, the elven city stretched away towards the sea.

'The dragon hasn't returned, my lord.' Drogor lowered the spyglass from his eye and bowed to the dwarf beside him. Morgrim was silent for several minutes, only the fingers slowly pulling at his greying beard betraying any sign of the sombre deliberations unfolding inside his mind.

Morgrim finally glanced over at his old friend. 'The High King's deception has drawn it off,' he agreed, 'but will it stay away?' He reached out, taking the spyglass from Drogor. It was a cunningly contrived instrument, fashioned by the engineers of Barak Varr for their once mighty fleet of ships. It would take a long time for the sea hold to recover, but it would recover. The damage wrought upon it would be repaired.

The same would not be said of the elf city Morgrim stared at through the glass. The walls would be cast down, the towers toppled, the streets pulled up and cast into the sea. When the dwarfs were through, there would be nothing left to mark the trespass of the elves. Only in the bitter grudges of the dawi would the existence of the city be remembered.

Athel Toralien, standing against the rolling sea, the golden domes of its towers blazing like fire in the setting sun. The white stone of its streets and walls seeming to glow in the encroaching darkness. It was a captivating sight. Even the dwarfs were compelled to acknowledge the city's beauty. The oldest parts of the city were readily obvious to Morgrim's eye. Though built to an elven design, there was no mistaking the heavier construction and ponderous solidity of dwarfish labour. When the asur prince Malekith had founded the city, he'd called upon his friends, the dawi, to make his vision a reality.

Those days were long past, gone as though they'd never been. The old friendship between elf and dwarf would never rise again. There was too much hate, too much blood between them now. Morgrim recalled the confidence Imladrik had shared with him during that last, fruitless effort to negotiate peace. He'd claimed that Malekith yet lived, but that some great affront had driven him into discord with the asur, caused him and his followers to become a renegade people. Even now, Morgrim didn't know if he put any credence to the story. What he did know was that it didn't matter. The war wouldn't end until the asur withdrew to their island kingdoms. That was the only path to peace now.

'The dragon won't be back,' Drogor assured Morgrim. 'The elgi will be worried about the High King's army and Tor Alessi. They won't dare take resources away even when they learn of our attack here.'

Morgrim nodded as he returned the spyglass to Drogor. It was a brilliant piece of strategy the High King had conceived. He was exploiting the arrogance and pride of the elgi to bait a cunning trap. By showing himself at Tor Alessi, he would convince the enemy that the main attack would fall there. Forek and those dawi who knew the elgi best agreed that the elves would never consider the possibility that an assault led by the High King could be a feint because they could never imagine their own Phoenix King would be willing to engage in such a deception and let another take his glory.

The High King's army was considerable, but it was far from the strength it appeared. Dummies of wood and straw wearing armour fashioned from tin would be carried by the dwarfs when they sallied out towards the walls, metal rods lashed to the shoulders of each warrior supporting scarecrows to left and right. Phoney siege towers, catapults and bolt throwers would be hauled around the forest, furthering the deception. By night, the woods would be aglow with thousands of fires to heighten the notion that Gotrek had brought the full fury of the Karaz Ankor against Tor Alessi.

He would, in time, but that time was not yet. Gotrek was unwilling to leave the elgi their other coastal settlements, bastions from which they could stage their own reprisals against the dawi. Before the head of the elgi serpent was lopped off, the body would be cut asunder. Only then could Tor Alessi be finished.

The elgi would learn that they weren't the only ones who could trick their enemy with illusions. While High King Gotrek held them at Tor Alessi, Morgrim would bring a much bigger army crashing down into Athel Toralien. The city, more than any other, was ripe for conquest. It had, after all, been partially built by dwarfs.

Morgrim looked back to the cliffs behind him. They were pockmarked with old mine facings. The ore had been played out long ago, but the shafts remained. Brok Stonefist had been the first to conceive the idea of using the cliffs themselves to assault the city. His plan had called, first, for the old mines to be joined to the Ungdrin Ankor, a process that had taken almost a century of excavating deep underground to finally achieve. The second part of Brok's plan called for vast reserves of zonzharr to be piled within the shafts and used to blast apart the face of the cliff and send it smashing down into the city below.

It was a scheme that called for careful timing and exacting precision. The lower shafts, those nearest the coastal plain, had been shored up and reinforced to withstand the blasting that would demolish the upper heights. Once the top of the cliff was sent crashing down into Athel Toralien, demolishing its walls and razing its outskirts, the dwarfs would emerge from the lower tunnels and rush into the resultant breach. The asur would be unable to act swiftly enough to stop the surge of warriors into their city. The only real threat to the plan had been the dragons. With them gone, victory was assured.

'Now the elgi will understand why you are Elgidum,' Drogor said as he followed Morgrim back into the mineshaft. The two thanes passed the engineers and miners inspecting the barrels of zonzharr that had been placed through the passage as they made their way to the tunnels leading back to the lower workings. Drogor had proposed using an even more powerful explosive, but Morgrim had rejected the idea. For this to work, what was needed was precision, not power. Now wasn't the time to experiment with unknown factors.

Morgrim rested his hand on the elf sword hanging from his belt. 'They already know,' he told Drogor. 'They are just too proud to admit it. So we have to show them – for however long it takes to make them understand.'

Drogor nodded, a cold gleam in his eyes. 'Would it be such a bad thing if we had to kill them all?'

Morgrim didn't answer his friend. He didn't like to think about that question and how easily the answer would come for many dawi. The war was consuming them, becoming what defined them as a people. They were losing their identity. What would the dawi be, he wondered, when they no longer shared an enemy to keep them united?

The streets of Athel Toralien were abuzz with rumour, messengers hastening through the crowded streets to pass word from one house to the next. Lord Ilendril had left the city on his dragon! There was more – Ilendril had been sent away to help Tor Alessi. The High King of the dwarfs, the feared Gotrek, was laying siege to Tor Alessi, bringing with him an army a million strong and armed with siege engines that could pound the colonial capital into rubble. No less than Lady Aelis herself had sent the cry for help, begging Lord Gelthar to send the dragon.

Liandra wasn't sure how much of the rumours she believed. It was certainly possible that the High King had finally dared to poke his head from the mountains, but talk of an army a million strong was too much for her to entertain. As for the siege weapons, whether the dwarfs had them or not, there was nothing she could do about it. The fate of Tor Alessi was something beyond her now. She had her own quest to consider and her own goals to achieve. If anything, the dwarf attack was a boon to her, for it had drawn Ilendril away from Athel Toralien and left her free to confer with the informant she'd cultivated in his household. It had taken years to find an elf whose greed outweighed his fear of his master.

The informant was waiting for her in the shadow of a large alabaster fountain sculpted in the shape of a swan with outstretched wings. She hurried to the spy, joining him before he could reconsider and slip away. Liandra pressed coins into his hand. The elf quickly hid them beneath his cloak, twisting his fingers in a cabalistic sign to invoke the protection of Mathlann. After what he'd done, he'd be leaving Athel Toralien on the next ship he could find. He didn't want to be around when Lord Ilendril returned from Tor Alessi with his dragon.

'There will be a patch of wall at the base of his tower,' the spy told her. 'I've marked it with a sprig of holly pressed between the stones. Push one of the blocks an arm's length to the left of the holly and you'll open a passage into Ilendril's cellars. What you are seeking is there. May Asuryan watch over you.'

As she watched him hurry down the alleyway, Liandra couldn't keep the disgust from her face. What she'd been told went beyond the worst of her fears. Ilendril's filthy magic drew upon the fell forces of Dhar, the blackest shade of magic, but more than that, it was rooted in druchii sorcery. The highborn even had a witch locked away in the dungeons beneath his tower. Not just any witch – she was a witch known to Liandra. Someone she'd thought dead and dust long ago.

Drutheira, the druchii sorceress who had called up a black dragon and destroyed Kor Vanaeth. The witch who had brought about the death of Vranesh.

She'd thought Drutheira slain by the dwarfs when they conquered Oeragor. How the witch had survived, how she had come to fall into the hands of Ilendril, these were questions that didn't matter to Liandra. All that mattered was that the witch lived and she knew where the druchii was being held.

There was murder in Liandra's heart as she stalked towards Ilendril's tower. Once, long ago, she had spared Drutheira, kept her alive so that Imladrik could use her to convince the dwarfs it was the druchii, not the asur, who had fomented discord between their peoples. Now she could use the witch as evidence against Ilendril, to utterly discredit the elf lord's despicable magic. Yes, she could use Drutheira to do that, but she wouldn't. Liandra wouldn't take the chance that the sorceress would again slip through her fingers. This time she would die.

Liandra had just caught sight of the glazed cupola that topped Ilendril's tower rising above the streets when the entire city seemed to rise up a few inches from the earth and then come slamming down again. She saw the cupola collapse, raining shards of glass down into the streets. The walls of the buildings around her quivered, cracking as the tremors rumbled through them. She was thrown from her feet as the paving stones in the street split.

Any kind of audible sensation was drowned out by a titanic roar, a booming rumble that rolled into the city from the east. She could see stunned elves staggering out from their homes, their mouths open in screams of alarm, but whatever sound rose from them was silenced by the reverberations of that awesome crash. Then, even that sight was blotted out as a massive wave of dust came flooding through the streets, engulfing them in a grainy, choking fog.

Coughing on the dust in her throat, Liandra struggled back to her feet. Her heart hammered in her chest, shock and terror warring for mastery of her body. It was an effort to subdue the instinct to flee, to run in blind panic through the fog. That way lay certain destruction. The only path was to remain calm, to collect herself and use her reason, not unthinking emotion.

The echoes of that first roar were still ringing in her ears, but now she could hear screams and cries as well, muffled as though they came from some great distance. When her hearing cleared, the shrieks resolved themselves into a piteous din that rose from all around her. Wails of anguish and fright that sounded from every building and every quarter.

Liandra felt her heart crack as she heard those mournful cries, the image of Kor Vanaeth after the black dragon ravaged it rising in her mind. She had neglected to help the survivors then, choosing instead to slake her need for revenge.

Forcing herself to focus, she evoked a spell that let her eyes pierce the veil of dust. Through her magically enhanced vision, she could see dazed asur stumbling about in the street, blundering into one another and the rubble that had fallen from the roofs above. Veiled in mantles of dust, the elves looked like ghosts as they fumbled their way blindly through the destruction.

'Here! To me!' Liandra cried out, hurrying to the closest of the elves. When she reached for him, the asur seized her arm in a panicked grip, clinging to her like a drowning wretch seizing upon a bit of flotsam. Liandra tried to ease his fierce grip even as she worked more of her magic to allow his eyes to pierce the dust.

'We have to help the others,' Liandra told the elf when she saw her magic take effect. 'Bring anyone you can find to me.' She waited only long enough to get a nod of agreement, then hurried to reach another survivor and clear his vision with her magic.

Whatever was coming, whatever horror had fallen upon Athel Toralien, being blind and confused would only make it worse. Liandra didn't have time to think about the tower and Drutheira now. Survival was problem enough for the moment. And then, from the distance, from beyond the veil of dust, rose a fierce roar less deafening but far more malignant than what had come before. It was a sound every elf in Elthin Arvan had come to dread.

'Khazuk!' The dwarfish cry of war and battle. Whatever calamity had descended upon Athel Toralien, the dawi were hot on its heels.

Drogor lingered upon the cliff even after the last of the sappers had withdrawn into the tunnels. As they left, the other dwarfs shared knowing glances with one another. It would be hard for them to say it to Morgrim, but among themselves they weren't so sheepish. The thane from Karak Zorn was insane, and he was going to die because of it.

Drogor cared little for the scorn of the dwarfs. It would take more than a handful of miners to make him abandon his vantage. From the mouth of the mine-working, he could look straight down at Athel Toralien. He could see almost the entirety of the city, could watch the elgi down in the streets as they bustled about on their business, oblivious to the doom that hung over them – the doom Drogor had done his part to arrange.

When the explosives were detonated, the tunnel shook as though gripped by a seizure-suffering giant. Rocks pelted Drogor's helm, tore at his feathered cloak and ripped at his leathery skin. Dirt and dust rolled down from the ceiling, coating him from head to toe. Dimly he was aware of the roar and rumble of the passage behind him collapsing. It wouldn't reach him here, at the edge of the working – he could tell as much from the vibrations of the stone and the receding nature of the cave-in. It wouldn't have mattered if it had drawn towards him; his choice had been made. He was staying to watch the annihilation of the elf city.

Drogor watched the face of the cliff slide away, ripped clear as though by a gigantic axe. Thousands upon thousands of tonnes of stone rushed down at the city. The earth itself seemed to shiver in fear as the avalanche came rolling into Athel Toralien. Doubtless there were cries of alarm from the elgi, screams of terror and moans of disbelief, but any such sounds were utterly devoured by the gargantuan roar of the cascading rocks. As the avalanche smashed into the outer walls, the fortifications were blasted apart, great blocks flung hundreds of feet into the air only to come hurtling down again onto the houses below. A plume of grey dust erupted from the tidal wave of rock, flooding the streets in a rolling fog of dirt and debris.

The avalanche smashed past the walls, torrents of rock gashing Athel Toralien like enormous knives, slicing through the buildings and spilling rubble in every direction. Entire towers were lifted off their foundations and hurled like javelins across the streets to come slamming down in a deluge of broken stone. Drogor smiled when he imagined how many of the elgi were crushed beneath that grotesque rain. It was only the slightest taste of what was to come.

Through the deafening roar of the avalanche, Drogor strained his ears for another sound. Not the faint cries of dead and dying elves, but the war-cry of the dawi. Soon the warriors of the Karaz Ankor would swarm over the rubble, charge across the broken walls to take the stricken city. The elgi might stage some effort at defence, but it would be hopeless. The day was already lost to them.

Drogor glanced back at the fallen tunnel behind him. He'd have to find another way down the cliff now, but just as he'd been determined to watch the cliff come smashing down upon the city, so too he was determined to be there when the last elves were vanquished.

He'd waited too long for this to be denied that satisfaction now.

Forek wrenched his axe from the dying elf, letting the wretch collapse in a gasping heap at his feet. The steelbeard glared down at his latest victim. Merchant, artisan, whatever the foppish swine had been, he should have kept himself in Ulthuan where all elgi belonged. Rubbing his finger along the gory blade, he watched the torchlight glisten on the blood he'd shed. Elgi blood was thin, but it had a curious viscosity about it. Somehow it never failed to remind him of oil – the way light played about it. The sheen of fresh elf blood was something he would never tire of seeing. He lusted after it the way some dawi coveted gold.

'Lost your taste for glory, brother?' Forek barked out with a certain disgust when he found Rundin staring at him. The skarrenawi still eschewed armour and his powerfully built body was a mass of scars and wounds left by elgi blades.

'There's no glory in butchery,' Rundin told him.

Forek scowled and kicked the corpse at his feet. 'You were ready enough to kill the guards. I had to be satisfied with what you left for me.' He looked beyond Rundin to the other dawi warriors who had followed the two heroes into the devastated streets of Athel Toralien. The initial wave of destruction inflicted by the collapse of the cliff had battered much of the city, leaving behind many buildings with weakened supports and broken foundations. At every turn, facades might come crashing down or a house suddenly collapse into itself as its compromised structure gave out.

The elgi were there too. The dawi met persistent resistance, though never organised opposition. The enemy came at them in dribs and drabs: a few swordsmen here, the odd archer there. Not enough to satisfy either Forek's thirst for revenge or Rundin's need for atonement.

Rundin pointed at the elf Forek had killed. 'They did you a terrible dishonour,' he told the steelbeard. 'Don't let them take even more from you than they have.'

Forek shook his head. 'All I have left to give them is steel,' he snarled.

'If you believe that, then you are dead already,' Rundin said. He hefted his axe up onto his shoulder and started off down one of the broken streets. Forek watched him go, then turned to the warriors who had been watching the two heroes argue.

'What does an oathbreaker know of honour?' Forek cursed, giving the elf corpse another kick. He stared at the other dawi, holding them with his fierce gaze. 'Only a *wattock* would find any disgrace in killing an elgi.' Beckoning to the warriors, he led them away from the street Rundin had followed.

Athel Toralien was a big place and there'd be enough elves to kill without having the disgraced champion of Kazad Kro judging him, Forek decided.

His thoughts still on Rundin's berating words, Forek almost missed the asur swordsmen in the street ahead. Cursing under his breath, he braced himself as they came at him. For a moment he was by himself, struggling to fend off the furious attack of five elgi blades. The shriek of steel scraping against steel rang out as the elves struck his armour again and again. Several links from his beard of chain were torn loose, the faceplate of his helm dented by the bashing pommel of a longsword.

Then his comrades-in-arms were rushing in. Axe and hammer cracked against elven chain; shields were pressed before elven swords. Inch by inch and foot by foot Forek's attackers were driven back. Given the space to breathe, the steelbeard rushed at the elves, the murderous runes of his axe glowing as he cleft through armour and flesh alike. In the space of a few heartbeats, the momentum of the battle shifted. The elves were forced onto the defensive, pressed back into the rubble. The advantages of height and reach vanished as the elgi lost their footing on broken, uneven ground. The struggle soon dissolved into a massacre.

The last swordsman, the one the others had striven so valiantly to defend, leapt back when his last companion was brought down. Scurrying to the top of a rubble pile, the elf tried to clamber onto a roof and pull himself to safety. The tiles cracked under his hands, spilling him back into the street.

The dwarfs closed on the fallen elf, but stopped when he suddenly cried out to them in Khazalid. 'Spare me, dread axes of Karaz Ankor! Let me pay wergild for my life!' The elf reached to his belt, quickly removing a little casket of silver. Thumbing back the latch, he exposed a collection of gemstones that brought gasps of astonishment from the onlooking dawi. The quality of the stones was obvious at a glance, their value enough to ransom a king.

Forek pushed aside the warriors who started to reach for the elf's treasure. 'Who are you?' he growled in Eltharin. The elf blinked in surprise when he found the masked hero spoke his language. Perhaps he'd heard of the steelbeards. Perhaps he had some inkling of who it was he faced.

'I am Lord Gelthar of House Derreth,' the elf answered, turning his hand and displaying the gems for Forek alone. 'They are all yours if you call your warriors back and let me leave. I will return to Ulthuan. You will never see me again.'

'No,' Forek agreed. 'I never will.' With a speed that caught Gelthar by surprise, the steelbeard sprang at him. The hideous axe blazed as it was brought crunching down into Gelthar's skull, splitting his head from crown to jaw. The casket of gems fell from his hand, spilling into the rubble. Forek brought his boot stomping down on the hand of a dwarf who tried to retrieve one of the stones.

'We've rejected his ransom,' Forek declared. 'Let the stones rot with his carcass. Then the elgi will know the price of dawi honour.'

Grim nods greeted Forek's declaration. With a few of their number watching for any straying elgi, the dwarfs gathered up Gelthar's treasure and returned it to the silver casket. Scornfully, they dropped the casket onto Gelthar's chest. As much as they coveted the gems, they valued their honour more.

Between Forek and Rundin, the dawi had lessons enough on what it meant to live without honour.

Drutheira crouched down in her cage, shivering as the sounds of battle continued to drift down to her. After the hideous quake that had trembled through her prison and sent her guards fleeing into the tower above, the sounds of conflict had grown both louder and more frequent. She didn't know what was happening, of course, but she could guess well enough. The city was under attack and things were faring poorly for Athel Toralien. She didn't think a mere siege could have wrought the turmoil she was hearing. Was it the dwarfs? The dragons? Had Ilendril's foolishness finally brought him to his just end? Briefly she wondered if it might be her own people, but she discarded that thought. Malekith's eyes were on Ulthuan, not the colonies. Elthin Arvan was just a distraction, nothing more.

She pulled the shift she wore a bit closer to her, trying to fend off the cold, dank atmosphere of her lonely dungeon. Ilendril had been ungentle in his treatment of her, extending her just enough comfort to keep her alive. She'd wasted away down here in the dark, subsisting on the gruel her gaolers provided her with and such vermin as the length of her chains would let her catch. After so many years of this living hell, she had been looking forward to the day when she was of no further use to Ilendril and her son came to take her life.

A vicious smile fixed itself on her thin face. That, of course, had been before whatever calamity it was struck Athel Toralien. Now circumstances had given Drutheira very different ideas.

The sound of the dungeon door opening drew her attention. Blinking against the harsh light of a torch, it took Drutheira several seconds before she recognised the elf descending the stairs. She should have guessed it would be him. Nobody but Ashelir would trouble themselves over her when the city itself was beset.

'Checking up on your mother?' Drutheira mocked. 'How courteous of you.'

Ashelir set the torch into a sconce and turned towards her. Beneath his cloak he wore full armour, sword and quiver strapped to his lean body. His bow was strung, looped around one shoulder, and beneath his hood he wore a steel helm. The shadow warrior was kitted for battle. He was ready to fight and die, but first he had a bit of murder to attend to.

'The dwarfs?' Drutheira asked. 'This is becoming a habit with them, rescuing me from prison.'

'This isn't Oeragor and I'm not the Lady Liandra,' Ashelir growled at her. 'I'll let no one, dawi or asur, take your life. Killing you is the only dream left to me.'

Drutheira cringed, pressing herself to the stone floor. She watched as Ashelir marched across the dungeon, the tramp of his boots sounding like the drums of doom. She watched, studying the hate on his face. There was so little of his father there, so little of Nagarythe. He looked like one of the merciless Naggarothi, bleached of all compassion and pity until only spite and malice remained.

It was when Ashelir thrust at her with his blade that Drutheira sprang into motion. The quake that had shook Athel Toralien had loosened the staples binding her chains to the floor. She'd been able to draw them loose, hiding the chains under her shift. Now, as Ashelir came at her, she whipped one of the chains at him. The steel looped around his wrist, allowing her to tug his arm through the bars of her cage. Caught utterly by surprise, he didn't react quickly enough to keep the druchii from ripping his dagger from him.

Viciously, Drutheira thrust the captured blade up under her son's chin, pushing it with all her strength through the roof of his mouth and into his brain. 'I hope Slaanesh savours your soul for an age or two,' she snarled into Ashelir's dying eyes. 'I should be happy to know you were being tortured in the hereafter.'

Drutheira let her son's corpse slide down against the bars of her cage. Quickly she lifted the key from his belt and unlocked the door. She stripped the cloak from him before pushing his body into the cage. She regretted leaving behind his sword and armour, but she knew that her years of deprivation had left her too weak to manage either. She only hoped the cloak would be enough to conceal the warding tattoos Ilendril had marked her with. It would be bad enough trying to elude the dwarfs as she made her way from the city. She didn't need the added ordeal of trying to escape the asur as well.

Pausing only to pluck the torch from the wall, Drutheira hurried up the steps and to the freedom so long denied to her.

For Liandra, it was like Athel Maraya all over again. Handfuls of shocked, confused elves staggering about the dying city, lost and abandoned. She couldn't leave them. Whatever she wanted for herself, she couldn't forsake the need she saw all around her. Liandra turned her back on Ilendril's tower and began to gather the survivors of Athel Toralien to her.

The elf refugees skirted the main rush of the dwarfs. The dawi seemed intent on securing the waterfront and cutting off any retreat by sea, so by pressing landwards Liandra was able to lead the survivors away from most of the dwarf warriors. There were still small bands of roving enemies to contend with, gangs of looters for the most part who were easily dissuaded by any show of force. War brought out the best and worst in any people, and the dawi were no exception.

Fortunately, enough asur warriors had been drawn into Liandra's mass of refugees to make a decent show of force. With her came militia, Sea Guard, mercenaries and household soldiers, even a few knights. There was also a mage, who'd staggered out from a burning temple to join the exodus. He claimed his talents didn't lend themselves to martial applications, but Liandra suspected that had more to do with moral qualms than ability. If a crisis arose, she hoped he'd put the lives of his own people ahead of his pacifism.

The warriors and fighters she'd gathered were far outnumbered by the civilians, though. White-haired elders, soft-skinned artisans, haggard fisherfolk, pallid scholars, delicate courtesans and craftsmen – all had come stumbling from the chaos to join the exodus. Children, too, so many it pained Liandra to consider how few would have their parents among the survivors.

'Where will we go?' a merchant with blackened skin and charred hair asked Liandra.

'Away,' was the only reply she could give him. It was all she could think to do for the moment. To get them away, away from the fighting and destruction. Away from the enemy. Away to anywhere that might offer them a chance to escape.

Through the smoky streets, past the crumbling buildings and the broken towers, the refugees marched. With the dwarfs pressing their attack towards the harbour, Liandra felt their best chances lay in trying to reach one of the landward gates. Obsessed as they were with either loot or revenge, it would take time for the dawi to think about sealing off the lesser gates close to the cliffs. Or at least she prayed that it would be so. If they could gain the Jade Door, then perhaps they would have a chance of reaching the Loren Lacoi before the dwarfs came looking for them.

Little clutches of survivors continued to flock to Liandra, but they were far fewer in number than before. They were entering that part of the city the dwarfs had already struck, the periphery of the districts smashed by the falling cliff. Sometimes they would find the body of a dwarf lying in the rubble, but far more often it was the corpses of asur they passed. Occasionally a cry would ring out as someone in the column recognised a loved one, but most were too dazed to care about the dead.

Liandra wished she could slip into the same numbness. She wished the faces of the slain would stop haunting her for even a few moments. But they wouldn't. Over and again she saw Vranesh and all those who had perished at Kor Vanaeth. She found herself looking over her shoulder in the direction of Ilendril's tower.

And then, with a suddenness that shocked her, Liandra found her attention riveted upon an alleyway. A little ragged group of refugees was climbing through the rubble-choked street, striving to reach her column. She gave scant notice to most of them. Her attention was firmly focused upon one particular survivor in a grey cloak, a survivor whose aura was familiar to Liandra's magesight. Though dimmed and hollowed, subdued by guarding wards and eldritch tortures, it was unmistakable.

It was the aura of Drutheira.

Maybe if the witch's senses had been whole, if her magic hadn't been stripped away from her, she would have detected Liandra before her enemy had a chance to rush at her. Snarling in almost bestial exhilaration, Liandra lunged at the sorceress, seizing her cloak in a steely grip. Spitting like a cornered panther, Drutheira recoiled and drew her dagger. The refugees around her scattered, crying out in horror as Liandra tore the cloak from her enemy and revealed the warding tattoos.

Liandra's sword flashed out, striking Drutheira's hand, severing it at the wrist. The sorceress shrieked and turned to flee. In her panic, she turned not towards the alley but back to the column of refugees. Sight of the witch and the marks inked into her flesh provoked a dramatic change in the battered survivors. Faces that only a moment before had been lost and forlorn now became contorted with hate and outrage. Hands clenched about broken stones and loose rocks. From somewhere a voice cried out, giving a name to the hate that had galvanised the refugees and drawn them out of their dazed shock.

'Druchii!'

Even if she'd wanted to, Liandra couldn't have stopped what happened. A wave of shouting, cursing asur swept down upon Drutheira. Enraged fists brought heavy stones smashing onto her, spilling her to the ground. The mob ploughed her under, bringing their primitive bludgeons crashing down again and again. When at last they were through, what lay strewn along the street wasn't recognisable as anything any more.

Liandra didn't linger over the sight. There was no satisfaction in looking at that gory mess. The witch was gone, and in her death she'd managed to take one last thing from Liandra. She'd left a gaping wound inside her where her hate had been. It was strange how that hurt almost as much as losing Vranesh.

The refugees turned away from what they had done, as though they shared the sense of loss Liandra was feeling. But it was only a matter of an instant before they had something more to ponder than the slaughter of a druchii witch. Frightened voices cried out as grim armoured warriors appeared all around them.

Liandra had known their progress through the ruins wouldn't go unnoticed. She had only hoped they could be out of the city before any organised force moved to stop them. Now she saw how fragile and transitory hope could be. The streets around them were swarming with dawi, not the stragglers and looters they'd chased off before, but disciplined columns of warriors. A regiment of crossbows took position on their right flank, a detachment of bloodied axemen formed up at their rear. Ahead of them, Liandra was stunned to recognise the masked ambassador she'd spared at the Battle of Blind River. The hate exuding from Forek Grimbok was, if anything, even more potent now than it had been then.

A dwarf wearing a wild cloak of feathers appeared at the head of the warriors before Liandra's refugees. His demeanour was completely different from that of Forek. There was an expression of sadistic enjoyment on his face, a malignance that Liandra hadn't thought anyone, be they dawi, asur or druchii, could embody. Beside her, she heard the mage from the temple moan in despair. He covered his eyes and grovelled in the street.

'Kill them,' the dwarf in the feathered cloak snarled. 'Kill them all.'

Before the dwarfs could advance, before the crossbows could loose their bolts, a fierce bellow arrested them where they stood. Forcing his way through the throng was another dwarf Liandra recognised. Morgrim, the Elfdoom himself.

'Stand down!' Morgrim roared, casting a withering look at the dwarf in the feathered cloak.

'Don't sully a great victory with a senseless massacre.' He turned from his warriors and glowered at Liandra. 'I remember you. Imladrik's lady. You understand our tongue?'

Liandra matched Morgrim's glare. 'I remember,' she said. Her eyes fixed on the sword hanging from the thane's belt. The urge to fling herself upon him rushed through her. It was difficult to put it down, almost as though the idea was being forced into her from somewhere outside herself.

Carefully, she forced herself to relax. If she did anything, if any of them made one move against Morgrim, the dwarfs would slaughter the entire column. She knew that and so did everyone with her. Whatever benefit killing Morgrim might serve the overall war, whatever satisfaction she might derive from it, nothing could justify such a massacre.

'Surrender your arms,' Morgrim told her. 'Surrender and I will guarantee your lives.'

Liandra turned from Morgrim, looking at the dwarf in the feathered cloak and Forek in turn. 'Can you speak for all your people? You forget that I saw what was done when Kor Vanaeth fell the first time. I was there when Athel Maraya burned. I was there when you took Oeragor.'

Morgrim glowered at her. 'Your kind should never have come here at all. Everything that has happened was the doing of elgi.'

'You know that isn't true,' Liandra told him. She didn't need to remind him how Snorri Halfhand had poked and prodded to get his war. In the end, neither side could hold itself blameless. She turned and gestured to the bloody ruin of Drutheira. 'You saw what happened here? That... that was a druchii. You may recall that Imladrik tried to speak to you of them.'

A tinge of uncertainty crept into Morgrim's face. Briefly he consulted with a fur-clad dwarf, a scout who no doubt had been watching the refugees and had seen the mob execute one of their own.

'We have no interest in elgi feuds,' Morgrim declared, provoking grunts of approval from many of his warriors. He cast his stern gaze across his fighters. 'Neither do we have any interest in a massacre.' He fixed his attention on Forek for a moment before turning back to Liandra. 'Leave your weapons and go. None of my throng will assault you.'

Liandra shook her head. 'And what of all the other throngs? The land is filled with dawi, dawi who won't know of the clemency the great Morgrim Elfdoom has extended to the wreckage of Athel Toralien. If we are to be butchered by dwarfs, let it be here and now.'

Morgrim was pensive a moment. Liandra knew it could still go either way with him. He might use force to seize the refugees and lead those who couldn't fight into captivity. In the end, it was his conscience that won out. He could afford to allow the handful of warriors among Liandra's exodus to escape. They wouldn't diminish the victory he'd won or the damage he'd inflicted against the asur.

'You'll not be harmed by my army,' Morgrim said. He reached to his neck, ripping free one of the amulets he wore. 'Show this to any dawi you meet and they will know you tell them the truth when you say it is by the grace of Morgrim Bargrum that you are alive.' He cast the amulet at Liandra's feet. 'I can speak only for the warriors who have sworn fealty to me. Any others you encounter may not be moved to show you the same mercy.'

The dwarf lord watched as Liandra retrieved the amulet from the ground. 'Leave,' he declared, pointing his axe in the direction of the forests. 'Keep going until no dawi ever has to look at you again. Only then will the threat of our axes be gone from your necks.'

Liandra bowed her head, an act of obeisance an elf rarely afforded to a dwarf. She could imagine the discord Morgrim's act of compassion would sow among his vassals. Already she could see the feathered dwarf whispering something to Forek. Somehow, the sight brought cold dread closing around her heart.

'Hurry,' she told the refugees with her. 'They might change their minds at any moment.'

The elves didn't need to be told twice. With such haste as they could, carrying the wounded and dying with them, the last survivors of Athel Toralien filed past the grumbling, jeering ranks of the dwarfs.

It was only much later, when they were away from the city and deep in the forest, that Liandra would notice the mage was gone. None among the refugees had noticed the elf lying in the street as they hurried past the dwarfs. None had noticed while the mystic clawed out his own eyes and bled out in the gutter. None had heard the word he muttered as he died.

'Daemon.'

TWELVE

THE SCOURING OF SITH RIONNASC

536TH YEAR OF THE REIGN OF CALEDOR II

'They're coming.'

The words reached her in a subdued whisper that was more awful than any cry of alarm or scream of terror could be. It meant that the enemy was near enough that they had to be careful about not being overheard.

Liandra rose from the mossy rock she was sitting on and looked at the hardened scout who stood before her. He was whipcord thin, dressed in crude buckskin and wolf-fur, a brown pelt to better match the foliage. A cloak of woven leaves was stretched across his lean shoulders. His boots were leather reinforced with animal bone; the sheath of his sword was fashioned from wood and lined with weasel-skin. The bow he carried was yew strung with bear-gut, and his arrows were fletched with the feathers of shrikes and hawks.

Everything about him had come from the forest, even the hard cast of his face and the sinewy toughness of his skin. It was hard to imagine him as a child playing in a marble-walled hall in Athel Toralien. But, then, that had been long ago. Another lifetime.

When she'd led the refugees from the dying city, the path had seemed so clear to Liandra. She'd lead her people inland, use the forest for cover, and then strike out along the coast to Sith Rionnasc. From there, her people could find passage to Tor Alessi or Sith Remora or back to Ulthuan if they chose.

If only it had stayed that simple. From the start a pall had hung over their retreat. Morgrim had extended his clemency to them, but even among his army there were elements who demurred. It hadn't taken long before a regiment of dwarfs led by Forek Grimbok came looking for them. It wasn't hard for the dwarfs to guess what Liandra's intentions were, nor was it hard for them to block the way.

Every time the refugees tried to break out onto the coastal plains, the dwarfs had been there waiting. There was no question of fighting them; the only choice had been to retreat back into the forest and lose their enemies among the trees. Another enemy would have tired of the chase after a time, but the dwarfs were a stubborn and intractable people. Once they had an idea in their heads it was almost impossible to remove it. Even more so when their warchief believed himself to have been shamed by the refugee's leader.

Liandra realised how little she truly appreciated or understood the dawi mentality. Her act of mercy towards Forek had engendered a vicious resentment that had only festered and grown more malignant over the years. She'd magnified the shame he felt at what King Caledor had done to him, and the worst thing in the world that could be done to a dwarf was to make him feel shame.

'How far?' Liandra asked. The dawi disliked the forests and usually didn't penetrate too deeply when they took it into their heads to go looking for the elves. If they were far enough away, Liandra could pass the warning along to the camps, get her people to scatter.

Her people. She still wasn't sure how it had happened. Maybe it was simply because she'd led them from Athel Toralien or stood up against Morgrim. Maybe it was nothing more than her highborn station, the rank she enjoyed back in the courts and grandeur of Ulthuan. Maybe it was just that there was no one else willing to assume responsibility for five hundred refugees. Whatever the cause, she'd been accepted as leader of the elves who'd fled Athel Toralien. They looked to her for guidance, trusted her judgement, leapt at her every command. For Liandra, the faith her followers invested in her was a grave burden. They trusted her, but she had no such delusions about her own infallibility. The city her father had entrusted to her had been twice destroyed, she'd led her dragon to its death and she'd watched her lover die. There were so many mistakes and always it had been others left to pay for them.

The young scout shook his head. 'Not far enough. Maybe two miles. My lady, I think this time they mean to pursue us wherever we go. I've never seen them come into the forest in such numbers. The masked dwarf leads them.'

Liandra nodded. Of course Forek would be there, goading the dwarfs on. If he couldn't lead them, then he would shame them by reminding them of what he'd suffered. Insulting a dwarf's pride was dangerous, but it was the quickest way to push him forwards. Forek had become a shrewd manipulator of his own people since devoting himself to destroying the refugee asur.

'This is your trial.' The statement came from a wispy, frail-looking elf maiden with golden hair and strange amber eyes. Aismarr's eyes were the most striking thing about her. They were at once dull like an animal's yet at the same time impossibly wise. Liandra was always reminded of the way an owl or a raven looked, at once brutish and profound. Aismarr hadn't been in Athel Toralien. She and the mangy hunting dog that always crept by her side had joined them after they came into the forest. Whenever anyone asked her where she was from, she'd simply say, 'Loren Lacoi.'

Liandra looked at the elf maid, trying to find some recognisable emotion in her strange eyes. 'We have escaped them before,' she said. 'We will do so again.' She started to call out to the other elves in her camp. By design, the refugees kept themselves in loose groups of no more than thirty, using fleet-footed runners to maintain communication with each other. It was deemed a good way to keep the dwarfs from finding the asur – and if they did, from catching them all in the same trap.

Aismarr caught Liandra's arm before she could call out her orders. 'There is a season for flight and a season for fight. The time of the deer is over. Now you must be the wolf.' She looked up, staring at the trees with her strange eyes. 'You cannot escape this time. This is your trial.'

Something in Aismarr's voice made Liandra hesitate. She was right. They couldn't keep running away, sinking deeper and deeper into the forest. They were subsisting on roots and berries, on such game as the scouts could bring back to their camps. Their clothes were scraps stitched together from furs and skins, from leaves and vines. They were losing themselves, vanishing into this primitive squalor. They huddled in tents and lean-tos where once they had walked marble halls and slept upon silken sheets. The dwarfs didn't need to kill them to destroy them. The forest was already doing that all on its own.

'The dwarfs, are they scattered or do they march in a column?' Liandra asked her scout.

The youth was thoughtful for a moment. 'From what I could see, they have sent out pickets, but most of them are in a single body led by the masked dwarf.'

Liandra cursed. The pickets would be rangers and long experience had forced a grudging respect for those dwarfs upon her. They were as capable as any asur huntsman when it came to finding and following a trail. Forek had made good use of his rangers in his earlier searches, twice managing to catch one of the elf camps.

But for the rangers, Liandra would have tried an attack against the dwarfs. She could muster about three hundred fighters from her followers. Few had swords or any weapons of steel, it was true, but every one had a bow. If they could surprise the dwarfs...

She clenched her fists in a fit of frustration. If not for the rangers, they might have had a chance. If they could strike the dwarfs, fade back into the trees and then hit them again, victory would be achievable.

'Do not worry about their rangers,' Aismarr said. She was still looking at the trees, watching the branches swaying in the breeze. 'They will not trouble you.'

There was no reason for Liandra to believe the elf maid's words, yet she was more certain of them than anything she'd ever been told. How, why, she couldn't begin to guess, but somehow she knew the dwarf rangers wouldn't be there to help Forek's troops.

'Send runners to all the camps,' Liandra called out to the elves around her. 'Every asur able to draw a bow is to come here at haste.' A fierce smile spread on her face. 'We won't run any more. Today we show the dwarfs why they should keep to their burrows and holes!'

Liandra saw the excitement on the faces of her followers as they hurried away to carry her commands to the other camps. Maybe some of her own thirst for battle had passed on to them. She hoped so, for they would need all their courage and resilience in the fight ahead of them.

Aismarr reached down and stroked the neck of her dog. The animal licked her hand, then turned and raced away into the trees. She watched it until it was lost among the undergrowth, then she turned and looked at Liandra. 'This is your trial,' she repeated. 'When you fight the dwarfs, remember that.'

Overhead, Liandra could hear the branches swaying and creaking, the rustle of the wind through the leaves. Somehow, the sounds seemed sinister to her now.

Like the whispers of magistrates sitting in judgement of the accused.

Draukhain settled onto its perch just beneath the tower's spire, its great wings folding against its back. Thoriol's cloak whipped about him as the dragon's settling wings sent a hot breeze wafting down the drake's back. For an instant, the prince worried about his appearance, then laughed at his concern. No one was going to criticise the decorum of a highborn sitting on the back of a dragon.

They called it the Tower of Mathlann and it was the highest point in Sith Rionnasc. From the tower, Thoriol could look out into the vast fields and meadows that stretched away in every direction. Little fingers of sapphire water wound their way between vast gardens of brilliant flowers, fruit orchards and olive groves, crops of corn and wheat and millet, sunken ponds for rice. The lands around Sith Rionnasc were the richest in the asur colonies, the breadbasket of Elthin Arvan. Except for Tor Alessi itself, nowhere had been more fiercely defended by the elves. A ring of keeps surrounded the farmland. The great dam upriver that chained the Anurein and fed the intricate canal system was built like a fortress itself, with great towers and parapets, batteries of ballistae and one of the largest garrisons in the colonies. Seven times the dwarfs had tried to capture the dam; seven times they had been sent away to bury their dead and lick their wounds.

At the heart of the farmland was Sith Rionnasc itself, a sprawling coastal settlement that perhaps lacked the cosmopolitan flair of Tor Alessi and the grandeur of its noble houses, but which compensated for that lack of refinement with the buzz of enterprise. An endless stream of ships pulled into the city's harbour, taking on loads of grain, vegetables, fruits and flowers that would be carried throughout the asur empire. From dawn until well after twilight, the waterfront would be a bustling hive of activity as cargo was loaded onto vessels bound for Lothern and the ten kingdoms. Many a fortune was made by those who travelled the trade route between Sith Rionnasc and the shores of Ulthuan, and the fame of captains who could make that journey in the shortest amount of time was a thing of fascination in the courts and tea houses of the elves.

Such, Sith Rionnasc had been. Looking down from the Tower of Mathlann, Thoriol saw only the spoiled echoes of that past grandeur. The fields had fallen fallow, the meadows become overgrown. Most of the groves and orchards had been cut down, their shadowy expanses deemed inadvisable by a people who now had good reason to desire an unobstructed view of the approaches to their city. Here and there some of the flowers lingered on, going wild and expanding furiously beyond the acres they'd originally occupied. Tulips and roses were the most abundant, their red petals merging into a sanguine sea when seen from Thoriol's vantage. The ghosts of the warriors who had died defending these lands, perhaps. Many of the keeps that had guarded the breadbasket of Elthin Arvan were nothing but broken jumbles of stone now, beaten into rubble by the fury and tenacity of the dwarfs.

Now they had returned once more, in numbers he had never imagined to be possible. Like some colossal centipede of steel, the dwarfs came, tromping across the barren fields and wasted pastures, through the ruined meadows and desolate orchards. Their goal, of course, was to lug their catapults and siege towers close enough that they could bombard the city. They'd tried such tactics before, but never with enough strength to make their threat reality. That was different now. This wasn't just the king of some mountain hold trying to claim glory for himself. The banners Thoriol gazed down upon bore the device of Morgrim himself, the infamous Elfdoom, conqueror of Athel Toralien, destroyer of Athel Maraya.

Killer of Prince Imladrik.

We could swoop down and roast the vermin in their armour until their little champion shows himself. Then we'd take our time ripping him asunder.

Thoriol could feel Draukhain's rage flow through him. The wrath of a dragon was an awful, primordial fury that its rider could feel in his very bones. The prince reeled in his saddle, clenching his jaw against the painful psychic resonance.

'Today is not the day for revenge,' Thoriol told the gigantic reptile upon whose shoulders he sat. The regret with which he denied Draukhain's vengeful urges was more painful than the resonance that shivered through his spirit. He would have liked nothing more than to do just as the dragon wanted, to go down there and slaughter dwarfs until his father's murderer showed himself. He'd give almost anything for that. But the one thing he wouldn't surrender was his duty to his fellow asur. His uncle would never understand that, the kinship between highborn and commoner, noble and peasant. In King Caledor's view the king was above everyone and obligated to no one. Thoriol couldn't accept such a vision.

Then you intend to fight as this petty general would have you fight? You intend that we should fly... with them?

The general Draukhain mentioned was Prince Yverian, the latest noble to be dispatched to Elthin Arvan by King Caledor. Like all the others, Yverian had been chosen for his ambitious streak, his desire to take the battle to the dwarfs rather than sit behind walls and build up his defences. He'd been a cavalry commander fighting with the druchii in Naggaroth, but with that campaign fading so that it more resembled a boar hunt than a war, his family had petitioned the king to find a more auspicious battlefield. He'd been sent to replace Lady Kelsei and his first efforts had been to organise Lord Ilendril's dragons into a strike force that could hit the dawi wherever they mustered in great numbers. The only defence, in Yverian's eyes, was to attack the enemy before they came calling.

It was a tactic the dwarfs had exploited time and again. Much as they had when Athel Toralien fell, they would gather a huge army only to disperse once they had the dragons where they wanted them. While the wyrms were away chasing shadows, other throngs would spill from their tunnels to attack their real targets. Many lives had been lost before Yverian agreed that he had to change his tactics, to become less reactive and more strategic about where he would send his strongest warriors.

Thoriol looked out over the city. Three of Ilendril's wyrms were perched upon other towers, watching the dwarfs below. They represented almost half of his total complement – perhaps more than half since Ilendril himself and the great crimson beast he rode were among those present. Malok was a gigantic brute, only slightly smaller than Draukhain and perhaps a bit more massive in its overall build. The wyrm exuded an awful atmosphere of brooding malignance; when he gazed at Malok, Thoriol could think only of a seething volcano just at the edge of eruption. Despite his disgust for the noble, he'd even tried to warn Ilendril, cautioning him about how great his steed's enmity towards him was. The warning, of course, had fallen on deaf ears.

That is what they are, these dragons of the far lands. They are hate and greed and arrogance. They care nothing for anything except themselves, they think of nothing greater than their own hubris. That is why they can be chained, because for all their pride and strength, each of them is utterly alone.

Thoriol looked down at Draukhain. The enormous blue head had turned to stare at Malok. The drakes of Ulthuan acknowledged a kinship with the wyrms of Elthin Arvan, but that was as far as their connection went. Draukhain considered creatures like Malok to be raw, savage things. They lacked the introspection of those who slumbered beneath the Dragonspine, the perspective to see beyond themselves. The nearest comparison Draukhain could make for Thoriol was the difference between the asur and the human barbarians of the wilds. There was enough similarity between them in form and shape that the asur should be disquieted to see humans enslaved, but that didn't mean they held men to be equals or kindred souls.

'You will show wyrm and asur alike what real pride and real strength are,' Thoriol told Draukhain. He could feel the drake's amusement at his words.

It is impossible to show anything to the blind, but we will try, little one.

The blast of horns from the distant towers was the signal that sent Malok and the other wyrms rising into the sky. It was the command from Prince Yverian that the dragon riders should launch their attack against the advancing dwarfs, targeting their siege engines and then their heavy infantry – the foes the archers would have the hardest time keeping from the walls. Thoriol watched the wyrms for a moment, fanning their leathery pinions as they climbed, finding the thermals that would sweep them out and away towards the invaders. Even knowing the miserable magic that forced the reptiles to obey, he was impressed by the majestic spectacle of the thing. Ilendril's vassal riders fanned out until their dragons were in unison with Malok, taking up an aerial formation more perfect than anything he could remember the riders of Caledor attempting.

'Tricks taught to dogs,' Thoriol grunted, shaking his head and snapping from his reverie. He watched Ilendril's riders a moment longer. As the king's nephew, he was outside the command of anyone in Elthin Arvan, even Prince Yverian. He was under no order, no obligation to take any part in the fighting. He could stay here and watch and there would be none with authority to condemn him. Indeed, it was probably what the king would expect of him, to keep away from the battle and not expose himself to risk.

Knowing that made it all the easier for Thoriol to urge Draukhain into the air, to send the dragon flying out over the city, out towards the advancing dwarfs. Regiments of dour axemen, the horns of their helms capped in gold and silver. Vast companies of quarrellers, their crossbows resting against their mail-clad shoulders. Brigades of longbeards, their flowing white beards adorned with charms and amulets of ruby, jade and sapphire. Great axes from the far northern holds, wings of metal soaring out from the sides of their helms, their immense blades etched with the snarling faces of giants and dragons. Among the infantry came the dwarfs' artillery, grotesque bolt throwers carved to resemble wyverns and wyrms, huge catapults with buckets shaped like the talons of trolls and monsters. It was a grim and terrible host, an army such as only the Karaz Ankor could muster.

Obligations, orders and the regard of his uncle weren't the things that mattered to Thoriol. What mattered was his duty to the colonies and the asur – and that was something even the king wouldn't take away from him.

Draukhain was a powerful beast, but its wings had never healed properly after the battle for Oeragor. It lagged behind Ilendril's wyrms as the other dragons dived down upon the vanguard of the dwarf army, a phalanx of warriors in heavy plate and bearing great rectangular shields. They advanced slowly, even for dwarfs, but at first Thoriol didn't guess the reason for their ponderous tread.

As the dragons descended, the dwarfs raised their shields, presenting them with an unbroken wall of defiant steel. The wyrms drew up short just above them, spewing withering blasts of fire down upon them. For an instant all was lost behind a pall of writhing flame and billowing smoke. It was only as the draconic fury began to abate that Thoriol noted the runes shining upon the shields of the dawi. In past battles, he'd seen champions and thanes equipped with enchanted armour that could resist dragon fire, but he'd never suspected that whole regiments could be afforded similar protection. The art of crafting such devices must be tedious and costly, otherwise the dawi would have sent such warriors into every battle.

At once, Thoriol suspected that the dwarfs would not invest such expense simply to defend against dragons. He brushed his hand along Draukhain's neck, coaxing the drake to slow its flight.

In a matter of a few heartbeats, Thoriol saw the wisdom of such caution. At the heart of the dwarf formation, concealed and protected by the shields of the warriors, a compact, wheeled bolt thrower was suddenly exposed. The dwarf artillerists hastily aimed their already loaded weapon and loosed a great barbed bolt into one of the wyrms. The missile struck the reptile even as it tried to climb away, slashing through its side and pinning its left foreleg to its breast. The stricken dragon howled and roared, sizzling blood steaming from its wound.

See what befalls the rider now that he has lost control, Draukhain cautioned Thoriol.

The rider of the wounded dragon was screaming, his arm and side coated in blood. The elf gave no thought to maintaining command over his steed, of using the talisman hanging from his neck to demand the creature's obedience. So it was that he didn't stop the wyrm from slashing the straps of his saddle with its remaining foreclaw and sending the asur plummeting earthwards. Before he could hit, the elf's dragon dived down and snatched him in its jaws, biting him in half with a vicious snap of its fangs. In its rage, the wyrm ignored the dwarfs and their bolt thrower, and the fact that the weapon had been rearmed. A second missile speared through its neck and knocked the beast from the sky.

Ilendril and his remaining vassal peeled away from the dwarf dragon-killers, retreating into the sky beyond the reach of their missiles. The dawi cheered, hurling their derision at the fleeing wyrms. They reformed their ranks, pressing on towards the city. Behind them came the bulk of the dwarf force with their onagers and siege towers, a rumbling sea of glistening steel and sombre banners, the tide of the mountain holds made manifest. These were the dawi and they had come to Sith Rionnasc for blood and vengeance.

Thoriol clenched his fist in frustration. He knew that he couldn't risk taking Draukhain close to the dragon-killers. The drake's compromised wings would make him an easy target for the artillerists. They might be able to circle around, to harry the flanks, maybe destroy any supplies the dawi had stockpiled, but such tactics would hardly blunt the impetus of the advance.

Even as Thoriol urged Draukhain to swing around the dawi force and set upon it from the rear, Ilendril and Malok reappeared. The crimson dragon was carrying a great chunk of rubble in its claws, the broken side of an abandoned keep. The wyrm didn't descend to breathe his fire on the dragon-killers. Instead, it climbed high above them, far beyond the reach of their bolt thrower. Then, when it felt it was high enough, Malok let go of its burden. The massive stone crashed down upon the regiment, smashing their rune-inscribed shields, flattening their steel plate, pulverising their bones.

The dragon-killers were thrown into disarray by the vicious attack. Before they could recover, before they could defend the bolt thrower, Draukhain was diving down upon them, its fire shooting across their ranks. Some of the dwarfs were collected enough to lower their shields and guard themselves against the flames, but many more were too dazed by Malok's attack to remember their discipline. They collapsed as the flames consumed them, flesh and metal bubbling away in greasy threads of steam.

Draukhain landed full among them, its claws lashing out and smashing the bolt thrower, its tail whipping around to scatter the armoured dawi. Thoriol stabbed his lance into a bearded warchief, spitting him like a boar. A slash of the dragon's claw ripped the dying dwarf free so its rider could attack again. For several minutes, elf and dragon lost themselves in a frenzy of carnage, careless of anything but the enemies around them and the power to annihilate them.

The sound of dragon fire searing its way towards them was what drew Thoriol from the red mist of battle. He looked up and saw Malok winging its way through the sky. Nearby, a band of dwarfs lay burning, caught by the wyrm's fire. Thoriol wondered if Ilendril had deliberately allowed the warriors to draw so close, so that he might have an excuse to offer if the prince should accidentally be caught in his steed's fire.

Whatever the cause, it was clear to Thoriol that they couldn't remain. There were too many dwarfs to fight. Other bolt throwers were being hurriedly wheeled into range. Once they were, they would bring Draukhain down in a concentrated attack.

'Come, mighty one,' Thoriol told the dragon. 'We've done what we can for now. Let the dawi worry themselves over how we shall acquit ourselves later.'

Sweeping his claws across a last clutch of dwarfs, Draukhain climbed back into the sky, uttering a fierce roar as it swung back towards the city. From the dragon's back, Thoriol could see the vast army continuing its march. The dragons had massacred the vanguard regiment, but they represented only the smallest fraction of the whole, a speck of sand on the beach.

Even with a dozen dragons, Thoriol wondered if the asur would be able to hold back such a horde.

Sith Rionnasc rested against the shore of the northern sea on land the elves had laboriously reclaimed from the waves by means of clever spells and even more clever engineering. A wide crescent spread about the bay, circling the water on three sides. It was here that the storehouses, shops, homes and civic institutions had been raised. Out in the middle of the harbour a broad island stood, the only ground in Sith Rionnasc that didn't naturally belong to the sea. Here, in the oldest part of the settlement, the towers of the nobility had been reared along with the temples in which the asur paid homage to their gods.

The dawi assault against Sith Rionnasc had been exactingly prepared over the course of a hundred years. Ever since the siege of Barak Varr, the dwarfs had intended to make an example of the city that had once been the sea hold's greatest trading partner. It wasn't enough to simply take Sith Rionnasc; the city had to be obliterated, every trace of it smashed and destroyed.

Inside the shelter afforded by a broken elgi keep, Morgrim studied the battlefield. The fire-breakers had claimed one of the drakk, a grand omen for any conflict. The others had returned to avenge the fallen wyrm, and Morgrim mourned the loss of so many brave warriors. Their names would be recorded, entered among the grudges owed by both elgi and drakk. At the same time, they'd served a heroic purpose. They'd taught the dragons a lesson in humility. The monsters now knew they couldn't run rampant against the dawi. Now they knew that the dawi could fight back – and bring them down.

Archers on the walls took their toll from the dwarfs as the invaders closed upon the city. Elgi bolt throwers and catapults exacted their due as well. Thankfully there had been little contribution from their mages, a circumstance that caused Morgrim concern but one that he intended to exploit for as long as possible. He would almost feel happier seeing lightning flashing out from the towers or burning rocks shooting down at his warriors. It would mean that the mages hadn't divined the real nature of this attack.

Morgrim watched as the first of the bolt throwers loosed its missile at Sith Rionnasc's walls. More than simply an oversized arrow, the weapon hurled a great steel grapnel at the fortification. A thick chain unspooled behind the grapnel, but it wasn't there so that the dawi might climb up it and gain a presence on the wall. Instead, the moment the grapnel caught, a score of stout dwarf warriors began to work a great winch set behind the weapon. The chain soon became taut and then, as the strain steadily increased, the grapnel pulled down a section of the wall.

In half a dozen places around the fortifications of Sith Rionnasc, similar grapnels were performing the same function. A score of the machines, slowly pulling down the city walls. The army made no move to force or expand any breaches. Catapults lobbed boulders into the city, crossbows loosed bolts from the platforms of great siege towers, but these were to keep the elgi away from the grapnels. That was the real thrust of the attack and every effort was being made to prevent the thrust from being repelled.

'You sent for me, my lord?'

Morgrim looked away from his study of the battlefield, folding the spyglass he'd been given by King Onkmarr of Barak Varr. He thrust the contraption into his belt next to Ifulvin and turned to greet his visitor. He was surprised to find that High Runelord Morek wasn't alone. Beside him was the savage-looking Rundin Torbansonn. He gave the half-naked champion only a brief glance, then returned his gaze to the runelord. 'You needn't say it like that, Morek,' he admonished. 'We've been friends too long for that.'

'I suspect that it is duty, not friendship, that summoned me,' Morek answered.

Morgrim shook his head. 'Every time I see you, you get that little bit more dour and cheerless. If you start speaking in riddles, I promise that as a thane of Karaz-a-Karak, I *will* brain you.' He waved his hand towards the distant city. 'They are bringing down the walls. I think tomorrow night we will be ready. Do you think your magic has kept the elgi from spying out the plan?'

'Eight runelords from as many strongholds, each bringing with him an Anvil of Doom,' Morek observed. 'Such a concentration of magic hasn't gone unnoticed. The elgi know we are here. However, I am certain they don't know our purpose. If they did, they would have taken action by now. We have expended a great amount of energy to keep them blind to our intentions.'

'Then you foresee success?' Morgrim asked. He raised his hand in a concession of defeat when he saw the frown that appeared on Morek's face. 'I should know better than to ask a runelord about the future. That is how problems start. Prophecy is the worst riddle of them all.'

Instead of improving his disposition, the thane's levity only broadened Morek's scowl. 'One doesn't need the ambiguity of a prophecy to take bad counsel.' He stared hard into Morgrim's eyes. The question had vexed him for a long time now, but he was determined that he would ask it. 'What kind of advice do you take from Drogor Zarrdum?'

Now it was Morgrim's turn to scowl. 'He is a friend. I am not so feckless that position and power make me forget my friends. Whether they be a runelord or a wandering adventurer from Karak Zorn.'

'He was Prince Snorri's friend too,' Morek reminded him. 'You were there. Maybe you remember the guidance he offered the prince? Did his advice lead to wisdom or to tragedy?'

'That was a long time ago,' Morgrim said. 'Much has changed. For all of us. We've all become harder, less prone to mercy.'

'There is a difference between mercy and morality,' Morek said. 'To spare a warrior on the field of battle is mercy.'

Morgrim could see where Morek's words were leading. Somehow he found even the suggestion to be threatening. Dimly, deep down inside him, he felt an irrational anger flare up. 'Drogor has suffered more than most. If his counsel is sometimes unduly vicious, then the bitterness that makes it so is not so strange.'

'Strange,' Morek repeated the word, letting it hang in the air between them. He tapped his runestaff against the floor. 'Tell me, how well do you know your old friend from Karak Zorn? Would you say he is the same dwarf you knew from the days of peace?'

Before Morgrim could give the question any thought, an answer rang out from away to his left. The three dwarfs turned to see the subject of that question climbing down a set of crumbling stairs, his feathered cape rustling about his shoulders.

'War changes us all,' Drogor said, his tone neutral. 'What dawi of conscience could say it hasn't? Are you, Morek Furrowbrow, the same zaki who doted upon Ranuld in his senility, or has the war made you expand your horizons and think for yourself?'

'Mind your tongue, *ufdi*,' Rundin warned. 'That is a runelord you mock.'

Morgrim raised his hands, motioning all of his companions to calm themselves. If Drogor had been listening from the floor above, he could understand how the thane might be upset, but that was hardly an excuse for rudeness.

'Oathbreaker, be thankful I do not attend your words,' Drogor spat, savouring the flush of colour that swept through Rundin's face.

'Spying on your friend, Drogor of Karak Zorn?' Morek wondered, gesturing with his staff at the crumbled ceiling.

Drogor smiled. 'I am never far from my friends. They are not so numerous that I neglect them.' His eyes narrowed as he focused upon something in Morek's hand.

'Relent!' Morgrim barked out. 'This bickering is disgraceful. The elgi are the enemy, save your anger for them.'

Morek's voice was barely a whisper and within it was a quality Morgrim had never heard before, a sound of terror. 'There are older enemies than the elgi.' Morek held forth the artefact that had so caught Drogor's attention. It was something he'd retrieved from the darkest vaults of Karaz-a-Karak, something locked away among the trophies of Snorri Whitebeard. It was a simple thing, just a feather, but as he held it towards Drogor, the object began to pulse and vibrate with scintillating colours.

Drogor's face twisted into a monstrous leer. In a single bound he reached the bottom of the steps, not even seeming to feel the impact as his armoured weight cracked one of the flagstones beneath him. Another spring brought him before Morek. Deftly he snatched the feather out of the runelord's hand. 'What a clever maggot,' Drogor hissed in a voice that no longer even possessed an echo of the dwarf's tones.

Morek raised his runestaff, the metal rod already glowing with power, but a single blow of Drogor's hand sent the dwarf hurtling across the chamber.

He slammed into the far wall to crash in a heap among the rubble. Rundin rushed at him next, only to receive similar treatment.

'I thought I lost this somewhere,' Drogor said. He pressed the glowing feather against his cape. The feathers shifted, pulling themselves aside to allow the new one to join them. As it attached itself, the entire garment began to pulse and throb with a dazzling prism of colours.

Numb with horror, Morgrim couldn't find the voice to howl a war-cry as he charged the thing he had called Drogor. His foe slashed out at him with a hand suddenly tipped with vulturine talons and fitted to an arm three times its original length. The monstrous limb caught Morgrim by the neck and thrust him against the ceiling.

'Does this mean we aren't friends any more?' Drogor mocked. The dwarf's face was slowly melting, flesh dripping in obscene streams into his beard. 'To be honest, your compassion was becoming tedious. I was thinking you'd make a better martyr than a leader. A much better force to push the war forward.' He cocked his corroding head to one side. Clusters of eyes had begun to sprout from the gleaming bone of his exposed skull. These fixed Morgrim with a quizzical stare.

'What was that you asked?' Drogor wondered. He relaxed his grip enough that Morgrim was able to drag a breath into his gasping lungs.

'You did this,' Morgrim moaned. 'You goaded us into war with the elgi.'

A ghastly, bubbling laugh wheezed from the mush of Drogor's face. 'You did this to yourselves,' he cackled. 'I am simply… a spectator. It was your pride and stubbornness that brought war to your peoples. Now it will go on and on until you are both wasted, ruined shells of what you were. What delight more delicious than watching enemies destroy themselves? If only everything could be so obliging!'

As he laughed, Drogor's head spun completely around to glare at Rundin as the hill dwarf flung himself at the monster once more. The shimmering cape now became a set of immense wings, fanning out and smashing the skarrenawi to the floor. 'You should have stayed in your hole and died with your little king,' he sneered, as the feathers of his wings slashed and cut the tattooed champion.

Still gripped by Drogor's hideous arm, Morgrim looked longingly at his axe lying on the floor far below. Then his hand fell to the sword hanging from his belt. Without hesitation, he drew Ifulvin and raked the blade across the monstrous arm.

Drogor cried out in surprise as syrupy ichor drooled from the ugly gash. His hand released Morgrim, leaving the thane to crash ungently to the floor. His head little more than an exposed skull riddled with clusters of eyes, the monster stalked towards Morgrim.

'Thank you for reminding me,' Drogor hissed. 'It would be disgraceful to make a dawi of such noble rank die behind a lunatic from the hills.' The creature's claws flashed out, seizing Morgrim's arms. A brutal twist sent Ifulvin clattering to the floor. 'I will rend you into enough pieces that they can put a bit of you in each stronghold. Would you like that, Morgrim Would-be-King?'

A crackling bolt of amber lightning scorched across the daemon's twisted frame. Again, Drogor turned his head impossibly around to stare back across his shoulders. His myriad eyes focused upon Morek. Uttering a bestial shriek, the daemon unleashed a withering blast of unholy energy at the runelord. The glowing staff in his hands corroded, flaking away into little slivers of sludge.

'Wait your turn,' the daemon hissed.

Despite his injury, Morek managed to smile back at the monster. 'You first.'

Too late the daemon appreciated the limitations of its fleshy frame. Despite its myriad eyes, it had been too focused upon the runelord. It didn't see Rundin as the mangled dwarf limped across the floor to take up both Azdrakghar and Ifulvin. With elven blade and dwarfish axe, the champion of the skarrenawi turned and charged at the monster.

Morgrim's axe crunched through Drogor's armour, biting down to sever the spine. Imladrik's sword licked across the arms holding the dwarf lord, severing them at the elbow. Foul daemonic ichor spurted from the stumps, steaming as it struck the stone floor. The daemon howled, its cry reverberating through the souls of those who heard it. Only Rundin had the stamina to withstand that aethyric wail. Taking both axe and sword, he leapt upon the beast, driving the blades into its shoulders. The feathered wings went flopping away, shrivelling like burning parchment as they were detached from the daemon.

A fanged beak sprouted from Drogor's face, stabbing forwards and piercing the dwarf's breast. Defying the mortal wound, Rundin brought Azdrakghar shearing into the right side of the daemon's neck. A moment later, Ifulvin cut into the left. Throwing the last of his vitality into his powerful arms, he forced the weapons across Drogor's flesh.

As the daemon's head rolled free from its body, Rundin collapsed. There was a fierce smile, an expression of terrible fulfilment on the dead dwarf's face. In his last moments, he had known his death would be a worthy one. He had achieved what Morek promised him he would achieve: a name greater than Dragonslayer, a name that would blot out forever the stigma of the oathbreaker.

In life he had been Rundin Torbansonn. In death he was Rundin Daemonslayer.

Weary, wounded, shocked by his ordeal, Morgrim somehow found the strength to see to Morek. Fighting to maintain his own consciousness, he helped the runelord to his feet and led him away from the carnage within the ruins. As soon as they were in the courtyard, Morgrim's hearthguard came rushing over to attend them. He was stunned that they had failed to hear the sounds of so fierce a fight, but supposed it had just been another example of the daemon's powers at work.

As he let the guards take Morek from him, the runelord gripped Morgrim's arm. 'The attack,' he said. 'You will still attack?'

Morgrim shook his head. 'Nothing can stop it any more,' he said. 'When they tried to tell us about their druchii, we would not listen. Why should they listen if we tell them of our daemon? No, the only way this can end is with victory. There is no other way to find peace now.'

Away to the north, the lights of Sith Rionnasc were a dull glow. Some of those lights belonged to the elgi within their city, waiting for the dawi to come rushing through their shattered walls. Many more would be the fires set by the dwarfs as they held their ground outside those walls. For two nights, the dawi had been stealing back to their camps, tending their fires and awaiting the dawn before making half-hearted thrusts against the city. Tonight, however, there would be no dwarfs in those camps, only the fires they'd left behind.

King Onkmarr of Barak Varr turned away from his view of the hated city. How many times had he voyaged there as a simple trader? How many times had he walked those streets listening to elgi lies and bartering for cheap elgi trinkets? Nothing the tall-ears did was substantial; nothing they built could withstand the test of time. He would prove that soon with Sith Rionnasc.

'It is time,' the king growled, patting the handle of his axe. Around him, his thanes and champions, all of them veterans of the Siege of Barak Varr, muttered their agreement. They would stand by Onkmarr in everything so long as it repaid the elgi for what had been inflicted against the sea hold.

'Bring down Brynnoth's Wrath!' Guildmaster Strombak cried out. At the engineer's command, throngs of dwarfs came rushing down the slopes of the hill. They were divided into gangs of twenty and thirty, each team labouring beneath the burden of a massive beam of wutroth or an enormous spool of rope and wire. Some struggled under the heft of immense mattocks and hammers, great adzes and spanners. A huge mob over a hundred strong drew a gigantic sledge down from the forest, a great platform of oak, from the centre of which an enormous stone head glowered at its surroundings.

'Tromm,' Onkmarr intoned, bowing as the head was dragged past him and towards the valley below. The head had belonged to a colossal statue of King Brynnoth that had been partially demolished by the elgi during the siege. Great care had been taken to bear the decapitated head from Barak Varr, especially when the tunnels of the Ungdrin Ankor grew too narrow to allow its passage and its journey had to continue overland. Difficult as that journey had been, the avengers of the sea hold had seen the ordeal through.

'Now the old king will have his revenge,' Strombak declared. 'We will make the elves answer for the grudges of our people.'

Onkmarr stared past the sledge, looking down into the valley below. Eyes attuned to the darkness of the underground could easily spot Strombak's engineers directing the dwarfs as they brought their strange burdens down to them. 'The elgi will know what it is to lose their homes,' he declared. 'They will know the same horror our people felt when the great gates came crashing in.' A grim chuckle rose from the king. 'But they won't know it for long.' He looked over at his thanes. 'You have set your warriors to guard against the elgi?'

'Yes, my liege,' one of the thanes replied, rapping his fist against his breast as he bowed. 'But if the elves come at us in force, we may need help from Thane Morgrim's army.'

'We'll suffer no help beyond what we've already been given,' Onkmarr declared. Morgrim's army had done the hard part, breaking down the walls. Elgidum had also tasked nearly every runelord and runesmith in his host with employing their magic against elgi divinations. That was all Onkmarr could ask of his fellow dawi. If there was going to be any honour for Barak Varr this night, then the rest of it must be left to them alone.

'We are protected from their spells, but if one of their scouts should see us, then the plan could be thwarted before it begins,' Strombak cautioned.

Onkmarr scowled at the master engineer. It was an argument they'd had many times. The need for haste balanced against the care and caution that was ingrained into the engineers' guild. There was a place for prudence, but there was no time for it now. 'Your guildbrothers must do their part,' Onkmarr declared. 'They must get the machine ready before the sun betrays us or the elgi find us. Everything hinges on that. If we miss our shot, then all of us deserve no better than to wander Gazul's halls for eternity. We will have betrayed the trust and hope of our people. We will have failed our oaths to our ancestors and our gods!'

'It will be as you say,' a chastened Strombak said. He looked up anxiously at his liege. 'You are determined to...'

Onkmarr slapped his hand against his axe. 'It is the doom that has come for me. I would not cheat it for a lesser end.'

Strombak nodded. 'Then I would stand beside you, my liege.'

Onkmarr smiled and clapped his hand on the engineer's shoulder. Together they watched as the enormous machine began to take shape on the valley floor. Piece by piece, beam by beam, a colossal catapult was taking shape. It resembled a grudge thrower as much as a sword resembled a knife. The scale of the thing was nearly beyond compare, a cyclopean construction that strained the limits of dwarfish inventiveness and mechanics. Even Strombak was hard-pressed to understand all of the balances and counter-balances that allowed the weapon to function, the weights that would keep it from shaking itself apart when its titanic arm was loosed and it hurled its awful burden at the enemy.

By the standards of the dawi, the assembly of Brynnoth's Wrath was reckless and frantic. The engineers would have preferred to have days to set each part into its place. Instead, they only had a few hours. When they were finished, however, they had erected a monster of oak and wutroth and steel that stood two hundred feet in height. The wood was stained a grey-black, blending into the darkness around it. As the workers dispersed back into the wooded hills, the crew of artillerists who would work the catapult marched up to it, their armour blackened with soot to avoid any betraying reflection.

The last gang of labourers loaded the great stone head from the sledge, rolling and sliding it into the gigantic basket at the end of the catapult's arm. Once the scowling visage of King Brynnoth was set in place, the labourers turned and retreated to the heights.

'It is time,' Onkmarr said again, feeling the weight of his words press upon him. It was no easy thing to embrace one's doom, but if it were easy then there wouldn't be any honour to be had from it.

Onkmarr and Strombak strode down to the colossal catapult. The artillerists bowed as their king walked past them. 'All is in readiness,' their captain reported. He gestured to the notched wooden partitions that fronted the legs of the catapult and from which the artillerists had taken sightings and evaluated the direction and distance between themselves and their target. Everything had been calculated long before the catapult was erected; the artillerists had simply verified the range and that Brynnoth's Wrath stood in the exact spot it had been designed to stand.

'You can feel the anger of Barak Varr pulsing from Brynnoth's head,' Onkmarr said, pointing with his axe at the scowling effigy. The observation wasn't entirely imagination. Potent and terrible runes had been carved into the head, the most powerful and malignant the runelords of Barak Varr dared to employ. The eldritch letters pulsed with a crimson light, throbbing as though in sympathy to some spectral heart.

'The elgi give us reason enough for our rage,' Strombak said. 'They draw from us the very depths of hate and then demand even more.'

Onkmarr walked to the arm of the catapult. He glowered at the tautened chain that restrained the tensed arm. 'They will demand nothing from anyone ever again,' he said as he brought his axe shearing through the chain.

Despite all the precautions, Brynnoth's Wrath rose up as the arm slapped against the crossbeam and lobbed the gigantic head down the valley. One of the artillerists was crushed as a counterbalance tore free and smashed down upon him. Another had his leg reduced to pulp as the lower part of the arm splintered and snapped back at him.

Onkmarr was oblivious to the hurts of his subjects, however. Seizing his spyglass from his belt, he dashed to one of the observation posts and fixed the scope at the victim he'd chosen for Brynnoth's Wrath decades ago. He focused on the great dam the elgi had built across the river. An instant it stood there, vast and imposing. The next moment the stone head smashed into it. With a thunderous boom, the face of the dam was broken.

The runes of destruction carved into the stone erupted into ferocious, awful malignancy as the head struck. They conspired to magnify the impact a thousandfold. It was just possible the immense elgi dam could have withstood the crash of the stone by itself, but with the magical enhancement its demolition was assured.

Through the crimson flashes and whorls of the released rune magic, Onkmarr could see grand cracks snaking away across the face of the dam, rushing in every direction from the ugly crater the head had gouged into the meat of the structure. Streams of water spurted from the cracks, provoking still more fractures. On the wall above, in the little forts that guarded the dam, the elgi defenders could be seen rushing about in alarm and confusion. Onkmarr couldn't make out their faces, but he could well imagine the horror written across them.

'Now the elgi learn what it means when a dwarf takes revenge,' Onkmarr hissed, clenching his hand tight about the spyglass.

Strombak and the engineers had reckoned the exact spot that Brynnoth's Wrath would need to strike, the spot where the impact would be the most devastating. The spot where the pressure of the waters behind the dam would explode the compromised structure and bring the whole thing crashing down.

A vibrant roar of delight echoed from the hills as the dwarfs hidden there saw the distant dam break apart. Through the spyglass, Onkmarr could see the tiny figures of elves hurtling from the walls to be caught in the roaring cataract that had erupted from the shattered dam. A tidal wave of churning, rushing obliteration was spilling down the valley, roaring across the path the river had once taken before the elgi tried to chain it. The path that would lead back to the sea.

The path that would bring the flood smashing down upon Sith Rionnasc.

Onkmarr dropped the glass and turned to face Strombak. When they'd lobbed the head at the dam, they'd known they had invited death upon themselves. The engineers had timed the speed of the flood waters they expected to unleash with Brynnoth's Wrath. Their conclusions had been sobering: the crew of the catapult wouldn't have time to escape the deluge.

The king didn't even try. With his death, he would wipe out an entire city of elgi. What greater feat could he aspire towards?

'It is a good death, my liege,' Strombak told him.

'Aye, a grand death,' Onkmarr replied.

The floodwaters slammed down upon Brynnoth's Wrath, smashing the catapult to splinters and bearing its remains away with it towards the sea. Somewhere, in the boiling deluge, the corpses of Onkmarr and the others were borne away to the deeps.

The Anurein went sweeping through the countryside, uprooting forests and submerging hills as it ploughed its way towards the coast. The breadbasket of Elthin Arvan vanished beneath the deluge, the carefully cultivated soil washed out to sea, leaving behind a morass of silt and mud that would never again be anything more than a quagmire of marshes and fens.

Sith Rionnasc itself was obliterated by the floodwaters. Houses and shops simply disappeared. Sections of rubble from the walls were transformed into rolling, crashing, crushing juggernauts. The lofty towers toppled, their foundations shorn by the tide of debris. Many of the ships at anchor in the harbour were flooded, pitching to the bottom with all hands. Some few managed to ride out the assault, surviving to lend themselves to the rescue of those who'd been spared by the deluge.

From surrounding hills, the dwarfs were content to merely watch as the asur rowed out to drowned buildings and plucked wretched survivors from rooftops. They didn't move to intercept the ships as they sailed out to sea, escorted by a pair of massive dragons. They didn't do anything but wait until the floodwaters had receded and the ruins were exposed. Then and only then did they stir themselves. In a great troop they swarmed down into the ravaged port. With hammer and mattock they destroyed what remained, tearing the ruins down to their very foundations.

True to the promise they'd given their brethren in Barak Varr, when the dawi were finished there was almost no trace that Sith Rionnasc had ever existed.

The city had been erased from the world.

THIRTEEN

RETURN OF THE PHOENIX KING

596TH YEAR OF THE REIGN OF CALEDOR II

The walls of Tor Alessi had become a symbol of the tenacity and arrogance of the elgi. Foremost of the elven settlements in Elthin Arvan, Tor Alessi surpassed them all in size and grandeur. Its opulence was shabby and crude by the refined standards of Ulthuan, but to those born in the colonies it was inspiring. They took heart from the concentric rings of walls running clear down into the harbour. They marvelled at the wide streets and their tiled intersections, at the ashwood lampposts with their bronze lanterns that lined every avenue. They wondered at the soaring majesty of the great towers with their white walls and golden domes. They gazed in astonishment at the enormity of Founders' Square, the place where the asur had raised the very first stones of what would become a mighty city. An obelisk of red-veined marble stood proudly at the centre of that square, its shadow perfectly aligned with the sun to mark out the shifting seasons and the coming solstice. From the square, broad roads swept down to the always-busy harbour, where goods from Elthin Arvan were loaded onto ships bound for the ten kingdoms.

Again and again, the dawi had tried to smash their way through the barrier, only to be thrown back. Other elven settlements had been conquered and demolished. Athel Maraya was so much ash. Kor Vanaeth was overgrown ruins. The streets of Oeragor were smothered beneath desert sands. Athel Toralien was peopled only by rooks and rats. Sith Rionnasc was lost in the muck of marsh and fen. The dwarfs had evicted the colonists from most of their former holdings, but they knew that so long as Tor Alessi still stood, they could never claim any victory.

High King Gotrek felt the weight of his centuries like chains of iron bound tight about him. It seemed so long ago when he'd led his people to victory over the greenskins, when they'd at last driven the menace of urk and grobi from the realms of the Karaz Ankor. Such glory there had been, such a bright and shining future ahead of his people. But it hadn't been anything more than a dream. Maybe from the first there had been no chance of peace with the elgi. Two peoples could be no more different than dwarf and elf. The dwarfs were slow and deliberate, gruff and direct in their manners, pragmatic in their thinking. To most dwarfs, the elves were never more than flighty, foppish hedonists who pampered themselves with luxury and decadence. It was inevitable that they would go to war with a race with which they had almost nothing in common. As much as he'd tried to encourage coexistence with the elgi, Gotrek wondered sometimes how much of the blame for this war rested on his own shoulders.

Certainly there had been forces at work to bring dwarf and elf into conflict. There were the stories of renegade elgi called druchii who bore responsibility for atrocities like the murder of Runelord Agrin Fireheart. Then there was the chilling account related to the High King by Morgrim and Morek, the report that Drogor Zarrdum had actually been some kind of daemon, an unholy beast exuding his poisonous influence to speed the war to ever greater heights of barbarity and atrocity. The lorekeepers of Karaz-a-Karak speculated that the daemon might have been the fiend Htarken, a loathsome lord vanquished by High King Snorri Whitebeard and the elf prince Malekith nearly two thousand years past. A daemon was never truly destroyed and with time its essence could return to perpetuate its evil upon the descendents of those who had foiled its schemes.

Daemon or druchii, neither were the cause of the war. All they might have done was fan the flames, but the spark had come from the elgi king himself. Gotrek felt his body tremble as a wave of absolute rage coursed through him. The arrogant contempt of Caledor II had brought all of this about. First there had been the disgraceful mutilation of Forek Grimbok and the rest of the ambassadors sent to Ulthuan. Then there had been the Phoenix King's butchery of Prince Snorri. To have his son fall in battle would have been hurtful enough, but to have the body defiled by the elf king, to have his son's spirit condemned to wander Gazul's halls as a maimed thing, that was too great an insult to bear. True, wiser and more compassionate elgi had retrieved the 'trophy' their king took away and returned Snorri's missing hand to the dawi, but the damage was done. There could never be any reconciliation between their peoples. Peace and coexistence weren't even dreams now. They belonged to the world of fable and legend.

Gotrek stroked his long beard, feeling the little onyx beads as they slid across his leathery palm. For him, there would never be any peace. Not while the elgi king breathed.

The little spit of rock rising from the forest had become known as the 'Long Watch'. For centuries dwarf rangers had maintained a presence here, living in the caves beneath the rock while using its summit to spy upon Tor Alessi. It had endured, sometimes with only a single ranger occupying it for years. The Long Watch, devoted to one grim and terrible purpose: to call the dawi to the final battle.

Gotrek climbed down the cunningly concealed steps that had been cut into the side of the rock. There was nothing else to be seen by studying the elgi city. What he wanted wasn't there. Burying his disappointment under his stolid exterior, the High King joined his hearthguard waiting for him below. His thronebearers hurried forwards, straining beneath the weight of his stone chair. By long tradition, the High King could sit on no lesser seat than his Throne of Power. Whatever the obstacles and hardships, it was the honour of his thronebearers to always keep the ancient seat ready for him. Gotrek considered it a foolish custom, but even a king had to bow to the traditions of his people.

With a wave of his hand, Gotrek sent his thronebearers to precede him into the cave. The mammoth door was fashioned to mimic the rock around it and when closed, even a dwarf was unable to find any sign of its presence. The eyes of elgi, unused to the subtle differences exhibited by rock and stone, had never pierced the camouflage, nor had the spells of their mages, for the runesmiths had taken pains to inscribe potent symbols of concealment in the rock. The steps just within the entrance had been worked so that they seemed jagged and uneven, the product of nature rather than dwarfish pick and hammer. The cave beyond likewise betrayed no artificiality, but hidden in its deep shadows, shielded by stalagmites and stalactites, were tunnels that led down into vast vaults and chambers.

It was to one of these vaults that Gotrek and his entourage descended. Once past the outer cave, the tunnels lost their ruggedness. Great blocks of granite and limestone flanked the walls and ceiling while the floor was a smooth series of steps. The room at the end of the corridor was a great hall, its ceiling some fifty feet off the stone floor. Soaring pillars and archways supported the roof, the glowering visages of ancestors frowning down from the heights. Except for the lack of a hearth and a roaring fire, the hall wasn't so dissimilar from the sort that might be found in Ekrund or Kraka Drak, or some of the more distant strongholds. There were many, of course, who still grumbled that it was an unfit residence for the High King, but Gotrek had no patience for those mutterings. When he came to Tor Alessi, he didn't do so to be comfortable. He came to make war.

The thronebearers marched to the middle of the hall, hefting their burden to where a raised dais awaited them. Grunting, they lifted the throne up over their heads and set it back down again upon the platform. With a precision born of long practice, they withdrew the gilded poles from the sides of the pedestal beneath the seat, leaving it to stand on its own upon the dais.

Gotrek marched over and climbed the steps. Only when he was on his throne did he cast his gaze across the hall. A long table of wutroth, a relic salvaged from the rubble of Kazad Thar, stretched ahead of the dais and around it were gathered many kings and generals, drawn from every corner of the Karaz Ankor. The almost barbarous Norse dwarfs of Kraka Drak far to the north and the steely-eyed desert-dwellers from the lands beyond Ekrund sat beside the lords of Karak Izil in their silver-chased finery and the grim nobles of the Grey Mountains with their eagle-winged helms. Warchiefs from Karak Kadrin and Karak Ungor with their girdles of gold and their breastplates of gromril, commanders from Zhufbar proudly displaying jewels looted from vanquished elgi. Great or small, whatever matters they had been discussing had been forgotten when the High King entered the hall. One and all, they watched their king, waiting for him to speak.

Gotrek was silent for a long time. His eyes didn't linger on the generals or his subject kings. He stared beyond them, out across the hall to the silken banner that hung on the wall. Torches set to either side of the standard made it stand out from the gloom around it. It had been captured in Athel Toralien, found in the ruins of its great palace. Captive elgi had identified it.

A great dragon and a fiery bird, entwined about one another, both beasts rendered in crimson against a white field. It was a standard that had been kept by the governor of Athel Toralien against the possibility of a royal visit. It was the heraldry of one elgi and one elgi alone. It was the personal device of King Caledor II and would be unfurled only when the Phoenix King was in residence.

Gotrek could feel his hate burning inside him as he stared at the standard of his son's killer. How desperately he wanted to see those colours flying from the spires of Tor Alessi! It was what he'd commanded his rangers to watch for ever since Morgrim had brought the banner to him. It was what he'd dreamed about for decades, the message that the elgi king had returned to the Old World, had placed himself again within reach of the dawi.

By his own decree, Gotrek had allowed Tor Alessi to endure. The many sieges against the city had been half-hearted, probing attacks. They'd been staged to cover more important strikes elsewhere, such as Morgrim's conquest of Athel Toralien, or been used to forestall any fresh campaign mounted by their enemy. The elgi could always be depended on to come running back anytime Tor Alessi was threatened. They knew if the city fell, there would be no rebuilding their lost colonies.

With each siege, the dawi had diverted some of their resources towards the future. Beneath the plains, far from where they could be discovered by the enemy, a network of tunnels had been excavated, underground storehouses and barracks constructed. Traps by the hundreds had been prepared, all waiting for the day when the High King would declare the final attack.

The very momentum of their successes elsewhere had become burdensome to Gotrek. With the elgi reeling at every turn, with their people fleeing out to sea or into the forests, the dawi were riding the tide of victory. Ever since the destruction of Sith Rionnasc, there had been voices calling for a total assault against Tor Alessi. Gotrek had tried to argue against these voices, tried to quieten them until such time as he could end the war his way, but with each year the effort had become more onerous. The kings argued that the war had been fought long enough, that they'd spent enough blood and treasure. There was no need to prolong it when a single attack against Tor Alessi could end it all.

Even now there were some strongholds that seemed to think the war was over. Barrak Varr had sent only the smallest contingent to join Gotrek's throng. Karak Eight Peaks hadn't come at all, King Varnuf keeping his warriors in his own lands with condescending talk of maintaining a 'reserve' should the High King's plans go awry. Other holds, too, had offered their excuses. Everyone seemed to want Gotrek to capture the city, but none wanted to spend their own treasure and warriors to make it happen.

Turning his eyes from the elf standard, Gotrek studied the generals and kings who had come to join him. He knew he couldn't afford to demur. If he was to maintain the cohesion of the Karaz Ankor and the authority of the High King, this attack had to succeed. He locked eyes with Morgrim, motioning for his nephew to stand.

'Light fires to honour our dead and to draw the eyes of our ancestors,' Gotrek said. 'Call the grudge-keepers to reckon the accounts. We attack with the dawn. You, Morgrim Bargrum, will command my armies. Bring down the walls and let the elgi know that this time they will not escape vengeance.'

Morgrim Bargrum leaned against the craggy outcropping that topped the Long Watch and studied the elgi city stretching down to the sea.

The walls of Tor Alessi had changed since last Morgrim cast his eyes upon them. They'd been expanded, strengthened, rendered far more formidable than they had been in Imladrik's day. It was only natural. After thirteen sieges, the elves had taken pains to prevent a repeat of what they'd suffered during each attack. Walls had been heightened to defy siege towers and ladders, thickened to thwart catapults and bolt throwers. Gates had been strengthened to withstand battering rams. Jagged blocks of stone had been strewn about the approaches to the gates to spoil the momentum of any wheeled engine being rushed against them. In several places, elaborate earthworks had been established to interrupt any rush by an enemy approaching the walls. He could see the bolt throwers and catapults standing atop the towers, the archers lined up along the battlements. Somewhere, he knew, the dragons would be waiting, probably in their eyries deep within the city proper. The drakk would be nesting in the tallest towers, waiting for their elgi masters to send them into battle. It was an endless source of disgust and disbelief to him that anyone could dwell with such monsters, could accept the presence of such beasts.

There would be the mages to worry about, too. The dawi had taken pains to keep their advance secret from the elgi, but never had they achieved the sort of surprise they'd accomplished when he'd led his warriors here against Prince Imladrik. Morgrim suspected that the elgi must have entire covens of mages whose only purpose was to use their sorcery to keep a watch for dwarfs advancing upon Tor Alessi.

He let his hand fall to the hilt of Ifulvin. Whatever the dangers, they had to bring an end to this war. The elgi were too proud to leave on their own. The dawi were too stubborn to accept anything less than victory. Even the High King wanted to prolong the war. Morgrim knew Gotrek didn't care so much about conquering Tor Alessi and driving the elgi into the sea. He wanted the Phoenix King. Nothing less than the blood of Caledor II would satisfy him. All the campaigns, the capture of the other elgi cities, the decimation of elgi armies, all of it had been an effort to lure their king back to the Old World. None of it had worked. Now the High King's hand had been forced by his own subjects – they wanted the war over.

At least Gotrek was king enough to recognise the fact. He'd entrusted command of his armies to Morgrim, leaving it to the Elgidum to take Tor Alessi. He knew Morgrim would fight without restraint, without the hope that they might yet draw the elgi king back.

Morgrim looked over the armoured hearthguard who surrounded him. Each dwarf held his warhammer across his shoulders. Some of these warriors had been there from the very first, fighting with Prince Snorri at Angaz Baragdum. Old Khazagrim bore Morgrim's standard. Too old to wield hammer or axe, much less lead the hearthguard, the grizzled ancient had almost begged for the honour of carrying Morgrim's banner. Khazagrim had been the last dawi to cross blades with the elgi king, chasing Caledor off the field of battle after Snorri was cut down. His failure to take the elgi king's head that day was a burden that had crushed him, aged him beyond his years. It was a terrible thing for any dwarf to live with such a burden of shame.

Thoughts of shame drew Morgrim's eye away from his hearthguard. Most of the dwarf regiments were forming into ranks in the shelter of the trees, where they would be safe from watchers on Tor Alessi's walls. There was a distance of some two miles between the forest and the outermost wall, open ground that was devoid of any manner of cover. A killing field the elves had prepared long ago to receive the next wave of dwarfs to come against them. There wasn't so much as a stand of tall grass to provide an enemy with cover but that was of no concern to one group of dwarfs, who deliberately strayed out onto the field. They stood out at the edge of the woods, howling and jeering at the elves on the walls. From time to time an arrow would whistle out, usually falling well shy of the shouting dwarfs. Occasionally one would strike true, stabbing into naked flesh. In response, the stricken dwarf, unless mortally injured, would simply rip the shaft from his body and wave the broken arrow at his attackers in a fresh bout of bawdy derision.

There were thirty of them, drawn from across the Karaz Ankor. In appearance, they sought the same savage aspect as that of Rundin Daemonslayer. They wore little beyond their tattoos and chains, their hair dyed a bright crimson and shaved into a tall cockscomb. Those with beards wore them plaited and festooned with tiny runestones and golden talismans. Among them, however, were three who had no beards. Their faces were scarred and horrendously disfigured, only the odd tuft of hair sprouting from the wrecked skin. They were the last of the steelbeards, the survivors of the disgraced delegation to Ulthuan. Most of them had perished over the course of the war, but these three had persisted, driven on by their need to atone for the shame that had been inflicted upon them.

It was Forek who led them now. The former reckoner had spent years in defiance of Morgrim's command, hunting the refugees of Athel Toralien in the forests. By circumstances the steelbeard never explained, the warriors he'd led were wiped out. Only he had escaped and when he learned of Rundin's death it had unbalanced his mind. He'd gone away, wandering the mountains for a decade before one day appearing at Karak Kadrin. He'd walked to the shrine of Grimnir and in the sight of the astonished priests had stripped off his mask and armour, shaving his head while making dire oaths before the ancestor god. Then he'd left again, as suddenly as he'd appeared. Stories filtered back about a crazed, beardless dwarf fighting trolls in the high passes, challenging beasts and greenskins wherever he found them and whatever the odds. Forek Grimbok soon came to be known by a new name: Forek Trollslayer.

Morgrim knew the reckoner was seeking the same prize that had drawn Rundin from battle to battle: a noble death that would efface his shame. When he heard that Forek had challenged and destroyed the giant Yvnir near Kraka Drak, he was certain of it. No amount of reassurance from himself or even from his sister Elmendrin could sway him from his suicidal purpose. Other dwarfs, labouring under similar feelings of guilt, made the journey to Karak Kadrin and followed Forek's example, shaving their heads and taking up what was now called the 'Slayer's oath' – to wash away their shame by seeking a heroic death.

The Slayers were fierce fighters, but undisciplined. Morgrim had been tempted to refuse them a position in the battle line. It wasn't possible to depend on warriors already committed to dying to hold ground or occupy a position. Other fighters might be put in jeopardy if the Slayers charged off and left a flank exposed. In the end, though, he simply didn't have the heart to deny them. They'd suffered so much already, it would take a soul more callous than his own to reject them a place in the battle. He would simply have to make allowances for them and ensure those who fought beside them had reserves ready to support them if the Slayers proved unreliable.

'Why did we have to come to this?' Morgrim said as he watched the Slayers turn their arses to the walls of Tor Alessi, daring the archers to loose another volley.

'He blames himself for the dawi he lost in the forest.' Morek Furrowbrow leaned against his runestaff, his head cocked to one side as he spoke to Morgrim. Ever since the fight against Htarken, the runelord's body had become increasingly twisted, as though his spine were trying to inch its way around to his belly. Every year his shoulders became less even, and one arm was notably shorter than the other. Morek had grimly stated his own prognosis, that because he was attuned to magic the daemon's corruption had been able to taint his body. How many years it would take before he was completely crippled, Morek wasn't able to judge, but he wanted to find a different death for himself if he could.

'We've all lost dawi who were following our orders,' Morgrim said. Grungni only knew how many dwarfs had died under his command throughout the war. It was something that would snap any dwarf's mind if he allowed himself to dwell upon it.

Morek's head twitched, the closest he could manage to a sidewise motion. 'Forek confided to me that he let himself be goaded into pursuing the elgi from Athel Toralien by "Drogor". He'd become great friends with Rundin during their days under Brok Stonefist. They'd argued when they last fought together and to find his friend dead was a terrible shock to Forek. To find him dead at the hands of the daemon whose advice he'd taken was simply too much guilt for him to accept.'

'Now he seeks a hero's death,' Morgrim sighed. 'Haven't we lost enough heroes already? What is to be gained by dying?'

The runelord's answer came in a whisper, a whisper laden with piteous longing.

'Peace.'

In blocks of armoured warriors thousands strong, the dwarfs came marching out from the trees. The archers on the walls knew the range of the plain outside the city down to the last yard. There was none of the frustration and broken discipline that had caused a few of them to loose arrows at the Slayers. Captains and sergeants prowled the battlements, coldly warning their soldiers to hold back. Upon the towers, signalmen observed the advance, displaying flags as the enemy marched closer and closer.

The goal was simple enough – to draw the dwarfs well within range of the archers before loosing the first volley. The deeper the enemy was allowed to proceed within that kill zone, the more casualties the elves could hope to inflict. Once the dwarfs broke, they would have to retreat with elven arrows pursuing them every step of the way. The trick and the danger lay in deciding how close was too close. If the dwarfs were allowed to gain too much ground, they might be able to threaten the walls.

From the lofty vantage of the Tower of the Dragon, Thoriol could see the dawi creeping ever closer. The woods seemed to pulse with eerie life as the trees began to sway, then pitch and fall. With rapid strokes, the dwarfs were cutting paths through the forest from the hills beyond, felling trees that must have already been weakened and prepared weeks before. Through these paths, great war machines were rolled towards the city: battering rams, catapults, bolt throwers and siege towers. It was an amazing sight, watching the way the dwarfs cleared the obstacles and brought their weapons forwards. He was reminded once again of his father's warnings about underestimating the dawi race. By elven standards they were uncouth and crude, but it was a grave mistake to ever belittle their industry or determination.

Like lambs to the slaughter, Draukhain hissed in Thoriol's mind. *Their determination is that of a frightened rabbit who runs into the jaws of the fox.*

From his saddle, Thoriol stroked the dragon's scaly neck. It still amazed him how the reptile's body could feel both cold and hot at the same time. 'They know we are here, but I don't think they marched all the way from their mountains just to burn in your fire.'

That is their doom just the same. Look, you can see the killer's standard down there. He is proud of what he's done. It would be easy to make him swallow that pride. Before I swallow him.

The dragon's rage flowed through Thoriol's veins. He felt the drake's confidence, its ancient contempt for all the little creatures and lesser breeds. It was more than flesh and bone – it was elemental force unleashed. The dwarfs could no more stop it than they could a meteor. It would descend upon them and wreak such havoc that they'd never dare stick their heads from their holes again. It could take up his father's killer and squeeze the life out of him, feel it drip drop by drop through its claws.

Thoriol fought to regain his control. 'Not until the order is given,' he cautioned Draukhain. 'Not until Lord Eylrk gives the command.'

The latest of Menlaeth's generals, Draukhain snorted with contempt. *He cares nothing for justice, only for the glory he can win for himself here. How long before he too is called away in disgrace? We can leap down and claim our own from the dwarfs. That is the only glory you and I desire!*

The dragon's urgings appealed to the pain and hollowness inside him. Thoriol would have liked nothing better than to submit. Avenge his father and then he could go home.

It was his sense of duty and obligation that made him hold back. He couldn't let himself bring disgrace to House Tor Caled, to the memory of his father. He couldn't let the people of Tor Alessi believe he was less valorous than Ilendril and his enslaved creatures. Thoriol was surprised by the sense of embarrassment such thoughts provoked in Draukhain. The dragon understood that there was more to honouring Imladrik than avenging his death. It was ashamed to have forgotten that.

Without Draukhain urging him to the attack, Thoriol was able to focus on the tactical situation as it unfolded. So many centuries on the battlefield had given him more than a cursory appreciation of strategy. Looking down on the dwarfs he was confused at what he saw. He'd seen the craft and care with which Morgrim had deployed his forces at Sith Rionnasc. What he saw now seemed as subtle as one of the dwarfs' hammers. They advanced in great blocks, staggered like checks on a gameboard. The foremost regiments were heavily armoured with great shields; those following behind were arrayed in coats of mail and bore an assortment of ladders along with their weaponry. It seemed as if the armoured vanguard were there to cover the warriors following behind while they raised ladders against the walls.

It was an obvious deception. If the dwarfs meant to force the walls, they would use their towers, not climb ladders that left them exposed to arrows. There had been no barrage to soften the defences, no effort to use smoke to blind the bowmen, no concentration of crossbows to keep the elves from pushing back the ladders as soon as they were raised. No, this wasn't an attack, it was a feint, but no matter how hard he looked, Thoriol couldn't see the purpose behind the deception.

The archers held their arrows with exemplary discipline. Thoriol had stood where they now stood and he knew first-hand the strain of waiting for the command to loose, the fortitude it took to wait for the fighting to begin. Closer and closer the dwarfs came. At three hundred yards they hesitated, crying out in their gruff voices 'Khazuk! Khazuk!' before resuming their fearsome march. The captains on the walls were looking anxiously at the signalmen, watching for the command to strike the enemy.

It wasn't until the enemy was one hundred and fifty yards from the walls that the command was issued. The voices of the captains rang out sharply from every quarter of the outer wall. In response, archers stepped out from behind the embrasures and shot down into the dwarfish ranks. From the plain behind the walls, the massed ranks of bowmen deployed there arced a volley up and over the fortification, sending a rain of steel-tipped death showering down upon the dawi.

Thick armour prevented most of the volley from striking true, but as the dwarfs raised their shields to defend themselves from the arrows dropping down on them from above they left themselves exposed to the sharpshooters on the walls ahead. Taking direct aim at the enemy, the archers took their toll, skewering throats and transfixing eyes with expert aim. Mangonels and bolt throwers shuddered into action, hurling boulders and shooting spears into the massed enemy.

The barrage continued for several minutes before the dwarfs broke. First one regiment, then another turned to flee back across the field. Deep within range of the archers, they'd be vulnerable to attack to a distance of three hundred yards from the wall and a further two hundred yards before the sharpshooters on the walls couldn't reach them with any degree of accuracy. Scores of dwarf dead littered the ground around the walls and many more lay strewn in the wake of the retreating dawi, like the trail of some steel slug.

Another signal flag was raised, one that bore the device of a dragon rampant. Fierce roars shook the streets of Tor Alessi. From the spire of the Tower of the Sea, a great green-scaled wyrm rose into the sky and went soaring towards the fray. Rising from the Tower of the Winds was Malok, Lord Ilendril seated upon the red-scaled brute's back. These two were the last of Ilendril's wyrms, the others having turned on their masters or fallen in battle over the years since Sith Rionnasc. It was either a testament to Ilendril's hubris or the desperation of the colonies that his wyrms were still being pressed into service.

Thoriol waited only a heartbeat before urging Draukhain into the air. As they rose there sounded a woeful cry from the dwarfish ranks, a groan of despair as they saw the dragons take wing. That was only right. Let the dawi feel the terror of imminent death – let them curse the vanity that had made them march here to cross blades with the asur.

Ilendril's wyrms were already diving upon the retreating dwarfs. As they drew near, the volleys of arrows stopped, the artillery from the walls went quiet. The elves wanted to allow the dragons a clear field in which to operate.

The two wyrms spat fire onto the dwarfs, immolating scores of them in their first pass. They swung back around to make a second run. Thoriol noticed something in that moment, something that made him scream a warning to Draukhain. The blue dragon pulled back, climbing instead of joining the wyrms in their dive. So it was that he escaped the trap as it was sprung.

The advance and retreat of the dwarfs had been a ruse to draw out the dragons. For centuries the dawi had been making their preparations, preparing their traps. Right under the noses of the asur, their miners and engineers had been at work, burrowing beneath the plain, digging their tunnels in secret, hollowing out the earth below and constructing their fiendish weapons.

As the two wyrms swept down upon the dwarfs, the earth erupted. Great iron poles, long hidden underground, now sprang upwards, slicing through the layers of dirt that concealed them. Between each set of poles was a steel net. Dwarfs were old hands at snaring bats by laying nets across the mouths of caves. Now they applied the same tactics to catching dragons.

The two wyrms crashed into the nets, their wings becoming snared and dragging them down. As soon as they crashed to earth, the seemingly routed dwarfs turned. Screaming their war-cries they rushed at the fallen drakes. A blast of fire from Malok forced the dwarfs away as it used its claws to shred the confining net. The green drake wasn't so fortunate. Its anguished wails rang out as hundreds of dwarfs chopped at it with axes and picks. The elf rider was ripped from his saddle, his head pulped beneath a warhammer.

It was like watching ants devour a lion. Sharing Draukhain's disgust and fury, Thoriol offered no objection when the dragon dived down upon the dwarfs swarming over the green wyrm. The drake's flames consumed a hundred dwarfs in the first blast, sending them screaming, rolling and writhing on the ground in blazing heaps of agony. Draukhain landed among its victims, crushing dozens beneath its claws. Its great tail flashed out, swatting another score of dwarfs, hurling them into the trees. With a seething roar the dragon sent another gout of fire searing across the dawi warriors, burning down another score of the bearded foe.

The green wyrm thrashed about in its bindings, but it was clear the reptile was mortally wounded. Draukhain clamped its jaws around the creature's neck, breaking it with a powerful twist and ending the wyrm's suffering. Then it reared up, spewing more fire at the dwarfs still lingering around the trap.

Thoriol saw that Malok was back in the air, Ilendril urging the wyrm towards the walls. He urged Draukhain to do the same, but even as the drake started to respond, he saw something that riveted his attention. The standard of Morgrim. The dwarf hero's standard was close to where Malok had been trapped. Nearby... nearby stood the murdering dawi himself!

'He's here!' Thoriol snarled. Draukhain roared in reply. The dragon used its wings not to rise into the air but simply to propel itself across the field in a set of soaring leaps. The ground shuddered beneath the reptile's feet as it lunged at the dwarf.

Before they could close upon Morgrim, something shot out from the trees. As Draukhain howled in pain, Thoriol appreciated how cleverly the enemy had laid their trap. The display of bringing up their siege weapons had been ostentatious, meant to gull the elves into thinking the dwarfs had nothing heavier than crossbows and axes at hand. Nestled among the trees, trained upon those concealed nets, the dwarfs had already deployed several bolt throwers. The dwarfs had swarmed the green wyrm before the bolt throwers could be employed and Malok had escaped too soon. Draukhain, however, in its charge, had become easy prey.

The bolt slammed into the dragon's side. The dwarfs had had centuries to engineer weapons specifically designed to kill such monsters. The one that speared Draukhain had a cruel double-head, making it impossible for the dragon to pull free or tear loose without ripping its wound wide open. Vicious runes engraved upon the bolt's head caused it to penetrate thick scales as though they were made of parchment. Other runes sent pulses of eldritch pain rushing through the dragon's body, burning a creature who dwelled amidst volcanoes.

Draukhain's last leap became a graceless crash. The dragon slammed down upon its side, breaking its left wing. Its weight gouged a deep trench until the creature intersected one of the hidden dwarf tunnels. Partially sinking into the now exposed fissure, Draukhain came to rest, roaring in pain and bleeding profusely from its wound.

Thoriol was almost overcome by the sympathetic pain he shared with the dragon. It took all of his strength to loosen the straps of his saddle and free himself. He nearly pitched headlong into the tunnel, where angry dwarf miners shook their fists and hurled rocks up at him. Taking a firm hold of Draukhain's neck, he pulled himself up onto the dragon's shoulder.

His head still ringing from the disastrous descent, Thoriol barely saw the crazed, half-naked dwarf who charged across the field until the maniac had nearly reached Draukhain. It didn't take much awareness to guess what the dwarf intended to do with his upraised axe.

Shouting his own war-cry, Thoriol leapt down and intercepted the dwarf. Seeing the enemy up close, he found him to be a grim specimen indeed, with shaved head and scarred face. He thought of the beardless dwarf Liandra had spared, the ambassador Forek Grimbok who'd been disfigured by the king.

Whatever sympathy she'd shown the beardless dwarf, Thoriol knew he couldn't do the same. Charging at the Slayer, he brought his sword flashing out at him, slicing a shallow cut across his arm.

The Slayer turned, glaring at him with crazed eyes. He snarled something in Khazalid, punctuating the remark with a blob of bloody spittle. Then, the dwarf's fury was fully refocused against Thoriol.

In all his years, the elf prince had never encountered such a foe. The Slayer would fearlessly throw himself at Thoriol, accepting the cuts and gashes inflicted by his sword so long as he could bring his axe swinging around. It took all of his agility to avoid those sweeps of the axe. Once, when it glanced across his armour, he saw the mail split and shear away. What such a murderous weapon could do to flesh and bone was something he didn't want to learn.

Bleeding from a dozen wounds, the Slayer kept up his attack. One of Thoriol's slashes split the dwarf's nose and opened his jaw, yet the crazed foe paid his mutilation less notice than a stubbed toe. Spitting teeth and blood, he pressed his assault, and had the satisfaction of connecting with the elf's side.

It was a glancing blow. By rights it should never have penetrated Thoriol's armour, no matter how strong the dwarf himself might be. But whatever hideous enchantment empowered the axe made it slash through his mail and sink deep into his body. It felt like a lance of fire pressing against his ribs, the flash of pain almost blinding him.

The Slayer had no opportunity to press his attack. As he ripped his axe free and prepared to strike again, Thoriol thrust at him with his sword. The blade he had been given by his father, the sword Caledor had claimed was unfit for a prince of Tor Caled, split the dwarf's beardless face, punching through flesh and bone until it exploded from the back of his skull.

The Slayer crumpled, the terrible axe falling from his numbed hands. The light behind those crazed eyes faded.

Thoriol clamped one hand against his bleeding side and staggered over to rip his blade free from the Slayer. As he did so, a gruff voice called out to him in Eltharin.

'That is my friend you've killed, elf!'

Thoriol turned. Through the pain, he managed to focus upon the dwarf who cried out to him. For an instant, hate blotted out all sensation of pain. His accoster was Morgrim Elfdoom himself. Attended only by a wizened runelord and his standard bearer, the great hero of the dawi was almost within reach of Thoriol's blade.

Thoriol's eyes narrowed as he saw the sword thrust beneath Morgrim's belt. How many times had he seen that blade? The mud-eater hadn't just killed his father, he'd taken his sword for a trophy.

Pointing at the sword in Morgrim's belt, Thoriol snarled at his enemy. 'That is my father you killed, dawi.' He managed one staggering step before the pain of his wound brought him crashing onto his face. Then all was blackness.

Morgrim stared in astonishment at the elf as he collapsed. Was it possible that this truly was Imladrik's son? Part of him sneered at the idea. What did it matter if he was? He'd killed Forek, cut him down before Morgrim's very eyes. He was an elgi, one of their dragon riders, friend and companion of the drakk. He was vermin, just like the wyrms, and just like the wyrms he deserved no mercy.

Just as he started towards Thoriol, Morek cried out in warning. A nimbus of protective magic flared up around him as the runelord evoked some conjuration. The blast of fire that swept around him in the next moment made Morgrim's skin blister and singed the hair of his beard, but otherwise rendered him no harm. When the flames abated enough that he could see, the thane found that the blue-scaled dragon was standing between him and the injured prince.

'Draukhain,' Morgrim muttered, recalling the monster's name. Long ago he'd nearly ridden upon this beast, when invited to accompany Imladrik to Karaz-a-Karak. Long ago he'd spared this beast's life in the ruins of Oeragor, allowing it to bear Imladrik's body back to his people.

There could be no such compassion for the creature now. It had become a scourge to his people, preying on them as the Crawling Death. Even the merciless Malok was second to this drakk in the grudges levelled against it.

The dragon answered Morgrim with a low hiss. The reptile was wounded, both from the bolt and from its fall. It still carried the scars of Oeragor upon it. Yet even with all its injuries, it was still powerful enough to kill Morgrim almost without a thought.

Azdrakghar seemed to twist in Morgrim's hands, pulsating with excitement. The thane recalled his enraged oath during another attack against Tor Alessi, swearing vengeance upon Draukhain for its part in massacring his army. That oath had awoken the runes of his axe – the axe originally crafted for Prince Snorri Halfhand.

Now he would fulfil the weapon's purpose. It had been crafted for a Dragonslayer, yet for all the enemies it had claimed, no dragon blood had yet crossed the blade.

Draukhain reared back, spitting another gout of fire at Morgrim as he rushed the beast. Once more, Morek's magic preserved the thane, fending off the worst of the drakk's ire. Bulling through the incendiary blast, he brought Azdrakghar swinging out. The blade cracked against the dragon's snout, shearing through its jaw and sending ripples of crackling magic sizzling through the monster's face.

The dragon lurched back in both shock and pain. Before it could recover, Morgrim slashed at the exposed breast, cleaving a great gash across the beast's chest. Draukhain's claw came slamming down, nearly crushing the dwarf flat. Morgrim threw himself to one side. As he rolled across the ground, he delivered a back-handed cut that almost cleft through one of the drakk's claws.

Beast and dwarf glared at each other. The warning cry of Khazagrim alerted the thane just before the dragon's tail came slamming down. Morgrim replied by chopping at the tail, shearing it through and leaving a six-foot length of flesh writhing on the ground.

Draukhain came at him again, snapping at him with its jaws. The fangs missed Morgrim by inches and he felt the dragon's foetid breath wash over him. Again he lashed out with Azdrakghar, this time ripping open the brute's face and splitting several of its teeth in half. The dragon recoiled and brought its uninjured wing slamming down. Morgrim was knocked flat by the blow. For a hideous instant the leathery pinion settled over him like a shroud. He felt himself being smothered under the musky reek of the reptile.

Twisting the axe around in his hand, Morgrim pressed the blade against Draukhain's wing, slicing it down the membrane. The dragon raised its wing, bellowing in pain. As it did so, Morgrim was dragged up with it, his axe catching in one of the bones. He worried his weapon free, dropping down onto the creature's scaly back. Before the dragon was fully aware of his presence, Morgrim braced his legs and brought Azdrakghar down.

The blade crunched into the top of Draukhain's skull, just ahead of the dragon's horns. A froth of blood and tissue boiled up from the wound. The beast bucked and started to rear, but Morgrim brought his axe chopping down again. This time the reptile's legs went limp and it slammed back to the ground. Morgrim lost his footing, but managed to keep hold of the drakk's horn. Bracing himself again, he brought the axe slamming home for a third time. Now he could see the slime of the beast's brain clinging to the end of his blade. A terrible shudder swept through the beast. Except for the nervous twitches and writhing of its mangled bulk, the dragon was motionless. All purpose and motivation had fled from it with that last blow.

Morgrim had earned the title Snorri Halfhand had believed would be his and which had driven him to such a tragic end. Morgrim Bargrum had become the Dragonslayer.

Strangely, he didn't feel any sense of triumph as he dropped down from Draukhain's body. All he felt was a terrible weariness and an urge to wash the blood from his body. If the drakk hadn't been half dead when he fought it, Morgrim knew which of them would have prevailed.

Stumbling from his own wounds, Morgrim allowed Khazagrim to help him from the field. Before he returned to his own lines, however, he paused and pointed at Thoriol. 'Bind the elgi's wounds,' he ordered Morek. 'Stop the bleeding and send him back to his people.' He hesitated, then removed Ifulvin from his belt.

'Send this with him,' Morgrim said. 'Let him know I too remember his father.'

'The Council of Princes doesn't rule Ulthuan – the king does. And I am king!' Caledor's outburst rang through his throne room like a peal of thunder. Only a few of the king's closest confidants were present, those he felt he could depend upon for their devotion and loyalty.

Caradryel felt himself to be in strange company indeed. He felt like a lamb among wolves, waiting to be snapped up at any moment. Why the king had summoned him to this meeting was a mystery. It was no great secret that he was in service to Lady Yethanial, and he was certain that his patron's views of Caledor and his rule were no secret to the king. When Thoriol had been present at court, Caradryel's presence there had made sense. Now, he could only speculate why the king would want him around, and his speculations weren't venturing into comfortable territories.

Hulviar, the loyal seneschal, was the first to find his voice. 'There has been discord among the Council of Princes ever since Yverian was recalled from Elthin Arvan.'

Caledor glared from his throne. 'Is it my fault that he proved an incompetent commander? Is it my responsibility that he chose to fall on his sword rather than face up to his failures?'

Caradryel was careful to hide his own feelings on the matter. The king had dispatched a seemingly endless succession of generals to the colonies, commanders who had been chosen for their rank and position among the noble houses rather than their tactical capabilities. While such a strategy kept the best generals available for the campaign in Naggaroth, it also meant that the commanders sent to the colonies were ill-prepared for their duties. When they failed, when the asur suffered some new defeat, the king would recall them to Ulthuan in disgrace, a policy that was embittering the great houses. By trying to play up to his supporters, by sending their favoured sons and daughters to win fame and glory against the dwarfs, Caledor had instead fomented resentment and distrust. At every turn, the king was pushing more and more of the nobility away from him. Voices like those of Yethanial and Athinol weren't alone in questioning the king now. There had even been whispers that the king should abdicate in favour of his nephew.

The king had to be aware of the rebellious sentiment that was growing among the ten kingdoms. Yet still he persisted in flaunting his authority and acting in defiance of every council and advisor.

'My liege, caution is not cowardice,' Caradryel offered.

Caledor smiled at Caradryel. It was a smile devoid of anything approaching warmth. 'Did I ask your opinion on the matter?' the king snapped. He leaned from his throne, waving his hand at a great tapestry hanging upon the wall. The tapestry displayed the lands known to the asur, each settlement and colony cleanly depicted. Ugly splotches denoted the lands the dwarfs had seized. The defacement was deliberate, a sight to provoke revulsion in anyone studying the map. At a glance, the observer could share his king's displeasure.

'The druchii are finished,' Caledor declared. 'What is left in Naggaroth are a few pathetic holdouts. We have the core of our strength out there chasing shadows, defending the coasts from raiders who will never come again.' He snapped his fingers at Hulviar. 'When was the last raid against Tiranoc?'

'Three hundred and twenty years ago, my liege,' the seneschal replied.

Caledor turned from the map, shaking his fist in disgust. 'The druchii are finished! It's nothing but a rat hunt now. The only reason the Council of Princes is displeased is because each of them wants the glory of being the one to bring Malekith's head back on a pike. I'll not see the whole of my kingdom threatened by their vanity.'

Caradryel could have told the king several things about whose vanity was threatening the kingdom, but again he kept his thoughts to himself. What he'd already heard was enough to alarm anyone, much less the Council of Princes. The armies were being withdrawn from Naggaroth, leaving only a few scattered garrisons to prosecute the 'rat hunt' as the king called it. The rest were being drawn into a royal expedition to the colonies.

But the king wasn't stopping at simply recalling his army from Naggaroth, he was levying troops from Ulthuan as well. Caledor intended to gather the largest force ever seen in the ten kingdoms, a fleet and an army so enormous that its mere arrival in Elthin Arvan would have the dwarfs suing for peace. The mud-diggers would learn who was superior when they saw the true strength of the asur.

'My liege, perhaps it would be wise to offer the Council of Princes something to appease them,' Caradryel suggested. 'Maybe only take the forces from Naggaroth on your expedition...'

'That is out of the question,' Caledor said, giving a dismissive wave of his hand. 'I will need every sword and bow to impress upon the mud-eaters the hopelessness of defying me. With the drakes refusing to participate, I must build the strength of my army with asur steel and ithilmar.' A crafty gleam shone in his eyes as he leaned forwards and stared at Caradryel. 'You are right, however. I am going to offer something that should appease my detractors and keep them quiet until I return.' He pointed at the diplomat. 'I am going to appoint you as my steward while I am gone.'

There weren't many things in the realm of politics that could take Caradryel by surprise, but the king's proclamation was one. He stared dumbfounded at Caledor. He glanced over at Hulviar, knowing that the king's seneschal should be steward while the king was gone. There was resentment in Hulviar's expression, but no real surprise. Clearly he'd known about this decision for some time.

'I... I am not certain I am equal to such responsibility...' Caradryel began.

'Then make yourself equal,' Caledor said. 'I know how little affection you or your mistress bear towards me, but I know you are both loyal to House Tor Caled. I can trust you to protect my throne while I am gone because you will want to keep it safe for my heir.'

The king's expression suddenly darkened. He sank back in his seat, his fingers tapping against the jewelled arms. 'I have received a report from Tor Alessi. The dwarfs are attacking again. That is hardly news. What is news is the fact that Prince Thoriol has been gravely injured by the mud-diggers. The best healers in the colonies are trying to keep him alive.

'Thoriol is my heir, the one who will wear the Phoenix Crown after me. He is my legacy, the legacy of Tor Caled.' Caledor clenched his fists. 'I will not have the blood of Caledor Dragontamer extinguished by a gaggle of bearded savages. If I must bring every asur in Ulthuan against them, I will do so!'

'Then you intend to lead the army yourself?' Caradryel asked, still reeling from the news that Thoriol was wounded and possibly dying.

Caledor smiled, somehow making the expression even colder than before. 'I killed their prince – it should be no great ordeal to kill their king as well. I'll return to Lothern with my nephew and their king's head on a platter. Then we shall have peace in the ten kingdoms and in Elthin Arvan.'

Caradryel wondered if the king would have such confidence if he had any idea how strong the dawi truly were; if he'd seen the forces Caradryel had seen, and if he understood how many more dwarfs there were in the mountains.

'I shall do honour to the trust you have placed in me,' Caradryel announced. 'I will safeguard the Phoenix Crown until your return, my liege.'

A sharp laugh rose from the king. 'The crown? There will be no need of that. I shall take it with me. When I lead my armies into battle against the mud-eaters, I will wear the crown over my helmet. How else will the vermin know that they have the honour of dying upon the sword of a king?'

FOURTEEN

THE BATTLE OF THREE TOWERS

597TH YEAR OF THE REIGN OF CALEDOR II

The outer wall of Tor Alessi had been reared after the seventh siege against the city. Built on a colossal scale, the fortification was fifty feet thick at its base and stood one hundred and fifty feet off the ground. Running across the plains in a semi-circle, the wall was anchored at either end by the pounding waves of the sea. Every three hundred yards of its three-mile length, a broad tower rose, its covered roof harbouring deadly eagle claw bolt throwers and cauldrons of molten lead to spill down upon attackers. Between each of the towers, ramparts with stone crenellations stretched, affording hundreds of archers protection as they loosed arrows at the enemy.

For a further six sieges, the outer walls had held and prevented all but the most minor harm to the city they defended. Now, with the fourteenth siege against Tor Alessi, they found themselves outmatched.

Grudge throwers cast tonnes of stone over the outer wall of Tor Alessi, soaring across the empty plain beyond to smash sections of the older inner wall that surrounded the city proper. Smaller catapults had to be content with battering the defences of the outer wall itself, collapsing the parapets and obliterating the battlements, sending the elven defenders scurrying into the shelter of the guard towers. One of these towers had been reduced to a heap of shattered stone, its rubble laying strewn in all directions. The rubble itself was too extensive to afford the dwarfs an easy way past the barrier, but at least the bolt throwers housed in the fortification had been silenced.

Yard by yard, the dwarfs were making progress, though the elves couldn't see it. Runesmiths and runelords lent their magic to hiding that secret from enemy mages while the utmost care was taken to conceal the advance from more mundane scouts and spies.

Years ago the dwarfs had started their tunnels, reaching out to undermine the outer wall. The elves had learned to take precautions against such tactics, placing enchantments upon the foundations that would scorch any sappers before they could get close enough to undermine the walls. It was an obstacle the dwarfs had learned about only through the most devastating losses, but nothing could stand between a determined dawi and his objective.

Instead of digging close to the foundations, the miners had excavated forty feet beneath them, well past the enchantments, creating a great underground corridor running just ahead of the wall. At intervals of every ten yards, a little notch had been dug into the side of that corridor, and into each notch had been set a great steel spike twenty feet long and five feet wide. Placed at an angle, the spikes were aimed up at the wall. Charges of zonzharr lit behind the spikes would drive them upwards, skewering the walls from below. A further charge placed within each hollowed-out spike would then explode the barrier from within. When every sapper was in position, signals tapped against the walls of the tunnels would give them the command to light the charges and run to the side-shelters prepared for them.

Morgrim observed the assault from the top of the Long Watch. The siege was well into its second month. Snow glimmered from the roofs of Tor Alessi and ice caked the sides of the walls. He worried about how cold it must be down in the tunnels, wondered if perhaps it would be too cold for the zonzharr to catch fire. The same blasts that drove the spikes up into the walls were also expected to light the fuses leading to the secondary charges. If either should fail to catch fire then the entire attack would fail. There wouldn't be a question of trying again. Once the elgi had even a suspicion of what the dwarfs were about, they'd spare no effort to thwart it. That would mean magic, perhaps even their remaining dragon. Malok had proven how aptly it was named in the weeks since the other drakk had been killed. The list of the wyrm's victims swelled every time the beast flew out from the city. Either it or its master had grown quite shrewd about avoiding the precautions the dwarfs tried to take against them.

'Strange to think of this as the quiet before the storm,' Morgrim said. He handed his spyglass over to the dwarf standing beside him. High King Gotrek squinted suspiciously at the device. Most dwarfs were distrustful of anything new and the spyglasses had only been developed by the engineers' guild four hundred years before. It would be some time yet before they were accepted as a useful tool rather than an exotic contraption.

'The elgi have always built to please their eyes,' Gotrek said. 'I warned them about that. Who cares how pretty something is if it lacks the strength to endure?'

As Gotrek spoke, the rock upon which the dwarfs stood gave a mighty groan. A jagged crack snaked across its surface, sending an overhang crashing down into the forest. The two dwarfs were sent reeling, fumbling for handholds to stop themselves from falling after the overhang. Smaller stones and pebbles crashed all around the dawi as the quake knocked them loose. Fighting to keep his footing, the High King pressed the spyglass to his eye and nodded. He could see the spikes jutting out from where they'd stabbed their way through the base of the wall. Playing the glass across the length of the fortification, he saw scores of places where the spikes had ripped their way up from below to stab through the stone.

A moment later an even more tremendous shiver passed through the rock. The two dwarfs staggered, almost falling from their perch. Morgrim reached out to help steady his king, but Gotrek waved him off. He was too intent on studying the walls to be distracted.

Great plumes of smoke and dust rolled out from the walls. As they began to clear, Gotrek handed the glass back to Morgrim. 'You'd better get your warriors moving,' he advised.

Morgrim peered through the glass. He could see that the wall had been brought down in a dozen places. Dead elves were strewn about the heaps of rubble; on the battlements, stunned elgi were stumbling about in shock. Before they could gather their wits enough to try to defend the breaches, Morgrim wanted his troops well beyond those walls.

'They're your warriors,' Morgrim reminded the king as he started to descend the steps. 'They fight for the Karaz Ankor and their High King.'

'They fight for their leader,' Gotrek corrected him. 'They fight for the one who takes them into battle. That is you. Elgidum, the great hope of the dawi.'

Morgrim couldn't linger to reassure his uncle. He knew the doubt and pain behind Gotrek's words, just as he knew there was nothing he could do to ease that doubt. All he could do was to try and bring his king whatever peace victory over the elgi would allow him.

Volleys of arrows rose from Tor Alessi, raining down into the killing field between the outer and inner walls. Bolt throwers cast their spears at the advancing enemy, impaling dozens of them. Arcane fires swept about the invaders as the elf mages drew upon their magic to burn down scores of the foe.

'Khazuk! Khazuk!'

Roaring their fierce cries, the dwarfs charged across the killing ground, running the gauntlet of arrows, magic and spears. When sufficiently roused, the normally ponderous dawi could become a raging avalanche of flesh and steel. Such an avalanche stormed through the broken walls, dwarf warriors hurdling the piled rubble with the agility of mountain goats. Some of the elves who'd survived the explosive demolition managed to create a few pockets of resistance. The dwarfs didn't gain ground without paying a toll in blood though. Such a toll wasn't enough to stall the impetus of their attack, however. By the hundred and then by the thousand, the dwarfs rushed past the broken wall out onto the open plain. Others rushed up onto the walls they had breached, confronting the surviving archers with hammer and axe. In short order the last holdouts were eliminated.

'Khazuk! Khazuk!'

The thousands of dwarfs mustering on the plain grew into tens of thousands. Throngs of dwarfs cleared away the rubble piled about the outer wall, making a path for the great siege engines they'd brought to break the city. Now the catapults hurled their burdens over the inner wall and far into the streets; the grudge throwers cast their stones almost into the bay itself.

The inner walls were barely scratched, those same walls that had defied Morgrim the first time he'd laid siege to Tor Alessi almost four centuries before. Every dwarf knew they would be no easy obstacle to clear, yet they also knew that no wall was stronger than the warriors defending it.

A delegation of dwarfs under a flag of truce started to march towards the inner wall's great gates. They would offer to the inhabitants Morgrim's terms for surrender, a test to evaluate the resolve of the elgi inside the city.

The delegation had only proceeded part way towards the wall when a strange sound rose up from Tor Alessi. It was faint at first, but it steadily grew until it became a dull roar. Bells rang out from the temples and towers, gongs boomed from the shipyards, horns and trumpets flared. Out on the field, the dawi stared at one another in confusion, wondering what new elgi trickery this sudden celebration might portend.

The dwarfish delegation was stopped when a set of arrows flickered past their noses. Another arrow sheared through the flag they bore, sending them hurrying back to their own lines. Jeers in stilted Khazalid pelted them from the walls. The elgi were mocking them for their presumption.

The battle was far from decided. Because in Tor Alessi's darkest hour, their homeland had remembered them. The armies of Ulthuan had come at last.

Thoriol could hear the tumult echoing outside his chambers in the Tower of the Dragon. At first he mistook the sounds for those of battle and thought that the dawi had at last forced their way into the city. Then, as the fog of fatigue began to clear from his mind and he became better attuned to his senses, he began to wonder if his injury had driven him mad.

It wasn't the sounds of battle he was hearing but rather jubilant cheers. Gripped by confusion, bewildered beyond endurance, Thoriol forced himself from his bed. His entire body felt as though it had been scooped out and only a shell remained. From his talks with Liandra, he knew this was what it felt like to have the connection with a dragon broken. No one had to tell him Draukhain was gone; he'd known it the moment he regained consciousness. That feeling of emptiness was even worse than the pain in his side where the crazed dwarf's axe had struck him. That wound had only threatened his life – the hurt left by Draukhain's death was a scar against his soul. Flesh could knit and heal, but spiritual hurt lasted forever.

'My prince, you must rest.' The alarmed voice belonged to a servant in the livery of Tor Caled. The elf came rushing across the chamber to push

Thoriol back into bed. The prince was too weak to mount much of a resistance. Slowly he was forced back among the silk pillows and fur blankets.

'What is happening outside?' Thoriol demanded. 'Why do the people cheer?'

The servant smiled back at him, his face fairly glowing with delight. 'It is the fleet. The king's fleet has come.'

Thoriol blinked in amazement. He lifted himself back off the bed. 'Help me to the window. I must see for myself,' he told the servant. The other elf demurred for a moment, but then assisted his master to the balcony.

What he saw out in the bay was indeed wondrous. As far as his eye could see, the water was filled with ships, ships of every shape and description, with more cresting the horizon with each breath. It was an armada such as Elthin Arvan had never before witnessed. He marvelled at the spectacle, at the infusion of troops and weaponry that would soon be set against the dwarfs.

He felt a pang of guilt when he realised this was exactly what his mother and people like Caradryel had struggled so long to prevent. King Caledor had ordered the armies of Ulthuan to the colonies. The days of half-measures and limited efforts against the dawi were over. The full might of the ten kingdoms was now being set loose.

Amongst the fleet, Thoriol spied a gigantic white galleon and above it, snapping in the wind, was the dragon and phoenix standard of King Caledor himself.

After almost four centuries, the Phoenix King had returned to Elthin Arvan to put an end to the war.

'To the wall! To the wall!' Morgrim's command rang out as he led hundreds of his own retainers and hearthguard out across the open plain. His shout was taken up by thanes and captains throughout the dawi host. Every champion of that vast throng seized upon the cry, leading their warriors into a massed charge against the inner wall of Tor Alessi. Enormous siege towers and massive war machines were pushed by entire battalions of shouting dwarfs, rushed to where they could deal the most damage to the enemy fortifications.

The pride and hope of only an hour before had withered inside Morgrim's heart, replaced with a gnawing dread. He'd imagined that at long last the dwarfs were poised to claim a hard-fought victory – an end to the War of the Beards after so many centuries. Then, just as that vision was becoming reality, the elgi fleet appeared, disgorging a flood of fresh warriors to reinforce the city. From the very edge of triumph, the dawi were being thrown back.

'To the wall!' Morgrim bellowed once more, trying to force his warriors to greater speed by the sheer power of his voice alone. Beside him, as he ran across the field, Khazagrim waved the thane's banner frantically from side to side, trying to inspire the dwarfs who had sworn oaths of service and loyalty to that standard.

After so many centuries of conflict, now the matter of victory boiled down to this one instant. If Morgrim could only get his troops to the wall, if the dwarfs could force a foothold upon the barrier before the new elgi warriors arrived, they could still seize the day. The lesser walls within the city that guarded the Old Quarter and the Royal District were far less formidable than the walls that fenced the whole of the city. They would soon crumble once the dawi brought their onagers into Tor Alessi.

If only the dawi were given that opportunity.

Morgrim glanced to his right, watching as a heavy onager rolled towards the wall, hurling chunks of rubble from the outer wall at the turrets and ramparts of the inner. A regiment of quarrellers flanked the war machine, shooting bolts into the elgi archers who tried to harass the advancing catapult.

Looking to his left, Morgrim saw several bolt throwers thrown into position, their crews anchoring the siege engines with great spikes of steel before turning them up towards the walls. The machines cast iron grapples up at the battlements and as each hook caught hold, gangs of dwarf warriors rushed to pull the chains fitted to the grapples and tear down some of the tooth-like crenels, depriving the elven archers of their cover.

'The gate! The gate!'

Morgrim wasn't sure who first uttered the cry, but the shouting brought his gaze towards the main entrance into Tor Alessi, the great door through which Imladrik and his entourage had come to parlay with him in that last fruitless peace conference so long ago. Now, the gate was shadowed by a formidable keep, flanked by turrets from which elgi bolt throwers launched spears into the oncoming dawi.

The dwarfs who now rushed at the gate weren't repulsed by the punishing volleys. They were heavily armoured hammerers from far-off Ekrund, the fiercest warriors of that distant stronghold. They spared little notice for the elgi shooting at them, focusing instead upon helping a gang of engineers push a great bronze-roofed battering ram towards the gate. Smoke and steam spewed from the boiler that projected from the rear of the ram, feeding the engine that would provide the driving impetus of the mechanical juggernaut.

Morgrim caught hold of Khazagrim, pointing in the direction of the hammerers and the battering ram with his axe. 'We'll help them,' he told the old dwarf. 'They'll get us inside and then nothing will force us out.' Khazagrim nodded, waving the banner and dipping it towards the gate so that the following warriors would understand the change in their objective.

Morgrim had reason to question his bold claim that nothing would force the dawi back as he led his troops towards the gates. The full violence of the elf garrison had been unleashed. They recognised their peril and were determined to hold the dwarfs off until their reinforcements could arrive. Great eagles dived down from the sky, snatching dwarfs from the siege towers and releasing them to smash into the infantry far below. Griffons swooped upon the catapults, their snapping beaks and slashing claws wreaking bloody havoc amongst the dwarfish artillerists, while their elven riders demolished the siege engines with spell and sword.

Volleys of arrows arced up from hundreds of archers assembled in the courtyards and squares within the city itself, speeding over the walls to shriek down at the invaders. Again, sharpshooters on the walls themselves took their grisly toll from the advancing dwarfs, striking the weak points in their armour with lethal precision. Eagle claw bolt throwers shot their spears down into the enemy formations, impaling clutches of the close-packed dawi with each cast. Catapults added their brutal violence to the carnage, flagstones pulled up from the streets smashing down upon the dwarfs, pounding their armoured bodies into the earth like bloody nails.

The mages of Tor Alessi unleashed their magic now. Strange fires and lightning fell from the wintry sky, cooking a dozen of Morgrim's dwarfs as they ran towards the gate. Strange tempests erupted from the nothingness to writhe and rage about the ponderous towers, ripping away their protective skins of oak, canvas and copper plate. The winds shrieked still louder as they wrenched the frames of the towers apart, spilling dwarfs hundreds of feet to the frozen earth below. One by one, the mighty towers were broken apart by phantom claws and icy gales.

'Onward! To honour and vengeance!' Morgrim shouted, trying to spur his warriors ahead for the final effort. Through the riotous carnage inflicted by the elgi, the dwarfs pressed on. If they could only force their way into the city, then whatever sacrifices they made would be worth it.

While Morgrim led his followers towards the gate, other dawi were answering the elgi assault. Rune-lightning crackled up from the ancient Anvils of Doom as the runelords of the dwarfs forced their arcane power into violent manifestations. With each crack of their hammers, the erudites sent their magic snaking up at the walls, following the aethyric reverberations of their spells back to the mages who cast them. Some of the elven wizards, guarded by talismans and charms, endured the dwarfish reprisals, but others were reduced to smouldering carcasses by the malignant energies hurled at them by the ancient Anvils.

Companies of Ironbreakers, their armour engraved with runes of aethyric discord, formed protective cordons around the runelords, acting as a barrier against the magical assaults of the elf mages. Steaming showers of starfire sizzled harmlessly from their armour; pulsations of kinetic fury were reduced to naught but a faint breeze when they slammed into the Ironbreakers. Thus, it was from a different quarter that the elves attacked the dawi mystics. Roaring its reptilian wrath, the dragon Malok dived upon the Ironbreakers, ripping and crushing them in its claws. Its fiery breath licked out at the Anvil of Doom each company protected, washing over artefact and runelord alike. Then, before weapons could be brought against it, Malok would leap back into the sky, flying beyond the range of its foes until it was prepared to swoop down again. Anvils from Karak Kadrin, Karak Izor and Karak Norn were lost to the dragon, reduced to slag by its volcanic breath – further grudges to be levelled against the wyrm in the Dammaz Kron.

The steam-powered ram began its assault against the gates, crossbowmen trying to ward off the attentions of the elves shooting down at the machine. Thanks to its metal roof, the flaming arrows the elgi loosed at the machine couldn't burn it, but there was a chance the defenders might manage to hit the pipes and pistons that drove the steel-capped ram into the gate. The hammerers from Ekrund waited nearby, ready to force any breach the ram provided and be the first dwarfs in centuries to penetrate into Tor Alessi.

Slowly the dawi were making progress, but it was too little to counter the rapid, disciplined deployment of the troops from Ulthuan. While still at sea, the generals of the asur and their king had plotted their strategy. Aware that the city was already under siege, they drew up exacting plans for rushing their soldiers straight to the front. A system of coloured flags displayed by the king's flagship alerted every ship in his fleet of the situation they'd find in Tor Alessi and how they would be expected to respond. From a selection of fifty flags, each with its own meanings and associated commands, it was a red pennant with a white star that unfurled from the galleon's mast – indicating that the dawi were through the outer wall and staging an assault upon the inner one.

As soon as the ships drew into the harbour, the asur warriors disembarked, armed and armoured for war. Their commanders had given them exacting instruction on where they should deploy once they made landfall, showing them on intricate maps of the city where they needed to go and which streets they would use to get there. When the warriors entered the city, there was no hesitation or confusion. Like cogs in a well-oiled machine, they swiftly formed ranks and hurried to their assigned positions.

The first the dwarfs were aware of the reinforcements was when the volleys rising from behind the walls swelled, the flights of arrows becoming so thick that their shadows created a flickering twilight across the battlefield. The siege towers were suddenly no longer menaced by elgi magic, but as the first of them crashed against the wall and lowered its hooked ramp, the dwarfs were swarmed by fresh battalions of grim-faced spearmen and swordsmen. Far from gaining a foothold on the wall, the dwarfs were decimated in a display of such ferocious butchery that the towers were quickly withdrawn.

The steam-powered ram became the next focus of elven reprisal. A blinding glow suffused the machine and the dwarfs around it, an aethyric glamour that expanded and throbbed with magical power. As the dazzling light intensified, the dwarfs began to scatter, abandoning the machine. Some weren't quite fast enough and as they tried to run, the light overwhelmed them. In a howling flash, the light suddenly winked out, leaving behind it only a deep crater where the battering ram and its protectors had been. The dawi would never know that the ram had been translocated by the wizardry of asur loremasters, that the machine and the dwarfs caught with it had been transported out into the bay, there to sink and drown beneath the waters.

It was with a heavy heart and a bitter taste in his mouth that Morgrim finally gave the command to withdraw. Horns blared, runners were dispatched and signals flashed from mirrors. Gradually, the command was disseminated amongst the dwarfs. Sharing their general's reluctance, the dawi began to fall back, marching away from the walls to establish a perimeter just inside the outer curtain they had already captured.

Instead of cheers and trumpets, the asur marked the repulse of the dwarf assault in a different fashion. From the highest towers in the city, a new pennant was unfurled: a white flag upon which a red dragon and phoenix were emblazoned. It was all the elves had to say to their attackers.

The King of Ulthuan had come to save Tor Alessi.

King Caledor II threw open the doors of Thoriol's chamber, dispatching the healers and servants attending his nephew and heir. He waved an armoured gauntlet at the White Lions who surrounded him, motioning them to await him in the hall outside. Only Envaldein, the captain of his guard, remained, closing the door and standing with his back set against the portal.

The king removed his gilded helm, handing it to Envaldein as he hurried across the room. Nestled amidst the golden splendour of the helm and the ruby-encrusted dragon-wings flaring out from its sides, the glittering brilliance of the Phoenix Crown shone like a sliver of starlight. The king belatedly remembered his crown, turning after a few steps to snatch his helm back from the White Lion. Then, with slightly less haste, he resumed his walk to the chair in which his nephew reclined.

'Blood of Asuryan,' Caledor shouted. 'What do you think you are doing? Is this what you think it means to bolster the confidence of the colonials? To risk yourself in senseless battles against grubby, mud-slugging savages? I did not allow you to come here to take such chances.'

Thoriol smiled at the outraged king. For all the many reasons he had to despise his uncle, he couldn't help but feel a twinge of guilt at provoking such concern in him. 'If the dawi are such miserable creatures, why should there be any risk to me, a prince of Tor Caled?'

Caledor wagged his finger at his heir's impertinence. 'Don't think to turn my words back on me. A griffon can still get stung by a bloatfly. Just because something is contemptible doesn't mean it can't hurt you.' He looked around a moment, shifting his gaze from one chair to another, as though trying to decide which would inconvenience his royal dignity the least. Finally he drew a cherrywood chair with velvet backing towards Thoriol.

'By all the Cadai, I thought you'd be safe with that dragon,' Caledor said. 'I should have insisted you come home long ago, but I thought that creature would protect you. I didn't think there was any power in the world that could strike down that brute of your father's. I should have known better. It didn't save my brother, so how could it save you?'

'Draukhain,' Thoriol corrected the king. 'His name was Draukhain and he did save me. When Morgrim was ready to kill me, it was Draukhain who intervened. The garrison on the walls saw it all. He fought the dwarf lord to the very last. Maybe killing Draukhain quenched Morgrim's thirst for blood. For whatever reason, he had one of the dawi mages attend my wound and then bring me back to our people.'

'The mud-eaters did that?' Caledor scoffed. 'An empty gesture if they think they can win my forgiveness.' His eyes hardened. 'What about this Morgrim? That's the animal that struck down your father. What sort of brute is this creature? Before I leave this place, I intend to hang his beard from the yardarm of my flagship. It will be small recompense for my brother, but it will be a start.'

'Don't you see? That is why this war isn't going to end until one or the other of us can't fight,' Thoriol said. 'We're just going to keep battering away at each other. Morgrim killed my father, you killed his cousin. There's just too much blood on all our hands to ever see them clean again.'

'What would you have me do?' the king growled. 'I should forget that they killed Imladrik? I should forget all the cities they've razed to the ground? I should forget all the blood and treasure these animals have cost my kingdom? Do you expect me to forgive these beasts for all of that?'

Thoriol shook his head. 'No, I don't. It wouldn't matter anyway. The dawi don't feel they have anything they need to be forgiven for. They wouldn't accept it. I don't think they'd accept anything we could give them.'

'Then what do you advise?' Caledor asked. 'Should we let these creatures drive us from Elthin Arvan? Should we abandon everything we tried to do here? Should we cast aside what your father died for? Is that the legacy you would inherit – a legacy of compromise and retreat?' The king leaned forwards, clasping Thoriol's hands between his own. 'You are the future of House Tor Caled. In your veins burns the fires of our line. When I am gone, you are the one who will wear my crown. There can be no doubt about that. I would leave you a shining realm – strong, prosperous, reaching from sunrise to sunset. A new golden age of plenty for our people. If we are beaten here, if we do as your mother and those like her want, it will kill the pride of Ulthuan. We will lose our sense of destiny and purpose.

'No,' Caledor corrected himself, 'we won't lose them. They will still be there, the ambition of empire and the pride of accomplishment. But they will forever be tainted by the poison of doubt. We'll never again be so certain of our path, so sure of our purpose. Always in the back of our minds, in the depths of our souls will be that little voice reminding us that the dwarfs forced us from these lands. Like a cancer, it will bleed the strength from our people.'

The king rose from his chair and walked to the balcony, staring out over the bay and the vast fleet he'd brought to relieve the siege. 'I won't be the one to leave such poison behind me. I won't have that be my legacy. When the chronicles are written, I won't have my rule be a mockery of what came before. I am the son of King Caledor and I am worthy of that name. In my heart pumps the same blood as that of the Conqueror, the king who drove Malekith and his cursed followers from Ulthuan. I am the Phoenix King!'

Thoriol stared at his uncle in silence, startled by the passion in his voice. In his more candid moments, Imladrik had sometimes spoken of the great burden his brother bore and how onerous it must be. It was not the weight of the Phoenix Crown, but the strain of trying to measure up to their father's expectations. From the earliest age, Menlaeth had been pushed to carry on the legacy of King Caledor I and always the king had pushed him harder and harder. Never had Menlaeth been good enough in his father's eyes; never had he earned the king's regard. That was the real legacy he'd inherited.

'We can't always choose what it is we will leave behind,' Thoriol said. 'I don't think we can abandon the colonies. At the same time, the dwarfs aren't an enemy we can fight half-heartedly. It must be all or nothing.'

The king turned away from the balcony. 'All or nothing,' he repeated. 'If we could break the dwarfs here – one great battle. Then the animals would be forced to submit.'

Caledor turned as sharp knocking rattled the door. He nodded to Envaldein, who admitted the Lady Aelis and a pair of dour-looking generals. All three bowed as they approached their king.

'My liege,' Lady Aelis said, 'a dwarfish delegation is outside the wall under a flag of truce. They request–'

'Khaine take them and their requests,' Caledor snapped. 'If they don't have the stomach to fight then let them scurry back to their burrows.'

'Sire, their king is here – their High King, the lord of them all,' Lady Aelis explained. 'Gotrek Starbreaker wants to speak with you. He is offering terms for peace.'

A bitter laugh rang out as Caledor heard the news. 'You see, Thoriol. A show of force, real force, and these boastful animals start reconsidering things. By the gods, we'll put these mud-eaters back in the ground where they belong.'

The king settled his helm back onto his head, his crown still aglow with its enchanted brilliance. 'Assemble the Council of Five and all your generals. After we go through the formality of receiving and dismissing this request from the mud-eaters, we must make our plans. I don't want the dwarfs escaping here with anything that still looks like an army.'

As he passed Envaldein, Caledor motioned for the captain to remain. 'Stay and guard the prince,' he told the White Lion. 'See that he gets the best care. I want him looking his best when we bring these dwarfs to their knees and they come crawling to me for mercy.'

Thoriol watched his uncle leave. He thought about the king's talk of legacies and destiny, and like Caledor he wondered what it was that he'd leave when he was gone.

The gloom within the great hall beneath the rock of the Long Watch was more than simple darkness. It was a brooding malignance, an almost palpable atmosphere of doom that set fingers of ice raking down the spines of even the stoutest dwarfs. The source of that grim atmosphere sat at the head of his long table, ensconced within the ancient Throne of Power. The High King of the Karaz Ankor had withdrawn to the underground vault soon after the elgi reinforcements arrived and the colours of their king were unfurled. For many days, he had sat in the dark, centuries of hate turning his heart into a blackened cinder.

'He is here,' Gotrek snarled. 'After all this time, he is finally here.'

The High King glared at the captured banner, feeling the fury boiling inside him. The dragon and the phoenix, wings and talons spread. The heraldry of Ulthuan's current Phoenix King. The symbols of Caledor II. The same as the flags that now flew above Tor Alessi.

'All the death, all the carnage, all the centuries of strife, all the suffering and deprivation – all of it,' Gotrek declared, '*all of it* is because of him. Everything we have suffered is invested in that one miserable elgi.' In Gotrek's mind, in the minds of most dwarfs, the elgi king had become the face of the enemy, the cause of the war. The shame of Forek and the steelbeards, the murder of Snorri Halfhand – these were the crimes of Caledor, crimes that no dwarf could forgive.

Gotrek leaned forwards, cupping his head in his hands. Tears glistened at the corners of his eyes. 'I am weary of the killing. I only want an end to it all. After all this time, after watching so many die in the fighting, I only want it to stop. Taking Tor Alessi could have been enough.' Through his fingers, he lifted his gaze back to the captured banner.

'But now *he* is here!' Gotrek raged as he sat upright and clenched his fists. 'The bastard has come back! He's here! He's close enough that I can feel his rancid breath, hear his rotten heart. He's out there, just beyond the reach of my armies and my hammer. He's there, just waiting to be made to pay for what he's done!'

If it took every axe in the Karaz Ankor, if he had to draw every dwarf in the world from their mines and mountains, Gotrek would break Tor Alessi now. The whole of dwarfdom would march under his banner as they brought the Phoenix King's ruin.

His banner. Gotrek would lead his armies into battle when the fighting resumed. It was no slight against Morgrim or his ability to command, but the conflict had taken a new turn with the arrival of Caledor himself. It had become a conflict of kings now, Gotrek against Caledor, just as it should always have been. When he defeated the elgi king, it would be his own accomplishment.

'Vengeance will be mine,' Gotrek swore. 'No one, not even the gods themselves, will stay my hand.' The old king stroked his beard, letting his fingers linger over the beads of mourning nestled amidst his snowy hair, strung there so long ago in memory of his murdered son. Justice and recompense for Snorri were almost at hand. Gotrek had already set the boulder rolling that would become an avalanche such as the elgi had never dreamed of.

'The elgi have heard my demands now,' Gotrek said. 'They've had two days to think about them. But those demands aren't meant for the elgi. Word of my terms will be passed to every hold in the Karaz Ankor. From Kraka Drak to Karak Eight Peaks, every dwarf will hear of what I've offered the elgi – wergild to buy them peace.' The High King chuckled darkly at the cynical wisdom of his ploy. 'The smell of gold will draw out the other dawi kings, the ones who've sent only a token of support for this siege. Even kings weary of battle will come running when they see the promise of elgi gold and compensation for what their holds have suffered in the war. They'll bring their armies with them, a show of force to help strengthen their own demands against the elgi.'

A snort of bitter laughter wheezed from the High King. In a way, by making his journey to Tor Alessi, Caledor had not only brought fresh troops to the elves, he'd given Gotrek the best instrument with which to draw the full might of his kingdom into one great throng. Duty, honour, loyalty and obligation – these were all powerful, tremendous forces in the hearts and minds of the dwarfs, but they were slow, ponderous things that took time to stir and bring to a boil. Greed, however... greed was something that could make a grey-headed venerable as spry as a beardling.

The elf king had brought the might of his nation to Tor Alessi. Soon Gotrek would be able to do the same.

'Maybe the elgi will pay the wergild,' Gotrek mused. 'When they see the vast throng arrayed against them, maybe they will forget their pride. Grimnir forbid! Let them remain defiant and arrogant. Let them fight us!'

Gotrek swept his gaze across the empty darkness of his hall. Except for his memories, he was alone in the shadowy vault. It was to one of those memories that the High King spoke.

'Gold and treasure won't bring you back,' Gotrek whispered, 'but the blood of the elgi king will bring peace to your spirit, my son.'

FIFTEEN

DUEL OF KINGS

597TH YEAR OF THE REIGN OF CALEDOR II

The smell of burning wood hung heavy upon the air. The Loren Lacoi rang with the crack of axes and the gruff voices of dwarfs.

Liandra watched from the boughs of the oak she'd climbed, watching and waiting for the marching dwarfs to draw closer. Never before had such a vast horde of the dawi come tromping into the forest. They numbered not in the hundreds but in the thousands. Their march was like a raging tempest, smashing through the trees like a hurricane, careless and indifferent to the destruction they wrought. By axe and torch, they cut their way across the land, a great monster of steel and muscle crushing all in its path.

Dimly, Liandra wondered what had engendered such boisterous arrogance in the usually dour dawi. Surely something of great consequence to make them raise their voices in bawdy songs, to pass flagons of beer and mead from the hulking carts that accompanied them. Even in times of peace the dwarfs had been wary of the forests, and with the war they'd come to shun any stand of trees that might conceal asur bows. Something had changed, something that made the dwarfs contemptuous of the risks of forest trails and too proud to stalk their underground vaults.

Had the dawi finally claimed victory over the elves? Was it possible they'd captured Tor Alessi? Liandra was surprised to find how little she cared about either possibility. Those were concerns from a different time and a different world. All that mattered now was the forest, the sanctuary that had sheltered her people for so many decades. Whatever had happened outside, be it war or peace, the dwarfs made battle against the forest and that was all Liandra's people needed to know.

She had only seven hundred fighters between the camps. Their numbers had slowly grown through the years as children matured and stragglers from the outside found their way into the forest. There had even been a few more like Aismarr, fey elves with strange eyes and a weird air of wisdom about them. Many were veterans of the fighting against Forek Grimbok, and some had even taken part in the great battles outside. Many more were untested. She knew their skill with the bow – a few had even taken dwarfish stragglers before – but none of them had been called to fight in a real battle until now. It would be a baptism of fire, one that might burn them all if too many of the novices lost their courage.

The elves were arrayed along the flanks of the advancing dwarfs, slipping like shadows from tree to tree and bush to bush. Decades lurking in the wilds had given them a facility for shifting and fading into their surroundings that bordered on the mystical. Liandra had seen some of her best scouts steal so near to a buck that they brought the animal down with knives rather than arrows. The dwarfs, by comparison, were a simple adversary to hide from. Even their rangers, the only warriors among them with some knack for woodcraft, failed to sound the alarm.

Seven hundred against perhaps ten times their number. They were odds that Liandra would have shunned even with Vranesh at her side. Yet she didn't intend to give battle to the whole dwarfish host. To drive them from the forest, they need kill only one dwarf. Her scouts had already brought her word of the dwarf king with the tall, golden crown who marched with the dawi, borne along on a sort of stone palanquin by a dozen burly warriors. That was the dwarf they had to kill. Whether he was their High King or simply the ruler of a single stronghold, he was clearly the leader of the army. There were few things that could make dwarfs abandon the field of battle, but the death of their lord was one. They'd gather up the body and hurry to enshrine his remains in a crypt. Only after their dead hero was entombed would they begin turning their minds to reprisal and revenge.

On the bough just below her, Aismarr shared Liandra's vigil. Once again, the fey elf had dispatched her mangy hound on some obscure errand, and once again Liandra knew better than to ask her purpose in sending the dog away. There were no answers when Aismarr spoke, only more questions.

Still, Liandra never thought it hurt to ask. 'Is this part of our trial as well? Are we still being tested?'

Aismarr closed her eyes and nodded. 'Your trial nears its end,' she said. 'But whether for good or ill, I do not know.'

Liandra fixed her gaze back on the advancing dwarfs. She felt an unspeakable revulsion as she watched them clearing their road through the forest. Each tree they struck down, each bramble and bush they put to the torch, all of it filled her with a disgust she hadn't felt even when she watched them burn Athel Maraya.

'So long as there are dwarfs to kill, I do not care,' Liandra said. She waved her staff before her, a length of yew topped by a strangely gnarled knot that resembled some impish face. A grey light streaked from the end of the staff, shrieking up over the trees to explode in a spiral of shimmering embers. Before the invading dwarfs could react to the arcane flare, the elves lying in wait at either side of the path snapped into action. Arrows whistled out from the trees, stabbing into victims chosen minutes before. A hundred dwarfs were struck down in that first butchering assault, twice that number wounded or maimed.

The lurking elves didn't wait for the dwarfs to come rushing into the undergrowth looking for them. As soon as the first arrows were loosed, the asur were already in motion, fading to another vantage from which to attack the invaders.

Liandra knew that they had to be careful. If the asur proved too elusive, then the dwarfs would become frustrated and in their malice would simply try to burn the trees to root out their hidden foes. Deliberately, some of her people held back, exposing themselves and sacrificing their lives to encourage the dwarfs to pursue them into the forest. Even the most enraged dwarf wouldn't consider burning the woods while his kinsfolk were among the trees.

The dwarf king recognised the peril presented by the headlong rush of his warriors in pursuit of their shadowy enemies. Standing up from his stone throne, the silver-bearded dwarf howled at his subjects, raging at them to fall back and form ranks. Liandra was surprised that she recognised that voice and the ostentatious crown that circled the dwarf's head. He was Varnuf of Karak Eight Peaks, one of the more belligerent dwarf lords she'd met at that long-ago feast at Karaz-a-Karak. The years of conflict hadn't been kind to Varnuf. He'd lost an arm in some engagement, replacing it with a surrogate of gold. One of his eyes was milky and blind, and one of his ears notched where an arrow had almost ripped it from his head. Age had taken its toll as well, withering his limbs and curling his back. Yet there was still an air of command about the old dwarf and an imperiousness in his voice that made his subjects attend his every word.

Liandra drew the aethyric vibrations from the air around her. Since retreating into the forest, her old abilities had atrophied, the fiery magics that had once been as natural to her as breathing. In their stead had come strange, eerie patterns – conjurations that seemed to imprint themselves onto her mind. She was certain she'd never learned them from some hoary old tome, or heard them discussed by a loremaster. They were too raw and primal to be the magic of books and scholars, too wild to be bound by the strictures of theory and hypothesis.

At her instigation, Liandra formed the vibrations into a coruscating nimbus of amber light. With a word, the light leapt from her staff, expanding, twisting and writhing until it was sent streaming along the road the dwarfs had gouged from the forest. The trees the light passed through were left unharmed and untouched, but wherever it struck dwarfish flesh, the dawi burned.

Varnuf and his thronebearers were lost for an instant in the amber light, but only for an instant. When the glow faded, the dwarf king and his bodyguards stood unharmed, runes of protection glowing fiercely from their armour. A gnarled runelord glared out from among the king's entourage. Thrusting his staff forwards, he called upon his own magic to strike back at Liandra.

The fire the runelord called forth scorched its way through the trees. Barely had Liandra and Aismarr leapt down from the oak in which they perched before the thick boles and branches were transformed into a great pyre. Liandra raised her staff again, conjuring a roaring tempest to smother the flames the runelord had kindled. As she sought to quench the fire, the dwarfs were already charging towards her, determined to slay the witch who had tried to kill their king.

Aismarr drew her blade and struck down the first of the dwarfs rushing to confront Liandra. The armoured axeman fell, his throat opened from ear to ear. A second dawi dropped, then a third. Aismarr cried out as the fourth dwarf's axe ripped down her leg, opening it to the bone. A fifth dwarf smashed her ribs with his hammer. Then the warriors were surging past the dying she-elf to come to grips with the mage herself.

Fierce war-whoops sounded from amidst the trees. Arrows streaked out from the shadows to strike down the dwarfs closest to Liandra. As she turned from extinguishing the fires, her heart became heavy. Hundreds of her people were rushing out from the forest, rallying to her aid. They struck at the dwarfs with their swords and spears, heedless of the thick armour, and superior numbers, of their foe. Stealth and woodcraft, the greatest weapons the elves had at their disposal, had been abandoned in this vainglorious attempt to save their leader.

Liandra drew upon her powers once more. She couldn't let her people be massacred any more than she could let the forest be despoiled. She had to make the effort, had to try the only thing that might at least give them a pyrrhic victory. If they could yet strike down Varnuf, then they could still turn the dawi back. Even if none of them were alive to see it.

Even as Liandra focused her mind upon the grim conjuration, cries of terror rose from the dwarfs. From the edges of the forest, shapes now emerged, weird and monstrous figures that reached out with wooden talons to pluck dwarfs from the road. Ghastly creatures of wood creaked out onto the path, lumbering on trunk-like legs and flailing about with branch-like arms to rend and slay. Ghostly lights shone from knotted faces, glaring at the dwarfs with ancient malignance. The dawi, their faces pale with fright, closed ranks and pressed back towards the road they had been cutting. A palpable aura of fear rose from the dwarfs.

The forest itself had come alive, had roused itself to combat the invaders who would maim it with axe and flame.

A great, hulking thing stomped out from the woods, a giant of bark and timber with only the roughest semblance of a humanoid form. The hollows of its trunk formed the vaguest image of a scowling visage, jagged splinters lending the impression of a fanged maw gaping beneath its hollow eyes.

The wooden giant brought its clawed hands smashing down, pulverising several of Varnuf's thronebearers with a single blow. The stone seat lurched to one side, hurling the horrified king to the ground. The treeman loomed up above him while its lesser kin rampaged among his army.

Swiftly, Liandra refocused her spell, training her magic not upon the king, but against the runelord. Only the dwarf mystic could have the power to harm the gigantic treeman – and that was something she had to prevent, whatever the cost. Aismarr had spoken of trials and tests. At this moment, Liandra understood what the fey elf had meant.

How much was she willing to sacrifice to defend something greater than herself?

Liandra sent the roiling ball of shadow she evoked crawling across the runelord. The dwarf tried to banish the malefic conjuration, but as he strained to dispel it, Liandra focused more and more of herself into the attack. The magic of the dwarfs was more earthy than that of elves, more bound to things and objects. The runelord, for all his skill and experience, simply couldn't match the powers Liandra brought to bear. With a cry that was more resignation than despair, the runelord's counter-magic failed and the arcane blight his foe had called forth swept down upon him. The dwarf's armour corroded off his body, his beard withered to its roots, and his flesh crumbled and flaked away. In only a few heartbeats, all that was left of him was a little pile of ash.

Liandra reeled back from the tremendous toll of her conjuration. She was too weak to defend herself as the dawi warrior came charging at her. He thrust at her with the head of his axe, the spike fixed to its tip piercing her breast. Even as she felt her life pouring out from the wound, Liandra smiled. Beyond her attacker, she could see the treeman standing tall, Varnuf's aged body clutched in one of its great branch-like claws. As she watched, the giant closed its hand into a fist and burst the shrieking king like a blood-gorged tick.

As a warm, peaceful darkness washed over her, Liandra heard the cries of battle fading away, drowned out by a soft, inviting harmony. It was a sound strange to her ears, yet it seemed dear and familiar to her soul, as if it had always been there inside her, biding its time.

The voice of the forest.

Caradryel had ever been a light sleeper. A few too many dalliances with married ladies had impressed the habit upon him. Now, the uncomfortable weight of his new duties only added to his sleeplessness. Inveigled in the confidences of those opposed to the king, only to then be appointed steward by that same king! He had to hand it to Caledor – he was as cunning as a jackal. It certainly couldn't be lost on him that Caradryel's appointment would make his detractors assume the new steward had betrayed them. Given the intrigues Caradryel had been involved in before taking service with House Tor Caled, he had to concede that such suspicions weren't completely irrational. With a suspected traitor to worry about, the king's enemies would be taking pains to be as discreet and unobtrusive as possible.

While at the same time seeing what steps they could initiate to remove the elf who'd betrayed them.

That cheery notion focused Caradryel's thoughts on the sound that had awoken him. Straining his ears, he waited for it to be repeated. His vigilance was rewarded several minutes later when he heard a footfall sound from the direction of the door. The sound that had disturbed him was that door being opened. Now he listened as the intruder crept across the room.

Caradryel had taken up the practice of sleeping with a dagger strapped to his arm. He drew the blade now, holding it behind his back to conceal its presence. He wasn't skilled at throwing a blade, indeed he was doubtful of his facility with any weapon, but assumed his chances would be better the closer his enemy was. Holding his breath, he waited while the creeping steps drew closer.

When he judged the owner of those footsteps to be somewhere near the foot of his bed, Caradryel did something he was certain would take his guest by surprise. Although he wasn't a mage by any stretch of the imagination, he'd spent enough time visiting the courts of Saphery to learn a few small tricks, such as the cantrip he now evoked. Shutting his eyes, he conjured up a dazzling flare of light that instantly threw the darkened room into brilliance.

Caradryel felt the bed shiver as something violently slammed into it. Opening his eyes again, he found a dagger stuck into the sheets and a blinded elf standing beside his bed groping for the weapon. Outraged that this coward should steal in here and try to murder him in his sleep, Caradryel lashed out with his own blade, raking it across the would-be assassin's hand.

The intruder recoiled in both pain and surprise. Caradryel was shocked himself when his attacker lowered his arm to clutch at his injured hand. The elf's features were far from unknown to him.

'Hulviar,' Caradryel gasped.

The outburst was a mistake. Snarling, the seneschal turned towards the sound of Caradryel's voice and lunged at him. Hulviar's hands closed about Caradryel's neck, thumbs pressing against his windpipe.

Caradryel stabbed his dagger into Hulviar's breast, plunging it again and again into his attacker. Just when he thought he'd surely be throttled before the seneschal expired, he felt Hulviar's grip relax. With a groan, the assassin collapsed on top of him. Caradryel shoved the corpse aside, letting it crash to the floor.

The door to his chambers burst inwards a moment later. Caradryel found himself staring at a pair of armoured White Lions, the king's own bodyguard. He could imagine the spectacle he must present – covered in blood, a bloodied dagger in his hand and the blood-soaked corpse of the king's seneschal lying practically at his feet.

Caradryel started to speak, to offer an explanation for the grisly scene, but before he could, the White Lions were surging towards him.

'Are you unharmed, my lord?' one of the guards inquired, plucking at his nightshirt to check for wounds. 'The sentry outside your door is dead,' he added, answering a question that hadn't occurred to Caradryel until that moment.

'It is lucky you chose to check on me when you did,' Caradryel said.

The White Lion shook his head. 'It wasn't luck, my lord. We were conducting a messenger to see you.' He nudged the corpse of Hulviar with his foot. 'Lord Hulviar said he would awaken you, but the messenger said his report couldn't wait. It was at his insistence that we came when we did.'

Caradryel looked past the guards to the doorway. Once again he was shocked to recognise a visitor. First an assassin proved to be Lord Hulviar, then a messenger was revealed to be Lord Athinol.

The highborn bowed as he stepped towards the bed. 'Forgive my intrusion, but the tidings I bear are of the utmost urgency.' He looked down at Hulviar. 'Maybe more urgent than any of us know. A fleet has been spotted sailing out from the Sea of Chill. A fleet of black sails and floating fortresses. A druchii fleet.'

The news sent a thrill of horror through Caradryel. He stared down at Hulviar. At first he'd thought the seneschal had tried to murder him in accord with some orders Caledor had left behind. Now he knew it was a different master Hulviar had served. Not all who believed in Malekith's right to the Phoenix Crown were druchii. There were still some in the ten kingdoms who thought the Witch King was their rightful lord and master. How carefully Malekith must have plotted to get one of these traitorous asur so close to Caledor. Hulviar, always at the king's shoulder, dispensing his poisoned advice and encouraging the king's excesses.

The War of the Beard, this thoughtless, wasteful conflict with the dawi – It was nothing but a scheme concocted by Malekith to weaken Ulthuan, to give him time to rebuild his forces and invade. While the asur struggled against the dawi, the druchii had been given the time to build their ships and armies. Feigning weakness, pretending to be on the verge of defeat, Malekith had hidden his real strength until now, until the moment when Ulthuan was most vulnerable.

'There is no time to waste,' Caradryel declared. 'All defences must be readied against invasion. I'll need a fast ship and a dependable crew. The king must be informed and he must bring the army back from Elthin Arvan.'

High King Gotrek stood on the broken battlements of the outer wall, facing towards the yet unconquered city. It was the third time that the king had climbed up onto the structure and addressed the enemy inside the city. In the two weeks since the arrival of the Phoenix King, the dawi had yet to catch a glimpse of the hated Caledor. By his display, Gotrek wanted to let both dawi and elgi alike know that he wasn't afraid to show himself, unlike his foe.

'A hundred-weight of gold shall be the price for Karak Hirn. A hundred-weight of gold shall be the price for Karak Izor. A thousand-weight of gold shall be the price of Barak Varr.' High King Gotrek's voice boomed out from Tor Alessi's ruined battlements, hurled like a spear at the city before him by the great brass horns into which he spoke. Some connivance of the engineers' guild had led to the crafting of the device, an invention to both magnify and project the king's voice.

It was the third time, too, that Gotrek had read his demands – demands for the wergild that the dwarfs would have from the elgi. There had been no response to his prior readings, only the defiant silence of the inner wall and the city beyond.

As he read through the list, Gotrek stared up at the great towers of Tor Alessi, blackened by the smoke of war, cracked by the few stones that had managed to strike them. Above each of the spires flew the hated banners of the Phoenix King. From across the whole of the Karaz Ankor, Gotrek's subject kings had come, seeking restitution from the elgi. Only Varnuf of Karak Eight Peaks and Zar of Karak Zorn had failed to come. The kings had spent days debating how much wergild to demand from the elgi and how great should be the share of each stronghold. It had been a tedious process and one in which the king placed no faith.

The elgi would pay no ransom, no restitution. The only thing to be gained by such talk had already been accomplished – the gathering of a throng vast enough to tear down the city with their bare hands. By coaxing the other kings to Tor Alessi, Gotrek had assembled an army unlike anything seen since the days of Snorri Whitebeard.

It was an army that would bring him not gold, but the head of the elgi king.

Gotrek finished reading his list of demands and turned away from the array of horns. He saw the kings of the dawi waiting for him below, their expressions eager, goldlust smouldering in their eyes. Much nearer to him was his nephew Morgrim. His expression was far less eager. The High King hadn't been able to deceive his heir about his intentions.

'Ready the grudge throwers,' Gotrek told Morgrim. 'And tell Morek... Tell him he may do as he judges necessary.'

The last remark made Morgrim wince more than when the wound in his side pained him. 'There must be another way.'

Gotrek sighed and ran his fingers through his beard. 'There is. We can sit here for months, maybe years, trying to break the elgi. We can't starve them out – they'll just get supplies from the sea, so it will mean wearing them down, stone by stone. That will mean more dawi sent to wander the halls of their ancestors.'

'The elgi might pay,' Morgrim suggested. 'But would that satisfy you?'

'No,' the king confessed. 'But if the elgi pay, I am now obligated to accept. I have to abide by my word to them. To do less would be... like breaking an oath.' Gotrek pointed at the city, waving his finger at it. 'They won't pay,' he declared. 'Their king is too arrogant for that. He'd sooner see his whole kingdom burn than admit weakness. Such is the way of boastful braggarts with more pride than brains.'

Gotrek locked eyes with Morgrim. 'See that the grudge throwers are ready. Remind the crews of their targets. We'll give the elgi until sunset to answer our demands, then I will order the attack. The kings of the Karaz Ankor will simply have to content themselves with whatever plunder they can loot from the rubble when we're through.

'Tor Alessi will fall and the Phoenix King will die,' Gotrek decreed, clenching his fist. 'By Grungni and Grimnir, I'll hear Caledor draw his last breath and watch the light fade from his eyes.'

The council chamber of the Tower of the Winds was filled with the great and powerful of Tor Alessi – the nobles, mages, priests and warlords who commanded the respect and fealty of the asur colonists. Their numbers had been swelled by the generals and highborn who had made the voyage from Ulthuan with the Phoenix King. Lady Aelis sat in the old seat from which she had once adjudicated Elthin Arvan's Council of Five. Now, of course, her authority was superseded by that of Caledor. The king made that much immediately clear. Aelis called the meeting right after Gotrek issued his demands, but Caledor had kept them waiting until well into the afternoon before making his appearance and initiating the conference.

'If you were to pay the dawi, we could earn concessions from them. They would withdraw to their mountains and leave us to our lands,' Aelis appealed to the king.

From the high throne of Tor Alessi's council chamber, the same chair that had once been occupied by his brother Prince Imladrik, King Caledor scowled down at Lady Aelis. She had ever been too timid of temperament for the war, an asset that had been exploited by the barrage of generals the king had sent to the colonies over the years. The fact that she saw opportunity in the dwarf demands was something that seemed to Caledor to border on complete idiocy.

'You would have us pay these animals for burning our cities and killing our people?' Caledor's tone was sharp enough to cut steel. 'And what happens the next time one of their mud-eating wretches stubs his toe crossing our lands? Do we bend our knee and pay another ransom to these brutes?' He shook his head, incredulous at the idea. 'Are we the children of Asuryan? Are we the proper masters of the world? Are we the asur? Or are we dogs to grovel and cringe at the grumbling of a mole-king?' Caledor smacked the flat of his hand against the arm of the throne. 'By all the gods, we will not pay this bastard or his dirty mob of badgers. He'll get no gold from me, only steel!'

'Then what, my liege, are your plans to lift the siege? The dwarfs have had us encircled for almost a year and show no signs that they intend to leave of their own accord.' The question came from Lord Ilendril. The grey lord had arrived at the meeting of Tor Alessi's high and mighty arrayed in his finest cloak and robes, resplendent in the finery his exile in Elthin Arvan had enabled him to acquire. He'd wanted to attract the king's attention by displaying his wealth and prestige. As he felt the king's eyes turn to him, Ilendril immediately regretted his decision. The monarch's gaze was like having a dagger pressed to his throat.

'My plans are just that,' the king growled. '*Mine*. Do not think that I have not heard your claims of mastery over the dragons. It reminds me that my father cast you out of Ulthuan for such ideas. It reminds me that when Prince Thoriol, my nephew and heir, lay alone and bleeding on the battlefield, you and your wyrm flew away. I wonder, then, Lord Ilendril, are you a charlatan? Is your mastery perhaps less firm than you claim? I would hope such is the case. It would pain me to think that you abandoned my heir of your own accord.' The king sneered as he watched the arrogant poise wilt off Ilendril's face. 'Your beast is undependable, Ilendril. Your role in my plans is to safeguard the refugee ships. See if you can manage at least that much.'

Thoriol looked up at his uncle from where he sat among the Council of Five, in the seat that had once been Lord Gelthar's. 'Refugees? Do you mean to abandon Tor Alessi?'

Caledor laughed. 'Not one inch are we abandoning to these moles,' he declared. 'But we will evacuate the city. My warriors will fight better without the confusion of panicked civilians getting in their way. The people will be moved to the ships and taken to Sith Remora or some other settlement.' A cunning gleam shone in his eye as he raised one finger. 'But they won't be the only ones to leave. Under cover of the evacuation, half the warriors I've brought will likewise board ships. They will sail a few leagues down the coast, far enough to be beyond the notice of the dwarfs. Then they will make landfall and march with all haste to assault the besiegers from the rear. As soon as the attack is under way, I will lead a sally from Tor Alessi. The mud-eaters will be caught between us.' Caledor laughed again. 'It was very obliging of this High King of the short folk to bring so many of his brutish subjects here. It affords us the chance to wipe them out in one go, rather than ferreting them out of their holes in the mountains.'

'It is unwise to underestimate them, my liege,' Thoriol warned.

'Ever the voice of caution,' Caledor declared. 'You are much like your father. That is why you shall have the honour of leading the contingent that takes the dwarfs from behind. I can depend on your judgement. If you do not think there is a real chance for success, then you are to hold back. Unless your forces attack, I will keep my troops inside the walls.'

The king's expression was almost benign as he nodded at Thoriol. 'Be wary of the dwarfs if you like, but do not let that wariness dull your eyes to the strengths of your own people. A king must have pride in his kingdom if it is to be prosperous.'

Whatever else the king might have said was forgotten as the entire chamber suddenly began to shake. Dust spilled down from the ceiling and cracks snaked across the walls. A dull, monstrous groan shuddered through the Tower of the Winds, almost drowning out the cries of shock and alarm that echoed through the halls.

Caledor's face was livid as he rose from the throne and brushed marble dust from his hair. He didn't join the rush of generals and nobles who flocked to the balcony to see for themselves the validity of the screams and shouts sounding all around them.

He'd expected the dwarfs to keep up their demands for wergild a few days more. That would have allowed the king time enough to bring his own schemes to fruition. The one time he needed the brutes to behave like stubborn children, the miserable creatures decided to play against type and take swift action.

'Aelis!' Caledor shouted. 'Get your people to their ships. Thoriol, embark your troops. The filthy beard-sniffers have forced an acceleration of my plans, but the strategy remains the same.' The king stumbled as the Tower of the Winds was slammed once more by one of the huge projectiles the dwarfs were hurling at the structure. His eyes blazed with outrage as he regained his footing.

'The dwarfs are so fond of their hammers and anvils – let us see how they like being caught between the two.'

The colossal grudge throwers growled as their arms snapped upright, casting tonnes of stone far into Tor Alessi. Raised by the dawi just behind the outer wall, the immense trebuchets had no shortage of ammunition, hurling rubble from the wall itself at the city. With expert aim, the artillerists lobbed their projectiles at the targets High King Gotrek had chosen for them – the three tallest towers in the city, the soaring spires of Winds, Sea and Dragon. Hundreds of feet higher than their closest neighbours, the towers were readily visible landmarks, ones that the artillerists had spent months demolishing in their imaginations.

Now they were turning that vision into reality.

Gotrek watched with grim satisfaction as the great blocks of stone slammed into the towers, raining rubble and debris into the streets below. With each impact, he could see the hated banners atop the towers tremble. It amused him to think of Caledor himself shivering away inside whatever hole he'd taken refuge in. Wherever it was, the dawi would drag him out into the light of their vengeance. His only real fear was that the elgi king might escape back to his island realm. The grudge throwers were the only weapons that could strike out into the harbour and menace the ships there, but to do so would mean diverting them away from their demolition of the towers, and that was something too crucial to Gotrek's battle plan.

While a few of the smaller onagers and mangonels attacked the inner wall, they weren't expected to batter a path for the dawi. Entry to the city would come from a different quarter, but to hold that breach, the dwarfs needed to keep the elgi from rushing reinforcements to the crucial zone.

The key to accomplishing that purpose was an especially satisfying one for the onlooking throngs of dwarfs. The great towers of Tor Alessi would be brought crashing down. So many centuries they had stood firm and defiant, mocking the warriors who waged thirteen sieges against the city. They wouldn't survive the fourteenth. The grudge throwers would see to that.

While Gotrek watched, one of the massive stone blocks crashed through the walls of the Tower of the Sea. Flashes of light played about the stone moments before it struck, the reaction of the runes etched into each missile by the runelords to dispel any enchantments the elgi cast to try to fend off the attack. As the stone struck, a cloud of dust exploded from the side of the wounded tower. Already holed in half a dozen places, this last impact was too much for the structure. Roaring like a dying god, the Tower of the Sea went crashing down, spilling its tonnes of stone across the outlying district, smashing neighbouring buildings and blocking entire streets with its enormity.

Gotrek turned his gaze from the fallen tower to watch as the attacks continued against the others. The grudge throwers aimed low, trying to cut the buildings off around their bases, ensuring the most destruction possible when they fell. It was a boon to the dawi that elgi construction owed more to aesthetics than durability. Tor Alessi was suffering now for the fragile compromise its people had made between pragmatism and artistry.

The city would fall, Every dawi assembled outside the wall knew it now. As the Tower of the Dragon came crashing down, the demolition was nearly drowned out by the fierce cries of 'Khazuk!' that rose from the mighty throng.

Gotrek looked towards the main gate leading into the city, at the strange crater where the elgi mages had destroyed the battering ram. Without knowing it, the enemy had helped the dawi with their sorcery. They'd made the job of bringing down the gate much simpler.

The High King descended from his view on the captured wall, climbing onto the Throne of Power and letting his hearthguard carry him out onto the field.

When the gates fell, he wouldn't be found lingering at the rear. Gotrek might not be the first inside Tor Alessi, but he was determined that both dawi and elgi would know that the High King of the Karaz Ankor was there for the final battle.

Lord Ilendril fumed as Malok lifted away from the trembling spires of the Tower of the Winds. The arrogance and temerity of King Caledor was a bitter pill to swallow. Far from the glory and acclaim he'd expected for his contributions to the war, he instead was subjected to the king's suspicious insinuations.

Looking out across Tor Alessi, Ilendril could see the devastation wrought by the Tower of the Sea as it came smashing down. Entire blocks were smashed flat, buildings crushed like bugs beneath a boot. Chunks of masonry, even entire walls were thrown into the air to come hurtling onto the heads of panicked survivors. The evacuation had started, but far from the orderly enterprise Caledor had planned, it was a chaotic rout, mobs of panicked elves streaming to the waterfront, herding themselves onto the ships designated to bear them away. It was only the presence of the Sea Guard that kept them from mobbing the vessels that were to take Thoriol's army down the coast to attack the dwarfs from behind.

Thoriol's army! Ilendril struck his fist against Malok's scaly neck as he thought of the glory and honours that awaited the feeble prince when he led that attack. An unaccomplished, insignificant nobody whose only achievement was being sired by Imladrik. By all the Cadai, it was insufferable. That whelp leading an army while Ilendril was squandered playing nursemaid to a refugee rabble.

Distracted by his ire, Ilendril didn't notice when his dragon shifted slightly in its flight. His control over the wyrm was almost complete, but there were slight gaps in his domination – limits that Malok had learned over its centuries of enslavement. If the dragon openly defied Ilendril or tried to rebel, the elf would know it in an instant. So the wyrm was much more cautious than that. It knew it couldn't expose its master to danger, but the same rule didn't necessarily apply to itself.

Before Ilendril was aware of what was happening, Malok had flown not out towards the bay, but across the lines of the dawi. Ballistae cast their spears at the huge wyrm, great iron lances with rune-inscribed heads. One of the spears raked across Malok's side, gouging a deep furrow in the creature's scaly flesh. Fiery blood spilled from the wound, pelting the walls as the dragon roared in pain and hastily pulled away.

Ilendril screamed, clutching at his own bleeding side, his body suffering the sympathetic stigmata that was the side effect of his enslaving magic. The elf lord's endurance was considerable, but it was paltry beside the primordial constitution of a dragon. While the asur was yet debilitated by the agony surging through him, the dragon was exploiting the resultant loss of control.

Malok threw its powerful body into a spinning dive. The ferocious drive of wind and gravity caused the straps of the saddle, already weakened by the dwarf spear, to snap. Ilendril was flung from his seat and sent hurtling through the sky.

The wyrm was after Ilendril in an instant, snatching him up in its mighty claws like a hawk swooping on a dove. Malok raked one of its long talons down Ilendril's body, splitting the elf's armour and slashing the body beneath. The fang hanging about Ilendril's neck, the talisman that allowed him to control the dragon, was ripped loose to plummet to the earth far below.

Malok's baleful eyes glared at the maimed elf who had enslaved it. Tightening its grip, the dragon held the screaming asur tight as it flew towards the refugee ships Ilendril had been tasked to defend. Helpless, Ilendril watched as the wyrm spat its fire onto one of the packed vessels. Hundreds of elves were consumed as flames erupted across the ship, as its sails became fiery shrouds and its decks became a blazing holocaust.

Bellowing its wrath, the dragon set upon a second ship and then a third. As Malok approached a fourth vessel, it noticed that no more screams sounded from the mangled elf it held in its claws. Glaring at Ilendril's corpse, feeling cheated of its revenge, the dragon cast the body down onto the deck of the ship it had been stalking. The elf lord struck with such force that the body bounced overboard, sinking into the waves.

Malok shrieked, a sound of terrible, bestial triumph, and wheeled away. The horror-struck elves below watched as the rampaging beast winged its way towards the south.

Enslaved for so long, Malok was seeking a lonely place far from dawi and elgi, a place in which it could sleep and brood and nurture its bitter hatred of both.

The best tunnellers in the miners' guild had excelled themselves, forcing the passages that led from behind the outer wall to the crater left by the elgi wizards. The need for secrecy, the speed with which the shafts had to be cleared, the pressure of working right under the noses of the enemy, all of these had added to the difficulties of their task. Should a single elf scout notice them, should any elgi mage divine their presence, then the entire plan would be undone – most likely in a way that would see the very tunnels they were digging collapse on their heads.

Morgrim reflected on the ghastly moments when it had seemed just such a thing must happen, when the beams overhead appeared to sag beneath the weight of the dawi warriors on the battlefield above. It would have been too conspicuous to leave any gaps in the dwarf lines, too suspicious for a clear path to exist between the dawi and the gate. The miners had accepted the added burden, compensating by using wutroth beams rather than common oak for the tunnel supports. Some of the diggers had even relished the novelty, employing wood commonly reserved for only the most prestigious projects on so mundane a purpose.

Yet, truly, could there be anything more prestigious than helping to break the walls of Tor Alessi and bringing an end to the War of Vengeance at last? Morgrim certainly didn't think so. There would be honours and glory enough to share when the victory was done and he was determined that the miners' contribution wouldn't be forgotten.

From a side passage, Morgrim could see Runelord Morek ambling out into the crater lying before the main gates of Tor Alessi. Morek's staff hummed with the arcane vibrations of his magic, cloaking him from the eyes of the elgi on the walls above. In the dark of night Ironbreakers had already brought forward one of the Anvils of Doom, depositing it at the far end of the pit. It stood there, black with age, pulsing with the uncanny forces that were the runelord's art. A feeling of dreadful anticipation pulsed through Morgrim's veins. Even Gotrek wasn't privy to the details of what Morek was going to do. All they knew was that the runelord had promised to bring down the gate.

Morek had asked one further thing of Morgrim and Gotrek – that when all was done, when the battle was recorded in the annals of the dawi, that his own role should be forgotten. He offered the key to victory, but the price was his own anonymity. There might be glory for Gotrek and Morgrim, but Morek said there would only be infamy for himself if his role were made known. He would be the lowest of oathbreakers in the eyes of his fellow runelords, a criminal without compare.

Drawing close to the Anvil, Morek slammed his runestaff into the earth beside it. Raising his arms as best he could, the twisted dwarf began to call out in a strange tongue, an ancient variant of Khazalid that was unknown to any outside the order of runesmiths. Eerie letters of fire flashed before his hands, speeding away from his fingers to stream down into the Anvil. The blackened surface of the relic began to glow a dull crimson, turning to a flaming orange as the fiery runes continued to seep down into it.

Morgrim had to shield his eyes when the Anvil turned white-hot. An afterimage of Morek with his hands upraised lingered in his vision. The next instant, the passage was shaken by a tremendous explosion. A thunderous roar rolled down the tunnel, assailing the ears of every dwarf. Mephitic odours wracked their senses, and a sorcerous chill plucked at their beards. Many of the warriors with Morgrim made the signs of Valaya and Grungni, invoking the ancestor gods for forgiveness and protection from what they'd unleashed.

When Morgrim could see again, Morek and the Anvil were gone, obliterated by the forces the runelord had summoned. So too was the gate, ripped asunder by the arcane explosion – not so much as a splinter remained between the immense columns that flanked the once-door.

'Ladders!' Morgrim shouted to his troops. At their thane's command, waves of dwarfs surged out from the side passages and into the crater, raising their ladders and scrambling into the breach. A few arrows shot down at them from the elgi on the walls, but far too few to turn back the tide.

As he rushed through the crater to join his warriors, Morgrim reflected sombrely on the terrible sacrifice Morek had made. Deliberately destroying an Anvil of Doom, risking the unending infamy of his name and the shame of his entire line. It was a hideous prospect, one that Morgrim hoped he would never face. The choice between shame and the welfare of the dawi race.

Balanced against what he'd done, anonymity was the kindest reward Morek Furrowbrow could have hoped for.

From the crater, the dwarfs spilled out into the city. Detachments of crossbows flanked the walls, picking off elgi archers from behind. Axes and hammers rushed to clear the gatehouse, cutting down the garrison before they could mobilise and try to close the breach. Already a great throng of dwarfs was charging across the plain, cascading towards the shattered gate, thousands of warriors eager to at last seize the city that had defied them over so many sieges.

The elgi were waiting for them at every turn, contesting every street. Each building, each square became a scene of unspeakable carnage – a red ruin of heaped bodies, splintered mail and broken blades. Griffons and eagles soared down from the roofs, tearing at the dwarfs with beak and talon. Archers infested every window, loosing arrows until dawi fighters smashed their way into each strongpoint and wrought a final reckoning upon the bowmen with axe and hammer. Phalanxes of spears blocked entire avenues, defying the determined dwarfs, forcing them to smash their way through the stabbing, thrusting steel to close upon the elven warriors.

The dwarfs fought on, paying no heed to their own hurts, forgetting for the moment the dead and dying comrades they left behind as they burrowed their way ever deeper into the city. Grudge throwers smashed a breach through the old wall separating the New City from the Old City, opening the way for the dawi to the harbour and the market districts, to the hill where the great temple of Asuryan stood with its marble roof and gilded columns, to the opulent manors of the merchants and sea-traders who had once brought such prosperity to the city.

Morgrim led his hearthguard through the thick of the fighting, Azdrakghar flashing out in great cleaving blows that left elgi torn and maimed wherever the thane found them. It was when he was bringing his warriors against a regiment of spearmen trying to defend a barricade thrown across the Street of Autumn that Morgrim first heard the cries and shouts rising from dawi outside the walls. He forced himself to focus on the fight at hand, to forget the promise that lay behind those excited shouts, those vengeful roars.

Only when the barricade was taken, when hundreds of elgi spearmen had been killed or routed, did Morgrim really listen to the voices of the dwarfs. The colours of the Phoenix King had risen once again, the dragon and phoenix flying above the great square at the heart of the Old City – the Founders' Square, where the elgi had set down the first stones of what would become Tor Alessi.

'Caledor,' Morgrim growled, wiping the blood from his axe with a cloak he'd ripped from the corpse of an asur captain. 'The maggot is making a stand.' In his mind he could see again the elgi king as he duelled Snorri Halfhand and brought the prince to destruction.

'Beware, Morgrim,' Khazagrim cautioned. 'It could be a trick, bait to lure us into a trap.'

Morgrim shook his head. In his gut he knew Khazagrim was wrong. He'd seen the elgi king, seen the arrogance and contempt with which he had fought Snorri's army. Thick in the fighting, Khazagrim hadn't taken away the same impression of the Phoenix King that Morgrim had. Caledor wouldn't try to trick them because the elf didn't think he needed deceit to conquer enemies so far beneath him.

'He'll be there,' Morgrim declared. 'He'll be there to challenge us, to prove himself our better. He thinks he'll teach the dawi a lesson about his own superiority. That is why he shows his flag, why he tells us where he is.'

Morgrim brought his axe sweeping around, shattering a marble column standing before a herbalist's shop. 'We'll teach the dog a lesson instead, a lesson he can take away with him when he goes down to elgi hell!'

Founders' Square was a vast expanse sprawling at the centre of the Old City. Markets and workshops fronted onto the square, as did the halls of the various artisan associations and craft-schools. Diamondsmiths and sculptors, enchanters and armourers, silk-weavers and conjure-workers, all had their businesses facing in upon the birthplace of Tor Alessi. The immense municipal hall and the colossal High Library stretched along much of the northern perimeter, their mighty towers staring down upon the market below.

The square itself was tiled with mosaics depicting the legends and heroic history of the asur. Lavish fountains with golden statues and alabaster basins were scattered about the expanse, each fountain devoted to one of the elven gods. The waters bubbling from each statue were coloured to match their respective deity – dark crimson for bloody-handed Khaine, rich azure for the creator-god Asuryan, sombre emerald for the wild huntsman Kurnous.

In the middle of the square, a massive obelisk of granite rose, towering a hundred feet in the air. Down the sides of the obelisk, etched in glyphs of ithilmar, were the names of those asur who'd first settled Tor Alessi. Once, other symbols had flanked those glyphs, sharp dwarfish runes of gold to remember the dawi who had befriended the asur and helped them raise their city. The Khazalid runes had been effaced long centuries ago, carefully excised when the news came to Tor Alessi that Imladrik had been slain.

King Caledor looked up at the obelisk. It was from the summit of that memorial that the king's banner now flew, declaring to his brutish enemies where he was. Even a dwarf would have enough wit to find him with such a marker to guide them onwards.

The king leaned back in the saddle of his steed, a white charger named Torment. The horse was of the blood of Tiranoc, sired by one of the few remaining stallions of the royal herd of that battered kingdom. The royal stallions of Tiranoc stood sixteen hands high, broader and stouter of build than any other horses in Ulthuan. Their hooves had a hardness to them that was like iron even before they were shod. The bold hearts and sharp minds of the animals were unmatched by any steed born of common stock. Fiercer than a tempest, Torment was the only horse Caledor would deign to ride into battle. When the royal bloodline of Tiranoc's herd was spent, it would indeed be a sorry day for the highborn of Ulthuan.

'Soon,' Caledor whispered into his steed's ear, feeling the animal's restlessness. Around him, the chargers of his knights stamped and snorted anxiously. They could smell the smoke and blood on the air. The war horses were dependable enough once battle was joined, but like the warriors mounted upon them, it was the anticipation of conflict that made them uneasy. It was the mark of lowborn blood – the same in horse as it was in elf. It took nobility to truly appreciate war, and the higher the quality of the blood, the more keen that appreciation. Caledor and Torment didn't feel anxious. No, they looked forward to the coming fight, secure in their understanding that no foe could be their equal, no enemy their master. Doubt was a vice of the common stock, not royal blood.

There were hundreds of knights and horsemen gathered in Founders' Square. The best and boldest cavalry from Caledor's fleet and Tor Alessi's army had been put directly under the king's command. Supporting them were hundreds of archers positioned in the towers of the municipal hall and the library, scattered across the roofs of the markets and shops. Regiments of swordsmen crowded inside the buildings, ready to join the fray when they were given the signal.

Caledor doubted he would need the infantry. His knights would be enough to cut down the dawi. The filthy mud-eaters seemed to recognise that fact. A few had appeared at the southern end of the square, but they'd withdrawn fast enough when they saw the force arrayed against them. The miserable moles were bold enough in their talk of fighting the Phoenix King, but when they had the opportunity, they soon lost heart.

'My liege,' Lady Aelis addressed the king. She'd adopted a mantle of silver chain and ithilmar plate over which she wore a silk surcoat bearing the heraldry of Tor Alessi. The stallion she rode was a decent-enough example of colonial stock, though far inferior to the herds of Ulthuan.

'My liege,' Aelis repeated until the king deigned to look at her. 'I advise that you position more warriors to protect the streets leading down to the bay. The dawi know you are here and they will certainly try to cut off any avenue of escape.'

Caledor glared at her, his face twisting into a sneer. 'Escape? That sounds like the sort of thing a defeatist might suggest. No, I am here to fight these animals, not run from them. My legacy will be one of courage, not retreat.' He slapped his armoured hand against the golden breastplate he wore. 'The Skin of Vaul,' he declared, 'forged in the fires of the gods themselves and entrusted to the kings of Ulthuan.' He tapped a finger against his helm with its great dragon-wings and snarling reptilian face. 'The Dragonshard,' he named the ancient relic, 'sculpted around a scale from Indraugnir himself.' His hand raised to point at the gleaming crown wrapped about the helm. 'The Phoenix Crown, the glory of our people and the ten kingdoms. These are the symbols of my power. I did not carry them across the sea to flee at the first twitch of a mud-eater's whisker!' He pointed his mailed hand towards the seaward streets. 'Join your people. Help them escape if that is your intent.'

The king looked away smiling as he saw a great body of dwarfs tromping towards the square. This time the dawi weren't darting back the way they'd come. This time the enemy was marching to battle.

'Leave the fighting to warriors,' Caledor dismissed Aelis. 'Leave the glory to those worthy of it.'

The warriors of Morgrim Elgidum were the first to march out into the Founders' Square. Though a few scouts had been there before him, it had been generally agreed that the attack against Caledor should be led by the mighty hero of the dawi.

Despite his conviction that Caledor was too arrogant to run, Morgrim couldn't shake a sense of unreality when he led his hearthguard out across the tiles, past the bubbling fountain of Isha and towards the waiting line of elgi cavalry. After so long dreaming of this moment, it was hard to come to grips with the fact that the dream had become reality. He, Morgrim Ironbeard, was getting his chance to bring down the king of the elgi.

The elves waited until the dwarfs were a hundred yards out onto the square before launching their attack. Caledor raised his armoured hand, the jewels set into each joint gleaming in the sunlight. Boldly he dropped his hand and gave the signal to charge. With a thunder of hooves, the knights and horsemen galloped across the square. Morgrim could feel the mosaics shivering beneath his boots as the vibrations of the charge shook them.

'Set shields!' Morgrim bellowed out. Khazagrim dipped his standard, alerting the hearthguard to their leader's command. The warriors closed ranks, locking arms and shields with the fighters beside them, forming a single block of dwarfish steel and muscle to oppose the onrushing cavalry.

Arrows whistled down from the towers and roofs on the opposing side of the square, a furious volley designed to break the dwarf formation. A few of the dawi fell to the descending arrows, struck in face or throat. Most of the arrows, however, simply clattered off the thick steel plates of their armour or got caught in the sturdy oak of their shields.

Just as the elves tried to undermine the dwarf strategy, so too did Morgrim loose his own plans to blunt the elgi attack. 'Give the sign,' Morgrim shouted into Khazagrim's ear. The old warrior hefted the thane's banner high, thrusting it up and down several times in the air. In response, trumpeters hidden in the buildings on the left flank of the square blew a blast of monstrous noise from their instruments. The roaring cachinnation struck when the charge was still many yards away from the dwarf formation. Assailed by the noisy tumult, many of the horses were thrown into panicked confusion. They reared back, stamping their hooves and kicking at the air. Some were bowled over by the horses coming after them, spilling across the square in a miserable tangle of injured mounts and riders.

Not all of the cavalry were undone. The boldest of the steeds managed to maintain their charge, rushing at the dwarfs in a wave of steel barding and silk tabards. At their head, an ivory-gripped lance held before him, was Caledor himself. The Phoenix Crown was dazzling, almost blinding as the king brought his knights smashing into the dawi ranks. Morgrim conceded a grudging respect that the Phoenix King had ensured his foes would recognise him even in the fury of battle.

The elven knights slammed into the dwarfs, slaughtering a dozen in their first rush, the steel-tipped lances driven clean through their thick armour by the momentum of the attack. The locked shields and stubborn resistance of the dawi prevented the charge from punching through to the rearward ranks, however. After that first horrendous crash, the elves found themselves pinned in place by Morgrim's warriors. The elves didn't waste time trying to free their lances, but cast the weapons aside the instant their charge faltered. With almost machine-like synchronisation, the knights drew their swords and cast about them at their foes.

Morgrim fended off the blade of one knight, blocking it with the haft of his axe before bringing Azdrakghar swinging around to cleave the leg from the elgi's horse. As the animal collapsed, he brought the axe chopping down into the knight's head, splitting helm and skull like a melon.

Turning from his vanquished foe, Morgrim was barely able to avoid the downward slash of another elgi blade. He jerked back, almost stumbling over the horse he'd killed. The thane blinked in shock when he saw the elf behind the slashing blade. 'Caledor!' he roared, spitting the name as though it were the vilest of curses.

'You are the vaunted Elfdoom?' the elgi king taunted, his words rolling off his tongue in a precise if stilted Khazalid. 'You are the maggot who killed my brother?' The king's blade flashed out once more, slicing across Morgrim's pauldron and nearly splitting the steel in half. Forged for the Great War against Chaos, Dawnkiller was meant to spill the essence of the mightiest daemons. Before the enchantments woven into the blade, Morgrim's armour was little more than paper.

'You are the scum who killed my prince,' Morgrim snarled back. He lunged at the elf lord, but Caledor kicked his horse, causing Torment to rear and lash out at the dwarf with its steel-shod hooves. One of the flailing hooves cracked against Morgrim's helm, staggering him and forcing him back.

Caledor moved to exploit the opening, stabbing down with Dawnkiller. The ithilmar blade pierced Morgrim's shoulder, drawing a ragged cry from the hero, but instead of reeling, he brought Azdrakghar swinging back around. The axe cracked against Caledor's shield, almost splitting it in two. Morgrim grunted as he tried to pull his blade free, then his breath caught in his throat. The axe was stuck fast, refusing to budge from the rent in the shield.

The elf king cried out in pain – the impact of Morgrim's axe had nearly broken his arm. Digging his spurs into the flanks of Torment, Caledor brought the animal spinning around, dragging Morgrim after it. The dwarf was battered as the horse's stomping hooves pounded against him, but he held fast to the haft of his axe. Even as the hooves knocked teeth from his mouth, turned his nose to pulp and crushed one of his ears, he maintained his hold. At last, as the animal's fury waned, Morgrim set his feet and, exerting the full limit of his strength, wrenched his axe free.

Or so he thought. As Caledor turned to face him once more, Morgrim saw that he hadn't freed Azdrakghar at all – the elf king had simply released his shield, leaving it caught on the axe. Glaring at the thane, Caledor prepared to ride down the dwarf.

The thunderous roar of hundreds of voices howling the dawi war-cry boomed across the square. Dwarf warriors in their thousands had converged upon the battle. They swiftly spread out, surrounding the elgi king and his knights. More dawi drove in from the sides of the square, pushing before them the infantry Caledor had kept in reserve. Defying the arrows still whistling down at them from the roofs, the dwarfs were forcing their foes out, pushing them towards the fountains and the obelisk.

Caledor arrested Torment's charge, managing to maintain control over the horse even in the fury of the dwarf war-cry. The elf king kept Dawnkiller pointed at Morgrim and slowly turned his head, staring with consternation at the masses of bearded warriors all around him. Morgrim's bloodied face pulled back into a smile. Caledor was trapped and he was being forced to face that fact.

'So this is how it ends,' Caledor growled at Morgrim. 'A lion brought down by jackals.'

'No, a dragon felled by a king,' a grim voice called out from the direction of the broken gate. Both Morgrim and Caledor turned to see the hearthguard forcing their way through the press of dwarf warriors. Behind them, carried aloft upon the shoulders of his thronebearers, seated upon his ancient Throne of Power, was High King Gotrek Starbreaker.

When his thronebearers reached the square, Gotrek bade them lower him to the ground. Tightening his hold on the haft of his axe, the king stepped out from among his hearthguard.

Caledor sneered at the dwarf king. 'I had imagined that the High King would be taller,' he mocked. 'Am I to understand that you mean to challenge me?'

'If you have the spine for it,' Gotrek snarled back in the rudimentary Eltharin he'd learned from Forek many years ago. The way the elf smiled at his pronunciation only fed the fury boiling inside him. 'You killed my son, elgi. If you'd paid the wergild demanded by my kingdom, I would have been obliged to let you live.' Gotrek spat at the ground beneath Caledor's steed. 'Now I am under no such obligation.'

Caledor slowly dismounted. He looked into Torment's eyes, then with a shout and a swat of his hand against the animal's flank, he sent the horse galloping back towards the municipal hall where the elgi still held command. He watched the horse for a moment, then turned back towards Gotrek. 'What are the terms you offer, dwarf? What do I gain when I kill you, other than the pleasure of removing one more mole from this world?' He looked around at the glowering faces that lined the square. His surviving knights had withdrawn into a circle, presenting swords and shields to their enemies, but the dwarfs were making no effort to close upon them. Around the fountains of Mathlann and Vaul, hundreds of elgi soldiers were being squeezed by a ring of dawi axes. Even there, the fighting had stopped. All eyes were turned towards the two kings.

Gotrek unlimbered the axe strapped to his back. It was the most potent and venerable weapon in his armoury, a relic from the time of legend. The Axe of Grimnir, an heirloom from one of the ancestor gods, an artefact hoary with myth and history. As the High King took the weapon up in his hands, the ancient runes etched into its blade began to pulse with a violent crimson glow.

'Kill me, and there will be no grudgement,' Gotrek declared. 'You and your people will be allowed to leave with your lives.' He raised his hand, stifling the protest he saw in Morgrim's face. 'No dawi will defy the words of their High King.'

Caledor nodded, then abruptly sprang forwards. Dawnkiller licked out, raking across the meteoric iron of Gotrek's mail and striking sparks from the rune-etched armour. 'Fair enough,' the elf said. 'Let's have this done, shall we?'

Gotrek cracked the butt of his axe against Caledor's leg, driving the enemy king back. Then he tried to press his attack, bringing the Axe of Grimnir spinning about in a whirling sweep. The elf nimbly darted aside, retaliating with a gruesome jab that notched the dwarf's ear and sent blood coursing down his neck.

'Surely you can do better than that?' Caledor said.

'I intend to,' Gotrek growled back. The Axe of Grimnir flashed out in a murderous arc, striking for the elgi's legs. Caledor leapt over the strike, slashing down at the dwarfish axe. The impact unbalanced Gotrek, causing him to stagger forwards. The elf cracked Dawnkiller's pommel against the back of Gotrek's helm, provoking a further stagger.

Gotrek could feel the eyes of his ancestors, the eyes of Snorri, watching him as he reeled from Caledor's strike. The thought brought him spinning back around, slashing out with the Axe of Grimnir even as the elf king moved to exploit his foe's loss of balance. Caledor twisted to one side, fright on his features as the axe ripped across his waist and tore away his silk surcoat.

The High King of the Karaz Ankor would not be humiliated by this elgi. Gotrek wouldn't dishonour his ancestors in such fashion. He wouldn't allow the memory of Snorri Halfhand to become a mockery, to force his son's spirit to wander Gazul's halls lost and unavenged!

With a bestial roar, Gotrek turned his stagger into a charge, rushing at Caledor. A furious cascade of blows forced the elf into retreat, driving him back across the mosaics. Gotrek sneered as he watched Caledor's boots scrape across the face of ancient elgi heroes. That was the difference between elgi and dawi: the dawi honoured their ancestors, the elgi stepped on them.

The Axe of Grimnir raked down the blocking blade of Dawnkiller, both weapons seeming to scream as sparks flashed from them. Gotrek felt the tremble of Caledor's resistance rush down his own arm. Agility, finesse, these were the assets of the elgi, not strength and endurance. That failing would seal the fate of the Phoenix King.

With a hiss, Caledor swung away from Gotrek, freeing Dawnkiller and twisting away before the dwarf could bring his axe chopping back around. The elf leapt away, hopping onto the alabaster basin of one of the square's many fountains. The water that lapped about his armoured feet was dyed a vivid crimson and the golden statue that loomed above him was a grisly, savage-looking god with red water spilling from his snarling mouth.

'Do not look to your gods for help, tall-ears!' Gotrek snarled. He thrust up at Caledor, his axe missing the elf as he twisted away and instead cleaving a great gouge in the side of the basin. Gotrek cried out in sudden pain as Caledor brought Dawnkiller flashing back around, slashing the sword across the back of the dwarf's helm.

The meteoric iron was gashed by the blow, but even Dawnkiller was unable to penetrate the protective runes that defended the High King. A few wisps of hair were all that clung to Caledor's blade when he pulled it out from Gotrek's helm.

Bellowing in fury, Gotrek brought the Axe of Grimnir crashing against Caledor's shin. The gilded plate, despite the vaunted enchantments woven into it, split apart beneath the blow. The dwarf grinned when he saw blood boil up from beneath the cleft armour.

The next instant, Gotrek was knocked back, his nose split by a kick from Caledor's steel boot. He blinked as red pain seared across his vision, spat as the taste of his own blood streamed down into his mouth. He glared up at the elf, now circling above him on the rim of the basin. Caledor matched his gaze with one equally savage.

'That was almost admirable,' Caledor said, dabbing at his injured shin with a strip torn from his surcoat. Wincing in pain, he stuffed the silk down the rent in his armour, trying to stop the blood leaking from his body. When he spoke to Gotrek, however, it was with a scornful bravado. 'This duel might be interesting after all. Much more memorable than the one I had with your son. What was his name again?'

Hearing the elf mocking his dead son sent daggers of hate stabbing into Gotrek's brain. He trembled, feeling every muscle in his body engorged with the magnitude of his fury. Snarling, he lunged at his enemy, all craft and care abandoned in his bloodthirsty urge to kill.

Caledor was ready for him. Spinning around, he raked Dawnkiller across Gotrek's arm, slashing across the meteoric iron. The armour of Gotrek's gauntlet, however, wasn't so thick and ancient as the rest of his vestment and when Dawnkiller reached it, Caledor gave it a vicious twist. The turning steel ripped open Gotrek's hand, sending two of his fingers leaping in the air.

'Ah, yes,' Caledor grinned. 'Halfhand was what they called him.'

The elf had expected Gotrek to reel back in pain after his mutilation. He wasn't prepared when the dwarf spun back around and brought the Axe of Grimnir licking at his belly. Caledor was able to turn aside, but the blow caught him just the same, cleaving deeply into his knee. He cried out in agony as his leg crumpled under him.

The High King glared up at his reeling foe, vicious satisfaction in his eyes as he watched Caledor's blood dripping down into the fountain. 'Snorri Halfhand, son of Gotrek Starbreaker,' Gotrek snarled at his enemy. 'Felled by a treacherous elgi king unworthy to cross blades with a grobi.' He brought his axe flashing around once more.

Even injured, Caledor was able to bring Dawnkiller flashing out to intercept the descending axe. Again, the two weapons shrieked as the kings ground them against one another, striving to overwhelm the might of their foe.

'Your people are unworthy of *us*,' Caledor declared. 'What right have you to dare to contest the destiny of the asur? You should be honoured that we thought enough of you to let you see the majesty of our accomplishments!'

Gotrek ducked as Caledor brought Dawnkiller slashing at his head. The enchanted blade ripped across his helm once more, this time carving a deep notch in its side. Clenching his teeth against the pain from his mangled hand, fighting to keep his fingers firm on the haft of his axe despite the blood streaming down them, Gotrek struck back at his foe.

Caledor again tried to twist away. Even with his injured leg, the elf's agility might have served him once more if his foot hadn't settled in the notch the Axe of Grimnir had carved into the basin. Gotrek felt a thrill of anticipation when he saw his enemy unbalanced. It was only a heartbeat, only the briefest of moments, but it was enough. The Axe of Grimnir, impossible to dull, impossible to defy, slammed into Caledor's side. No glancing blow but a solid impact that made Gotrek's arms quiver. He could feel the golden armour break beneath that impact, he could hear the sharp crack as he split the elf's ribs.

Caledor slumped from the lip of the basin down into the crimson waters of the fountain. Now a darker red stained the mouth of Khaine as the Phoenix King's blood dripped down into the pool and was drawn up into the golden statue. Caledor stared in shock as Gotrek climbed into the fountain after him, the king's blood splashed across the Axe of Grimnir.

'You've drowned both our kingdoms in blood,' Gotrek growled at his enemy. 'But for your scornful pride, none of this had to happen.' He raised his axe on high, clasping it with both hands. Blood from his cut fingers dripped down onto the prostrate Caledor's face.

'Elthin Arvan is yours,' Caledor moaned. 'My kingdom will pay the wergild you ask. I will make full restitution for your losses.'

Gotrek glared down into the wounded king's eyes. He imagined the scene, that long-ago day when this villain had stood over his dying son and cut off his hand as a trophy to carry back to Ulthuan. Any semblance of pity was crushed in the High King's hate. 'Ask the gods for mercy. You'll find none in me.'

The Axe of Grimnir came chopping down, striking Caledor in the side of his neck. Bright arterial blood sprayed from the elf king's wound. The dying monarch clutched at his neck as though he might staunch the ebbing of his life with his own hands. It was a futile effort. Soon the gushing blood slowed to a trickle and Caledor II, Phoenix King of Ulthuan, collapsed in the red waters of the fountain. Above him, the golden statue of Khaine spat out a stream of royal blood.

The awed silence that had held the onlooking elgi and dawi crumbled as Caledor fell. From the elves, a terrible wail arose. Staring in stunned horror, the elgi watched as Caledor's killer reached down and plucked the Phoenix Crown from the dead king's head.

'Let this be the end of it,' Gotrek shouted, holding the crown high in his maimed hand. 'Let this be an end to the killing! I claim the crown of Caledor as restitution, as recompense for all that the Karaz Ankor has endured, for all of our dead, for all of our crippled!' The High King looked over at

Morgrim, cast his eyes across the throng of dwarf warriors gathered in the square. His gaze hardened as he looked again at the elves. 'Go to your ships, elgi. Leave the Old World. There is no place for you here.

'There never was.'

EPILOGUE

Thoriol stared back at Tor Alessi from the deck of his ship. Smoke billowed from the burning buildings. The broken stumps of towers reared into the sky like shattered teeth. The palaces on the hill overlooking the bay were little more than heaps of rubble, smashed to ruin by the dwarfish siege engines. He could see elves still making their way down to the harbour flanked by escorts of armoured dawi. The dwarfs were taking no chances, it seemed, that any asur would try to stay behind. Whatever their own feelings, they were following the decree of High King Gotrek to the letter. No elf would be harmed as long as they didn't try to remain in Elthin Arvan.

Elthin Arvan. Despite all the blood and treasure that had been spent trying to maintain the colonies, in the end they'd been lost just the same. Bitterness and regret tried to seize him, but all he could manage was a woeful weariness. He felt like a mourner watching as the body of a loved one was consigned to the flames.

More than just the colonies had been lost, however. Ulthuan had lost its king. Caledor II, the great warrior, cut down by Gotrek Starbreaker, the Phoenix Crown taken away as a trophy by the dwarfs. Briefly, Thoriol had entertained the idea of landing the warriors his uncle had placed under his command far down the coastline and trying to intercept the dawi before they could return to Karaz-a-Karak. The thought of losing the Phoenix Crown, of having such a priceless relic captured and carried off by an enemy, was almost too much to bear.

His fellow asur thought so too. They'd urged him to strike back, to carry the fight back to the dwarfs, to reclaim the crown whatever the cost. However suicidal the effort, reclaiming the crown of the Phoenix Kings was worthy of the effort.

Thoriol had almost laughed at that. The Phoenix Crown was naught but a symbol, the symbol of the ten kingdoms and Ulthuan. What good was the symbol if what it represented were brought to ruin?

The prince turned from his last view of Tor Alessi and faced the emissary who had journeyed from Lothern to bring tidings to Caledor that his kingdom was under attack. Not the far-flung colonies of the wilderness but the homeland itself.

When the galley from Ulthuan encountered refugee ships fleeing out to sea, when it found Tor Alessi being evacuated, the vessel had brought about and flown the pennant of Caledor's steward. The hulking troop ship Thoriol had embarked upon came about and rendezvoused with the galley, taking aboard the messenger from Lothern. The prince was surprised to find that the king's steward had come in person. Lord Caradryel of House Reveniol.

'Can we return in time?' Thoriol asked the steward, not for the first time.

Caradryel's face was grim. 'I don't know,' he confessed. 'There are certainly more optimistic ways to describe the situation, courtly words I could employ to downplay the catastrophe, but I respect you too much for such games. Besides, there isn't time for the usual courtesies.'

'Malekith.' Thoriol hissed the name, his fingers digging into his palms. It had been centuries since the usurper had dared threaten the shores of Ulthuan. The menace posed by him and his druchii traitors had seemed a dwindling one, as they faded from a renegade nation to small cabals of pirates and marauders. The asur had hounded them ever deeper into the wilds of Naggaroth, a land of such malignant hostility that it seemed nothing could survive there.

Caradryel nodded. 'The druchii have survived. No, more than that. In their own twisted way they have flourished in the Land of Chill. Their numbers have grown. They've raised new generations of traitors out in the wilds.'

'While we fought the dwarfs, Malekith was watching and waiting,' Thoriol said. 'He feigned weakness, letting us think him beaten. All the while he was raising new armies in secret, biding his time until Ulthuan was fully engaged against the dawi. Then, like a slinking serpent, the host of Naggaroth struck our homeland.'

'The druchii have raised the fortress of Anlec once more with their foul magics,' Caradryel said. 'They have landed warriors on the Blighted Isle. Even the loudest voices crying for calm, claiming these are naught but pirates, have been forced to admit it is a full-out invasion.' Caradryel fingered the ring he wore, the emblem of the Phoenix King emblazoned upon it. 'When we need him most, Caledor is lost to us. Who will lead the asur into battle without him? Who will stand up to the malice of Naggaroth?'

Thoriol shook his head. 'My uncle wasn't the kind to lead anyone. He could command, he could coerce and demand, but he couldn't lead. All his life he lived in the shadow of my grandfather and, in the end, it was as a shadow of my grandfather he died. A warrior like him has courage and he has determination, but he lacks the vision and the wisdom to be a conqueror.'

'You are wiser than your uncle,' Caradryel said. 'You have his courage, but you have your father's wisdom.'

'Do I?' Thoriol asked. 'Even if I were certain, even if I were everything you believe me to be, I couldn't take the crown. The people would see me as naught but my uncle's shadow. They would see in me the echo of the failures that brought us to this calamity. Ulthuan needs a new king to lead her, not Caledor III. I wonder if there isn't a curse against the blood of House Tor Caled, if the Witch King's spite hasn't infected our souls and made us poisonous to all we hold dear.'

'Fear the things you know and let the unknown attend itself,' Caradryel advised. 'Ulthuan needs a king. We need the unity and determinacy that only a king can provide.'

'I agree,' Thoriol said, smiling as he set his hand on Caradryel's shoulder. 'That is why when we return to Ulthuan I shall advise the Council of Princes, and any others who might care to listen, that in these dark times we need a king who can unite, not simply one who can win battles. I will advise them that there is only one highborn to my knowledge who can bring together the factions and divisions in our society that were caused by my uncle. That asur is you, Caradryel. You have the confidence of my mother and her supporters, but as my uncle's steward you will also have the loyalty of the late king's court.'

The colour drained out of Caradryel's face. He was clearly horrified by the prospect. 'But... I... I am no king.'

'That is why you must become one,' Thoriol said. 'It is those who covet the crown most who are least worthy of it.' Bitterness gripped the prince's features. 'But you'll need a new crown. Leave the old one to the dwarfs. Let its loss be a lesson to our people that pride has its price.'

Morgrim tipped his tankard as a regiment of axemen passed him in the street. A bit of the amber liquid sloshed down the side of the pewter cup, spilling onto his boots. The thane frowned as he considered the wasted ale. Before capturing the elgi city, the dawi warriors had ransacked their own baggage train, fortifying themselves with beer until the stores were all but depleted. Too many novices among the army – they thought to replenish the stores with what they captured from the elves. Morgrim hoped they had a taste for thin elven wines, otherwise it was going to be a terribly dry march back to the Karaz Ankor.

When the axemen passed, Morgrim continued his march towards the harbour. Every step he looked at the crumbling splendour of Tor Alessi. More than simply the ruin of war, the city seemed to be visibly withering before his eyes. The beauty and lustre of its palaces and pavilions were wilting, unable to suffer the harsh glow of conquest. Morgrim had seen it happen before, in the other cities the dwarfs had conquered. Once the elgi were gone, they seemed to take with them the essence of the places they'd built. The glamour, the wondrous enchantment dissipated. It almost seemed that Tor Alessi was ageing in front of him. Soon it would be just another lifeless, haunted place, like Oeragor and the others. Even if the dwarfs wanted to preserve them, to keep the elgi cities for their own, they wouldn't be able to stop the decay. When the last elf abandoned them, the soul was cut from their cities, leaving behind only a dead shell.

Morgrim reached the end of the street, the harbour opening out before him. A great throng of dawi warriors was gathered about the docks. Earlier this district had echoed with cheers and catcalls, the boisterous revelry of the victorious. Now, however, there was only a sombre silence. The last of the elf ships was pulling out into the bay, her sails unfurled to catch the wind that would speed her back to her island kingdom.

The dwarf who'd been christened Elgidum could readily appreciate the mood of the warriors. The thrill of victory was leaving them. As they watched that last elf ship depart, a new thought had entered their minds. Perhaps it had occurred to some of them before, but for many of them it was the first time they'd been forced to confront the question. The war was over – what would they do now? Many of these warriors had been born and raised in conflict; they knew nothing else. So long had they been focused on driving the elgi from the Old World that now they held that dream in their hands, they didn't know what to do with it. None of them had planned for what sort of future lay beyond this day.

The war had changed the dawi. Morgrim recognised that fact every time he looked into the faces of the new generations. They'd been tempered upon the anvil of battle and suckled at the teat of hate. If anything, they were more dour and unforgiving than those who had come before. The Slayer Cult Forek Grimbok had founded was emblematic of what the dwarfs had allowed themselves to become: more obsessed with atoning for their mistakes than recognising and fixing them.

Such would be the kingdom Morgrim would one day inherit from his uncle. Would he be able to lead it into a new golden age, or would he simply be there to watch it as it continued to fade?

As the sword wound in his side sent a new flare of pain coursing through his body, Morgrim wondered if Imladrik had foreseen all of this that day so long ago when they'd met outside the walls of Tor Alessi for one last pathetic try at peace.

How different it all might have been if he'd allowed himself to listen to his friend that day.

Am I dead?

The thought echoed through Liandra's mind. It seemed an absurd question to ask. Simply being able to form the thought should have been answer enough. Yet she couldn't be certain. She felt detached from her own body, and what little sense of it she possessed was cold and distant. She could see and she could hear and she could smell, but these sensations appeared removed from her body. She seemed to be staring down at herself, watching as she was carried down a winding forest trail. Strange shapes flickered among the trees, recalling to her the grisly things that had risen from the forest to destroy King Varnuf's army.

Through her haze of confusion, she focused upon the one carrying her. He was a tall elf, arrayed in buckskin and a cloak of leaves, a deer-hide hood with attached antlers covering most of his head and face. It was more some uncanny instinct than anything about his appearance that sent hate surging through her body.

'Druchii,' Liandra hissed through her cold lips. She tried to twist out of the elf's grip, but found that the effort was beyond her numb body.

The elf carrying her stopped. He lowered his face, staring down at her. His features were hard, weathered by a life in the wilds. His eyes had the same fey quality as that of Aismarr, though with an even more pronounced remoteness about them.

'Druchii,' the elf repeated, as if trying to recall the meaning of the word. At last he nodded his head. 'Yes, I think I must have been.' He peered more closely at Liandra. 'I recall a sorceress named Drutheira. She was precious to me once, but somehow the memory of her refused to fade with all the rest. It was that memory which led me to you. I could sense you were there when she died.'

'Then you are druchii,' Liandra accused, yet even as she did she found it hard to remember the root of her hate. The memories of her mother dying in a corsair raid, of her own near-death at the hands of a druchii, these were less intimate now than they had been – like things she'd heard in a story rather than the trauma of her childhood.

'I am Sevekai,' the elf corrected her. 'Soon, perhaps not even that.' He nodded his head to the path ahead of them. For the first time Liandra noted the curious turns their route took, as though the forest were bending itself around them. Oaks would be replaced with ash and yew in a heartbeat, bushes would vanish, brooks would dissolve. It was less as if they moved along the path and more as if the path flowed around them.

'Am I dead?' Liandra wondered, this time articulating her question.

Sevekai smiled at her. 'We must all die to be reborn,' he said. 'Druchii and asur, we must all cut away what we have been. We must go beyond what we were and become what we must be.'

They reached the end of the path, entering a vast clearing. Liandra managed to lift her head, astonished to see so many elves gathered in this place. Most were arrayed in the same primitive fashion as Sevekai, and many had that same fey look in their eyes. Although nearly all of them were asur, here and there the odd druchii stood among them – apparently without distinction.

Ahead of them, a great wall of branches and thrones rose up, like the rampart of some fantastic fortress. There was a light beyond that barrier, a light profoundly warm and inviting. Somehow, Liandra knew that some of those gathered in the clearing around her had been waiting here for centuries to step into that light.

'Your trial is ended, Liandra of House Athinol. And with it, our journey begins,' Sevekai said. 'We will die and be reborn in the light of the forest.'

As Liandra watched, the wall of branches began to untwine, folding back upon itself to expose the light beyond. The heart of the forest.

'What will we become?' Liandra asked Sevekai.

'What the forest wishes us to become,' he answered. 'The protectors and watchers, the guardians who will preserve it against axe and flame. Defenders who can recognise danger with more cleverness than beasts and with more immediacy than spirits.

'We will become the asrai.'

ABOUT THE AUTHORS

Nick Kyme is the author of the Horus Heresy novels *Old Earth*, *Deathfire*, *Vulkan Lives* and *Sons of the Forge*, the novellas *Promethean Sun* and *Scorched Earth*, and the audio dramas *Red-marked* and *Censure*. His novella *Feat of Iron* was a *New York Times* bestseller in the Horus Heresy collection, *The Primarchs*. Nick is well known for his popular Salamanders novels, including *Rebirth*, the Space Marine Battles novel *Damnos*, and numerous short stories. He has also written fiction set in the world of Warhammer, most notably the Warhammer Chronicles novel *The Great Betrayal* and the Age of Sigmar story 'Borne by the Storm', included in the novel *War Storm*. He lives and works in Nottingham, and has a rabbit.

Chris Wraight is the author of the Horus Heresy novels *Scars* and *The Path of Heaven*, the Primarchs novel *Leman Russ: The Great Wolf*, the novellas *Brotherhood of the Storm* and *Wolf King*, and the audio drama *The Sigillite*. For Warhammer 40,000 he has written *Vaults of Terra: The Carrion Throne*, *Watchers of the Throne: The Emperor's Legion*, the Space Wolves novels *Blood of Asaheim* and *Stormcaller*, and the short story collection *Wolves of Fenris*, as well as the Space Marine Battles novels *Wrath of Iron* and *War of the Fang*. Additionally, he has many Warhammer novels to his name, including the Warhammer Chronicles novel *Master of Dragons*, which forms part of the War of Vengeance series. Chris lives and works near Bristol, in south-west England.

C L Werner's Black Library credits include the Space Marine Battles novel *The Siege of Castellax*, the Age of Sigmar novel *Overlords of the Iron Dragon* and novella 'Scion of the Storm' in *Hammers of Sigmar*, the End Times novel *Deathblade*, *Mathias Thulmann: Witch Hunter*, *Runefang*, the Brunner the Bounty Hunter trilogy, the Thanquol and Boneripper series and Time of Legends: The Black Plague series. Currently living in the American south-west, he continues to write stories of mayhem and madness set in the worlds of Warhammer 40,000 and the Age of Sigmar.

YOUR NEXT READ

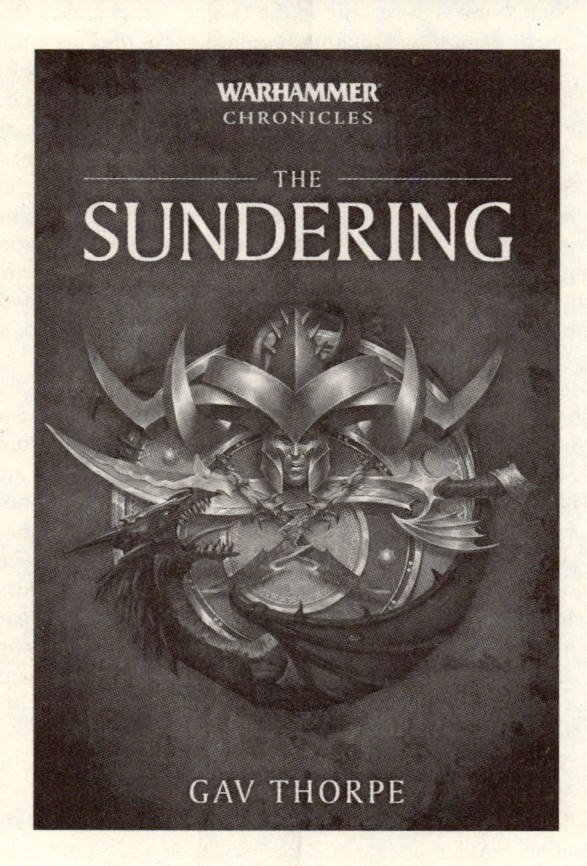

WARHAMMER CHRONICLES

THE SUNDERING

GAV THORPE

THE SUNDERING
by Gav Thorpe

When treachery strikes, the elven kingdom of Ulthuan is plunged into a bitter civil war that will change the destiny of the elf race – and the entire Warhammer World – forever.

Find this title, and many others, on **blacklibrary.com**